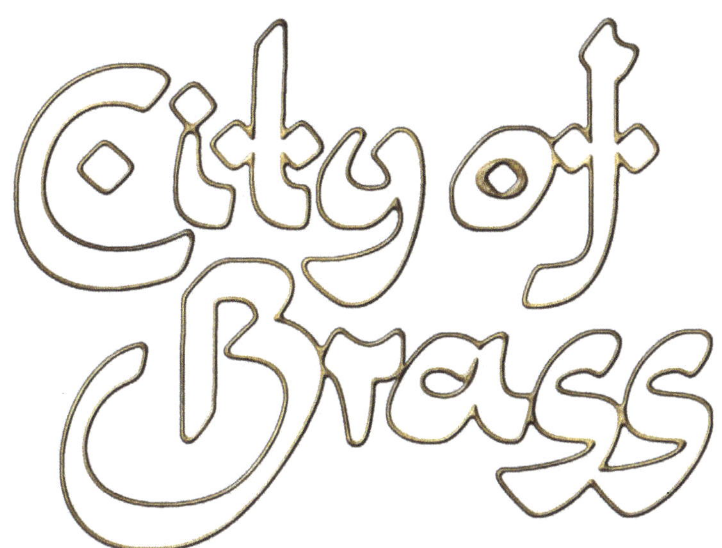

Authors: Casey Christofferson and Scott Greene

Additional Materials By:
Clark Peterson, Erica Balsley, Levi Combs, Kathy Christofferson, Charles Arthur Ford III, Skeeter Green, Chris Jones, Jeremiah Lasch, Patrick Lawinger, Nate Mcphail, Anthony Pryor, Robert Schwalb, Brenden Simpson, Rachel Tayler, Robert Mull, Kevin Walker, Matthew Wolph, and Jon Hershberger

Developers: Casey Christofferson and Edwin Nagy

Producer: Bill Webb

Editors: Jeff Harkness, Edwin Nagy, Scott Greene, Casey Christofferson, Patrick Lawinger, and Elizabeth Murphy

Content Editors: Scott Greene and Casey Christofferson

Art Director: Casey Christofferson

Fifth Edition Adaption/Conversion: Edwin Nagy with Eric Chapman, Meagan Maricle, Scott McKinley, Richard Meyer, and Michael Potter

Layout: Charles A. Wright

Cover Art: Artem Shukaev

Interior Art: Casey W Christofferson, Adrian Landeros, C. J. Allen Marsh, Michael Syrigos, Raashaad Jones, Brian Leblanc, Peter Bergting, Jeremy McHugh, James Stowe, and UDON Studios (featuring Chris Stevens)

Front & Back Cover Design: Charles A. Wright

Cartography: Robert Altbauer, John Auer, and Alyssa Faden,

Playtesters: Brooke Delano, Mark Davis, Greg Hamilton, Josh Martin, Kim Martin, Jeff Smith, Zach Kirkendoll, Roger Pierson, Clint Bennett, Kathy Christofferson, Ainsley Christofferson, Katie Wells, Menolly Crossett, Mack Crossett, Marcia Crossett, Brandon Rehse, Neil Dawson.

Dedication: This book is dedicated to the amazing fans and backers. 18 years in the game and still going strong because of you! You all made it happen!

[This book uses the supernatural for settings, characters and themes. All mystical and supernatural elements are fiction and intended for entertainment purposes only. Reader discretion is advised.]

FROG GOD GAMES IS

CEO Bill Webb	**Production Director** Charles A. Wright	**Special Projects Director** Jim Wampler
Creative Director Matthew J. Finch	**Chief of Operations** Zach Glazar	**Customer Relations** Mike Badalato

978-1-62283-648-2

Table of Contents

Book 1: Cult of the Burning One

Chapter 1
The City of Brass:
A City of Splendor, City of Evil

City of Brass: Preface

All of the greatest quests begin with something small. Those of us fortunate enough to have been around in the venerable "Old School" age of RPGs cut our teeth on the "T" series. While reading the "A" series, we were blown away when these were tied to the "G" series, then leading to the "D" series of adventures that finally led our characters from their humble beginnings to extra-dimensional travel in a cosmic challenge against the arachnid face of ultimate evil in the module "Q."

So we plotted and thought about it. Who better to do it again? With the venerable and deadly ***Rappan Athuk***, we have offered a lair of ultimate evil like none other. With ***Bard's Gate***, we have a cozy yet dangerous city du jour. With ***Sword of Air***, we explored the Shadows of the Lost Lands, and the horrors that naked ambition can unleash on the folk who dwell there. So what could we do to create another epic start-to-finish adventure within our properties that would take characters to the ends of the universe?

So here we are on a quest for the City of Brass. It all starts with something as simple as a village in need of aid. Maybe newly rolled player characters are informed that their childhood friends have gone missing. Perhaps there is an important message that has to be delivered to allies at all costs? These small adventures tend to reveal something greater hidden behind the curtain, and when that curtain is pulled, a new path is opened. Once that path has been followed, another curtain is discovered. Here a new, stronger enemy who was holding the strings the whole time is revealed.

In developing the new release for ***City of Brass***, we thought, "Why not offer an opportunity for an even greater adventure to unfold?" In revisiting this fantastic setting, we took the opportunity to tell a greater story, and to involve lower-level characters in a world of extra-dimensional travel. We thought it best to offer the players a chance to be part of the "big picture" and to save their world in a more streamlined and defined fashion. Or of course they could choose not to as is their right.

The adventures in this revision of ***City of Brass*** have the opportunity to begin with 1st-level characters solving a problem in their local neighborhood. Through the course of that adventure, they discover a greater menace and that their universe is much larger and more complex than they could have possibly imagined. Their pursuit of justice leads them farther down the rabbit hole to new cities and new foes. Their adventures culminate in the **The Path of the Prophet**, an adventure redrawn from the original piece that transports the characters to the Plane of Molten Skies, where the second leg of their journey begins.

The new material recognizes that ***City of Brass*** exists as its own campaign and sourcebook. For example, ***City of Brass*** is designed to be used in any campaign setting, and as an open and ever-growing resource for you to interject extra-dimensional adventure of high fantasy into your own preferred settings, be they home-brewed or our own favorite material: ***The Lost Lands***. For that reason, little has changed from the original material, save to add new places to explore, and to reorganize the material for ease of use at the gaming table.

We have instead added more. More places to explore, more adventure locations. More planes of existence, more legends to learn, and more dangerous foes to conquer.

City of Brass

The name conjures visions of magnificence and splendor, of mystery and timelessness. A place of wonder, a fable, an enigma, a magical fortress adrift in a sea of flame under a sky of fire, a fantasy and so much more. Home to the satrapy, final resting place of the Sultana, high kingdom of the efreet, treasury to all the races of genie, this is a place born of the dreams of the very gods of creation. This is a city unlike any found in the universe, with impossibly tall minarets, and impossibly impregnable walls guarded by the leering demon gates. Behind those gates, high adventure awaits those brave enough to test their mettle against the diabolical wit of the treacherous efreet.

The City of Brass is all of these things and so much more. Born with a single word as home to all efreet, the City of Brass floats forever on the border of the Plane of Elemental Fire and the Plane of Molten Skies, which alone is the sole dominion of the fabled city's cruel Sultan.

A bazaar at the crossroads of the universe, the City of Brass has long been rumored amongst mortal folk to be a repository of relics both fantastic and foul. Here is a place where your greatest dreams and worst nightmares may be granted with a wish if the price is right. Now, without further ado …

Why the City of Brass?

As you read this, you are saying to yourself, yes, this is all quite fantastic, but why on earth would I use something like this in my campaign? What is in it for me as the Judge, Referee, or GM? This sourcebook offers much in the way of a richly detailed campaign setting. Perhaps your characters have a need or desire for something that cannot be found anywhere in their home plane or the universe that they are familiar with. The City of Brass makes a logical storehouse for such an item or materials to create their own relics and magical artifacts. Possibly the greedy Efreet have raided their township, kingdom, or world, and laid waste to it, stealing family members and friends as hostages and slaves.

There is magic here, possibly greater and stronger magic than has been offered in most campaign settings you may find, but it need not be the crux of any campaign run in the City of Brass. *City of Brass* works equally well for low(er)-magic campaign settings where the theme is centered on a more sublime approach to magical power and its prevalence in the universe. Indeed, the City of Brass may serve as the only conduit of magical powers to a low-magic campaign setting. The city's secrets and mysteries could possibly be the wellspring from which other magic has somehow fallen into the characters' world, and thus rightly be a place sought by adventurers for its many treasures and vast areas of knowledge in ancient eldritch secrets and forbidden arcane lore. Weapons great and terrible, spells arcane and evil, items of wondrous power, and armor of legend are available here within the extensive soukss. If they can be haggled from their owners, that is.

Riches beyond imagining lie dormant within the vaults of the efreet, locked away from the greedy eyes of the masses behind a curtain of smoke and fire for untold centuries … until now.

A wealth of information is detailed within these pages. New foes, new magic, and new dangers are found here. So too are ways to incorporate the City of Brass into any campaign setting, be it a traditional dungeon crawl, or a futuristic campaign setting in a low-magic universe. The city's dozens of detailed shops, locations, and areas of intrigue and adventure may fill an entire campaign setting all in themselves and are not limited to the exceptionally high-level characters to play out their last great adventure … or the beginning of their next.

City of Brass is a campaign setting that seeks to capture a sense of immediacy, wonder, and excitement with every twist and turn. When used as a "drop-in" city for a high-level campaign, there is no limit to the places that the characterss' actions may take them. A few simple rolls of the dice and a quick summary of the text could catapult the characters along on their next great adventure. With very little prep time, adventurers could be off on a brand new grand epic in an alien city of power and magic. This great adventure could last many weeks or months of campaign time or be resolved in a single evening.

Extensive encounter tables were developed with the idea in mind that "anything could happen." Imagine being a Midwesterner suddenly transported to Katmandu or suddenly lost and penniless in a favela of Sao Paulo, and you have a small idea of that "anything could happen" attitude that permeates the City of Brass. Almost every seemingly random event that befalls the party as they explore the City of Brass has the potential to further them along on their quest, or lead them on prodigious side quests that could easily fill a lifetime of high-level campaigning.

No two visits to the City of Brass are the same. Like all good settings, there is no "fixed" conclusion for the adventures that take place here, merely more adventure seeds leading to even greater glories, or horrific death. The great white wizard is NOT likely to come to the rescue of the party should they get into a jam — although someone might — if the characters have made the right contacts or greased the right palms. It is of course preferred that the characters' actions guide their path to glory or destruction.

Even relatively low-level characters may find themselves trapped in the City of Brass or the Plane of Molten Skies. Perhaps they arrived as victims of a wish gone awry, or incurred the wrath of an angered genie or powerful wizard. Possibly, they have been sent on a quest by their representative temple or wizard guild to seek an item locked within the city's many extensive vaults. Quite possibly an entire campaign could be based on the characters being born into servitude in the City of Brass and their purpose is to escape slavery and seek the home plane of their parents — or to seek and reclaim their birthright from their efreet masters.

Many areas of the City of Brass are detailed in broad generalizations. This is done with a pure purposeful intent and respect for the product and for the source material of the Arabian Nights from which it is drawn. A broad brush to paint with assures that you are allowed to run your own version of the City of Brass as your campaign setting dictates, and not to structure the source material in such a way as to straitjacket you into running the material strictly as it is written here. A number of monsters and NPCs are given for each major location in the city, as is a framework to build encounters upon. Other areas are left to you to fill in your own vision of the City of Brass. The City of Brass is a city of wondrous magic and unsolved mysteries. Its story, ancient and rich in the retelling, belongs to everyone.

Other areas are drawn in greater detail. Owing to their fantastic nature, they deserve a more thorough accounting. For these, their rooms, their defenders, and their treasures, as well as general maps, are all laid out and ready to use by you on the fly, or as part of a well-planned gaming session.

Ways to Use this Book

You can use this book in many different ways. Below are just a few suggestions.

Exploration

A hallmark of the Lost Lands setting is the opportunity for characters to indeed "get lost" in the world. **Book I: Cult of the Burning One** offers a glimpse at new locations in the Lost Lands ranging from the tiny Barony of Lornedain to a preview of Freegate. From there, the adventure crosses the Sea of Baal before landing at the Port of Kirtius on the edge of the small Kingdom of Numeda in the Maighib Desert, tying it loosely to areas described further in **Dunes of Desolation** from **Frog God Games**. The work expands on other parts of the Lost Lands, providing new encounter areas and mysteries to explore.

Establishing a "Start-to-Finish" Campaign

Since their inception, role-playing games have had campaigns with a story arc that stretches from low-level fare to near super heroic and even deific levels of game play. **Book I: Cult of the Burning Ones** establishes the base levels of such an epic adventure and works as a perfect companion for tying the areas and characters detailed in **Books II** and **III** of *City of Brass* together with locations and characters of *The Lost Lands* in a logical manner. For example, several adventure modules written in the classic era of fantasy role-playing games started with a village located near a mega dungeon or a raid against local slavers. The early adventures introduced hidden villains and offered characters a variety of paths and activities to pursue. These adventures culminated with face-to-face battles against demon lords and demi-gods that are still spoken of in hallowed terms thirty years later and are republished and rebranded with every new release of the world's most popular role-playing game.

Not to be confused with a so-called shotgun or railroad style of adventure, these adventures are designed with player character freedom in mind. The beginning may be the same, but the "how" or even the "if" of the adventures and their conclusions lie entirely in the decisions of the characters as they proceed through the adventures. Likewise, there is plenty of room for the creative GM to introduce her own plot elements, add her own dungeons, and introduce her own non-player characters. This is in fact encouraged, as it creates a deep level of ownership for GM and player alike in the events of their shared gaming experience.

Get Lost in the Side Quests

Throughout the adventure threads, numerous side quests exist that the characters may participate in. These may be as simple as exploring a hidden island or hiring themselves out as bodyguards for an other-planar diplomat who is at the center of a major assassination plot. Story seeds and plot suggestions abound.

From Something Small, Something Big

The adventures that lead to the City of Brass start small. They are local affairs that grow into a larger cosmology of planes, events, and powers. Because they are small, their stories and events are largely relatable even to players who are new to role-playing games. The villains are bad to be sure, though some of the characters and creatures they meet along the way operate in a sort of gray area of moral and ethical ambiguity, much like the characters themselves.

As the characters gain levels of experience, the stakes get higher as new enemies are revealed and the full scope of the Sultan of Efreet's plans for their world become clear. The sultan intends to turn the characters' home world into one of his farm planets, enslaving the masses and slaying any who would deny his supreme authority. The only way to save their world may be a strike at the heart of his empire. Or maybe that isn't it at all. Maybe the important thing is rescuing friends and innocents from their imprisonment in the City of Brass? The choice is in their hands!

As an Ongoing Campaign

City of Brass includes introductory adventures and story hooks to get the characters to the city and optional goals to achieve to complete their quest. These introductory adventures are scaled for Tier 3 characters with objectives scaled to fit your needs. Completing the characters' quest may result in their eventual return to their home plane, with the option for return forays into the Plane of Molten Skies and the City of Brass. NPC contacts and alliances may be forged, giving you a ready-made excuse to bring the characters back again and again.

As a Break from the Normal Campaign

The various shops and locations within the City of Brass offer high-level characters a nice break and a series of diversions from their standard ongoing campaign. An efreeti bottle or magical portal in their standard dungeon may transport them to the Plane of Molten Skies, forcing them to find a way back home. Perhaps the player characters have found a hidden portal directly to the city itself, thereby giving them a place to explore and spend their money, or more importantly, a place for you to rob the them blind, relieving them of some of their more annoying possessions.

As an Epic Campaign

Many of the denizens of the City of Brass are extremely powerful. Simply storming into the Hall of the Sultan and demanding his head on a platter is likely to incur ridicule and lusty laughter from the Sultan's Court. Fourth tier characters are sure to find the City of Brass an adequate place to whet their appetites for high adventure. A GM who finds difficulty developing campaigns that challenge such powerful characters need look no further than the Grand Vizier for an idea of the sorts of nemeses that await their hardened adventurers. A run at the City of Brass can serve as a capstone to a lengthy campaign.

The Appendices

The back half of this book is filled with monsters, magic items, and spells. If it's not in the Fifth Edition SRD, we put it in the appendix. Appendix 1 has creatures. Lots of creatures. Appendix 2 has magic items. Appendix 3 has mundane items, diseases and poisons. It even has grenades and canons. Appendix 4 lists a bunch of new spells we thought would add flavor to the world you and your players create. Enjoy them!

A creature that is simply bolded, like **this**, can be found online in one of the many fine Fifth Edition SRDs. A creature that is bolded with a footnote, like **this**[1], is in Appendix 1. Magic items and spells are similar, except they are italicized rather than bold.

Scalable Adventure

Although *City of Brass* is geared toward a higher level of adventure than many GMs may be accustomed to running, everything within is scalable to meet the needs of any campaign setting. A reduction of hit dice for a powerful monster here, a reduction of level there is all that is needed to enjoy the atmosphere of adventure and excitement.

For Player Characters

City of Brass offers limitless potential for adventure for player characters. Listed below are but a few examples.

As a Base of Operations

The characters may find through their adventures in the City of Brass that they have come into possession of some property that they may use as a base of operations for forays into the other planes of the multiverse, or for continuing adventures within the Plane of Molten Sky and the City of Brass. Perhaps the party completed some quest on behalf of the sultan of efreet and were rewarded with a citadel in the Plane of Molten Sky. Perhaps the characters gambled extensively in a gaming house or the Circus of Pain and won a fortified house in one of the cities various foreign quarters.

Magical Research

Powerful wizards, clerics, druids and the like may seek the wealth of knowledge in artifacts and tomes that lay hidden within the many structures of the City of Brass. Complete quests may be developed around the acquisition of ancient lore or the study of mysterious artifacts. Of course, the characters must find a diplomatic or nefarious means of acquiring such knowledge, perhaps even seeking an audience with the Sultan of Efreet[1] himself.

A Plane of Opportunities

Both the City of Brass and its adjoining Plane of Molten Skies offer many opportunities for exploration and discovery. The Plane of Molten Skies is an extensive wilderness setting that should appease any fan of wilderness adventure. Rangers and druids may find a new home traversing the trackless wastes of the Plane of Molten Skies; rogues may find rich bazaars, hidden treasures and wealthy nobles of the City of Brass to be inviting targets for their underworld activities. Monks may seek enlightenment or redemption in physical challenges against the Order of Devils. Bards may find wealth and prestige of their own as performers and story tellers in the ancient capital of the genie races, possibly even catching the ear of the Sultan's Court, earning a position in the Orchestra of Ashen Thunder. Paladins may no doubt find much that is evil to crusade against, as the City of Brass is frequently a cruel place ruled by wicked folk and peopled by oppressed slaves.

Using This Book

This book is designed to be used with Swords & Wizardry, available free in PDF from Frog God Games, but can easily be used with many similar rule sets. Many of the magic items, creatures, and spells have been created particularly for this adventure; they can be found in the appendices at the end of City of Brass and in sidebars near where they are first encountered in the adventure. All the creatures have condensed stat blocks listed below the area where they are encountered. Many of these reference published creature compendiums for full details. These tomes can purchased if desired from Frog God Games. They include The Tome of Horrors Complete, Tome of Horrors 4, and Monstrosities. Magic items and spells that are described herein are typically found in the Swords & Wizardry Complete rulebook.

A Note on Words

In the City of Brass magic is driven by spoken and written words. In our world, words are used to soothe or to inflame, to praise or to denigrate, to build community or to connote otherness and fear. A different kind of magic, equally capable of creation and destruction. To be mindful of this power, and to guard against its misuse, is to wield magic responsibly. This respect for the power of words prompted the authors of City of Brass to ask me to review the book for cultural sensitivity. As my friend Edwin noted, a team of white Americans writing an adventure in a land flavored by "1001 Nights" offers many opportunities for inadvertently causing offense.

An important caveat: I am about as white as you can get, and I don't want to pretend otherwise. But I was married to a man from the Middle East for seven years. I became part of a large (to me) Arab family, and they accepted and loved me unconditionally, even after the marriage ended. I traveled around the world with an Arab last name on my passport, which got pretty complicated in the early 2000s. Perhaps most importantly I am mother (protector, tutor, cheerleader, annoyer-in-chief) to a daughter who is half Arab and fully Muslim, and I am keenly aware of the effect that words have on her. She was very young (second grade?) when someone on the playground called her a terrorist and I had to explain the "war on terror" and why she was being associated with it. She wasn't much older when she heard something strident on the radio about Christmas being only for Christians. I had to reassure my alarmed child that Santa (who had faithfully followed her all over the world her whole life) did not hate her for being Muslim. This life we have led straddling two civilizations is the main qualification I bring to my review of this game. To be clear, I represent only my own understanding. Reasonable people can and will hold legitimate opinions on these issues that do not match my own.

In reading City of Brass I looked for choices that might unintentionally offend people of the Muslim faith or people from the Near or Middle East both at a micro level (words, phrases) and a more macro level (story arcs, trends). I advised against using the word "jihad", for example, to describe wars. This word is frequently deployed in Western countries to describe a violent East vs. West confrontation. In Arabic, the word jihad represents three types of struggles faced by Muslims: a personal struggle against temptation, the struggle of a community to establish and maintain a godly Muslim society, and the struggle to defend Islam from attack by nonbelievers. Using that word to casually describe warfare (in my opinion) perpetuates Western usurpation of a beautiful and nuanced Muslim religious concept.

Similarly, the word "crusade" in our language and custom is commonly used to describe a campaign that can be political, military, or social in nature. "The Crusades" of course also specifically references a series of wars many hundreds of years ago in which European armies repeatedly invaded and eventually occupied Jerusalem and parts of the Holy Land. We in the West may use the word "crusade" without necessarily thinking about "The Crusades." But in the Middle East it carries the unmistakable baggage of European occupation and oppression. It's important to remember that what we think of as ancient history continues to have urgency and relevance for millions of people in that part of the world.

At a meta level I looked for signs that the overall story arc might reinforce a certain type of us-versus-them narrative. Plucky kidnapped children with European names being rescued from sneaky and diabolical villains with Arabic-sounding names strays dangerously close. As does the idea of a band of adventurers likely derived from the European folk traditions underpinning fantasy literature saving the oppressed Arab(ish) people of the City of Brass by overthrowing the evil Sultan. That being said, I was also reassured by the wide range of characters and settings. Evil abounds in the City of Brass, and it answers to both Arab and non-Arab sounding names.

There is no international convention which can certify a work to be free of bias and stereotype. The best any of us can do as writers is to try our best not to piss anyone off: to be conscious of the danger, sensitive to the effect our work might have on others, and genuinely humble in the face of legitimate criticism. But I would argue it is a risk worth taking; immersion in another culture, however loosely based on reality, gives us the opportunity to explore a world unlike our own, and to perhaps inhabit a skin very different from ours. Surely there is value in that, and an opportunity to learn from it if we want to.

Enjoy City of Brass. The words in this story are powerful, they will take you on a wild ride through a rich universe of good and evil. But as you travel the dank alleys and dim corridors, negotiating your passage with monsters both human and non-, I urge you to be aware of the preconceptions you bring to this almost-familiar world, and the ways in which the story may reinforce some of the unfortunate stereotypes we all carry with us. It's not the worst idea to do so out of game as well.

—Elizabeth Murphy, sensitivity editor and gamer

Chapter 2
History of the City of Brass

Of the Creation of the Genie

As the greater powers stepped forth naked from the void, they each in their own fashion set about forming that void into their own realms, filling each with shapes and sounds that they found pleasing to their divine ears. Among the creators in that time were many free spirits unleashed upon the universe: beings of fire, earth, water, and air. These beings were formless but seemed possessed of their own power and will. The creators found that those beings that seemed to intuitively shape the chaos into structure and shape were useful to their purposes. Some of the powers formed to themselves angelic choirs, while others shaped great hosts of demons and devils to do their bidding.

Anumon, a great being of law and order, chose one among these beings that seemed to show greater power and less willfulness in its ordering of the chaos, and ordained to give it a shape and form of its own. This being he called a genie and named him Sulymon. He set Sulymon to many great tasks, the first of which was the gathering of other like spirits. After Sulymon completed this first task, the first houses of the genie were formed.

Of the Crafting of the Mudawwarah Al Jin

The City of Brass has stood for eons unknown to the world of humans, elves and dwarves, created by the words of the gods as a home for their devoted genie servants. The city — a fortress recognized by all genie-kind as their true homeland — is a vibrant burning jewel of gleaming metal and wondrous magic. The City of Brass was given as a gift of gratitude sworn to them for all eternity in compact and oath to the gods in exchange for their unending service in matters of creation and intuitive command of the elements of which they were formed. The City of Brass was not always known by that name, however.

Sulymon, the great engineer and architect of the gods, devised for his children and kin a great city, the Mudawwarah Al Jin, for them to dwell within. He envisioned a homeland for all of the free spirits who had helped the gods. Thus, Sulymon proposed his case on behalf of the servitor genies before the greater gods.

In the forging of the city, not all of the gods were satisfied with their endeavor. Some argued that a city should be given to all the servant races, from which they could help the coming of the second children of the gods and work the elements in the shaping and creation of the universe to come. The wind lords for their part had little interest in such a place, as their servants found joy in the soaring of the winds and clouds, but they offered their winds to assist the lords of fire in super heating the metal. The gods of the lower waters saw no reason for any of their children to need a great city, owing that all of the rivers, lakes, streams, oceans, and seas of the newborn universe drained to them. Anything raised up above would eventually mix and flow into their kingdom, so they offered only to temper the gleaming metals with their waters to give them the hardness they would need to withstand the flow of time. The lords of earth and fire gave the most, providing the flame for the forge and the materials with which to craft it.

With the words of creation, a lifetime in a day passed and the gleaming city was made whole. The city was given to the genies as their new home for all time. Beautifully crafted of gemstone and jewels, of gold, silver, and lapis lazuli, the great city floated betwixt the four elements, a holy city to all races of genie-kind where they could congregate, worship, and trade.

The genie-kind, for their part, realized that in accepting this fantastic gift of the gods, they had bound themselves to time and mortality. Although living a lifespan far exceeding that of any of the newborn races of the universe, their free will made them aware of their loss of freedom and the true meaning of their bond to the gods of creation. In spite of their many gifts, this knowledge caused many of the genies to seethe with anger, especially the efreet, who ever after worked to cast off the shackles of the gods.

Sulymon placed Iblis, the first genie to whom he had given a true form, upon the throne of the Mudawwarah Al Jin to act as chief to the council of the round city. In Sulymon's mind, Iblis would give order to the chaotic servant spirits of the void and allow their successes and progress to ripple forth across the multiverse. So the city was made, and so it stood for a thousand years as the races of genie-kind lived together, peacefully floating on the elemental convergences of earth, air, fire and water. Like all cities, it grew and changed with the ebb and flow of its citizens, becoming rich in magic and material things.

As the Mudawwarah Al Jin grew in greatness, the clan of the djinn (of whom Iblis was master) became more arrogant. Long had they worked as taskmasters over the other genies during the Great Creation. As the creation grew to a close, the clan of Iblis began to make demands of their kinfolk among the djinn, the marid, and the jann.

Of the Great Purge and the Exodus of the Djinn

Iblis took many wives from the houses of the genies, siring a great host of efreet. His lusts seemed limitless and raised much consternation among the houses of jann, marid, and especially the djinn, whose women were known in that time for their chastity. It was in this time that a djinn princess found herself with child out of wedlock with Iblis as the father. Her own father, a great emir among the houses of the djinn in his own right, demanded Iblis marry the princess and take her as Sultana. He was rebuked before the entire court as Iblis struck him upon the face and cast him down the steps of the Sultan's Palace. Iblis' actions stunned many among the houses of genie, and they threatened to go to Sulymon with charges that Iblis was outreaching his authority as Sultan of the Council of Al Jin.

Fearing the judgment of Sulymon, Iblis gathered the loyal children of his clan together. In the dark of night, they struck out at those who had raised their voices against him, seeking to silence them forever. Many were the heads of houses slain in the night, the fresh blood of murder soiling the streets of their beloved city. Somehow, the Emir of Djinn and his daughter escaped the purge. They gathered what followers and allies they could find and fled Mudawwarah Al Jin for the sanctuary of the Plane of Air, their ancestral homeland from before the time of Sulymon. There did they continue to follow the teachings of Anumon which Sulymon had taught them. Ever after, they swore enmity toward their cousins the efreet. The efreet they now knew were ruled by passions that had become as hot as the fire of their making. Knowing that the wild winds of their own tribe only made those passions grow hotter and more uncontrollable, they sought ever after to protect their wives and daughters from the embrace of Iblis' host.

So too did the marid take their leave of Mudawwarah Al Jin, for they truly missed their brothers in the houses of djinn, and would not abide any longer the insults and violence heaped upon them by their weaker yet more numerous cousins the efreet. Fire and water, it is said, may never know friendship.

Of the Fall of the House of Iblis

It came to pass that the job of creation was all but completed and the gods set about to people the multiverse with elves, dwarves, and humans of every caste and description, which they had held secretly in paradise. Before doing so, they brought these creatures before the genie so that they could marvel at their final creation.

To the genie, the gods said, "All of your hard work is done children, and it was not in vain. Behold the stewards of this new and ever-changing universe."

Iblis and his host of efreet were nearly all that remained within the Mudawwarah Al Jin in those days after the purge. He gazed upon the meek creatures and was unimpressed. Were the gods to give the genie only a city as gift for all of their labors? How unfair it was that creatures of little more than mud should be granted a universe of their own, while he and his people should get only a city in it. With rage quivering in his voice did he challenge the gods' decision.

"These meek creatures made of little more than spit and earth with no powers, these are the chosen ones for which all of our labors have been squandered? I for one will never bow to such as these! Let them be our slaves and servants in this new universe to wait upon us hand and foot, in appreciation that they even draw breath."

The host of Iblis concurred with his statement, adding their voices to his protest.

This boldness took the gods aback. For his insolence, the gods cursed Iblis and cast him down from his high place.

In a thunderous voice did the gods speak as one, saying, "Since you have deemed to question the mind of the gods in this manner and declare our beloved creation to be beasts, so shall you be shriven of the beauty you once knew. Forever after, you and your kin shall bear the face of beasts and tear your meat with fang and claw. So prideful were you of your heritage of fire, let your flesh now burn of it so that all may see the scorching lusts that your greed hath made. That you sought dominion over your brethren through deceit, let your crown of rulership forever more be horns of the lesser beasts, a symbol of your lowly station."

As the gods spoke their judgment upon Iblis and his gathered host, each in turn felt the torment of their wrath in full force. Flames burst from their bodies that had long burned within, their faces becoming twisted and animal like, horns sprouting from their once proud brows.

The gods then turned to the children of Iblis and said. "As you have chosen to declare our chosen children to be nothing more than mud and spittle, know that forever will there be enmity and distrust between your houses. Each forever more shall seek always to make the other his slave. For them, life is short. Should you find one in your possession, know that their toil shall be rewarded with salvation in the afterlife. Should you in turn find yourselves bound to their will, remember that your servitude may prove unending, passed from father to son and mother to daughter as a possession."

"So were you glutted with the powers of creation, thus will you be required to grant their every desire should they ask it of you. As your life is tenfold ten the lives of these children, you will have many centuries to contemplate the choice you have made."

The gods again turned to Iblis. "Since you have sought to place yourself upon thrones that do not belong to you, and claimed rights which are not yours to claim, you may forthwith enjoy rulership of a throne in hell. Damned are you forever. Rule there as you wish. See how long you may keep it." With that, Iblis' throne was cast down, and the very pit of Hell opened beneath his feet.

Lastly, they again turned to the efreet host and said, "To the victors go the spoils. Since you have followed a fool and taken from your brothers and sisters that which was given each of you in equal part, the Mudawwarah Al Jin is yours." With that, the gods hurled the Mudawwarah Al Jin to the very edge of the Plane of Fire itself. "If the smokeless fire of your birthing is your preference to the universe we have created together, then, like your master, may you rule well in the place of your choosing."

All that was once gold did thus turn to brass, all that once glittered then did char and show the mark of flame. Thus did the efreet begin their sojourn within the Plane of Fire, forever more a distrustful lot of dealmakers and slavers constantly seeking to expand and regain the glory they had enjoyed under the rule of Iblis.

The Demise of Sulymon the Genie and the Rise of Sulymon the Prophet

Then did Sulymon the Elder know great shame. Much that he had wrought had gone awry. He wept for his children among the genie races, and strove hard to make right that which had been set wrong among his folk. Eons passed as Sulymon pondered what had gone wrong. Staring deep within himself, he searched for answers in solitude. He prayed and begged Anumon for guidance. Eventually his prayers were answered as Anumon granted him a great vision. In the vision, two great spirits contested within him, one a force of law and reason, the other a force of treachery and darkness. As the universe was crafted from equal parts law and chaos, so too he discovered the living spirit was the domain of good and evil.

Excerpt from the Song of Sulymon and the Birth of a Prophet

Long did we wrestle in the Ever-burning Flames, my Dark Genius and I. Hard was the Battle which raged within the chambers of my heart. Many were the wounds that we struck one another in that place, tearing my flesh to ribbon and annihilating my physical form as I blasted my foe with the power of Truth. Wracked was my spirit in the face of ultimate deceit and the purest black of hatred.

At last the evil one was cast from me, but truly who is to say if it was destroyed or still lives on there, tortured by the Fires of Eternity. To win the battle I chose forever the form of mankind, mixing my ashes with the waters of life, extinguishing the burning sins that had long haunted my soul.

Only then did I return to the City of Brass, my final task among the immortals fulfilled. From there did I close the Grimoire of Infinite Worlds upon my past and turn my face back to the beginning, retracing my footsteps to the world of mortals. It was there that I would work the miracles of Anumon for all to see, and remain, subservient to the will of He who keeps the gates and codified the laws till my dying day. I foresee that this day will not come quickly to me, for there is much to do, the beast that was within me has been beaten but not slain. Praise be to Anumon that I am blessed to the lifetimes of many men before my task is completed.

There within him all along was his dark half staring back at him, dogging his every step, secretly releasing evils into the universe he had helped craft. Surely, this dark half had allowed him to long ignore the evils of one such as Iblis.

When the vision expired, Sulymon wrought great magic to draw the dark one from him. The evil would not go quietly and contested him at every turn. Through the planes of existence did they battle until at last they stood within the Eye of Fire.

Upon the defeat of the Dark One, Sulymon returned to the City of Brass, intent on righting the many wrongs. Gathering many of the most evil efreet to him, he bound them each in a bottle of brass, stoppering the bottles with molten lead and sealing them with the seal of Anumon. He thus placed them well hidden within the Chamber of Bottles there to stay, he hoped, for all time.

Sulymon then sent for Cirrishade, one of his daughters and a princess among the djinn, and saw her wed to Ashur Ban, an efreeti who had abstained from the campaigns of slaughter Iblis had led. Placing them upon the Throne of Brass, he then left the city he had helped create.

Strolling to the Bab Al Baquarra, he cast open the great gates into the nothingness beyond. Calling upon Anumon's might, the Plane of Molten Skies formed over his princely head, scorched earth and sand now the path beneath his sandaled feet. There into the world of mortals, as a mortal, to spread the gospel of Anumon.

Of the City of Brass and the Coming of the Usurper

Many years passed and relative peace reigned again between djinn and efreet. A truce brokered by the marriage of the Sultana and Sultan brought great prosperity to the city. Here secrets were gathered, and great treasures piled high in the vaults of the efreet. But not all of the efreet were satisfied. Many despised the Sultana and saw Ashur Ban as weak compared to rulers who had come before him, yet they remained silent in their opposition, unable to deny their prosperity under his rule.

Despite their troubles, the love of Ashur Ban and Cirrishade grew stronger with each passing year. Theirs was a love to be recorded by poets and songwriters for all times. Many children were born to them; and to those children, many grandchildren. They were called the hawanar. A perfect blending of the djinn and efreet, their visages were not unlike the ancient genies from the days of the creation.

Unbeknownst to them, a great evil was taking shape within the Eye of Fire. A dark half, defeated and nearly destroyed, the wretched thing took the form of one it had once helped shape. It was a proud figure, beautiful and terrible to behold. It hid its chiseled features behind a veil of inflammable silk. Its massive form and unbreakable thews, it laid bare, save for a harness of gold and elemental gemstones. There in the Eye of Fire it forged its weapon for the taking of the universe … a brazen scimitar with which to set the very heavens ablaze.

In the Eye of Fire, many years passed as the creature grew stronger, gathering evil to its side. It whispered its summoning rituals through the planes for assistance in a grand scheme. At last, beasts of flame and fire, devils, and servants of darkling gods answered its call, offering their services to its fell plan.

Once gathered, the Usurper then struck out from the Eye of Fire, capturing efreeti fortresses throughout the plane. In each fortress, he offered the inhabitants a simple choice: join him or die. Many among them swore it was Iblis returned from Hell to lead them once again. He did much to foster this belief, and when he was strong enough to attack the City of Brass, he did so with much of the army once sworn to protect it among his ranks. He next attacked strongholds long held by the salamanders, slaughtering every one of them he met. Their plunder did much to fill his war chest, while the blood of his foes filled his forces with a thirst for slaughter.

When the Usurper finally arrived at the City of Brass, he cast down the gates and slew Sultan Ashur Ban in one blow, shattering the resolve of those efreet who still stood true to the Sultan's banner. Only the hawanar and their Sultana remained to oppose him. Soon she too was defeated, and the hawanar bound, slain, or cast to the four winds. At long last, the Usurper claimed the Throne of Brass and has sat there unchallenged ever since.

Claiming the title of Great Sultan, the Usurper freed the evil servants of Iblis from their bondage, breaking the seals of Anumon upon their prison bottles. He called forth for great construction projects and bound demons to the city's many gates. He set the efreet to work collecting numerous slaves for the many tasks, and bade them forge weapons of great destructive power to be sold to the highest bidder. Much wealth had once come to the City of Brass in the form of peddled magic and now much more still comes under his shrewd guidance.

The Great Sultan's armies now wage war against the djinn again. Each conquered territory in the Elemental Planes of Earth and Air extend the Plane of Molten Skies, which now serves as the staging ground for his numerous invasions. Already the azer number among the races conquered by the efreet, and the once great might of the proud salamanders may not last another assault. The salamander nation is rumored to seek a pact with Orcus himself to stave off their imminent annihilation.

The City of Brass as it now exists is a city ruled by a merciless despot. It is a city where evil walks freely in the light and, if nothing else, is openly welcomed. It is a city of strange magic and long-forgotten lore. However, it is also a city of rules and law, for the Sultan knows that law equals obedience to his will. Aided by servants of Set and The Lightbringer, the Sultan willingly seeks to place himself among the thrones of the greater gods of the multiverse. He will stop at nothing to achieve this goal.

Thus, as the quests begin, the Usurper has turned his veiled gaze to the realms of mortals, his clawed hand grasping at all the denizens of the Lost Lands hold dear.

Chapter 3
Lornedain: The Secret Flame

Lornedain: The Secret Flame is an adventure for 4–6 characters of 1st to 3rd level. The adventure takes place in a small village not far from a larger metropolitan area, but far enough away that the temptations of the big city should not be too much of a distraction from the adventure at hand. As written, it takes place near the city of Bard's Gate, offering an adventure for those who call the Lost Lands home. The Madness of Lornedain serves specifically to introduce low-level characters to a greater menace in the form of the ever-growing Cult of The Burning One. Designed to begin a much larger campaign, this adventure sets characters on a path that eventually leads to the City of Brass.

The adventure takes place in semi-civilized wilderness, a small village, and dungeons and subterranean crypts hidden beneath the various locations. As such, the party composition should include a cleric, an arcane spellcaster, a character capable of following tracks, a character capable of locating and disabling traps, and a decent contingent of fighters or other warrior types to handle melee combat with the various monsters and people who would do them harm.

The area is shown on the map ***Barony of Lornedain*** and detail maps ***1. Village of Lornedain***, ***9. Abandonded Tower***, ***12. Worg's Lair***, ***14. Old Rest***, and ***15. Lornedain Keep***.

Background

Madness has befallen the small barony of Lornedain. Recently, youngsters and others from the village and the surrounding area began to disappear in alarming numbers. The locals are at their wits' end trying to find their lost children, and the Lady Lornedain responded by offering a reward. None of this has helped. Strangers who normally pull their flatboats into the village for an overnight stay have been accused, and travelers are now avoiding the popular portage.

Locals have turned on one another. Farmers blame the Riverfolk; Riverfolk blame the farmers. Both blame the folk who live in the village, while still others blame wild beasts and monsters known to roam the countryside. What is clear is that something wicked has happened to Lornedain, and it is going to take brave heroes to cure the madness ailing the small community.

Adventure Summary

For whatever reasons, the characters are drawn into investigating the missing persons within the community of Lornedain. Through diligence, luck, and sleuthing, they discover a deeper plot hidden just under the veil of hearth and home.

As the characters explore the region, they find various threats such as worgs, river pirates, charnel croakers (a primitive tsathar), and a secret cult of fire brought to the restive village from a far-off land by the very baroness sworn to protect them. Characters complete the adventure when they uncover the plot that has cost the village its folk. They may then set out to rescue those still missing from the clutches of the Cult of the Burning One.

Getting Started

As the adventure begins, confer with the players and offer them options on how they are connected to Lornedain, and explain why the village and the happenings therein have an impact on their characters. As this adventure is designed for low-level characters, it is within the realm of reason that the characters' backgrounds may have some ties to the community without outright forcing characters into a plot straitjacket with which they are uncomfortable. Listed below are a series of possible options for introducing new characters to the campaign.

Characters are Natives to the Region

The characters could have been born in the region, trained elsewhere, and only recently returned upon gaining their first or second level of experience. For example, a wizard may have served as an apprentice to a member of the Dominion Arcane in Bard's Gate. Or a character could have ties to the Riverfolk, and gained experience as a thief or fighter plying the waterways as a merchant guard. A fighter may have earned experience campaigning for the Duke of Waymarch, or as an auxiliary in the City Guard, returning to Lornedain after being contacted about the current situation. Native characters gain a +2 on any checks related to rumors and Charisma rolls while dealing with natives aligned to their background. For example, a person descended from Riverfolk gains a +2 in their dealings with the Riverfolk of the Lornedain region. In this instance, the characters are personally familiar with 1d4 of the missing persons.

Characters are Relatives of a Missing Person

In this situation, a character is related to at least one of the folk missing from the village. Establishing a relative, nephew, cousin, brother, or sister, as one of the missing, creates a strong bond to the campaign as it moves forward. Care must be taken in this scenario not to overplay the "lost relative" angle, however, as it could backfire and create unnecessary tension among members of the gaming group. Proceed with care if this is an option you wish to explore with your players.

Characters are Investigators

Nobles or merchants who rely on trade from Lornedain hire the characters to investigate the disappearances. In this event, the characters are given a bit of the background of the region and are aware that the village and barony are suffering some sort of crisis but not much else. This offers the characters a bit more control over their backstory but doesn't necessarily afford them any personal ties to the village or the missing villagers.

Barony of Lornedain
N
1 mile

Characters are Just Passing Through

The characters also could simply be passing through the region and find the villagers in need. They hear the villagers' tale over dinner and decide to do what adventurers do best: jump in and help! Characters who had hired on to guard a barge of goods on its way to Bard's Gate suddenly find themselves embroiled in the deeper plot as desperate locals plead for them to return their missing loved ones.

Characters Stumble Across a Crime Scene

In this instance, the characters are traveling overland and encounter one of the crime scenes detailed in the adventure. They may find blood, an item, or some other signs of a struggle that leads them to question what has gone on. They may begin sleuthing on their own to discover what happened.

Part 1: The Madness of Lornedain

In the first part of the adventure, the characters explore the area looking for signs of missing persons, engage the locals, and explore the region.

1. The Village of Lornedain

Lornedain is located at the northern end of the Arendian Forest and to the south of the Plains of Mayfurrow. It is an independent barony outside the influence of the elves of the Forest Kingdoms to its south and is located a few hundred miles northeast of Bard's Gate. Lornedain is a community of small farms that dot the countryside, with a walled central village located on the banks of Glimmerill Run as it connects to the Talamerin River on its way to Freegate. For this reason, it has become an overnight rest stop for travelers plying the river. Much of the village's economy depends on river trade for transporting its goods, and from the coin that the travelers spend at the local inn.

The village proper is small and consists of roughly 15 buildings including the guardhouse, granary, boatwright, fishmonger, blacksmith, apothecary, and a shrine to Kamien, god of rivers and streams.

Running the Village

Aside from the local shops and homes of the folks living inside the wall, many people are usually outside doing laundry, cleaning game, or otherwise going about their daily lives. At least, that is how it is supposed to be.

Now, due to the missing children, 2d8 suspicious villagers (**commoners**) armed with clubs and pitchforks greet newcomers. Characters are asked their business and questioned as to whether they have seen any of the missing children. Depending on their answers, villagers may search or even assault the characters before guards arrive and repeat the line of questioning.

If the villagers decide the characters are there to help, they give them access to the local shops and passage through the gates during daylight hours. The typical villager may know one rumor as listed in the rumors table in **Area 8: The War Mallard Inn**.

If the **guards** arrive, they take the characters to the barracks to meet Sheriff Bolen. Bolen again questions the characters as to their motives and lays out the story of the missing children. Characters can hear rumors from him as well, and he may describe a location they might want to investigate. He offers a bounty of 50 gp if they discover any evidence of the missing villagers, and 100 gp for the recovery of any victim, dead or alive.

1-1. Village Wall

A wall 10 feet high, 5 feet wide, and edged by an earthen rampart covers three sides of the inner village. A village guard unit patrols each quadrant of the wall, keeping an eye out for bandits, river pirates, or monstrous threats. A unit is composed of 4 **guards**.

A gate pierces the eastern wall, affording access from the eastern farms. In times of trouble, the farmers make way to the village or to Lornedain Keep.

1-2. Guardhouse

The guardhouse serves as the barracks for Sheriff Bolen's deputies and as a temporary jail for lawbreakers before they are transported to the dungeon of Lornedain Keep. Often, those who are jailed are held temporarily and released after restitution is paid or after they sleep off their offense.

Jail Cell

A trapdoor from the main floor leads into a basement that contains a simple 10-foot-by-10-foot cell with manacles attached to the walls every 5 feet. A bucket and straw are on the floor. The bars are wrought iron, and the door is secured with a sturdy lock that requires a successful DC 16 Dexterity check with thieves' tools to pick. The door requires a successful DC 20 Strength check to break open. A single *continual flame* provides all the illumination for the cell.

Behind a tapestry depicting the coat of arms of Lornedain is a secret door in the wall that leads to the tunnels (**Area 5a**) on the **Abandoned Tower** map. Sheriff Bolen and his men known about the secret door. The secret door can be found with a successful DC 17 Wisdom (Perception check) once the tapestry is moved aside.

Note: The kidnapper Hafbert uses this tunnel to spring any of his men captured during a kidnapping attempt, or to escape should the characters bring him in for questioning.

Armory

A locked cabinet on the ground floor holds 6 spare suits of ring mail, 10 longswords, 10 spears, 3 light crossbows, and 6 boxes of quarrels with 20 quarrels per box. Picking the lock requires a successful DC 19 Dexterity check with thieves' tools.

Village of Lornedain
1,000 ft.
N

Bolen's Office

Sheriff Bolen's office contains a desk and several bookshelves filled with ledgers pertaining to writs, licenses, bonds paid, bonds due, arrests made, executions, investigative case files, and other interactions going back roughly 100 years.

A suit of chain mail, a shield, a great mace, and a pair of boots with the sheriff of Lornedain's emblem emblazoned on the surcoat hang from a rack in the corner. This suit is a spare to Bolen's normal gear.

Bolen seldom takes meetings here as he prefers to meet subjects of Lornedain from the saddle where he has a tactical advantage in martial prowess and intimidation.

A careful search of the ledgers and a successful DC 17 Intelligence (Investigation) check reveals that no open case file exists for the missing persons of Lornedain. If the Investigation check reaches a DC 21, it reveals that missing persons are nothing new to the area, though what that means is relatively uncertain.

Sheriff Bolen

Sherriff Bolen keeps watch over the village and its guards, typically drubbing drunks over the head with his cudgel, and ensuring that the good folk of Lornedain stay safe. Currently, the villagers are angry with Bolen as the missing children have become an issue. Ultimately, Bolen answers to the Baroness Aora, though like her, he is beholden to the authority of Bard's Gate for trade and regional protection. Bolen himself is unaware of the identity of the actual kidnappers. The sheriff isn't a bad person, but is instead mostly a tax collector inept at solving complex crimes, which suits the actual kidnappers quite well.

Sheriff Bolen[1] sports chain mail, a steel shield, a *+1 longsword*, and a dagger. He keeps 250 gp in his office, and wears a gold chain worth 30 gp affixed with a holy symbol of Vanitthu around his neck.

Barracks

The barracks proper is on the second floor of the guardhouse and has bunks for eight, though it currently serves six guards who work overlapping shifts from sunup to sundown. As many as 1d4 deputies (**guards**) may be sleeping or otherwise resting in the barracks at any given time.

1-3. Granary

The dome-shaped community granary stores sorghum and barley grown in the fields and farmsteads of the river plain. The granary currently stores a year's worth of grain. Portions of the grain are sold at the markets in Bard's Gate based on the assumption that the farms will replenish their stocks from year to year with enough food to continue to feed the folk and their livestock.

There is a concern this year that, with the children missing and the farmers spending time away from the fields looking for them, the crops may be short this growing season. Hanen (**apprentice druid**[1]) manages the granary on behalf of Lady Lornedain, and travels with Granwuld Sprague to sell items in Bard's Gate's markets.

1-4. Anselom's Boat-wright

Anselom Dubois' (**commoner**) shop near the river docks sells fishing supplies, and repairs flatboats, canoes, and small barges that ply their way along the river. Characters can find boating and fishing supplies for a 15% markup over standard costs at this shop. Anselom is an Arkaji by birth and is the uncle of the missing girl Simone Dubois. He is infuriated with the local farmers who accuse the Riverfolk of complacency in the disappearance of the children. Anselom has 100 gp he offers as a reward to anyone bringing him proof that his brother's daughter, Simone, is alive. Anselom's brother Henri lives in Backwater Landing a mile down the river.

It takes Anselom one day to repair 1 hp of damage done to a boat.

Anselom may send the characters to **Map Area 4: Backwater Landing** with his blessing to speak with Minoa DeLeon.

1-5. Natan and Folse's

Natan and Folse (**commoners**) buy freshwater fish from the locals. Their small compound is made up of a barn-like warehouse and a two-story home that consists of a kitchen downstairs and their living quarters above.

Natan is an expert at salting, smoking, and pickling fish, after which it is piled on barges and sent to Freegate to be served at taverns or sold by street vendors who have developed a taste for his recipes.

Folse is an expert cook known for plank-roasted and deep-fried fresh fish, fried freshwater clams, and boiled crawfish. He sells meals out of a side window for 2 sp each that are eagerly gobbled up by locals and those making stopovers during river journeys to and from Bard's Gate.

One-third of their profits are tithed to the Lady Lornedain as the cost of doing business. Currently, Folse's half of the business has been suffering. The couple's Arkaji ancestry is putting a strain on their relations with the local folk, whom they once considered close friends. The villagers suspect Natan and Folse's Arkaji kinfolk of being complacent in the mystery of the missing children from the Backwater settlement (**Area 4**), which is driving a wedge between the men and the villagers.

Natan and Folse pay a copper per pound for bass, sheep-head, catfish, gar, and other river fish.

1-6. Bellinza the Apothecary

Bellinza (**apprentice mage**[1]) sells curatives, teas, herbs, and unguents. Most common spell components can be bought at her shop for 15% over market value. She has components whose value is under 25 gp, as well as healer's kits, bandages, crutches, slings, and other items for the healing of non-life-threatening maladies.

1-7. Shrine of Kamien

This ancient house-sized structure is easily the oldest building in the village, and may be one of the oldest buildings in the region south of the forest. Not far from the river, a small stone moat surrounds the domed shrine. Within the building is an altar of cedar carved in the shape of a great fish. The fish's scales are made up of hundreds of silver coins carefully nailed to the altar by thankful fishermen who share a coin of their earnings to the goddess of the fresh waters.

Peg Van Knap (**missionary**[1]), priestess of Kamien, tends the shrine. She has scrolls of *cure wounds* available for sale for 40 gp.

1-8. The War Mallard Inn

The sign over the door of this three-story establishment features an ornamental kite-shaped wooden shield carved with a black duck with a green head and orange bill dressed in full plate and wielding a longsword.

The inside of the main room is cozy if a bit tight, and features half a dozen tables for six, and six stools at the bar. The bar is kept by a bald middle-aged man with thick fingers and a grizzled jaw who looks as if he has seen a thing or two. A battle-worn halberd hangs over the bar.

The War Mallard Inn is run by Ricio DuCanard (**footman**[1]), who retired here after campaigning as a footman for Waymarch for 20 years. The inn is popular with travelers and charges 1 gp per night per guest for any of the 10 double rooms he rents. He allows no more than four persons per room. He also charges visitors 5 sp a night to sleep on the floor near the hearth and allows only 18 in the common area.

The largest room on the third floor is his personal apartment.

Ricio's menu contains the following items:

Item	Cost
Hammer Hand whiskey	bottle, 2 gp; glass, 12 sp; shot, 4 sp
March Rye whiskey	bottle, 4 gp; glass, 16 sp; shot, 4 sp
Brin Zwiescher's Light Ale (bottled in Bard's Gate)	bottle, 1 sp
Arendian Red	bottle, 1 gp; glass, 5 sp.
Pot roast	3 sp
Bread and cheese	1 sp
Pork chops and wild rice	2 sp
Ham, steak and eggs	1 sp

Ricio employs a cook, a waitress, and a housekeeper (**commoners**) who cleans the rooms and takes care of the bedding. All are local villagers. One-third of Ricio's profit goes to Lady Lornedain's tax, which pleases him not one bit. There are usually 1d8 + 2 travelers and 1d6 + 2 locals (**commoners**) in the common room having an ale or getting a bite to eat. Due to the current troubles, however, travelers now avoid the town as the locals accost them for being "in" on the kidnappings until convinced otherwise.

Ricio has heard rumors and may part with some if a character spends at least 10 sp in his establishment.

Village Rumors

Throughout the village, characters hear an undercurrent of fear rising from the disappearances. A character looking to gather additional information can make a Charisma (Persuasion) check and add +1 for every 5 gp spent on bribes, drinks, presents, etc. Consult the table below for the results of the check. A character that casts *Legend Lore* or uses a similar spell or class feature can make an Intelligence (Arcana) check or other appropriate check with a +10 bonus.

Check	Result
1–9	"I tell you what … wait, what was I talkin' about? Strangers? You probably got them kids. I'm going to go tell the guard about you. Can't believe the Lady Lornedain hasn't closed the borders of her shire to the likes of you!"
10–11	"Filthy Pete the blacksmith did it! Of course the vagrant Filthy Pete had something to do with it! Don't you see how he hasn't been back to town since he was kicked off MacGovern's farmstead? And don't you just know how he is? We searched his shack, but of course he's nowhere to be found!"
12–13	"River pirates are tied into this somehow, which means the Riverfolk are somehow responsible!"
14–15	"Farmers did in the Macewan family because they were jealous of their successes. The lady was about to grant them another plot of land, and that was just too much!"
16–17	"The Riverfolk did in the Macewans. It was payback, pure and simple. You see, the Macewans did in the Riverfolks' kids for stealing from their fields. Certainly, the filthy Arkaji are mixed up in this."
18–19	"The beast of the forest has returned no doubt. Snatching the children up it is, and our cattle as well! We have complained to the Lady Lornedain, but her huntsman has not returned! Likely killed by the beast itself!"
20–21	"Nay, it isn't the beast, it's the lumberjacks! No doubt one of them was bit by a werewolf for certain!"
22–23	"Horrible spirits dwell at Old Rest Cemetery. The missing somehow disrespected the Old Ones under the mound, and we are all paying the penance for their sin."
24–25	"My kids told me that some masked and cloaked stranger offered them sweets over at the fork in the road down past the ruined watchtower. They ran and hid just like I taught 'em. The stranger chased 'em on horseback. Once they made it to the ruin, the stranger backed off."
26–27	"River pirates have a base hidden in a backwater about a mile north of town. I saw it through the trees, but we got away just in time."
28–29	"Old Rest is built atop a mound of the Old Ones. The ruined tower was part of their city in the days before days were counted."
30+	"It's said that a spider's web of tunnels, some collapsed, some not, ties certain parts of the shire together." (*Legend Lore* or similar actions only)

1-9. Wayne Home

This cottage is home to Matilda and Edwin Wayne (**commoners**), the distraught parents of Denton Wayne, one of the missing children. Edwin, a laborer, has missed work ever since his son vanished. His wife is a washer woman. At first, they thought their son had run off with Emile Anton. All Matilda and Edwin know for sure is that their child was last seen fishing the sandbar, where children have been known for years to fish, swim, and enjoy life on the river after their daily chores. The Waynes were friends with the Antons and are somewhat suspicious that Leon Anton has disappeared as well. They believe that he perhaps is in league with Filthy Pete, as neither man has been seen in about the same time.

Matilda Wayne offers the characters anything to hire them to find her son. Unfortunately, Matilda and her husband possess only around 10 sp and an heirloom silver locket worth 5 gp.

1-10. Anton Home

The Anton Home is empty, and appears to have been ransacked. In reality, Leon Anton tore his own home apart in frustration at the disappearance of his only child. He then headed out drunk to the area of the sandbar where the children went missing. He was reportedly cursing Riverfolk and saying he was going to take a piece out of Captain Lambert if he could get his hands on him.

A dagger stabbed into the wall pierces a scrap of vest commonly worn by Riverfolk.

1-11. Barony Trade and Loan

Riverfolk often find themselves in debt due to storms ruining their boats, floods, gambling, or just plain bad luck. To this end, the baroness, at the urging of Granwuld Sprague, has set up a trade house near the village docks where locally woven blankets, crossbow bolts, arrows, knives, handaxes, iron spikes, 10 foot poles, and the like can be bought. Locals may ask for loans of under 20 gp at 15% interest per year that are backed by the baroness.

Michele Sprague (**spy**) a sharp-eyed young woman who is Granwuld's niece, runs the Trade and Loan. She also secretly works as a fence for the river pirates, buying untraceable items such as bolts of velvet and silk, furs, alcohol, and other items destined for foreign ports that can easily be re-packaged and sold back on the black market.

A locked iron strongbox in the Trade and Loan contains 200 gp. Opening the lock requires a DC 15 Dexterity check with thieves' tools or a DC 19 Strength check.

The Trade and Loan building houses 2,000 gp worth of goods and materials, more than half of which were plundered by Captain Lambert and his river pirates.

1-12. Porter Home

Herrell Porter, his wife, Leaane (**commoner**), and his son, Mareal, lived in this house before Herrell and Mareal disappeared. Herrell and his best friend Gulllom Ferdinand took Mareal on a hunting trip, but none of them has been seen since. Leaane believes a werewolf took her family and friend and she openly blames the woodsmen camped to the north of town as the cause of the disappearances. She notes how they are always drunk and feral in town, and that she and her husband had an unwelcome encounter with a group of foresters outside of the War Mallard Inn before he vanished.

She can describe the wooded clearing north of town where scraps of bloody clothes and large wolf-like prints were found, though the bodies of her son, husband, and their friend were nowhere to be found.

The Missing: Where are They?

Several people are missing from the village of Lornedain and its surrounding environs. Even an experienced GM may have trouble keeping track of who is found and who is lost. Below are the locations throughout the Lost Lands and the City of Brass where various missing persons may be found. Although locating them all may not be part of the characters' ultimate quest, it is a thread that can be pulled on whenever players get distracted by possibly less important details.

Children of Lornedain

Emile Anton, *Lornedain: The Secret of the Flame* **(Chapter 3):** She is located in **Cell G** of the **Lornedain Keep Dungeon (Area 15-30).**

Denton Wayne, *The Brazen Spires* **(Chapter 4):** He is located in an enchanted bottle in the Brazen Spire of Freegate.

Mareal Porter, *The Great Ziggurat* **(Chapter 28):** He is located in the slave pits.

Adults of Lornedain

Guillom Ferdinand, *Lornedain: The Secret of the Flame* **(Chapter 3):** He is located in **Cell D** of the Lornedain Keep Dungeon **(Area 15-30).**

Leon Anton, *Lornedain: The Secret of the Flame* **(Chapter 3):** He was immolated in a sacrifice by the baroness of Lornedain.

Herrell Porter, *The Brazen Spires* **(Chapter 4):** He is held in **Cell Block A2** of the Spire Dungeon.

Children of Backwater

Fergie and Marie Laroushe, *Lornedain: The Secret of the Flame* **(Chapter 3):** They are being held in **Cells A and B** of the Lornedain Keep Dungeon **(Area 15-30).**

Simone Dubois, *Ard's Sanctuary* **(Chapter 17):** She is being held in a cell in the City of Brass.

Woodsmen

Kent Chenar and Thod Greae, *Lornedain: The Secret of the Flame* **(Chapter 3):** Dire wolves ate the pair. Their remains can be found in the worgs' main lair **(Area 12-8).**

The Macewan Family

Yeoman Jon Macewan, *The Brazen Spires* **(Chapter 4):** He is in the hold of *The Sand Dancer*.

Maggie Macewan, *Numeda: The Caliphate of Flames* **(Chapter 5):** She was burned in the fountain of the Palace of Massini.

Linsey Macewan, *Numeda: The Caliphate of Flames* **(Chapter 6):** She is a slave in the Palace of Massini.

Grendle Macewan, *The Circus of Pain* **(Chapter 23):** He is being held in the Circus of Pain.

Aelish Macewan, *The Sultan's Palace* **(Chapter 31):** She is a servant in the Palace of Concubines.

2. Lambert's Lookout

This river pirate camp is well hidden in a wooded area on the western bank of the river about a mile north of Lornedain. The hideout moves from time to time as men-at-arms from the baroness's forces are constantly in search of Captain Lambert's forces. Lambert (**scout** with Str 14 and a *+1 longsword*) also keeps a two-hulled barge at his camp that is used for smuggling operations.

A dozen river pirates (as **bandit** and **sneakthief**[1]) ply the waterways in a pair of swift 25-foot canoes each capable of carrying 4–8 men. The tactic of Lambert's pirates is to coast in quickly on slower-moving and unsuspecting river traffic, then overpower the merchant guards and steal their loot. Lambert and his men keep and divide the gold and divide larger items into smaller cargo to be sold off in various markets along the river.

If captured and questioned about the missing, he suggests that the characters search the foresters' camp, or check farther inland. He is distant cousins with the folk of Backwater Landing and is insulted at the idea that he would do anything so cruel against his own kinfolk, regardless of their feelings toward him and his business ventures.

Captain Lambert is actually on the payroll of the baroness through Michelle Sprague and shares profits from things stolen near the barony in a privateer capacity. It is because of this secret relationship that he has been able to avoid capture by Sheriff Bolen for so long.

Also on behalf of the baroness, his men smuggle items a day's sail down the river on his barge. Sir Hafbert (**footman**[1]) and two of his goons (**bandits** with AC 14 from chain shirt and shortswords) always accompany these missions. Lambert is preparing for another trip down the river and merely awaits delivery of the new stock from Hafbert. Lambert does not suspect that this cargo has been of the human variety as the cargo has always arrived pre-packaged in medium-sized crates.

Lambert and his pirates are careful not to attack any Arkaji boats that have paid their tax on his portion of the river, and they tend to avoid larger vessels such as the Northmen's longships, especially those that are heavily armed and swelling with barbarians.

The pirates' hideout holds a cache of stolen loot in a small flatboat. The hoard contains 3 kegs of ale, 4 empty ale barrels, a case of fine wine, 4 yards of pink silk worth 400 gp, two barrels of salted pork, and two crates of dried beef. Each pirate has 15 gp. Captain Lambert has a *+1 longsword*, 245 gp, a gold chain worth 25 gp, a silver bracelet worth 10 gp, and 2 *potions of healing*.

3. The Sandbar

A little less than half a mile north of the city in the center of the river is a narrow sandbar that appears in midsummer. It is a popular location for youngsters to fish and play.

Scene of the Crime

The water is shallow on the eastern side of the sandbar. Flags are posted on the north and south sides of the island to advise river traffic to steer west when the waters are low. It is nearly impossible to find any signs of a struggle. The characters might discover a lunch basket left behind by Denton Wayne when he and Emile Anton went missing.

What Happened Here

The banks along the eastern side of the river near the shallows collapsed in the manner that sometimes happens when a person or rider tries to get out of the water quickly. A successful DC 16 Wisdom (Survival) check notes that hoofprints similar to those found in other areas of the duchy both enter the river at this location and leave in the same direction at a high rate of speed. The children Simone Dubois, and Fergie and Marie Laroushe were fishing along the stream when they witnessed a wagon led by the men in black pull up and off-load crates to a barge. When one of the crates dropped, they overheard a howl from within that belonged to one of the Macewan children.

The dark riders saw the witnesses and immediately charged after the children, scooping up Fergie, Marie, and Simone.

4. Backwater Landing

Backwater Landing is a small Arkaji (Riverfolk) settlement about a mile south of the village. It is made up of several houseboats lashed together and connected by plank bridges in an actual backwater pool sitting under the drooping branches of black willow, river birch, and cottonwood trees. Currently, two barges are tied up here to block entrance to the river cove due to the tensions between the Arkaji and the villagers of Lornedain.

The folk of Backwater are a generally peaceable and tight-knit group trading and offering barge service up and down the river for a price. Their barges are less frequently attacked by Lambert's pirates due to familial ties. This does not mean that Lambert's river pirates won't attack the Arkaji of Backwater; it simply means that they are more likely to take a bribe or a "tax" on the goods that the Backwater residents are hauling.

Three children are missing from Backwater: Fergie Laroushe and Marie Larousche, and Simone Dubois.

Running the Backwater Riverfolk

The Backwater Riverfolk (**sneakthiefs**[1] and **bandits**) are suspicious of strangers who approach their settlement. Any intruders are met with an armed response, though the Riverfolk are willing to parley so long as visitors are calm and bear no weapons against them.

If they like what they hear, Minoa de Leon (**scout** with *+1 saber*, as scimitar), the elder of Backwater, tells the party of the children missing from their band: sisters Fergie and Marie Laroushe, and Simone Dubois. The youngsters are between the ages of 9 and 13 and had taken a boat full of fish up to Lornedain to sell to their kinfolk Natan and Folse. They had not returned as night fell, so their parents went to Lornedain to inquire about them, only to find that the children had never arrived. Their canoe was found submerged along the eastern bank of the shoreline less than a quarter mile from Backwater between the Macewan farm and Filthy Pete's shack.

Henri Dubois (**sneakthief**[1]) is the father of Simone Dubois and is desperate to get his daughter back. He has a string of pearls worth 50 gp that he offers as an additional prize should he get his daughter back alive. He offers to join the party if necessary to keep the focus on rescuing his child.

Some among the Backwater clan at first suspected the Macewans, but after the Macewans themselves disappeared, blame shifted to Captain Lambert's pirates or Filthy Pete as possible suspects. Either way, the folk of Backwater are incensed at the lack of help from the villagers of Lornedain in recovering their missing kinfolk.

Minoa knows that his folk are not free to explore the farmlands due to the current attitudes of other locals and he knows that his folk would be damaged among other tribes of the Arkaji if they mounted an attack on Lambert and his goons. He sees a solution in using the party to search for their missing kin, and has 200 gp, two *potions of healing*, and a *+1 shortsword* to offer as bargaining chips should their kinsmen be returned to them.

Minoa can also direct the characters to the place where the sunken canoe was found.

5. Macewan Farmstead

The largest farmstead to the south of the village belongs to the Macewan family. Yeoman Jon Macewan was a very successful farmer and soldier who served the Barony of Lornedain in various campaigns, earning land and title before returning to work his piece of land and build his family. Recently, he petitioned the baroness for property to the south of Old Rest that happened to include Filthy Pete the Blacksmith's sliver of land. An enraged Pete threatened Yeoman Macewan publicly over the deal.

Though his threats were not taken seriously at the time, Pete's hard drinking and lack of fear of Yeoman Macewan or his association with the baroness led most in the region to speculate that he had something to do with the disappearances, especially of those who spoke out against the blacksmith.

Currently, the Macewan farmstead is overgrown with weeds, but neighbors have been caring for the livestock upon the orders of the baroness. Should the whereabouts of the Macewan family not be discovered within 30 days, their land is to be forfeited by the baroness, and their plots reassigned to other farmers of the region. This decree has left other farmers in the area with mixed emotions. They would all love a piece of the Macewan farm, but most are also terrified the fate of the Macewans might befall their own families.

Scene of the Crime: Signs of a Struggle

The main home of the Macewan Farmstead shows signs of a struggle. The front door was cut open with an axe, and bits of furniture and broken glass are strewn about the dining room. The family ledgers and account books all appear to be missing. A heavy wooden box in the master bedroom was broken open, but the valuables it contains were left undisturbed.

A simple search of the master bedroom finds ripped pages under the bed. These were obviously torn from a diary. The entry from a few weeks ago reads:

Peter confronted me outside the trade house today, and in front of the children no less! I wanted to tell him to hold his tongue lest our plan be undone and our plot discovered! But all I could do was sputter like a fool for fear of raising suspicions, all the while hoping beyond hope that he would not reveal our secrets to the entire village. Luckily, he managed to hold from the brink of ruin, but for how long?

I hoped after our campaigning together that I could trust him in our endeavor to get the ring, but the things we saw merely brought back worse memories for him. I remember well how he could not handle the horrors of combat, especially when magic and unnatural creatures were involved. He seems ill at ease these days, and was clearly drunk, swearing and cursing in front of the children as he did. I told the older children to steer clear of his property until all of this settles down.

An extremely thorough search of the home with a successful DC 18 Intelligence (Investigation) check, discovers a large amount of ash in the fireplace. Sifting through the ash uncovers a partially burned leather-bound diary with several pages missing.

Yeoman Macewan's Secret Diary

The first half of the diary is an account of Jon Macewan's campaigns in the Maighib Desert in far-off Libynos. Most of the entries describe daily soldiering, but one entry is a compellingly detailed account of a battle against the brave desert lancers of Numeda.

A page speaks of discovering a brass flask stoppered with lead and inscribed with a holy symbol that was found sticking out of the sand in the "Dark Oasis."

The eyes of milady's foreign wizard lit with glee when she discovered the bottle jutting as it was from the sand not far from the oasis. We had encamped not far from our quarry city, a walled Numedan privateer fortress that had thus far withstood all of our best plans.

The weasel-faced sorcerer spoke quickly to milady in a tongue that I have not yet mastered. She smiled and nodded to him and replied in his own tongue as she patted the strange vizier on his back like one would pet their prized hunting dog.

She drew off to the edge of the camp, near the waving fronds of the oasis. I followed, and I know not why. Something about the odd glimmer of the bottle compelled me. Fear for the safety of my liege drove me to be sure she would not spend more time than necessary with the desert jackal dressed in the skin of a man, cursed be the day he made her confidence! There at the edge of the oasis did I see her draw her sword and strike the stopper.

Suddenly a smoke of green and purple, red and orange, poured from the end of the brass flask, and I saw the most damnable vision I had ever seen. A demon no doubt, called an efreeti by local lore, rose above my mistress with eyes like a pair of gleaming hot coals and red skin licked with living fire. It grinned at her and demanded her name as I trembled awestruck and in fear.

My lady did not raise her voice but beckoned the being to crouch and listen as she commanded of it three wishes in return for the gift of freedom. I know not what she asked, for I fled the scene in terror.

When next I saw our lady, she looked easily ten years younger. She returned to the generals of the army that very morning and held closed counsel with them. By the afternoon, we had taken the city and plundered its treasuries in the name of our gods. The following morning, a great tower of brass, whose minaret burned like a torch, stood over the city, and we withdrew upon the ships of the harbor, set to return at last to our homeland.

For my part in the campaign, I was granted this fine farmstead, and I do my best to forget the strange happenings in that horrid desert land.

A later entry reads.

Old Rest has always been a peculiar, haunted place. Sometimes it seemingly has a life of its own that I think was unleashed from beneath the soil. This is likely why our folk returned to burying their kin on our farms rather than in that ancient graveyard. Once, Grendle and Aelish came home after playing hide-and-seek among the tombstones with a handful of charnel coins. I have since forbidden the children from playing anywhere near the mound, as there is no reason the children should have come into possession of the eyes of the dead.

It was a good thing I did! The halfling Fritz from Bard's Gate stopped by the farm on his way to explore the place for some chronology he was writing for the Sanctum of the Scroll in Bard's Gate. He seemed confident that any tales of danger at Old Rest were nothing more than wives' tales. No one has seen the fellow in over a week. We went looking for him, but were turned away by a number of ...

The rest of this piece of manuscript has been burned away.
Another entry reads:

They are hunting for something. I think I know what it is, and if my suspicions are correct, I can use the information to my advantage. I should tell Peter the Blacksmith and have him come with me to investigate.

The last entry indicates a growing concern on the part of Yeoman Macewan:

Sadly, my suspicions are confirmed. I do not think the seekers suspected the thing to still exist. After what we saw in the mound, I fear that poor Pete will never be the same. I have hidden what they seek. Gods help us if they find it. I gave it to the forester Kent to take to Andrigor in Bard's Gate. If he does not, it is no matter. At the least the ring will be out of their hands.

The broken chest contains 300 gp and a silver ring with emerald chips worth 25 gp. Also in the chest is a partial hand-drawn map of the region of Libynos showing the city of Kirtius and several pirate fortresses along the coast. There is a longbow, 20 arrows, a yeoman's breastplate armor, a longsword, and a helm in a dressing room off the main bedroom.

6. The Sunken Canoe

Along the wooded banks on the east side of the river between the edge of the southern flank of the Macewan property and Filthy Pete's pasture are the broken remains of the boat that the Arkaji children Fergie and Marie Larousche, and Simone Dubois attempted to row to the market.

Scene of the Crime

Many footprints and patches of smashed grass are found around the area where the broken canoe was hauled onto land. Fifty feet away from this mess is a fishing creel that belonged to Fergie. His name is embroidered on the broken strap. Faint tracks show hoofprints of at least two and possibly four horses that pass just past Filthy Pete's shack and head off in the direction of Old Rest. The tracks vanish along the well-traveled road.

Note: *Characters who have visited Filthy Pete's shack may recall that Pete drives a mule cart and owns no horses.*

7. Filthy Pete's Shack

Angry villagers ransacked and burned the shack of the maligned local blacksmith. The villagers arrived with rope, pitchforks, and torches, expecting to catch Filthy Pete and punish him for his alleged crimes. When they arrived at his cabin, however, Pete was nowhere to be found, though iron in his forge was still red hot to the touch. The locals arrived just at dawn, but quickly lost any trace of his footsteps as they stamped around his home, destroying his smithy.

Outside the shack are the remains of his forge, his anvil, and a handful of blacksmith's tools that were not stolen by the villagers when they left. Pete's mule cart has been left intact, though it is empty and his mules graze in their fenced-in pasture by the river's edge.

Scene of the Crime

A letter stabbed to the wall and splattered with blood and spotted with sooty fingerprints reads:

How dare you threaten my land? After all I've done for this community. Your greed, yeoman, is your undoing. While you are suffering everlasting torment, you and your family shall know the folly of trying to take what is rightfully mine!

Note: *The handwriting on this note is different from the handwriting found in Jon Macewan's diary and on the sheet found in the Macewans' bedroom. Characters who somehow come across any handwriting belonging to Baroness Aora Lornedain can match the handwriting, though this note was penned quickly and in anger.*

A thorough search of Pete's cart and a successful DC 16 Intelligence (Investigation) check discover a child's shoe tucked under the blanket that covers the seat. The shoe can be identified as belonging to Aelish Macewan, one of the Macewan children. How Filthy Pete ended up with the shoe is unknown.

A careful search of the area and a successful DC 15 Wisdom (Survival) check discover a series of hoofprints leading toward the overgrown road that runs around the north end of Old Rest.

Characters exploring down by the shore of the river note several boot prints here in the sand and mud along the edge of the banks and wagon wheel ruts where a wagon apparently backed up to the water. The wagon ruts do not match the width of Filthy Pete's cart, and the hoofprints do not match the hooves of his mules, though they are intermixed with them.

8. The Windmill

The third tallest structure in the barony behind the abandoned tower and Lornedain Keep is the windmill that stands a quarter mile from the village. The windmill grinds the wheat, corn, and barley into bread meal that is then transported throughout the region. The windmill is run by Old Man Elmer (dwarf **commoner**), a third-generation miller who is raising his grandson Wilmer (dwarf **commoner**) to take over the family business when he is gone.

Elmer's eyesight isn't what it was, but his grandson is sure that he has seen at least four riders at dusk galloping to the southeast near the abandoned tower. The riders were too far away to make out their colors, but they appeared to be dressed in dark clothes and riding horses that Wilmer did not recognize. Perhaps bandits, assassins, or worse have set up shop in the barony?

9. Abandoned Tower

A half mile from the village stands the hollowed out remains of a 200-foot-tall tower of ancient design. It predates the Lornedain family's arrival in the county by at least 1,000 years. It is believed that the tower was built during the time when Durendia's reach was larger, but this theory is flatly denied by long-lived elves themselves who date the tower as even older. The stone itself is sturdy and perfectly fitted, albeit with a significant 15-degree tilt. There is no obvious ground floor entrance to the tower, though open archways that begin 20 feet off the ground reveal that the tower is at least partially hollow and is apparently abandoned by all save crows who stare down at travelers with black-eyed ambivalence.

Climbing the outer wall of the tower requires a successful DC 18 Strength (Athletics) check due to the smooth, weathered nature of the stone and the lack of obvious handholds. Characters managing to climb into the window find a hollow tower shaft where wooden floors and stairs have long since fallen away. Nooks high above the ground are now home to crows' nests made from bundles of sticks.

A stone staircase descends below the tower and can be accessed from inside the tower.

9-1. Secret Entrance

A secret door is hidden at ground level and requires a magical password to enter. This password is known to the Lady Lornedain, Sir Hafbert, and Giza al Hofu.

Where is Filthy Pete?

The hermit-like blacksmith referred to as Filthy Pete (**bandit**) keeps a cabin in the woods down by the river. Many villagers suspect him of evildoing and ran him out of town for boozing and wild conspiracy theories about croaking dirt people, cannibalism, and wild plots. He spent a lot of time digging holes in various farmers' fields in search of "proof," often accompanied by village children helping him in his journeys into the unknown. These activities led him afoul of many of the local farmers.

Long before all of his recent craziness, Pete was an armorer for Baroness Aora Lornedain and traveled with Yeoman Macewan and others on wars in far-off Libynos. Most say Pete was not suited for battle, and that he came back a much different man than the one who originally left.

The Cult of the Burned One found a perfect scapegoat and patsy in Filthy Pete. Peter knows more than a bit of the truth, and he knows he is being hunted. Unfortunately, years of drink, avoiding his neighbors, and his experiences beneath the Old Rest Cemetery and abroad during the wars have combined to make him a wreck of a man whose only real goal is self-preservation.

Enough evidence exists to cast a shadow of doubt on Filthy Pete's involvement, but the baroness and her cronies are hoping that the sheriff or the characters conclude that Pete is the villain behind the missing villagers.

Filthy Pete's whereabouts should be a driving force of at least the first half of the adventure. You may decide on a location that best serves the narrative of the adventure based on the characters' actions, or simply place Filthy Pete ahead of time. Another option is to randomly roll 1d6 for an encounter with the blacksmith as the characters enter an area of the map where he may be hiding. If a 1 is rolled, Pete is indeed hiding in the area. Make sure the characters have had some opportunity to explore on their own before introducing Filthy Pete to the adventure.

Filthy Pete is likely to be encountered in the following locations:

Yeoman Macewan's Barn

Pete has occasionally been spotted down by the river not far from the Macewans' land. If the party finds him here, Pete is hiding in the loft of the barn underneath a pile of hay.

The Woods North of Old Rest

Villagers saw Pete in the southern end of the duchy poking around by Old Rest, but he ran into the woods when they gave chase. If he is found here, Pete is camping in the hollow of an old oak tree near Old Rest where he can keep an eye on the baroness's kidnappers and any croakers that may creep out at night in search of fresh meat.

The Abandoned Tower Tunnels

If he's here, Pete is lurking in the tunnels between the jail and the tower, or between the keep and the tower, as he keeps an eye on the comings and goings of the baroness and avoids the sheriff and his deputies.

Abandoned Cave

Villagers can tell the characters that they saw Pete crossing fields toward the woods to the west of the keep. Filthy Pete uses the cave just west of Lornedain Keep to hide from the authorities and angry townsfolk. There is a chance he is still hiding in the cave at any given time while he surveils the comings and goings of the baroness's forces.

Filthy Pete's Shack

It is always possible that Pete returned to his home hoping that the coast is clear. He may be looking to retrieve his mules, as their well-being is of great concern to him.

Old Rest

As terrified of the croakers as Pete is, he holds out hope that the troops will return with Yeoman Macewan in tow and that he may somehow rescue the fool.

Finding Pete

Once located, Pete draws his battleaxe and fights like a cornered badger. He is harried, his eyes are red and sunken, and he is indeed coated with ages of forge silt and the wear and tear of living the life of a hunted man.

Pete swears up and down that he is not guilty of the crimes he is accused of, and claims bandits using tunnels beneath the barony are to blame. He knows where the tunnels are and can take the characters to them, so long as they do not kill or arrest him. If the characters agree, he takes them to the tunnels beneath the abandoned tower. From there, he points them in the direction of the keep.

He knows nothing of the letter in his cabin, or the child's shoe in his wagon. He insists that he is being framed. Which he is.

Pete tells how Macewan came to him because of their time in the service of the baroness, and how he convinced him to help steal a ring from the tomb of the Lornedains in Old Rest. He says that Macewan believed some bandits were also searching for the ring.

While in the tomb, the pair uncovered a hidden cavern system before they were set upon by creepy folk with sharp claws and huge white eyes. They barely escaped with their lives after fighting off the creatures. Taking the ring, they fled back to their respective homes. Not days later, Pete discovered footprints of the things around his property. Believing the creatures sought the return of the ring, he confronted Macewan in town and begged him to return what they had taken.

Masked bandits carted off the entire Macewan family the very next day. Pete followed as best he could, but he lost them at the abandoned tower where the hoofprints of the horses simply vanished.

This is all that Pete knows. Now others have gone missing and he has seen the bandits on at least two other occasions. He tracked them and knows that the tower is key to their movements, and helps them remain hidden even during the day, though they seem mostly to attack during dusk and just before dawn.

The secret door is noticed on successful DC 16 Wisdom (Perception) check though a successful DC 15 Wisdom (Survival) check notes horse tracks that seem to proceed through the space where the door is located.

9-2. Staircase

A stone staircase descends into an underground cave hidden below the tower.

9-3 The Cave

A 10-foot-tall statue of a frog with bat-like wings dominates the center of the cavern. The frog's back is to the characters as they enter the grotto, and it is facing a large stone fly attached to the western wall. Menacing portcullises in the shape of demonic mouths full of fangs stand to the north and south of the cavern.

9-3A. The Frog God: This putrid statue is easily a thousand years old and is slick with an unknown slime. The statue weighs several tons and is immovable. A successful DC 15 Intelligence (Investigation) check notes that the altar rests upon a bed of small stone ball bearings that are seemingly locked in place. An inscription is written at the base of the large frog.

It requires *comprehend languages* to read the inscription, which states: *Two turns past as the sun doth rise, the fly does pass the Frog God's eyes.*

9-3B. The Fly: A stone fly roughly 2 feet in length is attached to the wall about 5 feet off the ground. A smooth circular groove in the wall follows the

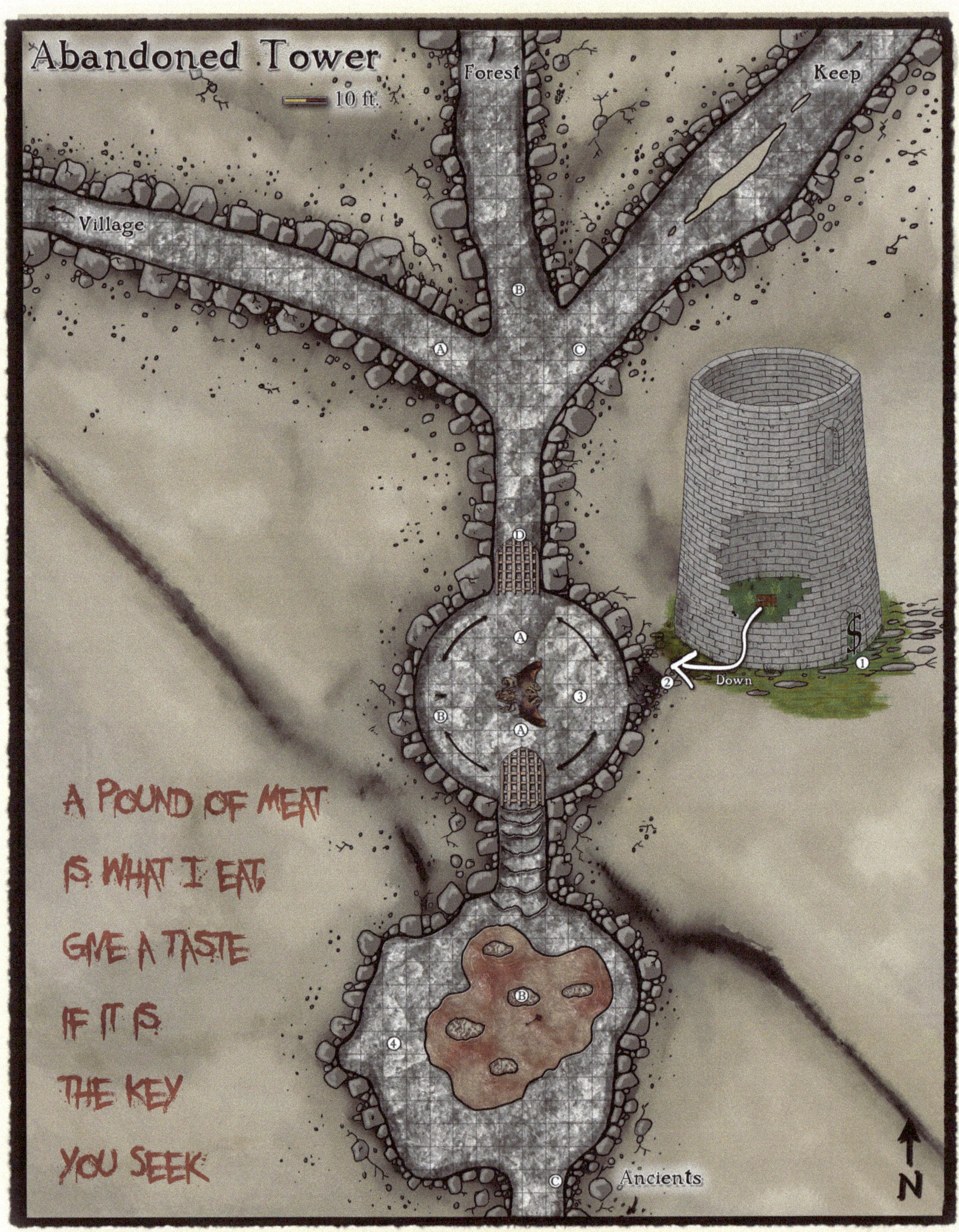
Abandoned Tower
10 ft.
Forest
Keep
Village
Down
A POUND OF MEAT
IS WHAT I EAT
GIVE A TASTE
IF IT IS
THE KEY
YOU SEEK
Ancients
N

circumference of the room. The fly can be unstuck with a successful DC 15 Strength check, though once moved it slides easily along the wall.

Sliding the fly around the frog twice counterclockwise and stopping it in front of one of the portcullises causes the frog statue to turn on its bearings toward the fly, and that portcullis immediately opens.

If the fly is moved into any other position, it triggers a *stinking cloud* that floods the room with noxious smelling gas. Any creature that starts its turn within the cloud of noxious gas must make a successful DC 15 Constitution saving throw or spend its action retching and reeling. The existence of the poison gas trap can be found if the frog statue is investigated and a successful DC 15 Intelligence (Arcana) check is made.

9-3C. Southern Portcullis: This portcullis leads to **Area 9-4A**. Opening the portcullis requires a successful DC 22 Strength check. There is no visible lock to open.

9-3D. Northern Portcullis: Once opened, this portcullis leads to the Turkey Foot (**Area 9-5**) Opening the portcullis requires a successful DC 22 Strength check. There is no visible lock to open.

9-4. Pool of the Key

The ceiling of this natural seeming cavern is high and domed. A strong stench of sweat and body odor billows up from the floor. A large, slimy pool resembling a bubbling blob of semi-liquefied flesh dominates this cavern.

9-4A. Entryway: A staircase roughly cut into the limestone descends to the cavern of the flesh pool. As characters approach, the sickly-sweet stench of wet, slowly souring meat assails their senses.

9-4B. The Flesh Pool: As the characters approach, the pool starts to bubble, forming claws, mouths, and eyes that stare at the characters as the mouths begin to speak:

A pound of meat is what I eat. Give me a taste if it is the key you seek. Ignore my request and we shall war, and you shall join me ever more.

The flesh pool is a slightly more intelligent **gibbering mouther** (with Intelligence 6) that has guarded the pathway to Croakers Hollow beneath Old Rest Cemetery for centuries since an ancient priest of Tsathogga enchanted it.

The gibbering mouther demands a pound of flesh from anyone who would pass through its lair. The pound (or more) of flesh that must be sacrificed to the gibbering mouther can be offered in a variety of ways. The offered flesh must be fresh, however, and weigh no less than 1 pound per character seeking passage. It may be the flesh of a freshly slaughtered animal or a slain enemy.

Alternately, characters may opt for cutting the required amount of flesh from their bodies. This option deals 1 point of Constitution damage and 1d6 slashing damage, all while carving a wound into themselves about the size of a decent steak.

Should the characters offer the gibbering mouther none of these delicacies, it becomes impatient and attacks. For a small party of 1st- to 2nd-level characters, this might result in a TPK. It may be wise to allow some form of lore check on behalf of party members to forewarn them of this possibility via some eldritch knowledge. Or not.

The brazen key that allows entrance to the shrine of the Qalb Al Nar beneath Old Rest lies within the folds of the gibbering mouther. The flesh pool ate a thief who made off with the key years ago, and other seekers have yet to uncover its location. The key may be uncovered by slaying the gibbering mouther, or by giving it its flesh treat. None who has attempted to pass this way since has survived the encounter. The mouther, for its part, long ago scared away any of the croakers attempting passage through its lair.

9-4C. The Runes on the Wall: The far side of the room contains a set of runes engraved into the wall and inlaid with silver. A successful DC 18 Intelligence (Arcana) check reveals that the runes contain a permanently

The Brazen Key

The brazen key unlocks a platform that raises the Qalb al Nar from the Cave of Flames into the Worship Dome without triggering the trap that spews fire into **Area 13** of the **Old Rest Dungeon**.

scribed spell that can be read once per day by an arcane caster. Upon reading, the caster can transmute a chunk of stone into a 9-pound chunk of "mystery meat" that can be cut from the stone and fed to the gibbering mouther. The mouth devours the strange pink flesh and politely slides to the side of the chamber to allow egress from the southern tunnels. Several holes line the wall next to the silvered script where others have used the ancient spell.

Once used, the runes require 24 hours to regenerate.

The passage beyond **Area 9-4C** leads to **Croaker Hollow** beneath **Old Rest Cemetery**.

9-5. The Turkey Foot

This tunnel not far from **Area 9-3D** branches off in three directions, with tunnels leading to the northwest, northeast, and north.

9-5A. Northwest Tunnel: This tunnel heads directly to the secret door in **Area 2** of the **Village of Lornedain Map**.

9-5B. The tunnel leads northward a mile and a half and ends in a natural shaft at the bottom of **Area 12-2A** of the **Worgs' Lair**.

9-5C. This tunnel leads a little over a mile to the dungeons beneath **Lornedain Keep (Area 15-28)**.

10. Abandoned Cave

This cave in a hill to the east of the worgs' lair about a half mile from Lornedain Keep shows signs of having recently been lived in. Ashes from a small fire, a dirty bedroll, and the leavings of a man are evident. Filthy Pete used this cave as a hideout in the past. There is a 1-in-6 chance that he is here.

11. Blood in the Woods

Characters investigating missing hunters or woodsmen find this clearing a half mile from the windmill. Characters diligently searching note several broken crocks, the moldy remnants of a wheel of cheese, dried blood, and a well-oiled wood axe hidden in the underbrush.

Two of the broken crocks smell strongly of over-proofed rum. The third smells of sugar and spices. The cheese was a variety popular to the area.

A successful DC 15 Wisdom (Survival) check reveals a set of large wolf (worg) tracks that lead north by northwest another quarter mile to the **Worgs' Lair (Area 12)** atop a wooded bluff.

As they investigate the area, they are set upon by 1d4 **worgs**. If overly wounded, the worgs set off for their lair. Any dead or unconscious characters are dragged off to the worgs' lair if possible.

12. The Worgs' Lair

This cave is home to a small pack of vicious worgs that only recently moved into the area and have thus far made off with a gang of unwary smugglers, a pair of woodcutters, and a handful of travelers that became lost in the woods north of the village. The worgs are intelligent and have spent time observing the folk of the farmland and the woodsmen gathering timber from the forest.

12-1. Entrance

The entrance to the worgs' lair is a crack in the rock face in the center of a wooded hill about a half mile from Lornedain Keep. Smugglers occupied the cave until the worg pack snuck into their hideout one night and devoured them.

The stench wafting from the cave entrance is harsh and charnel. A creature that enters the area must succeed on a DC 15 Constitution saving throw against poison or suffer nausea from the smell of decay, offal, and wet fur. Those failing their save have disadvantage to attack rolls and Stealth checks for the remainder of their time in the worgs' lair. Those that succeed are immune to the effects for 24 hours.

There is a 50% chance of a **worg** lying in wait not far from the entrance. The worgs may also move through the complex to get behind the party, with some of the animals taking out the rear guard while its kin challenge the front of the adventuring band.

12-2. Cavern of the Pit

This broad hall has a low roof, requiring characters taller than 5 feet to bend lest they hit their head. It is extremely dark and strewn with bones of deer, cattle, and humans.

12-2A: A natural pit in the southern end of the cavern is 10 feet across. A close observation of the pit notes iron handrails hammered into the wall of the of the pit. Descending the handholds leads to a miles-long tunnel that ends at **Area 9-5B** of the dungeon beneath the abandoned tower.

12-3. Smugglers' Lookout

This area once served as the lookout for the smugglers who used this cave. There is a 50% chance a **worg** is in this portion of the lair.

In the room are pieces of gear and broken bones that include an amulet of a wagon's wheel (indicating a member of the Wheelwrights Guild), an ironbound club, a rusted longsword, a crossbow, and 10 rusted crossbow bolts. Characters attempting to use *speak with dead* may converse with the broken skull, which reveals itself as Grandell Trane, a smuggler working with the Wheelwrights Guild who really doesn't know what happened to him.

12-4. Cave of the Stone

A large stone boulder sits along the northern wall. A pair of **worgs** lie on the floor of the cavern tearing apart a deer.

Etchings along the floor indicate that the stone has been moved frequently. A successful DC 14 Intelligence (Investigation) check looking for traps reveals that a heavy spring has been set and must be unlevered in order to avoid smashing whoever tries to lift the boulder out of the way. The trap can be disabled with a successful DC 15 Dexterity check with thieves' tools. If the boulder is moved without disarming the trap, the creature moving it must succeed on a DC 15 Dexterity saving throw, taking 14 (4d6) bludgeoning damage on a failed save and half as much on a successful one.

12-5. Freshwater Spring

Hidden behind the boulder is a deeper portion of the cavern complex that the smugglers used to hide their loot. The first hollow contains a pool formed by a natural spring. At the bottom of the pool are two dozen bottles of sparkling red wine. It has a fresh bouquet and is worth approximately 5 gp per bottle. The wooden crates that the wine was kept in are stacked along the southern wall.

12-6. Smugglers' Chests

This cave contains four, 2-foot-by-1-foot wooden chests. The first chest contains 400 sp, while the second contains 400 cp. The third contains 400 gp, and the fifth contains fine china plates apparently stolen from a noble house. The plates are monogrammed with a large "V" and were indeed intended for the Vinwood estate before they were stolen on the way from the porcelain potter.

12-7. This Weird Pool

This freshwater pool is fed by the same spring that feeds the pool in **Area 5**. With the smugglers missing for several weeks now, the pool has become home to a **water weird**[1].

12-8. Main Lair

The main worgs' lair is filled with bones and contains 1d4 **worgs** at any given time. A search of the remains finds physical evidence of the corpses of Kent Chenar and Thod Greae, as recognized by Thod's boots and Kent's armlet. The lumberjacks were heading back to their campsite with several jugs of rum, sarsaparilla, baloney, and wheels of cheese when they were surprised by the small pack of worgs. The beasts dragged them back to their lair to share with the rest of the pack.

There is no evidence of children's bones or missing children among the remains found in the cave. There is also no evidence of Herrell, Mareal, or Ferdinand among the bones and shredded clothes of the smugglers.

If the party returns to the woodsmen's camp (**Area 13**) and provide proof of Kent and Thod's deaths to the lumberjacks, the rest of the woodsmen

Ring of Qalb

This ring of iron and brass serves as a *ring of resistance* (fire) that is attuned to the fire elemental Qalb al Nar (literally the Heart of Nar, although he is also sometimes simply called "Sparque"). The ring does not necessarily control Qalb, but it makes the elemental friendly to the owner of the ring. The owner of the ring has a chance to entice Sparque's father, the fire elemental lord Nar al Nar, to leave his prison in the Ziggurat of Flame (**Chapter 28**). Currently, Sparque is transformed into a heart of flame in the Cave of Flames (**Area 14-14**). Only a character possessing the ring of Qalb can convince the elemental Sparque to transform from the heart-shaped fire to accompany the party.

The ring is the phylactery of Qalb al Nar's soul. So long as the ring exists, Qalb reforms within 24 hours of his defeat. The regenerated Qalb is always one HD weaker than it was before its defeat, however. If Qalb is ever reduced to zero hit dice, he truly dies, and the ring turns to dust. For example, if Sparque is destroyed in battle while he has 3 hit dice, he returns the next day as a 2 hit die elemental. If he is then defeated two more times before acquiring any new hit dice, he is lost forever.

Possibly among others, agents working for the following entities are seeking the ring: the Cult of the Burning One, the Basilica of the Lightbringer, Minions of Set, Jhedophar the Arch Lich, and the Phoenix Warriors.

reconsider their contract and withdraw from the barony. Returning the tails or furs of the worgs to Sheriff Bolen establishes that werewolves are not roaming the duchy eating cows and snatching children.

Scraps of a ledger indicate the general location of **Lambert's Lookout** (**Area 2**), a scheduled meeting time two days hence, and instructions to hire Lambert to raid a barge filled with wine, vinegar, and grain.

Three more wheelwright amulets are among the detritus scattered about the lair. If these are returned to the Wheelwrights' Guild in Bard's Gate, they net 20 gp each, but also place the characters under the surveillance of Duloth and his henchmen. Also found here are two shortswords, 2 working crossbows, 30 serviceable crossbow bolts, and 36 gp in various coins.

A pile of worg dung detects as magical should a *detect magic* spell be cast. Within the pile of dung is the *ring of Qalb*[2].

13. Foresters' Campsite

A group of foresters and woodcutters is camped about a mile northwest of Lornedain Keep. These woodsmen are working for Bayard (**scout**) via a contract with the baroness. The woodcutters have selected several areas in the forest for clearing to supply the lumber and cooking fire needs of the cities along the river.

Forestry work is always difficult and dangerous, and it is not uncommon to lose a lumberjack in the process. Lately, the foresters are on edge as two of their members are missing after making a run into town. Many of the foresters suspect that angry townsfolk had it out for the woodsmen after their own folk began disappearing.

Bayard leads the 13 or so foresters (**scout**) who cut lumber from the forest while they camp at the very edges of the barony. The foresters' work is hard, dangerous, and fraught with perils — such as having a druid turn them into a deer and set mountain lions on them, or simply having a large piece of timber flatten them like a pancake. Bayard's men occasionally make their way down to the village for supplies or to trade with farmers for milk, cheese, fresh bread, and other foodstuffs.

Bayard sent out an initial search party to look for his folk, but they were turned away by angry villagers who were dispersed by the sheriff and the baroness' soldiers. It was suggested at that point that Bayard handle any further shopping needs for his men personally, and that his woodsmen confine themselves to their camp until the case of the missing persons could be resolved. Bayard is close to filing a complaint with his logging company against the Lady Lornedain and the folk of her dominion for interference in his business.

The missing foresters are Kent Chenar and Thod Greae. Their remains, such as they are, are in the main lair of the worgs' den (**Area 12-8**). Bayard will pay 100 gp for proof of what happened to his men.

14. Old Rest Cemetery

Upon a hillock in the southern end of the barony is the ancient graveyard known by the locals as Old Rest Cemetery. The cemetery hasn't been used by the locals recently, as it is known for sinkholes and unsafe ground, and a generally unfriendly atmosphere. Long before the recent disappearances, it was rumored by the local folk to be a place where one could slip into a realm of shadows and be captured by the dark fey folk who would hold you for 100 years or worse.

The lords of Lornedain are said to maintain a crypt that serves as the burial ground for their long-departed ancestors, who grant them some ownership of the land.

Little do the folk of Lornedain know how close to the truth their superstitions about the place actually are. Old Rest was used as a burial site for thousands of years by ancient kingdoms long forgotten in the memories of humans and even dwarves. Prior even to their arrival upon the land, the mound was a site to an ancient culture that flourished and eventually faltered on its own.

The folk of the mound are now debased and twisted by unknown forces, their bodies accustomed to life among the roots and bones of the new societies that sprang up above them. They have stayed hidden from the eyes of surface folk for thousands of years, held prisoners in the remains of their old land, keepers of the hidden fire that boils at the root of their mound. Although their numbers have dwindled over time, they remain vigilant as always over the sanctum that burns at the pit of their lair.

The last person known to explore the deeper recesses of the mound in search of archaeological evidence of lost civilizations was Fritz Manfriend, a halfling archaeologist from Bard's Gate.

The cemetery is dangerous, not just because of the croakers residing underground. For every 10 minutes spent exploring among the tombs, roll 1d12 and consult the table below.

Old Rest Cemetery Dangers

1d12	Result
1	**Sinkhole:** Several of the graves now contain loose soil where croakers dug tunnels to get at the buried dead. Walking across one of the graves may cause a sinkhole to open beneath the feet of a random character. The sinkhole can be detected with a successful DC 14 Wisdom (Survival) check. If not noted, a creature that crosses the sinkhole must succeed on a DC 16 Dexterity saving throw or be swallowed up by the ground, sliding into **Area 14-3** or **14-4** while suffering 7 (2d6) bludgeoning damage.
2	**Loose tombstone:** A large obelisk or mausoleum wall collapses on a random character, dealing 7 (2d6) bludgeoning damage unless a successful DC 15 Dexterity saving throw is made. The loose or unsafe tombstone is noticed with a successful DC 14 Wisdom (Perception) check.
3	**Strange Blinding Mist:** A blinding mist rises from the ground. The mist is very warm, though not quite hot, and very damp. It reduces visibility to less than 5 feet. A creature walking in the area must succeed on a DC 14 Dexterity saving throw or tumble down the slopes of the hill, taking 3(1d6) bludgeoning damage.
4	**Landslide:** Ground loosened by the croakers' digging causes a portion of the hill to slide over the pathway. A successful DC 15 Dexterity saving throw must be made to avoid suffering 3 (1d6) bludgeoning damage and becoming restrained until an action is used to dig out from the soil.

1d12	Result
5	**Croakers (Night Time Only):** This is an encounter with 1d6 + 2 **croakers**[1] who attempt to drag one of the characters underground via one of the many tunnel sinkholes dug throughout the cemetery. Roll again if during the day.
6	**Baroness's Guard (Night Time Only):** Sir Hafbert set 1d4 of the baroness's **guards** here to kill any croakers that appear and to capture or chase away any villagers they find snooping around. The guards are not dressed in the tartan of the barony and instead wear black tabards with helms to obscure their faces. Treat as no encounter if rolled during the day.
7–12	No danger.

14-1. Crypt of the Lornedains

The largest and best maintained mausoleum still standing bears a bronze placard with the noble crest of the Barony of Lornedain upon it. The mausoleum is an ornate marble blockhouse with a peaked roof atop which stands an angel holding an upright flaming sword in its hand. The door to the mausoleum is a large bronze portal fastened with a large lock. The lock can be opened with a successful DC 17 Dexterity check with thieves' tools.

Beyond the door is a rectangular sepulcher with vaults lining the walls from floor to ceiling. Each vault bears the name of a lesser member of the baron's family. Five marble sarcophagi are placed in positions of importance in the center of the crypt. These include the baroness's father, grandmother, grandfather, and one labeled for her great grandfather, as well as an empty sarcophagus destined for the baroness herself.

Characters proficient in History, may note that the baroness's great grandfather Francois I was not in fact buried in Lornedain, but was buried somewhere in Mayfurrow at the site of a great battle.

A search of the room reveals several broken darts lying about the crypt. Their steel tips have not yet begun to rust.

Sarcophagus 1: Francois Lornedain: A close examination of Francois Lornedain I's sarcophagus reveals that it is built on sliding hinges. A successful DC 17 Intelligence (Investigation) check notes a carefully placed dart trap that fires spring-loaded darts from the walls at anyone attempting to move the lid without first depressing a button in the shape of a candle on the side of the crypt. If the trap is triggered, it releases a hail of darts in a 5 foot circle around the crypt. Each creature in the area must attempt a DC 16 Dexterity saving throw. Those failing take 2d4 piercing damage while those succeeding take half.

The sarcophagus opens to reveal an iron spiral staircase that descends into the darkness below (**Area 2**).

Sarcophagus 2: Francois Lornedian II: This sarcophagus is similarly trapped to release a hail of darts as Sarcophagus 1. The corpse inside is old and dry. A ceremonial set of plate armor covers the corpse. The armor is tooled in silver and gold with the crest of the family, a flaming key set inside a circle upon a kite-shaped shield enameled in a field of orange and black. The suit is worthless as armor, being only ceremonial.

Sarcophagus 3: Auguste Lornedain: The trap to this sarcophagus was apparently already sprung at some point in the past. Within the stone coffin is the fresher of the two male corpses. It is dressed in armor similar to that found in Sarcophagus 2. A search of the coffin reveals that the ring finger of the body has been broken off and lies at its side. A space where a ring was worn is missing.

Sarcophagus 4: Marie Aora Lornedain: This coffin is trapped similarly to the others. The body of a female baroness is adorned in a finely made dress of orange silk with a black fox stole and matching slippers. The back of the dress rotted over time, though the fox stole may be worth as much as 25 gp.

Sarcophagus 5: Baroness Aora Lornedain: This vault is empty, and the trap has not been set.

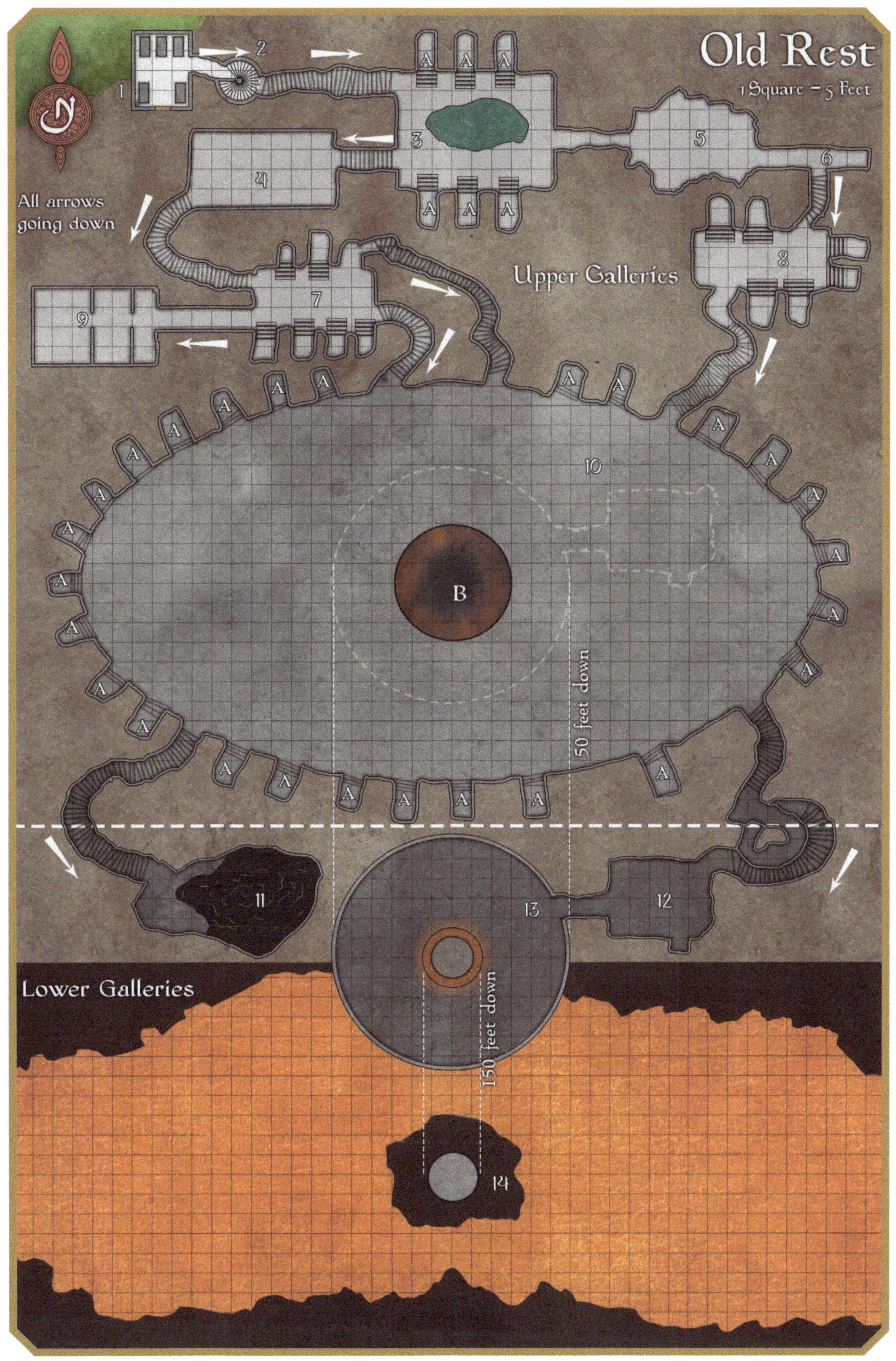

Old Rest
1 Square = 5 Feet
All arrows going down
Upper Galleries
1
2
3
4
5
6
7
8
9
10
11
12
13
14
B
50 feet down
150 feet down
Lower Galleries

14-2. The Stairwell

The stairwell below the crypt of the Lornedains is built in the fashion of an inverted tower descending downward into the depths. The stone is old and crumbling, giving a dwarf or someone with knowledge of engineering pause as they consider the dangers of this subterranean descent. The characters feel something soft and dusty brush across their faces as they descend. Light reveals a preponderance of cobwebs and thick dust.

As the characters descend, they are set upon by 1d4 **giant spiders** that dwell within the hollow shaft.

The floor is damp, though clear footprints in the dust of ages lead to a hole in the floor in the western wall. Rotting bodies of spiders are found here, as are three other rotting corpses. One is the corpse of a man in chain mail wearing a black tabard and carrying a sword. The other two are small and goblin-like, but with long clawed nails and strangely shaped skulls. Their bodies are basically husks, their fluids drained by the dog-sized spiders that dwell among the walls.

The hole in the floor leads downward to **Area 14-3**. The climb down requires rope to descend carefully for anyone without the ability to climb walls. Climbing without rope requires a successful DC 22 Strenth (Athletics) check. Spike marks in the wall indicate that others have descended this way using ropes in the past, though what happened to these ropes is unknown.

The Upper Galleries

The upper galleries are largely unused by the croakers who descended deeper into their lair after battles with the baroness's soldiers. They have laid several barriers and ambushes in these halls to alert them of any further incursions into their subterranean word, from herding beasts into the galleries to staking doors to impede progress.

14-3. Old Dwellings

This large hall appears to once have been part of some undercity area, for there are alcoves and apartments carved into the walls of what is obviously an expanded cave. Roots from trees have burst through the ceiling and some of the walls, giving the whole area a somewhat unsafe appearance. There are signs of a recent struggle here, as dried blood splatters are found along the pathways. Drag marks indicate that bodies were removed from the area and hauled off to the west.

14-3A. Alcoves: These six alcoves are strewn with small humanoid bones, as well as the bones of rats, large frogs, and other vermin.

14-3B. Scummy Waters: Muck and water appears to have drained into the base floor of the room, having brought with it an unholy smell. The croakers drove 1d4 **giant killer frogs**[1] into the dwellings. The frogs mostly feed on bats from **Area 14-5** or rats that make the mistake of passing through the chamber.

14-4. Smashed Catacombs.

This ancient catacomb is filled with hundreds of years' worth of broken coffins and piles of chewed-upon bones. The bones are organized into skulls, arms, legs, torsos, and pelvic regions, and are all piled about 10 feet high. A close examination of the bones reveals that most are fairly old, but all show cuts, as if from sharp tools, teeth, or claws that somehow stripped the flesh from the cadavers. A hole in the wall leads west.

Hidden among the refuse are a set of *bracers of defense*, a *+1 club*, and a *spell scroll* of *charm person*. They can be found with a successful DC 14 Wisdom (Perception) check.

14-5. The Bat Cave

This room squeaks with life when the door from **Area 14-3** opens. Shredding sanity with the echoing noise, the room is beset with a large **swarm of bats**.

Bat guano covers the floor of the room. Beneath the 6 or so inches of guano are the remains of shattered caskets and piles of bones organized like the ones found in **Area 14-4**. The bones also show tool marks.

A doorway to the north leads to **Area 14-6**.

14-6. Down or Out

A slippery natural stone staircase 30 feet down this tunnel descends to **Area 14-8**. Beyond the staircase, the tunnel continues northward to the **Abandoned Tower (Area 9)**.

14-7. Guard Gallery

This large gallery has several alcoves carved into the walls. Hiding within these alcoves are 1d2 + 2 **croakers**[1] who wait to ambush any who attempt further access to their underworld.

14-7A. Alcoves carved into the walls serve as nests for the croakers who dwell in the guard gallery. Two holes in the wall lead to ancient carved staircases. The first leads to **Area 14-9**. The second leads to the Grand Gallery (**Area 14-10**).

14-8. Guard Gallery

This gallery is identical to the one found in **Area 14-7** with the exception that a single staircase leaves this chamber and descends to **Area 14-10**. Here also are 1d2 + 2 **croakers**[1].

14-9. Old Study

This series of rooms must have once been some form of academic area, as evidenced by several broken clay tablets that lie about. Bits of primitive statuary also are in disarray here. A large statue of a frog-like beast similar to one found beneath the **Abandoned Tower** lies on its side here among other broken bits of statuary that are much less identifiable in form, though no less grotesque in execution.

Thorough exploration of the clay tablets reveals six unbroken tablets that act as spell scrolls. The spells contained are: *feather fall, greater invisibility, light, protection from evil and good, protection from energy,* and *sleep.* The tablets weigh 5 pounds each.

14-10. The Grand Gallery

This massive chamber located roughly 250 feet below the crypt of the Lornedains is the central hub to the croakers' lair. It is 190 feet across and 100 feet wide, with a 50-foot-high naturally domed ceiling of packed clay and limestone. The walls are lined with alcoves and dizzyingly narrow staircases that descend from the alcoves to the floor of the gallery. Other staircases lead deeper beneath the mound or up to areas closer to the surface. The room is dimly lit by a murky orange-pink light that glows from a large hole in the center of the floor.

The grand gallery is home to dozens of croakers who viciously guard their homeland from any surface invaders, making an assault on their lair unbelievably difficult. Passage through the area requires more stealth than the baroness's soldiers have managed to use so far.

Attempting to invade the gallery results in all surviving croakers moving to the area of assault as rapidly as possible to overwhelm the attackers. This means 1d8 + 13 **croakers**[1] from the gallery alone as well as any surviving croakers from **Areas 14-7, 14-8,** and **14-12** who arrive in 1d4 rounds. If more than half of their number is killed, the croakers flee, retreating if possible to the tunnels toward the abandoned tower, or they burrow into the loose earth in the upper galleries, returning when the invaders leave.

14-10A. Alcoves: The alcoves are home to 1d2 + 1 **croakers**[1]. Rat, frog, and bat bones and masses of wriggling grubs are piled on the floors of the alcoves, indicating a portion of the meals that make up a croaker's diet. Hidden among the refuse are small piles of 2d6 + 10 sp collected from the dead whose graves the croakers have long pillaged.

14-10B. Central Pit: This 30-foot wide opening in the floor of the gallery descends to **Area 14-13** 50 feet below.

Lower Galleries

The lower galleries are located deep beneath the Old Rest Cemetery and contain the **Submerged Cavern**, the **Worship Dome**, the **Cloister**, and the **Lair of Sparque the Qalb al Nar.**

14-11. Submerged Cavern

The stairway from **Area 14-10** is slick and requires a successful DC 16 Dexterity (Acrobatics) check to avoid tumbling headlong into the murky black pool found here. Falling down the stairs causes 3 (1d6) bludgeoning damage.

The pool of water is dank but warm, and the cavern is slightly steamy. The pool is home to 3 **giant killer frogs**[1] similar to the ones found in **Area 14-3**.

At the bottom of the silty, brackish waters are a *+1 warhammer* of ancient design and a disk-shaped bronze *+1 shield*, as well as a soapstone amulet carved in the shape of a crude humanoid figure.

14-12. Cloister of the Ancients

This room once served as the high priests' quarters for the guardians of the Qalb al Nar buried here deep in the earth. The room currently serves as the home of the **croaker chieftain**[1] (with AC 19 from *+1 chain shirt*) and his bodyguard (2 **croaker brutes**[1]), plus an additional 1d4 + 1 **croakers**[1] sitting among their piles of grubs and bones. The croaker chieftain wears a *+1 chain shirt* pilfered from the corpse of a buried hero.

A search of the room finds inscriptions on the wall written in the Ignan tongue that refer to a great veiled being bearing a flaming heart in his hands who arrived from afar. The being commanded the folk of the land to guard the heart with all their might, unto the last generation of their kin. The being granted great wealth and power to the folk, who used the power to create a vault below their city, setting a guard of trusted heroes around the vault. At last, the being entrusted their most powerful archmage with a burning key, and their wise king with a burning ring.

An alcove in the wall carved in the shape of a large key is painted and carved with bas-relief flames.

14-13. Worship Dome

This large hemisphere-shaped cathedral is hidden deep beneath the Old Rest Cemetery. A pinkish orange glow rises from a 15-foot-wide pit in the center of the room. A chimney-like hole in the 50-foot-high ceiling leads to **Area 14-10B** above.

Numerous charred skeletons lie half broken around the edges of the pit, their fate possibly a form of sacrifice as they either leapt or were hurled from the gallery.

Within 1d4 rounds, 4 of the charred **skeletons** rise from the ground and attack anyone within the room unless someone carries the *ring of Qalb*[2].

The skeletons attempt to push characters into the central pit, dropping them into the **Cave of Flames (Area 14-14)**.

The walls are inscribed in a script foreign to the lands and denote ancient symbols of worship from when the world was very young. A translation of the language, a combination of Ignan and dialects spoken in the Maighib, reads:

Here did we defend the gift of the wise one. Let they who are worthy bring forth the heart of fire from the confines of the earth that it may be joined with the flame of flames, and the truth can at last be told.

A keyhole is found in the wall on the opposite side of the room from the doorway. The key is found in the gibbering mouther in the Abandoned Tower (**Area 9-4B**). Picking the lock without the key requires a successful DC 20 Dexterity check with thieves' tools. The lock is trapped in such a way as to cause an explosion of hot gases from the Cave of Flames (**Area 14-14**) to fill the room. The trap can be detected with a successful DC 18 Intelligence (Investigation) check and disarmed with a successful DC 18 Dexteirty check with thieves' tools. If the trap is triggered, all creatures within the room must attempt a DC 18 Dexterity saving throw, taking 10 (3d6) fire damage on a failed save and half as much on a success.

The Key: If the key is used or the lock is picked and the trap disarmed successfully, the **Qalb al Nar**[1] rises upon a pedestal from within the Cave of Flames (**Area 14-14**).

The Qalb al Nar appears as a large beating heart made of pure fire that emits near-blinding light and heat. If a character possesses the *ring of Qalb*[2], the heart transforms into a small fire elemental that introduces itself as Sparque. The elemental addresses the bearer of the ring and asks if it is time to leave the Cave of Flames and return home.

Sparque, the Qalb Al Nar

Sparque is a unique fire elemental and the only begotten child of the Nar al Nar, Flame of Flames and King of the Fire Elementals who is currently held prisoner atop the Ziggurat of Fire in the City of Brass. Being born of the Heart of Fire, Qalb serves as an optional key to freeing the Nar al Nar from the Burning Ziggurat.

If Sparque joins the party, he "levels up" at a rate commensurate to that of the party, gaining one additional hit die for every level the average of the party gains. Sparque grows in size from Small, to Medium, to Large, to Huge with every 3 HD gained, to a maximum of "Huge" size.

If the party answers "yes," the elemental Sparque joins them as an intelligent henchman, similar to a familiar or animal companion of the bearer of the ring. If they answer "no," Sparque instead returns to its heart form and descends back on its pedestal into the Cave of Flames to await someone to return him to the City of Brass and reunite him with his father, the Nar al Nar.

If the party attacks Sparque, he fights back. If he is killed, he reforms within the Cave of Flames (**Area 14-14**) within 24 hours.

If the party did not find the *ring of Qalb*[2] in the worgs' lair but instead picked the lock to reveal the heart, Sparque creates a vision of the ring's current location, then disappears into the Cave of Flames. The ring's original location at the start of the adventure is in a pile of worg dung within the Worgs' Lair (**Area 12-8**).

The Scorched Gnome: Among the charred corpses along the side of the pit is the relatively fresh body of Fritz Manfriend. One half of his corpse is burned to ash, while the other is dried and well cooked. Fritz obviously failed his saving throw. His gear is likewise in shambles, though his body did protect most of his satchel. The bag contains maps showing the tunnel complex beneath Lornedain that leads to the keep, the jail, the Abandoned Tower, and Old Rest Cemetery, as well as maps of the galleries beneath Old Rest, and a contract for exploration stamped by the Authority of the High Sanctum of the Scroll, which grave robbers are known to use as a license to steal.

His pack also includes 2 *potions of invisibility*, 2 *potions of healing*, 1 set of thieves' tools, a *+1 shortsword*, a hand crossbow, 10 bolts, ten 10 gp gems and 50 gp sewn into a silk sash that is burned beyond worth.

14-14. Cave of Flames

The Cave of Flames is located 150 feet below the Worship Dome (**Area 14-13**). The cave is an opening in the earth where lava flows freely around an island of volcanic rock. In the center of the island is a pedestal that rises and lowers depending on the direction the key is turned in the Worship Dome. The cave is 250 feet across and is incredibly hot, dealing 7 (2d6) fire damage per round merely from the warmth of the air.

Anyone actually touching the lava flow beneath the pedestal is likely killed instantly, catching on fire and burning to cinders with all equipment.

Unless otherwise encountered, the **Qalb al Nar**[1] sits in the center of the pedestal among a wreath of flames, pulsing out its lonely heartbeat. The Qalb al Nar can be dealt with only by a character bearing the *ring of Qalb*[2]. Any character who enters the Cave of Flames without the ring sees images of the location of the ring in the Worgs' Lair (**Area 12-8**).

Completing the Old Rest Cemetery

If the characters survive the horrors of the croakers, undead, and the blazing heat, and leave the caverns with Sparque, allow them a day's rest before they are summoned to meet the baroness in her halls by Sheriff Bolen, Sir Hafbert, and a squad of 4 guardsmen from the keep. The characters can of course choose to go willingly, or fight, as characters are apt to do when they see a situation going south on them. If the characters fight, Bolen, Hafbert, and their men fight ably, attempting to subdue the characters so the baroness may question them before they are potentially traded to one of the nearest Brazen Spires.

If the characters entered Old Rest but were unable to free Sparque because they lacked the the key and the ring, they may end up revisiting the caves. Some croakers may have returned, but if the bats and frogs were cleared from the dungeon, it may be months before other critters replace them.

If the characters raided the cemetery at the behest of the baroness in search of any missing persons, they are expected to report their findings and return any treasures gathered back to her immediately. The *ring of Qalb*[2] was an heirloom of unknown value to the baroness. At the time of her father's passing, he was buried with it while she joined the foreign wars.

Information on the baroness and her inner circle are detailed in **Part II: Servants of the Burning One**.

The newly appointed court wizard Giza revealed the value of the ring to the baroness upon her return to Lornedain.

When Filthy Pete and Yeoman Macewan took the ring, it set about a chain of events that led to kidnappings, murder, and the enslavement of Baroness Aora's people in the name of the Cult of the Burning One.

Part II: Servants of the Burning One

The Lornedains have held the *ring of Qalb*[2] in their possession since they conquered the ancestors of the croakers and drove them underground hundreds of years ago. The importance of the ring was lost to subsequent generations that ended up inheriting the land, building a small but thriving barony in its place.

The Baroness Aora Lornedain rediscovered many of the ancient secrets of her homeland while crusading in the Maighib Desert. While there, the sorcerer Giza al Hofu (**theurgist**[1]) secretly converted her to the Cult of the Burning

One after her encounter with Emir Farphanes in the desert. Upon returning to her homeland, she was given a two-fold mission by Sheik Mutastir: find the *ring of Qalb*[2] and recover the Qalb al Nar for the Burning One. In return, more wishes and youth would be heaped upon her.

The Baroness and Her Confidants

Baroness Aora Lornedain

Baroness Aora Lornedain (**cult fanatic**) traveled extensively in overseas campaigns, bringing with her a contingent of her men-at-arms from her barony. Baroness Aora recently returned to Lornedain to take custody of her lands after completing her most recent fighting in Libynos. Those who have seen the lady note that she does not seem to have aged a day since the start of her travels, aside from a hardness in her eyes and a demeanor unknown before years of war and conquest.

Sir Hafbert

Sir Robere Hafbert (**footman**[1]) is a brute whose loyalty to Baroness Lornedain is absolute. He served as her bodyguard during her campaigns overseas. If Hafbert holds any jealousy over his lady's dealings with Giza al Hofu, he keeps it to himself. Hafbert is captain of the guard and overseer of the defenses of her estate. Hafbert is disliked by Sheriff Bolen, who in turn is somewhat intimidated by the boorish Hafbert. Rektor and Garault (**scouts** with Str 14 and longswords) serve as Hafbert's lieutenants and aides, orchestrating the kidnappings throughout the barony. The pair

of soldiers are treated little better than ruthless dogs. Rektor is small and trim with dark, far-seeking eyes, and a thick black moustache. Garault is broad and tall with a thick neck and piggy pink face topped with a shock of straw-colored hair. If encountered in the castle, there is a 50% chance that he is at least slightly drunk, which doesn't make him any less ill-tempered or violent.

Granwuld Sprague the Butler

Family servant to the Lornedains, Granwuld Sprague (**commoner**) is the husband of Lemitra and assists the lady with the ledgers and finances of her holdings. He is responsible for traveling to Bard's Gate to sell grain, hams, and salted fish. Nothing that goes on in the manor is beyond Granwuld's knowledge. That he has turned a blind eye to his lady's dealings with Giza al Hofu says much about his loyalty to the Lornedain clan.

Lemitra Sprague

Lemitra (**commoner**), the lady's handmaiden, is a sturdy matron in her middle years who keeps the confidence of Aora and does her bidding without question. Lemitra manages the day-to-day activities of the house, ruling over the housekeepers and cooks with an iron fist.

Giza al Hofu

Giza al Hofu (**theurgist**[1]) is Aora's court wizard, whom the lady brought back from her campaigns abroad. Giza is accomplished at the brewing of sleep draughts and is a great asset to Aora's current schemes. Giza is unknown to the populace of the village. He is a servant of the Cult of the Burning One in Numeda and has had a deep influence over the Lady Lornedain. Giza has 5 vials of *sleep potion*[2], 1 *potion of invisibility*, two *spell scrolls* of *magic missile*, and a *ring of protection*.

Navigating Part II

The second part of the adventure involves the character's interactions with the authorities of the barony and details the keep and its dungeons. Listed here are possibilities for how the second half of the adventure may play out, with suggestions on the baroness's actions and possible outcomes for the characters should things go awry.

Granwuld or Sheriff Bolen Offer Jobs

Through the course of the adventure, it is possible that the characters may take it on themselves to ride up to Lornedain Keep and seek an audience with the baroness. In this event, they are initially met by her butler, Granwuld Sprague, who directs them to speak with the sheriff about any sleuthing and suggests that the characters may in fact be interfering with the ongoing investigation.

Granwuld, like the sheriff, may also direct the characters to investigate any of the areas that they themselves have not yet explored. For example, if the characters have not gone in search of the wolves or to interrogate the woodsmen, he sends them in that general direction. If the characters have not gone looking for Filthy Pete, he sends them off to where he thinks the blacksmith may have last been seen. Ultimately, Granwuld seeks to keep the characters as far away from the baroness's operations as possible.

The Baroness Offers Reward
for a Job Well Done

If the characters find and slay Filthy Pete, or clear the worgs' den, they are invited to receive a bounty of 500 gp from the baroness herself, and the offer to investigate the area of the Old Rest Cemetery. She informs them that a ring buried with her beloved grandfather has been stolen, and she suspects a gnome from Bard's Gate who was seen nosing around the region. If the characters have already recovered the ring and are wearing it in her presence, she of course sees it and asks that it be returned.

Her hope is that the characters clear out the creatures dwelling under the cemetery or die trying. Once weakened by the characters, she is sure it will be an easy job for her troops to complete clearing the dungeon and finally take possession of the fire elemental Sparque.

Should they successfully return from Old Rest and bring her Sparque, the ring, or any of the things she desires, she gives them 1,000 gp. She also wishes them well and sends them on their way from the barony as heroes. The baroness may even make a big deal out of knighting the characters for their deeds, making them honorary knights of Lornedain.

Of course, her intent is to shuffle the characters off and away from their activities of searching for the missing persons. If the characters inquire about the missing villagers and indicate that they would seek to continue their quest, they are assured that the mystery is solved, and that no doubt the bodies were sunk in the river or devoured by worgs. If Pete was captured and turned over to the baroness, she informs the characters that he has confessed to the crimes and that she had Pete hung as a murderer. His body hangs next to her gate as a reminder to others that the punishment for murder in her holdings is death.

Things Don't Add Up

If the characters interrogated Filthy Pete or listened to his rantings during their encounter with him, they may have their own suspicions as to what is going on. Or they may have discovered that some of the clues don't add up, such as hoof prints or the width of wagon wheels at some of the crime scenes. They may have their own questions and concerns that they would like to further explore.

After speaking with the baroness, Sheriff Bolen, or Granwuld Sprague, and despite clearing out the worgs, defeating the pirates, or capturing or slaying Filthy Pete, the characters may still feel things still don't add up. They may decide to continue their explorations on their own. This ultimately leads them into direct conflict with the baroness and her forces.

Clearing Old Rest

Within a day of clearing out the Old Rest dungeon, the characters are approached by a contingent of the baroness's forces and invited to the keep for an audience. Should they refuse, they are attacked and hauled in chains before the baroness. If they come peaceably, they are offered a peaceable audience attended by the baroness and her lead henchmen.

The baroness may at this point suspect the characters of possessing the ring. This is confirmed if Sparque is with the characters. During this audience, the baroness demands her birthright ring in no uncertain terms but offers the characters her undying gratitude and 1,000 gp as a reward.

If the characters give up the ring, they are given their reward and escorted to the edge of the barony — without the ring and Sparque, of course.

Villagers soon stop the characters as they are leaving and ask where their missing family members are. The villagers appeal to the characters to keep looking for those who are missing.

If the characters refuse the baroness's deal, they are attacked by the baroness, Giza, Sir Hafbert, his goons, and whatever retinue of guards it takes to subdue the characters. If the characters are defeated (even reduced to zero and considered "dead"), they awaken days later, bound for the nearest Brazen Spire as a tribute to Sheik Mutastir. If the baroness is defeated, an exploration of her keep provides enough evidence to prove that she and her lackeys were behind the disappearances.

The Characters Get Suspicious

If the characters become unmanageable or suspicious of the baroness, or even hostile to the baroness and her retinue, their relations with the barony change from an unwelcome but acceptable annoyance to one of outright hostility. They are forbidden entry to the village and are openly hunted by guards and deputies of the barony. The baroness declares the characters are her enemies, as she did with Filthy Pete, and unleashes the full force of her troops to engage and apprehend them.

In order to halt the attacks, the characters may need to infiltrate the keep and defeat the baroness's command staff.

The Character Discover the Secret
Entrance to the Keep

It is quite possible that the characters find the secret passage below the tower and simply walk into the dungeon below the keep and there discover the few kidnapping victims who remain within the dungeon and other evidence to implicate the baroness. The characters may continue their infiltration of the keep and confront the baroness and her henchmen, or they may return the missing villagers to their families and explain to the villagers what their baroness has been up to. The second scenario results in torches and pitchforks as the villagers, farmers, Riverfolk, and even pirates who were once allied with the baroness rise up against her. You can play this scenario out as desired.

15. Lornedain Keep

At some point, the characters likely find themselves either as guests, prisoners, or invaders of Lornedain Keep. The keep is a rocky structure sitting on a lone flattened hilltop overlooking the farmland of the barony and is located roughly 1-1/4 miles from the village of Lornedain.

General Features

Doors: Locked unless otherwise noted. Opening them requires a successful DC 17 Dexterity check with thieves' tools or DC 19 Strength check. Lemitra and Granwuld Sprague have keys to all rooms save the baroness's personal bedchamber and Giza's study.

Walls and Parapet: The 25-foot-high walls are surrounded by a parapet that is 10 feet wide. The walls are straight, though the keep is old, and there are handholds here and there in the fieldstone stack of the outer walls. Climbing the walls requires a successful DC 18 Strength (Athletics) check.

Moat

A moat has been dug around the hill and is filled with runoff from rains, melting snow, and emptied bedpans of the keep's inhabitants. The moat is 30 feet across and about 20 feet deep. The servants' children are sometimes sent down to the moat to fish for smallmouth bass, bluegill, sunfish, and catfish that can be caught there in the summer months.

Drawbridge

The drawbridge has a simple stone guard post on the north side of the moat that houses a pair of guardsmen. The guards challenge any who approach the keep and ask them their business. If an armed party appears, they remain protected in their stone hut, leaving the drawbridge up until a larger party of defenders can ride down from the keep to assist. Granwuld or Sir Hafbert leads the larger group. Once the purpose of a visit is ascertained, the drawbridge is lowered and an armed force escorts guests into the keep.

Drive

This twisted gravel drive is well maintained and leads to the gatehouse at the top of the hill. It is wide enough for two riders to ride abreast or for one carriage bearing the baroness and her retainers to take a day trip to survey her lands. The hill is fairly steep, and those proceeding up it on foot do so at half their normal movement rate. Mounted riders progress at two-thirds their normal speed.

15-1. Main Gate

The gates of the keep are 10 feet wide and 20 feet tall. A blockhouse tower overlooks the road. A squad of guards is posted on the rooftop in **Area 15-2D** where the banner of Baroness Lornedain flies over the countryside.

15-2. Blockhouse

This tower stands at the nose of the keep, serving as the first line of defense against invaders approaching from the drive.

The main gate opens into a 30-foot-long hall having a 20-foot arched ceiling that is pocked with murder holes provided for guardsmen above to rain down arrows, hot sand, and other horrors.

15-2A. Gate Mechanism: This hall adjoins the hall beyond the gate and has an arrow slit piercing its outer wall, affording a view of the drive outside. A pair of **guards** is stationed here to operate the winch that opens and closes the gate into the keep, and the portcullis that leads to the courtyard (**Area 5**).

Another pair of arrow slits is located in the eastern wall, affording an opportunity for defenders in **Area 15-2A** to attack those in the entry hall with polearms. The door can be barred from the inside.

A stairwell on the north end leads to the second story of the tower (**Area 15-2C**).

15-2B. East Guardroom: This guardroom typically houses 2 **guards**. An arrow slit faces the drive, as well as two slits in the western wall that allow a view of the entry hall. A staircase in the north leads to **Area 15-2C**. A doorway off the main hall leads to the sergeant's quarters (**Area 15-4**). The door can be barred from the inside.

15-2C. Guard Barracks: The second floor of the tower serves as guard barracks for the baroness's men-at-arms. This 30-foot-by-30-foot room has 12 bunk beds to accommodate the warriors who serve at the keep. Three arrow slits line the south wall of the tower, accommodating a firing positions on the drive, and three arrow slits in the north wall offer positions on the inside courtyard.

Doors to the east and west lead out into the parapet of the wall surrounding the keep.

15-2D. Roof: The rooftop post is 30 feet by 30 feet and is patrolled by 4 **guards**. They are each armed with a longbow, 20 arrows, and a longsword, and wear ring mail. While standing behind the parapet they are afforded partial cover against enemies attacking from the ground.

The rooftop lookout gives a commanding view of the valley, and the watchmen are instructed to rotate posts watching the cardinal positions. The guards rotate every 6 hours with a fresh batch from the barracks.

Stones — each weighing between 20 and 30 pounds — are piled next to the parapet facing south. These can be hurled at attackers held at the gate and do 3 (1d6) bludgeoning damage to anyone they strike as they fall.

15-3. The Spragues' Quarters

The baroness may be the mistress and overseer of the subjects of Lornedain, but Granwuld Sprague and his wife rule the lives of the servants and staff of Lornedain Keep. This two-story apartment serves as their home.

15-3A. Main Quarters: A small table and chairs are here for the rare times when the Spragues dine by themselves. A cloak rack carries extra cloaks for rainy days, and a small barrel next to the door serves as a storage place for the walking sticks Granwuld is known to carry around to "manage" lazy servants. A walking stick with a silver head engraved with the crest of Lornedain is in the barrel. It was a gift from the baroness's father and is worth 25 gp.

15-3B. Bedchamber: The bedchamber has two dressers on the walls and a bed in the center. Small arrow slits overlook the southern end of the valley and north into the courtyard.

A locked wooden chest sits in one corner under a brass oil lamp. A banner of Lornedain adorns one wall, and a tapestry of a girl feeding an apple to a unicorn is on the other. The unicorn tapestry is worth 100 gp and weighs 10 pounds.

The chest can be unlocked with a successful DC 16 Dexterity check with thieves' tools. Inside it are 300 sp, 400 gp, and a ledger containing all of the current shipping and receiving documents for Granwuld's visits to the city. A second ledger is newer and shows deliveries of four crates weighing 250 pounds each to "the captain" on a date one week prior with a destination of "the boathouse." The records indicate that shipments were delivered to "money-grubbing pirates" off the river near Filthy Pete's home.

Note: *The boathouse is detailed in the adventure* **A Matter of Faith** *in the* **Bard's Gate** *sourcebook by* **Frog God Games***. Attacking the boathouse would be a foolish endeavor and likely results in the characters being imprisoned and shipped to Numeda.*

15-4. Sergeant's Quarters

This is the quarters of the keep's sergeant-at-arms (**guard**). He has a suit of studded leather for training purposes, and a weapon rack contains a boar spear, a spare longsword, a light crossbow, and 20 extra bolts. The sergeant has 200 gp in coins and a silver brooch with the crest of Lornedain on it worth 25 gp.

Parapet
11
10
9
8
7
6
5
3A
2
4
2A
2B
1
3B
2C
2D
15
14
12
13
18
17
16
22
20
19
21
23
A
B
C
G
30
F
D
E
26
23
24
28
25
29
27
Lornedain Keep
1 Square - 5 Feet

If the keep comes under attack, the sergeant moves to **Area 15-2B** or goes upstairs to organize defenses with reserves from **Area 15-2C**.

15-5. Courtyard

The courtyard in the center of the keep is used for training and is where the baroness's men take their meals during fair weather. A set of stairs in the western wall leads to the parapet above. The baroness's carriage is usually parked here. The carriage is finely made and worth 250 gp due to additional carving, tooling, brass inlays, and crystal lanterns. It seats four comfortably inside, with a seat for a driver and lookout atop.

A second larger wagon appears to be a general, over-road transport vehicle. Its tire width matches the wagon tread found near Filthy Pete's home.

15-6. Stables

The stables house eight light warhorses, and four carriage horses. Their tack and harness are all neatly hung and ready to be used. Typically, at least 4 light **warhorses** are in the stables at any given time, as well as Excelsior, the baroness's heavy **warhorse** (with 33 hit points).

Three stable hands (human **commoners**) sleep in the loft above the stables. They avoid combat if possible.

15-7. Keep Armorer

This is the smithy for the keep where arms and equipment are repaired, horseshoes are replaced, and any other items of need are managed on behalf of the baroness and her men-at-arms. The smith (**scout** with AC 16 from a chain shirt) also forges chains for the dungeon.

The forge contains 2 breastplates, 3 suits of ring mail, two longswords, and 4 spears, as well as the tips for 200 arrows, and a dozen horseshoes.

The armorer lives in a loft above his workspace, and has a small chest containing 35 gp, 60 sp, and a flask of honing oil.

Baron's Tower

This three-story found tower serves as the quarters for the baroness, and her guard and advisors, including Sir Hafbert and Giza al Hofu.

15-8. Main Hall

This hall at the base of the baron's tower is where the baroness and her chief advisors dine and have their important meetings. A set of double doors opens onto her throne room (**Area 15-11**) beyond. The doors are opened when the baroness takes audience with travelers or locals who come to make a proposal or ask for the baroness to intercede on a private or business manner. In the event of an assault on the keep, Hafbert's goons are moved from their lodging on the second story to stand guard in this hall.

15-9. Stairs to the Dungeon

This stairwell leads to the dungeon below the keep.

15-10. Kitchens

Lemitra Sprague (**commoner**) manages the kitchens and oversees the cooks. She makes sure food is prepared for the baroness and all the retainers who live within the keep. The stores in the cellar below the kitchen have enough supplies to stand a two-week siege of the keep and include potatoes, cured hams, and various pickled vegetables.

A ladder leads to two lofts above the kitchens that serve as homes for the keep's cooks and cleaning ladies (**commoners**). Each loft houses four servants.

15-11. Throne Room

A stone throne carved in the shape of a living flame occupies the far end of the room and a large stained-glass window depicting the crest of Lornedain rises from the back of the throne. The throne itself is cushioned with orange velvet. A stairwell in the southwest corner of the room leads upward to the trophy room (**Area 15-12**).

If the characters are invited to a meeting with the baroness, she sits on her throne, flanked by two guards and Granwuld Sprague (**commoner**), while Hafbert stands at the door.

15-12. Trophy Room

This room is decorated with the heads of various beasts slain on hunts, including the heads of beasts such as giraffes, apes, hyenas, and jackals that may appear foreign and odd to the characters. A single locked door is in the inner wall. Arrow slits point outward, affording a view of the courtyard and the parapet.

15-13. Stairwell

The stairwell leads to the sitting room (**Area 15-16**).

15-14. Rektor's Room

Rektor is a hawkeyed tracker who has campaigned with Sir Hafbert for several years. He is intensely loyal to Hafbert, and thus by proxy to Lady Aora as well. Rektor keeps his clothes, spare weapons, and armor here, and not much else. A search of Rektor's closet reveals a black suit of studded leather armor, a black leather mask, a black hooded cloak, and black boots that match the description provided by several witnesses throughout the barony of one of the strange riders.

A secret compartment in the dresser conceals a box containing 10 pp, 55 gp, 3 marble-sized opals worth 10 gp each, and a silver mirror. Finding the compartment requires a successful DC 16 Intelligence (Investigation) check.

His weapons rack contains a shortbow, 20 arrows, a shortsword, and a lasso.

If an alarm sounds, Rektor is located in the main hall (**Area 15-8**) or moves to a position in the windows of **Area 15-13** where he can put his bow to use.

15-15. Garault's Room

Garault's room is a general pigsty. His room is filled with empty wine and brandy bottles, scraps of meals, and soiled clothes. Garault is a big drinker when not on the job. Garault isn't a thinker, however, and he lets Sir Hafbert do the thinking for him. Garault is a doer, doing whatever Sir Hafbert orders him to. Once a month, Hafbert orders him out of his quarters so that cleaning ladies can come in and take care of the mess he leaves behind.

Among the trash in his room is a map to the port of Freegate and a ship named *The Sand Dancer* scribbled in barely legible text. This is found with a successful DC 14 Intelligence (Investigation) check.

A black cloak, mask, and surcoat hang in his closet, matching the description offered by witnesses of gear worn by dark riders.

15-16. Sitting Room

This room has a set of bookshelves and a southern view that affords good light. The masters of the keep use the room as a study and reading room. Stairs lead down to **Area 15-13**, and up to **Area 15-19**. A doorway on the north wall leads to **Area 15-18**, while a doorway to the west leads to **Area 15-17**.

A search of the books reveals a book titled *Flame of Lornedain*. This is a history book that tells of how the Lornedain clan came to the land and conquered it from a set of cannibalistic creatures of the night. In a great battle, Francois Lornedain slew the leader of the cannibals and took its ring of copper and iron. The following day, the creatures departed the land never to be seen again.

Further tales feature frequent times when the Lornedains participated in wars across the sea on the continent of Libynos and how they often came back burdened with riches that quickly vanished before the barony could use the coin to prosper and grow.

15-17. Sir Hafbert's Room

Sir Hafbert's corner tower room is small but tidy. The banner of Lornedain hangs proudly on the wall. His wardrobe holds a black cloak, mask, and surcoat similar to those described by witnesses of the highwaymen. Upon his nightstand is a gold locket worth 25 gp that opens to reveal a likeness of the baroness.

He keeps an iron chest at the foot of his bed that contains 250 gp, 2 *potions of healing*, a flask of Derendian brandy worth 25 gp, a silver knife, and a cat-o'-nine tails (as whip). A ledger indicates that Hafbert, Rektor,

Garault, and Giza were forced to retreat from an attempt to retrieve "the ring" from Old Rest Cemetery after "maggot eaters" were roused and slew six of their men at arms.

In the event of an attack, Hafbert takes command of forces guarding the keep, running operations from **Area 15-2C** or **Area 15-8**, depending on how much time he has to make it to his position.

15-18. Giza al Hofu's Room

This large room takes up half of the tower floor. It serves as Giza al Hofu's private bedroom, though he spends the majority of his time entertaining the baroness, much to the pain of Sir Hafbert.

Giza's wardrobe contains a set of black robes, a facemask, hose, boots, and gloves similar to those described by witnesses who mentioned highwaymen or bandits.

Giza's valuables are hidden in the laboratory he established for himself atop the tower.

If the fortress is attacked, he is found at the baroness' side. If things go south for the bad guys, Giza does whatever he can do to return to Sheik Mustatir in Numeda. Typically, the plan involves Lady Aora and Giza taking the secret path from the dungeons along with whatever treasure they can carry to Freegate or beyond

15-19. Third-Floor Landing

Two **guards** are posted here to guard the mistress's quarters. These guards never leave their post and are rotated with guards from elsewhere in the fortress every six hours.

A painting of a warrior in plate armor battling hordes of short, heavily clawed creatures with pale flesh hangs on the wall. The warrior is lit by the sun so that his flashing sword appears infused with fire. The painting is worth 300 gp to a collector.

15-20. Baroness Aora Lornedain's Room

This sumptuous room just below the crown of the tower serves as the baroness's private bedchamber. A large bed, a dresser, and a writing desk fill the room.

The bedclothes are satin and would fetch 200 gp on the open market. A large silver mirror worth 100 gp hangs on the wall opposite the bed. A stained-glass doorway to the north featuring double images of the crest of Lornedain opens to the baron's balcony (**Area 15-22**). A door in the southeast corner of the room leads to the baroness's private toilet.

15-21. Baroness's Boudoir

The room serves as boudoir and dressing room for the baroness. Among her gowns and dresses are her suit of armor, shield, and weapons when she is not girded for battle.

Five gowns here are worth 200 gp each, as they are stitched with golden thread and embroidered with pearls, garnets, and topaz. The dresses favor silks of yellow, orange, red, and black.

Five daily wear items are worth 75 gp each and are complete outfits from boots to collar. These include martial training outfits, riding gear, and hunting outfits.

A locked iron chest holds the baroness's treasury with which she pays her retainers and henchmen. The lock is trapped with a poison gas trap. Finding the trap requires a successful DC 16 Intelligence (Investigation) check. It can be disarmed with a successful DC 17 Dexterity check with thieves' tools. Opening the lock requires a successful DC 17 Dexterity check with thieves' tools or DC 18 Strength check. If the chest is opened with disarming the trap, gas is released in a 10-foot radius. Anyone within the area who does not succeed on a DC 17 Constitution saving throw takes 10 (3d6) poison damage.

Inside the chest are 3,500 gp, 100 pp, 4 emeralds worth 200 gp each, 2 rubies worth 500 gp each, 3 gold necklaces worth 100 gp each, 2 *potions of healing*, a *spell scroll* of *nondetection*, a *spell scroll* of *silence*, a *potion of invisibility*, a map of Kirtius' location, and several documents written in Ignan.

A second map details suggested locations for new Brazen Spires to be erected in Akados, with the first placed in Freegate, another in Bard's Gate, etc. A diagram showing a slender tower surrounded by divine beings and topped with a torch-like flame is also depicted.

Documents further indicate that the baroness and her henchmen had been taking captives of travelers "no one would miss" for some time, and only recently have they begun to snatch locals who had seen or knew too much, such as the family of Yeoman Macewan.

15-22. Balcony

This broad balcony overlooks the forest to the north of the keep.

15-23. Giza's Laboratory

This round laboratory atop the tower serves as the hiding place for Giza's magical and alchemical equipment. It is where he crafts the sleep draughts he uses to knock out the folk that get packaged off to construct a new Brazen Spire, or those sent to an existing spire.

The laboratory has a complete alchemical setup worth 500 gp, 3 flasks of acid, 2 *potions of sleep*, ingredients to make 5 more potions of sleep, and Giza's spellbooks containing ten 1st-level and four 2nd-level spells of your choice.

Documents in his laboratory describe an upcoming war of fire that will kick off shortly after the establishment of the caliphate of flames. No real indication of what either of these things is can be construed from the writings, as they are written in the gibbering thoughts of a true believer.

Lornedain Keep Dungeon

Below the keep is the dungeon that is used as a hidden base by the baroness's henchmen to go forth and capture prisoners who are then turned over to Sheik Mutastir at the Burning Spire of Freegate. The dungeon can be accessed via the path from the **Abandoned Tower (Area 9-5C)**, or via the staircase from **Area 15-9**.

Standard Features

Torches: A sconce in the wall every 20 feet holds a torch enchanted with *continual flame*.

Doors and Gates: As with all other doors and gates in the keep, they are locked unless otherwise noted. Opening them requires a successful DC 17 Dexterity check with thieves' tools or DC 20 Strength check.

15-23. Stairs Down

This staircase leads down from **Area 15-9** above.

15-24. Privy

This toilet is used by those castle staff allowed access to the dungeons. There are four seats.

15-25. Storage

Wine, ale, pickles, pickled fish, cured ham, pickled eggs, and hardtack are stored here along with several crates are partially filled with straw. The crates are roughly 3 to 4 feet square. They have holes drilled in the tops and are labeled "live animals" and they appear to have not been used.

There are 200 bottles of wine worth 10 gp each and 3 ale tuns with 50 gallons of ale each.

15-26. Shrine of the Burning One

Once a shrine to Arden, the area was re-consecrated by Aora Lornedain in the name of the Burning One, called the Veiled God and the Fire of Truth by his followers. The shrine now serves as a de facto torture chamber. A rack for pokers, heated tongs, and other instruments of heat-based torture stands along the western wall.

The room is filled with the undeniable smell of roasted flesh. A 7-foot-wide-by-3-foot-high altar stands at the north end of the room. The top of the altar burns with constant flame, much like that of a barbecue. Charred human bones rest upon a wrought-iron rack that hangs over the burning altar. The rack is slick and still dripping with the fat of a recent sacrifice. Small bites of his charred flesh have been removed along his legs and arms.

Brightly colored murals of a tall, veiled figure with flesh like molten bronze sitting atop a throne over a city in a dish have been painstakingly painted over the original artwork on the walls of the shrine. The old statues of the ancient sun god have been tossed aside and broken, though his brazen symbol has been repurposed in honor of the new fire lord.

The corpse atop the altar is that of Leon Anton, who fought his captors and was sacrificed in front of the other prisoners as a warning. This knowledge could be gleaned via a *speak with dead* spell.

A **fire drake**[1], a gift from Emir Farphanes, dwells within the coals atop the altar. It generally leaves others alone unless it is disturbed.

15-27. Underground Stables

Five black light **warhorses** are kept in this stable and are tended by the guardsmen in the dungeon.

15-28. Portcullis Gate

The portcullis gate is made of wrought iron and wood and is very heavy, requiring a successful DC 18 Strength check Strength check to lift. The winch to move the gate is operated by a sentry **guard** posted on the keep side of the gate at all times. The sentry is one of Sir Hafbert's goons.

The hallway beyond the gate extends into a tunnel that leads for miles to **Area 9-5C** of the **Abandoned Tower Dungeon**.

15-29. Dungeon Guardroom

The guardroom has two bunkbeds and a regular bed that is used by an officer known only as the "Boss" (**captain**[1]) who wears a hooded mask to hide his identity from his captives. Other hoods hang on hooks just inside the door are donned by guardsmen before going in to feed the prisoners in **Area 15-30**.

A winch on the wall opens and lowers the portcullis leading to **Areas 15-29** and **15-30**.

The 2 **guards** are roused at the sound of the war horn or by any other commotion they could realistically hear coming from the halls.

15-30. Prison

This circular room holds seven cells. The cell doors are a simple affair of wrought-iron bound oak doors on heavy hinges, barred from the outside with a barred window slot to peer in at the folk held hostage within their 5-foot-by-7-foot alcoves. The alcove floors are strewn with straw, and each alcove contains a bucket for waste and a bucket for food.

15-30A: This cell is occupied by Fergie Laroushe, (**commoner**) who was taken along the bank of the river after seeing black riders and a wagon loading crates onto Captain Lambert's barge, which he recognized. He has no idea where he is, only that he has seen horrible things. His eyesight is currently poor from being held in the dark. He has been well fed, however.

15-30B: This cell is occupied by Marie Larousche, (**commoner**) Fergie's sister. Marie is psychologically scarred from seeing a ritual where folk in red-and-black garb burned Leon Anton. She was further terrorized when the guards hauled her good friend Simone Dubois away in chains a few days ago. He has not returned.

15-30C: This cell holds Guillom Ferdinand, (**commoner**). He watched from his cell as Herrell and Mareal Porter, and Denton Wayne were hauled off the same day that Simone Dubois was taken away. Guillom was terrorized with the others and witnessed the torture and immolation of Leon Anton.

15-30E: Empty cell. A search of the cell finds writings on the wall in the script of Yeoman Jon Macewan.

I am held prisoner by the baroness of Lornedain, for I recognized her voice even under the red silken hood she wore. It was Hafbert and his men who raided our home. We were drugged by the wizard Giza and awoke in darkness. I fear we do not have long ...

15-30F: Empty Cell

15-30G: This cell holds Emile Anton, (**commoner**) who is nearly catatonic after watching the baroness and Giza burn his father alive.

Tying Up Loose Ends

The locations and temperaments of the baroness and her minions has been left largely to your discretion for this adventure. They should act as their intelligence dictates. The baroness and Giza for their parts are true believers in the Cult of the Burning One. They are smart enough to attempt to save their own lives.

Sir Hafbert is cruel and callous, and completely in love with his baroness. He and his men die at her command if necessary. As the GM, you may notice in the read-through of this adventure that several of the victims of the baroness's machinations are no longer in the Duchy of Lornedain. Some, sadly, have already been pounded into *living brass* to facilitate the construction of new Burning Spires across the cities of Akados. Others may already be on their way to the City of Brass or are being held for transport to the city where they are to become one with the Great Ziggurat.

Enough clues have been left behind during the adventure to lead the characters to Freegate or another city of your choice that has a newly minted Brazen Spire built within it. Likely, the characters found the name of *The Sand Dancer* in some documents or pieces of information they collected. They are definitely aware of a supernatural invasion plot that involves kidnappings, missing persons, and a cult whose origins are in far-off Numeda.

Family members of the missing beg the characters to pursue all leads and attempt to rescue any that they can. Those who are not invested in this endeavor may still find themselves at the mercy of the Cult of the Burning One in the near future. Their meddling in Lornedain has drawn the interest of Sheik Mutastir, who no doubt sends assassins to deal with those pesky characters. If the baroness and Giza survive the attacks against them, incidents of interference on behalf of the Cult of the Burning One are doubled.

But What About the Keep?

Within a week, members of the Lyreguard come to Lornedain and take custody of the keep, thanking the characters for their handling of the matter. The ownership of the barony will itself turn over to the suzerainty and the land is likely to be turned over to distant heirs. The characters are given another 500 gp as a reward for their deeds.

Offer the characters an additional 500 to 1,000 experience point reward for completing the adventure.

The adventure continues in ***The Brazen Spire***.

<h1 align="center">Chapter 4
Freegate: The Brazen Spire</h1>

Freegate: The Brazen Spire is an adventure for 4–6 characters of 3rd to 5th level. The adventure takes place in a city setting but is designed as a raid against the influence of the Cult of the Burning One, and possibly as a rescue mission. It requires the skills of a trap finder, arcane and divine spellcasters, and a plethora of warriors for absorbing damage and dealing out vengeance.

The main locations are shown on the map ***Freegate City***, and details are provided in maps for ***22. Safe house of Tegman Zekii***, ***The Sand Dancer***, and ***Brazen Spire***.

Background

The spires of the Burning One have spread across the Lost Lands from their initial appearance in Numeda like a prairie fire spread by a cloud of cinders. Rumors abound about the new Cult of the Burning One, led by those chosen by the Sultan, the hariphs, and guarded by the sacred order of the khalit, a powerful cult of elite warriors. It is difficult to separate rumor from truth as the cult's rituals and taboos remain secret to all save those who convert to their cause. One thing is certain: many who have been exposed to the cult's teachings bear witness to the miracles they have seen granted at the hand of the viziers of the Burning Spires.

New temples to the Burning One go up in as little as a day owing to the great sorcery used to raise them. They are typically built within the poorest parts of a city or in close proximity to the disenfranchised of a given land. The burnished brass spires gleam like massive arcane torches over the cities where they sprout. The Brazen Spires' open doors offer food and purpose to those undesirables who for many years have been offered the boot or worse at the hands of their fellow citizens.

The rise of the Brazen Spires and the burgeoning Cult of the Burning One are raising concerns among local priesthoods and nobles who fear the rapid spread of the new religion.

Adventure Summary

The adventure takes place in the port of Freegate or its environs, with the majority of the adventure played out in a tenement apartment on the south side of the wharf area and in the Brazen Spire itself. If played as part of an ongoing City of Brass campaign, the characters' experiences in Lornedain lead them in pursuit of kidnapped villagers. The characters quickly learn of a cult rising among the denizens of the Foreign Quarter near the city's poorest neighborhoods. The city's praetors seem oblivious to the threat, and citizens are becoming agitated.

Several of the city's officials recently have been ensnared by a *mirror of duplication*[2] that trapped them and produced doubles under the control of Sheik Mutastir, the leading hariph of the Brazen Spire.

The characters are told of missing persons and an influx of strangers not accounted for by the amount of ship traffic to the area. The characters are soon enlisted in a secret effort to find the truth behind the masters of the Brazen Spire and to determine if they are a threat or merely the rise of a new flash-in-the-pan religious movement that the city is all too familiar with.

Through the course of the adventure, the characters may investigate the ship *The Sand Dancer* and infiltrate the newly erected Brazen Spire that has appeared in the city. Characters eventually meet Sheik Mutastir, the nefarious **burning dervish**[1] who leads the Cult of the Burning One on behalf of the sultan of efreet. Mutastir has not forgotten the adventurers who thwarted his minions in the tiny village of Lornedain.

Part 1. Freegate

Freegate is a major port city with a population of about 15,000. Its governor is Praetor Axator Polides, a human Hyperborean. Along with the governor, there are several city leaders that the characters may want to talk to.

Peoples of Freegate

The following NPCs are found in and around Freegate. Some of them have been replaced by fakes created by Shiek Mutastir's *mirror of duplication*[2]

Praetor Axator Polides

Praetor Axator Polides (**captain**[1]) is from the Polides noble family, the most powerful of the nobles descended from the ancient stock. Axator is a strongly built man in his fifties, but with the stride and bearing of a man half his age. He is typically adorned in a toga of state. He wears silver governor's laurels that highlight the streaks of silver that run through his curly hair and pointed black beard.

As a shrewd diplomat, Axator recognizes the authority of Bard's Gate and the dominance of the Duchy of Waymarch, but he is also aware of the ancient traditions and martial pride of his galley fleet and phalanx of battle-ready hoplites.

Currently, Axator seems indisposed or incapable of handling the growth of the cult associated with the Brazen Spire that has appeared in his city. He is in fact a double produced by Sheik Mutastir's *mirror of duplication*[2]. To avoid having to expend too much energy, the sheik has arranged for the double to spend most of its time in a sick bed.

Praetor Machisus Lycurtay

Commander of the Freegate galleys, Praetor Machisus Lycurtay (**eldritch archer**[1]) is a leather-skinned mariner with stone gray hair and matching eyes. Machisus honed his skills at ship-to-ship combat over the years by battling pirates that harry the trade routes leading to the city. Although his fleet is typically coastal in nature, his ships are a comforting sight to merchant mariners who see their striped sails.

Machisus has some expertise as a wizard, which has helped his galleys remain dangerous against more modern and better designed craft.

Praetor Machisus was at the Lighthouse when Sheik Mutastir trapped his compatriots.

Machisus knows something is up and may be willing to enlist the aid of the party in determining what is going on with his fellow praetors. He wants to know why they would so lightly allow a new religion to spring up within the confines of the city.

Praetor Halixes Pemmanon

Grand General of the Phalanx of Apollon, Praetor Halixes Pemmanon is a hardened **veteran** of many armed conflicts and leader of the elite phalanx of Freegate. Her phalanx is assisted by mages and war priests who protect the phalanx from magical assaults.

The Pemmanon family traditionally manages the Agoge of Apollon on the banks of the Talamerin River. Several members of their family have previously served as praetors of the city.

Praetor Pemmanon has also been duplicated by the Sheik's *mirror*. The double is vague and dismissive, and short-tempered.

Zarius Medius

Zarius Medius (**arcanist**[1]), the High Magus of Freegate, sits on the governors' council and is a member of the Dominion Arcane. The Medius family is another of the great noble houses and is politically aligned to the Polides family through marriage and financial alliances. Currently, High Magus Zarius is missing, a victim trapped in Sheik Mutastir's *mirror of duplication*[2]. The magic-user's duplicate was recalled and destroyed after it served Sheik Mutastir's purposes.

Antolychus Ermes and the Children of Mirkeer

The local thieves' guild is interested in the goings on of the Brazen Spire, seeing a money-making opportunity. They are afraid religious zealotry will cause the opportunity to "go up in smoke." Some of their members warn of the customs of Libynos and are afraid that if the cult takes too strong a hold in the city, punishments could go horribly awry. Most members of the Children of Mirkeer much prefer a few months in Freegate prison to the thought of having their limbs lopped off with a burning sword.

Guildmaster Antolychus Ermes (**assassin**) is a youthful-looking thief who presumes to run a "legitimate shipping business" and owns a warehouse on the north side of the docks.

Locations in Freegate

Most citizens live in four- to seven-story apartments with two bedrooms and a common living area. The typical apartment building contains four to six apartments with the larger rooms on the ground floor and smaller rooms on the upper stories. Construction ranges from raw or fired brick to marble and stone.

1. Arena of Apollon

Located just outside of town, the arena is an immense structure nearly the size of the Praetors' Acropolis with seats for 4,000 spectators. Although bloodsport is not technically illegal in the region, it has fallen into disfavor due largely to pressures from Bard's Gate. Most of the fights taking place here are of the bare-knuckle variety.

2. Walls of Apollon

The city walls are 30 feet tall and 10 feet wide. Hoplites armed with javelins patrol the walls. Towers with a mounted ballista flank each of the city's three gates and house 30 **hoplites**[1] each. The three remaining guard towers house 20 hoplites[1] armed with javelins who patrol the walls to keep an eye out for trouble within and without the city.

3. The Agoge of Apollon

The Agoge of Apollon rests along the shores of the Talamerin River. It is divided into barracks of 200 **hoplites**[1] who train within the confines of its walled campus under the tutelage of Praetor Halixis Pemmanon, currently a double (as **veteran**).

4. Praetors' Acropolis

The north side of the Talamerin River is a large walled structure that stands atop the tallest hill within the city walls. Within this heavily defended castle are the Governor's Palace and the Bank of Sefagreth.

The walls and gate are manned by 20 **guards** armed with bows.

Governor's Palace

This fortress complex on the north side of the Praetors' Acropolis is the estate of Axator Polides (as **captain**[1]), the current governor. Two squads of 20 **hoplites**[1] each stationed at the Governor's Palace serve as guards to the praetor. They are selected from the ranks of the governor's own noble house.

Bank of Sefagreth

Part bank vault, part temple of trade, the Bank of Sefagreth stands within the governor's compound within its own walled fortress. The vaults of the Bank of Sefagreth are said to extend many hundred feet below the ground and are said to be encased in iron and lead. With the triple guard of the city, the keep, and the temple guard, the bank's defenses are considered some of the best in the region, with wealthy landowners from Bard's Gate keeping a portion of their wealth hidden here in case of emergency. The actual amount of coins and valuables is a closely guarded secret so as not to draw the attention of any greedy dragons.

Beyond the bank lobby is the Temple of Sefagreth, which is administered by Memes Trapezitis (**emeritus chaplain**[1]) and his 10 **acolytes**. There are normally 20 bank **guards** on duty at any time.

7. Tower of Zarius Medius

This tower next to the governor's palace is the home and center of study for Zarius the High Magus and his apprentices. The Medius estate is located on the same walled grounds as the tower, though Zarius conducts his wizard business separately from that of his family's affairs. The base of his tower serves as a shrine to Belon the Wise and is where Zarius' 4 **apprentice mages**[1] offer training to other wizards after the teachings of the traveling god.

Instruction in the arts is offered for a fee of 200 gp per spell level of spell learned, though they offer training only in spells of up to 2nd level. They also sell potions and scrolls of 1st- and 2nd-level for 10% over the standard fee. It's left to your discretion whether to limit access to such items.

Zarius himself has apparently been missing since around the time the spire arrived. Nobody knows for sure what that is all about, but he evidently was present when the visitors came to the city with their strange chest of treasures. Zarius has also been trapped by Sheik Mutastir. His double was used briefly before being dismissed.

8. Forum

The forum is an open-air amphitheater where folk gather to discuss current events, take part in philosophical debates, and vote on new praetors. Current discussion covers the quick construction of the brass tower within sight of the forum itself.

9. Shrine of Mithras

This shrine is attached to the northwest wing of the Agoge of Apollon, with its entrance facing the street so that visitors can pay homage to Mithras.

It is tended by Cleomine (**priest**), who offers his blessings to warriors and those set to face battle on behalf of righteousness.

10. Gardens of Zadastha

This garden next to the Agoge of Apollon stands in direct contrast to the warlike training endured by the phalanxes that practice behind the Apollon's martial walls. The garden encompasses several city blocks and has its own small lake. Next to the lake is the Temple of Zadastha. Temple acolytes wander the gardens, offering their succor to those in search of love.

11. Temple of Zadastha

The marble bathhouse dedicated to the goddess of love is enriched with gilt inlay and features bronze statues of the various guises of Zadastha, including passionate love, enduring love, eternal love, and unconditional love. The statues strike curious poses around the men's, women's, and unisex pools and grottos within the structure.

The temple is tended by 20 **acolytes**, male and female members of the primary civilized races.

The high priest of the temple is Briseis Minet (**preacher**[1]). Her temple offers *potions of healing* and *scrolls of protection from evil and good* for 15% over standard prices.

To Triereme
N
Freegate City
800 ft.

12. Port of Apollon

This extensive dock includes the navy pier that sits on the protected outer banks, as well as trade docks that pull right into the heart of the city itself. A small fortress sits on the outer docks overlooking the sea wall. The southern portion of the port is lined with warehouses for the storage and portage of goods into and out of the city, with fishermen occupying the docks on the northern end of the port, trading their wares to the folk at the Sea Market.

13. Wharf

Merchant traders and fishing fleets use this series of docks built on the inner part of the shielded harbor. The wharf is lined with rental tenements used by sailors, as well as dive bars and flophouse brothels. The wharf is considered relatively dangerous and seedy by locals, though they ignore its more undesirable aspects in favor of the splendors that the Sea Market offers.

14. Sea Market

This open-air market stands in the center of the harbor on an artificial peninsula. Citizens of Freegate come here to trade directly with ships' quartermasters for the riches brought from across the seas. This leads to a good deal of smuggling activity which the Children of Mirkeer oversee.

15. Navy Pier

This small fortress is the headquarters of the city's dozen triremes. They push off from the docks on their way to patrol the coast.

Captain Glyphos (**bandit captain**), Praetor Machisus' second in command, oversees patrol schedules and produces reports for the praetors' weekly meetings. Typically, three triremes are being outfitted or set for training purposes in the harbor or at the docks at any given time with another six on patrol along the coasts. Each trireme has a complement of 200 **hoplite**[1] marines.

16. Lighthouse of Apollon

The Lighthouse stands on an island at the mouth of the Talamerin River, and is home to Praetor Machisus Lycurtay (**eldritch archer**[1]), who has views of the Freegate Prison and the navy pier from this location. Praetor Machisus has a guard retinue of 20 **myrmidons**[1] who are also adept at spellcasting, and he keeps a small galley at the lighthouse docks to allow him quick access to much of the city.

17. Freegate Prison

This prison has room for 200 inmates, but currently houses only about 80 (**commoner, sneakthief**[1], or **spy**). Most are common thieves, captured pirates on their first offense, deviants, or belligerents who have spent the night in the city lockup for fighting one too many times. The rest are madmen whom the city saw no other place to house, but who are too dangerous to let leave on their own. Characters who break the law should be careful not to end up here.

There are 20 **guards** at the prison, and Warden Quaestor Attulkon (**bandit captain** with AC 16 from chain mail) is known for his strict severity.

18. Mausoleum of Apollon

This fortress-like structure on the southern end of the city is a mausoleum. Due to the low water table on the southern side of the city, it was necessary to bury the dead aboveground. A rocky outcropping was chosen and a round tower to the dead was built. Every true citizen has the right to be buried here free of charge. For others, the cost is 300 gp to secure a 3-foot-by-7-foot vault sealed with a bronze plate and blessed against any unholy return from the dead.

Some wonder at the need for the walls surrounding the tower if the blessings are supposedly so strong and the vaults so secure. All that can be said to that question is that there may have been "some incidents." A cleric of Mitra (**cult fanatic**) handles funeral arrangements, and a contingent of 20 **hoplites** faithful to Mitra serve as funerary guard to make sure the dead stay dead and that grave robbers are kept at bay.

19. Temple of Mitra, Mitras Isle

The island south of the Mausoleum of Apollon houses the Temple of Mitra. The temple is small by some standards but is one of the oldest temples in the region, established by the ancient Hyperboreans who claimed the land in the days before the city was built.

It is tended by 5 **acolytes** and Anolopsis the Elder (**emeritus chaplain**[1]), who serves as their leader. Anolopsis is one of the few clerics in the region capable of raising a freshly killed individual from the dead. This doesn't mean he will, however. Typically, he reserves such powerful magic for the most affluent and powerful.

20. Foreign Quarter Slums

The Foreign Quarter is the traditional name for the area of the city on the south side of the docks and to the northeast of the Garden of Zadastha. It is poorer and less well patrolled by the local authorities than the neighborhoods that border the river. The Foreign Quarter Slums are known for their petty street gangs, poverty, and violence. The folk who have settled here come from regions up and down the Gulf of Akados, as well as islands and continents beyond its tight confines. The neighborhood is one of the most populous in the city, with nearly 2,500 people who speak dozens of languages living within its small concrete and brick apartments. Nearly half of these folks have joined the Cult of the Burning One in recent months, leaving the others to dwell in a new sort of fear.

21. Brazen Spire

Rising above the Foreign Quarter Slums is a tall gleaming edifice of gilt brass that glows day and night like a 200-foot-tall torch. The Brazen Spire is detailed in **Area of Adventure: The Brazen Spire**.

22. The Safe House of Tegman Zekii

Zekii's hideout occupies an apartment building near the docks. It is fully detailed in **Cult Strongholds** under **The Safe House of Tegman Zekii**.

Random Encounters Freegate

Roll once at the start of every session.

1d12	Result
1	Sailor
2	Hoplite patrol
3	Cult of the Burning One religious procession
4	Protest
5	Street performer
6	Pickpocket
7	Gladiator, boxer
8	Wine seller (commoner)
9	Gang
10	Streetwalker (commoner)
11	Oration
12	Con man (spy)

Con Man: A con man (**spy**) sees the characters and their adventuring gear, and tells them how he was ripped off by a fellow to whom he sold jewelry. If the characters could simply retrieve the jewelry, he promises to repay them for their troubles. The con man works for the Children of Mirkeer, a local thieves' guild. The nature of the scam is up to you.

Gang: A gang of toughs (**hired thugs**[1]) calling themselves the Gladius of Fire is shaking down a store owner near their apartment. If the characters chase the gang members away without killing anyone, they are offered a free place to stay with the shopkeeper's family, or a discount on the shopkeeper's wares. If they murder the gang members in the street in front of witnesses, they probably go to prison or are hanged.

Gladiator/Boxer: A boozed-up **gladiator** has had his feelings hurt at not being recognized by one of the characters for the "big deal" that he is. He challenges the character to a few throws at the colosseum outside of town. If the character doesn't show up, it's a hit to the character's reputation and everything in town costs 30% more. Also, everyone starts calling the character nicknames that remind people of the character's cowardice.

Hoplite Patrol: This is a patrol of 10 **hoplites**[1] with short spears, shortswords, shields, and breastplates who are patrolling the streets. They are led by an officer (**captain**[1]). If the characters look as if they are up to no good or are intent on starting a fight, they arrest them on the spot. The characters are brought before a praetor for immediate judgment and sentenced to 1d6 days of incarceration in Freegate Prison as well as a forfeiture of at least 100 gp.

Oration: A political speech is taking place about the need to cast aside the old ways and embrace the new world that has grown in the last thousand years. The orator's (**commoner**) comments are being met by boos from the crowd of traditionalists who dominate Freegate's culture and society. It appears that the crowd is close to stoning the man.

Pickpocket: The party runs afoul of 4 pickpockets (**spy**) working for the Knaves of Apollon, a local thieves' guild. One knave distracts the party while the other three take turns snagging loot off a victim chosen at random.

Protest: Protestors (**commoners**) who are worried about how quickly fellow citizens have fallen for another new religion are invoking their right to speak their minds at the forum. A debate turns into a brawl as several hundred members of the Cult of the Burning One arrive and heated words turn to blows. You are free to determine how this event turns out.

Religious Procession: Members of the Cult of the Burning One (**commoners**) are walking in the streets in their own phalanx. They shout prayers to the coming of the Burning One and his righteous judgment, wailing about their wishes being granted and the riches he has provided. They toss handfuls of silver and copper coins into the streets to share their wealth with the townsfolk, causing a miniature riot as people rush to collect the coins. Others are not so impressed and hurl insults at the cultists. The streets in every direction are blocked for one hour.

Sailor: This encounter could be with 1d4 + 2 pirates (as **bandits**), marines (as **guard**), naval **hoplites**[1], merchant seafarers, or fishermen (**commoners**). There is a 50% chance that they see the characters as a form of entertainment (mistaking them for streetwalkers or gladiators).

Street Performance: A clown stands on the street corner scaring everyone. The clown is actually a cleric of Moccavallo (**priest**). Folk who do not tip the clown are cursed with bad luck for 1d2 days unless they make a successful DC 14 Wisdom saving throw.

Streetwalker: This could be anyone looking to make some extra coin and is typically found in the slums, the Gardens of Zadastha, or near the wharf. This encounter never takes place north of the river. The streetwalker takes no time in telling the characters how down on their luck they are after the rise of the Cult of the Burning One and hopes that the characters can "spare some coin."

Wine Seller: A wine seller standing on his corner with his wine cart is shouting back and forth with someone claiming the wine is watered down. The characters are invited to taste the wine and decide if it is weak or not. The wine is extremely strong, however, as is popular in Freegate, and causes the characters who tastes it to quickly get lost and wake up in another part of the city separated from their friends. Unless a successful DC 14 Constitution saving throw is made, of course.

Part 2. The Cult of the Burning One

Getting Started

If the characters played through ***Lornedain: The Secret Flame***, they likely came in contact with agents of the Burning One close to their own community and saw firsthand the diabolical nature of the cult's activities.

Perhaps in the course of that adventure, Baroness Aora Lornedain escaped with her wizard, Giza al Hofu. In this event, the pair's trail leads to Freegate (or whichever city you choose) and an escape aboard *The Sand Dancer*, along with a shipment of Lornedain's kidnapped citizens.

Possibly, the characters also have alliances with the Dominion Arcane who wish to know what secrets are found within a Brazen Spire. The mages are aware of the great magic required for a metal tower to form in such a short period and want to know more. Another option includes the local thieves' guild hiring the characters to plunder the alleged treasures hidden within the spires.

Characters allied with other agencies such as the Paladins of Muir or those associated with the sect of the Maiden's Cross are aware through their chapterhouse of the dangers of the Brazen Spires, having been told legends from Libynos of the Cult of the Burning One and its association with the City of Brass. Their very charter offers them reasons for revealing the threat that the Spires represent and eliminating it if necessary. The characters are dispatched to investigate.

Listed here is an overview of more detailed options for how the characters came to Freegate. These adventure opportunities are designed to get the characters into the action quickly. They may be used in any order or combination that works best for you or that meets the needs of the story as it has played out based on the party's actions.

Heavy-Handed Tactics!

Some GMs may feel that some of the ways of including the characters into the adventure are heavy-handed. The following facts are pertinent. The city guard and some of the clerics who serve them may seem slightly "off" compared to what some would consider standard actions and behaviors. This is because the praetors and wizards in charge of protecting the city have been replaced by doppelgangers in the service of the Cult of the Burning One! Because of this, the cult has flourished without direct interference by the guards or others who would immediately stand up to such a threat.

This obviously creates a strong challenge for the characters who find themselves diving headfirst into the jaws of the enemy. Indeed, the characters may actually start the adventure imprisoned. They may end up poisoned, weaponless, and left for dead at any point during the adventure. Does this mean the adventure is heavy-handed or overtly and purposefully cruel? Of course not. It merely means that the adventure rewards social skills such as role-play and problem solving over naked violence more so than other adventures.

Luckily, the characters can befriend plenty of allies in Freegate such as Tetrarch Niketas, Cleomides, Aeetes Kokino, and Skia, whose assistance may be used at any time to break them out of a tight situation. Feel free to use these NPCs any time the characters become overly stuck in a situation that the players find they cannot think themselves through.

Adventure Opportunities

1. Prisoners

If you wish to start the adventure with the characters as prisoners, several options exist. Perhaps they were captured during their encounters in Lornedain and ended up in crates and shipped off by the river pirates who navigate the riverways. The pirates then traded them to unscrupulous merchants with orders to get the crates aboard *The Sand Dancer*. The characters have been kept unconscious by sleep draughts poured into the airholes of their crates.

A few miles outside of town, bandits attack the merchants transporting the characters' crates. A struggle is overheard, and the characters find themselves un-crated and in the custody of Balisis the Bandit (**bandit captain**) and her band of 20 **bandits**.

Balisis sees that the characters are watered and fed but keeps them bound as prisoners until she decides what to do with them. She questions the characters at length about their captors and what happened to them, all the while keeping her opinions to herself. She sees the potential in selling the characters back to the baroness of Lornedain, though she also sees the possibility that she and her band may end up in the same predicament as the characters.

Offer the characters an opportunity to make their case for freedom and strike whatever offers they can with Balisis for their freedom. The characters can always attempt to fight their way out, though they are likely devoid of their daily spells, have their hands bound behind their backs, and lack weapons.

If the characters mention the Brazen Spires, Balisis' eyes light up, as the Brazen Spire of Freegate can be seen a short distance ahead.

If the characters mention the names of any of the missing persons from Lornedain, specifically Simone Dubois, and the characters declare their intention of rescuing her, they are immediately freed. The child is a second cousin to Balisis. In this instance, Balisis offers her full support to the characters, outfitting them as best she can with gear (basic spellbooks, holy symbols, basic armor, etc.) and any other support she has to offer.

Along with her armor and weapons, Balisis has 525 gp, 800 sp, a gold ring worth 30 gp, and an Arkagi pearl locket worth 40 gp.

Getting Free

If negotiation is off the table, characters can always attempt to slip their bonds with a successful DC 18 Dexterity (Acrobatics) check, and free other party members in the night.

Characters who start as prisoners are without gear, however, save for whatever they take off their captors.

Allow the characters whatever reasonable plan of escape they can come up with and assume that 1d4 bandits stand guard any given night. If the characters overpower the bandits, they can "gear up" with any equipment that the bandits possess.

To avoid an overly hostile gaming environment, you can rule that the bandits were paid with the character's personal effects and that the characters may retrieve everything save potions and expendable items that the bandits have already used.

Sold to the Cult of the Burning One

If the characters fail to break free, they are sold to members of the Cult of the Burning One. The cultists are looking for more souls to ship to other locations for the construction of more Brazen Spires, or for transport to the City of Brass where they are pounded into the foundations of the Great Ziggurat. In this event, they are smuggled via a barge into Freegate and taken immediately into the Brazen Spire. There, they may be given another opportunity to escape before they are shipped off to Numeda across the Gulf of Akados and the sea beyond.

2. Ambushed on the Road

Characters may have set out for Freegate on their own after having discovered a great deal of information that leads them to search for the ship named *The Sand Dancer*.

The characters may also be in hot pursuit of Giza al Hofu and the Baroness Aora Lornedain if they escaped the characters during the events of *Lornedain: The Secret Flame*.

Another option includes the characters' search for the missing children and families who disappeared from Lornedain and who were not rescued during that adventure. Clues they discovered should lead the characters to the Brazen Spire and *The Sand Dancer*.

However, a band of cultists intent on capturing the characters attack as they arrive in Freegate. Sheik Mutastir warned the cultists of the party's arrival. Giza al Hofu sent him their general descriptions in a message. If the characters have not played through the events of *Lornedain: The Secret Flame*, the cultists are merely assaulting travelers to collect souls for the Burning One.

The Ambush

Eight **cultists** led by a **priest** of the Burning One attack the characters from behind an outcropping of rocks. Allow the characters an opportunity to avoid being surprised before launching the ambush.

Among their personal effects are specific physical descriptions of the characters. If the characters possess the *ring of Qalb*[2], or if Sparque accompanies them, they are described as an object of interest. The descriptions are marked with the letters "TZ" by way of a signature. This is the mark of Tegman Zekii, an underboss of Sheik Mutastir.

3. The Trireme

The Trireme is a tavern that could serve as a good home base for characters new to the region, a place where they can learn rumors about the current conditions within the city of Freegate. (The Trireme first appeared in *The Book of Taverns* by **Necromancer Games**.)

See the rumors table in The Word on the Street sidebox.

While the characters are enjoying drinks and listening to the rumors, they become the purposeful or unwitting targets of an assassination attempt perpetrated by the Cult of the Burning One. They have either been chosen because of their previous adventures in Lornedain, or they have been mistaken for characters who interfered with those operations. Mistaken identity aside, the characters are now in the thick of it!

Assassination Attempt

Three assassins (**hired thug**[1]) hired by either Sheik Mutastir or the baroness and Giza al Hofu target the characters. This encounter does not have to take place within the Trireme, and could take place in any tavern, restaurant, or enclosed location where there is an opportunity to hit all of the characters' food and drinks at the same time. The assassins' plan is to poison the characters' drinks or food when they stop for a bite. Allow the characters any appropriate checks to notice their assailants.

The assassins are using a fish-based paralytic neurotoxin[3] distilled from native jellyfish of the region. A successful "assassination" with the appropriate failed saving throw results in the character falling "dead" for all intents and purposes. "Dead" characters are taken by authorities from the city to the Mausoleum of Apollon, where their bodies are held until funeral arrangements can be made.

Captured Assassins

If characters capture an assassin alive, they may learn that the Cult of the Burning One hired the killers to poison the characters. Their master is intent on seeing the characters brought to the Brazen Spire. The assassins' contact was Tegman Zekii[1], who is to meet them at a safe house near the docks when the mission is complete.

Escaped Assassins

Assassins who escape after the assassination attempt make their way to the **safe house of Tegman Zekii** where they plan to lie low until the heat is off. You can use this opportunity to proceed with a chase through the streets of the city. The chase may be constructed using whichever rules are helpful. The assassins are natives and know their way in and out of the city and use various shortcuts that the characters may not be aware of. This grants them an advantage in getting to their destination before the characters. How soon before should depend on the characters' actions and any advantages they have at their disposal such as an ability to fly, tracking, or telepathic contact with an animal companion or familiar.

At the Mausoleum

Any characters who are poisoned are taken to the Mausoleum of Apollon. Characters who resist the poison can visit them, but are allowed only so far as a chamber to say their last respects. The cleric of Mithras (**cult fanatic**) and the mausoleum's 6 hoplite **guards** politely ask the characters to leave after a short time so "preparations can be made." Within the hour, a retinue of 6 **cultists** led by **Tegman Zekii**[1] arrives and bribe a hoplite sergeant (as **veteran**) for the bodies of the characters. If the party keeps watch over the mausoleum, or if they sneak back inside, they see their friends' bodies wrapped in shrouds being loaded onto a wagon to be hauled across town to the Brazen Spire. If the survivors do not observe this event, they may re-encounter their friends later in the Brazen Spire dungeon.

Characters attempting to stop the transfer of their friends' bodies face Tegman Zekii[1] and his retinue.

4. Out on the Town

Immediately upon arriving in the city, the characters note the strange otherworldly spire that soars above the city's skyline. A tall, slender tower seemingly made of brass, it gleams like gold as it rises from near the center of town. The top of the tower glows with a brilliant arcane flame that can be seen for miles both day and night.

The city is experiencing an upheaval the likes of which has not been seen since the arrival of the church of Zadastha. New religions and an influx of new faces to the Foreign Quarter have the praetors of the city on guard and have left the hoplites and native citizenry nervous. Protests and counter-protests have begun taking place, and in some areas the atmosphere is near to rioting. The praetors are contemplating arresting members of the cult but have stopped just short of this decision. Rumors abound that the reason is due in part to the city's ancient laws. Most believe it is the bribes they took, and also the fear of greater destruction if the magic used to raise the Brazen Spire were to match that of the city's magus in sorcerous combat.

The Word on the Street (Rumors)

Characters are almost immediately beset with rumors as they enter the city. Give characters one free rumor and an additional rumor for every attempt to gather more or for every 10 gp in bribes and persuasion offered. Players can make an Intelligence (Investigation) or Charisma check of some sort to determine which rumor they get on the table below. If characters played through ***Lornedain: The Secret Flame*** and Baroness Lornedain or Giza Al Hofu escaped, they may have questions as to the whereabouts of the nefarious duo. If the characters ask pointed questions about the pair, feel free to use the 20+ results.

1d20	Rumor
1	"Look at the sky! Wow!"
2	"The fishing this year has been astounding!"
3	"Have you heard of Captain Bethany Razor? Naw? Me neither."
4	"The spire? It bothers me. Casts a light day and night. How in the hell are you to get any sleep? Another thing, who builds a tower in a day? Wizards sure, but this seems like the devil's work if you ask me."
5	"Foreigners! The praetors sold us out for certain. It started with a group of turbaned men who arrived aboard a ship that is anchored out in the harbor."
6	"Evidently all it took for the praetors of the city to sell us all out to this new cult was three chests. Wonder what was in them chests?"
7	"You know them turbaned men with the treasure chests? They put up a pavilion. From inside it came this gods' awful pounding. Enough to drive you mad. Then, a big golden spire out of nowhere I tell you! Built it right where that apartment burned down a few months before."

1d20	Rumor
8	"You would think someone would do something about that bright light that the thing gives off. I mean, we already have a lighthouse in the harbor. What if this thing draws a ship off course and it rams into the navy pier? Disaster!"
9	"So we all sat in wonder as a doorway opened at the base of the tower. Dancers and musicians poured fourth, as did servants bearing platters of food, flagons of wine, and jars of honey, oil, and fragrant perfume. All these gifts and more were handed out to the poor folk of the Foreign Quarter Slums, along with apologies for the noise. The festival continued for days. What a party! We got so wasted. Haven't seen most of my buddies since that night though…"
10	"Their leader is called Sheik Mutastir or something. They say he comes from across the sea. Have you seen him though? His skin is almost as shiny as that spire. Not human, that's for sure. Probably some kind of elf or something. Very generous though. Gives away food, and his folk are teaching the poor kids to read. That's what I heard."
11	"Something's up. That's all I know. People who used to be beggars are now running the streets in these black and orange robes embroidered with a golden flame. Covering their faces. Acting smarter than everyone else."
12	"I heard some of these followers of the 'Burning One,' as they call themselves, were chasing folk out of the Garden of Zadastha. Saying they could offer deeper pleasures in their spire. Wishes come true! Believe that? I may have to go check it out for myself, that's a fact! Hahaha! (Burp) …"
13	"So … I haven't seen Jazmer and Haemon since the festival. They were dancing with veiled beauties and drinking that golden wine. Lucky devils."
14	"I hear they let you in to show you their wonders. Those who enter seem very different afterward though. They have money for one, but they never seem to need to spend it. What's that all about? The Bank of Sefagreth is furious. Not getting any interest from new loans, I guess?"
15	"Heard they were training an army. A platoon of them left, walking in rank, bearing a banner written in some strange tongue. They all wore veils over their faces and headed off in the direction of Darnagal."
16	"What's with that boat? Strange looking jobber. Faster than our triremes, that's for sure. It just sits there anchored in the bay. Every so often some of those folks with the turbans and veils take a skiff out there full of supply crates, but we have a perfectly fine dock here. Are they too good for us?"
17	"Tegman Zekii and those bad folks he runs with are tied up in this scheme. What would you expect from a crook such as he?"
18	"So, I heard another spire just went up in Durendia, and they say one is going up in Bard's Gate before long. What's that all about? You ever see a religion move this fast? I tell you what though, there aren't so many beggars around these days, so there must be something to it."

1d20	Rumor
19	"I don't want to talk about the folk and the spire. Them who talk too much don't seem to stick around for very long."
20	"Where is Zarius Medius? The high magus hasn't been seen in some time. Certainly he wouldn't let such magic as an enchanted spire rise up in his city without some say?"
21	"A couple matching that description arrived a week ago. Haven't seen them since."
22	"A couple matching that description arrived in the city and immediately disappeared into the Brazen Spire."
23	"The couple arrived, visited the Brazen Spire, and then went to the docks."
24+	"The couple arrived, visited the spire, then took a skiff from the docks to the ship anchored in the harbor."

Note: These answers apply only if Giza or the baroness, or both, are still alive. Adjust them as needed.

Note: The city is only superficially detailed, as the city is not the focus of the adventure, but simply the setting for it. Contacts the characters make should impress upon them the immediacy of the situation with the rise of the cult. If the characters are off track, it is a simple thing to attempt to "assassinate them" again with jellyfish toxin[3], or to tempt them with the thought of riches hidden within The Sand Dancer or the Brazen Spires.

*If the characters arrived in the town with this goal in mind, it should be a simple matter to give them opportunities to do so. If the characters come to the adventure via means of mistaken identity, or as prisoners, their adventure of course begins in the bowels of the Brazen Spire and is further detailed under **Area of Adventure: The Brazen Spire**.*

Character Contacts

Soon after the characters make it into the city and begin investigating, various contacts approach them to enlist their aid in finding out more about the mysteries of the Brazen Spire. Listed here are contacts who may approach the characters with the intent of having them infiltrate the Brazen Spire or *The Sand Dancer* and report their findings. The point of the contacts is to get the characters moving toward looking into Tegman Zekii's operation and exploring the Brazen Spire itself. Feel free to use as many or as few of these contacts as is necessary to keep the plot moving along.

Tetrarch Niketas

Tetrarch Niketas (**greater commoner**[1]) serves as the chief of staff for Praetor Polides. If the praetors hired the characters to investigate the Brazen Spire, it is Tetrarch Niketas who does the hiring. Niketas serves as a point man for the characters and meets with them at Gyros Ki Alla, a restaurant just to the north of the forum. Niketas is a broad, strong man with a thick beard, bald head, and sharp greenish-gray eyes.

Tetrarch Niketas was not present when Sheik Mutastir offered gifts of treasure to his master, though he has noticed a certain change of resolve in Praetor Polides that he has never seen before. He believes it a weakness perhaps, or maybe an unwillingness to move against the dangers that Tetrarch Niketas believes are imminent.

Further, Praetor Halixes instructed Niketas to command city troops to stop any trouble between cultists and the citizenry, but not to interfere with any of the religious activities that the followers of the Burning One may be performing. He has been further forbidden from conducting any search or inspection on the grounds of the cult's "sacred spire." This is alarming to Niketas, as he personally knows of several missing persons from within the city's poorer districts as well as some other prominent folk such as

High Magus Zarius Medius, who has been missing since almost the time the Brazen Spire was created.

Tetrarch Niketas approaches the characters after word reaches him that they defeated an ambush outside the city. If the characters completed ***Lornedain: The Secret Flame***, word of their exploits has just reached his ears, and he arrives to "arrest them" with a squad of **hoplites**[1]. He frees them from custody only after extending an offer to have them work for him.

Tetrarch Niketas suggests a further meeting with the characters at the Shrine of Thyr so Cleomine may guard their conversations. He has a squad of loyal hoplites at his disposal who may be called into service should the characters find need to do so. He offers the characters 1,000 gp each if they take on the task of discovering the true activities of the Cult of the Burning One by infiltrating their tower. He is suspicious and wants the characters to understand that the survival of Freegate, and possibly all of Akados, may be at stake.

Skia Ithipio

Skia Ithipio (**scout**) is the second in command to Guildmaster Antolychus Ermes and is his "person of first contact" for outsiders to the Children of Mirkeer. She tests prospects and handles any new hires. Much of the more dangerous work for the guild is subcontracted to throw heat off its members in the event that a confidence deal, forgery, or robbery goes bad.

Skia approaches characters with a test of thievery: Make their way into the Brazen Spire and retrieve a fist-sized piece of ruby with a rune carved upon it. Called the *fire stone of Sulymon*[2], it is somehow used to construct the tower. She has heard that the stone is currently being held within the spire as the leaders of the Cult of the Burning One decide where they shall raise their next tower. Bring the stone to her, and they shall be awarded full membership in the Children of Mirkeer, as well as deep discounts at all guild retail outlet stores (aka fences). If that is not enough to sweeten the deal, she also offers them 500 gp each, though she can be talked up to 800 gp each for pilfering the *fire stone*[2].

Aeetes Kokino

Aeetes Kokino (**theurgist**[1]) is an apprentice of Zarius Medius who has become concerned over his master's disappearance. He knows that High Magus Zarius frequently leaves without offering a message of any sort to his apprentices, expecting them to "manage the shop" while he is gone. Normally that would be fine, but it has been more than a month now, and the graduating mages need to be tested for an opportunity to gain protection from the Dominion Arcane. Zarius is truly the one who must oversee the testing. Aeetes knows that his master was summoned late in the evening on the day that *The Sand Dancer* anchored offshore, and that he was present with Praetor Polides and Praetor Halixes Pemmanon. Praetor Machisus Lycurtay chose to remain at his watchtower that night. The visitors brought three chests to the meeting. One chest was left at the governor's palace, while another chest was hauled to the Agoge of Apollon. The third was taken back to the tent that the strangers built on the spot of the burned apartment complex.

Aeetes needs proof that his master was taken in the last chest. Aeetes is unsure if his master is still in the city, though his own magical search leads him to believe so.

Aeetes offers 1,000 gp worth of magic in the form of scrolls or potions to characters who help him find out what happened to his master.

The Safe House of Tegman Zekii

If the characters encountered Tegman's assassins and questioned them, their interrogation should lead them to this apartment complex on the south side of the city, just off the wharf.

The apartment (**Area 21** on the city map) shares the outward appearance of other slum-like buildings in the district, complete with bums and drunks sleeping in the street and curled up on the stoop. Tegman's gang occupies the topmost apartment in the complex and has closed off most of the top floor. They rule over the common folk dwelling in the lower two levels of the apartment and the rest of the block with threats, intimidation, and the occasional murder.

There is a lot of hidden space within the building. Characters who are actively mapping or who have a good spatial sense may notice this. Otherwise, of course, the usual options for searching for secret doors are available.

Standard Features

Doors: Unless otherwise stated, the doors on the first two floors are locked and require a successful DC 16 Dexterity check with thieves' tools or DC 18 Strength check to open.

Gates: The gates are bound and chained and require a successful DC 20 Strength check or *knock* spell to open. Tegman Zekii[1] and Gregiorie Kaj (**spy**) have keys to the gates and their chains.

Secret Doors: Unless noted otherwise, the secret doors require asuccessful DC 17 Wisdom (Perception) check to find and can be opened easily once found.

Ground Floor

The ground floor of the apartment complex is similar to others in the city, with entrances in the north, south, east, and west that lead to a central courtyard and fountain where the tenants get fresh water. The north, east, and south entrances to the tenement are locked and chained wrought-iron fences, leaving only the western entrance open to the street.

1. Western Entrance

A member of Tegman's Gladius of Fire gang (**sneakthief**[1]) who is also a new convert to the Cult of the Burning One watches over the entrance. He dresses as a half-asleep beggar with his alms bowl lying next to him and his staff propped on the wall. The spy lets any characters pass but signals those above with a tap of his staff on the second-floor ceiling when they go by. He then closes and locks the gate behind any suspicious persons and heads to **Area 2** or **3**.

2. Guardrooms

These rooms face the outside of the tenement. A typical apartment has a storefront where denizens of the apartment sell services such as laundry services or stalls selling prepared seasoned fish, meats, or cheeses, and the like. In the case of the tenement, however, these rooms are filled with tough-looking youths who drink sour wine, play cards, and watch the approach to the building from the north and south.

These gang members keep an eye on approaching strangers. They file out into the courtyard and actively threaten anyone who arrives unannounced. If the strangers are heavily armed, they brandish maces, daggers, and shortswords of their own. Tegman Zekii[1] pays them to guard the ground floor and to chase off intruders. They are not paid to die for him.

Each guardroom has 4–6 gang members (**bandits** with AC 14 from chain shirts, and **spies** of various races and nationalities.

3. Ground Floor Apartments

These are simple dwellings of the impoverished folk who live here. Typically, 4–6 people (**commoners**) live in a one- or two-room space. These civilians close their doors and hide if trouble breaks out.

4. Gang Clubhouse

This room serves as a clubhouse for the gang that runs the lower level. The gang was once called the Fighting Fish, but recently re-dubbed itself the "Gladius of Fire" so they sound more cool and can be associated with the new Cult of the Burning One.

The clubhouse has 2d4 gang members (**bandits** with AC 14 from chain shirts and **sneakthieves**[1]) in it at any given time. They are usually drunk on sour wine, or high on lotus petals that have been picked up from sailors at the wharf. Their inebriation gives them a –1 to hit and damage.

5. Fountain

This central fountain splashes clean and slightly brackish water that the tenants use for everything from cooking to laundry. The fountain features a series of cherubs pouring water on one another from an ever-full amphora. The cherubs have been defaced significantly over time to take on a deformed and slightly malevolent appearance. A long time ago,

a thief being chased by hoplites tossed his stash into the well where it has lain ever since. A golden idol of Mithras still clogs the drain and is worth 800 gp. Finding it requires a search and a successful DC 18 Intelligence (Investigation) check. If returned to the Temple of Mithras, the characters are given a *spell scroll* of *raise dead* as a means of a thank you.

Second Story

6. Residences

These residences are similar to the ones on the first floor. They have 3–4 **commoners** living as virtual prisoners in their own homes. Daily, a newly minted acolyte of the Burning One forces them out into the courtyard to preach the gospel of flames. The entire wealth of a residence is under 5 gp. If characters enter or approach a residence, the tenants flee in terror, their screams alerting the gangs and assassins who dwell here.

7. Biacolo's Residence

A locked secret door leads to the entrance of this apartment just off the landing. Unlocking it requires a successful DC 17 Dexterity check with thieves' tools. It is the home of Biacolo (**captain**[1] with *+1 spear*), an old fighter who pretends to be blind and hides in this apartment to avoid the gangs and the cultists. If the characters end up in a tight spot and need a place to hide, he secretly invites them into the home he shares with his old war-hound (as **wolf**) jokingly named "Victim."

Biacolo isn't actually blind, but he wears a scarf over his eyes so that the gang members and assassins leave him alone. He has a pretty hideous scar over his face that he got from being stung in the face early in his career by a giant wasp that makes his ruse of blindness quite believable. If the characters promise to drive out the gangs and their masters on the third floor, he offers to aid them.

8. Guardroom

This guardroom protects the upper-story entrances to the assassins' training chambers. The room is guarded by 3 assassins-in-training (**sneakthief**[1] with poisoned daggers that do an additional 3 (1d6) poison damage on a hit) culled from the neighborhood gangs. They keep the door barred unless they are given the secret knock. The assassins possess 2d10 gp each.

A secret door hidden in the western wall opens to **Area 9**.

9. Secret Corridor

This secret corridor has a ladder leading up to **Area 11**. Secret doors open to **Areas 8** and **10**.

10. Ikram Karh's Apartment

This apartment is divided into two chambers, with the front room used as lodging for a pair of cultists, and the back half used by their priest.

This room houses Ikram Karh, a **missionary**[1] of the Cult of the Burning One. He guards the secret entrance at **Area 9**, which leads up to the assassins' training room and outfitters.

Ikram Karh is assisted by 2 **acolytes** who received their training directly from Sheik Mutastir. All three of them have flasks of oil and flint and steel.

11. Hidden Hallway

This hallway has a ladder leading to **Area 9**. Secret doors to the east and west lead to **Areas 12** and **16B**

12. Chamber of Silence

Wooden staves hang from weapon racks on the walls. Broken pieces of glass and thin ceramic cover the floor of this room and give disadvantage to any Stealth checks made within the room.

On one side of the room, a key hangs from a silken cord that runs through a block and tackle hanging in the ceiling. The cord is tied off to a counterweight connected to a heavy ceramic tub. A successful DC 18 Intelligence (Investigation) check indicates that fiddling with the cord has a good chance of flipping over the tub. If the slack is taken off the cord, the trap triggers and the tub flips.

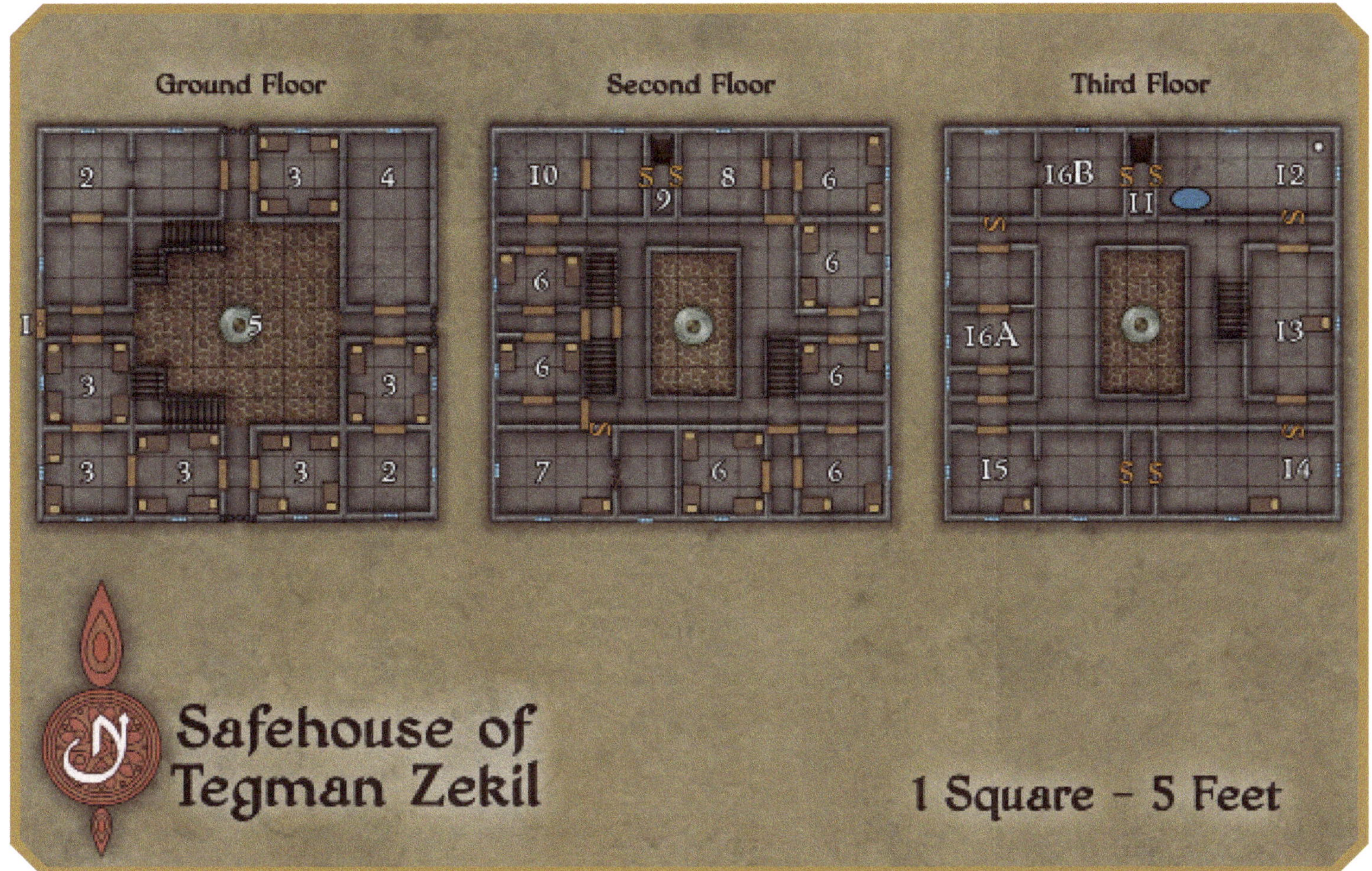

The objective for assassins-in-training is to creep across the room without making a sound and get the key off the cord without flipping the tub. This is fairly important, as the assassins captured a **rust monster** and keep it secured beneath the ceramic tub. Untying the cord and retrieving the key without triggering the trap requires a successful DC 16 Dexterity check.

13. Mr. Callipus' Apartment

Mr. Callipus (**assassin**) is a dealer in venoms and poisons imported from around the world. He sells shortswords, daggers, slings, hand crossbows, darts, and blowguns at standard rates, and various venoms per the table below. Many of the weapons are on display, along with a wild assortment of wigs, masks, and costumes ranging from dresses and attire for ladies or gentlemen, to rags worn by wharf rats and beggars. Disguise kits and other similarly knavish tools are also available. Mr. Callipus trains recruits for a standard fee, though the cost is deeply discounted for members of the Cult of the Burning One.

Poison Costs

Poison	Cost per dose
Jellyfish toxin[3]	500 gp
Assassin's blood	150 gp
Pale tincture	250 gp
Drow poison	200 gp

14. Tegman Zekii's Apartment

Tegman Zekii's dwelling is hidden behind secret doors in the southeast corner of the building. The room contains his bed, a wardrobe, and a footlocker. Tegman has a 25% chance of being in the room unless an alarm sounded. In that case, he responds to the commotion, and lends whatever assistance is necessary.

Tegman Zekii[1] is Sheik Mutastir's lieutenant in Freegate. Tegman is a half-elf wizard and assassin who has spent a great deal of time in and out of Freegate prison. Tegman has extensive knowledge of the underworld, and managed to convert a number of his old associates to the new cult. In return, Tegman Zekii[1] has been promised a seat of power in the world that follows the Sultan's conquest. Sheik Mutastir has filled his head with visions where he is the overlord of his former oppressors.

Tegman possesses a *brazen amulet*[2], which is given only to cultists who achieve the highest level of worship for a mortal convert. He also carries a *+1 shortsword*, a *spell wand*[2] of *sleep*, a *potion of invisibility*, keys to the partment building, and 3 doses of drow poison[3].

Tegman's footlocker is trapped with a poison gas trap. The trap can be discovered with a successful DC 15 Intelligence (Investigation) check and disarmed with a successful DC 17 Dexterity check with theives' tools. Failing the check by 5 or more triggers the trap. If the trap is triggered, all within 10 feet of the footlocker must succeed on a DC 16 Constitution saving throw or take 7 (2d6) poison damage. Inside the footlocker are 484 gp, 3 rubies worth 200 gp each, 2 *potions of healing*, 2 *potions of invisibility*, 2 *potions of flying*, and a strange phrase written on a scroll made from pounded copper. The words written on the copper are "Malik al Khabith." Its purpose is unknown without questioning Tegman Zekii[1]. The scroll is actually an invitation, and anyone speaking the phrase while wearing a *brazen amulet*[2] is invited to the sanctum of Sheik Mutastir (found on the 10th floor of the **Brazen Spire**).

A secret door in the western wall of Tegman's room leads to a hidden hallway between his room and Gregiorie Kaj's room (**Area 15**).

15. Gregiorie Kaj's Apartment

Gregiorie Kaj (**spy**) is Tegman's right-hand man and became leader of the Gladius of Fire gang after cutting the throat of the leader of the Fighting Fish. He keeps an eye on the safe house when Tegman is off doing the work of the Burning One. His apartment is opposite Tegman's and has a secret door in its eastern wall.

Gregiorie is a sloe-eyed killer who prefers to use his knife to gut his victims while covering their mouths with a strong gloved hand. Gregiorie is a sandy bearded dwarf who hails from the dunes of far-off Libynos. He converted to the Cult of the Burning One when Sheik Mutastir's ship arrived. He carries a *+1 dagger* and a *potion of invisibility*, wears *+1 studded leather*, a *brazen amulet*[2], and *boots of elvenkind*, and has keys to the apartment building on his belt.

A chest trapped with a poison dart contains his possessions:189 gp, a bottle of Numedan honey wine worth 100 gp, 3 emeralds worth 50 gp each. Discovering the trap requires a successful DC 17 Intelligence (Investigation) check. It can be disarmed with a successful DC 16 Dexterity check with thieves' tools. If triggered, the dart makes a ranged weapon attack at +6 to hit against one target within 5 feet. On a hit, it does 1 piercing damage, and on a failed DC 14 Constitution saving throw, 7 (2d6) poison damage.

16A. Assassins' Bunkhouses

Each of these rooms houses a trio of assassins (**hired thug**[1]) who converted to the Cult of the Burning One. If any assassins were killed or captured in previous encounters, they are taken from the number found here. Each assassin has roughly 200 gp worth of coins or jewelry, a disguise kit, forged documents with various identities, one costume, and a *potion of healing*.

16B. Bunkhouse

A secret door in this bunkhouse leads to **Area 11**.

Running Tegman Zekii's Safe House

If the characters are in pursuit of assassins who attempted to kill them, the assassins meet in the courtyard before moving to the gang clubhouse (**Area 4**) to report to Tegman Zekii[1] about their mission.

As the characters make their way through the safe house, any noise they make in a given area attracts the nearest Gladius of Fire gang members. The assassins move to positions where they can circle around the characters and attempt to pick them off one by one. Gang members fight to kill intruders unless Tegman tells them specifically to take their quarry alive.

Characters should be reminded of the residences in the stronghold and that they have no way of knowing if civilians are in the area or not until they investigate on their own. Spells that cause concussive or fire damage could turn a bad situation worse in a relatively short period of time! Ultimately, the fight may be as hard or easy as you feel is necessary to challenge the players.

Tegman is under orders to capture the characters if at all possible so that they may be remanded to further torture at the hands of Emir Farphanes for their interference in the Sultan's plans. For this reason alone, Tegman orders the assassins to use incapacitating venoms.

If things are going poorly for Tegman, he makes a break for the Brazen Spire to report his failure personally to Sheik Mutastir.

If the characters capture Tegman Zekii[1] or Gregiorie Kaj alive, they can use them to gain access to Sheik Mutastir via the sheik's invitation once they are within the Pillar of Fire inside the Brazen Spire. Tegman's presence may afford them passage through Paradise as well. Tegman likely attempts to warn the guards at any and every opportunity.

Area of Adventure: The Brazen Spire

Rising more than 200 feet from the center of a cluster of tenement apartments is this tower of gleaming brass polished to a golden hue. Atop the tower is a burning torch that lights the neighborhood with an orange glow, creating a second lighthouse that passing ships can see from miles away. The surface of the spire appears to be expertly embossed with dizzying patterns depicting faces and bodies captured in a swirl of stylized flames.

Outside the Spire

Hundreds of cultists dressed in black and orange robes gather at the base of the spire to pray and exalt the glory of the Veiled God, whom they also know as the Burning One, and the salvation of the purifying fire he promises. As strangers approach, priests break off from the praying throngs to determine their intent. Armed warriors — such as squadrons of hoplites — are almost immediately met by hundreds of cultists who form a human wall between the hoplites and the entrance to the spire. Within a short time, they are met by more than a thousand cultists (**commoners**) armed with stones, daggers, clubs, shortswords, torches, and flasks of oil.

Note: *If dispel magic is cast on a cultist, there is a 50% chance that the cultist is under the effects of a charm person spell and snaps out of it, fleeing combat and the Brazen Spire altogether.*

Gaining Entrance

Due to the watchful eyes of the cultists outside, entry into the spire may be difficult. The following methods of entry are some possibilities.

Disguised as Cultists

The characters arrive in robes and veils favored by the cultists and proceed to the front entrance. Typically, cultists come and go from the first few levels of the spire and are not questioned until they reach the inner entryway.

As Prisoners

If the characters are captured or smuggled into the city in crates, they are hauled directly to the cells for processing. In this instance, Tegman Zekii[1] and Gregiorie Kaj, if they are still alive, bring the characters to the prison.

Fight Their Way In

It is possible for characters to battle their way into the spire, but this involves slaughtering dozens of cultists who may or may not be willing followers of the Veiled One. Doing so probably eats up most of the *fireball* and *lightning bolt* spells the characters possess rather quickly.

Sneaky, Sneaky

Characters could sneak in using illusions, invisibility, or other magical distractions. Whatever is clever is worth a try. It is up to you to decide the success of such attempts.

The characters may have captured Gregiorie Kaj or Tegman Zekii[1]. If Gregiorie Kaj is in their custody, they may be able to get through the **Vortex of Purification** without having to disarm themselves so long as they also have the *brazen amulets*[2] from Gregiorie or Tegman.

Standard Features

Doors: Doors are locked unless otherwise noted. Unlocking them requires a successful DC 18 Dexterity check with thieves' tools. Otherwise, they can be battered down with a successful DC 20 Strength check or opened with a *knock* spell.

Pillar of Fire: A magical Pillar of Fire touches several floors that are contiguous from the **Mosque of Adoration** to the torch that blazes through

Brazen Spire
1 Square - 5 Feet
1st Floor:
Mosque of Adoration
2nd Floor: Sacerdotal Studies
Ground Floor: Paradise
Dungeon

Brazen Amulets

These amulets are made from the same living brass material as the tower itself and are attuned to the bearer. They allow access to the different levels of the Brazen Spire, including those areas not readily accessible by a staircase.

Hariph's Brazen Amulets: These amulets are worn by hariphs and high-ranking members of the cult. A set of *hariph's brazen amulets*[2] grants the bearer and anyone within a 5 foot radius immunity to the fires from the **Pillar of Fire** and the **Vortex of Purification**. They provide resistance to all other fire damage. The amulet allows access to all the floors of the tower save the personal dwelling of Sheik Mutastir himself. The sheik's quarters may be accessed only with his permission, or by speaking a secret password which is afforded only to select persons.

Note: The password to Sheik Mutastir's sanctum is "Malik al Khabith." This password could be gleaned from the metal scroll found in Tegman Zekii's apartment (**Area 14**), or through various means of divination magic.

Lesser Brazen Amulets

Lesser brazen amulets[2] allow access up to the **Alqamar Mulnajum** (the Hall of Moon and Stars), but otherwise function as a *hariph's amulet*[2]. It protects only the wearer from the fires and damaging effects of the **Vortex of Purification** and the **Pillar of Fire**, however.

Bearers of *hariph's brazen amulets*[2] or the *lesser brazen amulets*[2] are immune to the enchantment effects found in the **Mosque of Adoration**, though unlike the protections from the **Vortex of Purification** and the **Pillar of Fire**, these effects do not extend beyond the wearer.

the roof of the tower. The flames are used by the hariphs (leaders chosen to run the cult), Sheik Mutastir, and others to access the various floors of the spire instantly via a *brazen amulet*[2]. Those not possessing an amulet or other immunity to fire damage must attempt a DC 17 Constitution saving throw. Those failing suffer 21 (6d6) fire damage per round they are engulfed in the flame while those succeeding take half this amount. Casting *dispel magic* on the pillar quenches the flames for 10 rounds.

Ground Floor: Purification and Paradise

1. Entry

Double doors of burnished bronze open onto the inner spire. The doors open to a hallway flanked by a pair of guardrooms. At the end of the hallway is a circular portal of swirling flame.

1-A. Western Guardroom: A group of 4 **guards** in the western guardroom watch everyone through the barred doorway, making sure that only cult members or those brought in as guests of cult members may enter. They demand any weapons and armor from non-cult members, offering them a simple robe to wear. Characters are directed to remand their equipment to the eastern guardroom, where it will be returned upon request when they leave.

The guards are led by a **cultist** with a *wand of magic detection* that he uses to make sure that no one tries to sneak any dangerous items into the spire. The guards are thick-necked toughs armed with great maces. They dress in the black and orange garb of cultists, though they seem to be mercenaries from lands foreign to the characters. A locked door in the guardroom opens onto a stairwell that leads to the prison level below.

A clothesline holds dozens of ankle-length robes in orange and black. Once they change into a black or orange robe, visitors are instructed to purify themselves in the portal of flame.

1-B. The Eastern Guardroom: This guardroom serves as the de-facto coat check to get into the inner sanctum. Like the western guardroom, the 4 **guards** here wear orange and black robes, with black silken veils covering their faces. Several bronze-bound chests in this room are used to store the belongings of visitors to the spire. Oddly enough, most visitors never bother to come back for their things after their second or third visit, so the chests are full with all manner of mundane items. Examples include:

Chest 1: 4 daggers, 3 flasks of oil, 10 togas, sophisticated thigh-length black leather boots with polished silver toe and heel clip (unisex, 30 gp).

Chest 2: 3 Shadowmask masks, a cup made from agate worth 50 gp, 3 suits of leather armor, 3 scimitars, 3 punch daggers, 3 pairs of boots.

Chest 3: a cocobolo pipe, flea-ridden alms rug, copper cooking pot, rusted iron bracelet, small carving of a trireme, a flimsy nightgown, a rusty razor, 2 daggers, and a vial of holy water. Pearl prayer beads worth 200 gp.

Chest 4: 200 gp bottle of rare brandy, a silver holy symbol of Mithras, gold-embroidered toga (10 gp), perfume (20 gp), an ivory comb (20 gp).

Chest 5: Clay wine amphora (10 gp), sack containing 20 sp, a bag of apples, a silk evening gown (30 gp), 4 gold hair pins worth 20 gp.

Very valuable items such as magic items and significant treasures are cleared out of the guardroom at the end of every day.

1-C. Vortex of Purification: This swirling doorway is roughly the same size as the archway leading into the spire.

The vortex acts as a *wall of fire* cast with a level 4 spell slot (DC 16 saving throw) to anyone who is not invited through the gateway by a member of the cult. Characters who have been stripped of their gear and are wearing the offered robes are welcome to enter. Prisoners brought through by cult members are allowed entry and suffer no ill effects. Bearers of a *brazen amulet*[2] may bring up prisoners without question.

The vortex can be dismissed temporarily by a successful *dispel magic* spell, but it returns in 1d4 rounds.

2. Welcome to Paradise

The room beyond the vortex that greets characters is an interdimensional paradise heretofore undreamed of by the characters. The sky is lit with a brilliant yellow-green glow, with wafts of smoky white clouds. The floor is a soft powdery white sand that is hot to the touch but not uncomfortable. Copses of palm trees dot the inner landscape, and here and there are piles of silk pillows where 20 or so adorants (**commoners**) in orange and black robes lounge about while sipping wine from crystal decanters or smoking strange herbs from glass hookahs. Four servants (**doppelgangers**) in lewd attire consisting mainly of strings of pearls and beads of ruby, emerald, and sapphire bring plates of steaming meats and honey-dipped delicacies to the attendees. The servants greet new arrivals, welcoming them to Paradise.

2-A. Pool: This pool is filled with comfortably warm water that is 4 feet deep and mildly salty. Visitors and nubile servants splash playfully in the waters.

2-B. A burning statue 10 feet high stands in the center of the pool. It features a perfectly muscled humanoid figure with clawed feet and its hands raised to the sky. The figure is draped in a harness of jewels and a veil covers its face. Short horns protrude from its brow, which is adorned with some sort of monarchical diadem. The statue itself is covered in flames that continually lick across its metallic surface. Touching the statues causes 3 (1d6) fire damage.

2-C. Platform: A platform rises from the sands and appears to be part of some sort of bar and stage area. A quartet of performers (**entertainers**[1]) plays music with an oboe-like instrument, a tambourine, a long-necked lute, and a dancing girl in a tight orange gown with brass cymbals on her fingertips.

2-D. Bar: A bar built in the shape of a golden palace sits toward the back end of the platform. Seven seats surround it. A large well-muscled man (**illusionist**[1]) pours drinks that the servants carry out to revelers, and directly serves those seated before him with wine, brandy, and other libations poured into crystal and gold goblets.

Eamil is very likeable and friendly, asking folk what they like even as he gains information from them about their needs and desires. Once he feels satisfied that he "knows" what someone wants, he directs them to the object of their desire. Eamil has a *lesser brazen amulet*[2], a *spell wand*[2] of *major image*, and *potions of invisibility* and *flying*.

Brazen Spire
1 Square = 5 Feet
Roof
200 Feet
10th Floor: Sheik Mutastir's Quarters
9th Floor: Bottle Ritual Chamber
8th Floor: Apartments of the Ihariphs
7th Floor: Prayer Room of the Ihariphs
6th Floor: Moon and Stars
3rd – 5th Floor: Barracks
2nd Floor: Sacerdotal Studies
1st Floor: Mosque of Adoration
Ground Floor: Paradise
Dungeon

Behind the bar are 30 bottles of wine, 4 kegs of ale, 7 bottles of rum, 3 whiskeys, 6 bottles of brandy, and 10 bottles of other distilled spirits. Most bottles are worth 1d20 gp each, although some bottles of wine are worth up to 100 gp.

3. Eamil's Room

Eamil keeps a room next to the bar area. He hails from a village deep in the Maighib Desert and was an early convert to the faith of the Burning One after Emir Farphanes granted him a wish that saved the life of his mother and sisters. The doors to Eamil's room are magically locked and open only to his hand or that of Sheik Mutastir. A *knock* or *dispel magic* spell allows entry.

Eamil's belongings are locked in a dresser drawer where a small *bag of holding* contains 10 silver bars worth 10 gp each, a pouch of saffron worth 20 gp, a *potion of healing*, 2 golden topaz worth 250 gp each, and 2 flasks of alchemist's fire. Opening the drawer requires a successful DC 16 Dexterity check with thieves' tools.

4. Alhim and Dahish's Room

This room is shared by Alhim and Dahish, a pair of **ogres** Sheik Mutastir charmed and trained to serve as Eamil's bodyguards. They are slightly smarter than the local variety of ogre. More to the point, they are a pair of painted and coiffured pigs who do what they are told. If trouble breaks out in Paradise, Alhim and Dahish arrive with their large falchions (as longswords) to put a quick and bloody end to it.

5. Hall of Private Pleasure

For those insisting on discreet fantasy fulfillment, the rooms of private pleasure are where charmed **dopplegangers** — with Eamil's assistance — create whatever fantasy the visitor would seek. They do so in order to lure recruits to the Cult of the Burning One.

Each room houses a doppelganger that is capable of becoming the heart's desire of its visitors.

Running Paradise

Each Brazen Spire has its own version of Paradise, all of which are managed in much the same way although they may have a slightly different layout. Their purpose and execution are similar to that of a chain restaurant or a family amusement park.

The intent of Paradise is to lure visitors with a sense of wonder and sensual pleasure that keeps them coming back to find out what more the Veiled God has to offer. All pleasures are offered free of charge, with the open invitation to come back and enjoy Paradise again, or to seek joys unimagined when they become a true venerate of the Veiled God. Whatever dream or fantasy they have of the Veiled God, also called the Burning One, is fulfilled in the mind of the visitor as the charmed doppelgangers read the thoughts of the visitors and pass their desires on to Eamil to conjure illusions to match their fantasies.

After a few visits to Paradise, guests are invited to learn more about the Veiled God in the Hall of Adoration. They must simply take the stairs to the next floor where new revelations are visited upon them.

If battle begins, Eamil attempts to make his way upstairs where he can use his amulet to warn the hariphs and Sheik Mutastir about the party. If the doppelgangers read the characters' minds and discover their true intentions in the spire, Eamil tries inform his masters. If encounters in Paradise turn to combat, Eamil likewise attempts to flee to warn his masters. If he is captured, he can be intimidated or tortured into explaining how the *brazen amulets*[2] work.

Tower Dungeon

A prison is built below the ground floor to house slaves and others who displease the Cult of the Burning One until such time as they can be placed in bottles and shipped to the City of Brass.

1. Landing

Leading from **Area 2** of the ground floor is a landing guarded by a pair of veiled mamelukes (**guard** with scimitar and short bow) armed with short spears and shields.

2. Jailhouse and Pillar of Fire

The massive Pillar of Fire seen on most levels of the Brazen Spire flows from the center of the floor in this room. The room itself is surrounded by a series of doors that lead to guard outposts and the cellblocks holding the spire's prisoners. There are 1d4 mameluke (**guard** with scimitar and short bow) guards armed as the ones in **Area 1** here at all times. There is also a 15% chance that Sheik Mutastir (**burning dervish**[1]) is present and a 15% chance that one of the hariphs is preparing to lead a prisoner to the **Bottle Ritual Chamber**.

3. Cellblocks

There are five doors marked A through E in the Ignan script of the Plane of Fire. The doors are locked with a key kept by the jailor (**Room 5**) and by Sheik Mutastir. The doors to the cellblocks can be unlocked with a successful DC 19 Dexterity check with thieves' tools or broken open with a successful DC 20 Strength check.

3-A1. This cell is empty

3-A2. This cell contains Herrell Porter (**commoner**), a victim kidnapped from Lornedain. His son, Mareal, and Simone Dubois were taken away from him almost immediately upon arrival. He knows of no other survivors from Lornedain, nor does he know where he is. All he knows for sure is that his time is short.

3-B1. Sir Dalineish is a **knight** of the Lyreguard, and an emissary to the city of Freegate. Eamil the bartender and his doppelgangers captured the knight in Paradise. Dalineish is ready to ride back to Bard's Gate and alert Imril of the situation that has befallen Freegate, but he offers to assist the characters in any way necessary if they free him.

3-B2. Malwane Shebu (**sneakthief**[1] currently unarmed and with AC 12) was hired by Skia to retrieve the *fire stone of Sulymon*[2], but was instead captured. She now realizes she bit off more than she could chew on this job.

3-C1 and **3-C2.** These cells each hold six local miscreants (**commoners**) who showed up in Paradise, but like Ilokos in the **Bottle Ritual Chamber**, they were somehow immune to the power of the **Mosque of Adoration**. The locals could be instrumental in convincing others of the deceit and evils of the Cult of the Burning One should they be freed and allowed to speak openly against the cult in the Forum of Apollon. Among them are Jazmer and Haemon, two well-known partiers who have been missing since the first festival hosted by the spire.

3-D1 and **3-D2.** These cells are similar to those in Cellblock C, but hold a dozen children (**commoners**) scooped up from the slums and wharfs of the city.

3-E. The cells in this cellblock are empty but show evidence of recent occupancy.

4. Guard Bunkhouse

Stationed here at any given time are 6 **guards** who rotate with the others found in **Areas 1** and **2**. Four double bunk beds are found here. The guards each have 10 sp and one coin made of brass.

5. Jailor's Room

The hariph (**priest**) in charge of the dungeon is called Rathmosis, a particularly cruel cleric of the Burning One who hails originally from Khemit. She was a cleric of Sekhmet before being seduced with wishes granted by the servants of the Veiled God. Rathmosis has a *+1 mace* and a *+1 breastplate*.

Rathmosis has a jade inlaid chest trapped with flaming scorpion venom that injects the wrist of any who tamper with the lock without using the proper key. Detecting the trap requires a successful DC 17 Intelligence (Investigation) check. It can be disarmed with a successful DC 17 Dexterity check with thieves' tools. If the trap is triggered, it makes a melee weapon attack against an adjacent creature at +6 to hit. On a hit it does 1 slashing and 10 (3d6) acid damage, specifically to the hand and arm of the lock picker, possibly resulting in a permanent wound.

Within the chest are 300 gp, 2 *potions of healing*, a *spell scroll* of *lesser restoration*, and 3 *potions of resistance*.

First Floor: Mosque of Adoration

Located on the floor above Paradise, the Mosque of Adoration is an 80-foot-diameter open room with a domed ceiling surrounded by several doors. In the center of the room is the Pillar of Fire that extends from floor to near the ceiling, where a large veiled head floats. The head bears a striking resemblance to the burning statue located in the pool in Paradise. Worshippers surround the big floating head, kneeling before the Pillar of Fire. Each appears to be in a deep state of meditation. Figures in robes of orange, gold, and black walk like school teachers among those who bow to the veiled face.

Characters entering the Mosque of Adoration without one of the *brazen amulets*[2] such as those held by Tegman Zekii[1] or Eamil must make a saving throw vs. the enchantment effects of the floating head as detailed below.

The head is a reflection of the face of the sultan of efreet and emanates a continuous *hypnotic pattern* that implants *mass suggestion* in those who fail their DC 18 Wisdom saving throws. Those who fail feel obliged to do the will of the Veiled God, falling to their knees and bowing in contemplation before the vision of the Sultan. They follow the orders of his anointed servants for one year and one day.

Surrounding the central dome are 20 alcove-like rooms. Each room offers a rolled-out floor mat and blankets for a worshipper to rest after training and instruction.

There are 20–40 worshippers (**commoners**) in the mosque at any given time with an additional 1d4 **missionaries**[1] of the Burning One and one hariph (**priest**) overseeing worship. Their purpose is to make sure that the charms emanating from the image of the Sultan "stick" in the minds of the worshippers, or to remove any persons who succeeded in throwing off the indoctrination. The hariph has a *hariph's brazen amulet*[2].

Worshippers whose indoctrination sticks are examined for ability and usefulness. Those who truly feel the calling of the Veiled God are vetted for training by the hariphs to become clerics or wizards to further the cause of the Sultan in the Lost Lands. Those whose training sticks, but who are not considered cleric material, are taken to the Barracks of Blood and Fire, where they are trained as a cadre of the Sultan's own personal mamelukes to do the bidding of his commanders in the conquest of the plane. Those deemed unworthy to serve any other purpose are instead trained in the use of the torch, flask, and knife and sent out to the streets to await the command of their new god and master.

Note: A successful *dispel magic* cast against a level 5 spell slot on the giant head in the pillar grants a new saving throw for all the charmed worshippers in the chamber and dampens the effects of the pillar for 5 rounds. Those worshippers who succeed on their save are broken from the brainwashing and immediately attempt to flee the Brazen Spire. Most soon find themselves trapped in Paradise, where they must battle it out with the barkeep, ogres, or other surviving cultists.

Second Floor: Evocation and Sacerdotal Studies

This floor serves as a school for fledgling wizards and clerics. Central dormitories offer a place to stay for the few chosen ones who make it to this level of training. Access to this level is permitted only to someone bearing some form of a *brazen amulet*[2].

1. Stair

This set of stairs leads upward from the **Mosque of Adoration** and continues to the **Halls of Blood and Fire** on the floors above.

2. Blow Torch Font

This hallway ends in a false door. Pulling on the door handle or turning it in any way unleashes a gout of flame from a gargoyle face carved above the door. The trap can be noted with a successful DC 17 Intelligence (Investigation) check and disarmed with a successful DC 17 Dexterity check with thieves' tools. If triggered all creatures within 20 feet of the false door must attempt a DC 16 Dexterity saving throw. Those that fail take 10 (3d6) fire damage while those that succeed take half this amount.

3. Fresh Targets

Some who fail their indoctrination into the Cult of the Burning One are held in the dungeons until they can be transported. Important persons, children, and those with pure souls are taken to be transformed into living brass upon the **Soul Forge** in the City of Brass. Others are worked to death and then transformed into zombies that are used for training clerics to turn undead and for arcane target practice.

This room contains 6 **zombies** with targets painted on their torsos and foreheads. Bits and pieces of blasted skeleton and leathery flesh are strewn about the floor.

4. Who Watches?

The door to this room is locked to all save those possessing a *brazen amulet*[2] of some sort. The room is guarded by an **invisible stalker** instructed to protect against any intruders not bearing the correct amulet unless commanded otherwise by a hariph or Sheik Mutastir.

5. Balls of Brass

The hallway outside **Room 4** seems to rise at a slight angle that is noticeable to those with Stonecunning who make a successful DC 14 Wisdom (Survival) check.

At the end of the hall is a door leading inward to **Room 6**. The door is trapped to any who do not have permission to enter the training sanctuary (requiring a *lesser brazen amulet*[2] or better). Enchantments on the door trigger the trap, which releases a hidden door at the end of the hall. This second door opens to reveal a 9-foot-diameter brass ball that rolls swiftly down the hallway, smashing all in its wake. Discovering the trap requires a successful DC 19 Intelligence (Investigation) check. It can be disarmed with a successful DC 18 Dexterity check with thieves' tools. If the trap is triggered, those in the hall must attempt a DC 16 Dexterity saving throw. Those failing take 55 (10d10) bludgeoning damage from the ball while those that succeed manage to dodge back into **Room 4**.

6. Serpents and Flames

The door to **Room 6** is hot to the touch. Opening the door reveals a room that is a thin spot projected from the Plane of Molten Skies. The room appears to stretch on in infinite directions and features burning skies, a blasted glass ground, and white sands that lick with open pools of flame. Twenty feet away from the door through which the characters enter is another portal perpendicular to their entryway. The temperature is hot, over 140° F. The temperature causes intense discomfort to any who enter the room. Remaining for an extended length of time may cause heat exhaustion, especially if water is not available. Any of the *brazen amulets*[2] shield the characters from these effects.

Wandering: Characters who wander away from the doors find themselves walking for up to 10 minutes before the doors appear again, exactly in the orientation they originally appeared.

As the characters cross over to the standing door to **Area 7**, they are attacked by 1d4 **fire snakes**[1]. An additional 1d4 fire snakes arrive every 4 rounds. The snakes attack anyone who is not a native of the Plane of Molten Skies.

7. Outer Sanctuary

A **fire drake**[1] named Flare guards this room. The drake lazily sleeps on a pedestal in the center of the room. He expects to be fed a live fire snake from **Area 6** by anyone coming through from that direction and gets a little snippy if he does not get his treat. He attacks anyone entering the outer sanctuary who does not bear some form of a *brazen amulet*[2].

There is a 50% chance that any combat occurring in the room attracts the attention of others within the **Inner Sanctuary (Area 8)** or the rooms beyond.

8. Inner Sanctuary

The Pillar of Fire illuminates this 30-foot-diameter domed room. The fiery pillar rises from the center of the room and extends through a hole in the ceiling. There is a 50% chance that 1d2 **acolytes**, 1d2 **apprentice mages**[1], or a hariph (**magician**[1]) are in the room at any given time. The hariphs use this chamber to instruct their students on the powers of the Veiled God. There is a 10% chance that Sheik Mutastir is here overseeing the teachings.

If overwhelmed, they seek to escape using their *hariph's brazen amulets*[2]. They step into the Pillar of Fire and call out the floor that they wish to visit.

Dance into the Fire: Further access to the upper stories of the spire require characters possessing a *hariph's brazen amulet*[2] (or some other magical means of travel) to step into the Pillar of Fire and speak the floor they wish to reach.

9-11. Evoker Dorms

These dorms house 3 wizards (2 **theurgists**[1] and **apprentice mage**[1]) specializing in evocation and fire magic whom the hariphs are training. Each wizard dresses in robes of black and orange and has a ceremonial dagger made of iron with a brass cross-guard, a *lesser brazen amulet* and a *potion of healing*. One theurgist[1] has a *spell wand*[2] of *burning hands* while the other has a *spell wand*[2] of *scorching ray*.

12-14. Acolytes' Dorm

These rooms house newly minted **acolytes** of the sultan of efreet in his guise of the Burning One. There are 3 present at any time. These members willingly joined the cult, having found their salvation upon arriving in Paradise and being further vetted in the Mosque of Adoration. One acolyte has a *spell wand*[2] of *command* in his possession. All have been awarded *lesser brazen amulets*[2] and are armed with falchions.

Floors 3-5: Thakunat's Dam al Nar (Barracks of Blood and Fire)

These floors serve as barracks for those more violent converts to the faith who, like the clerics and evokers on the floor below, serve more freely and willfully than many of the faithful on the streets who are merely charmed by gifts and the powers of the Veiled God. These warrior slaves, or mamelukes (**guard** with scimitar and short bow), are trained to believe that they are chosen to live and die for the Burning God. They are taught that service to the new god in his conquest of the planes will bear them an eternity of paradise not unlike the joys they first experienced upon entering the Brazen Spire. They are loyal and furious, and fight to the death. Typically 2d6 are in the barracks at any time.

1. Stairwell.

This stairwell leads to the third, fourth, and fifth floors. Characters can descend all the way to the ground floor from here.

2. Mamelukes' Barracks and Training Room

This room in the center of the barracks hall is used for training in general hand-to-hand combat. Currently, the mamelukes training here are drilling in methods of flanking and overcoming the phalanx formations favored by the praetors of Freegate. This training involves a more sophisticated checkerboard formation.

There is a 50% chance of 1d10 mameluke trainees (**guard** with scimitar and short bow) being led through the paces by an officer who is a **khalit jinn**[1]. The khalit jinn are related to the burning dervishes of the Maighib Desert, and natural candidates to serve the Burning One. Each khalit has a *+1* scimitar, a *potion of* healing, and a *lesser brazen amulet*[2]. The troops attack anyone not bearing at least a *lesser brazen amulet*[2] or who is not in the company of someone they recognize who possesses one.

3. Mamelukes' Barracks

Barracks are located in the north and south ends of the training hall. Each barrack holds a dozen bunk beds. Each troop barrack has 2d10 mamelukes (**guard** with scimitar and short bow) in it at any given time. The mamelukes are praying, exercising, or doing the normal things soldiers do in their bunkhouse.

4. Khalits' Offices

Each office houses a **khalit jinn officer**[1] who oversees training the troops. If the khalit is not found in the office, it is found in the training room, disciplining the mamelukes. The khalit has a bottle of rare wine worth 2d20 + 10 gp, a sack holding 2d100 + 100 gp, 2 fire rubies worth 50 gp each, a longbow, a quiver of 20 *+1 arrows*, and a *potion of healing*.

A scroll case with Ignan writing impressed upon a copper sheet includes a map of the Gulf of Akados and portions of Libynos showing where Brazen Spires are located. A star is drawn around a coastal city in Libynos named Kirtius. Feel free to describe any other cities in the region currently possessing a Brazen Spire in your own campaign setting. This is an option that is useful to push the concept to the players that their world is in peril and that forces from other planes are intent on conquering their lands and kidnapping or enslaving their people.

Instructions are included to seek out an item referred to as the "Flask of the False One" in all the lands with details of a specially constructed bottle. This refers to the *flask of Sulymon*[2].

Floor 6: Alqamar Mulnajum, the Hall of Moon and Stars

The Hall of Moon and Stars is accessed by the Pillar of Fire. Its ceiling and walls are inlaid with astronomical symbols and a representation of the heavens as they are seen in the night skies. The inlay is made from diamonds, emerald, and sapphires. This floor of the spire is a known place of study for the evokers trained in the chambers below, and access to its tomes is granted as a form of a graduation gift. This room is lined with bookshelves around the outsides and features illuminated topographical globes.

Globe 1: This globe is a semi-mechanical representation of the cosmology of the inner planes with a globe of the Lost Lands built around it as a crystal shell. Various levers can be moved to show places in the Lost Lands where portals to the Planes of Air, Earth, Fire, and Water can be found. The levers have symbols representing the various elements. As the globe is turned and one of the levers is engaged, the globe produces certain special effects such as spritzing out water, a puff of air, or grains of sand. The fire lever for whatever reason does not appear to function correctly and is locked in place.

Globe 2: This is a globe of the world of the Lost Lands. Featured upon it are all the currently completed Brazen Spires as represented by 50 brass pegs shaped like Brazen Spires placed in peg holes on the globe. A brass bowl sitting next to the globe contains another 16 brass spire pegs that would fit in the remaining peg holes. If all 66 brass pegs are placed in their holes on this globe, the fire handle on **Globe 1** makes an audible click and suddenly unlocks. All the empty holes on the globe correspond with cities and holy sites in Akados.

The Moons: This mechanism is a representation of the planetary moons. A complex series of cranks and handles can be turned and adjusted to create a lunar alignment with **Globe 2**. This accomplishment requires a successful DC 19 Intelligence (Nature) check. A subsequent successful DC 17 Intelligence (Nature) check reveals that there is roughly one year

Brazen Spire

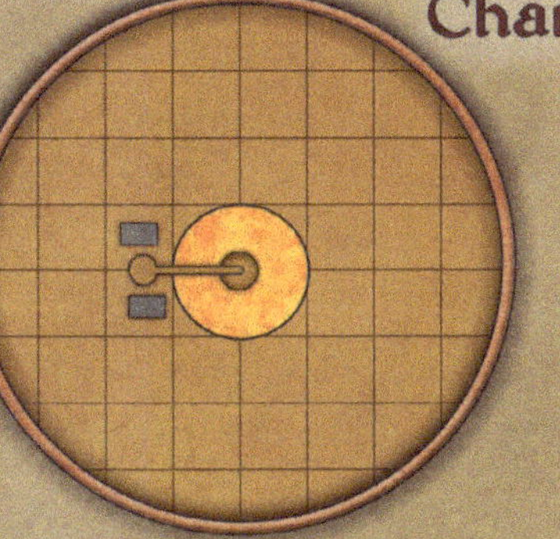

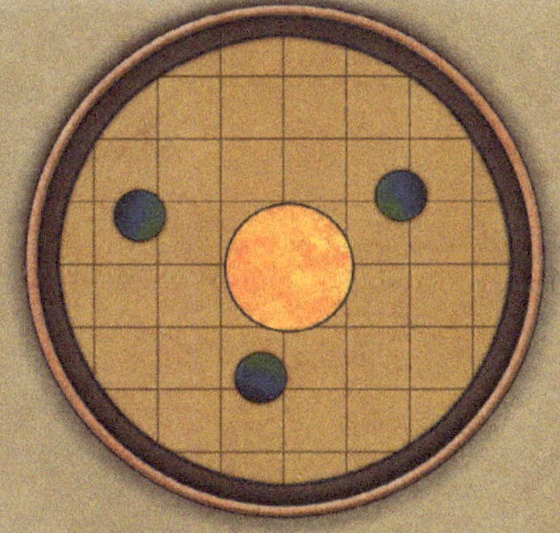

1 Square – 5 Feet

until a similar conjunction of the planets takes place. Failing the first Intelligence check jams the machine, making it impossible to move the moons into position.

If the pegs on **Globe 2** are all in place and the moons are placed in the correct lunar alignment, a flame fires out from the Spheres of the Inner Planes and bathes the second globe in fire. Anyone caught between the two globes must succeed on a DC 15 Dexterity saving throw or suffer 3 (1d6) fire damage.

A map on the wall features the triangular shape of the Plane of Molten Skies and an inset features a generalized map of the City of Brass, with its major temples, palaces, plazas, and markets named in the key.

A study of the books finds a series of illustrations that may be of some interest to the characters. The first show a pile of yellow ingots with anguished faces on them placed in front of a short-statured flaming dwarf. The dwarf is surrounded by figures in black and orange robes. The second image shows the figures standing before a representation of the Brazen Spire that now stands where the ingots were once piled. The flaming dwarf is being dragged into the tower in chains.

Among the books in the library are 2d6 arcane spells of 1st to 3rd levels found in a series of spellbooks. Also in the room is a book titled "*The Forge of the Holy Spire.*" This book contains instructions to create a Brazen Spire. Much of the esoteric material seems to describe a ritual overseen by burning dervishes and native planar worshippers of the Veiled God. The ritual calls for ingots of "living brass" forged by an azer native to the Plane of Molten Skies.

Floor 7:
Prayer Room of the Hariphs

This room is accessed via the Pillar of Fire.

The interior of the room features polished crystalline walls. A series of finely woven rugs lie on the floor in a circle around the Pillar of Fire. Sheik Mutastir and his assistants are able to use the powers of ritual to commune once per month with the Sultan of Efreet[1] or the grand vizier, and once per week with Emir Farphanes in the Palace of Kirtius.

Emir Farphanes can open a gate allowing passage between the spire in Kirtius and any of the other spires so long as the master of the spires and his attendant hariphs are still alive. Sheik Mutastir can use the power of the *fire stone of Sulymon*[2] to travel to any of the Brazen Spires once per week, so long as at least two hariphs or two other willing spellcasters assist him in controlling the stone.

If Sheik Mutastir or more than one of the hariphs are in the chamber, they are capable of entering a trance that allows them to see and hear what is happening in any of the other rooms of the Brazen Spire for as long as they maintain their concentration.

Emir Farphanes and the Sultan of Efreet[1] are capable of bestowing wishes through the Pillar of Fire. During deep meditation, they are also capable of seeing and hearing into the room with *clairvoyance*. The wishes are often used as payment to buy local authorities, to grant payment to faithful servants such as Baroness Aora Lornedain, or to prove the might of the Veiled God to suspicious would-be converts. There is a 25% chance that Emir Farphanes (**efreeti**) or the **Sultan of Efreet**[1] are viewing the room. If they see intruders in the prayer room, they summon a **fire elemental** into the room. The creature appears 1 round later and immediately attacks. There is a 50% chance that 1d4 **hariphs**[1] are in the chamber, and a 25% chance that Sheik Mutastir (**burning dervish**[1]) is present (roll separately for each).

Floor 8:
Apartments of the Hariphs

This floor is accessed only by the Pillar of Fire.

1. Entry

The Pillar of Fire halts in this narrow entry featuring doors in the north, south, east, and west.

2. Apartment of Nannos Daksos

Nannos Daksos (**magician**[1]) is one of the first converts to the Burning One from Freegate, along with Tegman Zekii[1]. Nannos was a student of Zarius Medius who was banished from Medius's tower due to his perceived greed and avarice. Nannos traveled the world, eventually finding himself in Kirtius. He entered the Brazen Spire and soon found himself enamored with the power he perceived in the Sultan. He led Sheik Mutastir to Freegate and suggested the trap that ensnared his former master.

Treasure: *+1 dagger*, *bracers of defense*, *potion of fire breath*, *potion of flying*, *spell scroll* of *augury*, pearl worth 50 gp, *figurine of wondrous power* (silver raven), 339 sp, 223 gp, a diamond ring worth 200 gp, spellbooks, *hariph's brazen amulet*[2], and two scrolls of *dispel magic*.

3. Hariph Tariq Mahmoud's Room

This is the room of Hariph Tariq, a **priest** of the sultan of efreet from the Maighib Desert. Tariq arrived with his master Sheik Mutastir and, like others, has been afforded wonders and glory in the service of the Sultan and under the direct command of Emir Farphanes. He helps to oversee instruction of the acolytes in the faith of the Veiled God. Among his possessions he has a *+1 mace*, *+1 chain mail*, a *spell wand*[2] of *guiding bolt*, a *hariph's brazen amulet*[2], a *spell scroll* of *protection from energy*, a *potion of healing*, and a *potion of flying*.

4. Hariph Jibade Thabin

Hariph Jibade Thabin (**priest**) is a follower of the sultan of efreet from far-off Khemit. Jibade is as clever as she is cruel, and is known to have the ear of Sheik Mutastir. She is most often encountered on the sixth floor teaching disciples about the history of the planes and the plans for expansion of the Caliphate of Flame. She has a *+1 scimitar*, a *spell wand*[2] of *scorching ray*, a *spell scroll* of *dispel magic*, and a *spell scroll* of *protection from evil and good*.

5. Teeks Regeern

This sorcerer attunes his rage into channeling the awesome power of flame imbued in his blood at birth and that the viziers of the City of Brass taught him to master. Teeks Regeern (CN human **pyromancer**[1]) is not native to the Lost Lands but traveled here from a world previously conquered by the Sultan. His magical aptitude saved him from the slave pits of the city, granting him an opportunity few others are allowed. He has a sling and 20 *+1 slingstones*, a *ring of protection* (giving him AC 15), a jade figurine worth 50 gp, 4 jet stones worth 50 gp each, 455 gp, 1,300 sp.

Floor 9: Bottle Ritual Chamber

A brass pot hangs by a chain from an arm next to the fire. A pair of chests sit on either side of the arm. The arm can swing, bringing the pot into the Pillar of Fire.

Chest 1: This chest contains 100 pounds worth of 2-ounce lead wafers.

Chest 2: This chest contains a dozen finely crafted bottles of the purest colored glass. A careful glance inside the bottle shows the reflection of a tiny prison cell.

When full, the bottles are transported to the City of Brass via a gate opened once per week by Emir Farphanes in Kirtius. Once there, they are transported to the Agony Forge below the Great Ziggurat in the City of Brass. The prisoners are freed long enough for them to be pounded into ingots of living brass.

There is a 50% chance that a hariph (**magician**[1] or **priest**) is in the chamber, and a 25% chance that Sheik Mutastir (**burning dervish**[1]) is present with one of the prisoners from the cells in the dungeon below the spire.

Six bottles in the room are currently stoppered. If the lead stopper is broken off, a shimmering mist pours out. In 1d4 rounds, the victim trapped within the bottle appears:

Bottle 1: For whatever reason, the young man named Ilokos, a **commoner**, was immune to the various charms that the cult uses to blast the "faithful" in the mosque and Paradise. Assuming his soul was pure or exceptionally strong, he was placed in a bottle for safekeeping.

Bottle 2: The child Denton Wayne (**commoner**) is a prisoner kidnapped from Lornedain. He is awaiting transport first to *The Sand Dancer* and from there to Kirtius.

Bottle 3: Praetor Halixes Pemmanon (**captain**[1]) was among the trio of leaders duped and taken by surprise when Sheik Mutastir arrived with his three chests of treasure.

Bottle 4: Fiore Martella (half-elf **killer**[1]), an assassin of the Red Blades, resisted the cult's influence over the gangs of Freegate. She was eventually captured and imprisoned here.

Bottle 5: Praetor Axator Polides (**captain**[1]) was caught in the glamour that overtook himself, Halixes, and Zarius Medius, the high magus of Freegate.

Bottle 6: Innez Fuentis (**entertainer**[1]), a member of the Greycloaks, was sent by Cyrilia to find out what was going on in Freegate but was caught snooping around. Once her thoughts were gathered by the doppelgangers on the first floor, it was merely a matter of charming her and leading her into the jail cells below the tower where she was eventually bottled.

Freeing Prisoners

Praetor Halixes Pemmanon and Praetor Axator Polides are grateful if they are freed. They ask to be escorted out of the spire so that they may gather troops and lead an assault on the spire and destroy it immediately. They believe that Sheik Mutastir has custody of the High Magus Zarius Medius. Halixes overheard that powerful wizards were of great use to the "Sultan and his vizier" but did not know what that meant.

Innez Fuentis offers to assist the party in any way she can, though she needs equipment as hers was stripped from her when she was captured. Ilokos and Denton Wayne simply want to go home. If Denton Wayne happens to make it back to Lornedain alive, grant the characters an additional 1,000 XP story award bonus.

Floor 10: Sheik Mutastir's Quarters

The tenth floor serves as the home of Sheik Mutastir (**burning dervish**[1]). It may be reached via the balconies that overlook the slums below, or by invitation of the sheik, who grants access to those bearing one of the various *brazen amulets*[2]. Figuring out how to get into Sheik Mutastir's room may prove difficult for some players. Luckily, several foes throughout the adventure have *potions of flying* as part of their treasure. Captured hariphs could be charmed or otherwise persuaded into giving up their password of permission from the sheik. Characters who took the time to explore the apartment of Tegman Zekii[1] may have uncovered the password written on a metal scroll hidden there. It may require a bit of role-playing, strategy, and creativity to gain access to Sheik Mutastir or his treasure!

Four balconies surround Sheik Mutastir's room, each with a crystal doorway that opens into the central chamber. These doors are magically locked, but open to the sheik's touch. They can also be opened with *dispel magic* cast against a level 6 spell. A large bed at the north side of the room is draped with silk netting.

The Pillar of Fire rises from the center of the room and disappears into the ceiling above. There is a 20% chance that Sheik Mutastir is in his chamber. If Mutastir has not already been encountered, he is definitely found here. If he is defeated but not killed, he first attempts to flee using the *fire stone of Sulymon*[2] to create a portal in the **Prayer Room of the Hariphs**. If this is not possible because too many hariphs have been killed, he makes his way instead to *The Sand Dancer* as quickly as possible, commanding the captain to take him to Kirtius.

Jeweled mosaics cover the walls. The mosaics show a tableau of images, including a mountain containing a portal of fire similar to the portal that allowed entrance into the Brazen Spire. It shows multiple worlds covered in spires. Each world is surrounded by golden flame. The flames are connected to a profile of a city that sits in the midst of flames and seems to rise up from a metallic bowl in a gleaming sea. The profile of the city features a pyramid or ziggurat rising up from its center with the fires from the different worlds aimed at the ziggurat. A torch-like flame sits atop the ziggurat. The flames

Sheik Mutastir

Sheik Mutastir's *spire master's brazen amulet*[2] allows him access to any floor of the tower from anywhere within the spire itself via the Pillar of Fire.

Sheik Mutastir is one of the **burning dervishes**[1] tasked with preparing the world for conquest by the Sultan of Efreet[1]. He answers directly to Emir Farphanes, who in turn answers to either the Sultan of Efreet[1] or the Sultan's grand vizier. Sheik Mutastir's goals in the conquest are the collection of souls from among the local populace to use in the creation of living brass in the Agony Forge. The living brass in turn is used in the creation of Brazen Spires and the prepping of gates to the Plane of Molten Skies for the Sultan's invasion forces.

Sheik Mutastir is the handler of agents of the Cult of the Burning One, including Lady Lornedain, Giza al Hofu, Tegman Zekii[1], Gregiorie Kaj and other unknown agents of the Veiled God. The sheik serves as a villain behind the curtain. As the curtain is slowly pulled back, it should reveal only new villains such as Emir Farphanes and ultimately the Sultan of Efreet[1] himself as a threat to life in the Lost Lands. As the characters begin killing off cultists within the spire, you may decide to move Sheik Mutastir and some hariphs into position to intercept the characters. Mutastir should not be expected to cower in his penthouse and await the characters' arrival to slaughter him out of hand, however. Sheik Mutastir fights the characters if confronted but attempts to avoid capture or his own death by any means necessary. If chased away, he flees for Kirtius where he is assigned a new spire to construct to replace the one that is lost. After being punished severely by Emir Farphanes, of course!

leading from the different worlds with Brazen Spires indicate the Sultan's power and dominion over these worlds. If Sparque is with the party, he agitatedly points at the flame atop the ziggurat and glows excitely, and then glowers angrily at the figure sitting atop the throne.

Another mosaic shows long lines of supplicants of various races, many unknown to the characters. Each carries great piles of treasure or leads a train of beasts or prisoners. They walk among tall, horned, red-skinned guards whose bodies are licked by golden fire. The procession leads to a huge, red-skinned figure wearing a veil who stares intently at the procession. A successful DC 17 Intelligence (History or Religion) check reveals that this is a procession of gifts granted to the Sultan of the City of Brass, worshipped colloquially as the Burning One or the Veiled God.

A trio of ornate treasure chests sit on the floor near the Pillar of Fire. The chests are 3 feet wide, 2-1/2 feet high, and 4 feet long, and are made of fine wood plated with gold and platinum leaf and silver sheeting. The chests alone are worth 200 gp each.

Chest 1: This chest contains 1,411 gp, 120 bp, 35 pp, 2,800 sp, a black onyx worth 100 gp, a bloodstone worth 50 gp, a moonstone worth 120 gp, and a chunk of quartz the size of a human heart.

Chest 2: This chest contains a bottle of *oil of etherealness*, a *potion of greater healing*, a *potion of heroism*, a *potion of resistance* (fire), a *spell scroll* of *dispel magic*, a *spell scroll* of *dispel evil and good*, and a bottle of firewine worth 300 gp.

Chest 3: This chest opens to reveal a large velvet cloth. Beneath the cloth is a *mirror of duplication*[2]. The mirror contains 12 cells, of which the first 10 are currently occupied. Once the mirror is filled with prisoners, roll 1d12 to see which cell empties to replace any additional characters who may fail their save against the mirror.

Mirror Occupants

Cell 1: The **sandman** in this cell is pretty unhappy with Sheik Mutastir and about being held captive in the mirror. It immediately attacks the nearest person.

Cell 2: Cobra-black[1], an inphidian, arrived on a mission to determine the purpose of the spires for its mistress, a leader of the cult of Set in the Maighib Desert. It was captured in Kirtius and has been a prisoner ever since. It is confused upon its release from the mirror and attempts to escape.

Cell 3: *The Sand Dancer* crew captured this **gray nisp**[1] at sea, and Sheik Mutastir placed it in the mirror. It attacks immediately.

Cell 4: Adeela (LG human **holy knight**[1]) is a paladin of Anumon in Numeda. She was part of a force that attempted to stop the Cult of the Burning One as it rose to power in Kirtius. She knows of Emir Farphanes and the cult's search for the *flask of Sulymon*[2] and its attempts to collect all of Sulymon's sacred stones.

Cell 5: This myrmidon (**captain**[1] unarmed and with AC 10) was a bodyguard to the leaders of the city. The myrmidon was in the room serving when he was captured by the mirror. He was horrified when the exact duplicates of Zarius Medius, Praetor Halixes Pemmanon, and Praetor Axator Polides stepped forth from the mirror when Sheik Mutastir called them.

Cell 6: Babak is an **azer** slave brought from the City of Brass. He is kept trapped in the mirror and is called forth only when Sheik Mutastir needs the fire dwarf to shape the living brass of the Brazen Spire. Babak has the power to undue the living brass, returning it back to the ingots of its creation. Babak knows the future of those souls transported to the City of Brass and allies himself with the party to free his folk from the chains of the burning dervishes in the Great Ziggurat.

Cell 7: Gahez is a **janni**[1] faithful to the teachings of the Prophet Sulymon. He was in the holy city of Dawaad when Emir Farphanes sent forces to eradicate the city and defile the prophet. He tracked Sheik Mutastir to Freegate but was captured trying to infiltrate the Brazen Spire.

Cell 8: This **air elemental** called Ruzgar of the North Wind was trapped not far from the Jazira al Alriya and wishes to return there so that it may make its way back to the Plane of Air. It has a 50% chance of fleeing the chamber via the balcony and a 50% chance of attacking whoever is in the room out of anger over its incarceration.

Cell 9: Zeva the **minotaur** is angry about its incarceration. Emir Farphanes gave the creature as a gift to Sheik Mutastir. It attacks immediately upon being freed.

Cell 10: After having been tricked before by the mirror and succumbing to its imprisonment, Zarius Medius (**arcanist**[1]) is ready, and comes out with spells blazing, so to speak. He casts any defensive spells he has memorized while taking a moment to determine friend from foe. This is not easy, as the only foe he knows for sure is Sheik Mutastir.

The Roof

1. Pillar of Fire

The Pillar of Fire erupts from the top of the roof, basking the area in bright firelight.

2. Catwalk

A catwalk surrounds the top of the spire and affords a view of the harbor and the slums below.

The Brazen Spires

The Brazen Spires serve as a toehold for the Plane of Molten Skies in the City of Brass. The Sultan can currently use his powers to open a gate through one Brazen Spire at a time, allowing for the transport of bottled souls to the City of Brass and living brass from the Agony Forge back to the Lost Lands. Living brass is then used to manufacture more spires. Each of the spires is itself an extension of the Plane of Molten Skies. Once the 66th spire is completed, parts of the newly conquered world are transported into the triangular plane and a new *farm world gate* forms in the Palace of the Sultan. As the Plane of Molten Skies expands its mass, the powers of the sultan of efreet grow, furthering his bid to become a greater god of the cosmos.

Note: The Lost Lands are unique among other universes that the Sultan has conquered in that Sulymon entered the Lost Lands via a naturally occurring portal and blessed the Lost Lands with his holy seal. The prophet dismantled the portal when he recognized the dangers that direct access to the Plane of Molten Skies could present to the mortal realms. Thus, the prophet distributed the elemental stones throughout the lands, hidden among portals to the inner planes in the hopes that they would protect the Lost Lands from any potential foes.

Sulymon's seal upon the Lost Lands — granted to him by the authority of Anumon — limits planar gates from the Plane of Molten Skies and the greater Plane of Fire, thus hindering the Sultan's ability to directly assault the Lost Lands for the time being. This would change if the Sultan's armies were to acquire the *carnelian idol*[2], *Sulymon's flask,* or complete the elemental gate hidden within the Secret Canyon along the Path of the Prophet.

Currently, the forces of the Burning One have recovered the *fire stone*, which is in Sheik Mutastir's possession.

With or without the stones of Sulymon, when the 66 spires are completed and the conjunction of the moons take place, each of the spires becomes a gate to the Plane of Molten Skies, allowing the full force of the Sultan of Efreet's armies to invade the world and flood it in fire.

Destroying a Spire

Study in the Hall of Moon and Stars reveals that the spires can be dismantled in a day by an azer smith or by four earth elementals, or devoured by a xorn in an hour. An azer in possession of two of the *stones of Sulymon* could unmake the spire in 10 minutes. The spires could also be dismantled with a *wish* spell, or it could be destroyed with violence. For example, being filled with the contents of the powder magazine of *The Sand Dancer* or shelled with cannon fire would take it down. The tower can withstand up to 10 direct hits with a cannon before it crumples and collapses.

The Sand Dancer

The Sand Dancer is anchored offshore just outside the harbor. It is a tri-masted lateen rigged blockade runner carrying ten short 6-pound guns[3] and a crew of 40, not including the command crew. The majority of the crewmembers were Numedan privateers who now serve as slaves, charmed by servants of the Burning One. The ship has a keel of 140 feet and a beam of 45 feet. The ship is quick and with its stowed sweeps it is not as susceptible as other vessels to being trapped in doldrums or shallows mired in sargassum. *The Sand Dancer's* 6-lb. guns deal 4d10 bludgeoning damage and have a range 180/360 feet. *The Sand Dancer* has 500 hit points, an AC of 15, and a damage threshold of 20.

Note: *If your interpretation of the game world does not account for cannons, you may substitute them for a ballista or Roman-style scorpions.*

Getting to the Ship: Characters have a variety of methods to get to *The Sand Dancer*, be it magic, hiring a small boat, or even attempting to swim and clamber aboard. Whatever plan the characters come up with, understand that simply sailing out in a galley in the bright light of day is also a possibility, but it is a possibility that could easily result in the characters' vessel catching a broadside from *The Sand Dancer's* guns.

1. Main Deck

The main deck holds four light 6-lb. guns. During the night, 4 **guards** patrol the main deck while 1 **guard** is in the crow's nest.

2. Quarterdeck

The quarterdeck at the aft is the ceiling of the cabins below and holds the ship's wheel. During evening hours, a lookout (**guard**) is posted here. His role is to guard the wheel at all costs.

There is a 50% chance that the captain or the first mate is on the quarterdeck at any given time.

Sand Dancer

1 Square – 5 Feet

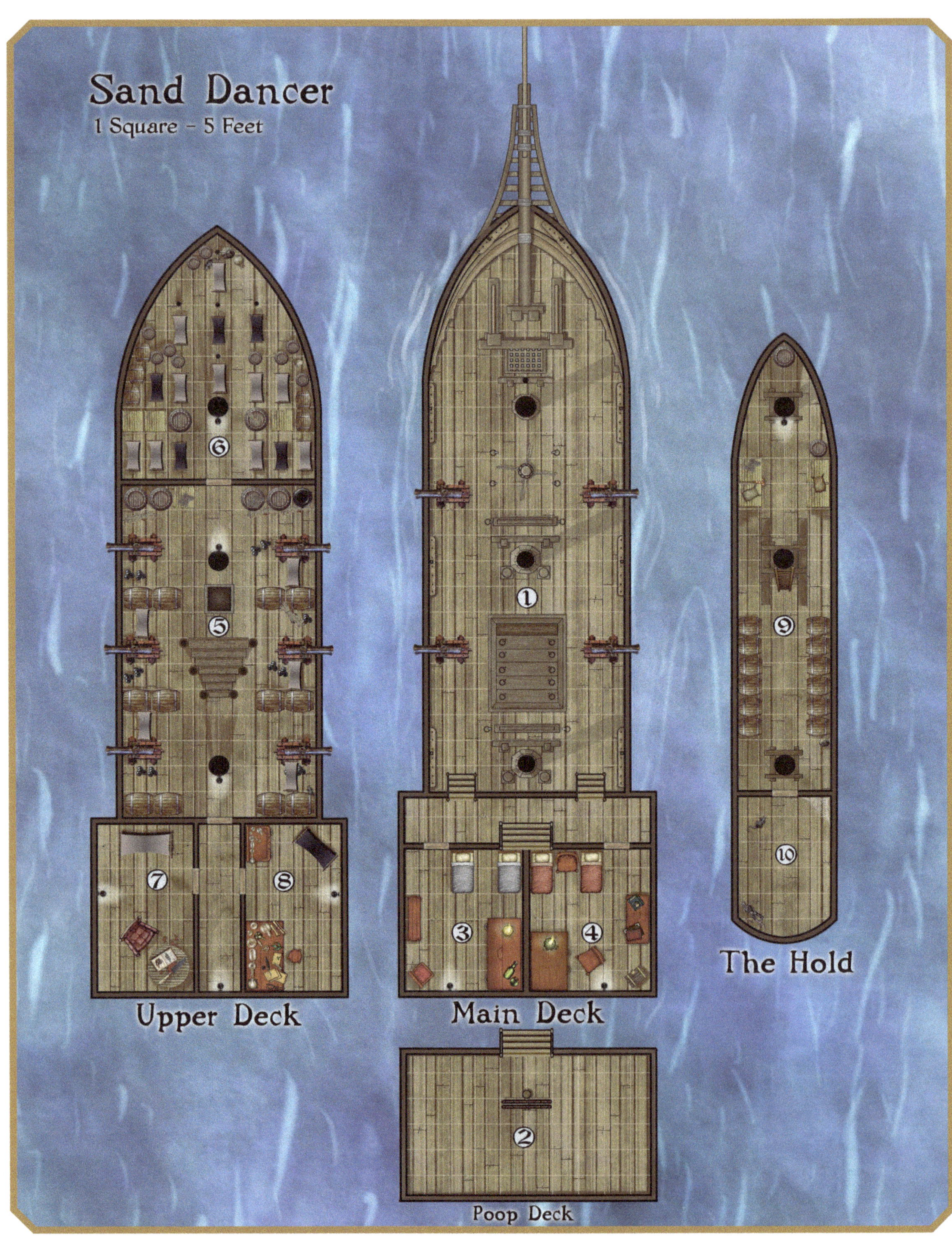

3. Guest Berth

The guest berth currently serves as the hideaway for Giza al Hofu (**mage**) and the Baroness of Lornedain (**preacher**[1]) if they eluded justice in the Barony of Lornedain. Sheik Mutastir uses the guest berth when he makes his journeys aboard ship across the seas to Numeda or to oversee the construction of other Brazen Spires throughout the Lost Lands.

If Giza and the baroness are here, they do whatever they can to defend their pathetic lives.

4. Captain's Cabin

Captain Quarash's (**bandit captain**) cabin is located across from the guest berth. His cabin is filled with nautical charts that detail several of the islands located in the Gulf of Akados and the Sea of Baal. The captain shares his cabin with the first mate (**captain**[1] with Dexterity 16, leather armor, AC 14 and scimitar instead of greatsword). There is a 50% chance that one or the other is in the cabin at any given time unless they are on deck piloting the ship or seeing to the crew's activities.

Treasure: The captain's chest contains 1,200 cp, 1,300 gp, 2,000 sp, a coral comb, a jade statuette of a dolphin, an ivory pipe, a pouch of dwarven tobacco, and a lady's silk dressing gown. The captain himself has a *+1 chain shirt*, a *+1 saber* (as longsword), 2 *potions of healing*, and a *potion of water breathing*.

Quarash and his first mate are not members of the cult, though they are fearful of Sheik Mutastir. They are distrustful of Tarkesh and Ramzi as well, but know that if they say or do anything against the sheik or his allies, their crewmen will suffer.

5. Ship's Hold

The ship's hold is filled with enough barrels of foodstuffs, wine, and supplies for the return trip to Libynos, and trade besides. Among its stores are bars of Akadosian steel. The hold also stores the ship's cannon shot, extra sail cloth, sweeps, tar, sand, and rope.

6. Crew Quarters

Beneath the foredeck of the ship is the crew quarters. Here, the crewmen sleep suspended from their hammocks. Twenty sailors (as **guards**) can sleep in the crew quarters at any given time.

7. Surgeon's Cabin

This cabin is used by Tarkesh, a **missionary**[1] of the Burning One who serves as the ship's surgeon. He handles injuries that don't necessitate magical healing with splints and bandages. He has 2 *potions of healing* and a *spell scroll* of *protection from energy*.

8. Wizard's Cabin

Ramzi (**theurgist**[1]) is a wizard from Libynos and a member of the Cult of the Burning One. Ramzi is tasked with keeping the Numedan corsairs "attuned" to their new roles as servants of Emir Farphanes and his master, the Veiled God. He has a *spell scroll* of *sleep* and one of *protection from energy*.

9. Powder Magazine

The powder magazine sits below the waterline. It holds enough powder to fire the 10 short guns of the ship 10 times each. If the powder is set off, it would be a catastrophic event that sinks the ship and deals 70 (20d6) thunder and fire damage to everyone within a 30-foot radius of the ship.

10. Prisoners' Hold

The prisoners' hold is reserved for those whom Sheik Mutastir wants to suffer throughout the journey to Numeda. Currently, the lightless room holds Yeoman Jon Macewan (**footman**[1], unarmed with AC 10, 10 hit points, and a speed of 10 feet). Yeoman Jon has no idea where his family has been taken, and is nearly mad with anger, hunger, and the desire to find them. Yeoman Jon is sick with scurvy at the moment and in need of healing on several levels.

He was brought before Sheik Mutastir when he and his family were taken some months ago. If he sees the baroness or Giza al Hofu, he goes into a murderous rage and attempts to kill them with his bare hands. Yeoman Jon stops at nothing in his attempt to find his family, and if he believes they are in Kirtius, he does whatever he can to find passage there so that he can retrieve them.

Completing the Adventure

The adventure is complete when the characters defeat Sheik Mutastir or chase him back to Kirtius. There are several times throughout the course of the adventure where characters are given access to maps and information that should lead them across the sea to Kirtius to deal with the ongoing threat that the Cult of the Burning One presents. Of course, the doppelgangers that replaced the praetors of the city still need to be rooted out. This could be a job for the characters as they contemplate their next move.

Should *The Sand Dancer* escape or the characters decide that they have need of passage to Numeda, the grateful praetors of Freegate offer a vessel for their use. The ship is equipped with a captain, crew, and supplies for the characters to use in pursuit of *The Sand Dancer*. This ship, *The Kataskopos*, is detailed at the beginning of **Chapter 5: The Sea of Baal**.

The escape of *The Sand Dancer* of course means that Baroness Aora Lornedain and her pet, Giza al Hofu, once again slip the noose of justice. They are next encountered somewhere in Kirtius as guests of the wicked Emir Farphanes!

Conditions for Success

- Characters kill or chase away Sheik Mutastir.
- Characters expose the Cult of the Burning One.
- Characters rescue the praetors and any remaining prisoners.
- Characters destroy the spire.

Bonus Experience Points

- Characters destroy the Spire: 500 bonus XP each.
- For each kidnap victim freed, offer the characters an additional 100 bonus XP.
- Giza al Hofu is arrested or killed: 500 bonus XP each
- Baroness Aora Lornedain is arrested or killed: 500 bonus XP each.

Chapter 5
The Sea of Baal

The Sea of Baal is a series of mini-adventures designed to move characters from the Lost Lands' traditional stomping grounds of Akados to the kingdom of Numeda on the continent of Libynos, and eventually on to the City of Brass itself. The mini-adventures are scaled to allow physical movement of the characters from the west to the east, while also allowing for some movement in within the Tier 2 levels. Appropriate challenges abound for all character classes.

The area is shown on the map **Sea of Baal**, and the detail maps *1. Mines of Azaadipur*, *2. House of Three Mysteries*, and *3. Isle of Winds*.

Local Background

The Sea of Baal that stretches beyond the Gulf of Akados is the shallow sea that traditionally separates the West from the East and the cultures of Akados from the cultures of Libynos. The sea is dotted with islands referred to as the Titian Isles, so named for their deep ore veins of bauxite and copper that give the islands a golden-auburn color. The majority of the islands are arid and volcanic in origin, though the volcanos that forced them from the bottom of the sea are long extinct. Sailors stop at the small ports throughout the isles to resupply, trade, and take on fresh water.

Ownership of the islands has traded hands over the centuries as their mineral resources and strategic significance often serve as a catalyst for the many wars between the East and West. These include numerous incursions, occupations, and raids of retribution perpetrated by Akados and Libynos against one another over hundreds and thousands of years.

As characters travel across the Sea of Baal, they are required to make several stops to resupply their crew with water and food, as the world of the Lost Lands is vast and travel across the sea takes significant time. Throughout their journey, they may be impeded by the forces of the sultan of efreet in the guise of the Cult of the Burning One. Their stops at islands such as the mines of Azaadipur may place them in possession of a first or even second of Sulymon's elemental stones. They may also find themselves transported to the Plane of Molten Skies earlier in their quest than anticipated, even if only for a short jaunt!

Possibly the characters are lost in their quest or need a shortcut to find enemies who escaped them, such as Baroness Aora Lornedain or Giza al Hofu. The crew of the party's ship may be aware of an oracle on the Isle of Sarmad Yazdg who can provide some answers. As the characters explore the various islands on their trek to Numeda, they may make new allies and uncover more information about the planes, the Sultan, and his plot.

The adventures and locations are listed with a suggested character level so you may use them in whatever manner they deem necessary to help the characters acquire new levels and treasures required for success in later chapters.

How many of these islands the characters visit, or how many encounters they face is at your discretion, as you know best the needs of your gaming group. They are by no means required to visit all the islands in order to complete their journey from Freegate to Kirtius!

Random Encounters and Events

By this point in the adventure, the characters may have made themselves the target of the Sultan of Efreet[1] after destroying his Brazen Spire in Freegate. The Sultan, or his agents, may seek ways to slow or capture the characters, including assault by pirates true to the Burning One, powerful storms, and sudden heatwaves. Depending on the timeframe of the journey, roll 1d20 on the following table daily or weekly.

1d20	Random Event
1	Heatwave
2	Rough seas
3	Storm
4	Meteor shower
5	Pirate attack
6	Marid
7	Efreeti harasser

1d20	Random Event
8	Doldrums
9	Siren
10	Merfolk and sahuagin
11–20	No Encounter

Heatwave: The Sultan causes a heatwave to strike the ship, doubling the consumption of water and causing discomfort among the crew, which increases travel time by 1d4 days. Water may run out, forcing a stop at the nearest port or island.

Rough Seas: Rough seas erupt around the ship due to the Sultan exerting his powers over the temperature of the waters. Characters must make a successful DC 18 Dexterity or Strength saving throw or be tossed overboard along with 1d4 crew members. They must be saved within 1d4 rounds or be lost at sea and drown. If the ship suffers a loss of more than half of its crew, there is a 50% chance of mutiny. Regardless of mutiny, the ship adds 1d6 days to its travel time due to the difficulties of running the vessel with a reduced crew.

Storm: A rough storm erupts due to the Sultan meddling with the weather over the Sea of Baal. The captain must make a successful DC 15 Intelligence check with navigator's tools or the ship runs aground and is damaged on one of the detailed islands in the chain. The storm also has the same effects as the rough seas event.

Meteor Shower: The Sultan hurls bolts of molten stone through the cosmos at the characters' ship. Characters must make a DC 20 Dexterity saving throw or find themselves struck by an exploding meteor for 10 (3d6) bludgeoning and fire damage. Additionally, the ship catches fire. The characters and crew have 1d6 + 2 rounds to put the fire out and save the ship. Failure to put the fire out adds 2d6 days to travel time as the listless ship floats to the shore of one of the Titian Isles. Repairs take 1d4 days.

Pirate Attack: A dhow crewed by Numedan corsairs who have converted to the Cult of the Burning One attack the ship. The ship is equipped with 2 cannons. There are 20 pirates aboard the ship. They are the equivalent of **bandits** and are led by a **bandit captain**.

Marid: A bottle floats in the sea. If the characters snag the bottle (perhaps with a DC 15 Dexterity check) and open it, they release Barak al Bahr, a **marid**[1] cast into the sea by servants of the sultan of efreet. Barak is grateful and offers to guide the characters to the location of one of the *stones of Sulymon*. There is a 50% chance that Barak can also grant a single *wish*. If the characters are disrespectful, Barak punishes them with a curse, casting them into the Plane of Elemental Water.

Efreeti Harasser: An **efreeti** sent by Emir Farphanes or the Sultan of Efreet[1] appears, casts *wall of fire* on the characters' ship, and summons a **fire elemental** to burn the riggings and sails. The efreet leaves when it expends its magical attacks and warns the characters to turn away from their quests.

Doldrums: The winds die completely, requiring the use of twice the provisions and water by rowers. This lasts for 2d6 days.

Siren: A **siren**[1] tries to pull the crew into a reef, causing damage that requires 2d6 days to repair, and the potential loss of life!

Merfolk and Sahuagin: Characters encounter a trio of wounded **merfolk** being harassed by 1d8 + 4 **sahuagin**. If the characters rescue the merfolk before any of them are killed, the merfolk tell them a story about the *water stone of Sulymon* that they heard from a passing water elemental. They suggest that it is trapped at the bottom of an oasis in the Maighib Desert not far from the city of Dawaad.

Titian Isles

The Titian Isles are so named for the rich copper ores that give their mountains a deep brown to greenish tinge. They have a Mediterranean climate, with many of the islands being arid and having sparse vegetation. Others islands are lush and fed by deep springs of fresh water and covered in groves of olive, cypress, and citrus trees. Among the isles are the following areas of adventure.

1. The Mines of Azaadipur

The Mines of Azaadipur is an adventure location for 4–6 characters of Tier 2. Their exploration involves role-playing with local officials, and subterranean exploration. Characters could potentially fall through the mines into the Plane of Molten Skies; you should be ready for such an event and read the section about the **Ash-Grinder's Arcology** in the Plane of Molten Skies in **Chapter 10**.

Background

Situated among the mountainous cliffs in the Titian Isles, the mines of Azaadipur are old by even the reckoning of the Hyperborean sages, dating back to the earliest civilized human occupation of the region. More than five miles of twisting tunnels run beneath the surface of the islands, spreading across nine different levels and reaching a depth of more than 250 feet. Some of the tunnels are so narrow that only small demihumans and children would be able to access them, which is exactly what happened when slaves of ancient Khemit once worked the mines.

For the most part, those ancient days have passed, however. The mines have been refitted and are actively being worked again, with several veins of rich copper already completely depleted and the mining of more veins well underway. Unfortunately for the mine's investors, an incursion of ankheg has broken through into the tunnels of the mine and excavations have ground to a halt.

Normally, an incursion of ankhegs would be not be too great a challenge for a well-armed group of soldiers or hired heroes to systematically take out, but the ankhegs have been acting erratically and unpredictably. Some would even say they seem organized and unusually aggressive. Several armored squads of soldiers have been sent into the depths but have not returned, leading the mine's investors to wonder what is truly going on at the heart of their once-prosperous dig.

After two failed attempts at clearing the mine, the investors are offering up to 500 gp to each character who can clear the mine, in addition to the gratitude of the local lords with interests in the mine.

The Truth at the Heart of the Mine

Miners working deep within the mine partially uncovered the buried *earth stone of Sulymon* and triggered its magical effects, suddenly opening an unstable portal to the Plane of Molten Skies. The portal leads to a location in the Plane of Molten Skies that rests in midair on the border

of territory controlled by the formians of the **Ash-Grinder's Arcology** (see **Chapter 10**).

The formian queen at the head of the Ash-Grinder's Arcology sent one of her own lieutenants through the portal to secure it and to make sure it is not discovered before a land-bridge is built to the midair portal on their side in the Plane of Molten Skies. To this end, her formian envoy enslaved a local group of ankheg lairing near the mine and used them to clear the mine of all workers. Furthermore, the formian envoy instructed the ankhegs to destroy anyone who should enter the mine, with the ultimate goal of keeping the portal as secret as possible from the outside human world … at least until the armies of the Ash-Grinder's Arcology can come through it.

If left alone and unopposed, the ankheg should be able to keep any party of normal soldiers without magical aid from breaching the inner work-areas of the mine where the unstable portal resides. With enough time the formians intend to create a stable, permanent gate to establish a secure two-way thoroughfare between the mines and the Plane of Molten Skies. If this is accomplished in secrecy as the formian queen intends, a massive danger looms on the horizon for the entire region … and possibly for the entirety of the Lost Lands!

Getting Started

The mines are currently managed by praetors from Freegate who sent galleys to conquer the islands and to take over the mining operation after surveyors indicated that copper was still in abundance among the isles. Gios Hermes (**commoner**), a merchant from Freegate, has taken passage aboard the characters' ship and offers them a sum of money to act as his bodyguards when the ship puts into the harbor. He understands the characters' haste and assures them that the expedition should take only a day.

The captain agrees, as his crew needs food and fresh water, and the ship needs a day of outfitting and repairs before it can be fully seaworthy again.

Once the characters arrive at the mine, the manager Epiketos tells Gios Hermes or Captain Airla how he personally sent two phalanxes of the mine's guards into the mines to clear out the problem. Unfortunately, none returned, and he now has only a single phalanx left to guard the mining camp. The miners who survive refuse to re-enter the mines until they are assured the mine is safe and clear of beasts.

1-1. Entrance to the Mines

The entrance to the mines of Azaadipur is roughly 10 feet in height and close to 20 feet wide. The access-point is bolstered by several thick, rough-hewn beams that have been used to bolster the stability of the entryway. The ground is relatively flat from all the traffic going in and out of the mine. To the right of the entrance sits a pile of excavated stone, perhaps 12 feet high at its tallest point. Several unlit hooded lanterns hang from iron spikes to the left of the entrance.

A successful search DC 14 Intelligence (Investigation) check shows that there has been much foot and wagon traffic in and out of the mine in the past, but none lately. It looks to have been at least a week since anyone passed through the entrance.

1-2. Exploited Veins

These tunnels end where the veins of ore have already run dry.

1-3. Chokepoint and Collapse

This chamber appears to be a collection area where the largest deposits of copper are separated from the outlying rock and then carried out toward the entrance. Unfortunately, a partial cave-in makes the only access point deeper into the mine somewhat of a chokepoint. A closer look at the scattered rubble in the room shows that at least two minecarts have been smashed to bits. The remains of several armored men lie crushed and partially covered by the fallen rocks. In all, eight bodies lie beneath the rubble.

This is all that is left of an armored squad of soldiers sent by the mine's investors to investigate the problems. They were crushed by a forced collapse and then finished off by the ankheg. A successful DC 14 Intelligence (Investigation) reveals two things. First, the bodies of the soldiers all show evidence of some sort of corrosive acid attack. Second, select bits of these soldiers were bitten off and carried away, presumably as a meal by the ankhegs. All the soldiers' gear, weapons, and armor remain behind; nothing was looted or taken.

The soldiers have a total of 8 suits of chain mail and 8 medium metal shields in poor condition (most show damage from an acidic attack), along with 4 usable spears (4 are broken or burned beyond use), 5 shortswords,

and 3 longswords. Four helmets remain behind in usable condition, but the heads of 4 of the soldiers are nowhere to be found.

The chokepoint from the fallen rubble is between 5 feet and 8 feet wide. A successful DC 15 Wisdom (Survival) check reveals large, strange, insectoid tracks going in and out of the chokepoint.

1-4. Lying in Wait

Just beyond the chokepoint, 2 **ankhegs** wait for any unfortunate victims to wander into the room. The ankhegs are in elevated areas, 8 feet above the tunnel floor, allowing them to deploy their acidic attack on anyone below them. In addition, they have the higher ground, enabling them to use their physical bite attack as well. They attack the first individual coming through the chokepoint and, if others make it through, they bombard them with acid. The ankhegs fight to the death and do not retreat.

1-5. Stalagmite Field

This cool, sloping cavern is an offshoot of the mine, having been discovered during its initial dig. Usually used to store supplies for the miners and their operation, the majority of this underground grotto is choked with stalagmites and stalactites. A few bats and small cave spiders can be seen flitting or dangling about, but the cave is otherwise quiet.

Near the entrance, two mine carts lie tipped over on their sides, spilling an assortment of mining equipment onto the floor. In addition to the usual mining picks and axes, several hundred feet of good, usable rope, 2 broken hooded lanterns, 3 bundles of torches, 8 mining pans, 3 sledgehammers, 4 leather pouches filled with iron spikes, 4 fine quality rock hammers, and 8 large canvas bags are scattered across the cavern floor.

A simply made, unlocked wooden chest sits on a pile of loose rocks behind the carts, wedged open with an iron spike. Inside the chest, a ransacked cache of moldering but curiously gnawed food can be found, along with 5 large bladders of water and 2 smaller bladders of strong wine. Aside from a few cave crickets and maybe a centipede or two, the water and wine are untainted and quite safe to drink. Not so much the food, which spoiled and was snacked upon by some unknown creature.

Unfortunately for intruders, this cavern is also home to 6 **darkmantles** who recently moved in after workers vacated the mine. Unable to attack or effect the ankhegs in any meaningful way, and being beneath the concerns of the formians, the darkmantles are starving and desperate. They attack any Medium or smaller creature that enters the cavern. Once characters enter the cavern, they use their darkness aura and descend from above.

1-6. Drop-Off

A natural crevasse divides this area of the mine, but the miners built a sturdy-looking wooden bridge over it. Normally, the bridge would be easily crossed, but the formians instructed the ankhegs to weaken the underside with their acid. The import of the damage can be noted with a successful DC 15 Intelligence (Investigation) check.

If more than 100 pounds is placed on the bridge, it immediately collapses, falling into the jagged crevasse below. Any character on the bridge must make a successful DC 15 Dexterity saving throw or fall into the breach. The fall is 60 feet deep, inflicting 21 (6d6) bludgeoning damage. A character that falls and survives can climb out of the chasm unassisted with a successful DC 19 Strength (Athletics) check or assisted with ropes by fellow characters without a check.

1-7. Formian Nest and Portal to the Plane of Molten Skies

This is the chamber where the unstable natural portal initially opened, causing this whole mess in the first place. A **formian warrior**[1] barricaded itself here with 2 **ankhegs** as a final measure to protect the portal.

This chamber is oblong, some 25 feet wide and 60 feet long. The formian envoy had his ankheg servitors build small barriers and obstacles throughout the room using rubble from the mine. Because of these obstacles and the uneven footing in the room, the area is considered difficult terrain and taking the Dash action requires a successful DC 14 Dexterity (Acrobatics) check.

The entire chamber has an odd, chemical smell to it — the result of the formian taskmaster[1] constantly sending reports and updates via pheromones through the planar gate.

The planar portal (**Area 7A**) is located at the rear of the chamber, against the north wall. The portal appears as a roughly circular, wavy plane of luminescence, distorted as if by waves of intense heat, hanging unattended in midair a few inches above an exposed piece of glowing rock. It gives off a magical aura under the scrutiny of a *detect magic* or similar spell and has a slight static sensation if touched. The portal can visually be identified with a successful DC 16 Intelligence (Arcana) skill check. A successful skill check also reveals the most obvious solution to closing it: a *dispel magic* spell cast against a level 8 spell.

The formian taskmaster[1] from the Ash-Grinder's Arcology is here, attended by 2 ankhegs. It spares no time attacking the characters. The formian does the bidding of its queen and fights to the death attempting to protect the portal from any perceived danger. The ankhegs fight to the death as well.

On the Other Side of the Portal

A few things are immediately evident to anyone passing through the portal.

First, the individual emerges onto the Plane of Molten Skies in all of its boiling hot glory. The first thing seen is the massive undertaking by the formians to build a land bridge from their hill to the midair portal. In the distance, massive anthills larger than anything than the character could have possibly conceived rise out of the ash of the plane while thousands of formians work as a single unit to keep the Ash-Grinder's Arcology rhythmically working at a perfect, steady pace.

Second, an individual that cannot fly — naturally or otherwise — immediately plummets to the ground. The portal rests some 1,000 feet in the air over a particularly remote and unimpressive patch of land on the borders of formian territory. Normal damage applies, but few living creatures could survive a fall of this magnitude without magical aid.

Any creatures that do manage to survive are immediately accosted and apprehended by the formians on this side of the portal. The formians' main purpose is to ascertain the danger the individual poses to the Ash-Grinder's Arcology as a whole and what danger they may pose to keeping the portal open and active. After a brief interrogation using their slaves or their bizarre alien pheromones, the formians either enslave or dispose of the intruder.

Ways to Close the Portal

As mentioned before, the natural portal to the Plane of Molten Skies is not an actual intended construct created by a spellcaster. It is a phenomenon that occurred when miners uncovered the *earth stone of Sulymon* and inadvertently activated it, creating the conduit between the Plane of Molten Skies and the Lost Lands, a conduit that the Sultan of Efreet[1] is as of yet unaware.

The portal can be closed if *dispel magic* is cast upon the *earth stone*[2], temporarily disabling it until its workings can be gleaned. This may be difficult, as the stone is partially imbedded in the bedrock next to the portal. Whoever removes the stone from the wall must do so without falling into the Plane of Molten Skies. If the characters have the *fire stone of Sulymon*[2] or the *air stone of Sulymon*[2] and understand their workings, they may touch either of these stones to the *earth stone*[2] to close the portal, allowing for its safe removal.

An alternate method of ending the immediate danger of the portal would be to collapse the mine. While this would work on the short term, once the formians complete the land bridge on the other side of the portal, they immediate begin excavating. Though it might take them months or even years to clear the way, the clockwork persistence of the formians and their queen eventually triumph.

Wrapping up the Adventure

As mentioned before, unless the portal is closed, serious problems could develop for the denizens living around the mine. Furthermore, if the situation is left unchecked, the formians complete their land-bridge and establish a secure two-way thoroughfare between the mines and the Plane of Molten Skies. The entire region (and possibly the entire plane, given long enough) could be in peril.

It is entirely possible that the characters may not have the benefit of a *dispel magic* spell (or better) on hand, or they may fail after multiple attempts. If this is the case, an entire campaign can be made out of thwarting the incursion of the planar-invading formians and their queen, which could have repercussions that reverberate through your campaign for years. Players might have to make a journey to find someone who can actually close the portal, or they may have to discover an alternate method of doing so.

2. Isle of Sarmad Yazdg-or: The House of Three Mysteries

This monastery located on the Isle of Sarmad Yazdg-or is often avoided by passing sailors due to the curious nature of the cult that dwells there. Rarely, those lost in a quest seek the monastery so that they may query the oracle Sarmad Yazdg-or[1]. Caught somewhere between religious fanatics and psychedelic oracles, the shaven-headed, lip-stained seers of the House of Three Mysteries have long been sought out by adventurers, courted by the wealthy, and consulted by kings for their far-seeing, divinatory powers.

In addition to their clerical spell-prowess, the monks gain their supernatural insight through consuming the petals of the rare purple lotus. The mythic desert flower causes excruciating death in most, but miraculously gifts a select few with powerful visions of the future. Through their ritualistic consumption of the purple lotus, these decadent prophets are capable of divining and predicting the oft-changing will of the gods themselves.

Using the House of Three Mysteries

The House of Three Mysteries may be used as a standalone adventure or as a side quest for characters who aren't quite ready to face the challenges of Numeda, the Caliphate in Flames. Other options include a place to stop and gain focus for adventuring parties that need a little more guidance.

Alternate uses of the House of Three Mysteries would be for thieves looking to steal sacred objects, assassins sent to murder the oracle, or as a religious crusade to drive the followers of Hecate from the island.

The following is a detailed description of the House of Three Mysteries.

Walls and Front Gate

The walls around this temple are roughly 25 feet high and in good repair. The gate is made of heavy timber and stands 20 feet high. Flanking either side of the gate, meticulously carved wooden idols of Hecate glare out and over those who come through the gateway, her triple-faced visage looking ahead and to either side. Two armored **guards** stand vigilant.

Guard Barracks

Inside the walls, on the east side of the compound, lie the barracks for the temple's guards. The barracks are a simple, one-room affair reflecting the utilitarian military discipline of the armed faithful who devote their service to this house of Hecate. Rows of simple bunks, with a small chest at the end of each bed, line the walls on either side. Three long tables dominate the middle of the room, where the guards take their meals or enjoy other pursuits during off-duty hours. At the north end of the barracks, several racks rest against the wall, each holding spears, bows, khopeshes (as battleaxe), and a variety of other weapons.

At any one time, 2d4 temple **guards** are here. There is a 50% chance that a guard **commander**[1] will be here as well.

The chest at the end of each bunk contains a variety of robes, clothes, personal effects, and 2d4 gp. Chests are usually unlocked, as the sentence for petty theft among this militant order is a swift death. The guard commander's chest holds identical contents, along with 4d6 + 4 gp.

Courtyard and Front Steps

The gateway opens onto a wide courtyard that runs the length of the front wall. Just inside the gate, several long wooden beams rest against the wall, ready in case the gate needs to be bolstered. Several hitching posts and water troughs for mounts can be found immediately to the right, along with a small covered stable appointed with all the usual saddles and tack.

The courtyard itself is well-groomed and attended by 2d4 shaven-headed devotees (human **commoners**), all of whom wear simple, unadorned garments and have the symbol of the third-eye painted on their foreheads. They tend to keep their heads down and not make eye contact unless directly engaged. Each is armed with a dagger. A number of blooming, well-pruned desert roses line the walkway leading to the front steps of the House of Three Mysteries.

The steps leading up to the entrance are wide and tiled with a colorful mosaic of artfully designed open, staring eyes. Above the entrance, the following words are carved into the archway:

At the crone's gate I stand, the maiden and mother on either hand. Let me pass, blessed and unshaken, eyes open to these visions forsaken. Grant me the mother's boon — maiden, crone, triple-faced moon.

The front entrance to the House of Three Mysteries is fashioned from bronze and carved with numerous images depicting large serpents entwined around three women, all of whom stare skyward at a gibbous moon. A temple **guard** stands to either side of the entrance.

2-1. Entrance Hall

Simple, yet elegant, the entrance hall rises a full two stories, serving as the gateway into this ancient temple and a place where the inhabitants of the temple may greet and speak with visitors. To the left of the door is a small stone basin containing clear, cool water so that any who wish may wash their hands and faces. Long, colorful carpets cover the floors, and several reclining couches covered in pillows and cushions rest against the west wall.

The entrance hall is 45 feet long and 20 feet wide. Three large pillars dominate the center of the chamber. The pillars are intricately carved with images of dancing, shaven-headed women whose eyes appear to gaze at something unseen in the heavens while a blazing third eye stares open and surrounded by flames on their foreheads.

The stone basin is carved with images of a wide, staring eye and benefits from a minor magic that keeps the water cool regardless of outside temperatures.

At any time, 1d4 devotees (human **commoners**) are in this room, all who bear the standard look of those who share their station: simple garb, shaved head, and the image of an open third eye painted or drawn upon their foreheads. They are engaged in cleaning or some other sort of simple labor. Each is armed with a dagger.

2-2. Gallery of the Ages

This is a gathering and discussion area, usually where visitors, delegates, or other travelers can be found in talks with the priests and attendants of the temple. Like the Entrance Hall, this chamber rises a full two stories.

Heavy double doors on the north, west, and east walls are bound with iron and sport large brass handles. The floor here is patterned with a large mosaic of white, purple, and red stones depicting the three faces of Hecate over which a blazing, open eye rests.

The interior of this chamber is decorated with many fine tapestries detailing important historic events such as the Hyperborean Crusades, the rise of the Northmen, and the arrival of the prophet in the ancient Maighib. In all the renderings, a subtle image of Hecate can be seen watching from the shadows or the sky, silently bearing witness.

2-3. Chapel of the Triple-Faced Moon

Used mainly by traveling worshippers of Hecate and other travelers, this domed chamber is lit by a spectral blue-white glow reminiscent of moonlight. It is dominated by a large, black, basalt altar carved with scenes of rampaging genics, coiled and striking serpents, and the triple-faced aspect of Hecate. An ornate brass offering bowl sits atop it and a jeweled golden ewer of wine worth 350 gp sits directly to its left. When the wine from the ewer is poured into the bowl, a simple glamour causes the wine to slowly swirl in the bowl until it depicts the image of a star-filled sky with a full moon at its center. This effect is a minor magical illusion. Priests and aspirants often cast minor magical divinations here, using the bowl as a focus.

Behind the altar, a large tapestry depicts the triple-faced aspect of Hecate amid the smoking carnage of a battlefield, the crumpled form of Lucifer the Lightbringer lying at her feet. One hand hoists the ghostly,

spectral form of that same god into the air by the throat. This represents Hecate's triumph over those who would deceive her or seek to deceive her all-knowing nature, even in death.

2-4. Ceremonial Vestry

This chamber holds numerous supplies and garb for the temple's decadent priests, such as robes, blocks of incense, ornate brass censers, and offering bowls.

A locked chest in the northwest corner contains a number of prayer books, along with a nonmagical crystal sphere (worth 100 gp) covered by a small black velvet sheet. The chest can be unlocked with a successful DC 14 Dexterity check with thieves' tools. The priests of the temple often cast minor illusions and *continual flame* spells onto the crystal sphere to bathe their surroundings in prisms of psychedelic light during services or divinations.

2-5. Immersing Font

A stone font filled with swirling, petal-filled water bubbles endlessly here, filling the air with the sweet smell of roses. The prophets and attendees of the temple anoint themselves here.

2-6. Chapel of the All-Seeing Eye

This grand chamber rises a full two stories to a fully painted domed ceiling that depicts the tri-fold aspect of Hecate among the celestial bodies of the heavens. Dominating the lower chamber is a large statue of the goddess, her arms outstretched and holding a glimmering sphere of crystal aloft in the open palm of one hand.

A minor magical illusion, along with a permanent effect similar to an *antipathy* spell, has been placed on the statue's glimmering green eyes so that they appear lifelike and seem to smolder if stared at. When characters gaze into the eyes of the statue for more than a few moments, they must make a successful DC 16 Wisdom saving throw or feel uneasy, then queasy, and finally — if they continue to stare and fail a second saving throw — be forced to leave the unnerving presence of the statue.

The statue's eyes are two large emeralds worth 3,500 gp each. The crystal sphere, if somehow dislodged from the palm of the statue, would be worth up to 2,150 gp on the open market. Unfortunately for any would-be looters, both the gems and the crystal sphere bear a powerful curse. If removed from the House of Three Mysteries without the divine blessing of Hecate, the thieves are afflicted with a magical malady that affects them as if they had contracted mummy rot[3]. All saving throws against this effect are made with disadvantage. Even if returned to the temple, the curse continues to take its toll. The priesthood of Hecate is not known to be particularly forgiving toward those who would loot their sacred mysteries.

The stone altar is oval-shaped and fashioned to resemble a bowl of sorts, with a raised pedestal rising from the center. The pedestal is adorned with images of open, staring eyes and coiled serpents. A shimmering crystal ball sits upon the pedestal. The water in the altar is clear and cool, full of floating, purple petals taken from the rare purple lotus flower. This altar is reserved for the temple's senior-most seers and is the spell focus for their most powerful divination spells.

On the west and east walls, long, burgundy-colored curtains lead to adjacent areas. These curtains are almost always drawn closed.

At any one time, 1d4 + 1 devotees (**commoners**), 2d3 temple **guards**, and 1d3 **missionaries**[1] of the sacred eye can be found here. In addition, there is a 75% chance that 1d2 **priests** will be found here, with an additional 35% chance that Harsham Amun Tul (**emeritus chaplain**[1]) will be present. Finally, there is a 20% chance that **Sarmad Yazdg-or**[1] will be in attendance. Roll for each separately.

2–7. East Long Hall

This arched hallway is adorned with numerous finely carved marble statues representing several saints and revered oracles of Hecate's faith. In total, eight statues line the walls, four to a side.

The statues are labeled as follows, clockwise from the top left:

Raamiz el-Saidi "of the Five Eyes"
Indas al-Siirah "the Black Seer"
Nashar al-Moghad "the Doom Prophet"
Shaamik el-Jabur "the Hand of Fate"
Anam el-Moustafa "of the Scarlet Eye"
Rahaan el-Dakar "of the Five Lost Lores"
Tamir el-Soltuuni "the Omenspeaker"
Argaat al-Mular "the Whisper of Hecate"

Numerous garlands of roses and assorted flowers adorn the necks and feet of each of these statues.

A minor magical effect fills this chamber so that anyone who lingers or stays for too long begins to hear murmurs and whispers, seemingly coming out of thin air. It has no practical effect but can be unnerving to non-worshippers.

2–8. West Long Hall

Much like the long hall to the east, this arched hallway is adorned with a number of superbly carved statues that represent the many saints and oracles of Hecate's faith. Unlike the east hall, only five statues line the walls here, four on the east wall and one on the west, just north of the grand stair.

The statues are labeled as follows, going clockwise from the top left:
Arkaan el-Sadek "of the Seven Sacred Mysteries"
Wajiid Shaam-dak "the Far-Wanderer"
Farduuk al-Damir "of the Brazen Eye"
Zaad al-Abdul "the First Son of the Wind Duke"
Mus'ab el-Uddin "of the One Thousand and One Murmurs"
Numerous garlands of roses and assorted flowers adorn the necks and feet of each of these statues.

A minor magical effect fills this chamber so that anyone who lingers or stays for too long begins to hear murmurs and whispers, seemingly coming out of thin air. It has no practical effect but can be unnerving to non-worshippers.

2–9. Grand Staircase

This wide stairway leads up to the second and third floors, and leads down to the subterranean lower level. The tiles on each of the steps are worked with numerous images depicting serpents coiled around the moon, open eyes staring into the void from the confines of a full moon or sphere, and crossed keys over an open eye. An engraved wooden handrail provides balance for those ascending the stairs.

2–10. Serving Room

This simple room serves as a washroom and food preparation chamber. A handful of new devotees (1d3 + 1 **commoners** each armed with a dagger) can be found working here. A set of well-balanced, swinging wooden doors on the west wall lead into the kitchen.

2–11. Kitchen

This smoke-stained chamber holds two hearths, a large stone tub, several small food preparation tables, and countless pots and pans that hang from racks on the ceiling. A small well some 50 feet deep in the east corner feeds into a small underground stream. This well provides most of the drinkable water for the temple.

A handful of devotees (1d3 + 1 **commoners** each armed with a dagger) can be found here, cleaning and readying meals for the temple's faithful.

2–12. West Food Storage

This relatively cool chamber is used for storing all sorts of meats, vegetables, fruits, and other types of perishable food. A small pit, more than 20 feet deep, contains a carefully cultivated and well-fed strain of deadly **brown mold** that the caretakers of the temple use to keep this chamber cool.

2–13. East Food Storage

This room stores dry foodstuffs such as grains, herbs, and breads, as well as a large assortment of wines.

The wines were mostly attained through trade with merchants or as gifts from those wishing to retain the services of the seers of the temple. While most of them are common, a small handful (1d4 + 1) of old and expensive wines could fetch as much as 200 gp from the right buyer.

2–14. Public Privies

These four rooms serve as small toilets and washrooms.

2–15. Private Privy

This room is similar to the public privies, just a bit larger and cleaner.

2–16. Back Stairs

These stairs are often used by higher members of the temple's priesthood who like to come and go as they please without the hassle of interacting with visitors or other members of the faithful.

2–17. Gallery of the Faithful

This tasteful, well-appointed chamber is decorated with numerous paintings, tapestries, sculptures, and other trophies that are treasured by the faithful of the temple.

The paintings and tapestries show various scenes involving either the worship of Hecate or the goddess herself, most often in her triple-faced aspect. The sculptures are varied and finely fashioned, representing aspects of the goddess attended by large serpents, nagas, or death dogs.

On average, each of the tapestries or paintings is worth 2d4 x 50 gp, while the sculptures — depending on their size and craftsmanship — are each worth 2d4 x 100 gp.

In addition to the objects mentioned above, a finely worked pedestal holds a smooth stone form upon which a *robe of eyes* has been draped. The pedestal is sealed with a *glyph of warding* that triggers if the robe is touched or moved, dealing 17 (5d6) lightning damage to anyone within 30 feet who doesn't make a successful DC 16 Dexterity saving throw.

A broad set of steps on the north wall leads down to a more sunken area: the temple's meditation area. The low guardrail here allows access to viewing areas below.

2-18. Meditation Chamber

A wide flight of steps leads down into this spacious chamber, which is more of a steam bath than a standard meditation sanctum. A thick haze of incense hangs amid the room's vapors. The interior is uncomfortably warm, but not unbearable.

Several **acolytes** and **priests** can be found here, cleansing their bodies and preparing themselves for the process of opening their minds to the psychedelic visions Hecate grants. The incense has a slightly euphoric effect on those who stay here for more than a few minutes, but also opens up the inhaler's mind. Unless a successful DC 14 Constitution saving throw is made, creatures take 1d3 + 1 temporary Intelligence damage, but gain advantage on any rolls involving the casting of divination spells. These effects persist for 1d3 hours after leaving the chamber.

2-19. Rear Gallery

This lower, open-air gallery is often used by the priesthood to entertain dignitaries and other visitors who have come long distances. Low, broad stairs at the west and east ends of the gallery lead upward into a beautiful room resplendent with padded chairs, comfortable couches, and long tables full of fresh fruits, palm fronds, and ewers of fresh water. Finely carved pillars line the outside of the room, depicting images of beautiful women staring to the heavens with a third eye open upon their foreheads.

At any time, 1d4 devotees (**commoners** armed with a dagger) are in this area, all who bear the standard look of those who share their station: simple garb, a shaved head, and the image of an open third eye painted or drawn upon their foreheads. They are engaged in cleaning or some other sort of simple labor.

2-20. Storage

This small room is used to store supplies for the Rear Gallery and for cleaning the lower floor of the temple.

Second Floor

2-21. Indoor Balcony Area and Additional Seats

This area overlooks the lower floors of the Entrance Hall, the Gallery of the Ages, and the Chapel of the All-Seeing Eye, connecting the beautifully painted domed ceiling to the lower floors and serving as a grand gallery to look down on the lower floor. The ledge is encircled by numerous padded chairs and long pews, so that privileged parishioners can observe services.

In addition to the extra seats and pews, this voluminous chamber also holds a small area on the north end dedicated to musical instruments, which are often used during ceremonies. In addition to the usual sitars, flutes, and drums, a number of mizwad (a type of bagpipes), mizmar (horns), riqq (hand drums), and sagat (hand cymbals) can be found.

2-22. Guardroom

This room is staffed by 4 well-armed **guards** and serves as the gateway to the temple's treasury. A double door on the western wall is worked with a grand image of the goddess Hecate in her triple-visage form, seated upon a throne with twin serpents coiled at her feet. Six arms hold aloft a sword, a wand, a dagger, an orb, a torch, and glowing star. A crown of fire hovers above her head. The door is fashioned from magically dweomered iron brought here from the City of Brass by the Burning Dervishes, who traded it to the priests of the temple for their services.

2-23. Armory

This chamber holds a small number of arms and armaments used in defense of this level of the temple and, most importantly, the treasury. Numerous wooden racks hold spears, polearms, swords (khopeshes, shortswords and greatswords), large and medium shields, and scale mail armor. Two tables hold items used in the upkeep of these weapons and armor, such as whetstones, oil, a grinding wheel, cold forge instruments, and numerous other tools of the trade.

2-24. Private Privy

This room is similar to the public privies on the first level and is used exclusively by the armed guards of the treasury.

2-25. Main Treasury

This chamber is where the collective wealth of the temple is kept, alongside assorted valuables and holy relics of the faith.

The chamber is guarded by a *glyph of warding* that triggers if the chamber is entered without saying the proper prayer, dealing 17 (5d6) thunder damage unless the trespassers make successful DC 17 Constitution saving throws. The glyph can be noted with a successful DC 17 Intelligence (Arcana) check but can only be deactivated with the proper prayer. The sound that emanates from the spell's effect also alerts the faithful, letting them know that someone is attempting to loot the temple's relics. The sound is the deep tolling of a bell, as if coming from far below ground. The **guards** do not know the prayer that allows safe entry to the chamber.

Inside the treasury, the chamber is a simple room, holding a wall of scroll racks, 4 large, iron-bound chests, and a long table holding a variety of items. Ringing the upper walls of the chamber are a dozen 2-foot-by-2-foot alcoves, each containing a human skull with a red rune emblazoned upon its forehead. These are **runeskulls**[1] that guard the chamber from those who would plunder it.

The scroll racks hold many finely detailed maps of Kirtius, along with additional charts and surveys of the nearby lands of Numeda. To a cartographer, sage, or royal official, these maps could potentially fetch upward of 450 gp as a collection.

The chests hold the majority of the temple's tithes and shared wealth. Each chest is locked and requires either the key or a successful DC 17 Dexterity check with thieves' tools to unlock. None of the chests is individually trapped. From north to south, the chests contain the following:

Chest 1: 5 medium leather sacks containing 350 gp each, a finely worked leather scabbard inset with jade and two small emeralds (worth 450 gp), a large silver dog's collar engraved with *runes of submission*[4] (worth 30 gp), a small wooden box containing 75 sp, and 4 golden trade bars stamped with the symbol of Numeda (worth 50 gp each).

Chest 2: A golden coffer worked with the image of serpents and snarling death dogs (worth 465 gp) containing 607 gp, 396 sp, 119 cp, and 80 pp; a finely made wooden ocarina inlaid with turquoise (worth 190 gp, or up to 250 gp to a discerning bard or collector); the fang of a young gold dragon hanging from a silver chain (worth 625 gp to anyone who recognizes it for what it is); and a small bag containing 5 carnelians (worth 50 gp each) and 2 chalcedonies (worth 65 gp each).

Chest 3: 14 stone tablets that if read and studied consecutively over a week's time act as a *tome of understanding*; a polished brass goblet inset with jewels (worth 550 gp) filled with a variety of gemstones, including a piece of highly polished amber (worth 100 gp), a square-cut chrysoberyl (worth 125 gp), 4 pieces of blue coral banded with red stripes (worth 100 gp each), a garnet (worth 80 gp), a smooth piece of jade (worth 110 gp), and 5 white pearls (worth 60 gp each); and an arcane *spell scroll* of *stoneskin*.

Chest 4: A nicely carved wooden scroll box (worth 10 gp) containing a *spell scroll* of *purify food and drink, cure wounds* (at 3rd level), and *lesser restoration*; 3 *potions of greater healing*; a *spell potion*[2] of *remove curse*; a double ivory scroll tube containing a *spell scroll* of *divination* and a *spell scroll* of *arcane eye*; and a wood and iron lockbox with the key in the lock that contains 120 gp, 50 sp, a silver and gold necklace (worth 90 gp), a cloak pin fashioned to look like an owl with tiny opal eyes (worth 155 gp), and an ivory full-face mask set with carnelian (worth 250 gp).

The table contains a set of adamantine scale mail; a *+1 shield* emblazoned with the symbol of Mithra; a fireproof bronze and leather belt inlaid with silver bearing the image of a snarling efreet (worth 250 gp); a silver platter holding 7 dried purple lotus petals[3]; a *potion of giant strength* (fire) in a jar of black basalt; and the *Damned Fragments of Wadji al-Moghaddam* (also known as the *Apocrypha of the Blinded Eye* to a handful of learned scholars), a large tome bound in toughened, cured leather with adamantine hinges and fittings that must be exposed to an open flame before it can be opened. It is a spellbook that contains the

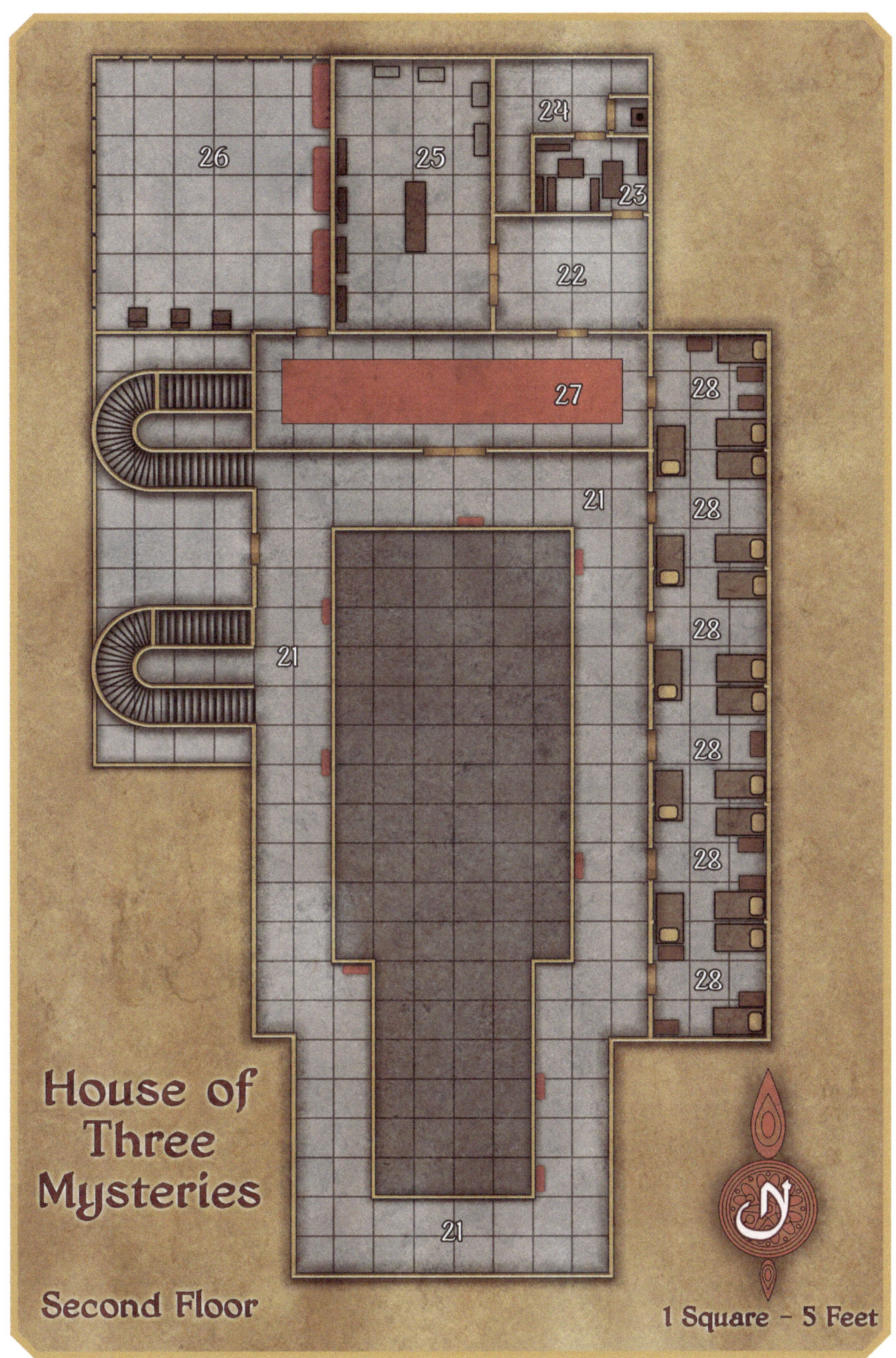

26
25
24
23
22
27
28
28
28
28
28
28
21
21
21
House of Three Mysteries
Second Floor
1 Square – 5 Feet

following spells: *confusion, true seeing, eyebite, fear, geas, hold monster, conjure invisible stalker*[4], *legend lore, project image, protection from evil and good, sending, conjure animals*, and *conjure elemental*. The spells are written in flowing, fiery runes evocative of the legendary fire mages of old.

2-26. Outdoor Balcony

This large, open-air chamber looks out over the back half of the temple and is often used by the temple's priests and oracles for relaxation and thinking. Compared with the rest of the temple, the area is fairly spartan and devoid of the finely carved pillars and elaborate tapestries that decorate the rest of the House of Three Mysteries. Several padded chairs and long, comfortable couches line the walls.

A minor, permanent magical effect causes a soft, cool wind to constantly blow through this chamber. The temperature is always comfortable.

2-27. The Portal of Dreams

A thick set of double doors leads into this long chamber. The floor of this room is covered with a long, fine burgundy carpet woven with images of wide, staring eyes, fanged serpents, and shining stars. The walls are covered in similarly worked tapestries depicting Hecate in all her heavenly glory and power. A single, heavy wooden door is on the northern wall.

An oval mirror of ancient construction stands at the east end of the hall, framed in ornate, polished silver and festooned with black adamantine cap-ends. The frame is worked with images of open eyes, ornate keys imposed over a full moon, and large serpents either set to strike or devouring their human victims whole. A coating has been applied to it, making it highly reflective.

Once each day, an individual who is a faithful worshipper of Hecate or who is beseeching the temple for assistance can look into the mirror for three full rounds and gain the benefits of a *divinitation* spell. However, if the viewer does not worship Hecate or has been hostile to those in the temple, the mirror instead bestows the effects of a *phantasmal killer* spell upon the viewer. The DC for the saving throw is 18 and the duration up to 1 minute.

2-28. Dormitory

This long hall houses the attendees, priests of the sacred eye, and lower-tier servants in the temple. These aspirants sleep upon a long row of bunks separated by chests and curtains for privacy. Thirty-two of the temple's faithful can reside here.

At any one time, 2d4 devotees (**commoners** armed with a dagger) and 1d4 **priests** of the sacred eye are here, either resting or preparing for the day.

Third Floor

2-29. Hall of Lore

This chamber is adorned with several reclining couches, chairs, tables, and crowded shelves, upon which records important to the temple are studied and perused.

The shelves hold many sacred stone tablets associated with the prophecies of the temple. Such works as *The Testament of Arjani-Ru* (the prophecies of Sulymon) and *The Dictums of Dal-Ahaj* (prophecies and teachings associated with Anumon) are found here, along with an assortment of other records dealing with the temple oracles and their prophecies.

A book titled *Jawahra min Alriya, the Jewel of the Winds* details the location of the Isle of Winds and suggests a hidden treasure is located there.

The west wall is covered in an expertly and meticulously painted mural that depicts the goddess Hecate clad only in a sheer garment made from the celestial bodies of the heavens standing upon a column of stars and surrounded by a swirling swarm of open, staring eyes.

2-30. Hall of Prophecy

A large stone podium holding an aged, similarly-sized tome dominates the center of the chamber. The tome meticulously records all the predictions and auguries made by the temple's oracles. A large chain of adamantine clasps the book to the podium.

A few sample prophecies follow:

"It shall be then, when stars fall from the heavens and the three sisters pass from the light, the accused shall mark an age of warlords and the overthrowing of reason."

"A forced marriage and a prophet — cut of tongue and blind to the world — heralds the reunion of friends but the coming of the man in gold."

"As soon as the brother becomes the father, the exiled one — forgotten but remembered — returns, marked by a burning eye in the sky and a boiling sea of blood."

Aside from the podium and its book, the chamber is unadorned and unremarkable.

2-31. Senior Priests' Quarters

These are sleeping quarters for the senior priests of the House of Three Mysteries. At any one time, 1d2 senior priests (**emeritus chaplains**[1]) are here, either sleeping, in prayer, or preparing for the day's duties. Otherwise, this sleeping area is very similar to the dormitory (**Area 28**). Each priest has a 50% chance of possessing a scroll with a clerical spell of 3rd level or lower.

2-32. Central Hall

This area is often used as a place of conversation, as it leads to several different areas of the temple. The floor here is decorated with several long, beautiful rugs depicting scenes from the fall of the efreet They show the transformation of the handsome race to a bestial one, with horned skull, tusked jaw, and cruel visage.

At any one time, 1d2 senior priests (**emeritus chaplains**[1]) and 1d2 oracles of Hecate (**priest**) are present. Each priest has a 50% chance of possessing a scroll with a clerical spell of 3rd level or lower. Each Oracle has a 50% chance of being under the effect of the mists in the Meditation Chamber: 1d3 + 1 temporary Intelligence damage, and advantage on any divination spells.

2-33. Oracles' Quarters

These areas (labeled from **A** to **T**) are where the temple's many oracles reside, one to a room. They are sumptuously furnished with rugs, fur coverlets, four-post beds, ironbound chests, and sideboards covered in folded, ornate vestments, along with 2 crystal wine decanters (worth 20 gp each).

Most oracles tithe the majority of any accrued wealth to the temple, though each personal living area contains 1d8 gp, 2d6 sp, and 1d20 cp, usually kept in a leather bag or in a chest.

At any time, 2d8 oracles (**priests**) are here, recovering from their visions within the temple.

Underneath a loose flagstone in the northeast corner of one room (**Area D**) is a velvet bag containing 100 gp, 2 small sapphires (worth 250 gp each), and a jade ring set with a moonstone (worth 250 gp). The secret niche is discovered with a successful DC 15 Wisdom (Perception) check. This particular oracle just happens to be a little greedier than the rest.

2-34. Privy

These chambers serve as toilets and washrooms.

2-35. Senior Oracles' Rooms

These five rooms house the oldest and longest-serving oracles of the temple. They are similar to the other quarters, though much more opulent. Each chamber is lavishly furnished with an assortment of fine rugs and tapestries, large four-post beds, locked ironbound chests, and sideboards covered in sacred temple vestments, prayer beads, silver incense burners (worth 10 gp each), and a crystal wine decanter (worth 20 gp).

The chests in each room are locked, though a successful DC 16 Dexterity check with thieves' tools grants access. Inside, an assortment of religious ephemera can be found, including robes, censers, small wooden icons, blocks of incense, and holy texts. The senior oracles are almost always greedier than their fellows, having become accustomed to the closet decadence and wealth that their services provide, and their hidden personal

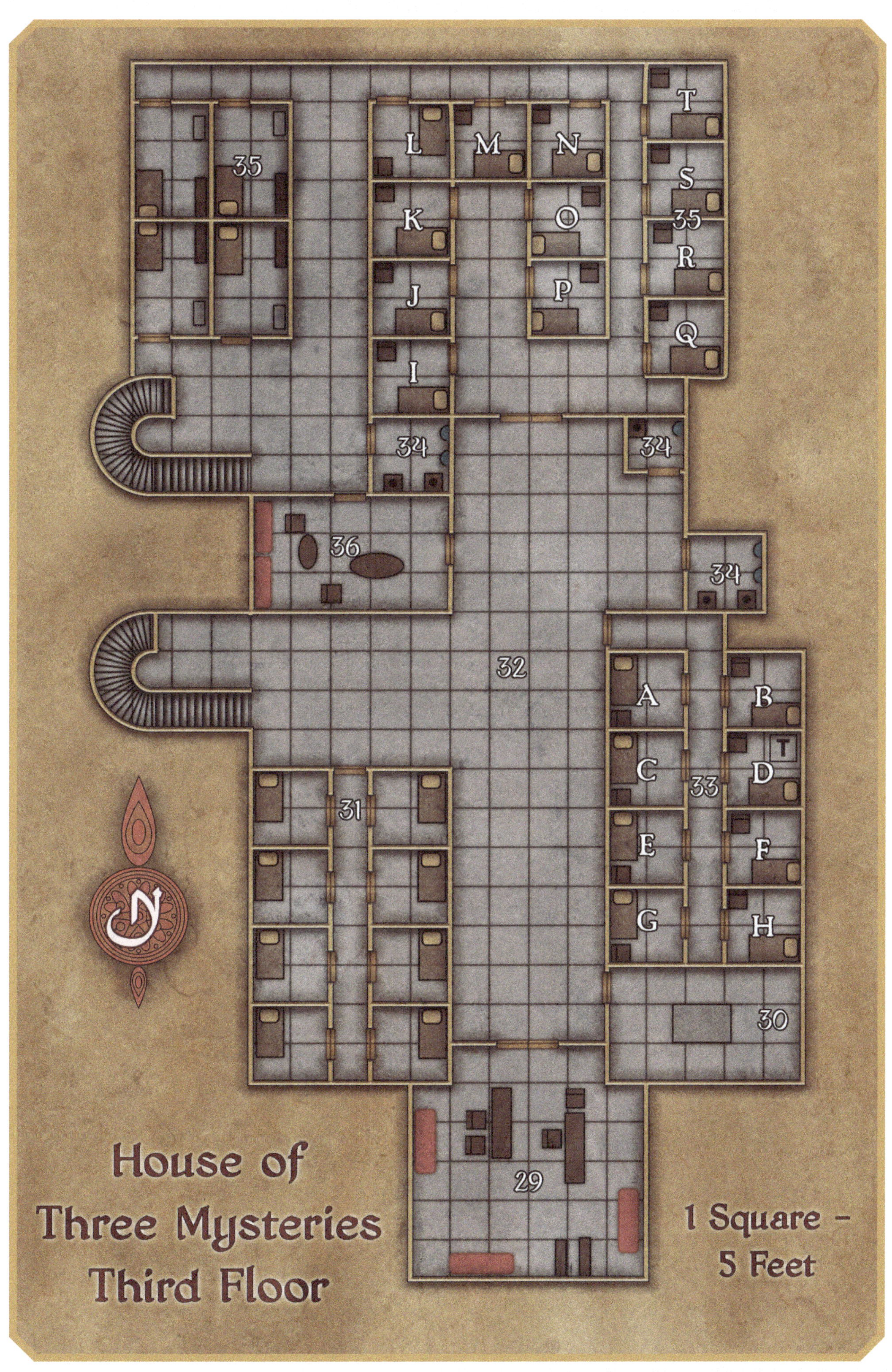

35
L
M
N
T
S
35
R
Q
K
O
J
P
I
34
34
36
34
32
A
B
T
C
33
D
E
F
31
G
H
30
29
House of
Three Mysteries
Third Floor
1 Square –
5 Feet

wealth reflects this. Each of the senior oracles' chests contains 1d10 pp, 3d20 gp, 4d20 sp, 6d20 cp, and gems or art objects worth 2d100 gp.

At any one time, 1d2 + 1 senior oracles (**preacher**[1]) of Hecate are present in personal meditation, attending to their daily duties, or conducting private affairs. Each has a 25% chance of being under the effects of the mists in the Meditation chamber:1d3 + 1 temporary Intelligence damage and advantage on any divination spells. Each has a sepll scroll with two spells of 4th level or lower and a 50% chance of having minor magical item of your choice along with their robes and finely crafted daggers.

2-36. Conversation Chamber

This open space serves as a lounge of sorts and as a place where the temple's oracles can come down off their drug-induced states in peace. Numerous chairs, lounges, and padded benches are found here, alongside several small tables containing ewers of fresh water and bowls of figs and other fruits. There are 1d2 + 1 Oracles of Hecate (**priest**) in the room at any time. They are under the effects of the mists in the Meditation chamber:1d3 + 1 temporary Intelligence damage and advantage on any divination spells.

Lower Level

2-37. Harsham's Quarters

This chamber is the personal abode of Harsham Amun Tul (**emeritus chaplain**[1]), the senior-most advisor and right hand of Sarmad Yazdg-or, the temple's foremost oracle. His chamber is identical to the rooms occupied by the senior oracles of Hecate, except that it contains a personal reflection pool, which he uses as a focus for his divination spells.

Harsham is a frequently cruel man who lacks upward ambition, satisfied in his current station serving Sarmad. The slave Al-Sheera (human **commoner** with 8 hp), one of the temple's many "conscripted" concubines, resides here, scantily clad and chained by her ankle to the bed. If intruders appear, she is extremely helpful in return for her freedom, pointing out valuables in the room and telling characters anything she thinks could help them, in addition to barbaric tales about her hated captor.

In addition to finely tailored robes, holy books, a silver and gold holy symbol of Hecate (worth 25 gp), and other assorted religious items, the ironbound chest in Harsham's chamber also contains a finely engraved wooden coffer (worth 20 gp) that holds 351 gp, 240 sp, 299 cp, 2 amethysts (worth 100 gp each), 3 large black pearls (worth 150 gp each), an *elixir of health*, and a *potion of mind reading*. Harsham has a *+1 dagger*, *bracers of defense*, a spell scroll with *banishment* and *dispel magic*, and a *wand of paralysis* on his person.

If Harsham Amun Tul has not been encountered before, or been roused by alarms from the temple, he is encountered here.

2-38. Privy

This room serves as a toilet and washroom.

2-39. Private Study

This finely appointed chamber is the personal study and private library of Sarmad Yazdg-or, where he comes to study the temple's prophecies, to write, or otherwise to relax in solitude. A scroll rack sits on the east wall, along with a shelf containing many rare tablets and old scrolls.

In addition to dozens of normal books, rolls of records, and personal ledgers, a number of interesting, nonmagical tomes line the study's shelves, including: *The Shards of Nethos-dul*, *The Testament of Vahab the Ashen-Eyed*, *Sharzeh's Tome of Devils*, *The Runes of Al-Awaadi* and *The Three Tablets of Bahador*. These books don't possess any special powers or hold any magical spells but are an example of the kind of flavor and text found in Sarmad's study.

2-40. Sarmad's Private Temple

This is where Sarmad Yazdg-or takes his personal prayers and studies in the dark arts of Hecate.

The private temple is lit with magical torches that glow behind a supple marble statue of the goddess of black magic. The goddess stands holding a sacrificial bowl stained with dried blood in her right hand and a wand in her left. The statue emanates a continuous *detect magic* effect. Once per day, a cleric of Hecate can call upon the statue to *identify* any magical items as the spell of the same name, so long as a sacrifice of at least 1 hit point of blood is offered.

Scroll cases placed carefully on a scroll rack contain 1d4 spells of levels 1–5. Their unique property is that they are usable by divine and arcane spellcasters even if the spell is not on their spell list.

2-41. Sarmad Yazdg-or's Personal Quarters

This is where Sarmad Yazdg-or[1], the prophet of Hecate and grand oracle of the House of Three Mysteries, resides when he is not in the temple proper.

The door here is made from thick, stout oak and reinforced with iron bands. It is warded with a *glyph of warding* that triggers if the chamber is entered without saying the proper prayer. Each creature within 15 feet of the door must succeed on a DC 16 Dexterity saving throw or take 17 (5d6) fire damage.

A long couch sits against the west wall, lavishly covered in cushions and pillows. A finely made, high-backed wooden chair sits next to it, with the hide of some sort of great cat draped over the back. The hide is worth up to 100 gp to the right art dealer.

A long table rests against the east wall. A set of damaged adamantine scale mail and a matching adamantine helmet sit on the table, in the process of being repaired. The chest plate is worked with a single open eye above which a crown of arcane fire smolders. *Runes of submission*[4] that are sacred to Hecate ring the eye in a full circle. This is Sarmad's personal armor, although he rarely wears it unless going into open battle. It is currently not wearable.

A bathing pool, ringed by square-cut stones and with wide steps descending into it, is on the right. A minor magical glamour keeps the water here warm and clear, so that the prophet may bathe in comfort.

In the far-left corner, a grand and plush four-post bed sits, with a small end table to its right side. Underneath the bed is a loaded and poisoned crossbow. The poison is wyvern poison and is good for one use.

A full-length dressing mirror rests on the east wall next to a clothing rack, on which hang several finely tailored vestments. The mirror conceals a secret door that leads to **Area 42**. The secret door is discovered with a successful DC 17 Intelligence (Investigation) check.

A small dais containing a reflecting pool is here as well, with an offering table before it. The table supports a ceremonial bowl and an incense burner. The air still carries the pungent scent of herbs.

If **Sarmad Yazdg-or**[1] has not been encountered before, or been roused by alarms from the temple, he is encountered here. He has a *circlet of telepathy* (as the helm), a *ring of superior protection*[2], *robe of armor*[2], and a scroll with *planar ally*, *dispel evil and good*, and *harm*.

2-42. Sarmad Yazdg-or's Secret Chamber

This is the oracle's personal escape route, leading to an underground earthen tunnel that he uses if in serious danger. The floor in front of the tunnel, right inside the door, is protected with a *symbol* spell (death) inscribed here by Sarmad. The save DC is 18.

The tunnel leads to an outcropping of rock in the boulder-strewn hills north of the House of Three Mysteries. If need be, Sarmad summons a *planar ally* or uses a *word of recall* to carry him away from the temple.

3. Qourrk: The Aerie of the Birhaakamen

This particular flock of creatures is an offshoot of the normal variety of birhaakamen, resembling vultures far more than the eagles with which standard birhaakamen are associated. These beings are an inherently uncaring and dispassionate sort, subsisting on carrion, opportunistic attack, and scavenging as their main sources of day-to-day life. The

House of Three Mysteries
Lower Level

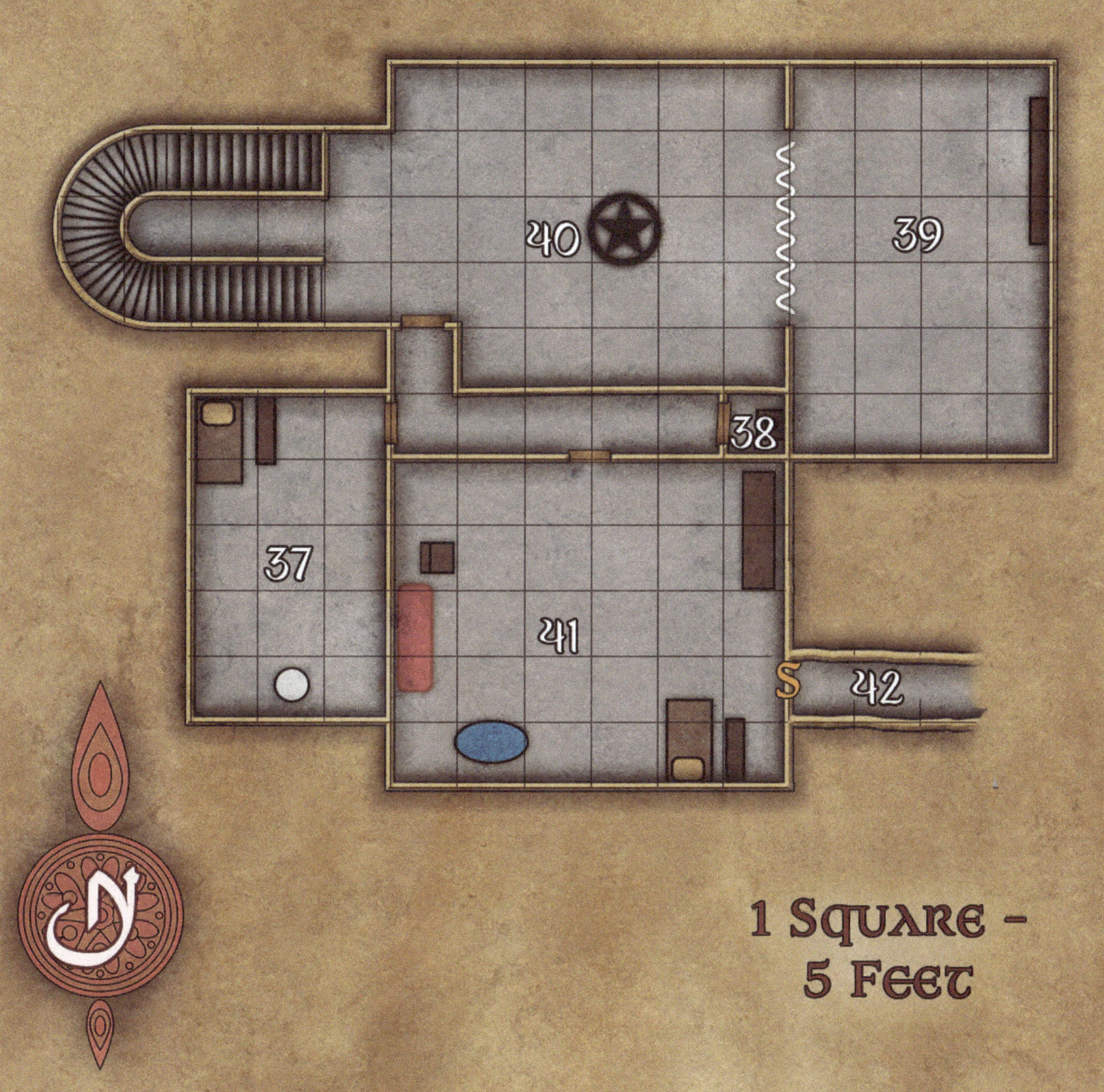

1 Square –
5 Feet

birhaakamen live in a windswept aerie that is nigh-inaccessible without flight or magic, and consort with vultures of both the normal and dire varieties. They care only for themselves and have absolutely no interest in the plight of local, innocent folk, much less the burning dervishes or the higher powers they serve.

Nest of the Birhaakamen

Located atop a windswept spur of rock among the cloudy peaks of the Titian Isles, Qourrk is a simple settlement built among high trees consisting of an extended series of protected nests that have been firmly woven from a variety of scrub brush, desert palm, mesquite, cedar, and knotty pine. On the whole, Qourrk is made up of 8 interconnected nests, with the birhaakamens eggs being protected in the centermost nest and flanked by the rest. The outermost nests have the most active defenses. Currently, the birhaakamen are looking over 5 eggs.

The birhaakamen of this aerie are by nature non-possessive, having no sense of property. Everything is owned collectively and could be in the hands of one being or another on any given day — if that being has the power to wrest it from the grip of another or the guile to take it when they are not looking. In the world of these scavenging, opportunistic beings, possession is the extent of the law.

Twenty-one **birhaakamen warriors**[1] are led by their eldest and mightiest warrior, Haark-Ek (**birhaakamen chieftain**[1]), a clever and cunning sky-fighter who ensured their survival after the entire flock was almost wiped out by an attack from several ravenous, marauding manticores. Haark-Ek led the flock to exact a brutal revenge against the manticores through a series of cleverly laid traps and a divide-and-conquer plan of attack.

Haark-Ek is served directly by the flock's shaman, a young birhaakamen named Serk-Kruuk (**birhaakamen shaman**[1]) who was the all-but-unprepared apprentice of the flock's former shaman. When his master was murdered during the manticore attack that nearly wiped out Qourrk, Serk-Kruuk hastily assumed the mantle of the flock's shaman at Haark-Ek's suggestion and has been learning on the job ever since.

At Haark-Ek's behest, the birhaakamen have built numerous platforms alongside the mountain from which they can land, perch, or take carefully aimed shots at intruders. The bird-men occupy several of these perches around the clock. They take advantage of their exceptional eyesight to locate trespassers and potential dangers in their lands.

In addition to the standard defenses of guards and sky-platforms, Haark-Ek's birhaakamen have fashioned 2 spike traps around the nest, using tail-spikes taken from the fallen manticores that once attacked the flock. These traps can be activated by any of the birhaakamen in defense of the flock and function just as a full tail-volley from a living manticore would. When activated, each trap makes 3 ranged weapon attacks at +7 to hit against one target, range 30/60 feet, and doing 7 (1d8 + 3) piercing damage on a hit. The trap can be used 3 times before it is out of spikes.

Treetop Armory

While not your standard armory from any sort of human sense, this area is where Haark-Ek and his birhaakamen stockpile their weapons and limited armor. The birhaakamen prefer to use spears and javelins when they attack, and their armory clearly reflects this. The armory holds a total of 90 spears, 50 javelins, 50 shields, and 35 breastplates that have been specifically designed and fitted for use by birhaakamen. In addition, the armory contains a small collection of weapons and armor that has been captured, taken, or outright stolen from enemies, intruders, carrion, or victims. These include 3 daggers, 2 shortswords, a longsword, a handaxe, 2 scimitars, a human-sized set of studded leather armor, a full helmet, and a *large +1 metal shield*.

The armory also contains 34 tail-spikes harvested from the bodies of the manticores that attacked Qourrk. While these are not immediately useful as weapons, they could be harvested as spell components or sold for as much as 25 gp each to the right buyer on the open market.

At least 2 **birhaakamen warriors**[1] are always on guard here at Haark-Ek's command.

Cliffside Prison

In the times before Haark-Ek's leadership, captives of the birhaakamen did not tend to live long, quickly becoming food for the nest. These days are more uncertain for the flock than they have ever been before, so Haark-Ek has taken a more measured approach to keeping captives. If the birhaakamen do take a prisoner, this cliffside prison is typically where they are placed. Nothing more than a lonely offshoot of rock sticking out of the side of the mountain, it offers no safe access or way to leave — just a sheer, unclimbable ascent or a deadly drop to the foot of the mountain thousands of feet below. Up to 2 medium creatures can fit side by side on the spur, but beyond that, there is not a lot of room for movement, much less a plan of safe escape.

A nearby roost provides a lookout for 2 **birhaakamen warriors**[1] to keep an eye on any prisoners who might languish here.

Carrion Field

While there is no clear landbound boundary for players to know when they enter birhaakamen territory, the appearance of numerous carrion fields should give them a pretty clear idea that they are in a potentially unsafe region.

These carrion fields result from the castoff debris and gnawed pickings of the birhaakamen nests. The bird-men have no use for the bones and castoff bits of clothing and miscellaneous human items, so these things usually end up strewn about in fields of debris and carrion. It is not unusual for characters making their way through a lightly wooded mountain pass or coming out of a desert region to find these vast fields of offal, carrion, filth, junk, and assorted remains scattered everywhere.

No valuables are located in any of these carrion fields, as they have been picked clean long ago.

Roost of the Dire Vultures

For security and defense, Haark-Ek and his birhaakamen allied themselves with 2 dire vultures (as **giant vulture**) that roost near their aerie. The bargain they struck allows the dire vultures the first pick of any large carrion or mega-fauna that dies or is killed in the area, while the birhaakamen take the smaller fare, such as humans and other Medium- to Small-sized creatures. When the birhaakamen took their revenge on the manticores who slew their kin, they allowed the vultures to feast upon the remains of their enemies.

The roost here is rather simple: a single, large nest located high among the trees and constructed in a fashion similar to the birhaakamens' aerie. The dire vultures currently have no eggs, but if they are defeated and their nest searched, the following items of interest can be found: a set of human-sized chain mail in poor but usable condition, a *+1 quarterstaff*, a splintered and barely held together wooden chest that still contains 24 gp in loose coins, 8 unused torches, a large burlap bag containing 14 silver bars (worth 50 gp each), a small golden brazier adorned with the leering faces of efreet (worth 275 gp) and a polished redwood statuette of a woman in full plate armor holding aloft a scepter (worth 120 gp). Aside from these items, nothing remains but gnawed carrion and castoff bones from the remains of unlucky travelers.

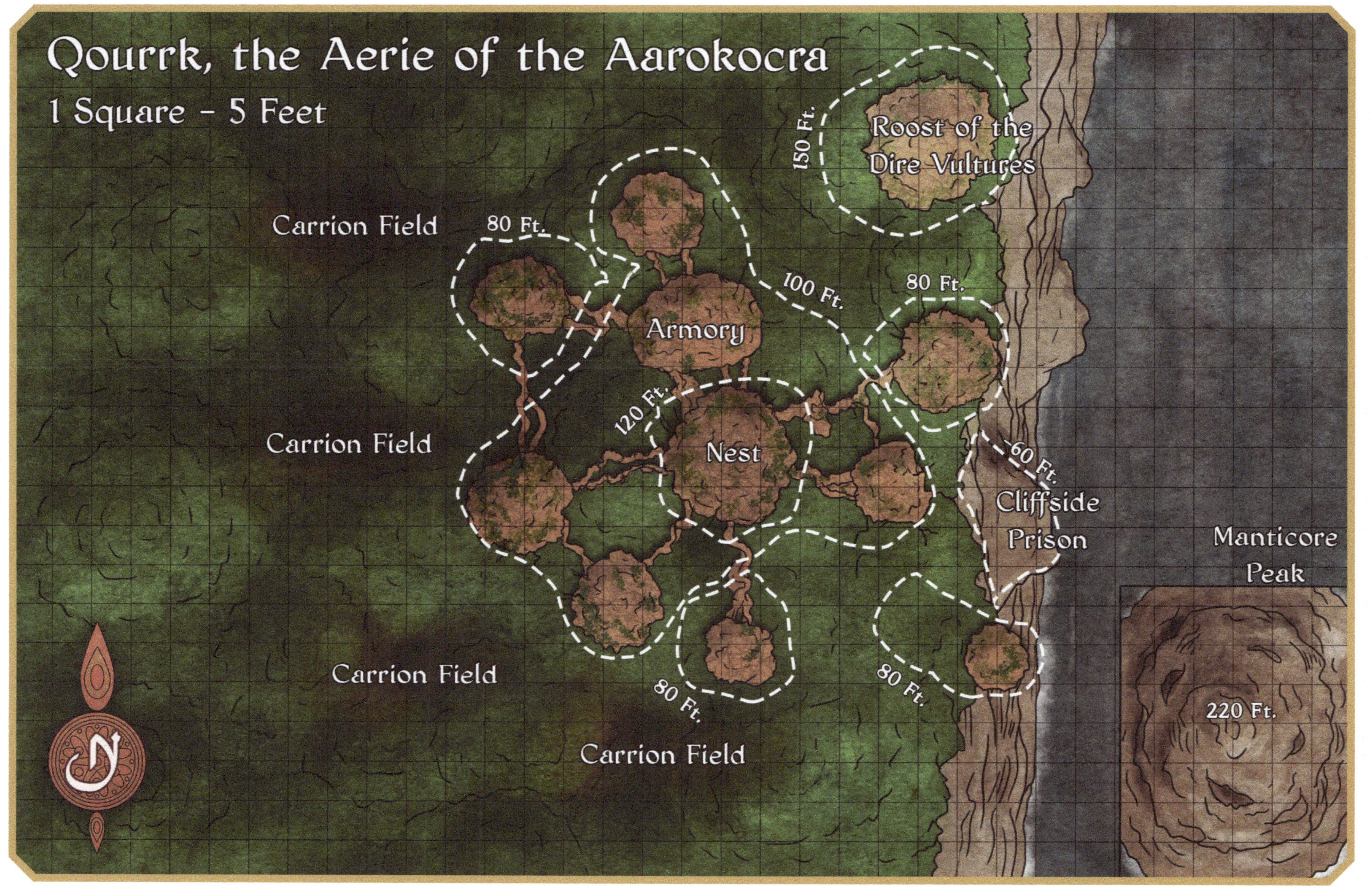

Qourrk, the Aerie of the Aarokocra
1 Square - 5 Feet
Roost of the Dire Vultures
150 Ft.
Carrion Field
80 Ft.
100 Ft.
80 Ft.
Armory
120 Ft.
Nest
60 Ft.
Cliffside Prison
Carrion Field
Manticore Peak
Carrion Field
80 Ft.
80 Ft.
Carrion Field
220 Ft.

Manticore Peak

This rocky outcropping rising from the sea is home to a pack of 4 vicious **manticores**. The manticores just recently recovered from their battle with the birhaakamen and are planning a new raid on Qourrk soon. Until then, the manticores attack passing ships but flee if they take more than 25% of their hit points in damage.

The manticore nest is atop a 1,500-foot-tall volcanic rock.

Treasure: 5 manticore eggs, suit of *+1 chain mail*, *+1 scimitar*, 3 vials of holy water, a *scroll of protection* (elementals), and a sapphire worth 200 gp.

Using the Birhaakamen of Qourrk

The side quest offered here affords an opportunity to gain a few more experience points before attempting the recovery of the *Jewel of the Winds* from the Isle of Winds. The characters may make advantageous allies with the birhaakamen, who could show up to rescue them at a later time.

4. Isle of Winds: Jawahra min Alriya, the Jewel of the Winds

The Jewel of the Winds is an adventure for characters of Tier 2. It is strongly suggested that the characters have an arcane spellcaster, a divine spellcaster, characters who are adept at finding and overcoming traps, and of course a good selection of sword swingers and meat shields to defend against whatever physical horrors the characters may face on their adventure.

The adventure takes place at sea and in the Plane of Air, where characters find themselves among a series of terrestrial air islands that serve as a hiding place for the *jewel of the winds*, one of Sulymon the Prophet's elemental stones.

Background

> Jewel of Wind in the ever storm's eye
>
> Along the paths of the prophets does it lie
>
> Through air and water, ice and sin
>
> A wish ever hidden, this prize of djinn.
>
> —So sing the Bahar of the Lost Seas

Perhaps treasure, perhaps death? None who still lives know for sure, and those survivors who claim to have set foot upon the Isle of Winds were driven mad from their experience or pour sour wine down their throats in an effort to forget the things they saw as their crewmates were stripped from them one by one.

For centuries, a great storm has blown around the Isle of Winds, drawing in ships to wreck upon its shores and stranding sailors upon its rocky beaches. From a distance, a great tornado can be seen ever grinding against the barren stone beach, its vortex reaching into the lightning-shot blue-black skies that glower above it.

Rumors abound as to the secrets of the blasted isle. Mariners from Numeda claim that it is one of the places where the Prophet Sulymon stopped on his pilgrimage of prayer before settling in the Holy City of Dawaad. Others say that it is a conduit to the Abyss and is ruled over by the warring sides of Demogorgon, who lays claim to the blood and souls of those who are drawn onto the island's rocky shores. Ultimately, it is suspected that the island is somehow home to one of the holy elemental artifacts hidden in the world to protect them from the grasp of the Burning One and his numerous minions.

Characters become aware of a rumor that states that passing through the Ever Storm of Jazira al Alriya opens a portal to other dimensions. The "how" of the journey is unknown, as the only alleged survivors who made

it off the island are a lunatic sorcerer and three sailors allegedly lifted to safety upon the backs of a powerful elemental.

These survivors spoke of a jungle in the sky, and above that jungle hovered a palace whose walls were of gleaming gold and alabaster.

For a time, treasure hunters or those seeking a portal to the magical bazaars of the City of Brass financed expeditions in search of the fabled island, hoping it would provide a key to reaching the magical city of wonders. After several failures, these expeditions dried up and interest in the Isle of Winds faded from memory.

Summary

Through the course of the adventure, the characters find themselves on the Isle of Winds and from there travel into the Plane of Air. While in the Plane of Air, they encounter, among other obstaacles, a giant squatting in the palace of Caliph Omar, a djinn relative of the slain Dead Sultana of the City of Brass.

As the characters overcome the challenges they face on the floating air islands of the Plane of Air and free Caliph Omar, they are awarded the *jewel of the winds*[2], one of Sulymon's elemental stones, and gain an ally in their quest to seek the City of Brass.

Getting Started

Characters may find themselves drawn to the island by the following means:

Connivance of the Sultan of Efreet: In an effort to gain Sulymon's enchanted stones, the Sultan and his minions manipulate the weather to blow the characters off course and into the path of the Isle of Winds.

Purposeful Exploration: Characters discovered a map to the Isle of Winds in the possessions of Sheik Mutastir or in one of the books located in a Brazen Spire. Various history checks indicate a potential gateway to the City of Brass where allies, friends, or loved ones have been hauled off as prisoners.

Characters may also have encountered the bird men of Qourrk and been told of their shaman Serk-Kreuk's vision of the characters bearing the *jewel of the winds*[2].

Elemental Plane of Air

Much of this adventure takes place on floating islands that are part of a chain of air islands composed of water, earth, and fire known as a caelispheres. These floating air islands are tenuously tied to one another through common material density, gravity, and magic. The chains are further tied to the material planes via thin spots between the walls of terrestrial and elemental reality.

These air island caelispheres float throughout the Plane of Air and serve as homes to semi-terrestrial beings such as the air caliphate of the djinn, storm and cloud giants, and certain aged dragons who have grown bored with the mortal realms of humans, dwarves, and elves.

The Plane of Air itself is of unknown size, though its borders with the other elemental planes are measurable, forming borderlands with one another that have similar, though extreme, versions of lands found in the material planes.

Wind: Winds in the Elemental Plane of Air can be furious, running the gamut from small gusts of 20–60 mph to cyclonic winds of more than 100 mph that make even magical flying impossible. Wind shear and cyclonic gusts can be deadly, dealing significant damage to those caught in them. Often these winds have been known to blow travelers far off course and to send groups of adventurers in different directions that may make it nearly impossible for them to find one another again.

Creatures: Innumerable creatures of the air are found in the Plane of Air. Many other volumes such as **The Tome of Horrors** from **Frog God Games** are filled with information regarding their types, numbers, and powers.

Magic: Magic functions normally in the Plane of Air, though spells that conjure air-based creatures automatically summon twice that number and afford a 50% chance that they turn on the summoner.

9
7
8
6
5
4
3
2
1
N
Throne Room
Treasury
Hall
Armory
Living Quarters
Isle of Winds
1/2 mile

Shipwreck: Characters fail hard at piloting and navigating their ship, and wind up shipwrecked upon the island, dodging the miniature tornadoes spinning off the main eye. Before long, they find themselves pulled through the planar portal and find themselves on Sky Beach.

4-1. Isle of Winds

Called Jazira al Alriya by the Numedan corsairs, this rocky outcropping is blasted by a constant storm and surge, leaving naught but bare rock where perhaps a fine volcanic island once stood. Stripped bare of its vegetation and soil, the isle is a forbidding place.

From a distance, the Ever Storm spinning above the outcropping appears to be a powerful tornado, but it is in fact a portal to the Elemental Plane of Air. Approaching the portal deals 9 (2d8) bludgeoning damage unless a successful DC 18 Strength saving throw is made. Characters who fail their saving throw must make a secondary DC 18 Strength or Dexterity (player's choice) saving throw or lose 1d4 random items to the wind.

Once characters lose their footing, they are immediately sucked up into the tornado where they next find themselves unconscious on the shores of Sky Beach (**Area 4-2**).

4-2. Sky Beach

This wide expanse of water and sand sits beneath a windblown but almost tranquil sky. The water surrounds the beach for about 100 feet before it pours over an invisible divide and dissolves into clouds. Characters attempting to swim beyond the edge of the waters are pulled off into the turbulent winds of the Plane of Air and are lost unless they can fly or can summon a being to return them to the Sky Beach. A thick jungle hangs in the puffy cumulous clouds above the island. On high clouds beyond the floating jungle, characters can just barely catch a glimpse of a heavenly palace with alabaster walls and gleaming golden domes that must be several miles away.

4-2A. Vortex to the Isle of Winds

Exploring the beach, the characters note a buffeting wind on one side of the beach, about a quarter mile from where they awoke. Peering down the vortex is difficult but reveals the broken rocks of the Isle of Winds as seen from the sky a mile above the ground. Attempting to enter this vortex results in the characters being blown back to the beach at the starting position and suffering 10 (3d6) bludgeoning damage as they are violently tossed and hurled.

4-2B. Vortex to the Lost Jungle of the Sky

The wind grows stronger at the opposite end of the beach away from the vortex, blowing upward in the direction of the palace hanging in the sky above. Entering the vortex requires a leap of faith. Characters who willingly leap into the vortex of wind are buffeted and swirled through the air as they are hauled up to the Dayie Adjhal Sama.

4-2C. The Tide Pool

A successful DC 15 Wisdom (Perception) check while searching the beach finds a conch shell with carefully drilled openings to add flute-like fingerholes to its side. The conch rests in a tide pool formed by a series of volcanic stones upon which are drawn a series of characters. There is a depression in the water that is the same size and shape of the *air stone of Sulymon*. Characters capable of playing a flute or other wind instrument recognize the markings on the volcanic rock as musical notes and could play the tune on the conch flute with a successful DC 17 Charisma or Dexterity (Performace) check.

Playing the proper notes upon the conch while the *air stone of Sulymon* is in place allows the characters to switch the direction of the winds on the Sky Beach, allowing escape from the isle back to the Isle of Winds below. The effect lasts for 10 minutes, and the *air stone* may be removed from its depression once the notes are played.

4-3. Dayie Adjhal Sama (Lost Jungle of the Sky)

Ten-square-miles of the Plane of Earth and a demi-elemental wilderness known as the Great Wild project into the Plane of Air here, providing a chunk of earth and soil that the jungle grows upon. The projection borders the Great Wild, and a portal here joins the island to the jungle of Oruk the Horned in the Freeman's Tower of the City of Brass.

Many beasts pass freely between the planes and may be encountered here at random. For each hour that the characters spend exploring the jungles, roll 1d20 on the following table.

1d20	Random Encounters
1–2	1d4 saber tooth tigers
3–4	3d10 water buffalo
5–6	1d4 woods apes
7–8	1d2 dire lions
9–10	2d4 axe beaks
11–12	Catoblepas
13–14	2d4 raptors
16–20	No encounter

Saber tooth Tiger: This is an encounter with 1d4 hunting **saber tooth tigers**. The pride stalks the characters, attempting to pick them off one at a time.

Woods Apes: These intelligent **woods apes**[1] hunt other creatures that pass into the jungle via the hunting lands. Their tribe consists of 20 members ruled by an **advanced woods ape**[1] who wields a two-handed ironbound club in one fist. A random encounter with the woods apes typically results in an encounter with 1d4 apes who wait in the branches of the trees to snatch foes from below, hauling them up into an arboreal lair above the forest floor.

Water Buffalo: This is an encounter with a small herd of water buffalo (as **giant boar**). The beasts are found near the Adjhal Sama River and can be quite aggressive if approached.

Dire Lion: This is an encounter with 1–2 **dire lions**[1] who see the characters as easy prey and stalk them instead of other, more dangerous prey.

Axe Beaks: 2d4 **axe beaks**[1] stalking the forest attack the characters.

Catoblepas: The **catoblepas** lies in wait, with merely its eyes and nose above the waters of the river. It attacks any smaller creature that passes by.

Raptor: This encounter is with a pack of 2d4 raptors (as **bloodhawks**) hiding in the jungle. They pick off characters from the rear of the marching order first, attempting to drag them into the underbrush and kill them quickly before moving on to their next target.

4-3A. Portal to the Sky Beach

The cyclone of air rising from the Sky Beach deposits characters in a windblown circle of greenery at the edge of a jungle. Beyond the patch of greenery stands a giant stone eagle. Its mouth is open as if to make a great call. A depression carved in the back of its head is the size of the *air stone of Sulymon*.

Placing the *air stone of Sulymon* into the back of the eagle's head causes it to let out an earsplitting screech. The screech summons Araalo, a **roc** whose aerie is built upon a floating boulder not far from the Jawahra min Alriya. Araalo lands and proffers its back, allowing the characters passage to the Sky Beach before flying back to its lair.

4-3B. Edge of The Jungle

The edge of the jungle drops off into the ever-blowing winds of the Plane of Air. Characters going off the edge are lost in the vortex of the winds unless they can fly, walk on wind, or have some other means of safe travel in the strong winds.

4-3C. The Cavern of Oruk the Horned

A cavern in the jungle highlands serves as a passage to the primeval pocket plane of Oruk the Horned. Oruk is further detailed in the **Freeman's Tower of the Lower City** (*see* **Chapter 22**) in the City of Brass.

4-3D. Adjhal Sama River

A river meanders through the center of the jungle before cascading off into the winds of the Plane of Air.

4-3E. Pillars of the Sky

The Pillars of the Sky is a temple to the spirits of the air. However, a **belker prince**[1] cast out the air elementals who dwelt within the temple. The belker attacks any beast or intelligent being that approaches the pillars.

Once per day, the Pillars of the Sky can be used to summon the aid of an **elder air elemental**[1]. The elder elemental performs one task before returning to the freedom of the ever-blowing sky.

4-4. Sky Isle of Yunfakh, Palace of the Wind

This island holds an enormous palace that is oversized by any standards. Originally, it was the castle of Caliph Omar, but a cloud giant named Imlaq has taken possession of the structure in the years since Omar has gone missing. The cloud giant first came to the castle many ages ago to steal the treasures of the abandoned palace, but ended up trapped upon the island by a curse Omar left to protect his treasury: Anyone seeking to steal his treasures cannot leave the grounds of the Palace of the Wind until Caliph Omar returns to free them. Since Omar remains in meditation with the *air stone of Sulymon* — and since no one seeking the stone has yet survived to awaken him — the caliph still waits high above his palace amid the islands in the clouds, oblivious to the current situation.

Imlaq made good on the time he has spent trapped upon the island. Shipwrecks, adventurers, and even servants of various powers and agencies have come calling in that time, filling his coffers with gold and his larders with meat and bone meal as he sends them up, one after the other, to attempt to break the curse that holds him in the abandoned palace of a djinn prince.

4-4A. Outer Island

Like other islands floating in this particular caelisphere, the edges drop off directly into the Elemental Plane of Air. Those who arrive on this island are held here by intense gale force winds that blow up from below, returning any who attempt to fly back to the jungle or the Isle of Winds to the shores of Yunfakh, battered and exhausted. A creature taking this round trip suffer 16 (3d10) bludgeoning damage and 1 level of exhaustion.

Several pools of water are here, and a broad grassland seems well tended. A fenced garden grows enormous fruits and vegetables, and an orchard grows pears and apples the size of a human's head. A herd of 20 **giant goats** roams the grassland. The goats leave well enough alone if they are not bothered.

4-4B. Portal to the Broken Isles

The portal to the Broken Isles is protected from entry by a fence with a huge silver gate whose bars are too narrow to cross. The air portal to the Broken Isles works only if the gate is opened with the proper key. Otherwise, those attempting to step through the portal are blown into the Plane of Air.

High above, a series of broken islands can be seen, along with the flicker of lightning and a preponderance of angry black clouds. The key to the gate is currently in the possession of Imlaq. Using the silver key of Caliph Omar opens a vortex of wind that draws any who cross the threshold of the opened gate to **Area 4-5A**.

4-4C. The Palace

The gates and outer wall of the palace are tall and graceful and appear to be made of powdered alabaster inlaid with fine gold patterns representing the swirling winds. The domes and minarets of its halls are also overlaid in gold leaf and swaying palm groves appear to sway behind the 20-foot-high walls. The gate opening to the palace stands wide open and unattended. No guards can be seen, nor is there any sign of servants to till the fields outside the palace or to cultivate the fruits of the trees growing on its grounds.

The palace is filled with outsized furniture that would be more comfortable to beings between 10 and 20 feet tall. Huge tapestries adorn the walls, and large overstuffed cushions and piles of silks that could be used as tents are found in abundance, though all seem slightly timeworn and threadbare. Within the palace are gigantic chambers and broad halls depicting the daily life and magnificence of djinn caliphs.

Great Hall

A mural painted inside the large central hall shows the islands of this caelisphere as they once were, peopled by the djinn who hunted the jungles of the Dayie Adjhal Sama, and who played tricks on sailors who came too close to the Isle of Winds.

The stratospherically highest islands in the chain are featured in the mural. Upon each are the mirror images of a falchion-wielding djinn who stands over a stone set with a gleaming blue jewel. The two figures mirror one another in every detail save that each holds the falchion (as longswords) in the opposite hand and touches the jeweled stone with the other. An inscription written between the two islands reads: "Let he who knows the true hand of the prophet bear the Jawahra min Alriya from the Isle of Winds. Let he who does not suffer the fate of those who are on the wrong side of Anumon."

Throne Room

The throne room is 150 feet wide by 50 feet long and features a throne fit for a person 15 to 20 feet tall. The walls and domes are coated in mother of pearl carved from massive oyster shells and feature a blue skinned djinn with a golden crown, wielding a gleaming silver scimitar while defeating a red-skinned efreet who is bathed in flames.

For every hour spent exploring the palace, there is a 25% chance of encountering Imlaq (**cloud giant**). Imlaq tires of his imprisonment upon this caelisphere and has at long last devised a plan to escape. Imlaq introduces himself as the ruler of the land, and a kindly follower of Sulymon's teachings. He invites them to a feast of giant mutton, fruits, and grains grown upon the palace grounds.

Imlaq offers the characters access to the wind tunnel that leads to the Shattered Islands above the palace, if they would but return with the *stone of air*, so that free passage could be had to and from the palace. He explains that he is lonely, and that the caelisphere of the Jawahra min Alriya has become a lonely place.

The Treasury of Caliph Omar

Written across the lintel of the room in golden script are the following words: "Let those who would steal from the faithful Caliph Omar be cursed forever to walk the grounds of his realm, until such time as he returns to forgive them of their sleight. So sayeth Sulymon, faithful servant of Anumon, lord of the gates."

A silver gate seals the treasury. Its bars are only a handbreadth in width from one another but offer a glimpse of fantastic wealth. The locked gate could be opened with magic or via the silver key Imlaq carries.

Within the treasury is the following: a golden holy symbol of Sulymon worth 100 gp, a *+1 suit of half plate*, *+2 chain mail*, a *+1 chain shirt*, 3 *spell scrolls* of *greater restoration*, a *spell scroll* of *raise dead*, a platinum coffer worth 2,200 gp, 6 ivory drinking horns with platinum inlay worth 200 gp each, a *sword of hunting*[2] (greatsword, genies), a *spell scroll ofpolymorph*, a *potion of flying*, an *arrow of slaying* (blue dragon), a *sword of speed*[2] (scimitar), 2,500 gp, 400 pp.

Imlaq wears the silver key of Caliph Omar around his neck. The key opens the treasure vault and operates the silver gate that leads to the Broken Isles.

4-5. The Broken Isles

This series of stone fragments is formed from the remains of a shattered caelisphere. The area is in the center of constant lightning storms and is hyper-charged with static electricity. Travel through the Broken Isles is dangerous — if not outright deadly — as it involves hopping from stone to stone across a floating field of unstable earth. The broken isles are ruled by Easifa the **voltar**[1] (**Area 4-5C**), who denies passage to most who would seek to cross through his realm to the Jazira Min Jalid.

1d20	Random Encounters
1	2d4 lightning mephits
2	Mihstu
3	Air elemental
4	Niln
5	Lightning elemental
6	Aerial servant
7	Voltar
8	2d6 volts
9	Lightning weird
10	Wind walker
11	Hurtling stone
12	Lightning strike
13–20	No Encounter

Lightning Mephits: These creatures claim this piece of rock as their own. The **lightning mephits**[1] attack from a distance, discharging their hypercharge of electricity without any actual malice, intent instead on chasing away intruders. They flee if injured.

Mihstu: This evil creature dwells upon this broken piece of rock. Its air is composed of thick fog. The **mihstu**[1] uses the uneven ground and thick fog to its advantage, murdering travelers and sorting through their magic items for loot to add to its strength and power.

Niln: The weather upon the niln's isle is splatters of icy rain. The **niln**[1] sneaks through the rain looking for prey.

Air Elemental: The **air elemental** demands a magic item from anyone passing through. If it is not given what it asks for, it grabs characters and hurls them into the windy void of the Plane of Air.

Lightning Elemental: The **lightning elemental**[1] is hypercharged by the static energy field of the Broken Isles, discharging it wherever it can make a positive to negative connection.

Aerial Servant: An **aerial servant**[1] lairs upon this shard of earth and stone, awaiting the summons of some powerful wizard or priest of the material planes.

Voltar: A **voltar**[1], one of Easifa's lesser folk, dwells upon this stretch of stone. It looks to test its skills against visitors.

Volts: A flock of **volts**[1] fly through, swarming whomever they feel has the most negative charge (selected at random).

Lightning Weird: The **lightning weird**[1] attacks as characters are crossing from one floating stone to another.

Wind Walker: The **wind walker**[1] is allied with Imlaq. It begins following the characters, assisting them as they are on their way to collect the *stone of air*, and attempting to murder them and steal the stone for its master should they achieve their goal.

Hurtling Stone: This stone hurtles through the air at a random character. A successful DC 16 Dexterity saving throw must be made or the character suffers 14 (4d6) bludgeoning damage from the projectile as it flies through the eternal sky.

Lightning Strike: A lightning bolt from the disturbed skies zaps an individual, with the electricity spreading out in a 10-foot radius from its target. Each creature in the area must attempt a DC 15 Dexterity saving throw. Those failing take 21 (6d6) lightning damage while those succeeding take half this amount.

Common Features

Uneven Ground and Dangerous Passage: Leaping from stone to stone requires a successful DC 15 Dexterity (Acrobatics) check. Failure means the character falls into the wind. The character has one final opportunity to grasp another piece of earth floating in the caelisphere before being sucked out into the ever-sky of the Plane of Air. This requires a successful DC 15 Dexterity or Strength (player's choice) saving throw.

All Charged Up: A high degree of positive and negative electrical energy exists in the air around the characters. Roll 1d4 for each character before any encounter and 1d4 for the monsters or environmental effects. On a 1 or 2, the being is positively charged, while a 3 or 4 means they are negatively charged. Monsters and random lightning strikes are automatically attracted to characters with the opposite charge.

4-5A. Entrance to the Broken Isles

This archway rests on one of the most stable pieces of stone in the Broken Isles and is connected one way from **Area 4B**.

4-5B. Floating Stones

The main area of the Broken Isles are stones ranging from several feet to several hundred yards wide. Static electricity and lighting are thick in the air. Crossing these fields carefully takes twice the standard amount of time due to uneven surfaces and the constantly moving ground. A minimum of three Dexterity checks are required to cross the field without falling directly into the Plain of Air and becoming lost forever. This can be avoided by using belaying tactics.

Allow 1–2 rolls on the random encounter chart as the characters cross the Broken Isles. If there are no encounters, play up the danger of the moving stones and the constant flashes of lightning and spurts of rain that appear from nowhere. Heighten the excitement in this area with lots of meaningless rolls and serious looks as the characters pass. Describe how they narrowly miss their footing and "just" avoid head-sized bits of earth and stone hurtling past their heads.

4-5C. Exit from the Broken Isles

The **voltar**[1] Easifa guards the exit. He is charged with denying passage to the Isle of Ice by Sulymon, but he may allow a cleric or paladin of Anumon passage should either possess at least one *stone of Sulymon*. Otherwise, he fights until he loses 90% of his hit points, at which point he yields and offers passage.

4-6. Jazira Min Jalid (The Island of Ice)

This frozen caelisphere is thin with oxygen, making travel across it perilous due to reduced energy on the part of travelers. For each 10 minutes of activity on the island, each character must succeed on a DC 13 Constitution saving throw or suffer one level of exhaustion. Resting does not cause exhaustion. The outside of the caelisphere is a mix of ice, dirt, and broken rock that grows with lichens. Peryton frequently land here to hunt the yeti who dwell within the frozen ice caves that dot the land. The yeti in turn hunt the flying peryton, forming a symbiotic circle of life and death.

The **young white dragon** Afiqueea lives at the heart of the icy isle. It is believed that her presence accounts for the great cold, and that if she were slain, Jazira Min Jalid may in time unravel and join the Broken isles as they hurtle through the Plane of Air.

1d12	Random Encounters
1	2d4 frost men
2	Ice elemental[1]
3	2d4 perytons
4	Yeti
6	Frost Giant
7–12	No encounter

Frost Men: This is an encounter with 2d4 **frost men**[1] who were stranded here when they crossed from their home plane to the Plane of Air and became trapped in the Jazira Min Jalid. They fight an unending battle for survival with the perytons, frost giants, and yetis. They may see the characters as allies or prey depending on the characters' actions.

Para Elemental Ice: This is an encounter with 1d4 **ice elementals**[1] who maintain an existence on this section of the snowball. They are drawn to warmth and food, but disperse if any of their members are slain.

Perytons: This flock of 1d4 **perytons**[1] is out hunting for meat, with their favorite prey being frost men and yeti. They may assume the party is easy prey.

Yeti: These beasts of ice and snow roam the windswept outer snows as well as their own ice caves. The **yeti**[1] tend to be hunting by themselves when encountered outside of their lairs. They stalk characters through the frozen lands, attempting to pick them off one by one and drag them back to their lairs to devour.

Frost Giant: This is an encounter with Bjorngolf, a **frost giant** who like the frost men crossed over into the Jazira Min Jalid during a whiteout. If he is killed, treat this result as no encounter.

4-6A. Passage from the Broken Isles

A monolith of broken standing stones marks the location where the swirling vortex of wind deposits characters from **Area 4-4B**.

4-6B. Yeti Lairs

Large boulders requiring a Strength of 18 to move block these icy cavern entrances where the yeti live. Beyond the boulders, deep tunnels lead to caverns holding 1d4 **yetis**[1]. The bones of perytons, frost beasts, and assorted travelers litter their lairs.

4-6C. Lair of the Yeti King

The **yeti**[1] (with 140 hit points) king lives in a large cavern with his family of 3 **yetis**[1].

A few random items from the yeti king's victims lie strewn among the refuse, fur, and bits of animal hide on the floor. These are a *spell scroll offire storm*, 3 *potions of resistnace* (acid), a *+1 harpoon*, 5 perfect amethysts worth 200 gp each, and a folded map. The map depicts an island in the sky covered in pools. A portal on the far end of this island points to two smaller islands. A question mark is drawn over each island along with a drawing of a brilliant blue and white jewel encased in a crystal box.

4-6D. Afiqueea's Lair

Deep in the heart of the Jazira Min Jalid is an ice cavern whose walls and floor are spherical, smooth, and slippery. Glittering white frost covers the massive bones of a huge dragon. Those who enter the cave without using crampons or some other means to keep their footing move at half their movement rate and must make a successful DC 17 Dexterity (Acrobatics) check before every action to avoid falling prone.

The **young white dragon** Afiqueea hides within the spherical cave, waiting for characters to enter her domain. She is wily and hides if she hears the characters coming.

Afiqueea keeps her treasure hidden in the ribcage of her mother, who was dealt a deadly blow by Sulymon in some bygone age. The treasure hoard contains a suit of *+1 splint*, a set of prayer beads, a *spell scroll* of *resistance*, a *spell scroll* of *heal*, a *potion of vitality*, a *potion of greater healing*, 2,400 gp, a spinel worth 50 gp, a diamond worth 300 gp, a silver cup worth 5 gp that is filled with 100 ruby chips worth 2 gp each, a *ring of protection*, and *gloves of thievery*.

4-6E. The Ice Wall

A wall of ice 5 feet thick forms a circular pattern at the far end of the dragon's cavern. Characters who make a successful DC 16 Wisdom (Perception or Survival) check note the difference between the depression and the surrounding ice instantly. Melting the ice opens the wind vortex to **Area 4-7A**.

4-7. The Poisoned Land

The poisoned land is a barren rock covered in pools of toxic liquids, as well as living patches of oozes and slimes. The toxic air is thick, causing creatures trying to breathe it to suffer a −2 to all skill checks, saving throws, and attack rolls for the duration of their time crossing through this floating wasteland. Vortices to other planes exist here, not the least of which are passages to the Abyss that lead to realms ruled by Jubilex, the demon lord who claims the poisoned lands as his piece of the Plane of Air.

1d12	Random Encounters
1	Ochre jelly
2	Brown pudding
3	Black pudding
4	Tarry demodand
5	Acid pool
6	Noxious cloud
7	Acid elemental
8–12	No encounter

Tarry Demodand: This is an encounter with a **tarry demodand**[1] who passed through the portal to Jubilex's Abyss and now dwells on the poisonous windswept rock known as the Poisoned Land.

Acid Pool: This lake of acid is hidden by a sheen of ash, making it appear as just another part of the desolate landscape. Characters must make a successful DC 16 Dexterity saving throw or tumble into a hidden acid pool, suffering 14 (4d6) acid damage per round of exposure. Nonmagical equipment and items that are worn or carried by the creature have a chance of being damaged each round they are within the acid pool. A creature can attempt a DC 14 Dexterity saving throw to save any particular piece of equipment.

Noxious Cloud: A cloud of foul gas rolls over the characters, forcing a DC 15 Constitution saving throw. Those who fail suffer 14 (4d6) acid damage and disadvantage on Constitution saving throws until they are magically healed.

Quasi Elemental Acid: This **acid elemental**[1] sees what is happening in the caelisphere and beyond and is fearful that outsiders are bent on bringing about its destruction. Quick-thinking characters may be able to convince it otherwise.

4-7A. Venom Island

The vortex from **Area 4-6E** deposits the characters in a 1-ftoot-deep depression that stands on a low hill above a quarter-mile-wide caelisphere covered in pools of venom and acid. The air is thick and acrid and burns the throat. Beyond the island, two identical but smaller islands hang high above it in the sky. These smaller islands revolve around one another in the blustery skies.

4-7B. Portal to the Abyss

This portal in the center of the wasteland leads to layers of the Abyss ruled by Jubilex, the Lord of Slimes. The portal opens randomly and remains open only for one minute per day. A **shaggy demodand**[1] guards the portal. If the demodand is defeated, the portal opens for 1 minute.

4-7C. Portal of the Divergence

The path into the sky divides here, with a pedestal standing at the point of the divergence. Inscribed upon the pedestal in Sulymon's script are the following words, "As I faced my dark half, I knew his treachery by the difference in his eye. In that instant, I knew all that is right may ultimately be left to burn in ashes."

4-8. The Island of the Ghirru

The right-hand sky path from **Area 4-7C** transports characters via a current of wind to an island covered in ash. At the center of the island is a large figure whose skin is burned and charred. The creature here is a **ghul efreeti**, the ghost of an efreet, left here as a test to the faithful. It immediately attacks with its *flaming weapon*[2] (greatsword) that it wields in one hand.

4-9. The Island of Caliph Omar

The left-hand sky path from **Area 4-7C** leads to a barren island. A 10-foot-tall man with ice-blue skin sits cross-legged as if in sacred meditation in the center of the island. The figure sits within an impenetrable magical sphere with a clear blue sapphire floating above his head. The sapphire itself rests inside a crystal cube.

If characters touch the *fire stone*, *earth stone*, or *water stone of Sulymon* to the sphere, it dissolves immediately and the caliph awakens. The sphere is otherwise impenetrable and unbreakable save by *dispel magic* successfully cast against an 9th-level spell.

Completing the Isle of Winds: If the characters' intentions seem righteous, or if Sparque accompanies them, Caliph Omar (**efreeti**) greets them warmly and thanks them for his freedom. He asks the characters if they have been in his castle, and how things are there. If the characters tell him about Imlaq, his brow furrows, for he knows of this plundering giant and his wicked ways. Caliph Omar then grins and offers the characters a deal. If they help rid his castle of the cloud giant, he grants them the *stone of air* and one additional treasure from his fabled treasury.

If the characters agree, Caliph Omar uses the stone to reverse the wind vortices and uses *wind walk* to return the characters to the Isle of Yunfakh (**Area 4**).

5. Isle of Bliss

This small fishing island is inhabited by a mix of descendants of marooned ships and peoples native to it. The sea currents have caused more than its fair share of brass genie bottles to migrate to its coves. No map is provided for this island, but if it is time for the adventurers to learn about the City of Brass and a route to it, you can include the following scene.

The Party Finds the Isle of Bliss

The characters are getting provisions on a small island inhabited by the descendants of a shipwrecked naval vessel and native inhabitants. While there, the party spies a fisherman breaking open a brass bottle found in his net and releasing an efreeti trapped within. The efreeti howls with glee and fills the fisherman's otherwise empty net with fish. The fishermen mention that this sort of thing happens from time to time as Sulymon was known to bind any genie he encountered in a bottle of brass. Sulymon then sealed the bottle with molten lead and cast it into the sea exclaiming, "Let you find peace with thy brothers of the deeper waters." The islanders indicate that once freed, the genies tend to leave the world forever not wishing to run across Sulymon again. It is said that they return to their home in the City of Brass, a place known for its opulent wealth. They also add that Sulymon knows the path to the City of Brass and that the characters should sail southeast to Dawaad and ask him if they are curious.

Chapter 6
Numeda: The Caliphate of Flames

The Caliphate of Flames is an adventure designed for 4–6 characters of Tier 2. It continues the adventure that started in **Lornedain: The Secret Flame** and continued in **Freegate: The Brazen Spires**. The adventure takes place in a city during a violent religious uprising where existing government and societal norms have collapsed. Many have fled the War of Flames. Supernatural other-planar powers and their vengeful native allies are now hunting survivors who could not escape as they remain trapped in their homes.

The adventure has a high likelihood of street fighting, role-playing encounters, and other hazards as the characters negotiate the dangerous streets of a desert city descending into madness. It is suggested that the party include a healer, an arcane spellcaster, a character skilled at finding and disabling traps, and a decent collection of frontline fighters capable of close-quarter combat in the narrow streets of Kirtius.

Maps for this chapter are **Kirtius City**, and **20. Massini's Fortress**.

Adventure Background

Numeda, a proud kingdom in the greater Maighib Desert, has become the frontline for the Sultan's invasion of the Lost Lands. It is now the focal point in his attempts to spread his power, expand the Plane of Molten Skies, and establish himself as a greater god of the cosmos.

A year ago, a Brazen Spire appeared within the city of Kirtius, just as they have in other lands. The strange, veiled priests offered relief and succor to the beggars and the poor of the streets, and began instructing them in the laws of the deity they referred to alternately as the Burning One and the Veiled God. Eventually, this influence grew to others in the capital, causing alarm and distress to King Massini and his court.

The characters are aware of Kirtius as a center of activities for the Cult of the Burning One and have been dispatched to end the cult's reign of terror once and for all. It has been suggested by clerics and leaders from around the Lost Lands that a strike against the cult's leadership in Kirtius may sever the head of the serpent and end their War of Flames.

As the characters arrive, they find themselves faced with a terrified populace lorded over by cultists of the Burning One led by the efreeti Emir Farphanes. The brainwashed citizens seek to exact vengeance on their perceived former oppressors with the help of burning dervishes, hariphs, and monsters from the City of Brass itself. While exploring the beleaguered city, the characters' investigations uncover the fate of King Massini and his royal family. Emir Farphanes has declared the whole of Numeda to be the capital of a newly established caliphate of flames. Their intention is to bring about a spiritual and fundamental kingdom of fire in service to the Veiled God of the City of Brass.

Further adventure reveals that the Brazen Spire of Kirtius now serves as a nexus connecting the other spires throughout the Lost Lands. Emir Farphanes uses the city as a base of operations while seeking the remaining *elemental stones* and overseeing the construction of new spires.

A search of the city concludes when the characters defeat Emir Farphanes and discover the location of the Holy City of Dawaad, setting them on the final part of the adventure, **The Path of the Prophet**.

Numeda

Numeda is the largest of the independent Bedouin Kingdoms of the Maighib Desert region, though it is heavily influenced from the influx of Hyperboreans during the heyday of their expansionist wars. Numeda developed as a camel and horse culture of nomads that has only settled into cities and villages in the last few hundred years, since the arrival of Sulymon the Prophet. These towns are culturally built around the oasis of the desert, or religious sites dedicated to the old gods as they were worshipped in the time before the rise of the worship of Anumon and later the coming of Mah-Barek.

The Numedan light cavalry are considered some of the best of the Maighib, if not the bravest light horse in all Libynos, and their soldiers often serve as mercenaries for the other city-states of the desert. Since the coming of Sulymon, many began to worship Anumon, god of the gates, and are paladins in his holy orders.

Numeda's port city of Kirtius serves as the capital and is a center for inland trade in jewels and precious metals gathered from beyond the deep Maighib Desert. Caravans of raw materials flow here from the desert, while trains of pilgrims seeking the Holy City of Dawaad often begin their travels here.

It is no secret that Kirtius is also known in other parts of the world as an outpost for privateering licensed by Numedan nobility. This particular fact has brought about harsh reaction from nobles of the Kingdoms of Akados who have fought the Numedans for centuries over control of trade in the Titian Isles.

Currently, Numeda is a kingdom in turmoil, whose surviving nobles have fled across the Maighib Desert to the smaller nation-states around Numeda after the rise of the Cult of the Burning One resulted in the immolation of their king and the declaration of a caliphate of flames under the command of the twisted efreeti Emir Farphanes.

Kirtius

Kirtius is the capital of Numeda, and now serves as a toehold for the armies of the sultan of efreet. Many of the citizenry fled the takeover, running across the wastes of the Maighib desert only to find more Brazen Spires rising up in civilized lands as far away as Akados. Others are hunted by Lotus Eaters who have pledged their sword arms to the Cult of the Burning One.

Currently, Emir Farphanes sits upon the throne of Numeda, in the palace of Massini, where he rules as the Sultan's voice in the new realm of conquest. With agents throughout the lands such as Sheik Mustatir and the Cult of the Burning One, he oversees the placement of Brazen Spires of living brass in cities throughout the Lost Lands.

Although Kirtius is a conquered city, pockets of resistance against Emir Farphanes' forces and the Cult of the Burning One search for new people who seek to depose the foul efreet, tear down his Brazen Spire, and re-institute the Massini royal family. A legend among members of the resistance persists that a flask containing the spirit of the prophet Sulymon may somehow aid in their quest.

Entering Kirtius

Kirtius may be approached by sea or land, or characters may arrive by one of various magical means such as being befriended by Caliph Omar or other djinn or jann able to provide them with transportation.

By Sea: Characters arriving by sea may be aboard a galley provided by the grateful praetors of Freegate, the captured *Sand Dancer*, or on another vessel they gained during their journey across the sea.

If the characters are aboard *The Sand Dancer*, they are allowed to dock with no difficulties. Problems begin when they get off their ship, however. Any time *The Sand Dancer* docks, it is expected that plunder or slaves from one of the provinces under the eye of a Brazen Spire has arrived. If the cleric Tarkesh and the wizard Ramzi are not aboard the

N
North Lighthouse
1
Docks
4
Bastion Battery
10
8
7
5
8
9
6
17
Gate of Morning Star
18
12
Silk Street
17
13
14
11
15
18 Gate of Sunrise
16
17
Fishing Village
2
South Lighthouse
3
Dock & Warehouses
Palace Fortress
20
19
Kirtius City
500 ft.

ship, conversations with the dock masters are likely to go south quickly. For more details on The Sand Dancer and its crew, see *Freegate: The Brazen Spire*.

If characters approach in an unknown vessel — such as *The Kataskopos* — a ship is sent out to intercept them. At the same time, cannons at the harbor bastion are loaded and sighted in on the intruding vessel. The characters are escorted into the harbor, then given directions by one of the hariphs of the Brazen Spire of Kirtius. The characters are presented to the caliphate of the Burning One and instructed to visit the Brazen Spire for prayer and purification, after which they are free to find lodging at the Fanduq near the Gate of the Morning Star.

By Land: The city could be reached via travel through the Maighib Desert after having separate adventures there. Hobgoblin mercenaries faithful to the Cult of the Burning One patrol the outskirts of the city and are likely the first inhabitants of the city that characters encounter. Their riders are currently sequestered in the Oasis Aljania (**Area 19**) outside of town.

Through the Brazen Spire: Characters capable of manipulating the *fire stone of Sulymon*[2] may find themselves stepping into the seventh-floor prayer room of the hariphs in Kirtius, which is analogous in layout and defenses to the Brazen Spire of Freegate. This, of course, would mean that the characters would have to figure out how to escape the spire before any further adventure within Kirtius could take place!

Running the City

Characters may arrive as pilgrims, as folk swearing allegiance to Emir Farphanes, or as an insurgent force. The more violent the characters are in the streets of the city, the more likely they are to attract the attention of stronger enemies. See the Open Encounters table for details on what occurs as characters get noticed.

Open Encounters

Open Encounters are events that take place at one of the gates, or in the streets where the characters battle Emir Farphanes' forces in full view of citizens or other cultists. The danger ramps up considerably as the characters engage in more encounters in the streets.

Cumulative Encounters	Result
After 1 encounter	50% chance of attracting 2d6 mamelukes (**guard** with scimitar and short bow) accompanied by a **magician**[1] and a **priest**.
After 2 encounters	Automatically attract 2d6 mamelukes (**guard** with scimitar and short bow) and there is a 50% chance of triggering the next encounter level unless they retreat, hide, and regroup. There is an additional 50% chance that a hariph (**magician**[1] or **priest**) from the spire of Kirtius is summoned to the scene.
After 3 encounters	2d6 mamelukes (**guard** with scimitar and short bow) arrive in 2d4 rounds accompanied by a hariph (**magician**[1]), and there is a 50% chance that Sheik Munimin (**burning dervish**[1]) is present.
After 4 encounters	The characters are actively hunted. Sheik Munimin (**burning dervish**[1]), or one of the other burning dervishes, 1d2 hariphs (**magician**[1]), and 2d6 mamelukes (**guard** with scimitar and short bow) seek out the characters in 2d4 rounds. The hunters go door to door searching for them and executing any civilians who do not give them up.
After 5 encounters	Emir Farphanes (**efreeti**) himself flies over the city in search of the characters while a patrol similar to the one listed in encounter level 4 above stalks the city, going door to door in search of the characters. If the characters are out in the open, Emir Farphanes directs troops to surround the party. He demands their immediate surrender and has them taken to the jail beneath the spire of Kirtius to await transport to the slave markets of the City of Brass.

Making Alliances

Should the characters free Prince Nidjal and his men and arm them, or if they ally themselves with Sir Al-Furusiyya Muniq, the liegemen of the king comport themselves as best they can so long as the characters keep the more serious threats of burning dervishes and Emir Farphanes away from them.

Destroying the Spire

The spire can be destroyed in the same manner as detailed in *Freegate: The Brazen Spire*. If Babak the azer is with the party, they have a distinct advantage in destroying the spire. It should be noted, however, that Babak refuses to destroy a Brazen Spire unless he is certain that any prisoners have been freed, as its destruction instantly kills all those inside the tower at the end of his ritual.

Locations within the City

1. North Lighthouse

The 100-foot-tall north lighthouse is a beautifully painted domed spire lit with an enchanted leaded crystal lamp whose magnification can be seen from 8–10 miles away. Two watchers (**guards** with scimitar and short bow) live in the base of the lighthouse and take turns keeping an eye out for incoming ships.

2. Fishing Village

Idzagen seafarers, cousins to the desert-dwelling Numedan tribes, live here. The Idzagen have thus far stayed clear of the horrors happening in the city, and were quick to swear their allegiance to Emir Farphanes, recognizing him as a herald of the genie princes of old and keepers of the ancient faiths of the old gods of desert and sea. As with their desert-dwelling cousins, the Idzagen blow with the wind, and tend to take the faith of the winning side over the loser, or simply disappear into the desert or the sea before any great calamity strikes their own house.

The village is home to roughly 30 families (**commoners**) who make their living taking their skiffs out to sea to gather fish in their nets to sell in the markets of Kirtius. They make no move against any characterss unless ordered to do so by Emir Farphanes' minions.

3. South Lighthouse

The south lighthouse is exactly like the north lighthouse, and is home to 2 watchers (**guards** with scimitar and short bow) who observe the southern coast and 10 or so miles inland for sign of land-borne raiders.

4. Docks

The docks are located outside the walls of the city proper and are accessed via the northern coastal channel. Currently, a pair of swift sailing coastal dhows are in port.

The Port Master

If characters have not engaged in an all-out sea battle with the dhows and cannon from the city's batteries, their first encounter is with Port Master Aeidi (as **spy**).

Aeidi inspects ships that come into the harbor, charges a 10 gp docking fee, and informs those docking of the costs of unloading and warehousing their goods. Aeidi is new to his job and not very good at it. He is also a member of the Cult of the Burning One and is familiar with Tarkesh and Ramzi, the cult members assigned to keep an eye on the captain and crew of *The Sand Dancer*. Aeidi is assisted by a small squad of 4 mamelukes (**guard** with scimitar and short bow).

Dhows: These lateen-rigged ships are small and swift, carrying two 6-pound guns[3] each and crews of 12–18 sailors (**bandit**).

5. Dock Warehouse Market

Before Emir Farphanes and the Cult of the Burning One took over, the warehouse market teemed with throngs of travelers and visitors from other kingdoms and potentates of the surrounding desert tribes of the Maighib Desert. Visitors traded in silk, jewels, rare herbs, spices, and other sundries. With the coming of Emir Farphanes, most of the riches brought to the city now fill the greedy emir's coffers, while the remainder is carried in tribute to the City of Brass to be lain at the feet of the Sultan.

A squad of 1d6 + 4 **cultists** patrols the warehouse market. Along with their weapons, they carry torches and flasks of oil. At least 50% of the cultists were exposed to the influence of *charm* and *mass suggestion* enchantments by the hariphs of the Brazen Spire of Kirtius.

6. Dock Gate

The dock's gate is fitted with four 6-pound guns[3] pointed out to sea on twin towers that face the docks and the inlet between the fisherman's isle and the mainland. The dock gates are 40 feet tall and guarded by 12 mamelukes (**guard** with scimitar and short bow) each who rotate shifts manning the guns and acting as lookouts.

7. Foreign Quarter

The foreign quarter of Kirtius was a dangerous place in the best of times. Crime and thievery were rampant due to the constant ebb and flow of foreign trade. Gambling dens, liquor shacks, and hookah lounges occupied the lower floors of mud and brick apartments while the upper stories housed squatters and other residents of the city.

Despite its reputation, the local guardsmen under King Massini kept the troubles of the foreign quarter slums confined to a few blocks of the north end of the city where they could be easily managed. Nonetheless, the neighborhood proved easy prey to the enticements of the hariphs and the wishes granted by Emir Farphanes upon his arrival to the city.

Now, the foreign quarter is occupied by gangs of faithful cultists who prey on the rest of the citizenry, driving them from their homes, looting the buildings, and burning the people as sacrifices to the Veiled God.

Travel through the foreign quarter almost guarantees an encounter with a gang of **cultists** led by a mameluke (**guard** with scimitar and short bow) or an **imam of fire**[1].

8. Foreign Quarter Checkpoints

The quarter is surrounded by a 9-foot-tall concrete and stucco wall, and is pierced on its north and south ends by gates that were at one time managed by Massini's guardsmen, but now serve as cult checkpoints. The checkpoints are managed by 4 **cultists** each who shake down anyone who isn't wearing the garb of the faithful, which consists of black and orange robes, a turban, and a veil.

Foreign Quarter Random Encounters

1d12	Encounter
1–2	Cultist gang with mameluke
3–4	Cultist gang with imam of the Veiled God
5–7	Scavengers
9–10	Resistance survivors
11–12	No Encounter

Cultist gang with imam of the Veiled God: 2d6 + 2 **cultists** armed with scimitars, torches, a flask of oil, with a **missionary**[1] armed with an iron mace, 3 flasks of oil, and a *potion of resistance* (fire).

Cultist Gang with Mameluke: 2d6 + 2 **cultists** armed with scimitars, torches, and a flask of oil, with a **captain**[1] wearing chain mail and bearing a shield (AC 18), a spear, and a scimitar acting as a leader.

Scavengers: This is an encounter with 1d10 terrified locals (**commoners**) seeking food and sustenance while avoiding an encounter with a cultist gang. Scavengers are just as likely to flee from characters as they are to offer shelter.

Resistance Survivors: This is an encounter with 2d6 members of King Massini's royal guard (**captain**[1] with AC 16 from chain mail and wielding a longsword two-handed instead of greatsword) who escaped the massacre. They hide now among the ruins of burnt buildings and in houses not under the control of the Cult of the Burning One. They ambush the Burning One's forces in a dangerous guerilla war. Resistance survivors may offer the characters shelter or offer to team up for an attack on Emir Farphanes. Resistance survivors can offer the characters whatever information you feel is pertinent to furthering the adventure.

9. Hookah Bar

Few of these remain open as the Paradise of the Brazen Spire provides for all the needs of the cultists. That said, a few still remain, as smoke is considered an affectation to the Burning One, and flavored smokes are believed to transcend the cosmos and reach their master's nostrils with prayers and pleasure.

The tobacco offered at these bars is very strong and would be highly sought after by imbibers in Akados.

10. Brazen Spire of Kirtius

The Brazen Spire of Kirius has a similar floor plan and purpose as the Brazen Spire of Freegate. It is occupied by a cabal of 6 hariphs from throughout Libynos who have sworn their allegiance to the Veiled God. The spire is administrated by Sheik Munimin, a burning dervish[1] who answers directly to Emir Farphanes. Use the floorplan for the Spire of Freegate (**Chapter 4**) for the purposes of running any raids into the Spire of Kirtius. Also, the spire can be destroyed by similar methods to the spire of Freegate, such as by using the cannons ringing the city to bombard the tower.

Ground Floor

This floor has its own version of Paradise. There are 6 **doppelgangers** here doing their part to seduce and befuddle those sent to the spire for their education in the teachings of the Veiled God.

First Floor: This floor contains a mosque of adoration as described in *Freegate: The Brazen Spire*.

Second Floor

This floor contains a training center for sacerdotal studies and is laid out similarly to the spire in Freegate.

Munimin and the Hariphs of Kirtius

The hariphs of Kirtius have ridden to the cause of the Veiled God, and seek to expand the caliphate of flames so they are guaranteed a place of power once their world is merged with the Plane of Molten Skies.

Hariph Ayize the Sharp (male human **magician**[1]), has a *ring of protection* and a *spell wand*[2] of *scorching ray*.

Hariph Saidi Efie (male human **priest** of the sultan of efreet) has a *flaming weapon*[2] (mace), *+1 chain mail*, and innate resistance to fire damage.

Hariph Hondo Kush[1] (male hobgoblin) has a *flaming weapon*[2] (falchion, as longsword), *+1 breastplate of fire resistance*[2], and a *potion of healing*. Hondo is part of Ergat Shem's tribe and was the catalyst that led his folk to accept the Burning One as their new master.

Hariph Nathifa (female human **priest** of the sultan of efreet) has *+1 chain mail*, *+1 mace*, *boots of striding and springing*, and a *hariph's amulet*[2].

Raziya Witch Eye[1] (female, mostly human) has a *wand of fireballs*, *bracers of defense*, a *potion of flying*, and a *hariph's amulet*[2]. Raziya is from the deep desert, and claims efreeti blood from her elder ancestors.

Hariph Mother Umaya Gamba (female **priest** of the Sultan of Efreet) has a *+2 shield*, a *+1 mace*, a *staff of healing*, and a *hariph's amulet*[2]. Umaya Gamba hails from the far south and was steeped in dark studies long before the Sultan of Efreet[1] discovered her. She sees the coming purge of fire as a welcome rebirth to a land long beset by chaos and uncertainty.

Sheik Munimin (male **burning dervish**[1]) has a *+2 falchion* and a *spire master's amulet*[2]. Sheik Munimin is a rival of Sheik Mutastir and has long sought to supplant him in the eyes of Emir Farphanes and their master the Sultan of Efreet[1].

Place the hariphs and Sheik Munimin wherever necessary throughout Kirtius or the palace. They are typically in the company of mamelukes, clerics, or fire wizards. If the characters create a great deal of havoc entering the city, the hariphs and their forces are out actively hunting them.

Third through Fifth Floors

These floors serve as training ground and barracks for mamelukes trained as shock troops in the armies of the sultan of efreet. Each floor holds 3d10 mamelukes (**guard** with scimitar and short bow) led by a **khalit jinn**[1].

Sixth Floor (Hall of Sun and Wind)

Like the Hall of Moon and Stars in Freegate, the Hall of Sun and Wind is a study containing spellbooks, history books, and astrological data. The location of the *Jawahra min Alriya* is located in a book here, as is the true name of the djinn who guards it. Another book details the location of the Holy City of Dawaad and how one must march directly into the rising sun and ride three days from the gate of Dawaad to reach the place of prayer.

Seventh Floor (Prayer Room of the Hariphs)

When Emir Farphanes contacts his master in the City of Brass or speaks with the sheiks of the other Brazen Spires, he does so from the spire of Kirtius' prayer room.

Eighth Floor (Apartments of the Hariphs): These dorms serve as homes to the hariphs of Kirtius. They have similar treasures, traps, and layout to those found in Freegate.

Ninth Floor (Guardians Lair): This floor holds a furnace golem (**clay golem**) lent to the spire by the Sultan. Hidden within the mouth of the furnace is a strange key. The key unlocks Emir Farphanes' treasure chest hidden in the palace of the king.

Tenth Floor (Sheik Munimin's Penthouse): This floor is similar to that of Sheik Munimin's rival Sheik Mutastir, with the exception that no *mirror of opposition* is in the room. Instead, an ironbound chest contains 2,500 gp, 200 bp, 100 pp, 3 diamonds worth 1,000 gp each, two *potions of greater healing*, and 2 *potions of resistance* (cold).

The chest is trapped with an **iron cobra**[1] that obeys only Sheik Munimin. The cobra does not move until the chest is opened.

Spire Dungeon

The dungeon beneath the spire of Kirtius is set up and guarded similarly to the dungeon found beneath the spire of Freegate. Its cells contain the remaining 100 soldiers (as **bandits** unarmed and with AC 11) who have not yet been immolated for the amusement of Emir Farphanes. Also locked away is Prince Nidjal (as **bandit captain** with AC 13, no weapons or armor), whom Emir Farphanes holds captive as a hostage to ensure that no further insurrections take place during his reign.

Prince Nidjal

The surviving son of King Massini, Nidjal swelters in the jail, dreaming only of liberation and revenge. Prince Nidjal believes that Emir Farphanes and his master, the so called Veiled God, seek relics related to the prophet Sulymon in the Holy City of Dawaad across the desert to the east. He is convinced that their activities must be stopped before they set the world on fire.

11. Burned Neighborhoods

Throughout the city are areas that are charred and burned to rubble. These neighborhoods were scorched by the faithful of the Cult of the Burning One, leaving naught but cinders behind. Piles of bodies lie among the burned area where whole families were slaughtered in the name of the Veiled God.

There is a 25% chance that 1d4 corpses encountered rise as **cinder ghouls**[1].

12. Silk Street

This street was once lined with boutique shops whose owners lived in the apartments above their businesses. Clothiers, cobblers, perfume merchants, hookah lounges, tea shops, spice sellers, and the like all kept shops along Silk Street as it faced the wall of the noble quarters.

An enslaved **firefiend**[1] now patrols Silk Street, challenging any who have not accepted the brand of the Burning One. It makes way only for mamelukes, imams of the Burned One, hariphs, burning dervishes, and the like. All others are instructed to surrender or face death.

Note: If Sparque is with the party, he knows the firefiend's true name — Cebu — and can negotiate passage without need of combat.

13. Noble Quarter

This garden-like walled neighborhood of palatial estates is largely abandoned now. Several of the fine palaces have burned to the ground. Others serve as armed camps for those who converted to the cause of the Burning One.

14. Tariq the Mummawil's Palace

This was once the home of a wealthy banker. A small band of thieves who once ruled the slums — before the construction of the spire of Kirtius chased them away — now occupy the home. They have taken up residence among the houses they once preyed upon. The thieves have no love for Emir Farphanes' despotic rule, however, and even less for the mad cult that dismembers its members for not swearing allegiance to their primordial "god."

The band, once known as the Silk Shadows, is made up of Hirsiz Alb (male **assassin** with *+1 scimitar,* a pair of *+1 daggers*, and a *cloak of arachnida*[2]), Al Alquatu (male **spy** with 31 hit points, *boots of striding and springing*, a pair of *+1 daggers*, and a *bag of holding*), and Al Altayir (female **spy** with 31 hit points, a *potion of invisibility*, and *wings of flying*). Their other members have since joined the cult or been crucified and burned. The trio would be interested in teaming up with the party if it means getting some revenge against Emir Farphanes, but they know for certain that they cannot take him on their own. There is always a chance they betray the party if offered a better deal.

15. Emir Yama's Estate

This was the palace of King Massini's bravest general. The estate was ransacked of its valuables, and the emir died at the foot of his king's throne defending his liege lord to his last breath. Members of his family fled the purge, but some of his loyal soldiers returned to the city. These brave few took up refuge in the remains of General Yama's estate, and use it as an observation post to record the comings and goings of those who have sworn faith and allegiance to the Burning One.

Hidden in Yama's estate are 30 resistance rebels (**bandits**) led by Sir Muniq, a knight of Massini's court. Sir Muniq uses the statistics of a **holy knight**, except that he wears a set of *+1 chainmail*, which makes his Armor Class 19 with his shield, and a *+1 tulwar* (which functions as a longsword), giving him a +6 to hit with it, and deals 8 (1d8 + 3) slashing damage, or 9 (1d10 + 4) slashing damage when wielded with two hands.

Sir Muniq seeks to rescue his betrothed Yesmilla from the clutches of Emir Farphanes. He is aware that Emir Farphanes and his allies are searching for secrets left behind by the Prophet Sulymon, and that Sulymon's holy city is to the east of Kirtius. He knows that Emir Farphanes sent an army against the city not long ago to uncover these secrets, which they consider to be key to their War of Flames. He is also aware that Prince Nidjal is being held captive in the spire of Kirtius.

Another 150 members of their cavalry (also **bandits**) are hidden in an oasis 20 miles from the city, waiting Muniq's orders to return.

16. Burned Mansions

The Cult of the Burning One torched several estates when they overwhelmed the city. A portion of the wall separating the noble district from Silk Street collapsed when basalt columns rolled downhill and smashed through the brick and stucco wall.

Like the burned areas in the city proper, there is a 25% chance that the deceased homeowners or their servants rise from the ashes as 1d4 **cinder ghouls**[1].

17. Bastion Batteries

The three Bastion Batteries are large walled embankments facing the rolling deserts to the east of the city. The batteries are topped with a trio of trebuchets equipped to hurl 80-pound stones a great distance against any siege engines brought to bear by hostile tribes or neighboring kingdoms. The trebuchets are each ready to be manned by 5 loaders and 5 firers who are normally garrisoned in the bastion tower below their feet. Currently, the troops are prisoners in their barracks (15 per bastion) while a skeleton crew of 5 mameluke (**guard** with scimitar and short bow) cultists man the towers.

If freed, the troops (as **bandits**, currently AC 11 and unarmed) gladly fight, though they know such a fight is folly and would ultimately lead to the destruction of the city at best, and their deaths at the worst. The lock to the garrison barracks requires a successful DC 18 Dexterity check with thieves' tools to open. The garrison troops' weaponry is in the hands of cultists and mamelukes either in the Brazen Spire or on the streets.

18. City Gates

Two sets of gates lead into the city from the desert. The easternmost facing gate is known as the **Gate of Sunrise** as it is situated in such a way that the rise of the morning sun lifts above its lintel. The gate points the way to the holy city of Dawaad. The northernmost gate is called the **Gate of the Morning Star**, as it faces the first star to be seen in the night sky. A squad of 5 mamelukes (**guard** with scimitar and short bow) trained in the Brazen Spire is currently stationed at each of the city's gates.

19. Oasis Aljania

The Oasis Aljania rests on the southern edge of the city outside of its gates but directly facing the fortress palace of King Massini. The oasis is currently overrun by a warband of 100 **hobgoblins** that has ridden in from the deep desert. The band has sworn its allegiance to Emir Farphanes and the efreeti's Veiled God.

The band is led by Egrat Shem, a notoriously cruel **hobgoblin captain**[1] who revels in the finery of silks and fine linens that his new abode provides. He has 10 **hobgoblin lieutenants**[1] to support him. He awaits captured ships to carry his band to new lands where he can bring the cleansing War of Flames to the enemies of his newfound master, little knowing that service to the Veiled God is typically short lived, ending in servitude or a pile of ash.

20. Massini's Fortress

This palace located on a smaller island across a drawbridge from the noble quarter was home to Massini al Dawaad, a human descendent of the aged prophet. His grandfather established this port after his father founded the kingdom of Numeda at the behest of the prophet himself.

20-1. Bridge

The bridge crosses from the noble quarter into King Massini's private island palace. The bridge ends in a strongly built guardhouse whose four towers are topped with burnished golden domes.

20-1A. Massini's Gate

The gate is made from polished bronze and heavy hardwood. The gates once featured the handsome visage of King Massini sitting astride a powerful Numedan warhorse with his lance piercing one of the heads of a recoiling chimera. The face has been melted from the bronze relief by a great heat.

The gates are a foot thick and barred from the inside when closed. Breaking through them requires a successful DC 30 Strength check.

Anyone approaching the gate is hailed by a **guard** who calls down from the towers.

20-1B. Guard Towers

The guard towers are each guarded by 4 sentries (human **captain**[1] without Leadership ability). The sentries allow hariphs, fire imams, and burning dervishes free admittance to the fortress.

20-2. Massini's Garden

A beautiful garden surrounds the royal residence, complete with waving palms and terraces of rare tropical flowers.

20-2A. Fountain

The fountain licks with burning embers and a glowing yellow orange flame. Polished marble mermaids are charred black by the heat that rises from the fountain's pool.

The fountain is now home to a **fire elemental** enslaved to Emir Farphanes. The elemental rises from the fountain to challenge any who would seek entrance to the buildings. If the characters are not escorted by one of the hariphs of Kirtius or a burning dervish, the fire elemental rises and attacks.

The fountain itself is clogged with charred bones and piles of skulls, the remains of those who stood against Emir Farphanes when he arrived to take command of the city and begin the War of Flames. Among these charred remains are the bones of Maggie Macewan, wife of Yeoman Jon (see ***Lornedain: The Secret Flame***). There is no way of knowing her body is among the others who were burned here save for a partially melted golden ring on the finger of one of the charred bones that reads *"From J to M: 8"* that Jon would recognize. It can be found if a thorough search is made of all the burned and charred remains found here. The search takes an hour, although with a successful DC 18 Intelligence (Investigation) check, the time can be cut in half.

20-2B. Garden of the Palms

The gardens of Massini are filled with flowering fruit-bearing palms brought from throughout the region. These include coconuts, date palms, and acai berry trees brought in abundance to the table of Massini and his guests. The palm garden was patrolled by a pack of 4 **saber tooth tigers** patrol the palm garden. They were originally trained to ignore the royal family and certain staff members, but to devour all others. Emir Farphanes charmed the felines, and they now serve him.

20-3. Gun Emplacements

These towers are affixed with three 6-pound guns[3] each. The guns are manned by 4 mamelukes (**guard** with scimitar and short bow) loyal to the Veiled God who keep an eye on the horizon for any flotilla that would bear threat to the fledgling caliphate. Shot and powder are stationed at the gun emplacements to fire each cannon four times, with more stored in a magazine 20 feet beneath the base of the tower.

20-4. Throne Room of Massini

Massini's throne room is lavishly adorned with velvet curtains of royal purple. Simulated date palms crafted of red marble once hung with fist-sized jewels — jewels that now adorn the throats of the Sultan's noble court in the City of Brass. The ceiling is pierced with crystals that replicate the stars in the sky directly over the palace. Interestingly, the stars are lit during the daylight, showing the stars hidden when the sun is overhead.

The floor of the throne room features a large-scale mosaic map of Libynos, the sea, and the coastal regions of Akados. Brass oil lamps have been placed over cities and religious sites across both continents. Some of the oil lamps are lit, while others are not. An examiner of the placement of these lamps could deduce that areas where oil lamps are lit are areas where an active Brazen Spire is located, and areas where the lamps are not lit are areas where new spires are intended to be built. If the characters destroyed the Brazen Spire of Freegate, its lamp has been removed from the map.

Farphanes now uses the throne room as a military command center, where he summons local tribespeople to submit to the authority of the Throne of Brass, and to himself as the new caliph of fire in the Lost Lands. Their options are always to join or burn. Those who refuse to join hide in the deep desert, and are hunted by desert-dwelling hobgoblins and Lotus Eaters loyal to the Burning One. There is a 50% chance that the characters encounter Emir Farphanes (**efreeti**) in the Throne Room, either awaiting their arrival or overseeing plans for the expansion of the caliphate and the eventual conquest of the Lost Lands by the sultan's forces.

A pair of charred skulls are affixed to the outsized throne. The skull on the left hand is that of a woman and belonged to Queen Batheera. The right-hand skull has the melted remains of a golden turban pin fused to the frontal bone and is the skull of King Massini.

20-5. Advisor's Tower

The advisor's tower was once occupied by Massini's vizier, Juwanza Bin Hadath. After the coup and otherworldly invasion that conquered Numeda, the vizier was sent in chains to the City of Brass. Juwanza is currently being held prisoner in the Bayt al-Najoom by Sheikh Azul Bin Berith, in the Noble Quarters of the City of Brass. He is slowly being drained of his magical powers by an efreeti noble.

His tower contains crates of books that have not yet been shipped to the Great Repository. Within is a wizard's spellbook containing four spells of 2nd level, three spells of 3rd level, two spells of 4th level and one spell of 5th level.

A second book, *Paths of the Prophet*, details the exploits of Sulymon, and his arrival in the Maighib Desert by way of a mystic passageway hidden in the Dark Oasis. A successful DC 22 Intelligence check could deduce directions to the Dark Oasis from the text.

20-6. Servants' Tower

The servants' tower houses 50 slaves (human **commoners**) who previously served as courtiers to King Massini. Their reversal of fortune is complete, as the courtiers now serve slaves who joined the Cult of the Burning One, their wish fulfilled. The slaves serve little purpose in the regime of Emir Farphanes, save as entertainment for him when he immolates one for his amusement. They variously serve wine, fruits, and meals to guests of the emir.

Among the slaves is Linsey Macewan (see *Lornedain: The Secret Flame*). If Yeoman Jon is with the party, he instantly recognizes his child, and they have a tearful reunion. Linsey was separated from her brother Grendle and her older sister Aelish, and she believes that Emir Farphanes sold them. Her mother was burned in the fountain by Emir Farphanes to punish Grendle for trying to fight. Emir Farphanes threatened to burn his sisters if he did not submit. She has not seen Aelish or Grendle in some time.

20-7. Knights' Tower

The Knights' Tower served as the barracks for Massini's own personal retinue and royal guard, with its first floor serving as the royal stables. Those knights who survived the arrival of Emir Farphanes are now hiding in nearby palaces, or at Yama's estate awaiting a sign to rise against Farphanes' forces.

The **burning dervish**[1] Jin al Waamplir, who now serves as Emir Farphanes' bodyguard, occupies the old barracks and enforces order among the mamelukes who guard the palace. Hidden among the belongings of the burning dervish are a set of *marvelous pigments*.

20-8. Royal Sahir's Tower

This tower served as the shrine of Hakiim Oban, the court fakir of Massini. Hakiim was taken prisoner during the assault on the palace and forced to lead Emir Farphanes's army to the Holy City of Dawaad in search of holy relics related to the mortal life of Sulymon.

The tower now serves as the quarters of Fahd, a **burning dervish**[1] (with a *+1 glaive*) under the command of Emir Farphanes.

20-9. Massini's Family Courtyard

The family courtyard is a garden within the garden, filled with beautiful flowing roses, daffodils, and other flowers fed through a complicated irrigation system. A gilt marble table sits in the center and was used by Massini and his family to dine and enjoy quiet time with one another. Emir Farphanes uses the garden as a kennel for his favorite pair of **hellhounds**.

20-10. Queen's Chambers

The queen's chambers were an apartment used by the queen and King Massini's children. The area has been all but stripped of its valuables, all of which were sent as tribute to the City of Brass. There is a bed with silk sheets, a dressing bureau, and a desk covered in a stack of scrolls and books. A richly painted mural that surrounds the bedroom depicts a beautiful oasis marked with a pair of crossed palms. The oasis is dominated by a glorious lake of deep blue waters upon which float brightly painted lotus flowers. A strange symbol of two waved lines appears engraved on a brick-like stone which rests at the bottom of the lake beneath a marble pillar guarded by a turbaned figure of bluish green. The mosaic depicts the Dark Oasis (**Area 7** in *The Path of the Prophet*) and shows the location of the *water stone of Sulymon*.

If Baroness Aora Lornedain (now a **preacher**[1]) and Giza Al Hofu (now a **mage**) survived *Freegate: The Brazen Spires* and *Lornedain: The Secret Flame*, they are found here where they serve Emir Farphanes in whatever role he demands of them. Giza Al Hofu has 5 vials of *sleep potion*[2], a *potion of invisibility*, *bracers of defence*, a *staff of fire*, two scrolls with *maggic missile*, and a *ring of protection*. The Baroness has *+1 plate*, a *+1 shield*, a *flaming weapon*[2] (mace), 2 *potions of healing*, and her signet ring of Lornedain (200 gp).

20-11. King Massini's Royal Apartments

Massini's Apartments now serve as the harem and bedchambers of Emir Farphanes.

Harem

Emir Farphanes' ground floor harem is composed of three daughters of the royal families of Kirtius, and daughters of the wild tribes who have ridden to the banner of the Burning One.

Yesmella (**entertainer**[1]) was promised to Al-Furusiyya Muniq. Farphanes keeps her in a gilded cage for his amusement and forces her to sing to him like a pet bird, even going so far as dressing her in a cloak of golden feathers. Yesmella hates Emir Farphanes with a burning passion and would murder the efreet if she could somehow figure out a way.

Haadiyah (**hobgoblin lieutenant**[1]) is the daughter of the hobgoblin chieftain Egrat Shem and was taken to seal the deal between the two. Haadiyah is loyal to Emir Farphanes and whiles away her days torturing the other girls of the harem and ruling it as if she were a chosen queen.

Jimiyah (human **noble**) was the daughter of a southern prince defeated in an early battle with Emir Farphanes' armies. Like Yesmella, Jimiyah seethes with hatred for the foul efreet. Anyone who returns her to her people in the grasslands just north of the Maighib Desert is awarded with as much ivory as they can carry.

A seraph eunuch named Al Samath guards the harem. Al Samath is marked upon his face with the sigil of the sultan of efreet and is forced into slavery by the mark. He was a prisoner of war captured when the seraphs rose against the Veiled God who had usurped the Throne of Brass. Al Samath uses the statistics of a **seraph genie**[1], except that he cannot disobey the wishes of Emir Farphanes nor raise a hand against the Sultan.

Bedchamber of the King

This chamber remains opulent, though the large bed is almost too small for Emir Farphanes' huge frame. Carven elephants of alabaster flank the bed. A mosaic of semi-precious materials displays the cycle of the sun and moons taking place above a gorgeous desert landscape. Featured in the mosaic is a holy city set among mountains in the distance, and footprints leading through the desert to the shores of the sea. From the shores, a ship awaits a man dressed in white robes who carries a stone that glows like fire in one hand, and one that seems to blow like the wind in the other.

If Emir Farphanes (**efreeti**) has not yet been encountered, there is a 25% chance he is found here.

Farphanes' Treasure: The locked ironbound chest wrapped in iron chains is actually a transformed **chain devil**. If the lock is attempted without Farphanes' key, which is hidden within the furnace golem in the spire of Kirtius (**Area 10** on the ninth floor), the chain devil is released and immediately attacks. Once destroyed or if the command words are spoken, the chain devil turns back into a box. Noting that something is odd about the trunk requires a successful DC 20 Intelligence (Investigation) check.

In the chest, Emir Farphanes keeps 1,000 bp, 5,000 gp to pay his armies, a war mask of gold, brass, and iron inlaid with emeralds worth 1,000 gp, a *potion of giant strength* (cloud), 3 blue spinels worth 500 gp each, and a *staff of healing*.

Documents found in the chest detail a search for Sulymon's *elemental stones*, and the conquest of the Holy City of Dawaad deep in the desert. He also notes that he dispatched the Lotus Eaters in search of the Cavern of Secrets where they hope to take control of a hidden planar gate that would accelerate their invasion and break Anumon's wards. The importance of the cavern to the Sultan's schemes is not to be ignored. There is a strong chance that the characters have already collected some of the stones and should now have a good idea as to their purpose. If they do not, it would be a good time for an NPC reveal this information to the characters.

Running Farphanes

Farphanes is a newly minted emir of the Bayt Al Sikkyn. He is arrogant and cruel, as are the majority of his race. Seen as an early supporter of the Usurper, Emir Farphanes knows he cannot in any way fail his master in the absorption and conquest of the Lost Lands. For this reason alone, Farphanes is unlikely to use his plane shift ability to flee the characters when confronted, choosing death before dishonor. He is, however, not above offering a single *wish* to the characters in exchange for his life.

Emir Farphanes is as likely to hunt the characters in the city if he discovers their presence as he is to wait for their attack in the palace. Of course, there is a chance he is surprised by the characters due to their clever use of stealth and diplomacy in making their way into the city without incident.

Farphanes tends to monologue throughout a battle, making arguments on behalf of his master. He argues that the doings of the greater beings of the cosmos are beyond the reckoning of mortals and that they should either join him or stand out of the way. Joining him offers its own rewards. Emir Farphanes suggests that they could become masters and rulers of the New Lost Lands that is to be forged in the fire of his master's conquests.

The Wish

Should combat turn against Emir Farphanes, he offers a parlay to find out what indeed the characters want. If the characters have pursued the story since Lornedain, he is likely aware of their search for the missing citizens of the village. Foolish as he believes it is for mortals to put so much stock in their worthless lives, he may offer the characters a *wish* while slyly suggesting they could save the ones that they seek to rescue.

But What Can You Wish For?

Rescue of the Missing: The characters could indeed wish for the return, alive and healthy, of all the missing persons from Lornedain and Backwater. This would by no means stop Emir Farphanes' minions from continuing their assault against the characters, nor would it stop the Sultan's planned invasion.

Farphanes to Depart: Characters could wish for Emir Farphanes to leave and never return to the Lost Lands. Farphanes would be banished for 1 year and 1 day from the Lost Lands. This would not stop the Sultan from elevating another minion from a different noble house to assume his place.

Riches and Power: Riches and power are limited by the strength of the wish as written in its spell description. Attempting to get more than the limits has a 50% chance of failing and resulting in the character who makes the wish ending up in the slave markets of the City of Brass.

Destruction of a Brazen Spire: The wish is powerful enough to remove one spire from the map, but not all of the spires. This would not stop the Sultan from simply attempting to build more, and would no doubt put his attention and everlasting ire on the party.

Assess the Location of the Remaining Missing Persons: Long shot. Players don't always make the best choices. Instead of wishing for the return of their missing friends from Lornedain, they may end up wishing to know where their friends are. They can be given a detailed account of the remaining missing children of Lornedain and Backwater. At this stage, Mareal, Simone, Aelish, and Grendle are still missing. See *The Missing: Where are They?* in **Chapter 3** for their locations.

Standard Uses: Standard wishes include bringing a dead comrade back to life, removing a disfigurement or debilitating disease, curse, or wound. Wishes must be carefully worded!

Farphanes is clever in his assessment of wishes during the "ask," and follows the wish request to the absolute letter of the law, for he knows far better than the characters do that failure of a wish results in the enslavement and imprisonment of the asker within the City of Brass!

Completing the Adventure

The adventure concludes with the characters on the trail of the Holy City of Dawaad.

It is not absolutely necessary to defeat Emir Farphanes in order to set out for the holy city, but it offers another opportunity for some level of closure in finding answers to the missing persons hunt that set them on their quest. Depending on how you are calculating XP, this might be a good time for the characters to gain half a level or so. Depending on how many of the success conditions listed below they have achieved, this may between 6000 and 8000 XP each.

Conditions of Success

- Characters Kill or Defeat Emir Farphanes
- Characters Rescue Prisoners hidden within the spire dungeon of Kirtius
- Characters Discover location of the Holy City of Dawaad.

Chapter 7
The Path of the Prophet

Introduction

The Path of the Prophet is an adventure to get characters to the Plane of Molten Skies, and from there allow them to eventually find the City of Brass. The adventure is designed to challenge 4–6 characters of Tier 2. However, the adventure may be scaled up or down depending on the composition and makeup of your group. Several plot hooks are offered to get the characters right into the action with little preparation time on your part.

The adventure may be used to kick off a high-level campaign in the City of Brass or merely as a tool to get the characters to the city where they may find their own adventures as characters are often wont to do. **The Path of the Prophet** may also be used as a stand-alone adventure offering the party a final prize where they find a stationary gate leading to alternate planes of the universe. During the course of the adventure, the characters discover an abandoned city where they must slay a horrific evil, and then follow the footsteps of the great prophet Sulymon to the Plane of Molten Skies. During their journey, they pass landmarks important to the prophet's miracles before reaching the gateway to the Plane of Molten Skies.

Maps for this section include **Numeda**, *2. Oasis of Ghobad-Usk*, *5. Holy City of Dawaad*, *7. Dark Oasis*, and *9. Secret Canyon*.

Adventure Background

The city of Dawaad has stood for many centuries as the center of worship for the god Anumon on the characters' home plane. The prophet Sulymon, a mortal possessed of a lifespan beyond that of normal men, ruled this ancient theocracy. Sulymon led his followers from the barren deserts to the east of Dawaad, where he proved his worth in the eyes of Anumon by achieving many miracles. Most recently, a great festival was planned within Dawaad as Sulymon was at last to rejoin his god Anumon in a richly deserved afterlife.

A great pilgrimage was undertaken, and thousands of Anumon's worshippers traveled to Dawaad from all corners of the world to observe the miracle of ascension. During the course of the ritual as Anumon was to reveal himself to his followers, a trio of strangers appeared in the midst of the celebrants. One placed a flask of brass to the lips of the aged and dying prophet as the others set loose a great evil within the temple sacred to the god of gates and the codifier of the laws of gods and men. Temple guardians fought a great battle, and succeeded in destroying one of the two summoned beasts, but at the cost of their own lives. In the midst of the fray, the trio of men whose flesh burned like fire escaped into the eastern desert with the brass bottle containing the spirit and flesh of the prophet.

In anger, the god of gates sealed many of the passages between the worlds of the living and the dead, so that no souls may travel on to their respective afterlife. He immediately dispatched a cordon of djinn princes to seal off the city and forbade the exit of the beast that defiled his temple with its presence. Anumon decreed that no soul shall meet its just afterlife until his temple is set right and the body and soul of his prophet are returned to him.

It is into this desperate struggle between gods and men, prophets and outsiders, heroes and villains, that the characters find themselves inexorably drawn. For their part, the party may take up the struggle for no more reason than that they themselves may wish to have a decent afterlife, rather than find their soul entombed in rotting flesh forever.

Be aware that this adventure does not lead characters to finding the magical bottle holding the prophet, nor does it end with the characters returning everything to rights in their world. Instead, it is the start of a great adventure set against the backdrop of the Plane of Molten Skies and the cruel grandeur of the City of Brass.

Plot Hooks

Listed below are several plot devices that may be used to bring the characters into **The Path of the Prophet**.

Characters Have a Vision

A dream reveals apocalyptic events taking place across the characters' world. In the vision, souls are unable to reach the afterlife and are returning as shadows and wraiths, with whole villages being attacked by their newly buried dead. Ever so slowly, the vision leads the characters to a once gleaming white city on the edge of the sea. Huge princes of the air wielding gleaming tulwars in their massive fists seal the city's gates, but the vision leads the characters beyond these guardians to a great temple in the center of the city. The temple is blackened, however, and an aura of pure evil emanates from the ruined structure. A being of great evil stands astride a mound of charred bodies in the midst of the temple. The vision changes again, and suddenly the characters are flying across the desert, stopping first at a moonlit oasis, and finally flying past a statue of a horseman forged of solid brass who points to a darkened cavern among a spine of bare rock. The vision ends before a swirling portal surrounded by engraved stones.

Upon waking, characters may attempt Intelligence (History) or Intelligence (Religion) checks to determine the meaning of their dreams.

DC 15: The character determines that the abandoned dream city is a holy city that closely correlates to one on a map in their possession. The city is located not far from their current location.

DC 20: The character recognizes the city as Dawaad and the guardians as noble djinn.

DC 25: The character further determines that the temple in their vision is the Temple of Anumon, holy seat of worship to the god of gates and codifier of laws. The character readily know that the worship of Anumon is led by Sulymon, a powerful prophet rumored to be more than 1,000 years old. If something happened to Sulymon and the temple of Anumon is desecrated, then an event of great portentousness has happened or is about to take place.

Rise of the Living Dead

For every day that the characters spend avoiding the city and going about their own business, they are visited by another such dream and are attacked by 1d6 **wraiths** (but neutral and immune to being turned), 1d4 **shadows** (but neutral, immune to being turned, and not vulnerable to radiant damage), and 1d2 **specters** (but neutral and immune to being turned). These incorporeal undead moan and howl for the characters to end their suffering, begging as they attack for the characters to appease the god of gates so that they may pass on.

The Party is Pursuing Missing Persons

Characters who played through **Lornedain: The Secret Flame** and **The Brazen Spires** may be hunting the remaining missing persons from Lornedain. The party may have just defeated Emir Farphanes and learned of the plight of Dawaad from Yesmella and Al-Furusiyya Muniq. At this point, the characters should have a pretty strong idea of the Sultan's plans for the Lost Lands and should suspect that their remaining friends and kinsfolk have been sent to the City of Brass. The Holy City of Dawaad should have the answers they seek.

At the onset of the adventure, the characters may be aware that Emir Farphanes directed followers of the Burning One to set forth to Dawaad days before the characters arrive in Kirtius.

A Messenger of Their God Visits the Characters

A messenger of one of the Characters' gods appears and points the party in the direction of Dawaad, explaining that it is of the utmost importance to appease Anumon, the god of gates, and to find out what happened to cause him to seal the portals between the realm of the living and the dead.

If the characters refuse the messenger of their god, their own god punishes them, stripping priests of clerical spells, sending divine totem creatures to attack the party, denying them healing, and the like until they take up the quest.

A Character Finds a Djinni Bottle

The characters locate a djinni bottle in one of their recent treasure troves. Upon rubbing the bottle, a djinni prince appears and speaks:

Alas for the love of Anumon and the blessings of his ever-faithful servant Sulymon, freedom is at last granted but too late to warn my master. At the edge of the desert stands the city of Dawaad. Great is the wrong that has been done there, and for one year and one day shall I, Qaanit Al Sharrade, serve thee freely if you first help me upon my quest!

Qaanit tells the party that three beings known as burning dervishes captured and forced him into this bottle after he followed them from the Plane of Molten Skies. He identifies the burning dervishes as assassins in the service of the sultan of efreet, who seeks to kidnap or murder the prophet of Anumon. If the characters are not convinced, Qaanit offers them great but vaguely defined riches.

Qaanit can easily shorten travel time to Dawaad through use of *wind walk*, carrying up to ten individuals to the very gates of the city.

Characters Find a Treasure Map

The characters find a treasure map etched into the bottom of a brass bowl. The treasure map is inscribed with the following passage:

From the eastern gates of the city of Anumon, follow the footsteps of the prophet through the moonlit oasis to find the brass horseman. Beyond his spear ten leagues lies the Cavern of Secrets, there the passage to the Plane of Molten Skies, and through his path to the gates of the City of Brass.

The map iterates numerous items of wealth and power found within the City of Brass.

This option works best for characters motivated by need or greed, and for GMs not comfortable with an extended high-level adventure campaign in the **City of Brass** campaign setting.

Anumon, God of Gates, Keeper of the Laws, Overseer of Creation

Alignment: Lawful Neutral (good tendencies)
Domains: Creation, Law, Protection, Travel
Symbol: A locked gate and seven keys.
Typical Worshippers: Artists, judges, nobles, teachers, loremasters.
Favored Weapon: Bronze Mace

Anumon wears many guises and many faces when he appears to his subjects. Most representations of him are of a noble and just king with a plaited beard. Upon his head is a helm wreathed in a crown, and light springs forth from eyes that burn like twin suns. He bears a huge bronze scepter (a great mace) with which he smites his foes. Known as one of the beings present at the original creation, he is known as a creation god and bringer of knowledge and justice to his worshippers.

Known as the keeper of the gates, he oversees transfer between the different planes so that demons do not run free to ravage the homes of the faithful, and that the unworthy are barred access to the homes of the gods.

Creation Domain

At 1st level, you gain proficiency in two types of artisan's tools. You gain the *mending* cantrip if you don't already have it. You gain proficiency with the great mace[3].

At 2nd level, you can use your Channel Divinity to tap into your powers of creation. For 1 hour, you have proficiency with any type of artisan's tool. If you already have proficiency, your proficiency bonus is doubled.

At 6th level, when you use a transmutation spell, you can create or affect twice as much material. For spells that affect a single creature, the duration is doubled instead.

At 8th level your words have physical force. As a bonus action, you can make a verbal attack against a single creature using your spell attack modifier. If the attack succeeds, the creature takes 1d8 force damage and must succeed on a Strength saving throw against your spell save DC or be pushed 5 feet. The damage increases to 2d8 when you reach 14th level.

At 17th level, choose one Domain spell of 4th level or lower. You can cast this spell without using a spell slot.

Creation Domain Spells

Cleric Level	Spells
1st	False Life, Fog Cloud
3rd	Alter Self, Enlarge/Reduce
5th	Animate Object, Blink
7th	Polymorph, Stone Shape
9th	Passwall, Wall of Stone

Great Mace

This two-handed mace has a head usually cast in solid iron and is heavily weighted, offering it massive damage-dealing capability and the power to shatter armor.

Great Mace: Heavy, two-handed martial melee weapon; Cost 40 gp; Damage 1d10 bludgeoning; Weight 12 lb.

The Characters Find the Isle of Bliss

The party is getting provisions on a small island inhabited by the descendants of a shipwrecked naval vessel and native inhabitants. While there, they spy a fisherman breaking open a brass bottle found in his net and releasing an efreeti trapped within. The efreeti howls with glee and fills the fisherman's otherwise empty net with fish. The fishermen mention that this sort of thing happens from time to time as Sulymon was known to bind any genie he encountered in a bottle of brass. Sulymon then sealed the bottle with molten lead and cast it into the sea exclaiming "Let you find peace with thy brothers of the deeper waters." The islanders indicate that once freed, the genies tend to leave the world forever not wishing to run across Sulymon again. It is said that they return to their home in the City of Brass, a place known for its opulent wealth. They also add that Sulymon knows the path to the City of Brass and that the party should sail northeast to Dawaad and ask him if they are curious.

Getting Started

Traveling to Dawaad from Kirtius should take the party about a week. Random encounters should be infrequent, possibly consisting of more wraiths, specters, or shadows as detailed under the "Characters Have a Vision" story hook.

Dawaad may be approached from the north via rugged hill country, from the south via the southern savannah, or from the east via the vast sea of sand that is the Maighib Desert. Use wilderness encounter tables appropriate to the terrain according to the route that the characters take to arrive at the city.

The Maighib Desert

This desert is detailed at length in **Dunes of Desolation** by **Frog God Games** but feel free to substitute any desert environment you desire as the characters travel across this forbidding wasteland.

Trek Across the Maighib

The deserts to the east of Dawaad are treacherous. Sudden sandstorms, lack of water, bandits, and other dangers await those who travel there. Refer to the sidebox for random encounters while traveling across the desert.

Numeda
10 Miles
Holy City of Dawaad
Secret Canyon
Refugee Camp
Brass Horseman
Dark Oasis
Kirtius
Tomb of Dawaad
Oasis of Ghobad-Usk
Ruins of Mati-Alamul
N

Maighib Desert Random Encounters

Roll 1d20 for every 3 miles traveled. Since visibility in the desert is clear, allow Perception checks before any encounter not involving creatures hidden under the sand.

1d20	Encounter
1	Sandstorm
2	1d6 + 4 refugees from Dawaad
3	2d6 sand ghouls
4	1d6 + 1 desert nomads
5	1d4 jann
6	2 ant lions
7	2d4 sand spiders
8	2d4 desert bandits plus leader
9	1d4 + 1 giant scorpions
10–20	No encounter

Sandstorm: A sandstorm reduces visibility to 1d10 × 5 feet and provides disadvantage on all Perception checks. A sandstorm deals 1d3 bludgeoning damage per hour to any creatures caught in the open. It leaves a thin coating of sand in its wake. Driving sand creeps in through all but the most secure seals and seams, chafing skin and contaminating carried gear.

Refugees from Dawaad: These refugees (**commoners**) need water and tell of the horrors visited upon them by the horned devil Izkandr (area **5-8**). If they are assured that Izkandr is destroyed, they point the party toward the Brass Horseman.

Sand Ghouls: This group of sand **ghouls** are the risen remains of bandits who preyed upon the desert nomads and continue this tradition even in undeath. They frequently ride undead camels and pretend to be desert nomads. They may also disguise themselves as water traders.

Desert Nomads: Wanderers (**sneakthief**[1]) who make their homes in the dunes and blowing sands of the desert.

Ant Lions: A pair of **ant lions**[1] have constructed a 40-foot deep camouflaged pit trap in the sand and await unwary travelers at its base. Noticing the trap requires a successful DC 20 Wisdom (Perception) check.

Sand Spiders: These **sand spiders** make their home in the desert. They are carrying the dessicated remains of some nomads.

Desert Bandits: Human outlaws (**spy**) who ply their trade across the sandy terrain. Some ride horses while most operate from camels. The leader is a **bandit lord**[1].

Giant Scorpions: Camouflaged by the sand, the **giant scorpions** attempt to ambush passers-by.

1. Kirtius

Kirtius is fully detailed in **Chapter 6** of **Book I: Cult of the Burning One**.

2. The Cursed Oasis of Ghobad-Usk

Long known as a reliable stop and watering hole for caravans, trading companies, and various desert tribes, the Oasis of Ghobad-Usk is now a silent tomb of death and mystery littered with fresh skeletons picked clean in the desert sun. The water remains fresh, the figs and olives delicious, but a quiet aura of menace hangs over the oasis.

History of the Oasis

Although the oasis has changed hands many times over the centuries as a strategic point between competing desert tribes, it originally began as a remote, deep pocket of subterranean water that eventually bubbled to the surface. This was followed by slow growth over the centuries as migrating birds and animals passed seeds with their droppings, causing vegetation to slowly sprout up around the water's edge. These days, the borders of the oasis support a verdant field of lush and carefully cultivated vegetation — a rarity in Numeda. The oasis has a healthy supply of date palms, along with apricots, plums, and olives that grow in small gardens underneath the protection and shade of the larger trees. As assortment of desert cacti, scrub brush, and low grasses round out the vegetation at the oasis.

Several months ago, a group of desert reavers and bandits known as the Sons of Al-Saheed took over and occupied the oasis. The slavers arrived after a recent deal with Farphanes and the burning dervishes went sour over the price of slaves, resulting in the death of most of the reavers. The few Sons of Al-Saheed who were left fled into the desert to escape. They hid out in the Oasis of Ghobad-Usk, licking their wounds and planning their next move. At times, they waylaid caravans passing through or exacted a steep toll for use of the oasis.

Four nights ago, an earthquake shook the Maighib, rolling through the deserted hills and valleys and over the Oasis of Ghobad-Usk. The earthquake initially appeared to have no effect on the oasis, though it silently dislodged a portion of the substrata beneath the oasis, opening up a formerly isolated cavern. Unfortunately for the sleeping and off-guard inhabitants of the oasis that night, the cavern was home to a large colony of ochre jellies that — sensing movement on the surface above them — slowly oozed their way to the surface through the newly opened tunnel. When they bubbled to the surface of the oasis, they moved in on its current occupants with a ravenous, primal hunger. Over the course of an hour, the ochre jellies killed and devoured the Sons of Al-Saheed to the last man.

The Oasis Now

By day, the Oasis of Ghobad-Usk appears as it always has — a lush watering hole surrounded by shade from the date palms that hug its boundaries in the middle of a harsh wasteland. As one draws closer, the oasis appears unguarded and unoccupied. Carts are overturned. Hitching posts for mounts are empty, though reins, saddles, and ties remain behind. Several tents flap lazily in the breeze, their contents undisturbed. Closer inspection reveals the truth: Some sort of struggle occurred here, resulting in one side being completely overwhelmed. The skeletal remains of more than a dozen men — their bones completely picked clean of all flesh and sinew by the horrid digestive enzymes of the ochre jellies — lie haphazardly strewn across the sand and rock, some bent at odd angles. The clothing, armor, and accoutrements of

Finding the Oasis

Here are some options for how the party finds the oasis

Sandstorm: An unexpected sandstorm delays the party by more than a week and their water supply is running low. Through cracked, bloody lips, their guide insists that a stop at the Oasis of Ghobad-Usk is unavoidable if they want to live, even if they may have to pay a heavy fine to use its waters.

Wild horses: As they trek through the desert, the characters see several wild-eyed **riding horses** run by, each frothing at the mouth and in obvious distress. One has a saddle and all appear to be branded with the mark of a local desert tribe. If these sad, scared beasts are chased down or somehow subdued, one is revealed to have a curious and altogether strange burn on its left flank.

Missing caravan: A trading caravan full of fine silks, rare herbs, and expensive dyes disappeared on its way through the Maighib Desert more than three weeks ago and is long overdue at its destination. The party is hired to find out what happened to the caravan and to recover what they can.

Oasis of Ghobad-Usk
Protected Gardens
1 Square – 5 Feet

these unfortunate souls show no recent damage from combat. Their weapons and valuables lie scattered across the oasis, un-looted and unused.

The waters of the oasis continue to be safe to drink and are unaffected by the presence of the jellies' protoplasmic biology. The ochre jellies merely use the waters of the oasis as a means to travel to and from their next meal. They became aware of the oasis only because of the earthquake opening the tunnel.

The ochre jellies do not come out during the day, being unable to last long in the oppressive desert sun. They come out in droves at night, seeking anything that moves, be it desert rat, migratory bird, or thirsty human. Within an hour of the sun setting and the air cooling, the ochre jellies silently bubble up from underneath the waters of the oasis. Because of these creatures' unearthly, protoplasmic form and weird biology, any characters attempting to detect a danger from the waters of the oasis have disadvantage on their checks.

When the ochre jellies make their move, they are motivated solely out of hunger and biological impulse. They come in waves, bubbling up from beneath the oasis and then moving onto land to grapple and dissolve their potential meals. The first wave is only 1d2 **ochre jellies**, but 10 rounds later 1d3 + 1 ochre jellies follow. Every ten rounds after for the next sixty rounds, another 1d3 + 1 ochre jellies emerge from various corners of the oasis and move in to devour any living creatures up to and including characters, mounts, familiars, and followers.

The jellies are utterly fearless but do not pursue fleeing characters out into the desert, preferring the sure meals and aquatic comfort of the oasis.

Treasure in the Oasis

As noted earlier, the oasis appears to have been swiftly and prematurely abandoned. In all, the bodies of 15 humans and 13 horses litter the sands around the Oasis of Ghobad-Usk. The corpses are ghoulishly stripped of all flesh and blood, leaving nothing but white bone shining brightly under the desert sun.

If the characters pick through the skeletal remains and abandoned tents of the Sons of Al-Saheed, they can salvage 490 gp, 405 sp, 110 cp, 10 pp, a small bag of goat skin containing 4 polished opals (worth 150 gp each), 9 scimitars, 11 shortswords, 2 greatswords, 9 breastplates of various sizes and condition, 4 sets of studded leather armor in decent condition, 13 spiked helmets of the desert nomad style, 17 daggers or long knives, 9 shortbows, 3 longbows, a total of 131 arrows, 15 spears, a lightly jeweled scabbard worked with images of desert horses running wild (worth 235 gp) containing a *+1 scimitar*, a finely wrought silver ring inlaid with a tiger's eye (worth 150 gp), and a small, squat basalt idol depicting a broad, crouching demon with an oversized head and jeweled emerald eyes (worth 500 gp).

3. Ruins of Mati-Alamul, "The Moaning King"

Deep within the inhospitable wastes of the Maighib Desert lies a forgotten relic of the past long shrouded in fearful whispers and superstitious dread. Known to the tribal folk of the region as Mati-Alamul — "the Moaning King" in old Numedan — this rubble-choked ruin appears as a large statue of basalt rising out of the ground. The statue has the sleek body of a sphinx, but the statue's face is in a sad state, its features all but blasted clean by the harsh desert sands. The apprehensive tribespeople say the gods themselves wiped clean the visage of whatever awful being it once represented.

"The Moaning King" gets its name from the horrible, droning wails that emanate from deep within the ruin on certain moonless nights. These harrowing moans sweep through the desert, scaring away local tribespeople and making the old women mark themselves with signs of protection as they take refuge in their tents. The place is almost universally avoided — even by uncivilized folk — with only creatures such as **harpies** or **death dogs** being reported in the area.

In truth, nothing is particularly supernatural or dreadful about the ruin other than the frightful rumors that surround it. Now fallen into severe ruin, it was once the tomb of a long-dead and now-forgotten warlock whose resting place was plundered centuries ago. With its riches gone and the area being of no strategic importance, the place passed from memory and became just another desert legend whispered around campfires. Over the centuries, it has served as a meeting place for burning dervishes passing through the region, a safe house for a despot in hiding, and even as a staging point for the summoning of several bound and controlled elementals. The keening is the result of desert winds whistling through the crumbling structure via carefully crafted vents that were purposely built to simulate the dreadful wails of the beast whose visage the ruin once carried.

These days, the **barbed devil** (with AC 16 and +1 to all saving throws) Helvuk, Mati-Alamul's current occupant, values the place for its reputation as a demon-haunted ruin, which keeps outsiders and superstitious tribespeople from approaching too closely. Before claiming the abandoned tomb, Helvuk had been magically imprisoned inside an *iron flask* carried by an evil outlander sorcerer named Tur-Bolen. A handful of desert raiders waylaid Tur-Bolen on the open wastes, however, and as the sorcerer attempted to use the *iron flask,* it was accidentally sundered, thus releasing the barbed devil trapped inside. Helvuk, now free of his decades-long imprisonment, murdered Tur-Bolen and the desert raiders in a fit of rage. Free-willed and unsure of his exact location, Helvuk recovered his former captor's valuables from the carnage and struck out for the nearest landmark, which happened to be Mati-Alamul. Helvuk now plots his next move from the old, crumbling edifice.

An Overview of Mati-Alamul

"The Moaning King" is little more than a desolate ruin now, a place avoided for its superstitious legacy but serviceable as a shelter from the harsh desert. The statue is a little over 40 feet tall and some 25 feet wide on each side at its base. A door-less opening yawns wide on its south side. A low, crumbling wall surrounds the whole structure, but the harsh desert elements have almost completely worn it down. It bears no flags or banners, and its simple stone walls are unadorned.

The Interior

The doorway on the south side opens into a single 20-foot-by-20-foot room choked with windblown sand. The chamber is bare and unadorned, as the barbed devil neither intends to stay here long nor has he had time to settle in. Aside from the scattered bones and bloody feathers of a lone harpy unlucky enough to run across Helvuk as he sought to feed, the only things of interest in the chamber are a crumbled canvas sack in the north corner of the room and a set of stairs near the east wall that descend into the earth beneath the ruins.

A crypt was once located beneath this room, but centuries of neglect caused most of it to crumble. Sand now chokes the stairwell. Even if all the sand and rubble were removed and the chamber below somehow cleared out, nothing of value remains as the crypt was plundered long ago.

Helvuk delights in physical combat, preferring to tear his foes to pieces and sting them with his deadly stinger. If he finds himself overmatched, he uses his hurl flame ability from a distance and retreats if necessary. He uses *telepathy* if he needs to parlay with intruders. After years of imprisonment inside Tur-Bolen's *iron flask*, he has no plans to throw away his newfound freedom on this plane by fighting a losing battle. Still, his devilish nature rules the day, and he truly enjoys inflicting pain and torment on any intruders should he have the opportunity.

Helvuk's only treasure is what he took from the ravaged corpse of Tur-Bolen. He wears a *ring of protection* and has a medium canvas sack containing 45 cp, 69 sp, 81 gp, 12 gold trade bars stamped with the symbol of the king of Numeda (worth 50 gp each), a small bag containing a polished lapis-lazuli (worth 350 gp), and a plain ceramic scroll tube containing a wizard scroll with *arcane eye, comprehend languages, passwall*, and *sending* inscribed upon it.

4. Refugee Encampment

About a half day's journey from Dawaad is a rough encampment of nearly a thousand refugees fleeing the horrors that befell Dawaad. Many of the refugees are starving, and all are fearful of outsiders; the Lotus Eaters and mamelukes savaged them mercilessly for whatever valuables they carried during their escape from the city. The refugees have no priests among them, as all of Anumon's clerics in the temple were slain during the assault. This is an encampment of forlorn **commoners** awaiting the apocalypse, fearful that their god has forsaken them. When characters approach, a dozen youths armed with spears (**bandits** with spear instead of scimitar and no crossbow) come out to meet them. The youths demand to know the party's purpose and ask them to leave. They claim that Anumon has forsaken them, leaving them to repent in the desert as the prophet did in the days of old. If any priests of Anumon are among the party, they are greeted with guarded caution. Priests of other gods are treated with outright aversion, for the people of Dawaad accept only Anumon as their one true god.

If the characters share with the refugees that the Temple of Anumon has been cleansed of evil and that it is now safe to return to Dawaad, the youths lead the party to an elder. Ranmaash the Elder (as **hardy commoner**[1]) thanks the characters, questioning them how the temple was cleansed. Getting a positive reaction from Ranmaash requires a successful DC 15 Charisma check. If the characters' story does not inspire him, he says nothing more and asks them to leave as soon as possible.

However, if characters give satisfactory answers (by passing the the Charisma check) and ask for the location of the Bronze Horseman, Ranmaash provides them with directions. But he also warns them to keep an eye out for the Lotus Eaters, allies of the burning men and mamelukes that assaulted the temple.

If a character asks about the "Path of the Prophet," Ranmaash shares the tale of how Sulymon came to earth from the heavens, reborn as a man, bringing water to the desert and gathering the people to him. The story tells how he convinced the ancient Bedouins of the glory of Anumon, and how he cast out the idolaters and sinners among them. Mighty were the feats of Sulymon, and so was the path he trod. Brass horsemen placed in the desert led Anumon's devout followers along Sulymon's path. Pilgrims once followed the route of the horsemen to better understand the prophet's miracles and his sacrifices to bring Anumon into their lives. It has been a long time long since any made that pilgrimage; most now simply pay their respects at the Temple of Anumon. The way of the horsemen fell into disuse and has since been lost.

If the party attacks the encampment, the majority of the refugees flee farther into the desert without putting up a fight.

5. The City of Dawaad

As the party approaches Dawaad, they see hundreds of huge, powerful djinn flying about the city in a swirling counterclockwise pattern. A pillar of blue light bathes the center of the city. As the characters approach one of the two gates, a djinn prince named Hamash Al Habash (**djinni**) appears before them. Read or paraphrase the following as the djinn addresses the party:

> The city of Dawaad has fallen under a grave curse, and none who are faithless may enter its gates. Only those strong enough to consecrate the Temple of Anumon in his name may leave the city again. The evil within the city is mighty, and even we princes of djinn are forbidden to enter. The will of Anumon dictates that it is now our lot to guard and await heroes to take up the cause of our lord.

A zone of *forbiddance* surrounds the city of Dawaad and keeps the devil who has taken residence within the Temple of Anumon from escaping. Only those swearing an oath to remove the "beast" from the temple may enter the city. They must further swear to take no plunder from the city lest they suffer the wrath of Anumon — to be visited upon them by the princes of djinn.

Should the characters decide to brook the wrath of the princes of djinn, they are attacked by 1d4 **djinn** princes per round until a maximum of 20 djinn princes either defeat them or they beg Anumon's forgiveness for their thievery.

If the characters defeat all 20 djinn princes, they may have the run of the city, plundering it for up to 10,000 gp worth of magical and nonmagical treasure as determined by you.

The city itself is apparently devoid of life. Signs pointing to a hasty escape can be found everywhere, radiating outward from the centrally located Temple of Anumon. Many folk were obviously trampled in the rush to escape, and shops now lie open, their wares hanging in the windows untouched. Not even a single cat, dog, or bird can be found in the streets. An ominous silence covers the entire city, so that the footfalls of those walking its flagstones echo like a distant thunder.

5-1. Ramp

A twisted ramp rises 300 feet from the desert floor, winding like a snake to the gates of the city. During normal times, the guard towers and gatehouse fired on would-be attackers. Corpses now litter the ramp. The djinn princes slew the cultists of the Burning One as they ran the gauntlet. Characters can collect 100 arrows, 10 scimitars, and 3 *potions of healing* from the bodies.

5-2. Gates

The great gates of Dawaad stand wide open, the guardians dead and desiccated. They rise as 6 **cinder ghouls**[1] and attack.

5-3. Guard Towers

Like the rest of the city, these 50-foot-high spires are completely empty. Each contains a guardroom on the top floor and a cage for jailing troublemakers on the bottom floor. The cages lie open in each tower, with no prisoners present. The guardrooms contain 20 heavy crossbows and 2,000 heavy bolts. A ballista firing position with working ballista stands concealed atop each tower.

5-4. Pilgrims District and the Souk al Dawaad

Beyond the gates at the top of the ramp are numerous inns and apartments whose doors have been blown open. Bodies of cultists, priests, and pilgrims lie here. Some appear to have been trampled to death; others died of unseen marks

The buildings in the pilgrims' district generally consist of warehouses, casbahs, taverns, and inns catering to foreign visitors and merchants who find the other districts of the holy city to be a little too "religious" for their liking.

The Souk al Dawaad is an open-air market filled with many tents and shops lining its outer walls. Not a living soul is found here. However, the bodies of people trampled in the rushed exodus may be found here and there. The shops are full of such objects as one would expect in a large city, including armor, weapons, gems, jewels and a healthy business in holy symbols of silver, platinum, and gold.

5-5. Abedin District

This portion of Dawaad served as dwelling spaces and lodging for pilgrims visiting the city. It consists of rows of dormitory-style buildings with small centrally located courtyards, each with a shrine to Anumon set in the middle. Like the other areas of the city, it is completely abandoned as if those who stayed here fled in a great hurry, leaving the majority of their possessions behind.

A thorough search among the homes finds a passage in an old scroll that reads, *"To the South and West of the Dark Oasis, for a half a day seek the caves that hide the last house of Noble Dawaad."*

5-6. Khoury District

The Khoury were the priests of Anumon. Most lived contemplative lives ever reading the prophecies of Sulymon and the other sacred texts of their faith. Their abodes are large stucco family living structures, with the father and mother of the home serving as clerics in the temple. Their district is located outside the gates of the gardens of Anumon. Like the other districts of the city, these homes are abandoned.

5-7. Gardens of Anumon

These lush gardens surround the Temple of Anumon and are themselves surrounded by a 15-foot-high wall of limestone coated with white stucco. A bluish light pouring down from the sky above bathes the entire area in an eerie light. The divine light forbids the 4 **bearded devils** who stalk its gardens from escaping farther into the city.

One bearded devil arrives to attack the party for every two rounds they spend in the gardens of Anumon, until all four join the fight. The horned devil Izkandr (area **5-8**) summoned these creatures before Anumon's minions locked the city from further summoning.

Dawaad
1 Square = 20 Feet
8
7
6
5
4
3
3
2
1

The temple itself is a blackened ruin and piles of dead and immolated figures lie about as if some great explosion laid them flat in a blast fanning out from the temple's door. An unnatural aura of pure evil wafts through the air, so strong that it supplants the power of law and order that once pervaded this mighty edifice to the god of the gates.

Izkandr the **horned devil** waits in the center of the temple's assembly hall, fat and bloated upon all the souls he has devoured. Restless from his imprisonment within the holy city of Anumon, he has whiled away his time inscribing the walls and floor of the temple with an infernal encyclopedia of his sins. As the characgters make their presence known outside the temple, he beckons them to enter. Izkandr recounts the number of his sins to the party should he be given ample time to do so, swearing and cursing Anumon for trapping him upon the mortal plane, so far from his palace in Hell. Read or paraphrase the following for the players:

A thousand blessed virgins did I sacrifice upon the altar of the gatekeeper. One thousand more of his brave warriors did waste themselves upon my sword and I am not sated, for their souls tasted as ashes upon my tongue. Imprisoned I may be upon this wretched world and for this slight do I curse the gatekeeper's children. I fear his waning powers not. I am Izkandr, of the house of the Light-Bringer, and much glory is promised unto me. So when the dead outnumber the living, my palace in Hell shall be great beyond compare. I shall be anointed with the blood of the innocent for my deeds as surely as your world will perish in the coming of the great fires. Devils and efreet shall rule in your stead when the time for the sons of Sulymon is expired upon this pathetic plane.

The temple of Anumon lies more or less in ruin, defiled by Izkandr with the blood of the gatekeeper's minions. If the characters take the time to clean and consecrate the altar and help remove the corpses piled around the temple itself, Anumon shows his pleasure by granting each participant in the cleansing a 200 XP bonus. A holy symbol of Anumon made of adamantine appears upon the altar for each character who helps clean the altar.

As the characters leave the Temple of Anumon, a most curious sight awaits them. Sitting outside the temple is a large, ruined throne. Astride the throne is a venerable man of large stature, somewhat twisted and bent with age. Skin that perhaps once glistened like gold is now drawn and weathered. The man fixes his pale eyes upon the characters as if appraising their worth, and his claw-like fingers curl around an ornate rod. The city of Dawaad is gone, and there is naught but sand and wind for as far as the eye can see. The sky has taken on an unnaturally dull pallor, for the stars that were once bright and full now appear dim and changed in their constellations, beyond the reckoning of even the keenest astronomer. Read or paraphrase the following for the characters:

Greetings, heroes. I stare back at you through the sands of time, and I know as surely as the doom that awaits me that you are the last hope to a dying universe. Before you stands the true ruin of your world, and a billion other worlds like it. Observe, if you dare, the twilight of our epoch and the true end of ends. The alpha is passed into dream and myth; now the omega looms large before all is cast into entropy and nothingness.

Foolishly did I grasp the reins of the universe and attempt to guide it with my 'infinite' wisdom. A billion worlds did I command, and yet my lusts for power were not sated. Law did I seek to bring to the lawlessness, only to find in the end that my laws were for naught. My ambitions were too great and, without my other half, my light genius, I was nothing. My hubris and rage did hide this fact from my senses for far too long.

I, flush with the thrill of victory after victory as I laid the very gods of creation low with my brilliant sword and invincible tactics, did not see the destiny I had made for myself.

I, who thought that by destroying my light half I would find my own godhood.

I, who sacrificed his family and laid low his house in order to bribe the lords of death and the dukes of Hell for my ascendancy. No matter now, for they too are laid low and their houses in ruin just as surely as is mine.

I, who committed innumerable sins in my quest for true greatness.

I, who mastered the Grimoire of Infinite Worlds, did not heed the fate of those who had delved too deeply of its secrets.

Indeed, in this end I have found my dominion, my true kingdom. For that which I thought I had craved the most now stands before you. Master of the many planes am I, and master of nothing as well. I am the steward who sits alone in despair at the edge of oblivion. Yet even here I may not die, but instead watch powerless as all the things I have wrought come to pass. Immobile beyond this throne to change the fate I have made for myself.

I, who should have been we. I, the lonely one, missing my twin, the half that would make me whole again.

If you do not wish to see this future come to pass, then I charge you to rejoin me to my true half so that my wrongs may be made right. I bid you take this quest so that I may finally have true death so that the universe may live on. Failing that, I ask that you find and destroy me so that this course may never come to pass. Follow the Brass Horseman in the Blowing Desert along the Path of the Prophet. There shall the future lead you. Let the path lead you to he that is as I was, and to mine light half.

With these final words, the vision fades and the characters are again in the city of Dawaad upon the steps leading to the Temple of Anumon.

The characters have no way of knowing it yet, but the vision was a decreased and worn version of the Sultan of Efreet[1] sending them a message from the future. Without the unity granted by Sulymon to his soul, the evil machinations of the Sultan have come undone, leaving the planes blasted and the universes they hold on the edge of extinction. Having delved too deeply into the *Codex of Infinite Planes*[2], the Sultan managed to tie himself into the tome's final curse and bring along the rest of creation with him. Too late, he has realized that in order to avoid the ultimate dissolution of everything, he must indeed rejoin with his soul brother Sulymon to avoid his fate. Explaining this to the Sultan of Efreet[1] in the party's "current" time may be difficult, and they may be forced to find other options for "changing" fate.

It should not be obvious to the characters at first who they were talking to, be it the Sultan, or Anumon, or Sulymon. Let this bit of the mystery remain a mystery to the characters no matter how many Intelligence checks they take or spells they cast. Indeed, the characters have many options for saving their world. And perhaps even the you don't wish to run such an earthshaking campaign. In this case, the fate of "worlds" that the vision refers to could easily mean just certain planes, or the Plane of Molten Skies. A little mystery and intrigue either way never hurts anything.

6. The Brass Horseman

Roughly 10 miles outside Dawaad stands the first brass horseman, or rather what remains of it. The horse appears to be complete and intact, its nostrils flared as its mighty head pokes through the sand. The remainder of the statue is buried. Upon excavation, however, it is revealed that the torso of the horseman broke off and is missing. The entire statue is set upon a pivot and blows somewhat like a slow-moving weathervane in the wind.

Once the statue is uncovered, characters find these words written in Ignan upon the base of the statue: "*Strike the flank and verily call forth for the Path of the Prophet. I shall lead thee, for upon this path did the prophet bring life to the desert.*"

Unfortunately, the horseman is broken into three parts. Each part must be found and returned to the base, then held in place until it magically reattaches to the whole.

The horseman's torso and head are located in Shameek's yurt in the dark oasis (**Area 7**). The horseman's missing staff, which fits into the outstretched right hand, is hidden in the tomb of Dawaad (**Area 8**).

If the flank of the horse is struck while the brass horseman is incomplete, it turns to point toward one of its missing pieces. It points first toward the dark oasis (**Area 7**) where the torso is located. Once the torso is reattached, it then turns toward the tomb of Dawaad (**Area 8**) and the horseman's staff.

Once all of the pieces are returned to complete the statue, striking the rump of the horse statue and calling out for the "path of the prophet" causes the entire statue to steady and pivot on a hidden mechanism. The statue slowly turns to point through the desert toward the location of the secret canyon (**Area 9**). Those who seek the path of the prophet day or night also now see faintly glowing footprints that lead through the desert sands toward the canyon.

7. The Dark Oasis

The dark oasis is hidden between two giant sand berms. Beyond the berms, a trail leads through a forest of palms. A pair of crossed palms, tied together in the past by Sulymon's hand, mark the trail. It was here that Sulymon, upon coming to the world of men, first encountered other folk. Among the shifting sands of the blowing desert, he found a tribe of simple desert people dying of thirst. Sulymon spoke to the people about the glory of Anumon, but at first, they shunned him, fearing his fervor. It wasn't until he performed a great miracle, transforming a dry well into a deep blue lake of purest water, that he won them over. It was here that he anointed Dawaad, son of Adad, as the ruler of the people of the sands. It was Dawaad who decreed that his city be built forevermore to hold the temple of the great Anumon, and the days of its construction were but a year in the lives of men.

The dark oasis has lost much of the grandeur of ancient days. A horde of bandits known as the Lotus Eaters has taken control of the oasis and uses it as their base of operations to plunder the belongings of the Dawaad refugees. Most of the members of the band are permanently under the effects of the desert lotus[3]. During their visit to the dark oasis, the characters may find information about who assaulted the temple and stole the spirit of Sulymon. With luck, they may also uncover the horseman's torso or quite possibly discover the water stone hidden at the bottom of the Lake of Miracles.

Entering the Oasis During Daylight Hours

During the day, encounters occur quickly in the dark oasis, usually with 2d4 **Lotus Eaters**[1] arriving to question or challenge the characters every 1d6 rounds. Characters may role-play their way through the challenges or fight it out.

Entering the Oasis at Night

If characters enter the grove at night, most of the Lotus Eaters are too caught up in their drugs and drinks to notice much of anything. A couple of sentry patrols made of 1d4 + 1 **Lotus Eaters**[1] wander about the dark oasis, watching for intruders but wishing they were part of the nightly revelries. If characters attempt to sneak into the dark oasis, allow the patrols to make Perception checks against the Characters' Stealth checks. If a fight breaks out, most of the Lotus Eaters pay it no mind, as such things happen frequently. They are fully alerted only if explosive magic such as *fireballs* are tossed into the tents where they sleep. Such actions bring the wrath of the whole (drugged) force and summon Shameek (**burning dervish guard**[1]) from his slumber, with an invisible Moad (**efreeti**) in tow. See **Area 7-3** for more on Shameek and **Area 7-5** for details on Moad.

7-1. Date Palm Grove

Sulymon himself planted this grove of date palms. It is said that he brought the original seed with him from another world, and their planting is one of his many miracles for they have long fed the people of the desert. Anyone climbing one of the palms can easily pick a pound of dates per tree per day. They bloom year-round and are always bountiful with fruit. Eating a handful of these dates also protects the eater from the pangs of hunger or the need to eat for 1d4 days. The dates and their special qualities are unaffected by being dried, jarred, or otherwise preserved. The dates detect mildly of divine transmutation magic.

7-2. Yurts of the Lotus Eaters

The Lotus Eaters are a barbaric tribe of desert folk who found a new master in the burning dervish Shameek. He converted the wild desert folk into a cult who worship a burning idol they keep locked within a tabernacle of brass and sandalwood. The tribe earned its name — the Lotus Eaters — from the desert raiders' predilection for eating handfuls of narcotic lotus before battle to add to their ferocity and to keep them fighting even after defeat.

Each yurt houses 1d6 **Lotus Eaters**[1] and their slaves (**commoners**). Typically, each Lotus Eater dwelling contains 2d20 + 10 gp worth of treasure, 1d4 various pieces of masterwork arms and armor, 1d4 doses of desert lotus, 1 slave, and 1d4 camels staked outside the yurt. The slaves typically are the children of desert nomads slaughtered by the Lotus Eaters, or refugees from Dawaad.

7-3. Shameek's Yurt

The burning dervish Shameek (**burning dervish guard**[1]) lives in this large tent located near the sandalwood tabernacle. Shameek has spied upon the city of Dawaad for the Sultan of Efreet[1] for many years now and guided the feyhda, or assassin priests, of the Sultan to the elemental portal hidden within the secret canyon. Of course, he will not willingly share this information with the characters.

Treasures: A pile of silks and satins, gems, jewels, and other sundries Shameek accumulated also hides the upper half of the brass horseman (**Area 6**). The total value of the silk is 3,000 gp. The party also finds 6 fire opals (600 gp), 2 fire rubies (1,200 gp each), and 30 clear pearls (50 gp each).

7-4. Lake of Miracles

This lake of pure azure blue water is roughly 80 feet deep and feeds the date palms as well as many parched souls who thirst in the desert. Mellow-tasting, rainbow-colored fish swim in the clear water. The *water stone of Sulymon* is lost at the bottom of the lake. When commanded, the *water stone* opens a conduit to the Elemental Plane of Water and pours forth pure water like a faucet. The stone itself weighs approximately ten pounds and is carved with Elvish writing and the Aquan rune for water. Speaking the word in Aquan causes the stone to either produce or stop producing water. If the stone is removed, the oasis dries up within six months.

Growing along the edge of the lake are hundreds of desert lotus plants whose blossoms the Lotus Eaters consume. An individual attempting to harvest the desert lotus could easily collect 2d12 mature flowers in an hour. Of course, the Lotus Eaters are not likely to give them hours to harvest their precious drug.

7-5. Sandalwood Tabernacle

This tent of sandalwood and brass holds an ancient 10-foot-tall idol that the Lotus Eaters worship as a god. The idol is in fact hollow, and an **efreeti** named Moad resides within it. Moad is a liar and deceiver who allows the folk to believe he is indeed their god, even though they have no priests of their own save Shameek. If exposed by a *true seeing* spell or some other magic, Moad fights to the death. The Lotus Eaters turn upon Shameek and eventually one another in the ensuing power vacuum.

8. Tomb of Dawaad, Son of Adad

Dawaad was the first secular ruler of the desert people that Sulymon converted to the worship of Anumon. Over the years, Dawaad fought many wars to unify the folk of the desert in the name of Anumon, and he even built the holy city that bears his name, all in honor of the prophet and god who led his people to greatness. Despite this, his tomb is a simple one, a sepulcher hidden among some standing stones in the desert.

A tablet is affixed to each of the seven standing stones. Written upon the tablets are verses that sing the praises of Dawaad as a great ruler in the eyes of Anumon. The blowing winds and scouring sands have erased much of what was written here.

The Dark Oasis
1
5
2
3
4
1 Square - 10 Feet

A character making a successful DC 20 Intelligence check or casting a *comprehend languages* spell determines that the tablets are written in the form of a song. The song details the conversion of Dawaad to the worship of Anumon and his great deeds as Sulymon's right-hand man before founding the city that was to take his name.

A bard or other performer making a successful DC 20 Charisma (Performance) check while reciting the song written on the tablets causes the stone door to the tomb of Dawaad to open. Learning the song requires at least 10 minutes of study on the part of the performer.

Without learning the song and performing it, finding the door to the tomb requires a successful DC 25 Wisdom (Perception) check. The door is trapped with an *earthquake* spell that triggers if anyone seeks to open the tomb without first performing the song. The ensuing earthquake lasts for one minute and has a save DC of 20. Unlocking the door without the song requires a successful DC 25 Dexterity check with thieves' tools or a DC 30 Strength check.

Inside the Tomb

A sarcophagus of gold-covered mahogany, perfectly preserved due to the utter lack of moisture in the desert air, sits inside the tomb. A staff of pure mithril with seven keys hanging from a loop in one end lies across the chest of the king.

The king is adorned with a simple golden ring about his head, which may have once been a headband to a turban that has rotted away. A single large sapphire emblazons the golden circlet. A greatsword rests against the hip bone of the king and not a single speck of rust can be found upon it. Canisters and urns hold old wine, oil, incense, and dried foods to be offered to the gatekeeper as sacrifice for the afterlife.

Sulymon himself placed the staff once borne by the brass horseman (**Area 6**) upon the breast of the king when he was buried in order to hide the location of the cavern of the path from infidels and non-believers.

If a character of lawful neutral alignment or any worshipper of Anumon enters the tomb after the entry song is performed, the spirit of Dawaad appears and offers the sword to the likely candidate, saying, "Use my sword on your quest in the name of Anumon. May it serve thee as it did me in my time." If no such candidate enters, or if the tomb is opened by force, the spirit does not arrive and instead anyone trying to steal the sword must make a DC 25 Wisdom saving throw when using the weapon. Failure means the character's alignment changes to lawful neutral.

Treasure: Besides the *sword of Dawaad*[2], the tomb houses numerous earthenware jugs set around the room. Characters searching these jugs find gold coins in some (for a total of 2,000 gp), while others contain vinegar that was once a fine wine. A few jugs contain rotting olive oil and fish oils. Besides the jugs, a *headband of intellect* rests upon the brow of Dawaad's corpse. However, touching any of these gifts to Anumon — including the spoiled wine and oils — forces the would-be tomb robbers to succeed on a DC 20 Wisdom saving throw or be cursed with a 50% chance for loss of action per turn until the curse is removed.

9. The Secret Canyon

A *hallucinatory terrain* spell hides this canyon from prying eyes until the brass horseman (**Area 6**) is restored with all of its missing pieces. When characters follow Sulymon's footsteps from the brass horsemen to this hidden location, they find that the secret canyon itself is deathly silent. At the far end, a fissure of rock opens to reveal a cavern. Two sets of untouched footprints lead out of the canyon, and four pairs lead to the cave.

9-1. Cavern of the Path

The cavern is large and very dark, and the narrow path leads to the elemental portal (**Area 9-2**).

9-2. The Elemental Portal

A misty black portal about six feet across is set into the floor. A painting on the wall depicts a yellow city built within a bowl floating on a sea of fire. Lines of stones surround the portal, but four stones appear to be missing from the collection. These are the *elemental stones*, and all four are required before the portal can be opened. The characters should arrive at the portal with one or more of the stones already in their possession.

Each of the missing stones is marked in the tongue of the elemental plane where it was crafted. The first is the *earth stone*, and it is marked with the Dwarven alphabet and the Terran symbol for Earth (found in *The*

Using the Elemental Stones

If characters place the stones in their proper places in the row of stones around the misty portal, they can activate the portal by touching various stones. Different combinations lead to different areas in the Plane of Molten Skies (see **Chapter 10: The Plane of Molten Skies**). Here are a few suggested locations where characters may end up.

Air	Earth	Fire	Water	Destination
●	●			The Palace of Dust (see **Chapter 10: The Plane of Molten Skies, Area 1-1**)
	●	●		The Glass Maze (see **Chapter 10: The Plane of Molten Skies, Area 5-2**)
●		●		The Shattered Peak (see **Chapter 10: The Plane of Molten Skies, Area 7**)
●	●	●		The Hall of the Vulcan Lords (see **Chapter 10: The Plane of Molten Skies, Area 20**)
●	●	●	●	The Obsidian Bridge at the Bazaar of Beggars (see **Chapter 10: The Plane of Molten Skies, Area 23**)

Combinations with the water stone may open portals to other places in other planes, as you please.

Sea of Baal adventure). The second stone is the *air stone* and is marked with the Draconic alphabet, and the Auran symbol for air (also found in *The Sea of Baal* adventure). The third stone is the *fire stone* and is marked in the Draconic alphabet and displays the Ignan symbol for fire (found in *The Brazen Spires* adventure). The fourth is the *water stone*, which is marked with Elvish writing and the Aquan rune for water (see **Area 7-4**).

Touching any of the stones when they are placed in their respective places causes the stones to light up with a strange eldritch glow. If all four stones are present and put in their proper spots, merely touching one of the stones opens a direct portal to the Elemental Plane corresponding with the selected stone. When two stones are touched, the portal opens onto the Plane of Molten Skies. Depending on the stones selected, the characters are afforded a glimpse of the area beyond, but there should be no doubt that this indeed is a portal to the Plane of Molten Skies and eventually to the City of Brass itself.

The Finale or Just the Beginning?

The characters have found a way to reach the Plane of Molten Skies and, from there, the City of Brass itself. So what's next? Certainly, the party has many options for epic adventures ahead of them, not the least of which is the potential for a grand and sweeping campaign that pits the characters against the Sultan of Efreet[1] and his many nefarious cohorts. These adventures and more are detailed in **Books II: The City of Brass** and **Book III: Tales of Brass**.

9-1
9-2
Secret Canyon
1 Square – 5 Feet

Book 2:
The City of
Brass

Chapter 8
Introduction to Book 2

Book II: The City of Brass details the general locations of the Plane of Molten Skies, the Bazaar of Beggars, and the City of Brass itself.

The section begins with the general planar traits and features of the Plane of Molten Skies, where the City of Brass is found at the gateway to the Plane of Fire. It is a convocation, formed at a point where earth, air, and fire meet in the elemental nexus. The Plane of Molten Skies is ever-growing and serves as the Sultan's physical kingdom among the planes.

Even still, the vast plane is filled with mysteries unknown to the usurper of the Throne of Brass. It is home to the Fire Sea Corsairs, tribes of massive giants, and the hidden lairs of ancient wizards and priest kings.

Hidden there are wonders such as the Ash-Grinder's Arcology, the Caverns of Abdul-Shihab, The Sulfur Mountains, and The Plains of Kush. Exploring this vast and dangerous world may lead the characters to new powers.

The Bazaar of Beggars is located here, standing at the foot of the Obsidian Bridge. The line of tributes to enter the city is vast and the bazaar offers diversions for those forced to wait in line. Here are found wine tents, water sellers, merchant emporiums, and intrigue as would be expected of one of the largest markets in the elemental planes.

Lastly, within its great bowl stands the City of Brass itself. This book contains descriptions of its various palaces, towers, apartments, and markets. The city description details the various factions behind the scenes from the nobles of the Upper City to the imprisoned azer slaves dwelling in the Basin below.

The Upper City is filled with broad thoroughfares. It is the home of the Shining Pyramid of Set, the Cathedral of the Lightbringer, the Sultan's Palace, as well as the palaces of the efreet nobles who assisted his rise to power. It is also home to the most expensive souks in the city.

The Middle City is home to the infamous Bazaar of Sins and restaurants serving strange delicacies appealing to the palates of the denizens of the universe. Here, too, are strange jewelry shops, mercenary hangouts, and baths for foreign visitors who have need of the rarest commodity in the Plane of Molten Skies.

The Lower City hides many of the city's less savory characteristics. It is home to hidden cults, pirates, and assassins. It is also home to the oppressed azer population that serves as slaves and builds the omnipresent Great Ziggurat, dedicated to the glory of the Sultan by his faithful burning dervishes.

In total, **Book II** serves as a backdrop for many great adventures. Most of the characters encountered here have a story to tell or a quest to offer, all providing unending adventure opportunities for characters and GMs alike. For ease of use, a faction guide has been included. Also included is a guide to the sorts of shops, stores, and markets found on the various levels.

Chapter 9

Agents, Factions, and Foes

The following are independent operators, cults, factions, or heroes who either stand with or against the Sultan of Efreet[1]. Each can be used in their own way to create new quests, or to give characters a push in starting an epic adventure in the City of Brass.

Rah'po Dehj

The agent known as Rah'po Dehj is none other than the **lich** Jhedophar who dwells in the cursed tower. Jhedophar keeps an apartment in the City of Brass. He is currently searching for several items kept at the temples and fortresses of several other powers, in hopes of using them against the Sultan in an undead coup at the behest of his true mistress, the Demon Queen Beluri.

Rah'po Dehj sends his goblin assistant Dawzin[1] the Handsome to offer the characters sums of cash, magical items, or information in exchange for the relics and items he seeks.

If the characters crossed paths with Jhedophar in the past and sided against the lich, it is likely that he is quite cross with the party. In this event, he assuredly has Dawzin[1] send the characters on adventures far too difficult to achieve in hopes that they can thin the guardians before being snuffed out themselves. Being a rather lazy lich, or a truly wily one, Jhedophar assumes that even if the characters are destroyed, they should soften up any enemies, hexes, and traps in an area to better allow him access to the loot without any undue expenditure of energy.

Jhedophar, in his guise as Rah'po Dehj, appears only while wearing a gold and ceramic mask that hides his deathly visage. He dresses differently and acts "friendlier" — so long as his true identity is not recognized. That said, he is not above using *geas* spells to force characters to accept his quests if it seems necessary to give them a little extra motivational "oomph." That said, *geas* spells should be used sparingly, unless you really don't mind pissing off your players.

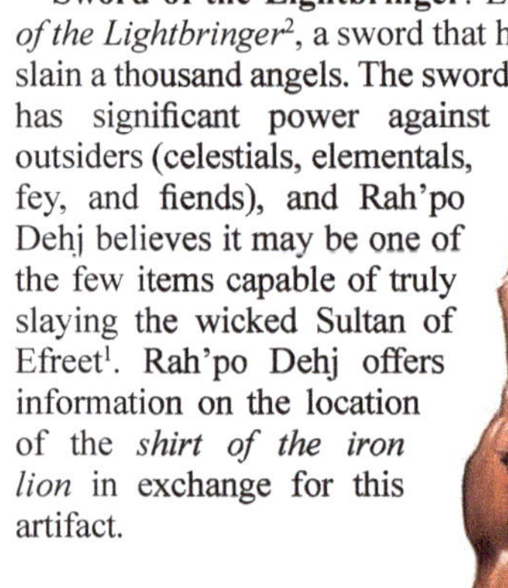

Dawzin the Winged Goblin

Dawzin[1] is an apprentice of Rah'po Dehj. He is a resourcefully clever winged goblin who has served Rah'po Dehj for many years in the capacity of apprentice, personal valet, messenger, and stooge. He is faithful to his master and takes on the lich's many jobs in hopes of one day learning his secrets of immortality and gaining a piece of the master's power.

Dawzin[1] has greyish skin and small beady red eyes. Golden velvet robes cover his body but leave room to expose his leathery bat-like wings. Dawzin[1] carries a staff and wears no boots or shoes upon his taloned feet. Dawzin[1] is the go-between for Rah'po Dehj and the characters, offering them jobs and quests on behalf of his master, and delivering any treasures they may have been promised in exchange for their service.

Dawzin[1] carries a *staff of necromancy*, a *wand of lightning bolts*, a *ring of greater protection*, *bracers of defense*, a *cloak of greater protection*, and keys to the sanctum of Rah'po Dehj.

Jhedophar's Quests

Rah'po Dehj is searching for the following items to boost his chances to challenge for the Throne of Brass.

The Carnelian Idol: Jhedophar has scried the location of the idol, which will grant him power over a great undead army. He wishes for the characters to retrieve it for him and offers magic items in exchange for the idol. If the characters have not yet found the idol, this is an opportunity to let them know where it is hidden. The idol is further described in **Chapter 16**.

Mask of Ankev: Like many liches, Jhedophar craves to show the world his greatness. To that end, he feels the mask held in the Pyramid of Set will help him accomplish his goals. The lich offers characters a magic item (chosen by you) in exchange for the *mask of Ankev*[2]. He does not indicate its actual value or what use he intends for it.

The Book of Al'Hazrad: Hidden in the great repository (see **Chapter 21**), this ancient tome is highly sought by wizards and sorcerers, both living and dead. Jhedophar likely already has a copy, but being a collector and a completist, he won't rest until he has them all. Jhedophar is also interested in finding a secret way into the repository and pays handsomely for such knowledge.

Sword of the Lightbringer: Engrin the **pit fiend** possesses the *Sword of the Lightbringer*[2], a sword that has slain a thousand angels. The sword has significant power against outsiders (celestials, elementals, fey, and fiends), and Rah'po Dehj believes it may be one of the few items capable of truly slaying the wicked Sultan of Efreet[1]. Rah'po Dehj offers information on the location of the *shirt of the iron lion* in exchange for this artifact.

Jhedophar's Gifts

Jhedophar is not one to give things away lightly. The items he offers as gifts for a "job well done" refuse to work against the lich in any capacity. In fact, these items turn to dust if raised against the lich in any way.

The Iron Shirt: The *shirt of the iron lion*[2] is an exception to Rah'po Dehj offering valuable information when it comes to valuable magic items. Rah'po Dehj will gladly trade the location of the *shirt of the iron lion*, a holy relic allegedly crafted by Muir and given to her chosen few in battles against the forces of darkness, for the *Sword of the Lightbringer*[2] that he seeks. The *iron shirt*, as it is often called, offers untold protection against the powers of demons and devils, and is currently hidden within the vaults of the KhizAnah. Rah'po Dehj is aware of the name of the efreeti noble who possesses the container holding the shirt. It would be a simple matter to walk into the bank, use this information, and simply call the shirt up for the taking.

If the *Sword of the Lightbringer*[2] is recovered and handed over to Rah'po Dehj, he delivers the bank code to the characters, leaving them to their own devices as to how they may gather the *iron shirt* for themselves.

Ard

Leader of the People

Ard leads the People, a cult of worshippers who venerate the Church of the Lightbringer. The People are slick and cunning, always seeking to lift the banishment of the Prince of Darkness from the City of Brass. With Ard's guidance, they successfully rebranded the outright idolatry and devil worship into a fad that is easier to digest for greedy self-absorbed youths to rally behind. For their newly minted scheme to work, however, Ard and his masters at the Cathedral of the Lightbringer need a goodly number of items stashed in the Plane of Molten Skies. Ard is working in concert with Engrin the **pit fiend** and **Dark Cardinal Paz Amare**[1].

The Church of the Lightbringer seeks the following items or events from throughout the city and its environs.

The Assassination of Thane Brihnda: If the People succeed in assassinating the thane, they might close off the alliance the Sultan of Efreet[1] currently holds with Brihnda' father, Surter. The removal of Surter's support means that the fire giant mercenaries serving as the police force for the City of Brass walk off the job. The loss of the fire giants would force the Sultan to rely on other means such as the devils from Infernis to do the job, increasing the Lightbringer's footprint in the city.

Furthermore, Surtur's withdrawal is the first step in a possible war between the god of the fire giants and the Sultan.

Ard offers the "adulation" of the People in the form one suit of *armor of resistance* (cold), a pair of *boots of the winterlands*, a *frost brand* (any type), a *ring of resistance* (cold), and a *staff of frost*.

Raid on the Pyramid of Set: Set complicates things for the Lightbringer. Ard would hire the characters to destroy Retep Inkusad so that Set, too, would remove his support of the Sultan in his bid to join the ranks of the greater gods. Ard gifts the party with a set of six *+1 silver steak knives* (as *+1 daggers*) if they accept the mission and tells them to help themselves to whatever they wish to steal from the pyramid. He also offers them access to his bodyguard Tienan as a fence for any stolen materials. He would ask only that the characters bring him the *mask of Ankev*[2] as proof that they completed their mission.

Great Repository: Within the repository, Ard and the People seek the copy of the Viscerterica so that their lord, the Lightbringer, may seek answers to the enigma of the n'gathau and their weird plane of existence. If he could somehow draw their plane into Infurnace and dominate its lords, they would serve as a great tool for his reconquering of the Nine Hells and the Heavens.

The Underbasin: Access to the body of Ashur Ban is very important to the People. They seek to swap the body and replace it with Engrin himself, thus allowing close access to the Sultan for an attempted assassination.

The Circus of Pain: Ard and the People have been ordered to discover anything they can about the Circus Master and his origins. They assure characters willing to "join the circus" for purposes of information gathering that they will buy their freedom once things get a little too hairy. He is lying.

The Revolutionary: Chufa Um Sophanie

Hidden from the watchful eye of the Great Sultan, **Chufa Um Sophanie** has quietly worked behind the scenes to find heroes ready to rise against the depredations of the usurper. If the characters' actions upon arrival to the Plane of Molten Skies reveal them to be goodly and just, she seeks them out. Chufa Um Sophanie implores them to join in the resistance against the Sultan and his cruel priesthood of burning dervishes.

Chufa is quick to declare that Ard of the People, the Grand Vizier Tarbish, and Jhedophar's goblin assistant Dawzin[1] are not who they appear and that all represent darker forces. She is unsure of who their actual associates are, but she is certain that they are up to no good. If you wish to avoid the complications of a character-driven plot where different factions are out to frame one another using the characters as unwitting pawns you may choose to have Chufa Um Sophanie and her sect hire the characters to raid the cathedral in order to close its portal to Infernis. Chufa Um Sophanie believes that the *Sword of the Lightbringer*[2] is in fact a weapon devised to slay angel, devil, and genie alike and that it would indeed serve as a great tool against the Sultan's forces. She is also aware that the *shirt of the iron lion*[2] is held somewhere within the city and that it would offer great protection against the forces of evil.

What Chufa Seeks

Chufa seeks weapons and allies in the fight against the Sultan. If the characters have not yet located the *flask of Sulymon*[2], she has a clue as to its whereabouts, as well as clues to the whereabouts of the *carnelian idol*[2].

Great Repository: Chufa Um Sophanie needs access to the Book of Justicars located within the repository. She feels there is a secret within the book that would provide a new strategy to help fight the Sultan.

City of the Dead Sultana: Chufa seeks access to the body of the late Sultana Cirrishade, and an alliance with Oriazier, the great wyrm solar dragon.

The Underbasin: Chufa seeks access to the body of Ashur Ban.

The Circus of Pain: Chufa Um Sophanie is aware of the prophecy of the Diya al Din and the *Heart of Flame*. The *maul of Hezoid*[2] is one of the most powerful weapons known throughout the city. She believes that if the maul can be put in the Diya al Din's hands, the city can be freed of the tyranny of the burning dervishes and their living brass abomination.

The Waters of Mukphat the Blind: Chufa has no idea where the oasis of Mukphat hides, but seers have told her that the waters may grant life to the dead. She surmises that the waters would be strong enough to raise Sultana Cirrishade.

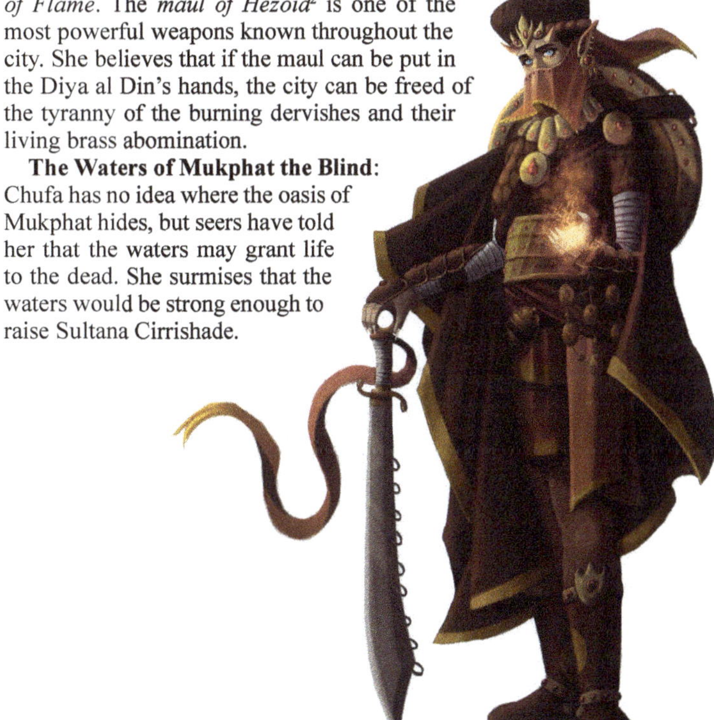

Cult of the Burning One

The Cult of the Burning One or, as it is also known, the Cult of the Veiled God, is the name given to the terrestrial worship of the Sultan of the City of Brass. Through his own connivance, the Sultan established his dominance over the Plane of Fire. With his terrestrial invasions and the conquests of various worlds, the Sultan has seen to the expansion of the Plane of Molten Skies. These triumphs have seen the Sultan's ascendancy from a power of the Elemental Planes to lesser godhood, giving him the ability to grant clerical powers to clerics of his cult, or to serve as patron to those sorcerers and warlocks who wield arcane fire.

Burning dervish sheiks administer the cult on the planes where it operates. An efreeti prince appointed governor general of the new world by the Sultan of Efreet[1] himself commands the dervish sheiks. Below the dervishes are a series of hariphs who are clerics or arcane casters who have sworn their allegiance to the Sultan. The hariphs are humanoids native to the world that is chosen for invasion and were among the first to convert to the new faith. They themselves often came from wealthy or privileged backgrounds but were not in a line of succession to their families' riches.

The dervishes are a sect of janni that have sworn their souls to the Sultan and now serve as his priesthood and secret police. Their very existence is tied to the Sultan and to the Great Ziggurat that occupies the center of the City of Brass, an omnipresent monument to his might and power. The ziggurat of the City of Brass is the headquarters of their sect and is said to house legions of the burning dervishes, most of whom devote their days to prayer and training.

The cult is active in regions where a brazen spire has been erected. New converts to the cult are either forcibly or willingly coerced into listening to the teachings of the Sultan. Burning dervishes and the priests they have trained proselytize the faith of a coming cleansing fire and judgment of the veiled god over the false gods that have come before. They "prove" the power of their faith through wishes granted to the most obedient converts by the local governors.

The truth behind the Brazen Spires and the indoctrination of the cult is to prepare an area for invasion by the Sultan's forces when new worlds are conquered. Destitute and forgotten folk are invited to the spire and given food, clothing, and a purpose. Many are trained as mamelukes for the Sultan's armies, while the more receptive of the converts are trained in the use of magic or the worship of the veiled god. These newly trained forces serve as the forward base for the attack that inevitably comes as they destabilize local governments and cities. The invasion itself is often swift and is usually accompanied by efreet, squadrons of burning dervishes, enslaved fire elementals, and armies of mamelukes gathered from other planes to fight at the behest of the Sultan.

The cult can be used to motivate the characters into getting to the City of Brass in the first place. Once there, the characters find the ultimate power of the cult in the form of the Great Ziggurat and the watchful eye of the burning dervishes.

The Fahd al An'il

This interdimensional clan of thieves, assassins, and mercenaries ranks with the Underguild as one of the more dangerous organizations in the known universe. They may become intrigued by the characters' successes and seek to siphon off some of their ill-gotten gains through intimidation, extortion, or even an offer of membership. The Fahd al An'il has ties with the Bayt al Sikkyn, however, and prefers not to overturn the status quo and hurt their business interests.

The Efreet Nobility

The noble class is made up of those efreet who rose up against their former Sultan at the behest of Nomylus. They are petty and cruel, representing the lion's share of the more decadent and evil virtues of the efreeti race. The various nobles are extremely wealthy and distrustful of one another. Their spheres of influence may encourage them to reach out to characters in an attempt to quell the strength of a rival house. They may offer wishes in exchange for work, though one should be careful of wishes granted by the efreet, as they are as often as not a gateway to personal slavery as they are a path to power and riches.

The Grand Vizier

Rahib al Tarbish Zafir's goal is to remove the Sultan and take the throne of the City of Brass for himself. Tarbish is a frequent quest giver, appearing in the guise of a friendly if slightly buffoonish wizard who seeks the return of the old ways before the usurper arrived. He and his motivations are more thoroughly detailed in **Book III: Tales of Brass**.

Fatavdra, the Dark Elf Emissary

Fatavdra and her brood are further detailed in **Book III: Tales of Brass**. Their goals and aspirations are to act as an assisting hand to the Sultan, while also figuring out a way to seize his power for their own patron demon lord or lady. They recently took an interest in the doings of the Freeman's Tower and see Oruk's device as a weapon that could be used against their enemies. They may attempt to use the characters as patsies in their schemes. Likewise, her agents may be encountered in the middle of adventures, swooping in with the intent of stealing loot the characters fought hard to retrieve.

Nomylus al Kabith, The Sultan of Efreet

The Sultan of Efreet[1] is further detailed in **Book III: Tales of Brass**. He is the "Big Bad" of the City of Brass and the absolute ruler of the Plane of Molten Skies and several other worlds beyond. His intent is to elevate himself to the status of a greater god. His aspirations are huge, as are his powers. The characters eventually become a fly in his ointment, and a nuisance that must be dealt with. Nomylus has numerous allies, and each must be countered by an alliance of his enemies for the characters to succeed in removing the usurper from the Throne of Brass. The Sultan of Efreet[1] is a muscle-bound manipulator who is constantly pushing his agenda forward while maneuvering his enemies into battle against one another for his own amusement. Have fun with the thought of the Sultan casually impeding the efforts of the characters, as he feels that they are ultimately inconsequential to his own plans.

Numerous other allies, enemies, agents, factions, and foes can be found within these pages. Those listed here are but a few that you can use to keep the adventure and excitement flowing along.

Chapter 10
The Plane of Molten Skies

A nexus connecting three planes formed of elemental air, earth, and fire, the Plane of Molten Skies is a legendary waypoint for planar races who wish to do business with one another away from the confines and consequences of a hostile elemental plane.

Planar Geography

The skies are ablaze on this plane; its upper atmosphere seems to be perpetually in a state of consumption by a gigantic ball of flame and liquid fire. The air is stuffy and warm, breathable, but uncomfortable to those not used to it. The ground is formed of cracked obsidian and basalt, warm to the touch, but comfortable enough to walk upon. Mountains and hills formed of basalt and small pools of lava dot the landscape. Volcanoes scattered throughout the planar landscape belch forth blasts of molten elemental fire and rock at random intervals. Rivers and streams of liquid flame wind through the landscape, emptying into a raging sea of liquid elemental fire. Desert-like areas covered in blowing, burning sand are prominent near the nexus and conjoining points of the Elemental Plane of Earth.

The Plane of Molten Skies contains the road to the infamous and fabled City of Brass and serves as the native home of the fiery efreet wishwardens who view themselves as the peculiar realm's absolute masters, bar none (including the gods).

Traits

Traits unique to the Plane of Molten Skies are detailed below.

Normal Gravity: Gravity on the plane functions for travelers and visitors as it does on the Material Plane; up is up, and down is down. The usual rules for ability scores, carrying capacity, and encumbrance apply.

Normal Time: Though the plane is constantly bathed in heat and light, and night never falls, time passes as it does on the Material Plane. One hour on the Plane of Molten Skies equals one hour on the Material Plane.

Finite Size: The Plane of Molten Skies, as a nexus point, is finite in size. The plane itself is triangular in shape, with each side connecting to a point on the elemental plane that forms this nexus. So, one side of the triangle touches the Elemental Plane of Earth, one side touches the Elemental Plane of Air, and the third and final side touches the Elemental Plane of Fire.

Morphic Traits: Alterable morphic. Objects remain where they are (and what they are) unless affected by physical force or magic. You can change the immediate environment as a result of tangible effort.

Dominant Elemental Trait: None are dominant, though certain areas may be fire-dominant or earth-dominant.

Enhanced Magic: A creature using a spell or spell-like ability invoving air, earth, or fire within a mile of a portal or gate to the respective elemental plane, may, at your discretion, choose one of the following Metamagic options to apply: distant spell, empowered spell, extended spell, or heightened spell. Spells cast within the walls of the city have their own rules. See **Chapter 12** for more details.

Impeded Magic: Spells and spell-like abilities that use or create water or water elementals are impeded. The caster must succeed on a DC 15 spell attack roll each time the caster attempts to cast such a spell. If the check succeeds, the spell functions normally; if it fails, the spell fizzles away just as if it had been cast.

Heat Dangers: Though the skies are ablaze with fire, this plane serves as a waypoint for inter-planar travelers. Therefore, heat dangers caused by the plane itself are less threatening than one would expect. (Some suspect the Sultan of the Efreet controls this feature.) Creatures resistant to fire or immune to fire suffer no ill effects of heat from this plane. The plane itself, unless otherwise noted, is always between 85° F to 90° F.

A character wearing medium or heavy armor must attempt a Constitution saving throw for every 4 hours spent on this plane. The DC starts at 15 and increases by 1 for each previous check. Characters wearing heavy armor have disadvantage on their saves. A character proficient in Survival may apply their proficiency bonus to this save and may be able to apply this bonus to other characters as well. Creatures failing the saving throw lose 2 hit points from their maximum hit points and receive a level of exhaustion. Characters wearing light or no armor do not suffer any ill effects from general heat exposure on this plane (unless the temperature is raised above 90° F).

Within 1 mile of a nexus to the Plane of Fire, the saving throw must be attempted every 2 hours for creatures wearing medium or heavy armor, and creatures withlight or no armor must attempt the saving throw every 4 hours.

Within the city itself, the temperature is usually a "comfortable" 101° F. Though the temperature within the city can be raised much higher, the Sultan controls it so that extraplanar travelers may visit his fair city in relative comfort. See the **Overview of the City of Brass** for more information. Axam, a merchant within the **Bazaar of Beggars** (**Area B10** in **Chapter 11**), sells amulets that offset and negate the natural effects of heat exposure. *Brazen amulets*[2] (as they are called) are detailed in **Appendix 2: New Magic Items**.

Features

Volcanoes, the burning sky, rivers and seas of liquid fire, ground made from obsidian and basalt, and the oppressive, sweltering heat — the Plane of Molten Skies offers all of these as natural wonders to those who visit the place. The air is breathable here, but it is warm and uncomfortable to inhale for those unaccustomed to it.

Light is always prevalent, and darkness is nowhere to be found naturally (except perhaps inside fortresses, conjoined planar areas, outposts, citadels, and other structures). One of the few exceptions to this is the City of Brass, which boasts artificially imposed darkness on a 30-hour cycle thanks to a group of wizards who call themselves the Nightfall Concordance. The Sultan sponsors this service in an effort to draw more outsiders to the city in order to increase the size of his coffers through taxation and trade.

Though the ground is warm to the touch, it is not particularly deadly to those that contact it. The rivers of flame, volcanoes, heat storms, and other natural wonders of this plane on the other hand are not quite so friendly (especially to those not protected from or immune to fire and heat).

Ash Storms

An ash storm generally occurs within 1 or 2 miles of an active volcano or where the Plane of Earth meets the Plane of Fire. A typical ash storm comes on suddenly and ends 2d6 minutes later just as suddenly as it began. An ash storm consists of grayish-brown ash raining from the sky that obscures sight and raises the temperature in the affected area and deas damage to those caught in it.

The ash obscures sight, including darkvision, beyond 10 feet. Creatures and objects 10 feet away are lightly obscured. Creatures and objects farther away are heavily obscured. Further, a creature caught in an ash storm takes 3 (1d6) fire damage per round of exposure. Wind has no effect on an ash storm.

Flame Geysers

The dry, cracked, obsidian ground of the plane is networked with underground rivers of fire that feed the lakes and seas on this plane. Every so often, pressure builds in these underground rivers, forcing the magma to erupt through the parched surface. An eruption resembles a steam geyser, but billows forth shards of obsidian and blasts of liquid fire, spraying each randomly into the air over a 30-foot radius. A creature within the area must attempt a DC 15 Dexterity saving throw. Those that fail take 11 (2d10) fire damage and 11 (2d10) piercing damage while those that succeed take half these amounts. Further, the magma sticks to a creature that fails its saving throw and deals 5 (1d10) fire damage per round for 1d3 rounds.

Flaming Rivers

Many flaming rivers are found beneath the surface of the plane, but a few small rivers and streams of liquid fire are on the surface. The liquid fire can be deadly to creatures not resistant or immune to fire. A creature contacting the liquid fire in a flame river takes 11 (2d10) fire damage and must succeed on a DC 15 Dexterity saving throw or catch on fire. A creature on fire takes 4 (1d8) fire damage per round until an action is used to put the fire out. A creature foolish enough to submerge itself in liquid flame or stand in a lake, pool, or river of fire takes 110 (20d10) fire damage for each round of contact. Damage continues for 1d3 rounds after exposure but only half that dealt during contact: 5 (1d10) or 55 (10d10) points per round.

Magical protection reduces the damage and creatures immune to fire do not take damage but can still drown if they sink underneath the surface.

Heat Storms

Randomly occurring across the plane, these storms appear out of nowhere in most cases, though at times they can be predicted by watching the fiery sky. A potential heat storm threat can be seen by a brightening of the sky, similar in ways to a darkening of the skies on the Material Plane before a thunderstorm or rainstorm moves into the area. A heat storm brings a sudden rise in the ambient temperature to the affected area. A typical heat storm covers an area 1d2 miles in radius and lasts an average of 20 + 1d10 minutes.

Heat storms are deadly to those caught in the area. Breathing the air in a heat storm deals 3 (1d6) fire damage per minute (no save). In addition, an exposed creature must make a Constittion saving throw save every 5 minutes (DC 15, +1 per previous check) or take 2 (1d4) fire damage and gain a level of exhaustion. Characters wearing any sort of armor have disadvantage on their saves. Those wearing metal armor or creatures touching metal exposed to a heat storm are affected as by *heat metal*.

The best defense against a heat storm is to seek shelter inside a structure where the ambient temperature is cooler or use magical protection to shield against the heat.

Lava Pools

Lava pools pockmark the landscape of the plane. Many are lairs to such creatures as magmin, lava children, magma oozes, and various sorts of mephits. A creature contacting a lava pool takes 11 (2d10) fire damage and must succeed on a DC 15 Dexterity saving throw or catch on fire. A creature on fire takes 4 (1d8) fire damage per round until an action is used to put the fire out. A creature foolish enough to submerge itself in a lava pool takes 110 (20d10) fire damage for each round of contact. Damage continues for 1d3 rounds after exposure but only half that dealt during contact: 5 (1d10) or 55 (10d10) points per round.

Magical protection reduces the damage, and creatures immune to fire do not take damage, but can still drown if they sink beneath the surface.

Magma Storms

One of the deadliest features spawned by the plane is a magma storm. Thankfully, they occur only in areas within 1d3 miles of the City of Brass or a portal leading to the Elemental Plane of Fire, and even there are a rare occurrence.

A magma storm is a torrential downpour of liquid fire loosed by the fiery atmosphere. Its only warning is an ever-growing roar coupled by a loud crack; then the sky opens up and rains liquid fire down on those unfortunates caught in the area.

Creatures and objects caught in a magma storm take 16 (3d10) fire damage per round of exposure and must succed on a DC 15 Dexterity saving throw to avoid catching on fire. A creature on fire takes 4 (1d8) fire damage per round until an action is used to put the fire out. Creatures and objects immune to fire do not take damage. Structures not protected against fire melt into piles of slag. A typical magma storm lasts 1d10 + 2 minutes and covers an area of less than 1 mile in radius, however the destruction it unleashes is often enough to destroy unprotected travelers and unfortified buildings.

Volcanoes

The great basalt volcanoes are a particularly fearsome feature of the landscape. Spewing their contents miles into the air and raining fire and debris down to the surface, they are quite beautiful to behold, despite the enormity of death and destruction that they literally rain down upon hapless, unwary souls. Even long-time and native residents have trouble predicting with any accuracy where and when the volcanic fallout will land.

A typical volcano spews its contents high into the atmosphere, forming a living column of debris, ash, and liquid fire. Fallout consists of the aforementioned materials and covers an area with a radius of 1d6 miles around the volcano. A typical eruption lasts 1d2 hours.

Creatures caught in the area must succeed on a DC 15 Dexterity saving throw or be pounded by elemental rock and liquid fire. A new save must be made every minute a creature remains in the area. On a failed save, a creature is struck by debris and fire and takes 11 (2d10) fire damage and 11 (2d10) bludgeoning damage and must succeed on a DC 15 Dexterity saving throw to avoid catching fire.

Another danger associated with an eruption is the unmitigated flow of lava. An erupting volcano spews forth lava, streaming it down the basalt surface and destroying everything in its path. A typical lava flow has a speed of 50 feet per round and travels 1d2 miles away from the source. Creatures contacting the lava take 11 (2d10) fire damage. A creature submerged in the lava sustains 110 (20d10) fire damage per round. Damage continues 1d3 rounds after exposure ceases, but this damage is only half that dealt during contact: 5 (1d10) or 55 (10d10) points per round. Magical protection reduces the damage, and creatures immune to fire do not take damage, but they can still drown if they sink beneath the surface.

Inhabitants

Since this plane serves as a waypoint and nexus for three elemental planes and the road to the City of Brass, it is a busy place. All manner of odd and unusual creature can be found here: elementals, devils, salamanders, azer, djinn, jann, and efreet, and even travelers and merchants from the Material Plane.

Creatures, especially those from the adjoining elemental planes, frequent the Plane of Molten Skies to trade, barter, buy, and sell their goods and wares (including slaves, information, valuables, foodstuffs, etc.). Some, like djinn, jann, elementals, and devils, build outposts and citadels on this plane. Most such creatures build their fortresses and citadels near portals and gates that lead to their plane of origin or near a source of elemental material that they themselves are formed of or find to their liking (for example, the elemental earth citadel is built into the mountains of basalt in the west and the fire elemental outpost seated near the curtain of flames that links to the Elemental Plane of Fire).

Efreet are a common occurrence on this plane, though their numbers and encounter frequency are not quite as great away from the City of Brass or curtain of fire.

Locations in the Plane of Molten Skies

The following are some of the plane's more prominent places. They are shown on the **Plane of Molten Skies** map.

1. The Parched Expanse

The Elemental Planes of Earth and Air conjoin here, but quite unlike the violent, bastardized conjunctions at the opposite corners, it is a sedate and peaceful union. It is the most commonly traversed part of the Plane of Molten Skies, where the mated planes become a flat, dusty, barren landscape known only as the "The Parched Expanse." More often than not, it is the first sight that greets itinerant travelers to the realm of the efreet. The sky is colorless, existing only in shades of black, white, and the entire spectrum of gray in between. The ground is covered in a thick, deep layer of dust — not ash or soot, but rather the dust of decay accumulated over ten thousand millennia, dust of past and future generations, dust of all things dead and forgotten.

The portal by which entry to and exit from the plane can be made is a great, towering, mountain-high keep — the Palace of Dust — sealed by a gleaming steel door that, unlike everything else on the plain, does not seem to have aged at all. The door swings open effortlessly, perfectly balanced upon oiled hinges that make nary a sound.

Road markers rise from the dust, connoting a path leading deeper into the plane. This byway is the Highway of the Damned, and if followed all the way, can guide travelers straight to the City of Brass.

Parched Expanse Random Encounters

Roll 1d20 for every hour spent traveling in this area and consult the table below.

1d20	Encounter
1	Dust spiral
2	2d4 air mephits[1] or dust mephits
3	1 invisible stalker
4	1d2 + 2 wind walkers[1]
5	1d4 greater air elementals[1]
6	1d2 + 2 belkers[1]
7	1d3 elder arrowhawks[1]
8	Atomization zone
9	1d4 + 1 dust ghouls[1]
10	1 elder air elemental[1]
11	1d4 noble djinn
12	1 ancient dust dragon[1]
13	1 air elemental dragon[1]
14-20	No encounter

Effects of the Parched Expanse

Creatures moving across the Parched Expanse do so at half of their normal movement rate. In many places, the dust covers deep, treacherous pits that many an unwary traveler have fallen into, especially in heated moments of fight or flight. Spotting one of these pits requires a successful DC 20 Wisdom (Perception) or Wisdom (Survival) check. The utmost care must be taken lest a person suddenly sink out of sight, asphyxiating and choking to death on the collected dust of fallen generations. Sound on the Expanse is also muted, making it difficult to hear much beyond 20 feet and impossible to hear anything beyond 50 feet. Creatures relying on sound for Wisdom (Perception) checks have disadvantage and all Stealth checks are made with advantage.

Plane of Molten Skies
80 miles.
Sea of Fire
City of Brass
Earth
Air
N

Dust Spiral: A dust spiral springs up suddenly and unexpectedly. It appears as a moving column of whirling dust and debris. A typical dust spiral covers a 10-foot radius and stands about 20 feet tall. A dust spiral moves at least 10 feet in one direction before shifting and moving randomly in another direction. A creature caught in a dust spiral takes 7 (2d6) bludgeoning damage each round and must succeed on a DC 18 Dexterity saving throw or be knocked prone. A dust spiral obscures vision as a *fog cloud* spell does.

Atomization Zone: This immobile area of the Expanse is alive with negative energy. An atomization zone appears as a part of the landscape and is almost indistinguishable from the surrounding area. A character can attempt a DC 25 Wisdom (Perception) check to notice the small, shifting motes of light that wink in and out of existence in this area. A typical atomization zone covers a 30-foot cubic area.

Upon entering an atomization zone, a creature's physical structure quickly breaks down, and must attempt a DC 18 Constitution saving throw each round it remains in the area, taking 70 (20d6) force damage on a failed save and half as much on a successful one. A creature reduced to 0 or fewer hit points in an atomization zone is essentially disintegrated, leaving behind only a trace of fine dust.

Creatures of the Parched Expanse

While there is not much in the way of native flora or fauna that travelers must worry about, there are still predators: **dust ghouls**[1], risen, animated corpses of creatures that have died on the Expanse. They move swiftly through the powdery murk, releasing terrible, paralyzing shrieks that cut through the silence like a razor-sharp obsidian knife through flesh. As they close in for the kill, ghostly apparitions materialize out of the swirling dust at their command, pinning their prey in place while they tear the flesh from its bones with sharp teeth and claws.

Creatures of pure earth, such as earth elementals, avoid the Expanse as it causes their structure to slowly break down, reducing their maximum hit points by 1d2 each round they spend in this area.

Other creatures encountered on the Expanse include air elementals, air mephits, belkers, dust mephits, invisible stalkers, wind walkers, djinn, and air elemental dragons. See the Random Encounters sidebox for details.

1-1. Palace of Dust

At the point where the Elemental Plane of Air and the Elemental Plane of Earth meet stands a black colossus of a building, the former palace of Kush, one-time ruler over all mortal creation, son of Shaddad, son of Id the Greater. The palace, now chained by the dust of ages past, is one of the few portals that cross directly into the Material Plane.

Despite the building's immense size, little is left of its rooms. Just the first two floors have survived the ravages of time eternal. Dusky gray light pierces the innumerable holes riddling its onyx-colored walls, streaming through arrow loops and shattered windows like an invasion of dust motes. The air is harsh and dry. As with the Parched Expanse, sound is hindered by some natural or magical feature of the building. Unlike the Expanse, absolutely nothing lives within the building's interior.

Strangely, many of the palace's original accoutrements are still in intact. Tapestries, rotted through and tattered, hang from the walls in many of the keep's galleries, paintings, threatening to crumble at the slightest touch, lean against the walls and sit on the floors of rooms where they long ago fell, and porcelain plates, vases, and tableware still decorate the tables where the lord of mortal man once supped with adversary and ally. Many a creature has tried to take from the palace, but never to any lasting success. As soon as one crosses the threshold, pilfered treasures turn to dust, and reincorporate to their places in the building.

The main entry hall is a long, wide chamber with a ceiling 30 feet from the floor. Every square inch of stone is inscribed with poems decrying the fate that befell Kush, commenting on his hubris for thinking he could defeat the army of Sulymon, the prophet of Allah, the All-Mighty Creator. In the next room, a long table that would have been truly majestic in better days awaits travelers. There are no seats around it.

Like the entry hall, the dining hall table bears an inscription:

At this table have eaten a thousand kings blind of the right eye and a thousand blind of the left and yet another thousand sound of both eyes, all of whom have departed the world and have taken up their sojourn in the tombs and the catacombs of the City of Brass.

And a second inscription carved by a different hand reads:

Be wary, o' seekers. Death is the inescapable conclusion to all tales.

GM Note: If the characters are arriving for the first time to the Plane of Molten Skies through the Palace of Dust, give them a chance for a quiet respite. This portal should be a safe haven, especially if they fought long and hard to get to it. Reinforce this in your descriptions and abstain from throwing any random encounters at them for the time. The palace should afford the opportunity for the characters to reflect on where they have been and what awaits them on the road ahead.

2. The Brass Horseman

A small hill supports a large brass statue of a heavily armored rider and his equally heavily armored horse, both of which stand nearly 15 feet high. Pointing westward, held in the rider's right hand and supported under his arm, is a lance with a broad, silver tip that shines brightly under the fiery sky. The rider's left hand tightly grips the reins of his mount.

Closer examination of the lance tip reveals the following inscription written in the Common tongue:

He who seeks the brass horsemen seeks the way to the City of Brass. Let he who desires such knowledge rub the reined hand of the horseman for then the way shall be shown to him.

Rubbing the horseman's left hand causes him to turn slowly clockwise, creaking and groaning until his lance points eastward.

3. Dahish al A'amash, the Obsidian Angel

A 12-foot-tall block of perfectly cut volcanic glass emerges from the ground here. Trapped in it, sunk up to his midsection, is a jet-skinned man with four arms (two of which end in leonine paws), a pair of razor-sharp obsidian wings outstretched up and away from the glass pillar imprisoning him, flowing black locks of hair bound with brass circlets, and blazing coal-red eyes. A third eye inset in the middle of his forehead constantly weeps liquid fire discolored by black smoke. He greets the party as they approach, initially using the High Speech of the Efreet, then switching to Common if the characters do not understand him.

The obsidian angel turns to face you, an almost beatific smile on his perfect features. He says something in a lilting dialect foreign to your ears. When he notices your lack of comprehension, he says again in the common speech of humankind:

There is no God but the All-Mighty Creator, and Sulymon was his prophet! Repent, friends, repent and atone for the error of your ways if you are not initiates of the True Faith! Fill your hearts with the greatness and glory of the All-

Dahish al'Aamash (**efreeti sardar**[1]) was once the guardian of the *carnelian idol*[2] of Iblis, the original efreeti who rebelled against Sulymon and the All-Mighty Creator. If asked, the imprisoned general relates his tale. He claims he once inhabited the Idol and spoke with the voice of Iblis to a proud, arrogant king into whose possession the idol fell. One day, Sulymon came to the king and told him to abandon his worship of the false idol or face his ire. The devil Iblis was no master of men, and Sulymon would not tolerate any of his children worshipping him. When the king consulted the idol about the temerity of the prophet's commandment, Dahish became livid, believing quite arrogantly that the prophet was nothing more than a "has-been." He told the king to bring a righteous holy war to the tyrant Sulymon. If he did this bidding, Iblis would provide him with an army of 10,000 elite janni soldiers to lead into battle. The king, heartened by these words, returned to his palace whereupon he decreed that the prophet was no longer welcome in his lands. Sulymon left, vowing to return with a host of marids to quench the upstart idolater's treachery. In time, the king and Sulymon joined one another in battle. Dahish emerged from the idol to lead half of the janni army, while the king led the other half. Sulymon's marids, however, beat them easily. Sulymon slew the king, taking his daughter for his wife, and for the Dahish's complicity mired him for eternity within the pillar upon which the *carnelian idol*[2] once stood.

Since that day, Dahish has regretted his betrayal of Sulymon and the All-Mighty Creator and his choice to serve Iblis. He eagerly tells any and all travelers who come upon him his story in an effort to dissuade them from going to the City of Brass. The Sultan, he believes, is Iblis reincarnate. If he had his freedom, he would indeed raise an army to lead against the city. Dahish dreams of the day he can press his boot against the Sultan's throat and hear him beg for the forgiveness of the All-Mighty Creator.

The obsidian pillar possesses an enchantment similar to a *dispel magic* or *antimagic field* in that it disrupts and prevents Dahish from using his *change size* ability, any of his spell-like abilities, or otherwise escaping from the fate with which he has been saddled. It also prevents such magic cast by anyone else from freeing him. If the efreeti dies while trapped in the pillar, the slayers do not gain any XP and Dahish returns to his original state within 1d4 hours. The only way to kill Dahish permanently is to first free him from the pillar. Not even the Sultan can kill Dahish, and he has tried repeatedly (sometimes he comes to the pillar after a particularly frustrating day just to kill Dahish over and over again until he feels better).

If the characters recover the *carnelian idol*[2] and destroy it upon the sides of the pillar prison, Dahish is set free. He grants his rescuers any three unconditional *wishes* and then leaves to gather his army of 10,000 undead janni skeletons that he plans to use to lay siege to the City of Brass. These undead soldiers are the restless souls of the army he and the unnamed king originally led against Sulymon.

4. The Great Rock Wall

A colossal wall resembling an unending mountain of jagged obsidian and steaming basalt divides the boundary between the Elemental Plane of Earth and the Plane of Molten Skies. It rises from the ground as far as the eye can see, appearing to disappear into the haze of a horizon that will never be reached. Several portals leading to the Elemental Plane of Earth are located along the wall, some within small caves and caverns.

Movement beyond the wall is impossible (except perhaps by magical means). A character can climb the Great Rock Wall by succeeding on a DC 20 Strength (Athletics) check and using the normal climbing rules. Note however, that the wall stretches infinitely into the sky above, so anyone hoping to climb up and over the wall will be sorely disappointed.

Creatures of the Great Rock Wall

The wall is home to various beings, most of which are outcasts from the Plane of Earth. **Earth elementals** are frequently seen roaming the area, often in contest with **xorns** and indigenous **stone giants** for the precious minerals that the unyielding stone protects within its nearly impregnable bosom. See **The Great Rock Wall Random Encounters** table.

The Great Rock Wall Random Encounters

Roll 1d20 for every hour spent traveling in this area and consult the table below.

1d20	Encounter
1	Rockslide (see below)
2	2d4 earth mephits[1] or salt mephits[1]
3	1d4 + 1 caterprisms[1]
4	1 greater earth elemental[1]
5	2d6 gargoyles
6	1 elder earth elemental[1]
7	1d3 elder xorns[1] or 1d4 + 2 xorns
8	1d3 stone giants
9	1 adult blue dragon or copper dragon
10	1d4 Haidar[1]
11–20	No encounter

Rock slide: Rocks come crashing down from the wall above in a 30 foot wide strip 200 feet long. Creatures within the area must attempt a DC 18 Strength saving throw. Those that fail are knocked prone. Creatures must then attempt a DC 15 Dexterity saving throw, with those that are prone having disadvantage. Creatures failing the Dexterity saving throw take 33 (6d10) bludgeoning damage while those that succeed take half this amount.

4-1. Splinter-Rock Clan

The Splinter-Rock Clan of stone giants makes its home among the cliffs of the Great Rock Wall. Though they have extensively mined the region for almost a hundred thousand years already (approximately 200 stone giant generations), they are nevertheless always on the lookout for new and interesting sources of minerals and precious gemstones, especially rubies, emeralds, adamantine, mithral, gold, silver, and living brass, which they are eager trade to merchants who later sell it for outrageous sums of money in the City of Brass.

The Splinter-Rock Clan is currently made up of **26 stone giants** including the chieftain and the shaman. There are 13 non-combatants including elderly and children. Their chieftain, **Thunderhead**[1], is a druid of no small repute. Their shaman was given the name **Mossknee**[1] because of a large dark green birthmark located on his right knee. A mated pair of tattooed gorgons guards the giants' extensive network of caverns, primarily stalking the upper halls and keeping unwanted visitors at bay (usually by using their unusual abilities to turn them into attractive new décor for the fortress). A tattooed gorgon is a **gorgon** that can cast the following spells once per day without material components: *magic missile, lightning bolt* (gorgon 1), *fireball, blur* (gorgon 2). The spells have a save DC of 17. Within the clan's caves are 14,000 gp and 6 bloodstones (50 gp each).

The Splinter-Rocks dress in the loose-fitting tan and brown robes typical of desert nomads. Unusually colored woven hemp ropes that identify their clan to those in the know bind their headdresses. Thunderhead's headdress is further decorated with polished stone beads. He often travels "downhill" to the Obsidian Angel, with whom he shares an abiding friendship. They often while away the hours smoking quarry tobacco and discussing the glory and teachings of Sulymon.

4-2. Wall of the Petrified Dead

After Sulymon defeated Dahish's army, he banished the dead enemy soldiers to the Great Rock Wall, embedding their corpses in it as a horrific reminder to future rebels and as punishment — as long as they are a part of the wall, their souls will never know peace. The remains of a thousand dead jann can be seen in the gray basalt, from a distance resembling skillfully carved statues half-emerging from the stone. Up close, they possess disturbingly life-like visages. When Sulymon cast them into the wall, he brought them back to life in the process as part of their punishment. Thus, the agony evident on their faces was felt as they merged with the wall, and it is one they continue to feel to this day in the hell that has become their existence.

An effable sense of madness pervades the region near the wall out to a distance of 5 miles. Anyone within this area must succeed on a DC 20 Wisdom saving throw each hour or be affected as by an *confusion* spell each round until it succeeds on its saving throw. This does not affect sleeping characters or characters that cannot hear.

There is an epic spell seed in the Great Repository of the City of Brass in a book called *The Analects of Sulymon the Wise, Vol. 23*. Both Dahish and Thunderhead of the Splinter-Rock Clan know of this seed, but neither surrenders this information until Dahish is freed. If the ritual is correctly performed, all 10,000 dead soldiers crack free of the wall, becoming animated skeletons whose bones and withered flesh are encased in a jagged stone firmament (grants natural armor bonus). The **janni skeletons**[1] follow the orders of none but Dahish however.

Treasure: In the gaps in the rock wall left by the animated janni soldiers is a small hoard of valuable treasure left over from the king whom they once served. It consists of 21,000 gp, a fire opal on silver chain (1,700 gp), a brass mug with platinum inlaid rim (400 gp), a brass plate with sapphire inlay (2,100 gp), 10 white emeralds (1,000 gp each), 5 purple corundums (1,100 gp each), *potion of greater healing*, a *staff of abjuration*[2], a *carpet of flying* (6 foot by 9 foot), a *staff of conjuration*[2], a *ring of x-ray vision*, a *mantle of faith*[2], and a *spell scroll* of *nightmare*[4].

The undead soldiers do not let anyone take these items without a considerable fight, since they intend to sell them off and use the money to re-equip themselves for their imminent war with the City of Brass.

5. The Black Plain

Where the elemental planes of Earth and Fire converge, the ground changes from cracked rock to black, banded, smooth obsidian. A faint orange glow can be seen on the eastern horizon. The northern horizon ends in a wall of solid rock that stretches into the fiery sky above, disappearing in a thick haze of smoke, boiling water vapor, and flame. As one travels north, the ground slowly changes from obsidian to solid stone, eventually terminating in a massive stone wall stretching upward and disappearing into the haze and smoke of the boiling sky. As one travels east, the ground eventually "melts" into an oozing plain of magma as it nears the border to the Elemental Plane of Fire. Somewhere on the Black Plain lies the **Tomb of Y'Cart** (see below).

Black Plain Random Encounters

The area where elemental earth and fire meet are home to many creatures of one or both of the aforementioned subtypes as well as several unique phenomena. General encounters are with creatures of obsidian, earth, and magma, the latter being more prevalent as one nears the border of the Plane of Fire. Obsidian elementals, obsidian minotaurs, purple worms, efreeti, and xorn are common encounters on the Black Plain.

Roll 1d20 for every hour spent traveling in this area and consult the table below.

1d20	Encounter
1	Ash storm
2	2d4 magma or fire[1] mephits
3	Fissure
4	1d4 greater obsidian elementals[1]
5	2d4 xorn (break through surface)
6	Fossilization nexus

Obsidian Weapons

Weapons fashioned from obsidian increase the die size of the damage (from 1d4 to 1d6 or 2d6 to 2d8, for example) and increases the critical range of the weapon by one (from 20 to 19 and 20, for example).

Only weapons normally made of metal can be fashioned from obsidian.

Obsidian weapons are incredibly fragile. If its wielder rolls a 1, the wielder must succeed on a DC 14 Strength saving throw or the weapon shatters into thousands of immeasurably sharp shards that deal 2 (1d4) slashing damage to the wielder.

Obsidian weapons may be purchased in some of the markets of the City of Brass. See the table below for cost modification from a standard weapon.

Obsidian Weapon	Cost Modifier
Ammunition	+4 gp
Light weapon	+30 gp
One-handed weapon	+130 gp
Two-handed or heavy weapon	+250 gp

1d20	Encounter
7	1 adult brass dragon
8	1d4 + 1 efreet
9	1d4 obsidian minotaurs[1]
10	1 purple worm (breaks through surface)
11	1 adult red dragon
12-20	No encounter

Effects of the Black Plain

The Black Plain is the result of the two elemental planes joining in more or less equal parts. The glass landscape is blistering hot to the touch and deals 1 fire damage per round to any unprotected character touching it or walking upon its surface. (An unprotected character is one with light or no armor or a natural armor bonus of +3 or less.) Protected characters or those resistant to or immune to fire take no damage.

This vast swath of obsidian plate is at least 10 feet thick and extremely dense. However, it can be cracked and chipped because it is quite fragile despite its mass. When broken, it forms conchoidal chunks that can be fashioned into incredibly sharp weapons (see sidebox).

Ash Storm: A typical ash storm comes on suddenly and ends 2d6 minutes later just as suddenly as it began. An ash storm consists of grayish-brown ash raining from the sky that obscures sight and raises the temperature in the affected area (dealing damage to those caught in the storm).

The ash obscures sight, including darkvision, beyond 10 feet. Creatures and objects 10 feet away are lightly obscured. Creatures and objects farther away are heavily obscured. Further, a creature caught in an ash storm takes 3 (1d6) fire damage per round of exposure. Wind has no effect on an ash storm.

Fissure: The ground cracks open, creating several long fissures in random locations within a 100-foot-radius area. A fissure is about 20 feet deep.

Each creature standing in the area must make a DC 20 Dexterity saving throw or fall into one of the fissures taking 27 (6d8) slashing damage from the razor-sharp obsidian and 7 (2d6) bludgeoning damage from the fall.

Fossilization Nexus: One of the greatest dangers to those traveling across this area is a fossilization nexus. This is a web of cracks and fractures emerging from a central fissure. A successful DC 23 Wisdom (Perception) check reveals a fossilization nexus, though characters unfamiliar with a nexus may not recognize it as anything more than cracks in the plain. A typical fossilization nexus covers a radius of 10 + 1d20 feet.

A creature touching any part of a fossilization nexus must succeed on a DC 18 Constitution saving throw or immediately be transformed into an obsidian statue. The condition can be removed by casting *greater restoration* or *wish*. If a fossilized creature is removed from the Black Plain while fossilized, it immediately crumbles to dust, only recoverable then by a *wish*.

5-1. Lost Tomb of Y'Cart

A bizarre perfectly square slab of stone roughly 10 feet tall and 200 feet on a side stands somewhere upon the Black Plain although its exact location is unknown, and none who have reached it have returned. There is only a 1% cumulative chance per visit to the Black Plain that the slab may be encountered as anything other than a mirage caused by the roiling fires of the sky and the sheer gleam of obsidian glass. Characters climbing up the sheer slab find that the gleaming blackness seems to flicker with and reflect disturbing alien starlight. A single stone staircase flanked by jet black stone sphinxes with the skeletal faces stands in the center of the slab. The staircase descends into virtual nothingness.

Characters descending into the darkness are magically teleported into the afterlife of the vile God-King **Y'Cart Chi'Namk**[1]. This demi-plane is populated by the souls sacrificed in Y'Cart's name. The plane is relatively small, encompassing only 10 square miles, the majority of which is a lush jungle filled with venomous fiendish serpents, crocodiles, hippopotami, and apes. Rising from the center of the jungle stands the cyclopean pyramid housing the Lost Tomb of Y'Cart the Eternal, surrounded by the dwellings and temples of his shadowy slaves. A black hole floats in the sky above the pinnacle of the pyramid, devouring the god-king's universe and casting a hellish pallor over the jungle as star after star is consumed for this ruler of the end of days. It is said that none who enter Y'Cart's realm may escape except by his leave, which of course is never offered. The treasuries of Y'Cart are believed to be filled with the malevolent artifacts of his reign, including perhaps the undead steeds and harness of Narmer himself.

5-2. The Glass Maze

The planar portal at the convergence of Fire and Earth is known as the Glass Maze. The maze stretches for miles and miles before finally breaking down upon the Black Plain. There are many entrances to the Plane of Molten Skies that open first within the Convergence of Fire and Earth. The maze also contains a direct conduit to the Elemental Plane of Earth. The Glass Maze is very complex, consisting of hundreds of layers of cracked obsidian shelves shot-through with deep fissures that are hard to make out among the reflective surfaces. Travelers seeking the City of Brass via the Elemental Plane of Earth typically starve to death before ever finding their way out of the maze. To make matters worse, marauding bands of obsidian minotaurs who are nearly impossible to see against the sheer cliffs and twisting pathways continually stalk the maze's maddening corridors and shafts. The grand vizier of the City of Brass constructed the minotaurs to guard this entrance to the Plane of Molten Skies.

There is a 25% chance that 1d4 **obsidian minotaurs**[1] are encountered for every hour that the characters spend within the Glass Maze.

5-3. Pits of the Crystal Queen (EL varies)

At the heart of the Black Plain, **Queen Widushka**[1], a wicked drider noble woman living on the Plane of Molten Skies in exile for some unimaginable transgression against the Spider Goddess, reigns supreme. Her domain is a broad piece of land fives mile in length and two miles deep. It looks, at first glance, like any other part of the elemental conjunction. However, her hybrid **drider-goblin**[1] warrior slaves have in fact riddled it with hundreds of "trapdoor" pits, which they occupy in rotating shifts, waiting for unsuspecting prey to come within range. Then, much like the mundane trapdoor spider, they leap forth from their pit to capture it, drag it down below ground, and then bind it with their fetid silk.

The pits extend far belowground, forming a decidedly confusing network of tunnels, tubes, and chambers all lined with polished volcanic glass. Some portions of the network are designed explicitly for wall-walkers, and thus appear to pedestrian travelers as being inverted or upside down.

Queen Widushka has a voracious sexual appetite. When she and her slaves are not eating captured prey for dinner, she can usually be found satiating her bizarre appetite in her private chambers. The drider-goblins, when they are off duty, entertain themselves by creating new and interesting sports using the various body parts yanked from the queen's leftovers.

The queen and her "subjects" (such as they are) have no interest in the world beyond the borders of their pits. She couldn't care less about the Sultan in his ugly brass bowl, nor does she care about the fire giants servicing Thane Brihnda. She does not yet know about the xill or the formians, not that it would matter. Hidden within the maze are 5,000 gp, 11 moonstones (75 gp each), and a *wand of binding*.

5-4. Caves of the Glass Wyrms

The Black Plain is home to an expanse of subterranean caves, accessible through a large shaft or tunnel. The tunnel descends 200 feet at a 45-degree angle, its make-up gradually changing from the dark obsidian rock of the Black Plain to smooth polished glass. Climbing up the tunnel requires a DC 30 Strength (Athletics) check, at least in the area composed of smooth glass. The tunnel eventually opens into an expansive complex of glass caves interconnected by massive corridors, all formed of smooth polished glass. Scattered about the caves and corridors are glass statues of various humanoids and other creatures, some wholly intact, some chipped or shattered. The statues are in fact the "petrified" remains of explorers that entered the caves and couldn't get out.

The glass caves have an effect on creatures that stay too long within their confines. For every 5 minutes spent in the caves, a creature must succeed on a DC 15 Constitution saving throw (+1 per previous save) or take 1 point of Constitution damage as its body slowly transforms into glass. A creature reduced to Constitution 0 dies and changes into solid glass, becoming one of the many statues littering this lair. All carried or worn items other than legendary magic items transform with the creature.

The caves are home to a family of 3 **glass wyrms**[1] who spend most of their time here and rarely venture out into the surface world. The wyrms sustain themselves on a diet of glass or flesh, either eating the glass statues scattered throughout the caves or devouring creatures that enter the caves (or sometimes journeying to the surface and actually hunting prey). Often, the glass wyrms simply wait for some foolhardy adventurer to stumble into the cave complex, become lost, and eventually succumb to the "glassing" effect of the caves. Once a creature is glassed, it is either devoured or placed somewhere in the caves as a decoration. Lying within the cave are 8,000 gp, 23 silver pearls (150 gp each), *spell wand*[2] of *magic weapon*, and a *+3 greatsword*.

6. The Eternal Storm

A massive, impossibly-sized sandstorm forms the border between the Plane of Molten Skies and the Elemental Plane of Air. Known locally as the Eternal Storm, this maelstrom's winds can be felt up to 20 miles away. Only the hardiest souls live along this border. Life here is exceedingly harsh by local standards; for outsiders, it is an impossibility at best and a death sentence at worst. The fact that the Sultan from the City of Brass exiles many of his worst political enemies to this deadly borderland is a testament to just how bad it can be — it is, as they say, a fate worse than death, and everyone knows just how fond the Sultan is of the death penalty for those who irritate him or otherwise get in his way.

Eternal Storm Random Encounters

The Eternal Storm is home to air elementals, belkers, wind walkers, aerial servants, lightning elementals and the like, who flirt within the banks of whirling wind and sand. Occasionally, heavily armored airships can be seen traversing the borderland on their way to and from the City of Brass, inevitably carrying exotic goods from deep within the Elemental Plane of Air and other far away worlds.

Roll 1d20 for every hour spent traveling in this area and consult the table below.

1d20	Encounter
1	2d4 air mephits[1] or dust mephits
2	1 invisible stalker
3	1d2 + 2 wind walkers[1]
4-5	2d4 lightning elementals[1]

1d20	Encounter
6–7	1 elder air elemental[1]
8	1d4 greater air elementals[1]
9	2d6 belkers[1]
10	1 aerial servant[1]
11	Airships
12–20	No encounter

Airships: Sailing on the wind unimpeded through the Eternal Storm are ships that resemble normal waterborne craft save they are heavily armored … and flying. Almost all airship encounters are with 1d2 galleys escorted by 1d4 wargalleys.

Airship fleets come from various planes and worlds, and just about any intelligent race can be encountered at the helm.

Airship Galley: This three-masted ship is 100 feet long and 20 feet wide. It has a total crew of 150 and can carry up to 120 tons of cargo. Most are fitted with rams and ballistae mounted on firing platforms. It moves at a speed of 6 miles per hour (60 feet per round). *Airship Galley:* AC 15; hardness 10; hp 300; damage threshold 10.

Airship Wargalley: This single-masted ship is about 90 feet long. It does not carry cargo but can carry up to 150 soldiers or troops. A wargalley is used as an escort for airship galleys. All wargalleys are fitted with a ram and ballistae mounted on firing platforms. It has a speed of 4 miles per hour (40 feet per round). *Airship Wargalley:* AC 18; hp 320; damage threshold 15.

Effects of the Eternal Storm

Any creatures standing within a half dozen miles of the Eternal Storm feel as if they are staring into an infinite wall of roiling sand, dust, and detritus. Attempting to cross into the Plane of Air through the storm is suicide for all but a very few creatures. The winds constantly blow in excess of 200 miles per hour, laced with grains of blazing hot sand capable of slicing to shreds any creature without adequate armor, thick skin, or magical protection. Creatures entering the Eternal Storm are affected as if by tornado-like winds. Standing against the wind requires a successful DC 16 Strength check and moving into it a DC 20 Strength check. Failing a check causes the creature to slide 15 feet downwind and become prone. Further, a creature takes 3 (2d6) slashing damage each round from the blistering and burning sands unless it has a non-Dexterity based armor bonus (natural or from armor) of +8 or higher.

6-1. The Eye of God

Many say the Eye of God is a mere myth or legend, but in fact it is a very real and prominent part of the plane. Every once in a great while, a ten-mile section of the Eternal Storm calms down, becoming a gentle wall of refreshing wind and, at times, rain. The last time people report the eye forming was over two thousand years ago. Some say it was put there as a sentinel by the guardians of the Elemental Plane of Air, others believe it is a temperamental puncture in the fabric of the plane, a gateway to other worlds yet to be discovered, and some academicians claim it is the part of Sulymon that died when he sheared his dark genius away from his being, eternally destitute, confused, and alone until such a time as it can be rejoined with it. Whatever the case may be, the eye is a rare occurrence few people are willing to let themselves believe in. However, one oddity that actually supports belief in the eye is that the region where it is said to form is always free of sand. Instead, the winds blow smooth and clean there.

A minor cult devoted to the eye exists, with temples established in a few of the border towns.

6-2. The Great Sand Sea

A desert of shifting sands and towering sand berms, the Great Sand Sea extends for miles into the Plane of Molten Skies out of the borderlands around the Eternal Storm. It is an inhospitable region to those not protected against the natural temperatures of this area.

The Great Sand Sea Random Encounters

The Great Sand Sea is home to air elementals, sandlings, sandmen, and death worms, and it contains the berm fortress of the Haidar[1], a barbaric tribe of sand giants who serve Ilgomaxag[1] the dust dragon.

Roll 1d20 for every hour spent traveling in this area and consult the table below.

1d20	Encounter
1–2	2d4 sandlings[1]
3	2d6 sandmen
4	1d4 greater air elementals[1]
5–6	1d6 death worms[1]
7–8	1 elder air elemental[1]
9	1d4 djinn
10	1 adult blue dragon
11	1d4 Haidar
12	Sandstorm (see below)
13–20	No encounter

Effects of the Great Sand Sea

Movement through the sand sea is one-half normal for all creatures not of elemental earth. Frequent sandstorms also pose a considerable threat. The greatest danger, however, is the sweltering heat.

A character must succeed on a Constitution saving throw once every 10 minutes or take 1d4 fire damage and gain a level of exhaustion. The DC starts at 15 and increases by 1 for each previous check. Characters wearing heavy armor of any sort have disadvantage on their saves. A character with the Survival skill may add their proficiency bonus on this saving throw and may be able to apply this bonus to other characters as well.

Sandstorm: A sandstorm reduces visibility to 1d10 × 5 feet and provides disadvantage on Perception checks. A sandstorm deals 1 (1d3) bludgeoning damage per hour to any creatures caught in the open, and leaves a thin coating of sand in its wake. Driving sand creeps in through all but the most secure seals and seams, to chafe skin and contaminate carried gear.

6-3. Nest of the Gray Wyrm

On the edge of the Great Sand Sea and the Parched Expanse lives **Ilgomaxag**[1], an ancient dust dragon who makes his lair in a subterranean burrow formed of saliva-hardened layers of dust and wind-blasted sand. Three tunnels connect to his lair, with one emerging below the Palace of Dust, another in the heart of the Haidar Fortress to the east, and the third not far from the Highway of the Damned. **Dust ghouls**[1] haunt the tunnels (the initial 50 feet of each tunnel goes straight down into the earth) and can be encountered in groups of 3d6. Adventurers unlucky enough to find themselves in the dragon's lair do not last long. Once the dust ghouls begin shrieking, Ilgomaxag comes rushing to defend his home from the intruders. Most creatures he simply eats on the spot; some he toys with for a week or two before killing.

When the time is right, Ilgomaxag plans to go after the Sultan of the City of Brass (whom he hates with an abiding passion). As much as Ilgomaxag dislikes the upstart Sultan, he realizes the Sultan is a more than a match for him. As such, he is content to bide his time until someone else can weaken him enough for the dragon to strike.

Ilgomaxag considers himself the sovereign lord of the entire southwest side of the Plane of Molten Skies, but he does not really expect fealty or obeisance from anyone other than the Haidar giants, whom he saved from a particularly ignoble fate a few generations ago. The one group he truly hates is the nomads of Kush, the self-styled descendants of the hedonist king from millennia past.

Treasure: 15,000 gp, 10 clear quartz (50 gp each), 17 alexandrites (500 gp each), 5 blue diamonds (3,500 gp each), *ring of blinking*[2], *spell scroll* (*antimagic field, create undead, dispel magic* at a 6th level spell slot, *wall of stone, planar binding*), *manual of bodily health,* and a *thundering great mace*[2].

6-4. Haidar Fortress

The high walls of this sand berm resemble a child's sand castle, albeit on a massive scale. This fortress is home to the wild **Haidar**[1], a tribe of barbaric sand giants who serve the dust dragon Ilgomaxag unquestioningly. The tribe consists of 22 adults ruled by a triumvirate of **Macyn**[1], a barbarian chieftain, **Rannyn**[1], a sorcerer, and **Glaen**[1], a cleric of Loki. The Haidar despise the nightmare-riding nomads from the Plains of Kush, and often ambush their caravans, ruthlessly slaying everyone they encounter before returning to their fortress. One of their favorite tactics is to open pits beneath the nomads using their innate ability to manipulate the earth, and then slice the heads off their enemies while they are trapped and immobilized.

Treasure: 5,000 gp, 1,300 pp, 11 onyx (50 gp each), 12 black pearls (500 gp each).

7. The Shattered Peak

When the Plane of Molten Skies first formed, this volcano stretched all the way up into the sky, as perfect a cone as ever seen on any world. Clouds completely enveloped the peak. Some local cultures believe that the All-Mighty Creator once lived atop it, and Sulymon lived at its base. When Sulymon severed his dark genius away from his soul, the peak exploded with such force that it was felt on every material plane. The land cracked and the barriers between the bordering plains thinned, punctured in one place where the Sea of Fire spilled in from the Elemental Plane of Fire. The sky became angry. Molten rains fell. The former paradise became a living hell overnight, and the efreet had their new Sultan to thank for that.

Today, all that remains of the once glorious peak lies in pieces across the landscape. Towering mesas, jagged buttes, and crooked pillars of stone and sand rise from the earth like so many groping skeletal fingers. Winds from the nearby border with the Elemental Plane of Air howl through the crevices, picking up unbelievable speed capable of hurling giants and dragons to their death against the rock walls. The southern half of the Highway of the Damned wends a careful path through the walls of the colossal canyon.

Shattered Peak Random Encounters

Travelers on this road must contend with overpowering gusts of wind and the unusual inhabitants living within its confines: chimeras, greater abyssal basilisks, oblivion wraiths, pyrohydras, barbed devils, and, some people claim, the Tarrasque (though it has never actually been seen, apparently existing solely in their fevered imaginations). Roll 1d20 for every hour spent traveling in this area and consult the table below.

1d20	Encounter
1–2	1d4 chimeras
3	1 spirit naga
4–5	1d4 efreeti
6	1 greater pyrohydra[1]
7	1 young red dragon or young silver dragon
8	1 oblivion wraith[1]
9–10	1d2 bone devils or 1 barbed devil
11	1 abyssal greater basilisk[1]
12–20	No encounter

8. The Ash-Grinder Arcology

These seven huge anthills serve as entrances to the labyrinthine, underground fortress housing a formian city-state that calls itself the Ash-Grinder Arcology for reasons only they truly understand. No greater threat to the authority of the Sultan of the City of Brass exists upon the Plane of Molten Skies than the one posed by these hyper-organized planar invaders. Defended by its distinctly singular hive-mind, the formian fortress has proven impregnable to the Sultan's forces since the discovery of their hills several years ago. This colony is further fortified and filled with captured slaves of every race and creed dedicated solely to defending the lives of their insect-like masters to the death.

Formian War Crawler

The formians of the Ash-Grinder Arcology have used the heat of the Plane of Fire and access to minerals from the Plane of Elemental Earth to craft a cadre of ant-shaped war crawlers that they intend to use in perpetrating an invasion of the City of Brass. These 160-foot-long craft stand 60 feet tall. The six-legged machines are made of steel plate. Their hooked feet are capable of scaling even sheer stone walls with relative ease. The mechanical and magical technology involved fits the sharp minds of the formian queen and her myrmarch officers.

The war crawler is commanded via its head, which is fixed with pincers that are capable of slicing through tree trunks up to 10 foot in diameter. A pair of stalks atop the head can be aimed in any direction and are affixed with lightning blasters that can fire every other round at +8 to hit at a range of 120 feet, dealing 35 (10d6) lightning damage on a hit. See the map in this section for details of locations.

The war crawler can still actively move so long as it has at least one operative leg on each side.

War Crawler

Move 50
Armor Class 20
Legs: 100 hp each, damage threshold 10
Carapace, Head, and Thorax: 150 hp per 10-foot section of hull, damage threshold 15
Antenna Weapons: 50 hp each

The members of the Ash-Grinder Arcology stumbled across the Plane of Molten Skies quite by accident several decades ago. The formian queen's first taste of the realm was a mouthful of disgusting ash, a byproduct from the convergence of the Elemental Plane of Fire and the Plane of Molten Skies' own landscape. The hyper-logical part of her brain immediately calculated the exact number of ash particles in her mouth, then calculated a rough estimate of the number of particles within eyesight, and then came to the sudden realization that the entire plane was covered in enough ash to fill six thousand formian citadel-cities on the Plane of Law. That, she decided, was unacceptable. Ash was, in her mind, the pure unadulterated incarnation of chaos. It had to go. She commanded her workers to lay down the foundation for a new hive, telepathically feeding them plans to build new factories that she and her people would use to grind the ash into an expression of pure logic. Since then, the hive has grown enormously. She is constantly in an egg-laying state, frantic due to the fact that her people just cannot possibly keep up with the influx of filthy ash. Her warriors spend the majority of their time fending off raids from fire elementals, the Sultan's dervishes, and Haidar bandits, in addition to capturing slaves to augment her workforce.

Deep below the hive, miles underground where the Plane of Molten Skies transforms into indeterminate nether materials, are twenty thousand vaults filled with the product of the formian efforts to rid the realm of ash. No non-formian has ever seen them. The hive has 1,200 **formian workers**[1], 120 **formian warriors**[1], 21 **formian taskmasters**[1], 32 **formian myrmarchs**[1], and Dryzyxxl, the **formian queen**[1].

Treasure: 20,000 gp, 15 moss agates (10 gp each), 2 black diamonds (4,000 gp each), *ring of evasion, ring of djinni summoning, staff of necromancy*[2], *shocking sword of law*[2], *rod of flailing*[2].

8-1. Troop Transport (Abdomen)

The abdomen of the machine holds gear and equipment for two full formian platoons. A formian platoon is led by a **formian myrmarch**[1], and contains two **formian taskmasters**[1], eighteen **formian warriors**[1], twelve grunt **formian workers**[1], and their equipment. The abdomen opens completely so that the troops can fan out, using the top half of the shell as cover from incoming fire.

A locked iris door separates the abdomen from the Thorax. The door is controlled by the control panel in area **3**. It can otherwise be picked with a successful DC 16 Dexterity check with thieves' tools, or a *knock* spell.

Battle Crawler
10 ft.

8-2. Thorax Gear Works

The central portion has a walkway that connects the head and the abdomen so that commanders may pass back and forth between the two sections. The gearworks is sophisticated, with redundant hydraulic systems based on the physical features of formians themselves. The gears, however, be sabotaged with a successful DC 25 Intelligence check with thieves' tools. Such sabotage brings the entire war crawler to a grinding halt that takes 1d4 hours to repair.

A locked iris door separates the thorax from the head. The door is controlled by the control panel in area **3**. It can otherwise be picked with a DC 20 Dexterity check with thieves' tools, or a *knock* spell.

8-3. Command Module (Head)

The command module is in the ant-shaped head of the crawler. It is occupied by a **formian myrmarch** commander and a quartet of **formian warriors** who operate the weapons systems and relay commands throughout the system.

8-3A. Eye Screens

These eye screens are polished screens of cut quartz crystal. Each eye affords a broad view of the area in front and to the side of the crawler. The eye screens are 5 feet across and can be aimed independently of one another at a 45-degree front-facing angle.

8-3B. Lightning Cannon Emplacements

A pair of gun turrets located on the back of the command module's head are occupied by **formian warriors** who operate the lightning blasters powered by arcane crystal energy units located inside the armored thorax.

8-3C. Pincer Controls

A set of hydraulic controls are located near the front facing pincers of the head. They are operated by a **formian warrior**[1].

8-3D. Crawler controls

The formian is driven from this location by a **formian myrmarch**[1] or a **formian taskmaster**[1] from the thorax if the myrmarch is otherwise engaged. Refracting mirrors made of polished quartz and silver from the eye screens afford the driver a 180-degree panoramic view of the battlefield.

As many as 10 war crawlers are in the bowels of the formian nests. The characters may be hired by forces representing the Sultan to eliminate the threat that the formian force represents, bringing back the head of their queen as tribute to the Sultan. Alternately, the characters may be sent by Chufa Um Sophanie, the forces of the Lightbringer, or Rah'po Dehj as a means of raising an additional army for an assault against the usurper.

9. The Blasted Land

As one moves farther east toward the borderlands with the Plane of Elemental Fire, the ground gradually changes into a wasteland of dry and fragmented rock covered in a thick layer of ash. A bright, blistering orange glow can be seen on the eastern horizon, but it is thickly clouded with smoke and cannot be seen completely. A rolling cloud of gray smoke obscures most of the sky above, with a sporadic hellish glow peeking through every once in awhile. Thick clouds of gray or black gases and smoke roll across the plain at random intervals.

Moving closer to the conjunction of the elemental plane, the haze grows thick, burning the air from the lungs of creatures not accustomed or immune to it. Closer still, flesh and bone begin to spontaneously ignite. The transition from the Plane of Molten Skies to the Elemental Plane of Fire is a subtle one for non-elemental creatures. It is also a change very few survive.

At times, some say, the fiery borderland seems to be a sentient being. Many an efreeti and janni has attempted to build a castle or citadel inside its barriers, but always to no avail. Something seems to destroy such structures shortly after construction is completed. One academic living in the City of Brass reportedly saw an army of 10,000 marids lay waste to one such fortress. (How this could even remotely be possible is anyone's guess.) Strangely, natives to the Elemental Plane of Fire seem to have immunity to whatever force guides the destructions of efreeti citadels, their own lairs floating safely in the flaming curtain they call the **Phlogiston**.

Blasted Land Random Encounters

Efreet from the City of Brass often come here to hunt in large boisterous groups, immensely enjoying the sport of hunting the endangered flame-spawned rocs (which they call ruknar). Further encounters in this area are with efreeti, burning dervishes, and various flame-spawned creatures.

Roll 1d20 for every hour spent traveling in this area and consult the table below.

1d20	Encounter
1	Superheated ash cloud
2	Hot spot
3	1 greater fire elemental[1]
4	1d4 + 1 fire elementals
5	2d4 flame-spawned trolls+
6	1d2 flame-spawned rocs+
7	1d4 + 1 flame-spawned dire bears+
8	1 elder fire elemental[1]
9	1d4 + 1 efreet
10	1d4 fire giants
11	1 adult red dragon or adult brass dragon
12–20	No encounter

+Immune to fire damage, add 1d6 fire damage to successful attack, and a creature within 5 feet takes 3 (1d6) fire damage at the start of its turn.

Effects of the Blasted Land

The Blasted Land is the derivation of elemental fire and elemental air burning and sweeping across the landscape. The ground is scorching hot to the touch, dealing 1 (1d3) fire damage per round to any unprotected character touching it or walking upon its surface. (An unprotected character is one with light or no armor or a natural armor bonus of +6 or less.) Protected characters or those resistant to or immune to fire take no damage.

Further, a character must succeed on a Constitution saving throw once every 10 minutes or take 2 (1d4) fire damage from the heat and gain a level of exhaustion. The DC starts at 15 and increases by 1 for each check. Characters wearing heavy armor of any have disadvantage on their saving throws. A character proficient in Survival may add their proficiency bonus to this saving throw and may be able to apply this bonus to other characters as well.

Superheated Ash Cloud: A superheated ash cloud is a mixture of thick, billowing smoke and superheated atmospheric gases. An ash cloud is gray or black in color and occasionally bursts with an orange glow as it rolls across the ground. Such a cloud is typically 50 feet across and moves in a random direction across the ground at a speed of 30 feet. Creatures caught in or entering a superheated ash cloud must succeed on a DC 20 Constitution saving throw each round they remain in its confines or take 5 (1d10) fire damage and lose 3 (1d6) points of Constitution from the choking ash.

Hot Spot: A hot spot is formed in an area where a blast of elemental fire detonates. The superheated gases and resulting fire intermingle to actually liquefy the ground in the area. As it cools, the ground hardens again, but remains superheated for a time. A typical hot spot covers a 20-foot radius and deals 16 (3d10) fire damage per round to creatures contacting it.

10. Phlogiston

A shimmering, psychedelic curtain of fire separates the Plane of Molten Skies from the Elemental Plane of Fire. This barrier, called the Phlogiston, appears to onlookers as a rolling sheet of flames, a slow-moving waterfall of liquid fire that inexorably reaches into the boiling sky. Creatures foolish enough to wander too close or actually enter the Phlogiston sustain fire damage from the scorching elemental fire.

Phlogiston Encounters

The area around the Phlogiston is home to fire elementals, magmoids, fire and magma mephits, rast, salamanders (who often build floating fortresses on the fringes), efreet (who often build outposts near the Phlogiston), and many other fire creatures.

Roll 1d20 for every hour spent traveling in this area and consult the table below.

1d20	Encounter
1	1d6 + 4 magmin
2	1 magmoid[1]
3	1d6 + 4 fire[1] or magma mephits
4	1 greater fire elemental[1]
5	1d4 + 2 rasts[1]
6	1d4 + 1 fire elementals
7	1 elder fire elemental[1]
8	1 greater pyrohydra[1]
9	1d4 + 2 efreeti
10	1 adult red dragon or adult brass dragon
11–20	No encounter

Effects of the Phlogiston

Within 100 feet of the Phlogiston, a character takes 16 (3d10) fire damage each round (no save). Within 30 feet of the Phlogiston, a character takes fire damage and also must succeed on a DC 18 Dexterity saving throw each round or catch fire. A character coming into contact with the Phlogiston takes 110 (20d10) fire damage and must succeed on a DC 20 Dexterity saving throw or catch fire. Fire resistance offers protection against the effects of the Phlogiston, while characters immune to fire are completely unharmed.

11. Citadel of the Fire Thane (Surtur's Thane)

Rising mirage-like from the Blasted Land stands this cyclopean fortress of charred iron. Called the Citadel of the Fire Thane, it serves as an outpost to one of Surtur's trusted lieutenants upon the Plane of Molten Skies. Surtur is the main god in fire giant culture, and the patron lord of all fire, flame, smoke, and ash.

A force of 32 fierce **fire giants** — they typically hire themselves out as mercenaries to the Sultan in order to bolster his army and city watch — occupies the fortress and the lands around it. They also frequently work as bodyguards to the various amirs, beys, and pashas who make up the ruling class of the City of Brass.

The smiths of the great forge in the bowels of the citadel work day and night, hammering out huge weapons and armor for trade within the Bazaar of Arms in the City of Brass.

Thane Brihnda[1] rules the citadel. Devastatingly beautiful and unimaginably cruel, she is a daughter of Surtur. Thane Brihnda serves the purposes of her immortal father by ingratiating her servants into the good graces of the Sultan of the City of Brass. Surtur seeks to eventually topple the Sultan, thus furthering his dominion beyond his kingdom in the Elemental Plane of Fire.

The Sultan, of course, has his own designs and seeks instead to dominate Thane Brihnda's heart and mind. He hopes to use her as his means for ensnaring and destroying Surtur and for claiming the divine mantle of fire for himself as well as extending his domain deep into the Elemental Plane of Fire. These deceptions and machinations are very far reaching, so it would not be surprising in the least if they somehow reached the characters.

If the characters can impress Thane Brihnda with their martial prowess, she may give them a *writ of passage*, using them to do her dirty work in removing the Sultan from the throne of the City of Brass. On the other hand, if they catch the Sultan's attention (and survive the experience), he may decide to send them against the fire giants as a distraction while he quietly prepares his army for a full-fledged invasion (though he must first rid himself of the fire giants patrolling the streets of his City).

Treasure: 20,000 gp, 300 pp, sapphire pendant on platinum chain (1,000 gp), 3 brass and platinum goblets with ruby inlay (3,000 gp each), brass idol of Surtur (7,000 gp).

12. Efreeti Outpost

A spiraling fortress of basalt and brass rises against the baked landscape. This fortress serves as an outpost for the efreeti of the City of Brass. The ground floors serve as a feasting hall, kitchen, servants' quarters, and stables. The upper floors house the guard barracks and commanders' quarters. Beneath each tower is a catacomb of passages and chambers that serve as detention areas, armories, and smithies (where djinni slaves forge weapons and armor for the outpost's troops and commanders).

Each outpost is more or less identical in size, structure, and force size. An outpost houses about 30 efreeti troops and a single malik who acts as the outpost commander. Each malik reports to his regional commander (an amir). One amir controls the northern regions of the Plane of Molten Skies, while the other controls the southern region. The amirs are usually found residing at one of the fortress outposts within the area they control.

Most efreeti patrols on the Plane of Molten Skies originate from one of these fortresses.

All djinni slaves are fitted with a brass collar (see **Appendix 4: New Spells**).

13. Xigla Xaltaz, Fortress of the Xill

The xill maintain this fortress on the mud flats just beyond the Black Plain, an effort on their part to covertly observe the activities of the various forces who vie for dominion of the plane's resources and eldritch qualities. The pod-shaped fortress, called Xigla Xaltaz in the rumbling language of the xill, is heavily shielded from the intense heat of the Plane of Molten Skies by various magical protections of xill origin. The fortress has no apparent opening, as the xill who dwell within it simply use their *planewalk* ability to enter and leave. Bands of xill hunters often ambush small groups of travelers from the Ethereal plane, killing most whom they encounter in this manner. They occasionally take prisoners to Xigla Xaltaz for torture, for food, or to be used as slaves.

Fifty **xill**[1] hunters reside in the fortress. They travel the Plane of Molten Skies in hunting gangs of five. These hunting bands are made up of 4 normal xill and one powerful **xill leader**[1]. **Xilyat Xaygon Xill**[1], a large brute of a specimen, commands the fortress with an iron will. He is prone to having his soldiers gather on the plane outside the fortress on a daily basis to listen to him lecture about the xill's manifest destiny. As the months wear on, it is becoming increasingly obvious that Xilyat is insane. He demands more prisoners, hoping to pump them for any and all information on the hated City of Brass. His other primary enemy is Thane Brihnda and her clan of smelly, sulfur-stinking giants, but he is less worried about her than the Sultan. Xilyat doesn't yet know about the Ash-Grinder Arcology on the opposite side of the plane. If he did, he would probably lose his mind entirely. A three-sided war is one with which he cannot cope at this time.

One prisoner recently captured by the fortress's hunters is Hasan bin Hamani, a **burning dervish**[1] (currently at half hit points) merchant who worked for house Quahari. The xill captured Hasan and murdered all his bodyguards as they journeyed back to the City of Brass from the Elemental Plane of Earth. His *writ of passage* — which allowed Hasan and any persons in his company admittance to house Quahari — is currently in the fortress treasury. If provided with the opportunity, Hasan tells the characters that house Quahari is willing to offer 10,000 bp as a reward for his rescue. Other slaves and prisoners inside the fortress are of various races and character classes. Feel free to add any NPCs you feel appropriate or use xill prisoners as replacement characters for any characters that have died.

Hasan bin Hamani does not have any of his possessions (the xill confiscated them when he was captured). His *+1 falchion* (as *+1* *longsword*) and *+1 leather armor* lay in the treasure chamber with the xill's hoard. Hasan is fitted with a pair of xill *inhibitor bands*[2] (clasps around his wrists) that suppress his spell-like abilities, plane shift ability, and ability to assume flame form. The bands are constructed of an unknown metal and require a successful DC 30 Strength check to break.

Treasure: 13,000 gp, 12 smoky quartz (60 gp each), *spell wand*[2] of *enhance ability* (*owl's wisdom*), *cloak of displacement*.

14. Thalana's Lavaquifer

Mournful singing rings through the air long before a person sees the beautiful maiden who appears to be made of smoke and fire sitting atop a steaming stone in the midst of the lava pool. Oily, smoldering tears mar her enchanting face as she sings a sad lament.

Thalana is a **fire nymph**[1]. She is singularly uninterested in combat as she has much more important problems occupying her thoughts at the moment. Wyrthil, an elemental fire dragon, kidnapped her sister Yismina recently. If the characters approach Thalana peacefully, she begs them to rescue her sister. Should they accept her entreaty, she gives them 3 potions of *resistance* (fire), and an *icy burst glaive*[2]. If they take her treasures and do not return with her sister within 4 days, she goes in search of them. If the characters cheat her, and she suspects it or knows it for sure, she enlists the aid of a **greater fire elemental**[1] to get her things back.

Unbeknownst to Thalana, Wyrthil has already sold her sister to the owners of the Purple Veil in the City of Brass. If the characters return to Thalana with this news, she implores them to rescue Yismina and gives the characters a *ring of resistance* (fire) as additional payment. Should the characters succeed in returning Yismina, Thalana gives them a *necklace of frost*[2].

15. The Spire of Hazrad the Mad

This extinct volcanic cone is home to Abul al'Hazrad (**spellbinder**[1]), known more commonly as the Mad Wizard. Al'Hazrad can seldom be found within his fortress, however, as he often wanders the Elemental Plane of Fire in other guises or is off traveling the planes gathering the secrets of the universe. There is a 20% chance that he is actually in the spire. The spire is guarded by a bound **balor** named Velech and a bound **glabrezu** named Azinor.

Dangerous magical and mechanical traps designed to ensnare or destroy outsiders protect al'Hazrad's spire (it's up to you to determine the exact type and number of traps); he is quite paranoid, deathly afraid that demonic and infernal lords, as well as every servant under their command, is stalking him. He has already captured several of these demonic assassins. They are bound by his obscenely powerful magic and set to the task of guarding his abode at all times. Although al'Hazrad is not really evil, he is truly insane. If he is at home, he may invite the characters in only to try to murder them under suspicion of being spies for the demon lords. Or he may just deny them admittance altogether, preoccupied as he is by a horse of a different color.

Al'Hazrad once kept a tome containing all arcane conjuration and abjuration spells known hidden within his inner sanctum sanctorum. A horrible curse on the book requires that all who read from it must make a DC 20 Wisdom saving throw or be struck permanently mad as if by an *confustion* spell. Agents of the sultan of efreet stole this famed tome some years ago. Al'Hazrad offers to give the characters the bound **balor** Velech if they return the tome, though being fully insane, there is a 50% chance that he turns on the characters and attempts to murder them should they succeed, believing them to be agents of the same fiends who tried to destroy him in the past.

Treasure: 20,000 gp, 3 yellow topaz (500 gp each), 14 red garnets (100 gp each), 1 black emerald (1,200 gp).

16. Wyrthil's Lair

Wyrthil the **elemental fire dragon**[1] lives within the bowels of a great volcano known as the Ghoul's Mountain. The volcano is active, and vomits forth smoke, ash, and fire at regular intervals (20% chance per hour that an eruption occurs). See the description under **Features** earlier in the chapter for details on what happens when characters are caught out in the open during a volcanic eruption.

Wyrthil is a vicious predator, often hunting nomadic bands of jann and small bands of travelers. He has been known to capture important-looking individuals and ransom them back to their families or sell them into slavery. Characters seeking Wyrthil in order to rescue the fire nymph Yismina from his clutches may learn that she was sold into slavery at the Purple Veil in the City of Brass if they parlay with him.

Mechanical traps guard the dragon's lair, the most common being covered pit traps and chutes that drop characters into deep pools of red-hot magma. This type of trap can be found with a successful DC 18 Wisdom (Perception) check and the cover jammed in place with a successful DC 16 Dexterity check with thieves' tools. A creature that triggers the trap must succeed on a DC 18 Dexterity saving throw or fall 50 feet into the lava-filled pit. A creature that falls takes 17 (5d6) bludgeoning damage from the fall and 70 (20d6) fire damage per round in the lava and 35 (10d6) fire damage for 1d3 rounds after leaving the lava.

Twenty **lava children**[1] serve Wyrthil. They dive deep into the molten stone beneath his volcanic fortress to pull up the *elemental diamonds*[2] he covets so much. The dragon spends much of his time wallowing in his impressive hoard, enamored by their inherent magic.

Treasure: 27,000 gp, 14 *elemental diamonds*[2], *volcanic longsword*[2], *armor of resistance* (chain mail, fire), *wand of fear*, *gem of seeing*, *bracers of superior defense*[2], *staff of fire*, *potion of vitality*, *potion of resistance* (poison), *oil of paralysis removal*[2].

17. The Salamander Warren

A craggy outcropping of rocks and lava tubes functions as the basis for this outpost of fiery salamanders. They despise the efreet and their ilk, mainly because the efreet are so annoyingly arrogant and bloodthirsty. The Sultan's mad lust to wage war against the King of Salamanders, who rules his own section of the Elemental Plane of Fire, disturbs them greatly. After all, their plane is practically infinite in scope, so they cannot fathom why the Sultan wants their particular piece of territory.

Prince Asmyr (**salamander monarch**[1]) is the master of this salamander listening post on the borderland between the Elemental Plane of Fire and the Plane of Molten Skies. He is a competent sorcerer. Five other **salamander nobles**[1] serve beneath him. Each of one of them has a squad of 10 **salamander** soldiers, whom they use to scout the plane. The salamanders avoid direct confrontation with the Sultan's forces and his various teams of dervish assassins. Other creatures are fair game, however, and the salamanders think nothing of capturing and slaying any they catch snooping around their base. Hidden within the base is a portal that opens directly onto the Salamander King's court on the Plane of Fire, and another portal that leads to **Level 10: The Lava Pit** in *Rappan Athuk* by **Frog God Games**. Both are well-hidden and trapped with an array of runes and spells (they deal no damage to the salamanders).

The prince makes contact with another group of insurgent salamanders embedded inside the City of Brass called the Samaghar. They hail from a different clan, one with a grudge against the Sultan that is even deeper than the one his king bears. The Samaghar have proven themselves time and time again, so he trusts their leaders implicitly.

Treasure: 14,000 gp, 500 pp, 17 fire opals (600 gp each).

18. The Steel Garden

Acrid plumes descend from skies above the plain, burning paths through the flame-drenched sky. Light sputters in mute roars consumed immediately upon issuance by the fury of the sky fires. A canopy of mercurial clouds and fumes of caustic haze drapes over this great metal forest, a dazzling canvas of turgid colors and swirling infernos. The volcanoes scattered throughout the steel jungle erupt continually to contest the anger of the sky. Dragons and other awe-inspiring magical beasts inhabit these burnt skies, soaring through the noxious vapors and wading through the macabre silvered trees, mighty trees whose leaves are made of ultra-fine growing metal, leaves that blow in the fetid breeze and rust in the autumn, swaying trees that lurch up in the inhospitable environment, thriving off the heat and stagnant air.

This is the Steel Garden, and a secretive tribe of fandir (as **commanders**[1] with darkvision 60 ft., Dex 16 (steel elves) known as the Qadir Nizar rules it. By all accounts, the Nizar are regarded as little more than bandits by the efreet Sultan, who covets the living metal growing in this bizarre jungle. Those who enter the garden find the eyes of the Qadir Nizar are always watching them, awaiting some subtle cue from their Steel Mistress to strike with a primal ferocity born of this harsh climate.

Besides the Nizar, several other creatures are indigenous to the Steel Garden, including **bulettes**, **gargoyles**, and poisonous snakes known as **cobalt vipers**[1] with eyes that mirror that of the roiling sky above and whose venom is so deadly that just being in proximity to it can cause death. These serpents slither through the rusted underbrush, carefully stalking their prey. Brass vines tug at leather armor, iron-brush scrapes gashes in boots, and intermittent pathways twist and weave through the dark heart of the forest.

A typical Nizar hunting party consists of 2 archers, 2 swordsmen, and 1 spellcaster (usually a beastshifter[1]). They use the cover of the steel forest to conceal their approach. If their queen orders the death of those trespassing in her metal paradise, they strike swiftly and mercilessly.

The Qadir Nizar number nearly 200 individuals. They are led by the Steel Queen Sunthelia (**heirophant**[1] with darkvision 60 ft. and Str 18), who is said to be a living embodiment of the twisted metal jungle, and as such is immortal for as long as it stands. The Sultan's forces have found it impossible to dislodge the Qadir Nizar from their home, as every raiding party and assault force sent to invade the jungle has been destroyed utterly.

Sunthelia's animal companion is a **dire tiger**[1] named Steelfang. He is by her side at all times.

The Steel Garden Encounters

Roll 1d20 for every hour spent traveling in this area and consult the table below.

1d20	Encounter
1	1d3 + 2 common cobalt vipers[1]
2	1 giant cobalt viper[1]
3	1 elder xorn[1]
4	2 bulettes
5	1 greater earth elemental[1]
6	1d3 + 2 xorn
7	1d12 + 4 gargoyles
8	1d4 + 1 earth elementals
9	1 elder earth elemental[1]
10	Fandir hunting party (2 champion warriors[1], 2 eldritch archers[1], 1 beastshifter[1])
11	1 adult blue dragon
12–20	No encounter

19. The Sea of Fire

The Sea of Fire is an inland sea, except unlike those found on any of the material planes this one is a blasting, roaring, inferno of boiling oil and fire. A portion of it extends into the Plane of Molten Skies, while the majority of it is actually found on the Elemental Plane of Fire. The City of Brass floats upon the Sea of Fire in its great brass bowl and is anchored to the Plane of Molten Skies by an obsidian bridge.

Much of the time, the Sea of Fire is a roiling maelstrom of liquid fire. At other times, it is a calm sea of boiling oil with demi-flames dancing across its surface just waiting to ignite the entire lake. Hundreds of different species of creatures make their home beneath the waves, while other beings make their living plying this vast burning sea gathering raw materials from the Elemental Plane of Fire or bringing trade and piracy to the other demi-planes touched by the sea. The most powerful of the beings sailing its surface are the Fire Sea Corsairs, a band of roving efreet pirates, reavers, and ne'er-do-wells.

Likewise, salamander raiders also dwell deep within the Sea of Fire. They lie waiting to ambush the cogs and caravels of merchants bearing loot-laden cargos to the City of Brass. The salamander raiders take particular delight in hampering or hindering the Fire Sea Corsairs.

The Sea of Fire Random Encounters

Roll 1d20 for every hour spent traveling in this area and consult the table below.

1d20	Encounter
1	1d4 + 1 azer fishermen
2	1 greater fire elemental[1]
3	1 fire whale[1]
4	1d4 + 1 fire elementals
5	1 elder fire elemental[1]
6	1 adult red dragon
7	Salamander pirates
8	1d4 + 1 volcano giant[1] fishermen
9	Salamander traders
10	Fire Sea Corsairs (burning dervishes[1])
11–20	No encounter

Fire Sea Corsairs: An average-sized fleet consists of 2d4 galleys, 3d4 oil skimmers, and 1 warship. The crew consists of **burning dervishes**[1] who oversee the enslaved rowers. All answer to the captain of each ship (an **efreeti** with maximum hit points).

Salamander Pirates: A roving band of pirates in a seized corsair galley. The crew consists of 5d4 + 10 **salamanders** led by their captain (a **salamander noble**[1]).

Salamander Traders: A small fleet of galleys hauling goods and slaves. Each galley has 10 crewmen (**salamanders**), a retinue of slaves that function as rowers, and a **salamander noble**[1] captain.

Effects of the Sea of Fire

A creature making physical contact with liquid fire takes 33 (6d10) fire damage and must succeed on a DC 15 Dexterity saving throw or catch fire. A creature who is on fire takes 4 (1d8) fire damage until an action is used to put it out. A creature foolish enough to submerge itself in liquid flame or swim in liquid fire takes 110 (20d10) fire damage for each round of contact. Magical protection reduces the damage, and creatures immune to fire do not take damage, but can still drown if they sink beneath the surface.

Creatures swimming in areas where the oils of the Sea of Fire are unlit take 17 (5d6) fire damage per round if completely submerged or 3 (1d6) fire damage from being splashed with the boiling oil.

The Fire Sea Corsairs

The Fire Sea Corsairs are burning dervishes[1] that sail in brass-plated galleys under an efreeti captain across the rolling flames and burning oils of the Sea of Fire. Most of their ships possess some sort of magical shielding to protect their rowers, hulls, and sails from the intense heat emanating off the water. Corsairs frequently make forays into the Elemental Plane of Fire to hunt the Salamander King's privateers and trade ships. Corsair captains often purchase foreign slaves from the Slave Bazaar in the City of Brass to row their great vessels. Life is short aboard these vessels as the brutal efreeti captains and their burning dervish crewmen achieve new levels of cruelty and contempt.

The Corsairs are separated into three distinct types, each of which is responsible for different tasks:

The Corsairs of Transport: These are used to transport slaves and living brass collected on missions on the Sea of Fire. These monstrous vessels can carry up to 150 tons of cargo over large distances, primarily because of strong magical enhancements placed on the hull by the Sultan's wizards. If the need arises, these galleys can be used to transport up to 200 medium creatures with enough provisions to last one month.

A full galley crew consists of one captain, 10 overseers, and as many as 50 rowers. The rowers are generally azer slaves who are made to row until they drop from fatigue, at which point they are replaced by a backup and allowed one hour to rest. Many azer slaves have rowed themselves to death on journeys that were meant to collect more slaves.

The Corsairs of Travel: Their small sizes and unique hulls allow them to travel swiftly over the fiery sea. These skimmers also perform as scouts, and usually a patrol group of ten travels in a predetermined route in order to keep an eye out for invaders. If such an invasion occurs, then the skimmers first notify the commanders of the Corsairs of Arms. Each skimmer is equipped with a ballista.

The Corsairs of Arms: This is the Sultan's fleet of warships. They remain docked most of the time unless called upon to defend the city against attacks from the Sultan's numerous enemies. Each warship is nearly 150 feet long, has a single gargantuan mast, and is propelled by up to 250 rowers. The bow of each warship boasts a heavy catapult that can take aim at any target in front of the ship. Two ballistae are on the port and starboard sides of the ship, each of which can take aim at any target on their respective sides. A typical crew consists of one captain (efreeti), 3 burning dervish wizards[1], 6 burning dervish guards[1], and 250 burning dervish[1] rowers. These vessels can, if the need arises, carry up to 50 additional soldiers, but only with enough provisions for one week.

The hulls of the warships and galleys are composed of living brass, making them resistant to the heat of the Sea of Fire and also capable of repairing themselves at the rate of 1d4 hit points per hour.

20. Hall of the Vulcan Lords

Deep within the recesses of an active volcano located near the shores of the Sea of Fire, a network of interwoven tunnels and subterranean caves houses a tribe of **volcano giants**[1]. The tribe consists of 15 adult males and 5 adult females. A powerful warrior chieftain, **Ahi Mau Haka**[1], lords over them.

The volcano giants spend their leisure time fishing on the banks of the Fire Sea. On occasion, small hunting bands use fireproof canoes to maneuver across the sea in order to find the best fishing spots. Other activities include hurling volcanic rocks at ships or creatures in or on the Sea of Fire (though they do not hurl such rocks at the Fire Sea Corsairs or other efreet for fear of incurring the wrath of the Sultan).

The giants despise the salamander raiders that live in the sea, as they have lost more than one canoe and hunting party to their trickery and evil. Volcano giants attack the salamanders in the Sea of Fire on sight. Those that are slain are carried back to the giants' lair, where their hides are used to make clothes or household decorations.

Treasure: 19,000 gp, 1,100 pp, 22 rose quartz (70 gp each), 5 star rubies (1,000 gp each), 5 tanned salamander hides.

21. Bazaar of Beggars

See **Chapter 11** for information on the Bazaar of Beggars.

22. Caverns of Abdul-Shihab

The cracked ground in this area covers a well-hidden trapdoor that opens to a set of blackened stairs winding down. Finding the trapdoor requires a successful DC 24 Wisdom (Perception) check. The stairs end in a large chamber of blackened rock with hallways venturing off to the north and south. The hallways in turn lead to many interconnected underground passages and chambers. Most all of the passages and rooms are coated (walls, ceilings, and floors) with a 6-inch layer of molten brass to prevent trespassers not immune to fire from wandering around down here. The entire complex is hot, and characters spending any time down here are subjected to the effects of extreme heat. Touching the walls, ceilings, or floors deals 7 (2d6) fire damage per round of contact. Each hour in the tunnels, a creature must succeed on a DC 16 Constitution saving through or gain one level of exhaustion.

This underground network of passages and rooms serves as the base of operations for the Abdul-Shihab, the Servants of Flame. The cult is relatively new (in elemental terms) and consists of many like-minded individuals of varying races who all have one thing in common — their dislike of non-fire creatures, particularly creatures from the various material planes. To Abdul-Shihab, such creatures are trespassers and interlopers and are unwelcome for they jeopardize the balance of the planes and the way of life of the denizens of the Plane of Fire. Likewise, creatures aiding or befriending such interlopers are despised as well, perhaps even more. Abdul-Shihab's ultimate goal is to close all portals leading to the other elemental planes and the material planes, thereby sealing the planes to creature not of the Plane of Fire.

Abdul-Shihab's members consist of **azers, salamanders**, a few **fire giants**, some **efreet** (including one or more noble houses of the City of Brass), and various other fire races. Flame-spawned and cheitans[1] are not accepted as members; both are considered an abomination and are killed whenever possible. Likewise, burning dervishes are shunned for their racial heritage and their beliefs (most of them anyway).

Abdul-Shihab members despise the Sultan of the Efreet and would like to see him killed. Accordingly, while enmity exists between this cult and the burning dervishes, they sometimes work together to accelerate the downfall and destruction of the Sultan. Such alliances are extremely short-lived at best. Other alliances with like-minded earth and air elementals exist, but they too are generally short-lived. Abdul-Shihab never associates with creatures of elemental water.

To the general populace of the City of Brass and the surrounding planes, Abdul-Shihab is relatively unknown. They would like to change this in the near future, however. Recent activities include waylaying travelers, kidnapping of a prestigious member of a noble house of the City of Brass (the noble was eventually ransomed back to the family), and the burning of various tents within the Bazaar of Beggars. As their numbers grow and expand, their activities are likely to increase as well.

The current leader of the Abdul-Shihab is Sabir Qudamah, a **salamander monarch**[1] of great strength and evil.

Characters wandering the halls here are very likely to encounter several members of Abdul-Shihab.

Caverns of Abdul-Shihab
Random Encounters

Roll 1d20 for every 5 minutes spent in the passages and chambers.

1d20	Encounter
1	2d4 + 2 azers
2	2d4 azers, plus salamander

1d20	Encounter
3–4	1d4 + 2 salamanders
5	1d4 salamanders plus 1 noble[1]
6	2d4 efreet
7	1d4 fire giants
8	Sabir Qudamah (salamander monarch[1]) plus 1d3+1 salamanders
9–20	No encounter

23. The Obsidian Bridge (Kubri al Azim)

The Obsidian Bridge, or Kubri al Azim, is a massive 20-mile-long bridge of solid obsidian that stretches out like a blackened tongue from the last chunk of solid earth upon the Plane of Molten Skies toward a burnished brass bowl floating upon a sea of boiling oil off in the horizon. Towering over the lip of the brass bowl, gleaming minarets and glittering jeweled domes appear to shimmer like a mirage upon the horizon.

Here, the sky appears to have an almost greenish tinge to it, as if alchemical fire licks the very edges of the sky with its curious light. An almost endless stream of travelers makes its way to and from the Obsidian Bridge; many appear from thin air in front of the bridge itself before turning toward the brass bowl and determinedly making their pilgrimage to the city of wonders, flame, and death.

Wealthy petitioners usually cross the bridge riding in ornate sedans as large as houses. They are so large, in fact, that they require the services of the enigmatic **tusk lords**[1] to carry them. The tusk lords are towering, intelligent elephants that hail originally from a world destroyed ages ago. Only a dozen of these creatures are left in all the realms of existence: Six work the eastern end of the bridge, while the other six work the western end. As they carry petitioners on their backs to the City of Brass, they chant in an unknown language, their voices deep and rumbling. The reasons for their service here are unknown. Perhaps they owe a great debt to the residents of the Plane of Molten Skies. Or, as some people speculate, they are the last of Aspsis's hierophants. Whatever the case maybe, one thing is certain: everyone, including the Sultan, leaves them alone.

Wealthy petitioners pay a nominal fee of 2,000 gp per person for the privilege of jumping ahead in line. An efreeti "tax" collector stationed at the entrance of the bridge receives the gold. The fee for riding on the tusker sedans is another 3,000 gp per person.

The tusk lords treasure whale songs. If one can present a tusker with a reasonable facsimile or reproduction of one, it grants the person who gives it to them a single *wish*. Only one wish will ever be granted to a single character in its lifetime.

As the characters approach the City of Brass, the immensity of its structures undoubtedly fills them with a sense of awe, wonderment, and dread — it affects everyone that way, even the exalted gods, as they see its shining towers and demonic gates reach high into the molten sky. The line before them seems choked with visitors and diplomats cut from every cloth and description. Strangely formed denizens of the lower planes here on the official business of their archduke or demon lord travel the same bridge as powerful arch mages and high priests. Turbaned jann and burning dervish merchants drive throngs of porters and bearers hauling goods from a dozen planes for trade and barter among the city's many bazaars. Most that travel this bridge walk its long expanse. Others are borne upon exquisite sedan chairs hauled by a dozen slaves.

The throngs of slaves and prisoners to be offered to the Sultan are driven before their masters with the lash or by some unseen command. Plodding ever closer to the gargantuan spires and leering gates of the city of the efreet, a great rasping moan like that rising from split lips and parched throats can be heard on the wind.

Once across the Kubri al Azim, petitioners stand before the Bab al Baquarra (or Great Gatehouse).

24. The Blackened Range

Against all odds, this arm of earth extends from the Elemental Plane of Earth straight into the Plane of Molten Skies, where incredible fires blast its surface to no avail. In fact, neither scorching flames nor shuddering earthquakes can bring it down. Moreover, because the range has an extremely high carbon content, it is uniformly colored an unusual silvery-black and many of its boulders are roughshod plated with a form of naturally occurring chrome.

The Blackened Range possesses few natural types of flora or fauna, and most encounters are with creatures of the earth subtype.

The Blackened Range Random Encounters

Roll 1d20 every hour spent in this area.

1d20	Encounter
1	1d3 + 1 xorn
2	1d3 bone devils
3	1 greater earth elemental[1]
4	1d4 + 1 earth elementals
5	1d8 + 4 gargoyles
6	1d3 + 2 xorn
7	1 elder earth elemental[1]
8	1d4 + 1 stone giants
9	1d4 fire giants
10	1 adult blue dragon or copper dragon
11–20	No encounter

25. The Sulfur Mountains

This squat range of mountains consists mostly of active volcanoes. They constantly belch forth sepia-colored sulfur vapors, roiling black clouds of ash, and bright burning lava. Traveling through the Sulfur Mountains is an extremely risky endeavor. The land never stands still for an instant. At any given time, at least one volcano is in the process of erupting. If the quakes don't kill travelers, then the ash and lava undoubtedly will. For all the dangers these mountains are fraught with, they are home to a variety of monsters that include fire elementals, magmoids[1], fire giants, ash specters (creatures killed in the Sulfur Mountains by ash or volcanic activity), red dragons, lava children[1], and a multitude of other ash and fire creatures.

Sulfur Mountains Random Encounters

Roll 1d20 for every hour spent in this area.

1d20	Encounter
1	1d2 magmoids[1]
2	1d3 specters
3	1d3 + 3 lava children[1]
4	1 greater fire elemental[1]
5	1d4 + 1 fire elementals
6	1d4 + 3 burning dervishes
7	1 elder fire elemental[1]
8	1d2 + 2 hawanar[1]
9	1d4 fire giants
10	1 adult red dragon
11–20	No encounter

26. Hecate's Fathom

Eons ago, a vast expanse of water populated with all manner of fertile life covered this part of the plane. Though it was an insignificant outcropping from the Elemental Plane of Water, it was highly regarded as one of the few truly tranquil places on the Plane of Molten Skies. One of the few exceptions to this seemingly preternatural tranquility was an area known as "Hecate's Fathom," a stretch of water notorious for swallowing ships in their entirety, never to be seen again. It lay at the heart of the most heavily traversed sea-lane. Storm clouds often occluded its skies, monstrous sea creatures assaulted many an incautious ship, and indecipherable, infernal magic often played havoc with local reality. In short, it was a devil's playground and any sailor worth his salt knew better than to take his ship across it. Yet, there were always those captains who thought they could outrun Hecate's wrath, pressing their luck despite the horror stories and sailing across the Fathom in vain attempts to beat their competition to port. Few ever made it out alive, and those who did rarely did so with their sanity intact.

No one knows when or how the sea dried up. Today, this landscape is as harsh and as inhospitable as it is dry, populated only by roving bands of undead (those who drowned in the Fathom) and by priests from the Seekers of the Ebony Moon[1].

The Seekers of the Ebony Moon[1] who now claim these lands believe Hecate drowned Marduk at the bottom of the Fathom, hiding his body in an impossibly deep canyon where none would ever find it again. The story goes on to describe how Enki banished Hecate to the moon and then swallowed the sea as he sought his son's body. Only dusty-robed desert sages and nomad storytellers remember the tale at all, and even then, most do not take it too seriously. The ship graveyard buried at the center of the desert, however, is a testament to its veracity. The Seekers maintain a single fortress of rock and stone located somewhere in the heart of this wasteland. From here, they await the return of Hecate and during the full moon make blood sacrifices to her (believing such sacrifices will hasten her return). Hellhounds, being the favored animals of Hecate, freely roam the grounds of the Seeker's fortress temple. The high priest is a mysterious figure of unknown power who never ventures forth from the temple. His lesser priests and agents often journey to the Bazaar of Beggars or the City of Brass.

Hecate's Fathom lay safely buried under the sand until recently, when a massive sandstorm uncovered a small part of it. The skeletal remains of hundreds of ships jut from the sand, and the undead of everyone who drowned in that part of the Fathom haunt it. Desert wanderers and itinerant adventurers often find themselves in the midst of the Fathom before they realize they were somehow pulled off course.

Hecate's Fathom Random Encounters

Roll 1d20 for every hour spent in this area.

1d20	Encounter
1	10 zombies
2	1d4 + 1 wights
3	1d2 ghasts plus 1d6 + 6 ghouls
4	1 shadow captain[1]
5	1d6 + 5 shadows
6	1d2 + 2 specters
7	1d6 + 4 mummies
8	1d4 Seekers of the Ebony Moon[1] plus 1d4 hellhounds
9	1d6 + 5 wraiths
10	1d2 + 2 mohrgs
11–20	No encounter

27. Queen of the Serpent People

One thousand years ago, the serpent people who lived in this area went insane. Their queen, a beautiful serpentine humanoid named Liithkii built an army the likes of which rivaled that of the City of Brass. Rather than invade the efreeti home as many expected, she instead opened a magic portal inside a continent-sized fortress on a remote plane ruled by arcane-warriors. Her snakeman warriors were charged with finding the lord of the realm, a pale, straw-haired man known only as the Wicker King. The battle between her people and his lasted exactly seven hours. The Wicker King's high mages sent a minor artifact back through the portal to explode, completely destroying the serpent people's lands. Reverberations from the explosion were felt across the entire plane. When the Sultan learned of what had happened, he sent three platoons of his most elite troops into the Wicker King's lands, permanently sealing the portal behind them. While he never bore any love for the Serpent Queen or her people's disturbing preoccupation with the chemical arts, he could not tolerate the existence of an enemy people capable of damaging his world with such impudence and ease. Six weeks after the Sultan's troops entered the enemy world, the Wicker King and the walls fortifying his continent fell.

These days, all that's left of the serpent people's once impressive empire is a horribly scarred, magic-blasted plain. Standing at its exact center is the petrified form of the Serpent Queen. The Sultan resurrected her and transformed her into a monument, a reminder to him and others. The twisted, winding statue stands 500 feet high. The queen's body is approximately 100 feet thick. Over the centuries, many creatures and peoples have covertly dug homes from her stone flesh, cave dwellings camouflaged from casual sight with canvas and wood. Serpent folk from other worlds (primarily benign, good-hearted serpent fairies) who have heard the story of the queen's dead empire often make pilgrimages to the statue to pay their respects. No less than six temples can be found inside the stone queen's various hollowed-out appendages. A small temple populated by 30 gem-encrusted **gargoyles** inhabits the queen's head. The gargoyles are mendicant priests, strangely enough, who devote their lives to sustaining the One Song of Existence (a droning chant they can never let stop, for they fear that if they do so, existence will end altogether).

28. The Plains of Kush

On the western side of the Plane of Molten Skies, bands of roaming horse lords reign. They are a tribe of grim-faced, steely-eyed humans, allegedly descendants of the great King Kush who was destroyed during his foolish war with Sulymon. The horse lords' ancestors were the only surviving refugees of the slaughter. As the centuries fell by the wayside, they built a new civilization for themselves. Many powerful beings on the plane, namely Ilgomaxag the Dust Wyrm, still have long memories regarding King Kush, and have stopped at nothing to hunt down his progeny. As a result, Kush society became nomadic. They are always on the move, always one step ahead of their enemies. Their powerful, muscular horses transformed gradually over the generations into the tall, proud, noble beasts they are today, the **kathlin**[1]. This special breed of 6-legged horses possesses immunity to fire. The kathlin of the horse lords are so renowned across the multiple layers of the splintered universe now that traders come from all over just to purchase them from the horse lords. (Horse lord traders typically sell a kathlin mount for 2,400 gp or more.)

The Plains of Kush are covered with a fine, hairy coat of ashen wheat, the grain that sustains the horse lords and their steeds. It is dry and a deep jet black in appearance. Though it might seem brittle to the touch, ashen wheat is difficult to free from its earth moorings much less cut. Stone stelae that mark the territories of individual horse lords rise intermittently from the hazy, wavering landscape. The nomads (as **spy** and see below) are quite unforgiving of trespassers. Only those with permission of one of the horse lords (as **bandit lord**[1] and see below) may cross the plains here. Trespassing usually receives an immediate death sentence. A few clever individuals have managed to talk their way out of such punishment.

Horse lord encampments are constantly on the move. While they don't usually wage war against one another, when the oases begin drying up, the pressure for decent watering holes grows too great and they cannot help it. The horse lords are a patriarchal society. Women are expected to serve and be utterly obedient. Any transgression is enough to warrant death at the hands of a Kush male. The Kush trade hides and meat of the plains animals they hunt to the Splinter-Rock clan of stone giants for steel and granite.

Typical Kush nomads have heat resistance which grants them advantage on Constitution saving throws to avoid damage from heat dangers. There are also all proficient in Survival. Otherwise, they follow the rules for normal humans.

Random encounters on the plains are with Kush nomads and horse lords. These warriors keep their lands well patrolled and clear of monsters.

29. The Gulgomak Mountains

This range of jagged and sharp mountains stretches across the landscape resembling upward-curved stone daggers in many places. The northern portion of the mountains is dotted with portals and gates connecting to the Plane of Elemental Earth. There is no natural flora or fauna found in the Gulgomak Mountains, but random encounters with denizens from the Plane of Earth are not uncommon.

Gulgomak Mountains Random Encounters

Roll 1d20 every hour spent in this area.

1d20	Encounter
1	1d3 + 1 xorn
2	1d3 bone devils
3	1 greater earth elemental[1]
4	1d4 + 1 earth elementals
5	1d8 + 4 gargoyles
6	1d3 + 2 xorn plus 1 elder xorn[1]
7	1 elder earth elemental[1]
8	1d4 + 1 stone giants
9	1 adult blue dragon or copper dragon
10–20	No encounter

The Stone Tablet

This tablet was constructed and engraved by ancient priests who served Grashnak. The tablet measures 10 inches wide, 15 inches tall, and 2 inches thick. Covering its surface are runes inscribed in Terran. A character deciphering and reading the runes (taking 1 minute to fully read them all) gains a permanent +2 bonus on all Strength checks, checks using mason's tools, and on Charisma checks made to influence earth creatures.

29-1. Temple of the Stone Maidens

Within a secluded cave that requires a successful DC 18 Wisdom (Perception) check to notice, dwells a group of 4 **stone maidens**[1], beautiful female elementals formed of living rock. Their features are exquisite and well-defined, seemingly carved by delicate hands. The cave in which the stone maidens dwell is an ancient shrine dedicated to Grashnak, one of the Elemental Earth Lords. The stone maidens remain here as guardians and protectors (even though the temple is no longer in use). The shrine itself is a large multi-chambered series of caves carved into the mountains. The largest chamber houses the main worship area and is dominated by a crumbling stone altar. Upon the altar lies a stone tablet, flanked on either side by a stone candelabrum. See the sidebox for a description of the stone tablet.

The stone maidens jealously guard this temple. Any creature entering this area and paying homage to Grashnak is unmolested. Creatures defiling the area or touching the stone tablet are immediately attacked.

Treasure: Under a pile of rocks and debris behind the crumbling altar is a rotted leather sack containing 600 gp and 3 amethysts (150 gp each). Near the sack is a *wand of magic missiles*.

30. Plains of Smoke

This area is a blackened plain of soot and earth. It is a bleak, flat, featureless land. Puffs of smoke rise from the ground at random intervals and blacken the sky above. Overall, this area is dark and clouded, and the sky above is thick with smoke. As a traveler nears the east, the smoke begins to clear and gives way to a shearing wall of elemental fire. Travelers journeying southwest find the smoke turns to wisps of fog and eventually dissipates all together. The ground likewise gives way to air as one nears the Elemental Plane of Air.

The smoke covering this area usually remains close to the ground and is generally thin and breathable, but it obscures vision beyond 20 feet. Creatures more than 20 feet away are heavily obscured.

Characters adventuring here are likely to encounter one or more of the area's inhabitants or natural features. Encounters in this area include cinder ghouls[1], smoke mephits[1], smoke elementals[1], smoke giants[1], air pockets, holocaust portals, incendiary clouds, and smoke clouds. See the Random Encounters table.

Within the Plains of Smoke lies the Tempest of Embers.

Plains of Smoke Random Encounters

Roll 1d20 for every hour spent traveling in this area and consult the table below.

1d20	Encounter
1	Smoke cloud
2	2d4 smoke elementals[1]
3	2d4 smoke mephits[1]
4	Incendiary cloud
5	Holocaust portal
6	1d2 flame-spawned dire bears[+]
7	1d4 + 1 salamanders

1d20	Encounter
8	1d4 greater air elementals[1]
9	1d4 greater fire elementals[1]
10	1d2 + 2 belkers[1]
11	2d4 smoke giants[1]
12	1d4 + 2 cinder ghouls[1]
13	Air pocket
14–20	No encounter

[1] Immune to fire damage, add 1d6 fire damage to successful attack, and creature within 5 feet of creature takes 3 (1d6) fire damage at the start of its turn.

Air Pocket: Relative to the darkness common to the Plains of Smoke, an air pocket appears as a light gray, almost translucent cloud of billowing air or steam. An average air pocket covers a 10-foot area. It is immobile. Some air pockets contain portals to the Elemental Plane of Air. Anyone stepping into a space covered by an air pocket has a 25% chance of being immediately transported to that plane. The two-way portal inside an air pocket remains open for 10 minutes.

Holocaust Portal: This appears as an immobile, hovering globe of bright yellow light. If a creature approaches within 10 feet of a globe, it explodes, dealing 35 (10d6) fire damage to all creatures and objects within a 20-foot radius. There is a 20% chance after a globe explodes that it opens a portal to the Elemental Plane of Fire. Anyone stepping through the portal is instantly transported to that plane. The two-way portal remains open for 10 minutes.

Incendiary Cloud: This cloud of roiling smoke is shot through with white-hot embers. Each round it moves 10 feet in a random direction. A creature that starts its turn within the 20-foot radius of the cloud or enters the area on its turn must attempt a DC 16 Dexterity saving throw, taking 21 (6d6) fire damage on a failure and half as much on a success. The area within the cloud is heavily obscured.

Smoke Cloud: A smoke cloud is a billowing cloud of black smoke. A typical smoke cloud is 20 feet high and covers a 20-foot area. It moves along the ground at a speed of 10 feet. Creatures caught in a smoke cloud must succeed on a DC 20 Constitution saving throw or take 7 (2d6) points of Constitution damage immediately. Additionally, those failing a second DC 20 Constitutin saving throw 1 minute later take another 3 (1d6) points of Constitution damage. Those who succeed on either saving throw are nonetheless disabled by coughing and choking (treat as stunned) for 2d6 rounds. A smoke cloud obscures vision as a *fog cloud* does.

30-1. Tempest of Embers

This is a gigantic windstorm filled with swirling and burning bits of elemental fire. The tempest is unmoving and unyielding, affecting anything that enters this area as a Material Plane tornado does. Any creature within the tempest trying to remain still or move with the wind must succeed on a DC 30 Strength check. On a failure, the creature is knocked prone, slid 30 feet, and takes 7 (2d6) bludgeoning damage. A creature attempting to move against the wind has disadvantage on the check. Additionally, creatures and objects caught in the tempest take 14 (4d6) fire damage each round until they are expelled or escape.

31. The Oasis of Mukphat the Blind

This small unusual oasis is surrounded by a copse of hearty coconut trees. Beyond the coconut trees and the thick, coarse grasses that grow among them is a rather small patch of wet looking sand. Several inches under the sand is fresh potable water, unusual in the extreme for a place such as this.

A small herd of camels sits lazily munching the grasses. Near the edge of the wet sand stands a small sandstone shrine perhaps 10 feet wide by 5 feet high with greenish bronze door. Sitting before the shrine is an old toothless camel herder wearing a gray turban and smoking from a rather long pipe. The camel herder is Durb (**greater commoner**[1]). He serves as guardian of the shrine for which the oasis is named and has done so for as long as he can remember.

Mukphat was a high priest of Anumon who displeased Iblis during his reign and was blinded for questioning the judgment of the first ruler of the City of Brass. It seems that Mukphat had said of Iblis "I have seen much that is wrong with your method of rule, sire." To which Iblis replied, "And you shall see no more that displeases you," before plucking the priest's eyes out with his own hands. He then cast Mukphat out into the wastes that would become the Plane of Molten Skies.

There Mukphat remained for many decades, gathering a following of those genies who had become dissatisfied with the cruelty of Iblis' rule. Mukphat was buried here within this shrine. A cistern was placed beneath his corpse to collect his body's precious waters so that they may feed those who had a thirst for the truth.

Few know of this strange oasis and most efreet who know of it shun the place for its bad luck and the reminder of Mukphat's warning to Iblis before he was cast down. Durb knows a bit of the tale of Mukphat but does not allow entry into the shrine (nor will its door open) unless a riddle he was trained to remember is first solved.

The Riddle of Mukphat

I am triumvirate in my many faces. My works may tear down even the mightiest of mountains and lay waste the oldest of temples. In their place do I allow life to thrive. I seek always to join my many disparate parts no matter which of my faces I choose to reveal. No solvent is stronger than me, nor is there any glue which may bind me, though I may be contained and manipulated by those who know my secret. Who am I?

The answer, of course, is "water" and its many attributes. Easy enough, and should the answer be given, Durb steps aside and the bronze portal opens.

Note: Should the players fail the riddle but really work at it, allow one or two party members to make Intelligence checks (against DC 18) or other die rolls to keep your gaming session moving along. Nothing is worse than three hours of game time spent frustrated over a riddle or other puzzle that the players find too difficult.

Should the characters for some reason attempt to attack poor Durb and force their way into the shrine or achieve entrance by some other means (such as *teleport*, *passwall*, etc.), the ground begins to rumble. An **elder water elemental**[1] then erupts from the sand and moves to defend Durb, as the old man's camels transform into 6 **androsphinxes**. To put it mildly, the battle is on.

Tomb of Mukphat

Within the sandstone shrine stands a large sarcophagus whose lapis lazuli lid is carved in the likeness of a 10-foot-tall man wearing a turban affixed with the symbol of Anumon. A larger symbol of Anumon rests upon his breast between his folded hands. The sarcophagus stands on four bronze pillars beneath which lies a small silver cistern. Ever so slowly, water drips from a tiny hole carved in the bottom of the sarcophagus, catching in the cistern with an audible splash. As the water overflows the cistern, it rolls gently down four golden channels branching from the sides of the receptacle before disappearing down holes a mere two inches in diameter that eventually feed the oasis beyond.

There is enough of the pure blue water in the cistern to fill one small flask. Water outside of the cistern is merely normal water. Water inside the cistern is a special liquid derived from the blessed waters of Mukphat the blind. Once these waters have been collected, it takes 100 years for the cistern to produce enough water to again fill a flask.

> ### Water of Mukphat
>
> The water grants the power of *resurrection* when poured upon any body, piece of a body, undead, or portion of once-living matter. The water cannot however restore life to that which has died from old age.

Chapter 11
The Bazaar of Beggars

The Bazaar is located at **Area 21** on the Plane of Molten Skies map. The area is detailed in the ***Bazaar of Beggars*** map.

The Bazaar

Located on the scorching plains just beyond the bridge leading to the City of Brass, this sprawling, ramshackle collection of tents is where those queued up waiting to be admitted to the city can purchase much needed supplies or take a respite from their journey. The lines of slaves, slavers, knowledge seekers, adventurers, and those who are simply lost move exquisitely slow. Some say it can take years to be allowed admittance (with the obvious exception of diplomats, and their families and entourages), while others are admitted within minutes of arrival, especially if they carry a *writ of passage*. Regardless, there will always be those who cannot get inside in a timely manner, and this bazaar caters to their needs.

The bazaar is a mile long and one-and-a-half miles wide. The queue for the city runs through it via a winding, and at times confusing, 50-foot-wide lane known to the bazaar's residents as "The Highway of the Damned." Slaves are not allowed to step off it lest their masters whip them to death. Leaving the road is a good way to lose one's place in line, and experienced travelers do not do it. Fortunately, hundreds of stalls line the roadway, turning it into a hellish gallery where anything can be bought, sold, or traded, though at such exorbitant prices it drives many would-be customers into debt and slavery if they are not careful. A person who doesn't mind paying the high prices can hire a professional placeholder to stand in line while she or he enters into the bazaar's confusing interior. Placeholders gladly work for their clients until they reach the Obsidian Bridge, at which point the fire giant guards turn them away if their clients have not yet returned to resume their own march toward the city.

The bazaar's thousands of tents exhibit an incredible range of styles, shapes, colors, and functions from almost as many worlds. One of the few exceptions is the regional office for the Bureau of Taxation. While the city does not officially have authority over the bazaar, few of the people living here have the wherewithal to argue with the efreeti and fire giant tax collectors. The building is made from a block of weathered basalt standing three stories high. The senior-most official working in it is a beautiful woman named Lady Fatima Umau. Her soldiers make weekly rounds through the crowded bazaar demanding "expatriate tax" from the tents; if nobody pays for a particular tent, they simply burn it to the ground.

Smoke from cooking fires, forges, and incense tents constantly drifts through the narrow alleys, lending it a hazy patina. The myriad scents filling the air are exotic, mostly unfamiliar, and sometimes homey. The sounds of haggling and money exchanging hands fill the air. Sahoduin nomads from one of the material planes work as enforcers, keeping the law, and generally trying to prevent the whole place from falling into utter anarchy. Because they are an extremely patient people, slow to anger or take offense, people generally don't bear them any resentment, despite the unpleasant job they perform. The Sahoduin keep to themselves in their own camps south of the bazaar when not on duty. Camels, workhorses, donkeys, bulls, and oxen are kept in public corrals, their dung collected, dried, and later sold for fuel. At night, after the shopkeepers close up, large public tents become packed with people looking for a good time. Alcohol, though proscribed by the local religion,

may be consumed in these tents with impunity, hookahs for smoking tobacco and other addictive (often dangerous) substances may be rented, and veiled dancing girls may be hired for private performances. Meanwhile, the garish and noisy Beyanni clan tents are the places to go for playing games and gambling if one can afford the steep entry fee. Finally, exotic music from a many a tent, public and private, gently intermingles with the other sounds of nightlife in the bazaar.

The vast majority of the bazaar's residents either speak a harsh, guttural form of Terran, a consonant-laden version of Ignan, or a headache-inducing pidgin mixture of both.

To the obsidian bridge
and the City of Brass
Bazaar of Beggars
1 Square - 40 Feet
Smoke Tents
Water-Maker Tent
10
11
5
4
7
7
1
3
8
2
The Highway of
the Damned
6
N
9

Bazaar of Beggars
Random Tents and Stalls

Use the table below to randomly determine the nearby tents and stalls as the characters explore the bazaar.

1d20	Type of Tent/Stall
1	Basket weaver
2	Moneychanger
3	Bordello
4	Leather goods
5	Cartographer
6	Fruits and vegetables or smoked and dried meats
7	Rugs
8	Mounts (horses and camels)
9	Gemstones and jewelry
10	Herbalist

1d20	Type of Tent/Stall
11	Potter
12	Rope maker
13	Lamp and oil
14	Barber
15	Animal trainer or furrier
16	Water-maker (**cult fanatic**) or **smoke merchant**[1]
17	Tattooist
18	Healer
19	Metalsmith
20	Fortuneteller or scribe

1. The Mendicants' Chapter House

The largest and most successful mercantile guild (if it can be called that) is an organization of professional beggars, cripples, pickpockets, snatch-

satchels, cat burglars, lepers, and whores known simply as the Mendicants. Their main meeting spot is a burned-out part of the bazaar where an elemental mage once had a nasty run-in with the Sahoduin peacekeepers. It is widely believed his and the dead peacekeepers' ghosts haunt the area, and no one wants to anger them by erecting new tents in it. This story isn't true. The beggars began spreading the rumor soon after the battle so they could claim the lot. They turned the long adobe stable building that survived the blaze into their chapter house. Gordon the Mouse, a blind pickpocket, leads the Mendicants, styling himself the "Pontiff of Poverty." Gordon the Mouse uses the statistics of the **housebreaker**[1], save that he has blindsight out to 60 feet, as the result of rigorous training (or, depending on whom one asks, an expensive treatment bestowed on him by a spellcaster). Ranks in the guild are fashioned after religious titles from the region's churches. His two lieutenants are Haru Yoro (**performer**[1]), a human bard, and Burgundy Rose, a **half-ogre enforcer**[1] who specializes in collecting protection money. No other illegal organization in the bazaar has as much clout as the ubiquitous beggars. They are masters at blending in, at obsequiousness, and at disappearing into the maze of tents when trouble (or Lady Umau) comes calling.

The chapter house is divided into 4 large rooms: the altar, where the guild holds its general assemblies; the baptismal, a ritual magic chamber for initiating new recruits; the pontiff's quarters, where Gordon and his 2 lieutenants reside; and the bishop's quarters, used by everyone else as a common dormitory.

The Well

The guild wealth lies at the bottom of an old well in the courtyard. It was destroyed in the fire and subsequently covered. Now, it looks like any other part of the burned-out landscape. Finding the cover requires a successful DC 25 Wisdom (Perception) check. It is locked and trapped. Furthermore, every 10 feet of the 70-foot-deep shaft is also trapped. A person who does not know the proper sequence of keystones to press undoubtedly has a difficult time avoiding the traps. The exact sequence of keystones to be pressed is left to you. The treasure is kept in a secret room dug off the shaft's bottom. Within the secret chamber is the treasure's guardian, a captive **roper**.

Chain Lightning Trap (on well lid): Anyone other than Gordon or his lieutenants who touches the lid of the well triggers the chain lighting trap. The trap can be detected with a successful DC 17 Intelligence (Arcana) check and removed with *dispel magic* cast successfully against a 6th level spell. Any creature within 10 feet of the well is struck by lightning. In addition, any creature within 10 feet of a creature struck by lightning is struck, up to a possible range of 80 feet. Any creature struck by lightning must attempt a DC 17 Dexterity saving throw. Those failing the saving throw take 28 (8d6) lightning damage, while those succeeding take half this amount.

Well Shaft Traps: various traps located in the shaft can be chosen or randomly determined using the table below.

1d20	Trap

1–8 Burnt Othur Vapor Trap: Three rounds after a creature first moves by this location, a 10-foot cube of poisonous burnt othur fumes develops around the location. Detecting the trap requires a successful DC 16 Intelligence (Investigation) check and it can be disabled with a successful DC 16 Dexterity check with thieves' tools. A creature caught in the area when the trap is triggered must succeed on a DC 17 Constitution saving throw or lose 1d6 points of Constitution. The points are recovered after a long rest.

9–12 Deathblade Wall Scythe: When a creature puts weight on this protruding stone, a scythe cuts out from wall making a melee weapon attack at +8 to hit, one target, and doing 7 (2d6) slashing damage on a hit and target must succeed on a DC 17 Constitution saving throw or lose 1d6 points of Constitution from the poison. The points are recovered after a long rest. Detecting the trap requires a successful DC 18 Intelligence (Investigation) check and it can be avoided or it can be disabled with a successful DC 18 Dexterity check with thieves' tools.

13–15 Incendiary Cloud Trap: When a creature enters the area around this trap, an incendiary cloud fills a 10-foot cube and remains for one minute. Any creature that starts its turn in the cloud or enters the cloud must attempt a DC 17 Dexterity saving throw. Those failing take 14 (4d6) fire damage while those succeeding take half this amount. The trap can be detected with a successful DC 20 Intelligence (Arcana) check and disabled with *dispel magic* or a successful DC 20 Intelligence (Arcana) check. Failing either check by 5 or more triggers the trap.

16–20 Poison Wall Spikes: This trap is triggered by creatures putting weight on the walls of the well. When triggered, the trap makes ranged weapon attacks against two targets within 10 feet at +8 to hit. On a hit, a spike does 3 (1d6) piercing damage and the target must succeed on a DC 14 Constitution saving throw or become paralyzed for one minute. A paralyzed creature can repeat the saving throw and the end of each of its turns, ending the effect on a success. The trap can be detected with a successful DC 17 Intelligence (Investigation) check and disarmed with a successful DC 16 Dexterity check with thieves' tools.

Treasure Chamber Secret Door: A hidden switch in the wall opens the secret door. The secret door and its itch can be found with a successful DC 20 Wisdom (Perception) check. The door swings inward to the right when opened.

Treasure: 3,000 gp, 1 violet garnet (700 gp), 1 black pearl (300 gp), *+1 shield, potion of hide from undead*[2]*, potion of greater healing, wand of paralysis.*

2. Water-Maker Tent

Like the City of Brass, water in the bazaar is semi-legal. While most non-efreeti creatures require it, the efreeti overlords nevertheless want to keep it under tight control, as it is deadly to them. In the bazaar, all water must be had through sanctioned water-makers, clerics in the thrall of the Sultan who *create water* for those who pay, and even then, they only make enough to get a person through the day. Water-maker tents are scattered all over the bazaar. The few wells that have been successfully dug more often than not get "accidentally" destroyed or corrupted. Thus, the average person relies even more on the water-makers for survival. Each water-maker tent houses a single water-maker (**cult fanatic**) and at least 2 **burning dervish**[1] guards.

A water-maker uses a bone knife to draw a pint of blood from each customer, which is then transformed into 2 pints of water through magic. A single person can buy as many as 6 pints of water, though that means sacrificing 3 pints of blood. The cost is 1 cp and the willing sacrifice of 1 point of Constitution per pint of blood. Constitution damage can be healed normally or magically.

In times of need, water-makers serve the community as midwives and generalized healers. However, if another deity's temple is in the neighborhood then they defer to its priests. A water-maker may cast *create water* but rarely does so without receiving a willing blood sacrifice (1 pint of blood for 2 pints of water). The quantity of water created like this is always passed out in pints with any excess being kept for the water-maker. (For ease of reference, a *create water* spell creates 16 pints [2 gallons] of drinkable water per caster level.)

Water-Maker Goods and Services: The table below lists the typical goods or services that can be found at a water-maker's tent and the cost associated with each.

Service	Cost
Water	1 cp + 1 pint of blood
Cure wounds	60 gp
Prayer of healing	80 gp
Mass healing word	100 gp
First aid	2 gp
Midwifery	10 gp

3. Regional Bey of Taxation

This is one of the few real buildings in the bazaar made of proper stone and more or less permanent. A few years ago, when it became evident that the bazaar that had coalesced out of the desert around the queue for the city was not going to disappear any time soon, the Sultan commanded the chief bootlicker (another unfortunate adoption) at the Bey of Taxation to set up an office here. The bootlicker (who has since been killed for insubordination, his soul later forged into currency) couldn't imagine how he was going to tax the bazaar's residents, considering that according to an ancient treaty with the area's other native residents, the city technically had no authority over the land on which the bazaar sits. So he made up the Expatriate Tax, reasoning that the bazaar's residents service citizens and guests of the City of Brass and therefore could be considered expatriates of the city, who are still required by obscure city law to pay taxes. The logic was spurious, at best, but it made the Sultan happy. Shortly thereafter, azer construction gangs built this simple basalt building in the middle of the bazaar, a constant reminder of who their true master would forever be.

The current regional tax administrator is **Lady Fatima Umau**[1], a distant second cousin of the Sultan. She is a stunningly gorgeous cheitan (half-efreeti) possessing skin the color of coffee, large hazel eyes, and a smile that effortlessly melts men's hearts. The fact that she has been assigned to such a desolate, dead-end job means she somehow angered the Sultan. It could be worse, though; she could be dead. Despite the circumstances that brought her here, she still does an excellent job. As long as the bazaar's residents pay, she leaves them to their own devices, unless, of course, something major happens that requires her soldiers' intervention. A total of fifteen conscripts (both **fire giants** and **efreet**) serve under her. They, like Umau, did something unfortunate to warrant such a hellishly boring assignment. All of them tend to be corrupt, often shaking down bazaar residents for money above and beyond simple taxes. As long as it doesn't get too out of hands, Umau lets it pass. As soon as the soldiers' behavior begins stirring dissent, especially if the Sahoduin peacekeepers get involved, she comes down hard on them. Getting removed from this post means certain death.

It is widely thought that the building's top floor holds all the collected tax money. It seems, from a distance, to have the highest security. This is indeed the truth, with the room containing 50,000 gp + (1d20 x 1,000 gp) at any time. The second floor is the barracks, and the first floor contains

Umau's offices and residence. At any given hour of the day, two soldiers stand guard at the building's only entrance. Nobody is admitted without an appointment or an invitation. Once a month, Umau invites the bazaar's most prominent citizens and visiting VIPs to take afternoon tea with her and discuss current bazaar events, politely air grievances, or beg for favors. Her social and political connections in the bazaar are rock solid as a result.

4. Kanbatsu's Tattoos

The first thing a person notices about this garishly colored tent is the thick scent of incense wafting out through its flaps. It can be smelled a good five minutes before actually seeing it. The tent is woven from fine silk threads imported from the proprietor's homeland, adorned with a kaleidoscopic assault on the eyes that shows a horde of fanged, red-faced demons battling bamboo-armored warriors who wield wickedly sharp, curved swords. **Kanbatsu Ieyau**[1], the proprietor, claims to have been with the warriors in the picture that day, of which there were only seventeen survivors. The battle was lost. The warrior ended up here in disgrace, where he makes a living now with the tattooing awl rather than the sword.

The tent is crowded with clay pots of varying sizes. They all contain different kinds and colors of ink. Along one wall there is a rack and tray holding about a hundred types of tattooing awls made from a wide range of materials such as fire beetle chitin, obsidian, and whalebone. There are also mallets for tapping the awls into a customer's flesh. Kanbatsu, a wiry outlander with gentle, almond shaped eyes and a broad smile, is covered in tattoos. As a matter of fact, every part of his body except for his hands, feet, and head is hidden beneath ink depicting demons, warriors, and white-faced noble women in the same style as the art on the tent's outer walls. He has a tale for every situation and occasion, which he gladly relates while he works. He treats everyone with the same amount of deference and respect, except for the efreet whom he absolutely detests. They remind him too much of the demons that murdered his comrades.

Kanbatsu has 3 *magic tattoos*[4] inscribed on his body: one on his chest and one on each arm. The tattoos allow him to cast *mage armor*, *magic missile*, and *hold person* once per week.

Kanbatsu's Goods and Services: The following are some of the services Kanbatsu offers.

Service	Cost
Tattoo	10 gp per color
Magic tattoo[4]	100 bp per spell level
Information, local gossip	5–10 gp

5. Azi's Dubya Tent

An old tradition in the bazaar is that of *dubya lafama*, or "the art of standing still" as it is sometimes jokingly known. A dubya (as **commoner**) is a work-for-hire placeholder, someone who stands in line on behalf of another person. Without the dubyas, outsider commerce would cease to exist inside the parts of the bazaar off the Highway of the Damned. Azi Khadeem, an enterprising **djinni**, owns this tent. His dubyas are indentured servants working off their contracts in his employ. People in the queue for the City of Brass are obviously his most frequent customers. His good reputation is widespread. He charges fair rates, and his dubyas are reliable and trustworthy (unlike other agents). In all his years in business, he has only ever had 2 runaways. Bounty hunters caught them within a week of their flight, and then he had them drawn-and-quartered as an example to others. Azi Khadeem is always guarded by at least 5 **djinn** bodyguards.

According to tradition more so than law, dubyas wear brass-forged torcs the color of blood. The torcs cannot be removed, and many believe them to be enchanted with magic that allows easy tracking of them should they run. Furthermore, dubyas are not permitted on the obsidian bridge, so if they come to it while standing in line for someone, they must turn around and go home. In such instances, Azi and the dubya retain their fees, which are paid upfront on a daily basis. If a payment is missed, the dubya returns home or to the tent and the person who hired them is out of luck. Dubyas can be hired for 5 gp per day.

One peculiar side service provided by Azi is water collection. A person who, for whatever reason, needs more than 6 pints of water from a water-maker (see **Area 2**) can hire a dubya to donate blood to be turned into water. This costs 10 gp per pint.

Treasure: A wooden chest buried underneath the tent holds 1,100 gp, 2,000 sp, 1 black pearl (800 gp), 1 silver pearl (1,100 gp), and 1 deep blue spinel (400 gp).

6. Osawi's Wine Tent

This is one of the larger so-called "public" tents in the bazaar, a massive tent that, if it were a proper building, would stand approximately 2-1/2 stories tall. The tent's canvas is a plain, unadorned tan color and is supported by three pillars made from petrified sandalwood. Hooded lanterns distributed evenly throughout the interior hang from smaller, thinner posts. Half of the tent possesses creaky tables and chairs made from inexpertly hewn wood, while the other half has cushions for sitting on the floor in front of low, wide tables. There is one hookah for every table, as well as the assorted hookah-smoking accoutrements. Built haphazardly along the back wall is a makeshift kitchen. Crates for storing barrels of wine, ale, mead, water, tealeaves, and coffee surround it. At night, when the place gets crowded (mostly with foreigners, since locals tend not to drink alcohol or go to such low-class environments), smoke hangs so thickly that it becomes impossible to see more than 10 feet. Dancing girls (**commoners** with Dexterity 16, Charisma16, and Performance +5) wend through the crowd, charming gold coins from those who can afford their entertainment or cutting the purse strings on those who are too cheap to afford it. Other women, properly veiled though wearing no less scanty clothing than their cohorts, serve patrons (**hardy commoner**[1]). Small, private tents out back are available for rent on either an hourly or nightly basis. They are decorated with low-rent bedroom furniture, threadbare cushions, and serviceable but rather unclean toilet facilities.

The tent's owner and resident cook is a great big garrulous mountain of a man named **Osawi al Mujaheba**[1]. He loves interacting with foreigners, often buying drinks for anyone he deems worthy of conversation. His food is excellent by bazaar standards, a synthesis of local cuisine and well-known foreign dishes. His drinks, which are imported at great expense, are some of the finest around. Lady Umau even graces the establishment occasionally, albeit in disguise. Though a genteel, well-mannered lady, she still enjoys braving potential scandal to come here, primarily to meet foreigners she considers potentially beneficial to her.

Osawi carries a dagger and 200 gp and wears a gold ruby ring (1,200 gp) and a platinum chained pendant with a violet garnet stone (800 gp). The servers and dancers typically each have 1d6 x 10 gp.

Osawi's Goods and Services: Services Osawi offers include:

Beverages	Cost
Wine, low quality	5 sp per carafe
Wine, good quality	7 gp per carafe
Wine, high quality	12 gp per bottle
Ale, light	5 cp per mug
Ale, dark	8 cp per mug
Mead	4 gp per mug
Food	**Cost**
Pickled turnips	2 cp
Chickpea soup	3 cp
Cucumber yogurt	1 cp
Chicken with olives	1 sp
Potato and beef kebabs with yogurt	3 sp
Eggplant and lamb stew	9 cp
Other Services	**Cost**
Dancing girl courtesan	25 gp
Hookah tobacco	5 sp
Room (hour)	3 gp
Room (night)	10 gp

7. Beyanni Clan Tent

These tents are made from jet-colored goat hide and have a broken circle painted across the flaps connoting that they belong to the Beyanni clan. The Beyannis (male and female human **burlgars**[1], typically) are notorious for their fondness of gambling and visitors to any one of their thirty-some-odd tents in the bazaar are more than welcome to gamble with them, provided they can pay the ridiculous entrance fee. The members of the Beyanni clan are dark, swarthy individuals who favor long, curling moustaches, festive clothing, and speak Common with a decidedly exotic lilt. They are loud, raucous, cheerful folk, as well as notorious cheats and thieves. Anyone who gambles with a Beyanni clansman is definitely taking a chance. Regardless, people still flock to their tents in droves as soon as darkness falls, burning their money on every sort of betting game imaginable. Dice games are by far the most common, but it is the card games that have the largest pay-offs. See the **Gambling** rules below for details on various games played here.

The clan patriarch is Ibrahim Fuwaad (NE human **infiltrator**[1]), a very short man with a very large personality. Rumors persist of a secret love affair between him and the matriarch of the Eshe clan of assassins. If this is indeed true, then he is undoubtedly still involved with her, because if he weren't, he'd be dead like the eighteen men who came before him. The Beyanni clan pays three times as much on taxes as any other tent in the bazaar, presumably because they somehow raised Lady Umau's ire. Her fire giants periodically raid Beyanni tents to collect additional taxes from the patrons. Lately, the Sahoduin have been providing the tents with early warning of the soldiers' imminent arrivals, not because they especially like Ibrahim's people but because the good lady from the city is overstepping her bounds by persisting in her design to destroy his clan.

Beyanni Goods and Services: Goods and services offered at the Beyanni Clan Tent include:

Service	Cost
Entrance fee	80 gp
Cinnamon-spiced water	2 gp per cup
Dried dates	10 gp
Wine	20 gp per cup
Ale or Mead	25 gp per cup
Private game buy-in, dice*	100 gp
Private game buy-in, cards*	250 gp

*A winning pay-off in a private dice game is triple standard, while in a card game it is quintuple standard.

Gambling

Gambling is a staple at the Beyanni Clan Tents. There are two ways to handle any games the characters decide to join: playing the games out or simply requiring a Dexterity, Charisma, Intelligence or other appropriate checks from each participant to use as a contest. You as GM should decide which to use. Characters trying to cheat might use Dexterity (Sleight of Hand) while those bluffing might use Charisma (Deception). For a strategic game, Intelligence (Investigation) might be the way to go. If a character is playing a game of pure chance, like War, and not cheating, you can flip a coin, although certain people are better tied into the streams of chance that run through the universe and may well have advantage even on these games.

Playing the Games

Common gambling games (and the rules to play them) are detailed below.

An'sas: The object of this game is to have the highest "hand" of dice; 1s are low, 6s are high. Players agree upon a stake (amount to be bet) and throw their money in the center of the table. Each participant takes 5d6 and rolls two dice. Additional bets are placed or players can drop out (they do not get their money back if they drop out). Each remaining player rolls two more dice. Additional bets are placed or players can drop out. Each remaining player rolls one last die. The player with the highest "hand" wins. Use the table below to determine the winner.

Highest to Lowest	Dice Rolls
Five of a kind	All 1s, 2s, 3s, 4s, 5s, 6s
Four of a kind	Four 1s, 2s, 3s, 4s, 5s, 6s
Full House	Three dice match and two dice match (such as 5–5–5, and 3–3)
Straight	All dice are sequential (1–5 or 2–6)
Three of a kind	Three 1s, 2s, 3s, 4s, 5s, 6s
Two of a kind	Two 1s, 2s, 3s, 4s, 5s, 6s

Note: If players have identical hands, the player with the highest set of numbers wins. For example, if two players have three of a kind, one player with 3–3–3, and the other with 2–2–2, the player with 3–3–3 wins.

This game is a combination of luck and probability — knowing when to drop out can certainly affect the outcome.

Blackjack (Twenty-One): One player is the dealer. Use a standard 52 card deck. Each player (including the dealer) is dealt two cards, one face-up. The object is to have a hand whose total is closest to (but not over) 21. Each player in turn can ask for additional cards, but a player cannot have more than five total cards. The winner is the player closest to, but not over, 21. Luck and math are important here, but there is really no room for bluffing.

Dragonbones: All players agree upon a stake (amount to be bet) and throw their money in the center of the table. Each participant rolls 4d6 and totals the roll. The highest total wins the stakes. A variation of this game allows each participant to roll all the dice more than once, keeping the highest total. Barring cheating, this game is pure chance.

Hazard: One player (called the caster or shooter) places a bet by tossing coins in the middle of the table. All other bettors do the same. This establishes the pot. Once all bets are placed, the shooter throws 2d6 to establish a "main point." The main point must be a total of 5, 6, 7, 8, or 9. A shooter who fails to roll one of these totals keeps rolling until the dice come up with one of these numbers.

Once the main point is established, the shooter throws the dice again to establish a "chance point." The shooter can win or lose immediately based on this throw. Use the table below to determine the results of the throw.

Main Point	5	6	7	8	9
Shooter wins	5	6, 12	7, 11	8, 12	9
Shooter loses	2, 3, 11, 12	2, 3, 11	2, 3, 12	2, 3, 11	2, 3, 11, 12

If the shooter neither wins nor loses on the chance roll, the shooter continues to roll until winning (by rolling the chance point again) or losing (by rolling the main point). (Subsequent bets can be placed between rolls.) A shooter who wins gets the entire pot. Otherwise, all bettors take their money back plus an equal share of the shooter's bet. The dice pass to the next player.

For the shooter, this game is only chance. Side bets once the main and chance points are set can be improved with Intelligence.

High-Low: All bettors make wagers that the total of the dice (2d6) will add up to 6 or less (low), exactly 7, or 8 or more (high). Once all bets are placed, the dice are thrown. Winners take back their own bets. The losing bets are split evenly among the winners (with leftover or uneven amounts going to the high winners). In a variation of the game, the house increases the winning odds on a 7 being rolled, often paying up to 4x the amount wagered. The odds of this game of chance can be improved by betting later than the other players.

War: This game uses a standard 52 card playing deck. The cards are dealt evenly among all players, face down. Players do not look at their cards but instead arrange them face down in a stack. One player takes the top card from and throws it face up on the table. All other players do the same. The highest card wins and that player takes all cards thrown during that round and places them face down on the bottom of his or her stack. Play continues until all players, except one, are out of cards. That player is declared the winner. Wagers are usually placed on who will win the game, who will win the round, who will lose first, and so on. A game of pure chance on the whole, side bets can be made based on a good memory, and of course it is rife with possibilities for cheating (odd how many aces there are in this deck…).

8. Tent of 1,000 Illusions

Probably the second largest tent in the bazaar, the Tent of 1,000 Illusions caters to those people who want temporary relief from the struggle of daily life. Most of the bazaar's residents are dirt poor, despite their trade and crafts, and cannot afford the finer things in life. This tent, owned and operated by a crafty elf illusionist, caters explicitly to them. It is fairly wide, subdivided into almost fifty smaller rooms and alcoves. Each one contains a purple amethyst mounted in granite. Customers enter a room and Ambiresh Kelgalla the Illusionist (male elf **master illusionist**[1]), or one of his assistants (male or female elf **illusionist**[1]), activates a *mirage arcane* spell embedded in it. He designs the illusions to meet the customer's desires. The fifty amethyst shards come from the lair of the notorious master illusionist Wadozijec the Unseen. Ambiresh stole them from their previous owner, who in turn stole them from the one who was responsible for slaying Wadozijec. Altogether, the shards are considered a minor artifact that grants their owner the ability to cast *mirage arcane* at will. If one stone is moved more than 20 feet from any other, the artifact no longer functions. As such, Ambiresh employs a small retinue of **half-ogre enforcers**[1] mercenaries to guard them at all hours of the day. To keep people from suspecting the truth about the stones, he performs an elaborate, and fake, illusion summoning ritual. If anyone asks, he claims the stones are merely decorations from his homeland.

The illusions, called *personal dreamscapes*, are very popular with bazaar residents. Some people are so addicted to them that they have resorted to petty theft in order to feed their habit.

Ambiresh keeps his wealth in a collection of *secret chests* buried in the Ethereal Plane 20 feet beneath the tent. A person can get access to them only by finding the trap door that opens on the stairs descending down into the "cellar" under the tent. The trapdoor and the room containing it are at the center of the tent, permanently under the effects of the *mirage arcana* spell to make it appear like five additional rooms with stones. From the Ethereal Plane, the pit is hidden under a mound of discarded bones left by ethereal marauders that wander the plane in this area.

Tent of One Thousand Illusions Goods and Services: Typical services Ambiresh offers include:

Service	Cost
Personal dreamscape, alcove	5 gp per half hour
Personal dreamscape, small room	10 gp per half hour
Personal dreamscape, large room	15 gp per half hour

Treasure: Within the chests Ambiresh keeps hidden on the Ethereal plane are 8,000 gp, 42 carnelians (50 gp each), 10 deep green spinels (100 gp each), and 4 *potions of greater healing*.

9. Sahoduin Camp

At the south end of the bazaar is the Sahoduin camp. These stalwart nomads found their way to the Plane of Molten Skies two generations ago while on a quest for one of their chieftains. At the end of the quest, they elected to stay here, intrigued by the lands and their peoples. They have been here ever since, assuming a peacekeeping role for the beggar's bazaar since it suits their temperament and because no one else wants the job. The Sahoduin living here have forsaken their nomadic heritage, though not to such a degree that anyone would mistake them for natives. They are calm, affable, and deadly when provoked. Most are martial, though the occasional sorcerer crops up now and again. Some Sahoduin, after coming of age, move on to seek their kin in the hinterlands. The "city nomads" they leave behind hold those who do in high esteem. Not all in the camp act as peacekeepers. Many weave carpets and rugs, others mine for water on the dusty plains, and some hire themselves out as mercenaries for good causes. However, they never aid or abet anyone they consider evil.

Sahoduin Goods and Services: Services the Sahoduin offer:

Service	Cost
Water	2 sp per pint
Sahoduin rug	700 gp
Meal, common	1 sp
Meal, good	3 sp
Meal, poor	6 cp
Mercenary, (captain[1]**)**	500 gp per day
Mercenary, (eldritch archer[1]**)**	600 gp per day
Mercenary, (commander[1]**)**	750 gp per day
Mercenary, (sorcerer[1]**)**	1,050 gp per day

10. Axam's Forge

One of the first things a person notices about this tent are the puffs of smoke rising through a hole in the top. The tent itself is made from the skins of several animals that have been crudely patchworked together. The tent is stained dark gray, and no other features adorn its surface. The clang of metal on metal can be heard emanating from within it as one draws closer.

Axam (**theurgist**[1] with Charisma 16, Deception +7, and Persuasion +7), the owner and proprietor, makes his living selling various trinkets and jewelry of fair to good quality. However, he is most noted for the fabled *brazen amulets*[2] that his **azer** assistants forge in the back of the tent and that he enchants. These amulets offer planar visitors — particularly those from the Material Plane — relief from the sweltering heat of various locales, including that of the City of Brass. For these amulets alone, his tent is often one of the first places visited in the bazaar (by those who have heard of him or his rings).

The tent is divided in half by a large flap of goatskin stained the same gray color as the outside of the tent. The front half is crowded with small wooden tables filled with various necklaces, torcs, rings, and other bits of jewelry made of gold, brass, bronze, and silver. Prices and quality vary, though none are of below average workmanship.

A large slit in the dividing goatskin grants access to the rear half of the tent, which is dominated by a large iron forge and a similarly large vat of water. Various tools lie on several wooden tables or hang from ropes tied to the tent's walls. Axam's assistants spend most of their time crafting trinkets and jewelry. One azer paces the area instructing the others and inspecting their work.

For the longest time, Axam alone knew the secret to constructing a *brazen amulet*[2]. As the popularity of the amulets grew, Axam was forced to teach his assistants the secret in order to meet demand. One assistant, Hajjaj, has recently taken to "contaminating" an amulet every so often. He is a member of Abdul-Shihab (see **Area 22** in the Plane of Molten Skies) and believes, much like his fellow members, that those not native to the elemental planes, particularly the Plane of Fire, have no business being here. There is a 5% chance that any *brazen amulet*[2] purchased works normally until exposed to a temperature of 101° F or higher, at which time it automatically fails and becomes forever after worthless.

Axam is a friendly and talkative person, chatting with anyone who listens. He is of dark skin and middle-age with black hair and a thick black mustache. He enjoys talking with customers and always tries to sell a *brazen amulet*[2] to each one, warning them of the dangers of the plane and of the city without such protection. He usually sells these below "market value" in order to sell more. It is believed he either possesses an unknown magic item or is in some way protected or blessed by his god in that he can mass produce these amulets expending spell slots or requiring quite the length of time normally required.

Treasure: Buried underneath the floor in a locked chest in the back portion of the tent is 9,000 gp. Unlocking the chest requires a successful DC 18 Dexterity check with thieves' tools.

Axam's Goods: A sample of services Axam offers:

Item	Cost
Brooch	1 gp[+]
Necklace	3 gp[+]
Ring	2 gp[+]
Bracelet or anklet	2 gp[+]
Brazen amulet[2]	4,000 gp

[+]Price is based on silver as the material. For other materials, multiply the cost as follows: for brass, x 2; for bronze, x 5; and for gold, x 10. Thus, a bronze necklace costs 15 gp and a gold necklace costs 30 gp.

11. Smoke Merchant

An unusual and sweet scent wafts through the air from this brightly colored tent, noticeable as the characters approach. Smoke merchant tents are scattered throughout the bazaar. Each contains 1d3 + 1 argeeli (waterpipes) from which patrons smoke purchased tobacco. A smoke merchant "rents" an argeeli for a price and also rents each group of patrons a tube from which to smoke their tobacco. Most smoke merchants have a variety of tobaccos for sale.

Smokers can take a single draw or sit and smoke all day if they wish. A single draw reduces the benefits of the tobacco: the alchemical bonus is halved and the duration is in minutes rather than the number of hours listed. A single draw does not reduce the penalties associated with the tobacco (but the duration is reduced to minutes as well). A character must smoke the tobacco at least 10 minutes to gain the full effects.

Most smoke merchants also sell cinnamon tea that smoking patrons can buy at a rather high price. Each smoke merchant tent houses a single **smoke merchant**[1] and 2 **burning dervish**[1] guards. At any given time, 2d4 + 2 patrons are present enjoying the benefits of an argeeli. Patrons can be of any race: human, dwarf, elf, djinni, efreeti, the list goes on. Note that tobacco must be purchased from the smoke merchant to be used in an argeeli.

Smoke Merchant Services: Typical services and goods the various smoke merchants offer include:

Service	Cost
Argeeli rental (single draw)	1 gp
Argeeli rental (all day)	5 gp
Hannan[3] (tobacco)	70 gp
Jena[3] (tobacco)	100 gp
Najala[3] (tobacco)	50 gp
Shun[3] (tobacco)	10 gp
Cinnamon tea	6 gp per mug

City Overview

Population: 6,000,000 (approximately)

Physical Features

The City of Brass is built within a great brass bowl that floats on the Plane of Fire. Those entering the city are granted a majestic view of the Upper City with its many sights and sounds. Built into the bowl, the Upper City sits atop floating platforms connected by broad thoroughfares and walkways that lead to one another and deeper into the Middle or Lower City, or "Basin" area. A broad ramp circles the city's singular gargantuan feature: the Ziggurat al Nar. The ramp leads to each level of the city below the Upper City.

The Ziggurat al Nar dominating the cityscape is a new public works project started after fighting between the current Sultan's armies and the forces of his predecessor, Ashur Ban, and the Sultana Cirrishade destroyed much of the middle of the City of Brass. Each year, the entire structure rises one inch from its foundations as new plates of living brass are fitted to it. On the far end of the great Sultan's Boulevard stands the Palace of the Sultan in all its regalia and splendor. Temples to fell gods also have their place here.

The Middle City is home to many of the most famous bazaars and a rather large population of foreigners who dwell within the Souk Dhimi. An expatriate attitude dominates the flavor of this section of the city, tinged with fear of what the Sultan might do if he decided to expel them all. Many visitors to the city are drawn to the Bazaar of 1000 Sins and the Bazaar of Arcana, or to the mysteries of the Great Repository and its more accessible annex.

The Lower City, or the Basin as it is commonly called, is the true underbelly of the City of Brass. Foreign fugitives and Fire Sea Corsairs press shoulder to shoulder with throngs of new slaves and the indigenous slave population of azer who toil at the Ziggurat al Nar day in and day out

Temperatures Within the City of Brass

Within the City of Brass, the temperature is usually a "comfortable" 101° F. Though the temperature within the city can be raised much higher, the Sultan controls it so that extraplanar travelers may visit his fair city in relative comfort.

Without some form of protection, a character within the city must make a Constitution saving throw each hour or take 1d4 fire damage. The DC starts at 10 and increases by 1 for each check. Characters wearing armor of any sort have disadvantage on their saves. Characters trained in Survival may add their proficiency bonus on this saving throw and may be able to apply this bonus to other characters as well.

Merchants within the city or the Bazaar of Beggars on the Plane of Molten Skies offer *brazen amulets*[2] to those willing to pay their price. These amulets offset and negate the natural effects of heat exposure.

for the length of their miserable existence. Here, rogues run the warrens and neighborhoods. The great Caravanserai and its Slavers Bazaar dominate the lives of folk who come here as surely as the Ziggurat al Nar dominates the skyline. A combination of ash and a peculiar acid rain fall daily near the sides of the bowl, giving the Lower City a strange orange-black overcast look that only adds to the crushing despair so tangibly in the air.

Rumors speak of layers carved into the brass and bedrock beneath the basin and even into the walls of the bowl itself. Only the most fell of creatures may find solace and rest in places such as this so far from the hustle and bustle of the city's many thoroughfares.

Races and People

The City of Brass is a complex city as any of its size would be. While the Sultan of Efreet[1] himself commands total authority over his subjects, he leaves the city be as long as his few absolutes are obeyed. Many organizations and forms of worship that would find themselves outlawed upon other planes are freely embraced in such places as the District of Foreign Gods, the Souk Dhimmi, and certain areas of the Lower City.

Although all efreeti consider themselves superior to each and every other sentient creature in the cosmos, they are not equal among themselves. Many castes of efreet exist, from the common to the noble. Efreeti nobles command respect from their clans and retainers but are in turn required to supplicate themselves before the might of the Great Sultan. Efreeti tricked by normal mortals into giving away their wishes or who are enslaved by them are the lowest form of efreeti, especially in the City of Brass. However, a distinction is made for willing servitude or gratitude for freeing an efreeti versus imprisonment and being duped into lifelong slavery. Such foolish efreet are referred to as *tatari* or *nawar*, and are scorned by their own people, who heap upon their names many insults.

Efreeti nobles hold the most rights, followed closely by the Sultan's military and the burning dervishes, a cruel sect of jann who sold their souls to the Sultan of Efreet[1] for power over fire. Unholy ambassadors from the Hells and domains of other planar powers are regarded in the same caste as the nobility as far as their legal rights are concerned. Following the Sultan's priesthood and military are the common efreet affiliated through familial ties to the noble houses.

The "common folk" are all associated with the surviving nobility through familial ties after a tribal fashion, denoting them as descendants and supporters of the original genie races cast down by the elder gods during the time of Iblis' fall from power. Common efreeti are required to report their successes and offer tributes to whomever they owe allegiance once per year. Furthermore, any efreeti may seek audience with a pasha or one of his designated representatives in the bureaucracy over disputed matters. If arbitration cannot be reached in this matter, they have the right to take their case before the Great Sultan.

Amirs are the military representatives of the nobility and serve as generals and officers in the family's personal armies. The Great Sultan has many amirs who are under the command of Khan Jihadi.

Many half-efreet who are mixed with mothers or fathers from nearly every dimension live in the Middle City and Basin, working menial jobs or living off funds left for them by their efreeti parent. Half-efreet are curious as they are "citizens" with the rights of foreigners.

Foreigners living within the city are common, especially in districts that cater to their needs. Most are from any number of material planes that adjoin the Plane of Fire. Others are outsiders from the Hells, the Astral Plane, and the like drawn here for the wealth and entertainment. Foreigners have few rights in the city and are generally ignored by the

efreeti's common populace unless they attempt to kidnap an efreeti in order to force wishes from him.

Lowest of all are the slave castes, those without rights.

Religion

The current state religion of the City of Brass is the worship of the Great Sultan as the War God of Fire and the resurrection of Iblis. All citizens are expected to pray to the Sultan. A sect of jann who sold their souls to the Great Sultan for power over the element of fire serve as his religious police and the priests of his worship. This fact does not sit well with many of the noble efreet, though none would dare speak against it.

The Grand Bureaucracy

Everything within the City of Brass revolves around the Grand Bureaucracy. Class, caste, and station are all governed by the ability of members within it to move up to the next level of power and responsibility. Thus, many of the noble efreet plot against one another and constantly seek to undermine their equals and take them down a peg, in turn making themselves shine in the eyes of He Who Rules. It would be foolish of an efreeti to undermine a lesser efreeti; instead, he would merely destroy a lesser for impudence, and raise up another in his place. This is a frequent occurrence, meaning there is always room for advancement within the Grand Bureaucracy. It is the goal of every efreeti to raise his house to that of the nobility.

Coin of the Realm

Although standard coins such as gold, silver, copper, electrum, and platinum hold a similar value to their worth in other planes, the common coin of trade used in the City of Brass is the brass piece or bp. Brass pieces are roughly the same size and weight of a gold piece and are emblazoned with the magically enchanted profile of the veiled Sultan of Efreet[1] upon one side and an image of the city as seen from the Kubri Al Azim wreathed in flames that seem to swirl and flicker when viewed on the other. Various moneychangers and tax authorities are willing to convert the coin of other realms into brass pieces. All of course take a 2% to 15% or more cut of the overall value of the original coin in the trade. A brass piece is the equivalent of five gp in the characters' home plane.

Barter and Trade

Although many objects and items detailed within the City of Brass are given a fixed price for purposes of ease of use and calculating the value of magical items, it should be noted that nothing in the city has an actual fixed price. Rather, everything has a "relative value" as decreed by the masters of mercantile trade. Bartering is an art form among the shopkeepers of the various soukss. Prices are always negotiable as the shopkeepers try to get the best deal for their products. It should be noted however that shopkeepers also enjoy being taken in a deal as they appreciate a negotiator who can outwit them in the trade.

Such instances can be fun to role-play during gaming sessions. If role-playing for each and every deal becomes overly burdensome, you may have the players pay the standard price or break the negotiations down by Wisdom or Charisma contests, allowing for Deception, Insight, and other possible skills or backgrounds. Allow a 2% decrease in cost for each point by which the purchaser wins, or a 2% increase for each point by which the merchant wins the haggling.

The terms of a sale are always final and bound by the Sultan's Law.

The Sultan's Law

Whosoever of foreign nation that comes as a visitor to my lands and hath the ill presence of mind to lay hands upon the noble personages of the efreet in a manner of violence shall find half of his belongings confiscated and he shall be banished forthwith from the Sultan's Domain through the Maw of Righteousness. Know that I protect my people and rejoice!

Any who would slay an efreeti within his own lands know that this is a great offence, for the Sultan so loveth his people. If such an unthinkable act should take place at the hands of a foreigner and it be an accident of misadventure, the guilty shall serve for one year and one day in the house of his victim as a slave to his family. They are forbidden to slay thee for your crime, but they are the ones who may choose the manner of your punishment and servitude. The Sultan is wise!

Should a foreigner take the life of one of my glorious subjects with malice and intention, he shall be beheaded upon the Plaza of Emirs by a family member of the one whom he slew unless this foreigner shows great prowess and would please the family members to serve as their combatant in the Cirque du Pain. All that the being possessed becomes the property of the victim's family forevermore. So sayeth I. In extreme cases, the foreigner may be cast into the Minaret of Screams. Let his name never be spoken again in my fair city.

Should one of my subjects quell the life of another of its ilk without my sanction or leave, he should pay the family of his victim five thousand pieces of brass and give to them one of his children as slave. Should he have no children, he must give himself to their service for one year and one day in the house of their victim.

Should a foreigner slay another within the confines of my domain without my sanction, and with malice, he shall have the corpse of his victim strapped to his back. There it shall be bound like the collar of a slave yet the corpse rot and poison him with its ichor. Thus shall he know the foolishness of breaking my commandments unto his own death. Should he survive one year and one day bearing the dead upon his back, he shall be absolved of any crime of wrongdoing.

Should any foreigner commit his crimes of murder or violence using the arcane arts, let him be stripped of all belongings and cast into the Minaret of Screams.

Whosoever shall take the belongings of another through grievous theft in a value of one hundred and fifty pieces of brass or less shall face imprisonment of one day per brass piece value, and must pay in restitution double the value which they sought to steal. Such a fool shall be branded a thief upon his body forthwith for all to know.

Should this dastard be again caught with the possessions of another within his holding or on his person, he shall have his left hand cut from his body and spend two days imprisoned with hard labor for each brass piece value of his crime. Triple the value must be paid to the victim of his crime. Should this person be caught a third time, he shall face life as a slave sentenced to row upon my war galleys. Know ye that my mercy is great and my word is justice!

Those who would commit grand theft of more than one hundred and fifty pieces of brass in value within the domain of the mighty efreet be forewarned. You shall be branded a thief and have your left hand cut from your body. You shall serve for one year and one day as a slave to those from whom you have stolen, and all of your wealth and worldly possessions shall be given to those whom you have wronged. So it is written. Should you foolishly endeavor to steal again within my domain you shall be sold into the Cirque du Pain. Again, I show my mercy for there you may fight for your freedom. The Sultan is just!

Those who would seek to counterfeit the coin of my land and disrupt the free flow of commerce shall suffer seizure and forfeiture of all their belongings and be cast into the Maw of Righteousness. Know my word for it is law!

Those seeking to impersonate my lawful servants and anointed administrators for illicit gain shall be fined twenty thousand pieces of brass and be sentenced to the Cirque du Pain or the Minaret of Screams depending on the gravity of their crime. In lesser cases, three months of hard labor aboard a war galley will suffice.

Those who would lay hands lasciviously upon a citizen of the City of Brass without my leave shall be blinded and castrated within the Plaza of Amirs. The Bazaar of One Thousand Sins provides any such pleasures of the flesh one could seek without the desecration of our sons and daughters. Am I not just? Are not all thy wants and needs provided for?

The Sultan's Law

Adulterers who perform their amorous activities without my leave or consent shall be stoned to death by their own families. I am wise and see all and know all!

Conspiracy against my kingdom shall not be tolerated. Assassins and conspirators who would undermine my great nation shall be executed and their families put to the sword, their property reduced to ash and their names stricken from memory. My virtue is the standard and to conspire against my virtue is to conspire against one's self.

Let all merchants deal fairly with their customer and let the buyer beware. Not all is as it seems. No lien may be laid against a merchant without proof of misdealing.

See how my wisdom rings like peals of silver with the truth.

A merchant caught misdealing to a customer may be called upon by the customer to give free that which was misdealt.

Let no item be constructed nor any magic be wrought within my domain that uses the force of water or ice magic. We are the smokeless flame ever-burning and pure. Let not our might be diluted by such whimsy.

Those who would question my law in the face of my priesthood shall be hurled into the Maw of Righteousness forthwith for I am the way and the path.

The efreeti will strive always and evermore to occupy the idols of false gods and speak my will so that it be done on all planes of existence and further my supreme divinity. Efreeti shall always seek to enslave the lesser races of the universe and deliver them unto my service. Efreeti shall grant a tithe no less than one-fifth of their monthly earned wealth unto me when asked, for the administration of the city, its public works, its defenses, and its armies.

When called upon, all citizens will raise arms against my enemies and strike with swiftness and great ferocity, raining destruction down upon the heads of our foes.

The master of a slave may treat his slave as he desires. It is a very foolish or very wealthy master who would destroy his own property. So do I treat you, my children, so too shall you treat your slaves.

Any slave indentured for crime will be freed of his collar upon completing his tasks and time. Let the fetters fall from they who survive their torments.

Should one slay the slave of another, he must provide in return slaves to the owner of double the value of what was lost. If there is a challenge to the value of these slaves, they who hold the grievance may seek counsel from the delegations of my court.

Those born into slavery are the property of their parents' master. In such a case where the slaves each belong to a different master and were bred for some service payment of stud service shall be granted the owner of the male, and the child be property of the mother's owner. Thus do I impart my wisdom in fair dealings.

Should a wife of a prince lay with slaves, so should she be stoned and the slave destroyed by the husband's hands. Any progeny of theirs is outcast to walk the trackless wastes of the Plane of Molten Skies.

Should a prince lay with slaves of the harem and beget a child, that child shall be common born and his mother freed and they given one thousand pieces of brass. Many are the tales of the father slain at the hands of the bastard for mistreatment of the mother. Great is he who has a great harem, and none are greater than mine! Father you not nameless bastards, princes of the city, lest you can afford to pay the penalty.

Should any man slay the beast or destroy the property of another be it of malice or hazard, he shall pay the victim double that which was lost be it in animals of like ilk or in compensation of living brass and elemental jewels for the properties laid to waste.

No wish shall be granted which should bring about harm to my loyal subjects.

All efreeti bound to grant wishes must abide by the rules of law to the exact letter. No wish may be wrought that would make anyone the master of the universe. No wish may cause love to well where there was none. No wish may grant more wishes. These are the rules of the cosmos and even I, Master of the Plane of Molten Sky and Sultan of all Efreet, cannot break these rules for they are scribed within the Grimoire of Infinite Worlds and are absolute. Lest all that was wrought before come undone and the universe be stricken void these rules thus stand. Wishes will be granted upon the exact wording of the one making the wish. An efreeti may not grant a wish to another efreeti even if he be that efreeti's slave.

No foreigner nor beloved citizen may deny my will, nor the will of my anointed advisors and priesthood. Although they may worship other gods within my realm, my power is absolute and my laws must be obeyed and respected.

Slavery and The City of Brass

A famous arch-mage once asked of an efreeti noble: Where do all of these slaves come from? "From a mortal's failed wishes," was the answer given him. Thus, the efreeti's greatest granted power is also its most successful form of gathering slaves for its palace within the City of Brass. Foolish mortals granted wishes by an efreeti in their own plane seldom understand the level to which an efreeti will twist their wish to its own desires. To an efreeti, a great stable of slaves raises his prominence in the eyes of a bey or pasha, and thus increases the efreeti's chances of promotion within the Sultan's Grand Bureaucracy. As the efreet often joke among themselves, an efreeti is not born, he is made.

Sold into Slavery

Characters captured by burning dervish or efreeti slave patrols in the Plane of Molten Skies, or those convicted of minor crimes within the confines of the City of Brass, may find themselves sentenced or sold into slavery. The slave market is open non-stop. Beings of nearly every race and description are put on sale within the Slavers Market and sold to the highest bidder.

Captured individuals are stripped of all their worldly possessions and goods, which are in turn sold at the Auction House within the Slavers Bazaar. Once stripped and examined by the efreeti Shaik Abdul Gazi, the master of the Slavers Bazaar, prisoners are marked in gold paint with a number indicating the value of their starting bid.

Calculating a Slave's Value

To calculate the value of a slave, multiply the creature's Strength x Charisma x Hit Dice. This sets the starting bid in bp (brass pieces). Thus, a 14th-level fighter with Str 18 and Cha 12 has a starting bid of 3,024 bp (14 x 18 x 12 = 3,024).

As the efreet have no real way of knowing how powerful an individual is, they may be tested through combat with one another or other captured slaves to determine their ability to fight or think.

Characters found with spell components are marked separately and sold in a separate auction from other slaves, as their value must be determined by a representative of the burning ones. Such characters may find themselves purchased by a noble house or a merchant in the Bazaar of Arcana. They will likely be set to crafting magical items until their worthiness is expended. The value of an arcane spellcaster is the standard value of a slave multiplied by 1.5.

Places to Stay

The Walls

The terraced walls of the inner bowl of the City of Brass are a district unto themselves, though they follow the general socioeconomic standards of the level of the city to which they are in the closest proximity. They make up upper, middle and lower rings, with rent and amenities reflected accordingly.

The walls are where the vast majority of efreeti and their families live and include the dwellings of wealthy foreigners who pay vast sums of money for permanent housing outside of the typical short-term inn or stodgy low-rent apartment in the Lower City.

The typical dwelling carved into the walls of the city has 9–15 rooms, including a common area, dining area, kitchens, bathrooms, servant quarters, guardroom, bedrooms for family members, and a guestroom for visitors. The rooms can, of course, be designated for whatever purpose comes to mind.

Wall Apartment Rent

Upper City Wall: These apartments are the most highly sought after by the lesser nobility of the efreet such as thirdborn and their spouses and are typically reserved for them. There are a few exceptions such as associates of dignitaries and ambassadors who need a residence outside of the massive palace complex. The terrace neighborhoods are patrolled by 1d4 **fire giants** and a **burning dervish** who assure that any riffraff are chased out of the area.

Rent: 500 bp per month.

Middle City Wall: These apartments are slightly less sought after and are occupied for the most part by fourth-born nobles and lower as well as wealthy merchants and visiting wizards. They lack most of the polish of the outer edifices of the Upper City, showing a bit more tarnish and a little less care in their upkeep. The terraces are also patrolled, though less frequently than the Upper City walls. Guard patrols typically consist of 1d2 **fire giants** or **fire** and **earth elementals** paid by the neighborhood association.

Rent: 250 bp per month.

Lower City: The dinge of soot and corruption is most obvious on the outer entryways of these apartments where the statuary has almost always been defaced or vandalized in some fashion. Guard patrols are infrequent in these neighborhoods. The homes here are often rented by slavers or merchants, or kept as a second home by nobles wishing to conduct clandestine activities away from the pervasive view of the burning dervishes. These homes are frequently burglarized.

Rent: 100 bp per month.

Typical Wall Apartment Layout

Here's a typical apartment dwelling that can be found to rent on the wall.

1. Entrance

A walkup entryway, typically featuring a pair of statues of the owner's ancestors.

2. Entry Hall

The entry hall features murals and mosaics depicting the feats of the apartment's owner. There may be a trap designed to chase away or secure unwanted guests. There might also be a pit in the floor that drops an intruder into a prison cell or something deadlier.

A sentry may be posted here to ward against assassins.

3. Guardroom

The guardroom is where the house mamelukes or lesser efreeti soldiers keep an eye on the comings and goings of visitors.

4. Guard barracks

This is the bedroom of the guards. There may or may not be a secret passage to the master's bedchamber with an alarm or ward. If a secret passage exists, it is surely trapped with a deadly trap such as a crushing

wall or some magical ward to keep unwanted visitors from creeping into the master's room.

5. Servants Quarters

There may be 2–4 or more small bedrooms for the house slaves who do the cooking and cleaning for the family. They are typically mortals who worded a wish incorrectly during an encounter with an efreeti noble.

6. Common Garden

This semi-interdimensional space has a fountain, date and coconut palm trees, and weather that is always perfect. It is where the family spends the majority of its time together.

7. Dining Hall

This indoor dining room is designed to be a showcase for the house. Revelers who begin in the garden retire to the dining hall to sit and eat from plates of steaming meat, couscous, sugared dates, and other delicacies.

8. Kitchen

This is a kitchen and storage area used by the servants to prepare the family's meals.

9a. and 9b. Guest Quarters

These rooms sleep 2–4 guests of the owner. They have beds, cushions, silks, towels, and the like for the master's guests.

10. Restroom

Guests and children use this communal bathroom.

11A. and 11B. Family Quarters

The master's family occupies these rooms. Alternately, they may be used as additional guestrooms should the owner not have a family.

12. Harem

This is where the master keeps his harem, or it serves as a private residence for the spouse of the master.

13. Master's Chambers

A. This is the greeting room of the master for entertaining family or private guests. It is filled with the master's private possessions, all designed to impress important visitors.

B. This is the private bedchamber of the master of the home.

Inns

Inns are infrequent, as most visitors are expected to stay in the Caravanserai outside the city walls where they may rent or buy a tent. Others who come to the city do so as either guests of the denizens of the city or as slaves. Notable exceptions include the Freeman's Tower and the Ubaydulah Tower, detailed in **Chapters 19** and **15**, respectively.

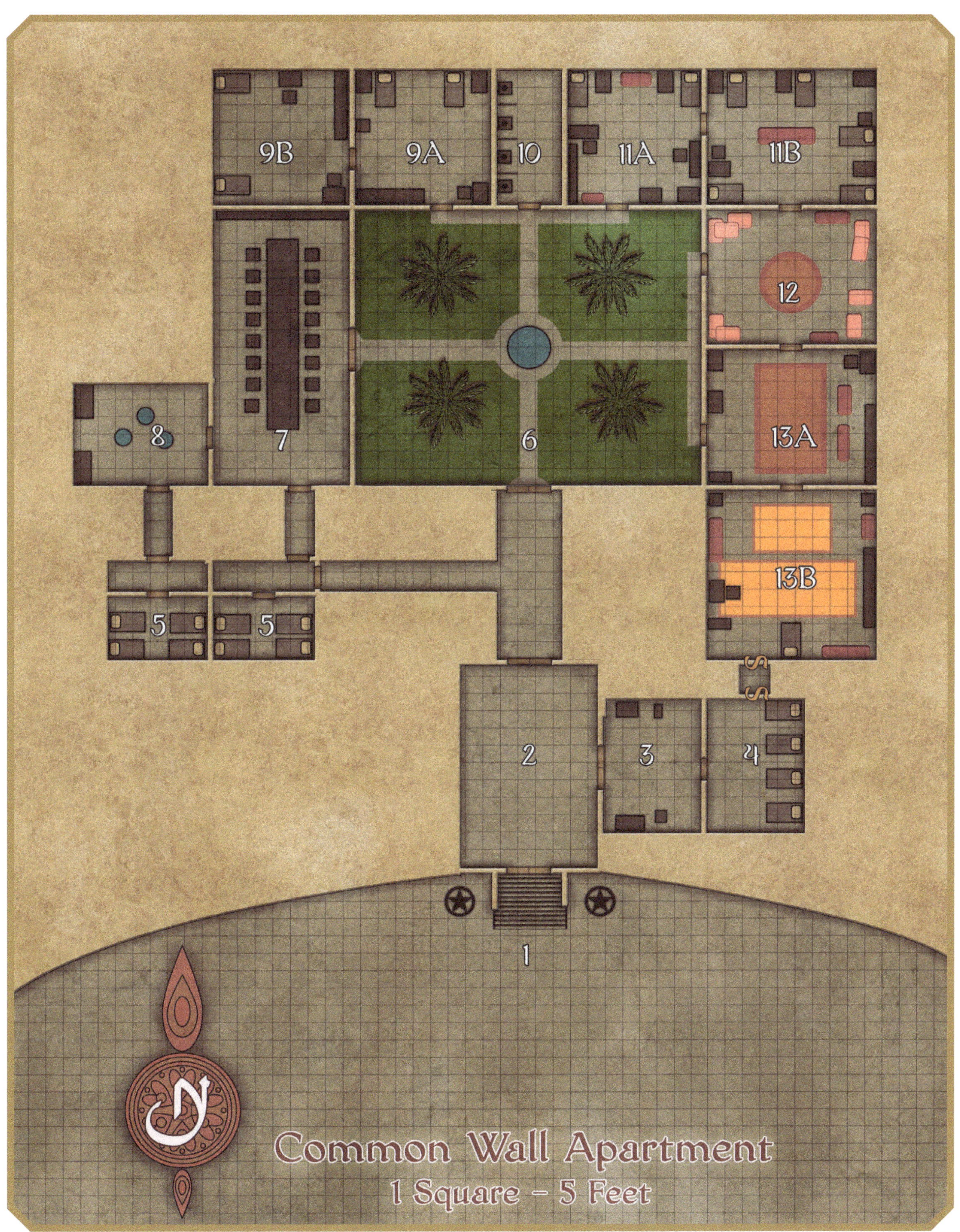

9B
9A
10
11A
11B
12
13A
13B
8
7
6
5
5
2
3
4
1
Common Wall Apartment
1 Square – 5 Feet

Chapter 13
The Upper City

Beyond the high gate towers of the Bab al Baquarra stretches the burning grandeur of the City of Brass. Living brass towers and needle-like minarets stand amid the ziggurats and domes of the various temples to foreign gods. Broad terraces curve and descend down the edges of the brass bowl on nearly all sides for miles to where the foundations of the city's great pyramids and gargantuan palaces rest.

Nearly every edifice is embossed or cast with arabesque ornamentation of a dizzying, swirling design. The twisting scripts of arcane wards offer curses and warnings to those who are foolish or brave enough to read their otherworldly secrets.

As seen from the Sultan's Boulevard, skyways and twisting staircases lead up and down to broad plazas and heavily thronged souks upon every level. Many of these walkways end in the gruesomely grinning faces of the demon gates, which grant or deny passage to those who seek the secrets hidden beyond their gaping maws.

The skies above the city seem to swirl and pulse, glowing with every color of flame from green to white hot. The airways above the city are equally thronged with flying demons and devils, and even an occasional dragon. Wealthy merchants ride upon flying carpets. Wizards borne on the backs of wind elementals avoid the streets below them entirely, knowing much faster routes to their destinations.

In the distance is the shimmering curtain of elemental flame that separates the Forbidden City of the Great Sultan and the royal enclosures of the noble efreet from the rest of the City of Brass.

The map **Upper City of Brass** gives all the locations, and some additional details are provided in the map for **District of Naibs**. While many of the areas are described here, several have their own chapters in **Book III** and are only referenced here.

Upper City Random Encounters

Roll 1d10 for every hour spent in the Upper City.

1d10	Encounter
1	Incantor[1]
2	Efreeti merchant
3	Burning dervish[1] squad
4	Fire giant guard patrol
5	Lich
6	Devil (your choice)
8	Pilgrim (commoner or other)
9	Emeritus chaplain[1] (deity of your choice and entourage)
10	NPC from the appendix, your choice

Districts

Districts are loosely aligned by the sort of civic buildings and services that may be found there. In the City of Brass, most of the districts occupy a single platform of their own or consist of one or two floating platforms attached by a foot bridge or other walkway.

Upper City District

The following are some of the area's more prominent places:

1. The Kubri al Azim (The Obsidian Bridge)

For more information on the Kubri al Azim, see **Chapter 11**.

2. The Bab al Baquarra (The Great Gatehouse)

At the far end of the Obsidian Bridge is the Bab al Baquarra (or Great Gatehouse). These towers of living brass are nearly a mile wide at the base and stretch nearly six miles into the sky. Five platoons of **efreet** and **fire giants** who work in rotating schedules during the City of Brass' 30-hour day are garrisoned in the gatehouse. The platoons are led by one sergeant, an **efreeti malik**[1], who in turn reports to **Sinsurab**[1], the Bey of Keys, who oversees the entire garrison. At all times, at least 10 efreeti, 10 fire giants, and 1 malik will be here. If under attack, Sinsurab raises an alarm, and up to 50 efreet and fire giants answer the call within 1 minute.

Efreeti gate guardians of the City Watch halt all visitors who seek entrance to the City of Brass here for inspection. These guardians inspect merchants for contraband items such as water, cold or frost magic, or large amounts of good holy items. It is not that the efreet fear good influences, rather they welcome folk of good alignment within their city as they figure the temptations of the Bazaar of 1,000 Sins and the many foul artifacts kept within the City of Brass should be enough to cause such beings to destroy themselves. They would however find fault with attempting to bring a thousand gallons of holy water into the confines of the city itself. When in doubt, the gate-guardians simply turn away individuals whom they feel will be too much of a bother.

No more than 3 gallons of potable water or drinking liquid per non-native may be brought into the city, and this merely for personal consumption. Most who come to the City of Brass subsist on fluids created by clerics and licensed water or wine merchants who charge a heavy price for their services, and in turn pay a substantial tax to the offices of the Bey of Taxation.

3. The Sultan's Boulevard

This broad thoroughfare runs the length of the City of Brass, from the Great Gates of the Bab al Baquarra to the Curtain of Flame and the demon gates that lead to the Palace of the Sultan. The Sultan's Boulevard is thronged with visitors entering and leaving the city, the majority of them being pedestrians from the inner and outer planes. Although the Sultan's Boulevard is always busy, the foot traffic seems to move at an orderly pace as if all who come here have a good idea of where they are going and how to get there. Loitering is not allowed, nor is it a common occurrence. Efreeti patrols keep the folk walking or standing in orderly lines that are as efficient as possible.

Entering the City

Whatever the reason for entering the City of Brass, all who seek passage beyond the Great Gatehouse may do so by one of four methods:

Efreeti Guide: The visitor is in the presence of an efreeti. One of the most common forms of travel to the City of Brass is by using the granted *wish* of a bound efreeti to whisk one away to the fabled city. Persons brought to the city in the company of an efreeti may not be turned away, nor may they be threatened with any violence unless they themselves bring violence against the gate wardens. Their gear and equipment, however, are still subject to search and possible seizure.

Official Writ of Passage: An official writ of passage granted by Surtur's Thane (**Area 11** on the Plane of Molten Skies) or written by any efreeti of the rank of Bey or higher. These writs are common among merchants, slave traders, and jann who do frequent business among the efreet.

A Substantial Bribe: A bribe of at least 2,000 gp worth of magic items per person to one of the Gate-Wardens suffices to allow an unbidden visitor passage into the City of Brass. As many areas of the city are open to visitors from throughout the universe, this is one of the most common methods of passage into the city.

Rod of Embassy: A character bearing a rod of embassy, granted by one of the noble houses of Efreet, the grand vizier, or the Great Sultan himself, is considered under the official protection of the Sultan and is untouchable by any official or bureaucrat of the City of Brass. Gaining one of these rods is considered nearly impossible as they are granted only to those diplomats and dignitaries who are held in the highest esteem by the Sultan or a pasha of one of the ruling families. These include emissaries of arch devils with business in the City of Brass, extremely powerful mages, lich lords, hag queens and the like. Of course, characters that somehow come into possession of one of these rods may be able to fake their importance through use of Deception skill checks or the use of magic to hide their true identities.

A strong patrol presence is seldom needed as folks traveling to the City of Brass do not do so to see its many-splendored sights. Most have business at one of the souks; others seek the knowledge locked within the Museum of Wonders or the Library of Secrets.

The Sultan's Boulevard is more than a mile wide and crosses through the Ziggurat of Flame located in the center of the city. Many skywalks and platforms branch off from the Boulevard itself leading to the various edifices of the upper city.

The City of Brass is often described as having the greatest souk in the entire universe. This is both true and not. The efreet, being a very organized race of beings, actually have several different bazaars to satisfy their needs and the needs of their relentless otherworldly customers. Nearly everything that can be bought and sold may be found within one of the many bazaars. The stalls and shops are most often run by the slave of an efreeti and in the rarest of occasions by a poor efreeti of the lowest caste.

4. The Nightfall Concordance

Built along the rim of the bowl are a series of 20 towers owned by the Nightfall Concordance, a group of mages, sorcerers, and clerics whose explicit purpose is to bring night to the City of Brass at regular intervals. Because the Plane of Fire is uniformly bright from the ever-burning fires, the city never had a true day/night cycle. All that changed 1,000 years ago, when the Sultan Sharif Madar established the group because emissaries from other lands complained constantly about being plagued with the inability to get a real night's rest. One emissary, in a moment of extremely bad judgment brought on by sleep deprivation, declared war on the city in his emperor's name. At first, Sharif thought the emissary was joking. A week later, when an army of 500,000 sweltering bugbear warriors from the emissary's home world showed up outside the city gates, Sharif realized the gravity of the situation. He apologized to the emissary in an uncharacteristic show of humility, asked that the bugbear army move away from the city (the stench alone was enough to choke an ancient dragon!), and promised to implement a magical day/night cycle. The emissary, appropriately mollified, accepted the terms and had the army withdraw. Since then, the Nightfall Concordance has brought a twelve-hour night to the City of Brass every 30 hours, though not exactly like clockwork. Like people everywhere, its members are susceptible to greed and bribery. Once in a while, the city might be cloaked in darkness for days or even weeks on end; at other times, the sun never seems to set. It all depends on who paid them, and how much. If the Sultan gets particularly fed up, he summons the leader of the Concordance to his palace for a little discussion. That invariably returns the day/night cycle to its original schedule. Night typically lasts 12 hours, but sometimes lasts as long as 30 hours during festival season. Even though efreet, azer, and to a lesser extant djinn, don't require night (or day for that matter), they have become used to it. And while they don't especially care about the opinions of outsiders, they discovered long ago that humanoids were much more agreeable if their sleep cycles were properly regulated.

A typical Concordance tower stands five stories tall. It is always made of living brass plated in pure silver. The first floor contains a common room, a kitchen, and a garderobe, and is decorated quite plainly. The second floor is the library, where the spellcasters in residence do research or spend their idle hours writing treatises that will one day be published in the Great Repository by Necromancer Grimes, a wizard who dabbles infrequently in book selling. The spellcasters' private residences are on the third and fourth floors. Finally, the fifth floor is a ritual space used by the spellcaster when they bring nightfall to the city.

The Nightfall Concordance admits spellcasters who are of at least 10th level, though they won't be ready to participate in the Ritual of Night until at least 18th level. The Concordance is a guild in everything but name. Most mages are **incantors**[1], but the more senior ones are **spellbinders**[1]. They all wear *rings of immunity* (fire)[2] and carry a *staff of power* and wear *bracers of superior defense*[2].

District of Foreign Gods

As surely as supplication solely to the will and power of the Sultan grants great power to the burning dervishes, so too does the Sultan respect the right of visitors to his city to seek worship within shrines dedicated to their own gods — as long as the god's worship does not become a civil disturbance. Most prominent among the temples and shrines to other gods are the Shining Pyramid of Set and the Infernal Cathedral of the Lightbringer. The Dome of Gates is also located in the District of Foreign Gods.

5. The Shining Pyramid of Set

This area is fully detailed in **Chapter 18**.

6. Pagoda of Devils

This area is fully detailed in **Chapter 29**.

7. The Cathedral of the Lightbringer

This area is fully detailed in **Chapter 24**.

8. Dome of Gates

The Dome of Gates is a useful stop for visitors to the city who decide that it is time to leave and wish a quick egress to their home. That is, of course, as long as they are not wanted for any major felonies within the city.

The structure holds powerful permanent portals that allow passage from the City of Brass to other planes of existence, as well as different times. Travelers with the proper coin may book passage to these otherworldly destinations from an efreeti gate-warden. Guides to the other planes may also be hired here. Terms of their service vary greatly from one efreeti to the next. Most efreeti tour guides take on a traveler with the ultimate intent of enslaving them or betraying them somewhere down the road. Such is the fate of those who seek service with the efreet; this has been said many times and bears repeating!

Travel through time is possible within the Dome of Gates but is, of course, conditional. Generally speaking, altering time is not allowed and those who travel through time are allowed to do so purely in a tourist capacity. This rule is strictly enforced. A time traveler may be allowed to view the unfolding of events in the past or future, but not participate directly in them without the use of powerful time-bending magic such as *wishes* (such as the efreet have). Their use to change histories and universal outcomes may however be restricted or vetoed by the Lord of Time or the fates at any point.

Prices for one-way travel to any of the planes are as follows:

Destination	One Way	Round Trip*
Home Plane	1,000 bp	1,500 bp
Inner Plane	1,500 bp	1,800 bp
Outer Plane (Lower)	2,000 bp	2,500 bp
Outer Plane (Upper)	2,500 bp	3,000 bp
Elemental Plane[1]	1,000 bp	1,500 bp
Energy Plane[2]	2,500 bp	3,000 bp
Travel Forward in Time[+]	6,000 bp	7,000 bp
Travel Backward in Time[+]	5,000 bp	6,000 bp
Efreeti Tour Guide	200 bp/day	300 bp/day

*Although the efreet have the power to return instantly to the City of Brass at any time (as long as they are not enslaved or bound), returning visitors must again pass through the Bab al Baquarra, as *teleportation* directly into the city is prohibited to all save efreet themselves.

[+]Requires an efreeti tour guide. All round-trip affairs require a guide. Upon returning, the traveler is deposited at the Bab al Baquarra (Great Gatehouse).

[1]This includes any of the para-, quasi-, or demi-elemental planes. Efreeti guides do not travel to a plane they consider hostile, such as the Elemental Plane of Water or Plane of Ice.

[2]An efreeti guide won't travel to the positive or negative energy plane unless the travelers procure adequate protection for him or her.

9. Shrine of Kal'Ay-Mah

Small and unassuming, the shrine to Kal'Ay-Mah has little to offer any but the truly faithful. There is no donation box to assuage the wary believers, no great displays exposing the might of the goddess. There is only dust, shadow, and silence — all maintained by a lone guardian

Kal'Ay-Mah (the Black One, the Black Mother)

Alignment: Lawful evil.
Domains: Death, Destruction, Law, Knowledge.
Typical Worshippers: Assassins, religious scholars.
Favored Weapon: Longsword.

The goddess Kal'Ay-Mah, the Black Mother, bringer of destruction and preserver of order. She is called patron by assassins and those seeking greater understanding, an often confusing set of extremes to those who fail to truly grasp Kal'Ay-Mah's divine role. The Black Mother is described as a truly fearsome creature by those who have claimed contact with her avatar — a black face wetted with blood, the heads of those she has slain hanging about her neck and their severed arms as a girdle about her waist. Four great arms stretch from her body, a bloody sword gripped in her upper left hand and the head of a demon gripped by the lower left. If these grotesque features alone had failed to capture attention, the eyes surely would — dark, ruinous, raging.

that sits quietly to the side of the room, head bowed in contemplation, seemingly ignorant of the presence of either pious or curious patrons of the shrine.

To the far end of the building is an unadorned altar, an ever-burning lamp on either side. Just out of reach of the full intensity of the lamp flames, its main features obscured by deep shadows, is an idol of Kal'Ay-Mah. On immediate examination, it appears to glisten in the light more than glow, wet and slick with red.

The idol of the Black Mother is eminently simple in craftsmanship — a plain thing carved out of ash wood, decorated by black stones and coated with thinned blood. Neither the greediest appraiser nor the keenest observer will find any great value in it, quick to find it is possessed by no mystical or otherwise extraordinary features. Despite this, any attempt to touch or abscond with the idol results in the guardian, a **Handmaiden of Kal'Ay-Mah**[1], rising from its resting place and attacking until either it or the offender are dead.

10. Aerie of Pazuzu

Atop this narrow 100-foot-tall pillar, carved with the faces of thousands of demons, is a single chapel chamber. The chapel is straddled by a gargantuan statue of a four-winged, four-armed demon with the head of a hawk, whose crotch is matted in filth. The chapel may be accessed only by flying to it. Within the large chamber stands an altar of gold covered with blood and entrails. The altar is guarded by 3 **vrock demons** and is serviced by Sargon the Bearer, half-fiend **archpriest**[1] of Pazuzu.

Pazuzu, Demon Prince of the Air, Thrice Cursed of the Rotting Genitals

Alignment: Chaotic evil.
Domains: Air, Chaos, Evil.
Typical Worshippers: Evil aerial creatures, evil humanoids.
Favored Weapon: Greatsword.

Pazuzu is the Demon Prince of the Air and maintains a healthy status of respect even among lawful evil lords such as the arch-dukes of Hell. He seeks dominion over all the airs in all the planes of existence and is not above negotiating to get what he wants. He frequently appears as a great bird-like man with a greatsword, with a head that may alternately be that of a lion, jackal, or hawk. A great stench of death wafts from his mouth and between his powerful legs. The air around him becomes plagued and spoiled immediately and he is known to be the father of many diseases.

Military District

The Military District is a pair of large platforms on the "western" side of the Upper City. It encompasses the **Bazaar of Arms**, the **Plaza of Amirs**, and the **Palace of the Khan**. The area is thronged with foreign visitors to the City of Brass, mercenaries, and the marshaled forces of the Sultan's Army.

11. Palace of the Khan

This huge palace, found completely within the upper city, overlooks the Military District. The Palace of the Khan serves as home to the Sultan's Secret police and internal security forces for the City of Brass. It has a garrison of **burning dervish wizards**[1], **fire giant** enforcers, and **efreeti amirs**[1], all under the direct command of Khan Jihadi (**efreeti amir al-umara**[1]). Khan Jihadi is the second most powerful single efreeti in the entire City of Brass after the grand vizier, and answers only to the Great Sultan himself. Khan Jihadi is a proud and brave efreeti who serves the Sultan without question, often personally leading the khan's expeditionary forces on wars of conquest and slave taking throughout the multiverse.

Many of these campaigns are spearheaded by the **Legion of Mamelukes**, a shock-trooper force of soldier-slaves *geased* to follow orders and fight the battles of the Sultan without question. These legionnaires come from all races and home planes, but all are foreigners to the Plane of Molten Skies and the City of Brass. They are distinctive in that they are dressed in oil-shark armor and have the brass circlet of a slave soldered around their neck.

The Legion of Mamelukes is divided into three divisions, each numbering more than 1,000 troops. The three divisions are further divided into three companies, each composed of siege engineers, footmen, and bowmen. The footmen, often foreign barbarians or fighters, bear large shields, spears, and hand weapons of their choosing. Siege engineers bear satchels filled with mage fire, vials of poison gas, and other such nasty weapons that are hurled into the midst of enemy forces. They also operate and repair any siege engines that the legion takes into battle. The mameluke bowmen are armed with composite longbows and carry arrows tipped with living brass.

The khan assigns and oversees the city defenses and the police activities within the city itself. The khan and his staff of military bureaucrats also act as judge and jury to those arrested for various crimes, assigning punishment to those foolish enough to break the laws of the City of Brass. For a detailed listing of crimes and their various punishments, see the section titled **The Sultan's Law**.

12. Officers' Quarters

These fine estates house the officers and war wizards that serve in the Sultan's armies. Located "north" and "south" of the Palace of the Khan, these fine homes are granted as sumptuous gifts to those who prove themselves worthy to the will of the Sultan.

Bazaar of Arms

Molten metal and burning coal fills the air with its pungent odor as the ears of visitors are assailed with the sounds of hammer and tongs. Vendors and arms merchants call out in a thousand languages bidding travelers and arms buyers to come and test their wares. Many forms of weapon and armament may be found within the Bazaar of Arms — with one notable exception. Frost weapons and cold-based items are strictly regulated, and the use of one by any non-efreeti is tantamount to instant execution at the hands of the Sultan's not so secret police.

The Bazaar of Arms is considered one of the greatest weapon markets in the known universe. Weapon forgers and masters of every race and description manufacture and trade their wares here upon this broad plaza. The resounding ring of hammer on metal fills the air, but only barely drowns out the gibbering mishmash of languages uttered from the hundreds of races represented. Many of the weapons and armaments found here seem of an alien origin even to experienced otherworldly travelers. Most items are unique not only to the merchant selling them, but also in their make and manufacture. It is not uncommon to see an azer slave hammering out weapons whose metallic components are superheated by a bound fire elemental. Powerful wizards and clerics of evil deities imbue these strange and unique weapons with deadliest of magic as they too work off time with their various efreeti masters.

The majority of stalls and tents trade in arms brought by traders who deal with craftsmen from throughout the universe. Characters may easily find a high-quality version of any armor or weapon found in the fifthe edition SRD, and magical versions of several items, up to +3 in total enhancements may be found as well, although they are sold at a minimum of 20% markup due to exorbitant taxes and the general greed of merchants found within the city.

Several shops of note exist within the Bazaar of Arms, these being the ones having the most lavish and powerful of weaponry allowed within the confines of the City of Brass. Other shops are known for their unique and exotic weapons and armaments, items not seen or even comprehensible to most.

13. Muhannad al Nar (The Sword of Fire)

The Muhannad al Nar specializes in scimitars, falchions (as longsword), longswords, greatswords, and other bladed weapons. Junyad ibn Tarriq, a powerfully built **efreeti**, keeps a staff of **azer** slaves under him who do the majority of the weapon crafting for his shop. Tarriq specializes in only the finest of swords, and sees that Kip al Jier (**arcanist**[1]), the wizard bound to his service due to a backfired *wish*, constructs each weapon to the specifications called for by his customers. Tarriq generally charges 1-1/2 times the standard value for magic items sold within his shop. As haggling is considered a standard method of purchasing items in any souk or bazaar within the City of Brass, good negotiations could increase the chances that the characters get what they are looking for at a considerably discounted price. The azer craftsmen can create high quality versions of every simple and martial sword, falchion, or scimitar.

14. Executioner's Edge

The Executioner's Edge is operated by **Al Fatik**[1], a burning dervish who sells axes whose blades are said to be able to slice through stone and armor as easily as they cut flesh. Whether this is propaganda or truth remains to be seen, but one thing is certain: Al Fatik's axes are of very fine quality and exotic craftsmanship, covered in detailed scrollwork and scribed with powerful magic. Al Fatik has the power to enchant his axes up to a +3 bonus. He carries a *staff of fire* and keeps 3 Fire Sea black pearls (550 gp each) in his pocket.

15. The Gleaming Panoply

Armor of nearly every make and description may be found within the Bazaar of Arms. Especially popular are breastplate, scale mail, and chain shirts crafted from adamantine, mithral, and living brass. The denizens of the City of Brass, whose masters seldom wear any armor at all because it is below their station to do so, similarly consider heavy armor unfashionable. This is not to say that the smiths of the Bazaar of Arms would not craft such items, merely that it would draw a certain amount of attention to the wearer upon completion, and the heat factor for wearing heavy armor may be unbearable even for those protected from the heat of the Plane of Molten Skies and the Plane of Fire.

The best armor shop within the Bazaar of Arms is the Gleaming Panoply. Here, the **efreeti** (with Charisma 20, Deception +11 and Persuasion +11) merchant Tahiq sells armor both magic and fantastic. His prices are high, being a minimum of 25% over market price, but his quality is assured. There is a 30% chance that any armor the characters may be seeking can be found within his shop. Exceptional armors may be crafted by Tahiq's azer slaves or ordered from the fire giants within the Citadel of the Fire Thane for a nominal handling fee. Tahiq may offer to knock off a portion of his price should the characters offer to go to the Citadel of the Fire Thane or the Spire of Abul al'Hazrad the Mad and bring back items he needs.

16. Qadir's Arms

Pole arms are notoriously difficult to make and use in the great heat of the city, but **Qadir**[1], a burning dervish sorcerer with a somewhat mad disposition, employs a variety of **azer** and **arcanist**[1] slaves to create polearms using special metal alloys for the haft, and adamantine blades. While these arms are still twice as heavy as standard polearms, they easily withstand the constant heat without stressing or weakening. Qadir can have these blades ensorcelled with a variety of different spells.

Qadir has a *+2 falchion* and a *potion of flying* with him at all times, along with a bag of 6 aquamarines worth 500 gp each.

17. The Burning Link

Narliv Al'Ora, a squat, powerfully built **efreeti**, rules over a team of **azer** slaves and two elven **incantors**[1] as they create fine links of chain mail from a special alloy of adamantine and mithral that is reddish-black in appearance. The wizards can enchant the chain shirts and suits of chain mail up to +3 enhancements with a variety of special magical abilities available. Al'Ora's normal mark-up of 50% can be significantly reduced with the offer of a suitable slave, or a round of heavy negotiation.

18. Baracus' Blades

Baracus[1] seems out of place in the City of Brass: a blonde-haired, bearded barbarian from snow-clad lands. The sole survivor of a disastrous longboat raid into warm southern climes, he was captured by genie warriors and brought to the City of Brass as a slave. After winning his efreeti master a small fortune in gold, gems, and magic items, he was granted his freedom and enough money to start his own business. The only condition of his freedom was that he could never leave the City of Brass.

Baracus realizes that he is stuck in the City of Brass for a long time, so he has spent the intervening years building up a successful blacksmithing enterprise, producing fine metal goods as well as masterwork arms and armor. His old master, the efreeti lord Mudeen al Sharir, is actually one of his patrons, employing the barbarian to craft weapons and armor for his gladiators. Baracus has become a wealthy man, taken a wife — another one of Mudeen's former slaves whom Baracus bought from his old master.

Baracus has grown weary of life in the City of Brass, and wishes to leave, despite the fact that he will be returned to slavery if he is caught. He offers up his finest creation, a *frost brand greatsword*, in exchange for aid in escaping the city. He wants his wife Najima (**sorcerer**[1]) to come as well, for he knows that she will be punished should he successfully escape and leave her behind.

Treasure: Hidden in several locked chests is 20,000 gp, 5,000 pp, 6,500 bp, 30 bloodstones (50 gp each), and 5 fiery yellow corundum (1,000 gp). Unlocking the chests requires a successful DC 25 Dexterity check with thieves' tools.

19. The Bone Forge

Within the Bazaar of Arms is a massive warren of forges run by hundreds of **efreeti skeletons**[1], **fire giant skeletons**[1], and **azer skeletons**[1]. This network is responsible for the majority of the Sultan's armies' weapons and armor. **Sim ral Marla**[1], a rather young lich, and his servants operate the forges. Note that Marla's undead servants have 20 additional hit points and and do an additional 8 points of damage when they hit with a weapon attack. In addition to mundane weapons and armor, they also create numerous magical and wondrous items. Many are immediately available. Other weapons can be special ordered. Sim ral Marla has a *staff of necromancy*[2], a *spell wand*[2] of *greater invisibility*, a *brazier of commanding fire elementals, bracers of defense*, and 25,000 gp in gems, jewels, and coins.

20. The Green Tiger

This casbah on the edge of the Plaza of Amirs is the secret headquarters of Nam'Umun Na, a **maharaja rakshasa**[1] who wanders the planes acquiring thousands of objects that are considered hard to acquire or are outright illegal. He has a small house behind the Executioner's Edge. Those who make a successful DC 25 Charisma (Investigation) check are able to arrange a meeting with one of Nam'Umun's agents. For the right price, usually twice the typical cost, he can acquire anything that would otherwise be impossible to find within the confines of the City of Brass.

Nam'Umun Na's agents (**assassins**) typically blend in with the rest of the crowd. They could be anyone or anything.

21. Plaza of Amirs

Efreeti war masters have perfected the craft of magical siege engines and huge war weapons. In the Plaza of Amirs, they sell them to otherworldly leaders to use in their constant ideological warfare. From foundries and workshops manned by azer slaves within the bowels of the Ziggurat al Nar come efficient death-dealing machines of slaughter and destruction. Magic battering rams, soul engines, war golems, and missile weapons that hurl powerful bolts of magical fire and screaming death may be found in this quarter of the Bazaar of Arms. Each of these powerful weapons has been specially charged to fail if ever used against the efreet and their beloved city, and their charter as arms dealers throughout the lower and inner planes guarantees that any who raise arms against them can be assured to lose contracts for the construction of such items for their forces in the future.

Many of these powerful weapons of destruction are far out of the reach of a normal party of adventurers to purchase, and the restrictions on their use in their home plane by the gods may be severe. There is always the possibility that you may be running a high-level campaign and wish to send the characters in search of one of these items as a plot device, or for use in large-scale combat scenarios. Some samples of what can be found here are detailed below.

Magic Missile **Ballista:** This functions as a standard ballista but fires oversized *magic missiles*. Each *magic missile* has a range of 240 feet and deals 13 (3d8) force damage. Unlike a standard ballista, this device can be fired for five consecutive rounds before it needs to be "reloaded." Reloading a *magic missile* ballista simply requires the firing crew wait two full rounds while the device "recharges." Price 30,000 bp.

***Shattering* Ram:** This battering ram is magically charged with a *shatter* spell (usable twice per day, cast with a 9th level spell slot, spell save DC 20). When the ram strikes a solid surface (such as a gate or wall), it releases a *shatter* spell targeted at whatever it struck. Price 20,000 bp.

War Golems: War golems are stone or iron golems fitted with an array of weapons including lightning blasters (fires a *lightning bolt* once per round, 17 (5d6) lightning damage, spell save DC 17) and *fireball* or *cone of cold* cannons (both can fire once every other round, cast with a 7th level spell slot, spell save DC 17). A weapon can be used instead of a slam attack in the golem's mutiattack. Some war golems are fitted with weapons taken from other worlds and can include modern or futuristic weapons. Price 50,000 bp.

Government District

The government district includes **The False Palace of Wonders, Palace of Commerce, Parliamentary Dome, Bureau of Magic**, the **KhizAnah**, and other symbols of the Grand Bureaucracy that makes up the civil authority of the City of Brass.

22. The Palace of Commerce

The Palace of Commerce contains the offices of Weights and Scales, offices of the Magistrate of Finance and Trade, Office of Slave Registration, and the like. These hundreds of offices are each variously administrated by a ranking noble efreeti bureaucrat. In essence, the Palace of Commerce is the center of the efreeti Grand Bureaucracy, as it is where the money is. The Palace of Commerce is also the location of the city's nonmagical treasury known as the KhizAnah.

Individuals seeking exclusive trade agreements with the City of Brass for some of its more exotic materials such as living brass or *elemental diamonds*[2] and the like must first get license from the offices of the Palace of Commerce. Slave traders seeking notarization of their cargo of misery register their wares here, as do crafts-folk not dealing in magic or some other trade good dealt with by another office. These licenses do not come cheap and the price may not always be in the form of hard currency. Such is the nature of doing business in the City of Brass.

23. Bureau of Magic

The Bureau of Magic works closely with the Sultan's security forces to see that illegal magic such as cold- and water-based spells and magic items are not illegally used or smuggled into the City of Brass. Their authority extends to and includes overseeing security of the Palace of False Wonders, the Great Repository, the Dome of Gates, and the Mosque of Smokes. The Bureau is overseen by Faseeha al-Halaby, an **efreeti sorcerers**[1] appointed from the Council of Viziers whose headquarters is within the Mosque of the Burning Ones. The Magistrate of Magic sets minimum prices for the trade of magical items sold within the Bazaar of Arcana.

The Bureau of Magic is also the first cog in the engine for those not connected to the nobility who seek to peruse the efreet's massive collection of spells, relics, and rare magic items. For a fee, the Magistrate of Magic may find it within her power to see that an individual finds what he or she seeks within the City of Brass. Depending on the bribe she takes, this help may be in the form of a lesser pass to view spells or magic items within the Great Repository or the Palace of False Wonders. A larger donation or appropriately difficult Charisma check and she may have the name of someone who can get them better access, such as nobles with whom she is on good terms.

24. Bureau of Taxation

The Bureau of Taxation sees that the Sultan gets his share of every trade, deal, and purchase made within the City of Brass. Efreeti tax collectors working under the Magistrate of Taxation filter throughout the city making spot audits of every stall, every shop, every brothel, and every casbah. It is not uncommon for these lesser bureaucrats to stop wealthy looking foreign visitors to assess the value of their goods and apply a 15% tax to the worth of any possessions beyond those that are worn on their person. For example, the armor, necklaces, rings, amulets, and sheathed weapons are tax exempted. The contents of a person's pouches, sacks, and bags, however, are taxable, as is the estimated value of any pack animals, or trains of slaves or porters and their belongings. Once taxed, a person is given a magical ivory chit bearing the seal of the Great Sultan that disappears after nine days. Displaying a tax exemption chit to a tax official allows an individual to avoid paying a second tax until their nine days pass, at which time they are considered taxable again. A person bearing a rod of embassy is exempt from taxation, or any other molestation while within the City of Brass.

25. Parliamentary Dome

This huge domed structure acts as the negotiating body between efreeti commoners, the governing royal families, and the Sultan. Meeting once every three months or whenever a special assembly is called, the parliament is little more than a sham of a government as everyone knows the Sultan rules the City of Brass absolutely. In essence, the parliament is no more than a kangaroo court as the Sultan handpicks each "elected" official to further his own wishes and desires. For their part, most efreet are too frightened to stand up against the Sultan or could care less who rules the City of Brass. Few of their number actually toil, save for those who have foolishly allowed themselves to be enslaved to other masters.

26. The KhizAnah

This area is fully detailed in **Chapter 25**.

District of Naibs

This district is directly above the infamous Bazaar of Arcana and has entrances to many of the most prodigious and powerful institutions in the universe of magic. Most of the homes and towers in this district are the "vacation" dwellings of famous wizards, sorcerers, and liches from across many worlds.

27. The Mosque of Smokes

The Mosque of Smokes is a large structure whose foundations are laid within the middle city. It rises to the level of the upper city where smokes of strange color seep from beneath its hammered brass eaves. Etched double doors of solid iron lead into the mosque on the upper and middle levels of the city. The interior of the mosque has the luster of highly polished black hematite, its floor a swirling mosaic of multi-colored semi-precious stones.

The Mosque of Smokes is famous throughout the planes as a center for gaining and bending of the second sight and for receiving powerful oracles. Efreeti sages have been delving into the hidden secrets of the oracles that flash across the huge domed ceiling of the Mosque of Smokes for thousands of years. Through its kaleidoscope of swirling images, the efreet find amusement in observing powerful mortals whom they then seek to ensnare with wishes before binding them to eternal slavery.

Many are the foreign visitors who seek the oracle of the Mosque of Smokes. They come in search of secret lore and forgotten secrets. Many who find what they seek are driven mad by what they see. The whirling vortexes of multi-colored smoke djinn who power the oracle are often too awesome to behold. A visitor staring into the dome for the first time must succeed on a DC 23 Wisdom saving throw or become permanently insane, as if affected by a *confusion* spell.

A character that succeeds on its save can ask a question about the future and wait for the oracle to answer. This is similar to a *divination* spell, but the question does not have to concern a specific goal or event and can be up to 1 year in the future.

To do so, the character must make a DC 10 Charisma of Intalligence (Arcana) check (the player chooses). The answer revealed functions as a *divination* spell, so the exact results of the portent are left up to you, as is how much information is revealed concerning whatever the players ask. The base chance that the oracle answers correctly is 70% + 1% per point by which the player succeeded on the Charisma of Intalligence (Arcana) check. If the check failed, the chance for a correct answer is 70%.

The 5 enslaved **djinni** that make up the oracle of the Mosque of Smokes are bound to the stone and metal of the building itself. The mosque even seeps smoke that is the essence of these djinni oracles. Freeing them from their bondage results in their instant death.

The smoke djinni are in turn protected by no fewer than a dozen **efreeti loremasters**[1] who are immune to the maddening effects of the swirling smokes, having grown accustomed to it after several thousand years. Anyone attempting to harm a smoke djinn is attacked immediately.

The middle level of the Mosque of Smokes houses the various efreeti loremasters in their personal quarters. These loremasters keep a stable of scribes within the lower level of the mosque who studiously pound out details of the visions granted to their masters upon leaden plates. Those recorded visions and prophecies deemed of greatest worth and importance are locked within vaults at the very base of the mosque. Here, their secrets are protected from would-be thieves. Unlike the treasures within the Great Repository, information kept in the Mosque of Smokes is often knowledge related. Thus, studying the many revelations pounded into lead slabs in the bowels of the Mosque of Smokes for a month grants the character proficiency on any one of the following skills: Animal Handling, History, Medicine, Nature, Relighion, or Survival. Gaining permission to study these leaden tomes may prove a difficult task as the efreet tend to guard their secrets jealously. Leaden volumes weigh an average of 200 pounds, with each page-plate weighing about 8 ounces.

28. Tower of the Burning Ones

This tower is the center of power for a group of efreeti fire priests and evokers known as the burning ones, taking their name from the Cult of the sultan of efreet. They specialize in empowered fire-based spells or summoning magic. The Burning Ones are a secretive lot who are themselves separate from the commoners and the noble classes, owing allegiance only to their sect, and those who would hire them for their skill and power. Burning Ones often hire themselves out to noble families and powerful merchants as mercenary muscle for expeditions on other planes. Although the Burning Ones may serve in the retinue of other noble houses, professionalism dictates that they leave any personal grudges with other members of the Burning Ones when they are within the confines of the tower itself.

The inner circle of the Burning Ones, known as the Council of Viziers, is composed of 12 powerful efreeti spellcasters. The four **efreeti**[1] and eight **efreeti sorcerers**[1] of the council command dozens of apprentices, **iron golems**, **fire elementals**, and summoned monsters who do the bidding of their various masters.

29. Palace of False Wonders

The Palace of False Wonders extends from the very Basin of the city to the highest cityscapes of the Upper City. This heavily guarded fortress-like palace contains numerous replicas of powerful unique relics held here in state treasury by the masters of the City of Brass. The upper levels of the Palace of False Wonders contain many forgeries of true relics, which are then displayed, museum style within the palace, to show off the power of the Sultan and his people. Beings known only as sentinels (as **iron golem**) stalk the halls ensuring that troublemakers think twice before attempting any skullduggery. The actual relics possessed by the efreet are held within heavily protected vaults on the lower levels of the true Palace of Wonders, guarded by the deadliest of traps and the wickedest of guardians. Access to these relics may be granted to some few special visitors by the Great Sultan or the grand vizier, and this only to a selected few relics, and for the right price.

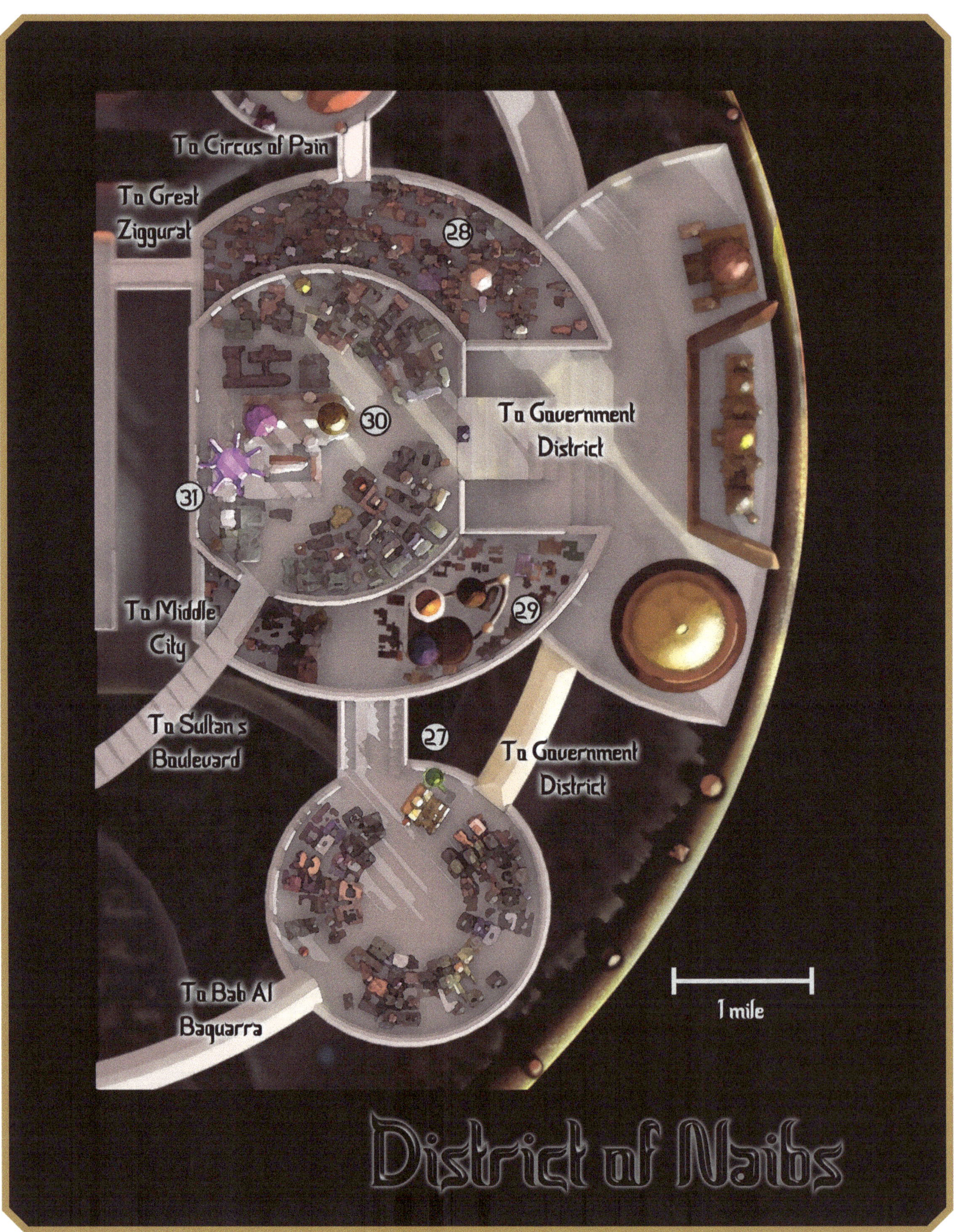

To Circus of Pain
To Great Ziggurat
28
To Government District
30
31
To Middle City
29
To Sultan's Boulevard
27
To Government District
To Bab Al Baquarra
1 mile
District of Naibs

30. Great Repository Annex (Upper Stories)

For more information on the Great Repository Annex, see **Chapter 14: The Middle City** (**Area 9**).

31. Great Repository (Upper Stories)

This area is fully detailed in **Chapter 21**.

32. Minaret of Screams

This area is fully detailed in **Chapter 20**.

33. Terrace of the Petitioners

The Terrace of the Petitioners is a broad curved terrace divided into three lines of waiting petitioners. The petitioners are drawn from every form of arch-mage, lich, and dweller of the lower planes imaginable, many with dozens and even hundreds of slaves and porters bearing gifts for the Great Sultan or one of his attendant pashas.

The eastern and western lines are each nearly two-and-a-half miles long curving toward the sixty-foot-tall grinning skull edifices of the Lesser Demon Gates, which lead to the palaces of the various pashas who serve the Great Sultan. A central, much shorter line leads to a broad staircase, and an even longer line crosses through the Sultan's Military District to the horrible countenance of the Greater Demon Gate.

The heat from the Curtain of Fire that separates the Exalted Enclave from the rest of the city is oppressive here. The Curtain of Fire, almost a half-mile high, ripples with waves of heat that cause the gleaming brass dome and high towers of the Sultan's Palace to appear as if they are a mirage wreathed in hellfire from this distance. The blast furnace environment feels like a slap in the face and is such a palpable force that even beings native to the Plane of Molten Skies but foreign to the actual Plane of Fire feel a certain degree discomfort.

The Sultan's cadre of bureaucratic efreet administer the various lines leading to the demon gates. These efreeti amirs are selected for their efficiency and efficacy in dealing with troublesome visitors; their job is to determine the business a petitioner has with any of the noble efreet. The petitioners line up in order of importance before the gates, where they must again state their reason for desiring an audience with one of the nobles of the City of Brass. An efreeti amir handles this duty. These efreeti in turn control the flow of foreigners into the Sultan's Military District, or directly into the Exalted Enclave itself. The most important visitors, such as visiting planar dignitaries (invited Demon Lords, ambassadors with a rod of embassy) of course are moved past the line and directly through whichever demon gate leads to their destination.

As is the law of the City of Brass, any visitor within the confines of the City of Brass has a right to seek audience with the pashas or the Great Sultan. This does not mean that petitioners will get an audience with either; it merely means they have the right to try, as the Sultan likes to think of himself as a "benevolent" despot.

As petitioners bring their gifts and documents forward in line, they can expect to wait up to 1d6 hours before they meet their first official who demands to know what business they have with the nobles of the City of Brass. Impressing one of the maliks or amirs requires at least one of the following:

• The petitioner is bearing an official and authentic invitation from one of the pashas, the Grand Vizier of Flames, or the Great Sultan himself. Individuals attempting to pass off a forged document must have scribed the document upon a paper-thin sheet of gold, imbued with *arcanist's magic aura*, and scribed in salamander blood. Even if all of these requirements are met, the bureaucrat who reads it still has advantage bonus on its Intelligence (Investigation) check to determine its authenticity.

• The petitioner is a bearer of a rod of embassy. If the rod of embassy was freely given, the bearer need make no further claim as to her reasons for passage. Rather, upon presenting the rod to a bureaucrat, the petitioner is immediately escorted to the proper demon gate. Bearers of a zinc rod are allowed free passage to the Noble Quarters. Bearers of a nickel rod are allowed free passage to the Plaza of Flame and the Noble Quarters. Bearers of a brass rod are allowed passage anywhere they wish to go.

• The petitioner offers a bribe. The petitioner makes an opposed Charisma (Deception or Persuasion) checks against the bureaucrat's Intelligence (Investigation) or Wisdom. The petitioner must offer a bribe of 10,000 bp minus 500 bp per point by which the petitioner wins the opposed check. If the bureaucrat wins the check, the bribe is still accepted if the petitioner pays 10,000 bp + 500 bp per point by which the bureaucrat won the check. Petitioners who fail the check by 10 or more are escorted off the platform and back to the Travelers Quarter and none too politely told to, "not bother coming back again." Petitioners who merely fail their check must wait 1d6 hours plus 1 hour for each point by which they missed their check.

Each **malik**[1] is escorted by 4 **efreeti** guards. Two **maliks**[1] and 1d4 **efreeti** assist each **amir**[1]. Should anyone be foolish enough to attack one of the bureaucrats or their attendants, 2d4 **efreeti** guards join the fight every round until the attackers are subdued or slain.

34. The Curtain of Flame (The Phlogiston)

A mile-high wall of flame marking the actual boundary of the Plane of Fire and the Plane of Molten Skies surrounds this section of the City of Brass. The flames are intensely hot and the only passage into the Noble District is restricted by a series of demonic gate guardians. This wall of fire is called the Curtain of Fire, Curtain of Flames, the Phlogiston, the Burning Wall, and a host of other names.

Wreathed in the Curtain of Flame itself, which rises from the tops of these grinning, horned skulls like a nightmarish halo of hellfire, stand the portals to the Upper City known as the Demon Gates.

Effects of the Curtain of Flame

Within 100 feet of the Phlogiston, a character takes 16 (3d10) fire damage each round (no save). Within 30 feet of the Phlogiston, a character takes fire damage and also must succeed on a DC 18 Dexterity saving throw each round or catch fire. A character coming into contact with the Phlogiston takes 110 (20d10) fire damage and must succeed on a DC 20 Dexterity saving throw or catch fire. Fire resistance offers protection against the effects of the Phlogiston, while characters immune to fire are completely unharmed.

The Noble District

The palaces of the ruling efreeti nobles flank the Palace of the Sultan. Trees of living gold and silver sprouting fruit of precious jewels stand in perfectly manicured groves before the large domed palaces. Within each palace, the noble efreet keep their personal armies of efreeti warriors, burning dervish assassins, bound demons, and constructs.

These palaces are all covered in magical traps and protections to keep rival houses from easily assassinating one another. Each noble house pays allegiance to the Sultan, although it could be said that none truly love him and that all seek to topple him and place their own pasha on the throne of the City of Brass. The efreeti ruling class is prevented from rebellion by binding magic that the Sultan placed upon many of the efreet of the lower castes and by the failed rebellion of the Dead Sultana. The ominous presence of the City of the Dead Sultana within view of many of the noble houses is a constant reminder of the fate that awaits those who betray the Sultan or think lightly of his might.

Although the Noble Houses are of roughly the same size, composition, and organization, they all have their own unique flavor and differences. For example, each of the noble houses has a unique dominion over the efreeti and a unique specialty to their powers and abilities.

The Houses

The population and powers of each noble house is left for you to decide. In general, most of the noble houses have the following population: 3d6 **efreeti amir**[1], 3d10 + 20 **efreeti** retainers, 4d10 + 40 slaves of various sorts, typically CR 1 to 6, 1d3 **burning dervish master assassins**[1], 1d3 **efreeti sorcerers**[1], an **efreeti amir**[1] house captain of the guard, and a majordomo (**efreeti amir**[1]). Numbers should be adjusted higher for more powerful houses and lowered for weaker ones. Houses may reflect more assassins, wizards, slaves, or retainers depending on the noble house's spheres of influence.

35. Bayt Al Sikkyn (House of the Knife)

The Bayt Al Sikkyn are feared as notorious patrons of assassins and sellswords. Unless a house assassin is employed by one of the other noble houses, the Sikkyn are likely to know about it. The assassins' guilds within the City of Brass must buy their sanction from the Al Sikkyn or face their wrath. This is equally true for any visiting assassin who seeks to ply his or her trade within the confines of the City of Brass. The Al Sikkyn have an extensive library of assassins' tactics and a notoriously thorough collection of poisons and antidotes.

Above all else, the Al Sikkyn despise a sloppy assassination. The more elaborate and well planned the murder, the more pleased the Al Sikkyn tend to be with the assassins in their stable. Finesse is the order of the day. An assassin who infiltrates the home of a mark and slowly feeds him a deadly poison makes more of an impression on the caliph of the Al Sikkyn than one who savagely cuts the throat of his target in a crowded souk. This is not to say that a dramatic public assassination is not sometimes required for shock effect, but rather the manner in which it is performed should be deliberate and well planned enough to ensure that the killer(s) escape and the blame is squarely placed upon one of the contractor's rivals.

Visitors seeking audience with Caliph Fatik (**efreeti amir**[1]), the master of the Al Sikkyn, most often do so with the intent of hiring one of his many assassins. Caliph Fatik charges a high price for the use of his Al Sakkyn killers, usually in the form of magical items, information, slaves, and rare gemstones. Naturally, the more difficult the target of the Al Sikkyn assassins, the more expensive the contract for assassination.

Caliph Fatik is a ruthless, calculating patriarch who likes to test the resolve of those who seek his house's services. It is not uncommon for him to take hostages of a new contractor's associates or family members, and keep them until the job is finished, to ensure the contractor does not lose her nerve.

Prestige: Well-known, well established.
Influence and Power: Political Assassination, mercenaries.
House Ruler: Caliph Fatik.
House Wealth: 4,000,000 gp in assets; 100,000 bp cash on hand.

36. Bayt al-Bakr (House of the Firstborn)

Of all the noble families in the City of Brass, the Bayt al-Bakr is believed to be the most ancient and powerful. It is commonly held that they are descendants of the first races of genie, those who were created by the gods in the time before time. Whether this is true or the product of long-term efforts to spread this belief is not entirely certain. Despite their noble ancestry and supposed power, al-Bakr is a house in steep decline. Al-Bakr's influence and authority fades as the Sultan claims ever more power for himself. With all their might dissipating before them, there is a growing sense of hopelessness that seems to pervade the core of the house. Many members of the clan have grown to accept the decreased status of al-Bakr with a touch of melancholy.

The Sheik Fahd bin Khalil bin Hashim (**efreeti amir**[1]) is not one of those. Since his ascension, the young sheik has quietly gathered his forces, reacting as best he can to this gradual erosion of power. Forging pacts with the other houses, notably the al-Waswas, Sheik Fahd has done everything he can to increase the flow of wealth to the family vaults and influence to the family loyalists. These efforts have achieved minor success by all accounts.

An added burden to these efforts has been the Sultan's secret police forces that seem to keep a constant watch over al-Bakr. Indeed, Sheik Fahd has been having some trouble of late guarding against hearsay that a secret plot is brewing to oust the Sultan and al-Bakr is at the center of it.

Prestige: Well-known, well established.
Influence and Power: Merchant Exchange, political, diplomatic.
House Ruler: Sheikh Fahd bin Khalil bin Hashim.
House Wealth: 8,000,000 gp in assets; 200,000 bp cash on hand.

37. Bayt al-Najoom (House of Stars)

Magic had always been the realm of al-Najoom before the arrival of the Sultan and the rise of his grand vizier. Now the House of Stars has fallen into a steady decline, losing their merchant wealth and public influence, slowly falling victim to a campaign by the Burning Ones to erode their power to dust. However, as sorcerers and masters of the forgotten lore, they have managed to keep their own secrets. This hidden wealth of magic has allowed Sheikh Azul bin Berith (**efreeti sorcerer**[1]) to maintain his position in the great noble houses of the City of Brass, thus keeping the most direct threats to the al-Najoom at bay.

These secrets have also made him a great number of enemies in the Council of Burning Ones and a considered threat to the grand vizier. Sheikh Azul bin Berith himself is the most stable of all the leaders of the noble houses, ruthless in his destruction of dissent from within. Bristling with arcane magic, few are willing to challenge him directly and those who do are quick to learn that his soft features are not indicative of his true nature. He alone protects the darkest secrets of the al-Najoom, the only living soul with access to a pocket dimension that allows the sheikh unlimited access to the vaults of the Great Repository unseen and undetected by the grand vizier or his many minions. This access does not come without a price. Azul is marked each time upon his back with demonic claw marks. He must cover these wounds for days afterward to hide his sacrifice from the spies of other houses.

Recently, Azul's daughter Maheen disappeared. He quietly seeks information as to her disappearance and fears she may have been captured by the Burning Dervishes to extract arcane information from his family. He offers a reward of wishes for her return and offers destruction to those who took her.

Azul purchased Vizier Juwanza Bin Hadeth (**arcanist**[1]), formerly the advisor to King Massini of Numeda. He is being held prisoner by the al-Najoom to learn more about the new world the Sultan is invading.

Prestige: Well-known, well established.
Influence and Power: Magic, Lore, Booksellers Guild.
House Ruler: Sheikh Azul bin Berith.
House Wealth: 4,000,000 gp in assets; 40,000 bp cash on hand.

38. Bayt al-Waswas (House of the Whisperer)

A long-standing tradition of mistrust in the doings of Bayt al-Waswas dates back to the times of their ignominious founder, the half-fiend efreeti now called Shezbeth (Liar), his true name forgotten. The common conception of them as worm-tongued advisors and sycophantic aides to Sultans has been woven deeply into the collective memory of the efreet. These beliefs about the al-Waswas are so ingrained that they are blinded to the reality before them. Indeed, the truth is that in council and in private, the noble efreet of al-Waswas rarely speak, content to quietly observe the doings of the other houses. They do not capitalize on the troubles of others nor do they seek power for themselves. They have not held a true advisory position to any Sultan in living memory. When Sheikh Fahd of Bayt al-Bakr came to them for aide, they offered it passively, selling them no hidden secrets, offering no known weaknesses of the Sultan for the firstborn house to exploit.

The Bayt al-Waswas seem undisturbed by common sentiment, and their lesser status leaves them free to quietly fade into the background of most meetings or conversations. Their social invisibility is their protection, their greatest trick upon the efreet and their ancient adversaries among the other noble houses. As none approach them, none see the secret doings of al-Waswas. The Liars need not ever speak for their intentions to be concealed; the distortions of common minds keep their truths buried under a thousand layers of accusation.

Prestige: Well-known, widely mistrusted.
Influence and Power: Merchant Exchange, diplomatic.
House Ruler: Rafiq al-Waswas (**efreeti amir**[1]).
House Wealth: 5,000,000 gp in assets; 400,000 bp cash on hand.

39. Bayt al-Ghaib (House of the Unseen)

Old spirits are the things that make Bayt al-Ghaib, their lingering presence all that keeps the House of the Unseen from fading into the past completely. Do not assume this is a figurative manner of speaking — it is not. Bayt al-Ghaib, while the youngest of the noble houses, is also the oldest of them all, its ranks filled by the spirits of those dead efreeti who would not let go of their ties to the living.

The public agents of the al-Ghaib are living efreeti relatives who would seem to possess little immediate interest in the outside world or the politics of the City of Brass. Their appearance at council and their presence walking the grounds of their estate is even rarer than outside visitors. The rumor that they are hiding secrets and power easily spread through the community of efreet. In truth, they are of passing interest only to anyone with true power, including the Sultan, who is more than willing to allow their survival.

The most public of the al-Ghaib is Abdul-Bari (**efreeti**), not a sheikh or a member of the Burning Ones. His status can be credited only to his odd relationship with Rafiq al-Waswas and the noble house al-Waswas, the pack of them seeming to be greatly indebted to him and reverent in his presence.

The rumor that he has somehow contacted Shezbeth on their behalf has not gone unnoticed, driving some of the most desperate to seek al-Ghaib's aid in contacting their own dead families.

Prestige: Minimal.
Influence and Power: Spirit World.
House Ruler: Abdul-Bari.
House Wealth: 500,000 gp in assets; cash on hand minimal.

Other Houses

You may create other houses to add flavor to your campaign. You may also assume that several of the estates remain vacant after one of the Sultan's many purges or await granting to a particularly efficient efreeti or burning dervish who shows promise in the eyes of the Sultan.

40. Tower of the Grand Vizier

This area is fully detailed in **Chapter 30**.

41. Circus of Pain

This area is fully detailed in **Chapter 23**.

42. City of the Dead Sultana

This area is fully detailed in **Chapter 22**.

43. Palace of the Great Sultan

This area is fully detailed in **Chapter 31**.

44. Sanctum of Rah'po Dehj

This area is fully detailed in **Chapter 27**.

Chapter 14
The Middle City

The districts of the Middle City make up many of the most famous bazaars in all the planes of existence. For this reason, they are titled by the name of the bazaar that they are part of rather than by an official district title.

Locations in the Middle City

The following are some of the area's more prominent places.

Middle City Encounters

Roll 1d8 for every hour spent in the Middle City.

1d8	Encounter
1	Thief
2	djinni merchant
3	Burning dervish[1] squad
4-5	Fire giant guard patrol
6-7	Wild champion warrior[1]
8	Hag (your choice)

Bazaar of 1,000 Sins (Middle City)

Roll 1d8 for every half hour spent in the Bazaar of 1,000 Sins.

1d8	Encounter
1	Pimp (djinni or efreeti)
2	Drug peddler (housebreaker[1])
3-4	Devil or Demon (your choice)
5	Street Walker (race of your choice; Cost = Charisma x HD x 10 bp)
6	Extortionist (**gladiator**, race of your choice)
7	Courtesan (race of your choice; Cost = Charisma x HD x 100 bp)
8	Torturer for hire (race of your choice, Cost = 100 bp)

Bazaar of 1,000 Sins

Located within the Middle City, the Bazaar of 1,000 Sins is a popular destination for otherworldly travelers who seek something a little different from their visit to the City of Brass.

Those who come to the City of Brass in search of their darkest desires and most perverse of delights may find them here. They may consume powerful and magical narcotics, partake of pleasure slaves, or possibly enjoy themselves at the hands of a highly skilled torturer. Anything is possible and probable if the consumer can afford to pay the price.

The air within this district is hot and sultry, and filled with the scents of sandalwood, jasmine, scorched garbage, and rank sweat. Incense and colored narcotic smoke mix and swirl to give the whole platform a mirage-like quality. A wavering sense of seduction and pain here is at once horrifying, exotic, and stimulating.

Pimps and pushers call out from the corners of tarnished or garishly annealed buildings offering their wares to passersby. Powerful illusions project images of the various pleasures each brothel, flophouse, gambling hall, or drug den has to offer upon the constantly roiling curtain of smoke that hangs like a pall over the Bazaar of 1,000 Sins.

1. The Purple Veil

The Purple Veil is an upper-class brothel located in the northeast corner of the Bazaar of 1,000 Sins. The Purple Veil charges a 100 bp membership fee to non-efreeti who seek admittance beyond its heavily guarded doors. The interior features a spacious dome high above bejeweled pillows of gold cloth, each of which is valued at nearly 100 bp. Lying astride the sumptuous pillows, slave men and women tempt and entice travelers to join them in private rooms hidden behind dazzling arabesque tapestries and polished basalt pillars carved in lewd forms that support the spacious ceiling. Painted upon the dome are coupling forms of wonder and degenerate perversity far too maddening for the mortal mind to fathom.

The Purple Veil is run by Master Futuh, a morbidly obese **efreeti** who keeps his harem drugged and docile for his high-class clientele. It is said that his slaves (as **hardy commoner**[1] with Performance +6) are second only to the harems of the noble efreeti themselves and trained in the finer arts of administering carnal pleasures to their jaded customers. Master Futuh wears a white gold ring with ruby (900 gp), a platinum bracelet (800 gp), and 2 additional gold rings (200 gp each).

2. Harem of the Bound Dancer

The gilt image of a dancing girl, with her hands tied over her head and a cruel leather gag stuffed into her mouth, stands atop the domed structure of the Harem of the Bound Dancer.

Visitors are greeted by a pair of **chain devil** eunuchs who direct them inside an establishment that is stark in comparison to the Purple Veil. All around are torture racks and devices for those interested in the darker side of life. Bare walls of blackest black and whitest white show the splattering of blood upon them. Nine doors lead from the central chamber, where would-be masters and those specifically trained and paid by the masters of the Harem meet with their chosen clientele for their evening of pain and degradation.

The nine doors each lead to nine hallways, each with nine more doors. What goes on beyond these doors is not spoken of, nor does such knowledge come cheap. A minimum price of 500 bp per hour offers the masochist the opportunity to spend some quality time with either a **chain devil** or **erinyes** of their choice. Observing such torture costs 300 bp an hour. Individuals with this particular perversion are escorted to finely adorned viewing chambers and treated to meals consisting of fine wine, and their choice of the victim of the day or something more civilized. A visitor to the Harem of the Bound Dancer wishing to participate as a master may do so for a price of 1,000 bp per hour. Prices are non-negotiable. Persons causing problems within this place ultimately face a retinue of **chain devil** guards and Ayasa al Shatan, the **horned devil** who rules over the Harem with a cruel passion for his work.

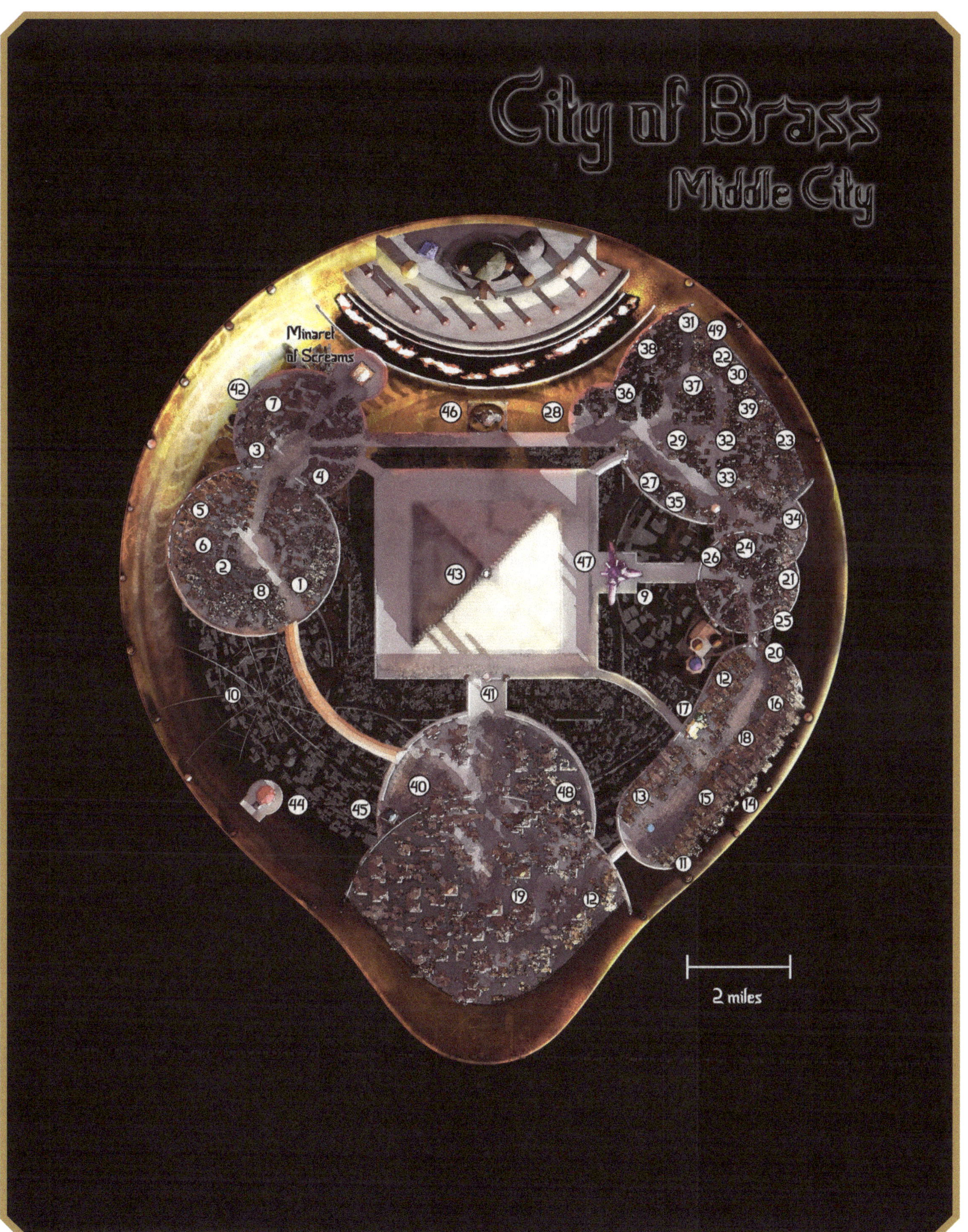
City of Brass
Middle City
Minaret of Screams
2 miles

3. Argeeli's Dream

This domed structure is primarily a smokers' casbah. Within its chambers are luxurious silk hangings and fluffy overstuffed pillows coated in cloth of gold. Exotic drugs of all sorts are procured and smoked from the huge argeeli pipes of pure crystal. Some such argeeli stand more than 12 feet tall and are filled with various substances from lotus-laden water to the floating corpses of demons, or the occasional water and air elemental. Cleolori Krimpz, a **night hag**, operates Argeeli's Dream. Her smoked drugs range from common tobaccos to the wildest narcotics of the material planes to more exotic flavors such as the larvae of evil folk and pineal glands of aboleth. She pays well for strange and exotic substances with which to ply her customers. Good characters should note that smoking any substance derived from a sentient being is an evil act. Evil characters should note that passing out from taking one of her substances means that Cleolori could very well be selling their essence to the next fool who comes along. Caveat emptor indeed!

Argeeli's Dream Services: The following are a sample of some of the unusual substances and their costs available from Argeeli's Dream. You are also encouraged to create your own.

Substance	Cost
Cannon[3]	50 bp
Ergos[3]	40 bp
Hannan[3]	25 bp
Higdne[3]	20 bp
Jena[3]	30 bp
Kesh-aath[3]	2 bp
Modron[3]	30 bp

4. The Gorger's Feast

As not all pleasures of the flesh are of the same genre, the Gorger's Feast seeks to serve those with the most varied and exquisite tastes in fine dining. This large banquet and dining hall boasts the indubitable distinction of being able to "cook anything you kill." Big-game hunters from throughout the universe bring their catch here to be prepared "any way they like it" — for an exceptional fee, of course. Others who are merely in the mood to "taste" something different are welcome to sample from the exotic menu. **Rewonek**[1], a drow, is the proprietor of the Gorger's Feast. Slim as a rapier and tall for his race, Rewonek knows exactly what wine to serve with whatever happens to be on your platter and is quick to see his wait staff refill your glass as soon as a draught is taken. Many of the more "refined" guests prefer to slay their own dinner before it is prepared. For that, a special "dinner theater" of sorts is a frequent draw for an evening's dining. The customer is placed within a cube-shaped *wall of force* with the prospective dinner and allowed to fight it out to the amusement of the Feast's many guests. If dinner wins, it is immediately set free and all of the customer's gear becomes the sole property of the establishment.

5. The Assassin's Moon

A slim crescent moon denotes the entryway of this dark structure on the corner of the Necropolis Way. The Assassin's Moon is actually owned by the nobles of the Bayt Al Sikkyn. Many of their assassins collect information on their next mark from this building, which poses as a shop selling rare and exotic poisons to would-be murderers from a thousand dimensions. **Raakham Al Abash**[1] is the proprietor of the shop. His knowledge of poisons and rare alchemical materials is second only to the cruelty with which he extracts them from the rare creatures he keeps caged in the back of his shop (just about any poisonous creature, extraplanar or not, can be found here at one time or another).

6. Al Shallaam's Coiffures and Beauty

This small shop caters to those who seek the perfect hairstyle and makeup to match any ensemble. Al Shallaam employs a dozen skilled hairdressers and makeup artists who for a price (and occasional use of magic) can perform true miracles of beauty and wonder. The shop is owned by Asima al'Madr (N human **orator**[1]). She wears a living brass necklace with emerald stones (7,000 gp), 3 gold rings (150 gp each), and a *ring of comfort*[2].

Getting a trim and a style from one of these expert beauticians grants the character +2 on Charisma-based checks when dealing with members of the appropriate sex (of a race the character's race finds attractive) for 2d6 days. An Al Shallaam beauty makeover can increase the bonus to +4, but it lasts only 1d4 days. More intensive work such as age defying skin treatments cost extra but can knock 2d10 apparent years from the flesh of any recipient. It is even rumored that unwanted fat can be magically removed or "redistributed" to more appealing areas of the body.

Al Shallaam's Coiffures and Beauty Services: Services offered by Al Shallaam's include:

Service	Cost
Trim-n-Style	10 bp
Al Shallam Beauty Makeover	50 bp
Skin treatment	70 bp
Body reconfiguration (fat redistribution)	2,000 bp

7. Hori's Boutique

This boutique serves to siphon the funds earned by the many prostitutes, temple virgins, and pleasure slaves who ply their trade within the Bazaar of 1,000 Sins. Owned and run by Khafi Jazeer (an **erinyes**), this shop offers boudoir wear and dancing attire made of the most unique and fashionable materials. A few of the items sold here possess unique magical properties. Khafi Jazeer wears 3,400 gp worth of various jewelry.

Hori's Boutique Services: Items for sale here include:

Item	Cost
Boudoir wear, average	20 bp
Boudoir wear, fine	150 bp
Dancing attire, average	20 bp
Dancing attire, fine	100 bp
Slippers of seductive dancing[2]	2,000 bp
Girdle of touch me not[2]	11,400 bp

8. Faakhira's Conservatory

Many of the slaves and daughters of deposed nobles who find themselves in the Bazaar of 1,000 Sins need some training before being turned loose upon the unsuspecting masses who throng to the bazaar. It is at Faakhira's Conservatory where they are trained in the arts of seduction, dance, music, and the physiology of beings from many strange worlds. A course in training at Faakhira's Conservatory usually entails getting the prospective pleasure slaves addicted to kesh-aath, an addictive, inhibition-numbing drug frequently used by the masses that swarm the bazaar. Once the addiction is complete, the training truly begins. **Faakhira**[1] is a believer in the "spare the whip" philosophy and has been known to beat more than one of her more willful charges to death. On rare occasions, she has horribly scarred the faces or bodies of those whom she perceives are more beautiful than she is.

Faakhira must be careful in this however, for the masters of these pleasure slaves have been known to exact a high price for damaging their property. Despite her shortcomings, Faakhira is good at her job, for the pleasure slaves of the Bazaar of 1,000 Sins are renowned throughout the multiverse as the best at what they do.

Faakhira wears a diamond ring (2,000 gp), ruby earrings (1,500 gp pair), and a ruby and sapphire necklace (5,000 gp).

9. The Repository Annex

While the Repository itself is, for all intents and purposes, off-limits to just about everyone in the known universe, the Annex is open to any who can afford the price of admission. Unlike the great tower beside it, payment does not mandate the sacrifice of any body parts or memories. The building housing the Annex hangs from the underside of the Palace of the Khan by a single enchanted, unbreakable strand of hair taken, according to popular legend, from the flame-witch Madani Jahani. A wobbly bridge made from living brass and obsidian connects it to the same platform as Indizhar's Bridge on the opposite side. Deeply colored crimson veins bore through the flesh-colored marble stone making up the building's walls. Unlike the Repository, the Annex appears to be built according to perfectly ordinary architectural doctrines — it is box-like, with thirteen broad levels supported by ornate arabesque columns. However, like the Repository, the Annex just does not seem to belong in the City of Brass — and yet it does. It continually exudes an ineffable sense of otherworldliness.

The Annex is a storehouse for spellbooks, scrolls, and other arcane and divine magical writings taken from spellcasters who've become slaves within the City of Brass. A perpetual queue of spellcasting petitioners extends out from the doors (which have not closed in more than 2,000 years), across the black glass bridge, onto the platform, and then down a spiral staircase that descends to numerous platforms in the Lower Levels and Basin. It is said that some mortal wizards have undergone the sickening transformation into lichdom as they have waited for the Sultan's or Grand Vizier's permission to access the Annex's tomes, many of which are severely restricted. More than a few of these stalwart knowledge-seekers continue to wait and have taken up residency among the crypts of the Basin within the Great Ziggurat. Others, impatient with the decades-long wait in some cases, have broken down in the end and made the requisite sacrifice to interact directly with the scholars in the Repository. Most have lived to regret the experience. A squad of **fire giant** soldiers and **efreeti** guards the building's entrance. Inside the foyer, an **efreeti** clerk and a gaggle of **azer** assistants manage access to everything inside.

Admission to the Annex requires payment of a magical item with a value of at least 1,000 bp (5,000 gp). Upon paying this admission price, the efreeti clerk or his assistants takes the petitioner into the stacks where piles of magical tomes are located. Individuals seeking to learn new spells find that they may learn any arcane or divine spell of up to 6th level by studying the tomes found within the stacks. This of course excludes cold-based and water-based spells (none of which are available; scrolls with such spells are destroyed, while the pages within a spellbook or tome are erased). Scribing spells from the stacks costs the seeker an additional 20 bp per spell level, which is paid to one of the assistants upon selection and scribing of the spells. The tomes and scrolls in this place are for reference, scribing, and learning only — none are for sale. Any enslaved character spellcasters find their spellbooks, scrolls, and such stored in this place. A character slave that buys freedom (or escapes) can buy back a lost spellbook (or scrolls, and so on) upon proof of prior ownership and payment of the asking price (usually total spell levels x 5 bp).

10. Nyissa's Web

In the Middle Levels, strung between the Pagoda of Devils, a residential tower, and the Bazaar of 1,000 Sins, is a web woven entirely from hemp and brass thread. Each strand is as thick around as a fire giant's arm. It is the home of **Nyissa**[1], the self-proclaimed head priestess of the spider goddess. The web lies flat, looking down on the city beneath it. It is a complex, dizzying array of shapes purported to be sacred to the goddess, shapes that symbolically represent her true name — the name by which her chosen few shall know her — in a hundred different languages. The center of the web supports Nyissa's lair, a spherical basket made from brass-reinforced wicker and the nexus of the web's numerous strands. She never leaves her home, which is roughly the same size inside as a three-story house, nor does she receive many visitors. Those who seek an audience with her must enter through a difficult entrance in the bottom of the basket. Many would-be seekers of the spider goddess's wisdom have died attempting to see Nyissa in person, falling to their deaths in the City Basin.

Navigating the web requires a successful DC 20 Strength (Athletics) check per round and it takes 10 rounds minimum to reach the center. Anyone attempting to climb around the basket to get to the door underneath it must succeed on a DC 25 Strength (Athletics) check each round.

Nyissa is a peculiar woman, to say the least. She is of elven heritage but tries to make people believe she is a drow. As her pale white skin and golden locks belie such a fanciful heritage, she dyes her skin and hair with indigo woad on a weekly basis. A successful DC 15 Wisdom (Perception) check while viewing her reveals the truth quickly enough. Moreover, she is not truly a cleric of any spider goddess known to the people of the City of Brass. She's simply another crazy person with way too much time and rope on her hands. But that doesn't stop some people from coming to her. In fact, a small cadre of disciples (as **hardy** and **greater commoners**[1], various races) has attached themselves to the high priestess, hanging their own meager baskets from the web in an attempt to live near her sacred presence. Every once in a while, unfortunately, a visiting wisdom seeker climbing through ropes inadvertently knocks one of their baskets loose and sends it plunging toward an ignoble end in the City Basin.

The monks in the Pagoda don't mind the web being attached to it, as they see Nyissa's folly as a harmlessly amusing distraction. Meanwhile, the patrons who visit the bazaar are generally so filled with lust and mind-altering chemicals that they more or less regard her as an amusement and curiosity.

Souk Dhimmi

This foreign quarter sits on an iron and steel platform that emerges from the city's inner wall. Houses are built from different grades of steel, mostly because the foreigners living here (called *dhimmi* by the locals) are not allowed to live in brass buildings. Even slaves are allowed to have brass housing, if their masters so will it, but dhimmi are not. In fact, it is against the Sultan's law for a foreign guest of the City of Brass to live above his station, though there are notable exceptions. Dhimmi caught with brass furnishings or constructions must pay a stiff fine; those who are caught with living brass are summarily executed. The dhimmi are those foreigners who are engaged in official business with the Sultan's administration, such as trade offices, embassies, and other members of foreign government.

Foreigners in the city on unofficial business — that is, the ones who came in through the normal channels, uninvited, can live wherever they can afford. The only stipulation placed on such foreigners is that they pay a unique tax that is supposed to guarantee their protection while in the City of Brass. The parameters of this protection are such that the sultan's officials almost never have to act on it, nor are they willing to reimburse the tax in the event the city's so-called protections fail. The dhimmi, on the other hand, are tax-exempt due to their diplomatic status, which gives them a whole host of fringe benefits not available to other foreigners. Of course, being tax-exempt means they suffer considerable drawbacks, as well, such as not being allowed to enter any part of the city outside their souk without the proper paperwork. Guards love nothing more than hassling dhimmi who don't have their papers. Many make several times their regular monthly salaries collecting bribes from such unfortunate foreigners.

One nice thing about the souk is that things normally proscribed in the city proper can often be acquired in it. Technically speaking, the souk is off-limits to the Sultan's people due to various treaties with foreign and other planar governments, though that certainly does not prevent them from entering it when they really need or want to. However, they generally leave the souk alone in order to not rock the diplomatic boat too much. As a result, many illegal things enter the city on diplomatic wagons. The foreign black market thrives in the souk. It always seems to be three steps ahead the sultan's dervishes, whose informants somehow manage to give them outdated information every single time.

The souk's most prominent citizen is a human named **Noman al-Ajadi**[1], once a caliph in a desert kingdom on a mortal plane. His house sits atop an artificial hill, looking down on both the souk over which he rules and the Lower Basin below. Rumors run rampant that he and the Sultan are very close friends and that someday he may be allowed to move to the city's upper levels, a first for a dhimmi. Any time foreigners run into trouble with the law, they tend to go to al-Ajadi for help. He never gives assistance for free, although he gladly takes payment in the form of favors if a petitioner has enough power or influence to pique his interest.

The least prominent citizen residing in the souk is the dwarf poet everyone knows simply as Ydnar of Looh (CN **hardy commoner**[1]). How he got to the Plane of Molten Skies — much less the City of Brass — is a mystery to everyone who has ever had the misfortune to encounter him, especially given that he is so incompetent at everything he does. One story currently circulating in the night markets is that Erkath Bal, a goddess on his native plane, cursed him with madness and displacement after he offended her with his ill-chosen words and loutish speech. As a poet, he failed miserably. In the City of Brass, he has sunk to lower depths; he can be found walking around the streets in tattered swaddling, carrying a threadbare teddy bear in one hand and ringing a brass bell with the other, crying at the top his lungs about a conspiracy to discredit his art. He also believes the demon-lord Orcus spends every waking moment plotting to kidnap **Grumby the Bear**[1] so he can sell it to Lucifer for 1,000,000 bp and a bone hairbrush. To say Ydnar of Looh is insane is something of an understatement.

Souk Dhimmi maintains its own watch, paid out of taxes on items sold in the black market. These mercenaries hail from all planes of existence, but most are human. They tend to be adventurers who live in the district and who take a percentage of pay to work a few days a week patrolling it.

11. The Iron Fortress

This fortress built upon the corpse of an iron giant serves as the headquarters for **Noman al-Ajadi**[1]'s diplomatic mission and financial enterprises in the City of Brass. The oddly shaped structure is heavily guarded by al-Ajadi's private mercenary force (**commnder**[1], typical) and warded against magical intrusions by those who would seek to rob him. Meetings with al-Ajadi are by appointment only if he knows you, or not at all if he doesn't. Rumors abound that the iron giant is not truly dead and that one day it will awaken from its slumber. Nobody knows what to expect when that happens. Until that day, however, Noman al-Ajadi is content to make it his home.

The lower half of the fortress sits atop the dead giant's folded arm and chest. There are three towers and one barbican gateway here. It is where most of the daily traffic passes through. Inside, a crooked staircase climbs to the giant's shoulder and back, where there is a second wall, another heavily guarded gate, and two more towers. Behind the second wall is al-Ajadi's residence, as well as barracks for his soldiers, and storehouses that allegedly descend into the giant's body cavity. The back of the fortress has a small servants' entrance, but no formal gates. Seven more towers line the rear and lateral walls. Rumors say there is a secret door in the giant's left foot along with a narrow tunnel that bores through the leg bones and deposits a person in the main residence's food pantry.

Al-Ajadi wears silk robes (5,000 gp), salamander-scaled boots (1,000 gp), and 3 platinum rings (600 gp each). He carries a *+3 longsword* and 400 bp.

12. Black Market

There is no single black market per se, unlike the countless day and night markets sprouting up in every alley wide enough to support a stall or three. Instead, the black market has fixers (**burglars**[1], **sneakthiefs**[1], and **commoners**) in every major market who are willing to do business with people whom they consider trustworthy. Fixers engage in normal market business as a cover, but are distinguished by a small red hand inside a red circle, usually placed discreetly in the corner of their shingle or standard. One must approach the fixer with the words "'Salam ala'kham!' cried the water-seller." (This is a line from a not-so-well known tale about a thief who stole everything from a rather doltish sultan.) Once in a fixer's good graces, a person can purchase just about anything. Something illegal or rare is typically sold above market value; common items are typically 60% of market value and invariably stolen property. Specialty illegal goods arrive on diplomatic wagons. If there is one thing al-Ajadi forbids, it is organized thievery in the souk itself, not that the really desperate or determined are swayed by his edicts.

13. Mastaba Well

One of the larger public wells in the souk, the Mastaba Well is so named because of the inordinately large number of *mastabas* (stone benches) surrounding it. Old men and women frequently gather at the well, sitting on the benches all day long while they drink tea or coffee, gossip, and play games. Up to 2 pints of water can be freely taken from the well (this is a person's daily ration). After a person's daily limit is reach, each additional pint of water must be purchased by that character at a cost of 1/2 bp (or 2 gp, 5 sp).

Other people from the surrounding neighborhoods come here to claim their daily ration of water, which is overseen by an **efreeti** named Dafydd Hezekiah. Hezekiah is unlike other efreeti in that he is not a native of the Plane of Fire — not of this timeline anyway. He comes from another time in another dimension where the entire efreeti race is enslaved to powerful and terrible azer lords.

At night, when Hezekiah goes home, he closes the steel lid on the well and locks it; he has the only key and he keeps it with him at all times. An enterprising burglar can pick the well's lock with a successful DC 20 Dexterity check with thieves' tools. If patrolling guards catch someone stealing water, they throw the thief off the city's wall.

Investigation or other checks made to gather information at the Mastaba Well have advantage due to the gossipy nature of the people who frequent the place.

14. Old Sewers

Nobody can remember what used to sit near this section of the city's inner wall, but whatever it was, it must have been huge. At their smallest, the abandoned sewage tunnels inside the city wall are large enough for hill giants to comfortably move around inside, and as big as a dragon's cavern at their largest. In theory, the sewer system could conceivably descend the entire length of the wall, as well as go all the way around it. The last time a brave soul attempted to map it, she managed to document 15 square miles of it under Souk Dhimmi alone before getting eaten. A cartographer in the City Basin currently owns her maps, though how he got hold of them is unknown. Today, the tunnels are sealed off. Magic employed by the souk's mercenary wizards takes care of most sewage (for a fee, of course). Iron grates cover the few obvious sewer mouths that still remain. The thieves' guild has a candlemaker's shop over one prominent grate that gives access to one of three tunnel nexuses. Noman al-Ajadi is supposed to have an entrance somewhere near his home. Other hidden entrances also exist.

Nobody in their right mind goes into the old sewers anymore. If they do, then they are either foolhardy or suicidal. Strange creatures live in them, including, according to popular myth, an elemental crocodile that eats anything that comes near it, a colony of pacifist formian artisans, a chthonian elder god, and blind, bat-winged dinosaurs well adapted to the dark conditions. No one has ever returned to the souk with firm evidence of anything living in sewers, usually because they don't come back at all after they enter.

Old Sewers Random Encounters

Roll 1d20 once every 10 minutes the characters spend prowling the sewers.

1d20	Encounter
1	Flame-spawned giant crocodile[+]
2	1d3 + 1 bodaks[1]
3	1d4 + 1 vrocks
4	Roper
5	1d4 + 2 blind fiendish megaraptors[1]
6	Fiendish purple worm[1]
7–20	No encounter

[+]Immune to fire damage, add 1d6 fire damage to successful attack, and a creature within 5 feet takes 3 (1d6) fire damage at the start of its turn.

15. Si'la Market

This is one of the greatest markets in all the planes, stretching the entire length of Souk Dhimmi down Si'la Boulevard. Law and custom forbid efreeti and djinni vendors from selling their wares to dhimmi without prohibitively costly licenses. As such, many other vendors (**Si'la Merchant**[1], typical) of varying races have set up shop here. Thousands of vendors maintain tents, stalls, caravans, and pushcarts in the market, hawking any mundane item a person can imagine, as well as a host of magic items. Most any mundane item imaginable is available. Prices may vary widely amongst vendors. The Ibari Consortium — owned and operated by one of the Sultan's lazy, adopted nephews — acts as the Si'la

Market's **efreeti** police force; they are the one group in the souk beyond Noman al-Ajadi's control, much to his disgust. Even though the group's mandate is to ferret out thieves and black marketers, its members spend most of their time shaking down the vendors for bribe money. Despite the exorbitant prices, the market still makes money hand over fist. Nobles come from the city by permit to the market on a daily basis so they can shop, and they are more than willing to spend as much money as it costs to get goods they can't normally get in their own markets.

16. The Silver Kettle

This tiny little shop is on an insignificant byway off of Si'la Boulevard. Clusters of wool-scrubbed pots and pans hang from a hammered iron awning at the store's front. A wide window below the awning opens on the workshop within, which is crammed with hundreds of assorted cooking and kitchen implements in varying degrees of completion. Jack Shue (**greater commoner**[1]), the youthful half-elf proprietor, can always be found straddling an imported dragonwood bench, hammering away at something and muttering happily to himself about the "good old glory days of High Adventure."

Jack lives in a world of his own making. He's crazy with delusions of grandeur and has been since the day he woke up one day five years ago here in the City of Brass. He vaguely remembers finding a magic lantern once, but that's pretty much it. Calling himself "Diamond Jack," he firmly believes he is a notorious adventurer who has already conquered the greatest dungeons the multiverse has to offer. Unfortunately, he was forced into early retirement, he says, in order to keep things on an even keel for the other adventurers out there, you see. Rappan Athuk? No problem. In his world, he singlehandedly went from top to the bottom in less than 2 days' time. Remember the Hall of the Rainbow Mage? Easy as pie. He did it twice, the second time just for the hell of it. It doesn't matter what name a person throws at him; Diamond Jack has a surprisingly accurate-sounding tale about it. And don't even get him started on the City of Brass. As far as he is concerned, the Sultan rules by his providence alone. Jack fancies himself a grizzled scoundrel and lady's man. He is neither, just a simple pot maker. However, if you let him talk long enough, you just might start thinking there is a shred of truth in his words.

Jack's Goods: Jack has an assortment of goods he offers to the would-be buyer. A sample of them is listed below.

Service	Cost
Pot or Pan, iron	2 cp
Pot or Pan, brass	2 sp
Pot or Pan, living brass	3 bp
Utensils, iron	1 cp per 4 utensils
Utensils, living brass	1 bp each
Maps, Sultan's Palace*	500 bp
Maps, Ziggurat of Flame*	100 bp
Maps, City of the Dead Sultana*	200 bp
Maps, Rappan Athuk*	100 bp
Maps, Tomb of Abysthor*	100 bp
Information, souk gossip	1 bp
Information, city gossip	1 bp

*These maps are fakes with absolutely no basis in reality, though they are of exceptional quality. Characters who have seen these places firsthand immediately know the map is fake.

17. Bobbit of Sharidesh

Bobbit (**commoner** with Deception +6 and a *ring of immunity*[2] [fire]) is not so much a shop as he is an institution. This little, brown-skinned street urchin sits on the same street corner every single day, plying his trade, such as it is. He wears stained cotton trousers that are two sizes too large and a ratty, cotton turban (inside which he hides an incredibly long braid of hair). He loudly offers his services to any and all passersby. If someone doesn't require anything, he resorts to flat-out begging. Or, he plays the sympathy card by telling a sad story about how his parents and 13 older siblings died unfortunate deaths when the ferry to the Middle City capsized, dumping passengers and crew fifty stories. Above all else, Bobbit is polite in his interactions, especially if people are rude to him. He might be dirt poor and stink to heaven, but by the gods he's still got his manners.

Bobbit's Services: Bobbit offers the following to his customers:

Service	Cost
Earwax removal	1 cp
Nostril cleansing	1 cp
Hair cutting	2 cp
Fingernail cutting/cleaning	1 cp
Toenail cutting/cleaning	2 cp
Tooth brushing	1 cp
Praise and adoration	1 cp
Manservant	5 sp per day
Street guide	3 cp per hour
Spying	2 sp per day
Message running	2 cp
Errand running	4 cp per errand

18. Jewel of Beshevar

Hami al'Hazred, an elderly **cheitan**[1], started this shop 100 years ago after he was discharged from the city's militia. He had always wanted to sell the exquisite rugs made in the outlying towns and villages, places where he was stationed for much of his military career. Just before he left the military, he wisely married a woman whose entire family did nothing but weave rugs. She had a terrible disposition, the kind that never let her speak a kind word to or about anybody. Hami felt quite relieved when she died. As was her village's custom, he cremated her. As a final farewell, he fed her ashes to the goats outside their house. Today, he and his six children (**cheitan**[1]) run the Jewel. His eldest son, Hami II transports new rugs from their grandparent's workshop in their home village on a weekly basis, using the family wagon (pulled by the family's two flame-spawned oxen and a flame-spawned bull borrowed from the kindly neighbors). Unbeknownst to the others in the al'Hazred family, Hami II has been having a secret affair with a young elf girl in the service of a minor noble.

The average rug is made from a combination of silk, wool, cotton, and goat hair, and is typically large enough to cover the floor of an entire room. One in ten rugs is actually a *carpet of flying*.

Jewel of Beshevar Goods: The following can be purchased from Hami al'Hazred:

Item	Cost
Rug, ghadar	100 bp
Rug, khosujay	200 bp
Rug, asab	300 bp
Rug, bopal	400 bp
Carpet of flying (4 feet by 6 feet)	5,000 bp
Carpet of flying (5 feet by 7 feet)	8,000 bp
Carpet of flying (6 feet by 9 feet)	14,000 bp

Ghadar Rug: This style of rug is distinguished by its reliance on the different shades of red to create patterns. It is generally used for telling tales about a family's prominent ancestors.

Khosujay Rug: This is a prominent style found in the households of minor nobility and the moderately wealthy. The patterns woven into it tend to show fanciful gardens and buildings in paradise.

Asab Rug: Marked by a predominance of tan and black hues, this style once enjoyed fame as the rug of choice among previous sultans. It is also one of the most durable rugs, taking a very long time to wear out.

Bopal Rug: The most expensive rug one can buy, it is characterized by the filaments of gold, platinum, copper, and brass running through it.

Some varieties are known to have living brass, which can dynamically change the patterns according to the owner's whimsy.

19. Servants' Quarter

The vast majority of the households in Souk Dhimmi have servants (tiefling **greater commoner**[1], typical) of some sort, usually of the tiefling variety. Though tieflings are *persona non grata* in the City of Brass, they are allowed in the souk strictly as second-class citizens in the employ of foreign diplomats, their friends, and families. In truth, practically anybody can get a permit for a tiefling servant. They can be recruited from agents in the Si'la Market. Tiefling wages are fixed by law at 2 sp per month, unless their masters require they find their own accommodations in which case they get 5 sp per month. The Servants' Quarter is where they live, not because they must but because it is the only place in the souk with housing they can afford. Tiefling-only markets abound, as do other shops owned and operated by azer slaves that cater to their specific needs (such as food and clothing). Every second weekend, tiefling servants are allowed one day off, and so fill the quarter, gathering in large groups to exchange news, gossip, gifts, and generally just enjoy the company of friends they haven't seen in two weeks.

Merchants in this quarter don't often sell to outsiders, not that outsiders would really want to buy their goods, as it is very shoddy. More often than not, it's secondhand or stolen from the households of their masters.

20. Sa Qahweh

Also know in Common as "Three Pounds of Coffee," this comfortable, spacious shop is owned by **Musa Ayoub**[1], who once served the Sultana in his childhood as a kitchen boy. During his time in her palace, he was always getting into trouble for talking with strangers. As such, when he finally retired, he decided to open a traditional-style coffee shop, not because he was an aficionado but because he wanted the opportunity to meet all kinds of new people. In the days before the current Sultan, things were much different. The foreigners living in it were of much better breeding than they are today, so it was only natural for him to open Sa Qahweh in their district.

The shop is situated in such a way that the sun always finds a way into the main sitting room. Cushions lie scattered all over the floor, turning the intermittently spaced wooden tables into small islands. Each table has one hookah, a bronze pot for dirty hookah water and expired tobacco leaves, and a tiny charcoal burner. Ayoub makes the coffee at a bar along the back wall, serving it in ornately carved stone cups. The coffee of his homeland is very rich and served with a healthy dollop of sugary tree sap. Most foreigners find it much too sweet for their liking, in fact. Learned men from the souk temples congregate here to debate religion, philosophy, and politics (though the latter not too loudly, for fear of dervish informants reporting their potential sedition).

Musa Ayoub Goods and Services: The following are a few of the coffees and items available from this shop:

Service	Cost
Coffee, local	4 sp
Coffee, imported	1 gp
Coffee, royal	1 bp
Dates	1 gp
Olives	4 sp
Rice pilaf	3 sp
Goat milk	3 sp
Lamb stew	1 gp
Hookah tobacco	1 bp

21. The Minter's House

This tiny, unassuming building is pressed up against the city's outer wall by just one of many barracks for the Sultan's elite soldiers. The mint is where the city's money comes from. It is surprisingly small considering the volume of brass pieces that come out of it. In truth, the mint doesn't really make the brass coinage, for that is done in the Agony Forge at the bottom of the Ziggurat of Flame, where azer slaves stamp captured souls into them. The coins are then enchanted by **Thunderheel Anger**[1], a minotaur sorcerer

from a world that no one remembers any more. The coins are not brought to the mint either, as Thunderheel can perform his magic from a distance. Also, he being here and the coins being in the Agony Forge ensures their security. Thieves would be harder pressed to rob the ziggurat, which is protected by the burning dervishes and the Sultan's head priest, than they would be trying to rob the mint itself. (Most thieves don't realize the coins aren't in the mint, and when they attempt to rob it end up finding a simple old minotaur playing chess with a **skeleton** named Zebediah.) Thunderheel has a *ring of immunity*[2] (fire), and a *staff of fire*.

Twice since assuming the job of master minter have adventuring companies kidnapped him and held him for ransom. Both times, the elite soldiers supposedly protecting him were summarily executed for their sloppiness. The burning dervishes recovered Thunderheel with little problem. The heads of the offending parties were filled with molten brass and then hung from the gates of the Sultan's palace as a warning to others. Today, the soldiers watching Thunderheel go out of their way to protect him, fearing a fate similar to their previous comrades.

The Bazaar of Arcana

The Bazaar of Arcana is crossed by the broad Sultan's Boulevard and flanked by the awesome edifices of the Great Repository and the Minaret of Screams. The stalls and structures of this souk are filled with strange merchants hawking wands, staves, rods, potions, rings, scrolls, and wondrous items, as well as reagents and components of nearly every type imaginable needed to craft whatever an arcane master would desire.

A magical bazaar is a strange and wondrous place, but it can easily become unmanageable for you to run. Should you wish to put some brakes on your characters, you can use the following suggestions to control the flow of magical items into their campaign:

• No magic item worth more than 80,000 gp value is sold to visitors to the Bazaar of Arcana, and no items of frost or water may be sold here by law.

• Limit the characters' knowledge of magical items to their in-character knowledge. To determine if a magic item is available, the character must first know what they are looking for. It is unrealistic to assume that characters have knowledge of every sort of magic item. Therefore, it may be surmised that through magical research and study of ancient text, a character trained in Arcana may have uncovered some knowledge of strange and obscure magic items that they have not personally come into contact with. To exhibit prior knowledge of such a magic item, the character must make either a successful Intelligence (Arcana) check with a DC of 15 + 1 per 10,000 gp value of the item in question. A character who makes a successful check may indeed have knowledge of the item being sought and may thus go seeking it within the Bazaar.

• Set a percentage chance that sought-after magic items are found within the bazaar. Despite the plethora of magical items present and traded at the bazaar by the various efreet, dervishes, jann, and foreigners, there should be only a 25% chance that specific magic items are found within the bazaar. Just because it is a Bazaar of Arcana, filled with fantastic wonders, does not mean that it has every wonder instantly or readily available for purchase. You may adjust this percentage up or down based on the rarity of the item in question.

• Roll on a random magic item table, disregarding or rerolling any items over 80,000 gp in value.

Several of the shops and stalls found within the Bazaar of Arcana are more permanent in their nature and are thus the highest sought after of any other shops within the souk.

22. Ayasa al Nar (The Staff of Fire)

A traveler from the material planes, Halif (**archmage** with a *staff of transmutation*[2], a *staff of fire*, and a *ring of fire immunity*[2] [fire]) crafts exquisite magical staves. His djinni noble slave, Gha'Bi, functions as his assistant.

Whichever material components Halif should need for crafting various staves are brought to him by Gha'Bi (male **djinni**) in short order or are brought by those seeking the creation of a mighty staff. Halif is careful to follow all the laws of the city, as he is wise enough to know that the time may come when Gha'Bi somehow frees himself and the tables become turned — the slave becomes master and the master becomes slave.

23. Bel a Din's Jewelry

The great sorceress Bel a Din (elf **sorcerer**[1] with *bracers of superior defense*[2] and a *staff of defense*[2]) crafts amulets, necklaces, charms, bracers, and rings of all sorts. Due to their great beauty and fantastic craftsmanship, the prices for her wares start high and go higher. She may be inclined to craft something at a reduced price if jewels, pearls, lapis lazuli, and the like valued at more than 1,000 bp are brought for use in the item's construction. Being one of the Halifi, she enjoys the protection of the Sultan, but is more apt to be friendly with foreign visitors to the city.

24. Wands of Wonder

Jahiz, an **efreeti sorcerer**[1], crafts various wands for sale to those with the coin to purchase his wares. He enjoys haggling over a price and always starts at double the standard price for his wands. Characters can usually find any wand here; and if not, Jahiz can usually craft it. Jahiz keeps three wands on his person at all times: a *wand of fireballs*, a *spell wand*[2] of *darkness*, and a *wand of lightning bolts*.

25. Mu-Duvac's Teahouse

Decorated with peaceful flowers and fountains of boiling oil, Mu-Duvac's is popular with efreeti nobles, merchants, and wealthy visitors from many planes. Those who can withstand the heat of his sweet, oil-based tea are treated to the delight of pleasant hallucinations, wild sensory pleasures, and a wide variety of magical side effects that make every drink unique. Customers somehow incapacitated or made foolish by the tea's effects are ridiculed and abused by their fellows, becoming part of the entertainment. Many visitors come not only for the chance to see others making fools of themselves, but for the excitement created by the risk of being the fool. Mu-Duvac (**efreeti sorcerer**[1] with AC 19 from his *ring of greater protection* and a *wand of lightning bolts* and a *+1 quarterstaff*) and his slaves (human or elf **greater commoners**[1]) serve tea, and the resulting entertainment, for a mere 30 bp per cup.

Far from the ordinary tea, this tea has a base of pale, light oil heated until it boils rapidly. Various magical herbs and substances are placed in each cup in random amounts before the oil is poured in, making each cup unique. The customer is then expected to gulp the tea down, willingly enduring 10 fire damage for those actually subject to heat. Once swallowed, the tea bestows upon a person a calm, comfortable feeling while at the same time heightening all the senses (+2 to Listen, Spot, and Search checks) and causing minor hallucinations (–4 to saving throws against illusions). The tea's effects last for 1 hour. Customers who experience ill effects are expected, though not required, to remain in the teahouse to endure ridicule. See the sidebox for various effects.

Mu-Duvac has no set recipe for his tea; the very randomness is what makes it attractive to customers. He is unwilling to discuss with anyone the exact nature of the magical substance he places into the cups, claiming it is a family secret.

26. Amar bin Silah's Pets

Caged and chained fiendish animals of all types fill this small shop with a din that echoes off the carefully engraved walls. Amar bin Silah (**senior druid**[1]) is a skilled breeder, guaranteeing the fiendish nature and trainability of his pets. Visitors to the shop include distant merchants and archmages looking for particularly unique pets; some visitors make special breeding requests that Amar does his best to fulfill.

27. Bahija al Farah's Glass Souls

Where but the City of Brass can one purchase such a variety of questionable items? **Bahija's**[1] half-dragon heritage gives her a strange, wild beauty as well as a mysterious ability to connect with the souls of ordinary mortals. Using her knowledge of necromancy, and her special talent, Bahija traps souls in special small glass vials that can be created only here in the fabled City of Brass. Although horrendously expensive (100,000 bp), these souls can be used in the creation of magic items, reducing the cost and time of crafting magic items by as much as 50%. A soul used to create a sentient magic item is no longer available to help create other items. Bahija loves to entertain guests, particularly mortals from the various material planes.

28. Al Bekar's Carved Brass

The Al Bekar clan, owners of the largest privately held group of azer slaves, keeps their slaves working in the furnace-like heat of a massive smithy doing nothing more than making statues and engravings on living brass for various nobles and merchants. The clan claims to know secrets of working the living brass that give their statues and carved decorations special powers. Whether or not this is true, their work has garnered them some favor with the Sultan and therefore among any hoping to maintain a good standing.

29. Azra bint Zarif's Jewels

Although low-caste, Azra (**efreeti**) is one of very few with the ability to work with zuristone, that rare form of rock sometimes found floating in the Sea of Fire or in remote spots on the Elemental Plane of Fire. Although unable to enchant the fine, delicate jewelry she creates here, her beautifully carved rings, amulets, and chains are extremely valuable to those hoping to enchant them (1,000 bp each). Her shop receives visits from a wide variety of archmages and liches hoping to create powerful, indestructible magic items. Azra carries 6,500 gp worth of jewels in an embroidered pouch.

30. House of Gates

This small house and shop holds many secret portals to other planes from the City of Brass. It is also a shop where the smart can find almost any magic item that allows planar travel of any kind. One can also find item that uses an inter-dimensional space, such as *bags of holding* or *portable holes*.

The shop has a policy that seems to be enforced often: If you arrive through an item, you just bought it. Saala (**efreeti sorcerer**[1]) is a former guide in the dome of gates and sports a pair of diamong rings (1,200 gp each), diamond earrings (600 gp each), and a platinum armband (400 gp). The shop has a small retinue of **efreeti** guards that patrols its boundaries, keeping an eye out for any would-be thieves.

31. Tsvi bin Darik's Collars

While most slave owners are content with the standard brass collar, some prefer their pleasure slaves to be more ornately adorned. Tsvi (male **efreeti**) and his **azer** craftsmen create slave collars of extraordinary design, from ornate and delicate to thick and imposing. Such collars cost their owners 10% to 25% more than normal, but they guarantee that a slave's owner can easily be identified. Tsvi carries 3,500 gp in jewels.

32. Horum's Emporium

The wizard Horum (human **incantor**[1] with a *ring of resistance* (fire)) sells magical baubles, weapons, and potions out of the back of a rickety red cart. Due to an unfortunate curse laid upon him by some god irate over Horum's pretentious manner, he rarely stays in one place after he's made a few sales.

The curse causes any item he magically fashions to be horribly flawed. The curse or flawed item registers normally if *detect magic* or the like is used. No trace of the curse or flaw is noticeable until the item is used, however. They either fail to work properly or result in strange side effects (such as in the case of the traveler who gained 500 pounds the day after he bought a *ring of sustenance*[2] from Horum). When a character uses an item crafted by Horum, roll on the table in the sidebox to see exactly what happens.

Horum is now just a shadow of his formerly arrogant self. Still, he flies into a rage when anyone dares to question the quality of his work. Horum wears a *ring of resistance* (fire).

33. Hansiq's Library

This small library contains books and scrolls from all over the planes and the Material Plane. If the book is an obscure text that has some connection to the city, the Plane of Fire, the efreet, the djinn, or the jann, any magic tome, or spell of up to 4th level allowed within the city, it is found within this bookstore. Most of the spells have been copied from the Repository Annex.

The store is run by an extremely old chaotic neutral male **djinni** named Hansiq bin Fatima. Spells can be copied from books in the library for a cost of 100 gp x the spell's level.

34. Al'Fabin's Tattoo Parlor

The crafty human **archmage** Al'Fabin inscribes magical tattoos for his clients here in a nondescript shack. His work is renowned for its superiority, and he takes advantage of his fame with drastic markups. A typical Al'Fabin tattoo costs 150% of the base price. The quality of the finished product is indeed superior, not only functionally, but also visually as well. Many visitors have come to Al'Fabin simply for his skills with the ink.

Al'Fabin is a cunning fellow, and often adds a unique touch to his tattoos that adds a +2 bonus to the spell's save DC for as long as the tattoo remains in place.

Al'Fabin's Goods and Services: His tattoos are priced as follows:

Service	Cost
Tattoo	20 bp per color
Magic tattoo[4]	150 bp per spell level

Horum's Emporium

Any magic item crafted by Horum is automatically flawed. Each time the item is used, there is a chance it malfunctions. Roll on the table below to randomly determine what happens each time the item is used.

1d20	Malfunction
1	Item is powerless against one type of creature (choose one or roll randomly).
2	User takes 17 (5d6) force damage (DC 15 Constitution saving throw for half).
3	User loses voice for one day; spells with verbal components cannot be cast.
4	User gains 1d6 x 20 pounds.
5	User loses 1d6 points from one random ability score until after a long rest.
6	User's Proficiency Bonus is reduced by 1. Attempt DC 18 Constitution saving throw after each long rest to regain.
7	User struck blind or deaf (50% chance of either) for 1d4 x 10 minutes.
8–10	Item functions normally.
11–13	Item fails to work.
14	User's hair turns white (permanently).
15	All liquids within 10 feet foul; magic liquids (such as potions) must make a successful DC 15 generic saving throw or foul.
16	User changes sex for 1d2 x 10 minutes.
17	User permanently loses 1 point from a random ability score.
18	User switches between incorporeal and corporeal for 1 minute.
19	One random gem or piece of jewelry within 10 feet tarnishes or turns dull gray, becoming worthless.
20	User teleported 1 mile away in random direction.

35. Flame on the Wall

A tall slender elf greets customers who enter this tidy shop. He is well over 6 feet in height, with jet-black hair slicked back into a long ponytail, and dresses in well-oiled, tight-fitting dark leather, elaborate golden jewelry, and rose-tinted spectacles.

Fazaad (**sorcerer**[1] with *bracers of defense, wings of flying,* and a *ring of comfort*[2]) is the proprietor of the Flame on the Wall. The walls of the establishment are covered in all forms of paintings and there are stands with various works of art from sculptures of efreeti and fire elementals, to glass objects with swirling infernos inside them, and other ornaments of various mediums, some of which are said to have magical properties (ranging in price from 1,000 bp to beyond 50,000 bp). Some of the best works of art are the paintings made with fire oils, a painting medium infused with the essence of the Plane of Fire, which allow parts of the painting to move and flux as if they beat with life themselves. These are known as fire prints.

Fire prints vary in quality and cost, but usually sell for a price of 50 bp x the painting's length in inches x the painting's width in inches. For example, a painting that measures 12 inches by 12 inches costs 7,200 bp (12 x 12 x 50 = 7,200). Each fire print radiates magic and, if mounted on a solid surface such as a wall or door, offers an immunity to fire to all within 30 feet (so long as they remain within 30 feet of the painting). A painting cannot be mounted on a shield, armor, or the like. It must be mounted on a stationary surface such as a wall or door to activate the magic.

Fazaad does commissioned work for a slightly higher price. His works are known to adorn the Sultan's Palace along with many other places in the city and are sought after by those from other planes. A **fire giant** guard sits in the back of the store with a wicked barbed *+1 scimitar* sitting across his lap. He says nothing and is not spoken to by Fazaad, but he attacks if provoked.

36. The Burning Stones

If gems need to be polished or shaped, this is the place to take them. Two twin dwarves named Idlen and Neldi (**archmages**) run the business. One of the dwarves (Idlen, they think) has long, thick, dark dreadlocks and a completely shaven face (he says he shaved his beard when it got in the way while polishing an emerald and caused it to crack straight through). Conversely, Neldi has a long, braided beard that almost reaches the floor, but his head is shaved bald. Their skill with gemstones is rarely matched and those who want the best gemstones possible seek out their services. If armor needs to be adorned with gems, if pommels of swords need to look special, if an amulet needs to look more majestic, then the twins make it happen. The twins also imbue gems with magic to give them incredible power and amazing value. These stone are called *burning stones*[2], though in reality they can be imbued with a variety of abilities.

By polishing gems and increasing their luster with the addition of facets, the twins can increase the worth of a gemstone by 150%. The dwarven brothers are the only craftsmen in the City of Brass who can properly work the elemental stones mined from the lava vents of the Plane of Molten Skies.

37. The Living Whim

This rather extravagant establishment is a combination of a brewery and a tavern with a few little-known extras. The Whim is run by an elder **efreeti** known simply as Vin. Vin oversees the work of a whole host of **azer** slaves who have proven remarkably talented at brewing various ales and liquors that are known for their fiery potency and unique taste. With names such as Red Death, Fire Opal Nectar, and Liquid Inferno, and with each brand packaged in a high-quality, unique bottle, Vin's creations have an undeniable appeal to those with expensive taste. A bottle of Red Death generally costs 100 bp, Fire Opal Nectar runs 150 bp, while Liquid Inferno costs a staggering 800 bp. Prices for other drinks and liquors range from 30 bp to 800 bp.

Aside from all that, there is a large common room and bar area where visitors to the bazaar can sit for a meal and fine spirits. Vin doesn't tolerate obnoxious behavior, and his squads of bouncers (consisting of 2 **fire giants** and 4 **burning dervishes**[1]) are always more than happy to quell any potential skirmishes.

What truly gives the Whim its name is the unspoken service that Vin is willing to provide for a hefty cost. If asked in the proper manner (usually 5,000 bp worth), Vin takes a customer to the backroom and grants one *wish*. As efreeti are wont to do, Vin generally twists the wish to suit his own desires, and leaves the victim wondering what went wrong.

38. The Melting Anvil

This is no ordinary blacksmith; this one deals only with exotic metals such as mithral, adamantine, and the silver found from the trees in the Steel Garden. The sturdy dwarf named **Feldspar**[1] hammers these precious metals into weapons and armor of wondrous quality for a hefty fee. His cost is generally 200% over market price plus the buyer must supply the raw materials or at least the cash for them up front. On the plus side, Feldspar is a master of his trade, and his work is quick, accurate, and possessed of extremely high quality. Items created by Feldspar have resistance to all damage and any saving throw made to prevent damage to them has advantage.

He is more than happy to construct magic weapons for those who can afford it. He does not, however, craft any weapon with cold-based special abilities (no matter how much he is offered).

39. The Lapis of Luxury

This is the most sought-after brothel in all the City of Brass. The women and men who work here are beyond the scope of beauty. They emanate an almost angelic grace, which is the wonderful irony of the Lapis. The small palace is filled with all things of beauty: statues, silks, velvets, lush pillows, fragrant plants, scattered gems, fountains that spew liquid silver, and of course the intoxicating workers. The workers are all **succubi** and **incubi**. The matron of the house is a **marilith** by the name of Fel'wieri. The bodies of those who fall into the trance of the succubi are teleported to the Abyss where they become slaves and servants of the demon hordes. Not all who come here become servants, however; some resist the Charm and Draining Kiss and those who do, survive, and pay twice the rate to come back.

40. The Nest

A ragtag network of child thieves and assassins (typically **spy** and **sneakthief**[1]) permeates the back alleys and corridors of the Middle City. They are constantly on the lookout for unsuspecting fools on whom to practice their trade. If the victim looks too powerful, then one member follows them. If noticed, the rogue blends into the street and finds a new quarry to prey upon. If unnoticed, the thief follows the victim to his place of rest and reports to his cohorts in the Nest for support. While the victims are asleep, a small group gains entry to their quarters and attempts to rob (and possibly kill) each one of them. It is said the Nest is so abundant in the Middle City that they have a safe house on every street. Most professional criminals, especially the Fahd al An'il, regard the Nest urchins as nothing more than meddlesome toddlers, if that.

41. The Towering Inferno

This burning spire stands between two pillars of living brass. It has a single iron door at the base, which stands 30 feet high and which can only be opened magically. The tower is rumored to be a gateway to the Abyss. Anyone within 20 feet of the Towering Inferno must make a successful DC 20 Constitution saving throw or take 7 (2d6) fire damage each round. Actually touching the tower deals 35 (10d6) fire damage per round of contact.

Fire[1] and **magma mephits** frequently leap from high upon the tower to fall upon passersby. They then run back into the flames, cackling and giggling. Any attempt to open the door automatically summons an **elder fire elemental**[1]. Upon successfully opening the door (and after dealing with the fire elemental), there is a 10% chance a very angry **pit fiend** appears to deal with the intruder.

42. Maw of Righteousness

Prisoners convicted of especially heinous crimes are sent here for spiritual purification. The **Smoldering Judges**[1] track down the guilty and call down the wrath of the gods upon them. A small flat one-story brass building marks the entrance to the Maw, which descends toward the Lower City in an ever-narrowing spiral. Five **emeritus chaplains**[1] in black robes lead prisoners to the bottom, chanting ritualistically. At the

The Smoldering Judges

These clerics are a mercenary group of law-keepers in the City of Brass. They are magically fortified humans clothed in sleeveless, hooded, white robes with matching veils that cover the lower halves of their faces. The High Judges wear black robes, while the absolute head of the order, the Grand Judge, wears crimson robes. Each carries a *flaming weapon* (halberd)[2], which can be turned into a *frost weapon*[2] (halberd) with a command word. They also have *belts of giant strength* (fire), *spell wands*[2] of *power word stun, hold person, force cage,* and *sleep.* They answer to no one outside their immediate circle. The Sultan's burning dervishes have orders to kill every judge they encounter on sight, no questions asked.

terminus is a great gaping portal. A mass of spinning, razor-sharp blades frames it. When the High Judges utter an incantation, the portal flares to life, forming a one-way gate to the Plane of Fire. All items are removed from the guilty before they are cast into the maw. For those who are of a fire-based nature, such as azers and efreet, the head cleric instead opens the maw to the Plane of Water or the Plane of Ice.

43. Great Ziggurat

This area is fully detailed in **Chapter 28**.

44. Pagoda of Devils

This area is fully detailed in **Chapter 29**.

45. Worshippers of the Great Pyramid

Beneath the Shining Pyramid of Set is a small community of "crazies" (as **commoners**) who worship the pyramid itself — not the god Set, but the pyramid. They wait for the day their god calls them home (which to them is the day the pyramid falls from the sky and crushes them all). Various races are represented here, all degenerate and somewhat insane. The area is covered in ramshackle houses and buildings. A larger building in the center serves as their temple, where they pay homage to the Shining Pyramid floating above them.

46. Tower of the Grand Vizier

This area is fully detailed in **Chapter 30**.

47. Great Repository

This area is fully detailed in **Chapter 21**.

48. The Traveler's Baths

This large structure serves as a privately operated spa filled with swimming pools, plunge pools, fountains, showers, and saunas. The finer needs of the customer are cared for in luxuriant fashion by **water elementals**, **nymphs**, and their master Sabil the **marid**[1]. Sabil makes a pretty penny offering the luxury of water to a parched foreign populace, and in turn pays a healthy tax for the right to do so. Sabil has few problems with his efreeti cousins, as they understand the need for his services within their great metropolis.

Services within the Traveler's Baths range from the opulent to the sublime. Simple common baths in a large pool suffice for most travelers; however, for the wealthiest there are private massages and near boudoir-like spa treatments. The entire structure is sealed in double airlocks that do not let even a drop of moisture out into the city itself. Some say that this is because of the disdain the efreeti have for anything water-based, while others claim it is merely to keep the escaping humidity from tarnishing the polished upper levels of the Ziggurat Al Nar.

49. Ard's Secret Sanctuary

This area is fully detailed in **Chapter 17**.

Chapter 15
The Lower City

Unlike the eye-popping grandeur of the Upper City, and the bustling wheeling and dealing of the Middle City, the Lower City, or Basin as it is sometimes called, is indeed the gritty, grimy underbelly of the City of Brass. Being at the very bottom of the bowl within which the city is built, the Basin is home to teeming gangs of azer slaves constantly working on the city's great building projects. The azer continually hammer and toil, taking on shiploads of raw living brass brought aboard the galleys of the Fire Sea Corsairs even as dark practitioners of magic in the employ of the burning ones bind the metal with the souls of those who have displeased the Great Sultan.

Looking up from the Basin, one marvels at the magic and engineering that has gone into creating the City of Brass. Buildings soar high into the glowing sky as tiny figures may be seen aboard *flying carpets* or flying of their own volition, while pedestrians travel along the broad ramps that connect the various structures and platforms of the city to one another.

The Lower City consists of many low-rent taverns, brothels, casbahs, and inns. These are places where even the poorer casts of efreeti refuse to come without good reason for fear of being seen by their brethren and being mocked or laughed at. Notable exceptions to this rule include merchants who own freight and shipping interests, and the cruel overseers of the azer, who ensure that their whips remind them of their fate of endless toil.

Sealed entrances leading to many of the great buildings of the city are also found within the Basin. The bindings and enchantments on these portals is so great that only the bearer of a magical key or password specific to these doors can pass into the bowels of these magnificent structures.

Lower City (Basin) Encounters

Roll 1d10 for every hour spent in the Lower City.

1d10	Encounter
1	Slave master (efreeti)
2	Master thief[1]
3	Azer slave gang (1d10 azer +2 efreeti guards)
4-5	Press gang or slavers (1d6 burning dervish[1] Fire Sea Corsairs)
6	Fire giant patrol (1d4)
7	Smuggler (sneakthief[1], any race)
8	Devil Monk[1] (Order of Devils)
9	Bounty Hunter (eldritch archer[1])
10	Demon (your choice)

Locations in the Lower City

The following are some of the area's more prominent places.

1. The Caravanserai

This district is the common destination for the beasts that haul the large caravans that bring trade and tithe to the masters of the City of Brass. The Caravanserai contains literally hundreds of pens and hostels joined by a common wall for the drovers and beasts of burden that are brought into the city daily. After dropping their wares off at their destination, the beasts are driven down the staggering platforms from the Upper and Middle City into the Caravanserai to be tended until such time as their master's business has been completed.

Nearly any beast or monster that can be imagined may be found picketed in one of the massive paddocks located in this section of the city. The animals are well tended by azer slaves. Patrols of mercenary guards in the employ of the beasts' owners frequently war with one another in the Caravanserai as they attempt to steal the beasts from their masters' business rivals.

More often than not, beasts that escape from the Caravanserai rampage through the Basin before being brought down. Occasionally they find their way to one of the crowded bazaars of the Middle and Upper City. Beast owners whose animals escape are required by efreeti law to repay double the damages done by one of their creatures. In the event of death, monies must be paid to the family of the deceased for a *raise dead* or *resurrection* spell. In a strange twist to the law, anyone other than a city guardsman who kills the beast of a merchant must repay the merchant double for the loss.

Lodging and accommodations are available at 1 bp per week for drovers and the like in any of the numerous hostels that lie against the outer wall of the Caravanserai. Rates for beasts are based on the size of the creature.

Size	Cost (per week)
Up to Small	1 bp
Medium	2 bp
Large	6 bp
Huge	12 bp
Gargantuan	24 bp
Colossal	50 bp

1A. The Slavers' Bazaar

Nearly one-quarter (or more) of the City of Brass' population is believed to be slaves. Powerful magicians from other planes often come here with their terrestrial bodyguards in search of knowledge and ancient magic, but their visits are generally short and direct. They report shock at seeing the hundreds and thousands of bound slaves of every race and permutation imaginable doing the bidding of their cruel efreeti masters. The various slave races serve in every capacity, from crafting the fine goods that the efreet greedily sell to the highest bidder, to polishing and cleaning the gleaming edifices of the city itself.

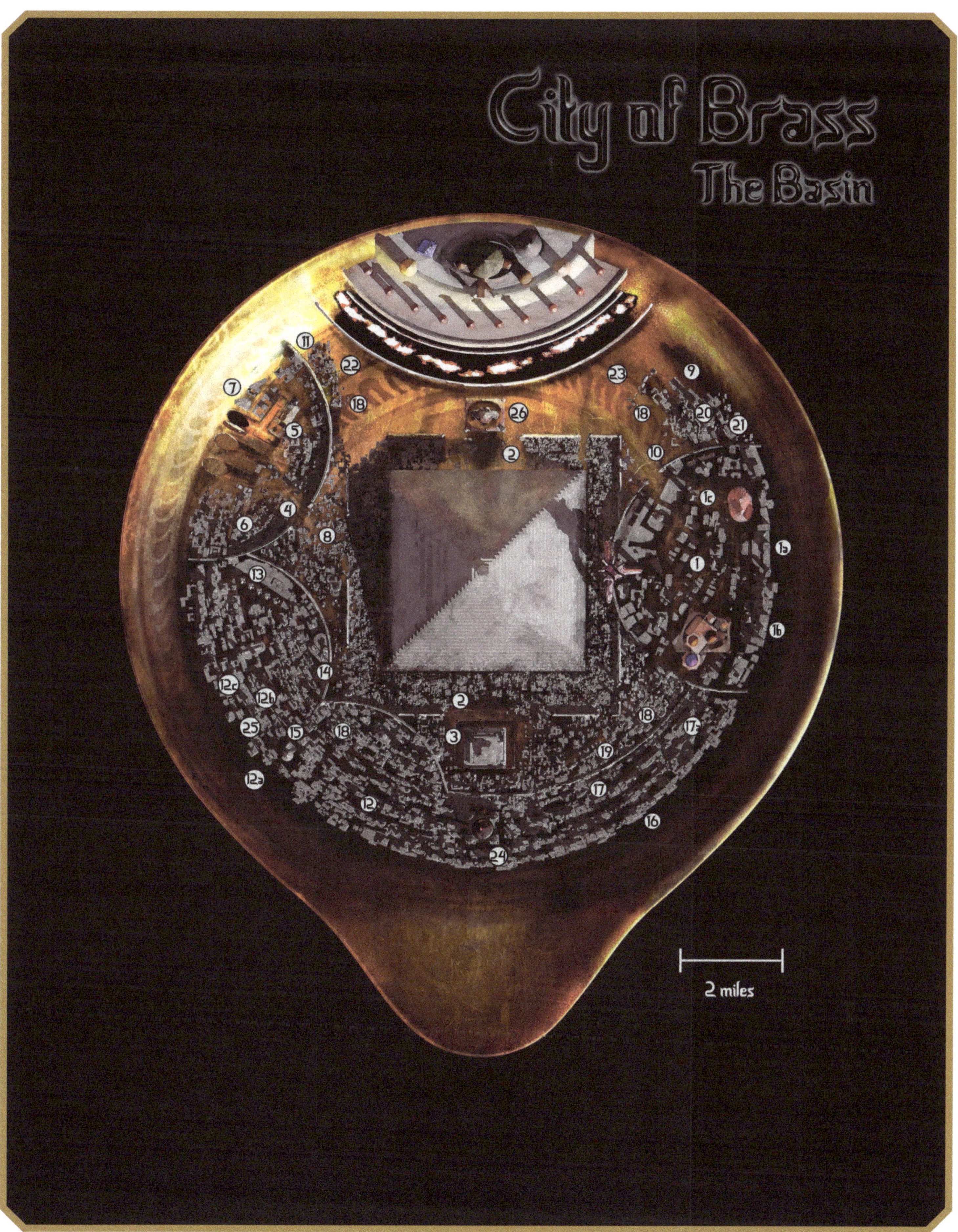
City of Brass
The Basin
2 miles

Calculating a Slave's Value

To calculate the value of a slave, multiply the creature's Strength x Charisma x Hit Dice. This sets the starting bid in bp (brass pieces). Thus, a 14th-level fighter with Str 18 and Cha 12 has a starting bid of 3,024 bp (14 x 18 x 12 = 3,024).

As the efreet have no real way of knowing how powerful an individual is, they may be tested through combat with one another or other captured slaves to determine their ability to fight or think.

Characters found with spell components are marked separately and sold in a separate auction from other slaves, as their value must be determined by a representative of the burning ones. Such characters may find themselves purchased by a noble house or a merchant in the Bazaar of Arcana. They will likely be set to crafting magical items until their worthiness is expended. The value of an arcane spellcaster is the standard value of a slave multiplied by 1.5.

Wealthy efreet frequently send professional buyers to the Slavers' Bazaar to make purchases on their behalf. Often these buyers are slaves themselves.

1B. Slave Pens

The slave pens of the City of Brass are always full. These naked prisoners are the beaten and degraded forms of hundreds of souls who await their sale and binding to their new master within these iron cages. The cages are six feet tall and are stacked two high and go on in rows for many city blocks. The bars of each pen are made of iron. Tougher slaves are kept in cages with reinforced iron bars (some are even *arcane locked*). Breaking open normal bars requires a successful DC 22 Strength check, while reinforced bars a DC 26 check. A cage lock can be opened with a successful DC 23 Dexterity check with thieves' tools.

No food is granted to those who wait within these slave pens, as, typically, less than 30 hours elapse from the time of capture or sentencing to the time of sale.

1C. Auction House

The auction house is home to the guards and auctioneers who oversee new slaves and the fitting of brass collars to every being sold in the Slavers' Bazaar. Hallamabath the Auctioneer (male **efreeti** with a *ring of mind shielding*) oversees a staff of 50 **efreeti** auctioneers and 50 **fire giant** guards who see that the constant flow of slaves goes uninterrupted from their arrival to their bondage. Hallamabath carries 260 bp, 2 bloodstones (55 gp each), and 1 black emerald (1,000 gp).

2. Azer Slave Quarter

The majority of azer that live within the City of Brass dwell in hovels surrounding the foot of the Great Ziggurat. Their existence is bound to their efreeti masters and the constant construction work in building up the Great Ziggurat. Beyond this massive and ongoing labor, the azer, being bound with brass collars, are free to move about the Basin, living in small family groups and working 24-hour days. The azer were the first beings to be subjugated by the Sultan's wars of expansion. Those azer not fully engaged in construction projects and the reinforcement of the dizzyingly tall skyscrapers of the city busy themselves polishing every inch of the city's many metallic edifices. They do this job invisibly however, so that none who visit the city ever notice their presence in the Middle or Upper City, unless they see one as a visitor to the various bazaars where some few work crafting weapons, armor, chariots, and shields.

A holy man named Amin al Anumon (**azer cleric**[1]) leads the azer. Amin is a very old, very humble azer, and a devout cleric of Anumon, despite his servitude and the worship of Anumon being banned in the City of Brass. He keeps the spirits of his people high in their toil for their cruel masters, promising them that Anumon has not forgotten their plight and will someday send saviors to free them.

3. The Overseers' Keep

This fortress — small by the standards of the City of Brass — houses the overseers who manage the affairs of the azer. They ensure that the fire-dwarves work hard and cause no problems. Umuyad the Beast (**efreeti amir**[1]) is the chief overseer of the azer slaves and lives up to his name in every way, commanding **efreeti** overseers and a host of 500 mercenaries of various races and ilk to beat, harass, and otherwise manhandle the azer at their work. Umuyad leads by example, frequently lashing out with his magical whip that crackles with electrical energy.

4. The Corsair Docks

Massive circular portals in the northwestern end of the Basin make up the docks that bring commerce and slaves and booty looted by the Fire Sea Corsairs from the Sea of Fire to the City of Brass. This rough-and-tumble area is home to many of the lowest forms of scum and villainy that may be found in the Inner Planes. The Corsair Docks is where the Galleymaker, the Flame Maiden's Voyage, the Oil Shark Cantina, and the actual portals that open into the Sea of Fire are located. There are various dwellings, warehouses, and flophouses in this district to give the crews of the massive efreeti war galleys ample ways to spend the spoils of their raids against the Sultan's enemies.

5. Shipyard of Hermes the Galleymaker

This large warehouse-like structure is constantly bustling with activity. Azer slaves move to and fro hauling plates of living brass to be bolted to the bulwark of a massive efreeti war galley currently under construction. Hermes (**efreeti malik**[1]), the efreeti overseer, commands all with a leaden whip and greatclub of bronze. Hermes is an able shipwright who learned the trade from his father. Two hundred **azer** slaves toil in his factory, forging the living brass into daunting vessels of destruction that the Fire Sea Corsairs use in their raids across the Sea of Fire. Hermes can craft any oil skimmer, transport ship, or war galley for the right price. Construction of such a war galley usually takes three months, while oil skimmers can be had in a month or less, and transport galleys take roughly two months to complete. Half payment is expected at the start of work, the rest on completion.

Hermes wears a *ring of evasion*.

6. The Flame Maiden's Voyage

This rough-and-tumble brothel and flophouse near the edge of the Corsair Docks serves those marines and sailors who ply their trade on the Sea of Fire and deeper into the Plane of Fire itself. Beautiful dancing girls undulate to the buzak, daff, and tablah music of skilled cheitan bards. Kul'soon (male **efreeti**) is the boisterous proprietor of the Flame Maiden and named the place after the war galley he once served upon. Kul'soon is a good source of information about the goings-on within the Docks District. His pleasure slaves are of average beauty but are well treated. For a mere 5 bp a night, a guest can have a room and a pleasure slave to waste away the hours. Liquor and other refreshments are of course extra. Many of the corsairs spend their entire pay during shore leave without ever stepping foot out of the Flame Maiden. The Flame Maiden is a good place to hide out if the characters attract too much attention in the Middle or Upper city.

7. The Oil Shark Cantina

This tavern and gaming hall is owned and run by Bazik al'Kadar (**efreeti malik**[1]) and is frequented by some of the more interesting characters one

would meet in the Basin. Often, it is a place used by folk seeking the employ of rogues, pirates, assassins, smugglers, or the casual magician for a difficult and frequently illegal job. The air is thick with smoke, and musicians from around the multiverse play for tips on a low stage. Tables are carved with game boards for playing seega, senet, chess, backgammon, and games of chance. Strange and exotic liquors line the shelves behind the bar, which are magically enchanted to ensure that a stray bottle or knife does not shatter the precious liquids held within. It isn't uncommon for a body to wind up on the floor after accusations of cheating. For whatever reason, the doorman dislikes familiars and constructs and they are barred from the place out of hand.

8. The Hidden Shrine of Orcus

Deep within the bowels of the Lower City is a hidden shrine dedicated to the Demon Prince of the Undead. **Livesha**[1], a lich priestess of Orcus, maintains the shrine. The shrine is secret only in that it is mostly ignored by the other denizens of the City of Brass and tolerated merely because Orcus has interest in many of the powerful weapons crafted and sold in the Bazaar of Arms. For more information on the shrine and Livesha's lair see **Chapter 26: The Underbasin**.

9. The Fahd al An'il Safehouse

Nestled inconspicuously amid the filth and bustle of the basin, the headquarters of an extraplanar guild of thieves, spies, investigators, and assassins known as the Fahd al An'il stages operations here. Made up of skilled rogues and spellcasters of nearly every civilized race, and with contacts spanning the universe, they are truly the masters of their trade. Their sigil is an illusory cerise leopard that is left behind at the scene of their jobs to mock their victims and those who would attempt to capture a member of their order. They remain otherwise unseen and unnoticed. The badge of acceptance into the order is a cursed *ring of invisibility* that can be removed only upon the death of the wearer.

Their meticulous attention to detail and relentless efficiency is surpassed only by their unyielding discipline. The guild follows a strict hierarchy that is based on sheer skill and has no place for petty intrigue. Each member of the guild must pass a test to gain admittance, and then must ascend through the ranks by further testing. Speaking of the tests of ascension is strictly forbidden and is punishable by death to both parties. The rule of the Fahd al An'il is simple: once in, never out.

Quarrels within the guild are not tolerated and the attempted or successful assassination of a higher-ranking member gains the offender a merciless death, regardless of their current rank.

The Fahd al An'il is run by a crafty efreeti known only as **The Wahid**[1]. He keeps meticulous records of what services are performed and makes absolutely certain that taxes are paid properly. The Wahid also creates and oversees the tests of ascension but leaves most of the contracting up to his clever human assistant, Zaki Husam (**grand master assassin**[1] with a *+3 shortsword*, a *ring of greater protection*[2], and a *ring of invisibility*). The Wahid possesses a powerful amulet that allows him to shapechange once per day.

The guild is split into four factions, each of which performs a certain array of tasks. These include thievery, assassination, spy work, and bounty hunting. Each faction is overseen by one sayyid (prince) that has up to five khalafi (lords) and ten faris (knights) working beneath him. The number of members is strictly limited to this pyramid of training, so at any one time there are never more than 64 "open" members. The only way to ascend the ranks is if a new spot opens up as a result of the permanent retirement of one of the existing members. Ascension to a superior slot in the organization is typically chosen from among the ranks by The Wahid through a series of complex tests and nearly impossible tasks.

The guild's rates are dependent on the rank of the member doing the job. Generally, a faris charges 200 bp per HD for a standard job, and only rarely performs tasks outside the city. A khalafi charges 500 bp per HD, while a sayyid charges 1,000 bp per HD for services. This base rate is often adjusted based on risk or abnormal difficulty.

The guild has loose connections with the Bayt Al Sikkyn, more as a formality than for any other reason. They hold a license to carry out assassinations within the city, but since most of their work is done outside the City of Brass, they usually do not fall under the direct dominion of the noble house. The Wahid does his best to maintain good ties with the other houses as well, especially the Bayt al Najoom, for their knowledge of the obscure has been useful on many occasions.

10. Razi's Rest

Razi (**champion warrior**[1]), an ancient, beardless dwarf, toils night and day behind the counter of this small inn. While his rates of 5 bp per night are outrageous, he asks no questions and his tongueless slaves (**greater commoners**[1]) certainly can't ask questions or reveal information. Slapped beneath the towering creations stretching into the Upper City, Razi's is considered one of the few discreet places in the Lower City.

11. The Meme Merchant

Devra[1], a succubus driven partially mad by the many scars crisscrossing her body and the torture that put them there, operates this strange establishment. Devra implants false memories of happiness through the use of hypnotism and drugs, charging only a fraction of the customer's life energy in exchange for the service. Slaves and servants of the Lower City seem eager to come here, trading what little life they have left for a small piece of happiness. Devra is rarely seen in her true form because it embarrasses her, and she uses her *alter self* ability to temporarily regain her former beauty. Rumor has it that her ability to implant memories can also be used to recover memories lost due to pain, madness, or mental manipulation.

Devra carries a *spell wand*[2] of *charm person,* two *spell scrolls* with *suggestion,* a pink diamond pendant necklace (5,000 gp), a purple corundum platinum ring (1,500 gp), and a black opal bracelet (1,500 gp).

12. Heyyab District

Along the side of the city's Basin is a villainous nest of deceit, corruption, poverty, and death. The Heyyab District differs little, in fact, from the other districts in the Lower City. Slave pens crowd the streets nearest the wall, with their accompanying flesh markets nearby. Towering residential buildings cast long shadows over the crowded, fetid-smelling streets, providing moderately affordable rooms for freemen and indentured servants. The district's residents scurry about during the daylight hours, casting fearful glances over their shoulders and into every shadow, wary of blackjackers, thieves, slaver pressgangs, and every other imaginable bogey monster, for they all thrive in the Lower City's cesspool of human and efreeti flesh. At night, only the bravest or the most foolhardy venture forth. Patrolling the larger streets are city guards who are heavily armed and ready for almost anything. They don't interfere when they can help it, though, afraid of the inevitable retribution that will come from the district's criminal element. Life in the district is the hardest it gets in the city, and that's saying quite a lot.

That said, Heyyab does provide adventurers a place where they can easily disappear from the eyes of the city's omnipresent bureaucracy. Few officials assigned to the district pay much attention to its goings-on. They'd just as soon let the people living here deal with their problems themselves. Crime is just organized enough to make the lives of the bureaucrats and their soldiers hell. Fortunately, the anarchy of everyday life also works against the criminal element like it does everyone else. Fighting between rival gangs occupies much of their time and activities, offering the average person a slight reprieve from fear at times. While it is true that the average citizen living here is distrustful, suspicious, and wary, it is also true that, once gained, friendship is maintained for life. Residents lead hard lives, and so take what few pleasures they can when they get it, including the simple pleasure of honest friendship.

A constant feature of the Heyyab closest to the city wall is that it always seems to be raining. It isn't; it is merely the filthy run-off from the ore-smelting factories in the Middle City above. As a result, the air in this part of the district always smells and tastes like rancid chalk. Breathing becomes laborious to those unaccustomed to it, and the slaves forced to live here invariably develop severe respiratory problems. The moisture is categorically non-potable, hence the city's lack of concern about the presence of so much of it, despite it being illegal. Efreet, azer, and other fiery creatures still avoid the area if they can help it, regardless. As such, most slavers in the district are humanoid.

12A. The Samaghar Bathhouse

This building is a meeting place and safe house for Samaghar infiltrators, a band of salamanders from the Plane of Fire who seek to bring about the downfall of the Sultan and the City of Brass. It is ostensibly a bathhouse for creatures not native to the Plane of Molten Skies or the Elemental Plane of Fire. Despite its location, the bathhouse maintains a façade of exclusive membership in order to keep everyone but the Samaghar and their allies out. Besides, neither the efreet nor the djinn dare to be seen in this part of town, and the city's fire giant guards would just as soon not bother with anyone in this area than intervene in any perceived violations of the law.

The bathhouse looks inconspicuous from the outside. It is made from heavy slabs of blueschist and gneiss, both durable enough to handle the Lower City's environment. Bands and bolts of brass hold the building together, often glowing white-hot in the ambient heat shed by surrounding buildings. The front entrance consists of a pair of wide double doors made from tempered iron and steel. Engraved above it are the words "The morally unclean shall be purified by the righteous." The doors are always locked.

A small, eye-level panel in the door slides open when the bathhouse caretaker answers, allowing him to see and question clients waiting on the other side. If a person is not on his list, he does not grant them entry under any circumstances, even if they claim to bear a writ of entry given to them by a member. The caretaker is an elderly human named Ephesius. He has been performing his duty for the better half of six decades and knows all there is to know about the Samaghars' plans for the city and the Sultan. He is careful, inscrutable, and eminently trustworthy. In sixty years, the city's efreeti masters have never once suspected the bathhouse was the nexus of the Samaghar insurgency.

Aruj Khayr leads the Samaghar. He is a young, proud, **salamander monarch**[1] recently arrived from his home plane. Serving as his counsel and the Samaghars' resident holy man is Malazgirt (**salamander noble**[1]), who has been operating out of the bathhouse for nearly a decade now. He oversees the local ranks of filthy flamebrothers. As such, he does not garner much respect or trust from Khayr, though the other Samaghar seem to trust him implicitly. Nevertheless, he and Khayr both hate the efreet with such ferocity that they easily manage to see past their personal differences and cooperate with one other. The Samaghar regard azer slaves with heartfelt pity because in the salamander homeland the fire-dwarves are accorded much respect and prestige. In fact, the azer there are generally the priests and sorcerers, roles that bind them closely to the generous salamander caliph. Finally, there is Malikshah (**salamander noble**[1]), the leader of the salamander death squads. He is a vicious, bloodthirsty creature who lives only to murder efreet. He and his assassins (male and female **salamanders**) are responsible for the gruesome string of serial killings that have been plaguing the Middle City for months.

Samaghar infiltrators possess magical cloaks that allow them to disguise their true forms while they are abroad in the city. The cloaks are very difficult for them to come by, being this far removed from their homeland, so the salamanders go out of their way to protect them.

Refer to the **Samaghar Bathhouse Map** for the following locations.

12A-1. Foyer

Built into the walls on either side of this entranceway are 8 ornate cubicles. The Samaghar use them to store their magical cloaks and weapons. It is considered very bad form to enter the main bath prepared for bloodshed or deceit. To the immediate right of the front entrance is a small wooden table, atop which sits a tiny charcoal brazier, a brass water pot, a clay urn filled with fresh tea leaves, a second urn filled with coffee beans, and three triangular brass cups. The table has two wooden seats. This is where **Ephesius**[1] whiles away much of his time, sipping either tea (in the morning) or coffee (in the afternoon), and reading books. The corridor terminates at the end opposite the front entrance in a beautifully frescoed archway leading to the main baths.

During the daylight hours, only four cubicles contain Samaghar cloaks, steel spears, scimitars, and daggers. At night, all except one are filled with the salamanders' gear. Ephesius reserves one cubicle for his own possessions. Usually, one can find 1d3 jars of fresh tea and coffee and a stack of 2d4 books and scrolls inside it.

Samaghar Bathhouse

1 Square – 5 Feet

12A-2. Main Baths

This is the predominant chamber in the building. It is the steam bath proper, but unlike the kind used by humanoids, the salamanders' bath is disturbingly cold. Decorative frescoes painted in cold-resistant plaster adorn the walls, which are 60 feet long. They depict images from Samaghar mythology of a young salamander hero who cast aside the shackles of slavery and slew his efreet masters. An elaborate, three-tiered marble fountain at the center of the room stands 16 feet high. Mounted atop it is the horrible visage of a frost giant, mouth opened wide, an icy wind and water emerging from inside it. In the fountain's water basins float deep blue chunks of preternaturally cold ice, formed in the wake of the wind's passage across it. The air here is thick with steam, a reaction to the wintry air mixing with the normally hot building walls as well as the salamanders' fiery bodies when they sit around the fountain on marble benches, sweating liquid heat. Other pilloried stone heads emerge from the tops of marble pillars spread evenly through the room, exhaling additional blasts of super chilled air.

12A-3. Private Baths

There are six private baths, all more or less identical in form and function. Each room is 10 feet across, with a single-tiered marble fountain in the center. Benches line the walls. As with the main bath, the water is frigidly cold and the private baths quickly fill with steam when the salamanders use them. Solid wooden doors seal the room, lockable from inside with slide bars to ensure privacy if required.

Each contains a secret door in the floor that opens into a short tunnel that leads to a disguised sewer egress two streets away. The secret doors require a successful DC 20 Wisdom (Perception) check to find.

Aruj, Malazgirt, and Malikshah often meet in the room farthest from the foyer to discuss their plans for murdering the Sultan.

12A-4. Storerooms

The salamanders keep their equipment as well as mundane supplies such as extra towels, replacement frost giant visages for the various baths, and so on safe in these three large storerooms. Each room is 20 feet wide and long, with a sturdy iron-banded door that can be locked from inside with a heavy brass bolt. The middle storeroom can be used in a pinch as a safe room for anyone who needs to go into hiding suddenly. The doors can be broken in with a successful DC 23 Strength check.

12A-5. Ephesius' Room

This is a small room that was never part of the original building. It was added 30 years ago when Ephesius — fed up with having to use the middle storeroom as his living quarters — threatened to retire unless given a real room of his own. The salamander in charge commissioned the room's construction that night, embarrassed at suddenly realizing he and the Samaghar had been so discourteous to the old man for so many decades.

A very expensive bed is pushed against the back wall, while a mahogany writing table and wardrobe, and a rather crudely built wardrobe, sit to the left of the door along the north wall. A well-built chest sits at the foot of the bed, inside of which Ephesius keeps his belongings: 5 books of popular lore and stories from his homeland, 2,201 gp, a *+1 dagger*, and a *cloak of charisma*[2]. The chest is not locked.

12B. The Freemen's Tower

The Freeman's Tower is fully detailed in **Chapter 19**

12C. Serpentis Alley

Named not so much for its shape but rather for its hissing, slithering merchandise, Serpentis Alley exists in a half-mile-long gap between the Lower City guard barracks and the Lower City prison. Hundreds of stalls, pavilions, tents, and carts offer passersby a bevy of snakes for sale. Any kind of known snake is presumably available here. Hawkers come from all the myriad lands. Many wear the traditional blue turbans of the local culture, which connotes a venomous snake handler. Others wear nothing but swaddling wrap, leaving their arms and legs exposed to proudly show off innumerable bite scars. Still, the majority of the hawkers dress more conservatively in flowing robes and keffiyeh, encouraged by local religion to be modest.

One peculiarity of the snake market is that while many vendors sell live snakes, many also sell a wide variety of dead snakes and snake parts. Dried rattler tails are said to drive off evil spirits, while coral snake venom diluted with raw alcohol and blueberries brings down a person's body temperature, a very popular drink during the heat of the day.

Serpent folk revile the market, refusing to have anything to do with it or its vile trade for obvious reasons. Occasionally they raid it, attempting to drive the hawkers out of business by destroying their stands and goods.

Serpentis Alley Goods and Services: A sample of what can be found here:

Animals	Cost
Lizard, monitor	4 bp
Snake, constrictor (Small to Huge)	1 bp x HD
Snake, viper[+] (Tiny to Huge)	2 bp x HD
Poisons	
Black Mamba venom	30 bp
Boomslang venom	20 bp
Cottonmouth venom	10 bp
Other Services	
Gall bladders and blood	1 bp
Rattler tail	1 sp
Coral snake tonic*	3 bp
Grilled snake meat	4 cp
Boiled snake eggs	2 cp
Snakeskin leather clothing	Special

[+]There is a 30% chance any given poisonous snake has already had its venom sac removed and sold.

*If consumed, the imbiber doubles the time required before having to make a Constitution saving throw when exposed to heat dangers. The effects last for 1d4 + 1 hours.

Black Mamba Venom: A creature subjected to this poison must succeed on a DC 17 Constitution saving throw or lose 2d4 points of Strength and begin to suffocate. The target cannot breathe until at least one point of Strength is recovered.

Boomslang Venom: A creature subjected to this poison must make a DC 16 Constitutions saving throw, losing 2d6 Constitution points on a failed save and 16 on a successful one. A creature that fails the saving throw by 5 or more is nauseated for 2d6 minutes. The nausea can be cured by magical healing or a successful DC 16 Wisdom (Medecine) check. While nauseated, a creature is incapacitated.

Cottonmouth Venom: A creature subjected to this poison must succeed on a DC 15 Constitution saving throw or lose 1d6 points of Constitution until after completing a long rest. A creature that fails the saving throw by 5 or more permanently loses 1 point of Constitution as well.

Snakeskin Leather Clothing: Finely crafted clothing made of snakeskin. The cost is the clothing's regular price + 60%.

13. Lower City Guard Barracks

These hardened guardsmen are a far cry from the highly-burnished soldiers that patrol the Upper City and Middle City. This barracks houses 90 **fire giants** and half that number in lowborn **efreeti** seeking to make names for themselves. Some merely like the action that they are sure to find down here in the guts of the city. They work in patrols of 1d4 giants and 1d2 efreet and are divided into three watches of 30 giants and 15 efreet.

The ward captain is a highly efficient **efreeti malik**[1] named Tayyib um Azzah, who apparently has a soft spot for Serpentis Alley. People say he receives a hefty bribe each month from its hawkers to ensure their business remains unimpeded. Whatever the case may be, it enjoys special privilege in the Heyyab district. He is armed with a *+2 falchion* (as *+2 longsword*) and wears a gold ring (300 gp) and a black pearl pendant gold necklace (1,400 gp) and carries 300 bp.

14. Lower City Prison

Those folk imprisoned for misdemeanor charges or lesser crimes and serving less than one year are placed in this prison. Visitors are welcome to the prison so long as they bring sufficient bribes for guards and do not try to spring the prisoners. Prisoners who have wealth and station are frequently in the "lap of luxury" and stay in the more influential Paradise Tower prison block. Undesirables who are doing hard time for petty crimes get the enjoyment of manning the massive bilge pumps that pump refuse from the city into the Sea of Fire where it is immolated by the intense heat. Few attempt to escape down the pipes as the great pressure from hundreds of prisoners cranking on the pumps could kill as easily as the heat of the Plane of Fire or drowning in boiling oil.

The prison is guarded by 20 **fire giants**, 10 **efreet**, and 4 **burning dervish wizards**[1]. These guards are culled from the normal city watch patrols and rotate every five days to avoid developing personal bonds and attachments with the prisoners. Occasional uprisings and riots within the prisons more often than not result in a newly emptied prison being repopulated with more docile prisoners.

15. The Ubaydulah Tower

This is one of the more notorious residential towers in the Lower City because it caters exclusively to women. It is an eighteen-story structure built from brass-reinforced gneiss and basalt. The outer walls are colorfully tiled with intricate mosaic patterns split occasionally by thin, arched windows. Bracing the building at each of the cardinal directions are the main courtyard, the main garden, the *chahar taq*, and the public mosque. The tower's domed roof is particularly noticeable as it is made from brightly shining leaves of living brass. All the rooms on the outer walls have balconies and glass windows. There are two entrances to the building, on the western and northern sides. Women generally enter through the north, while men are permitted entry only through the west. Free **azer elite**[1] ensure these rules are not broken. Furthermore, men are not allowed beyond the first floor. If a man is caught on any floor above the first, he is summarily executed (usually by being thrown from the nearest balcony).

The tower was built many decades ago at the late Sultana's behest, though nobody outside her immediate circle of handmaidens knew this. She channeled funds through her senior handmaiden's family to construct a place for women to feel safe in the City of Brass, where they could go to get away from cruel or vindictive husbands, jealous lovers, or simply the arrogant men who consider women their property. The Ubaydulah Tower strictly adheres to local religious tenets regarding the occasional segregation of men and women, providing an inviolate shelter for women at a time when many of them need it the most, given the current Sultan's predilection for cruelty toward the opposite sex.

The tower's council of elders, made up of women who have spent the better part of their lives residing here, manages the tower. Nobody knows their identities because they conceal their faces behind veils in public, which is proper behavior for a traditional, upstanding woman of their particular religious sect. The ornate headdresses the elders wear also set them apart from the other women living in the building. Any woman who desires to rent a room in the building must interview with one-third of the council first. Upon their approval, she is granted a room of their choosing. Only women of humanoid origin are accepted. Goblinoids are viewed as abominations, and outsiders (celestials, elementals, fiends, and fey) are considered untrustworthy. Moreover, the only kind of spellcasters they allow to live here are clerics. Wizards and sorceresses are black magicians in their eyes, and therefore most certainly not allowed (if the council had its way, arcane spellcasters would be stoned to death on sight.)

Seven staircases give access to sixteen of the eighteen floors. Only a select few of the residents know how to get into the uppermost two. Rooms and corridors are arranged and decorated according to traditional standards. If a woman didn't know better, she might think she was in her grandmother's country estate rather than high up in an unnaturally tall, magically supported building in the legendary City of Brass. Each floor has a small courtyard with arched windows opened to the city, a garden, and a mosque.

15-1. Main Courtyard

A spacious area at ground level, the courtyard is not really an integral part of the tower. It is built along the south side, a comfortable place audibly isolated from the rough-and-tumble hubbub of the Lower City streets by minor divine enchantments placed on the entry archways. Benches surround an elegant fountain that spills liquid bronze down the step-like tiers to the main basin at the bottom. Potted plants adapted to the intense heat of the plane give the courtyard a small, even comfortable, sense of otherworldliness. Male visitors are expected to behave themselves in the courtyard, where they are required to wait.

An elderly **griffon**, Lubna, makes the courtyard her home. Generally, she just sleeps in the southeastern corner and leaves everyone alone. When there is trouble, and there undoubtedly is when men are involved, she stirs from her torpor long enough to growl menacingly. If the rabble-rousing persists, she might work up the energy to bite the (likely male) offenders' face off or something.

15-2. Main Garden

The garden is on the eastern side of the tower. It is filled with a thick jungle of exotic and locale foliage. Orchids grow all year round; pink, yellow, purple, and white blossoms thicken the artificial landscape with their heady fragrances. Narrow paths wend through it, pausing intermittently at secluded stone benches. Chaperoned women come here to have some privacy with their male friends or lovers. Non-chaperoned women may freely enter the garden, but without male companions.

Jaida Malak[1] a resident of the tenth floor, has a secret stash of opium plants hidden in the thickest part of the garden. She comes down every night to harvest the bulbs after most of the women retire to their chambers. If the garden on her own floor were large enough to grow the plants without anyone noticing, she would use that, too. She waers a gold bracelet (400 gp) and uses her trowel as a dagger if needed.

15-3. Chahar Taq

This domed pavilion has four arched entrances, one of which connects with the tower. The inside of the dome is gilt with leaves of gold, the arches are colorfully tiled, and the floor is lined with ceramic plates that keep it cool despite the omnipresent heat of the city. The tower's female residents enter through this side of the building, though they are by no means required to do so; it is simply tradition and keeps them from inadvertently running into unpleasant males, who must confine themselves to the main courtyard. When the tower receives important visitors, they are allowed entry through the chahar taq, which is decorated for the event. Often, beggar women and their children can be found here, offering to wash the feet of the women entering the tower for a pittance.

15-4. Public Mosque

This temple is part of the tower's west side. A tall minaret rises from the outer wall, its hammered bronze bulb-shaped dome coming to a point just above the tower's roof. Though a public mosque, few traditional men come to it during prayer or other services because of its connection to the all-female residence next door. As such, the floor in the prayer hall is more often than not deserted. Women, according to tradition, may worship from the upper galleries, of which there are seven in order to accommodate them all. Male guests of the women sometimes come to the mosque to pray, though not very frequently and usually then just to impress the women. If word gets out a man does pray in the mosque, he is quickly stigmatized. The holy man who presides over prayer services is an ancient dwarf named Pudush bin Duba (**emeritus chaplain**[1]) from the outlying territories, an ultra-conservative who approves of the Ubaydulah ladies' lifestyles. Women, in his backward-thinking mind, should neither be seen nor heard. Living in the tower keeps them from tempting the males of the city, which is a good thing, according to his doctrine.

Ubaydulah's Tower

15-5. The Handmaiden's Palace

Chufa um Sophanie[1] is the second cousin of the late Sultana's senior most handmaiden, and the last surviving member of not just her family but her entire clan. She is a beautiful, bronze-skinned cheitan who escaped the vindictive burning dervishes' notice because she was raised anonymously in the Ubaydulah Tower. When the Sultana was executed, along with her entire household's retinue, Chufa received a message by courier telling her how to access the two topmost floors of the tower.

There she discovered the truth of her heritage and the tower's purpose. According to an obscure page in the *Prophecies of Sulymon*, known as the *Phoenix Legacy*, an army of female warriors will arise from the ashes of the Sultana's household. Once trained, the warriors are to abandon the City of Brass, for upon the Sultana's death the city had become irrevocably defiled. Their destiny is to rescue the hostage princess, and then charge forth until they come to the Elysium Fields where they shall spend a century driving the devils from those hallowed grounds. Afterward, the prophecy says the Phoenix warriors shall establish a millennium of peace under the rule of the hostage princess with which to build a great city of djinn to rival the City of Brass. At the end of their millennia, they shall launch a final apocalyptic assault against the corruption of the Usurper.

These two floors contain the last of the Sultana's wealth, which the heir to the Phoenix Legacy is charged with using to build and train her army. The lower floor contains training rooms, libraries filled with martial knowledge, a private mosque, armories with magical arms and armor (some of which seem to be of alien design and are water-cooled inside so the wearer can function in extreme heat without suffering any of the effects of wearing heavy armor in those conditions), and vaults filled with a king's ransom in coin, tapestries, rare artwork, and nonmagical artifacts. The upper floor is where Chufa and the council of elders live, their apartments' grand affairs worthy of the Sultana herself.

The women in training (as NG human **paragon knights**[1]) have smaller apartments of their own on the first sixteen floors. The elders of the sect choose potential warriors from the other residents, secretly approaching them with their tale and their offer. If the woman refuses, she is killed, for they cannot risk word of their existence reaching the burning dervishes. It should be noted that they do not share the secret of their mission up front but instead use a series of tests of faith, charity, humility, and valor to determine the worthiness of a prospect. Fortunately, they are very good at picking women who fit their ideology and temperament. In all the years of the tower's existence, they have only had to kill three who turned against their offer. None has ever defected after recruitment as their loyalty to Chufa unswerving.

The Ubaydulah Tower Rooms: The following rooms are available at the Tower:

Rent[+], all floors	Cost
Small room	12 gp
Medium room	30 gp
Large room	40 gp

[+]Rent is paid on a monthly basis. The council refuses to rent rooms on a weekly or daily basis, no matter much money they may be offered. Before renting a room to a woman, the elders must first interview her (sometimes repeatedly over the course of many weeks).

16. The Run

Surrounding the Basin is a ditch about 6 feet wide and 3 feet deep with four main pathways crossing it. The stones on the edges of this ditch are scarred and burnt from flame. The ravine is filled with a clear sticky fluid. Every half hour, the fluid ignites into a blaze for one full minute and then diminishes. Anyone caught within 5 feet of the ditch during a half hour mark takes 3d10 fire damage, although those succeeding on a DC 18 Dexterity saving throw take only half.

It has become an underground game of skill and stamina to make "The Run" around the circuit between blazes to earn brass pieces. Bets can be made in the House of the One-Eyed Jack. Based on the apparent speed and physical condition of the runner, the odds against success range from 3–1 to 10–1, but the runner always receives 50–1 payout if successful. The entire circuit is roughly two miles and the thick clear liquid is difficult terrain.

17. House of the One-Eyed Jack

The odds are in favor of the house at this rough-and-tumble joint. The owner of this place is **Morhidd**[1] the Jackknife, a large, thick, half giant who wears a patch over one of his eyes and carries a wickedly barbed dagger at his side. There are all sorts of gaming events here from dice to cards and from arm wrestling to knife throwing contests (an unfortunate slave generally being the target of choice). There are always three to four roaming **troll** bouncers. These trolls have found it in their best interest to swallow a gem that grants them immunity to fire. The house dealers (CN male or female **master spy**[1], with no weapons or armor, which makes their Armor Class 14) are cheaters all, and they're very good at what they do. The dice are magically weighted to roll in favor of the house 70% of the time and are enchanted with an *arcanist's magic aura* spell to register as nonmagical. Morhidd is no fool, though, and instructs his employees to hand out at least one big take per hour. Anyone who openly accuses the house of cheating is offered the chance to play Morhidd himself under virtually any conditions set by the accuser, at 20–1 odds. Anyone who accuses Morhidd himself of cheating is unceremoniously tossed out on the streets deprived of their clothing and instructed in no uncertain terms to avoid the premises in the future.

17A. The Gambit

The Gambit is a magically altered arena that can be accessed only through a door in the back room of the House of the One-Eyed Jack. The arena is relatively small but is much larger than it would appear to be from the outside. It can house roughly 2,000 spectators who sit on rows of shoddy wooden benches. The benches are organized around a 30-foot pit (15 feet deep) ringed with sharpened brass stakes. A railing surrounds the top of the pit where people can watch combatants fight one on one to the death. Anyone can enter the Gambit for a shot at fame and glory. The first fight wins the entrant 100 bp, which doubles every match after that. The matches become more and more difficult, and the combatant is allowed a mere five minutes of rest between matches (start with an "easy" opponent, and increase the Challenge for each subsequent match until the combantant gives up or dies). The combatant may leave after any fight won. If ten fights are won, Morhidd enters the Gambit himself offering the lease to the House of the One-Eyed Jack as the grand prize. The combatant does not get an option to leave once Morhidd challenges him; to quit results in a lynching from Morhidd and his bouncers.

18. The Corners Four

These are four identical buildings located throughout the Basin that offer the best in comfort in the Under City. The walls are made from a cheap stone and are chipped and broken in several places, but the prices can't be beat. Each room consists of two luxurious beds made from pillows half filled with feathers and a ratty blanket on old molding hay. These rooms are not without their charm, however, since the noise of the Basin with its screams, yelling, and magical explosions can lull even the mightiest beast to sleep. Typical rooms cost 5 sp per night.

19. The Hovel

The Hovels are groups of small houses and living quarters spewed all over the city in no organized fashion whatsoever. Citizens of the Basin live in absolute disarray. Houses missing windows, ceilings, and sometimes walls line the streets. People who live here beg in the streets, sit on the steps of their homes, and fight one another for scraps of foods. The smell of dried blood and stagnant urine emanate from the depths of a hovel. If someone wanted to hide from something, the place no one would want to look would be in the streets and alleys of a hovel. The authorities come here only during dire circumstances, and if they do, rest assured that the object of their search can expect nothing less than a tortured, miserable end.

20. The Venom Den

A two-story building of dilapidated wood sits on one of the dingy blocks of the Lower City. Inside, the smell of incense fills the air, causing anyone breathing it to succeed on a DC 20 Wisdom saving throw or be affected as by a *hypnotic pattern* and have disadvantage on saving throws to avoid being charmed. Near-naked women (actually **night hags** in disguise) greet the patrons and offer their exotic services to them upon entry. If the patrons accept, the women give them a drink (called a *resilugia*), which is a fiery amber liquid containing venom that grants an extreme sense of euphoria, followed by a deep sleep. A creature who drinks any amount of resilugia must succeed on a DC 17 Constitution saving throw or lose 1d6 points of Strength and fall asleep for 4 hours. The women strip the belongings of those who succumb to the sleep effects and give their possessions to runners who fence them in various parts of the city. The sleeping patrons are then taken to the Infirmary for a few extra brass pieces. The matron of the house is Palldafin, a **fiendish guardian naga**[1]. She rests in a lower room filled with plush pillows and luxurious sheets and perfume. She casts heavy alteration magic on the women to make them appealing to the men as well as altering her incense to make it more potent. If Palldafin's room is breached, she uses her *amulet of allies*[2] and tries to talk her way out of any situation. If combat ensues, all the females come to her aid. Palldafin has an *amulet of allies*[2] and *bracers of superior defense*[2] crafted as a circlet on her head.

21. The Infirmary

This is a small stone building with the only viable entrance in a dark alley off one of the winding streets of the Lower City. Not many people come here to receive healing but rather they drop off bodies they find passed out in the streets or unconscious from other means, receiving a few coins in recompense. Inside the dimly lit building are a few scant tables covered in dried blood and a few people who call themselves the Clerics of the Basin (male and female **emeritus chaplains**[1]). The clerics here heal the wounded and the people are never heard from again. Occasionally, some may notice them in slave quarries around the city. Those who do notice these unfortunate wretches know enough to keep their mouths shut lest they suffer a similar fate. Each cleric wears a brass ring (200 gp) and a platinum necklace (1,100 gp) and carries 6d20 bp.

22. House of Ill Repute

Untouched by the efreet, these young women have quite a business going for their master in the Basin. Youthful women (typically **greater commoners**[1]) of a variety of races offer services to the higher-class citizens of the Upper City who venture into the vile Basin for a sample of the beauty these women possess. The girls each have a brass collar that binds them to their own master. None of the women has ever felt the whip of their master for the simple fact that they have never met him. Their master is a powerful **maharaja rakshasa**[1] sorcerer by the name Velinari, who moves silently through the city pulling the marionette strings of his unknowing subjects.

23. The Shattered Spire

Standing almost 7 stories high is one of the former great structures of the City of Brass. This spire lies in ruins from some long-forgotten catastrophe. The spire is made of white alabaster and still remains quite clean even with the dirt and squalor of the Lower City. There is a single door made of cast iron covered in faint green runes. The first 5 stories of the building are windowless, a pure white stone stuck in the grime of the underbelly. It is rumored that great magic still awaits those brave enough to test themselves against the horrors that wait inside. Adventurers and thieves have gained access through the iron door, but none has made it past the first floor. And those who do escape tell stories of statues coming to life to attack them, ooze falling from the ceiling to dissolve their companions whole, and spheres of light that exploded in a blaze of energy consuming those it touched. Reaching the windows requires flying or climbing. Climbing the sheer surface requires a successful DC 30 Strength (Athletics) check per 10 feet. The windows are not glass but are made of swirling violet and crimson smoke. No one who has entered through these windows has been heard of again. The door can be sundered with a successful DC 30 Strength check or destroyed with 60 points of physical damage.

Within the Spire are 3 **balor demons** under a form of stasis. Whenever the spire is entered, the stasis effect is broken and they attack. Once the intruders are slain, they return to their post, and the spell takes effect again. They cannot leave the spire (including being dismissed, banished, etc.). There are also 4 **black puddings** awaiting potential intruders.

24. The Widow's Nest

The Widow's Nest is a dome of obsidian, framed in a crisscrossing silver faceted frame. A bright red light pours out through a small skylight in the center of the dome. Eight winding roads of the same polished obsidian as the Kubri Al Azim connect to the Widow's Nest, making it look even more like a giant spider, before the other roads of the Basin work them into the "web of the forgotten." Two **stone golems** chiseled of polished stone guard the main door to the most lavish bar in the entire Basin. The first thing a person notices is that the inside is much larger than the outside would warrant. Booths stretch around the perimeter of the bar with a host of tables and chairs scattered throughout. Two more **stone golems** are posted on each side of the building. Cages hang from the ceiling with nymphs and elven maids dancing, while a band plays music on the side stage (their instruments are enchanted to induce thirst and lust), and barmaids whirl in and out of traffic trying to wait on the throngs of patrons. The bar itself stretches across the back of the room where a mammoth human named Xell Danno (**champion warrior**[1] with a *+3 longsword*, *2 +1 daggers*, a *+1 spear*, a light crossbow, 10 silver bolts, and 20 cold iron bolts) fills tankards of assorted ales. Xell looks armed to the hilt as if he was going off to battle any second. His drow waitresses (**commoner** with 12 hit points, 120-foot darkvision, and the ability to cast *dancing lights* at will) flirt with him as they return empty mugs and await refills. Xell houses the most ales of any drink house in the city since he has his stock magically transported from the best breweries across the planes.

25. The Pagoda of Devils

This area is fully detailed in **Chapter 29**.

26. Tower of the Grand Vizier

This area is fully detailed in **Chapter 30**.

Book 3: Tales of Brass

Book 3
Tales of Brass

Within this tome are the most guarded secrets of a Sultan's empire. Places of treasures often sought but never gained. Used as a campaign setting, each of the fantastic locations found within offer hiding places and suggested relics and treasures to be discovered by heroes brave enough to walk the Path of the Prophet. Secrets of the ancients and gifts from the gods lie hidden in the gardens of the City of the Dead Sultana, which only the brave may know. An impenetrable bank sits behind the walls of the City of Brass, calling any doughty rogue to plot her most daring heist. Sages, hierophants, and kings of every design would give their left eyes to peruse the documents hidden within secret stacks of the Great Repository, while a secret scrawled upon its outer walls may very well hold the key to the destruction of the Sultan himself. Allies or adversaries may be gained within the Pagoda of Devils or the Shining Pyramid of Set, as surely as blood spills sizzling to the molten floor of the arena floor of the Circus of Pain. Remember, that which is won upon those hallowed disks may break the backs of the fell priesthood of the Sultan and cast down their Great Ziggurat once and for all.

Tales of Brass takes your game to new and exotic locales within the City of Brass itself, fleshing out in great detail the lairs of some of the most powerful foes that the City of Brass has to offer. It includes the resting place of many of the city's most fabulous treasures. Also found here are the powerful guardians of its various relics. *Tales of Brass* contains many new monsters as unique and deadly as the fiends who command them.

Tales of Brass includes unique adventure locales in the Plane of Molten Skies and the City of Brass. Played as a sweeping campaign, *Tales of Brass* takes the characters on an adventurous tour of each one of the adventure locales, introducing its denizens and treasures in detail. GMs wishing to use their own plot or campaign scenario may find the materials presented in *Tales of Brass* invaluable to any City of Brass adventure campaign. GMs wishing to use the materials located herein as place-settings for other short planar adventures need do nothing more than select an adventure location suited to the challenges of their home campaign and their own individual tastes, set up a premise for their party to investigate the location, and begin.

Characters who cut their teeth on the adventures of **Book I** may continue their quest for answers and possibly vengeance against those who wronged their homeland. The factions detailed in Chapter 9 offer the chance for various interested parties to place the characters on their quest of glory or infamy depending on the choices they make and the dice they roll.

Ultimately, it is what the characters do in the adventure locations detailed here that are the true tales of brass that will be spun around gaming tables and shared between friends in convention halls for years to come.

An Adventure Setting in Overview

Below is a brief list of the chapters and appendices found within *Tales of Brass*. Chapters are organized in progressive order as they would take place in a campaign, and more or less from the easiest set of challenges to the hardest.

Chapter 16: Prologue: This section of the book is designed to introduce the character of Rahib al Tarbish Zafir to the party in order to use this book in conjunction with the *City of Brass Campaign Setting*. Tarbish and his *geases* serve as the motivating force for the characters to gain great power and eventually either defeat or join forces with the Sultan of Efreet[1].

Chapter 17: Ard's Sanctuary: This secret sanctuary is best served after the characters have had a few encounters with the viceroy of the Lightbringer!

Chapter 18: The Shining Pyramid of Set. The Shining Pyramid offers the characters the opportunity to plunder an extraplanar temple to the god of evil and night. Great treasures and fabulous relics offer great rewards should characters be willing to make the ultimate sacrifices. Written for characters of Tier 3, this adventure location offers hours of role-play for more lawful or evil bending characters, as well as the opportunity to affect the destiny of a dozen universes by thwarting the priesthood's malevolent plans. The characters may find themselves on the good side of the Sultan of Efreet[1], or outlaws in his realm who must cling to the shadows, hunted by his squads of burning dervish feyhda[1].

Chapter 19: Freeman's Tower. The characters may be looking for a good hideout. This one isn't it, but it certainly serves as an adventure they will never forget.

Chapter 20: The Minaret of Screams. Suitable for characters of Tier 3, the minaret, like every chapter, is scalable for higher- or lower-level adventurers. Here the characters may find the ankle of *Tlaunehc Tnek, the Wyrm of Bones*[2]. Should the characters dare to free this wicked bone from its prison, do they dare awaken the nefarious spirit of the wyrm found in the Museum of Wonders? Perhaps the characters have found themselves prisoners here? Certainly no one would willingly enter a glistening tower of death?

Chapter 21: The Great Repository. Suitable for Tier 3 play, the Great Repository offers the characters an opportunity to explore the greatest collection of the written word in the universe. To peruse these tomes invites danger and sacrifice. Some may wish to unlock great powers scribed in forbidden tongues, while others may wish they had never turned their eye upon the baleful scripts hidden here. As much a prison as a storehouse of forbidden knowledge, there are those entombed within its stacks that the Sultan would prefer remain there forever.

Chapter 22: The City of the Dead Sultana. Designed for characters of Tier 4, the City of the Dead Sultana allows characters to explore a piece of the history of the City of Brass. The gardens of Cirrishade hold many secrets, secrets no doubt that the current Sultan would prefer remain hidden from the knowledge of his devoted followers. Here the characters may find a way to gain the *eyes of the Sultana*[2], or to activate the jade colossus with the *ruby star of law*[2] and set about events which could ultimately bring about the destruction of the Plane of Molten Skies itself.

Chapter 23: The Circus of Pain. Designed for characters of Tier 4, the Circus of Pain affords countless opportunities for adventure and role-play. A nearly unlimited cast of NPCs may do battle with or offer their allegiances to the characters depending on the outcomes of the games. The Circus Master rules all within the circus, dishing out and feeding on the torment of those who are part of the spectacle. Characters seeking to free themselves from imprisonment here should be warned: Failure in the games may be worse than death itself. Characters following the **Tales of Brass** as an adventure campaign would do well to recover the *maul of Hezoid*[2] from the circus champion before departing.

Chapter 24: Cathedral of the Lightbringer. For characters of Tier 4. This is what happens when the Sultan owes the devil a favor.

Chapter 25: The KhizAnah. Designed for characters of Tier 4, the KhizAnah is the impenetrable bank every rogue worth their garrote and *ring of invisibility* has longed to crack. A banking facility that even the gods use to store their loot, the KhizAnah has a reputation of efficiency and death. None who has tried to breach its tight security has lived to tell the tale. Perhaps it is the fiendish tigers that dwell the middle levels; perhaps it is the traps that guard its many vaults. Characters using the **Tales of Brass** as a campaign setting must find the *mymr stone*[2] itself if they hope to stand a chance against the KhizAnah's guardians.

Chapter 26: The Underbasin. Designed for characters of Tier 4. This small dungeon is as deadly as they come. Hidden secrets lay beneath the great bowl.

Chapter 27: The Secret Tomb of Rah'po Dehj. Jhedophar is at it again. Suggested for characters of Tier 4 level. His hidden lair in the City of Brass is at last revealed. Or were the characters just invited for tea and crumpets? Side trips to the Plane of Shadow, Styx, and the Astral Plane may be on the menu.

Chapter 28: The Great Ziggurat. Designed for characters of Tier 4, characters seeking to join the Sultan and worship him as their deity must survive the ash baths. Those seeking to dismantle his empire must find the humble high priest of Anumon among the slave pits below. There they must bring to him a mighty weapon with which to reap holy ruin upon the burning dervishes.

Chapter 29: The Pagoda of Devils. Written for characters of Tier 4 level and beyond, the Pagoda of Devils offers an interesting side quest for high-level characters. Victory against the masters of the Pagoda of Devils could very well sever ties between Geryon and the Sultan of Efreet[1], or at the very least create a new feud between the Lightbringer and his former prince.

Chapter 30: The Tower of the Grand Vizier. For characters of Tier 4, the Tower of the Grand Vizier offers great challenges that may result in characters gaining a new ally against the Sultan, or in crippling the Sultan's powers by removing an ally from his own right hand.

Chapter 31: The Palace of the Sultan. For characters Tier 4. This is the place for the final showdown between the characters and the Sultan's forces. Hopefully they have made some friends along the way.

Appendix 1: New Monsters Listed here are the statistics and descriptions of new monsters and characters with which to challenge your characters. Ranging from the normal to the extremely bizarre, these unique new creations are assured to add some shock and awe into any high-level campaign. They include both generic creatures and named individuals

Appendix 2: New Magic Items Placed here are new feats and magic items, including artifacts that are found within these pages.

Appendix 3: New Mundane Items This appendix details poisons and tobacco, automatic weapons and hand grenades. It includes items found throughout the adventure that are not detailed in the Fifth Edition SRD.

Appendix 4: New Spells This appendix details new spells found within the pages of this book.

Appendix 5: 101 Adventures and Encounter Seeds This appendix gives short seeds from which you can spin great adventures.

Running the Campaign

If the characters have already made entry to the Plane of Molten Skies or the City of Brass itself, a sweating abasheen genie named Tarbish approaches them. Perhaps some daring deed that the characters participated in caught Tarbish's interest. Tarbish tells a tale of horrors committed by the Sultan of Efreet[1] and swears the characters to secrecy hoping to connive, beg, convince, and, if all else fails, charm the characters with magic and place a powerful *geas* upon them to serve as his agents in a revenge plot against the Sultan of Efreet[1] himself.

Tarbish speaks of an ancient time when the City of Brass was ruled by efreet and djinn alike who followed the rules of law as set down by the god Anumon himself. Once Tarbish convinces the characters to join upon the endeavor, he sets them (based on their current party levels) on a quest to recover pieces of various tomes of knowledge, relics, and powerful entities who could serve as a force to thwart the Sultan's plans. More details about Tarbish and using him to further an ongoing mega-campaign are detailed in the prologue.

Aside from Tarbish, any other faction member save the Sultan or the Cult of the Burning One may approach the characters and offer them details on a quest. Perhaps the characters have come across the charming cult known as "the People" and been approached by their leader Ard. Possibly they have met with the trio living atop Freeman's Tower and are asked to clean house for them.

As with any RPG product, levels may be dropped off monsters, and other modifications may be made to any part of this book to easily fit it into your own campaign, following your own creative preferences. **Tales of Brass** is yours; use it as you see fit.

Chapter 16
Prologue

Shortly after arriving at the Kubri Al Azim in the City of Brass, the characters are approached by a tall, thin abasheen genie who introduces himself as Tarbish (**Rahib al Tarbish Zafir**[1]). Tarbish is handsome and well spoken, yet fast talking. He invites the characters to the shade of a tent he has placed upon the Kubri Al Azim along with his valets and retainers and entreats them to stay and enjoy a sumptuous feast.

Should the characters refuse his offer, Tarbish appears before them again later, more insistent than the time before, again inviting them to join him at the Caravanserai, where he has an encampment, and offers to share with them the secrets of the City of Brass.

Should the characters refuse a second time, Tarbish appears a third time as determined by you. This third meeting, should the previous two fail, should somehow come at a time when the characters are in danger of being arrested, enslaved, or slain in a battle, where he saves them from their fates and whisks them away to his tent in the Caravanserai. Alternately, Tarbish may purchase the characters as slaves and set them on the course of epic adventure — offering them only death if they should fail him in their endeavors.

Tarbish tells a tale of a fallen genie and a time of relative peace between those of the City of Brass and the tribes of the djinn who rule empires upon the Plane of Air. He speaks of Anumon and Sulymon and the days when a beautiful Sultana tempered an efreeti's innate cruelty with compassion and a sense of fair play. He speaks of a usurper who stole the throne and slew the former Sultan, releasing his prisoners and repopulating the bureaucracy with former criminals of the state. Tarbish speaks of a formation of gangs of burning dervishes, a tribe of jann driven mad by the powers of the usurper. Of how a Sultana, smote a deadly blow, remains perfectly preserved somewhere in the city. He tells of alliances between the Lightbringer, ruler of Infernus, and the Dread Lord Set. He speaks of how their minions have free rein over a city built for the races of genie alone to rule. He salts the tale with marvels of magic and blades of famous name, relics of the old ones in the time between the birth of gods and the dawn of men.

Should Tarbish's tales fall on deaf ears or should the characters attempt to attack Tarbish, he casts a *greater geas*[4] on the entire party, telling them that since they did not take the task willingly, they are now condemned to fulfill his desires for good or ill.

Tarbish is actually none other than the Grand Vizier of efreet, though he takes great steps to conceal his identity, for the traitorous path that he takes would mean his ruin at the hands of the Sultan. So secret is his task of revenge and so great is his desire for the Throne of Brass that he has shared the elements of his plot with no one, although perhaps his clone knows a bit of his mind. The Vizier secretly plots to depose the usurper and, being of the last true bloodline of efreet going back to Iblis, intends to wed the daughter of Cirrishade and Ashur Ban and solidify his control over the dominions of djinn and efreet alike; failing this, he would raise Cirrishade and force her to marry him. Something in the characters' demeanor or their previous victories has piqued the Vizier's interest. It was with the characters in mind that he set assassins to waylay the Sultan's burning dervishes and attempt to capture the iron *flask of Sulymon*[2].

Tarbish or one of the other interested parties should be introduced at the beginning and end of each foray into an area of adventure. Such encounters should begin shortly after the end of each adventure area that the characters explore. You may guide their search in this manner without totally leading the characters by the nose. Merely suggesting areas of adventure fitting their level range should allow for rapid level advancement. Use Tarbish or the other agents, alliances, and factions to motivate the characters when they are stuck or find themselves otherwise incapable of discovering clues, secrets, and sub-plots on their own.

Do not abuse the use of this NPC and allow yourself to steal the thunder from the characters. In all circumstances, they should be allowed every chance to learn and grow. Tarbish is best suited for making suggestions to the characters when it becomes a matter of "What's next?" or "Why should we go there?"

With the exception of the *maul of Hezoid*[2] being gained before giving it to the priest of Anumon in the Great Ziggurat, most other areas of adventure serve to challenge characters of the appropriate Tier. Eventually, the characters should be led to the Tower of the Grand Vizier, and either discover at that time or at some time right before that their benefactor or slave master Tarbish is none other than the Grand Vizier himself. What ensues upon their climactic meeting could very well seal the fates of the characters or send them upon the greatest challenge of their careers. It may very well seal their doom, or with luck and great heroism, lead them to face the Sultan of Efreet[1] himself.

The Flask of Sulymon and The Carnelian Idol

Two powerful artifacts could play an important role in your campaign if you desire: the *flask of Sulymon*[2] and the *carnelian idol*[2]. Both are described below.

Through use of the random table included below, at the start of any adventure in the City of Brass first roll and determine the location of the idol and flask. In this way, chance encounters or happenstance exploration of the Plane of Molten Skies may result in the characters coming into possession of an item of fantastic power without them knowing that they own it.

Imagine their surprise when they peddle the idol or flask off in one of the city's many bazaars — only to have to purchase the item back from the vendor or merchant at ten times its original sale price.

The Carnelian Idol

Wondrous item, artifact

Like the *flask of Sulymon*, the *carnelian idol* is a mysterious magical item that was lost in the ever-shifting terrain of the Plane of Molten Skies as a great curse bound Dahish into a pillar of obsidian. This curse may be broken only through the device of the *carnelian idol* itself. Having passed through many hands for centuries unknown, the idol was somehow lost in the Plane of Molten Skies itself. Again, like the deific powers which blind the Sultan of Efreet's eye to the whereabouts of the flask, so too does the great curse deny any scrying as to the whereabouts of the *carnelian idol*.

By smashing the *carnelian idol* upon the sides of the pillar prison in **Area 3** on the Plane of Molten Skies, the characters may release Dahish from his prison.

The Flask of Sulymon

Wondrous item, artifact

The flask and its holy contents could prove the Sultan's undoing or grant him a station among the thrones of the greater gods. Currently, the Sultan of Efreet[1] is scouring the universe for the magical flask that a trusted troupe of his burning dervishes was tasked with returning. It is believed by many that the flask contains the body and soul of the Prophet Sulymon who, it is said, founded the City of Brass itself. It is believed that the Usurper sought to prove his dominion once and for all to any doubters by producing Sulymon in the flesh. No doubt he has other diabolical schemes in mind. Due to the powers of the God Anumon, however, the flask and any details as to its whereabouts remain clouded in mystery.

The flask can be unstoppered and opened only in the presence of the Sultan, and only then if his true name is spoken as the seal is broken. This knowledge is not readily apparent, and even an *identify* spell will only provide some information about its true nature. A *wish, legend lore,* or other sources of information may provide more, at your discretion.

Determining the Location of the Flask and Idol

To randomly determine the location of the *flask of Sulymon*[2] or the *carnelian idol*[2], roll 1d12 for the flask or 1d20 for the idol on the table below. Note, the flask cannot be located within the City of Brass.

1d20	Location
1	Lost Tomb of Y'Cart (**Area 5-1**, Plane of Molten Skies, **Chapter 10**)
2	Pits of the Crystal Queen (**Area 5-3**, Plane of Molten Skies, **Chapter 10**)
3	Caves of the Glass Wyrms (**Area 5-4**, Plane of Molten Skies, **Chapter 10**)
4	The Shattered Peak (**Area 7**, Plane of Molten Skies, **Chapter 10**)
5	Citadel of the Fire Thane (**Area 11**, Plane of Molten Skies, **Chapter 10**)
6	Xigla Xaltaz, Fortress of the Xill (**Area 13**, Plane of Molten Skies, **Chapter 10**)
7	The Spire of Hazrad the Mad (**Area 15**, Plane of Molten Skies, **Chapter 10**)
8	Wyrthil's Lair (**Area 16**, Plane of Molten Skies, **Chapter 10**)
9	Hall of the Vulcan Lords (**Area 20**, Plane of Molten Skies, **Chapter 10**)
10	Caverns of Abdul-Shihab (**Area 22**, Plane of Molten Skies, **Chapter 10**)
11	Fortress of the Seekers of the Ebony Moon (**Area 26**, Plane of Molten Skies, **Chapter 10**)
12	The Oasis of Mukphat the Blind (**Area 31**, Plane of Molten Skies, **Chapter 10**)
13	Shining Pyramid of Set (**Area 5**, the Upper City, **Chapter 18**)
14	Pagoda of Devils (**Area 6**, the Upper City, **Chapter 29**)
15	The KhizAnah (**Area 26**, the Upper City, **Chapter 25**)
16	The Minaret of Screams (**Area 32**, the Upper City, **Chapter 20**)
17	Tower of the Grand Vizier (**Area 40**, the Upper City, **Chapter 30**)
18	City of the Dead Sultana (**Area 42**, the Upper City, **Chapter 22**)
19	Palace of the Great Sultan (**Area 43**, the Upper City, **Chapter 31**)
20	Tomb of Ashur Ban (**Area 7**, the Lower City, the Underbasin, **Chapter 15**)

Chapter 17
Ard's Secret Sanctuary

Introduction

The Viceroy of the Lightbringer keeps a secret apartment along the bowl's edge of the Middle City. The inauspicious looking exterior belies the lavish opulence and twisted horrors hidden within.

The general "rundown" quality of the Middle City is evident when compared to the opulence of the Upper City just a few hundred feet above, though it still stands in stark contrast to the Lower City and the squalor of the Basin. There is still wealth in the terraces of the Middle City, though it is masked by the general inattentiveness of its residents.

Using Ard's Secret Sanctuary

This adventure location is not intended as a "first stop" for the characters, but to serve as a location the characters may seek out if they find that Ard has double-crossed them, or that they have indeed been in league with the Lightbringer by mistake. Perhaps at some point they are hired by Rah'po Dehj or Chufa Um Sophanie to take Ard out. Possibly they are not yet strong enough to take down the Cathedral of the Lightbringer but feel as if Ard's Secret Sanctuary is a good place to go looking to weaken the presence of the Lightbringer in the City. The difficulty of the adventure is dependent on whether or not Ard[1] or Tienen[1] are present at the time of the raid. Overall, it is probably appropriate for characters of Tier 3.

If the characters have interacted with Ard, or if Chufa Sophanie convinces them of Ard's absolute evil, they may find it necessary to track down this hidden lair and raid it. Characters playing through the adventure started in ***Lornedain: The Secret Flame*** no doubt have a special interest in recovering Simone Dubois from Ard's hidden jail before he decides to sacrifice her to the Lightbringer.

If Ard is encountered and defeated in other areas on the Plane of Molten Skies, his magical contingency spells deposit him in his summoning chamber. Ard is further detailed in **Chapter 24: The Cathedral of the Lightbringer**.

1. Entrance

The entrance to Ard's Apartment is found on Khan Sarai, a road that runs the circumference of the bowl and is built into the great bowl itself. The entrance is flanked by two great statues of barbed devils that appear well worn from the general heat of the region and the occasional acrid and oily rains that slick the city.

The statues are in fact **barbed devils** that trigger to attack unwanted visitors to the apartment but are immediately returned to stone when the threat passes. The devils can be dismissed, banished, or destroyed, requiring Ard to summon and bind new ones.

The door is locked with an arcane lock triggered to Ard's voice. It can be bypassed with *dispel magic* or *knock*.

2. Bridge

The bridge leading into the inner dwelling is 15 feet long and is trapped with a weight-based trap. The trap is set so that if more than 400 pounds of weight is on the bridge without the proper latch being locked in place, it falls away, dropping all who cross into the Run within the Basin, possibly as flames are beginning to rush through the trench. Characters thus falling suffer 35 (10d6) bludgeoning damage as they are battered down the long refuse chute. Detecting and understanding the trap requires a successful DC 18 Intelligence (Investigation) check and it can be disarmed with a successful DC 18 Dexterity check with thieves' tools.

3. Guest Toilet

This is a lavish restroom with a gold-plated toilet seat, a silver mirror inscribed with the words "Because You're Worth It" upon the shining surface, and hot and cold running water in the sink basin. The toilet seat is worth 100 gp, and the mirror is worth 200. There are 20 individual rose-scented soaps worth 1 gp each.

4. Tienen's Room

The door to his room is trapped with a deadly venom needle trap that fires a needle into the face of anyone attempting to pick the lock. The trap can be noted with a successful DC 20 Intelligence (Investigation) check and disarmed with a successful DC 20 Dexterity check with thieves' tools. If triggered, the needle makes an attack against the nearest target within 10 feet at +10 to hit. On a hit, the needle does 1 point of piercing damage and the target must attempt a DC 18 Constitution saving throw. On a failure, the target takes 99 (18d10) poison damage. On a success, the target loses 1d6 points each of Dexterity and Strength that can be recovered after a short rest and takes 22 (4d10) poison damage.

This seldom used room is one of many hiding spots held by Tienen[1] throughout the city and among the planes. He keeps a bed, dresser, spare weapons and armor, and a respectable amount of loot here in a small *bag of holding* hidden behind a painting of a tavern recognizable by visitors to Bard's Gate as the Inn of the Fallen Tree.

The safe that the bag is hidden in has a difficult lock requiring a successful DC 22 Dexterity check with thieves' tools to unlock.

The safe contains a *sword of speed*[2] (rapier), *boots of elvenkind*, a *cloak of resistance*[2], a *bag of holding* containing a northern king's regal chair worth 300 gp, ten 1,000 gp diamonds, 200 pp, a diamond bracelet worth 500 gp, 3 *potions of healing*, and a suit of *+2 studded leather armor*.

Two smaller rooms off the main living room area contain a private restroom and bedchamber.

5a. Kitchen

The kitchen is filled with wondrous appliances, including an icebox, a potbelly stove, and fine cooking utensils. The kitchen is maintained by Pepin, a **hellstoker devil**[1]. Pepin is an excellent chef, but arrogant, cruel, and self-absorbed. His creations make Ard's dinner parties legendary among the nobility of the City of Brass for his use of exotic spices and even more exotic meats. Pepin is assisted by a staff of 3 **imps** who do his will lest they are returned to the confines of Infernus. Pepin scours the markets of the City of Brass for unique combinations of meat, seasoning, starches, fruits, and vegetables.

His concoctions have gathered the attention of the Sultan's chefs who have hired spies to follow the Hellstoker and attempt to copy his recipes. For this reason, he has taken to hiring decoys or paying strangers to the city to collect unique specimens from the planes for his menu. He would pay 10 bp per pound for the flesh of a celestial dragon, and 100 bp per egg

Ard's Apartment

for any dragon egg to make a casu marzu and dragon egg omelet for Ard and his guests.

5b. Larder

The larder currently contains 100 pounds of unicorn meat, 100 pounds of gold dragon meat, 20 pounds of kirin meat, three angel hearts, and two glazed elf suckling babes. He also possesses 20 pounds of casu marzu, two dozen balut eggs, a gallon of live escamol, two gallons of lutefisk, and a semi-sentient haggis (as **flesh pudding**[1] with Intelligence 4).

6. Ard's Grand Hall

Ard's grand hall is divided into three parts, creating a multi-purpose entertainment venue.

6a. Dining Area

The dining area features a 12-foot-long table made of polished vermillion surrounded by high backed vermillion and gilt chairs carved with the likenesses of devils torturing and murdering angels. The table can seat 12 guests. The walls hang with paintings of a high neoclassical nature showing the virtues of the Lightbringer offering knowledge to mortals in the form of weapons, technology, and business. The subtext of the paintings is greed, impiety, violence, and immorality. Despite this, their quality is unbridled, and they would be worth at least 1,000 gp each to a collector of fine art.

6b. Ballroom

A billowing red velvet curtain separates the dining area from the dancefloor and the stage. The dance floor is a roughly 30-foot-by-40-foot area with a gorgeous wooden floor featuring a raw umber and ivory inlaid chevron design. A marble statue of Lilith stands in one corner pointing as if its arms are placed on the body backward. The statue weighs 300 pounds and would be worth 2,000 gp to the right collector. It also exudes an unmistakable aura of evil. Celestials, elementals, and fey cannot enter the area nor can they charm creatures that are within the area and creatures that are not undead or fiends are vulnerable to necrotic damage while in the area.

6c. Bandstand

A stage stands at the end of the room. The band, known as Angelo's Cursed 13 Orchestra, is made up of 13 **wraiths** who sold their soul to Old Scratch for success in life. They play the violin, viola, cello, bass, trumpet, tuba, clarinet, flute, horn, xylophone, harp, drums, and piano. They are led by Angelo, a **cambion demon**[1] who thrashes the restless spirits of his orchestra with hell-born fury.

7. Trapped Closet

This supply closet doorway is actually a mechanical trap made of a powerful conveyer belt that runs into a steel thresher that spits any remains into the city's sewer system.

Anyone standing on the floor within 10 feet of the trap must succeed on DC 16 Dexterity saving throw or be drawn into the thresher. The thresher deals 21 (6d6) slashing damage per round until the victims are dead or pull themselves free. Escaping the trap requires a successful DC 16 Strength check. The trap requires a successful DC 18 Intelligence (Investigation) check to locate and a DC 18 Dexterity check with thieves' tools to disable.

8. Torture Chamber

Ard handles most of his own torturing, though he does keep a pair of **bearded devils** as thugs and enforcers to transfer prisoners from his private jail to the torture chamber and back again.

The torture chamber has all the common staples: tongs, braziers, a rack, a bed of nails, an iron maiden, and various cages. A rack of rubberized white scrubs hangs along one wall, all of them fitted to Ard.

Ard's Enchanted Mirrors

Ard's torture chamber, library, bedchamber, and summoning room each have a mirror enchanted to allow traveling between them in a manner similar to *dimension door*. Standing in front of the mirror, one sees oneself as if licked with hellfire. A pair of handprints on the mirror are about chest high and shoulder width apart.

Placing ones' hands on the mirror and repeating the magical words allow the viewer to travel to any of the rooms that currently hold a copy of the mirror. Ard uses the mirrors to quickly step through various rooms of his apartment.

The magic words are *"Tu Mori, Ea Mori, Vos Mori."* They can be gleaned by successfully intimidating the devils, through a *legend lore* spell, a successful DC 25 Intelligence (Arcana) check, through some other contact with a higher plane that could provide the answer, or by successfully reading Ard's mind. Speaking these words and thinking of the location one wants to travel within Ard's apartment reveals the image of the space and allows direct passage similar to *dimension door* to the location.

Removing a mirror from the wall triggers a *fireball trap* and destroys the mirror. Anybody within 40 feet of the mirror when the trap is triggered must make a DC 18 Dexterity saving throw, taking 28 (8d6) fire damage on a failed save and half as much on a successful one. The trap can be noted with a successful DC 20 Intelligence (Arcana) check. While the trap can be deactivated with *Dispel Magic* cast against an 8th level spell slot, the magical properties of the mirror are still destroyed if the mirror is removed from the wall.

There is a 15% chance that **Ard**[1] is occupying himself with one of his prisoners in the torture chamber.

A silver, full-length enchanted mirror hangs from one wall.

9. Ard's Prison

Ard has a small jail where he keeps choice guests. Currently, he has few prisoners, though characters who cross him may find themselves held here, awaiting torture at his hands.

The cells, like the torture chamber, are guarded by a pair of **bearded devils**. The cells are locked with a magical lock, but open to Ard's touch. The current prisoners are:

9-A. Maheen al Azul (efreeti)

The missing daughter of Azul bin Berith, sheik of the house of the Bayt al-Najoom. She has been largely unmolested by Ard, who knows she cannot be despoiled if he is to gain access to the Great Repository through her father.

9-B. Princess Yelsinia Jarlax of Parnuble

The elves of Parnuble, fearing an invasion by the forces of the Sultan, sent a party to the City of Brass to gather information and to see what they could do to stop the extra-planar assault. They were rooted out almost immediately by Fatavdra's people. Wounded in an ambush, with her allies slain, Yelsinia (NG elf **knave adept**[1]) unfortunately encountered Ard, who offered her succor and a place to hide within his apartment. She has been his prisoner ever since.

The princess is resilient in the face of her ongoing torture, however, and has taken it upon herself to incite torture to herself rather than allow Ard the satisfaction of torturing his new pet, the child Simone Dubois.

9-C. Empty

9-D. Empty

9-E. Empty

9-F. Simone Dubois (commoner)

One of the missing persons from Lornedain, she slipped through the fingers of many before finding herself in the custody of Ard. Due to her age, innocence, and purity, Ard intends to sacrifice her to the Lightbringer when the time is right.

10. Ard's Sanctum

This study is occupied by huge bookshelves featuring treatises on history, astrology, astronomy, physical sciences, engineering, mathematics, and, of course, magic. Studying these books for one month per subject grants proficiency in an Intelligence check related to the relevant field. The bookshelves contain all of Ard's known spells including all 1st- to 3rd-level conjuration spells, and 5 spells each of levels 4–9, with the predominant number of spells coming from the school of conjuration.

One wall holds one of Ard's enchanted mirrors.

Also included in this collection are a number of scrolls, as well as ink, paper, and materials to scribe 20 more scrolls. The following scrolls are available: *call lightning, chill touch, cone of cold, detect evil and good, disguise self, grease, heat metal, identify, inflict wounds, magic weapon, vampiric touch.*

The symbol of a large eye is emblazoned in the center of the room and is surrounded by stars and lunar alignments that are considered sacred to the Lightbringer. While concentrating, Ard can see whatever is in this room through the symbolic eye, thus alerting him to any would-be thieves or invaders.

11. Ard's Summoning Chamber

The summoning chamber is a spotless chamber dedicated to the idolatry of the Prince of Darkness. The various posts and lintels are hung with the masks of various devils, some even made from leather flayed from the flesh of lesser fiends. The room itself is octagonal in shape with one wall featuring a silver-backed mirror that licks with hellfire when gazed upon. There are eight masks. Seven devil masks appear to be worth anywhere between 200 and 1,000 gp each. The eighth mask is a cursed clown mask that turns the wearer into a red jester[1] unless a successful DC 20 Wisdom saving throw is made.

The floor of the room is inlaid with pentacles, summoning circles, and sigils of magic in polished silver. A music stand holds amulets, gemstones, and holy symbols from scores of religions that have fallen to the fork of the Son of the Morning. Conjuration spells cast within the circle after a successful DC 18 Intelligence (Arcana) check have a duration of 8 hours and do not require concentration to maintain (although without concentration, the conjured creatures may act in unpredictable ways).

12. Ard's Bedroom

Ard has a bedroom here, though he is as often as not found in the Cathedral of the Lightbringer. The room is lined with paintings of Ard in his capacity as the envoy of the Prince of Darkness. One painting shows him supporting an emperor known for massacring his people. Another painting shows Ard as witness to the execution of an innocent man, with a sly grin on his face. The dark shadow of his horned master is seen in Ard's cast shadow or as a shadowy figure just over Ard's shoulder. One wall has an enchanted mirror.

A dresser is lined with dozens of bottles, some of which are filled with expensive colognes valued at 100–400 gp. each. Others are filled with the following potions: *oils of etherealness, sharpness,* and *slipperiness,* and *potions of clairvoyance, dimunition, flying,* and *gaseous form.*

A chest locked with an arcane lock summons a **horned devil** when opened to protect Ard's treasures. The lock can be openend with *dispel magic* cast against a 9th level spell slot. The summoning trap can be detected with a successful DC 20 Intelligence (Arcana) check. It is disarmed along with the lock.

Within the chest are 500 gp, 100 bp, 50 pp, a *+2 sling*, a coral ring worth 200 gp, an ivory horn worth 500 gp, a moonstone worth 100 gp, 10 opals worth 50 gp each cut like dice, and a *spell wand*[2] of *identify*.

The room contains a closet and private bathroom with indoor plumbing.

The closet contains dozens of robes in silk and satin, mostly in red and black with gold brocade featuring finely woven yet monstrous images of devils and hellscapes too disturbing to describe.

Among the robes are a *robe of powerlessness*[2], a *robe of vermin*[2], a *cloak of resistance*[2], and a *cloak of etherealness*[2].

There are ten additional silk robes worth 300 gp each.

Chapter 18
The Shining Pyramid of Set

The Shining Pyramid of Set

This huge pyramid — the entire surface of which is seemingly constructed of glass — hangs suspended in midair about 700 feet above the Upper City. It is 750 feet square at the base and rises to a height of 479 feet. Its glassy surface reflects the nearby buildings, minarets, and burning skies. The only means of entrance seems to be a platform about 100 feet up from the base, 700 feet from the ground of the Upper City.

Through covenant and treaty with the Sultan of the City of Brass, Set's worshippers are allowed to practice their faith freely and are even granted preferential treatment through the offices of the Unholy Order of Venom. In return, they are expected to follow the laws of the Sultan and respect the sovereignty of the Sultan within his city. Servants of the dread god Set are welcome to stay within the Shining Pyramid as guests of the pyramid's high priest.

This respectable arrangement with the Great Sultan proves beneficial to the Sultan and Set, and keeps communications open between the two powers at all times. The Jackal-Lord is constantly looking for new ways to

Standard Features

Access: The Shining Pyramid of Set may be entered through **Area 1** of the main floor, 700 feet above the ground. The platform is accessible only to those who can fly or procure means of flying.

Exterior Walls: Though appearing to be made of glass, the exterior walls are actually constructed of an alien and unknown metal akin to highly polished steel. Given the temperatures of the City of Brass, the outer walls of the pyramid are extremely hot. A character touching the wall takes 16 (3d10) fire damage per round of contact.

Doors: The doors in the Pyramid of Set are made of living brass. Most doors to the public areas are either open or unlocked. Those leading to private chambers are always locked. Breaking down a living brass door requires a successful DC 28 Strength check. The locks can be picked with a successful DC 20 Dexterity check with thieves' tools. Living brass doors repair themselves at the rate of 1 hit point per minute and have a maximum of 60 hit points. A door reduced to 0 or fewer hit points cannot repair itself.

The doors in **Areas 14**, **15**, and **16** are made of thick, smooth stone. Unless noted otherwise, they can br broken through with a successful DC 24 Strength check or picked with a successful DC 20 Dexterity check with thieves' tools. They have 30 hp each and do not repair themselves.

Shielding: *Teleportation, plane shifting, passwall,* and the like automatically fail if used to attempt access into the pyramid. Such abilities function normally inside the pyramid's confines, but do not allow access from the outside, nor do they allow access from the inside out unless the caster possesses a *black ankh of Set*[2] that has been *blessed* by one of the high priests within the pyramid.

spread death and destruction throughout the planes. Set has a particularly keen interest in the more powerful weapons fabricated within the Bazaar of Arms and keeps a steady flow of such items from the craftsmen within the City of Brass into the hands of his minions throughout the planes.

Potential quest givers include Rah'po Dehj, Chufa Um Sophanie, Tarbish, Mistress Fatavdra and Ard, each of whom seeks random rare items hidden within the pyramid.

This adventure is suggested for Tier 4 characters.

Shining Pyramid of Set as Part of an Ongoing Campaign

For lower-level parties, Tarbish suggests infiltrating the Shining Pyramid of Set as their first mission to "prove their worth." He spins a tale of treachery upon the part of Set's agents in the City of Brass. Currently, Set's emissaries Sss'ashisth, and Retep Inkusad stand as representatives of Set's support of the Sultan of Efreet[1]. They seek the weapons and knowledge of the efreeti while the Sultan in turn seeks Set's assistance in completing his grand scheme. Tarbish surmises that a blow against the Shining Pyramid would bring about the ruin of the Sultan's plan and deal a mighty blow to Set's own designs in eventually claiming the City of Brass for himself. Tarbish indicates that a powerful relic known as the *mask of Ankev*[2] is in the possession of Retep Inkusad, and although the Viceroy of Set fears to use it himself, it could be combined with even greater relics to bring about the return of the arch lich himself. For evil parties, the potential of coming into possession of a powerful evil relic may be all the urging required. For good-aligned parties, the possibility of helping defeat the forces of evil should serve as excuse enough to take on the challenge. Alternately, the characters could run afoul of the priests of Set elsewhere in the City of Brass and set about for revenge. A naturally occurring series of events may be all that is needed to get the characters into the adventure.

1. Entranceway

Midway up the side of the Shining Pyramid stands the cursed portals that lead into the depths of Set's worship and priesthood here in the City of Brass. A staircase leads to the entrance.

Flanking the entrance at the top of the stairs are 2 stone sphinxes (as **ginosphinx**) standing upon gleaming pedestals. One sphinx bears the head of a jackal, while the other has the head of a vulture. A skull set with the device of a grinning face sits in the center of the 20-foot-wide stone door.

Anyone approaching the sphinxes without an unholy symbol of Set or a *black ankh of Set* animates the stone sphinxes, which attack instantly. The portals open to anyone bearing an unholy symbol or *black ankh* at a touch. Otherwise, a *power word stun* trap is triggered. Any creature within 30 feet of the door when the trap is triggered must succeed on a DC 18 Constitution saving throw or be stunned. The creature can repeat the saving throw at the end of each of its turns, ending the effect on a success. The trap can be noted with a successful DC 18 Intelligence (Investigation) check. It can be disabled with a successful DC 18 Intelligence (Arcana) check, but a failure by 5 or more triggers the trap.

2. Temple of Set's Pilgrims

This sanctuary to the left of the entrance within the Shining Pyramid serves as the main worship chamber for Set's minions in the elemental

The Shining Pyramid

1 Square –
20 Feet

planes and especially the Plane of Molten Skies. A high priest of Set administers to the needs of the faithful. Several acolytes assist in performing services and sacrifices and taking collections. The chamber is quite large, with worship space for more than 100 pilgrims. Those not able to display an unholy symbol of Set or *black ankh* are captured for sacrifice, their blood anointed upon true worshippers, and their bodies transformed into undead protectors of the pyramid.

There is a 50% chance that a **high priest of Set**[1] and 2d4 **acolytes of Set**[1] are here when the characters enter the area.

3. Temple of the Brides of Set

Respected members of the Temple of Set take their worship in pain and death here in the private worship chamber. Similar in size to the main sanctuary, this portion of the Shining Pyramid is administrated by the priestesses of Set. These priestesses, known as the brides of Set (human **preacher**[1]), perform various functions within the pyramid, from ritually torturing sacrifices brought in by elite worshippers to torturing the worshippers themselves should they require atonement, punishment, or just feel the need to be humiliated and lashed with the tails of giant scorpions.

Braziers burning exotic lotus and jasmine fill the chamber with a lush purplish black fog that gives those unused to the vapors a sense of numbness. Characters entering the chamber must succeed on an initial DC 15 Constitution saving throw or take a –2 penalty on Dexterity and Wisdom checks and saving throws for as long as they remain in the area plus 1d2 hours after leaving the area.

The brides of Set are assisted by 6 female black jackals of Set (**jackelwere**[1]) whose methods of killing and perverse wiles are renowned and feared wherever the name of Set is uttered.

The walls of the chamber are decorated with symbols of decadence and death, their hieroglyphics exploring aspects of mutilation that, as always, portray Set as larger and more powerful than his peers among the greater gods. Various torture tables and racks of whips, scourges, and lashes are arranged within this huge chamber. Contrasting this are numerous couches, divans, and chairs designed for the utmost in comfort. Most are in use. The floor of the temple fairly writhes with the activity of the intermingled bodies contorting in their ecstasy of pain.

Most perverse functions within this temple are attended to by the High Priestess Ak'Ton Val'tary (**high priest of Set**[1]), author of the *Slithering Scrolls*, a diabolical text dedicated to the dark rituals of Set. Only possessors of a *black ankh of Set* are allowed to take services within the temple of the brides of Set.

Interrupting services here results in an all-out assault by the revelers and priests. At any given time, 2d4 (or more) brides of Set (**preacher**[1]) are here, as well as 6 black jackals of Set (**jackelwere**[1]).

4. Temple of the High Priest

This colossal chamber is dominated by a 40-foot-tall statue of the dread god Set in his jackal aspect. The statue appears to be carved from a single piece of polished ebony and dressed in armor and weapons of pure gold. The pedestal at his feet is caked with the blood of thousands of sacrifices. This chamber serves as the central worship point for the various sects of the priesthood of Set as administered by the Unholy Order of Venom. There are 1d4 + 1 **high priests**[1] of the Unholy Order of Venom within this chamber at all times, and a 20% chance that Imthep the Ancient (**mummy lord**) is here performing some dark ritual at the foot of the statue of Set. Individuals entering the temple of the high priest who do not possess and prominently display a *black ankh of Set* are immediately attacked.

Statue: The statue of Set has AC 16 and 300 hit points. It ignores any attack that does less than 10 points of damage. It emanates an aura of despair that gives disadvantage on all saving throws to all good-aligned creatures and advantage on all saving throws to all followers of Set in the temple area. The statue of Set has a total value of 200,000 gp. If stripped of the gold and jewels embedded in its form, they fetch a total of 100,000 gp on the market.

5. Angled Passageway (down)

The shaft beyond the doorway descends into the lower areas of the Temple of Set. The doorway leading to the platform is trapped with an acid fog trap that only triggers when an attempt to open it is made by one not bearing a *black ankh of Set*. The trap can be detected with a successful DC 18 Intelligence (Investigation) check and disarmed with a successful DC 20 Intelligence (Arcana) check. If triggered, a cloud of acid fills a 30-foot square in front of the door for 1 minute. A creature that starts its turn in or enters the cloud must make a DC 14 Dexterity saving throw, taking 22 (4d10) acid damage on a failure or half as much on a success.

6. Angled Passageway (up)

This ramp beyond the trapped doorway climbs to **The Tomb of Retep Inkusad**. Only Retep and his trusted advisor Sss'ashisth may pass this portal without the invitation of Retep himself. Those attempting to gain access to the tomb without his permission manifest the curse of Set (see sidebox) upon themselves.

Curse of Set

Any being failing a DC 20 Constitution saving throw is cursed to be painfully transformed into an undead minion of Set upon their death. The type and sort of minion is left to you. Removing this curse requires divine intervention and likely a quest in the name of a deity or power opposed to Set's doctrines.

Those affected by the curse of Set are known to the god's worshippers. Worshippers of Set instantly recognize the curse scrawled upon the victim's face and know that Set has chosen this being as one of his own. To fulfill the wishes of their deity, these worshippers have been known to manipulate individuals bearing the curse of Set upon their face. They seek to place such beings into positions of power and prestige in their native lands so that when they die, they arise again as a faithful minion and servant of the Slithering Orders. Alternately, followers of Set may kill an afflicted individual on sight, and then command them as undead minions for their own use. These damning hieroglyphics are invisible to anyone else viewing the afflicted person, including the cursed individual, except through the use of *detect magic* accompanied by a successful DC 20 Intelligence (Arcana) check, *true seeing* accompanied by a successful DC 20 Wisdom (Perception) check, or greater magic (such as *wish*).

7. Priests' Quarters

This huge chamber houses the bulk of the acolytes and high priests of Set. Those who do not have other quarters within the City of Brass reside here free of charge and dine from the sumptuous banquets prepared for them in the kitchens. There are always 1d4 **high priests of Set**[1] accompanied by their undead minions (1 **mummy**, 4 **wights**, and 1 **wraiths** per priest) here. Non-priests entering the chamber are attacked on sight. This is not to say that disguises could not be worn, as there are frequently priests from other planes who visit the City of Brass for business or worship. Each priest has a locked iron box where he stores his valuables. The locks can be opened with a successful DC 18 Dexterity check with thieves' tools. Most priests sleep on sumptuous stuffed cushions covered in satins and silks. Sarcophagi are available for visiting liches, vampires, and mummy lords.

Treasure: Each iron box contains 2d6 x 100 bp, various articles of jewelry (totaling no more than 500 gp), and texts and books on Set's religion.

8. Sss'ashisth's Chamber

This chamber is similar to the temple of the high priests above. A statue of Set in his serpent aspect supports the ceiling. Slithering upon the floor are the children and mates of Sss'ashisth. There is a 20% chance that

Beyond the doorway lie, neatly piled, the riches of the priesthood of Set within the City of Brass. Found here are various unholy symbols, statues, canoptic urns, jugs, rugs, silks, furs, satins and the like left in the various upper temples as sacrifice to Set or earned as spoils from conquered foes. Items in the treasury are frequently used to buy favor among the bureaucrats of the City of Brass or to reward heroes of Set for their deeds in his name.

The treasure includes: carved bone statuette (20 gp), jeweled gold crown (5,000 gp), large wool tapestry (400 gp), golden circlet with four aquamarines inset (3,000 gp), gold and topaz bottle (1,000 gp), harp of exotic wood with ivory and zircon gems (1,000 gp), brass mug with jade inlays (600 gp), gold idol (1,000 gp), bejeweled gauntlet (700 gp), finely crafted silk rug (500 gp), painting of Set destroying the good-aligned deities (900 gp), gold cloth vestments (130 gp), gold bracelet (30 gp), silver chalice with lapis lazuli gems (100 gp).

10. Dining Hall

This oblong rectangular chamber is reserved for meals for the priests and dedicated followers of Set ranging from visiting slayers, assassins, kings, and generals. There is a 40% chance that 1d10 **acolytes of Set**[1] and 1d2 **high priests of Set**[1] may be found in the dining hall, eating on shift from the sumptuous banquet laid out for them. The banquet is a feast of strange delicacies to feed the rare and jaded tastes of the chosen of Set. Anyone entering the dining hall unaccompanied by a priest of Set and not bearing a *black ankh of Set* is immediately attacked by the diners who seek to kill them and give them to the cook for use on the pyramid's menu.

11. Kitchen

The kitchens of the Pyramid of Set are administered by **Chuadak the Knife**[1], a kobold assassin in the service of Set, and his 10 assistants (**kobold assassins**[1]). They take the slaves, prisoners, and various sundry sacrifices collected by the jackalweres at the various altars of Set and prepare them with seasoning, salt, and spice to create extravagant meat and rice dishes to be served to the priesthood and guests of the Shining Pyramid. Huge ovens and grilles are set with pots filled with bubbling mixtures of flesh and rice cooked in spicy sauces. When not in the kitchens preparing meals, Chaudak is frequently out in the City of Brass on temple business. This business includes and is not limited to the assassination of key members of the efreeti bureaucracy.

12. Scroll Room

This chamber contains a wealth of knowledge that the Unholy Order of Venom has gathered throughout its tenure within the City of Brass. It is filled with *spell scrolls* containing divine spells relating to Set's domains of law, evil, knowledge and death (your choice of spells). The chamber is constantly filled with 2d6 **acolytes of Set**[1] who prepare low-level scrolls for the priesthood, halting only when they have become too exhausted to

Sss'ashisth (**ha-naga**[1]) is present (but see the sidebox). Otherwise, he serves as the mouthpiece of Set at the Court of the Sultan of Efreet. There are 4 **dark nagas**[1] and 2d6 **giant fiendish vipers**[1] in this chamber at any given time. The gold-coated statue of Set has AC 17, 200 hit points, and ignores any attack that does less than 15 hit points of damage. It emanates an aura of despair gives all good-aligned creatures disadvantage on all saving throws and advantage on all saving throws to all followers of Set in the temple area. The statue of Set is worth 100,000 gp. If stripped of the gold and jewels embedded in its form, they fetch a total of 40,000 gp on the market.

A locked iron chest contains 1,000 bp, 6 amethysts (100 gp each), a *spell scroll* with *lightning bolt*, *spell potion*[2] of *darkvision*, *spell potion*[2] of *enhance ability* (*bull's strength*), a *spell scroll* with *enhance ability* (*bull's strength*) and *shatter*, and a *spell scroll* with *false life*, *enhance ability* (*fox's cunning*), *touch of idiocy*[4]. The chest can be onlocked with a successful DC 18 Dexterity check with thieves' tools.

9. Temple Treasury

The door to this chamber is guarded by 4 menacing **jackalwere guards**[1]. The door itself is trapped with an incendiary cloud trap. The trap can be noted with a successful DC 15 Intelligence (Investigation) check and disabled with a successful DC 18 Intelligence (Arcana) check. If triggered, the trap creates a cloud of burning air for 1 minute in a 30 foot radius of the door. A creature that starts its turn in or enters the area must make a DC 16 Dexterity saving throw, taking 13 (4d6) fire damage on a failed save and half as much on a successful one.

make more, at which time they take their rest, and go out to spread the gospel of Set as missionaries.

13. Black Jackal Society

This chamber is used by members of the House of Black Jackals. They attack anyone not bearing an unholy symbol of Set or a *black ankh* that enters their barracks. At any given time, 1d6 + 1 lower ranking black jackals of Set (**jackalwere**[1]) are here tending to guild business and 1d2 greater black jackals (**jackalwere guard**[1]) are here overseeing their progress.

14. Grand Hall of the High Priests

This large chamber is used as the council chamber for the priests of Set. Priests accused of heresy are tried here as well under a full concordance of Set's minions. The chamber is empty the majority of the time. An honor guard of 4 **jackalwere**[1] guards stands watch here at all times. This guard is doubled when a priest is on trial.

15. Burial Crypts of the Former Priests and High Priests

This crypt contains 30 stone sarcophagi inlaid with gold and precious jewels. Within the crypts are 2 **mummy lords** and 25 **mummies**. They remain undisturbed, occasionally raising their moldering bandages and creaking bones from their crypt to attend religious rites in the name of their god Set, whom they serve even from beyond the grave.

Treasure: 1,000 gp, 1,500 sp, 6 gold urns (500 gp each), 3 ivory statuettes (300 gp each), 6 silver chains (150 gp each), 14 broken pieces of ruby (50 gp each), *spell scroll* of *animate dead*, *spell scroll* of *fireball*, *spell scroll* with *bless* and *divine favor, wand of lightning bolts, ring of protection.*

16. Tomb of Retep Inkusad

This huge chamber at the pinnacle of the Shining Pyramid glows with unholy light for it is the personal sanctuary of Retep Inkusad (**greater mummy**[1]), the Viceroy of Set. The walls are a gleaming silvery incandescent crystal reflecting the varied colors of the Plane of Fire and the Plane of Molten Skies. A solid gold sarcophagus stands in the center of the chamber and emanates evil (if detected for). Unless encountered earlier, or if encountered earlier and he escaped, the Viceroy of Set is absorbing the focus of Set's power here. If the characters enter after having mopped the floor with his followers, Retep is willing to cease hostilities and offer a deal. If the characters entered this chamber by accident, or if Retep is assaulted, he attacks.

Retep was once known as the Sorcerer of the Sands in his native land of No'Tnar where late in life he built a great kingdom situated near the oasis of Teg'pu. In these ancient times, the Old Gods walked the material planes gathering faithful worshippers to them. So it was that Retep and his wife were taken into the worship of Set, who blessed his new priest and priestess with long lives. Theirs became a civilization of pain and sadism unseen in the ancient times. Retep, following the lessons of his master, soon betrayed his wife by taking as concubine several of the temple maidens and instructed them in the ways of a bride of Set.

Outraged at his infidelities, Retep's wife laid a death curse upon her husband and took her own life. Her curse, called forth with such power and conviction, slew Retep instantly. He was found dead by his followers the next morning and was quickly embalmed. On the sixth night after his embalming and entombment, he arose and revealed himself to his followers. The folk of his land stared with shock and horror as their risen lord once again ascended the black throne of the priest-kings. The screams of the brides of Set were heard long into the night as the salacious appetites that had brought about the death of their lord were brought to horrifying fruition, the queen's curse fulfilled.

Bored with the crown of eternal rule, it is said that Retep sold his entire kingdom to a wandering janni toymaker and peddler for a pittance and set out across the planes of existence, raising army after army for Set, establishing his cults where there were none and gathering hordes in the tens of thousands to his banner. Currently, his armies have suffered several rather crushing defeats against the foes of Set on various planes and are recruiting mercenaries in the City of Brass. They use whatever treasures they unearth to barter with the Sultan of Efreet[1] for more powerful weapons with which to outfit their armies assembling in the planes still under Set's rule.

Currently, Retep seeks the iron *flask of Sulymon*[2], and what hidden treasures are held within the dying plane of Y'cart.

Characters may find themselves bartering with Retep for the *mask of Ankev*[2] if they are able to gain other items for Retep in trade.

Treasure: In addition to Retep's personal possessions, there are 3 gold urns (1,500 gp each), 6 small ivory statues (500 gp each), and 17 emeralds (1,000 gp each) scattered in this chamber.

Completing the Shining Pyramid of Set

Depending on the goal the characters were tasked with when taking on the Shining Pyramid of Set, they may alternately need to slay Retep Inkusad or somehow bargain for the *mask of Ankev*[2] and then escape again with their lives. If Retep or Sss'ashisth are slain and the mask taken and his temple defiled, Set calls down three plagues upon the City of Brass that should cause enough confusion and disorder in the otherwise lawful city to allow more freedom of movement for the characters. On the flipside, defiling the pyramid causes the burning dervishes and any surviving members of Set's clergy to hunt the characters to the ends of creation if necessary.

Chapter 19
The Freeman's Tower

Built entirely of imported wood and treated with magical creosote, iron rebar, banding, and bolts, this multistory high tower is home to freed slaves, stranded visitors to the City of Brass, and permanent residents who can't seem to manage a better life for themselves. Freeman's Tower is a squalid guesthouse of epic proportions when compared to the average inn or guesthouse of most worlds. When the wind from the Middle and Upper levels is high, the tower sways disturbingly. Yet in the 500 years it has been here it has never fallen. It has also survived many a battle stemming from internecine feuding. All the floors have shuttered windows. If they ever had glass or oiled parchment, they are long gone, either destroyed or stolen. Eight sets of stairs ascend through the tower's interior, but stairs on various levels are unusable because they are filled with centuries' worth of detritus from the residents. Trash, excrement, discarded furniture, dead bodies, and anything else imaginable have all been thrown in the stairwells over the years.

This adventure is suggested for a party of Tier 3 characters.

Politics of the Tower

The tower's ownership is murky at best, but ultimately resides in the hands of Oruk the Horned. Doc, Orey, and Hick, a trio of corrupt elf wizards who live on the floors above him have transformed the upper floors into a laboratory and manufacturing facility for their burgeoning criminal business empire. Unfortunately for them, the mercenaries and their ongoing feud are bringing too much heat to their operations. The trio recently allied themselves with Ambassador Fatavdra who sees their operation as a means of seizing the Throne of Brass by destabilizing the populace of the city at its literal and figurative base.

Oruk for his part has several rooms of his own to rent, but for whatever reason, hasn't been around lately. This is not an unusual circumstance, and the wizards have thought to sweep the tower free of Oruk's renters and make a move to take the entire tower for themselves, only to have Oruk return and put them back in their place time and again.

The Scorpion League, a ruthless gang of mercenaries and assassins, manages a warren of rooms and currently controls the first several floors of the tower. The gang is known to provide muscle for various entities of the city's underworld, most notably crime lords who manage the many black markets and those who supply slaves to the battle arena.

Currently, the Scorpion League is in the midst of a leadership battle after burning dervishes enslaved its former captain, Jhadam the Half-Dwarf, and sold him to the Circus Master in the Circus of Pain. Sadly, Jhadam had an unfortunate encounter with Hezoid during a match and is no more.

How and why the burning dervishes captured him is currently a matter of hot debate between the two factions of the Scorpion League. One side accuses the other of setting up their boss. This has pitted the mercenary factions against one another in a bloody war of attrition. This internecine conflict is causing issues for the residents of the tower's upper floors who have money to make. Unfortunately for them, the overall landlord, Oruk the Horned, hasn't been answering his door, leaving the mages to consider hiring outsiders to clear up their "scorpion" problem.

Adventure Summary

Often characters need a place to hide out and collect themselves when the going gets tough. Rest, recuperation, and resurrection are often in the cards for our intrepid heroes as they seek to plunder the riches of the City of Brass, or to thwart the agents of the upstart Sultan of Efreet[1]. To that end, Freeman's Tower provides a perfect hiding place for adventurers on a budget. Like many places, however, Freeman's Tower is a fixer-upper. Currently it suffers from an infestation of bandits, murderers, and thieves that the owner doesn't seem to care about and that other residents currently don't have the time to bother with.

Characters are enlisted in an effort to deal with the Scorpion League, to locate Oruk, and ultimately to secure permanent lodging for themselves in Freeman's Tower. If the characters are successful, they may end up with partial ownership of the tower, a revenue stream, and a permanent base within the Lower City from which to continue their operations.

Getting Started

A Place to Stay

As the adventure begins, the characters may realize, or you may have smoothly implied, that they may need a home base to operate from within the City of Brass. As the characters go looking, they find few inns within the city from which to operate, and having no established "residency," they may not have the brass pieces just yet to outright purchase one of the homes built into the sides of the bowl.

As the characters ask around, they are directed to a notice for "Rooms to Let, Freeman's Tower, 5th floor and above, inquire within."

Hired Guns

If the characters don't take the bait, they are directly contacted by either Orey, Doc, or Hick, who offers them an apartment with a month's free rent if they clear out the lower five floors of the tower where a band of mercenaries has taken up residence and refuses to leave. Of course, they demand discretion in the matter. They give no additional warning as to what the characters may face there, other than they ask that the characters attack only those wearing scorpion emblems on their gear or bearing scorpion tattoos.

A Beef in the Streets

Characters may find themselves involved in an imbroglio in the streets with members of one of the Scorpion League factions or robbed by a thief making his home in the tower. Pursuit leads the characters into the tower, and the adventure begins.

Accidental Arrival

Characters who were stranded at some point on the Isle of Winds and accidentally found passage to Oruk's jungle while passing through the Dayie Adjhal Sama — the Jungle in the Skies — discover a door leading to one of the middle levels of Freeman's Tower and the City of Brass itself!

Scorpion League Factions

The Scorpion League is currently divided into two warring factions. The Red Scorpion League is led by a vicious vampire and is said to have ties with the Underguild, while the Black Scorpion League is a band of former slaves turned cyborg mercenaries.

Red Scorpions

The Red Scorpion faction is led by Nikolai, a lecherous **vampire** who was ousted by members of the Underguild and fled to the City of Brass. Nikolai brought his knowledge of criminal empire building to Jhadam's mercenary band and helped establish it as a resource for slavers, assassins, and strong-arm robbery. Nikolai is believed to be the child of Charity Bigh and Lord Tork, a skeletal warrior cursed to guard the Maze of Jhedophar. The Red Scorpions occupy the lower stories on the west side of the tower.

Nikolai brought many intelligent monstrous beings into the gang, a fact Draninko[1] uses against him among the humanoid and enhanced humanoid members of the Scorpion League.

Nikolai relies on his coven of vampire spawn to maintain order among the rest of the Red Scorpions. Many of his vampire spawn until recently were Black Scorpions, a fact his foe Draninko[1] knows all too well.

Red Scorpions include Nikolai (**vampire**), **Red Scorpion lieutenants**[1], **Red Scorpion assassins**[1], Red Scorpion **flind**[1], Red Scorpion **blood orcs**[1], and Red Scorpion **bugbears**.

The Red Scorpion **blood orcs**[1] have one **elder warrior**[1] among them. They prefer to use their greataxes, but enjoy the destruction and havoc wrought by fragmentation grenades[3], often carrying 2 (1d4) per blood orc.

Red Scorpion **bugbears** are a villainous lot, and find great delight in the destructive weapons they add to their arsenal. Most bugbears carry with them at least an automatic pistol, but some prefer the longer range of the rifle or the scattered mayhem of the shotgun. They can make the following attacks with these weapons.

***Automatic Pistol* (single shot).** *Ranged Weapon Attack:* +4 to hit, range 50/100 ft., one target. *Hit:* 6 (1d8 + 2) piercing damage.

***Automatic Pistol* (burst).** The bugbear fires a burst of bullets in a 20-foot cone. Creatures in the area must make a DC 12 Dexterity saving throw or take 6 (1d8 + 2) piercing damage.

***Automatic Rifle* (single shot).** Ranged Weapon Attack: +4 to hit, range 150/300 ft., one target. Hit: 7 (1d10 + 2) piercing damage.

***Automatic Rifle* (burst).** The bugbear fires a burst of bullets in a 30-foot cone. Creatures in the area must make a DC 12 Dexterity saving throw or take 7 (1d10 + 2) piercing damage.

Shotgun. *Ranged Weapon Attack:* +4 to hit, range 60/120 ft., one target. *Hit:* 6 (1d8 + 2) piercing damage, or 11 (2d8 + 2) piercing damage if both barrels are fired.

Black Scorpions

The so called Black Scorpions are led by Draninko[1], a cruel enforcer who was once the number two man behind Jhadam before the leader's capture. Draninko[1] has been "enhanced" by his experiences in the City of Brass, having technological pieces embedded in his body, including an eye he lost in a bar fight on his home world and the left hand that went missing after an unfortunate event involving a complicated trap. The Black Scorpions occupy the lower floors on the east side of the tower.

Draninko[1] has always wanted the monsters and non-humans removed from the Scorpion League and sees this feud as an opportunity to finish it once and for all. His folk have barricaded their half of the tower, and spy on those who enter the west entrance, assuming they are in league with the Red Scorpions.

Draninko's Henchmen

Ruslam

Ruslam is an **arcanist**[1] (with longsword proficiency, a *staff of frost*, *boots of the winterlands*, a *+2 dagger*, and a *frost brand* (long sword)) from the cold steppes of a world conquered by the Sultan of Efreet[1]. He has a disdain for genies bordering on maniacal, with those feelings running toward murderous when it comes to efreet in particular. Despite the warmth of the Basin, he wears a fur cap at all times and tends to summon cold-based creatures into combat.

Guldasta

Guldasta is an **emeritus chaplain**[1] (with a *flail of wounding*[2], *boots of striding and springing*, *+2 chain mail*, *+2 shield*) of the Master. Guldasta works connections in the city's massive slave markets, often taking squads of Scorpions on slave-taking missions into the Plane of Molten Skies and even to other planes. Guldasta specializes in gathering non-humans for use in the Circus of Pain. Other missions include collecting prisoners for the needs of exclusive clientele and for providing live sacrifices for Dark Cardinal Paz Amare[1].

Guldasta recently had custody of Simone Dubois and sold her to Ard, Viceroy of the Lightbringer and leader of "The People." Ard keeps the girl in his personal prison and plans to sacrifice her personally to the Lightbringer in the future.

Freeman's Tower: Standard Features

The Wall: A wall of rubble has been built out of multiple castings and re-castings of *wall of stone* on the first through fifth floors to divide the tower roughly down the middle between the two factions. The wall is built from rubble left over from the fighting, which at times has involved anti-personnel munitions and dangerous magic. The makeshift walls currently keep the peace, making the battle for control of the Scorpion League a battle of attrition that for the most part takes place off-site in dingy alleys in the bowels of the Basin. The wall between the two sides of the tower is roughly three feet thick.

Doors: Unless otherwise noted, the doors to the various rooms are lock requiring a DC 15 Dexterity check with thieves' tools to open.

Stairwells: As mentioned, many of the stairwells are stuffed with trash, timbers from destroyed rooms, and other rubble, making it impossible to use those stairwells to gain access to floors above and below. They could however be cleared with *disintegrate* spells, or the blockage bypassed with a *passwall* spell. Blocked stairwells are shown on the map filled with rubble.

Ground Floor

1-1. South and West Entrances

The south and west entrances open into territory ruled by the Red Scorpion faction of the Scorpion League. It contains a pair of staircases leading to the first story of the apartments, and has eight small apartments that are in various degrees of occupation by members of the league. A group of 4 **Red Scorpion assassins**[1] hides in the stairwells to keep an eye on the comings and goings of visitors to the tower. Visitors who are not readily known by the Red Scorpions are dissuaded from entry. Black Scorpion members enter at their own peril, as they are almost immediately captured, tortured, flayed, and returned to their brothers on the east side of the complex, or stuffed into the staircases on the upper floors.

If a group looks too difficult to handle — as noted by durable looking equipment and a hardened demeanor — they send one of their number to warn their allies on the upper floors. If intruders arrive in the presence of a burning dervish, fire giant, or efreeti constable of sorts, the assassins clear out, warning others in the upper floors as they go that a raid is in progress.

1-2. Occupied Rooms

These small dorms are large enough for a bed, a dresser, and not much else. They are as often barred from the inside by occupants as they are locked from without. The typical room is home to 1d3 members of the Scorpion League (**killer**[1] with *+1 shortsword*, automatic pistol[3], 2 magazines, 1 potion of healing or **bandit captain**, with longsword, automatic rifle[3] or shotgun[3], 2 magazines, 1 *potion of healing*, 1 fragmentation grenade[3]).

1-3. Abandoned Rooms

These rooms are largely abandoned. Typically, they are filthy, containing smashed furniture, or a bedbug-infused mattress stuffed with axe beak feathers and a beat-up brass oil lamp. There is a 50% chance that a dead body of a young slave has been stuffed under the mattress of one of these rooms, and a 25% chance that the body is actually one of Sascha Illwain's victims (a **vampire spawn**) that has been locked into the room by members of the Scorpion League who long ago stopped asking questions.

1-4. Spyhole

This room is used by members of the Red Scorpions to spy on the comings and goings of members of the Black Scorpions who enter through the north entrance to the tower. Aditya the **salamander** peers through a tiny spyhole drilled through the creosote infused wall. Aditya has no love for the efreet and less for the burning dervishes. He kills them when presented with the opportunity to do so.

1-5. Sybaruis' Room

This is the room of Sybaruis, a **lamia** (with AC 19, *wand of lightning bolts*) in charge of the Red Scorpion's first line of defense. Her room smells like nothing less than a filthy catbox. She is the first to appear in the event any alarm is sounded by her brethren in the Red Scorpion's faction.

Sybaruis has a *wand of lightning bolts*, *+2 splint*, and a *bag of holding* containing 30 gems worth 50 gp each.

1-6. North and West Entrances

The circular inner hall is divided like many of the lower floors by a breastwork, false wall, or magically created wall separating the warring factions of the Scorpion League.

These rooms are occupied by low-level operatives of the Black Scorpion faction. Like their foes on the other side of the tower, they keep an eye on visitors, and dissuade those they don't know from entering the tower.

Black Scorpion cyborgs keep an eye on things from the shadows of the stairwells.

1-7. Bravlik's Bunkhouse

This small watering hole serves Scorpion League members strong drinks and cheap information. The place seats only six or seven members of the Scorpion League and looks more like the kind of bar a fun-loving uncle would have in his basement than a place where assassins and mercenaries receive orders and get debriefed. The Bunkhouse is currently off limits to members of the Red Scorpion faction as **Bravlik**[1] has sided with Draninko[1] against Nikolai. Dozens of bottles of distilled spirits and tapped kegs of magically chilled beer and ale line the walls of the Bunkhouse. Bravlik has an automatic pistol[3], a *+3 bastard sword*, and a disguise kit, wears *fire armor*[2] (studded leather) and has 2200 gp locked in an iron box beneath the bar. The box can be opened with a successful DC 17 Dexterity check with thieves' tools.

There are up to 1d6 members of the Black Scorpions (**killer**[1] with *+1 shortsword*, automatic pistol[3], 2 magazines, 1 potion of healing or **bandit captain**, with longsword, automatic rifle[3] or shotgun[3], 2 magazines, 1 *potion of healing*, 1 fragmentation grenade[3]) in the room at any given time.

Second Through Fourth Floors

Rooms on the second through fourth floors share much in common with rooms on the ground floor and have similar occupants. There are noted exceptions on each floor depending on where the larger inner rooms fall along the makeshift walls that separate the warring mercenaries.

Second Floor Rooms

2-1. East and West Entrances

These hallway areas contain at least one working and one fouled stairwell.

2-1A. Stairwell of the Dead

This stairwell is the home of a **corpse orgy**[1] spawned from the murdered Scorpion Leaguers and their various victims. Nikolai is aware of the creature and invites foes whom he wants to dispose of without a hassle to take **Stairway 1a**.

2-2. Occupied Rooms

As ground floor.

2-3. Abandoned Rooms

As ground floor. No vampire spawn are in areas occupied by Black Scorpions.

2-4. Secret Access

This first-floor room contains a secret door that allows access to the opposite side of the tower. The secret door is trapped with a bundle of hand

6
2
4
2
2
2
2
3
1
6
5
3
2
2
2
3
1
2

S
1
2
3
4
5
6
5'

grenades hanging from a silk string. If the trap is not detected, it detonates. Finding the trap requires a successful DC 16 Intelligence (Investigation) check. It can be disarmed with a successful DC 14 Dexterity check with theives' tools. If triggered, all creatures within 30 feet of the door must make a DC 16 Dexterity saving throw, taking 21 (6d6) force damage on a failure and half as much on a success.

2-5. Ohan the Scorpion Man

A true scorpion in the Red Scorpions' cabal, Ohan the Scorpion Man (**scorpionfolk**[1]) guards the secret passage between the two warring halves of the tower.

2-6. Riasia the Rakshasa's Lair

Riasia (**rakshasa**) serves as a powerful second in command behind Nikolai. If alarmed or called for, Riasia leaves her lair and moves to nearby encounter areas. Riasia uses intense illusions to twist the combat zone where any fight takes place. Her magic causes lush green jungles with gripping vines to spring up out of thin air or beautiful maidens in distress to appear to trap and dominate foolish mortals into destroying their own friends. Meanwhile, she hunts those who become separated and confused one by one. Riasia joined the Red Scorpions to gain access to Oruk, who killed her in a previous life. Riasia seeks to once and for all return the favor and may follow the characters into Oruk's demiplane. If the characters make it into the plane and Riasia is still alive, she follows in order to exact her revenge.

Among the treasures hidden in her teak and silk adorned living quarters are a *spell scroll* of *hold portal, jump, chill touch*, and *fly, potion of healing*, a *spell potions*[2] of *levitate* and *spider climb*, a *spell wand*[2] of *animal friendship*, 145 pp, 450 gp, a pair of 100 gp tiger eye gems, a saltwater pearl worth 50 gp, a moonstone worth 200 gp, a malachite holy symbol of Kali-ma worth 200 gp, a half devoured corpse with a black scorpion tatoo, a suit of *+2 half plate* belonging to the corpse, and a *+2 war hammer*.

Third Floor

3-1. East and West Entrances

As ground floor. There is a 50% chance that spies are observing an unblocked stairwell.

3-2. Occupied Rooms

As ground floor.

3-3. Abandoned Rooms

As ground floor. No vampire spawn are found in areas controlled by the Black Scorpions

3-4. Ruslam's Suite

This pair of connected rooms serves as Ruslam's personal apartment. The door is trapped with a *cone of cold* trap. The trap can be detected with a successful DC 16 Intelligence (Investigation) check and disarmed with a successful DC 16 Intelligence (Arcana) check. If triggered, all creatures within a 60-foot cone must make a DC 16 Constitution saving throw. A creature that fails takes 36 (8d8) cold damage while a creature that succeeds takes half this amount.

The chambers are enchanted to be nearly ice cold. The walls are covered in mammoth hides, and a motif of carved mammoth ivory permeates the chambers. There is a 50% chance Ruslam (**arcanist**[1] with longsword proficiency, a *staff of frost, boots of the winterlands*, a *+2 dagger*, and a *frost brand* (long sword)) is here unless an alarm somehow sounds or the sounds of fighting attract him to the location of conflict.

3-4b. Ruslam's Bedchamber

The bedchamber of the ice wizard follows a similar décor as the outer chamber with the exception of bookshelves containing a collection of spellbooks, including a *manual of bodily health* that the wizard recently procured.

2
3
4
4b
2
2
3
1
1
5
2
2
3
6

Ruslam's spellbooks include all his memorized spells and 1d4 spells each of spells from 1st–4th level.

These books contain every cold-based spell from 1st–5th level in known existence. Among his other treasures are a *potion of remove fear*[2], *potion of giant strength* (cloud), *potion of greater healing*, a *spell scroll of levitate*, a *spell scroll of enlarge*, a *spell scroll of sleep*, a *spell scroll of unseen servant*, a *spell scroll* of *conjure swarm*[4], a *spell scroll* of *rope trick*, a 50 gp onyx, a red spinel worth 100 gp, a 450 gp grey pearl, 6 ivory mammoth tusks, carved, worth 500 gp each, that are 6 feet long.

3-5. Armory

Guarded by a cyborg (**thug** with 1d4 enhancements from the Black Scorpion Enhancements Table) and locked from within, access to this room requires the password "ledger" to be spoken into a speaking pipe outside the door. The password is known to Ruslam, Draninko, and Guldasta. Within is a crate of 20 grenades[3], 30 loaded magazines for rifles, 30 loaded magazines for pistols, 10 falchions (as longsword), 5 suits of studded leather, and 4 suits of splint.

3-6. Guldasta's Apartment

The door to this apartment is trapped with a mechanical guillotine trap that cuts off the arms of whoever tries to open the door. The trap can be noted with a successful DC 16 Intelligence (Investigation) check and disarmed with a successful DC 16 Dexterity check with thieves't ools. Failing the Dexterity check by 5 or more triggers the trap. If triggered, the trap makes a melee weapon attack at +8 against a creature within 5 feet. On a hit it does 7 (1d8 + 3) slashing damage and the target must make a successful DC 16 Dexterity saving throw or lose an arm.

This suite is kept by Guldasta (**emeritus chaplain**[1]), priestess of the Master. Guldasta's apartment is an opulent affair of gorgeous oil paintings, fine furniture, decorative carvings, and all the riches that a life lived off of the backs of slaves can provide. All of this is set in a backdrop of creosote-stained walls, iron spikes, and roughhewn furniture.

A rack covered in chains stands as a shrine to the Master.

The shrine holds a *necklace of prayer beads* and a *candle of invocation* (lawful evil). One of the items hanging on the wall is a *+1 spiked chain* (as *+1 whip* but base damage is 1d6) that hangs with Guldasta's *bands of binding*[2]. A silver coffer holds 100 bp, 200 pp, and 100 gp.

Fourth Floor

4-1. East and West Entrances

As ground floor.

4-2. Occupied Rooms

As ground floor.

4-3. Abandoned Rooms

As ground floor. No vampire spawn are found in areas controlled by Black Scorpions.

4-4. Doctor Eolytus' Room

This is the room of Doctor Eolytus (**arcanist**[1]), the resident mad scientist who assists Draninko[1] in enhancing Black Scorpion henchmen. Among items in the room are Eolytus' finely crafted medical kit, which contains bone saws, scalpels, and a variety of painkillers.

Treasure: An oil sea pearl worth 450 gp, a 100 gp onyx, two 100 gp fire rubies, one vial of *oil of magic weapon*[2], a *spell scroll* of *fear*, and a *spell scroll* of *hold person*, *charm person*, and *ray of frost*.

4-5. Draninko's Apartment

Draninko's apartment is no different from the apartments of his cohort. As he was a lieutenant of Jhadam, he chooses to continue living as if he is "one of the brotherhood" in order to maintain their respect. His door is trapped with a buzz saw trap that lifts a mechanical blade from the floor directly in front of the door if anyone interferes with the handle or lock.

Detecting the saw requires a successful DC 16 Intelligence (Investigation) check and disarming it a successful DC 16 Dexterity check with thieves' tools. If triggered, the blade makes an attack at +10 to hit against all creatures within 5 feet of the door, dealing 14 (4d6) slashing damage to anyone caught by the blade. The blade deals double damage on a natural 20, alternately sawing off a leg in the process (your choice).

Within the apartment, a collection of knives adorns one wall. A bookshelf contains various volumes on poison, knife making, knife fighting, and hand-to-hand combat. One book with the word "*tattoos*" on its spine is filled with the bound collection of tanned and treated tattoos of Draninko's victims.

Draninko's ironbound chest is locked and trapped with a poison needle. Finding the trap requires a successful DC 16 Intelligence (Investigation) check and disarming it a successful DC 16 Dexterity check with thieves' tools. If triggered, the needle makes a ranged weapon attack at +10 to hit against the closest target within 5 feet. On a hit it deals 1 piercing damage and the target must make a DC 14 Constitution saving throw, taking 55 (10d10) poison damage on a failure and 14 (4d6) on a success. Unlocking the chest requires a successful DC 18 Dexterity check with thieves' tools.

Within the chest are 4 vials of deadly poison, 4 *potions of greater healing*, 4 *potions of antidote*[2], a pair of *+1 daggers*, a *+1 chain shirt*, a *potion of invisibility*, a *potion of flying*, 500 bp, 250 pp, 2 diamonds worth 2,000 gp each, 10 rubies worth 300 gp each, directions to the Palace of Dust, and a disguise kit.

4-6. Cyborg Lab

This room is filled with medical gurneys, and strange metallic equipment is attached to buzzing machinery that lines the outer edges of the room. The equipment includes various saws, syringes, tubes, and wires. Racks of mechanical limbs, legs, arms, hands, and feet are here as well, with enough parts and pieces to replace ten arms, five legs, and four hands with prosthetics.

At any given time, 2 Black Scorpion cyborgs (**thug** with 1d4 enhancements from the Black Scorpion Enhancements Table) are in the room guarding the equipment from members of the Red Scorpion faction.

Schematics for operating the machinery and performing the surgeries required to create cybernetic enhancements are scribed on a series of gold plates. Warnings caution that cybernetic organisms are at a greater risk for electric shock. Characters who study the manuals for 1d4 months could learn how to operate the equipment properly to create enhancements.

Characters undergoing the procedure suffer 4d6 slashing damage per enhancement, and 1d4 points of temporary Constitution damage. The effects must be allowed to heal naturally for the enhancements to take effect.

4-7. Jhadam's Apartment

The room has been ransacked and divided in half by the warring factions. Posters on the wall depict Jhadam in his heyday when he was billed as "the Chain," a mutant half-dwarf gladiator before winning — and subsequently losing — his freedom.

An undiscovered secret door in the floor uncovers a case containing Jhadam's old gladiator armor (a *breastplate of free action*[2]). Finding it requires a successful DC 24 Wisdom (Perception) check.

S
7
1
1
2
3
3
3
3
3
3
4
5
6
2

4-8. Wahawk Deathbear's Room

Wahawk Deathbear[1] is a mighty bugbear chieftain. Wahawk's hair is shaved along his back from waist to forehead in a giant mohawk-like cut that is dyed with tiger-stripe colors. Where he is shaved, he is covered in tattoos featuring illustrated details of his greatest exploits and most vicious kills. Wahawk fought alongside Jhadam in the pits before Jhadam won his freedom and later purchased Wahawk and set him free. In appreciation of his freedom, Wahawk has brought his tribe to the Scorpion League, and claims this room as his own. With Jhadam's apparent death, Wahawk is looking to the future and is already in talks with the trio of wizards about switching sides and helping them against the remainder of the Scorpion League. He figures to strangle Hog Face[1] and Grashen[1] soon and take command of their clans, folding them into his own. Wahawk has a *+2 great mace*, a *+2 breastplate*, and *boots of speed*.

Fifth Floor

The Red Scorpion faction controls much of the fifth floor.

5-1. East and West Entrances

As ground floor.

5-1B.

All staircases leading upward to property controlled by Oruk are clotted with **assassasin vines**[1] and the corpses of those who tried to climb though the vines to raid the druid's chambers without his permission. They attack anything that attempts to climb the stairs.

5-2. Occupied Rooms

As ground floor.

5-3. Abandoned Rooms

As ground floor.

5-4. Collapsed Wing

The timbers and bricks of this section of apartments were reduced to broken rubble when the Scorpion League factions fought and divided the lower floors.

5-5. Grashen's Apartment

Grashen[1], a boss flind, keeps an apartment here close to Nikolai's lair. Grashen[1] is wildly loyal to Nikolai and hates Draninko[1] for his treatment of the non-human members of the league. He also keeps his apartment here so he can keep an eye on Hog Face, the orc boss who keeps an apartment on the opposite side of the tower. Grashen[1] lets none enter the crypt of Nikolai during the daylight cycle of the city. Grashen[1] has a *+3 morningstar*, an automatic rifle[3], and 2 magazines.

5-6. Hog Face

Hog Face[1], a brutal blood orc brought into the gang by Draninko, keeps his apartment here so he can be ready for whatever the boss needs of him. Hog Face doesn't particularly like the flinds, and thinks his orcs are better mercenaries. But he would love to have access to Draninko's cyborg lab so he can enhance his brood. For now, he and Grashen[1] find themselves on the same side. Like Grashen[1], Hog Face[1] lets no one enter the crypt of Nikolai under any save the gravest circumstances. Hog Face[1] has a *+3 greataxe*, an automatic rifle and 2 magazines, and *+2 ring mail*.

5-7. Nikolai's Crypt

A secret door is trapped with a necrotic blast trap. The door can be discovered with a successful DC 20 Wisdom (Perception) check, the trap with a successful DC 16 Intelligence (Investigation) check. Disarming the trap requires a successful DC 20 Intelligence (Arcana) check or *dispel magic* successfully cast against a 5th level spell slot. If the trap is triggered, all within 30 feet take 21 (6d6) necrotic damage).

The door opens to a central chamber filled with finely made hardwood coffins. The coffins are silk lined, but beneath the silk is the silty graveyard dirt brought to the city from Nikolai's homeland. Nikolai (**vampire**) rests here during the day cycle of the Nightfall Concordance, sharing his crypt with 1d3 **vampire spawn**.

Among the treasures found in the chamber are a suit of *+3 chain mail* worn by a corpse in one of the coffins, a *frost-brand* (longsword), a *potion of giant strength* (fire), a *potion of healing*, 500 bp, a 2,000 gp diamond, and a *spell scroll* of *greater restoration*.

Using the Scorpion League

The two factions of the Scorpion League are so fractured that only a strong leader could unite them again. To do so would involve removing Nikolai and Draninko[1] from the equation, so a strong leader could replace them. Perhaps one of the characters is up to the challenge?

Each faction leader may attempt to recruit the characters to take out the other, suggesting sub-bosses and bosses to take on. Worse-case scenarios include an all-out battle with both factions raiding one another's bases.

If the factions discover that Jhadam has been "recreated" at the hands of the Circus Master on behalf of the trio, this adds another wrinkle to the mix, and the factions may call a truce long enough to raid the upper stories of the tower with vengeance on their minds.

Oruk's Levels

The sixth through tenth floors belong to Oruk the Horned, though he is seldom present. Many of his apartments are abandoned or occupied by renters who don't care to be bothered.

Sixth Floor

The sixth through eighth floors share a common floorplan as they are the property of Oruk the Horned who did little to change the original builder's design, unlike those who live above and below him. This is largely because Oruk doesn't actually "live" in the building, but in a pocket dimension attached in its way to a primitive corner of the Hunting Lands, a dimension of reality ruled by great wild beasts and plants whose sentience is beyond the understanding of most mortals.

Access to this strange dimension is desired by Hick, Doc, and Orey, as the trio have begun distilling a new elixir of lotus from flowers they found growing in Oruk's garden chambers. They now seek an unending supply of the plants from Oruk's wild new world.

6-1. Lobby

The lobby hall is circular, with four outer doors and four inner doors. All four tower stairwells are located here. Descent to the fifth floor is clogged by the magically enlarged **assassin vines**[1] described in **Area 5-1B** on the fifth floor. The floors above the fifth are clear up until the tenth floor, which is currently controlled by the trio of wizards.

6-2. Central Plaza

The central plaza consists of a magical garden with a water fountain of clear clean water in the center of it. It is accessed by the doors that lead to the lobby hallway outside. Tall palms grow with dates and fresh coconuts all year round. 1d6 **monkeys**[1] chitter around in the branches of the trees. The monkeys detect as magical and throw fruit and coconuts at the party while at least one of them tries to pick the characters' pockets.

The monkeys are actually thieves who attempted to break into Oruk's apartment (**Area 9-2**). The curse upon the door permanently turned them into monkeys and teleported them to one of the plazas on the sixth through eighth floors. Anyone who is returned to their natural shape thanks the character, and promptly attempts to flee the tower by whatever means are available, never to return.

6-3. Emmerich's Apartment

This apartment is rented by a former gladiator named Emmerich who survived long enough to win his freedom and retire from the arena. He never made enough money to find means to escape the City of Brass and return to his homelands, however. If bothered, he is friendly enough but

6b
5b
5
c
c
6
1
2
3b
4b
3
4
c
c

6b
c
c
5b
5
6
1
2
3b
4b
4
3
c
c

asks the characters to leave him alone and indicates he didn't write the note requesting tenants. His landlord is Oruk and he hasn't seen the "Horned One" in quite some time. If asked why he calls Oruk by that name, he tells them, "because he has horns, of course." If asked where Oruk's room is, Emmerich points up and says, "ninth floor," and wishes them good luck.

Emmerich is currently annoyed with the Scorpion League and Oruk as he has to pay Malean to get food for him since he cannot fly, and access to the lower floors has become complicated due to Oruk's safeguards. Plus, there's the general violence on the lower level because of the feuding Scorpion League factions.

Emmerich isn't interested in helping or fighting, and he told Jhadam the same when the Scorpion League came calling. He does offer to buy food and wine from the characters if they happen to have any and would be satisfied with a week or more supply of both.

6-3B. Emmerich's Bedroom

Emmerich keeps his old *+1 trident*, a *+1 net*, and a bronze *+1 breastplate* here in his room. He sleeps on a hard mattress stretched out on the floor.

6-4. Empty Apartment.

These apartments offer a large living room/kitchen combo with a smaller bedroom (**Area 6-4B**) and a balcony (**Area 6-4C**). The furnishings include a sofa, a small kitchen table with two chairs, and a cotton-stuffed mattress. Normally, the apartments rent for 3 bp per month, whereas when the rooms on the lower floors are actually for rent, they go for a mere 1 bp per month.

6-4B. Bedroom

The bedroom is a small room with a shuttered window and a mattress on the floor. Many of them show signs of previous occupants on the floor and walls.

6-4C. Balcony

Each room has a small balcony that allows those with magic carpets or the ability to fly to forswear the lower levels of the tower altogether and avoid the collateral damage that monster vs. cyborg war tends to cause.

6-5. Malean's Room

Malean is a housekeeper of sorts. She is a freed **azer** who still dresses in the bronze cloth of a house slave to avoid conflict with the secret police, fire giants, and other denizens of the Basin who would cause her grief. Malean lives rent free in her apartment as she keeps the halls and common areas clean. She offers to clean apartments for the dwellers of the middle sections of the tower for a brass piece per month. Malean has a *rope of climbing* and uses it to get down to street level without having to worry about the fighting between the Scorpion League factions.

Malean knows of the Chufa Um Sophanie and any friend of Chufa's is a friend of hers. She, like all azer, seek freedom from the tyranny of the efreet.

6-6. Empty Apartment

As Room 4.

Seventh Floor

The seventh floor shares a layout with the sixth floor.

7-1. Lobby

As the sixth floor.

7-2. Central Plaza

As the sixth floor.

7-3. Empty apartment

7-4. Miercoles Mason's Apartment

This apartment is home to **Miercoles Mason**[1], a successful cat burglar who has kept free from notice by the Fahd Al Anil. The door to her apartment has been locked with a complex mechanical lock and trapped with a poison gas trap. Detecting the trap requires a successful DC 17 Intelligence (Investigation) check and disarming it a successful DC 17 Dexterity check with thieves' tools. If triggered, all creatures within a 10-foot radius must attempt a DC 17 Constitution saving throw, taking 99 (18d10) poison damage on a failure and 21 (6d6) on a success. Unlocking the door requires a successful DC 20 Dexterity check with thieves' tools.

Within the apartment are a series of fine oil paintings, small sculptures, and other objects of art nearing 14,000 gp in value. The rare collection has been culled from the houses of wealthy merchants living in the upper ring of the bowl. A high bounty exists on the head of the burglar, who leaves behind the calling card of an origami Bactrian camel in place of the stolen artwork.

Miercoles has a 50% chance of being present in her apartment at any given time.

7-5. Al Hazwir the Forger

Al Hazwir (NE human **housebreaker**[1]) is a known forger. His skills include forging coins, letters, badges, documents, and other small items. His main room has been transformed into a workroom where he keeps various inks, papers, coin blanks, coin dies, engraving equipment, inks, parchments, and sundry other pieces of the trade.

Al Hazwir works only by appointment. If someone knocks on his door, he calls through to ask folks to go away and leave him alone and that he has already paid his rent! If asked where the landlord is, he merely exclaims "upstairs."

7-6. Empty Apartment

This apartment is similar to the other empty apartments.

Eighth Floor

The eighth floor shares a similar layout to the sixth and seventh floors.

8-1. Lobby

The lobby hall is circular, with four outer doors and four inner doors. All four tower stairwells are located here.

8-2. Garden Plaza

As with the sixth and seventh floors.

8-3. Empty Apartment

8-4. Harir Al Quarakah's Apartment

This is the apartment of Harir al Quarakah, a **janni**[1] merchant of silks and satins. Al Quarakah has a decidedly desperate problem with strong wine and gambling that has left him nearly destitute. He once had a decent apartment in the bowl of the Middle City but lost it gambling at the Circus of Pain. He now dwells in the Freeman's Tower but travels to the Material Planes to trade for silk that he sells in the markets. He usually ends up losing most of the money he makes immediately. Thus far, though, he has made sure to pay his bills on time lest he feel the wrath of Oruk. If asked where Oruk is, all he says is that there's a slot in the door where he drops the rent through. Al Quarakah currently has 500 gp worth of silk and satin in his room.

8-5. Shazier the Crusher's Apartment

Shazier[1] is a retired warrior and dwarven strongman. Like many others, he survived the Circus of Pain, earned his freedom, and lives a quiet life in the Freeman's Tower. He accumulated enough wealth to keep him off the streets. He is often sought out by those who own battle slaves to serve as a strength trainer and a doctor of fighting beasts. Training with him for 3 months raises a character's Strength by +1 and gives them advantage on attack rolls when fighting while mounted on beasts. For this honor, he

6b
c
c
5b
5
6
1
2
3b
3
4
4b
c
c

charges 3,000 bp, and asks to be returned to his home world. He wears *+3 studded leather* and *slippers of spider climbing* and sports a *+3 warhammer*.

8-6. Apartment for Lease

A note on the door suggests inquiring by note at apartment 9A. The room is similar to the other empty apartments, with a large living room/kitchen combo with a smaller bedroom and a balcony. The furnishings include a sofa, a small kitchen table with two chairs, and a cotton-stuffed mattress. The apartment rents for 3bp per month.

Ninth Floor Oruk's Apartment

Oruk claims the ninth floor for himself and changed the floorplan to incorporate one large room in the center. This is because Oruk found a way to fuse his own personal demi-plane to the tower and to the mythic Hunting Lands of the outer realms. Oruk spends increasing amounts of time in the demi-plane looking for ways to connect his world to others where he can more completely become one with nature and live among the great beasts of time and space.

9-1. Lobby

The lobby of this level is filled with jungle flora, though the creosote walls, floors, and ceiling can still be seen. An aura of powerful magic can be felt in the air, almost overwhelming any active castings of *detect magic* that may be in effect. The Jungle of Oruk the Horned has truly begun to seep through into the reality of the tower on this floor. Grass grows up from the wooden floor in spots, and a jungle-like mist fills the lobby. There are no windows on this floor and no balconies.

The stairwells leading up are clogged with 6 **assassin vines**[1] as in **area 5-1B** and each is guarded by an **earth elemental** that allows passage only if Oruk wills it. A person delivering a rent check is allowed passage.

9-2. Apartment 9A. Oruk's Apartment

A single door decorated with the skulls of strange beasts has a sign upon it that reads "Apartment 9-A. Rent is due on the 30th Concordance of each cycle of the molten sky." A slot beside the door indicates where rent is to be paid. Another sign warns to enclose a note with the rent to ensure there are no "incidents," and that late payment is unacceptable and will result in immediate eviction.

The door to the apartment is actually not locked with anything other than a standard lock for the complex. However, the door is trapped with an unusual trap that polymorphs anyone within a 10-foot-radius into a monkey then teleports them to the plazas (**Area 2** on the sixth through eighth floors) to be with the other thieves who attempted to plunder Oruk's secret plane. Detecting the trap requires a successful DC 20 Intelligence (Investigation) check and it can be temporarily disabled with *dispel magic* cast successfully against a level 8 spell slot. A creature who is within 10 feet of the door when the trap is triggerd must succeed on a DC 20 Wisdom savig throw or be permanently polymorphed into a monkey and teleported to **Area 2**.

If the door and trap are overcome, the door opens onto a misty portal beyond which a thick jungle can be seen. This section is described at the end of the chapter under **Oruk's Wilderness**.

Tenth Floor "The Operation"

The tenth floor of the tower is the heart of where Orey, Doc, and Hick run their large-scale drug manufacturing operation.

10-1. Prisoner Barracks

These rooms house shifts of charmed workers whom Orey, Doc, and Hick made from potential renters. At any given time, 2d4 prisoners (humanoid **commoners**) are in the barracks resting or sleeping off the effects of the distillates of lotus. There is a 50% chance that one of the victims has died from an overdose.

The prisoners think nothing of strangers walking through the area. They have been charmed repeatedly, and their will to flee is depleted. The prisoners have all been shaved from head to toe save eyebrows and are dressed in a simple white cotton smock that stretches from collarbones to ankle.

10-2. Supply Room

This room contains crates filled with dried flowers, leaves, powders, and dried and sliced pieces of fungus folk butchered by the trio and shipped here to be mixed and distilled in the laboratory. There are enough supplies to make 100 doses of blue lotus[3] extract, 30 doses of distillate of nightmare[3], and 10 doses of death flower oil[3].

10-3. Distillation Facility

This room is filled with lab tables, large vats, beakers, drain tubes, distillation apparatus, burners, rings, condensers, ring holders, and large glass carboys. Several shaved humanoids dressed in long white smocks operate the various pieces of equipment, packaging the end products — either oils, powders, or elixirs — into flasks or wrapping them into waxed paper packages.

A **shield guardian** stands at each end of the room observing the activities of the charmed workers. The guardians are imbued with a *blight* spell in case things go wrong (each can cast *blight* with a level 6 spell slot and spell save DC of 17 as an action once).

Currently there are 20 doses of blue lotus[3] extract, 5 doses of distillate of nightmare[3], and 2 doses of death flower oil[3] completed.

The shield guardians are programmed to instruct any intruder to leave the premises immediately or face annihilation.

A large steel rack holds Moungus, a **fungus folk monarch**[1] (with half hit points) who is tied with copper bands that poison its flesh. A rubber sheet covers its head to prevent spores from filling the air. Glass tubes run into its brain stalk and torso, draining its fluids into a glass flask. Valter (as **mask wight** without Single-minded Purpose or Wail of the Forgotten) an undead chemist who runs the lab for the trio of wizards, is slowly torturing Moungus. Valter has a lair in the room south of the lab, though there is a 50% chance he is in the lab at any given time. If freed, Moungus tells the characters about the other imprisoned fungi and offers to assist the characters as best it is able.

10-4. Squeal's Apartment

This apartment belongs to Squeal (**wereboar** with *+2 great mace*[3]), a street dealer in the basin who helps peddle the trio's wares to buyers. As their operation is fairly new, they have thus far been able to avoid interference with any of the Sultan's enforcers, or even the notice of Oruk, who would most certainly forcefully "evict" everyone from the tower.

Squeal's street name is a bit of a misnomer, as he is wereboar who lets out a powerful snort as he transforms from his human form to his hybrid form. He has 10 doses of blue lotus extract on his person.

10-5. Overseer's Apartment

Valter (as **mask wight** without Single-minded Purpose or Wail of the Forgotten) the chemist oversees the day-to-day operations of the laboratory. He has 4 *spell scrolls* of *charm person* to use if it seems like any of the prisoners are on the verge of having their programming become unhinged and carries 4 vials of blue lotus extract antidote and 500 bp.

10-6. Fungus Folk Holding Pen

There are 6 **fungus folk**[1] here, each imported from a pocket of the Plane of Earth that bordered the realm of the dark elves. Moungus, their king, is being tortured by the wizard trio in **room 10-3**.

Eleventh Floor Hickshier's Floor

This floor serves as the lair of the dark elf **incantor**[1] Hickshier, commonly known as Hick. The eleventh through thirteenth floors are kept purposefully dark to accommodate the eyes of the dark elves who frequently visit the trio. Dim magical lighting is found in rooms where slaves and servants need light to see. Hick carries 500 bp, a *wand of fireballs*, a *potion of flying*, and a *ring of resistance* (fire) and has a *carpet of flying* (5 feet by 10 feet).

Stairwells

All stairwells descend to the tenth floor from here. Only two stairwells ascend to the twelfth floor.

The Freeman's Tower
Tenth Floor

11-1. Room to Rent Inquire Within

A sign on the door indicates a room for rent. The door is unlocked and opens into a nicely finished studio flat. The floor of the room is strewn with flower petals that give off a fresh aromatic odor. An elf (Hickshier, **incantor**[1]) in brightly colored wizard robes waves the characters over from the corner of the room, inviting them to come in and look around.

Characters entering the room are quickly overwhelmed with the orange poppy blossom[3] pollen that coats the room.

11-2. Watch the Floor

An animated carpet (**rug of smothering**) lies on the floor of this landing. It has been programmed to ignore guests of the trio and their servants but lies in wait to attack anyone else walking across it.

11-3. Study

The study contains volumes of intelligence the trio have collected on the City of Brass, its rulers, troop strengths, and weaknesses. The books speak of a hidden area in the Basin where the trio has not yet had an opportunity to explore and offers directions to locations within the Plane of Molten Skies, including the Ash-Grinder Arcology, the fire giantess's fortress, and the hidden base of the salamanders.

11-4. Goene's Apartment

This is the apartment of Chef Goene (**performer**[1]). It contains a small locked iron chest holding 100 bp, 100 pp, 121 gp, and several cookbooks written in the dark-elven tongue, including the infamous "*To Dine with Demons: 666 Recipes Worth Selling Your Soul.*" The copy is worth 2,400 gp to collectors, though reading it for more than six consecutive days summons a horned demon who offers additional recipes to be delivered monthly at the chef's convenience if only the chef is willing to exchange his mortal soul for a shot at mortal fame. Unlocking the chest requires a successful DC 17 Dexterity check with thieves' tools.

There is a 25% chance that Goene is in his apartment.

11-5. Haulman Coul's Apartment

Haulman Coul[1] is a bodyguard the trio keeps to oversee operations and to take care of things that are more easily solved with a blade than a spell. He spends the majority of his time practicing his torture techniques on the prisoners in **Area 7**.

There is a 25% chance he is found in his apartment. Otherwise, he is found in **Area 7**, or with one of the trio. Coul has *bracers of greater defense*[2], a *+2 rapier*, a *ring of greater protection*, a *+2 hand crossbow*, 3 doses of distillate of nightmare[3], and 2 doses of death flower oil[3].

A locked iron chest trapped with a poison needle trap smeared in distillate of nightmare[3] contains 300 bp, a 500 gp ruby, a 1,500 gp diamond, emerald earrings worth 200 gp, and 1,200 gp. Noting the trap requires a successful DC 17 Intelligence (Investigation) check and it can be disarmed with a successful DC 17 Dexterity check with thieves' tools. If triggered, the person opening the chest must succeed on a DC 16 Dexterity saving throw or take 1 piercing damage and succeed on a DC 16 Constitution saving throw or take 55 (10d10) poison damage. Unlocking the chest requires a successful DC 17 Dexterity check with thieves' tools.

11-6. Pentagram Landing

A silver summoning circle is embedded in the floor. Anyone crossing the pentagram without the mark of the trio becomes trapped within it unless a successful DC 18 Wisdom saving throw is made. The trap requires a successful DC 18 Intelligence (Arcana) check to notice and can be disarmed with *dispel magic* cast successfully against a level 6 spell slot. A **kytha**[1] demon is instantly summoned and attacks the victim trapped within the circle.

11-7. The Cells

The trio of mages use this area as their private jail. The bars of the cells are inscribed with runes that keep prisoners from using magic to escape.

11-7A. Occupied Cell

Currently, this cell is occupied by Ibn Al Almuhaqawq, a **burning dervish**[1] who got close to discovering the trio's operation. The revelation of their association with the dark elf ambassador Fatavdra would cause a potentially devastating rift between the Sultan and the dark elf representative.

11-7B. Unoccupied Cell

This cell is empty.

11-7C. Jhadam's Cell

This cell holds the shattered but revivified body of **Jhadam**[1] whom Fatavdra purchased from the Circus Master after Hezoid annihilated the half-dwarf in the Circus of Pain. The Circus Master took the soup that remained of the famous half-dwarf gladiator and poured him into a mold suitable for the n'gathau.

Jhadam's head has been rebuilt — more or less — though it now bulges in some areas and is held together with barbed wire. His left arm has been replaced with an enchanted length of chain and his right arm has retracting blades buried in the forearm. The rest of his body was broken beyond repair; his pulverized bones and organs were poured into a leather and rubber outfit that holds the haunted pain-filled sluice of material that Jhadam has become.

The trio, with the help of Haulman Coul, continue their tortures, training Jhadam to eventually clear out the infestation of Scorpion League members that infest the lower levels of the tower.

11-7D. Test Subjects

This cell contains a pair of slaves (as **captain**[1], unarmed with AC 10) bought at the market for use in testing drugs and poisons produced in the lab.

11-8. Hickshier's Suite

The door to this room is locked and guarded with magical wards. Opening them requires first *dispel magic* cast successfully against a level 7 spell slot and then *knock*. Alternatively, a *wish* would get the door open. Trying to open the door physically triggers *glyph of warding* (*explosive runes*) with a DC 17 saving throw with a different type of damage (acid, cold, fire, lightning, thunder) each time the attempt is made.

11-8A. Main Living Quarters

This room has a locked double door leading to the balcony beyond. It features furniture and the like for comfortable entertainment. There is no light in this room save a simple phosphorescence. A rug on the floor features various spider motifs and is woven from the thick silk of large spiders. The rug is worth 400 gp. Two doors open to the restroom in **Area 11-8B**, and the bed chamber in **Area 11-8C**.

A bookshelf holds Hickshier's spellbooks, and the following *spell scrolls*: *detect magic* x2, *identify* x3, *dispel evil and good, flame strike, enlarge/reduce*.

There is a 20% chance that Hickshier (**incantor**[1]) is in his room at any given time (unless an alarm has been sounded, in which case he is out looking for trouble). He may otherwise be found observing operations, torturing prisoners, or away on business elsewhere in the city.

Hickshier is known for his extravagant tastes and shares samples of the blue lotus extract[3] with members of the lesser aristocracy and merchants at Argeeli's Dream and other locations about town. He typically disguises himself as a grey elf during these visits, so as not to compromise the mission of Mistress Fatavdra among the court of the Sultan.

11-8B. Shower

Hickshier has a luxury shower built here with an enchanted fountain attached to one wall that pours water that is as hot or as cold as he needs it to be. A silver mirror on the wall in a golden frame is worth 500 gp.

11-8C. Closet

This closet contains a variety of robes, formal wear, hose, capes, and the like made from silks, satins, and sable. In all, there are 10 robes worth nearly 1,000 gp each, 4 capes worth 400 gp each, and a *cloak of resistance*[2].

The Freeman's Tower
Eleventh Floor
1
2
3
4
5
6
7
8
8b
8c

Twelfth Floor, The Doctor is In

This floor is where Doctor Rynithaz (elf **arcanist**[1]) keeps his apartment. Doc also has rooms to rent and is the source of notes throughout the Basin offering a place to stay within the Freeman's Tower, though in actuality, he is merely looking for either slaves to put to work in the laboratory or patsies to clear out the infestation of mercenaries on the lower floors.

Stairwell

The stairwell marked "A" is the only stairwell that affords access to Orey's floor. The stairwell marked B offers access to Hick's floor, going down, but is trapped with a smashing wall trap going up. Notcing the trap requires a successful DC 15 Intelligence (Investigation) check. I t can be disarmed with a successful DC 15 Dexterity check with thieves' tools. If triggerd, all creatures with 100 or fewer hit points on the stairwell must succeed on a DC 12 Dexterity saving throw or be instantly reduced to 0 hit points. There is no further "way up" aside from a *passwall* spell.

12-1. Luxury Suite

This luxury suite is reserved for special guests of the trio but would be rented to like-minded associates for 20 bp per month. The door has an *arcane lock* affixed to a special key. Currently, the trio save the room for ambassador Fatavdra's people whom she would prefer to keep secret from her standard retinue.

12-1A. Living Quarters

The living quarters are furnished with overstuffed divans and leather-bound chairs.

12-1B. North Master Suite

The room has an overstuffed king-sized canopy bed and dresser, and a bronze chest with a lock and key. If the key is missing, the lock requires a successful DC 15 Dexterity check with thieves' tools to open. The chest is empty.

12-1C. South Master Suite

As the north master suite.

12-2. Great Hall

This large central room is shared by the trio for their meals and planning sessions. A large table sits in the center of the chamber with sideboards of fine china, mirrors, and candelabras affixed with phosphorescent candles that please the eyes of the masters of the upper floors of the tower.

12-3. Kitchens

This section serves as a kitchen where meals for the delicate dark elf palate are prepared for when the trio's secret guests arrive. Their chef, Maestro Goene (drow **performer**[1]), is rivaled only by Chef Pepin and the Sultan's cooks for his indulgence in preparing meals for those with nightmarish palettes.

Among the delicacies being prepared here are ankheg eggs soufflé, halfling stuffed with minced mushroom man and baked in a puff pastry, brined sahuagin eggs, and mock dragon braised in night wine.

There are 10 bottles of night wine worth 100 gp each within this room. Hanging to dry are the corpses of a high elf, a baby copper dragon, and a halfling. Characters can also find 1,000 gp worth of rare spices.

There is a 50% chance Goene is in the kitchen preparing meals at any given time.

12-4. Doc's Suite

Doctor Rynithaz, the brains behind the operation, keeps his suite on this side of the tower.

12-4A. Sitting Room

This room serves as the suite for Doctor Rynithaz (male elf **arcanist**[1]). Doc likes to test various drugs, poisons, and concoctions in a controlled environment, using magic and science to distill the essence of their creations. Rynithaz rarely entertains guests, and his living room area is instead lined with volumes of books on anatomy of various creatures, their natural habitats, and their weaknesses. Studying the books in his collection for one month gives characters advantage in dealings with one type of creature.

A portrait-sized mirror of polished silver hangs on the wall. Doc carries 200 bp, an emerald (800 gp, a *+1 quarterstaff*, a *ring of resistance* (fire), and has a *carpet of flying* (5 feet by 10 feet).

A balcony opens to the outside of the tower from this room.

12-4B. Doc's Laboratory

This lab is where Doc performs the majority of experiments. Currently, Doc is experimenting on Xue Gong a tough **guardian naga** that the trio purchased in the market. Doc prefers to keep his victims heavily sedated and has concocted a distillate from orange poppy blossom and pixie dust for just such purposes. He would love nothing more than to get access to more of the lotus blossom, especially a primitive blend that he knows Oruk has access to.

If the naga is freed, it offers its services to the characters.

On the shelf are a *potion of heroism* a *potion of healing*, a *spell potion*[2] of *mage armor*, and a *potion of resistance* (fire).

12-4C. Doc's Bedchamber

Doc's treasures are hidden behind a strong door behind a tapestry, The door is trapped with a teleport trap that sends characters to the KhizAnah. Detecting the trap requires a successful DC 15 Intelligence (Investigation) check and it can be disarmed with *dispel magic* cast against a level 7 spell slot. Creatures within 10 feet of the door when the trap is triggered are teleported to **cell D** of **Area 22** of **KhizAnah**. The lock on the door can be opened with a successful DC 15 Dexterity check with thieves' tools. Inside the safe room is a silver coffer worth 100 gp that is filled with gemstones including a 100 gp diamond, a 250 gp opal, a 3,000 gp ruby, a 2,400 gp sapphire, and 300 tiny citrines worth 10 gp each. He also has his spellbooks and *spell scrolls* of *wall of stone*, *flesh to stone*, *remove curse*, and *animate dead*.

12-5. Servants Quarters

The servants' quarters hold 4 house slaves (as **captain**[1], unarmed with AC 10) charmed by the trio to serve them at their table. The house slaves are unaware of their hardship as the trio repeatedly charm them. They have become accustomed to the darkness of the upper stories. Their only recollection is having found a genie in their homeland, making a wish, having it go awry, then finding themselves in the markets of the City of Brass and meeting their new masters.

Thirteenth Floor, Orey Reish's Penthouse

The thirteenth floor serves as Orey Reish's (male elf **arcanist**[1]) domain where he attempts to replicate the flora brought through the portal from Oruk's jungle.

13-1. Barracks

Ambassador Fatavdra deems the work of the trio worthy of a small garrison of troops to help them further explore Oruk's plane. Garrisoned in this room are 4 dark elf warriors (**captain**[1] with AC 20). They wear *+2 chain mail*, carry a *+1 longsword*, a *+1 hand crossbow*, and 2 doses each of distillate of nightmare[3]. The warriors are under orders to watch the trio closely. If they show any indication of disloyalty to Mistress Fatavdra, they are to murder them instantly.

13-2. The Vats

This room contains a series of large glass vats containing various creatures that the trio use to create new poisons and drugs.

13-2A. Mandrakes

Held in a nutrient-rich environment within their terrarium are 4 **mandrakes**[1]. They are poked and prodded under extreme duress to get them to produce pollen that is used in powerful drug concoctions.

The Freeman's Tower
Twelfth Floor
2
1b
a
b
5
1
4c
4b
3
4a
1c
3b

6a
1b
6
1
4
6t
5a
5b
5t
2
3

13-2B. Flumph Tank

A **flumph hunter**[1], its tendrils clamped to electrically charged cables, is tortured inside this tank. Its stench glands are siphoned of ichor, and it is milked of its acids. The distillate of each is collected in beakers.

The concentrated stench gland acts as a stink bomb. If it hits a target, the target has disadvantage on Charisma and Stealth checks for 1 day.

13-2C. Vampire Spawn

Exeis, a **vampire spawn** and one of the Red Scorpion League, was recently captured by the trio and placed in this vat to drain away whatever essence they can capture for their drug and poison production. So far, they have not come upon a necromantic unguent that does not produce ghouls or wights.

13-2D. Gelatinous Tube

This vat appears to be empty save for a thick gelatinous solution.

The vat actually holds a **gelatinous cube**. The trio collects the acidic drippings for use in the distillation process of other drugs.

13-3. Silver Cages

Four silver cages hang from the ceiling, each containing an abused **pixie**[1]. The pixies are being farmed for their dust so the trio can experiment with it. The pixies are bound and gagged so that they cannot use their magic.

13-4. Trio's Hall

This hall features silver sculptures in the likeness of the trio. Each holds aloft his staff, orb, or wand. A gleaming beam of silver light connects the three. Crossing the beam of light without receiving the mark of the trio causes 36 (8d8) necrotic damage. The beam can be reflected with a mirror. Beams reflected at the original statue causes the statue to become inoperative for 1d10 minutes.

13-5. Penthouse Suite

This suite is similar to **Area 12-1**. The suite is available for rent so long as arrangements can be made with Orey (male elf **arcanist**[1]) or the other members of the trio. This might involve ridding the trio of their mercenary problem, or by capturing Oruk's jungle on behalf of the trio. Once achieved, rent for this suite is 10 bp per month. Orey carries 150 bp, 500 gp, 100 pp, and a *ring of resistance* (fire) and has a *carpet of flying* (5 feet by 10 feet) and a *crystal ball of telepathy*.

13-6. Orey's Penthouse

The locked secret door behind Orey's statue leads to his living room. The secret door can be seen with a successful DC 18 Wisdom (Perception) check. The door is magically locked and can be opened only with *dispel magic* cast against a level 5 spell slot followed by *knock*.

13-6A. Living Room

Orey has several statuettes carved from the ivory of murdered tusk lords that are worth 1,000 gp each. There are no chairs, only large cushions arranged around a *crystal ball of telepathy* in the center of the room. Curled atop a large cushion is a grey and white cat with piercing blue eyes and an extremely soft pelt. The cat is actually a greymalkin tether named **Frankie**[1]. Frankie is soft and as friendly as can be. He may even ignore his own master Orey if the opportunity to murder one of the characters in its sleep presents itself.

Frankie is Orey's familiar; if he dies, Orey's maximum hit points are reduced by 20 for one month.

A wine rack contains 20 bottles of fine elven wine of dark, grey, wood, and high elven varieties each more than 500 years old. The bottles are valued at more than 500 gp each.

Crystal Ball (Telepathy): The trio uses this *crystal ball* to "suggest" to the people Hog Face meets that they buy his drugs. Their meddling over snacks and wine has increased their sales exponentially.

13-6B. Bedchamber

The bedchamber is a simple affair, with silk sheets, a washtub, a mirror, and a wardrobe containing six robes and three capes, valued at around 200 gp each. A locked bronze box engraved with the image of Baccus Dionysus drinking from a kylix with Bowbe sits at the back corner of the wardrobe. The box is trapped with a chain lightning trap. The trap can be detected with a successful DC 17 Intelligence (Arcana) check and removed with *dispel magic* cast successfully against a 6th level spell. Any creature within 10 feet of the box is struck by lightning. In addition, any creature within 10 feet of a creature struck by lightning is struck, up to a possible range of 80 feet and a maximum of 8 strikes (the same target can be struck multiple times). Any creature struck by lightning must attempt a DC 17 Dexterity saving throw. Those failing the saving throw take 28 (8d6) lightning damage, while those succeeding take half this amount.

The trap must be dispelled or a password spoken before the box can be opened.

Within the box are 3 aquamarines worth 600 gp each, 1,000 bp, 200 pp, and a *spell scroll* of *resurrection*.

13-6C. Gargoyle Study

This room serves as a private study for Orey to contemplate the business operations as he observes one of the few unobstructed views of the Middle and Upper cities that can be found in the heart of the Basin. Bookshelves are lined with his spellbooks, scrolls, and enough inks and scroll-making materials to draw 13 additional pages.

Upon the shelf are *spell scrolls* of *chill touch*, *charm person*, *identify*, *invisibility*, and *passwall*.

The doors are locked just like the secret door into Orey's apartment.

On the balcony beyond are 2 **advanced margoyles**[1] that stand to either side of the balcony proper.

Using the Trio

Orey, Hick, and Doc are obviously bad guys. But so are most of the other denizens of the City of Brass. They may seek to use the characters to "handle situations" for them that arise through their business operations. Part one of that is handling the situation with the Scorpion League. If the characters successfully handle that situation, they are likely to be hired for a second mission. In this case, they make up a good story about Oruk the Horned being a psychopath who is endangering the integrity of the planes with his experiments. The trio say he must be stopped and that they must be allowed into the plane to "fix" his mistakes. This bit is partially true in that Oruk is somewhat out of his gourd but not in the way that the trio portray it.

If the characters defeat Oruk on behalf of the trio, the wizards instantly move up a rank in the underworld by assuming full control of the Freeman's Tower as they gain access to more powerful raw materials for their drug and poison enterprises. This may have a long-term effect on security in the city as their actions are personally masked by Fatavdra and her henchmen.

If Oruk convinces the characters that the trio are up to no good, or if they figure this out on their own, Orey, Hick, and Doc use whatever allies and means they have at their disposal to stop the characters. That may include unleashing Jhadam on the characters, summoning lots of monsters, or turning the characters over to the burning dervishes on a heresy charge.

Oruk's Wilderness

Beyond the portal to Oruk the Horned's living quarters is a vast pocket dimension. Partially spilled over from the planes of Elemental Earth, Air, and the Great Wild, this dimension is disk-shaped and covered in swamps, grasslands, and dense jungle highlands teeming with life from various eras of prehistory.

It is within this plane that Oruk the Horned rules as a semi-benevolent chieftain to a tribe of sentient ape folk who revere him as their god-king. Oruk has become less involved in the affairs of mortals outside his demi-plane and more engaged in this world within the world. He has not noticed that his own plane has begun to leak out into the Freeman's Tower. Nor is he aware that the expansion of the plane may in fact leak beyond the Freeman's Tower and into the Plane of Molten Skies itself. This event is sure to draw the attention of the Sultan's burning dervishes, who are sure to seize control of his demi-plane in the name of the Sultan himself. Only force of habit and a certain righteousness in his being as it pertains to the

Oruk's Wilderness

payment of universal debts ensuring universal balance has brought him back to collect rent from his leaseholders in the first place.

For their part, Oruk's upstairs neighbors have become increasingly interested in the primitive flora he brought back to the Freeman's Tower on his early expeditions into the jungle.

Though only 14 miles across, the demi-plane is wild and dangerous, and Oruk defends it mercilessly against any invaders. Recently he has taken note of strangers entering his jungle and has taken steps to guard against further incursions. Although the harsh vegetation and ferocious beasts of his domain kill intruders almost instantly, he has not yet realized that their purpose in visiting his realm is simply to harvest the plants that the trio uses in their secretive narcotics operations being run from the upper floors of the Freeman's Tower.

Oruk's jungle contains several areas, each with its own flora and fauna. Each of the sections below includes a random encounter table and descriptions of possible encounters. The regions are shown on the map *Oruk's Widerness*.

1. Portal Plateau

A permanent dimensional portal back to Oruk's apartment is located here. The portal stands on a plateau that overlooks the surrounding jungle highland area. The plateau is 80 feet high and the climb down is moderately difficult. The portal is in the shape of an arch standing 8 feet high and 6 feet wide. The stones are within 50 feet of the monolith. A pile of envelopes with apartment numbers written on them lies on the ground next to the archway. Each is filled with 2d6 bp.

Plateau Random Encounters

1d8	Encounter
1	1d4 pteranodons[1]
2	2d4 megaloceros[1]
3	2d4 + 1 perytons[1]
4	1d4 + 2 advanced woods apes[1]
5	1d4 + 1 saber tooth tigers
6	Blue lotus patch[3]
7–8	No encounter

Pteranodons: Pteranodons swoop down from the sky and attack the smallest party members, hoping to fly off and have them for a quick snack. They flee if their wounds are in danger of keeping them from flight.

Megaloceros: These megaloceros graze the plateau, avoiding larger predators.

Perytons: This flock of evil beasts roams between Oruk's demi-plane and the Great Wild, searching for prey.

Advanced Woods Apes: A group of Oruk's ape warriors arrive. They speak decent common, and demand the surrender of invaders. The apes are armored in heavy leather armor and wear the horns of musk ox and red deer upon their headdress. If the characters surrender, they are carried through the jungle via the treetops to Oruk's Encampment (**Area 7**).

Saber Tooth Tiger: A cat and her young prowl nearby, looking for stragglers to feed upon.

Blue Lotus Patch: A patch of prehistoric blue lotus grows here and is enough to be distilled down into 10 doses of the drug. A successful DC 13 Constitution saving throw must be made during harvesting to avoid accidentally being drugged by the plant's potent pollen.

2. The River Haya

The river runs from one edge of Oruk's demi-plane to the other, repeating in a never-ending cycle. As the river reaches the edge of the dimension, travelers and beasts alike find themselves transported to the opposite side of the river to continue the journey over again. The river is 24–40 feet deep in most places and is roughly a half-mile wide in most places. The river teems with life.

River Encounters

1d12	Encounter
1	1d4 diplodocus[1]
2	Piranha school[1]
3	1d2 + 1 giant crocodile
4	Giant gar[1]
5	1d4 giant crayfish[1]
6	1d2 swarms of mosquitoes[1]
7	2d4 cackle birds[1]
8	Algoid[1]
9	Giant leech[1]
10–12	No encounter

Diplodocus: A pod of diplodocus grazes by the riverside. The bull may make threatening moves toward the party but attacks only if threatened.

Piranha: A school of piranha lurks just below the surface of the waters. They feast for 1d4 rounds before swimming away satiated from their lunch.

Giant Crocodiles: These prehistoric crocodiles look for an easy meal.

Giant Gar: A giant gar takes a bite out of whatever swims by.

Giant Crayfish: These hard-shelled horrors lurk in the silty mud along the riverbanks.

Giant Mosquitos: These swarms of rather large mosquitos are thirsty.

Cackle Birds: These birds are fishing by the shore. They keep to themselves unless trifled with.

Algoid: This creature slinks along the banks of the river, appearing to be no more than a pool of goopy green algae. It uses its mind blast and attempts to make off with at least one character to study and absorb more "humanity" from.

Giant Leech: Things you find sticking to you when playing around in primordial ooze can be rather unpleasant. Really unpleasant.

3. Jungle Lowlands

The thick jungle lowlands are vast, encompassing the largest portion of the disk-like plane. They are covered in wild, primitive fauna, and thick rainforest. The rainforest is filled with dangers for those who do not know the paths.

Lowlands Encounters

1d20	Encounter
1	Amphisbaena[1]
2	Ant lion[1]
3	Giant rhinoceros beetle[1]
4	Blood bush[1]
5	Bloodsuckle[1]
6	Forester's bane[1]
7	3d6 mandrakes[1]
8	Memory moss[1]
9	Ankylosaurus[1]
10	3d4 deinonychus[1]
11	Woods ape patrol[1+] (2d4)
12	Saber-tooth cat[+]
13	Woolly rhinoceros[1]
14	Hadrosaur[1]
15	Orange poppy blossom patch[3]
16–20	No Encounter

[+]See sections above for description

Amphisbaena: The creature is looped in the low-lying canopy of the jungle, resembling for all the world a thick vine.

Ant Lion: The ant lion dug its pit in the thick debris of the jungle, waiting for prey to fall into its waiting jaws.

Giant Rhinoceros Beetle: Something annoys the beetle, and it comes charging through the thick fern forest. Lead, follow, or get out of the way.

Blood Bush: The blood bush decides to take a sip of passersby.

Bloodsuckle: Really just a bigger, meaner blood bush. This demi-plane is really unfriendly.

Forester's Bane: The forester's bane attacks living things that pass within its range. Scattered bones may offer a clue to their location.

Mandrake: Packs of these strange creatures hunt monkeys, birds, small lizards, and occasionally gang up on solitary woods apes. Humanoid characters may be just the thing.

Memory Moss: The memory moss is growing up under an old stump. Good luck finding your way back to your apartment.

Ankylosaurus: These creatures are rooting for wild pineapple and blue lotus that grows in a patch nearby.

Deinonychus: This pack of bird-like reptilians is out for a warm-blooded meal.

Woolly Rhinoceros: These creatures are munching on ferns.

Hadrosaurs: These large creatures feast on the fern trees. They are easily spooked by creatures seeking to devour their tasty flesh.

Orange Poppy Blossom Patch: This patch of orange poppy blossom has is much stronger than normal, and requires a successful DC 21 Constitution saving throw to avoid falling comatose.

4. Wetland

The wetlands of Oruk's wilderness encompass just over 20 square miles of marsh that stretch from the river to the edges of the disk, repeating again at the edge of the plateau and lowland jungle.

The wetlands, like other parts of Oruk's wilderness, are teeming with bizarre life drawn from the corners of the cosmos and the conduits to the Great Wild, and the planes of Earth, Air, and Water.

Wetlands Encounters

1d12	Encounter
1	1d4 bog beasts[1]
2	Bog creeper[1]
3	1d4 + 1 diplodocus[+]
4	Gutslug[1]
5	2d4 marsh jellies[1]
6	Living lake[1]
7	Swarm of giant mosquitoes[1+]
8	1d3 giant crocodiles[+]
9	Black lotus patch[3]
10–12	No encounter

[+]See sections above for description

Bog Beast: These cousins to the evolved woods apes are brutal and reclusive. They use the tall fern trees of the swamp to set ambushes.

Bog Creeper: These deadly plants lurk in the patches of soil and weeds that rise from the mucky waters of the swamp.

Gutslug: If it hasn't been mentioned before, playing in primordial soup has consequences.

Marsh Jelly: These creatures float along the surface of the bog snatching up small animals and insects.

Living Lake: The apex predator of the wetland is the **living lake**[1] that has taken up residency here.

Black Lotus: Ancient black lotus grows on a muddy island. It could be distilled down into 10 doses of the drug. A DC 15 Constitution saving throw must be made during harvesting to avoid being accidentally drugged and killed by the plant's pollen.

5. Clear Lake

This lake of pure fresh water occupies roughly 18 square miles and is dotted with small islands. The lake teems with fish.

Lake Encounters

1d12	Encounter
1	1d4 crocodiles[+]
2	Giant snapping turtle
3	Water weird
4	Water elemental
5	Whirlpool
6–12	No Encounter

[+]See sections above for description

Giant Snapping Turtle: This creature lurks just below the surface of the waters, dragging its prey to the bottom of the lake where it stores it beneath a rotten stump. As **dragon turtle**[1] without Steam Breath.

Water Weird: The water weird has found its way here through a whirlpool to the Elemental Plane of Water and has found it enjoys the hunting.

Water Elemental: Like the water weird, it can often be found near a whirlpool that acts as a portal to the Elemental Plane of Water.

Whirlpool: Deep near the bottom of the lake are whirlpools that connect Oruk's wilderness to the Plane of Water. Swimers who fail a DC 14 Strength (Athletics) check are sucked into the Elemental Plane of Water and had better find some air very quickly!

6. Grassland

This patch of grass is home to a pride of 2d8 **saber tooth tigers**. A large rocky outcropping near the center of the grassland contains the portal to the Great Wild. Any animal may cross through the outcropping and find its way into Oruk's wilderness.

7. Jungle Highlands

The jungle highlands are the domain of Oruk (**heirophant**[1]) and his tribe of woods ape folk that he discovered long ago and brought here so they wouldn't be wiped out by humans and elves. They dwell among the trees in small family groups of 3–12 apes with all adults serving as warriors. The family groups have an alpha leader who is a druid trained in the ways of natural magic by Oruk.

Simply entering the highlands guarantees a meeting with the apes should you wish to have an encounter. As it is their own jungle, they may merely take to the trees to avoid contact with invaders until Oruk can find a way to arrange a trap for the intruders.

The apes are savage meat eaters, but have been educated, trained, and awakened by Oruk's magic and the emanations of the Monolith of the Wild. They are at least as smart as the common orc but are far wiser and more attuned to the world around them. They treat Oruk as a god and chieftain, though he tends to ignore them much of the time. An encounter is typically with 3d4 **advanced woods apes**[1] and a **woods ape druid**[1]

8. Cave of the Dayie Adjhal Sama (Lost Jungle of the Sky)

This cavern found in a crack in the wall of a highland forest cliff howls with supernatural wind. Crossing through the crack allows entry into the Plane of Air, specifically to the Lost Jungle of the Sky featured in the adventure *The Jewel of the Winds* (see **Chapter 5**). Most creatures passing back and forth through the portal may not even realize that they have left one dimension and entered another. Creatures often pass frcely between the two dimensions. Characters entering Oruk's jungle from the cave in the Jungle of the Sky may find themselves in the City of Brass.

9. Monolith of the Wild

This strange 10-foot-tall monolith of glass, metal, gold, and stones of unknown origin flashes and hums with a dangerous-looking light. It is warm to the touch and seems to have a life of its own. Wildflowers have begun to grow on the surface of the monolith, seeming to draw their sustenance directly from it.

Oruk located the shattered parts of this ancient monolith during his adventuring days and began the arduous process of its restoration. Eventually he found his way to the City of Brass where he located the capstone of the Monolith of the Wild in one of the city's souks. Oruk built the monolith within a barren pocket plane for fear of what it may do when activated. When deployed, the cigar-shaped device reshaped the landscape of the plane. Its power was so great that it also opened rifts between the pocket dimension and the Great Wild, and several other dimensions. Because of this, the pocket plane is now somewhat unstable and parts of it have begun to leak into near dimensions, most notably the Freeman's Tower.

The monolith required a great ritual on the part of Oruk himself to begin its life-generating properties and disturbing the device without performing a similar ritual of powerful magic causes the plane to collapse upon itself, killing everything in it within 30 minutes. Determining the ritual without Oruk's help requires at least a week of study and a successful DC 30 Intelligence (Arcana) check.

Oruk lives in the presence of the monolith with his enchanted **tyrannosaurus rex** named Teef as his animal companion. When intruders are reported to Oruk by his faithful ape tribe, he rides out upon the back of Teef looking to punish the intruders.

Oruk keeps a wooden chest near his hut containing 1,000 bp, a *spell scroll* of *greater restoration*, a *spell scroll* of *earthquake*, and a flat silver card that fits into a slot on the monolith. What the card does is anyone's guess.

Encountering Oruk

As Oruk's jungle is his own, it is quite possible that he could be encountered anywhere in the demi-plane. Most likely he is encountered here, in the clearing where he stays close to the monolith.

If the characters willingly come with the apes, they are brought before Oruk at the clearing of the monolith and he respectfully listens to what they have to say as he sits astride his magically enhanced 40-foot-tall tyrannosaurus rex. He asks the characters their purpose in his lands. If Oruk doesn't like their answers, he and his tribe of apes attack.

Oruk is likely to listen to the characters if they say that they have Oruk's rent money. Oddly, the only thing really keeping Oruk rooted in a reality outside of his pocket jungle are the monthly rent payments. Oruk is serious about his rent and makes sure it is collected on time every month.

If the characters are there to warn Oruk about the trio's business, they may be disappointed. Oruk could care less if the trio poisons everyone in the City of Brass with their drugs. Unless he is given concrete proof of their duplicity and actions against him, he may be unwilling to listen, and simply asks the characters to leave his land and not return. If some proof is provided, however, he is all ears. Proof may include Moungus or other prisoners held by the trio.

Oruk has a problem with sentient creatures being tortured. Since torture has become a part of the trio's manufacturing process, this may stand as all the proof Oruk needs to agree to an eviction notice. Oruk further doesn't like any activities taking place within his tower that may bring undue attention to the Freeman's Tower and result in the Sultan discovering his little slice of the universe. For this reason, Oruk may decide to hire the characters to bring the Scorpion League to heel and to sort out the upstart trio. The fact that the trio has been hiring thieves to steal from the natural wonders of his land and assassins to kill him is a further insult to Oruk.

Oruk also listens to characters if they cross through the portal to the sky jungle. In this case, he is more likely to be amicable toward them and sympathetic of their quest. He sees the Sultan's ambitions as ultimately disruptive to the balance of nature. If it is pointed out that his use of the monolith is also disruptive of the balance, he agrees and

The Great Wild

The Great Wild is a vast plane encompassing many biomes and containing samples of flora and fauna from throughout known time. The eras spread from outside in, with the most primitive of life forming a warm ocean sea of primordial soup in the center of the plane. It is from this pool that life emerges, moving outward from the central source of life as it evolves and changes.

The Great Wild is ruled by neutrality in the sense that it is both chaotic and follows the laws of the jungle. It is a kill-or-be-killed realm where predators and prey follow a consistent cycle of life, death, and rebirth. As death is part of this cycle, a tributary of the River Styx passes through the Great Wild on its way to the Underworld. Due to its neutrality, those who touch the Styx here only temporarily lose their memories and are not permanently damaged by contact with the river. Charon and his minions can however be summoned at the shores of the tributary, and a destination in the underworld selected.

The plane is home to the Kingdoms of the Beast Lords. It is here that they keep their kingdoms and guard their portals to the Material Planes. Like anything in the Great Wild, the Beast Lords could be helpful or harmful to visitors to their realms.

Occasionally, projections from the Great Wild's more primitive realms breach into the Material Planes, allowing for pockets of extinct life to find their way back into worlds from which they have long disappeared. This escape from the Great Wild often accounts for strange sightings of cryptids in worlds where magic is on the wane.

As death is part of the life cycle, those things who die and are devoured are reborn. Those that die and are not devoured are reincarnated at dawn of the following day.

points out the quandary he is in. Oruk needs a dead world or empty plane where he can allow the monolith to generate and summon life.

Oruk may become upset when he discovers that his demi-plane is beginning to leak into the City of Brass as he knows this new development is sure to draw the attention of the Sultan. He realizes that something is wrong with the monolith and that it has become unstable. Oruk fears his monolith falling into the hands of the Sultan, as the Sultan would surely use the Monolith of the Wild as a weapon that could disrupt the fabric of nature.

If the characters manage to peaceably deal with Oruk, they are given the options of taking out the Scorpion League if they have not done so already. If Oruk is convinced of the trio's treachery, he offers the characters the trio's lease for the upper stories of the tower if the characters can evict the mages. Making allies with Oruk should award the characters an equal amount of experience points as they would receive for killing him.

Wrapping up the Adventure

As the characters complete the adventure, they may very well find themselves involved in a real-estate venture. If they work for the trio and take out the warren of mercenaries on the lower floors, they are offered a job going after Oruk the Horned. If they take out Oruk, they are offered his floors of the tower, and a cut of the rent for those rooms so long as they can help make sure the burning dervishes steer clear of the Freeman's Tower.

If they take out the trio on Oruk's behalf, they are offered a chance to take over the upper stories and a cut of the real estate. If the characters manage to find a new home plane for Oruk and his apes, Oruk may just hand over the deed to the entire tower to the party as payment.

The Freeman's Tower Rent: The following are offered by the Freemen's Tower:

Rent*	Floors 1–4
Small room	1 bp
Medium room	2 bp
Large room	4 bp
Rent*	Floors 5–6
Small room	1 bp
Medium room	1 bp, 1 gp
Rent*	Floors 7–10
Small room	1 bp, 3 gp
Medium room	2 bp
Rent*	Floors 11–13
Small room	2 bp
Medium room	2 bp, 2 gp
Large room	2 bp, 3 gp

*Rent is paid on a monthly basis. If a person needs a room on a weekly or a daily basis, then they pay the appropriate fraction of the total rent. If Oruk is still alive, rent must be paid on time. He is a real stickler about that.

The Minaret of Screams

Little is known to the outside world of the tortures that take place within the quivering, moaning tower known as the Minaret of Screams. The minaret appeared within the City of Brass shortly after the fall of Iblis. It is a dark and wicked place, avoided by visitors to the City of Brass and its denizens alike. The strange upper chambers of the minaret are used by the insane warden Rylon the Cruel; those banished to the lower chambers of the minaret are never seen again. For this reason, an enterprising Sultan decided to employ the strange minaret as a means of punishment, banishment, torture, and imprisonment for those beings who managed to displease him beyond measure.

The reality of what exactly the tower is baffles reason. The Minaret of Screams is actually an alien entity from the void. Having assumed the form of a worship tower, the creature was drawn to the City of Brass, attracted to the psychic energy produced by the beings who had helped the gods steal the building blocks of creation from the void itself. Since its arrival, the horrid entity has been well fed by the rulers of the Efreet. Servants of the Sultan of Efreet live in symbiosis with the entity, feeding souls of their torture victims to its black heart and their bodies to its undulating bowels.

This adventure is suggested for Tier 3 characters.

Adventures in the Minaret of Screams as Part of an Ongoing Campaign

Tarbish may approach characters after they complete a previous adventure and ask them to rescue an efreeti prince named Abdul al Azul. Alternately, Tarbish could announce that the key to finding the true name of the Sultan of Efreet[1] is by traveling through the bowels of the Minaret of Screams. The irony of this task should be lost upon the characters until they actually venture within the alien tower itself. If not using the Minaret of Screams in an ongoing City of Brass mega campaign, you could merely use the minaret as any alien prison or area of adventure that involves strange terrain and portals to other dimensions.

Other potential associates seeking power from the Minaret of Screams include Rah'po Dehj, Chufa Um Sophanie, Ard, and Fatavdra.

Standard Features:
Upper and Lower Gut

Access: Only the burning dervish guards, Nyal'oz, the Warden, Rylon, and the torturers enter and leave the minaret freely through the main doors. Unless Nyal'oz is slain or banished, or passage is found from the bowels to the Great Repository, individuals who enter the minaret are generally trapped until they are digested in both body and spirit.

Walls and Floors: The walls and floor of the interior of the Minaret of Screams are rubbery and elastic yet firm and almost solid to the touch. The walls have a yellowish wrinkly appearance from the rugae (folds and wrinkles). There is a 25% chance every 10 minutes that one of the elastic folds along the walls attempts to engulf any creature within 5 feet.

The wall makes an attack against a single creature within 5 feet at +10 to hit. On a hit, the target is grappled and restrained. A creature takes 1 acid damage at the beginning of its turn each round it is grappled. A trapped creature can escape by succeeding on a DC 20 Strength (Athletics) or Dexterity (Acrobatics) check.

Walls and Floors: Walls have 200 hit points per 10-foot section and ignore any attack that does less than 10 points of damage. The walls and floors repair themselves at the rate of 10 points of damage per minute. If a section of wall or floor is reduced to 0 hit points, it repairs itself at the rate of 5 hp per minute until it has been fully repaired for 8 hours. If the heart of Nyal'oz is destroyed, the walls and floors cannot repair themselves.

Acid: The floors and walls of the Minaret of Screams are mildly acidic. Any item not made of stone, gold, platinum, or bone slowly dissolves, taking 1 acid damage each hour it remains in contact with the Maw, Upper Gut, Lower Gut, or Bowel.

Howl: The Minaret of Screams emits an ear-shrieking howl at various times of the day and night (generally once every 1d4 + 4 hours). When the minaret howls, all creatures within the minaret weighing less than 1,000 pounds that are not strapped down or anchored in some way to the wall or floor must succeed on a DC 15 Dexterity saving throw or be knocked prone. In addition, creatures hearing the scream must succeed on a DC 20 Wisdom saving throw or be affected by howling madness for as long as that creature remains in the minaret. See the Howling Madness sidebox for more information.

Light: The minaret is completely dark in all areas unless otherwise noted. The only light present is from the everburning torches born by torturers in the Upper Gut and guards in the Maw.

Esophageal Passages: These peristaltic openings lead to the Upper and Lower Gut. Stepping into the odd fleshy disk causes one to be sucked down the tube (taking 10 (3d6) bludgeoning damage from constriction). Getting up one of the tubes is another matter and requires either a DC 18 Strength (Athletics) check while moving at one-quarter speed (movement any faster is not possible) or waiting for the minaret to howl, at which time the reflexive muscle jerk pushes a creature along at its normal movement rate (no check required).

Guards and Torturers

Guards: All guards in the minaret, unless noted otherwise, are under the command of the warden. Guards are burning dervishes[1] and all are completely deaf (having been made so by the silaaal[1] torturers), thus rendering them immune to the effects of the minaret's howling. The guards have grown accustomed to their deafness and suffer no penalty to spellcasting. All can read lips easily (Ignan and Common).

Most guards spend their time rounding up insane prisoners or battling the various slimes spewed up from the Lower Gut.

Burning dervishes stationed within the Minaret of Screams carry a flask of pink fluid that gives them resistance to acid damage for 1 minute and immunity to the crush damage from going up and down the esophageal passages. They pour this substance upon themselves before entering an esophageal passage.

A successful DC 18 Intelligence (Investigation) check with alchemist's supplies reveals that this nonmagical fluid is a mixture of powdered calcium, aluminum, bismuth, magnesium, and a milky substance that tastes mildly like strawberries.

Further, all burning dervishes in the minaret wear protective "hip waders" made of a specialized rubber that grants them immunity to the acidic floors of the minaret. The waders do not grant the wearer immunity to any other type of acid. Characters not proficient in their use have their movement reduced by 5 feet.

Minaret
of Screams
Side View

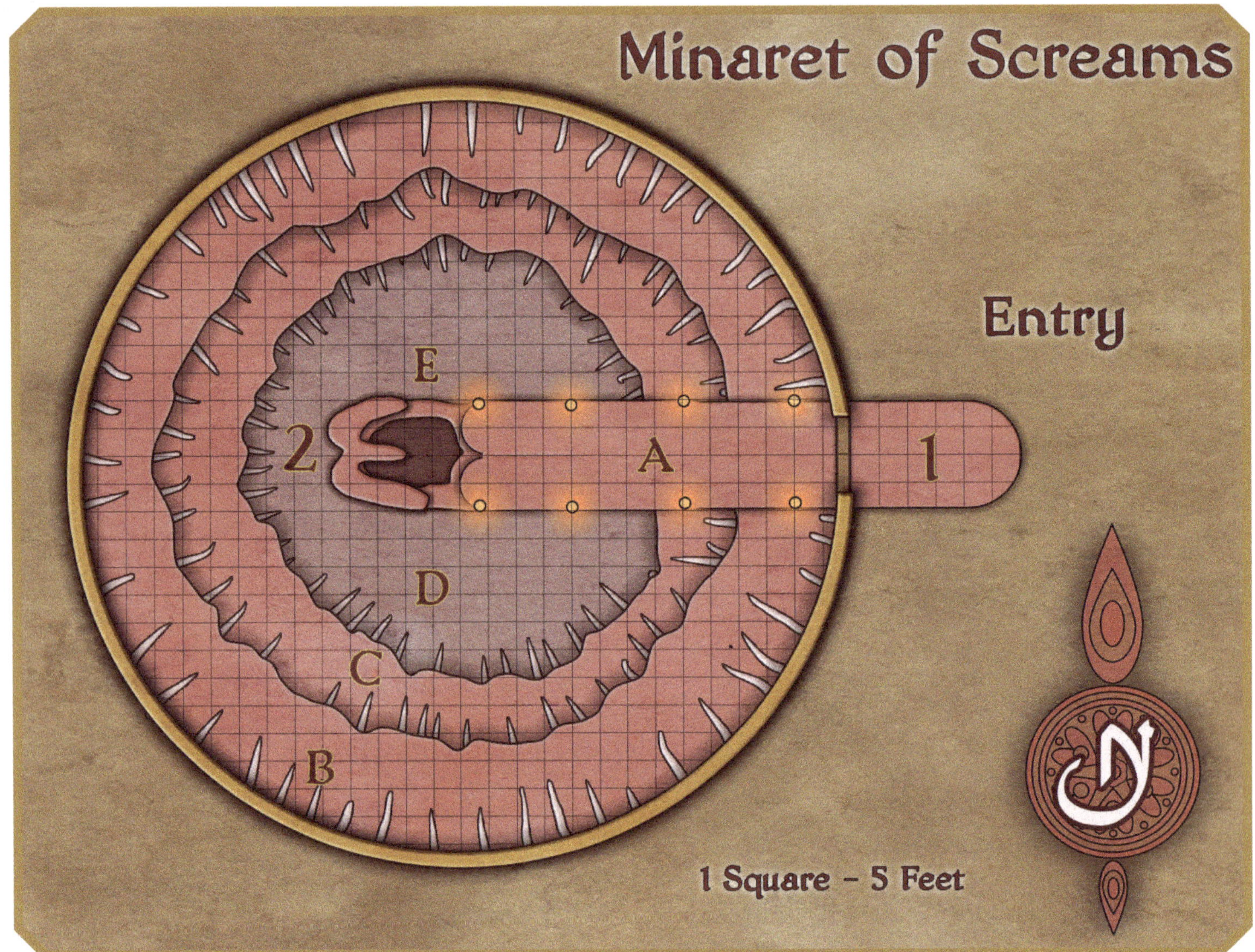

Torturers: The torturers are crimson-clad individuals and are feared and dreaded throughout the City of Brass. They are a race of creatures known as silaaal[1]. Believed to be genies at one time, they were captured by the n'gathau and taken to the Plane of Agony where they were reconfigured into their current form before being released back into the planes of existence. Standing 8 feet tall, these beings are lithe and slender under their voluminous robes. Their eyes glow an odd violet in the darkness and their surgeon-like fingers end in long, sharp claws. Their faces are veiled under black turbans, and they wear serrated kukris at their belts. Torturers appear to be immune to the acidic quality of the alien minaret as well as the howls and screams that emanate from within. Torturers may pass freely from within the minaret, suffering no damage from the crushing effects of the esophageal passages. Rarely seen outside of the minaret itself, those who have encountered them say that they have no mouth or ears under their veiled turbans and communicate via telepathy; they know the thoughts of any with whom they make eye contact.

1. Entrance

The entrance to the Minaret of Screams is a window-shaped aperture off a platform near the dome of the minaret. Two **burning dervish guards**[1] stand on the platform to either side of the aperture. These guards usher prisoners condemned to the Minaret of Screams into the gullet beyond.

2. The Gullet

This strange chamber is quite surprising to visitors who first enter the smooth serpent-like outer skin of the minaret. It has the look and feel of

Howling Madness

A creature subjected to the maddening howls of the Minaret of Screams must succeed on a DC 20 Wisdom saving throw or succumb to the effects of the howls and screams. The ability scores of an affected character are modified as follows: +4 Strength, +2 Constitution, –4 Wisdom, –4 Charisma, and –6 Intelligence. An affected creature also gains a +1 natural armor bonus.

Further, such a character cannot cast any spells or use any spell-like or supernatural abilities it possesses. In combat, a character affected by howling madness prefers natural attacks (claws, unarmed strikes, bite, and so on) to weapon attacks and refuses to use any sort of weapon in battle.

A character affected by howling madness remains so until it leaves the minaret. An affected creature that leaves the minaret must succeed on a DC 20 Wisdom saving throw to remove the effects of howling madness. If the save succeeds, the effects disappear in 1 hour; otherwise, the character becomes insane (treat as a permanent confusion spell). Howling madness can be removed through the successful casting of a *greater restoration* or *heal* spell or equally powerful (or greater) magic.

stone, and the interior of the minaret is gray, wet, and cancerous looking. Despite the presence of 1d4 **burning dervish guards**[1], this is a vault of **madmen**[1]. They wander aimlessly, occasionally beating one another with their bare hands, or stare blankly into space; bored burning dervish guardsmen often toss these unfortunates down the esophagus.

The gullet is arranged in three ringed tiers with a ridged bridge that runs from the entrance of the minaret to the first esophageal portal leading to the Upper Gut. The rings are covered in spikes ranging in size from 6 inches up to 20 feet long. These spikes are as sharp as the teeth of a shark and point out laterally from the walls. The ceiling of the gullet is also covered in razor-sharp spikes and rises 60 feet above the pallet. A creature running into the walls must succeed on a DC 14 Dexterity saving throw or be pierced by 1d4 spikes and takes 3 (1d6) piercing damage per spike.

2-A. The Tongue of Nyal'oz

Beyond the doorway leading into the Minaret of Screams is a 90-foot-long bridge that leads directly to the Maw of Nyal'oz. The tongue is guarded by 1d4 + 2 **burning dervish guards**[1]. Scones with *continual fire* stand every 20 feet along the length of the bridge, casting a strange orange-pink aura across the alien terrain.

2-B. Upper Ring

A group of 8 human **madmen**[1] wander the upper ring of the Gullet, mumbling to themselves and occasionally fighting with one another, or impaling themselves upon the spikes to stop the insanity that numbs their minds.

2-C. Middle Ring

The middle ring is 10 feet below the upper ring and is patrolled by 1d4 **burning dervish guards**[1] who beat down any madmen they encounter. There are also 4d4 half-orc **madmen**[1] who have escaped from the Upper Gut and wander aimlessly here.

2-D. The Soft Pallet

This ring of the gullet is spongy and uneven with a slight grayish pink color to it. Attempting to cross the pallet requires a successful DC 15 Dexterity (Acrobatics) check to avoid falling prone. Those failing their check are knocked prone and slide 20 feet toward the gaping maw that leads to the Upper Gut.

Wandering around the soft pallet are 4 human **madmen**[1] who hurl insults at the deaf ears of the burning dervishes upon the tongue above.

2-E. Maw of Nyal'oz

Standing at the end of the Tongue of Nyal'oz is the throat-like aperture leading to the Upper Gut. Prisoners consigned to the Minaret of Screams are hurled down this portal by the burning dervish guards. Flanking the Maw of Nyal'oz are 2 burly **burning dervish guards**[1]. Beings hurled into the Maw are sucked by peristaltic muscle action into the Entry Chamber of the Upper Gut.

The Upper Gut

The Upper Gut serves as the headquarters of Rylon the Cruel and the Warden. There are several irregularly shaped chambers. In the center of the Upper Gut is the pulsing organ known as the Hidden Heart of Nyal'oz. Many of the chambers here are used as prisons or for torture, with victims stuffed into the folds of rugae along the walls to be slowly eaten alive.

1. Entry Chamber to the Upper Gut

Those beings hurled down the Maw of Nyal'oz find themselves deposited within the Entry Chamber. Four **burning dervish guards**[1] grapple prisoners and usher them into one of the many cells that surround the torture chamber.

2. Torture Chamber

This chamber is where Rylon the Cruel works some of his most heinous experiments upon the woeful individuals sent into his custody. The large chamber in the top end of the Upper Gut is constantly filled with torturers and their victims who have been attached to the rugae.

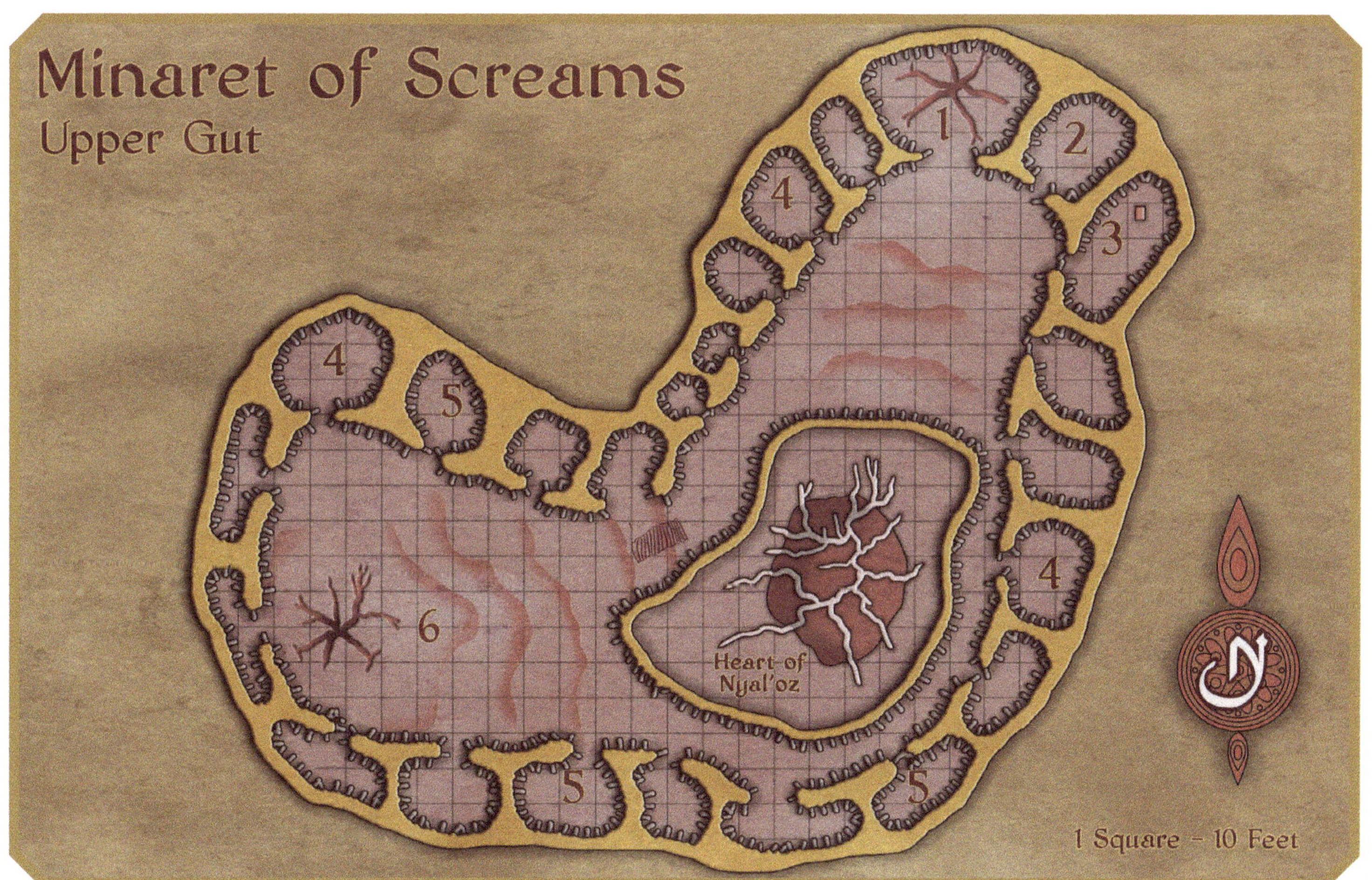

Torturers work upon the condemned through various means, whether they be long thin blades and saws or magical and mental powers that extract pain from their victims. There are 2d4 **silaaal**[1] torturers, 2d10 prisoners (as **greater commoner**[1] with Intelligence and Wisdom 3), and a 50% chance of **Rylon the Cruel**[1] being present within this large chamber at any one time. It is assumed that anyone entering the chamber not in the crimson garb of a torturer or stripped naked after the fashion of a prisoner is a foe to be attacked on sight. Frequently, creatures and prisoners tortured to the point of madness wander around the torture chamber mumbling and gibbering mindlessly. Those who become too annoying are cast into the Lower Gut from the Valve Chamber below the torture chamber.

3. Rylon's Chamber

This chamber serves as **Rylon's**[1] personal office and private torture chamber. The room is mostly bare, with the exception of a living brass chest filled with his personal belongings. Hanging from the rugae of the wall is Rylon's current prisoner, Abdul al Azul (**efreeti amir**[1] currently at 30 hit points and with three levels of exhaustion) of the house of Bayt al Najoom, an efreeti prisoner of interest. He is a noble who was an outspoken opponent of the Sultan's policies of alliance with Set's minions and Lucifer's progeny and was secretly abducted and sentenced in proxy to imprisonment and torture in the Minaret of Screams. As of yet, even Rylon's great prowess has been unable to break the spirit of this brave efreeti noble.

The rugae holding Abdul is extremely strong and requires a DC 30 Strength (Athletics) check to break. Abdul himself is too weak to do so. Further, the section of rugae holding Abdul has been enchanted with a permanent *antimagic field*.

If somehow freed, Abdul offers his services to the party for one year and one day or offers them the secret of passage into the Great Repository used by his father to gain knowledge in combating the Sultan's nihilistic policies.

If Rylon is not found within the torture chamber, he may be found here using his foul skills upon the immobile form of Abdul.

These chambers are home to the minaret's torturers. As not performing their services within the torture chamber, 2d4 **silaaal**[1] torturers have hung themselves within their private cells to regenerate their energies. When so cocooned, the torturers naturally regain hit points at twice the normal rate.

The cocoon holding a torturer is has 50 hit points and can be smashed open with a successful DC 20 Strength check. Each cocoon is resistant to slashing or piercing damage from nonmagical weapons. If a cocoon is attacked, it takes a silaaal[1] 1d4 rounds to break free.

5. Guards Quarters

These guard posts are resting areas for **burning dervish guards**[1]. The guards work 15-hour shifts and take their breaks and store extra gear here before returning to their natural quarters in the Ziggurat of Flame. Guards frequently do battle with the slimes, oozes, and other creatures that crawl

The Heart of Nyal'oz

Actually located in a hidden chamber within the Upper Gut, the **Heart of Nyal'oz**[1] may be reached only by means of the Digestive Crypts or by cutting through the wall of the Upper Gut. The chamber holding the Heart of Nyal'oz is filled with fluids and thus any combat occurring within must be performed following underwater combat rules unless the characters find a way to drain the fluid. The Gargantuan object pulsing in the center of the chamber is the Heart of Nyal'oz itself. The nerve center of the creature, the heart vaguely looks like a bloated cow heart covered in gaping lamprey-like mouths and dull frog-like eyes. The Heart attempts to devour any being that enters its chamber, using its powerful mental and magical attacks as well as the animated tendrils of the veins and arteries sprouting from it.

from the Lower Gut and keep supplies of *potions* of *healing* and *spell potions*[2] of *lesser restoration* here to heal themselves after battle.

Treasure: 500 bp, 300 sp, various gold cups and trinkets (total value 1,500 gp).

6. Valve Chamber

There are 1d4 + 2 **burning dervish guards**[1] in this chamber at any given time. There is a 30% chance that the Warden (**burning dervish sorcerer**[1]) is in the Valve Chamber, overseeing the dumping of prisoners into the Lower Gut for disposal or helping his guards fight the slimes, jellies, and oozes. The current fight is against an **advanced ochre jelly**[1] and a **stone pudding**[1].

Lower Gut

The Lower Gut is the domain of Samiij the Unclean, an **emeritus chaplain**[1] of the Brotherhood of Ooze and master of the *saddle of ooze riding*[2]. Rylon originally cast Samiij into the Lower Gut after he could not break the high priest's insane spirit. Samiij, for his part, frequently sends oozes, slimes, and jellies through the esophageal passages to wreak havoc upon his former torturers. The chaos of this situation pleases the foul spirit of the minaret, creating more negative psychic energy for it to devour.

Lower Gut Random Encounters

Roll 1d20 for every 10 minutes spent in the Lower Gut.

1d20	Encounter
1	1 black pudding
2	1 stone pudding[1]
3	1 brown pudding[1]
4	1 dun pudding[1]
5	1 advanced ochre jelly[1]
6	1d4 gelatinous cubes
7	2d4 gray oozes
8	1d2 arcanoplasms[1]
9	1 advanced gray ooze[1]
10	1d3 ochre jellies
11	2d4 madmen[1]
12	Trapped burning dervish guard[1]
13–20	No encounter

Trapped Burning Dervish Guard: This burning dervish guard[1] accidentally fell into the Lower Gut and is fighting for his life. Of course, he attempts to enlist the characters in rescuing him — only to betray them at the first opportunity.

1. Entry Chamber to the Lower Gut

The peristaltic reflex from the Upper Gut deposits individuals passing through it into this chamber. Beyond is a pathway leading deeper into the Lower Gut. A dim luminosity permeates the Lower Gut, offering vision out to about 20 feet.

2. Chamber of Oozes

This chamber of the Lower Gut secretes oozes from glands in the walls. The oozes are of various sorts and eventually join to form huge versions of their type.

The Glands

Each gland within the Lower Gut produces a single ooze whenever a living creature comes within 10 feet of it. It takes 3 rounds for a new ooze to materialize. A single gland can produce 1d6 oozes in a given day.

Each gland has 150 hp. Each gland heals damage at the rate of 5 hit points per day. A gland can be cauterized (rather than destroyed) by dealing at least 50 fire or electrical damage (or a combination of both) to it. A cauterized gland ceases to produce oozes and heals fire or electrical damage at the rate of 2 points of damage per day.

It takes the minaret one year to regrow a destroyed gland.

These occasionally divide and make their way to the entry chamber and eventually into the entry and up to the Upper Gut.

There are three glands upon the wall that secrete various oozes. Typically found here are 1d4 **gelatinous cubes** and 1d3 **advanced gray oozes**[1].

3. Chamber of Puddings

Like the chamber of oozes, this chamber contains several glands that produce various puddings. There is one of each of the following puddings found within the chamber: **black pudding**, **brown pudding**[1], **dun pudding**[1], and **stone pudding**[1].

4. Chamber of Jellies

This chamber, like the chamber of oozes and puddings, secretes jellies from glands in the walls. The difference between this chamber and others is that the walls are slick with 2d4 **stunjellies**[1]. There is an **advanced ochre jelly**[1] here as well.

5. Chamber of Arcanoplasms

Similar to the other chambers in the lower gut, this chamber secretes **arcanoplasms**[1]. The 2d4 arcanoplasms[1] are attracted to magic and attack any arcane casters instantly.

6. Hall of Samiij the Unclean

This large chamber in the Lower Gut is the prison and residence of Samiij the Unclean (**emeritus chaplain**[1]). Samiij was a high priest of the Brotherhood of Ooze and a faithful servant of Jubilex before he was cast into the Lower Gut many years ago. He quickly saw this as a blessing, for the oozes and slimes of the Lower Gut were indeed his goal in coming to the City of Brass in the first place. He has since completed construction of his ultimate item: the *saddle of ooze riding*[2]. Only Samiij knows the secret of making a *saddle of ooze riding*, and he isn't telling.

Samiij spends most of his time in meditation atop the saddle, which is affixed to an **elder black pudding**[1]. From here, he commands the various oozes and jellies of the Lower Gut to travel forth into the Upper Gut and attack the minions of the sultan of efreet. He has also spent much time traveling the gates found within the Crypts of the Bowel and mapping them. Samiij has made alliances with various powerful demons and can commune with his recently freed master Jubilex via the Crypt of Charonademons. Due to certain restrictions placed upon him by Nyal'oz, Samiij may only travel the planes through the Elder himself and may be gone from the Tower for only up to three days at a time before he is automatically gated back to the Lower Gut. Should Samiij be faced with destruction, he flees down the passage leading to the Bowel. Once there, he makes his way to the Crypt of the Charonademons and on to the Styx. Unless captured or killed, he returns to this hall again in three days.

Samiij is completely mad and for this reason is unaffected by the howls of the minaret. He may approach the characters peacefully one moment and then try to viciously attack, only to then suddenly break off his attack and fall into weeping and shuddering. Aside from that, he is keenly intelligent and wily with a strong sense of self-preservation and survival.

Treasure: In addition to Samiij's personal items, a carved stone box holds the following items: 1,000 bp, 550 sp, 4 white pearls (100 gp each), 30 bloodstones (40 gp each), and several finely-sewn gold and gray vestments (120 gp total value).

A map located in the box shows the location of the various Crypts in the Bowel. The portals leading to other planes are marked and noted by Samiij on the map. The back of the map holds a crude map of the City of Brass's upper levels with markings showing the Shining Pyramid, the Repository, and the Pagoda of Devils.

7. Entrance to the Bowel

This chamber contains a portal that uses peristaltic reflex to deposit individuals passing through it into the Bowel.

The Bowel

Most beings that make it to the Bowel do so in acid, slime, or ooze-dissolved pools of yuck. The Bowel is packed with bones, rocks, and remains, and many crypts along its length serve as storage places for the effluence that cannot be destroyed by the normal digestive process of the minaret. While walking on the smooth oily floors of the Bowel, characters must succeed on a DC 15 Dexterity (Acrobatics) check to avoid falling prone when attempting anything more complicated than moving at their normal movement speed.

1. Crypt of Cacodemons

This crypt points outward from the main turning passage of the Bowel. At the far end is a strange fleshy portal that undulates with an unholy stench. Once the crypt is entered, 2 **cacodemons**[1] immediately appear. Unless bargained with by an evil priest or if Samiij happens to be with the party and discourages the cacodemons[1], they attack the party in an

The Crypts

Crypts and capillaries within the Bowel feed directly to the Heart Chamber in the Upper Gut unless otherwise noted. While the crypts are fairly "standard" size chambers, the capillaries are accessible only to those of Tiny or smaller size. Creatures of Tiny or smaller size may pass freely into the capillaries. Several of the capillaries serve as portals that lead to other planes of existence. One in particular, the **Appendix** (see below), is actually a conduit by which persons may pass through the Minaret of Screams into a secret library known as the Great Repository.

These portals can be sealed by means of a *flesh to stone* spell. Such information could be gained via *commune* or other such spells or magic. Should all the portals be sealed, Nyal'oz is effectively asphyxiated and dies within hours. The latter information should not be readily available to the characters, though they could discover it by various means (through deductive reasoning or perhaps Abdul knows this and informs the characters of it, for example).

attempt to kill them all. Every 1 minute spent in this chamber causes another cacodemon[1] to appear until the party is slain, leaves the crypt, or enters the capillaries and thereby triggers the portal.

Portal: A portal in this chamber serves as a conduit to the plane of Gehenna, the outer planar home of the mighty Oinodemon.

2. Crypt of Derghodemons

This crypt, like the others, points outward from the main passage of the Bowel. At the far end is a fleshy portal. Once the crypt is entered, 4 **derghodemons**[1] appear. As with the Crypt of the Cacodemons, unless

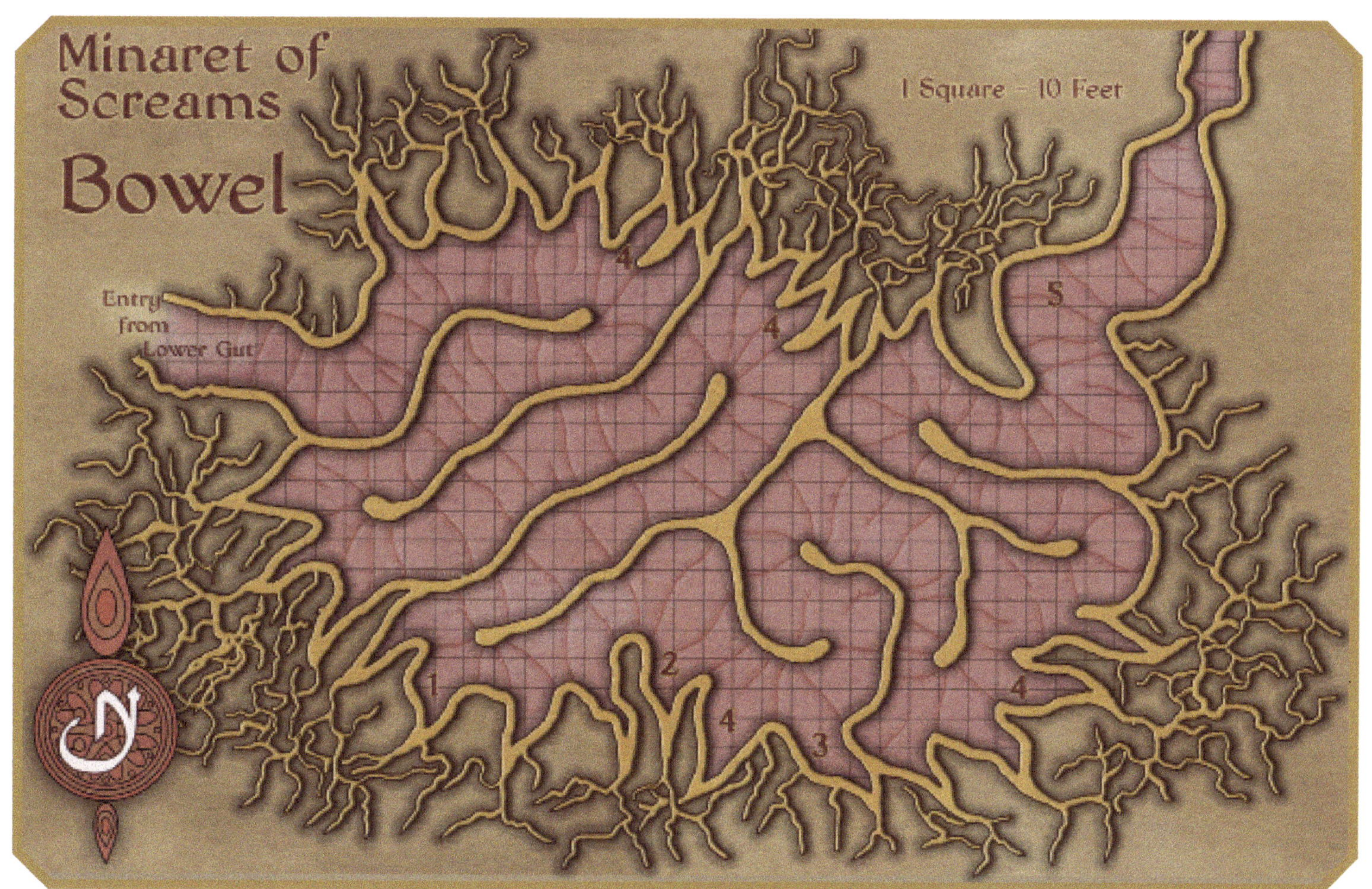

bartered with by Samiij or an evil priest of equivalent caliber, the derghodemons attack. A new derghodemon[1] appears every 1 minute spent in this chamber until the characters leave, are slain, or enter the fleshy portal.

Portal: The portal in this chamber leads to the plane of Tarterus (or alternately to the plane of Hades).

3. Crypt of Charonademons

The base of this crypt is filled with a noxious water. The scum-covered backwash is actually a tributary of the Plane of Styx (a recently discovered outer plane awash with the River Styx itself and controlled by those born of and blessed with its powers). A creature contacting the waters in this chamber must succeed on a DC 15 Intelligence save or lose its mind (treat as *feeblemind*). The effects can be restored through the casting of *greater restoration*, *heal*, or *wish*.

Several rounds after entering this crypt, a skiff appears bearing a **charonademon**[1]. It simply waits, making no sound or movement toward the characters. Should the characters attack the charonademon[1], it summons (no chance of failure) 1d4 **hydrodemons**[1] to its aid and all five creatures attack the characters.

Portal: The portal in this chamber leads to the Plane of Styx (or alternately to the Abyss, Nine Hells, or Hades).

4. Digestive Crypts

These crypts lead to the Heart of Nyal'oz itself via the digestive process. Creatures of Tiny size or smaller may actually pass through the capillaries into the bloodstream that feeds the heart. Floating through the bloodstream requires some means of breathing without air (such as *water breathing*) or holding one's breath, as those beings not so equipped drown in Nyal'oz's plasma. All objects, slimes, oozes, and chum is drawn through this mad bloodstream to the Heart of Nyal'oz within 1d2 minutes.

5. The Appendix

This crypt is larger than many of the others. Its innards appear to be tattooed with nonsense words in various languages. Attempting to read the words by means of *comprehend languages* results in the character immediately taking 1d4 points of Charisma and Wisdom damage. Unless the character succeeds on a DC 20 Wisdom saving throw the damage is permanent.

Continuing along the length of the Appendix eventually leads to the **Great Repository: Wound of the Haruspex** (see **Area 14** of **Chapter 21: The Great Repository**).

Completing Adventures in the Minaret of Screams

Characters may have been captured and forced into the Minaret of Screams for breaking laws in the City of Brass, or for proving to be difficult slaves. Characters following the advice of Tarbish may have sought entry into the Minaret of Screams in order to rescue Abdul al Azul or to seek the forgotten passages of the Appendix. From this point, they may find a secret means of admittance into the Great Repository, the key to uncovering the true name of the Sultan of Efreet[1].

If a simple rescue mission is in order, then the characters succeed once Rylon, his torturers, and the Warden are destroyed. Making their escape with Abdul still alive is of course an important requirement for success. This sets up a meeting between Abdul's father and the characters that allows them secret entry into the Great Repository.

If Nyal'oz is destroyed, the tower collapses upon itself as if it were a boned fish, slumping limply into the Basin and crushing anything located below it (dealing 77 (20d6) bludgeoning damage). All portals to various planes close, as does the passage back through Nyal'oz from the Great Repository. A horrible stench fills the City of Brass for days afterward as the thing rots, eventually bringing a plague of elemental vultures that devour the rotting remains. Characters within the Minaret of Screams are vomited forth from the minaret as it writhes in its death throes suffering any subsequent falling damage for the distance thrown and the distance fallen (unless magical precautions are used to save their lives; the fall is more than two miles down after all).

Chapter 21
The Great Repository

The Great Repository is a towering monstrosity of a library planted right in the heart of the city. While it is true that it possesses the sum of efreeti knowledge (though others say the sum of *all* knowledge), accumulated over hundreds of thousands of millennia and harvested from nearly as many worlds, it is also something so disturbing that every one of the city's residents, from the most worthless slaves languishing in the gutters at the bottom of the Basin to the Sultan himself, would rather it never have existed. Yet exist it does, and there is nothing anyone can do about it, as much as they might wish otherwise. In a place where wishes are the currency of dreams and are traded as freely as gold in the mortal realms, that is no small feat.

The Repository is the City of Brass' tallest building. It is constructed entirely from royal purple marble. Depending on the angle from which one looks at it, it seems to have between three and seven sides and its middle section seems to bulge outward like a sickly, cancerous tumor. Three colossal marble arms reach down like flying buttresses from the tower walls, stone fists firmly clutching the city floor. A thick layer of black and crimson filth that seems to be congealed blood covers them. In fact, it coats the entire tower base as high as the Middle Levels. Atop the tower are marble arms, a crown of seven ever grasping toward the molten fire sky. Unlike the much larger ones anchoring the library to the ground, these are pristinely free of muck. The Sultan would never normally allow any other building to look down upon his own palace, but this is the one exception. In the past, many tried to bring down the library. All failed. A dark magic inhabits it, making it immortal, indestructible. It is said with hushed whispers and fear-filled hearts that the only deity to ever come close to destroying it ended up obliterated from existence.

The Repository has no windows other than skylights built into the roof between the arms. Its single entrance opens at the City's Middle Level, where the tower swells to its widest girth to join an ornate brass bridge built 16,000 years ago by the eminently despicable Sultana Indizhar Nishwan Radhwa. All who enter do so as equals with one another and as inferiors to the scholars inside — no exceptions. The scholars kneel before no one, if only because there is no one else alive who understands the peculiarities of the tower.

The Great Repository in an Ongoing Campaign

The Great Repository may serve many purposes in an ongoing City of Brass campaign. Most importantly are the freeing of the builders, a trio of prophets whose engineering genius brought about the construction of the Repository in the time of the rule of Iblis. Equally important to a campaign run in the City of Brass would be the unraveling of the Words of Creation. Each circumstance has the potential of uncovering the true name of the Sultan of Efreet[1], greatly undermining his plans for planar dominion. Characters have various means of gaining entry to the Repository, be it through passage from the Minaret of Screams or by freeing the efreeti prince Abdul al Azul from his tortures at the hands of Rylon the Cruel. Once entered, the characters are exposed to many traps, treasures, and wonders that may warp the mind of all but the strongest heart. When played outside a City of Brass mega campaign, the Repository makes an excellent storehouse for knowledge with challenges easily applicable to any setting.

The characters may be introduced to adventures within the Repository by efreet nobles in the Bayt Al Azul, by Tarbish, Ard, Rah'po Dehj, or Chufa Um Sophanie.

For the following locations, refer to **The Great Repository** map. This adventure is suggested for Tier 3 characters.

Standard Features

Shielding: The Great Repository is shielded against any means of magical transport. Spells such as *teleport, dimension door, plane shift, etherealness,* and so on automatically fail if used to attempt to gain entrance to the structure.

Additionally, no spells or powers involving extraplanar contact such as *conjure elemental, gate,* or *commune* operate within the Repository. The structure is further shielded against *clairvoyance* and *scrying* (except when using the scrying bell, see below).

Flora and Fauna

The Great Repository has a miniature ecosystem that is ultimately the result of accidents from poorly understood or spontaneous summoning magic (though how summoned creatures get through the tower magic is unknown; most scholars assume they get through because the tower *wanted* them to get through). A wide variety of molds, mosses, and slimes make the damp, dark interior home. Birds have turned the Lightbringer's Highway into an aviary, all sorts of reptiles slither in and out of the stacks, and strange plants grow from the wall seams, the darkness behind bookshelves, and anywhere else their roots can take hold.

A Tower Possessed

Of all the mysteries on the Plane of Fire, the Great Repository is the king. It has been here since before the city was built, and in all likelihood will stand even longer. It is impervious to magic, both mortal and deific. Weapons cannot scratch it, fire cannot burn it, hammers cannot dent it, and the wind cannot topple it. Some people believe it is multi-planar nexus to other worlds, dimensions, and lifetimes.

There is just one public entrance into the tower, the Petitioner's Hall, but it does not grant access to the tower's interior. Even though the tower roof contains ornate skylights, the tower's magic makes them impossible to bypass. Not even the gods are allowed inside. How the scholars, creatures, and items that dwell or are located here get inside is the greatest mystery of all.

Occasionally a scholar or two escape (or are ejected) through the Exile Gate; unfortunately, the effects of the gate are so severe that most choose to remain within the structure. While it is physically impossible for creatures to get inside, a determined character can gain mental access in a rather unusual manner, but only by making a sacrifice (see the **Petitioner's Hall** below).

There is also a back entrance through the Minaret Screams for the truly hardy adventurer.

1. The Whispering Walls

A character who stands within 5 feet of the exterior walls of the tower and listens carefully hears an infinite chorus of faint, disembodied voices whispering maddening and indecipherable words. Characters who listen for more than 5 rounds must succeed on a DC 20 Wisdom save or take 2d4 points of Wisdom damage. Even if the save succeeds, the character takes 1 point of Wisdom damage. A character who rolls a natural 1 (regardless of modifiers) on the save suffers 3d6 points of permanent Wisdom drain. A

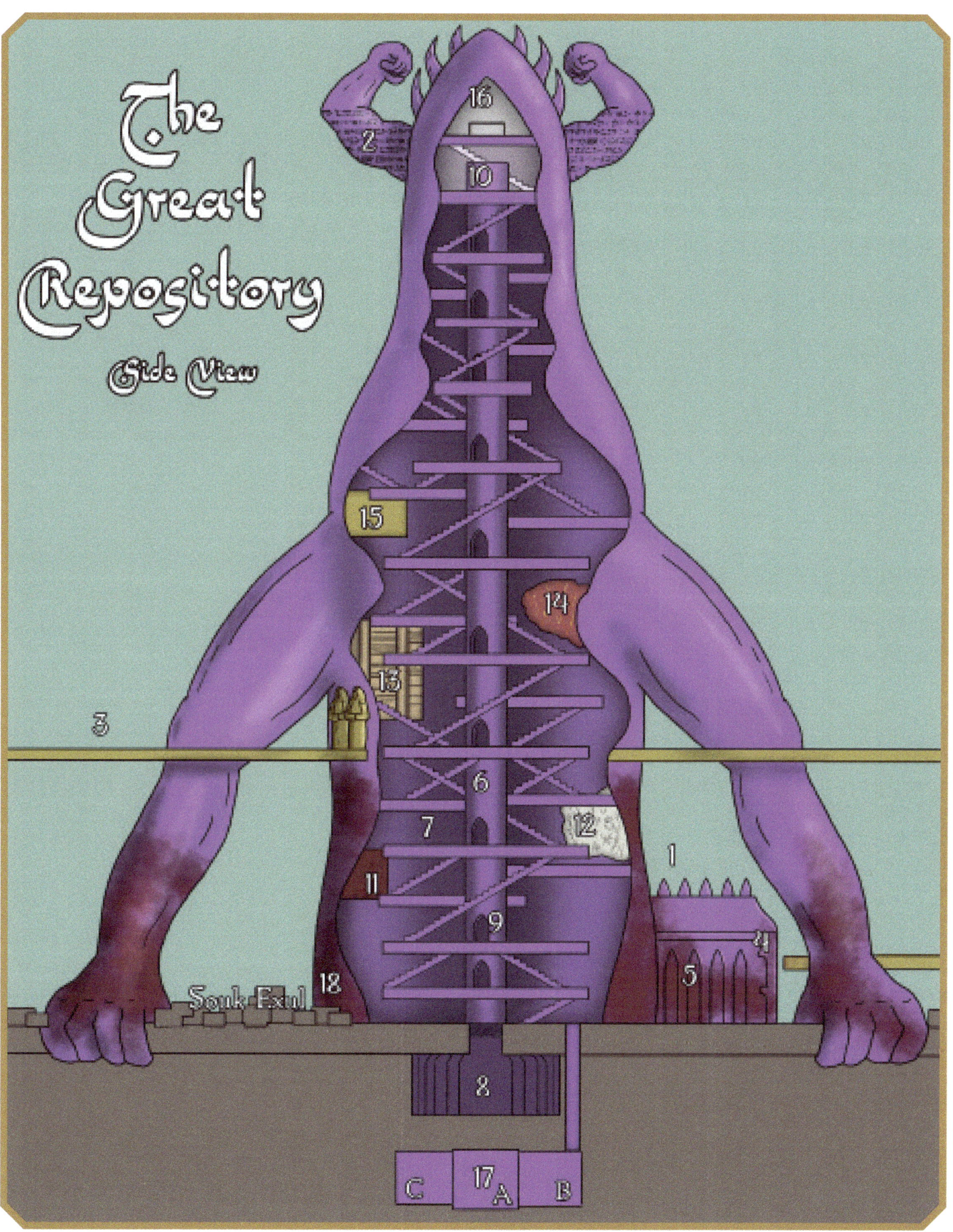

The Great Repository
Side View
16
2
10
15
13
14
3
6
7
12
11
1
9
5
4
18
Souk Exit
8
C
17
A
B

character reduced to Wisdom 0 slips into a coma for 5d4 years. A *wish* or a bard playing upon the *durbakke of wakefulness*[2] (found within the vaults in the KhizAnah) breaks the coma and allows the restoration of lost Wisdom points.

A character can be affected only once per day by the walls; a character who survives the first time does not need to make another save for the next 30 hours (remember, one day within the City of Brass is 30 hours).

No one can interpret the words being spoken. The words, despite being indecipherable, are mentally indelible; they can never be removed from memory once they've been heard. Such affected creatures suffer nightmares and restless, intermittent sleep for the rest of their lives. An affected character has a permanent 5% chance of not being able to gain the benefits of a long rest (roll each time the character attempts to rest).

2. The Law Code of King Horadin

The seven arms rising from the top of the Great Repository are tattooed with cuneiform inscriptions between the wrists and elbows. All together, they comprise the Law Code of King Horadin, a fool of a man who sought to rule the world but instead destroyed it through his own stupidity and arrogance. A captive efreeti gave the law code to him in fulfillment of the first of three *wishes*. Horadin never had the opportunity to make use of the subsequent two *wishes*, though. Upon receiving the efreeti-written law code and distributing it to his subjects, his empire fell within a fortnight. Within a year, his entire world succumbed to the fires of destruction. In the end, his subjects hung him from the palace gates by a noose of his own entrails.

The language of the law code is lost except to the builders, a trio of ancient prophets imprisoned within the Kiln of Sorrows deep below the bowels of the Repository. It is believed that anyone who can translate it will unleash the apocalypse upon the entire plane. Attempts to cover the inscriptions fail, as the tower magically destroys the coverings within hours of placement, and destroying the inscriptions is physically and mystically impossible. The Sultan would like nothing better than to murder the scholars, but has found, as Iblis did, that attempts on their lives arc fruitless. Thus, they remain forever burning within the Kiln of Sorrows. The Exsul (exiles) refuse to entertain any questions regarding the scholars or the inscriptions.

One rumor is currently running rampant among the city's conspirers of a fire giant magician who discovered a stone tablet on the Plane of Earth that contains text written in the Horadin cuneiform as well as in two other ancient, yet decipherable, languages. They believe this stone is the key to unlocking the text of the Law Code.

3. Indizhar's Bridge

The brass bridge that joins the tower with the rest of the city is called "Indizhar's Bridge" after the Sultana who commissioned its construction. It is a true work of art, but its position next to the tower makes it hideous by association. The end away from the Repository entrance supports two 60-foot-tall statues. One represents Indizhar's husband, Narif, sitting astride a war elephant; the other is a stylized depiction of Indizhar's crippled lover, a soldier known only as the Bodyguard. Legend has it his leg was crushed beneath the foot of her husband's elephant.

Where the bridge meets the tower stand two more statues. In ages past, they depicted the proud visages of the two greatest scholars in all the planes, but their long proximity to the library has distorted them. The pair no longer resemble the opulent, aristocratic intelligentsia they once did. Instead, they wear tattered robes, and their heads are covered with hoods very similar to those of the scholars inside. Their eyes have neither pupils nor irises. Flowing, cursive script on their robes changes on a daily basis, usually with disturbing quotes from the books stored in the library. Occasionally, they display a piece of the Muhaim Prophecy, which was recorded 700 years ago by the prophet Kheturus al Muhaim and details the downfall of the City of Brass at the hands of a heretic army from a desert kingdom ruled by the undead.

The prophecy was lost fifty years later when the ruling Sultan had both it and the prophet destroyed. Today, there are very few known, verifiable fragments in existence. Small crowds gather every day at the statues' feet, waiting expectantly, hoping for additional text from the prophecy. One watcher, Fayyad Mazin (**archpriest**[1]), has all the text recorded over the last 333 years, as well as a few snippets from earlier times.

Indizhar's Bridge does not actually touch the Repository proper. Rather, a 3-foot-wide gap separates them. This is one of the few places in the city not watched by guards.

4. Front Entrance

Two 15-foot-tall iron doors open into the Great Repository. Though they appear to weigh two or three tons apiece, an ancient enchantment makes them practically weightless. They do not possess locks of any kind, nor do city guards stand watch either inside or out. Carved into each door is a stylized eye. The left one has no iris.

A tiny river of blood constantly slips out from beneath the doors, cascading into the gap between the tower and the bridge like a miniature crimson waterfall, ultimately spilling against the wall below. It is the source of the coagulated grime clinging to the lower half of the tower. Sloppily painted graffiti above the doors reads in the common tongue, "Ignorance is Bliss."

5. Petitioner's Hall

At first glance, this massive, granite-lined chamber looks like a castle feast hall. It is 200 feet deep and 100 feet wide. A 4-foot-wide trough cuts through the middle, running the length of the hall from front to back. Numerous smaller troughs run perpendicular to it, coming in from the sides. Blood fills the troughs, flowing slowly toward the iron doors. Bits of rotting flesh spatter the walls, floor, and ceiling. Poorly constructed tables are haphazardly placed around the room, though there are no chairs other than a wooden throne sitting alone at the back of hall. The stench of offal, viscera, and vomit rotting in the extreme heat that permeates the entire city fills the air. It is truly nauseating, especially when mixed with odors of hundreds of unwashed bodies. Except for the entrance, the hall contains no doors. In fact, there is no apparent physical means at all to access the rest of the library's interior.

Hundreds of creatures can be found milling about the hall at all hours of the day. They are petitioners who come from all walks of life seeking answers. Once they cross the threshold into the tower, their stations in life become irrelevant. All are treated the same.

No random encounter tables are given for the Petitioner's Hall because of the multitude of possible encounters here. You are encouraged to let characters encounter pretty much whatever you desire, though oozes, mindless undead, and vermin are not found in the hall. Also keep in mind that everyone is here for a purpose, thus fighting it out with a petitioner seeking knowledge is probably not the best course of action because the city guards respond to any sort of disturbance immediately.

The Attendants

Attending the petitioners is small army of Repository slaves (**corpulent attendants**[1]), immensely corpulent men and women who wear little more than filthy cotton swaddling. Tight, leather collars armed with iron spikes pointed inward encircle their throats, constantly pricking the flesh there, and rusty manacles brace their wrists and ankles. A glossy sheen of fresh blood always seems to coat their skin. Once human (or at least believed to be), centuries of servitude in the Great Repository have altered their physical and mental state.

Attendants carry long, wickedly shaped daggers, for knowledge is never without its price and in the Great Repository that price is paid in blood. Upon presenting a request to an attendant, a petitioner is given a choice: sacrifice an eye to see firsthand the knowledge or allow the scholar to inhabit his or her body for seven days in order to imprint the knowledge onto the petitioner's soul where it is never lost or forgotten. Most people choose to lose their eye, as stories abound regarding the depravities committed by scholars on the loose, and the subsequent, merciless punishment inflicted on the petitioners who allowed their bodies to be so used.

Losing an Eye

A corpulent attendant can swiftly cut a petitioner's eye from its head as a standard action. This deals 1 point of Constitution damage to the petitioner and renders the petitioner partially blind. A partially blind creature has disadvantage on Wisdom (Perception) checks that rely on sight and on ranged attack rolls.

Furthermore, the petitioner experiences "double vision," seeing both from the remaining eye (as normal) and through the eye in the scholar's possession. This makes concentration and spellcasting almost impossible. All Concentration checks have disadvantage, and spellcasters must succeed on a DC 10 + spell level check using their spell attack modifier to cast a spell; if the check fails, the spell is wasted. This lasts until the question is thoroughly answered and the double vision goes away.

Once the eye has been cut out, the attendant takes great delight in consuming it. This is the ritual that delivers the eye to one of the innumerable scholars farther inside, who begins his research immediately upon receipt. Within half an hour of the sacrifice, the petitioner sees an image of everything that the scholar does — pages, books, scrolls, and so on. The time required to get an answer depends on the nature of the question. Some petitioners claim they are still receiving visions from inside the tower to this day, and these are people who placed their requests two or three centuries ago.

The lost eye can be restored by magic, but if it's restored before the petitioner's question is answered, the double vision is permanent until cured by *greater restoration* or *wish*.

Scholarly Possession (Soul Swapping)

If a petitioner allows a scholar to possess his or her body, then the scholar assumes control as soon as he finds the answer to the question. This effect is similar to a *magic jar* spell, except the duration is a maximum of seven days and it is not blocked by things such as *protection from evil and good* or similar wards. Soul swapping is not subject to *dispel magic*, *Antimagic field*, or the like.

Petitioners who soul swap with a scholar find themselves chained to the Wailing Walls in **Area 8** inhabiting the broken and misshapen body of a scholar restrained by rusty manacles. While imprisoned, they are subjected to the normal rules for starvation and thirst. An imprisoned petitioner can attempt to escape the bonds with a successful DC 25 Dexterity (Acrobatics) check or DC 25 Strength check. Once freed, a character can move around the Repository. See the **Amok in the Repository** sidebox.

While switched, each soul keeps its Intelligence, Wisdom, Charisma, level, class, saving throws, alignment, and mental abilities. The body retains its Strength, Dexterity, Constitution, hit points, natural abilities, and automatic abilities. A body with extra limbs does not allow either to make more attacks (or more advantageous two-weapon attacks) than normal. A switched soul can't choose to activate the body's extraordinary or supernatural abilities. The switched soul's spells and spell-like abilities do not stay with the body.

A scholar who possesses a character's body typically runs amok, experiencing every delight he can imagine. There are exceptions, naturally; some, unable to cope with the outside world, become plagued with overwhelming psychological disorders (the most prominent being agoraphobia). In the city's entire history, more serial killers have come from the Repository than not. As a result, the city guard does what it can to discourage petitioners from choosing the possession method of payment, generally by killing anyone they suspect has performed a soul swap with a scholar. Some of the scholars, too, have finally gotten the message and so do not always take a petitioner up on their offer. Unfortunately, the lure of the outside world is all too frequently impossible for them to resist.

At the end of the seven days, the character regains control of his or her body and wakes up with all pertinent information requested permanently imprinted in the character's mind.

If a petitioner's body dies while in the possession of a scholar, the petitioner's soul stays inside the scholar's body. Similarly, if the scholar's body dies, the scholar's soul remains permanently within the body of the petitioner.

Inside the Repository

6. The Lightbringer's Highway

This the largest and most important hall inside the Great Repository, extending from the top all the way down to the bottom. It is the tower's hollow core. The room gains its name from a creation myth that speaks of an archangel of law who fell from the heavens beyond the world of mortal man down into Hell. This room — indeed, the entire building — is a tribute to him, and the information within it is considered his greatest gift to the sentient races.

A thick stone pillar rises up through the center. Both the pillar's and the Highway's walls are lined with a knotty tapestry of bookshelves, balconies, and study cages. The staircase winding up the pillar's length (all one hundred or more stories of it) creaks loudly under each footfall. An untold number of doors lead into the dizzying, claustrophobic nest of corridors and rooms surrounding the hall. Pillar doors, on the other hand, lead farther inward to private rooms containing forbidden, fragile, or especially dangerous books.

Bars of natural light fall through the clear skylights in the roof, dimming gradually as they descend the hall's impossible height so that by the time they reach the bottom of the tower they barely have the collective strength of a candle. Bright fireflies move somnolently along the walls — scholars carrying hooded lamps which they use to peer into the shadowy nooks of the seemingly infinite book collection as they go about their research.

Random Encounters: Lightbringer's Highway

Roll 1d20 for every 20 minutes spent in the Lightbringer's Highway

1d20	Encounter
1	Lich
2	2d20 animated books[1]
3	1d4 swarms of eye spiders[1]
4	Repository scholar[1]
5	Corpulent attendant[1]
6	1d6 giant spiders
7	Horned devil
8	Salamander noble[1]
9	Normal petitioner[+]
10	Crazed petitioner[+]
11	1d4 violet funguses
12	2d4 gargoyles
13	1d6 + 1 harpies
14–20	No encounter

[+]The exact race and class of petitioners is left up to you to suit your campaign and personal take on the Repository and its petitioners.

The Repository Scholars

The Repository scholars[1] are the masters of the Great Repository. They wear heavy cotton, crimson-dyed robes trimmed with cracked leather imprinted with mystical symbols or fanciful aphorisms. Their skin is white to the point of translucence. Scholarly bodies are bent from a lifetime poring over thick tomes, and they have arms that are disproportionately sized, depending on which one the scholar uses for pulling books down from the shelves. Gnarly, brackish fingernails jut claw-like from the tips of their hands. Emerging from the scholars' flesh like so many abscesses are 10 to 100 petitioner-sacrificed eyes; each one is alive and moist, and all of them clearly filled with a delicate combination of fear and curiosity. Scholars are their own best company, always muttering or singing aloud regardless of who else may be within earshot. Some recite poetry in dead languages, while others tend to calculate impossibly complex mathematical formulas (one poor fellow actually does this in reverse).

When a scholar dies, his body is taken to the Kiln of Sorrows in the tower's lower levels. The smoke from the fire drifts out of the arm stretching the highest from the roof. Exactly one year later, another scholar appears in the library to take his place. The new one has no memory of previous lifetimes, nor does he have any of the memory or knowledge of the scholar he replaces. In fact, in the entire known history of the tower, there is just one scholar with any recollection of a life before coming to the tower: al'Hazrad (see **Area 15** in **Chapter 10** for more on al'Hazrad), the author of the *Book of al'Hazrad* (see **Chapter 21** for more information on the book). Coincidentally, al'Hazrad is also the only scholar in recent memory to escape from the tower without being affected by the Exile Gate. A scholar's life is filled with craving; they suffer an insatiable urge to learn. The aphorism "knowledge is power" is an absolute truth in the Great Repository, and the scholars exemplify this better than anyone.

Many scholars secretly hope to discover the key to their salvation from this prison of books. The only two practical ways they can leave offer no satisfaction: possession of a petitioner's body, or through the Exile Gate. Possession is a short-term solution as the scholars running around outside invariably end dead or hopelessly insane. On the other hand, the Exile Gate allows a scholar to leave the Repository on his own terms but the damage it does, both physically and mentally, make this an option few are willing to seriously consider.

The Eye Spiders

When a scholar answers a petitioner's question to the fullest extent of his ability, it no longer becomes necessary for him to continue wearing the petitioner's eye. The eye still functions, and, after it has been sewn together with a bunch of others and kept alive with magic, finds new life and purpose as an eye spider. An eye spider only vaguely resembles a real spider, with its long chains of haphazardly strung-together eyes acting as legs, and the lopsided, bloodshot globe made from the eye of a Huge or larger creature acting as its body.

Eye spiders help scholars (though never one who didn't create it) or are found crawling throughout the towers and shelves of books and papers. Individual eye spiders are easily dispatched; a **swarm of eye spiders**[1] on the other hand …

7. The Stacks

Books, scrolls, tomes, and parchments resting on their dilapidated, much-abused shelves collectively constitute the "stacks." Manuscripts come in all shapes, materials, sizes, and colors and they hail from practically every known plane of existence. Just about any mundane book ever published can be found here, as well as copies of most magical books, including spellbooks from especially renowned casters. The most powerful books can be found in the private rooms inside the pillar.

Books kept in the Repository tend to develop bizarre quirks over time (the scholars believe the tower liberates their innate personalities). Some quirks include bleeding, talking through a tiny *magic mouth* on the front cover, bat wings growing from the spine that allow it to fly about unless chained down, ever-smoldering pages, an embedded eye that always weeps liquid brass, covers bound in leathery human flesh, coarse animal fur, dusty reptilian scales, or all at the same time, and mirrored pages that reflect a reader's past lives back at her.

Encounters and Books

Roll 1d20 for every 10 minutes spent perusing the stacks to determine what encounter or type of book is discovered.

1d20	Encounter or Book
1	Corpulent attendant[1]
2	Repository scholar[1]
3	Normal petitioner[+]
4	Crazed petitioner[+]
5–12	Tome of general knowledge
13–16	Tome of high knowledge
17	1d4 swarms of eye spiders[1]
18–19	1d10 animated books[1]
20	Mimic

[+]The exact race and class of petitioners is left up to you GM to suit your campaign and personal take on the Repository and its petitioners.

Tomes of General Knowledge

Tomes of general knowledge are ordinary books on subjects such as war, religion, music and history. They are the sum of most mundane knowledge found throughout several planes as to the nature of the universe and the inhabitants within it. Studying one of these *tomes of general knowledge* thoroughly for one week grants advantage on future Intelligence checks related to that field of study.

Roll d10 on the following table to determine what sort of knowledge is found within a *tome of general knowledge*.

1d10	Text
1	Arcana
2	Architecture
3	Dungeoneering
4	History
5	Local lore (choose a region)
6	Nature
7	Nobility and royalty
8	Religion
9	Geography
10	The planes

Tomes of High Knowledge

Several sample ancient texts found within the Repository are described below. Many of these tomes are nonmagical, but extremely valuable and useful. They grant bonuses on certain skill checks and rarely grant bonuses higher than +1 or +2. Some contain a few spells (generally of 7th level or lower). Arcane spells contained within these texts can be learned by arcane casters.

You are encouraged to create their own tomes of knowledge.

Madness and Weakness: Ancient texts may be mind-warping, mentally stressful, or physically weakening due to their subject matter, the way they are written or crafted, or because of some powerful unknown curse associated with the text.

Sample Tomes of High Knowledge

Tomes of High Knowledge

The books follow the general format described below. Sections not pertinent to a book are omitted.

Title: This is the title of the book.

(Author): The author's name, if known, is listed beside the title in parenthesis.

Language: This lists the language (or languages) the book is scribed in. Some ancient texts require a successful Decipher Script check to read. These are noted in the text.

Saving Throw: Next is the saving throw to resist any damaging effect triggered by reading the text. Stat losses given for success/failure on saving throw.

Areas of Knowledge: The general area of knowledge covered by the tome. Characters reading this book gain the listed bonus on related skill checks (most often Intelligence) after reading the book. Such bonuses can be gained only once from a book (including its copies).

Spells: This area lists any spells contained in the tome.

Weight: How much the tome weighs

***The Analects of Sulymon the Wise, Vol. 23* (Prophet Musad):** Ancient Common (DC 18 Intelligence to decipher); History +2; contains *raise dead, resurrection,* and the epic spell seed *animate dead.* This seed can be used to construct a spell to free the janni skeletons of Dahish trapped within the Walls of the Petrified Dead on the Plane of Molten Skies; 4 pounds.

This massive tome contains various works, writings, prophecies, and teachings of Sulymon as penned by the Prophet Musad.

The Book of al'Hazrad (al'Hazrad): Ancient Common (DC 18 Intelligence to decipher); Wisdom DC 16 (2/1d6 Wis); The planes) +2; contains *planar ally* and *planar binding;* 3 pounds.

This tome is one of the most sought after books of occult lore found here. Its voluminous writings span just over 900 pages. Its author, al'Hazrad, is believed to be one of the few mortals who directly contacted the Elder Gods and survived the experience. The author is still alive and makes his residence on the Plane of Molten Skies.

The book begins with al'Hazrad's essays and ramblings on the Elder Gods, who are described as entities of great power who passed forbidden knowledge to mankind (knowledge of such things as fire, weapon-forging, war, magic, and so on). In exchange for this knowledge, the Elder Gods seek a channel into the universe where they can gain control and dominate the multitude of planes, worlds, and dimensions. Scholars disagree as to who the Elder Gods really are. Some say they are a collection of powerful races of efreet, djinn, jann, and marid, all evil, all in existence before time — the true genies. Others argue that the Elder Gods are in fact Iblis and his fallen angels, cast down from Heaven when they refused the commands of the gods of law.

The book is bound in soft brown leather; its page written on yellowed vellum with darkened ink. Adamantine straps keep the covers locked tight (requiring a key or a DC 25 Dexterity check with thieves' tools to open).

There are 14 known copies of this book.

***The Book of Eldritch Wizardry* (various):** Ancient Common (DC 18 Intelligence to decipher); Arcana +3; contains all known arcane spells of levels 0 through 9th; 5 pounds.

When the formulae in this book are used to craft magic items, determine cost and time based on an item of one lower level of rarity.

Few books in the mortal worlds are as much sought after as this one. Contained within this book's pages are ancient formulae for constructing and deconstructing spells, rituals, powerful and mundane magic items, and some say, artifacts. It said that everyone who has ever owned a copy has contributed to the original in some way or another. Adding pages to a copy creates a corresponding page in the original. As might be expected, the original *Book of Eldritch Wizardry* is thousands of pages thick, though to all appearances it looks like a small book. Its cover is made from supple, white leather. Inscribed upon it is a stylized ink sketch of a scantily clad sorceress kneeling in a magic circle before a rune-inscribed altar.

There are seven known copies of this book, five in the Repository, and two scattered across the planes in unknown locations.

***The Book of the Justicars* (various):** Common and Celestial; Planar knowledge +1, Religion +1; contains the spells: *antimagic field, chant[1], dispel evil and good, divine favor, flame strike, freedom of movement, hold monster, holy aura, magic weapon, mind blank, power word kill, power word stun, protection from energy, protection from evil and good, protection from poison, sanctuary, shield of faith, spirit guardians, spiritual weapon,* and *stoneskin;* 3 pounds.

This ancient text is the holy book of Muir, the Goddess of Virtue and Paladinhood. Several copies are known to exist.

The Book of Luminique (Lavorian): Fey; Nature +2; contains *entangle, barkskin, conjure woodland beings;* 2 pounds.

In addition gaining a bonus on Intelligence checks related to nature and the fey, the reader gains advantage on Charisma-based checks when dealing with fey creatures.

This tome was written by the magician Lavorian at the request of his wife, Luminique, the Fey Queen. It records the history of many of the races of fey, their treaties and wars with the unseelie fey, and other such bits of information.

***The Book of Jabb bin Jabaar* (Azul bin Berith):** Efreeti; Wisdom DC 16 (0/1d6 Wis); Planar knowledge +2; contains the spells *planar ally* and *greater planar ally;* 40 pounds.

This large tome bound in heavy bronze is actually one of two copies that serve as permanent gateways for passage between the two books, no matter their plane, location, or any shielding toward planar or magical travel. The other copy of this book currently resides in the possession of Sheikh Azul bin Berith of the Bayt al Najoom (see **Area 37** of **Chapter 13**), but knowledge of this fact is a strict secret known only to himself and his eldest son Abdul al Azul (who is currently imprisoned in the Minaret of Screams).

Travel through the book is not without its dangers. Each time the passageway is used for travel between the two books, the travelers are subjected to two effects. First, travelers are subjected to the Wisdom damaging effects of the book if they fail a Wisdom save. Second, they are subject to attack by the demon imprisoned within the book, Jabb bin Jabaar (**Hezrou Demon** with barbed scourge that deals 19 (4d6 + 5) slashing damage each time it hits. Damage taken by his scourge cannot be healed by any means of magic save for a *wish* and must be healed through natural rest.). The soul of a creature slain by bin Jabaar is devoured by the demon and the physical body is spit out the other side of the book. The body rises as a zombie under the control of Jabb bin Jabaar in 1d4 rounds.

If Jabb bin Jabaar is slain, his form dissipates in a puff of acrid black smoke. His body reforms at full strength 1 hour later. Only by destroying both copies of the book can Jabb bin Jabaar be truly slain.

***The City of Pillars* (Talib):** Ancient Common (DC 18 Intelligence to decipher): History +1, Planar knowledge +1; 3 pounds.

This ancient text was written by Talib, a muqarribun (wizard), and details the mystic City of Pillars; a city constructed by the Arna (djinn who came before mortals) and believed to be an extraplanar gateway between this multiverse and the Void where the Elder Gods (or Old Ones) dwell. The book records the name of one of the Elder Gods: Abduxuel.

***The Dreaming Scrolls* (Kalath):** Common; Wisdom DC 15 (1/1d6 Wis); Planar knowledge +2; contains *astral projection, etherealness, teleport;* 1 lb.

These four scrolls detail the Realm of Dreams — an extraplanar dimension existing solely in the space of sleep. The scrolls tell of the Moth King, a prisoner in the Manse of the Red Cenobite, who encourages his minions in the real world to do what they can to keep sleep at bay — not just for themselves, but for all creatures. By planting the seeds of nightmare and insomnia, they seek to bring about "The Sleepless Night" — a moment in time when no single creature sleeps. By doing so, the Realm of Dreams collapses and the Moth King will be set free.

There is a 1% chance that anyone reading these scrolls is plagued with visions of the Realm of Dreams. A plagued creature who sleeps pulls a creature from that realm into the real world. Choose an aberration, monstrosity or some other creature of your desire. The summoned creature attacks anyone in sight and disappears when slain.

There are 12 known copies of these scrolls. All copies are in the Repository.

Gone with the Djinn (Margell): Auran; History +1; contains *expeditious retreat, planar binding, magic jar, wind walk*; 4 pounds.

This heavy book tells the tale of forbidden love between an efreeti princess and a djinni prince, the ensuing wars between their races, and their ultimate flight from it all. The pages are thin and light while the cover is formed of hardened leather stretched tight over wooden planks that serve as its covers. Bronze locks seal the book closed requiring a DC 17 Dexterity check with thieves' tools to open.

The Plane of Molten Skies (Khazzid): Ignan; Wisdom DC 12 (0/1d4 Wis); Planar knowledge +2; contains *plane shift* and *conjure elemental*; 3 pounds.

This fabled tome penned by the mad mage Khazzid details the path to the fabled City of Brass.

Tome of the Undead (Magden the Black): Common; Constitution DC 16 (1/1d4 Con); Religion +2; contains *animate dead, create undead, hallow, magic jar, banishment*; 4 pounds.

A recent addition to the library here, this book is an extensive treatise on creating and animating skeletons and zombies, transforming corpses into undead, creating mummies, and trapping freshly slain souls before they reach their afterlife destination. Formulae on becoming a lich are also contained within the pages. (The exact formula is left up to you to suit your campaign).

This tome is written on blackened flesh bound by the bones of slain humanoids. The cover is formed from the burned flesh of a vampire.

Viscerterica (Reynan): Common; Wisdom DC 16 (1d2/1d6 Wis); Anatomy +1, Torture +1; contains *symbol* (pain); 2 pounds.

This rare tome was written several hundred years ago by a n'gathau spellcaster. The book's contents describe in great detail the art of torture, self-mutilation, sadism, and masochism.

The reader gains expertise (allowing a doubling of the proficiency bonus) in one weapon with which the reader is proficient. Further, the book opens a passageway to the Plane of Agony (home of the n'gathau). Passage through the book and into the Plane of Agony requires the traveler to mutilate his or her body with a single-bladed weapon for 1 full minute (taking 1 point of damage each round). After 1 minute, the creature loses 1d2 points of Charisma and 1 point of Constitution (both caused from the act of self-mutilation). The passageway then opens for that creature only.

The book's covers are hammered flat pieces of steel covered with blackened and scarred flesh that has been crudely stitched together. The pages are bound by sinew and corded muscle and are written on the dried skin of a thousand tortured creatures.

Perusal of a book generally does not trigger the effect. Studying or copying text (including spells) from it does, however. Maddening effects damage the reader's Wisdom score and require a Wisdom saving throw to avoid. Weakening effects damage the reader's Constitution score and require a Constitution saving throw to avoid.

Wisdom damage is listed as follows: "x/y" where "x" is the ability damage taken (if any) on a successful save and "y" is the ability damage taken on a failed save. A few tomes deal permanent ability drain rather than damage. These are noted in the text.

8. The Wailing Walls

Before a scholar can undergo a soul swap with a petitioner from the outside world, he must first descend to the bottom of the tower where it is darkest. Here, all the walls are cleared of all books, bookcases, and detritus, and heavy iron manacles are bolted to the walls. The sounds of ghostly whispering fill the air, the same ones that can be heard outside the tower.

A scholar must be chained for the duration of his soul swap so that the petitioner inhabiting his body cannot run amok within the Repository walls. Chained soul swappers manage to break loose every once in a while, causing the scholars incredible distress. Chained soul swappers, unaccustomed to the sights and sounds of the tower, often weep, wail, scream, shout, and laugh maniacally.

A soul-swapped character chained to the wall must make a DC 22 Wisdom save once per day or be adversely affected by the whispers, the effects of which are described in the **Whispering Walls** above. A character who leaves the vicinity of the Wailing Walls no longer needs to make saving throws against the whispers as the tower's magic shields against them.

9. The Private Stacks

These are the rooms inside the pillar in the library that contain tomes and papers meant only for specific people. Only one scholar has the

keys to all the rooms. When a certain room needs to be accessed, he judges the petitioner's merit. If deemed worthy, and the petitioner makes an additional sacrifice of 2,000 bp to 10,000 bp, she is granted access to the knowledge within. Payment can be made in the form of coin or magic items donated to the library. Once the petitioner has made the appropriate donation, a high-ranking and trusted scholar is assigned the case, under *geas* that he immediately forgets information gathered once the petitioner's demand has been met.

The entrances to the private stacks are caged with a permanent force cage. Scholars are immune to the effects of the force cage and may enter and leave the private stacks at will but others must cast *dispel magic* against a Level 9 spell slot or in some other way dismiss the magical barrier. A pair of **corpulent attendants**[1] stands before each entrance, barring the passage to all except scholars.

Tomes of Forbidden Knowledge within the Private Stacks

These tomes are similar to the tomes of knowledge found in The Stacks (see above), but unlike the others, these books are highly magical in nature and some could be considered (or are in fact) relics and artifacts. They are powerful books, often granting great power to those who read their pages. But with power comes a cost, and most of these tomes have some powerful side effects that affect those delving into them.

They follow the same general format as the previously detailed tomes of knowledge.

Cultes de Ghuls (**Klarkazton Wormious**): Ancient Common (DC 18 Intelligence to decipher); Constitution DC 16 (1/1d4 Con); Religion +2; contains *ghoul touch*[4]; strong necromancy; CL 20th; 5 pounds.

This tome is a treatise on ghouls as written by the insane necromancer Klarkazton Wormious. The first part of this volume contains general information on ghouls, their habits, techniques used to combat them, and so on. The second portion of the book contains ghoul-related magic and rituals that grant the reader ghoulish benefits.

Each ritual requires a sacrifice when first performed. Note that Constitution points sacrificed for a ritual do not heal naturally and cannot be healed magically short of a *wish*. The book contains the following rituals.

Command the Dead: The reader gains the ability to *command* up to 5 ghouls within sight with a DC of 8 + Charisma modifier + proficiency bonus. This ability can be used a number of times per day equal to 3 + the character's Charisma modifier. *Sacrifice:* 2 points of Constitution.

Eater of Flesh: From this point forward, by consuming the flesh of a living creature, the character heals as if affected by a *cure wounds* spell. It takes 1 minute to cut away and consume enough flesh to gain the healing benefit. A character can heal a maximum number of hit points per day equal to the character's level x Charisma modifier. *Sacrifice:* 2 points of Constitution.

Bite of the Ghoul: The character gains a bite attack that deals 1d4 + Strength or Dexterity modifier and delivers *ghoul fever*[4]. A person bit by this attack must succeed on a DC 14 Constution saving throw or succumb to the disease. The bite attack is gained as a bonus action. *Sacrifice:* 2 points of Constitution. The character also gains +1 to Charisma from this ritual.

Empower the Grave: When casting *create undead*, the character can create a number of ghouls equal to 1 + Charisma modifier. Further, ghouls created by the spellcaster have maximum hit points for their Hit Dice and have advantage on saving throws to resist being turned while the caster is in sight. *Sacrifice:* 4 points of Constitution. The character also gains +1 to Charisma from this ritual.

Death to Undeath: A caster that slays an opponent using necromantic magic can use one spell slot of 6th level or higher to immediately raise that opponent as a ghoul under the caster's command. The risen ghoul is a standard ghoul but has maximum hit points for its HD, +4 Strength, and advantage on saving throws to resist being turned while the caster is in sight. It retains none of the abilities the opponent had in life. The ghoul remains under the character's command until slain or the caster dies. *Sacrifice:* 4 points of Constitution. The character also gains +1 to Charisma score from this ritual.

A character that dies by sacrificing all Constitution points for the rituals contained in this book rises in 1 hour as an **iron ghoul**.

This is the only known copy of this book.

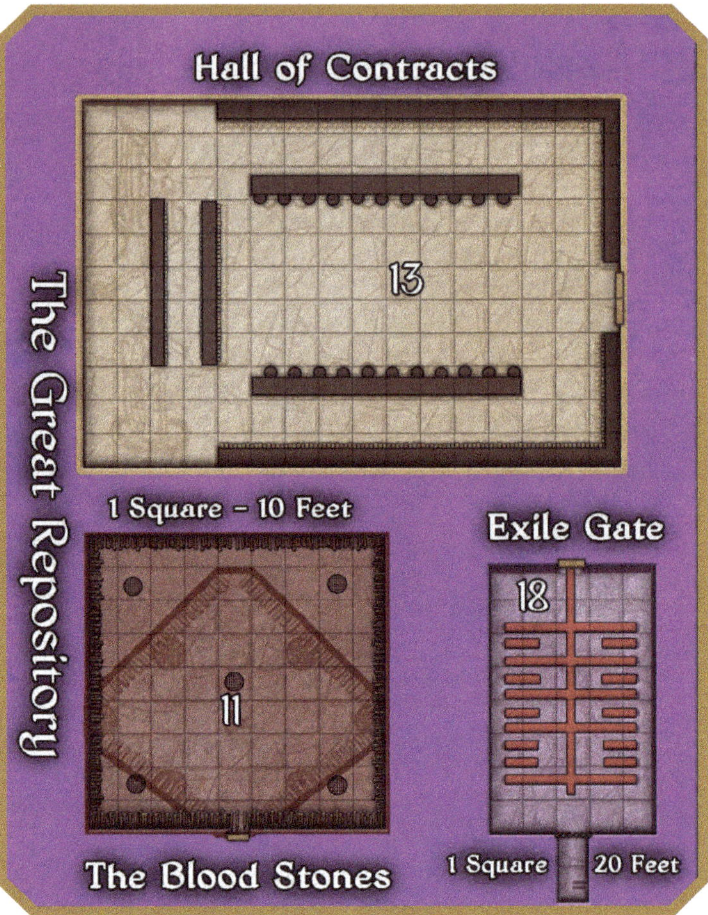

10. The Scrying Bell

This room is made entirely of crystalline glass. Any sound made while within it sets off a chain reaction of musical tones. A person proficient in Performance can attempt to control the tones by making a DC 25 Charisma (Performance) check. If successful, the character can control the room, thereby tapping into the innate scrying magic contained here. The scrying bell can show a person any event at any point in history on any plane.

However, using the bell comes at a price. For each round spent *scrying*, a character must make a DC 18 Constitution saving throw or be blinded and deafened for 1 day (this applies to a petitioner experiencing the room through a scholar's body). Moreover, as soon as the character leaves the room (or in a petitioner's case, as soon as the scholar bearing the character's eye leaves it), the character must succeed on a DC 22 Intelligence saving throw or forget everything seen and heard while scrying.

There is a cumulative 5% chance per round of scrying that the Sultan becomes aware that someone is using this particular instrument of his power. In this instance, the Sultan causes a reflection of himself to appear upon the walls of the Scrying Bell. This reflection appears exactly as the Sultan himself does, resplendent in his jewels of office and diaphanous veil. On the next round, the image steps from the bell and attacks. The image has the same HD, classes, special abilities, feats, and so on of the one who triggered the image. Any damage done to the image is actually taken by the one who triggered the image (that is, the last one to use the Scrying Bell).

The attacks cease when the individual who triggered the image flees the chamber. Characters are allowed a DC 20 Intelligence saving throw to recognize that the image is a partial illusion and that they are actually battling one of their own. Creatures who are knocked unconscious or die here (and not retrieved by allies) are eventually cremated in the Kiln of Sorrows.

11. The Blood Stones

Some tales can only be told in the blood that was spilled during their creation. This area is a perfectly square room with thick, heavy, granite walls that are stained a dark black color from millennia of blood running down them. Grilled gutters line the bases of the walls, their holes clogged with dried, clotted blood. Hundreds of rusty levers cover the walls. Moving a lever requires a DC 24 Strength check. Each lever can be moved into thousands of different positions, in either direction, and each position relates one tale. As soon as a lever moves, fresh blood pours down the walls from tiny holes in the ceiling. To a person with the knowledge or magic for reading blood, this room is a veritable treasure trove of knowledge and secrets.

The blood of the late Sultana can be found here, but only two people know both the lever and position to call it forth. Who those two are has been forgotten. There is a 1% chance per 8 hours spent working the levers that a character actually finds the correct position and lever to call forth the blood of the Sultana and relate her tale to the characters. Otherwise, feel free to develop any stories applicable to your campaign from whichever direction the lever is turned.

12. Bone Room

While some things can only be learned from blood, other kinds of information come from the salt of life: bone. This rough-hewn cavern seems endless, though that isn't so much because of its raw size (it's actually rather cramped). The sheer volume of bones permeating the winding, narrow corridors is endless. Skulls are embedded in walls. Arm bones hang from the ceilings. Leg bones line the floors. Rib bones stand or hang as stalagmites and stalactites. To a person with the knowledge or magic for reading bones, this room is a veritable treasure trove of knowledge and, more importantly, secrets.

Among the many bones within this chamber is the ankle bone of Tlaunehc Tnek. Should it ever be returned to its place among Tlaunehc Tnek's other parts guarded within the Palace of Wonders (see **Chapter 31**) Tlaunehc shall rise again. Woe to the universe should that day come.

The Bone Room is protected from theft by Ishapsip the Demilich (**advanced demilich**[1]). Ishapsip does not bother with scholars and those seeking knowledge from the tangled bones of his lair. However, any attempt to remove one of the bones causes him to instantly attack.

13. Hall of Contracts

This is the realm of legality. Every contract ever made, whether written or verbal, implicit or explicit, has a copy written on papyrus here. The room is made from beautifully cut sandstone inscribed with swarms of hieroglyphs describing the Ten Great Law Codices taken from all over the multiverse. Scroll and bookcases bearing the contracts are set firmly between the long lines of sandstone pillars supporting the unusually high roof. A **pit fiend** named Maximillian and a **planetar** named Handrizael stand at the rear of the chamber atop a large platinum scale suspended from the arched ceiling.

The two dire foes see that no piece of law is stolen from this chamber and that only copies are ever made. The two despise one another but are compelled by rule of law to defend this chamber from violation. They cannot under any means (magical or otherwise) be forced to fight each other.

When the answer to a legal question cannot be found among the limitless volumes lining the walls of the hall of contracts, the angel and devil may be approached with the question. The two debate the issue and each gives an equally logical legal argument in defense or opposition of the question.

There are 30 ghostly scribes within this chamber who — as well as being legal experts one and all — also hold the job of copying every document within the Repository onto copper sheets.

Spending at least one full week studying the contracts and legal documents within this chamber grants the reader advantage on future Intelligence checks related to law.

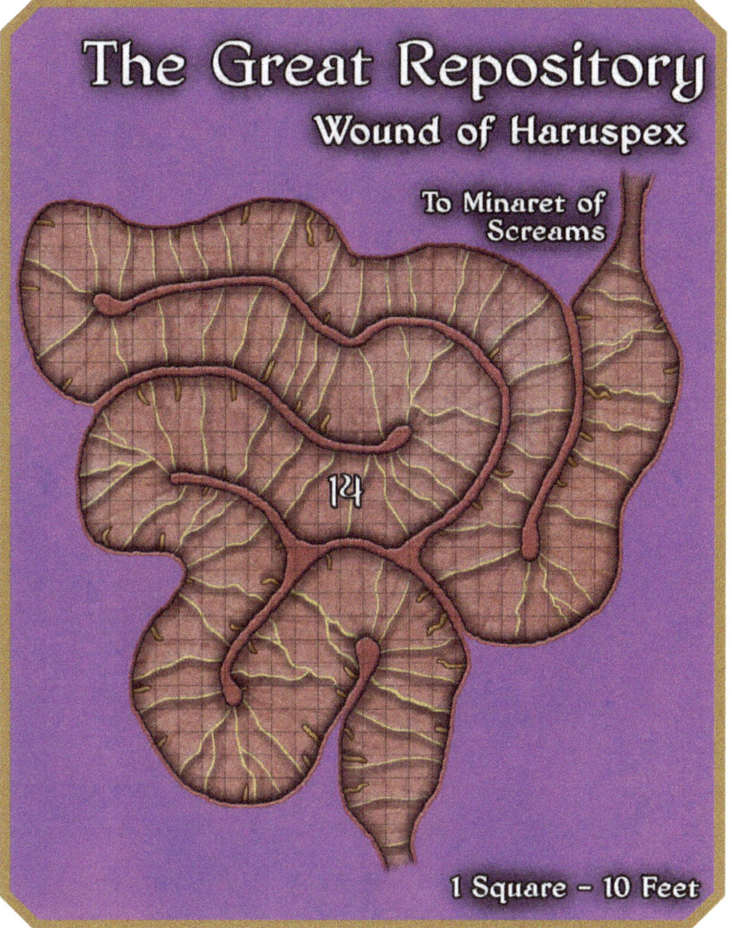

14. Wound of the Haruspex

The entry to this room is a long, fleshy, and moist tunnel. A person who actually enters the room itself is covered in fluid and blood. Dim light pierces the dense tissue making up its walls, casting a very weak glow into the chamber. Long, ropey tendrils of intestine, anchored to the walls, float languidly throughout the chamber. Wispy crimson veins, threads of yellowish fat, and pale white membranes cling like haloes to them. Occasionally, a chubby, baby-sized golem made of air-inflated intestinal segments tied crudely together in humanoid form swims past. These creatures are unapproachable, and their purpose here is an utter mystery to everyone, including the scholars.

A character does not need magic to breathe here, since the fluid magically lets a character acquire oxygen through the skin. A character with knowledge or magic that allow the reading of intestines may make use of this room. Somewhere within the Wound resides a **purple worm** who feasts on fools who enter here. The worm was created by a maddened scholar and soon became its first meal. There is a cumulative 10% chance per minute spent in the Wound that the purple worm appears and attacks. At the end of the chamber lies a passage that leads to the Appendix within the **Minaret of Screams.**

15. The Brass Mirror

Before the current Sultan took over the reins of power, each leader before him held a private ritual on the eve of his ascension wherein he would look into the large brass mirror hanging in the entry foyer of his palace to reflect on his deeds and actions for the past year. This room possesses an exact duplicate of that mirror, magically recording the Sultan's reflections for both posterity and for the benefit of future generations. The mirror doesn't record the Sultan's every thought, but instead just those he has while performing the aforementioned ritual. The one exception to the rule of payment that the Repository has is with regard to this room. A Sultan may come to the Petitioner's Hall any time he deigns with the express purpose of consulting the Brass Mirror. Rather than sacrifice an eye, or make a donation, he instead places a crude brass circlet upon his brow (said to be the first crown of the City of Brass) and consults the mirror directly. This works only for the Sultan. The circlet usually sits on the empty throne at the back of the hall. The current Sultan has not yet worn the circlet.

16. Words of Creation

According to legend, when Iblis was cast down from the heavens, he took with him the Words of Creation, sacred utterances made by the Creator in the first moments of the universe's existence. Some scholars say you can still hear faint echoes of those Words as they continue to ring down through time. Others concur, adding that when the Words finally fall silent, existence will cease. Not even Iblis can verify the truth of these conceits, but then neither can he debunk them. This room, occupying an entire floor at the very top of the Great Repository, has the ten words written down on parchment made from the flesh of archangels, cured in the blood of the Creator's first progeny, and preserved with light taken from the souls of the ten messiahs.

The room is made from the purest ivory taken from the mouths of star whales. The floors, walls, and ceilings are pristine, unmarred by time, unaffected by weather, and unscathed by mortal hands. A fountain made from solid mithral is in the middle of the room. Ornate etchings display the 10,000 lesser names, listing the Creator's favored sentient humanoid species across the fabric of the multiverse. A continuous stream of crisp, ice-cold water flows through the fountain. Drinking it grants the imbiber a single unconditional *wish*. A mortal may benefit from the fountain only once per lifetime. *Wishes* cannot possibly be given to petitioners by means of the scholars drinking on their behalf. This wish may be used to discern the true name of the Sultan of Efreeti, which is Nomylus, Ibn al Kabith, Ibn al Nar, Ibn al Shaitan, Ibn al Fajarah, Ibn al Munkar, Ibn al Maakir, Ibn al Dajjal

Standing vigil around the fountain are 10 **mithral golems**[1], their eyes burning with the fire of intelligence. The etchings covering their bodies, like so many fanciful tattoos, provide them with immunity to all divine magic. Embedded in the chest of each one is a single dark gemstone upon which is inscribed a single Word.

Words appear unique to every individual who has ever seen them. Scholars have spent many lifetimes staring at one Word only to be frustrated but their inability to decipher even a part of it. In all of history, only three Words have ever been unlocked. The individuals who succeeded couldn't cope with what they learned and were driven to a state far worse than death.

The first, a wizard whose name has been lost over time, slowly "unraveled" until he became nothing. The second was a midwife known only as Fira who transformed into a new world, her soul possessing it to this day. The third, a dragon from the First Age of Man, suffered the unmaking and ceased to exist for all time.

Some scholars think the only way to control the power imparted by the Words of Creation is to decipher them all simultaneously. As such, it is not unusual to occasionally find a scholar with nine simulacra staring intently at the golems' chests in their vain attempts to learn them (often they do this at the behest of petitioners.)

Living in the room are 4 **solars**. They, too, spend time studying the Words, but their real purpose here is to ensure that the scholars don't get up to any mischief, especially the ones possessed by outsiders (outsiders here meaning those not native to the Repository). In fact, it is not entirely unheard of for them to deny access to the fountain because of their suspicions.

The Words of Creation cannot be moved from their cradles, though that hasn't stopped people from trying. Presumably, the statue guardians are there to act as deterrents, but in all the centuries the golems have been in this room, they haven't budged a single inch.

17. The Kiln of Sorrows

This series of chambers within the bowels of the Great Repository serve as crematoria of deceased scholars and as a disposal place for various trash cast down the disposal chutes from the Upper and Middle cities. Within the actual blast furnace of the Kiln itself is the Firebox, which serves as the prison of the Builders.

17-A. The Defrayed Stacks

Old tomes deemed unusable by the scholars due to wear and tear are piled here for disposal in the Kiln of Sorrows. Each has been painstakingly copied by scribes in the hall of contracts before its disposal. 1d6 **corpulent attendants**[1] push hand cars along an iron track to the Kiln of Sorrows from here. Occasionally, a corpse from the Repository belonging to a beast or dead scholar is brought here to be disposed of. Among the documents to be destroyed are some *spell scrolls* containing cold-based spells and those spells used to create water or control weather.

Treasure: *spell scrolls* of *cone of cold* (x6), *sleet storm* (x4), *control water*, *control weather*, *create or destroy water* (x3), *ice storm* (x2), *protection from energy* (fire).

17-B. Rubbish Heap

Similar to the Defrayed Stacks, this room is piled with rubbish cast down shafts built along the walls of the outer walls of the Repository along the Upper and Middle cities. All trash is ground and sliced before reaching the rubbish heap by a series of razor-sharp blades lining the shaft that deal 70 (20d6) slashing damage, most likely ensuring that whatever (or whoever) reaches the bottom of the shaft is quite destroyed or dead upon impact. The entrances to the shafts are further guarded by **fire giant** patrols that make sure that the shafts are not used to dispose of murder victims unless properly bribed. 1d6 **corpulent attendants**[1] haul the tons of trash poured down the shaft in pushcarts along the iron track to the Kiln of Sorrows.

Treasure: Piled among the rubbish and trash are a *frost brand* (longsword), 2 *+1 daggers*, *boots of speed*, and 500 bp.

17-C. The Kiln of Sorrows

This chamber is intensely hot. Literally a blast furnace with a gated Firebox in the center, tomes and refuse dumped here fuel the flames produced by 6 **elder fire elementals**[1] and 66 **fire mephits**[1]. The mephits and elementals stoke the fires surrounding the Firebox to ensure the heat of the chamber is constantly concentrated upon it and the prisoners locked within.

The firebox serves as the prison of Shad, Mesh, and Abed (**The Builders**[1]), the ancient architects of the Repository, known to those few who have heard of them as the Builders. These antediluvian seers and wise men were the first among humans to understand and begin worship of the gods. As ancient folk, they were blessed with long lives and great wisdom. Tricked by Iblis, they were brought to the City of Brass to construct the Repository. They

labored long in the process before recognizing the evil of his intent. It was these seers who inscribed the Law of King Horadin upon the outer surface of the Repository as a reminder to Iblis to keep his pact with the gods. Upon seeing their sleight, Iblis threw the seers in chains and constructed the Kiln of Sorrows with which to burn the upstart sages. The first fuel he chose to power the Kiln was the Builders themselves. After depopulating their home plane, he burned every religious text and every living creature. Opening the firebox, he expected to find only ashes, but much to his horror the Builders remained untouched by the heat of the flames. Slamming the door upon them, he fled the Repository never to return.

The Builders are unable to escape on their own, and still reside within the firebox to this day, untouched by the flames, having only their faith in the gods to feed and protect them.

The doors to the firebox may be opened only by a *holy aura* uttered by a cleric of at least 20th level. The firebox itself, however, may be shattered by the following series of events:

If no fuel is added to the Kiln, the fire elementals and mephit are destroyed, and the chamber flooded with water, the firebox breaks apart, freeing the wise men.

Once freed, the Builders are thankful to their rescuers and proclaim that they will fulfill one single desire (a *wish* given them by their gods to grant to their rescuers) of the characters before ascending to their souls' rest among the gods. Whatever this desire may be is up to the characters. It could be as simple as resurrecting a fallen comrade or offering them the true name of the Sultan of Efreet[1]. Likewise, the Builders may read aloud the Law of King Horadin scribed upon the outer walls of the Repository and bring down the apocalypse upon the City of Brass. See Finishing Adventures in the Great Repository for further details.

18. The Exile Gate

As everyone knows, only one door leads into the Great Repository's interior. It is the door through which exiled scholars leave. It is built into the tower on the opposite side as the door to the entry foyer and doesn't so much resemble a gate as it does a fine line drawing of one. While yellow lines connote where the entrance should be, there is naught but the image of one. Nobody can remember ever seeing the gate let someone in, although plenty of people remember seeing it let a scholar or two out. It glows brightly, like a small sun, and then the light winks out of existence. Moments later, the exile comes tumbling out. If he is lucky, a passing merchant on a flying rug catches him, or he is not so disoriented that he can still manage to fire off a *fly* or *levitate* spell. Those who do live still end up enslaved to it, as described below. Those maddened scholars who have swapped souls with a character may very well flee the Repository through this gateway.

The room behind the door is a mirror image of the Petitioner's Hall. However, unlike its counterpart, the Exile Gate is completely uninhabited. Scholars provide light with their magic when they must come here. None like to, because their presence in the room means one of them will be cast out before the meeting concludes. Invariably, a scholar who loses his mind and becomes a threat to the sanctity of the Repository's knowledge can no longer be trusted. So rather than kill one of their own, the scholars banish him to the outside world. Other scholars recognize early on that they can't live inside the tower, so it is not unusual for them to ask for banishment. The presence of every scholar is required to open the gate. They must all speak the key word simultaneously. When they do, the door in the outer wall opens as described above. A pair of scholars then escorts the exile to the door. When the exile steps into it, it shuts behind him and the tower itself casts him out. The congregated scholars then return to their routine, most grateful to be away from the hated room though there are always one or two newly created malcontents, who, after seeing the city so closely, yearn for freedom.

Exile from the Great Repository is not as simple as being thrown from it, unfortunately. The gate transforms an exile's soul, stripping from it the experiences and memories of the person's time inside. A side effect of this is that the exile craves proximity to the tower. He cannot physically exist away from the tower for more than a couple of days, at best. The farther an exile goes from it, the worse he becomes until he eventually dies. An exile can wander up to 2,000 feet from the tower before suffering any ill effects. After that, the exile becomes ill and dies in 2d4 hours unless he comes back within 2,000 feet of the Great Repository.

Souk Exsul

The city's Basin is a virulent, disgusting morass of buildings, shanties, and slave pens. Only those with the worst lot in life live down there and usually for not very long. Strangely enough, the area immediately surrounding the base of the Great Repository is utterly devoid of any normal inhabitants. If there ever were any, it is widely presumed that the whispering walls drove them insane and ran them off. Even the nastiest slave owners are reticent to keep their slaves anywhere within 500 feet of the tower. However, a small collection of refugees from inside the Repository lives in and around the tower's base. They are scholarly men, women, and other sundry things that managed to escape. The tower's mystical connection to them is much too strong to deny for very long. Therefore, they live as close to it as possible, feeding their addiction from inside caves carved out of the bloody ordure coating it. The few who try to get farther away from it invariably suffer wracking mental anguish. The refugees (**master bard**[1]) call themselves "The Exsul," or "exiles" in the ancient scholars' language. They wrap their bodies and heads in tattered black garments. Just their eyes remain visible, disturbing, milky orbs that know no focus.

Their territory, known as "Souk Exsul" (The Exile Bazaar), is a place where people come to reclaim forgotten memories and forbidden knowledge — for a price. Despite the fact that the exiles no longer live inside the Repository, they are still able to leech power from it for their own purposes. They are master information brokers, and information is a valuable commodity in the city. A person who wants to recover a lost or forgotten memory must permanently sacrifice an existing one (of the Exsul's choosing … and there are very few things in life more disgusting than having the Exsul sift through your head). If someone requests knowledge to which he or she has no right, or desires a memory taken from another person, then negotiations are heavy and the price is always steep.

At seemingly random times, the Exsul articulate the whispers shed by the tower walls loud enough for the whole neighborhood to hear. Their malformed singing, agonized shrieking, and hypnotic chanting drive lesser people insane. Slaves have been known to hammer spikes into their ears in futile attempts to stop the sound from entering their heads, while others have ripped out their own tongues rather than ever risk repeating the alien words burnt into their brains. The Exsul, of course, are immune to the effects of the Whispering Walls.

Listening to an Exsul as it speaks the words of the Whispering Walls is the same as listening to the walls themselves.

---

*Note: See **Area 1** for details.*

Completing Adventures in the Great Repository

If the characters' goal was to uncover the true name of the Sultan of Efreet[1] and they succeed, Tarbish is pleased and suggests they use this knowledge to explore the City of the Dead Sultana, where great weapons may be gained by those who know the name of the Usurper. As part of a standard campaign, the Repository may also serve as a storehouse of knowledge for any information the characters have been seeking. You could offer the Repository and its strange guardians as a means by which to uncover this forbidden lore.

Chapter 22
City of the (Dead) Sultana

This chapter details the dead zone surrounding the tomb of the former Sultana of the City of Brass, a lifeless platform within the purview of the Walls of the Palace of the Sultan. It is a place where efreeti won't tread for fear of repercussion and instant death. Demon gates bound by the Grand Vizier keep thrill-seekers out as best they can. None who has entered its demesne since the darkening has returned to tell the tale. As part of an ongoing City of Brass campaign, the City of the Dead Sultana offers characters the chance to explore the Sultana's cursed gardens, to parlay with the spirit of Saaid al Djinn[1] and to acquire the *ruby star of law*[2] or the *eyes of the Sultana*[2], or to possibly activate the jade colossus, which is fashioned in the likeness of the Dead Sultana herself.

Characters may be sent to the City of the Dead Sultana by Chufa Um Sophanie, who seeks to resurrect her mistress. Others include Ard who seeks to pollute or possess her body, and Tarbish, who would resurrect the Sultana then force her into marriage with him, tying the bloodlines of true efreet and djinn. Rah'po Dehj sees the opportunity to use the eyes, brain, and jade colossus as a super weapon.

This adventure is suggested for Tier 4 characters.

The City of The Dead Sultana

High walls guarded by demon gates surround this darkened platform that never sees the light of the brilliant fires of the Plane of Molten Skies and the Plane of Fire. Plants with tall silvery fronds rise above the edge of the walls, unusual in the fact that they seem to grow and thrive despite the fact that they receive no light. Beyond the dense foliage, the tips of an onion-domed palace reach shadow-like over the oppressive walls. Nearest the wall, the dark outline of a colossal figure can be made out, but any detail of its surface is lost in benighted mystery. It is noted that the efreeti and others who live in the City of Brass avoid the City of the Dead Sultana like the plague, swearing that it is a place of ghosts and death. Under no circumstances will a citizen of the City of Brass enter the City of the Dead Sultana; rather, if trouble seems to be coming from that section of the city, they wait a safe distance away to apprehend anyone brave enough to pass its demon gates.

The City of the Dead Sultana encompasses an entire platform of several square miles and is filled with night palms and overgrown with other flora and fauna that grow magically despite the darkness hanging over the region.

Demon Gates

Like other **demon gates**[1] in the city, these are each bound with the trapped spirit of a balor. The demon is reduced to its purest essence of evil, contorted and conformed into a massive horned head upon a thickly corded neck. A demon gate is immobile but strikes with its wickedly long tongue. If the tongue grabs a character, the character is reeled in and bitten by the gate's demonic visage.

The demon gates may be passed only by someone bearing the *demon key*[2], which is currently in the possession of the Grand Vizier. Otherwise, the gates must be defeated in order to gain passage. A defeated demon gate reforms into a new demon gate within 30 hours.

Within the City

Beyond the demon gates rise a darkened wilderness, overgrown and jungle-like with vegetation from what once must have been a fantastic hanging garden. Artificial streams fall from mermaid-shaped spouts in the sides of a fortress-like palace that stands atop a tall hill in the center of the overgrown district, their water eventually captured in unseen reservoirs and pumped back through the structures. The outlines of ruins rise to the southwest and a tall conical spire rises from the foliage to the northeast. A red glow from the top of the spire casts the only light outside the dimmed fire-orange of the city that can be seen rimming the edges of the entire platform. Dominating the skyline of the southern section of the City of the Dead Sultana is a colossal solid jade statue nearly 100 feet tall. Its empty eye sockets stare impassively across the City of Brass.

Gardens of the Sultana

Overgrown plants, long left untended, tangle and knot the lower slopes of the hill that marks the palace grounds. Characters moving through the gardens do so at one-half their normal movement rate. Neither bird calls nor the sounds of animals are heard in the brush. The silence is unnerving to those accustomed to the sounds of primeval forest and jungle.

These gardens were once rich and vibrant with life, built by the previous sultan to please his new bride. Abundant fruits grew here, and songbirds of every color flitted from tree trunk to tree trunk. Now everything seems to possess nothing but shades of gray, as if everything green and healthy has been leeched away to leave only memory and decay of the grandeur that was once evident.

The gardens are now a place where dead things hunt for the living, and grumble in their hunger. Even some of the plants themselves are undead, waiting for any living thing to lie itself down upon the loam and rot for their dinner. Some of the plants do not wait, but actively seek to snare any would-be explorer of the Sultana's garden. A roving band of undead hyaenodons haunts this area, feeding on those foolish enough to wander into their domain.

Random Encounters: The Gardens of the Sultana

Roll 1d20 for every 10 minutes spent exploring the Gardens of the Sultana.

1d20	Encounter
1–2	1d4 ghul efreet[1]
3	1d4 oblivion wraiths[1]
4–5	1d4 night terrors[1]
6	10 specters
7	1d6 bodaks priests[1]
8	2 vampiric treants[1]
9	2 glabrezu demons
10	1d4 + 1 undead hyaenodons[1]
11–20	No encounter

The Jade Colossus

Towering over the foliage before an overgrown walkway in the south-central section of the City of the Dead Sultana is the **jade colossus of the Sultana**[1]. This statue, nearly 100 feet tall, is carved to show the exquisite beauty of the stately princess of djinn. A closer inspection of the colossus reveals a fist-shaped pit in the center of her forehead that must have once held a beautifully carved tiara. The eye sockets of the statue are empty, as if beautiful jewels the size of an ogre's head once stood in their place.

A shattered jade statue lies in a pile of valuable rubble next to the colossus of the Sultana. Pieces indicate it was once a statue of the former Sultan of the Efreet.

Characters placing the *ruby star of law*[2] in the colossus's forehead cavity or the *eyes of the Sultana*[2] into the eye sockets cause the colossus to awaken from it slumber.

If both the ruby and the eyes are placed in the colossus, the construct ventures out into the City of Brass of its own accord, seeking vengeance and retribution for the Sultana's defeat. The colossus is fully intelligent and aware, as if the spirit of the Sultana herself animates it. The colossus responds to spoken words and may even take suggestions. It is impossible to truly command, however.

If only the *eyes of the Sultana*[2] are placed into the eye sockets, the colossus goes berserk, striking out at any living beings within reach. Once they are destroyed, it goes in search of other beings to lay its revenge upon, after the chaotic fashion of the djinn. It easily steps over the walls of the City of the Dead Sultana, breaking the enchantments that deny others the ability to *fly* over, climb, or *teleport*, and exacts a horrid vengeance upon all efreet who failed in their loyalty to the Sultana's husband.

With only the *ruby star of law*[2] in place, the colossus remains inanimate unless commanded by a priest of Anumon who must succeed on a DC 20 Wisdom (Arcana) check to complete the complex ritual that breathes life into the colossus. Clerics of other non-evil faiths may attempt to command the colossus with a successful DC 25 Wisdom (Arcana) check. A failed check results in the colossus attacking the infidel before returning to

passive mode. Without the *eyes of the Sultana*[2], the colossus is blind and suffers all of the same penalties as a blinded character.

In the event that the colossus attacks the city on its own, feel free to run a large-scale tabletop battle, or resolve the damage and destruction the colossus creates before it is toppled and destroyed any way you see fit. Use whichever rules system you find appropriate for running such encounters.

Note: If the jade colossus is destroyed, the *eyes of the Sultana*[2] and the *ruby star of law*[2] are destroyed as well (if either or both are part of the colossus when it is destroyed).

Ruins of the Awanar

These once sumptuous palaces are little more than rubble. These were the last remaining strongholds of those who fought in the Sultana's rebellion. Only the sacrifice of the Sultana herself and that of Saaid al Djinn[1], her trusted advisor, stopped the Usurper's forces from demolishing the entire platform. The ruins are a place of great pain and resentment due to their failure to spur an all-out popular attack against the Usurper, and the spirits who dwell within these ruins have great resentment towards the living.

Six ruined palaces are within this section of the City of the Dead Sultana. Each is home to a **ghul noble**[1], the children of the Sultana who did not escape the fighting and died defending their beloved mother. (Only Ashazarade survived the purge and remains to this day hidden in the hostage tower of the Sultan of the Efreet.) Each of the princes and princesses is guarded by 2d4 **ghul efreeti**[1] followers.

Treasure: Each palace's treasure is listed below.

Palace #1: 380 bp, platinum locket with sapphire inlay (1,400 gp), gold anklet (100 gp), *spell scroll* of *enlarge/reduce* and *stone shape*, *spell scroll* of *lesser restoration* and *thunderwave*.

Palace #2: 400 bp, gold scepter with Fire Sea opal inlay (1,800 gp), platinum armband with 2 Fire Sea opals inlaid (1,000 gp), Fire Sea pearl brooch (1,500 gp), *spell wand*[2] of *enlarge/reduce*.

Palace #3: 200 bp, 100 pp, medallion with lapis lazuli (100 gp), bronze choker with diamonds (1,300 gp), *ring of climbing*[2].

Palace #4: 500 bp, silver necklace (500 gp), solid gold idol of Anumon (700 gp), *potion of resistance* (fire), golembane scarab[2].

Palace #5: 550 bp, exotic wooden headband with Fire Sea pearl embedded in center (800 gp), ruby tiara (5,100 gp), *philter of love, spell wand*[2] *of light*.

Palace #6: 200 bp, 1,000 sp, 500 pp, bronze and platinum statuette of the Sultana (5,000 gp), *potion of superior healing, spell scroll* of *burning hands*.

Barracks of the Mamelukes

These barracks once housed the Sultana's personal army of guards drawn from the most powerful of mortal slaves. Now their collapsed roofs are all that remains of their once ostentatious housing and parade grounds. The area surrounding the barracks is crawling with **skeleton warriors**[1] of the once brave fighters who attack any living beings that enter their turf. Unlike normal skeleton warriors, these beings are not possessed of a collar or circlet (and therefore do not have the normal skeleton warrior's *find target* ability) but were formed by the curse laid on the grounds by Saaid Al Djinn[1] to continue their defense of the Sultana's holdings even unto death.

Characters exploring this area are attacked by 1d4 **skeleton warriors**[1] every 2d6 rounds until they retreat a mile from the barracks, or until 100 such skeleton warriors are destroyed. The skeleton warriors ignore parties containing a priest of Anumon who openly bears his holy symbol.

Lighthouse of the Faithful

This conical tower in the northeastern section of the City of the Dead Sultana glows with a faint red glow cast by an enormous glowing ruby that floats at its top. The 200-foot-tall tower is surrounded by a spiral staircase that skirts its outer wall. Holy symbols of Anumon are evident in the tower decorations. The tower is protected by a strong aura. A chaotic or evil character that starts its turn or comes within 10 feet of the tower must make a DC 18 Wisdom saving throw, taking 21 (6d6) radiant damage on a failed save and half as much on a success. A creature that is both chaotic and evil takes twice as much damage. Those who speak the proper password can pass unhindered.

Guardian of the Stairs

Halfway up the staircase rests the dusts of **Saaid al Djinn**[1], guardian of the Lighthouse of the Faithful, and one-time advisor to the Sultana of the City of Brass. Saaid was a great wizard of djinni heritage, and brother to the Sultana. Some claim he was once even greater than the current Grand Vizier, although none utters this speculation too loudly.

Through intense ritual and powerful magic, Saaid fashioned this conical spire in the name of Anumon, showing to all he had accepted the rule of the creator of genie. As a gift for his faithfulness, he was given the guardianship of the *ruby star of law*[2], a gleaming relic said to have the ability to destroy faithless genie with an arc of red light. That Saaid attempted to destroy the Usurper with this gem is truth. That the gem failed is fact, and because of this failure, many of the efreet saw this as a sign that Anumon had turned his back upon them. Thus did many flock to the banner of the new Sultan as their true ruler, and joined in the attack upon the Sultana and her claim to the throne.

Retreating to the Lighthouse of the Faithful, Saaid defended the walls of the Sultana's city, even as Sultana Cirrishade led a counterattack. Cirrishade fought a bitter fight, but she fell in battle in the end. Her lieutenants gathered her body and whisked it from the battlefield to her waiting tomb, although many fell in the brave maneuver.

Saaid was well prepared for this possibility. His final rituals sealed his queen within her tomb. He then returned to the tower and reduced himself to the very salts of his creation, so that he could forever guard against the defilement of her body by the Usurper. From his lips, and through the will of Anumon, no race of genie would again enter the confines of her city, and all who died in its defense would rise again to defend it forever.

Saaid himself rises into a swirling resemblance of his once noble form and addresses characters who have managed to take the stair of the Lighthouse of the Faithful. He demands to know their business and their reason for being in the city of the dead queen. The only answers sufficient to avoid the wrath of Saaid are that the characters are enemies of the Sultan and that they seek to vanquish him, or that the characters are serving the will of Anumon and would right the wrongs committed upon the denizens of the City of Brass.

Should they answer truthfully or at very least bluff him in a manner that he finds reasonable, he may offer to aid them. However, they must first prove themselves to him by deeds rather than words and oaths. Saaid would see the Great Ziggurat destroyed, and suggests ways that this goal may be accomplished, such as gaining the *maul of Hezoid*[2] and granting it to one he refers to as "the penitent master of fire and forge." He is of course referring to Diya al Din, the Azer priest of Anumon, held prisoner in the bowels of the ziggurat. If this fails to pique the characters' interest, he suggests another seemingly impossible test of faith. He suggests that if the characters can retrieve a vial of water from the Oasis of Mukhphat the Blind in the Plane of Molten Skies and return it to him, the water may actually be used to restore Saaid to a portion of his former self, raising him from the dead … but much weaker than he was in his previous life. If the characters have been respectful to him and the tomb of the Sultana, he may join their cause and work to help them against the Sultan and his forces.

If the characters accomplish either of the missions, Saaid is impressed and allows them to take the *ruby star of law*[2] from the top of the Lighthouse of the Faithful.

Saaid is reluctant to speak about the tomb of his beloved sister and says merely that she is dead and that the dead should rest in peace. Any attempts to find her corpse send Saaid into a rage, causing him to attack the characters to thwart any tomb robbing.

If the characters blow their negotiations with Saaid, he attacks, attempting to force them from the stairwell and away from the *ruby star of law*[2]. This goes double for characters who are intent on merely stealing the *ruby star of law*[2] and using it for their own selfish interests.

The Ruby Star of Law

Floating at the top of the Lighthouse of the Faithful is the *ruby star of law*[2]. The *ruby star of law*[2] was handed down from Anumon to his prophet Sulymon then to Saaid al Djinn in order that the faithful of Anumon be saved and the wicked among all genie-kind punished for turning their backs upon the creator.

The final two stairs leading up to the platform over which the ruby floats are trapped with a *prismatic wall* trap. The trap can be detected with a successful DC 19 Intelligence (Arcana) check. It is triggered by a character stepping on or passing over and within 10 feet of either of the top two stairs. The Spell save DC for all of the trap effects is 19.

From its vantage point atop the Lighthouse of the Faithful, the *ruby star of law*[2] remains active to this day, firing a bolt of red energy at any genie that enters the confines of the City of the Dead Sultana, and slaying them instantly should they fail a DC 25 Constitution saving throw. So long as the ruby is atop the Lighthouse, the bolt of energy may reach anywhere inside the City of the Dead Sultana where a genie appears. See the sidebox for more details about the *ruby star of law*[2].

Curtain Wall

A curtain wall standing 50 feet tall and lined with thin minaret-like towers standing 130 feet tall marks the hill holding the Palace of the Sultana as well as her private lake. Date palms, banana groves, and coconut trees flourish impossibly in the sunless environment. A broad double causeway leads from the curtain wall to the gate leading to the palace. Three magnificent gatehouses lead to the palace grounds. Each gatehouse is flanked by a pair of high minarets, except for the central gatehouse that actually features two sets of gates, but only two minarets.

The gates are magically locked and are nearly impossible to break, though they may be easily bypassed by scaling the walls with rope and grappling hook and a successful DC 15 Strength (Athletics) check, or via magical means. Unlocking the gates requires *dispel magic* cast against a 9th level spell slot or a *wish*. Breaking the gates requires a successful DC 30 Strength check. The gates have AC 16 and 150 hit points and ignore any attack that does less than 10 hit points of damage.

Drains

Drains let water flow from the Sultana's lake through 6-inch-thick pipes that pierce the curtain wall in four places to form glorious waterfalls. The pipes are protected by a *disintegrate* spell that is intended to destroy any clogs that may plug the copper grating midway up each pipe. Characters attempting to shrink themselves or that change into fish and swim up the pipe trigger the *disintegrate* effect when they come within 5 feet of the copper grating. A creature passing through thte pipe must succeed on a DC 18 Dexterity saving throw or take 96 (16d6 + 40) force damage. A creature brought to 0 hit points by the effect is disintegrated. Large or smaller nonmagical objects passing through the pipe are automatically disintegrated.

Minarets

The minarets jutting from the curtain wall are dust filled and devoid of any standard life. The interiors of each minaret may be reached only from large bronze doors on the inside of the curtain wall. The doors are locked with *arcane lock* spells. There are nine such minarets. Breaking open a door requires a successful DC 22 Strength check or 60 points of damage.

The interior of each minaret is virtually identical. They all have guardhouses located in the domed tips of the towers. Each guardhouse contains 1d4 solid bronze statues of **Hawanari**[1] guards (half-djinni/half-efreeti soldiers) resplendent in flowing robes and each bearing a huge falchion (as longsword). These 8-foot-tall statues are indestructible by any magic the characters know. The expression upon the faces of the statues is that of grim determination as they stare from their watch portals out over the glittering city that shines beyond the darkness of the Sultana's platform.

These statues are in fact the remnants of the Sultana's elite bodyguard — the Hawanari — each turned into a metallic statue with the power of Saaid's final rituals, and each bound to the fate of the Sultana's corpse. Saaid's ritual served a two-fold purpose, for it spared the noble Hawanari the fate that awaited them at the hands of the Sultan and offered an additional protection of his beloved sister's body by those most loyal to her. Should her corpse be molested in any way, tomb robbers soon find that the statues have awakened as angry living Hawanari soldiers. Indeed, those seeking a hasty escape from the Sultana's hidden tomb soon find that they have more to reckon with than they had once thought.

A *wish* may free a Hawanari from its metallic state. The freed Hawanari, of course, questions the characters thoroughly as to their purposes in the Palace of the Sultana, attacking if they suspect the party to be nothing more than thieves, dissuading them from any search for the Sultana's body. The Hawanari may even go so far as to offer its services to the characters in a different venture if helps turn them away from any corruption of their beloved queen's final resting place.

The inner curtain wall is similar to the outer curtain wall. The minarets of the inner curtain wall are shorter than those of the outer wall, being only 100 feet tall. Each of the four minarets contains 1d4 bronze statues of **Hawanari**[1] guards affected by Saaid's ritual. Each minaret is accessed by a locked bronze door secured with *arcane locks*. Breaking open a door requires a successful DC 22 Strength check or 60 points of damage.

Lake Sultana

This crystal-clear lake is completely darkened due to the curse upon the platform, but in full light would be of unsurpassed beauty. Sitting in the center of the lake is an exact replica of the Palace of the Sultana, carved of the purest alabaster. Characters can swim to the palace in miniature with a successful DC 15 Strength (Athletics) check, yet they'll find there are no handholds on the palace, and that there is no land upon which the palace sits for them to climb onto out of the water. Beneath the waters is a solid rock wall that extends 40 feet beneath the waterline. Hidden within the miniature palace is the **Tomb of the Sultana**, which can be reached only by means of the magical gate accessed through the camera obscura in the **Sultana's Chamber**. The entire false palace is shielded from *scrying* and *teleportation*.

Swimming within these waters are 2d10 **ghoulish merfolk**[1]. These merfolk were once happy servants of the Sultana, sent as a gift from one of her marid cousins. Now, they are lowly and base, having had nothing to feed upon in all of these years. Any swimmer brave enough to test these waters soon knows their folly.

Palace of the Sultana

1. Front Door and Curse of the Sultana

A pair of domed towers flank this large circular, domed structure. The central domed palace is 130 feet tall, while its adjoining towers are shorter by nearly 30 feet. The curse of the Sultana lies upon the doors of the palace. A successful DC 25 Intelligence check or use of magic gleans the following words:

Turn back thee of no faith, for I, the Sultana Cirrishade, do command it. Faithful was I to he, the creator of all races of Genie. Faithful am I even onto my death, and forever will mine and the followers of the Keeper of his Truth wage war against usurpers and sinners who have turned their back upon the truth of the Gatekeepers Word.

Let any who enters this palace bearing ill will of my faith be set to the four winds, as if pulled by teams of thundering horses. Let them be struck blind by the Truth, and deafened by its resounding within their skull.

Let those who know the Words of Truth pass beyond these portals.

The doors to the Palace of the Sultana open only if *holy aura* or *divine word* is cast upon them. Otherwise, they remain forever sealed to those who would attempt to plunder their riches. Anyone attempting to bypass the walls or break down the portals in any other way must attempt on a DC 16 Constitution saving throw. A creature that fails takes 67 (15d8) radiant damage and blinded and deafened for one hour. A creature that succeeds takes half this damage is not blinded or deafened. In addition, if the creature is chaotic evil, it must succeed on a DC 16 Wisdom saving throw or be completely and irrevocably destroyed. The doors are impervious to all physical and magical assaults (other than the bypass spells mentioned above).

2. The Rotunda

As the door opens to the rotunda for the first time in many decades, the darkened chamber springs to life as if the sun had just risen over a false horizon, and the air fills with the fresh sounds of life. A character making a successful DC 20 Intelligence (Arcana) check determines that a form of temporal stasis has just been dispelled over the area of this chamber.

This huge circular chamber stands in the very center of the Sultana's palace and features a huge fountain in its center. A statue of Cirrishade stands here, water pouring freely from empty eye sockets to fill a huge basin at her sandaled and jeweled feet. So fantastic is the statue, which appears to be covered in pure gold, that the nails of the fingertips glitter with rubies. The fountain is surrounded by a colonnade of 30-foot-tall palm trees with golden boughs, having platinum fronds and fruits hanging from the tops that appear to be glittering jewels the size of a man's fist.

The ceiling is airy and high above the polished rose marble floor and painted to resemble the swirling skies of the Elemental Plane of Air. Twittering of arboreal creatures and jungle birds can be heard throughout the chamber. Massive double doorways of polished silver lead to the east and west of this huge chamber.

If the trees or statue within the chamber are tampered with, the 8 **magical monkeys**[1] hidden within the trees and a 6 **swarms of mechanical birds**[1] attack. The mechanical bird swarms swoop to peck out the eyes of characters as the monkeys hurl the gem-like "fruits" down upon the party. A fruit that strikes a solid surface (including a character) explodes upon contact. All within 20 feet must succeed on a DC 14 Dexterity saving throw or take 9 (2d8) force damage. There are 1d4 fruits per tree and 30 trees in the grove.

Although the radius of exploding fruits is not tall enough to reach the fruits already hanging in the trees, there is a 30% chance that the explosion knocks more fruits from trees within the radius of the blast. In such an event, 1d4 fruits fall from the tree, exploding where they land and dealing only 4 (1d8) force damage to those throw within a 20-foot radius who fail a subsequent DC 14 Dexterity saving, thus continuing the chain reaction until all of the fruits have exploded or the explosions cease.

2A. The Fountain

The water in this fountain are the pure tears of the Sultana. Anyone touching the water is cured of 3d8 + 10 points of damage; however, they are filled with a melancholic sadness that gives them a −2 on attack rolls, skill checks, and saving throws for the next 1d4 hours.

Treasure: Each magical fire fruit tree is worth more than 30,000 gp as it has golden bark growing over a living silver core. The trunk of each tree weighs more than 1,800 pounds, however, the fire fruits, if harvested, are worth 750 gp each on the open market, and may be hurled as grenade-like weapons. The water from the fountain may be preserved in a container for one week before losing its magical powers.

The eastern and western tower doors are each enchanted with *arcane lock* spells. They can be broken down with a successful DC 25 Strength check or hacked through with 80 points of damage. The doors have AC 15 and ignore any attack that does less than 10 points of damage.

3. Western Tower: The Chamber of Air

This chamber glitters with azure jewels and pearls an inch across from floor to ceiling in a swirling pattern that starts in a pinwheel at the center of the floor, swirls like wind, and ends in a pinwheel at the top of the ceiling. A character that makes a successful DC 20 Intelligence (Investigation) check notices that the swirling patterns actually reveal writing in the Auran language of the Sultana's home plane.

The swirling pattern spells out the musical notes of *The Song of the Sultana*. The song is impossible to sing for any but a bird as the notes stretch far beyond the range of humanoid vocal cords. A character proficient in a stringed instrument using *Oriazier's key*[2] (**Area 5**) can play the song with a successful DC 25 Dexterity (Performance) check.

Of the gems that are different from the rest, one gem is a blue diamond, while the other is a white diamond. Depressing the white diamond causes all of the other gemstones to rip free from the walls and begin swirling around the room like a cyclone, tearing at anything and everything within the room. A creature that starts its turn in or who enters the room must attempt a DC 20 Dexterity saving throw, taking 35 (10d6) slashing damage on a failure and half as much on a success. The effect lasts for 10 rounds, at which time the gems return to the walls and everything returns to normal (except of course for any dead bodies that may be lying around the room). Attempting to pry any of the gemstones from the walls triggers the cyclone effect as well.

Depressing the blue diamond lowers a brilliant silver staircase from the upper half of the tower that leads to **Area 4: The Silver Dome**.

Treasure: If by some miracle (e.g., using a *wish* spell to stop the magical effect of the cyclone) the characters manage to peel any of the gems, pearls, and the like from the wall, there is a full 100,000 gp worth of treasure here.

Upper Palace
1 Square – 10 Feet
4
6
5
Lower Palace
3
2A
2
5
1
Tomb
7
Palace of the Dead Sultana
N
267

4. The Silver Dome

This dome is perfectly polished silver and appears to have no opening at all other than the staircase that leads to **Area 3**. The walls and ceiling have a mirror-like effect that is very disorienting to those who enter the chamber, as up looks down and down looks up. The curved dome causes everything above to look distorted and multiple images of each person in the chamber reflect infinitely upon one another. Characters first entering the chamber must succeed on a DC 18 Wisdom saving throw or become disoriented (–4 on attack rolls, skill checks, and saving throws) for 1 minute. A successful DC 18 Wisdom (Perception) check reveals a small bowl-shaped depression in the center of the silver floor. Filling the bowl with tears from the statue in **Area 1** causes a vision to appear, reflected upon the walls. The characters' visions begin with reflections of their own innermost thoughts before shifting to the memories of a dead queen, and the bitter sadness that was her life. Each person seeking passage to the Sultana's private audience chamber must place a tear from the fountain into the depression.

The visions afford the characters a glimpse of the tragedy of the Sultana, starting with her marriage as a princess of the djinn to the former Sultan of Efreet[1], and her longing for the familiarity of her homeland. A young human traveler, a timelessly wise king among men, appears to have arranged the marriage, at the behest of the god Anumon. Their marriage was set forth by the rulers of the heavens to show the union of the faithful genie races to the gods who created them. Her life is peaceful for many years, and she bears the Sultan many children. Despite this peace, many of the efreet detested her co-regency of their emblazoned city. It was then that the time of troubles arose. A usurper arrived from deep within the Plane of Fire to lead a rebellion against Cirrishade and her husband's rule. This usurper was exceedingly powerful, far outstripping the might and abilities of any efreeti ever seen before. He destroyed her husband and forced her into a civil war with the efreet who denounced the gods and those who would support her. They saw the new Sultan as the reincarnation of Iblis, who was cast from the heavens for questioning the creators themselves. Iblis, they claimed, was a god that the efreet could respect, a god who brought his own laws. In finality, she is struck a deadly blow at the hands of the usurper and can only stare on as her children are destroyed or scattered to the four winds.

If characters place the *ruby star of law*[2] into the bowl with the tears from the fountain, or if a character proficient in stringed instruments makes a successful DC 20 Dexterity (Performance) check using *Oriazier's key*[2] to play *The Song of the Sultana* from the Chamber of Air (**Area 3**), the outline of the silver door appears before the characters, allowing them entrance into Cirrishade's Chambers (**Area 6**). Characters who do not place tears within the depression cannot pass through the door.

5. Lair of Oriazier

The doorway opens, and the room illumes with a flash as if dispelling some long-forgotten magical effect. A successful DC 20 Intelligence (Arcana) check indicates that a temporal stasis effect has just been dispelled. A loud anguished roar echoes through the chamber beyond as it is filled with light and fury. A massive blackish-silver dragon with platinum-tinged scales turns its mercury eyes toward the characters and demands to know who defiles the chambers of his mistress! This is **Oriazier**[1] the solar dragon. He is somewhat disoriented from his decades' long rest and does not know what changes have been wrought upon the City of Brass. Oriazier was Cirrishade's private mount and personal confidant, having been with her since her birth, serving as a bodyguard even as she was raised in the Plane of Air. His failure to save her life does not sit well with him, and to him, the pain of her death is still fresh in his mind. He does not realize friend from foe for the first one or two rounds of the encounter, and depending on the characters' actions, he may decide merely to slay them as tomb robbers deserving of a quick end. If the characters hold off battle or seek to subdue Oriazier and attempt to calm him, they may make opposed Charisma checks to halt him long enough to talk.

If the characters succeed in convincing Oriazier that they are enemies of the Sultan and allies of the Sultana's memory, he may be convinced to give up his "key" to her chambers. This may be a very difficult sell, however, and one that no amount of dice rolls may resolve.

Treasure: *Oriazier's key*[2], 3,200 bp, 11,000 gp, fire opal (1,400 gp), 12 green alexandrite (500 gp each), 22 violet garnets (400 gp each), silver brooch (700 gp), 4 bronze statuettes of the Sultana (600 gp each), sapphire and moonstone inlaid chalice (1,200 gp), 4 golden goblets (120 gp each), *+3 mace*, *+3 siangham* (as *+3 dagger*), *holy avenger*, *crystal ball of telepathy*, *cloak of resistance*[2], *potion of vitality*, *spell scroll* of *find steed* and *slow*, *staff of illusion*[2], *staff of defense*[2], *spell wand*[2] of *inflict wounds*, *spell wand*[2] of *false life*.

6. Cirrishade's Chambers

The door from **The Silver Dome** opens into a lavishly appointed chamber of immense size. The room is partitioned by finely painted silk screens and is complete with a large overstuffed bed designed to look exactly like a triple canopy jungle when it is lain upon. Lady's vanities of large size are found behind one of the screens, as are trunks filled with jeweled gowns and dancers' dresses, all tailored to fit a woman at least 15 feet tall. The wall is hung with beautiful tapestries depicting castles floating among pink and yellow clouds, peopled by realistically rendered djinn princes and princesses making gifts of lotus, pearls, and silk to one another. Steaming baths of jasmine scented water and highly polished marble floors covered with finely crafted rugs woven from cloth of gold accentuate the femininity of this room.

Set behind a silk screen stands an odd metallic box fitted with a fine clear jewel on one side and a slot in the top. The box is on a tripod and faces the north wall of the chamber. A latch on the side of the box opens it to reveal a space large enough for a thick candle. A second box of gold lined with velvet sits next to the first. It contains twenty-four plates of a cool smooth black stone-like material a quarter-inch thick. The plaques cannot be removed from the box unless a character declares how many the character wishes to view. Written upon the side of the box are these words in way of instruction:

Of plaques there are twenty-four to view and see not a number less or more. Twenty-two plaques offer blessings and doom, while two alone may gain entry to my tomb. You may draw as many plaques as all and as few as none. Once a number is called, the drawing is begun.

These plaques are none other than a special *deck of many things* created specifically for the Sultana to guard her tomb. By placing a magical light source within the camera obscura, and then inserting one of the plaques into the camera's slot, the picture upon the card is projected upon the wall. Whoever places the plaque into the slot is thus affected by the action upon that card. Unlike a normal *deck of many things*, this particular deck has two extra cards, but they must be drawn from the deck, like any of the others in order to discover their mystery. For purposes of game play, add a three of diamonds and a three of spades to the cards listed.

Drawing the three of diamonds from the deck projects a golden key upon the wall. This key is substantial, and real, and may be taken down from the wall. The key is the only key that allows entry into the **Tomb of the Sultana**. Drawing the three of spades causes a gated doorway to appear before the characters. The key fits into the lock upon the gate and the doorway opens into a hall that leads to the Tomb of the Sultana, which can be reached only by passing through this magical portal. Note that however many cards are called upon to be drawn, once the key is used to open the gate, the cards all disappear. Unlike a standard *deck of many things*, the same card cannot be drawn twice during a single use. The deck recharges 30 hours after being used.

Treasure: A thorough search of Cirrishade's chamber finds the following items of value: 2,300 bp, 10 aquamarines (400 gp each), 6 silver pearls (150 gp each), 3 fire opals (1,200 gp each), platinum decanter (1,100 gp), *mace of ultimate disruption*[2], *staff of frost*, *manual of bodily health*, *rod of spell enlargement*[2], *oil of greater magic weapon*[2], *ring of wizardry*[2], *spell scroll* of *halt undead*[4] and *silence*.

Note: Stealing items from Cirrishade's chamber awakens every restless spirit within the City of the Dead Sultana to the presence of the characters. They move at their fastest movement rate toward the Palace of the Sultana and await the thieves with the intent to destroy them when they leave the palace.

7. Tomb of the Sultana

Once the key and the gate are discovered from the *deck of many things* (**Area 6**), the characters are able to open the portal that leads to the actual Tomb of the Sultana hidden beneath the alabaster model of the palace in the center of the lake.

The room beyond the gateway is large and crafted of highly polished marble. Lying on a raised bier in the center of the chamber is the perfectly preserved corpse of a beautiful djinni princess, fully 18 feet tall. Her eyes stand open and appear to have a lifelike glint to them, as if she is staring intently at the swirling pattern of gemstones imbedded in the ceiling above her. Standing stock still on either side of the corpse are two huge men with withered, dried skin the color of mahogany. Each man wears the headdress of a priest of Anumon, and bears a huge falchion, held point down between its feet.

Unless a priest of Anumon or an individual bearing the *ruby star of law*[2] approaches the corpse, the **mummy djinn**[1] priests of Anumon animate and attack, hurling curses and wielding their *falchions of law*[2] with a vengeance.

Parties with the Ruby Star of Law

An individual bearing the *ruby star of law*[2] may approach the body of the Sultana and summon her spirit to speak. The lilting voice of the Sultana fills the chamber as her spirit blows through the room like a warm spring wind, and asks, "Who bears the ruby star of law and calls Cirrishade from her eternal slumber?"

The Spirit of Cirrishade

Bringing the *ruby star of law*[2] near the corpse of Cirrishade summons her spirit and allows the characters to commune with her spirit similarly to the spell of the same name. Through careful role-play, the characters may be granted a *wish*, granted the *eyes of the Sultana*[2], or find advice on any other predicament that they may currently face. For example, characters asking to be granted her eyes shall be denied and the spirit leaves never to return. Making a case that the *eyes of the Sultana*[2] could be used as a mighty weapon against her destroyer, on the other hand, may sway her decision if the characters give some further detail on how they might be used.

None of these things may be granted without clever and intelligent role-play on the part of the characters. Don't make it easy on them to get whatever they wish, however. If the characters want something from her, the Sultana's spirit may very well ask them to undertake other quests on her behalf. Such quests could include the destruction of the Great Ziggurat, or the assassination of the Grand Vizier.

Remember, the Sultana is a spirit and she has no love for thieves who would desecrate her burial chamber, but she also has a score to settle with the Sultan of Efreet[1]. Due to the nature of the wound upon her, she may not be raised through any action less than a *true resurrection*. Should the characters manage to raise the Sultana, she seeks to have the characters help her escape from the city and return to the Plane of Air, where she may seek refuge with her family.

Parties without the Ruby Star of Law

Characters who do not have the *ruby star of law*[2] may either stand awestruck at the sight of the perfectly preserved body of Cirrishade, or they may settle down to some serious tomb robbing. Once the mummies are dispatched, the only thing protecting the body of the Sultana and her treasures is an imprisonment trap set upon her body that is triggered by anyone who touches her noble personage. Discerning the existence of the trap requires a successful DC 17 Intelligence (Arcana) check. Removing it requires *dispel magic* successfully cast against an 8th level spell slot. A creature who touches her body without disabling the trap is imprisoned far beneath the ground for one thousand years. While imprisoned, the creature does not age or otherwise have any awareness of the passing of time. An imprisoned creature can be freed with a *wish*.

Treasure: Adorning the body of the Sultana are a *ring of elemental command* (air), a *rod of thunder and lightning*[2], a *ring of evasion*, *bracers of superior defense*[2], a *brooch of shielding*, a *headband of intellect* (fashioned like a queenly crown), and a *cloak of charisma*[2]. Most stunning of all these items are the *eyes of the Sultana*[2], which appear to be glittering pools of mercury yet maintain a lifelike aura over them, unglazed by the rigor mortis of death.

Completing the City of the Dead Sultana

Characters may have taken many routes in exploring the City of the Dead Sultana. Should they deal successfully with the spirits here, they may find it a serviceable hideout within the City of Brass, a place where the efreeti fear to tread and as a good base of operations for continuing their campaign. Gaining the *eyes of the Sultana*[2] and the *ruby star of law*[2] could unlock the very powerful jade colossus for their use against the Sultan and his forces. Forays into the City of the Dead Sultana may therefore be repeated, with side quests to the Plane of Molten Skies or other areas of the City of Brass before all its secrets are uncovered.

Should the characters follow the path of pure plunderers, the treasures located in the City of the Dead Sultana should make them wildly wealthy or kill them in their tracks depending on the outcomes of their actions.

It may be noted that Tarbish never visits the characters within the walls of the City of the Dead Sultana, preferring to meet them at a location of his choosing outside of it. He offers assistance in the form of information that the characters may need to further along the quest and keep the plot moving. Once the relics within the City of the Dead Sultana are gained, he suggests that the characters seek the *maul of Hezoid*[2] from the Circus of Pain, indicating that a combination of freed azer slaves, destroyed burning dervishes, and a raging jade colossus could be just what is needed to help dethrone the Sultan. Astute characters may begin to suspect that Tarbish is not all he appears to be.

Chapter 23
The Circus of Pain

Dominating the southeastern corner of the Upper City, almost in the shadows of the Palace of the Sultan and lit always by the glow of the curtain of fire, stands the Circus of Pain. This coliseum complex of white marble pillars, floating stages, a molten lead racetrack, teleporting arena floor, and rotating stands is a major draw for visitors from the planes of evil as well as visitors from throughout the universe who find themselves drawn into the grandeur and spectacle of the games of death and blood played out upon its four floating platforms. Here, the characters will find all sorts of activity and danger to get themselves caught up in. Audience participation is the order of the day and allows for interesting role-play and the chance to win fantastic prizes, including the *maul of Hezoid*[2] from the current Circus Champion should their adventures in the City of Brass place them upon this course. The characters could easily end up a crisped pile of ashes, but that is for good decisions, exemplary role-play, and the dice to decide.

The Circus of Pain travels from plane to plane every 3,000 years, most often coming to rest on a plane where it may fulfill the needs of a jaded populace. The Circus Master, a mysterious character who revels in gambling and combat, has always run it. The circus's dimensions vary depending on which plane of existence it is encountered in; in some places, it may be as small as a large tent with three rings and a dirt floor. Never in its history has the circus had such a dominant and opulent incarnation as is found in the City of Brass.

After the fashion of a true circus, the stadium seating is arranged in such a manner as to allow viewers a clear glimpse of activities going on in each stadium at once. Main events taking place at any one time are projected by powerful illusions to megalithic size over the center of the stadiums, affording a better view of the highlights of the action taking place below. Stadium announcers hawk like carnival barkers, directing the attention of the masses to the various events, giving colorful commentary to the life-and-death action taking place below.

Characters entering the Circus of Pain as part of an ongoing City of Brass campaign may have been sent here in search of the *maul of Hezoid*[2] by Chufa Um Sophanie or Tarbish. Characters adventuring in the City of Brass may have been arrested and sold to slavery at the circus. Finally, the Circus of Pain may be used as an extraplanar arena in any campaign setting, proving a challenging role-playing adventure for the characters.

This adventure is suggested for Tier 4 characters.

The Circus Master

Within the confines of the Circus of Pain, the Circus Master is at his most powerful, able to perceive everything going on within the confines of the circus. The Master can extend his senses to three remote locations at once and still sense what's going on nearby. Once the Master chooses a remote location to sense, he automatically receives sensory information from that location until he chooses a new location. This remote sensing is not fooled by *mislead* or *nondetection* or similar spells, and it does not create a magical sensor that other creatures can detect.

The Master controls just about every aspect of the circus. Very little goes on that he is not aware of (or quickly made aware of). He can adjust the landscape, seating, ground, lighting, sounds, etc., at his whim. Some believe the Circus Master can even bend the laws of magic in his realm.

Security

Fire giants patrol the stands, as do vendors and **efreet** carrying *spell wands*[2] of *dispel magic* (in the event that some errant visiting wizard or cleric starts casting spells that could cause the deaths of an uncomfortably large number of fans). An *antimagic field* surrounds each of the fighting platforms, so they have little concern that fans may disrupt the games.

Vendors

Vendors patrol the stands offering up various snacks, delicacies, and rental goggles, which they carry in *bags of holding*. The vendors are usually enslaved **djinn**; however, they can be of any race and description. They flee from trouble and notify guards if customers get out of hand.

Bookmakers

Licensed bookies, generally **burning dervishes**[1] and **bearded devils**, patrol the stands, soaking up any spare wealth as the announcers work the crowds into a frenzy of bloodlust and anticipation. They hand chits to the bettors that indicate the amount of their bet; these may be cashed at the betting windows.

1. Grand Causeway

A huge, heavily pillared gateway of pure white marble leads to a huge, cavernous causeway that affords entrance to the various seating sections that surround the floating stages. A colossal iron statue of a hero impaling his foe on a trident stands before the gateway in a fountain of fire. Broad causeways are lined with posters featuring the various heroes of the circus, painted in vibrant colors upon sheets of tin. Many of these posters are animated with illusions to repeat famous scenes of the sorts of activities that take place here. Pairs of **fire giant** guards are posted at the main gates and at the foot of the stairwells leading to the stands, acting as stadium security. Beings of every race, size, and description make their way to and from the stands, and form long queues before concession stands, betting windows, and restrooms.

If trouble breaks out here, or anywhere else in the causeway or stadium, 2 **fire giants** handle it first. If the problem is too severe for the fire giants, two more join them every round up to a maximum of 20 fire giants. If they cannot handle the issue at this point, 2 **efreeti sorcerers**[1] join them. If the combined force of efreeti wizards and giants cannot quell the problem, **Faa'Thasht the Circus Master**[1] is called with his retinue, and city guards eventually join them. Troublemakers are not turned over to imprisonment or sold at the slave bazaars as is normally the case for lawbreakers. Instead, they are stripped of their belongings and entered into the games immediately.

2. Betting Windows

Like other casinos and gambling houses found in the Bazaar of 1,000 Sins, odds are laid for various events that take place within the Circus of Pain at the betting windows. Each window has 1d2 **efreet** clerks working at all times. The Circus Master and his cronies adjust the odds on different events based on the previous successes of a competitor versus the likelihood that they can conceivably overcome the challenge dreamt up. The only real rule on betting here is that there is *no limit* to the wager that can be made, and an individual may always put him or herself up as

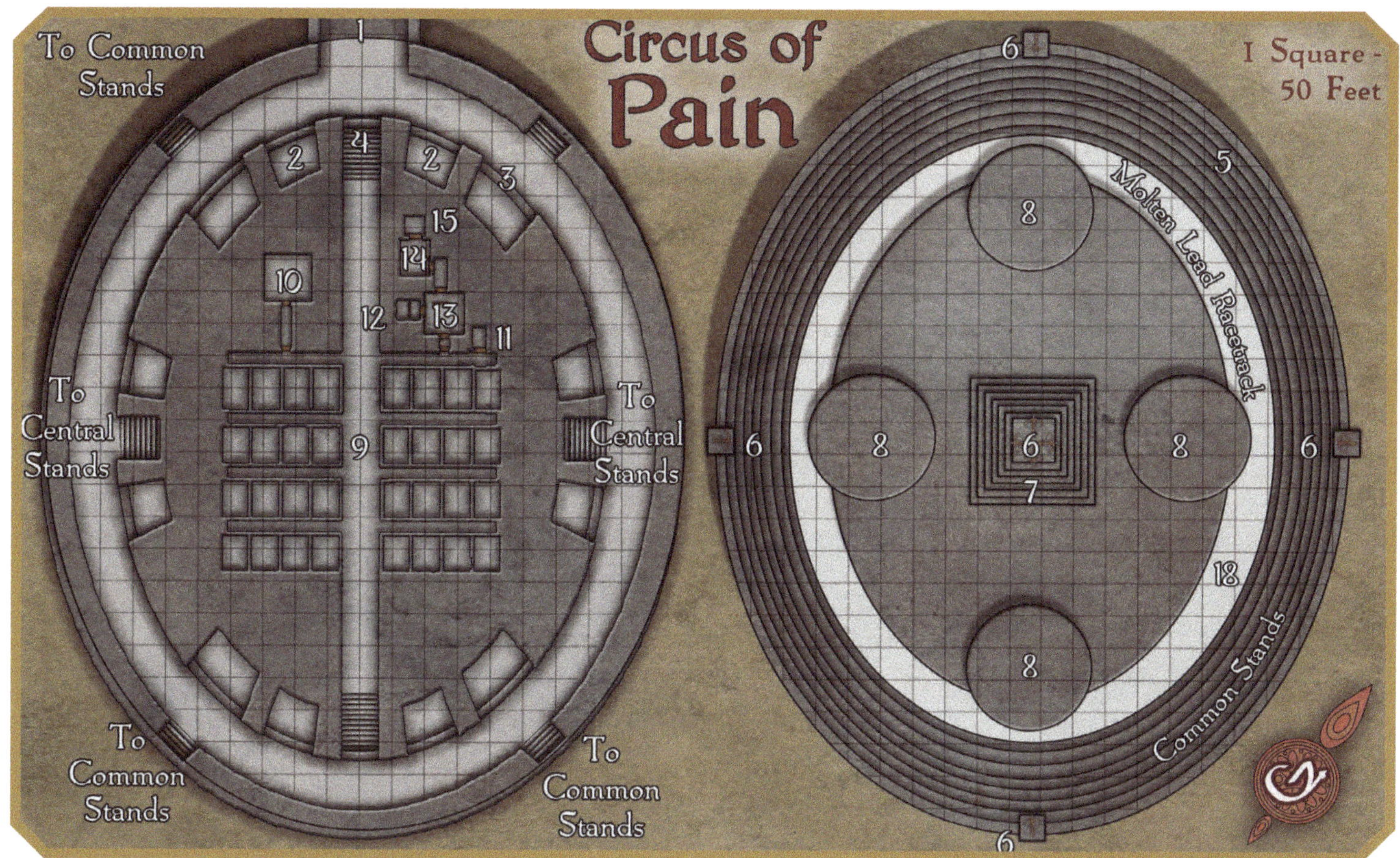

collateral. Bookmakers in the City of Brass are confident enough in their ability to handicap an event in the arena, or for that matter anywhere in the City of Brass and the Plane of Molten Skies, to be able to match any wager offered. The bookmakers take any bet no matter how insane or ludicrous it sounds, and since they are virtually immortal, the records of their bets may be held forever, or until the City of Brass and the known planes of existence cease to exist, whichever comes first.

Private, licensed bookmakers take individual bets; however, this is generally reserved among the high rollers only. The minimum bet for a high roller is 20,000 gp whether that amount is in slaves, magic items, material wealth, or any combination thereof.

The bookmaking and betting licensing is heavily organized through the Grand Bureaucracy and administrated through the Bureau of Organized Gambling, a branch of the Offices of Finance and Trade. Wealth collected here, usually in excess of 5 million gp, is magically teleported to the KhizAnah in an amount of 1 million gp every four hours.

There is no outside access to the drop where monies are collected and dispensed except via the drop slot and lifts. Instead, notes are sent down pneumatic tubes similar to the ones found in the KhizAnah to indicate how much wealth in coin and gems need be brought up to pay off lucky bettors. These notes are collected by 10 **homunculi** who use specially crafted permanent *rods of telekinesis*[2] to move the loot into treasure chests and to the lifts. The *rods of telekinesis* are attuned to the counting room and do not work outside of it. The shaft leading to the drop is 50 feet deep and 2 feet by 10 inches wide with a permanent *antimagic field* located 20 feet down the shaft. The drop is shielded from *teleportation* and planar travel into or out of the chamber by anyone save the Circus Master, or the *teleportation* of cash to the KhizAnah. The Circus Master created the homunculi, and they are connected telepathically to him.

Treasure: 1d6 x 1,000,000 gp in nonmagical treasure.

3. Concessions

Every food and libation imaginable is available at double the market price. Creatures that live off minerals such as gold and gems generally get their food by exchanging for it at the betting windows. Other humanoid types may feast at all-you-can-eat buffet lines featuring roasted yak or camel, side by side with sizzling slave meat. "Fast food" usually means fruits and vegetables and meat on a stick. Clay pitchers of wine and bottles of ales and spirits are also available.

4. Stairs to the Lower Levels

Iron gates lead down to the **Battle Slave Pits (Area 9)**. The gates are locked but have a smaller door set in them like a camel's eye to allow passage of up to Large creatures without much difficulty. The small door can be unlocked with a successful DC 18 Dexterirty check with thieves' tools or smashed open with a successful DC 22 Strength check. A pair of **fire giants** guard the gates.

5. The Commoners' Stands

The outer ring of seats slowly rotates to afford a view of all the various events taking place upon the arena platforms. This can be disorienting to first-time visitors, requiring that they make a DC 12 Constitution saving throw or become sickened for the duration of their visit at the circus and for 2d6 minutes afterward. This effect only occurs the first time a visitor comes to the circus, after which they become accustomed to the vertigo. Sickened creatures have disadvantage on attack rolls and ability checks.

Lesser events taking place on the various platforms must be viewed with the naked eye, which can be difficult to say the least, requiring a successful DC 16 Wisdom (Perception) to really see what is going on. Stadium goggles, which are no more than *eyes of the eagle*, are rented by hawkers and vendors making their way through the stands. The goggles offer a better view of activities, but one must be forewarned — the cheaper goggles may become permanently attached to the viewer's eyes, denying them any close-up vision. These may be removed only by offering one's self into the circus as fodder for the various traps, monsters, and combatants in one of the games or by a successful *remove curse* spell. This of course can prove to be a death warrant for those not prepared for the cruel perversity of the games. Goggle rental averages 30 bp per day and there is a 5% chance that the renter gets a cursed pair. If the *eyes of the eagle* are removed from the stadium, they cease to function.

General seating in the Commoners' Stands averages 1 bp per person. Seating closer to the action averages about 5 bp per person.

6. Ballista Firing Decks

Huge ballistae mounted on tall firing decks stand at the cardinal points encircling the arena. Four additional ballistae mounted on similar firing decks look out over the central stands. Each firing deck is attended by 3 **azer** slaves who are chained to the deck. They load and wind the ballista for stadium visitors who wish to take a shot at a combatant or at another ballista operator.

Each firing deck can hold up to 8 Medium creatures plus its azer slaves.

A firing deck can be rotated 90-degrees in a single round. A Medium creature firing a ballista takes a –4 penalty on attack rolls; Small creatures take a –6 penalty on attack rolls. It takes three azer slaves one action to reload a ballista. If fewer than three load a ballista, it takes two actions over two rounds.

These oversized ballistae have a range of 180/360 feet, score a critical hit on 19–20, and deal 18 (4d8) piercing damage on a hit.

For a mere 5 bp, a fan can purchase a single shot with one of the ballistae. For 10 bp, a fan can purchase three shots. Shots can be taken at game participants or other ballista operators.

Each firing deck has a small brass target on its side about the size of a buckler. The target is AC 18. Three successful shots from a crossbow or bow in the same round that hit the target causes the deck to lurch upward and forward. Each creature not attached to the platform must succeed on a DC 16 Dexterity saving throw or go hurling into the arena. Individuals falling to the arena floor are instantly teleported to the Battle Slave Pens beneath the stadium, stripped of their gear in the process.

A single shot from a firing deck-mounted ballista triggers the platform as well. The chained azer slaves avoid being hurled into the arena and end up dangling from their chains until the platform resets in 10 rounds.

7. Central Stands

The central stands are where the high rollers come to watch the games. This slowly rotating deck of stands is pyramid-shaped and has four ballista firing decks on it. The top tier consists of private boxes used by the Sultan (when he deigns to come to the games), the Grand Vizier, and the Circus Master. These boxes may be entered only through *teleportation*, and then only to those who know the proper password as they are guarded by *forbiddance* spells cast with a 9th level spell slot. The viewing portal to these stands is a permanent *wall of force* cast with a 9th level spell slot and the seating is luxurious to say the least. Below them are private boxes that may be rented by high rollers for 1,000 bp per hour. The doors are guarded by 4 **efreeti** elite guards and may be entered only with the proper password, a successful DC 20 Dexterity check with thieves' tools, or a DC 22 Strength check. General seating in the central stands averages 20 bp per person.

8. The Platforms

Each of these four platforms is a 500-foot-wide disk that floats in a circular pattern around the central stands. Each platform is enchanted with powerful magic that lets it morph and change into any sort of terrain upon which combatants do battle. The platforms float above the racetrack so as not to obstruct the spectators' views.

Each platform is surrounded by a special *antimagic field* that allows magic to take place normally on the platform but prevents magic from getting into or out of the area. The *antimagic fields* are designed to keep spellcasters from aiding their battle slaves during combat.

A platform generally hovers 60 feet above the molten lead racetrack, but its height can be adjusted by the Circus Master from within his private seating box.

Victory Points and Earnings

Each event offers a reward of Victory Points and brass pieces. Coin is either added to the victor's spoils or, in the case of battle slaves, added to a "pot" that can eventually be used to purchase the slave's freedom.

A combatant that earns 50 Victory Points can fight the Circus Champion for freedom. Victory Points are awarded as follows.

Event	VP Award	BP Winnings
Hit firing deck target with bow or crossbow	1	100bp
Win gladiatorial battle	2	1000bp
Win the golem smash	2	1000bp
Win nightmare race	2	1d4 x 5000gp
Win chariot race	2	1d4 x 5000gp
Win Tower of Pain	5	1000bp
Win Fire and Ice	5	1000bp
Win Ballista Blast	7	2000bp
Win Brain Ball	10	3000bp

Note: For team events, each surviving participant on the winning team gets the amount listed.

Games and Events

Various games are played upon each of the four floating platforms simultaneously. The platforms are changed magically, and combatants placed upon any given platform are generally done so via *teleportation*.

As the City of Brass generally never sleeps, there is a 50% chance that a major event is being held at the Circus of Pain at any given time. Admission to the arena is free for general seating. Individuals seeking more desirable accommodations, such as the private boxes overlooking the arena platforms, pay anywhere from 10 bp to 1,000 bp for the superior seating. When major events are not taking place, standard events such as racing or one-on-one gladiator style combat take center stage.

Getting into an Event

Most events are closed to the public, meaning that you cannot just sign up and jump right in. Noble Houses and certain extraplanar visitors have their own stables of battle slaves whom they send to the games for profit and amusement.

Being sold to a training facility is the most common way of getting sent into the games. Bribes can be made, however, and simply jumping onto the floor of one of the arenas has the result of an individual giving up all rights, gear, and freedom. Certain events, of course, may lead to fans "accidentally" being tossed into the arena by other fans, or hurled there by angry beasts who make their way up into the lower stands on occasion.

Jumping onto the floor or falling from the stands results in the creature being instantly *teleported* to a holding cell without any belongings, and then instantly *teleported* back to the arena with the proper gear and equipment for the games. If they survive the game, stable owners bid over the creature to decide who gets to keep the new combatant. All former gear becomes the property of the Circus Master, who keeps the items he likes and, after its former owner dies, sells the rest in one of the many bazaars of the City of Brass. If, however, a battle slave should win her freedom from the Circus of Pain, she claims the prize for the event and can reclaim her equipment as well.

Battle Slaves and Racers

It is important to differentiate between battle slaves and racers who participate in games. Battle slaves are generally slaves bought by various training facilities in the City of Brass, with the sole intent of using their combat skills for the amusement of the fans that throng to the circus. All battle slaves are fitted with a brass collar. The brass collar *geas* of a battle slave dictates that they honor their master, and fight in the arena with the purpose of becoming "Circus Champion," and upon becoming champion, to remain champion for life. Of course, it is possible to buy one's freedom before facing the Circus Champion; however, this is such a rare circumstance as to be unheard of. Slaves winning their freedom or being freed by their slave master break the *geas* and any further magical compulsion to take part in the sport.

A slave can purchase its freedom from the circus by earning enough brass pieces in winnings equal to twice his or her slave value. (Remember, a slave's value is Strength x Charisma x HD; arcane casters multiply this total by 1.5 to arrive at their value.)

Racers, be they nightmare jockeys or charioteers, are commonly free folk. They compete purely for sport and profit and are not bound to the rules that battle slaves must face, unless of course they happen to be owned by a noble house or wealthy visitor who compels them to participate as a form of "honoring their master." Free-folk racers come from all walks of life and all planes of existence.

The exception to the rule on entering and joining the games is among the racers, both mount and chariot. These games are open to any who can afford a racing chariot or a swift mount capable of riding over the grueling molten lead track and who are willing to risk their life for the fortune and glory that entails. Most racers are professionals who live for the sport and go for broke on every turn, knowing that the riches they earn are more than the sum of some entire kingdoms on their home worlds. The noble houses, featuring a younger prince of the house as a rider or driver, sponsor several of the racers. For more information on the races and how to run an event, see the section on races below.

To enter a race, a person must have 5,000 gp value of purse money to put up for themselves or their racer to cover licenses and to buy into the circuit.

The Games

Listed here are various games that you can use in the event that the characters wish to battle or compete their way through the games for a chance to face Hezoid, Champion of the Games, and attempt to wrest his maul from him. Also, if the characters find themselves prisoners of the fighter pits, these games afford their only chance at gaining their freedom from the circus.

Nightmare Races

These races are run by jockeys riding **nightmares** that spiral around the molten lead track in an effort to reach the finish line first. Nightmares are "grounded" in these races and do not fly. A rider who takes to the air is automatically disqualified (unless a special stipulation says otherwise).

One variation of the standard nightmare race allows the riders to use weapons as they circle the track. Riders that fall suffer the full effects of the arena's molten lead surface.

Another variation allows the audience to take shots at drivers with one of eight huge ballistae in the stands for 5 bp per shot, three shots for 10 bp. The audience likes this version of the race best as they think it gives them an advantage by helping their nightmare win. Of course, nothing really stops a fan from shooting at the person firing on their nightmare either.

See the sidebox for rules on running races.

Equipment: Many races forbid the use of weapons. As such, the jockeys in these events rarely wear armor. In races where weapons are allowed, jockeys usually wear light armor and carry hand or light crossbows and shortswords.

Sample jockeys might include Afzal, Male Human **commander**[1] and Stigandr, a **babau**[1] demon.

Molten Lead Racetrack

The molten lead racetrack circles the entire arena. An iron railing separates it from the stands and the inner arena floor. Touching the molten raceway deals 16 (3d10) fire damage per round of contact. Further, a character contacting the surface is exposed to the deadly fumes given off by the molten lead and must make a DC 16 Constitution saving throw or take 1d2 points of Constitution damage. All such characters must make a second save 1 minute later or take another 1d6 points of Constitution damage. Note, characters riding nightmares or riding in chariots do not suffer the effects of the fumes unless they fall from their mount or chariot and actually contact the molten lead.

An immunity or resistance to fire serves as an immunity or resistance to molten lead.

Conducting the Nightmare Races

The rules below can be used to conduct the nightmare races. The system is simply a number of Wisdom (Animal Handling) checks made by all participants and is designed for ease of use. (It's much easier than rolling 50 or so checks to get around the track.) The player that wins the most opposed checks wins the race.

To complete one lap around the track requires five checks (one entering each turn, one exiting each turn, and one at the halfway point on the end of the track opposite the starting gate). If a race runs more than one lap, an extra check is needed when the riders cross the starting line each time.

1. Opposed Ride Checks: Each participant makes a Wisdom (Animal Handling) check; the highest result wins that portion of the race and is considered to be in the lead. If the results are tied, the rider with the higher skill modifier wins. If these scores are the same, the riders are "neck and neck." On a natural 1 (regardless of modifiers), a rider must make a DC 10 Dexterity saving throw or be thrown from his mount. The rider can remount and get back into the race but has disadvantage on the next two checks made at the designated points in the race.

2. Winning the Race: The winner is the rider who wins the most checks during the race. If two or more riders have an equal number of wins, the one with the highest skill modifier wins. If these scores are tied, each rider in the tie makes another Ride check to break the tie.

Conducting the Chariot Races

Chariot races are conducted just like the nightmare races and use the above rules system substituting Dexterity checks with Vehicle (Land) proficiency for Animal Handling checks. Since chariot races are always more than one lap, six checks are needed to completely circle the track.

A charioteer that rolls a natural 1 on her Dexterity check must immediately make a DC 10 Wisdom (Animal Handling) check. On a failed check, she loses control and the chariot either crashes into a wall or flips over (50% chance for either). The driver and marksmen (and anyone else riding with her) take 7 (2d6) bludgeoning damage from the crash plus fire damage dealt by the molten raceway. A crashed chariot cannot get back into the race. A chariot that flips over can usually be flipped upright and continued in the race, but the chariot team has disadvantage on the next two Dexterity checks made at the designated points in the race.

Chariot Races

Chariot races pit charioteers in **nightmare**-drawn chariots against one another on the molten racetrack. Two-person teams (one driver, one marksman) ride the chariots while two nightmares pull each chariot along the raceway. The driver navigates the turns and avoids other chariots and drivers attempting to throw them off the track while the marksman takes aim at the other participants. A variation of this race allows the audience to take shots at drivers with one of eight huge ballistae in the stands for 5 bp per shot, three shots for 10 bp. Remember though, the marksmen can return fire at the stands if she so wishes. Three laps around the track wins.

Equipment: Drivers and marksmen usually wear medium armor. Drivers rarely carry weapons, and those that do usually carry nothing more than a shortsword or dagger. Marksmen wield a shortsword and heavy or light crossbow.

Listed below are three chariot teams.

Driver	Marksman	Weapon
Lil, **Succubus**	F'resnik, **vrock**	heavy crossbow
Celene, **nymph**	Lorelei, **nymph**	light crossbow
Human **bandit lord**	Human **assassin**	light crossbow

Gladiatorial Combat

Two or more combatants face off against one another with or without weapons, and with or without magic. The combat takes place on one of the large platforms hovering about the arena floor. Often, the winner of the contest is the one that finishes off her opponent by knocking him from the platform to the arena floor or molten lead track. This is the most common form of entertainment, and battles of this sort happen all the time.

Have characters participating in such combats face opponents appropriate for their level and abilities to make the battle interesting. Battle slaves are *teleported* from the pits to the arena, dressed in armor and weapons of the choosing of the Circus Master. Common accoutrements include oil shark armor and various melee weapons in which the combatants are proficient.

The Circus Master assigned Grendle Macewan (as **spy**) to gladiatorial combat. He loves the boy's spunk but doesn't see a long future for the youth among the horrors he concocts. So far Grendle has managed to survive and has developed a small following among the denizens of the city that frequent the circus. Grendle has also earned the respect of his fellow gladiators who know that when the boy graduates from fighting monsters, he will likely die gruesomely at the end of one of their swords.

Flame Spawned

A flame-spawned creature is immune to fire damage, adds 1d6 fire damage to a successful attack, and creatures within 5 feet of them take 3 (1d6) fire damage at the start of their turn.

Occasionally, beasts and monsters are brought into the arena to fight one-on-one or against a group of armed (sometimes unarmed) humanoids. Such pairings include fiendish dire tigers[1], fiendish death dogs[1], dragons, and various flame-spawned creatures (see sidebox).

Variants of the gladiatorial event have the disk rotating slowly, tilting, terrain morphing (for example, changing from plain dark slag to slippery ice or dirt or mud), or spikes rising and sinking from the surface as the combatants duel. Other variants have the platform lined with spell-laden traps that spring when an opponent steps on or is thrown onto a space occupied by a trap. The winner of a gladiatorial battle is the one left standing.

Golem Smash

This event pairs a wizard and an **iron golem** against a similar wizard and iron golem. Each wizard wears a special circlet that allows him to direct and control his iron golem. The golems battle each other in an attempt to destroy one another. The winner is the wizard whose golem smashes his opponent's golem into pulp. Wizards are not allowed to use spells or magic to aid their golem. The losing wizard of this event is usually slain

Masters of Pain

Popular combatants draw more people to the circus, and the Circus Master knows this; hence, he devised a way to (usually) keep his best combatants from being killed at the whim of some upstart challenger.

A combatant (or team) that wins three consecutive battles gains the title "Master of Pain." Masters of Pain may be granted mercy from a deathblow based solely on the reactions of the crowd. To determine the crowd's decision, the Master of Pain makes a Charisma check with a +1 bonus to the check for every 3 Victory Points she has (a team can have the member with the highest Charisma make the check; use the team's average number of Victory Points as a bonus on a team roll). The exact DC of the check can be set by you depending on how bloodthirsty or friendly you want the crowd to be that day. (The standard check is against DC 18 — it is the City of Brass, after all.)

If the check succeeds, the crowd decides the Master of Pain should live. She still loses the battle, but at least she is still alive. On a failed check, the bloodthirsty crowd decides they want blood; the challenger may finish off the Master of Pain however he sees fit.

(by the opposing wizard and/or remaining golem) unless he wins mercy from the crowd.

Equipment: No magic items. Wizards can carry any nonmagical weapons with them and can elect to wear armor.

Sample wizards and other spellcasters for use in this game can be found in **Appendix 1** under Humans and the Like.

Tower of Pain

A 100-foot-tall tower resembling little more than twisted iron scaffolding covered in sharpened spikes and traps is erected in the middle of one of the floating platforms. This is the Tower of Pain. Above it floats a *ring of three wishes* surrounded by a 20-foot *antimagic field*. The object of the game is simple: Climb the tower and recover the ring. After retrieving the *ring*, the character doing so has 1 minute to make a single *wish* before the *ring* vanishes.

This game features 2 or more teams of six combatants each, positioned on opposite sides of the platform. Each team is made up of two climbers, two fighters, and two snipers whose objectives include providing covering fire for their team's climbers and attempting to pick off the opposing teams' climbers. Climbers may face an additional threat from the firing decks if fans decide to participate.

Climbing the tower requires a successful DC 13 Strength (Athletics) check per round. A climber that takes damage must succeed on a Dexterity saving throw or fall from her current height and take appropriate falling damage. The DC for the saving throw is 10 or half the damage taken, whichever is higher.

To determine if a climber enters a space with a trap, roll 1d20 and consult the list below each round of climbing. Searching for and disabling traps follows the standard rules.

The first member of a team that reaches and secures the ring wins the game for her team.

Tower of Pain Traps

Each trap is listed with the DC to discover it with an Intelligence (Investigation) check followed by the DC to disable it with a Dexterity check with thieves' tools. You may decide that checks made to disable a trap that fail by 5 or more automatically trigger the trap.

1. Poison Wall Spikes (DC 15/DC 18)
Spikes attack closest target in each of two adjacent 5-foot squares at +8 to hit, doing 8 (1d8 + 4) piercing damage on a hit and target must succeed on a DC 13 Constitution saving throw or take 55 (10d10) poison damage.

2. Ungol Dust Vapor Trap (DC 17/DC 15)
Two rounds after the trap triggers, all creatures within 10 feet of the trap must succeed on a DC 12 Constitution saving throw or suffer the loss of 1 point of Charisma and 44 (4d10) poison damage.

3. Fusillade of Spears (DC 18/DC 18)

1d6 spears attack each target within a 10-foot square centered on the trap. Attacks are made at +8 to hit and do 4 (1d8) piercing damage on a hit.

4. Deathblade Wall Scythe (DC 11/DC 20)

A poisoned scythe makes an attack at the creature that triggers the trap. The attack is at +12 to hit and does 13 (2d4 + 8) slashing damage and target must succeed at a DC 18 Constitution saving throw or take 99 (18d10) poison damage.

5. Wall Scythe Trap (DC 11/DC 16)

Four scythe blades attack up to four targets within 5 feet of the trigger. Each attack is at +8 to hit and does 13 (2d4 + 8) slashing damage on a hit.

6. Fusillade of Darts (DC 16/DC 18)

1d8 darts attack each target within a 10-foot square centered on the trigger. Attacks are at +6 to hit and do 3 (1d4 + 1) piercing damage on a hit.

7. Wyvern Arrow Trap (DC 16/DC 12)

A poisoned arrow shoots at the nearest target making an attack at +10 to hit. On a hit, the target takes 4 (1d8) piercing damage and must succeed on a DC 14 Constitution saving throw or take 44 (8d10) poison damage.

8. Insanity Mist Vapor Trap (DC 18/DC 16)

Gas shoots forth one round after the trap is triggered filling a 15-foot square centered on the trap. All creatures within the area must succeed on a DC 14 Constitution saving throw or be confused as if affected by the spell for up to one minute. A confused creature may repeat the saving throw at the end of its turn, ending the effect on a success.

9. Scything Blade Trap (DC 14/DC 12)

A scything blade makes 3 attacks against a single creature within 5 feet. Each attack is at +6 to hit and does 4 (1d8) slashing damage on a hit.

10–20. No trap.

Equipment: No magic items except magic weapons. Fighters are usually heavily armored, and magic weapons are allowed. Snipers tend to wear lighter armor and carry either longbows or heavy crossbows. Climbers wear light or no armor and some don't even bother with weapons.

Fire and Ice

A large portion of the platform is converted into an ice maze. Prowling through the ice maze are packs of winter wolves and several frost minotaurs. A few areas of the maze are trapped as well. At the heart of the maze is a *brazier of commanding fire elementals*. The first team to get a member to the center of the maze and summon a fire elemental wins. When the fire elemental is summoned, the maze, winter wolves, and frost minotaurs vanish. One round later, so does the fire elemental and brazier.

This game is played by two opposing teams of two to four members each. Teams start on opposite ends of the maze.

For each four rounds spent in the maze, roll 1d20 on the table below for random encounters.

1d20	Encounter
1–2	1d3 + 2 winter wolves
3–4	1d2 + 2 frost minotaurs[+]
5–6	Opposing team member
7–8	Cone of Cold Trap[++]
9–20	No encounter.

[+]As **minotaur** with immunity to cold damage and a Challenge Rating of 5 (1,800 XP).

[++]DC 15 Intelligence (Investigation) to notice, DC 15 Intelligence (Arcana) to disarm. All creatures within 30 foot cone must make DC 15 Dexterity saving throw, taking 21 (6d6) cold damage on a failure and half as much on a success.

Equipment: Varies; can or cannot include magic items. Fire-based items, effects, and spells are outlawed, as are any magic items that grant an immunity or resistance to cold.

Ballista Blast

One team of eight members works to assemble the pieces of a heavy catapult, all the while being assaulted by the circus-goers who fire on them from the various firing deck-mounted ballistae located throughout the stands. It takes 10 rounds to fully assemble the heavy catapult and get it into firing order. A team member with a related proficiency (like tinker's tools or a soldier's background) can reduce the time needed to build the catapult by two rounds. Victory is achieved when the catapult is fully assembled and fired, hitting at least four different ballistae firing decks once. (There is a 20% chance that any hit on a firing deck hits the small brass target, thereby launching its occupants into the arena.)

This event is quite popular, because it requires crowd participation and also because it is one of the bloodier events the circus holds.

To fire a heavy catapult, one person acting as the crew chief makes a DC 15 Intelligence check, adding a proficiency bonus if appropriate. If the check succeeds, the catapult stone hits the space the catapult was aimed at, dealing 21 (6d6) bludgeoning damage to any object or character in the space. Characters who succeed on a DC 15 Dexterity saving throw take half damage. Once a catapult stone hits a space, subsequent shots hit the same space unless the catapult is aimed again.

If a catapult stone misses, roll 1d8 to determine where it lands. This determines the misdirection of the throw, with 1 being back toward the catapult and 2 through 8 counting clockwise around the target. Then, count 1d6 x 5 feet away from the target.

Loading a catapult requires a series of actions. It takes a DC 15 Strength check to winch the throwing arm down; most catapults have wheels to allow up to two crew members to use the Help action, assisting the main winch operator. A DC 10 Dexterity check latches the arm into place, and then a DC 12 Strength check loads the catapult ammunition. It takes four actions to reposition a heavy catapult (multiple crew members can perform these actions in the same round, so it would take a crew of four only 1 round to reposition the catapult).

Victory is achieved when the catapult is fully assembled and fired, hitting all of the ballista firing decks at least once.

Equipment: Ranged weapons are outlawed. Team members can choose between a large *+3 shield* and *oilshark armor*[2].

Brain Ball

This is a crude game of dodgeball played with the lime-hardened brain of a deceased battle slave. The "ball" has been enhanced to include a special version of a *power word kill* spell on it. To win, a team must kill all members of the opposing team. Teams consist of five members each.

The brain ball is a thrown weapon that deals 1d4 bludgeoning damage plus the attacker's Strength modifier on a successful hit. It has a range of 10/40 feet and scores a critical on a 19–20.

To trigger the *power word kill* effect, an attacker must hit her opponent in the head with the brain ball. To make a head shot, the attacker makes a normal attack roll with a –8 penalty. Unless the target is wearing a helmet (or similar protection), she does not get her armor bonus to AC against a head shot. If the attack succeeds, the attacker hits the target's head with the brain ball. The opponent takes damage and must succeed on a DC 14 Constitution saving throw or die. Even on a successful save, the opponent takes 20 (3d6 + 10) force damage.

Victory is achieved when one team kills all members of the opposing team with the brain ball.

Equipment: No magic items allowed, except armor and shields. No weapons are allowed. Generally, nonmagical armor is used. Helmets are allowed and are almost always worn (granting a +1 bonus to AC against head shots).

Circus of Pain

Fire and Ice Maze

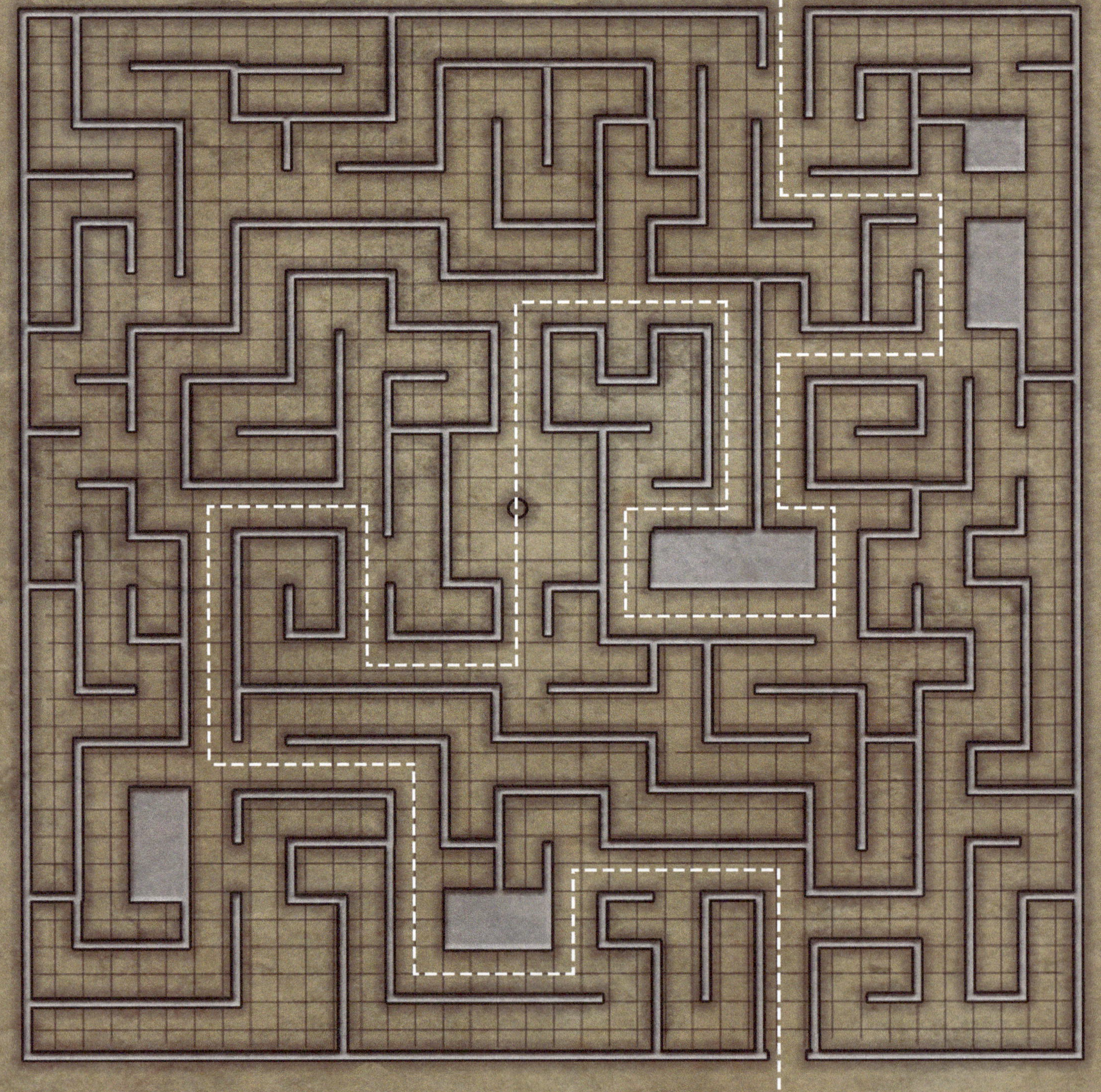

The Circus Champion (The Champion of Pain)

The goal of many battle slaves and competitors is to become Circus Champion. To do this however, one must defeat the current Champion of Pain: **Hezoid**[1].

Hezoid, a rather brave and foolhardy titan, came to the City of Brass many years ago and demanded the *Codex of Infinite Planes*[2] from the Sultan of Efreet[1], threatening to lay waste to the city unless he was given satisfaction. The Sultan and the Grand Vizier merely laughed at this rather large infidel, and after a lengthy and auspicious, if somewhat lopsided battle, they beat the titan into submission, and promptly bound him with a brass collar, then turned him over to the Circus Master. During the battle, Hezoid was shriven of his memory and became maddened by battle lust. He is well kept by the Circus Master, and although by the law he could have demanded his freedom long ago, feels no real reason to give up his current position, and rather enjoys the cheers that go along with it.

Hezoid has no memory of his former life, and now lives only to kill and appease the crowds in the Circus of Pain. Standing nearly 25 feet tall, the mere sight of him is enough to make the bravest of warriors cower. Fighting him alone is considered suicidal by most who have seen him, as he enjoys repeatedly smashing an opponent with his massive hammer while peppering them with his magic.

Facing Hezoid

To face Hezoid in battle, a team or individual must have accumulated at least 50 Victory Points or gone through all the events and won each at least once. Upon doing so and making the challenge, the individuals or team are transported to one of the platforms with all their original gear. The stadium announcer calls out that a challenge has been laid down, and the illusion screens above the stadium flicker to life as Hezoid is *teleported* from his chambers to the platform. Hezoid wastes no time and immediately attacks his opponent(s).

Defeating Hezoid

There are essentially three ways to defeat the Circus Champion of Pain, gain the *maul of Hezoid*[2], and escape the Circus of Pain. Clever players will probably invent others.

Restoring Hezoid's Memory with the *Mymr Stone*: Though he remembers nothing of his former life, Hezoid's memory could be restored if his brass collar is removed and the *Mymr Stone*[2] shown to him. Upon viewing the stone, his memories rush back and he becomes angry at his imprisonment, seeking retribution against his enslavers. He immediately steps into the stands and attacks every efreeti, fire giant, and burning dervish in sight, fighting his way out of the Circus. Fire giant guards and efreeti move to battle him. At the same time, 1d4 + 1 **efreeti** elite guards are *teleported* to the characters' location (if they are still on the platform) to subdue them. If the characters do not get off the platform 1d6 rounds after the chaos erupts, the Circus Master *teleports* them to their holding cells.

Further, every single creature in the arena viewing the *Mymr Stone*[2] has a very good chance of being affected by it. Rather than roll several thousand saving

throws (though you are free to do so if you wish), the easiest way to deal with it is to make a save when Hezoid or the characters encounter an opponent. Simply make the opponent's Wisdom saving throw. On a failed save, the encounter is with a fascinated creature that stands and does nothing (unless attacked).

Should the characters help Hezoid regain his memory and escape the Circus of Pain, he grants them the use of his mighty hammer, the *maul of Hezoid*[2], for one year and one day, and then returns to Olympus to regain his strength and plot his revenge.

Note: Using the *Mymr Stone*[2] can be dangerous as it reveals to the masses that the characters are the thieves who conquered the KhizAnah. Burning dervish bands and efreeti death squads are quickly assembled and the characters are marked and hunted.

Freeing Hezoid with Wishes or Magic: If the characters remove Hezoid's brass collar, his madness can be cured with a successful *greater restoration or wish*. His madness removed, his memories return and he attacks the efreeti as above.

By the letter of the law, Hezoid forfeits the fight to the characters when he turns on the crowd, thus making them the new Circus Champions, and allowing them to request their freedom.

Slaying Hezoid: Certainly not the easiest way to gain the *maul of Hezoid*[2], but it can be done. After defeating Hezoid and becoming the new Circus Champion, a character can request freedom.

Aftermath

If the characters defeat Hezoid, they are hailed as the Champions of Pain and can stay on with the circus, defending their titles, or they can take their winnings and depart. Staying with the circus grants them several perks. First and foremost, the characters gain fame and prestige in the eyes of the circus-goers. Second, they gain wealth by getting a 15% cut of all bets placed on them (if they win).

If the characters opt to take their winnings and leave, they are hailed as celebrities in the City of Brass, possibly opening new doors for them and perhaps gaining them discounts and perks they normally wouldn't otherwise have available to them. Freed characters collect all their earnings and get a 5,000 bp bonus from the Circus Master before they depart.

9. Battle Slave Pits

The Battle Slave Pits are accessed via the stairway to the lower levels, and the locked iron gates (**Area 4**). The gates are opened only for beast and slave traders, stable owners, or those given a pass by the Circus Master.

The Battle Slave Pits are 10-foot-by-10-foot pits dug into the floor. Larger creatures are contained in larger, more accommodating pits. The room is divided into two sections. One contains pens for various beasts that are *teleported* to the fighting platforms; the other is for humanoids, monsters, and outsiders who find themselves sent to this bleak existence. Literally hundreds of cells are in each section. Each cell is "locked" with a *wall of force* that allows visitors to walk around and view the contents of each pit. The entire area is surrounded with an *antimagic field* (that allows the *walls of force* to remain active but nullifies all other magic).

Battle slaves contained in each cell can be chosen from **Appendix 1** under Humans and the Like. Monsters in each cell include giant scorpions, giant wasps, manticores, medusas, demons of all types, devils of all types, a frost giant, a gold dragon, two brass dragons, several werewolves, dire animals of all types. You are encouraged to expand the list.

10. Hezoid's Cell

Unlike the battle slave cells, this is a finely ornate room full of oversized furniture and weapons. There is a 70% chance at any given time that Hezoid is in his cell.

The door to this cell is made of reinforced iron and locked with a *greater arcane lock*[4]. No guards stand before his cell. Hezoid's brass collar prevents him from smashing the cell door into a heap of iron and escaping. From the outside, once the magical lock is removed with *dispel magic* cast against a level 8 spell slot, the mechanical lock can be opened with a successful DC 20 Dexterity check with thieves' tools. It can also be smashed with a successful DC 30 Strength check or by doing 120 points of damage to it.

Hezoid has accumulated the following things over his years as the Circus Champion, but finds little use for any of them, content to drink and fight. Piles of brass, gold, and other loot won in the arena litter the floor. Several 50-gallon casks of wine, both full and empty, line the walls or lie broken on the floor.

Treasure: 3,000 bp, 12,000 gp, 12 brass mugs (200 gp each), 7 rolls of silk (150 gp each), platinum ruby ring (7,000 gp), *staff of abjuration*[2], *ring of telekinesis*, *+3 greatsword*, *+3 lifestealer*[2], *oil of magic vestment*[2], *staff of the python*, *cloak of charisma*[2], and *eyes of charming*.

Chambers of the Circus Master

The following areas are the private quarters of the Circus Master.

11. Entry Way

The portals are made of solid bronze and engraved with the seal of the Circus of Pain: a stylized rendition of the arena above. An ornate bronze gong stands nearby.

A pair of **fire giant** guards stands watch here. One bears a huge mace that he slams into the gong to sound an alarm before wading into combat. After 1d4 rounds, 3 **efreeti** elite guards appear to assist the fire giants.

12. Crystal Pool

A crystal-clear pool of liquid quartz dominates this chamber. Mist and steam fill the chamber, making the entire area lightly obscured. This chamber is home to a pair of crystal **nymphs** (with *bloody daggers*[2]) that tend to the Circus Master and his honored guests. Unwanted visitors are attacked and drowned.

Treasure: Three silver and bronze necklaces lie at the bottom of the pool. Each is valued at 350 gp.

13. Audience Chamber

It is here that the Circus Master takes meetings and entertains special guests. The audience chamber is guarded at all times by 4 **efreeti** elite guards that were granted as gifts to the Circus Master by the Sultan himself. The walls of the chamber are covered from top to bottom with *symbols of pain* that are triggered as soon as a character enters the chamber. The *symbols* require a DC 18 Constitution saving throw. The efreet know and use the password to avoid triggering the *symbols*. When entertaining guests, the Circus Master either covers the *symbols* or dispels them.

Treasure: Twelve inlaid silver engravings featuring arena combat line the walls here. Each is worth 2,000 gp, and weighs about 200 pounds. A throne-like onyx chair sits here (3,000 gp). It weighs about 300 pounds.

14. Treasury

Great iron portals lead to this large chamber containing all the booty stripped from battle slaves when they fall into the arena. By law, this booty is returned if the battle slave ever gains its freedom (this rarely happens). The door to the chamber is triple-locked and protected with a *greater arcane lock*[4] spell cast with a 9th level spell slot. Each mechanical lock requires a successful DC 23 Dexterity check with thieves' tools to open or a successful DC 26 Strength check to break. Smashing the door itself would require a successful DC 30 Strength check.

Once the doors are opened, the party must negotiate the pit trap just beyond the door. In the pit are 3 **giant fiendish yellow cobras**[1] that attempt to bite anyone who falls in the pit. The concealed pit can be noted with a successful DC 18 Wisdom (Perception) check and wedged shut with a successful DC 17 Dexterity check with thieves' tools. A creature that triggers the trap must succeed on a DC 18 Dexterity saving throw or fall in the pit with the cobras.

The snakes are critical to bypassing the last portion of the Circus Master's devious trap. An odorless, tasteless gas permeates the last 20 feet of the vault room. The gas is an inhaled form of black lotus extract that is countered by yellow cobra poison. Only if the characters make their saves or are bitten by the snakes (or happen to have some yellow cobra poison available and consume it) can they safely gather the treasure without suffering the effects of black lotus. A creature who is not inoculated with yellow cobra poison must succeed on a DC 18 Constitution saving throw each round the creature starts in or enters the area. A creature who fails loses 1d6 points of Constitution and is poisoned. The gas can be noted prior to entering the area with a successful DC 16 Intelligence (Investigation) check.

The entire vault area is encapsulated in an *antimagic field*.

Treasure: If any of the characters has become a battle slave, their belongings are found here. Additionally, the following is found here (a lot of this treasure belongs to the battle slaves). Gear or treasure not found here is contained in the Circus Master's private chambers:

Spell potion[2] of *darkvision, potion of climbing, spell potion*[2] of *jump,* 3 *spell potions*[2] of *haste,* 3 *potions of greater healing, spell potion*[2] of *blur, spell potion*[2] of *levitation, potion of flying, spell potion*[2] of *spider climb, potion of vitality, spell potion*[2] of *barkskin, potion of superior healing, potion of healing,* 4 *+1 studded leather armor, +2 splint, +1 plate armor, +1 chain mail, +2 chain mail, +2 chain shirt,* 2 *+2 leather, +1 greataxe, +3 maul, +1 great mace*[3]*, +2 longsword, +1 spear, +1 greatsword, +1 dagger, +3 quarterstaff, +2 shortsword, +1 shortsword, +3 dagger, ring of invisibility, spell scroll* of *lesser restoration, power word kill,* and *cure wounds, spell scroll* of *cure wounds* x2, *spell scroll* of *fireball,* and *lightning bolt, spell scroll* of *teleport, fire trap,* and *hold monster), spell scroll* of *hold person,* and *cone of cold, horseshoes of speed, silversheen*[2]*, bracers of defense, bracers of greater defense*[2]*, wand of lightning bolts,* 10,220 gp, 2,150 pp, 6,100 sp, 4,000 cp, 4 white pearls (300 gp each), 1 green ruby (700 gp), 10 red garnets (15 gp each), 8 amethyst (100 gp each), 2 emeralds (500 gp each), 3 fire opals (150 gp each), fire opal (700 gp), 2 amethyst (150 gp each), 2 sets of thieves' tools, white gold bracelet (400 gp), silver armband (100 gp), gold idol (600 gp), silver ring (10 gp), light crossbow, longsword, shortsword, longbow, longbow, small steel shield, 70 arrows, 8 daggers, 6 cold iron arrows, 30 bolts, 14 shurikens (as thrown dagger), holy symbol of Muir, unholy symbol of Set.

15. Boudoir of the Circus Master

This chamber serves as the Circus Master's nest and place of rest and meditation. A *greater arcane locked*[4] and trapped chest constructed of mithral contains a *portable hole* filled with a percentage of the Circus Master's great wealth. The *greater arcane* lock was cast with a 9th level spell slot. Aside from the magical lock, there are three mechanical locks on the chest, each requiring a successful DC 20 Dexterity check with thieves' tools or a successful DC 20 Strength check. If the chest is touched, an invisible *portable hole* hanging from the roof drops into an invisible *bag of holding* (likewise suspended). This tears a hole in the planar fabric that sucks the chest, the *bag of holding,* the *portable hole,* and all creatures within 10 feet into the Astral Plane. The *bag* and *portable hole* are destroyed. The trap can be noted by a creature that can see invisible objects or with a successful DC 25 Intelligence (Investigation) check.

The walls of the chamber are covered from top to bottom with *symbols of pain* that are triggered as soon as a character enters the chamber. The *symbols* require a DC 18 Constitution saving throw. Depending on the events of the circus, the Circus Master may or may not be present. If a major event is taking place in the arena or special guests, such as the Sultan, have made a visit to the circus, there is only a 10% chance the Circus Master is here. If nothing special is going on in the arena, there is a 60% chance the Circus Master is here.

Resplendent in its wickedness, **Faa'Thasht the Circus Master**[1] epitomizes the cruel pleasures of the pain trade. Faa'Thasht is neither man nor woman but embodies the most exquisite features of both, yet each finely chiseled feature of stunning beauty is malevolently sliced or pierced to reveal the pulpy wounds that are this creature's being. Unlike many of its fellows, Faa'Thasht encases its tortured flesh in the finest of accoutrements that emphasize the horrors of its creation thus framing them for the viewer's eye and capturing them in a stunning reverie of its self-inflicted torment.

The Circus Master is almost reed thin yet possesses the voluptuous curves and sensual moves of a harem dancer. Where its flesh is uninjured, it gleams like polished ivory. Its nails are the blackest of talons though its fingers are often gloved in glistening black and its eyes are the deepest pools of jet showing no iris or pupil. Faa'Thasht has full lips of blood red that are pierced here and there with rings and bars that strategically mar its angelic perfection.

Faa'Thasht is a n'gathau, a member of an alien race that derives immeasurable pleasure from inflicting pain and torture on their opponents and on themselves.

Faa'Thasht keeps a whip of braided alloy cable known as the *harmonious lash*[2] coiled in its belt. See the sidebox for details on this weapon.

Treasure: *Bracers of superior defense*[2]*, figurine of wondrous power (ebony fly), wand of fireballs,* 2 *rings of protection,* 3 *rings of greater protection*[2]*, spell wand*[2] of *charm person, spell wand*[2] of *sound burst*[4]*, 6 potions of greater healing,* 3 *potions of healing, sepll scroll* of *greater restoration* and *heal,* 7,500 bp, 9,000 gp, 50 black pearls (300 gp each), platinum and emerald ring (3,000 gp), 6 ivory statues (Zeus, Artemis, Hecate, Aphrodite, Hercules, Apollo) (850 gp each).

Escaping the Circus of Pain

There are several methods of escaping the Circus of Pain. For those seeking the *maul of Hezoid*[2] as part of an ongoing campaign, winning the maul from the Circus Champion and gaining their freedom is the key to their next adventure. How the maul is gained depends largely on their combat skills, abilities, and role-playing talents.

To escape the Circus of Pain, the characters must somehow manage to:

- Win their freedom in the games.

- Be set free.

- Gain the *ring of three wishes* on the Tower of Pain.

- Create or participate in a successful slave revolt.

- Create discord during the games by freeing Hezoid from his curse.

- Slay or banish the Circus Master.

If the characters are successful and survive the Circus of Pain, Tarbish appears to them, offering them a safe place to hide and recover for the time being until they can proceed to the next stage of their adventure and take the *maul of Hezoid*[2] into the heart of the Great Ziggurat, home to the burning dervishes.

Chapter 24
The Cathedral of the Lightbringer

The Cathedral of the Lightbringer is an adventure location within the City of Brass. The characters detailed here may be encountered in any portion of the City of Brass, though the cathedral serves as their headquarters and a base of operations for evil-doers in the city who are working their own conspiracy against the Sultan of Efreet[1] while pretending to be allied with Nomylus the Burning One. The adventure location serves as a hub for multiple plots and intrigues that the characters may become embroiled in as they explore the City of Brass. The adventure location affords you great freedom in how to incorporate the characters, location, and devious plots into your campaign.

This adventure is suggested for Tier 4 characters.

Background

As the Sultan of Efreet[1] is by the laws of the old gods required to pay homage to their might, so too is he required to respect Demogorgon and the Lightbringer as spiritual fathers after their own fashion. The Lightbringer himself has offered his aid to the Sultan of Efreet[1] through the agents of his faith and has placed this cathedral in the City of Brass as an embassy to the court of the Sultan. Unknown to most, the cathedral itself is a direct pathway to the Hell of Infernus, the structure serving as a permanent gate that works similarly to the ones Nomylus himself spread throughout the universe in the form of his Brazen Spires.

The truth behind any devil's embassy is as obvious as the horns upon its head: Old Scratch seeks an edge. The Fallen One was personally banished from the City of Brass by Sulymon and the power of Anumon during the fall. Since that time, he has coveted the addition of the Throne of Brass to his dominion, just as he craves the return of all the Thrones of Hell to his bejeweled hoof. Unfortunately, his physical banishment from the City of Brass lasts for several more centuries, unless his agents can somehow acquire several relics from within the city itself that could thwart the 1,000-year curse that the Lightbringer sits under.

The Sultan of Efreet[1] for his part would see himself lord god of the Plane of Fire, and all the mortal planes upon which his nation borders. So too would he see himself placed upon the throne of Infernus, carrying out his war of cleansing fire in the Heavens and Hells alike. The Prince of Infernus, being no fool, would see his influence spread to the Elemental Planes and the throne of the City of Brass used as a tool to enslave the genie races and the races of mortals once and for all.

Into this mix, the Lightbringer has sent several of his most trusted henchmen to the City of Brass as an ambassadorial corps of maleficence and evil. Among them are Engrin the **pit fiend**, trusted appointee of the court of Infernus, and official emissary of his power. Engrin is served by three near mortals who act as his agents as they travel the planes and watch visitors to the City of Brass for fools fit to steal the relics that the Lightbringer requires for his schemes.

Among the servants are Dark Cardinal Paz Amare[1], archpriest of the Lightbringer's faith who is assisted in his cause by a choir of lesser devils that travel with him whenever he leaves the cathedral on a fact-finding mission throughout the city.

Another agent of the Lightbringer is Viceroy Ard[1], a near mortal archmage and attorney whose ambition is to serve as chief counselor for the Lighbringer himself. The diabolist is conniving, charming, and gregarious. These traits make it all the easier for him to find souls to dedicate to his masters. If allowed to do so, Ard quickly insinuates himself as a party leader and spokesman. Ard revels in directing others to evil deeds, often without their knowledge. His current bodyguard is Tienen[1], a plane-shifting master thief and assassin with ties to the Fahd al An'il.

Using the Cathedral of the Lightbringer

Several potential plots are offered for you to use should you choose to do so, with most involving some element of role-play on your part and allowing the characters to engage in the collection of items throughout the city. These include being hired or befriended by one of Engrin's agents to steal items from elsewhere in the City of Brass. In the process of the theft, or in attempting to return the items to their client, the characters are made aware that the agents whom they have associated with are in league with the Lightbringer. It is also likely that an independent agent such as Tarbish or Jhedophar contacts the characters, suggesting that they steal *Phosphorus*, the *Sword of the Lightbringer*[2], from the cathedral to use as a weapon against Nomylus the Usurper.

Regardless of the selection the characters make, they likely end up in a confrontation with the agents of the Cathedral of the Lightbringer at some point during their adventures in the City of Brass. Their ultimate actions may have the outcome of removing the Prince of Infernus from the equation of great cosmic powers with a vested interest in seizing the Brass Throne. Of course, a party that decides to make a deal with the Devil may find a place at the table in a universe that has begun its slide into utter damnation.

The Devil's Due

A variety of story threads may bring the characters to the Cathedral of the Lightbringer. Listed below are options offered to them by various agents and authorities of the City of Brass who have their own web of intrigue that may ensnare the characters' interest.

Tarbish

Tarbish (**Rahib al Tarbish Zafir**[1]) is a proud efreet who covets the Throne of Brass for himself and foresees the coming tide of faith in the sect of Zahrahan as a path to power. Tarbish believes that among the many items that could be used to combat the Usurper is the sword *Phosphorus*, and he reveals that the *Sword of the Lightbringer*[2] is currently in the possession of Engrin, the envoy of the Lightbringer. The sword is believed to have significant power against demons, devils, and djinn, and is believed to protect its wielder from certain powers wielded by such creatures. Tarbish would have custody of the sword and would at the very least offer just compensation such as a *wish* to one who would recover it for him without drawing any undue attention to himself.

Rah'po Dehj

In his alias as Rah'po Dehj, the lich sees an opportunity to use the characters to gather powerful relics from this permanent gateway to Infernus without getting himself into any personal trouble with the efreeti authorities. Also, if the characters should happen to die in their endeavor, all the better as far as Rah'po Dehj is concerned.

Ard, Leader of "The People"

Of the various items strewn throughout the City of Brass and the Plane of Molten Skies, one of the most important items on the Lightbringer's list is the corpse of the former Sultan Ashur Ban that is hidden in the dungeon located in the Underbasin that is accessed through the Skull Gate. To this end, Ard is dispatched to offer a scheme for recovering the old Sultan's corpse from the Undercity. He claims his lord and savior may resurrect the body, and he is certain the presence of the newly reborn Sultan will spark a revolution among the disaffected efreeti nobles who have been slighted by the Usurper's burning dervishes in the takeover of the City of Brass.

Ard is dispatched by Engrin and Cardinal Amare to recruit the characters to navigate the Underbasin and recover the body of Ashur Ban and deliver it to Ard, where it may be raised by followers of his religious sect. Ard lies skillfully and never reveals his association with the Cathedral of the Lightbringer, Engrin, or Dark Cardinal Paz Amare.

Of course, the Lightbringer's true intention is to have Engrin use his *magic jar* power to possess the body of the dead sultan and assume his identity, thus controlling the old Sultan's former allies like a puppet master. Once "raised," the newly reformed "Sultan" begs the characters to recover other items to help in battling the Usurper.

Ard introduces himself as leader of "the People," a top-secret order of other planar mortals who seek to overthrow the Sultan of Efreet[1] and restore the old order. He coyly explains that their allies are many and that his associates have "legions" at their disposal, ready to slay the burning dervishes and confound the Sultan's own allies. In actuality, the organization is little more than a form of newfangled devil worship targeted at youth groups who feel angsty and alienated by the constraints of "established" faiths.

Chufa Um Sophanie

Chufa Um Sophanie may intercede either at the beginning or end of a quest offered to the characters by Ard and his associates, making claims that the characters are in fact serving an equal if not greater evil by associating with Ard and the cult known as "the People."

The Cathedral of the Lightbringer Overview

The cathedral exists in slightly different forms as it coexists in multiple dimensions. In Infernus, the Lightbringer's personal realm of Hell, the cathedral is a mockery of the finest cathedral buildings in all the known mortal realms, featuring gorgeous buttresses of marble, stained-glass, and beautiful landscaping. However, it is an inaccessible and unassailable space. Once the "Portal of Light" is crossed, visitors are deposited onto a quasi-plane that touches both Infernus and the realm it is also extant in at once. Denizens of Infernus who are capable of crossing the Portal of Light, such as archdevils with the Lightbringer's permission, pit fiends, and other high-ranking devils who have not been banned from a plane of existence, may pass freely into the cathedral from Infernus, and from Infernus they may enter the Plane of Molten Skies or another plane which the cathedral touches at your discretion. Weaker devils are denied such privileges, though this could change if the Lightbringer were to get his hands on the *Codex of Infinite Planes*[2] and bring it to his palace in Infernus.

The Cathedral Platform

To the local denizens, the cathedral is out of place amid the vast domed structures and sweeping arches of the rest of the city, whose burnished exterior gleams in the ever-present flicker of the phlogiston's flames. As visitors arrive upon the platform itself, they are often awestruck by the grandeur and power that the building presents, if merely that at first glimpse it appears as an austere palace of pure beauty with shining white marble surrounded by a finely manicured lawn of lush green grass edged along flagstones inlaid with semiprecious stone and crushed mother of pearl. Thick tangles of roses grow lovingly beneath the flying buttresses. The walkways themselves are lined with ripe fruit trees that offer succulent apples, pears, and oranges, each filling the air with a sweet, fruity fragrance.

Cathedral of
the Lightbringer
10B
9A
10A
9B
10C
To Infernus
12
9
11C
8
7
8
11A
6
11B
2
4
5
3A
5
3
1
1 Square – 5 Feet

The grounds can be explored, but the great bronze portal that leads to the sanctuary of the cathedral cannot be opened by any means without first crossing into the Portal of Light.

1. Portal of Light

A pair of beautifully carved marble angels support a portal of gleaming light that stands not far from the doors of the cathedral itself. The Portal of Light is held aloft in their outstretched hands as the statues seem to emanate a feeling of succor and peace. The light of the portal is similar to the great light those approaching the threshold of death might see as it invites them into the blessed afterlife. The grounds of the cathedral, as seen beyond the portal, flicker faintly as if the portal itself is not merely a disk of lifegiving light, but also a gateway to another world. From every angle outside the portal, there is the impression of serenity and beauty. Despite this, if the portal is ignored and simply walked around, the great doors to the cathedral remain firmly locked and closed.

The portal opens to the unholy Hell of Infernus, or more to the point, it is a crossing plane between Infernus and the Plane of Molten Skies where both realms co-exist but are not quite perfectly meshed with one another. Upon this particular plane, only the cathedral exists in full form, whereas the City of Brass in all its brazen glory is reduced to a ghostly reflection that can be seen but not touched by the denizens of the blasphemous portal realm.

Characters crossing the portal experience an unsettling sensation not unlike walking into a photographic negative. The normally brilliant fiery orange and gold skies turn to the rusty purplish color of a bruise that crackles with malevolent energy. The air is filled with a faint sulfurous odor.

Lawful good characters not protected by a *protection from evil and good* spell or those accompanied by a paladin of a good faith suffer an automatic 9 (2d8) necrotic damage.

2. Cathedral

Although the structure appears beauteous and divine before passage through the Portal of Light, the true horror is revealed once the passage is made. The roses drip with thick blood fed by the dismembered bodies of those who were offered a different form of salvation by the "Lord of Light." A buzzing fills the air as visitors approach, and they quickly realize that swarms of bloated gadflies crawl upon the lush fruit of the trees growing along the paved walkways, whose mother of pearl is now revealed to be the crushed bone of sentient beings.

The cathedral itself is protected with a *forbiddance* spell that denies the entry of celestials into its unhallowed walls.

3. The Narthex

The porch leads up from the gardens to a set of doors.

3A. The Doors to the Cathedral

The doors are 12 feet high and 8 feet wide and feature sixteen panels.

Before crossing the Portal of Light, the bronze panels seem to depict an angel coming down from the heavens and encountering mortals who are depicted as hairy, naked, and ignorant. The angel calls the ignorant masses together and instructs them in all manner of things. They soon appear shaved, clothed, and industrious as he instructs them in mathematics, reading and writing, engineering, construction, and industry, all of which results in a utopian betterment of the races.

When the portal into Infernus is crossed, the images on the bronze panels change, as does the door itself. Where once was a brilliant, polished bronze door now stands a red-hot iron door. The angel now appears sans halo, bestial horns protruding from its handsome forehead and sharpened claws springing from its fingertips. The story remains vaguely similar where the horned "angel" still instructs the mortals, though the teachings no longer show a utopian climax. Instead they are seen forcing slavery upon one another, committing murders, and forging increasingly devastating weapons. The final three panels depict the angel sitting atop a throne as the various mortal races savagely battle one another. The final panel shows a rift in the center of the world where flames lick at the feet of the angels while horned figured draw the souls of the dead down into the flames.

Any lawful good being other than paladins touching the door suffers 14 (4d6) necrotic damage. Any other being touching the door suffers 7 (2d6) fire damage due to the red-hot nature of the portal. The door swings open on its own if any honest prayer is offered to the Lightbringer and his infernal cause. It otherwise remains closed unless a *knock* spell, *dispel magic*, *dispel evil and good*, or similar spell is cast. *Strangely enough, paladins take no damage when touching the door and the door itself opens to their touch.*

4. Atrium

Beyond the doors is a high-ceilinged atrium with an archway that leads to the nave beyond. A gorgeous crystalline fountain stands in the center of the atrium. The water within the fountain is caustic looking and reeks of sulfur and the sickly sweet stench of slow decay.

The water is unholy water[3], and up to five flasks of it can be drained from the fountain before it must recharge for 30 hours.

A pair of stone statues stands to either side of the atrium. At first glance they appear as great angels of finely chiseled and polished marble, though they warp and transform into **reliquary guardians**[1] when the atrium is entered. They demand that those who enter bow and pay respects to the Lightbringer before being allowed access to the nave.

A mosaic on the floor between the atrium and nave features the tortured visages of goodly gods rendered in exquisite detail. Visitors are required by the guardians to prostrate themselves upon the floor, and crawl with their backs to the altar of the Lightbringer while spitting upon the images of the lords of the Heavens. To do so willingly is a blasphemy against these deities, which causes an immediate loss of level and connection to daily spells and powers to any cleric who chooses to act against his or her deity. To refuse results in an all-out assault as the guardians attack those who deny the might of their hellish lord. Paladins are beckoned into the nave with no interference by the guardians, nor are they required to kneel and back into the inner portions of the cathedral.

5. The Bell Towers

Flanking the door are the towers that lead to the great bells of the cathedral. Ten iron bells gong six times at six after six, cosmic standard mean time, and again at 3 a.m. The towers are home to 2 **chain devils** whose job it is to ring the bells and watch from the bell tower for those who would attempt to sack the cathedral in the name of "justice" and "good."

6. The Nave

Rows of seats face the altar here. The seats themselves are carved of fine wood covered in fine velvet. The seats are occupied by a host of 666 **lemures** who pray and prostrate their blobby forms before the altar. They generally ignore any who enter, other than to cower in fear from any powerful force of evil that enters the cathedral.

The nave is surrounded by high, imposing marble walls set with mighty stained-glass windows. The windows themselves are a horror to behold, as their imagery, although brilliantly lit and exquisitely crafted, features the tale of the Lightbringer's Crusade. Depicted upon the windows is a gorgeous angel butchering and impaling god after god in hideous manner. Eventually the angel appears crimson as it is bathed in the blood of the gods. The Lightbringer then casts down the heavens and forges a new realm from their slaughter. As his final act, he builds a golden throne from the skulls of his foes. He sits astride the golden throne with his blackened wings unfurled. The crowns of the heavens and the multitude of its hosts lay trampled beneath his cloven feet as the orb of the world rests blackened in his left hand and the bleeding crown of hell floats above his horned pate.

7. Chancel

A choir of 24 devils known as the **Choromos**[1] sing here for the ear of Engrin. These blind creatures are tall and thin and wear lush black velvet robes over their tattered and torn flesh. The Choromos ignore those who pass within hearing of their song, though the song may have its own unnerving effects upon listeners who are not followers of the Lightbringer.

8. The People's Transept

Pews line these large alcoves to the north and south of the chancel. The pews are filled during worship services with the Lightbringer's followers in the City of Brass, or those who wish to do business with the Prince of Darkness. At any given time, 2d10 worshippers (choose any lawful evil characters from **Appendix 1** under Humans and the Like) are here praying for guidance from the Son of the Morning.

Worshippers are members of Ard's Cult of the Lightbringer that is referred to as "The People." They are unlikely to involve themselves directly in conflict unless they themselves are attacked.

9. Sanctuary

The sanctuary drips with decadent opulence as every surface is covered in gold leaf and inlaid with precious jewels.

9A. Statue of the Lightbringer

A great statue of ivory and gold depicts the Lightbringer in his angelic form, his fork raised skyward, and his halo ablaze with an ever-burning fire atop his finely pointed horns. His face is beautiful, though there is a cruel turn to his lips. One cloven hoof rests upon the leaden skull of a defeated demon prince. Blood drips down the tines of the fork and splatters drip by drip upon the altar where they sizzle gently, filling the area with an incense of fried blood.

The statue itself has AC 15, 120 hit points, and ignores any attack that does less than 10 damage. It may be permanently destroyed only if a successful *dispel magic* against a 9th level spell slot, followed by *hallow* and a *wish* are cast upon the site. The statue otherwise reforms in 30 hours.

The Aura of Temptation

The statue of the Lightbringer fills those who see it with disturbing feelings of temptation. Listed here are a series of temptations designed to draw mortals to the various sins that Old Scratch has used to deliver souls into his domain since the dawn of time. No saving throw is listed for these visions, as each ends with a choice that may be made by the recipient of the vision. The character is afforded all the rights and benefits of free will, and the players are expected to role-play their way out of the situation.

Listed here are sample temptations that may be offered to various players at the table. No one knows your players better than you, who may choose other alternative temptations, or choose to ignore the temptations altogether as befits your running of the City of Brass and your ongoing campaign.

1. All the Power in the World

The character is filled with feelings of great power and glory. A handsome angelic being standing on their left side offers them the throne of the greatest kingdom of their home world. The folk cheer in adulation.

"This can be yours," the angel offers. "I can teach you the path. You just have to follow it."

A series of images of various murdered religious and political leaders is shown to them as a path to leadership. A contract then appears, with a feather quill that has a scalpel-like tip imbedded in it. There is no ink, and the contract asks only for the immortal soul of the signee, written in blood.

Characters accepting the contract are given a great tale of glory, and how a series of political assassinations leads them to control of a fantastic empire, until they themselves are assassinated by a rival. The character awakens to new life as a lemure on the outskirts of Infernus.

2. Undying Devotion

A cleric or paladin receives a vision where they wield great power as they slay devils, demons, efreet, and angelic beings in a massive conquest. They soon are a bishop or greater in a church whose laws and tenets award the strong, the motivated, and the aggressive with more power and prestige, including great basilicas and theocracies to rule over. Again, the only request asked is the immortal soul of the signee on a contract written on the flesh of a saint.

Any clerics or paladins who sign this document sign their soul over to Old Scratch. They lose any powers and abilities attributed to their previous deity and become a cleric or paladin of the Lightbringer with all the benefits and penalties thereof. A pair of bearded devils is bequeathed as immediate bodyguards to the signee. Upon their death, their soul is awarded status as a devil or death knight of Infernus, skipping the lowly ranks of lemures altogether.

3. The Eternal Mage

An archangel with jet-black wings reveals visions of power coursing through the veins of a wielder of arcane magic. Magic infuses their very flesh and bones as secret after secret of the arcane cosmos is exposed to their massive intellect. All these powers and more are offered should the infernal contract merely be inked in the signee's blood. Magic-users who sign this waiver instantly gain one full level of power as well as one full point of Intelligence and Charisma. Unbeknownst to them — at least initially — they are also transformed into a lich. Their phylactery and soul become property of the Prince of Darkness. No immediate outward appearance of their undeath is revealed at first, but their body begins to slowly decay. Their nose and ears fall off within a month or so, even as their flesh tautens and their blood slowly coagulates until their heart itself ceases to beat. The lich is forevermore in the service of the Lightbringer, forced to tempt others into sacrificing their own spirit and freedom in exchange for eternal servitude.

4. I'm Rich! I'm Wealthy! Yahoo! Oh Nuts.

The archangel to the left of the character shows chests of gold, diamonds, emeralds, and rubies flanking a fine hardwood desk behind which stand two shadowy figures. The character sits at the desk as a line of patrons awaits their chance to meet the new Godfather. Each in turn kisses his hand and lays a tribute upon the loot pile accumulating in the room. Wealth, power, and loyalty are all offered in exchange for favors that the character can proffer at the wave of his fingers or the nod of his chin. At a word, whole neighborhoods are taken over and city governments collapse. At a glance, foes die with a knife buried in their backs. A contract is offered by the dark-winged angel, and the character takes on the leadership of a highly renowned thieves' guild. The thirst for gold suddenly subsides as a thirst for blood takes its place. The new syndicate lord is quickly outed as a vampire, a member of the undead. He is hunted and destroyed by priest and brother in crime alike. They next find themselves risen as a bone devil in Infernus.

9B. The Altar of Deadly Sin

The altar itself appears to be made from a solid block of red marble 4 feet high by 6 feet wide and 4 feet across. Like everything within the cathedral, at first glance it is an ostentatious display of finery and opulence, but a closer look reveals the horrors of a sick and twisted worldview. The altar depicts the glory of the seven deadly sins with various mortals around the top edge of the altar feasting, fighting, fornicating, and otherwise showering themselves in greed, hate, pettiness, and ignorance. In the ring below, the angel of death visits the mortals and their souls are reaped and given over to golden rococo devils devouring the souls of the sinners and defecating out blobs of screaming lemures that cower in fear at the bottom of the altar piece.

The altar exudes a *hallow* effect. Any non-evil creature that approaches within 60 feet must succeed on a DC 17 Wisdom saving throw or be frightened of the altar. A frightened creature cannot approach the altar and will not willingly remain within 60 feet of it. A frightened creature can repeat the saving throw every hour, ending the effect on a success. A creature who succeeds on its saving throw is immune to the effect for 30 hours. Worshippers of the Lightbringer are unaffected.

10. The Apses

Three small, semicircular shrines occupy the area behind the altar.

10A. Chevet of Light

This shrine pertains to the wisdom that the Lightbringer grants his followers. A locked gate of red-hot wrought-iron bars denies access to a large book chained to a pedestal of gleaming white marble that exudes a bright light.

Touching the gate deals 10 (3d6) fire damage and opening the lock requires a successful DC 20 Dexterity check with thieves' tools or appropriate magic. The gate opens to the touch of a paladin or lawful good cleric. Within the chevet is a cursed *tome of understanding* that turns the reader to lawful evil unless a successful DC 17 Charisma saving throw is made. A reader who is already lawful evil and a worshipper of the Lightbringer gains one level immediately.

10B. Chevet of the Ancient Morning

This apse is protected like the other and contains a pedestal of red marble above which floats the *scepter of Attar*[2] which is made of petrified bone affixed with the head of a horned goat or ibex. The eye holes of the scepter glow like hot coals and a faint wisp of sulfurous smoke wisps from the nostrils. A quarter moon with points upturned is carved upon the skull, and a primitive pentagram is carved between the horns.

10C. Chevet of the Shroud of Truth

This apse is locked and chained like the others to protect the strange treasures held within. Floating in a pillar of light is the *shroud of truth*[2], a black and red cloak gives a yellow, sulfurous smoke.

11. Sanctum of Peace and Love

This tower attached to the cathedral serves as the personal sanctuary of Dark Cardinal Paz Amare[1].

The doorway is locked with a *glyph of warding* that deals 38 (11d6) thunder to creatures within 20 feet that fail a DC 18 Dexterity saving throw and half as a much to creatures that succeed. Noticing the glyph requires a successful DC 18 Intelligence (Investigation) check.

11A. Bodyguard Barracks

This room serves as the barracks for Dark Cardinal Paz Amare's two bodyguards, Sir Carlo and Sir Pedro, both fallen paladins infused with the glory of the Lightbringer.

Sir Carlo uses the statistics of a **fallen paladin**[1], save that he wears a set of *+3 plate armor* and wields a *+3 greatsword* with which he has +11 to hit, for 14 (2d6 + 7) slashing damage plus 4 (1d8) necrotic damage instead of a shield and longsword. Sir Carlo's Challenge Rating is 10 (5,900 XP).

Sir Pedro uses the statistics of a **fallen paladin**[1] as well, except that he wears a set of *+2 plate armor*, a *belt of giant strength* (frost), and wields a *+2 greataxe* that deals only necrotic damage on a hit, rather than slashing damage. Because of his magic items, his Armor Class is 20, Strength score is 23 (+6), he has a +12 to hit with his *+2 greataxe*, and deals 14 (1d12 + 8) plus 4 (1d8) necrotic damage when he hits. His Challenge Rating is 10 (5,900 XP)

11B. Second Floor

Dark Cardinal Paz Amare's Study

This library and study holds Cardinal Amare's papers, as well as various histories of the battles of the Lightbringer versus the angels of Heaven and his betrayal at the hands of the princes and dukes of Hell. Studying the books for at least one month grants a +2 bonus to History checks as they pertain to the Hells and the hellish hosts.

Among the items on the shelves are the following *spell scrolls*: *bestow curse, animate dead, protection from energy, spirit guardians, speak with dead, insect plague, raise dead, greater restoration, fire storm, plane shift,* and *earthquake*.

11C. Third Floor

The third floor is Cardinal Amare's private chamber. A velvet and silk adorned canopy bed occupies one corner of the room. Fine walnut cabinets hold the cardinal's vestments and robes. Cardinal Amare keeps his wealth on his person or in a pocket dimension hidden on the 666th page of his unholy scriptures that sit on the nightstand next to his bed. Entering the dimension requires access to Paz's password, which is "*phosphorus.*" Unless the characters are excellent at guessing or can read Cardinal Pax Amare's mind, it is unlikely they can access his demi-plane.

Within the confines of the secret plane are the amulets of five demons and the talismans of three horned devils, and unbeknownst to Engrin, a scroll with that pit fiend's true name.

A golden coffer (worth 500 gp) contains 1,000 pp, 5 hellfire diamonds worth 1,000 gp each and 500 bp. Dark Cardinal Amare keeps these items as a safety net in case things go wrong, as they are apt to do when dealing with fiends.

Engrin's Rectory, Hell's Back Porch

This square structure attached to the side of the cathedral proper serves as the lair of Engrin the **pit fiend**, guardian of the gate to Infernus. The large square room appears to be a charred, hollowed-out husk of a multistory structure where the upper stories have been torn out. A series of iron spears are embedded in the stone floor. Upon each is the impaled and charred corpse of other devils, demons, efreeti, djinn, and devas brought as tribute to the mighty pit fiend who serves as the eyes of the Lightbringer in the City of Brass. Engrin, the bearer of *Phosphorus*, the *Sword of the Lightbringer*[2], sits on a massive velvet and gold throne resting along one wall.

Engrin wastes little time mincing words. He demands that the party kneel and swear allegiance to the Prince of Darkness. If they do, he asks what business they have with him that could not have been handled by the mortal servants of the Son of the Morning.

Depending on their answers, he either fights or converses. Engrin is very intelligent, and with *Phosphorus* in his hand, is even deadlier than normal. Engrin tempts characters with treasures, power, and other opportunities. His mission is to act as friend to the Sultan of Efreet[1] while simultaneously destabilizing his empire. Engrin intends to become a duke of the reconquered Hells and the first step in his quest is the delivery of the City of Brass, the Plane of Molten Skies, and the Plane of Fire to his master. If he doesn't like the characters' answers, his options include — but are not limited to — eating the characters' souls or impaling their bodies upon iron spears.

Treasure: *Sword of the Lightbringer*[2]

Portal to Infernus

The exit to the courtyard reveals the drab Hellscape of Infernus where tortured souls are punished unendingly by hosts of devils. The portal is closed to any save those invited directly to the plane by its master, the Lightbringer himself. Those who have sworn fealty to him may pass freely into the Lightbringer's plane. Those who would enter unbidden must find some other means, such as the River Styx.

Closing the Portal

The portal can be closed if it is dispelled with a DC 22 *dispel magic*, a *wish*, or a *holy aura* spell. Closing the portal effectively shuts off access to the cathedral from Infernus until a new portal can be constructed from the cathedral side of the portal.

Using the Cathedral of the Lightbringer

The cathedral is a dangerous location. Dark Cardinal Paz Amare[1], Ard[1], and Engrin all represent difficult foes in their own right. Care should be taken by the characters when facing any of them, let alone trapping themselves in a situation where they may have to battle all of them at once. Ultimately, it is up to you to decide where you want to place Ard and Dark Cardinal Paz Amare[1], or if you need to have both members of the Lightbringer's retinue in the cathedral at the same time at all.

Agents such as Chufa Um Sophanie, Tarbish, and Rah'po Dehj may send the characters on a daring raid of the cathedral, hoping to close off the portal from Infernus, or to assassinate Engrin, Cardinal Paz, or Ard.

Chapter 25
The KhizAnah

The KhizAnah serves as the bank and central depository for the City of Brass. Its reputation for impregnability has not gone unnoticed to denizens of other planes who enjoy the security this place offers and often keep portions of theirt wealth within the mysterious vaults. Characters attempting to penetrate the stiff defenses of the KhizAnah as part of a City of Brass mega campaign do so seeking the *Mymr Stone*[2]. With this powerful relic, the characters may not only find a way to escape the unbreakable bank, but also use the stone as one of many tools to help them survive even tougher challenges that **Tales of Brass** has to offer.

The actual structure of the KhizAnah has the appearance of a bank perhaps found in a large, wealthy city anywhere. It is composed of a semi-circular domed structure of pure rose marble topped with a spiraling dome covered in red gold leaf. Finely fluted columns carved to look like stylized date palms offer a fantastic faux support to the front portico. Dates carved from clear blue quartz glitter brilliantly from the finely-chiseled palms. Magical inscriptions cover the entire structure, woven seamlessly into the design of the building.

Characters may wish to visit the KhizAnah to store their own loot, or they may be enticed to "rob the bank" by any number of NPCs suggested in Chapter 9. For example, the characters may have completed a mission for Rah'po Dehj, been awarded the *shirt of the iron lion*[2], and need to go collect it from the bank. Perhaps the Fahd al An'il has decided to test their prospects and determine if they are worthy of raiding one of the most dangerous and well-guarded banks in the universe.

This adventure is suggested for Tier 4 characters.

Standard Features

Circular Irising Doors: Unless otherwise noted, all doors are irising circular doors of solid adamantine, two inches thick and fitted with excellent locks, and protected by a *greater arcane lock*[4] spell. The doors can only be unlocked once the *greater arcane lock* spell is defeated. The magical locks were placed with a cast with a 9th level spell slot. The mechanical lock requires a successful DC 25 Dexterity check with thieves' tools, or the door can be broken in with a successful DC 30 Strength check. The doors have AC 18, 80 hit points, and ignore any attack that does less than 10 points of damage.

Shielding: A character who makes a successful DC 20 Intelligence (Arcana) check discovers that the entire structure is under the effects of powerful abjuration magic designed to deny extraplanar travel or teleportation into or out of the structure.

The KhizAnah is shielded against any means of magical transport for anything except inanimate metallic objects (with exception of the teleportation disks on Level 2 that allow teleportation to and from specific locations in the KhizAnah). Spells such as *teleport*, *dimension door*, *plane shift*, *etherealness*, and so on automatically fail if used within the KhizAnah or if used to attempt to gain entrance to the structure.

Additionally, no spells or powers involving extraplanar contact, such as *conjure* anything, *gate*, or *commune* operate within the KhizAnah. The KhizAnah is further shielded against *clairvoyance* and *scrying* by spells or magic items.

1. The Portico

The entry portal to the KhizAnah is protected by 2 **efreeti** elite guards armed with massive falchions who glare menacingly at all who enter. The portico leads to the foyer (**Area 2**).

Note: If the guards are attacked, an alarm automatically sounds throughout the KhizAnah. Two rounds later, the adamantine portal is

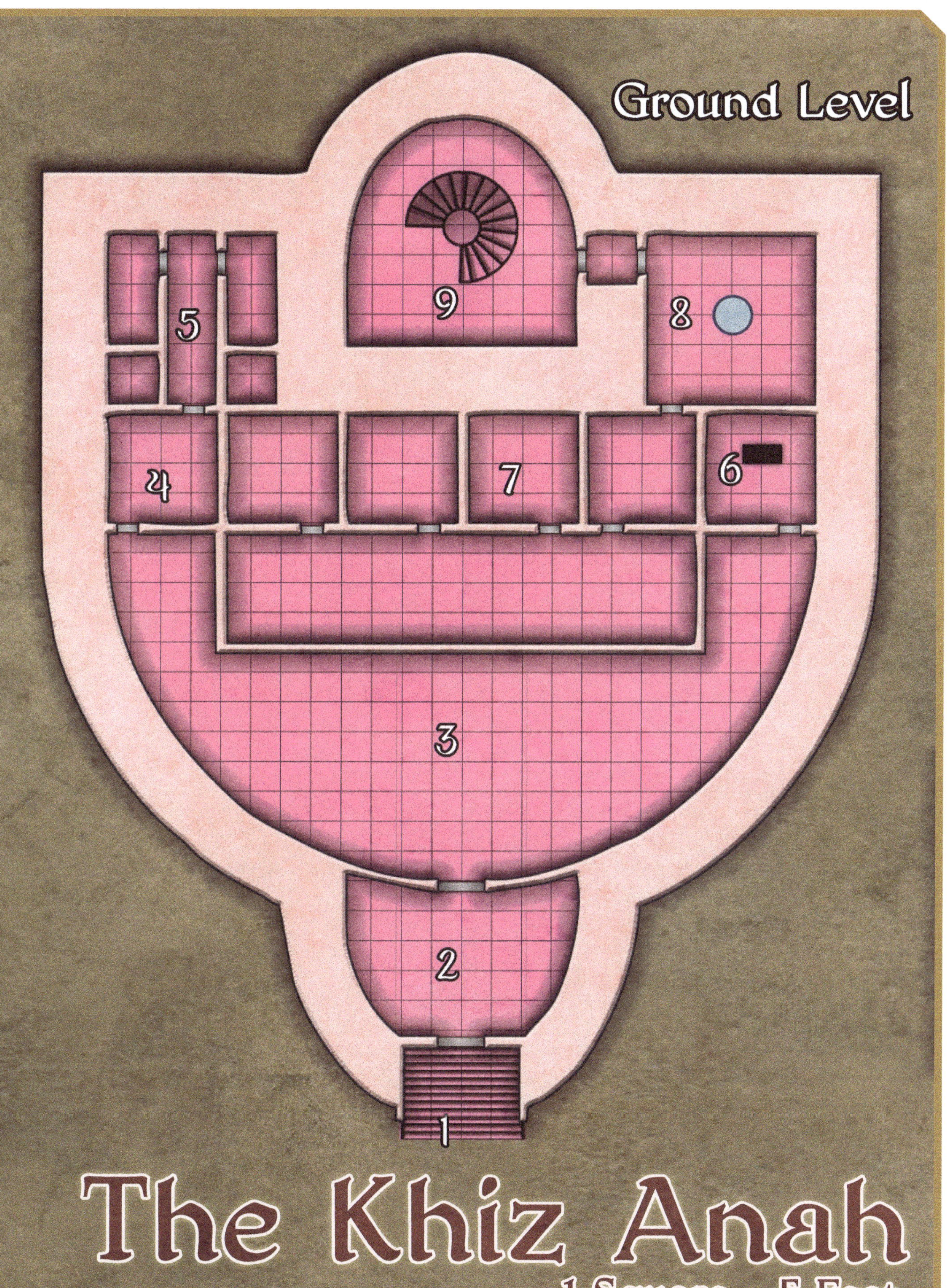

Ground Level
5
9
8
4
7
6
3
2
1
The Khiz Anah
1 Square – 5 Feet

sealed, a second adamantine door spirals shut atop the first set, and a *wall of force* spell is triggered. This *wall of force* is sandwiched between the two sets of adamantine doors. One of the guards is dispatched to gather a force to surround the KhizAnah. This force consists of a dozen more efreeti guards, a half dozen fire giants, an efreeti sorcerers[1], and a burning dervish feyhda[1], who form a protective perimeter around the KhizAnah. This force is readied to blast anyone who forces their way beyond the portals. A second force readies itself to override the defenses, go into the KhizAnah, and hunt down any intruders. See "Robbing the Bank" for details on the strike force sent to apprehend any would-be thieves.

2. The Foyer

Like the portico, the foyer is guarded by 2 **efreeti** bank guards. A second set of doors open into the lobby (**Area 3**). If the guards are attacked or an alarm is sounded, a second pair of adamantine doors and defensive measures as described above spring into effect.

3. The Lobby

The KhizAnah is nearly always open except on citywide holidays. Its lobby is filled at all hours with bank customers, messengers, and merchants from the city as well as other locales throughout the planes. **Efreeti** elite guards stand in the four corners of the lobby keeping a watchful eye on the comings and goings of the bank customers. Six teller windows staffed with **efreeti** bank tellers protected by 1-inch-thick adamantine bars stand before four counting rooms. The bars require a successful DC 28 Strength check to break out.

Banking

Individuals wishing to open an account at the KhizAnah may do so by depositing at least 100 bp (an account does not need to maintain a minimum balance, but a minimum deposit is required). Withdrawals may be done at any time during banking hours, and accounts are kept open indefinitely. Individuals opening a new account are given a numeric code to memorize to collect their cash or valuables from the bank and need only fill out a deposit slip scribed on a sheet of pure copper and hand this to the bank teller.

Safety deposit boxes are also available to bank customers. These are key-operated and each is a portable hole allowing the customer to come and go as they wish and collect their things. The safety deposit boxes cost 50 bp per month to rent, and items inside of them that go uncollected past the time the box has been rented become the property of the KhizAnah. Tellers ask only basic questions of the bank customers, which is one of the reasons for the success of the institution.

Four doorways lead from the teller area to counting rooms where the banking canisters are filled with valuables for delivery to the vault.

The Banker's Geas

All guards, bank employees, and slaves of the KhizAnah are enchanted with the banker's *geas*. This *geas* compels the employees to forget what is in the vault, or where it is located if they are asked or compelled to tell anyone other than another bank employee. Should someone attempt to read the minds of a bank employee or slave with a *detect thoughts* or similar spell or effect, a *feeblemind* spell is triggered that reduces the employee to a gibbering buffoon if the employee fails a DC 17 Wisdom saving throw. Likewise, the mind reader must also succeed on a DC 17 Wisdom saving throw or be affected as by a *feeblemind* spell.

4. Security Room, Deposit Boxes

A pair of large, gruff-looking **efreeti** elite guards similar to others found in the KhizAnah guard this room. An **efreeti** clerk is here as well, and conjures keys for customers coming here to use the deposit boxes. People just milling about are asked to wait in the lobby. Individuals with serious business pay their coin, are given their key, and are ushered into the deposit box vault.

5. Deposit Box Vault

The walls of this chamber are lined with safety deposit boxes from the floor to a ceiling some 50 feet above the ground. Polished bronze plates eight inches square with minute keyholes guard rare treasures for their owners in the strictest of confidence. Huge ladders on wheels and tracks allow access to some of the higher deposit boxes. Customers may optionally have the **efreeti** clerk fly them to the box, but many turn this down as they would prefer the bankers not know what is in their box.

Each of the deposit boxes is actually a portable hole and may be opened only with a specific key. Attempting to pry one of the brass doors from the wall triggers a crushing ceiling trap and an alarm begins to chime throughout the KhizAnah, bringing guards from the lobby, the guard barracks, and the security room to handle intruders. One round after the ceiling crushes the party and returns to its normal place, acidic gas flows into the area to cleanse the floors and walls of the vault. The residual gore seeps out through tiny cracks in the floor.

Crushing Ceiling Trap: One round after it is triggered, all creatures withing the 10-foot by 10-foot area beneath the ceiling suffer 88 (16d10) bludgeoning damage as the ceiling meets the floor. The trap can be found with a successful DC 18 Intelligence (Investigation) check and disarmed with a successful DC 25 Dexterity check with theives' tools.

Acid Gas Trap: One round after the ceiling resets to its standard position, the 10-foot by 10-foot area beneath the ceiling is filled with acidic gas from floor to ceiling for five rounds. Any creature that starts its turn within or who enters the area during the five rounds must make a DC 18 Constitution saving throw, taking 22 (4d10) acid damage on a failure or half as much on a success. The trap can be found with a successful DC 18 Intelligence (Investigation) check and disarmed with a successful DC 25 Dexterity check with theives' tools.

Treasure: The treasures held here are in a specially constructed inter-dimensional space that is inaccessible to anyone not having the corresponding key. If the characters happen to gain a key through pickpocketing or by some other means, feel free to insert any corresponding treasure you feel appropriate for the deposit box. The deposit boxes may serve as plot seeds if you wish to create your own adventures in the City of Brass.

6. Bank Manager's Office

Thaaman Ikla (**efreeti amir**[1]), the bank manager, keeps an office here on the ground floor of the KhizAnah. He alone knows the proper set of staircases to take to get to the vault-servicing chamber. However, he has a *geas* on him to forget this information should he ever be asked or forced to take anyone there. His *geas* further drains any knowledge of how to order treasure up from the vault if forced to do so by would-be robbers. A *contingency* spell placed upon him casts a heightened *power word kill* on him should his *geas* ever be broken. Thaaman's office is opulent with a fine onyx desk. His ledger is strangely blank, as the *Mymr Stone*[2] handles all the processing needs of the bank when it comes to retrieving treasure from the vaults (**Area 27**). His desk is empty, and the books on his shelves are more or less fiction or efreeti interest stories.

Thaaman's actual job is to oversee the upper counting rooms, and to make sure that the tellers do not try to sneak any treasure into their own pockets. He also handles transporting coins from the betting windows of the **Circus of Pain**. There is a 30% chance that Thaaman is in his office; otherwise, he is found in the teleporter room (**Area 8**) or in the upper counting chambers (**Area 7**).

Thaaman is a bureaucrat and was chosen specifically because he is weak enough to accept the *geas* placed upon him and a big enough ass to abuse the tellers and accountants mercilessly.

7. Upper Counting Chambers

An **iron golem** guards each of these four rooms and moves to slaughter any non-bank employee entering the chamber. There is the unmistakable sound of air being sucked into and spit out of this chamber, seemingly emanating from complex machinery set into the floor of the room, which is cared for by a team of 4 **efreeti** sorters.

Nine-inch-wide, two-foot-long metallic canisters inscribed over their surface with magical wards rise up from 9-1/2-inch-wide pneumatic tubes in the floor of these chambers, coming to rest on well-machined racks. The racks are then loaded and unloaded by industrious efreeti. The accountant works an abacus connected to a golden box set into the floor to enter the account number read from a deposit slip. This magically transmits the account number and amount of a deposit or withdrawal to the *Mymr Stone*[2] in the vault, which sends up the proper canister through one of the pneumatic tubes.

Once the canister arrives, the accountant (efreeti) gives a command word to unseal the lid. The contents are called for and recounted to ensure that it is the correct amount (which, because of the *Mymr Stone*[2], it always is). The amount and sort of treasure detailed on the copper deposit slip is then placed in a tray and sent directly to the cashier. The canisters are sealed just as swiftly and sent back to the vault. Returned canisters are quickly whisked away by some unknown engine in the bowels of the KhizAnah to the safety of the vault below. Accountants have a *geas* on them that causes them to forget any command words to open the canisters if they are "forced" to open them.

The fourth chamber has a doorway leading to the teleporter room (**area 8**).

Pneumatic Tubes: The pneumatic tubes are 9-1/2-inches wide. One sucks the canisters into it with powerful force; the other pushes the canisters out with a nearly equal force. Brakes are applied to the canisters as they come out of the tube, and they automatically fall onto a special holding rack until they can be processed by one of the accountants. A creature stepping in front of a down tube must succeed on a DC 15 Dexterity saving throw or be pulled into the tube (if Tiny or smaller size) or stuck against it (if Small or larger size) as the suction attempts to pull that creature into it. Stuck creatures can make a DC 18 Strength (Athletics) check to pull free. When freed, a creature is likely to have the biggest hickey of its life. A Tiny or smaller creature sucked into a tube takes 14 (4d6) bludgeoning damage each round for 1d4 rounds before being deposited in a middle level counting room.

8. Teleporter Room

This chamber has a permanent *teleportation circle* inscribed on the floor. It is two-way and only allows teleportation to and from the **vaults** of the **Circus of Pain**, and even then, only metallic objects are transferred. Rolling carts of coin and valuables are pulled from the *teleportation* pad and sent to the KhizAnah's vault (**Area 27**). In the event that someone bets the house and breaks the bank at the Circus of Pain, canisters from the State Treasury are brought up, and coin is matched to pay off the circus's debt.

Thaaman Ilka often observes this process, but the work is done by 4 **efreeti** sorters who take full containers to the counting chamber adjoining this chamber to deposit into the vault.

Separating the teleporter room from the secure access room (**Area 9**) are a pair of 6-inch-thick adamantine doors that are time locked and open for only 1 minute every 10 hours to allow for the guards in the secure access to switch shifts. The doors require a successful DC 30 Strength check to be forced open, or the lock can be picked with a successful DC 30 Dexterity check with thieves' tools. The doors have AC 20, 200 hit points, and ignore any attack that does less than 20 points of damage.

9. Secure Access to Lower Level

This portion of the main floor of the KhizAnah has the grandeur and security worthy of an extremely advanced and wealthy civilization. Everything about the rotating, vault style entry doors fixed with complex mechanical and magical locking mechanisms lead to this assumption.

The door is a foot thick and made from solid adamantine that weighs more than 16,000 pounds. The door is tubular in shape forming a semicircle that rotates when the proper combination of passwords and dial turns are completed. The doors are time locked, however, and may be opened only on the sixteenth hour of any given day. They remain open

Canisters of Holding

The KhizAnah uses specially magicked pneumatic adamantine canisters for delivering and retrieving treasure from the vault. These *canisters of holding* work exactly as a *bag of holding* capable of holding 1,500 pounds of material and weighing 60 pounds. The difference between a *canister of holding* and a *bag of holding* is that the *canister's* opening is only 9 inches wide. Nothing wider than that may be placed into a canister. Each canister is sealed with a special command word and its lid screwed tightly in place.

Once sealed, a canister is affected as if it had an *arcane lock* spell cast upon it. Further, a trap takes is placed on the canister when it is sealed so that if tampered with by force or magic without first speaking the second command word, the trap is triggered. The trap can be detected with a successful DC 18 Intelligence (Investigation) check and disarmed with a successful DC 18 Intelligence (Arcana) check. A creature that triggers the trap must make a DC 17 Constitution saving throw, taking 63 (18d6) necrotic damage as the creature's moisture is sucked from its body.

A canister can be smashed open with a successful DC 25 Strength check or by doing 60 points of damage against AC 18. Breaking a canister destroys its magic and causes all its contents to spill out in a rush, instantly filling the space around it.

If by some chance or quirk of fate (or really nasty GM) a living creature is enclosed in a canister, there is enough air for 10 minutes. After that, refer to the suffocation rules.

---

only for fifteen minutes before they seal shut again for another 30 hours. The door is affected by a *greater arcane lock*[4] spell cast with a 9th level spell slot, and the only person who knows the complex passwords for opening the time locked door is Thaaman Ikla. The walls on either side of the door are shielded against *passwall* spells, and the entire structure as is noted is shielded against *teleportation* or other means of magical egress. Smashing through the door requires a successful DC 40 Strength check or the mechanical locks can be picked with three successive successful DC 25 Dexterity checks with thieves' tools. The doors have AC 22, 480 hit points, and ignore any attack that does less than 20 points of damage.

For all this security, once the door is opened, it reveals a large nearly empty chamber with a spiral staircase leading down. Four **efreeti** elite guards attack any non-bank employee on sight.

The staircase leads down to the entry to the false vault.

10. Entry to the False Vaults

The spiral staircase ends in a large, brightly illuminated chamber. The walls of this chamber appear to be covered completely in gold leaf. Relief sculptures depicting bearers carrying burdens of treasure to give as tribute to the Sultan of Efreet[1] decorate these highly-polished walls.

Illusions hide secret doors in the eastern and western walls. These doorways lead to the eastern barracks (**Area 12**) and the western barracks (**Area 13**). *Detect magic* or a successful DC 20 Intelligence (Investigation) check may find the hidden alcove, but only a successful DC 22 Intelligence (Investigation) check will find the secret doors that lead to the barracks.

A huge double portal stands in the center of the southern wall. Its doors appear to be polished gold and are carved in the likeness of the Sultan sitting upon a throne of fire. The doors have no apparent hinges or keyholes. A character making a successful DC 23 Wisdom (Perception) check discovers a button that releases a four-handled doorknob that serves as a combination to open the door to the vault beyond.

The handles are coated in black lotus extract poison. The door is locked with an *arcane lock* spell that must be circumvented before any attempt to open the lock may be made. Additionally, the door is trapped with an acid fog trap that triggers if someone tampers with the lock.

The poison on the handles can be noted with a successful DC 20 Wisdom (Perception) check. A creature that touches the handle without

The Khiz Anah

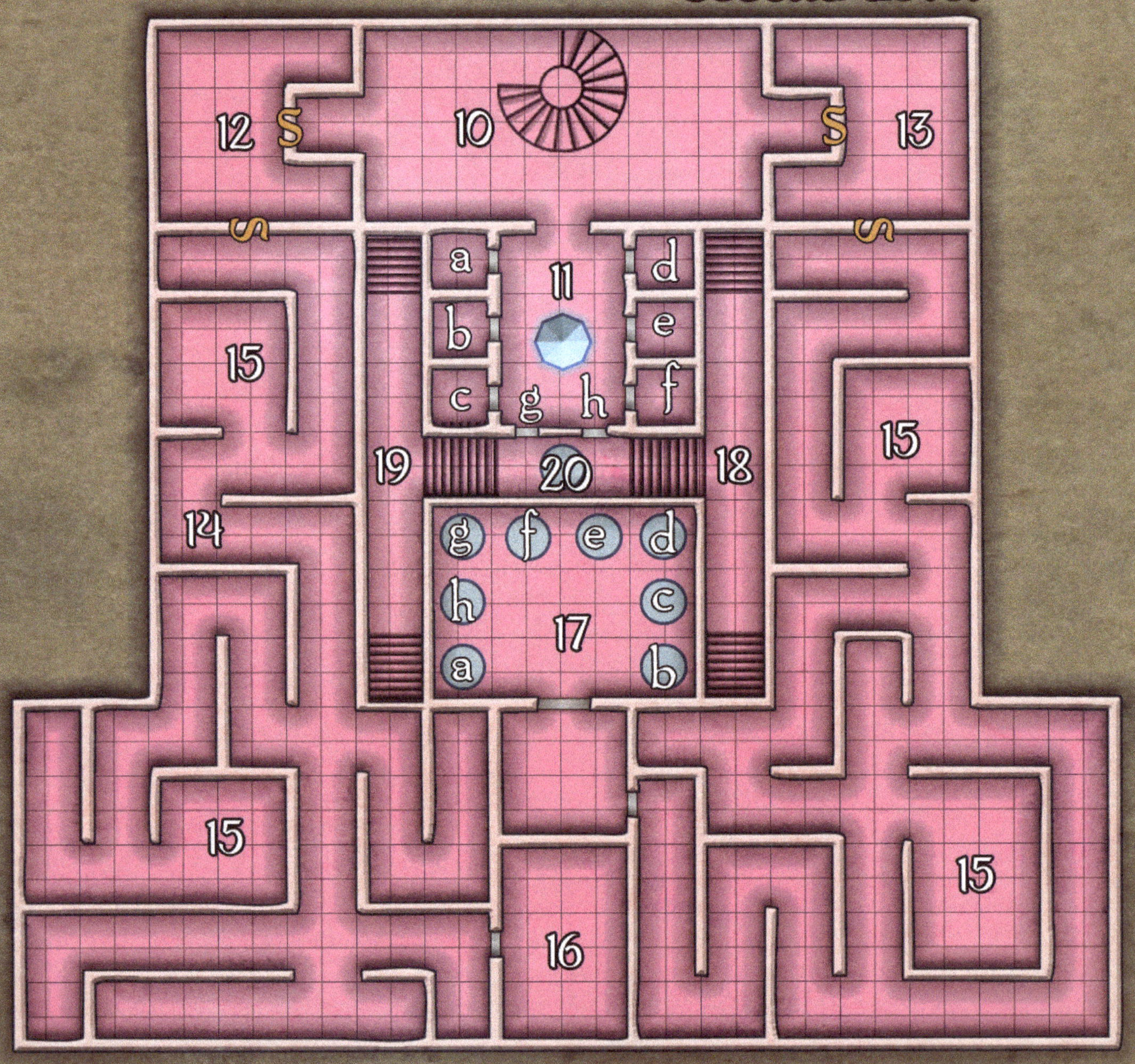

removing the poison must succeed on a DC 18 Constitutions saving throw or take 55 (10d10) poison damage. The trap on the lock can be noted with a successful DC 18 Intelligence (Investigation) check and disabled with a successful DC 18 Dexterity check with thieves' tools. If triggered, the trap releases an acid fog that fills the chamber for 2 minutes. Any creature that starts its turn in the area or enters the area on its turn must succeed on a DC 16 Constitution saving throw or take 7 (2d6) acid damage.

The lock on the door can be picked with a successful DC 18 Dexterity check with thieves' tools or the door broken in with a successful DC 23 Strength check.

11. False Vaults

A huge glowing crystal floats in the center of this chamber and draws strong emotions from individuals viewing it. The crystal is actually just a simple quartz crystal the size of a human head inscribed with a modified *symbol of discord* trap. A creature seeing the crystal must succeed on a DC 17 Constitution saving throw or be subject to the spell for 1 hour.

Eight large doorways line the eastern, western, and southern walls of this chamber. The doorways, lettered **A–H** on the map, are all false treasure vaults designed to destroy any would-be thief. Unless otherwise noted, each vault door is locked and requires a succesful DC 20 Dexterity check with thieves' tools to bypass.

11A False Treasure Vault

The door to this chamber is double locked (requires two successful Dexterity checks to open). Upon opening the vault door, the party sees a 10-foot-by-20-foot room and a bookcase filled with many scrolls and books. A loose sheet of paper near the door shows (false) ledger accounts of various safety deposit boxes.

Located in the central 10-foot-by-10-foot area of the room is a grid work of 2-inch holes covering the floor and spaced 6 inches apart. Closer examination reveals that each hole is about one-foot deep. The trap is actually hidden in the ceiling of this area. Sharpened iron rods strike down at anyone passing through the center 10 feet of the room. The trap can be discovered with a successful DC 17 Intelligence (Investigation) check and disarmed with a successful DC 15 Dexterity check with thieves' tools. Each creature within the area must succeed on a DC 20 Dexterity saving throw or be hit with 1d3 iron rods. Each rod that hits does 21 (6d6) piercing damage.

The books and scrolls are worthless gibberish.

11B False Treasure Vault

The door to this vault has a complex dial type lock that requires a successful DC 25 Dexterity check with theives' tools to open. Gaining entrance, the party sees a narrow, 10-foot-by-30-foot room with many shiny gems embedded in the farthest 15 feet of the room. Handling a gem reveals to the would-be thief that the gems are covered in a clear, touch-activated version of *sovereign glue*. Unless the party has *universal solvent* or some other powerful method of dissolving the *glue* (such as a *wish*), the thief is stuck. The glue can be noted with a successful DC 20 Wisdom (Perception) check. Two rounds after a gem is touched, an alarm sounds throughout the KhizAnah to alert all efreeti guards.

11C False Treasure Vault

Beyond the door of this vault is a brick wall. Carved on the wall opposite the door is a *symbol of stunning* with a save DC of 18. One round after the *symbol* is activated, a 20-foot deep, 10-foot-by-10-foot pit trap opens directly in front of the vault door to drop anyone standing in the area into a large pool of **green slime**. Finding the pit trap requires a successful DC 17 Wisdom (Perception) check.

11D False Treasure Vault

Beyond this door is a huge pile of brass, copper, gold, and silver coins, appearing to be valued at nearly 10,000 gp. The mound of coins is in fact 2 blade coin swarms. The swarms lie dormant, even allowing the characters to load several of the coins into their purses, sacks, chests, and so on. After 3 rounds, the coins project their deadly blades, cut their way free of

pouches and purses and whirl up with the rest of the coins into a cyclone of whirling bladed coins. A creature who starts its turn within 20 feet of the swarms must make a DC 16 Dexterity saving, taking 10 (2d6) slashing damage on a failure and half as much on a success. The swarms have AC 15, Speed 30, and 30 hit points.

11E False Treasure Vault

This vault door is made of solid silver (22,000 gp approximate value and weighing 4,000 pounds). A massive keyhole sits in the center of the door. Anyone inserting any device into the keyhole triggers a *chain lightning* effect. The trap can be detected with a successful DC 17 Intelligence (Arcana) check and removed with *dispel magic* cast successfully against a 6th level spell. Any creature within 10 feet of the door is struck by lightning. In addition, any creature within 10 feet of a creature struck by lightning is struck, up to a possible range of 80 feet. Any creature struck by lightning must attempt a DC 17 Dexterity saving throw. Those failing the saving throw take 28 (8d6) lightning damage, while those succeeding take half this amount.

Nothing else is in the room.

11F False Treasure Vault

This locked, plain riveted-steel door opens into a 10-foot-by-25-foot room. The farthest 10 feet of the room is stacked with iron chests and coffers, appearing to be weapons cases and treasure boxes. A character entering the room who succeeds on a DC 15 Wisdom (Perception) notices bits of frost on the containers. Approaching within 5 feet of the containers sets off a pressure plate-activated *hold monster* and *cone of cold* trap that affects everyone in the room. The pressure plate can be noted with a successful DC 18 Wisdom (Perception) check and jammed with a successful DC 17 Dexterity check with thieves' tools. If triggered, two spells occur immediately after one another. Each creature in the room must succeed on a DC 16 Wisdom saving throw or be paralyzed for one minute. Following right behind, a *cone of cold* fills a 60-foot cone. Each creature within the cone must make a DC 17 Dexterity saving throw, taking 49 (14d6) cold damage on a failed save and half as much on a success.

11G False Treasure Vault

This red iron door has 3 complex dial locks (requiring three Dexterity checks) on its face. Once the last dial is manipulated, a *phantasmal killer* trap is triggered. The trap can be noted before being triggered with a successful DC 20 Intelligence (Investigation) check but cannot be disarmed short of *dispel magic* successfully cast against an 8th level spell slot. When triggered, each creature who can see the door is subjected to *phantasmal killer* for up to 1 minute. Each affected creature must succeed on a DC 17 Wisdom saving throw each round or take 33 (6d10) psychic damage. On a successful safe, the effect is ended.

The door does not open in any case.

11H False Treasure Vault

This gold- and gem-studded door is covered in many nonmagical runes, seemingly in some long-forgotten language. There is no lock, nor is there any type of handle. When someone approaches within 5 feet of the door, a *magic mouth* speaks in a commanding voice, "To be transported to the vault, truthfully speak your name, quote three tasks completed, and touch the door." A character who complies with the request and touches the door is subjected to an *imprisonment* spell and must succeed on a DC 17 Wisdom saving thow or be imprisoned by burial. The door does not open. Touching the door activates an alarm that notifies all efreeti guards in the KhizAnah.

12. Eastern Barracks

This barracks chamber serves as the home of 4 **efreeti** elite guards. The guards work in shifts with the guards in the bank above. Their jobs include occasionally feeding the fiendish dire tigers and patrolling the maze areas. The tigers have been trained to recognize the guards' smell so they do not attack them when they enter the maze. The rest of the guards' time is spent gambling or resting. If an alarm sounds, they move up to reinforce the guards on the ground floor.

Treasure: Stored in an unlocked wooden chest are 1,100 bp, 8 lapis lazuli (15 gp each), and an *ioun stone (insight)*.

13. Western Barracks

The western barracks are identical to the eastern barracks (**Area 12**).

Treasure: Stored in an unlocked wooden chest are 1,400 bp, a small gold statue of the sultan of efreet (800 gp), 3 silver bracelets (60 gp each), and a *spell wand*[2] of *knock*.

14. Middle Maze

The middle maze is the lair of eight half-starved **fiendish dire tigers**[1]. Each tiger wears a *collar of invisibility* that functions exactly as a *ring of invisibility*. Owing to the fact that the efreet believe that not every treasure need be guarded with magic and mechanical traps alone, the tigers act as a certain physical piece of insurance for the wealth that the KhizAnah possesses.

For every minute the characters spend in the Middle Maze, roll 1d6. A roll of 1 indicates that a tiger has caught their scent and begins tracking them, reaching their location in 1d4 rounds. Continue these rolls in the event that combat breaks out, as other tigers may join in on the feeding frenzy.

The tigers do not roar until after they slay their prey.

15. Tiger Pens

These four chambers serve as the lairs of the 8 **fiendish dire tigers**[1]. If the tigers have not been encountered randomly in the maze, there is a 50% chance that 1d4 are here.

Treasure: The tigers have little in the way of treasure due to the fact that they generally feast on blind slaves brought to the KhizAnah on a weekly basis. However, one of the pens contains the remains of a thief who made it just this far on his journey. Strewn about this tiger's pen are 1,200 bp, 500 gp, a *scimitar of speed*, a *turban of intellect* (as *headband of intellect*), a *ring of greater protection*, 3 *potions of gaseous form*, *slippers of spider climbing*, *gauntlets of dexterity*[2], a *vest of escape*[2], and half of a map to the third level of the KhizAnah.

16. Gorgimera's Lair

The vault-like door to this chamber appears to be fixed with a complex locking mechanism. The door is trapped with a *prismatic spray* trap that triggers when the door is touched. The trap can be noted with a successful DC 17 Intelligence (Investigation) check and disarmed with *dispel magic* cast successfully against a 7th level spell slot. The spell save DC for effects of the *prismatic* spray spell is 18.

A **gorgimera**[1] waits behind this door, maddened in its desire for freedom. It instantly attacks anyone opening the door, starting with its breath weapons before closing in melee. A one-way teleportation disk in the center of the gorgimera's lair brings food to the creature from the teleporters. Six broken statues are all that remain of those unluckily to have found themselves in this chamber.

Treasure: 600 bp, *rod of spell empowerment*[2].

17. Teleporters

Doors trapped with an *incendiary cloud* trap open to a chamber set with eight teleportation disks engraved into the floor. When a creature enters the area around the trap, an incendiary cloud fills a 10-foot cube and remains for one minute. Any creature that starts its turn in the cloud or enters the cloud on its turn must attempt a DC 17 Dexterity saving throw. Those failing take 14 (4d6) fire damage while those succeeding take half this amount. The trap can be detected with a successful DC 20 Intelligence (Arcana) check and disabled with *dispel magic* or a successful DC 20 Intelligence (Arcana) check. Failing either check by 5 or more triggers the trap.

The disks allow the only teleportation travel within the KhizAnah. The teleportation disks are lettered **A–H** and teleport individuals to the areas indicated below. The circles glow green for one round after being used.

Teleporter	Destination
17A	Cell A (**Area 22**)
17B	Eastern stairwell (**Area 18**)
17C	Cell B (**Area 22**)
17D	Cell C (**Area 22**)
17E	Cell D (**Area 22**)
17F	Western stairwell (**Area 19**)
17G	Gorgimera's lair (**Area 16**)
17H	Central stairwell (**Area 20**)

18. Eastern Stairwell

The eastern stairwell is a long corridor with a set of stairs to the north and the south. These staircases lead to the third level of the KhizAnah and the **Maze of Mindlessness (Area 21)**. A *teleportation circle* set in the center of the stairwell leads to the teleporters.

19. Western Stairwell

As the eastern stairwell, one set of stairs is in the northern end of the corridor, one is in the southern end, and a *teleportation circle* is in the center. Both staircases lead to the **Maze of Mindlessness (Area 21)** of the KhizAnah.

20. Central Stairwell

The central stairwell runs east and west with a *teleportation circle* in the center that leads to the teleporters. The staircases are found in the extreme eastern and western ends of the corridor and both lead to the **Maze of Mindlessness (Area 21)** on Level 3 of the KhizAnah.

21. Maze of Mindlessness

The entire maze portion of the third level of the KhizAnah is filled with a gas that makes the area within 10 feet lightly obscured and any area farther away heavily obscured. A strong wind (21+ mph) disperses the gas in 1 round. A *fireball*, *flame strike*, or similar spell burns away the gas in the explosive or fiery spell's area. A *wall of fire* burns away the gas in the area into which it deals damage. The gas, however, refills the cleared area within 1d4 rounds.

The gas slowly drains the Wisdom and Intelligence of living creatures who pass through it. Living creatures must succeed on a DC 18 Constitution saving throw every 10 minutes spent wandering the maze. On a failed save, the creature takes 1 point of Intelligence damage and 1 point of Wisdom damage.

Nine **brass men**[1] are activated from their stations (**Area 23**) as soon as living beings set foot in the maze. See the map of the Maze of Mindlessness for the locations of the brass man stations. Brass men wander the maze randomly until they come in contact with a living creature. They attack it until the trespasser is slain or the brass man is destroyed. Brass men do not pursue creatures upstairs if they flee to the upper levels of the KhizAnah.

Any living creature killed in the Maze of Mindlessness rises as a **specter** in 1d4 rounds with a number of Hit Dice equal to its character level (but retains none of the abilities it had in life). If the body is removed from the maze before this time, it does not rise as a specter.

22. Cells

The cells (lettered **A–D**) are 10-foot square holding chambers made of solid stone accessible only via the teleporter in **Area 8**. Poor individuals dropped into one of these chambers are afforded no food or water and are left here until they die.

A trapped creature might be able to chisel its way out through the wall if it has the proper tools or equipment. The walls are reinforced masonry and about two feet thick. A section of wall large enough let a Medium creature

The Khiz Anah

1 Square – 5 Feet

pass hass 360 hit points and AC 14. The walls ignore any attack that does less than 5 points of damage.

Cells A and C have treasure from an unlucky band of thieves who made it this far into the KhizAnah before starving to death in the cells. The **advanced specters**[1] of the dead thieves remain in the cells where they were trapped, haunting the area of their demise.

Though incorporeal, the specters cannot pass through the walls of the maze or cells due to the various magicks placed on the KhizAnah. When their area is entered, they attack mercilessly, maddened by their hundred years' incarceration.

22A Touan Ibin Shar

Treasure: *Ring of resistance* (fire), *spell wand*[2] of *enhance ability, javelin of freedom*[2] (sentient: Int 17, Wis 12, Cha 9; communicates by empathy; neutral evil, detect opposing alignment at will), *potion of delay poison*[2], *armor of silent moves*[2] (studded leather), and 1,100 bp, 1,500 gp.

22B Empty Cell

22C Hawabi Ibin Shar

Treasure: None.

22D Treasure Cell

Treasure: *Figurine of wondrous power (bronze griffon), bracers of superior defense*[2], *wand of lightning bolts, ring of blinking*[2], *winged boots, a +3 shortsword, +2 light crossbow, 10 +1 bolts.*

23. Brass Man Stations

Each of these areas functions as a guard post for the brass men. Each contains 3 **brass men**[1].

The chambers are most likely empty as the brass men are out stalking the maze looking for intruders.

If the characters have not encountered a brass man while walking the halls, they find a malfunctioning one here. This **berserk brass man**[1] attacks with a +4 effective Strength bonus due to its malfunction.

Nothing of value is in these rooms.

24. Chamber of Azam al Ghul

Azam al Ghul, a maddened **ghul noble**[1], commands the specters that rise from those who die in the Maze of Mindlessness. Intensely cruel, he often stalks the corridors of his section of the maze looking for living treats that are occasionally sent down by Thaaman Ikla to keep him satisfied. There is a 50% chance that Azam attacks the characters on sight, but an equal chance that he sends them off on the wrong direction to the emergency vault access, and then follows them in hopes that they can win the *Mymr Stone*[2] and somehow help him gain his freedom from the KhizAnah. He had a *geas* placed on him by a necromancer that causes him to forget the direction to the vault if asked or forced to reveal its location.

Azam is always accompanied by 3 **specters**. He has the following possessions: *rod of absorption, ring of resistance* (fire), *spell wand*[2] of *vampiric touch, vorpal sword* (falchion).

25. Chamber of the Engineers

This chamber is home to 12 **gnomish engineers**[1] who make sure that the gears of the vaults and the pneumatic tubes work correctly. The gnomes have special slave collars that make them immune to the effects of the gas in the Maze of Mindlessness. A collar can be broken off with a successful DC 25 Strength check or by doing 40 points of damage against AC 16. Azam also sees that the specters and brass men ignore their presence in the maze. The engineers never actually get any closer to the vault than the engineering hatch.

The Khiz Anah

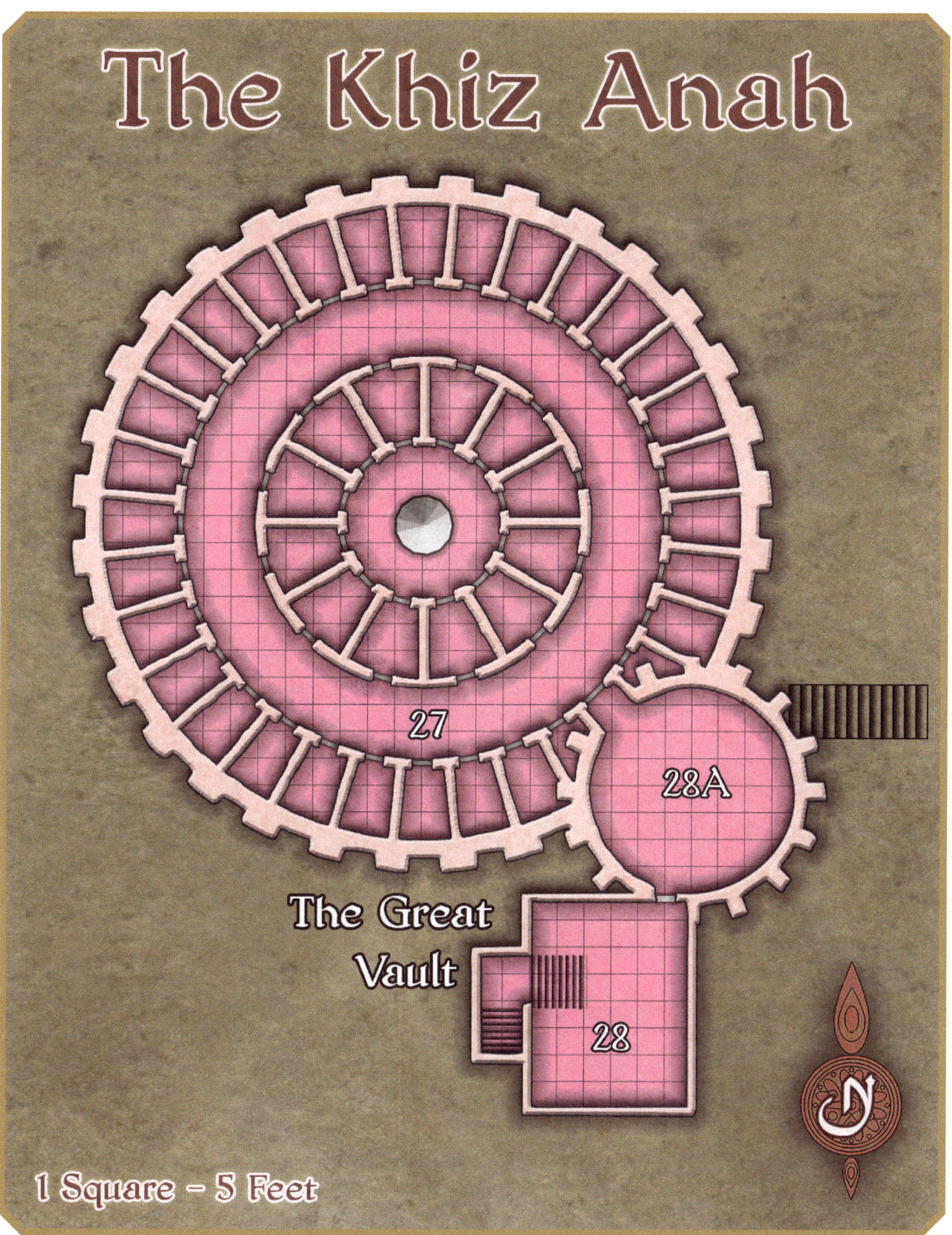

If the *banker's geas* (see the beginning of this chapter) can somehow be lifted from an engineer and its slave collar removed, it offers to help the characters get to the vault as long as the characters promise the gnome freedom and safe passage to the Dome of Gates whence it can make its way home.

Treasure: The gnomes have 40 doses of *oil of slipperiness* that they use to oil the gears of the vault mechanisms. Each also owns a set of engineering tools.

26. Descending Staircases

These two staircases, similar to one another, are hidden behind secret doors that require characters to make a successful DC 20 Wisdom (Perception) check to locate. The eastern staircase is trapped with a *sphere of annihilation* trap. After traveling 20 feet on the stairs, they transform into a ramp and dump the characters directly into a stationary *sphere of annihilation*. A character that makes a successful DC 14 Dexterity saving throw to avoid the trap finds a handhold or foothold to grab onto. A creature that fails is annihilated. The trap can be noted with a successful DC 17 Intelligence (Investigation) check.

The western staircase descends to the great vault and the engineer vault access.

27. The Great Vault

An *antimagic field* exists just above the great vault. This is designed to dispel any magical effects of individuals attempting to pass through the pneumatic tubes through use of magic. Such an individual, if naturally of larger than Tiny size, immediately assumes its natural size, and takes 35 (10d6) bludgeoning damage and is violently expelled into the vault.

The *canisters of holding*[2] are shielded from this antimagic effect.

The great vault itself is a huge chamber consisting of concentric rings of vaults spun by massive gears. One circle of vaults turns inside another like a gigantic clock. There are literally hundreds of vaults running from the floor to the ceiling some 50 feet above, each filled with *canisters of holding* that possess the nonmagical wealth of many who dwell within the City of Brass.

The pneumatic tubes from the main bank floor feed into this chamber and their contents are placed with great speed inside the appropriate vault by the magic of the *Mymr Stone*[2] that floats dazzlingly above the central vault cylinder.

Aside from the pneumatic tubes, the chamber may be entered only through the vault access gear (**Area 28A**).

Both the inner and outer chambers (walls and floors) spin at a dizzying pace. Anyone who enters the area without first disabling the gears and halting the spinning is flung against the outer walls and takes 35 (10d6) bludgeoning damage. Further, the centrifugal force of the spinning chamber pins a character to the wall requiring a successful DC 19 Strength (Athletics) check to break free. A character who breaks free must succeed on a DC 18 Dexterity saving throw each round or be flung and pinned to the wall (taking damage as above) each time it fails its save.

Anyone viewing the *Mymr Stone*[2] upon entering the chamber must make a DC 20 Wisdom saving throw or be fascinated at its beauty and ever-changing facets. Fascinated individuals may not move or take any actions as they stare mindlessly at the oddly humming stone. Of course, being flung against the outer vaults breaks this effect. A character that makes a successful saving throw against the stone cannot be affected by the *Mymr Stone's*[2] fascinating effect for one day.

The *Mymr Stone* floats 60 feet above the whirling floor of the vault and can be commanded to open any vault once it is possessed and its intellect defeated. The *Mymr Stone*[2] may only be accessed by passing through the inner vault and into the center of the chamber. Otherwise, the spinning vaults and antimagic field result in certain doom.

The Vaults

Each vault is locked with an ingenious lock that requires a DC 30 Dexterity check with thieves' tools to unseal. The vaults are also sealed with a *greater arcane lock*[4] spell cast with a 9th level spell slot and trapped with arcane disjunction traps that are triggered if anyone casts *knock* or *dispel magic* upon the locks. The *Mymr Stone*[2] is immune to the disjunction effect.

The vault doors have AC 20, 600 hit points, and ignore any attack that does less than 20 points of damage. They are immune to nonmagical damage. Breaking the doors with a Strength check is not possible. The arcane disjunction trap can be found with a successful DC 20 Intelligence (Investigation) check and disarmed with a *wish*. If triggered, each creature within 40 feet of the vault doors must make a DC 18 Wisdom saving throw. If a creature fails, all magic items that it is carrying or wearing lose their magic properties for one hour and all spells affecting the creature are permanently removed. All magic items in the room not being carried or worn and all spell effects not affecting a creature are automatically nullified.

Each of the 200 vaults contains roughly 500,000 gp worth of nonmagical treasures held in *canisters of holding*. Good luck hauling it all out alive.

One of the vaults contains a *durbakke of wakefulness*[2] that can be used to rouse a comatose creature put in that state by the whispering walls of the **Great Repository**.

28. Engineer Vault Access

This chamber leads to an area that accesses the titanic gears that turn the great vault. The gnomes from the chamber of the engineers use this one. A quickly whirling gear, 10 feet tall, occupies the northern corner of this chamber, which is filled with many tubes and pipes, levers, and wheels. There are 1d4 **gnomish engineers**[1] in the vault access at any given time. They oil the gears with *oil of slipperiness* to ensure its constant movement.

28A. The Vault Access Gear

The vault may only be accessed by passing through one of the sprockets in the vault access gear. A character must make a successful DC 20 Dexterity (Acrobatics) check to leap into the correct sprocket at exactly the right time. On a failed check, the character instead leaps into the gears and takes 70 (20d6) bludgeoning damage. On the next round, the character is spit out by the gears back into the engineer vault access room and takes 17 (5d6) bludgeoning damage from the 50-foot fall.

A *hasted* character should have advantage on the check. A *time stop* spell reduces it the DC to 10. Interfering with the gears mechanically or magically automatically sounds an *alarm* that summons city guardsmen to the outside of the KhizAnah where they await the thieves.

Escaping the KhizAnah

Characters who successfully gain the *Mymr Stone*[2] may actually be able to walk out of the KhizAnah and not be stopped or remembered by any beings who fail their save versus being fascinated by its ever-changing facets. Once gained, the *Mymr Stone*[2] may be used as any magic item or used as a replacement gear to activate the juggernaut of Kil Kath Kesh. Such weapons may prove useful if any challenge to the Sultan's authority is to be mounted. Upon successfully completing the heist, Tarbish comes to the characters. He may guide them to the Great Ziggurat if they have the *maul of Hezoid*[2], the Circus of Pain if they do not, or the Pagoda of Devils in order to topple the alliance between Lucifer's minions and the Sultan, an alliance that casts an unfavorable pall upon the rule of the efreet in their own city.

Chapter 26
The Underbasin

Traveling the alleys of the Basin, one notices large iron grates on the ground. The iron grates can be lifted or smashed with a successful DC 25 Strength check. Alternatively, doing 80 points of damage against AC 13 will allow entry.

These grates prevent people from aimlessly wandering into the Underbasin, a network of tunnels that runs almost the entirety of the Basin itself. These tunnels, which are essentially small waterways, become home to the trash and excrement of the people in the Basin and sometimes the bodies of the dead or the not so dead also find their way down here. Several carrion creatures roam these tunnels eating the trash and anything else that happens to find its way into the labyrinth. Deep within the wretched tunnels is a hidden door known as the Skull Gate.

The Underbasin holds secrets even from the various factions and agents who strive against the Sultan and is especially hidden from the Sultan himself. Its discovery should be secret, unless the characters have managed to gain the absolute trust of Chufa Um Sophanie, who only guesses at the tomb hidden below the Great Bowl.

This adventure is suggested for Tier 4 characters.

The Underbasin

Roll 1d20 on the following table every 10 minutes the characters spend wandering the Underbasin.

1d20	Encounter
1–2	1d4 + 2 greater barghests[1]
3	1d4 + 2 babau demons[1]
4	2d4 + 2 wraiths
5–6	1d3 fate eaters
7	1d2 + 1 bone devils
8	Greatrer abyssal basilisk[1]
9–20	No encounter

1. The Skull Gate

The gate is recessed into the wall of the tunnels and overlapped by a seemingly ordinary door. It has no unusual markings and does not appear to be fortified in any way. It is, however, guarded by a potent trap. Opening this door without speaking the proper magical words not only reveals the true Skull Gate, but also activates an audible *alarm* spell (immediately check for a random encounter) and sets off a hidden poison needle trap. The needle makes an attack at +10 to hit against the nearest creature within 10 feet. On a hit, the target takes 1 piercing damage and must succeed on a DC 15 Constitution saving throw or take 55 (10d10) poison damage and be paralyzed for 1 minute. The trap can be noted with a successful DC 19 Intelligence (Investigation) check and disabled with a successful DC 16 Dexterity check with thieves' tools.

Carved in the dank walls of the Underbasin's tunnels is the Skull Gate, a doorway covered with arcane writings and framed in humanoid skulls, a red rune scribed upon each forehead. There are 10 skulls in total, each of which bears a *symbol*, triggered by anyone passing through the Skull Gate without first speaking the proper password. A symbol can be found with a successful DC 18 Intelligence (Investigation) check, and the spell save DC for each symbol is 18.

Four skulls bear a *symbol of death*.
Two skulls bear a *symbol of fear*.
Two skulls bear a *symbol of hopelessness*.
Two skulls bear a *symbol of sleep*.

No less than two additional potent traps also protect the Skull Gate, as it leads to the inner sanctum of Livesha[1], the lich high priestess of Orcus.

***Glyph of Warding* (Explosive Runes–acid)**

Noting the glyph requires a successful DC 18 Intelligence (Investigation) check, and if triggered, each creature within a 20-foot radius of the gate must make a DC 18 Dexterity saving throw, taking 49 (11d8) acid damage on a failure or half as much on a success.

***Wail of the Banshee* Trap**

Noting this trap requires a successful DC 20 Intelligence (Investigation) check. If triggered, the trap releases a keening wail. The wail does 200 psychic damage total to up to 20 targets that can hear it within 40 feet. Starting with the closest creature, each creature within the area that can hear must succeed on a DC 20 Constitution saving throw or take the lesser of their current hit points or the amount of damage remaining to the effect (starting with 200 for the first affected creature). A wandering monster check should be made immediately after this trap is triggered.

2. The Courtyard

The normal heat of the city is somewhat hindered down here as cold emanates from the rock walls itself. The stairwell opens up into a stalagmite- and stalactite-riddled courtyard. Two **stone golems** guard a thick wooden door that lies at the end of the courtyard. The door is not locked but requires a successful DC 16 Strength check to open. The golems become active and attack anyone other than Livesha[1] who comes within 10 feet of the wooden door. They do not pursue intruders up the stairs.

3. The Warrens of the Dead

The Warrens of the Dead is a large room that slopes down to the south side. At the bottom of the slope, the ground is covered in a sea of bone, as hundreds of skeletons stand against the far wall in rows, awaiting the command of their mistress, Livesha[1]. Behind the mass of skeletons, the wall rises upward outlined by two massive pillars of dark stone. At the very top of the wall is a door with no viable route of access. To the west of the warrens are three more doors each protected by a *symbol of death* (spell save DC 18).

Non-worshippers of Orcus who enter this area are immediately attacked by 20 **black skeletons**[1], with 20 more animating within 1d4 rounds to attack. This cycle repeats until a total of 100 black skeletons animate. Within the warrens, the black skeletons cannot be turned.

3a. The False Door

This doorway, inscribed with the unholy symbol of Orcus, hangs near the ceiling between the two black pillars. The doorway radiates a faint aura of magic. Casting a *harm* spell and placing one's palm against the door causes the individual to be teleported instantly to the **Tomb of Ashur Ban** (see below). A paladin viewing the unholy symbols of Orcus must succeed on a DC 18 Wisdom saving throw or take 14 (4d6) necrotic damage. Whether the save succeeds or not, that paladin is then immune to the effects for one day.

Underbasin
1 Square = 20 Feet
1
2
3
3a
4
5
6
7

4. The Laboratory

The second door leads down a narrow corridor to a huge magical storeroom and laboratory. It is scattered with gems and wands and chemicals of all sorts. The gems are mostly broken, though pieces can be scraped up and collected totaling 1,100 gp. The wands are all either broken or burned out. The chemicals are various embalming fluids and other alien mixtures.

Humanoids in various states of decomposition sit in huge glass vats of green liquid and some lay upon tables with different cutting implements beside them. Scrolls and spellbooks litter the desks and tables. A successful DC 14 Intelligence (Investigation) check reveals pieces of parchment and scrolls detailing the Sultan's family line. Reading the document thoroughly reveals that Livesha[1] was the former Sultana's half-sister.

5. Nal'vun Akhan's Lair

The path leads into the remnants of a great hall with tattered red carpet still covering the ground, moth-eaten paintings hanging from rusty nails, and pillars of brass rising up along the sides to the ceiling. A throne stands here upon which sits a lone figure staring into nothingness. Nal'vun Akhan (**nightwalker**[1]), a once-powerful warrior priest and devout follower of a long-forgotten Sultan, now resides here. After his master was slain, Orcus summoned him and changed him into a nightwalker. Hating the light, he now waits silently in the empty throne room for his chance to return to power. He serves Livesha[1] without question.

6. Tomb of the Forsaken Mamelukes

The fourth door from the warrens leads to a twisting maze through an inner crypt. Icy water flows around the floor and between the large stone coffins. Deep in the back of the crypt rests the coffins of the Forsaken Mamelukes. Lifting any of the coffins' lids summons Livesha[1] to the premises primed for battle in 1d6 rounds.

The Forsaken Mamelukes are six men of courage whom time has forgotten. Livesha[1] brought them under her rule and entrusted them into the world of undeath. They are now **demonic knights**[1] under her complete control. Three of the soldiers were human, one was elven, one was a half-giant, and her most prized of the six was an efreet she manipulated into her services under the power of death. They sit at a round table that has eight chairs, two of which are empty. A *wall of force* protects the room, and the demonic knights cannot be reached or touched. If the *wall of force* is dispelled, they become active and attack.

7. Tomb of Ashur Ban

Anyone teleporting here from the door above the Warrens of the Dead arrives in a simple chamber with a stone dais upon which lies the husband of the former Sultana of the City of Brass, the former Sultan himself, Ashur Ban. The body is covered in a dome of rainbow colors (*prismatic wall* and *wall of force* spells) and the powerful magic keeps the body from decomposing. The *prismatic wall* spell has a spell save DC of 20. A successful DC 20 Intelligence check confirms the identity of the body. A solitary door stands behind the dais.

Behind this door is a model of the City of Brass on a marble table, a complete living model of the city. The Great Sultan, every ranking efreet, and nearly every resident (excluding slaves and travelers) of the city can be seen walking on the streets, flying on their magical carpets, or engaging in any of their other daily tasks. Several places leap into view, one being the Ziggurat of Flame now laid completely bare for all eyes to see, and the other is the City of the Dead Sultana.

Touching the model instantly teleports the user to the position touched and also summons **Livesha**[1] and 2 **demonic knights**[1] into the room in 1d3 rounds. Livesha[1] can automatically teleport to the exact spot the intruder did with 100% accuracy. This decreases 5% for every round after the teleportation took place.

Swatting at the flying efreeti, magic carpets, airships, or other flying creatures has no effect. Touching a flying creature instantly teleports the character to that location and requires an immediate DC 18 Dexterity saving throw to grab onto the magic carpet, flying efreeti, or whatever was touched. On a failed save, the character misses the mark and plummets to the city below. Attacking the model with magic (such as tossing a *cone of cold* or *gust of wind* spell at it) triggers an *imprisonment* spell that affects the caster. The caster must succeed on a DC 20 Wisdom saving throw or be restrained by chaining within the room. Success or failure, this too summons Livesha[1] and 2 demonic knights[1] into the room in 1d3 rounds. The trap can be detected with a successful DC 18 Intelligence (Arcana) check.

Chapter 27
The Secret Tomb of Rah'po Dehj

This apartment, built along the upper rings of the bowl in the Upper City, belongs to the elusive Rah'po Dehj (**lich**). His lair can be found if his minion Dawzin[1] is somehow tracked or followed after offering quests to the characters. The lair can also be discovered if the characters manage to impress Rah'po Dehj enough that he invites them for a private audience where he offers the final quest to the characters: join him in overthrowing the Sultan of Efreet[1] and establish him as the new ruler of the Plane of Molten Skies.

Rah'po Dehj's sanctum is nowhere near as complex as his tower in the Lost Lands. This is not to say it is without its own difficulties. Characters entering the lair of Rah'po Dehj should be prepared to face a lich in his own lair. More complex is that his phylactery is hidden in multiple planes of existence.

This adventure is suggested for Tier 4 characters.

1. Entry

Great iron portals lead into the sanctum of Rah'po Dehj. Unlike many of the portals in the city, it appears to steam and drip. This fact is not lost upon patrols of fire giants who march through the upscale neighborhood. Any attempts to question them about the master of the home end in confusion, forgetfulness, or death.

The doorway is locked with *greater arcane lock*[4] cast with a 7th level spell slot and trapped with a cone of cold trap. The trap can be detected with a successful DC 18 Intelligence (Investigation) check. If triggered, all creatures within a 60-foot cone must make a DC 18 Constitution saving throw. A creature that fails takes 45 (10d8) cold damage while a creature that succeeds takes half this amount. The trap can be temporarily dispelled with *dispel magic* cast against a 7th level spell slot.

2. The Grand Foyer

This room is dominated by the iron statue of a handsome half-elf wizard brandishing a twisted staff as he stands upon a short pedestal that itself is upon a 20-foot-by-20-foot dais. A locked iron door is beyond the statue. The door is enchanted and opens to the touch of Dawzin[1] or Rah'po Dehj, should he be inclined to leave off scrying from within the confines of his crypt. Unlocking the door otherwise requires a successful DC 18 Dexterity check witht thieves' tools.

Two secret doors flank the statue. Noticing them requires a successful DC 16 Wisdom (Perception) check. If either of the secret doors is touched, the iron statue activates and attacks (as an **iron golem**).

2A. Secret Door

This secret door leads to Dawzin's chambers within Rah'po Dehj's sanctum.

2B. Secret Door

This secret door leads to Rah'po Dehj's lounge, where he may entertain guests and dignitaries who happen to visit and have the power to compel him to converse "face to face."

3. The "L" Shaped Hall

This hallway runs beyond **Door A** and leads to Dawzin's laboratory and living quarters. The hallway is guarded by a **spellgorged zombie**[1] triggered to attack anyone not bearing the mark of Rah'po Dehj or in the company of Dawzin[1].

4. Dawzin's Laboratory

Dawzin[1] concocts his magical experiments, brews his potions, and tends to his master's spellgorged zombies within this chamber. The room is filled with bottles, beakers, burners, and jars of components such as sulfur, iron filings, bat guano, knucklebones of murderers, baby teeth, licorice whips, hemlock, dried venomous caterpillars, powdered silver, rat teeth, and live newts. Currently, the sawdust stuffed remains of four humanoid bodies lie on tables, fully utilized in the process of receiving their magical tattoos to become spellgorged zombies.

One particular jar on the counter actually contains a pocket dimension and holds a **glabrezu demon** prisoner. If the jar is lifted, the demon can attack with its pincers and magic abilities, running about on its human arms. It cannot fully escape the jar, however. The jar itself is magically hardened and can be broken only if it takes 50 points of damage from magic spells or weapons. The Type III demon retreats into its jar if it suffers more than half of its hit points in damage, though it wrecks the laboratory equipment, shatters the tables, and crushes the spellgorged zombie blanks in the process.

Items: The lab contains 3,000 gp worth of laboratory equipment and enough components to brew up to 10 potions of up to 3rd-level spells, or five potions of levels 4–6.

Spell potions[2] currently found in the laboratory include the following: *blur, protection from evil and good, resist energy* (fire), *detect magic, mage armor, heroism,* and *invisibility.*

5. Dawzin's Quarters

This room attached to the laboratory is the living quarters of the snarky winged goblin apprentice of Rah'po Dehj.

The room contains a golden roost that Dawzin[1] clutches with his clawed feet when he is at rest, a mirror, a bookshelf, and a clothing rack containing various shirts and robes cut to fit over his wings. His spellbooks are chained within their bookshelf with cold wrought-iron chains and locked with padlocks that are set with *magic mouths* to begin screaming if anyone other than Dawzin[1] touches them. Dawzin[1] keeps the keys for both on his person at all times.

If any attempt to pick the locks is made, the 4 chains animate (**animated chains**[1]) and attack.

Among the papers and spellbooks on his shelves are the following *spell scrolls*: *hold person, hypnotic pattern, invisibility, levitate, phantasmal killer, comprehend languages, identify, wall of stone, fear.*

Dawzin's spellbooks contain all his known spells of 1st–7th level.

The Tomb of Rah'po Dehj

6. Zombie Storage

This room stores 3 **spellgorged zombies**[1] for use if the others fail or are destroyed.

7. Hall of Portals

The Hall of Portals stands beyond a locked door affixed with a teleport trap. The trap teleports characters to the demon gate outside of the Tower of the Grand Vizier of the City of Brass unless a DC 16 Wisdom saving throw is made. The trap can be detected with a successful DC 16 Intelligence (Arcana) check and disarmed for 10 minutes with *dispel magic* successfully cast against a 7th level spell slot.

The door is locked with an arcane lock spell and is unlocked with a key that is in Dawzin's possession. Without the key, the mechanical portion of the lock requires a successful DC 16 Dexterity check with thieves' tools.

An altar-like platform stands in the center of the room and conceals a staircase under a secret door. The secret door can be found with a successful DC 14 Intelligence (Investigation) check. Portals stand at three cardinal points of the circular chamber.

Portal A leads **Area 9**, B to **Area 10** and C to **Area 11**.

8. Crypt

The staircase descends beneath the altar to a crypt. Carved around the outside of the crypt are panel images depicting an elderly man with pointed ears wearing a robe of stars and moons and bearing a crooked wooden staff that also vaguely resembles a man. In the first, the man buries what appears to be a robe. In the second panel, the man flays off his own skin, wraps it in a stone, and casts it into waters. The third section depicts the man carving away his own heart and feeding it to a demonic creature with the head of a crocodile and the body of a lion upon a field of stars. The final panel shows the being sitting upon a throne within a tower by the sea, his staff clenched in his right hand and his grinning skull staring into the cosmos. His left hand holds a globe. A city engulfed in flames is within the globe.

9. Plane of Shadows

The portal is black and swirling. A red-lipped mouth appears amid the darkness and recites DC following words:

The Shadow of Death has its price to be paid. Step carefully in the darkness, leaving that which our feet do tread behind, bringing back naught which can be held or carried. Nothing less than your sole may be paid for this dark treasure.

It smiles, licks its lips, and fades into the swirling dark.

Stepping through the Shadow Portal in the Hall of Portals transports characters to the Plane of Shadow. The characters can see the portal that returns to Rah'po Dehj's Hall of Portals as a sliver of light in the ever-present dark. Everything here is as a photographic negative, and the plane seems unending and familiar at the same time. In the mortal realms, it is a shadowy reflection of its nearest entry point. Here in the Plane of Molten Skies, however, where much is a field of fire, the darkness is exceedingly black and desperately cold and windy. There is an oppressive absence of light, and a fine dust seems to blow through the air. The ground itself seems to grip at the feet of wanderers.

The Plane of Shadow is described in greater detail in **Sword of Air** by **Frog God Games**. It is suggested that random encounter tables, spell changes, and planar differences from that work be used.

Not far from the portal to Rah'po Dehj's Hall of Portals is a hill. Upon the hill is a sarcophagus that is an exact double of the sarcophagus found in the center of the Hall of Portals. Standing astride the mausoleum is Lord Timor, an immortal **shadow captain**[1] tasked with guarding the sarcophagus by Rah'po Dehj.

Timor speaks as he is approached in a voice that sounds like cracked gravel:

I am Lord Timor, the Shadow of Death. Turn ye back those who would disturb the midnight shroud of my dread lord.

Lord Timor challenges any who approach, though he yields if bested. Due to his condition, he can be defeated, but he cannot be killed as he simply dissolves into a formless pool of shadowstuff and reforms the following day. If forced to yield, he explains that the crypt contains the *funerary shroud of Rah'po Dehj*. The *shroud* can be drawn from the sarcophagus only if the shadow of a pure sole is left in its place.

The instructions spoken by the mouth in the Hall of Portals are both a pun and a bit of a misnomer applied by the wily lich to protect his shroud and ultimately his phylactery from clever enemies.

The shadow must be carved from the sole of the foot of a willing being with the scythe of Timor. Doing so is painful, dealing 7 (2d6) slashing damage and 1d6 points of temporary Dexterity damage that lasts until the wound either heals naturally or is healed with a *heal* spell, as no other magic is strong enough to rectify the wound. The removal must be done within a *magic circle*, lest a wicked soul from the Plane of Shadow arrives and possesses the shadowless victim as an afya.

10. Riddle of the Styx

A salty and sulfurous breeze blows from the portal. Written around the edge of its stones are the following words.

The flesh of my body rests below the waters of forgetfulness; denied you who dwell among the living. Only the dead may know the spells scrawled upon my tattered skin.

The mists of the portal open to the shores of the dead. There the waters of the Styx flow high and fast. A skeletal boatman stands ready upon his skiff, which is tied off to a mooring stone. Characters must pay the **charonademon**[1] a magic item, 50 pp, or two gems worth a minimum of 100 gp for passage to their destination. They may ask to be taken anywhere that the ghastly waters touch. Asking to be taken to the skin of Rah'po Dehj elicits no effect, as the true identity of the foul creature is Jhedophar. Calling to find the skin of Jhedophar directs the boat to the center of the river where the boat sits and waits.

A locked bronze chest sits 30 feet below the surface of the roiling, sulfurous Styx. The lock on the chest requires a successful DC 18 Dexterity check with thieves' tools to open. The chest contains the mummified skin of Jhedophar the lich rolled up and wax-stopped in a canopic jar made of lapis lazuli.

The *death shroud of Jhedophar* protects its wearer from the adverse

Styx

Styx is the great river that flows between the dimensions as well as a great stream-shaped plane unto itself. Styx is the home of Charon and his various charonademons who serve as a sort of taxi service between the realms of the living and the lands of the dead of which Styx is the planar boundary.

The waters of Styx and its currents flow like a ribbon through space, time, and reality. In general, becoming immersed in the waters of Styx is a dangerous affair as the waters drain the memories of the living away from them so that they become like the dead, with no consciousness of their mortal life. Immersion forces a victim to succeed on a DC 14 Wisdom saving throw or suffer 1d6 points of Intelligence damage per round until their memories are completely erased. This effect is permanent unless the character is healed by using a *heal*, *greater restoration*, or *wish* spell.

A properly bribed charonademon can deliver a traveler to any of the lower planes that the Styx touches. These planes include Infernus, the Plane of Agony, the Hells, and the Abyss.

effects of the river, allowing one to swim to the bottom and open the chest. The swim is still very difficult, as the current is deep and powerful, requiring a successful DC 15 Strength (Athletics) check. Characters must also hold their breath lest they breath in the toxic waters of the River of the Dead. Failing the check washes the swimmer 30 feet down the river but allows a second check. Three consecutive failed swim checks results in the character being washed away on the Styx, where they are drowned, and their corporeal form washes up upon the shores of one of the planes that the Styx runs past determined at random.

If the characters successfully collect the skin of the lich (the *skin of Jhedophar*[2]), they may swim back to the boat and ask to be taken back to the portal to Rah'po Dehj's sanctum. This new direction of course requires a second payment, lest Charon himself be summoned to close the deal.

11. The Portal of the Scales

Written on the stones of the portal are the following words:

Beyond lies the weight and measure of a mortal soul. What worth is his flesh? Do his sins outweigh the burden borne by the righteous or the innocent? Let Ammit decide if my crimes of the flesh outweigh the sin that is the failure of the righteous heart.

Beyond the door is the glowing black vista of the Astral Plane, a glowing nothingness, where up and down, forward and backward, and movement are based purely on thought. At the edge of this nothingness floats a bit of sand and earth. A jackal-headed statue rises from the sand that is the beginning of the Duat, a portal where souls are assigned to Heaven or Hell, Elysium or the Abyss.

At the knees of the jackal sits a creature with the body of a lion and the head of a crocodile that stares intently at the characters with cold reptilian eyes. Before the creature are a set of golden scales.

If the skin of Jhedophar is placed upon the Scales of Justice, the statue of Anubis animates and asks them what they wish to weigh against such an evil soul in order to receive the thing they seek. If they fail, Anubis informs them that Ammit, the god at his feet, will be allowed to devour one of their number for the slight.

Items that would outweigh Jhedophar's crooked soul include a devil's talisman, the heart of an ancient or older lawful evil dragon, or an evil lesser relic. If any other evil item is placed upon the scales, Anubis states that the weight is equaled but is an unworthy payment, and that his friend Ammit hungers. They are allowed one more try to place one of the suggested items on the scale.

There is also a chance characters may be confused by the riddle, not relating the fall of purity to evil as the easiest hint.

Placing the proper lawful evil item upon the scale causes Ammit to disgorge the rotten heart of Jhedophar. Jhedophar's heart is his true phylactery. Destroying it allows him to be killed forever.

Chapter 28
The Ziggurat of Flame

This jagged pyramid dominates the city's skyline, its third largest structure and second only to the Palace of the Sultan in awe and splendor. The Ziggurat of Flame (called As-zug al Nar in the trilling, musical language of the city's masters) rises out of the Basin not far from the Great Repository, its majesty alone capable of keeping the darkness shed by that abomination from marring the beauty around it. Chained atop the ziggurat is one of the Nar al Nar, Lord of the Fire Elementals, who often howls with torment and rage at his imprisonment. The ziggurat's walls, which always shine resplendently in the molten light of day, are made from constantly expanding living brass forged deep in its bowels by an army of azer slaves. During the evening, when the Nightfall Concordance works its unusual brand of magic, the building seems possessed of a pale, golden light burning from within. Relief impressions depicting the deeds of the Sultan adorn their shimmering surfaces. Careful observation reveals two things: First, the Sultan's face is never shown, but rather is always depicted turning away from the viewer, or it is hidden behind a veil or somehow obscured; second, the stories on the wall move slowly, showing the events of the entire story they depict over the course of thirty hours and then beginning again when the cycle ends. Regardless of the tale, the Sultan always stands at least twice as tall as everyone else.

One section of the living bas relief is particularly famous, for it shows the Sultan holding in his left hand the chains of more than 30,000 humanoid slaves. Every day that passes shows an increase in the slave population by anywhere from 20 to 200 people. The slaves are unique individuals, representing those whose souls he now owns. In his right hand, he bears the Scepter of Set, a curiously bent ankh still in Set's possession as far as anyone knows. It isn't known why the mural shows the Sultan holding it.

Note: The Ziggurat of Flames is a huge location. Indicated below are the areas of "most importance" to you. The maps detail general locations and give more specific information on such locations as the Temple of the Sultan, the ash baths, the Emporium, the Agony Forge, slave quarters, and detailed maps of a common burning dervish's home and the priests' quarters. These maps by no way encompass the entirety of dwellings, homes, shops, parks, and other locations potentially found within the Ziggurat of Flame, which is more than 3-1/2 miles wide at the base and 2 miles high, indeed a mountain in the center of the City of Brass. You are encouraged to expand the ziggurat as you see fit to fulfill your campaign needs.

To assist the you in this endeavor, a table has been included to indicate whether a potential random room is a dwelling place of a burning dervish sheikh, priest, guardroom, or a trapped room designed to destroy intruders who would seek to invade the holiest of holies. Details of standard rooms are located within the text. Trap rooms are detailed below for ease of reference.

This adventure is suggested for Tier 4 characters.

Random Chambers

Roll 1d20 and consult the table below.

1d20	Random Chamber
1–5	Burning dervish[1] sheikh
6–10	Burning dervish[1] priest
11–17	Fire giant guardroom
18–20	Trapped room (see **Trapped Rooms and Doors Sidebar**)

The Ziggurat as Part of the Ongoing Campaign

Characters may enter the ziggurat through various levels and for various reasons. If the characters have retrieved the *maul of Hezoid*[2], Tarbish suggests that they get it to the Diya al Din, who could use it to destroy the Heart of Flame and thus break the stranglehold the cult of the Sultan has upon the City of Brass. If the characters have not overcome the Circus of Pain, or the adventures detailed there do not fit your campaign, Tarbish may suggest an assassination contract. In this scenario, the characters find the true name of the Sultan of Efreet[1] within the confines of the Great Repository that allows them to pass into the Temple of the Sultan through the Nar al Nar. In this instance, the death of the Husam al Din causes political and spiritual upheaval in the City of Brass, effectively taking the burning dervishes out of the picture as the mullahs fight one another for dominance within the spiritual hierarchy of the cult of the Sultan.

In your own campaign, the ziggurat may be used as a place to retrieve a hidden relic or for a rescue mission to free a current or potential ally from the clutches of the foul burning dervishes. Perhaps the characters have religious reasons to tackle the challenges of the great ziggurat, being sent by their deity as emissaries or spies. Pure thievery and greed is also a good motivator for entering the Ziggurat of Flame.

Due to its layout, the ziggurat may be accessed through the slave pits on the lower levels if the characters can somehow manage to circumvent the numerous demon gates. Another entrance to the Ziggurat of Flame is via the Mosque of Light. However, neither of these entrances allows access to the Temple of the Sultan or the City of the Burning Dervishes. These locations may be accessed only via passage through the Nar al Nar himself and then only by those able to glean the true name of the Sultan of Efreet[1], which are written in the Words of Creation within the Great Repository or gathered from the prophets entombed in the Kiln of Sorrows (also within the Great Repository).

Trapped Doors and Rooms

If a random roll to determine a particular chamber comes up 18 or higher on the **Random Chambers Table**, the room or door itself is trapped. Roll 1d8 and consult the list below. As appropriate, each listing gives the DC to discover the trap with a Intelligence (Investigation) check and to disable it with a Dexterity check with thieves' tools in parentheses after the trap name.

1. Test of the Sword Dance (DC 14/DC 18)

The floor, walls, and ceiling of this room are riddled with thrusting sword blades that a listener with a successful DC 18 Wisdom (Perception) check may hear at a range of 30 feet. A character viewing the area with a successful DC 16 Intelligence (Investigation) check may see a small gap between the blades near the edges of the room that can be used by someone less than 1 foot tall.

The blades spark with electricity. A creature attempting to move through this area must succeed on a DC 16 Dexterity saving throw every 10 feet or take 4 (1d8) slashing damage and 14 (4d6) lightning damage.

The room is occupied by an invisible **djinni** that attacks anyone attempting to fly across the room (including those in gaseous form).

2. Sonic Door (see below)

This obsidian door is under great pressure from the room beyond. A character succeeding on a DC 14 Wisdom (Perception) check notices a thin film of silvery liquid (mercury) running along the edge of the doorway. An astute character that succeeds on a DC 17 Wisdom (Perception) check can hear this door vibrate (the vibrations are otherwise undetectable). When the door is opened, a sonic blast and fine mist of mercury is released in a 20-foot cone affecting all within the area. Each character within the cone must succeed on a DC 16 Consitution saving throw or take 36 (8d8) acid damage and lose 1d6 points of Constitution until having completed a long rest.

The vapor is highly toxic. It causes severe respiratory tract damage. Symptoms include sore throat, coughing, pain, tightness in the chest, breathing difficulties, shortness of breath, headache, muscle weakness, ringing in the ear, liver damage, fever, and bronchitis.

The trap can be disabled by drilling a small hole in the door or otherwise relieving the pressure prior to opening it.

3. Chamber of the Bronze Lamp (DC 18/NA)

The room beyond this door seems bare save for a small bronze lamp. The lamp lies on its side near the wall, and any who inspect it notice that it is dented and a bit tarnished. Try not to laugh if they wish to rub it, for it matters not; upon entering this room, the character(s) committed themselves to finding a way out of this trapped chamber or die trying.

The room is under a continuous magnetic field upon every surface, which pull upon each other and can literally tear anything apart. This effect is nullified by the presence of the lamp. Anyone who tries to leave the room without the lamp is violently thrust backward into the room and smashes into the opposite wall for 10 (3d6) bludgeoning damage. When the lamp is picked up, it adopts the first person doing so as its owner in regards to effects that it provides while in this room. The new owner feels an odd sensation, which allows the owner and lamp to leave the room.

When the lamp leaves the room, however, all those still trapped inside take 21 (6d6) force damage each round from the magnetic forces pulling them in every direction. A trapped character can attempt to move but must succeed on a DC 17 Strength (Athletics) check each round to do so and can move only 5 feet per round. The only way to counter the effect is by having the owner toss the lamp back into the room for it to adopt another as its owner so that character might escape.

Doing this till all are out of the room still does not free the party. Two rounds after the last owner with the lamp leaves the room, the doorway acts as a vortex, drawing anyone within 5 feet of the door and with metal upon them (include those coated by the mercury from the sonic door, if it hasn't been washed off) to be pulled back into the room. Only the last owner tossing the lamp back into the room prevents this from happening. This trap may be quite deadly if the lamp is dropped outside the room and all party members are drawn in.

4. Hallway of Hot Coals (DC 16/NA)

This chamber appears to be a passage (about 120 feet long) littered with warm coals. Partly an illusion, the room beyond is actually covered in **brown mold**, with sharp rocks upon the floor (treat as caltrops).

5. The Blood Chamber (DC 16/NA)

Warm blood coats the floor here, which acts like glue when contacted. Characters moving through the area do so at one-half their normal movement rate.

In the center of the chamber stands a pillar of bronze covered in glyphs and sigils. The pillar is actually a **roper** that attacks as soon as the characters move within range.

6. Within a Lamp (DC 18/NA)

This chamber looks like the inside of a lamp: Every surface is gilded brass, and convex in the shape of a lamp. Plush cushions abound, as well as platters of food covering every surface of the floor. The walls are draped with silk curtains and beaded draperies. To all concerned, this room is a paradise from the hells found elsewhere, if you are not a genie. Trapped here by the powerful magic of the room are 13 **efreet**. They are not happy with their imprisonment and are very eager to do something to alleviate their boredom and rage; the characters provide just such a distraction.

The effects of the room are that everything repairs, cleans, and in all regards, replenishes anything damaged in this chamber. It is a room the

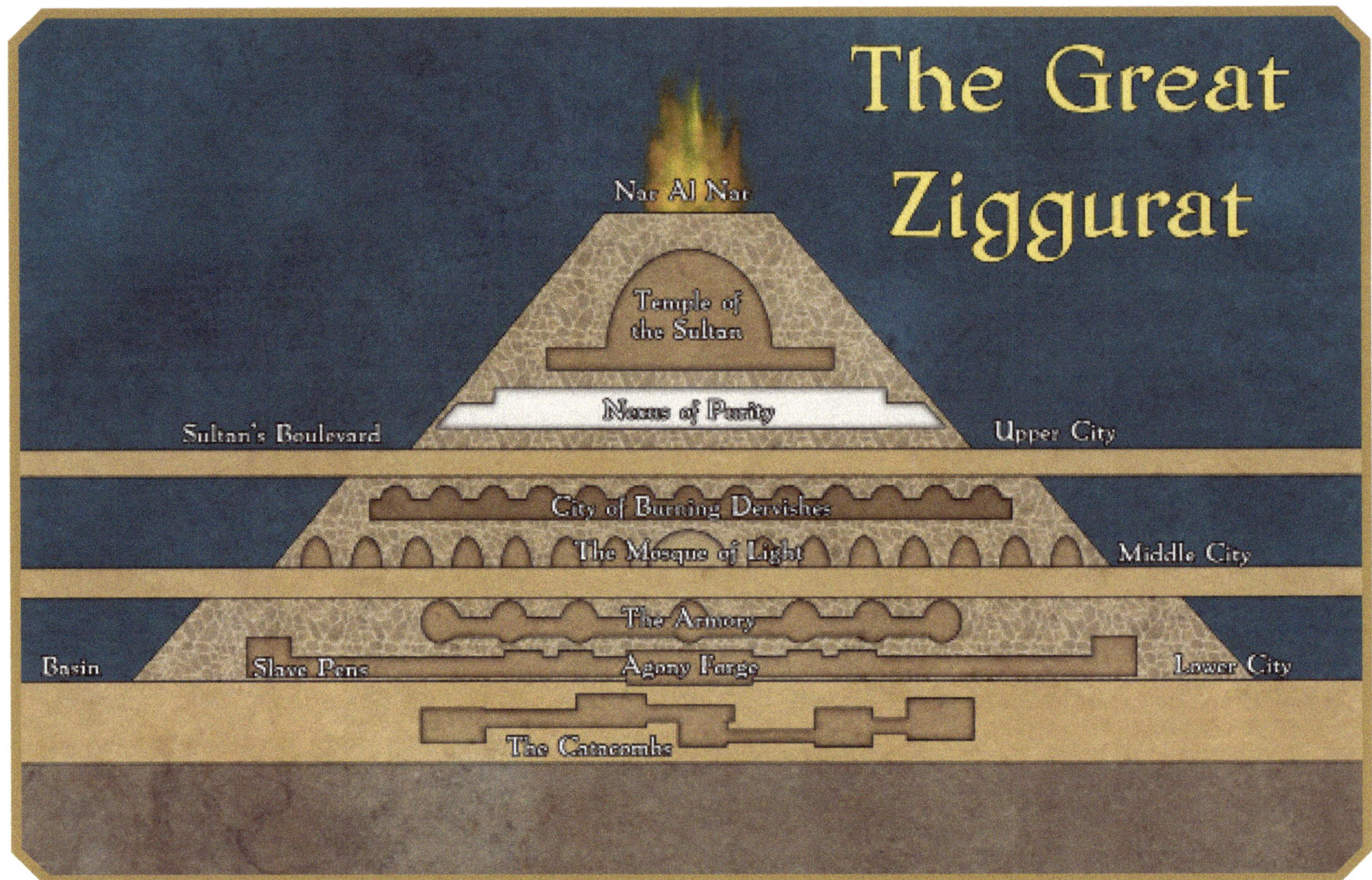

party may relax in if they clear out the trapped genies. Note however that any character who spends more than three days relaxing in the chamber must succeed on a DC 16 Constitution saving throw or thir soul becomes tethered to the room. On a successful save, nothing out of the ordinary happens. If the character leaves the chamber within the next three days, the bond is broken. A character who remains in the chamber beyond these three days must succeed on a DC 18 Wisdom saving throw or forever be trapped in this chamber. Nothing short of a *wish* can break the bond. (Killing the character and carrying the corpse out to resurrect it later does not work, as the character's form returns to this chamber as soon as it regains life.)

7. Elemental Nails (DC 14/DC 20)

Thirty sharpened spikes rise from the floor of this chamber. Twenty-six of the spikes are engraved with a letter (A through Z) in Ignan; the last four are engraved with a rune representing each of the four basic elements (air, earth, water, and fire).

To open the door and escape the chamber requires a character to wound herself (for at least 1 point of damage) using each of the elemental spikes (air, earth, fire, and water). Further, after each wounding, the character (or one of her allies) must *summon* a creature with that elemental subtype and wound that creature with the same spike for at least 1 point of damage. Once this process is complete, the door opens and the characters may leave.

8. Elemental Door (DC 17/NA)

The door to this chamber seems to pulsate and glow, slowly changing colors starting with red, moving to brown, then white, then blue. The first creature to touch the door triggers the elemental trap. The character feels his body heat up and burst into flames. No sooner do the flames extinguish when the character's form quickly transforms to stone in the next round. In the third round, his form shifts into wispy airy smoke, followed quickly (still in the third round) by his form changing into solid ice before returning to normal. The character who triggers the trap takes 14 (4d6) fire damage, 14 (4d6) cold damage, and 21 (6d6) necrotic damage from the rapid shifting of his body across the four elements. A successful DC 17 Dexterity saving throw (only one is needed) halves all the damage.

Locations within the Ziggurat of Flame

Nexus of Purity

The Boulevard of Sultans runs straight through the upper layers of the ziggurat. That tunnel is popularly called the Nexus of Purity, and 1,000 torches lit with *continuous flame* cling to the walls inside, which reflect their light a hundred times stronger. No entrance to the ziggurat may be had inside the nexus; it merely transits characters to the other side. Locals believe anyone who passes through the tunnel receives the Sultan's blessing; as such, it is one of the first places new pilgrims to the city visit. In truth, the Sultan commissioned the tunnel to honor his 1,001 greatest conquered enemies. Their names are inscribed in the wall beneath the torches. Just one torch does not burn, because the enemy whom it honors is no longer dead. His fate and whereabouts remain unknown. The real purpose of the tunnel is not widely known, as the Sultan does not want anyone mistaking him for a sentimental weakling.

Nar al Nar

The section of the ziggurat above the Nexus of Purity is reserved exclusively for the Sultan and the highest-ranking members of his bureaucracy. This consists primarily of those efreet serving directly below him and the burning dervishes. The dervishes were renowned warriors and assassins in their homelands many forgotten millennia ago, distinguished because they were the first to sell their souls to the Sultan. In return, the Sultan granted them unparalleled mastery over the sacred elemental flame called the "Heart of Flame." Since then, they have been his most fervent and loyal servants, spreading their faith and proclaiming his greatness wherever they travel. They were the ones who brought the priesthood of Anumon to its knees. To this day, they continue to hunt down its remnants, obliterating it at every turn. The only way into the Temple of the Sultan is through the elemental prince **Nar al Nar**[1]. Stepping into the flames of his body and commanding him in the true name of the Sultan allows a person to descend into it. The person speaking the Sultan's true name and any allies who join hands do not take fire damage; otherwise, passage is blocked for them and each character takes 16 (3d10) fire damage per round.

Nar al Nar, as you might guess, seethes with hatred for the Sultan and his cronies. The mystic chains binding him are exceptionally strong, so it is unlikely (but not impossible) that a party of adventurers will have it within their means to free him. Nor will they be able to con or deceive the elemental because it is just not possible given the strictures of the *geas* forcing him to guard the temple entrance. To make a long story short: Unless a character knows the Sultan's true name, she cannot enter the temple.

However, the elemental can be distracted by certain things from his home plane, things that let him experience (albeit indirectly) pleasures and sensations now lost or forbidden to him. If a party of adventurers brings him one of the following items, he is sufficiently distracted that they can sneak past him:

Mantle of Elemental Friendship: When the Sultan captured him, the Elemental Prince was wearing this liquid cloak. It was a gift given to him by the Elemental Princess Silisshanne from the Plane of Water as a token of peace when they agreed to end the hostilities between their two peoples. Since his capture and subsequent disappearance, the fire elementals of his home plane assumed water elemental assassins murdered him and renewed the war with increased fervor. The mantle currently hangs in the wardrobe of a high-ranking burning dervish named Raed Zis, given to him by the Sultan as a token of his appreciation for services rendered on a particularly dangerous mission. His residence is in the ziggurat's middle section. Anyone who dons the mantle is viewed as a friend and ally by all elementals, regardless of alignment.

The Black Blade: This is a weighty longsword that ends in a flat edge rather than a pointed tip. Inscribed along it length are the runes of the executioner, which claim the sword's rightful owner is Sovoran, royal high executioner to the emperor of fire. Sovoran was like a father to Nar al Nar when the elemental was young, and he was the only human ever allowed to enter the royal palaces of the ruling family, or even come within a thousand leagues of it. If Nar al Nar receives the blade, he is overcome with sadness, for the blade could not possibly have been taken from Sovoran unless he was dead. At the moment, the blade is owned by Al Fatik[1], proprietor of the Executioner's Edge, a weapons shop in one of the city's innumerable bazaars. The blade is a *vorpal sword* (longsword).

The Phoenix's Necklace: A beautiful agate pendant hanging from a sturdy platinum chain, this quaint looking piece of jewelry was once worn by the phoenix Nu-Shang, whose acquaintance Nar al Nar made when he was in hiding from the Sultan's hunters. It has no special properties, as far as anyone knows, but it does possess a lot of sentimental value for the prince. There was never a mortal creature more beloved by him than the beautiful phoenix. She gave him the necklace to remember her by right before she underwent her transformation. Two days later, the Sultan's brazen warhounds and huntsman captured him. The necklace is now in the possession of Bel A Din, a sorceress and jewelry store owner.

Qalb al Nar: If the characters brought Sparque with them from Lornedain and possess the *ring of Qalb*[2], they may instantly free the Nar al Nar from his chains as the great fire lord bursts his bonds to retrieve his son. The Nar al Nar, now free, offers his aid in whatever task the characters need, and with Sparque, he joins them in their raid on the Great Ziggurat if necessary. Grant the characters a significant experience point bonus in this event! Upon completion of the immediate task, the Nar al Nar whisks his son away to the heart of the Plane of Fire, with a promise to return and aid the characters at the point of their greatest need.

Temple of the Sultan

Inside the Temple of the Sultan stands a towering brass, gold, and platinum statue bearing his idealized likeness. It is rumored to be valued at more than 3 million gp. It is also the means by which he communicates with his faithful, usually by animating it, though occasionally he transforms it into a regal brass dragon (especially at those times he hands the burning dervishes new orders or directives). The head priest, a thin, balding weasel of a man named Husam al Din[1] ("Sword of Justice") lives in the temple with a retinue of efreeti and azer servants, fire giant bodyguards, and harem girls. Husam is the only person alive to have seen the Sultan's uncovered face. As a result, he is permanently blind. Though he could easily cure himself with divine magic, he does not, for he wears his blindness as a badge of honor and a point of pride. The areas described below can be found on the *Temple of the Sultan* map.

1. Worship Hall of the Great Sultan

This gargantuan chamber is large enough to hold 1,200 faithful worshippers of the Sultan. In the center stands the colossal statue of the sultan of efreet, flanked by two 50-foot-high pillars of fire that serve as portals for those burning dervishes entering the ziggurat by means of the Nar al Nar. There are 2d10 **burning dervishes**[1] and 1d6 **burning dervish priests**[1] in this chamber at all times.

During the Sultan's holidays and worship services, all the faithful are called to prayer by the banging of mighty gongs that hang at the north and south ends of the chamber. During worship service, the chamber is filled with two dozen priests, more than 1,200 burning dervishes, and a handful of efreeti clerics[1].

Treasure: The brass gongs on the north and south end of the hall weigh 2 tons each and are worth 5,000 gp due to their craftsmanship and the embossed image of the Sultan surrounded by stylized bronze dragons, the chains of their collars grasped in his outstretched hand.

The gold and bejeweled statue of the Sultan is worth 3 million gp. Smelted down, it weighs 10,000 pounds, as it is hollow inside, and has a value of 1 million gp.

2. Fire Giant Quarters

These six chambers each house 6 **fire giants** who serve as temple guardians. They are all slaves affixed with brass collars. Their existence and slavery are unproven but suspected by Surter's thain. Should they be freed, word quickly spreads among the fire giant population of the City of Brass as to the true nature of the cult of the Sultan and the cruelty of the burning dervishes, bringing not only the wrath of Thain Brindha but also likely causing an armed insurrection among the foreign mercenaries. A portion of the fire giants would remain within the ziggurat, slaying any burning dervishes or efreet they meet on sight.

Treasure (per chamber): 1,000 bp, *ring of invisibility*, 4 *potions of resistance* (fire), or *cloak of displacement* (roll 1d6 for each chamber: 1–2, *ring*; 3–4 *potions*; 5–6 *cloak*).

3. Azer Servant Chambers

These six chambers each house a dozen **azer** servants affixed with brass collars. These azer clean the temple and see to the needs of the Sultan's priests. Their chambers are spartan when compared with the opulence of the chambers of the priesthood, consisting only of woven copper sleeping mats and simple cooking utensils.

4. Chambers of the Lesser Priesthood

These chambers are identical to the burning dervish residences. The difference is that the "sheikh" is a **burning dervish priest**[1]. All guards found within the residence are **burning dervish guards**[1].

5. Chambers of the Mullahs

These chambers are larger versions of a normal priestly residence and similar to the burning dervish residences detailed earlier. They are home to the mullahs (**burning dervish high priests**[1]). There are double the number of **burning dervish priests**[1], wives, concubines, children, and servants (**burning dervishes**[1], **burning dervish children**[1], and **efreet** or

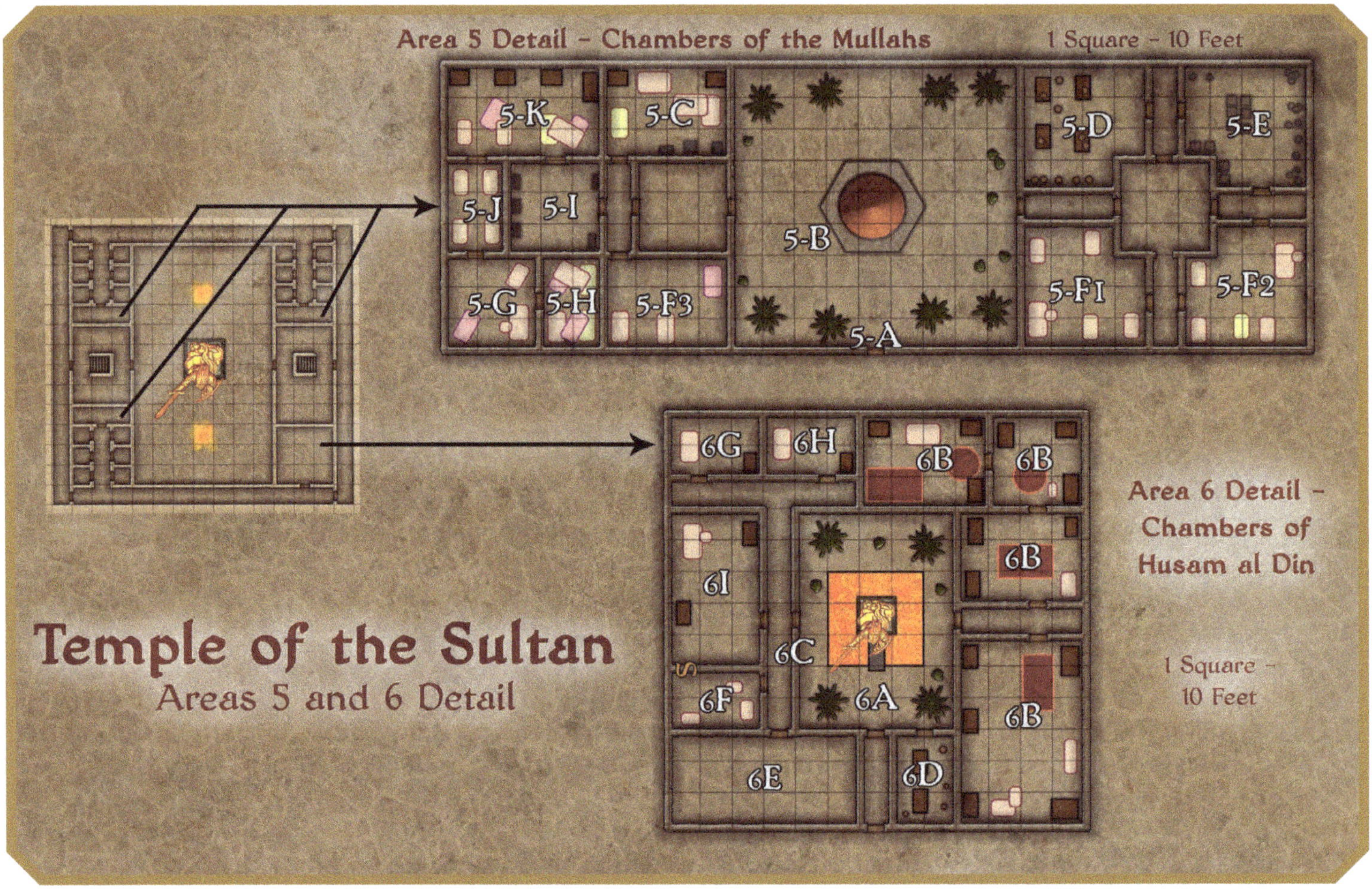

azers, respectively). The layout of their dwellings is similar to that of their High Priest Husam al Din[1] detailed below. These chambers are further detailed the *Chambers of the Mullahs* map.

5A. Entryway

The entry to a burning dervish's quarters is locked with an excellent mechanical lock and an *arcane lock* whose password is known only to the burning dervish and his family and servants. The lock requires a successful DC 18 Dexterity check with thieves' tools to open (DC 28 if the *arcane lock* is not first removed). As burning dervishes do not steal from one another, the doorway is seldom guarded by any other than an **azer** servant who escorts appointments to the courtyard that sits in the center of most dwellings.

5B. Courtyard

The courtyard of a burning dervish's private quarters has a small shrine to the Sultan of Efreet[1] in the center of it, often built beneath a domed gazebo. Tropical plants in magical planters bear fruits such as bananas, dates, and coconuts the year round and need no water to sustain their growth nor any sun to maintain them. The sheikh and his family and retinue take their meals in the gazebo. It is under this same gazebo where they also spend much of their time resting or praying to the glory and greatness of the Sultan.

5C. Guard Barracks

Every burning dervish sheikh has a complement of 1d4 + 1 **burning dervishes**[1] to guard his home and protect his family. Normally these guards are relatives of the dervish such as nephews or first cousins' sons. The barracks usually have several cushions, silks, and satins that serve as bedding for the guards. At least one burning dervish is within the barracks taking a rest at any given time unless an alarm sounds. The dervishes keep their weapons and cuirass on racks near their bedding, and each has a small iron chest with an excellent lock containing their personal belongings and private wealth that is not stored in the KhizAnah. The locks can be opened with a successful DC 18 Dexterity check with thieves' tools or a successful DC 20 Strength check. If the barracks are entered unbidden by an intruder, the dervish attacks should he notice the intruder.

5D. Kitchens

This large chamber is where azer slaves prepare meals for their burning dervish masters. There are 2d4 **azer** slaves within the kitchens from morning to mid-evening keeping busy with cooking and cleaning. If intruded upon, they ignore the strangers or seek to hide unless attacked. If assaulted, they retaliate with improvised weapons found around the kitchen and fight to the death. The head cook of the sheikh's family keeps a key to the storage chamber where foodstuffs, wines, and sundries are kept.

5E. Storage

Dried goods, wine, and other materials such as cleaning supplies needed to keep a home in working order are kept in this storage chamber just off the kitchen.

Treasure: 500 gp worth of saffron, cinnamon, pepper and other spices are kept on shelves along with flour, dried fruits, seasoned meats, barrels of fish, and other assorted dried goods. There is also an average of 1d20 + 5 jugs of fine wine worth 100 gp each as part of the sheikh's private stores.

5F-1 to 5F-3. Servants Quarters

These sparsely appointed chambers house the sheikh's various slaves who cook, clean, tend his children, and maintain the courtyard gardens. Each of the chambers houses 1d4 **azer** slaves, but a burning dervish sheikh may also have slaves of other races such as **salamanders**, **fire elementals**, or any of the various humanoid races depending on his personal wealth and tastes.

5G. Harem

The sheikh's lesser wives (**burning dervishes**[1]) and concubines (**varies**) occupy this chamber. A typical burning dervish sheikh has 1d4 + 1 wives or concubines. Due to the Sultan's law, sheikhs may only take female burning dervishes as wives; their concubines, however, may be of any race that suits their tastes. Children born to concubines become slaves within the households of other burning dervishes, while children born to wives become heirs with sons taking precedence over daughters due to the chauvinistic nature of the Sultan. Concubines are typically guarded by ogre-mage (**oni**) eunuchs. The rooms are decorated in the style of a boudoir with silks and satins piled upon the floor. Concubines will not battle intruders; however, wives and eunuchs attack on sight.

Treasure: 2,000 gp worth of silks and satins, 10 vials of exotic perfume (140 gp each), 5 masterwork disguise kits in jeweled makeup cases (300 gp each), each concubine has a courtesan outfit (200 gp each).

5H. Children's Chamber

Children of the burning dervish occupy these chambers until they are old enough to take service with the Sultan and survive the trials of the ash baths. These chambers are adorned with militaristic toys, sleeping silks and satins, and thin scrolls of burnished copper detailing the deeds of the efreet and Iblis, and the rise of the Sultan and the salvation of the tribes of dervish in his name. There are 1d4 **burning dervish children**[1] who occupy these chambers. They have not yet developed their powers and are considered noncombatants. A lone **burning dervish**[1] usually stands watch over the children.

5I. Master's Parlor

This chamber contains many of the trophies of the sheikh and his conquests, deeds, and holy reliquaries given him by the Sultan or the Sultan's priesthood. Most are items of decadence captured from infidels within the city during religious purges or the stuffed heads and skins of animals slain on hunting expeditions. The sheikh conducts his private business within this chamber.

Treasure: Silk tapestry (400 gp), 3 bronze urns (200 gp each), finely crafted rug (600 gp), bronze idol of the Sultan (900 gp), stuffed animal heads (1d6 heads, various animals or magical beasts; 1d10 x 100 gp each), animal skins (1d4 skins, various animals or magical beasts, 1d6 x 100 gp each).

5J. First Wife's Chamber

This chamber is home to the first wife of the sheikh and her children and is directly attached to the sheikh's own personal chamber. The first wife is always a **burning dervish**[1] and usually has 1d2 **children**[1] who are noncombatants. The first wife attacks any intruder on sight. Ornate carpets, overstuffed cushions, silks, satins, and furs line the sleeping area of the chamber. Heavily carved lapis lazuli and jade chests of drawers and wardrobes hold the first wife's jewelry and heavily beaded and jeweled finery. The first wife is the master of the harem and the household's slaves and guards, ruling the home with an iron fist in the absence of her husband.

Treasure: Sleeping silks (400 gp), 1d4 vials of perfume (80 gp each), finely crafted rug (200 gp), 1d3 gold chains (100 gp each), 1d4 gold rings (100 gp each), 1d2 bracelets or anklets (70 gp each).

5K. Sheikh's Bedchamber

This bedroom is where the sheikh (**burning dervish priest**[1]) takes his rest when he is not out patrolling the city looking for those who break religious law. Unless encountered elsewhere or out of the home within the ziggurat or the city proper, the sheikh may be found here. The sheikh of a burning dervish household's private bedchamber is opulent in the extreme and is often guarded by a **firefiend**[1] who dwells within a large brazier of burning coals.

6. Chambers of Husam al Din

Husam al Din[1] lives in a fine estate built within the confines of the temple atop the Great Ziggurat. His personal quarters are heavily guarded as his life is considered almost as holy as that of their living god, the Sultan of Efreet[1]. This area is further detailed in the ***Chambers of Husam al Din*** map.

6A. Courtyard of Husam al Din

This courtyard is a magnificent garden filled with magical planters from which grow trees that constantly bear succulent fruits such as pomegranates, pears, apples, bananas, dates, and coconuts. The center of the garden features a bridge leading to a likeness of the sultan of efreet similar to the one found in the main temple. It stands surrounded by a small lake of lava and may only be crossed without flight by means of a bridge of burnished iron. This smaller statue is only 20 feet high and is valued at 1 million gp, or 200,000 gp if melted down.

6B. Attendant's Chambers

These four chambers are nearly identical, featuring silks and satins, overstuffed goose-down pillows and lapis lazuli wardrobes containing the personal belongings of the priests who attend Husam al Din[1]. Each of the priests is a **burning dervish priest**[1] who would willingly sacrifice his own life in defending his blind master.

Treasure (per chamber): Sleeping silks (100 gp), 8 goose-down pillows (100 gp each), silk and satin vestments (500 gp each), priestly writings (150 gp if sold to a temple), bronze urn (200 gp), 1d10 x 20 bp.

6C. Entrance to Private Quarters

To the west of the courtyard is the actual residence of Husam al Din[1]. The entry chamber to his quarters is guarded by a pair of **efreeti** soldiers who are sworn to guard the blind priest to the death and beyond. The efreeti soldiers attack any non-burning dervish priest or other efreeti on sight who does not have a special pass to visit the venerable blind priest. Once slain, these efreeti immediately rise as **ghul efreet**[1] and fight again until slain a second time.

6D. Kitchens

These kitchens are similar to those found in the dwelling of any burning dervish, consisting of tables with which to prepare food and baskets filled with foodstuffs. The kitchen is maintained by a dozen **azer** slaves and 2 **efreeti** servants. All are fitted with brass collars.

6E. Servant's Quarters

These quarters house the two dozen house slaves (**azer**) kept by Husam al Din[1]. Unless their collars are somehow removed and they are armed, they remain noncombatants, fighting only to defend themselves.

6F. Harem of Husam al Din

Husam al Din's wives and concubines occupy this chamber. His thirteen wives are each **burning dervishes**[1] and his six concubines are **erinyes** and **efreeti** women given as gifts to him by the Sultan himself. The wives and concubines are easily able to defend themselves from any ravishment by outside forces. A secret door in the north wall requiring a successful DC 18 Wisdom (Perception) check to find leads to the private chamber of

Husam al Din[1] himself.

Treasure: Sleeping silks (100 gp), 25 silk pillows (50 gp each), 30 vials of exotic perfume (150 gp each), 1d6 x 10 bp, 2d4 x 20 sp, 20 satin bed dressings (100 gp each).

6G. Abdalla al Husam's Chamber

This chamber belongs to the second son of Husam al Din[1]. There is a 50% chance that Abdalla al Husam (**burning dervish high priest**[1]) is present at any given time. If not within his quarters, he is away somewhere in the city or traveling the planes on business for the Sultan of Efreet[1]. The chamber is filled with Abdalla's personal belongings. Among his personal possessions, Abdalla carries a *frostbrand* (falchion, has +2 bonus to attack and damage rolls) which he keeps hidden on his person for fear of reprisal by the City of Brass's police force. If engaged in battle, he usually relies on his natural attacks and spells.

Treasure: Sleeping silks (600 gp), 1,500 gp, 2,000 bp, ceremonial dagger with Sultan's likeness engraved on blade (1,000 gp), fire opal pendant (1,500 gp), bronze flagon with emeralds encrusted on handle (1,100 gp).

6H. Hasam al Husam's Chamber

This chamber belongs to the first son of Husam al Din[1]. Husam is currently grieving the disappearance of Hasam al Husam, who led the strike force that set out to capture Sulymon for the Sultan of Efreet[1]. Unbeknownst to the high priest, his son's bones are found with the flask containing the spirit of Sulymon, hidden from his father's view by means of the Grand Vizier's magic. As with his brother Abdalla, his many belongings line the walls and fill chests arranged neatly around the room.

Treasure: Sleeping silks (700 gp), silk vestments (500 gp), bronze chain with ruby pendant (3,000 gp), bronze chalice with lapis lazuli inlay (250 gp), *spell scroll* of *raise dead* and *commune*, *spell wand*[2] of *cure wounds*.

6I. Chamber of Husam al Din

The blind high priest of the Sultan resides within these chambers when not directly serving the Sultan on some mission or leading the faithful in prayer. The chamber is simply adorned due to the blindness of the high priest who needs no fantastic wall hangings or works of art. Instead, the chamber contains merely his wardrobe, sleeping silks, and toilet. Unless encountered elsewhere within the Ziggurat, **Husam al Din**[1] is found here. Should the gongs sound to alert the burning dervishes of intruders, Husam is found in the Worship Hall (**Area A**) with his mullahs, directing the defenses and attempts to capture the intruders.

Treasure: Sleeping silks (1,000 gp), 6 silk and satin pillows (500 gp each), bronze chain with three fire opals (2,500 gp), 4,000 bp, silk vestments (1,200 gp), bronze and emerald bracelet (800 gp), 600 sp.

City of the Burning Dervishes

Below the Nexus of Purity and the Boulevard of the Sultan is the City of the Burning Dervishes, accessible only through the Temple of the Sultan. At any given time, there are 1,200 members present. Their portion of the Ziggurat is a small city in and of itself, replete with azer-operated food and equipment bazaars, bathhouses, tea and coffee houses, pleasure houses, private parks, and bestiaries filled with all manner of exotic creature imported for training purposes. Each individual dwelling is occupied by a burning dervish sheikh (fighter, cleric or wizard level 5) and his family retinue of slaves, guards, wives, and children. Most notable of the locations within the City of the Burning Dervishes are the private residences, the ash baths, and the galleria and its shops.

The galleria is a gathering of shops that surround the ash baths in the center of this level of the ziggurat. These shops tend to the needs of the thousands of burning dervishes living within the ziggurat and are exclusive to the ziggurat itself. Several shop types are listed below. It is left for you to flesh out the shops with appropriate goods and proprietors for this section of the ziggurat. The majority of shops and markets within the galleria are maintained by burning dervish[1] sheikhs whose dwellings are located in the ring of homes directly outside the galleria itself and staffed and guarded by their collared slaves.

This area is shown in the *City of the Burning Dervishes* map.

1. Fawaki wa Khudra Souk

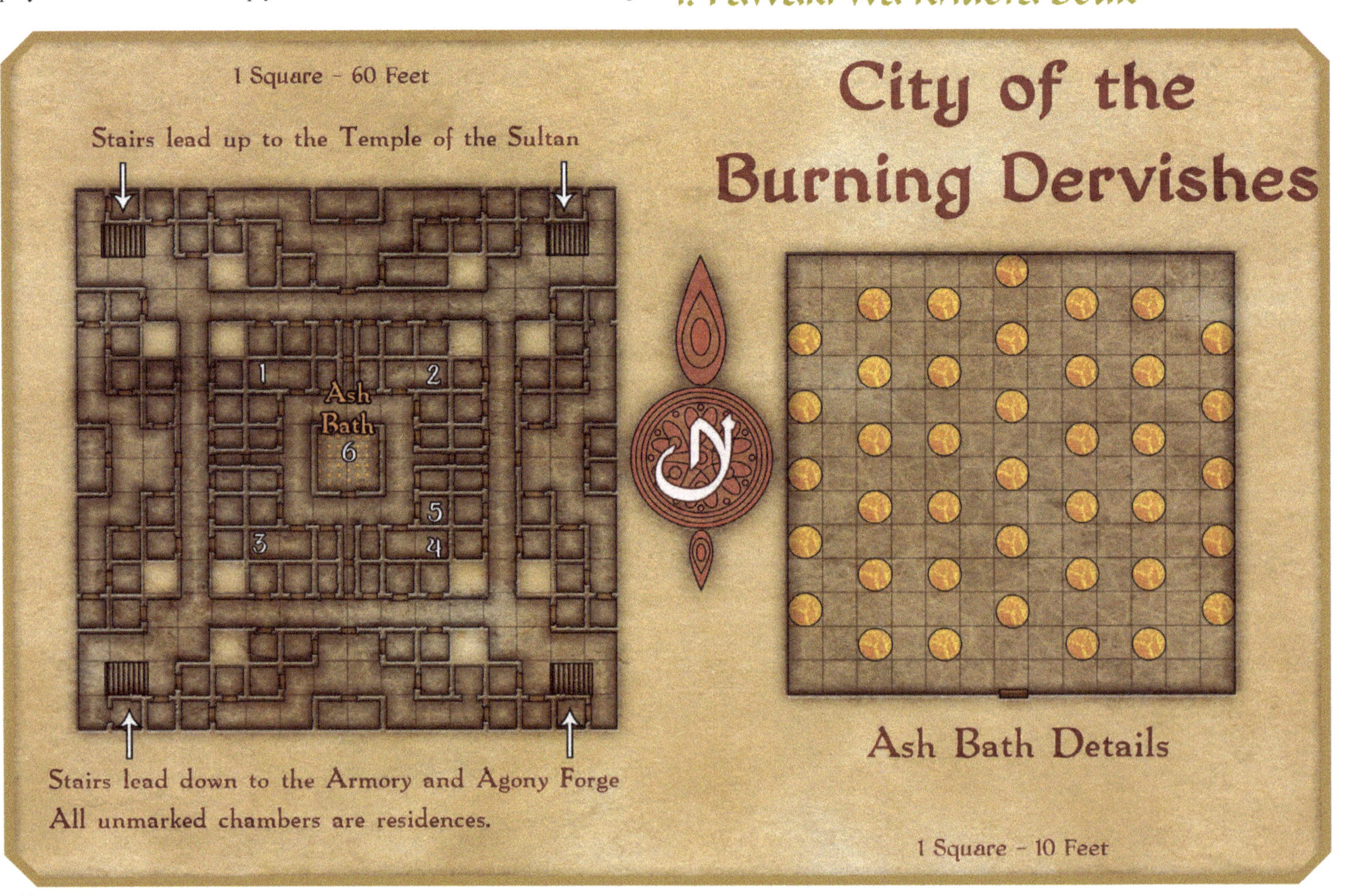

The fruit and vegetable shops. Levantine stuffed vegetables. More distinctly local are muhammara, a spicy paste eaten like hummus but made of the renowned Calidis hot pepper, pomegranate juice, and ground walnuts. Pistachios are creatively deployed in many sweets — rolled in dough and smothered with syrup or embedded in sweet gelatin.

2. Lahma wa Samak Souk

Lahma wa Samak Souk is a market restaurant serving many dishes popular to the burning dervishes. The cooks serve particularly tasty versions of kebab, kibbe (ground cracked wheat and lamb), mezze (appetizers), and a seasonal kebab in a sauce of stewed fresh cherries called kababbi-karaz, and varieties of kibbe made with sumac and quince.

The traditional dishes draw upon that which can be summoned: flocks of hardy fiendish dire sheep being a common meat source as well as having uses in textiles. Or things created upon this plane: orchards of fire treated olive, nut, and fruit trees being most common.

3. The Salleh Souk (Repair Market)

The Salleh Souk carries a wide range of items, including tools, spices, kitchenware, towels, shoes, fabrics, and watches. This souk is also well known as a place to get shoe and other leather repairs carried out. The Salleh Souk specializes in fabrics ranging from the incredibly cheap artificial fibers to the more expensive silks, linens, and cottons. A huge range of patterns and types of fabric is available

Buyers can purchase souvenirs such as khanjars and coffee pots, Bedouin jewelry, clothing (dishdashas, kummas (caps), massar (turban) and khanjar for the men; and dishdashas, surwal (trousers), and lihaff (shawl) for the women.

Wallets, antique jars, frankincense, silverware, antiques, and garments are the most sought-after items.

4. Feluus Souk (Money Market)

This souk is a cluster of shops selling masses of gold jewelry. Designs tend to be rather traditional, either devilish or in the efreeti style. Plenty of chains, earrings, bracelets, and rings can be found in comparatively plain styles. The gold used is a fiery metal from the plane of fire and is quite dense, valued at double the standard price in gold pieces.

5. The Infernal Sem (Demon's Poison)

This market is a good place to find tools that can inflict pleasure or pain, as well as secondhand slaves who have more likely than not lost their souls to their devilish masters.

6. The Ash Baths

The floor of this chamber is subdivided into hundreds of discrete "pools," all of them filled with white-hot smoldering ash. As part of their daily ritual, burning dervishes submerge themselves in the ash baths for up to 1 hour. Likewise, burning dervishes who have been away from the city come here to purify their bodies so they might reconnect with the Sultan's power.

The baths are extremely hot, dealing 7 (2d6) fire damage each round to any creature touching the ash. Burning dervishes take no damage from the ash.

The top edges of the walls dividing the pools can be used for walking, requiring a successful DC 10 Dexterity (Acrobatics) check every 5 rounds. The air is thick with drifting ash and smoke, and the stench of burnt flesh is overpowering. The baths' sandstone walls depict the assault on the Necropolis of Amun Ra by an army of burning dervishes. The figures are carved in relief and are well worn from the erosion of time.

Buried at the bottom of one bath is a rod of embassy. It used to belong to a high-ranking assassin who defected to Lucifer's camp a few years earlier after the Sultan, in a moment of whimsy, ravaged the man's daughter then had her beheaded for allowing herself to be thus despoiled. The rod is located under a loose sandstone tile and can be located with a successful DC 22 Intelligence (Investigation) check. Anyone who carries this particular rod is allowed free, unimpeded access to all levels of the ziggurat, including the Temple of the Sultan.

There are 1d10 + 10 **burning dervishes**[1] and 1d10 + 5 **azer** attendants within this chamber at any given time.

Mosque of Light

While the part of the ziggurat occupied by the Sultan's army has numerous mosques that receive worshippers at least 2 times daily, the Mosque of Light is special in that it is typically used but once a week. It is five stories tall and approximately 300 feet around. The outer walls are pierced through by hundreds of narrow windows similar in size and shape to arrow loops, allowing light from outside to pour in due to an intricate arrangement of polished mirrors throughout the level. When the dervishes and efreeti gather here, they kneel on their prayer mats around a piece of glowing amber set upon a pedestal in the center of the room. Embedded inside the amber are flame said to come from the heart of the first fire elemental. As the gathered congregation prays, the *Heart of Flame* glows increasingly brighter until it bathes the chamber in a blinding yellow-white light. The ecstatic high imparted by the ritual makes the truly faithful spontaneously combust into flame (this does not count against a dervish's daily allotment of flame form changes).

Rod of Embassy

A character bearing a rod of embassy is considered under the official protection of the Sultan and is untouchable by any official or bureaucrat of the City of Brass. Gaining one of these rods is considered nearly impossible as they are granted only to those diplomats and dignitaries held in the highest esteem by the Sultan or a pasha of one of the ruling families. These include emissaries of archdevils with business in the City of Brass, extremely powerful mages, lich lords, hag queens, and the like. Of course, characters who somehow come into possession of one of these rods may be able to fake their importance through use of Deception or Performance skill checks or the use of magic to hide their true identities.

Burning dervishes' traveling abroad place prayer mats on the ground, regardless of location, and direct their prayers toward the amber heart at least once a day, asking that the sacred fire guide them and inspire them. When they're not in the Plane of Molten Skies, they face the rising sun in lieu of turning to face the mosque, since that is physically impossible.

Should the *Heart of Flame* be "freed" from the amber, the resulting explosion is so enormous that the entire ziggurat collapses. Furthermore, every single burning dervish suddenly and violently combusts until nothing is left but ash and memories. To destroy the *Heart of Flame*, a person must use the *maul of Hezoid*[2], which is owned by the titan champion in the **Circus of Pain**. The magic contained in the hammer is sufficient that the amber shell around the *Heart of Flame* shatters upon being struck with it, but only by someone with acute knowledge of the artifact's singular weakness can do this. At this time, that person is Diya al Din, the penitent azer cleric imprisoned in the ziggurat's lower levels. Should the Diya al Din succeed in destroying the *Heart of Flame*, the characters have 10 minutes to flee the ziggurat or be killed themselves as the ziggurat collapses upon them. See **Finishing Adventures in the Great Ziggurat** at the end of this chapter for more details.

There are 1d6 + 2 **burning dervish priests**[1] attending the *Heart of Flame* at any given time of day or night. Worship times are at "sunrise" and "sunset" when the Nightfall Concordance alights and dims the city and the gongs from the Temple of the Sultan call folk to worship.

The Foundries

The ziggurat's lowest levels house the brass foundries, the slave pens, and the catacombs. None connect in any way to the levels above, as least as far as anyone in authority knows. Hundreds upon hundreds of alcoves pierce the walls of the lower levels, closest to the Basin. These are home to the wretched azer slaves who toil constantly, forging more and more living brass in the temple interior where unbelievable machinery fueled by incredible magic churns day and night in order to build the ziggurat higher and higher. The ziggurat is continually under construction from the bottom up, the living brass flowing into it to increase its overall height by one-half inch per month on average. The crypts buried within and below the building are accessed by means of the dense, confusing warrens of tunnels that house the azer. These crypts are purportedly filled with undead that have decided to make their stay in the city more or less permanent.

This area is shown on the ***Foundaries*** maps.

1. The Armory

Qussay al Nedjari[1] is a wizened old man with brown skin, white hair, and a face coated in a gristly layer of beard stubble. His smithy is the only one inside the ziggurat, taking up an entire level in and of itself. The burning dervishes get their weapons, armor, and unique magical devices from him, especially before heading off on their missions so they can get that special, decidedly deadly edge over their enemies and victims. Qussay has been doing this job for nearly 1,000 years now. Regardless of which "knucklehead" currently occupies the sultan's chair, he does his job and he does better than anyone else alive, politics be damned. In fact, he's not afraid to relay such sentiments to the Sultan himself when the big schmuck drops in for a surprise inspection. As such, the dervishes hide him in the Agony Forge until the Sultan leaves. Qussay lives only for his craft. He considers the dervishes a bunch of sheep, but they pay well and give him the highest quality materials with which to work. For that, he is slightly grateful (but not much). For their part, the dervishes pay the old man the utmost respect. Those who don't are likely to wind up with weapons that break at the most inopportune moments.

The armory has over 100 forges, with approximately 2,000 **azer** slaves working them. Unlike the slaves in the other parts of the temple, the blacksmith's assistants are truly loyal to him. He treats them exceptionally well, by modern City of Brass standards, allowing them to have their own beds, lockable chests, and the occasional day off in the city when they perform better than expected. The slaves love old Qussay like a grandfather. He in turn regards them like children — which in fact they are. Nine hundred years earlier he had a torrid affair with their ancestral matriarch (which almost led to marriage). She became pregnant with his twin offspring. Now, ten centuries later, the azer working the forges with him are the descendants of those two infants. They don't know this, and

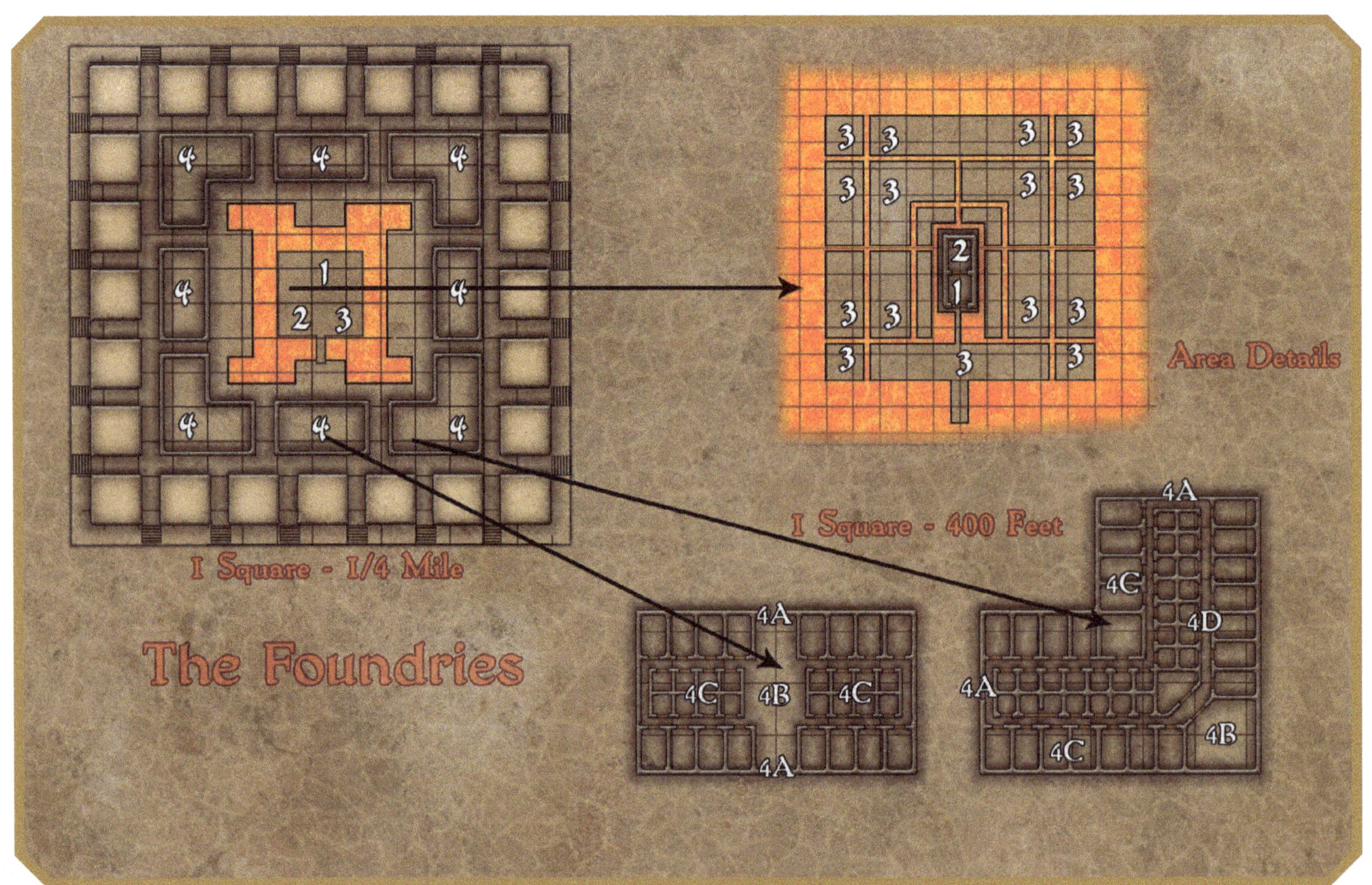

Qussay is surely not going to tell anyone. As much as the ziggurat enjoys his services, he's quite certain the head priest would throw him into the Agony Forge if his little secret escaped.

Qussay's immortality is a gift from the matriarch he befriended and nearly wed almost nine centuries ago. Though he will never die of old age or natural causes, he can still be killed. Qussay has a *robe of fire*[2].

2. The Agony Forge

At the center of the ziggurat's lower level is a vast foundry designed to transform captured souls into living brass. The mechanics of the forge and ore processors are beyond the ken of mortal minds. Suffice it to say they do their job exceptionally well. Hundreds of tons of brass are produced here on a weekly basis, all of which contributes to the temple's continuing growth. Hundreds of **azer** slaves work in the Agony Forge under the watchful eyes of **efreeti** elite guards and **burning dervishes**[1]. In the middle, a five-story-tall fountain spits out raw magma, which is then channeled into five separate smelting machines. Souls captured by the Sultan or his servants are "poured" from magic jars and soul gems into the magma flows by an army of 20 **fire mephits**[1], who seem to exist exclusively to deliver them to the ziggurat (when they're not sadistically dumping boiling pitch on participants in the arena). Mundane brass arrives by means of primitive conveyer belts through the 24 demon gates built in the outside walls; it comes from planes where copper and zinc are plentiful. An especially prized form of brass comes from a world in the midst of a techno-magical revolution; after it is processed, it goes straight to the top of the ziggurat to be added to the Temple of the Sultan.

The sounds of terrible, unearthly shrieking can be heard just beneath those of the thundering machinery. Souls that get transformed into living brass suffer the worst sort of agony in any of the known worlds.

3. Slave Pens

Before the reigning Sultan took over lordship of the city, the pens under the ziggurat held sacrificial lambs and cattle. All that changed with the new leadership, and the pens now hold thousands of **azer** slaves whose only purpose is to be pounded into living brass to build the temple ever higher. Slaves are crammed into tiny pens built from magma-reed. Most do not survive six months down here, either succumbing to starvation and thirst (there is *never* enough food or water for even half of their population) or violence (the slaves have a criminal hierarchy overseeing them that rivals the thieves' guilds of many a mortal city on other worlds). Many also give into overwhelming depression and apathy and either wither away to nothing or they commit suicide (though the **efreeti** slave drivers tell them the ones who commit suicide end up in the brass processors first). The warren of pens is so convoluted that the innermost portions have not been seen by the slave masters since the ziggurat's earliest days. Not so surprisingly, the azer resistance makes it their home and for the time being there is absolutely nothing the slave masters can do about it. Non-azers who attempt to find the inner pens almost always wind up dead for their efforts. Others find themselves hopelessly lost, or worse, in the catacombs dug out of the Basin floor.

Among these thousands of slaves is Mareal Porter (as **scout** with AC 12, no armor, and a dagger instead of a shortsword and longbow), one of those captured in Lornedain. He has grown much since his capture and, although still young, has learned the means to survive among one of the slave gangs. He has become accustomed to the blazing heat of the city and his skin has developed a certain toughness due to scars and conditioning.

Mareal keeps a living brass dagger hidden in his shirt.

If Mareal is liberated from the slave pits and reunited with friends and family, reward the players an additional 5,000 experience points for their efforts toward concluding the mystery of the missing persons from Lornedain.

4. Azer Slave Pits

Those **azer** forced to labor within the Agony Forge and the armories of the burning dervishes are separated from those who dwell and toil in the basin surrounding the mountainous ziggurat. Due to their special forging skills and mastery over the living brass, they are forced or compelled to work 25-hour days under the lash of their relentless **efreeti** and **burning dervish**[1] masters. Detailed below are common features of the slave barracks within which these unfortunate beings take their meals and what little rest their servitude has to offer.

4A. Entrance

The entrances to the azer slave pits are guarded with specialized *greater arcane locks*[4] cast with a 5th level spell slot that open to those bearing a slave collar, fire giant guards or efreeti overseers.

4B. Guard Tower

Built approximately six feet off the ground, these iron guard fortresses house a contingent of 4 **fire giant** guards and an **efreeti** elite guard overseer who work 10-hour shifts within the ziggurat. The guard towers are rigged with portholes and arrow slits that provide the maximum

firing coverage of the tower itself as well as polished silver mirrors set up throughout the slave pits. The mirrors allow viewing of any of the pits that the guards would wish to look into at any time and afford the azer no privacy. Keys to the individual slave pits are kept by the efreeti taskmaster on duty.

Bunks for fire giant guards and their efreeti overseers are arranged around a central brazier. Racks of Large and Huge weapons flank the doors into and out of the guard towers. As most of the guards live elsewhere in the city, they keep their personal possessions off site.

4C. Slave Pits

Each cell of the slave pit has a door ten feet off the ground accessible only by means of a ladder that is dropped with a crank and pulley system when the door is opened with its proper key. This allows the azer work gangs to leave their cell when their shift arrives but imprisons them within with little hope of egress when the door is closed.

The floors of the slave pits are covered with woven copper mats that the azer gain their few hours of rest upon. Any azer incapable of working due to fatigue or illness is immediately sent to the mercy forge to be pounded into living brass.

The slave pits each hold 20 **azer** slaves, each affixed with a brass collar. The added security is designed as an extra measure to ensure that they do not rise up against their efreeti masters. The azer slaves have no possessions of their own. They are known however to sing and pray to Anumon for release from their bondage.

4D. Slave Pit of the Diya al Din

An **azer cleric** named Diya al Din, a native of the azer homelands and not city-born like the majority of his brethren here, lives in the inner pens and leads a religious resistance movement. Gang boss Guth Bolixone (**azer elite**[1]) and his army of thugs (**azer soldier**[1]) protect him as he is the only person alive who understands the *Heart of Flame's* flaw. Given an "artifact of unmaking" such as the *maul of Hezoid*[2], he could bring the Sultan's pride and joy crashing down to its blood-soaked foundation. This reckoning is the moment for which every single azer in the city prays, loyalty to the Sultan notwithstanding.

You should feel free to place the Diya al Din within any of the slave quarters and add appropriate challenges for characters attempting to rescue the venerable priest of Anumon should their goal be the destruction of the Great Ziggurat and the foul menace of the burning dervishes. Alternately, a party bent on evil could use the opportunity to attempt to assassinate the Diya al Din. Both circumstances result in an azer uprising. See **Finishing Adventures in the Great Ziggurat** for details on running and completing whichever quest the characters choose to take.

The Catacombs

This section of the ziggurat is thought to be the original building, built centuries ago to house the then-ruling sultan's family after death. In the years since, it has been pushed lower into the bowels of the city by the oppressive weight of the temple above. With the new Sultan's urge to build the ziggurat clear to the roof of the sky, it has sunk to even more dramatic depths. Like the slave pens above, it is a tangled mess of narrow tunnels, alcoves, and funerary chambers. Living people do not enter the catacombs unless they have the mad desire to become one of the undead. **Ghosts**, **ghouls**, **specters**, **oblivion wraiths**[1], **deathwisps**, **shadow beasts**, **lavawights**[1], **shapes of fire**[1], and a few **vampires** make the dank, dark, fetid crypts their home. It is rumored that somewhere deep within the catacombs, the undead remains of a former efreeti noble rest — as an **advanced demilich**[1].

Eventually the catacombs lead to the **Underbasin**, detailed more fully in **Chapter 26**.

Finishing Adventures in the Ziggurat of Flame

Characters succeeding in the destruction of the *Heart of Flame* also succeed in the total destruction of the Ziggurat of Flame. The summative loss of the burning dervishes as a force of religious law to the citizens of the City of Brass damages the iron grip that the Sultan has on the city's populace. Should the characters manage to free the fire giant slaves from the Temple of the Sultan, an immediate civil war erupts between the mercenary fire giant guards and the efreeti officers who once commanded them. Should the ziggurat be destroyed and the azer set free, a general slave uprising begins, where azer slaves assist in the removal of slave collars from any slave they meet, arming them with whatever weapons they can muster. They hide in the Basin and Underbasin and stage guerilla-style attacks on any efreeti they come in contact with.

These events cause chaos and confusion to the otherwise well-ordered city of the efreet, allowing the characters to more easily move from place to place as guards and military forces such as the Legion of Mamelukes and infernal allies from the order of devils are called forth to quell uprisings and to fight pitched battles in the streets against rebellious slaves and fire giant mercenaries.

Should the characters succeed in taking down the Ziggurat of Flame, Lucifer's minions are called upon to take a greater role in establishing law and order within the city. This may offer an opportunity for Tarbish to send the characters against the masters of the Pagoda of Devils, further destabilizing the Sultan of Efreet[1]. Otherwise, Tarbish reveals himself as the Grand Vizier.

Chapter 29
The Pagoda of Devils

The Pagoda of Devils, home to the mysterious Order of Devils, stands ominously in the southwestern corner of the City of Brass. Although the curiously carved circular portals of the Pagoda of Devils are open to all comers, only two sorts of visitors ever enter: those who become members of the ancient sect, and those who are never seen again. The order is at odds with the Lightbringer, being a sect that follows the unholy teachings of his rival the archdevil Geryon. The pagoda is shown on **The Pagoda of Devils** maps.

This adventure is suggested for Tier 4 characters.

Standard Features

Entrances and Exits: The Pagoda of Devils may be entered through Area 1 of the first floor in the Lower City, or through the Devotional Hall on the tenth floor in the Upper City.

Doors: The doors in the Pagoda of Devils are made of kiln-dried wood imported from other worlds and are of a circular shape. The doors are never locked as the monks who call the pagoda their home are not terribly afraid of anyone or anything. Furthermore, the monks' absolute devotion to Geryon leaves them with little need for material possessions beyond those which they can carry upon their own back or atop their head.

Ceilings: The ceiling of each floor of the Pagoda of Devils is more than twenty feet high.

Shielding: *Teleportation* and *plane shifting* is denied to all save full members of the Order of Devils through powerful wards carved into the gargoyle-like devils that adorn the roofs of each floor of the pagoda. These wards are of an unknown origin and cannot be dispelled or negated.

Further, during the pagoda's creation, Geryon infused a portion of the plane of his layers of Hell into its foundation. As such, a lawful evil creature in the pagoda cannot be banished or dismissed (such as by a *banishment* spell), except by the creature who summoned it.

Ground Floor

1. Basin Entrance

This huge circular doorway is carved in the likeness of 1,000 devils of various castes and power. Their faces and expressions seem to change as they stare forward at any who approach the vault-like doorway. In unison, the devils ask what business they have in the Pagoda of Devils. Their question is only for their own amusement, as the doors open to any brave enough to enter the chambers beyond.

2. Foyer

This hallway is enclosed in a permanent zone of *darkness*. There is no light that guides those who would seek to pass deeper into the pagoda. The idea is that monks of substantial skill and power need not rely on their sense of sight to find their way to their challengers. Once travelers move 30 feet into the chamber, they find themselves facing 1,000 pairs of red eyes glaring at them. The eyes ask again the business of those who would enter the Pagoda of Devils. This time, the devil doors are more skeptical. They point out that each of them was once brought to visit the Pagoda of Devils, and none has yet left the shade of its twelve copper roofs. Nonetheless, the doors open to reveal a huge chamber beyond.

3. Dojo of First Challenges

Those who know a bit of lore about the Pagoda of Devils call this huge chamber the Dojo of First Challenges. The lowest caste of the Order of Devils keeps its barracks in the four surrounding chambers. Initiates seeking to join the order and learn their secrets spend their first three levels fighting and taking on new challengers who come to the pagoda. Surprisingly, many from the various planes of existence would seek to gain all the knowledge that the Order of Devils offers. New moves and new techniques are always sought by the martial artists, as are new defenses against such moves.

Upon entering this chamber, 6d4 human **devil initiates**[1] enter from their barracks and issue the initial challenge to characters. They demand to know if a "seeker of the path" is among them. If no monk is among the party, the initiates attack the characters with hellish fury while 1d4 additional **devil initiates**[1] arrive (up to a maximum of 40) and defend the Pagoda of Devils in an almost suicidal fashion. A particularly ugly monk named Yin Shi Yan (LE male human **devil mendicant**[1]) presides over the challenge … and if necessary, the subsequent attack.

If a monk is among the characters, this character is offered a challenge of single combat against one of the gathered host. A character who succeeds in easily defeating this opponent is offered a second challenge and given the opportunity to join the order as an initiate and, like the others within the chamber, take on newcomers and learn the basics tenets of the sect from Yin Shi Yan. A character who doesn't want to stay and learn may instead take on Yin Shi Yan in a fight to the death. Should the character defeat Yin Shi Yan in single combat, the other members of the

Order of Devils remain passive and indicate that the challenger may now proceed to the second floor of the pagoda. If attacked, the monks defend themselves and fight to the death.

A set of double doors in the northern wall reveal a broad staircase leading to the first floor.

4. Barracks of the Initiates

These large chambers each house 10 initiates who eat, sleep, and train here. Initiates are constantly exercising their skills or testing for advancement in the order and have little time to think of anything else. Even their current master, Yin Shi Yan, trains for his own advancement up the pagoda as he seeks to uncover all the mysteries of the Order of Devils. At any given time, 2d4 **devil initiates**[1] are found within these chambers.

First Story

5. Proving Grounds

This pillared and trapped chamber serves as the training ground for 4 lesser masters of the Order of Devils and their chosen students, each hand-picked from the initiates of the ground floor. The numerous pillars offer perfect hiding places for the monks who train by stalking one another through the chamber. Deadly traps ensure that initiates who are not up to snuff do not proceed any further in their training.

Characters entering this chamber find themselves face to face with one of the four masters and their disciples. As with the Dojo of First Challenges, monk characters are offered a chance to first fight a disciple and then to challenge the master. The disciples attack characters with no monk in their party, as the master rings a bell to alert the other three masters and their disciples to the intruders. These monks arrive in 1d4 rounds and fight to the death.

Central Spikes: These six-foot-high spikes occupy a 20-foot-by-20-foot square in the center of the chamber. Masters frequently attempt to hurl their disciples or any intruders onto this bed of spikes. Furthermore, masters of upper stories of the pagoda hurl their victims upon the spikes from above. Anyone falling or hurled atop the spikes is struck by 1d6 of the impaling shafts and takes 4 (1d8) piercing damage per spike.

Traps: The following traps are designed to trigger when an opponent steps upon a prescribed plate within the chamber. You may change the placement of the traps in the event that more than one encounter occurs within this chamber, or the Pagoda of Devils becomes a greater part of their campaign.

Listed below are four sample traps to use in the proving grounds. After the trap name, the DC required to locate the trap with an Intelligence (Investigation) check is noted followed by the DC to disable it with a Dexterity check with thieves' tools.

A. Floor Scythe Trap (DC 15/DC 16)

When triggered, a scythe springs up from the floor and attacks a creature within 5 feet at +10 to hit. On a hit, the scythe does 13 (2d4 + 8) slashing damage, or 28 (8d4 + 8) on a critical hit.

B. Flame Strike Trap (DC 17/DC 20)

Each creature within a 10-foot-radius, 40-foot-high cylinder centered on the trap must make a DC 16 Dexterity saving throw, taking 28 (8d6) fire damage and 28 (8d6) radiant damage on a failure, or half as much on a success.

C. Deathblade Arrow Trap (DC 17/DC 12)

Trap makes an attack against the closest creature within 20 feet at +12 to hit. On a hit, the target takes 4 (1d8) piercing damage and must succeed on a DC 17 Constitution saving throw or take 44 (8d10) poison damage.

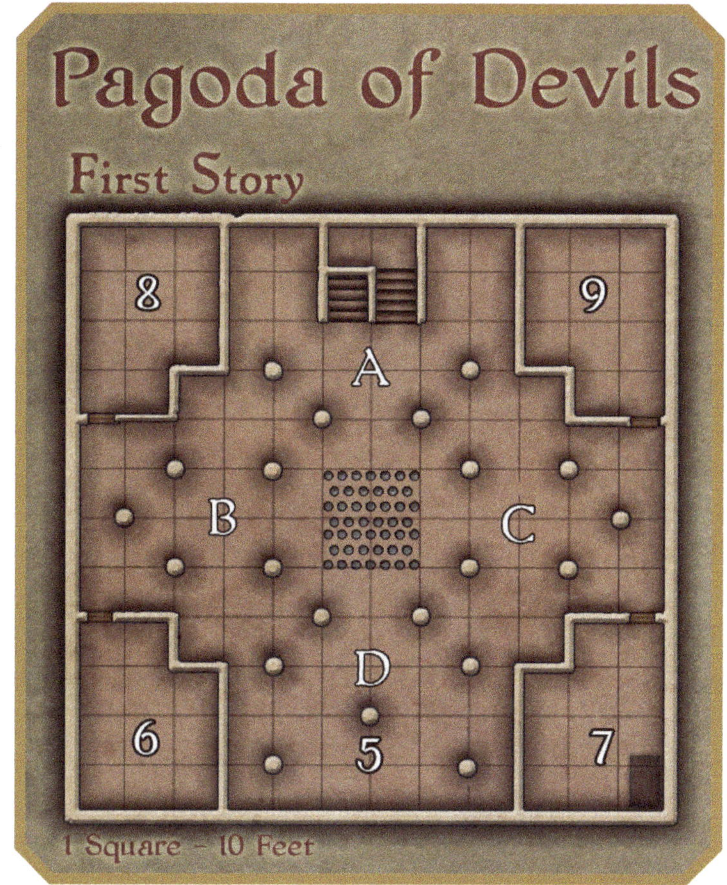

D. Fusillade of Spears (DC 14/DC 18)

Trap attacks each target within a 10-foot square centered in the trap with 1d6 spears. Each spear attacks at +9 to hit. On a hit, target takes 4 (1d8) piercing damage.

A staircase in the north leads down to the ground floor. A staircase in the south leads up to the second floor.

6. Master Qarid's Chamber

Master Qarid[1], a cheitan and member of the Order of Devils, keeps his quarters in this chamber. Qarid is intensely cruel to his new disciple Olerij (LE male human **devil mendicant**[1]) and tries at least once per day to impale him upon the spikes in the proving grounds. Qarid desperately waits for the day when he may move up in ranks of the order. Unfortunately, it is his own arrogance that keeps him from achieving this goal.

Olerij is a skilled martial artist, given the fact that he has moved up to a position of training with one of the masters. Olerij constantly plots a way in which he can defeat his master, for he knows now that only his victory will allow him to gain master status.

A locked chest sits in this chamber. Opening it requires a successful DC 18 Dexterity check with thieves' tools or a successful DC 20 Strength check. Contained in the chest are 8,000 cp.

7. Mistress Sialia's Chamber

Mistress Sialia (LE female human **devil mendicant**[1]) currently has no disciple, having broken her last one for playing too rough. She spends the majority of her time in her chamber meditating and practicing her skills. Eventually, she knows a new petitioner will work through the challenges that the other masters offer, and if the newcomer suits her, she will take the disciple on to train with her. Mistress Sialia beats her disciples to 0 hit points as often as she can. If they recover, she allows them to heal naturally before beginning again; however, she does not lift a finger to save them. Sialia enters the proving grounds only if a large force of intruders makes it this far into the pagoda.

Treasure: A low table of polished mahogany in one corner is worth 200 gp due to the quality of its carving. Sitting atop the table are seven platinum ewers worth 200 gp each. The perfume within them is worth 300 gp a dose. If a dropper of each perfume is mixed together, it forms a toxin more powerful than black lotus extract. There is enough perfume in each ewer to mix 10 applications of this aromatic poison.

8. Master Dasssar's Chamber

Master Dasssar[1] is from a highly civilized world dominated by lizard folk. Dasssar speaks in sibilant tones and is extremely articulate in his questions and his thinking. His disciple **Fas'ahad**[1] accompanies Dasssar at all times. Fas'ahad is actually an assassin sent to the Pagoda of Devils to recoup a slight offered to the leader of one of the noble houses by Pang Goy. Fas'ahad is unafraid to use any skill and weapon at his disposal to get close enough to Pang Goy to destroy him. If the characters manage to destroy the masters and disciples on the first floor, Fas'ahad may seek to join them, offering his blade in an assault on the other members of the order. Fas'ahad's deception is so complete that Dasssar has no idea an enemy is in their midst.

9. Master Tak's Chamber

A human monk named Tak (LE male human **devil mendicant**[1]) and his apprentice, a dwarf called Danrach (LE male dwarf **devil initiate**[1]), live and train within these quarters. Danrach only recently moved up and was accepted for training by Master Tak, who was impressed with the dwarf's cruelty and efficiency. Tak knows that moving up in the order is difficult at best and seems content to merely train new initiates in the ways of the order. Tak is too thoroughly interested in his devotion to the teachings of Geryon and the training of Danrach to worry about much else.

A locked chest sits in this chamber. Opening it requires a successful DC 18 Dexterity check with thieves' tools or a successful DC 20 Strength check. Contained in the chest is 400 bp, a small brass idol (500 gp), and two bronze candlesticks (200 gp each).

Second Story

The second floor serves as dormitories for masters who continually compete against one another for superiority and the opportunity to challenge one of the masters in the floor above. The central dojo is like the floor below, and contains dangerous traps designed to hone the skills of the monks who train here as well as to slay any not worthy of the title of master. Any monk of lower caste and thus stationed on a lower floor must face down and slay one of the four current masters who live on this floor. All of the masters of the second floor are **wang liang monks**[1]. Each of the wang liang masters are virtually identical in skill and power. For this reason, none has mastered the others and made his way to the third floor to face new challenges. All have chosen to refrain from speaking or using their names until one is strong enough to defeat the others and challenge the masters of the level above. For this reason, they are referred to as the Unnamed.

When new challengers arrive from the lower stories, they draw lots from an iron cauldron hanging on a chain near the northern staircase to decide which of their number shall accept the challenge. They are of course aware of any challenges coming from the lower levels, likely due to the sounds of battle and powerful *ki* strikes wafting up from the pit in the center of the dojo that leads to the central spikes in the first floor. If characters are completely silent and using the utmost of stealth to work their way up the pagoda, allow the wang liang monks to make Perception checks opposed by the characters' Stealth checks. If the monks fail, they are found individually in their own apartments.

Staircases leading to the second and fifth stories are found in the northern and southern ends of the dojo.

Large areas of the floor are trapped with pressure sensitive, sound sensitive, and heat sensitive traps that trigger when passed or moved across. These traps, like the ones on the second floor, help hone the skills of the monks and ensure that those not equipped to be a master don't move up in the hierarchy.

Traps: Listed below are four sample traps that may be moved or placed on the map as the you wish. If the traps listed below are too challenging

or not challenging enough, feel free to substitute any traps that you feel appropriate to properly challenge the characters. After the trap name, the DC required to locate the trap with an Intelligence (Investigation) check is noted followed by the DC to disable it with a Dexterity check with thieves' tools.

A. Fusillade of Acidic Darts (DC 14/DC 17)

Trap attacks each target within a 10-foot square centered on the trap with 1d8 acid-coated darts. On a hit, a dart does 3 (1d4 + 1) piercing damage and 3 (1d6) acid damage.

B. Blade Barrier Trap (DC 16/DC 16)

When the trap is triggered, a wall of blades springs into existence, filling a 20-foot square centered on the trap and lasts for 10 minutes. When a creature enters the area for the first time on its turn or starts its turn there, it must make a DC 17 Dexterity saving throw, taking 33 (6d10) slashing damage on a failure or half as much on a success.

C. Shock Spear Floor Trap (DC 17/DC 20)

A single magically electrified spear makes an attack against the nearest creature within 10 feet of the trap at +14 to hit. On a hit, the target takes 4 (1d8_ piercing damage and 3 (1d6) lightning damage and must succeed on a DC 14 Constitution saving throw or be paralyzed until the end of the target's next turn.

D. Glyph of Warding (DC 147DC 17)

Each creature within a 20-foot-radius must make a DC 18 Dexterity saving throw, taking 49 (11d8) thunder damage on a failure or half as much on a success. The noise from this trap is heard throughout the tower.

In the center of the floor is a pit trap. The trap can be noted with a successful DC 16 Wisdom (Perception) check and disabled with a successful DC 16 Dexterity check with thieves' tools. A creature who triggers the trap must succeed on a DC 16 Dexterity saving throw or fall 20 feet to the bottom of the trap, taking 7 (2d6) bludgeoning damage. A creature who hits the bottom is attacked by 1d6 spikes at +8 to hit. On a hit, the target takes 4 (1d8) piercing damage.

10. Weapon Chambers

These chambers that flank the northern staircase are used for training with monk weapons. At least two fantastically crafted monk weapons of every style and made from every imaginable weapons grade metal, including mithril, adamantine, brass, steel, and silver, line the walls.

11. Hot Mud Spa

This chamber contains four mud baths filled with scalding hot mud. Each mud bath is also home to a variety of **advanced mudmen**[1] that are immune to heat and fire. The mudmen massage the monks who take a dip in this bath to relax from their furious training regimen. The mudmen attack non-Order of Devils creatures who enter this chamber, unless they are accompanied by an Order of Devils' member.

12. Sand Spa

This chamber contains four huge pots filled with searing hot sand. Where monks of normal sects commonly stuff their hands and feet into the hot sand to toughen them, the masters of the third floor have a bit different take. Each of the pots is also home to a **sandling**[1]. The Unnamed like nothing more than to beat the sandlings into submission as a form of therapeutic rest.

13. Private Quarters of the Unnamed

These chambers in the southern end of the second floor serve as the quarters for the Unnamed. Each monk maintains his own quarters. Found here are a chest of drawers, a floormat, a neck board, and a small central fire pit with a cook pot. Chained to the wall are humanoid slaves whom the Unnamed feast upon. Any given chamber has 1d4 such slaves, most of which are **commoners** purchased in the Slavers' Bazaar.

There is little of value other than the slaves within these quarters as the Unnamed tend to keep their gear on their persons.

Third Story

14. Dojo of Missiles

This entire floor is laden with pressure sensitive plates that trigger spears, heavy crossbows, and ballista to rise from hidden platforms in the floor and fire upon those passing through it. Currently, it is used as the training facility for **Master Bagra**[1], a weretiger member of the Order of Devils. There is a 50% chance that Bagra is here. Otherwise, he is found in one of the levels above or meditating in his chamber on the eighth floor. Bagra challenges any single monk among groups of characters. If a large party attacks him, he attempts to escape the chamber by moving up to gather more allies from the dojos above. Stairwells in the north and south of the chamber lead to the second and fourth stories.

Bagra spends all of his time in hybrid form and is encountered in this form.

Traps: The traps are lettered with a **B**, **H**, or **S** on the map. After the trap name, the DC required to locate the trap with an Intelligence (Investigation) check is noted followed by the DC to disable it with a Dexterity check with thieves' tools.

Ballista Trap (B) (DC 10/DC 16)

A ballista rises and fires at a single target within the chamber at +14 to hit. On a hit, the target takes 13 (3d8) piercing damage and is knocked prone. The ballista scores a critical hit on a 19 or 20.

Heavy Crossbow Trap (H) (DC 14/DC 16)

A crossbow rises and attacks the closest target within 30 feet at +12 to hit. On a hit, the target takes 5 (1d10) piercing damage. The ballista scores a critical hit on a 19 or 20.

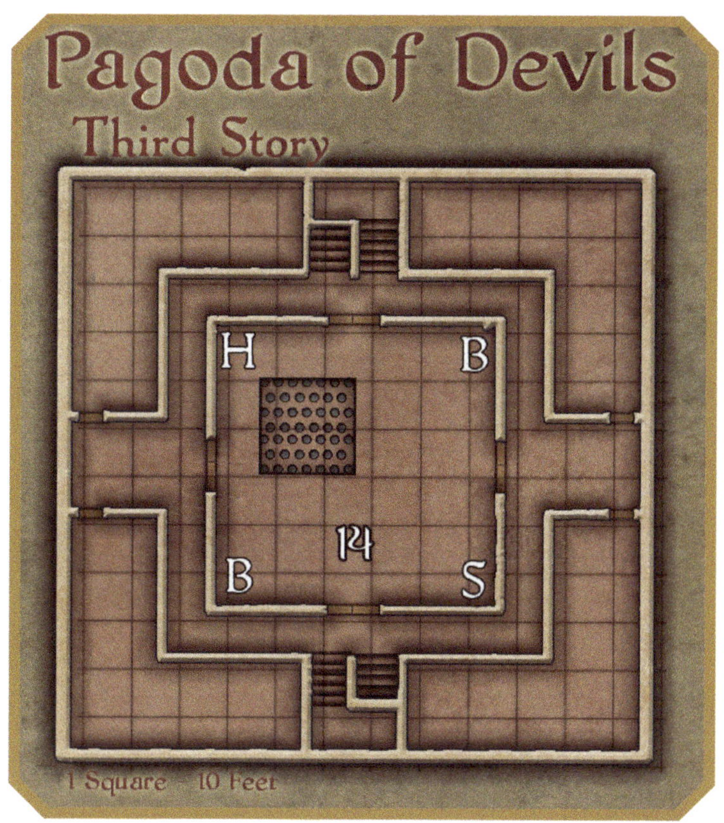

Poisoned Spear Trap (S) (DC 14/DC 18)

A spear makes an attack against the closest target within 80 feet at +10 to hit. On a hit, the target takes 7 (1d8 + 3) piercing damage and must succeed on a DC 16 Constitution saving throw or take 44 (8d10) poison damage.

In the center of the floor is a pit trap. The trap can be noted with a successful DC 16 Wisdom (Perception) check and disabled with a successful DC 16 Dexterity check with thieves' tools. A creature who triggers the trap must succeed on a DC 16 Dexterity saving throw or fall 20 feet to the bottom of the trap, taking 7 (2d6) bludgeoning damage. A creature who hits the bottom is attacked by 1d6 spikes at +8 to hit. On a hit, the target takes 4 (1d8) piercing damage.

Fourth Story

15. Dojo of Needles

Much of the floor of this chamber is covered with 1-inch-tall needles that glisten with some greenish poisonous ichor. The ichor is greenblood oil. A character can move through this chamber at one-quarter normal speed to avoid contact with the needles. A character moving faster than this contacts 1d8 needles per round. Each needle deals 1 point of damage and forces the target to make a successful DC 14 Constitution saving throw or take an additional 16 (3d10) poison damage. Additionally, a character contacting the needles has its movement reduced by one-half until it has completed a long rest or until the wounds are healed with a DC 17 Wisdom (Medicine) check or 1 point of magical healing. Monks and acrobatic characters find movement easier as they can tumble and leap through the chamber to avoid most of the needles. This is all fine and good until they come face to face with **Dagova Nix**[1], who trains here in the Dojo of Needles.

Dagova is a minotaur who has trained in the Pagoda of Devils since he was a calf and was raised by Pang Goy himself. For obvious reasons, he is thoroughly evil and particularly malevolent. Many would-be recruits and lesser masters of the Pagoda of Devils have fallen victim to Dagova's bestial lusts for sport and death. Although Dagova only recently begun

training in the Order of Devils, he makes up for that in sheer brute strength and deadly skill. Dagova attacks any who enter the chamber from below, unless they come with special permission from Pang Goy (with the exception of Bagra). If faced with overwhelming odds, he makes a fighting withdrawal to the upper stories to warn others and to seek reinforcements. He is loath to do this but is under orders after all.

Dagova can move normally through this area without contacting the needles. This is his "playground."

Dagova has a private chamber on the eighth floor of the pagoda.

Fifth Story

16. Dojo of Whirling Blades

The narrow catwalks of this dojo are suspended over the needles on the floor below. Anyone falling off one of these catwalks is surely impaled upon the millions of needles 20 feet below, taking 10 (3d6) piercing damage and they must save against the greenblood oil coating the needles. Four huge sets of whirling blades running on well-greased iron poles from floor to ceiling make passing through their sections of the catwalk treacherous at best. These blades appear to be from many different types of swords, axes, and edged weapons. The blades can be avoided with a successful DC 18 Dexterity (Acrobatics) check or disarmed with a successful DC 20 Dexteirty check with thieves' tools. A creature passing through the blades without making a successful Dexterity check takes 13 (2d6 + 6) slashing damage and must succeed on a DC 17 Dexterity saving throw or fall into the fire (50%) or the needles (50%) below.

Great flames rise from a 10-foot-deep trench in the center of the chamber, giving off waves of heat. Anyone falling into the flames who is not immune to fire or resistant to fire immediately catches on fire, taking 11 (2d10) fire damage each round until the fire is extinguished. A burning creature can use an action to attempt to extinguish the flames, succeeding with a successful DC 14 Dexterity check.

A small platform stands in the center of the chamber. A pit trap on the platform drops 80 feet down the central shaft of the pagoda onto the impaling spikes on the first floor. The pit can be noted with a successful DC 15 Wisdom (Perception) check and wedged shut with a successful DC 14 Dexterity check with thieves' tools. A creature who triggers the

pit must succeed on a DC 15 Dexterity saving throw or fall 80 feet into the pit, taking 28 (8d6) bludgeoning damage upon hitting the ground. In addition, a creature who hits the bottom is attacked by 1d6 spikes at +8 to hit. On a hit, the target takes 4 (1d8) piercing damage.

Sixth Story

17. Dojo of Anguished Souls

The dominant feature of this chamber is a vortex of fire surrounded by lesser flames rising from the floor below. Swirling within the vortex are the tortured souls of 100 **lemures**. The lemures cannot leave the flaming central portion of this chamber. Individually, the lemures are very weak; however, an unholy pact with Geryon allows the lemures to morph once per day into one gigantic beast (**lemure mass**[1]) of rubbery flesh and screaming mouths. The lemures ignore full members of the Order of Devils but may morph and attack any other entrant to the pagoda. Anyone killed by the gigantic lemure mass becomes a lemure and is absorbed into the mass.

Characters coming within 5 feet of the vortex must succeed on a DC 16 Constitution saving throw or be sucked into it, taking 14 (4d6) slashing damage and 7 (2d6) fire damage each round. After 1d10 rounds, a trapped character is sucked down the central shaft, falling 100 feet to the impaling spikes on the pagoda's first floor.

In the center of the floor is a pit trap. The trap can be noted with a successful DC 16 Wisdom (Perception) check and disabled with a successful DC 16 Dexterity check with thieves' tools. A creature who triggers the trap must succeed on a DC 16 Dexterity saving throw or fall 100 feet to the bottom of the trap, taking 35 (10d6) bludgeoning damage. A creature who hits the bottom is attacked by 1d6 spikes at +12 to hit. On a hit, the target takes 4 (1d8) piercing damage.

Seventh Story

18. Dojo of Master Mo Zhu

This floor consists of a large training chamber that is almost completely bare except for the two large flaming pits that lead to the sixth floor of the pagoda. Creatures falling into the flames suffer 7 (2d6) fire damage and must succeed on a DC 17 Strength saving throw or be sucked into the vortex on the sixth floor. On a successful save, they instead fall 30 feet to the fifth floor.

There is a 40% chance that **Master Mo Zhu**[1] is training in this chamber or has been warned of the approaching characters by one of the other masters. In this event, he hangs from the ceiling prepared for their arrival. Mo Zhu is a drider, and the entire ceiling of his chamber houses the webbed husks of his prey. Mo Zhu lies in wait for the characters, attempting to ensnare as many as he can with webs to reduce the numbers that oppose him. If pressed with incredible odds, he attempts to escape to the eighth floor to alert the other masters.

A locked and trapped chest in this room contains Master Zhu's personal treasure. The trap can be noted with a successful DC 16 Intelligence (Investigation) check and disarmed with a successful DC 17 Dexterity check using thieves' tools. If the trap is triggered, a needle makes an attack against the creature triggering it at +14 to hit. On a hit, the target takes 1 piercing damage and must succeed on a DC 14 Constitution saving throw or be paralyzed for 1 minute and take 11 (2d10) poison damage. The lock can be opened with a successful DC 22 Dexterity check with thieves' tools or a successful DC 25 Strength check. The chest contains 2,900 bp and 3 Fire Sea pearls (500 gp each).

Eighth Story

19. Hall of Masters

This floor of the pagoda holds the apartments of four of the masters of the Order of Devils. Two huge tree trunk battering rams hang from chains located on the ceiling of the room facing a huge bronze bell in the center of the chamber. The peal of this bell is so loud that it may be heard throughout the entire city and is rung only when a new master of the Order of Devils is chosen from among the ranks.

Any creature without proper hearing protection (such as wax ear plugs or being under the effect of a *silence* spell) who is in the chamber when the bell is rung must make a DC 18 Constitution saving throw or be deafened for 1d4 + 1 days.

Four chambers on this floor are the masters' dwellings.

20. Mistress Tang's Chamber

This simple chamber is the home of Mistress Tang (LE female human **devil cenobite**[1]), the highest-ranking pure human in the Order of Devils. Tang is most frequently found in deep meditation or intense training on the tenth floor of the Pagoda of Devils. There is a 40% chance that Tang is in her chamber. Tang is highly intelligent and is sought after by many of the rulers of noble houses in an advisory capacity or to serve as a temporary bodyguard should any of them choose to travel abroad.

Tang's few belongings are kept within an unlocked chest in her chamber or carried upon her person. Tang has become quite rich over the last several years working as a bodyguard and advisor, but the material wealth means little to her.

Treasure: 2,000 bp, 6 gold bars (1,000 gp each), platinum necklace with Fire Sea ruby inlay (7,000 gp), 4 white emeralds (1,500 gp each).

with a successful DC 17 Dexterity check. If the trap is triggered, a needle makes an attack against the creature triggering it at +14 to hit. On a hit, the target takes 1 piercing damage and must succeed on a DC 14 Constitution saving throw or fall asleep for 1 hour. The sleep can only be broken with magical means such as *lesser restoration*. The lock can be opened with a successful DC 22 Dexterity check with thieves' tools or a successful DC 25 Strength check. The chest contains 1,000 bp, amethyst pendant (200 gp), platinum eating utensils (500 gp), solid bronze egg (800 gp), electrum earrings (100 gp), 700 cp.

Ninth Story

24. Arches of Geryon

A pair of golden arches afford passage into the Hall of Devils through what are referred to as the Arches of Geryon. The arches act as a permanent *hallow* spell on the Hall of Devils. Further, two effects befall good-aligned creatures passing through the arches. First, several lacerations appear on the creature's body, as if cut by an invisible razor. An affected character takes 5 (2d4) slashing damage each time it passes through the arches (no save). Secondly, any liquids (other than potions) the character is carrying automatically foul and become poisonous (characters won't notice this change until the liquid is examined or consumed). A character who consumes such liquid must succeed on a DC 16 Constitution saving throw or take 55 (10d10) poison damage. One minute later, the character must succeed on another DC 16 Constitution saving throw or take 33 (6d10) poison damage.

25. Hall of Devils

Although this hall is open to all visitors, it affords no direct entrance to the pagoda compound itself, as the stairwells are sealed from the rest of the building. The ninth floor offers a glimpse into the world of the Order of Devils for common citizens and visitors to the City of Brass. It contains a huge open hall lined with statuary and murals depicting the various masters of the Order of Devils since the founding of the pagoda 1,000 years ago. There are frequently 1d4 + 1 **devil initiates**[1] meditating and keeping the peace in the Hall of Devils.

21. Master Dagova Nix's Chamber

Master **Dagova's**[1] chamber matches his bestial nature, consisting of a straw-covered floor. Dagova's walls are covered with intricate mazes that he draws upon the walls as a form of meditative reflection. If not encountered on the lower levels, most of Dagova's belongings lie strewn about the floor. Characters making a successful DC 16 Wisdom (Perception) check find 6 Fire Sea pearls (500 gp each) and 10 *potions of greater healing*.

22. Master Bagra's Chamber

Master Bagra's chamber is decorated in the style of a big-game hunter. Heads and skins of huge beasts ranging from young dragons to oliphants hang from the ceiling and line the walls, as do monk weapons of various sorts. An unlocked chest contains his belongings.

Treasure: 1,000 bp, a pair of white dragon-skin gauntlets (700 gp), 3 brass mugs with jeweled inlay (600 gp each), six doses of black lotus extract poison[3], 2 Fire Sea opals (100 gp each).

23. Master Cael O'Day's Chamber

Master Cael O'Day[1] is an unusual master of the Order of Devils, as he is a quickling whose natural speed and cruelty found an aptitude for the martial arts form. Cael is much sought after as an assassin as he is quite literally quicker than the eye can see, and deadly to the touch. Cael's chamber is filled with bouquets of flowers. There is a 70% chance that Cael is in the Pagoda of Devils. If in the Pagoda of Devils, there is a 50% chance that he is in his chamber; otherwise, he may be found on the eleventh floor of the pagoda.

A locked and trapped chest holds Cael's personal belongings. The trap can be noted with a successful DC 16 Intelligence (Investigation) check and disarmed

A huge statue of gleaming solid steel dominates the center of the chamber. The statue features a horned humanoid being of great physique and lithe grace. This is a statue of Pang Goy, the current Master of Devils, and a chosen champion of Geryon. The hall is cursed so that if any lawful good paladin, cleric, or monk enters, they are instantly attacked by 1d4 ghosts of previous masters (**ghost of a master**[1]). These ghosts attack the lawful good clerics, monks, and paladins mercilessly, ignoring any other targets until turned or destroyed.

Tenth Story

26. Dojo of the Quick and the Big

This large chamber serves as the training hall for Master Cael and the home of **Mistress Harthain Gursh**[1]. Spikes line the walls, but the majority of the chamber consists merely of a wide-open space with a lofty 40-foot-high ceiling. Sitting cross-legged in the center of this chamber is the large form of a powerfully built giantess.

Two conical tower-sized shields of solid gold, each a quarter-inch thick, hang from hooks on the wall. Curiously, the shields are attached together with four massive chains of burnished iron. The shields have no hand or arm straps attached and could likely fetch 5,000 gp on the open market.

The giantess issues a challenge to anyone who enters the chamber, offering monks an opportunity to face her in single combat. She is the personal

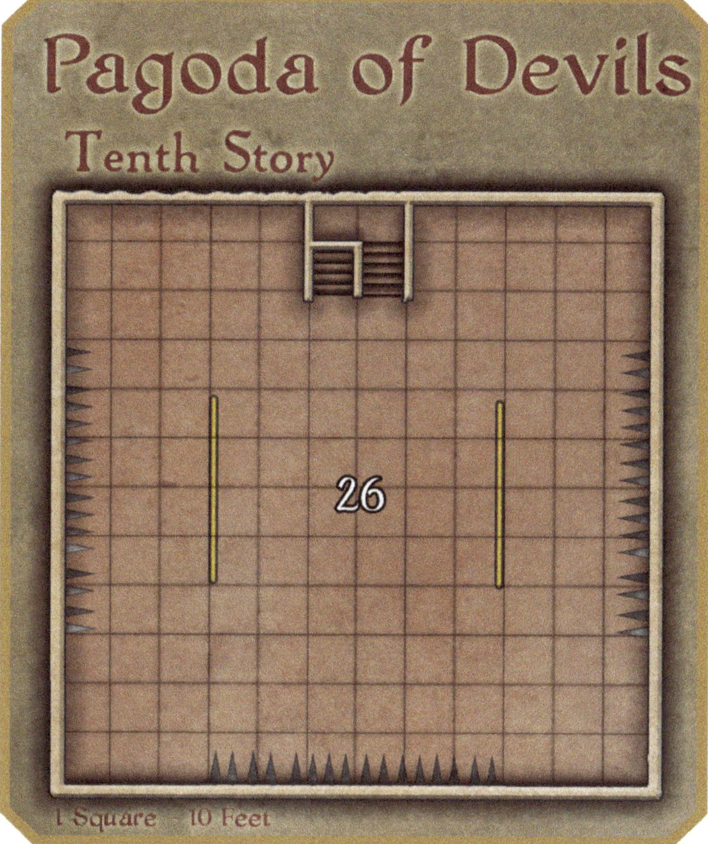

bodyguard of Pang Goy, despite the fact that he may not need her help at all. Master Cael frequently trains with Harthain, where they work Cael's speed versus Harthain's 11-odd feet of size and strength. There is a good chance Master Cael is also in this chamber with Mistress Harthain Gursh.

Tactics: Mistress Harthain's favored tactic is to grapple foes and hurl them into the spikes upon the walls of the chamber. A foe thrown into the spikes hits 1d4 of them, with each spike dealing 4 (1d8) piercing damage.

When working in concert with Master Cael, Harthain uses her prodigious strength to pummel fighter types, while Cael rushes through enemies to interrupt spellcasters.

Eleventh Story

27. Dojo of Pang Goy

Silk curtains hang from the 40-foot-high ceiling to the floor in this large chamber. The rich odor of incense and perfumes fills the air with multicolored smokes.

It is in this chamber that the Master of Devils makes his home and rules absolutely. The various smokes and odors have a mildly hypnotic effect, requiring anyone breathing them to make a successful DC 20 Constitution saving throw or have their mind filled with illusions and hallucinations. Such creatures have disadvantage on attack rolls as long as they remain in this chamber and for 1d4 rounds after leaving it. A character who succeeds on its Constitution save by 5 or more gains a +2 bonus to Wisdom checks while within this chamber. **Pang Goy**[1] is immune to the effects of the smoke.

As the characters explore the chamber, they are challenged by the tall, proud, handsome figure of Pang Goy (who looks exactly like the steel statue below). The figure appears as a human male, about 8 feet tall with dark hair and dark eyes, with small ivory horns on his brow. The most notable part of his body is his hands. They appear to be made of a gleaming greenish metal.

Pang Goy can transform his hands into any weapon with which he is proficient. His favorite transformations and adjusted attack and damage bonuses are listed below.

A locked and trapped chest contains Pang Goy's personal belongings. The trap can be noted with a successful DC 20 Intelligence (Investigation) check and disarmed with a successful DC 20 Intelligence (Arcana) check. If the trap is triggered, each cleric or paladin within 50 feet must succeed on a DC 18 Constitution saving throw or receive three levels of exhaustion. The exhaustion heals normally. The lock can be opened with a successful DC 25 Dexterity check with thieves' tools or a successful DC 25 Strength check. Within the chest are 10,000 bp, 6 Fire Sea pearls (1,000 gp each), brass inlaid platinum idol of Geryon (3,500 gp), jeweled sacrificial dagger (2,700 gp).

Pang Goy has an amicable relationship with the Sultan of Efreet[1] and is frequently sought for his wise counsel. Pang Goy's devotion to Geryon's will is absolute, however, and for this Pang Goy has been greatly rewarded. Pang Goy sacrificed his own natural hands to Geryon to show his faith and was given a pair of magical hands fashioned from an unearthly gleaming green metal. These hands, often referred to as the *hands of Pang Goy*[2], function as well as if not better than any natural hands could.

In the event that the characters reach the dojo of Pang Goy, there is a strong likelihood that Pang Goy is not alone, as one of the lesser masters may have joined him, or at the very least warned him. Any senior member of the Order of Devils who has successfully fled from the characters is found here. Those junior members who fled are killed by Pang Goy on sight for their cowardice, their bodies hurled from the window of the pagoda to be dashed on the streets of the Basin.

Due to his devilish heritage, Pang Goy has a plethora of spell-like abilities at his disposal to use in combat, but he prefers to engage foes with his monk skills.

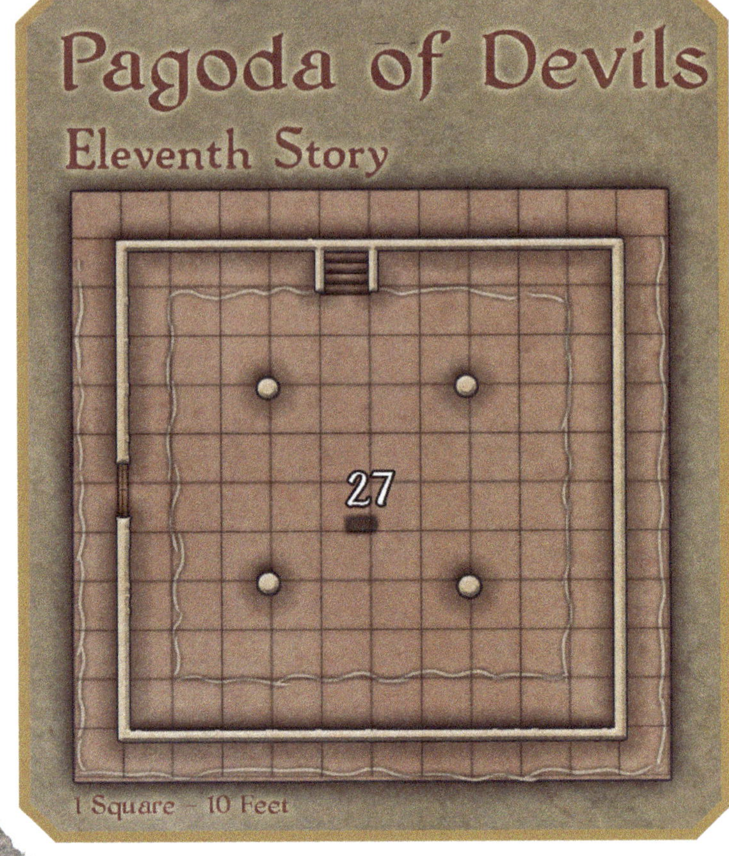

Chapter 30
Tower of the Grand Vizier

The Tower of the Grand Vizier

Stretching from the Basin to just below the height of the Palace of the Sultan, it is whispered that dark magic and ancient arcane experiments take place within the lofty spires of the hellish minaret fortress of the Grand Vizier of the City of Brass. The roots of the cursed tower find themselves in the Basin, where stout walls of white-hot bronze surround the base of the tower. A smaller tower stands in each corner of the four walls. Each of these towers is a replica of the central tower in miniature. A single demon gate opens into the tower compound from the Basin.

The central tower houses the Vizier's private chambers, laboratory, and harem, and a pocket dimension of clouds guarded by the cloud giant Norl[1]. The upper levels of the central spire require passage through this area and the acquisition of a magical key (from Norl's chambers) to open the doors that lead to the topmost parts of the spire. The Conjuring Chamber, the place the Vizier is most likely to be encountered, is accessible only by *teleportation* from a location within the central tower.

Characters seeking to defeat the Sultan of Efreet[1] or who are following the outlined Tales of Brass suggested campaign chronology would do best to face the Grand Vizier last. The dangers within his tower are deadly but none are deadlier than the Grand Vizier himself. In order to defeat the Grand Vizier, the characters may find that they must become him, an ordeal too gruesome to mention (were it not fully detailed later in this text.) Much will be revealed by completing the campaign portion of this area of adventure as the characters learn (if they haven't already) that **Rahib al Tabish Zafir**[1] was the one who arranged the ambush of the Sultan's assassination squad that originally set out to imprison Sulymon. Here they discover that the strange benefactor who set them on the course of retrieving the fell relics hidden throughout the city was none other than al Tabish Zafir, the Grand Vizier himself, and that he has been using the characters for his own purposes and has now discovered that they are perhaps more powerful than he bargained for. The outcome of this meeting may well determine the fates of the characters and the City of Brass itself! Draw closed the blinds to hide the rays of the rising sun so that the tale may continue uninterrupted.

This adventure is suggested for Tier 4 characters.

Standard Features

Doors: The doors of the Tower of the Grand Vizier are living brass and are locked with fantastic locks. Unlocking a door requires a successful DC 25 Dexterity check with thieves' tools. A door can be broken open with a successful DC 28 Strength check or by doing 60 hit points of damage against AC 16. The doors ignore any attack that does less than 10 points of damage and repair themselves at the rate of 1 point per minute. A door reduced to 0 or fewer hit points cannot repair itself.

Arcane Locked Doors and Chests: Some doors and chests in the Vizier's tower are *arcane locked*. Even after the *arcane lock* spell is

10
8 9
S
7
6
D B D
B 1 B
C
B A D
The Silver Door
5 4E 4D 4A 3 4B 4C
Fortress of Norl
E 4
Tower of the Grand Vizier
1 Square – 50 Feet
10
8 9
7
6
2
5280 Feet
E
D A

dispelled, the door or chest must be unlocked. Most are protected with locks constructed by the some of the best locksmiths the City of Brass has to offer.

Shielding: The Tower of the Grand Vizier is shielded against any *scrying*. Extraplanar travel and *teleportation* into or out of the tower may be achieved only if the password is known or if the traveler is in possession of a special amulet bearing the Vizier's personal seal. The Grand Vizier grants these amulets only to his special servants. Creatures attempting to fly into the compound are set upon by 1d4 **barbed devils**.

For the following locations, refer to **The Grand Vizier Map**.

A. The Demon Gate

Like other demon gates in the city, this **demon gate**[1] is bound with the trapped spirit of a balor. The demon, like other demon gates, is reduced to its pure essence of evil, contorted and conformed into a massive horned head upon a thickly corded neck. A demon gate is immobile and strikes with its wickedly long tongue. A character grabbed is reeled in and bitten by the demonic visage of the gate.

The demon gates may be passed only by someone bearing the *Demon Key*[2], which is currently in the keep of the Grand Vizier of Efreet. Otherwise, the gates must be defeated in order to gain passage. A defeated demon gate reforms itself into a new demon gate within 30 hours.

B. Walls

The walls surrounding the tower are 50 feet tall and made of blistering hot bronze. A creature touching the walls takes 7 (2d6) fire damage each round and must make a DC 17 Dexterity saving throw or become stuck to the wall as the heat burns away flesh. A stuck character takes 7 (2d6) fire damage each round and can break free with a successful DC 16 Strength check. Creatures immune to fire are unaffected.

Invisible *walls of force* encircle the compound from the tops of the bronze walls to the pinnacle of the central tower.

C. Courtyard

The courtyard is patrolled by 4 **barbed devils**. The barbed devils instantly attack anyone who enters the courtyard without permission of the Grand Vizier himself.

D. Lesser Towers

The lesser towers have no visible entryway and may be accessed only through the *teleportation* portals inside the central tower of the Vizier. They serve as a prison to the **afya**[1], or shades. These once great sorcerers were each trapped or captured by the Grand Vizier and imprisoned in one of these towers. They now serve as "batteries" of raw magical energy that the Vizier uses to command his most powerful magic without expending any of his own spells. The afya are bound with a permanent *resilient sphere* spell that can only be broken by a *disintegrate* spell cast with a 9th level spell slot, and under the effects of a permanent *spell siphon*[4].

Each of these towers is a hollow spire 80 feet tall containing a single chamber at the top of its crystal-domed tower. Trapped within each chamber is one of the afya. Rippling cords of magical energy knot and braid from a crystalline dome atop each tower as the magic of the sorcerers trapped within feed the mystic energies of the **Conjuring Chamber (Area 10)** at the top of the Tower of the Vizier. A creature touching one of these rays of pure magical energy must succeed on a DC 18 Constitution saving throw or instantly die as its body is flooded with raw magical energy. A creature that successfully saves gains the ability to manipulate magic or cast spells, dependent on character class. See the sidebox for details.

Freeing the Afya

If the **afya**[1] are somehow freed from their imprisonment, they offer their services in the characters' cause if they see the cause as just and especially if it includes the destruction of the Grand Vizier.

Characters Who Make Their Constitution Saving Throw

A character who makes its Constitution save against an energy ray from one of the towers gains one of the benefits below. A character can gain only one of these benefits once at a time. Touching the energy ray while still affected by one of the benefits does not bestow anything on the character and the character still must succeed at a Constitution saving throw or die each time the ray is touched. Multi-class characters use their highest-class level to determine the benefit gained. If one or more class levels are equal, you (or the player) decides which benefit is gained. Creatures without class levels (monsters, for example) are affected as non-casters.

Arcane caster: Spell slots are doubled for one (80% chance) or two (20% chance) spell levels for 48 hours. You can randomly determine the level(s) of spells affected. Roll 1d10: 1–4, 1st-level spells; 5–7, 2nd-level spells; 8–9, 3rd-level spells; 10, 4th-level spells.

Divine caster: A divine caster gains the ability to cast arcane spells of up to 4th level for the next 24 hours by substituting arcane spells for divine spells. When preparing spells, the divine caster can freely substitute spells from the arcane spell lists for divine spells on a 1-for-1 basis up to a maximum of one-half of the spells for a given spell level. For example, a 10th-level cleric can cast four 1st-level spells. Up to two 1st-level spells can be selected from the arcane spell list for that day. Arcane spells use the caster's Wisdom modifier (just like other divine spells).

Non-spellcasters: Non-spellcasters gain the ability to cast arcane spells up to 3rd level as a caster of one-quarter their character level for 24 hours. For example, a 10th-level fighter could cast arcane spells as a 2nd-level sorcerer. The non-caster must have a Charisma score equal to 10 + the spell's level to cast it. Non-spellcasters use their Charisma modifier for spell effects (save DC for example). They do not gain bonus spells per day, regardless of their Charisma score.

Each broken connection with one of the afya forces the Grand Vizier to succeed on a DC 20 Constitution saving throw or lose 1d6 points of Intelligence. To break the connection with the Vizier, the spells holding each afya must each be successfully dispelled. If the curse is then broken, the regain their former selves. Johora and Humam are **archmages**, Sirajha an **afya elemental overlord**[1], and **Mus'ad Camel Face**[1] has his own listing.

The Afya

The following beings are currently imprisoned in the towers and subjected to the *spell siphoning* of the Grand Vizier.

Johora the Lovely

Johora (**afya archmage**[1]) was an elven sorcerer princess who was long coveted by the Grand Vizier who observed her rise to power from afar. When she rebuked his entreaties of love, he turned his wrath upon her, making her the first prisoner of his tower. She sleeps ever within her containment sphere as the Vizier turns her powers, once used for justice and light, to evil and destruction.

Humam

Humam (**afya archmage**[1]) was a human sorcerer and follower of the teachings of Anumon. He sided with the forces of the Sultana and was imprisoned by the Vizier rather than slain outright as were many who joined her cause. Since then, Humam has languished in fitful sleep as the Grand Vizier siphons his magic off on a daily basis.

Sirajha the Brilliant One

Sirajha (**afya elemental overlord**[1]) was an azer sorceress who was renowned among her folk for her ability to bend and wield fire and light, and to shape metal alongside her husband the Diya al Din. When she was captured by the Grand Vizier, he placed an ancient curse on her, condemning her to the form of an afya. It is her imprisonment here in the tower that has kept Diya al Din from openly leading a revolt against the Sultan's forces from the Basin that would rock the City of Brass to its very foundations.

Mus'ad Camel Face

Mus'ad, a sage camel (**afya Mus'ad Camel Face**[1]), was sought by many denizens of his desert home plane as a keeper of secrets and speaker of lore. Tricked into slavery by an efreeti, Mus'ad was quickly snatched up by the Grand Vizier who saw the benefit of one as powerful as he. The Vizier uses Mus'ad's oracular skills when scrying the planes for relics of power and to further his command of all things arcane.

E. The Central Tower

There is no visible entrance to the Tower of the Grand Vizier, as his entry and exit are achieved through magic. Characters should somehow come across one of the Vizier's amulets or gain the secret password "Ain Al Nar." The password may be acquired from former agents of the Grand Vizier, who would see him destroyed. Or it may be set as a trap for characters by the Vizier himself to get them into his lair where he can slay them at his leisure. A *legend lore* spell may be used to figure out the password.

E-1. Bottom Floor

Any entrants other than those brought into the tower by the Vizier himself find themselves in a huge circular chamber of exquisite beauty. The ceiling of the chamber reaches 100 feet above the ground, and doorways and a platform can be seen there. Those who seek admission to the upper floors must do so by flight, as there is no obvious staircase or lift to reach them from the bottom floor. Located in the center of the chamber is a mosaic of a huge eye set in the center of an arabesque fire motif. Images of the Grand Vizier and the Sultan of Efreet[1] destroying their enemies and having them forged into living brass adorn the walls. The faces of both the Sultan and the turbaned Vizier are veiled.

As the characters enter, 3 **hellwasp swarms**[1] circling in the tower swoop down to attack in 1d4 rounds. Allow characters DC 15 Perception checks to notice the metallic insects descending on them.

E-2. Platform

A platform suspended in the center of the tower stretching the diameter of the shaft leads to two sets of staircases that follow the curve of the tower and lead to highly polished living brass doors. Each of the doors is locked as detailed in the Standard Features sidebox and is further trapped with a wail of the banshee trap. Noting this trap requires a successful DC 20 Intelligence (Investigation) check. If triggered, the trap releases a keening wail. The wail does 200 psychic damage total to up to 20 targets that can hear it within 40 feet. Starting with the closest creature, each creature within the area that can hear must succeed on a DC 20 Constitution saving throw or take the lesser of their current hit points or the amount of damage remaining to the effect (starting with 200 for the first affected creature).

E-3. Chamber of Clouds

The door to the eastern chamber opens to reveal a wide-open space that appears to be filled with nothing but great gray storm clouds. A large stone castle-like structure floats in the center of the chamber. The clouds appear to have some firmness to them, as if they are spongy ground.

Movement across the cloud cover is at 5 feet per round no matter what the character's normal movement rate is. Once the clouds are entered, vision is reduced so that objects beyond 10 feet are partially obscured. Some areas of the cloud cover are thinner than others, and some are so charged with static that they may unleash an electrical arc when a creature walks across them.

Chamber of Clouds Effects

Roll 1d8 for each minute the characters spend traversing this pocket dimension and consult the list below to determine what effects occur from crossing the clouds.

1. Static Electric Discharge: A creature makes a DC 18 Dexterity saving throw, taking 21 (6d6) lightning damage on a failure or half as much on a success.

2. Wind Shear: A massive gust of vertical wind lifts creatures of under 300 pounds total weight (including equipment) into the air, hurling them 1d6 x 50 feet in a random direction. If a character lands on the **Fortress of Norl** or back on one of the platforms flanking this area, they take falling damage. If they fall upon a cloud, they take no damage but are disoriented for 1d4 rounds from their ordeal and are unable to take any other actions as they catch their breath.

3. Thin Spot: A character must succeed on a DC 17 Dexterity saving throw or fall through a thin spot in the clouds. A character falling through the cloud cover is sucked through a vortex of wind and fire, taking 14 (4d6) bludgeoning and fire damage, and spit out over the Bazaar of Beggars in the Plane of Molten Skies.

4. Belkers: 1d4 + 2 **belkers**[1] rise from the clouds and attack the characters.

5. Air Elemental: A **greater air elemental**[1] rises from the clouds and demands tribute from the characters equal to 10,000 gp worth of magical items to escort them to the doorway on the other side of the cloudbank. Should they refuse, it attacks. Should they accept, the party arrives at the doorway without further rolls on this list.

6–8: No encounter or occurrence.

E-4. Fortress of Norl the Cloud Giant

In the midst of the great cloud stands this huge structure of stone and earth. From high atop its bastion, **Norl**[1] rules his tiny world of cloud and wind. Norl[1] acts as guardian and protector of the Grand Vizier's personal library, but not by his choice. The Vizier sees that Norl[1] is properly charmed and well stocked with wine, food, treasure, and slaves that he uses, tortures, and hurls from the fortress when he becomes bored with them.

Norl[1] is a priest of the Demon Lord Pazuzu, and as such gains access to his spells. Although his servant is a prisoner, the winged god of the skies sees the benefit of having someone "within" the Tower of the Grand Vizier.

Once characters come within 140 feet of Norl's fortress, allow both him and the characters Perception checks to notice one another, remembering that the partial obscurity applies until the characters set foot upon the island of earth from which the fortress rises. If Norl[1] succeeds on his check, he lets out a howl and a bellow and begins hurling stones at the characters.

E-4A. Gates

Huge iron bars protect Norl's property and keep his playthings from escaping. In the courtyard beyond the portcullis are several giant oxen. The bars can be unlocked with a successful DC 25 Dexterity check with thieves' tools or broken with a successful DC 30 Strength check. Wearing them down with attacks requires doing 120 points of damage against AC 18, and the bars ignore any attack that does less than 10 points of damage.

E-4B. Courtyard

The courtyard contains 12 **giant oxen**[1] and enough fodder to feed them all. If a running battle is taking place, the oxen are likely agitated, especially if magic is involved, and may trample folk who get in their way.

Broad stairs — with each step being 5 feet high — lead to the ramparts of the fortress. Climbing the stairs requires a successful DC 5 Strength (Athletics) check.

A keep standing in the center of the courtyard has a thick wooden door nearly 20 feet high. The door is barred from the inside and trapped with a *glyph of warding*. Detecting the *glyph* requires a successful DC 18 Intelligence (Investigation) check and disarming a successful DC 18 Intelligence (Arcana) check. If triggered, all creatures within a 5-foot-radius must make a DC 18 Dexterity saving throw, taking 36 (8d8) thunder damage on a failure or half as much on a success. The door can be unlocked with a successful DC 25 Dexterity check with thieves' tools or broken down with a successful DC 20 Strength check.

E-4C. Ramparts

Norl[1] spends most of his time standing upon his ramparts surveying his tiny pocket domain. There is an 80% chance he is on the ramparts at any given time. If not there, he is within his keep. The ramparts are stocked with many piles of stones for Norl[1] to hurl and afford him half cover as he stands behind the huge crenellations.

E-4D. Norl's Keep

The interior of Norl's massive keep consists of just two chambers, one upon the ground floor and a sleeping chamber on the upper floor. The ground floor chamber is filled with loot that has been granted him over the years by the Grand Vizier to keep him appeased. A huge dining table is covered with plates made of solid gold and silverware of pure platinum. Golden goblets as large as soup tureens and keg-sized bottles of wine are piled high upon Norl's dining board. Tapestries depicting beautiful cloud giantesses in exotic poses hang from the walls of the place. A large cage occupies one corner of the chamber.

Norl[1] keeps his slaves in the cage and lets them out when the mood strikes him. His current slave is Zabihsha (**entertainer**[1]), a halfling dancing girl snatched from the Bazaar of 1,000 Sins. Zabihsha was once in a band of adventurers who ran afoul of an efreeti, whose anger landed her and her companions in the slave pens. Zabihsha has been Norl's prisoner for a little more than three months and is in desperate fear for her life. Norl[1] forces her to dance atop his table while he eats. A golden chain is clamped around her leg while she dances, and Norl[1] jerks the chain to and fro if her moves displease him.

Zabihsha's cage is locked with a magical lock that can be opened only with one of the keys on the key ring Norl[1] wears about his neck. She pleads to be freed from her bondage if possible. Zabihsha knows of the other key (the silver key) that Norl[1] keeps in a hidden compartment beneath his bed that opens the doorway on the far side of the clouds, but she has no idea what lies beyond it.

In the northern wall is a huge spit capable of roasting an entire ox upon it and a chimney leading up and out of the fortress.

Treasure: The 20 golden plates and goblets are worth 200 gp each. The golden chain used to tie Zabihsha's ankle is worth 100 gp. The platinum silverware setting is worth 500 gp. Each of the ten massive bottles of wine holds 20 gallons and 1,000 gp worth of fine wine. Each of the tapestries weighs 300 pounds and is worth 2,000 gp.

E-4E. Norl's Loft

Norl[1] sleeps in a loft-like chamber built over his dining hall. His gigantic bed is covered with various silks, satins, and furs to keep him warm at night. A 14-foot-tall chest of drawers holds his many suits of clothing, and a weapon rack holds his spare armor and weapons, all sized just for him. The ceiling is painted with the realistically rendered image of a feathered demon of immense size, with two pairs of wings, one pointing up and the other down. The crotch of the figure is shown covered with maggots, blisters, and pustules. An altar cut in the shape of the same creature stands in one corner of the loft; it is covered in fresh and dried blood and emanates the effects of a *hallow* spell.

Characters making a successful DC 18 Intelligence (Investigation) check discover a secret panel hidden beneath the bed. Inside the panel is a velvet-lined lacquer box containing a silver key. The key itself is over a foot long and made of solid polished silver; its handle is covered in diamonds, and it radiates a strong aura of abjuration magic. The silver key may be used to open **The Silver Door (Area E-5)** in the western end of the Chamber of Clouds.

Norl[1] wears a keyring around his neck that holds the key to Zabihsha's cage in **Area E-4D**.

Treasure: The bedclothes of silks, furs, and satins weigh 10 to 50 pounds each and are valued at 1d4 x 100 gp each. There are 20 such silks and furs lying about. The lacquer box that holds the key is worth 200 gp. Ten *potions of superior healing* sit upon a nightstand.

E-5. The Silver Door

This magical door stands at the far end of the cloudbank. It is a freestanding door that one can walk around and look at from both sides. It glows magically and detects as highly magical. The door may be opened only with the silver key hidden in **Norl's loft (Area E-4E)**. Characters approaching with the silver key can unlock the door and step through the portal. Doing so deposits them into **The Brass Menagerie (Area E-6)**.

If the characters come within 10 feet of the door without the silver key in their possession, each character within the area must succeed on a DC 18 Dexterity saving throw or be sucked through the door and dumped onto the Astral Plane at a random location 1d10 miles away from the door. The exact nature of what happens to a character on the Astral Plane and how the character locates the door from that plane are left up to you.

E-6. The Brass Menagerie

This chamber is lined with row upon row of brass statues, most being lifelike representations of various creatures including humanoids, giants, centaurs, sphinxes, chimera, and, most impressively, a huge dragon that resembles a blue dragon though it is formed of brass. The dragon stands before a large door in the northern end of the chamber. There are exactly 100 such statues in the chamber. A character making a successful DC 17 Intelligence (Investigation) check notices that all of the statues are hollow except the statue of the dragon and a statue of a man in full plate armor, whose armor shows the markings of Muir.

The **brazen dragon statue**[1] animates after 1d6 rounds unless it is touched before that.

Tactics: The dragon breathes its antimagic breath upon the characters every 1d4 rounds and attacks anyone who comes near the doorway.

The solid statue of the man in full plate is actually **Sir Leobilus**[1], who was turned to brass by a *flesh to brass*[4] spell while questing to destroy the evil of the Grand Vizier. Sir Leobilus may be turned back to flesh by means of a *wish*.

Leobilus is eager to return to his quest but is unaware that nearly 50 years have passed since his imprisonment.

The exit from this chamber is a huge, red-hot iron portal trapped with a burnt othur vapor trap. Touching the portal deals 11 (2d10) fire damage per round of contact and triggers the trap (unless it has been disabled or discharged). Stepping through the portal triggers the trap (unless disabled or discharged) and deposits a character into **The Harem of the Six and Sixty-Six (Area E-7)**. Detecting the trap requires a successful DC 16 Intelligence (Investigation) check and it can be disabled with a successful DC 17 Dexterity check with thieves' tools. If triggered, the trap fills a 10-foot square centered on the portal with poisonous gas for 3 rounds. A creature that enters the area on its turn for the first time or who starts its turn in the area must make a DC 16 Constitution saving throw, taking 55 (10d10) poison damage and losing 1d6 points of Constitution on a failed save, and taking half as much damage and not losing Constitution on a success.

E-7. The Harem of the Six and Sixty-Six

This large circular chamber is littered with colorful divans, rugs, silks, furs, and pillows. Lounging about the chamber are 72 luscious female figures in various modes of dress and undress. These 72 creatures make up the demonic concubines of the Grand Vizier and consist of 6 **succubi** and 66 **alu demons**[1]. The succubi and alu-demons immediately turn the charm on to anyone entering the chamber, as it has been a long time since they have feasted upon any fresh souls. Prisoners here themselves, they may not necessarily attempt to kill the characters outright, as they also despise the Grand Vizier and would have their freedom so that they might go back to snaring mortals and eating their souls. Overt attempts to harm them in any way results in a massive attack by the alu-demons and succubi with claw and fang.

Treasure: The demons are draped with gold, platinum, and brass chains studded with precious jewels that make up the majority of their harness and girdle. Their arms and fingers drip with rings. Roll 1d20 x 100 gp to determine the total value of jewelry upon each defeated demon.

A spiral staircase in the center of the chamber leads to **The Grand Vizier's Bedchamber (Area E-8)**. The door to **Area E-8** is trapped with an energy drain trap. The trap can be spotted with a successful DC 25 Intelligence (Invstigation) check and disarmed with *dispel magic* cast successfully against a level 9 spell slot. If the trap is triggered, each creature within 5 feet of it must succeed on a DC 15 Constitution saving throw or receive two levels of exhaustion.

E-8. The Grand Vizier's Bedchamber

This chamber radiates immense heat and is occupied by a bed of pure flame that acts like a permanent *wall of fire* cast with a 9th level spell slot upon the floor. Characters walking upon or touching the floor take 45 (10d8) fire damage each round.

At the foot of the bed is a chest of pure gold. Curtains surrounding the chamber are made of woven gold and steel wire. A brass brazier stands in the center of a magic circle, with a book on a golden stand before it. The book is called *The Quarto Draconium of the Seven Flames*. It describes the admixture of seven alchemical elements that, when mixed in the brazier, may be used to summon and command an elemental dragon of fire.

The chest of pure gold standing at the foot of the bed of fire is trapped with a chain lightning trap. The trap can be detected with a successful DC 19 Intelligence (Arcana) check and removed with *dispel magic* cast successfully against a 9th level spell. Any creature within 10 feet of the box is struck by lightning. In addition, any creature within 10 feet of a creature struck by lightning is struck, up to a possible range of 80 feet and a maximum of 8 strikes (the same target can be struck multiple times). Any creature struck by lightning must attempt a DC 19 Dexterity saving throw. Those failing the saving throw take 35 (10d6) lightning damage, while those succeeding take half this amount. The chest is locked and the locak can be opened with a successful DC 20 Dexterity check with thieves' tools once the *arcane lock* has been removed. In the chest is a sack filled with brimstone, 10,000 bp, and enough expensive material components to use *The Quarto Draconium* two times.

An illusion over one wall of the chamber hides a locked door that leads to **The Grand Vizier's Laboratory (Area E-9)**. The illusion can be detected with a successful DC 18 Intelligence (Investigation) check.

The Quarto Draconium of the Seven Flames

This ancient tome, whose words are acid-etched upon beaten sheets of copper, contains great lore for the summoning and command of an elemental fire dragon[1]. Much of the book details the collection and refinement of the seven alchemical elements used in the conjuring. The elements include carbon, magnesium, sodium, sulfur, iron, copper, and tin. An ounce of each element, powdered and refined through alchemical means, is required for the summoning, and costs 1,000 gp per ounce to create, requiring a successful DC 20 Intelligence check with alchemists' supplies. To fully comprehend the remainder of the book and perform the summoning requires a successful DC 22 Intelligence (Arcana) check. If the check succeeds, an elemental fire dragon appears under control of the summoner and remains for 1 minute per level of the summoner. If the check fails, no summoning is made, and the summoner must start the process anew. If the check fails by 5 or more, an elemental fire dragon appears for 1 round per level of the summoner. The dragon is completely out of control, attacking all creatures within sight, especially the summoner whom the dragon attempts to destroy.

E-9. The Grand Vizier's Laboratory

Alchemical and arcane equipment of a design both eldritch and unusual packs this bizarre chamber. Four huge crystalline tanks fitted with hoses of braided steel occupy the corners of the chamber. Half-formed figures appear to grow within the tanks, many misshapen but one near perfect in every way, skin gleaming like molten metal, its eyes closed in a death-like slumber. Arcane writing lines the walls, ceiling, and floor, but is written in a haphazard fashion with some magical equations overlapping others. A large naked burning figure of an efreeti sits in the center of the runes.

His body is perfectly sculpted, but his eyes show signs of madness. When the characters enter the chamber, he giggles maniacally, and continues to draw strange sigils upon the floor. He suggests they stay where they are as he does not remember what is written upon the floor, giggling that approaching him "could be dangerous." The figure is Zanabar (**efreeti sorcerer**[1]), a failed clone of the Grand Vizier, who was awakened when his mind was only partially formed. The Vizier uses Zanabar as an assistant and guardian, abusing the clone constantly.

Other Features: Characters making a successful DC 22 Intelligence (Investigation) check find a formula written upon the wall by Zanabar that contains intricate details of how the wards protecting the Conjuring Chamber of the Grand Vizier may be breached only by the Vizier himself. A cosmic loophole that Zanabar realized in a maddened state ventures that since Zanabar is made from the flesh of the Grand Vizier himself that he may enter the chamber without being destroyed. Zanabar would try to wrest control of the Conjuring Chamber and steal the powers that the afya grant to the Vizier were it not for the fact that whenever he attempts such a ploy, he is struck with fits of madness or long periods of forgetfulness.

Zanabar knows how to get into the Conjuring Chamber but is forbidden to go himself on pain of death. If questioned as to how to get upstairs, Zanabar immediately falls into a catatonic state brought on by a *geas* lain upon him by the Vizier, gurgling, "only his flesh … only his flesh."

Zanabar is filled with hatred and fear of the Grand Vizier who created him in his own image, but who found him lacking during his initial experiments to create a perfect clone of himself. If attacked, Zanabar possesses a portion of his creator's powers but uses his abilities in a random and chaotic manner. Roll randomly every round to determine who Zanabar targets for his attacks. Unless fully engaged in melee, Zanabar uses spells and spell-like abilities to attack foes.

The distance between the characters and Zanabar is scribed with runes that may trigger deadly magical traps. Suggested spell traps are listed below. Each trap can be noted with a successful DC 18 Intelligence (Investigation) check and disabled with a successful DC 18 Intelligence (Arcana) check.

Acid Fog Trap

An acid fog fills a 30-foot-cube for 1 minute. When a creature enters the area for the first time on its turn or starts its turn within the area it must make a DC 16 Constitusion saving throw, taking 44 (8d10) acid damage on a failure or half as much on a success.

Chain Lightning Trap

Any creature within 10 feet of the box is struck by lightning. In addition, any creature within 10 feet of a creature struck by lightning is struck, up to a possible range of 80 feet. Any creature struck by lightning must attempt a DC 16 Dexterity saving throw. Those failing the saving throw take 24 (7d6) lightning damage, while those succeeding take half this amount.

Black Tentacles Trap

A 20-foot-square centered on the trap is filled with grasping black tentacles. When a creature enters the area for the first time on its turn or starts its turn within the area it must make a successful DC 18 Strength saving throw or be grappled and restrained. A restrained creature may attempt a DC 18 Dexterity (Acrobatics) or Strength (Athletics) check as an action on its turn to free itself.

Monster Summoning Trap

This trap typically summons a **glabrezu demon** or 1d3 **greater fire elementals**[1], but the exact summoning is left up to you (to suit your campaign).

Treasure: The entire chamber is a fully operational cloning facility used by the Grand Vizier to protect himself in the event the Sultan should destroy him, or through some magical experiment gone awry. The four tanks are of exceptional quality, valued at 10,000 gp each with another 2,000 gp worth of fluids and cloning materials located in the chamber as well. Although the cloning machinery is of a magical fabrication, its quasi-scientific components reach far beyond the skein of normal characters' experience. Any bit of flesh placed into one of the canisters grows within 1d4 days into a perfect replica of the original, lacking only the spark of life. The bits of flesh currently forming in the various containers are exact replicates of the Grand Vizier. If the flesh were somehow grafted to the characters, or even consumed by them, they would be able to *teleport* into the Conjuring Chamber above, thereby circumventing the Vizier's wards against intruders.

Becoming One with the Vizier

Eating of the Flesh: Eating a piece of the Vizier's flesh is enough to allow the characters to fake out the Vizier's wards but requires a successful DC 17 Constitution saving throw. On a failed save, the character is nauseated for 5 minutes. Whether the save succeeds or not, the character must wait 30 minutes for the effects to take (in other words, a character must wait 30 minutes before being able to avoid the Vizier's protective wards).

Grafting the Flesh: Pieces of the Vizier may be grafted to a character by use of a *regenerate* spell. First, an incision is made in the flesh of a willing subject and a piece of one of the Vizier's clone parts placed in the wound. Second, a *regenerate* spell is cast to graft the portion of the Grand Vizier's flesh to the character.

Individuals grafting a piece of the Grand Vizier to them must make a DC 17 Constitution saving throw. On a failed save, the piece of the Vizier retains a memory of the Vizier and may have one of the effects listed in the sidebox. On a successful save, the character has no ill effects from the graft. Whether the save succeeds or not, a graft falls off in 1d4 days as the body finally rejects it. Any benefits or hindrances resulting from a graft disappear at this time as well.

Grafting Effects

Roll 1d8 on the following list for each graft placed on a character.

1d8	Result
1	The subject grows an extra arm in 1 hour that constantly attempts to strangle or otherwise murder the host. The arm has a proficiency bonus equal to the character's, a Strength of 20 (+10), and deals 13 (1d6 + 10) bludgeoning damage on a hit.
2	The subject grows an extra leg in 1 hour that constantly tries to drag the owner off cliffs, or into dangerous situations, and kicks strangers in inappropriate places. Movement is either increased by 5 feet or decreased by 5 feet, purely at random.
3	The subject immediately grows a mouth in the affected area that constantly hurls insults at the host, yelling loudly and so on, thus making hiding and moving silently pretty much impossible. Additionally, the mouth attempts to bite anything and anyone within 5 feet of it, except efreet. The mouth has a proficiency bonus equal to the host's, Dexterity 17 (+3), and deals 5 (1d4 + 3) bludgeoning damage. If the host is a spellcaster, the mouth randomly depletes the caster's spells (purposefully miscasting beneficial spells so no benefit is gained; damage-dealing spells on the other hand can be cast normally by the grafted mouth). Only spells with a verbal component and no material or somatic component can be cast by the mouth.
4	The subject grows an extra ear in the affected area. The Vizier is able to hear whatever the subject hears.
5	The subject grows an eye in the affected area. The Vizier is able to see whatever the subject sees.
6	The subject's skin becomes scaled and a metallic-reddish hue in color. The subject gains resistance to fire damage but disadvantage on all Charisma-based checks.
7	The subject grows horns and gains a gore attack. The subject loses 2 points of Charisma (which return once the graft is removed or falls off).
8	Roll twice, ignoring this result.

Note: A graft can be hacked or burned off. A graft has one-tenth the hit points of the host. Damaging a graft does not deal hit point damage to the host but the host loses 1d6 points of Constitution when the graft is removed or destroyed in this way.

E-10. The Conjuring Chamber

This chamber, which sits atop the lofty pinnacle of the Tower of the Grand Vizier, is accessible only via *teleportation* from a location within the central tower. Entry into this chamber is denied to all save the Grand Vizier himself, unless an individual is brought here by the Vizier or has figured out Zanabar's workaround.

Anyone attempting to *teleport* from a location outside the central tower into the Conjuring Chamber (even by those who have grafted or eaten the flesh of a clone) automatically fails for all except the Grand Vizier, those with him, or those who have been given a special "key" by the Vizier. The "key" is a wound dealt by the Vizier's burning claws, willingly accepted, on the person's arm that leaves a permanent scar and lowers the target's maximum hit points by 2d6 points.

Entering the Conjuring Chamber

Characters who eat a portion of a clone and wait for 30 minutes or characters who graft a bit of a clone to their own body can access the Conjuring Chamber by *teleporting* into it from the central tower.

Those who haven't eaten the flesh of a clone or grafted a portion of a clone onto their body, or those attempting to teleport into the chamber from a location other than inside the central tower, suffer certain effects when trying to access the Conjuring Chamber. Each failed attempt results in increasingly "bad things" happening.

Attempt	Result
1st	Teleport fails; teleporting creatures take 35 (10d6) fire damage.
2nd	Teleport fails; teleporting creatures take 21 (6d6) force damage and loses 2d6 points of Intelligence.
3rd	Teleport fails; teleporting creatures diverted and arrive outside the Demon Gate (**Area A**).
4th	Teleport fails; teleporting creatures diverted and arrive midair, falling about 5,000 feet into the Basin taking 70 (20d6) bludgeoning damage.

The chamber is 80 feet in diameter and is topped by a crystal dome. A golden throne that rotates at the whim of the Vizier sits in the center of the chamber in the midst of a great magic circle 50 feet across. The circle acts as a *magic circle against good, evil, law,* and *chaos.* Four glowing portals generate an arcane light at the cardinal points of the chamber. They are permanent *teleportation* portals that lead to the four prison chambers of the afya (**Area D,** the **Lesser Towers**).

Unless the characters have some information as to the whereabouts of the Grand Vizier, **Rahib al Tabish Zafir**[1], there is a 50% chance he is in the Conjuring Chamber, unless they have taken no precautions to hide their identity and presence in the tower, in which case there is a 100% chance he is here.

The Vizier's Throne

The throne is attuned to the Grand Vizier and is permanently enchanted with *true seeing* and *clairvoyance* and allows him to trigger a *prismatic sphere* with a DC 19 spell save DC once per day at will. Anyone other than the Grand Vizier touching his throne takes 55 (10d10) necrotic damage per round with no saving throw.

Further, the throne acts as a conduit to the afya[1] prisoners that empower the Vizier's *spell siphon*[4] spell. While seated on his throne, he drains half again as many spell slots (rounded down) as normal each round. Also while seated on his throne, he does not need to concentrate to maintain the spell. He can also drain a higher level spell slot instead of a 4th level spell slot each round the afya have the slots available.

Bonus Spell Levels: The Vizier has 40 bonus spell levels drained from the afya imprisoned in the towers. He uses these to cast his spells, metamagic his spells, increase the caster level of a spell, or increase the save DC of a spell.

Tactics: The Vizier remains upon his throne for as long as possible, hurling magic upon intruders and using his bonus spell levels (drained from the afya) to supplement his assault. He uses *time stop, meteor swarm, imprisonment,* and whatever else he can do to destroy foes he feels most

threatened by, binding others with *charms* and *suggestions* to use them as he sees fit.

If given the chance, and if his bonus spell levels are depleted, the Vizier uses his *spell siphon*[4] to drain the prisoners and replenish his supply. Remember, while seated on his throne he can drain half again as many slots as normal, and the spell does not require his concentration.

If forced into combat, he wields the *Munir Seif al Shihab*[2] (Shining Sword of Flame)

Treasure: The Grand Vizier keeps his magic books hidden in a *secret chest*. Each page of his books is covered in *illusory script*. Readers of his books must succeed on a DC 20 Wisdom saving throw or be driven mad and permanently act as per the *confusion* spell.

The Vizier and His Tower

While within the tower and sitting upon his throne, the Vizier may view any room or chamber with his compound. The Vizier attempts to deal with intruders by using *conjure elemental* or other similar spells to thwart foes, intending that the summoned monsters deal with fools while he goes about the important business of creating new and powerful spells to aid his master, the Sultan. To conserve his power, the summoning spells are usually powered by spell slots drained from the afya. The Vizier may be somewhat shocked and entertained by the characters, as foes have never successfully infiltrated his tower.

Should the Vizier ever be pressed to the point of death, he does everything in his power to escape, including *teleporting* to the Palace of the Sultan to heal and gather reinforcements. Should the Vizier find escape impossible, he may attempt to halt combat and drop a bombshell on the characters. He reveals that he secretly detests the Sultan of Efreet[1]. Individuals powerful enough to defeat him are surely powerful enough to slay the Sultan of Efreet[1] — and he is willing to give them the keys to the Sultan's undoing! The Vizier has become increasingly uncomfortable with the presence of minions of Set and Lucifer at court and throughout the city, finding them an insult to pure efreet. Rahib sees himself as better suited to rule, and more or less the architect of the Sultan's rise to power.

The characters are of course unlikely to trust the Vizier's bargain, and you may choose to run this side plot any number of ways.

The Grand Vizier is Truthful: Rahib grants the characters access to previously unattainable areas of the city, possibly assisting them in secret with magic spells or weapons and items with which to battle the Sultan. Of course, if the characters rat the Vizier out to the Sultan, he denies it as skillfully as possible, claiming to have been "setting the characters up" all along. Furthermore, if the characters are losing in battle against the Sultan, he is more apt to throw in with the Sultan. Likewise, if the Sultan is losing to the characters, the Vizier may secretly use magic to deny the Sultan's ability to escape the characters.

Should the characters defeat the Sultan with or without the Vizier's help, the Vizier offers the characters a chance to work for him for up to a year and a day battling off members of the noble houses of efreet and consolidating his control over the City of Brass. After their year and a day of service, they are given vast riches (as determined by you) and asked politely to leave the City of Brass.

The Grand Vizier is Lying: The Grand Vizier would do or say anything to save his neck. He grants the characters numerous magic items to show that he is "keeping his word" and turns them over to the Sultan's forces at his earliest convenience.

The End?

Should they defeat Rahib and completed any number of the previous adventure locations within Tales of Brass, the characters have likely gathered sufficient allies and mighty artifacts to challenge the Sultan of Efreet[1]. If they choose this route (and who's kidding whom right?) and make a last great heroic stand versus the Sultan's remaining loyal legions, the outcome could very well create a great shift in the cosmic balance and place the heroes on the path of legends. How this turns out is entirely up to you. The Palace of the sultan of efreet is detailed in **Chapter 31** and a good summary of his entourage is given there.

Chapter 31
The Palace of the Grand Sultan of Efreet

The Palace of the Grand Sultan of Efreet stares dauntingly out over the City of Brass. The palace is a huge fortress and palace compound making up a major portion of the northern reaches of the City of Brass. The palace compound is easily the most massive structure in the City of Brass and is encompassed by an enormous bastion wall and enveloped in the Curtain of Flame. Quite literally, describing every cubbyhole, corridor, sleeping chamber, banquet hall, and servant's bunk in the Palace of the Grand Sultan would occupy a volume as vast as the one you are holding in your hands. For this reason, only the key areas of interest and a general overview of the palace compound and its contents are detailed here, that you may flesh them out as you see fit, fulfilling your own personal vision of the City of Brass.

Running the Palace of the Sultan of Efreet

The palace is a huge place filled with many powerful beings. Characters could seek admittance to the palace for any number of reasons. Quite possibly they have taken actions that have drawn the attention of the Sultan himself and have been brought before him so that he may see the characters in person and assess their powers and abilities with his own eyes. Possibly they have come as petitioners and seek a favor or boon of the Sultan. A frontal assault on the Palace of the Sultan could be run; however, such an action may quite easily destroy even the most fortified party of heroes. Information included in this chapter is designed to help you flesh out the palace to suit whichever need you may have for the palace or encounters with the Sultan of Efreet[1] within your campaign. This chapter could also prove invaluable should characters be searching for a means of destroying the Sultan or a way of unleashing the spirit of Sulymon upon the Lord of the Efreet as part of a sweeping high-level adventure.

Options for running encounters in the Palace of the Grand Sultan include but are not limited to:

- Stealing the *Codex of Infinite Planes*[2].

- Seeking to establish a business or stronghold in the Plane of Molten Skies.

- Participating in an assassination plot against the Sultan of Efreet[1].

- Bringing the flask containing the spirit of Sulymon before the Sultan.

- Offering a tribute to the Sultan in exchange for some favor (i.e. access to the Great Repository or the Palace of Wonders).

- Pulling off a (impossible) heist of treasures found within the Sultan's palace.

1. The Bastion

The walls of the Bastion consist of huge walls 80 feet thick that stretch down hundreds of feet to the Basin and are composed of magically hardened obsidian that gleams black-orange in the light of the Curtain of Flame.

2. Bastion Towers

Great towers divide the bastion wall into segments. Each tower serves as a barracks for a company of the Sultan's elite guard who man the walls in rotating shifts. The **fire giants**, **burning dervish feyhda**[1], **efreeti** elite guards, and **basalt warhounds**[1] offer a strong deterrent to otherworldly powers who would seek to seize the crown jewel of the efreeti state. As if this were not enough, the Sultan has personally gained the employ of Kalaxincynder the Emperor Wyrm to serve as commandant of the Bastion. The wyrm makes his lair in the Burning Gardens and rules the walls of the palace through fear and intimidation.

As if the strong guard presence of the Bastion towers were not enough, the Sultan and the Grand Vizier have devised a fiendish irrigation system of volatile acids and liquid nitrogen that is pumped through twin nozzles on turrets affixed to the top of each tower. The pump nozzles are aimed via a specially designed pump and crank apparatus.

Sultan's Turrets

According to design, the sprayers have the same ranged attack bonus of the turret gunner and fire their twin plumes of death in a cone to a range of 200 feet. The turrets contain enough fluid to spray continuously for 2d4 rounds before their toxic fuel is depleted. Any creature caught in the spray must attempt a DC 20 Dexterity saving throw, taking 35 (10d6) acid and cold damage on a faulre and half as much on a success.

The turret system has never been tested, and there is some fear among the Sultan's advisors that the acids and freezing nitrogen could crack or dissolve the floor of the Basin, sinking the City of Brass into the Sea of Fire. This scenario is highly unlikely due to the magical reinforcements of the bowl. However, the toxic rain spraying forth from the great jets would likely kill many of the denizens of the Basin, a prospect that does not bother the Sultan in the least.

3. Gardens of Fire

The Gardens of Fire fill the space between the Hanging Gardens and the city wall. Twisted and gnarled branches and oddly gleaming trunks give a glimpse at the weird flora of the Plane of Fire. Palms, vines, and gingko trees formed from living brass, steel, iron, nickel, and bronze twist in a manner considered quite hellish to otherworldly travelers. The foliage of the trees appears to be made up completely from smokeless fire. The fruits of these trees glisten as uncut gemstones of opal, sapphire, ruby, emerald, and diamond. A greedy person could pick an emperor's ransom from the boughs of these burning trees, were it not for the rumblings and noxious vapors escaping from a large temple-like structure standing at the foot of the Bastion wall.

This structure of 50-foot-high gleaming obsidian pillars is the lair of Kalaxincynder the Emperor Wyrm (**ancient red dragon**). Kalaxincynder is a great wyrm red dragon. He commands the forces that guard the Bastion wall. Well treated and well paid by the Sultan of Efreet[1], Kalaxincynder seeks to slay any who enter his gardens uninvited.

4. The Hanging Gardens

Growing up over half the side of the Sultan's Palace are the massive Hanging Gardens. These gardens grow with every known plant, each allotted its own special box which in itself is permanently magicked with eternal sustenance and immunity to fire. Fountains of molten lead pour down the terraced sides of this portion of the palace, running as irrigation ditches would flow in a terrestrial world. Among the many plants in the Hanging Gardens are several that have grown to enormous size.

The Hanging Gardens are tended daily by squads of humanoid slaves brought with the plants from their home world for just such a purpose. Most are druids, but all wear the collar of a slave.

Hilak of Hillhigh (**senior druid**[1]) is the most powerful druid among the gardeners. He is allowed the use of enough of his own powers to heal plants and to elicit plant growth and no more.

If somehow freed of his brass collar by use of the Vizier's Key or some other means, Hilak offers to join his rescuers in any venture they seek to take, on the promise that he be allowed to return to Hillhigh.

The gardens are also patrolled by packs of 2d4 **fiendish dire lions**[1] that attack any that walk these gardens who are not efreeti, burning dervish, or a slave wearing a brass collar.

Random Encounters: The Hanging Gardens

Roll 1d12 for every 10 minutes spent in the Hanging Gardens.

1d12	Encounter
1	1 forester's bane[1]
2	1d4 gardeners (druid)
3	1 assassin vine[1]
4	2d4 fiendish dire lions[1]
5	1 greater hangman tree[1]
6	Hilak of Hillhigh (senior druid[1])
7	1d4 + 1 sleeping willows[1]
8	1d4 + 1 witch trees[1]
9–12	No encounter

The palace side of the garden is covered by a carefully carved arcade of arches stretching the length of the lower face of the palace. This area has several entrances to slaves' quarters for the gardeners, and the occasional beast handler who goes out to check up on the fiendish lions. Other hidden entrances offer access to the **Palace of Exquisite Gluttony**, the **Palace of Blissful Acquiescence**, and the **Court of Indefectible Attainment**. Slaves, guards, and escorted guests may pass through these hidden entrances easily. Intruders attempting to stealthily bypass the portals must bypass the many traps that are disarmed only when a password is given to the guardians beyond.

Palace Grounds

The palace grounds are generally bustling with activity as servants, slaves, dignitaries, and guards move to and fro during the "daytime" hours, with only guard patrols and prowling beasts during the artificial nighttime as created by the Nightfall Concordance.

A large "reflecting pool" of liquid fire occupies a portion of the center of the palace grounds. A walkway over the pool leads the long lines of petitioners to the Grand Palace. At the far end of the grounds stands the Grand Palace. Flanking it to the left and right are the **Palace of Concubines** and the **Palace of Exquisite Gluttony**. Farther down the walls of the palace compound stand the **Palace of Blissful Acquiescence** and its Espial Tower, the **Palace of Wonders**, the **Court of Martial Magnificence**, and the **Court of Indefectible Attainment**.

Roll 1d8 for every 10 minutes spent in the palace grounds.

1d12	Encounter
1	2d4 **efreeti amir**[1] courtiers
2–4	Slave cleaning gang: Roll 1d4 on the **Slave Cleaning Gang** table to find the exact encounter.
5–7	A guard patrol (see below)
8	Petitioners: This encounter is with just about any race or intelligent creature you wish. The creature or creatures are awaiting an audience with the Sultan or a noble.

1d4	Slave Cleaning Gang
1	2d4 **azer** brass polishers with winged boots and buckets of brass cleaner.
2	1d6 human (**commoners**) food bearers
3	1d4 half-elf dancers (**entertainer**[1])
4	1d6 dwarf (**commoners**) porters carrying an empty sedan chair

A typical guard patrol consists of the following:
4 **fire giant** guards
4 **efreeti** elite guards
2 **basalt warhounds**[1]
1 **efreeti malik**[1]

5. Palace of Exquisite Gluttony

The Palace of Exquisite Gluttony houses the various kitchens and dining halls of the Sultan's palace. Hundreds of chefs and thousands of cooking assistants and slaves, valets, butlers, servers, and food tasters make their residence in the upper towers of the Palace of Exquisite Gluttony. The Sultan hosts the heads of noble families and heads of states from throughout the planes that come seeking counsel or aid.

The grand dining hall of the Sultan of Efreet is located here within the Palace of Exquisite Gluttony. The grand dining hall is actually three great dining halls that seat more than 2,000 persons. Each of the dining halls is connected to two huge kitchens. Wall dividers on hidden rollers may be opened to create one huge dining hall able to seat up to 7,500 diners.

The kitchens are overseen by Master Chef Semeer Sigalla (**efreeti**). Semeer is a barrel-chested efreeti known for his skill at cooking anything and everything that is brought to his board. Broiled, baked, braised, basted, roasted, tartar, or glazed, there is nothing that Semeer has not mastered in preparing. This of course includes the proper cooking and preparation of such delicacies as the jellied pineal glands of aboleth, shambling mound tossed salad, garlic roasted oilshark, and even rare poached dragon eggs.

Semeer personally prepares and serves every meal that the Sultan eats, knowing full well that his own life is on the line should the Sultan be displeased with his culinary efforts.

The stores and larders of Semeer's kitchens are located in the bowels of the Palace of Exquisite Gluttony, and contain chambers stuffed to the roof with grains, wines, liquors, and rare and valuable seasonings such as saffron and finely ground paprika. An extensive slaughterhouse and huge bakery are located near the stores, yet the only livestock found on the hook is there merely long enough to age properly before serving. The reason for this are the fantastic magical gates located in the stores. These planar gates tie the stores of the palace to farm worlds conquered by the Sultan's forces to provide a limitless food supply for his numerous guardians and guests.

Farm World Gates

The farm worlds of the Sultan of Efreet are bi-directional, meaning that one can enter and exit these gates at will. In most cases, the so-called farm worlds are conquered planes that have inferior technology. Anytime the beings living on one of these worlds raise themselves up to a status where they could challenge the authority of their masters, their culture is annihilated and they are cast back into an age of darkness. For the most part, these worlds are peopled by primitive individuals who are commanded by the "flaming gods" to cast sacrifices into the "eternal flame" which is no more than a gate leading into one of the slave pens or slaughterhouses. The efreeti communicate their needs for specific "sacrifices" through totems possessed by these primitive peoples, often standing atop one invisibly, or by animating the totem via a *programmed illusion* spell-like ability.

In other cases, humanoid beings upon the planets have been completely annihilated, leaving only the beasts and monsters of the world alive, thus allowing the Sultan the opportunity to host great safaris from the comfort of his own dining palace without ever really leaving the City of Brass. These safaris are hugely popular among the younger nobles of the various houses and being invited on one is generally either a sign of favor or an invitation to an assassination at the hands of one of the Sultan's various henchmen.

6. Palace of Nine Hundred and Ninety-Nine Concubines

This tower, attached to the Grand Palace, is the prison of the Sultan's 999 consorts. The Sultan is renowned for his salacious appetites. Here in the Palace of Concubines, the Sultan keeps his extensive harem. Although there are not always 999 consorts within this palace, the title refers to an old law of the City of Brass that states that a Sultan may have as many as 999 concubines but upon taking number 1,000 he must select from their numbers a wife to serve as co-regent of the City of Brass and share in his power. Needless to say, when the numbers within the harem grow dangerously close to the one thousand mark, concubines whom the Sultan has grown tired of are ritually strangled or their minds erased by Tatho and given over to one who has earned the favor of the Sultan.

The concubines in the harem range from mortal princesses and queens from conquered worlds and nations, to demonesses, captured angelic or celestial servants, and unique other-planar beings. So too, many are the daughters of efreet, djinn, and marid nobles over whom the Sultan has gained control. Being a creature of exquisite tastes, the Sultan's harem is populated only by beings with a Charisma score of at least 18.

Roughly 50% of the concubines may be considered willing prisoners or even allies of the Sultan. Their lives are of relative luxury and opulence, with most of their needs provided for. They are tutored in courtly talk, fed the best food and wine, given the finest of perfumes and clothing, and trained in dance, poetry, singing and the playing of musical instruments and storytelling. Most concubines are proficient or have expertise in Performance, and many have several areas in which they excel. All concubines can dance, having learned these skills soon after being added to the ranks of the harem.

A typical harem chamber acts as residence to ten or twenty concubines. The concubines are frequently but not always arranged by race, profession, and how well they get along. Being an orderly ruler, the Sultan sees the advantage of not placing concubines together that for whatever reason do not get along. A pair of **efreeti** eunuchs always guards the harem chambers.

Encounters in the Palace of Concubines

You are free to create your own encounters and plot hooks within the Palace of Concubines or use the following examples to populate the various chambers of the palace with inhabitants using the information provided to develop further adventures.

Ar the Groundskeeper

Formerly a high-ranking official in the Burning Ones, the once ambitious Ar (**efreeti amir**[1]) was brought low by the Bayt al-Waswas, his mind wrecked by dark magic that twists within his brain even now. A gibbering wretch of an efreeti, he has been assigned the duties of groundskeeper to the Palace of Concubines, using what little mind he has left to tend its many gardens and pathways.

Princess Jheelish

Princess Jheelish, an unwilling concubine of the sultan of efreet, seeks an escape from her bondage and servitude. She uses her stunning beauty and great intelligence to attempt to persuade characters to help her, but is discreet about her aid to the party, possibly hiding them or finding disguises for them so they can hide from the eunuchs. If Princess Jheelish can be rescued from the Palace of Concubines and smuggled away from the Plane of Molten Skies, her father, an amir of a kingdom in the characters' home plane, offers the party a magical item of at least 50,000 gp and a satrapy in his kingdom as repayment for their good deed.

Princess Jheelish uses the statistics of a **noble**, save that her Challenge Rating is 1/2 (100 XP), she has Charisma of 18 (giving her Deception +6 and Persuasion +6) and Intelligence of 16, she has 27 (6d8) hit points, and neither wears armor nor wields a weapon.

The Celestials

These three beings (**astral devas** with clipped wings and no fly speed) have been stripped of most of their powers by the heavy enchantments upon their chamber and the brass collar locked about their throats. The Sultan is immensely cruel to these poor glorious beings that, without their powers, cannot even will themselves to die. If their collars can be removed via the *Demon Key*[2] of the Grand Vizier or via some other magic, they immediately regain their powers and summon other celestial allies to bring their righteous wrath down upon the City of Brass for the sins visited upon them.

Efreeti Noblewomen

These female **efreeti nobles**[1] come from families who swore their allegiance to the Sultan when he came to the City of Brass as its conqueror. Although they are now more or less hostages to maintain control over their families, they were originally given over as gifts to the Sultan by their own mothers and fathers. Living in the harem, these noblewomen know nothing of any discontent or malice toward the Sultan and his rule, and instead consider themselves to be a step away from true wives. All vie and plot against one another to produce an heir to his throne.

Apalla the Blistered One

This demon princess is much reduced in stature and power since the Sultan of Efreet[1] conquered her in battle during an incursion she led into the Plane of Molten Skies. She possesses an unnatural beauty, until one comes close enough to see that her skin is flaked with a cracked, itching rash and raised pustules. Brought to the City of Brass as a tribute, resplendent in cold iron chains, she was sent directly to the Palace of Concubines as an example to other demons who would attempt to wrench control of the ever-growing Plane of Molten Skies from the Sultan.

Apalla[1] does everything in her power to charm the characters into freeing her. Once freed and away from the clutches of the Sultan, she returns to the Abyss to attempt to reclaim her power. She may occasionally visit the characters and offer them bounteous rewards in exchange for their help solving certain terrestrial problems. She fights to the death if attacked.

Eunuch Patrol

A patrol of **efreeti** eunuchs encounters the characters. They ask for identification and attack if the characters fail to produce the required documents.

Sabina the Titaness

Sabina[1] claims an entire tower of the Palace of Concubines for herself. Gorgeous beyond compare, she is the daughter of a greater titan who lost herself to the Sultan when she made a foolish wish to be "pampered and fawned upon forever." She is served by 100 human concubines of the Sultan and may not be freed or move against the Sultan until he is destroyed and the *wish* undone.

Aria the Nymph

Captured in a hunting excursion to the Material Plane by two sons of Sheikh Fahd of Al-Bakr, Aria the **Nymph**[1] was presented to the Sultan as a gift on his ascent to power. While first she was recusant, several years and many interesting encounters have changed her position, making her more than satisfied with the perks afforded her as a royal concubine to the all-powerful Sultan.

Zaynah the Lady-in-Waiting

Posing as a servant of the matron of the Palace of Nine Hundred and Ninety-Nine Concubines, the Espial Tower placed Zaynah (**efreeti** with Charisma 18) to keep watch over the activities of the Sultan while in the company of his concubines. She takes great pride in her work, ensuring that any problems that arise are quickly dealt with. She is more than willing to use a heavy hand to perform her tasks.

Fadilah

A great hedonist and deeply interested in the arts of love, the Lady Fadilah (**erinyes** with Charisma 24) has made a name for herself as one of the most favored in the host of concubines in the palace. In both study and practice, she has found countless new ways of provoking pleasure in her lovers and for herself, creating a legend of herself in the process.

Aelish Macewan

Aelish (human **commoner** with Charisma 18) only recently arrived in the Palace of Concubines. She currently works as a servant and groom to the 999 concubines. She is terrified, but strong, and hides her fears well, doing her best to avoid the gaze of the Sultan while avoiding the lash of Zaynah or some of the other more wicked members of the retinue.

If rescued from the palace, Aelish may have any information the characters need as to the strength and disposition of the Sultan's current forces at your discretion. Freeing her should award the characters an additional 10,000 experience points for rescuing the last of the prisoners from Lornedain.

7. Court of Indefectible Attainment

This large athletics structure is considered by many to be the ultimate in physical fitness facilities in the universe. Staffed by dozens of trainers, it is said that anyone willing to train under their extreme physical conditioning regimen would gain permanent benefits. A character allowed to train here for one month gains +2 to Strength to a maximum of 20. A character that trains here for another month gains a +2 to Constitution to a maximum of 20.

The various chambers of this court are filled with steam and magma baths, weighty clay oil-filled amphorae for lifting exercises, and odd other-worldly machinery such as giant-sized compound bows from which hang weights, steam-operated treadmills, wrestling pits, and lead barbells. Mirrors line the walls of every chamber so that those who work out here may gaze longingly upon their prodigious physiques. Vanity rules the day within the Court of Indefectible Attainment, and none is more vain or prodigious than **Ban Oook**[1], the Sultan's chief trainer.

Ban Oook serves as physical trainer, bodyguard, and advisor to the Sultan of Efreet[1]. There is a 20% chance that he may be found with the Sultan even when the Sultan is not training his body. Grossly fat and a supremely cruel taskmaster, Ban Oook is somehow extremely nimble and light on his feet, not to mention immensely strong. Lodged in Ban Oook's brain is the head of a crossbow bolt he took while defending the Sultan from an assassination attempt. Ban Oook's mind still functions basically the same, as does his body, but he is prone to fits of "hearing voices," with the voices frequently telling him to kill. Several unsolved murders in the

Basin and Middle City can actually be attributed to Ban Oook's madness. Ban Oook trained at the Pagoda of Devils and has many skills of the Order of Devils.

8. Palace of Blissful Acquiescence

This beautifully decorated palace has no windows and no visible doors. Within its walls are some of the most-dastardly torture devices and experts in administering pain this side of Hell or the Abyss.

Chambers for water torture, freezing, burnings, and solitary confinement are designed to discover and exploit the weaknesses and fears of those unfortunates consigned to the horrors and misery of this place.

The Sultan is an experienced torturer in his own right, and frequently comes to the Palace of Blissful Acquiescence to observe **Tatho the Mindwrack**[1] do his work. Tatho's expertise in torture and reputation as a bravura showman are legendary. Tatho is known not only to flay the flesh of a victim, but also to get inside a victim's head and make him believe he is actually torturing himself for some perceived wrong.

Those who suffer at Tatho's hands must succeed on a DC 20 Wisdom saving throw for each minute of tortured endured. On a failed save, the victim is driven mad as if by the *confusion* spell for 1d8 days.

Fadi Al Naifa[1], the Sultan's chief executioner, also keeps her quarters in the Palace of Blissful Acquiescence. Al Naifa is an expert in at least a dozen forms of execution, and an entire wing of the palace is set with devices such as pump-operated guillotines, impaling stakes, hangman's gallows and the like. Although the Sultan prefers public executions to set an example to his enemies, private executions are quite frequent as it is sometimes in the Sultan's best interest to make people "disappear" rather than explain to the bureaucracy his reasons for ordering the death of one of their number. This is not because the Sultan has any real fear of anyone within the City of Brass, but more because the bureaucracy would make having to give such explanations tediously long and boring.

The Espial Tower

The lone spire rising from the Palace of Blissful Acquiescence is known as the Espial Tower and is home to the Sultan's secret police.

The operatives of the Sultan never cease in their efforts to accumulate and sieve information about the population of the City of Brass, constantly working to keep the efreeti under surveillance and dissidents under wraps. To this end, the Espial Tower has been built, a great spire dedicated exclusively to the retrieval of information, using conventional and unconventional means to do so.

The primary tools used by the clandestine forces of the Espial Tower are clairvoyants and seers, talented magicians that use their powers to observe from afar and to predict futures. Their role is pivotal to the success of the Sultan in monitoring the populace, but they cannot always be effective, as they can be thwarted by either powerful counter-magic or other forces. Where the clairvoyants fail, the Asfar Mayia takes over.

The Asfar Mayia are spread throughout the city, none of them acknowledged by the tower as officials of the Sultanate, and few of them are aware of their colleagues. Each employs different techniques to complete missions assigned to them, with some preferring magic, some preferring brawn, and some preferring their wits alone. All are specifically chosen for callousness in their character and ruthlessness in their work.

When necessary, the Asfar Mayia send captured suspects to the Espial Tower, well aware that they will likely never return. It is understood that unlike the Palace of Blissful Acquiescence, the Espial Tower prefers to use the quickest means possible for extracting information. Disinterested in pain for its own sake, the Espial Tower uses mind-destroying magic and specialty tools provided by the n'gathau, including a pocket dimension filled by purified pain, both of which are commonly used when subjects are not immediately forthcoming.

Despite their intrusive and appalling activities, it is rare that the Espial Tower attracts any real attention from the public or the powerful; the city's efreet are resigned to surveillance by a paranoid Sultan. Fear that they might draw the ire of the Asfar Mayia or the tower itself is cause enough to pretend that neither really exists.

9. The Sultan's Stables

The Sultan's Stables takes up an entire palace all to itself. The stables house many of the prize nightmares, jockeys, and charioteers that make up the Sultan's own racing team for the Circus of Pain. Stabled within the Sultan's stables are 100 **nightmares** and 10 **cauchemar**[1] studs, as well as 300 grooms (various races and types), a **roc**, a herd of 12 **gorgons**, a **gorgimera**[1], and a pen containing the prize of the Sultan's stables: 4 subdued **ancient gold dragons** captured by the Sultan and the Grand Vizier.

The dragon paddock is guarded by 10 **efreeti** elite guards. Each of the dragons is tied about the neck by a braided strand of nymph's hair that may be cut only by an adamantine *vorpal blade*. The dragons pull the Sultan's chariot whenever he deems to personally lead his armies into battle. If the dragons are loosed and offered a chance at freedom, they may join the characters in any battle against the Sultan and his forces, preferring death in freedom to life in bondage.

10. The Palace of Wonders

This beautifully crafted structure of an ancient design is obviously left over from the time of the old city and the Mudawwarah Al Jin. With the new structures built around the Grand Palace, this building's almost alien design is quite out of place here.

The Palace of Wonders is a museum of sorts, for it is filled with many fantastic treasures. Most of the items within the Palace of Wonders are the nonworking parts of fantastic relics that have been gathered by the Sultans of the past and present. These relics are put on display here in the Palace of Wonders so the Sultans may gloat over their treasures before important visitors. The Palace of Wonders is as heavily guarded as any other palace in the complex, having restricted entry via *plane shift*, *teleport*, and other spells of its sort. Vaults below the palace are said to hold many mundane magical items from the Sultan's personal collection, given to him over the years in tribute and as payment for assistance and information. The grand hall of the Palace of Wonders itself showcases some of the more valuable pieces of magical memorabilia, the majority of which are little more than high-priced trash without their missing parts.

The display cases of this hall are guarded by numerous deadly traps, 10 **iron golems**, and 10 **efreeti sorcerers**[1]. The chief of security for the Palace of Wonders is Taleeb al Zaair, a NE one-handed, halfling **master thief**[1] who was once caught sneaking through the Vault of Tears within the Grand Palace. Taleeb suffers no penalties for the lack of a hand. The Sultan — who admired the rogue's bravery, unabashed skill, and lack of fear — noted that Taleeb had taken nothing and was only "looking." Thus, the Sultan only took the rogue's left hand and offered him a position as a counter-thief in his retinue.

The curator of the Palace of Wonders is the ghost of an ancient sage named **Baatina**[1]. She died hundreds of years ago when a powerful curse unleashed by one of the newly procured items for the palace that transformed her into a ghost, but she as yet seems unaware of her own demise. Baatina knows much of the properties and abilities of the items under her care and goes about her duties as if there is nothing odd at all about her undead state.

Traps

To determine which trap guards a certain relic within the Palace of Wonders, roll 1d6 and consult the following list, or select any trap from elsewhere in the *City of Brass*. The DC to find the trap with an Intelligence (Investigation) check and the DC to disarm it with a Dexterity check with thieves' tools are listed after the trap name.

1. Whirling Vorpal Blades (DC 14/DC 17)

A whirling magical blade spins across the location, making an attack at +12 to hit against a single creature. On a hit, the blade does 8 (1d8 + 4) slashing damage. The blade scores a critical on a 19 or 20, and a target hit with a critical that has a head loses one of them. A creature is immune to losing a head if it has legendary actions, is immune to slashing damage, or is too large to have its head cut off by a longsword. In this case, the creature takes an extra 27 (6d8) slashing damage.

Palace of Wonders

2. Power Word Stun Trap (DC 17/DC 17)

Each creature with fewer than 150 hit points that can hear within 40 feet of the trap must succeed on a DC 17 Constitution saving throw or be stunned. A stunned creature can repeat the saving throw at the end of its turn, ending the effect on a success.

3. Forcecage Trap (DC 17/DC 17)

A *wall of force* springs up in a 15-foot-square centered on the trap and lasts for 10 minutes.

4. Energy Drain Trap (DC 16/DC 20)

Each creature within 30 feet of the trap must succeed on a DC 17 Constitution saving throw of receive 3 levels of exhaustion.

5. Monster Summoning Trap (DC 18/DC 12)

1d4 + 1 **bone** devils are summoned and attack any creatures within sight of the trap.

6. Teleport Trap (DC 15/DC 15)

Any creature within 5 feet of the trap must succeed on a DC 15 Wisdom saving throw or be teleported outside the city gates to the **Bab al Baquarra**, **Area 2**, **Upper City**.

The Relics

Several relics are on display in the grand hall of the Palace of Wonders. Several of these are actual working relics that are used in time of war and conquest by the masters of the City of Brass, such as the *armament of aggression*[2] and the *chariot of Narmer*[2]. The workings of other items are a mystery even to Baatina, the Sultan, and the Grand Vizier. Still other relics appear to be missing pieces instrumental to their operation or work strangely of their own volition, such as the *sarcophagus of Ankev*[2], *Tlaunehc Tnek, the Wyrm of Bones*[2], and the *juggernaut of Kil Kath Kesh*[2]. The *Scepter of Anubis*[2] may even be a fake. Other lesser items are also on display. Any items that you seek to include in your campaign may be found here, as well as vaults of numerous magical items ranging from minor to major that the Sultan received in tribute and often grants as gifts to those who please him.

11. Court of Martial Magnificence

This squat rectangular fortress is dedicated to all things martial and warlike. Training halls whose walls are lined with masterwork armor and weapons of every make and description, a complete library of military tactics and histories of martial conflict, offices, and classrooms dedicated to the training of officers in the Sultan's army occupy much of this structure. The Sultan's elite bodyguards and field generals hone their skills within this edifice to destruction. A central parade ground is used on military holidays where the Sultan's armies march before his royal box. At least 50 **efreeti** elite guards and lesser officers (**efreeti maliks**[1]) are always within this building, with 1d4 officers (**efreeti amirs**[1]) and 1d2 efreeti generals (**efreeti sardars**[1]). A fighter, ranger, or barbarian invited to train among the Sultan's army for at least a month gains proficiency in a choice of the following: History (related to military only), Land Vehicles, Seige Engines.

12. Grand Palace

This huge domed structure flanked by two immense watchtowers occupies the largest area of the palace compound. The Grand Palace serves as the Sultan's home and symbolic center of his empire. The Grand Palace itself has hundreds of rooms and substantial chambers beneath the palace that stretch nearly to the Basin itself. Many are treasuries and chambers for servants and sycophants alike. Other chambers are completely empty, meant to house a large family. As the Sultan is an unabashed bachelor, these chambers may remain vacant forever.

Ruler's Archway

The smoldering red-hot living brass portals of the Grand Palace stand 50 feet high and are girded by a great archway of gleaming semi-molten stone. The roiling hot archway is inscribed with the Sultan's seal, and as such any being entering the Grand Palace for the first time must succeed on a DC 20 Wisdom saving throw or take a –6 penalty on Charisma-based checks when dealing with the Great Sultan.

The Rotunda

Centrally located beneath a huge domed ceiling, the rotunda is awe-inspiring in its size and grandeur. A huge panoramic mural decorates the lower dome, showing epic events from the Sultan's conquest of the City of Brass and the overthrow of Sultan Ashur Ban and his Sultana, painted in vivid detail. The high dome rising above it is decorated in swirling flame patterns of burnished copper, red gold, jet, and rubies. Standing in the center of the rotunda is a life-sized sculpture of the Great Sultan standing in a pose of conquest atop a 10-foot-high pedestal, his face veiled as always. He has planted a glittering scimitar firmly through the heart of a defeated enemy. His free hand points south in a direct line with the Sultan's Boulevard and the Plane of Molten Skies. The statue appears to change colors, revealing all the colors of flame in its countenance, depending upon the angle by which it is viewed.

The acoustics of the rotunda and dome are so perfect that a whisper may be heard from any point within the chamber as if the speaker were standing right next to the listener. Despite this, or perhaps because of this, the chamber is generally fairly quiet as throngs of petitioners wait along this final leg of their journey.

Petitioners frequently fill the rotunda during daylight hours, and with palace guards and slaves passing to and fro during the evening.

Beyond the statue of the Great Sultan stand a pair of huge doors of living brass decorated in exquisite detail as a map of the City of Brass done in jeweled cloisonné. The doors are guarded by a pair of massive efreet (as **efreeti maliks**[1]) in black veils. A smaller **efreeti** valet takes the names of petitioners, passing this on to Abded Al-Dar (**efreeti**) the herald, who announces the petitioner in grand fashion upon entering the Hall of Sultans beyond.

Hall of Sultans and the Sultan's Court

A half-circle shaped chamber nearly half the size of the rotunda beyond contains the Hall of Sultans, where the sultans of the City of Brass have held court since days long forgotten. During daylight hours, courtiers, nobles, sycophants, petitioners, and elite bodyguards flood this throne room. Frequently the Sultan himself sits upon the Throne of Brass in judgment of cases brought before him as well as accepting the gifts, tributes, and tithes offered him by visiting dignitaries.

Upper galleries facing the Throne of Brass seat favored musicians from the Orchestra of Ashen Thunder. Lower galleries house accommodations for each of the represented noble houses that have at least one delegate among the throngs of visitors to the Grand Palace any time that the Sultan holds court. A wide polished marble tile stands before the throne where the queue of petitioners and foreign dignitaries await their personal audience.

Veiled members of the Smokeless Fire, a secretive sect of 30 **burning dervish feyhda**[1], quietly patrol the throngs standing before the Throne of Brass, ensuring that no one brings a device along to make an assassination attempt of their god-king. Additionally, 10 efreeti guards (**efreeti malik**[1]) patrol the grounds.

Advocates' Throne

At the foot of the dais leading up to the Throne of Brass stands the Advocates' Throne. The Advocates' Throne is carved from a single block of pure alabaster and has three seats, one facing the Plane of Molten Skies, a second facing the Plane of Air, and a third facing the Plane of Earth. The three advocates are appointed from the royal families by the Sultan himself and stand in judgment or accept tributes on behalf of the Sultan should he be away. The advocates are trusted advisors to the Sultan, and each is chosen for their loyalty and for their wisdom in meting out justice.

Accepted gifts and tribute brought before the Sultan of Efreet[1] or his advocates are immediately hauled off to the appropriate palace, chamber, treasury, or slave pen. Rejected gifts are consumed immediately in fire, and the gift giver is subjected to base humiliation and berated before the entire court. Frequently a punishment is immediately administered, which could be instant execution, beating, enslavement, or a doubling of the tribute demanded. In the case of a doubling of the tribute, the petitioner is forced to submit to the casting of a *geas* upon their person to ensure that they strive hard throughout the next year to bring greater wealth to the Sultan's Court.

Throne of Brass

Standing atop a dais of 42 stairs in the center of the back wall of the Hall of Kings is the stately Throne of Brass[2]. High backed with armrests in the shape of dragons, the entire throne is cast from living brass and encrusted with thousands of elemental gemstones harvested from the volcanic fissures of the Plane of Molten Skies. The Throne of Brass is a throne built for an immense figure, a regal chair for an awesome planar power.

Most petitioners granted an audience with the Sultan stand before the Advocates' Throne, where they either make their offering to the Sultan or plead their case. The advocates then repeat this plea to the Sultan who makes his judgment known to the entire court. Rarely is a petitioner granted leave to climb the dais and stand before the Sultan himself. In this event, the petitioner must succeed on a DC 25 Wisdom saving throw for every six of the 42 steps climbed (thus it takes seven saves to reach the top). On a failed save, the petitioner succumbs to the awe and power of the Throne of Brass, crawling the remaining way to the top (no more saves are required). Further, on a failed save, the petitioner is subjected to the effects of a *suggestion* spell by the Sultan.

While within 5 feet of the Throne of Brass, the Sultan (and only the Sultan) gains the continuous effects of the following spells: *true seeing, globe of invulnerability, detect thoughts, shield,* and *zone of truth*. The Sultan is exempted from the effects of the *zone of truth*. By uttering a command word, the Sultan may reveal any permanent *symbol* spell (all are etched on the throne and currently hidden by magic) or globe-shaped *wall of force* spell once per round as a standard action.

Sultan's Court

The Sultan's Court is filled with intrigue and drama that should not be lost on the characters should they ever find themselves here. Generally, the chamber is abuzz with small private conversations as knots of courtiers, ambassadors, and their minions whisper among themselves at the Sultan's various decrees. It should be emphasized that for all his power and all his evil, the Sultan of Efreet[1] is a creature of law and discipline, thus his judgment, although cruel and despotic, is ultimately fair and evenly meted out.

As the characters wander the court, feel free to roll for random encounters using the table below.

1d20	Encounter
1	1d4 courtiers: efreeti nobles[1]
2	1d6 graceful dancers (burning dervish minstrel[1])
3	1d4 musicians (burning dervish minstrel[1])
4	Pit fiend ambassador and attendees
5	Ka-Shareech[1], Air Lord of Pazuzu
6	Yasiel[1], Herald of the Lightbringer
7	Sss'ashisth (ha-naga[1]), the Asp of Set
8	Petitioners: your choice; any race, any intelligent creature or character
9	1d4 Sultan's elite guard (efreeti malik[1])
10–11	30 burning dervish feyhda[1]
12	Ibn Al-Hasheik (**mage**), the Sultan's biographer
13	Masud the Fool (**spy**)
14–15	Efreeti[1] Bey and 1d4 efreeti nobles[1]
16	Fatavdra, ambassador of the drow
17	Slaves/attendees (various races and classes; your choice)
18	Bal-Shabiri[1], lamia princess and attendees
19	Master Qarid[1]
20	Fidelizzas, *charmed* adult brass dragon

Important Figures

Several important figures are almost always encountered here. They are detailed below.

Abded Al-Dar (**efreeti**) is the herald of the sultan of efreet. A charismatic **efreeti** (with Charisma 18) with a clear booming voice announces arrivals to the Sultan's Court and enumerates the treasures they bring with them so that all within the court may here. Abded is not above taking a substantial bribe to move petitioners up the lists of those wishing to stand before the Sultan. Whether or not bribing Abded really gets one any further along is subject to private debate among the noble courtiers.

Ha'Fiez Al-Sultan (**efreeti amir al-umara**[1]) is the chief bodyguard of the Sultan. Massive in frame and quick of eye, Ha'Fiez examines the petitioners, courtiers, and ambassadors warily for any sign that they may seek to assassinate the master whom he serves most faithfully, even sleeping at the foot of the Sultan's bed. Ha'Fiez cut out his own tongue to show his loyalty to the Sultan, proof that he would never speak a foul word against his beloved master. Ha'Fiez keeps a magical whistle that acts like an *alarm* spell, summoning others of the Sultan's bodyguard to his position in the event an attempt should be made upon the master's life.

Rahib al Tabish Zafir[1], The Grand Vizier, stands to the right hand of the Sultan when he is at court, fulfilling his role as chief advisor to the Sultan. In rare instances when the Sultan is away and the Grand Vizier is present, he stands upon the 41st step of the dais hearing cases called up from the Advocates Throne, and offering judgment in the name of the Sultan. If the Grand Vizier is not present, he is in his tower.

The Sultan of the Efreet

The Great Sultan of the Efreet, the Burning One, the Charcoal Lord, the Brazen Commander, Lord of the Fire Kingdoms.

The Sultan's true name is Nomylus, Ibn al Kabith, Ibn al Nar, Ibn al Shaitan, Ibn al Fajarah, Ibn al Munkar, Ibn al Maakir, Ibn al Dajjal.

The Sultan's full title is Grand Sultan of the Efreet, His All-Renowned Grandmaster of Elemental Fire, All-Seeing All-Knowing Caliph of the City of Brass, Arch-Regent of the Throne of Brass, Genius of Geniuses, Shah of Molten Skies, Pillar of the Faith, Khan of the Fire Sea, Destroyer of Worlds, Defiler of Nations, Pillager of Planes, Subduer of Azer, Binder of Demons, Vanquisher of Salamander, Administrator of Pain, Author of Suffering, Creator of Anguish, Distributor of Wealth, Acquirer of Wisdom, Punisher of Infidels, Purveyor of Justice, Bringer of Law, Keeper of Seals, Patriarch of Culture, and Majarajah of Space and Time, the Granter of Wishes and Revealer of Secrets.

If present, the Sultan is seated on the Brass Throne. He gains all the bonuses detailed above while seated on or close to his throne. When not in the Hall of Sultans, or somewhere within the City or Plane of Molten Skies, surveying his territory or inspecting his fortresses, the Sultan may be found in his quarters, library, Al Batani's lab, his sanctum, or the Chamber of Bottles. Each of these areas is detailed below.

Possible Encounters within the Hall of Sultans

While wandering around, the characters may encounter any or all of the following. This section details some of the possible encounters rolled from the table above.

Pit Fiend Ambassador and Attendees

An ambassador of an infernal power and an enemy of Lucifer's minions seeks sanctions against the followers of Lucifer for harassment within the City of Brass. The envoy includes Malikor, a male **pit fiend**, 4 **bone devil** attendees, and 8 **bearded devil** attendees.

Ibn Al-Hasheik

Ibn Al-Hasheik (**mage**) is the biographer and chronicler of the life and times of the sultan of efreet. Al-Hasheik tirelessly scribes the conversations held before the Throne of Brass with his adamantine-tipped quill upon an *unending scroll*[2] of pure gold. Al-Hasheik has three *floating disks*, each set with another *unending scroll*[2], and an animated quill that follow him around the Hall of Sultans, recording everything he hears. Al-Hasheik is careful to remain an impartial observer to the deeds of the Sultan and visitors to his court, avoiding conflict, but staying as close as he possibly can to any important activities. The Sultan frequently consults one of the *unending scrolls* for his own personal memoirs.

Ka-Shareech, Air Lord of Pazuzu

Although a demon, Ka-Shareech[1] is a notable and frequent attendee to the Sultan's Court. As Pazuzu claims the skies and winds as his domain, he keeps ambassadors among the courts of all evil powers. The Sultan is in the midst of a bargain to gain the assistance of Pazuzu's vrocks in his ongoing campaigns in the Plane of Air against the djinn. Ka-Shareech is never without at least four normal **vrock** attendants.

Sss'ashisth, The Asp of Set

Sss'ashisth, the Asp of Set, is a **ha-naga**[1] whose fangs constantly drip venom. A permanent fixture at the Sultan's Court, Sss'ashisth's sibilant tones are easily recognizable through the dull clamor of the Hall of Sultans. The Sultan has been known to call upon the ancient serpent's wisdom as it pertains to matters of theological debate. The Asp of Set is attended by a pair of **emeritus chaplains**[1] of Set at all times.

Yasiel, Herald of the Lightbringer, Fallen Planetar

Yasiel[1], acts as a go-between to the Cathedral of the Lightbringer and the Sultan's Court. He is beautiful and horrible to behold, like many of his kind. Nine feet tall, completely hairless, and having an emerald cast to his skin, Yasiel has coal-black wings like a crow that brush the ground when he walks. Small black horns protrude from his perfectly smooth forehead. He is fully subservient to Engrin who tortures him constantly whenever he is at the cathedral.

Masud the Fool

Masud is a mad gnome (**spy** but Small with Intelligence 16, darkvision 60 feet, speed 25 feet, and ability to cast *minor illusion* at will with spell save of DC 13) who captured the Sultan's attention when he was brought in a string of slaves given as tribute. Masud somehow managed to reduce the entire chain of slaves to gales of laughter as they stood before the Sultan with his quips, puns, and jokes in the face of instant annihilation. Masud's insults directed at the Grand Vizier and other notable members of the court and noble families struck the Sultan as funny and he has served as the court fool ever since. Masud scurries through the Hall of Sultans picking pockets, hurling insults, and zapping people with a *wand of wonder* that the Sultan granted him. Mostly harmless, Masud has been killed and resurrected more times than anyone can count.

Fatavdra Ambassador of the Drow

Why the Queen of Spiders keeps an ambassador in the City of Brass is anyone's guess. Assumptions may be made that she likes to keep her webs in everything, and the City of Brass is a place where everything and anything may be found. Her faithful high priestess Fatavdra (**archpriest**[1]) has been sent here on special assignment to retrieve a book from the Great Repository for her mistress. Upon arriving, Fatavdra and her entourage gifted the Sultan with 80,000 gp worth of precious stones mined from the Underdark, 80,000 gp worth of deadly poisons brewed from the venom of spiders and noxious fungi, and 80 slaves, trained by her own hand in the art of submissive compliance to command. Her gifts were well received by the Sultan, but her request has long gone unanswered. Mostly this is because the Sultan does not wish to reveal the true secret of the cursed Great Repository to foreigners and has tried to blow her off by granting her sumptuous quarters, lavish forays into the Palace of Blissful Acquiescence, and hosting wondrous feasts in her honor. Although the fickle high priestess is flattered by the Sultan's hospitality, time grows short and the Queen of Spiders grows impatient for her prize. Fatavdra may be in the market for powerful yet foolish adventurers to plunder the Great Repository on her behalf. Fatavdra is always in the company of a well-armed squad of drow **eldritch archers**[1] and **preachers**[1] and Trilia, a **succubus**.

Bal-Shabiri, Lamia Princess

Bal-Shabiri[1] is a lamia princess from a far-off plane where her mother rules as queen, keeping an entire desert planet in servitude. Bal-Shabiri was exiled after attempting a coup against her mother and has found a new home in the court of the sultan of efreet. Here she seeks the aid of the Sultan in raising an army to defeat her mother, offering the Sultan use of her home world as a staging area for further conquests of her plane.

Bal-Shabiri may be interested in hiring characters as mercenaries, or in outright charming them into serving her will, sending them through the Dome of Gates to assassinate her mother.

Bal-Shabiri is guarded by a trio of noble knights who lost their sanity in a failed attempt to destroy her. Eriel, Jaylan, and Dharis (NE human **fallen paladins**[1]) each guard her with his life, and all are now fallen paladins who have embraced their dark path.

Fidelizzas, the Charmed Adult Brass Dragon

Jokingly referred to by the court of the Sultan as "Fido," Fidelizzas (**adult brass dragon**) once served the Sultana, but was captured during the Sultan's conquest and charmed into obedience. No longer possessing a mind of his own, Fidelizzas fetches things for the Sultan, or does tricks to amuse the court attendees.

Should the charm on Fidelizzas ever be broken, he does everything in his power to slay the Sultan, fighting to the death.

Role-Play in the Hall of Sultans

As can be well imagined, a frontal assault against the Sultan of Efreet[1] in his throne room is tantamount to suicide. That being said, a visit to gain audience with the Sultan of Efreet[1] is likely the best option for lower-level characters to ever see or meet the Sultan of Efreet[1]. As an old efreeti tradition, any visitor to the City of Brass who brings gifts and tribute to the Sultan may seek audience with him, or at the very least have their petition heard before the Advocates' Throne. Should the characters bring great tribute for the Sultan, he may be more apt to rule in their favor, grant their request, or send them on a special mission on his behalf. Threatening the Sultan in his court generally causes the Sultan and the court to erupt in laughter, right before the characters erupt in flames.

If the characters decide to attack or do battle with the Sultan, refer to the area at the end of this chapter titled "Doing Battle with the Sultan."

Listed below are a few simple guidelines for making petitions to the Sultan and likely outcomes. Note that Charisma may turn the Sultan's favor, as can displays of skill.

Characters Come Before the Sultan Without a Tribute

Characters offering no tribute to the Sultan are awarded an audience with him only if they are invited due to possession of a rod of embassy or gained his attention through other means. Possible ways of gaining the Sultan's attention are: winning a chariot race, doing some great service for a noble house, stopping a calamity in the city, or bringing in the head or heads of one of the Sultan's enemies.

Characters Come Before the Sultan and Offer Their Services

The characters need not be lawful evil to offer their services to the Sultan of Efreet[1], or even be invited or commanded to gain an audience with him. However, it is unlikely that characters of any good alignment may receive anything better than an unfriendly or indifferent reaction from him.

Other Locations within the Great Palace

Detailed here are some of the more notable chambers or areas that can be found within the palace.

Vault of Tears

The adamantine door to this chamber is locked and protected by a *greater arcane lock*[4] spell cast with a 9th level spell slot. After the spell is dismissed, the lock still requires a successful DC 28 Dexterity check with thieves' tools to open. Further, tampering with the door triggers a trap within the chamber that coats the entire floor with dragon bile. Discovering the trigger requires a successful DC 23 Intelligence (Investigation) check. Disarming it requires a successful DC 25 Dexterity check with thieves' tools, and failing the check by 5 or more triggers the trap. If the trap is triggered, each creature in room must succeed on a DC 23 Constitution saving throw or take 132 (24d10) acid damage. Four rounds after the room is entered, unless a hidden bypass switch on the wall is depressed, an invisible globe in the center of the room unleashes multiple blasts of lightning. This is a chain lightning trap. Any creature within 10 feet of the globe is struck by lightning. In addition, any creature within 10 feet of a creature struck by lightning is struck, up to a possible range of 120 feet and 20 strikes. A creature can be struck multiple times by this trap. Any creature struck by lightning must attempt a DC 16 Dexterity saving throw. Those failing the saving throw take 49 (14d6) lightning damage, while those succeeding take half this amount.

A 10-foot-high mound of glittering diamonds (*dragons' tears*[2]) occupies the Vault of Tears, each one a tear shed from one of the noble gold dragons imprisoned in the Sultan's Stables when their eggs were destroyed and they were chained to draw the *chariot of Narmer*[2]. So many tears were shed that they once filled seven chambers of the Sultan's Palace. The Sultan foolishly gambled nearly all of them away at the Circus of Pain or paid them out to his mercenaries before their unique abilities were discovered.

The diamonds here total about 2 million gp.

Gallery of Kings

This awe-inspiring maze of brilliantly lit chambers has a magically controlled climate to protect the magnificent works of art gathered from thousands of planes. Perhaps a bit cool to the liking of the average efreeti, it is said that the Sultan frequents the Gallery of Kings to gloat over the portraits of Sultan Ashur Ban, his defeated Sultana, and their family. The value of the original paintings, sculptures, and assemblages held within the Gallery of Kings is incalculable, as each piece may be considered priceless in its own right. Wealthy indeed would be the rogue who could lift but one painting from these guarded walls. Many of the works of art are heavily trapped, and the collection has 10 **gynosphinxes** acting as curators and guards.

The Hall of Sound

This chamber of the Palace of the Sultan seats more than 5,000 guests. A bowl-shaped design decorated in brilliant scarlet and blue green hues, the Hall of Sound serves primarily as a practice and performance space for the Orchestra of Ashen Thunder, a gathering of nearly 200 fantastic musicians from throughout the planes. A treasure in its own right, the symphony's musical arrangements have been known to illicit tears from even the most hardened of arch-devils who have graced its plush seats. Every conceivable instrument, from the most arcane and audacious santur or rebab to the most common gaytah and daff, is represented by the symphony. Opera stars and vocalists also enjoy tremendous prestige for being invited to perform within the Hall of Sound. Sadly for many of these, they are asked to join the Orchestra of Ashen Thunder for life. Although great riches and praise are heaped upon those who take the Sultan's deal, such a life can prove to be a prison sentence to those who live a life of wanderlust.

Great attention was paid to the acoustics of the chamber during its construction, and even the lowliest bard gains a +10 bonus on any Performance skill check made within these halls.

Performers in the Orchestra of Ashen Thunder are generally bards of various races and backgrounds. The conductor of the orchestra is Maestro Farabi (human **master bard**[1] with a *ring of immunity*[2] [fire]). Farabi is an enigmatic human given high favor among the court of the Sultan, and much leniency in his comings and goings. His lifetime has been extended far beyond that of a normal mortal man due to *wishes* and magical elixirs bestowed on him by the Sultan and other admirers of the court.

The Laboratory of Al-Jabeer

Located in one of the many dungeons beneath the palace compound is this series of chambers and laboratories where the Sultan's alchemists craft their elixirs and potions, converting lead to other metals that fill the coffers of the Sultan's allies. Jars, beakers, and tubes of strange powders, viscous liquids, and raw materials fill this chamber from floor to ceiling. The contents of these jars should be selected at random, and could be any potion, oil, elixir, alchemical substance, or poisonous substance. To say

that there is an unlimited supply of such substances offers the challenge to characters with *bags of holding* and *portable holes*. Suffice it to say there is at least 1 million gp worth of alchemical supplies, equipment, potions, poisons, and the like.

No fewer than a dozen **efreeti alchemists**[1] are within the laboratory at any one time, headed by **Al-Jabeer**[1], chief alchemist for the current Sultan (and at least three past Sultans as well). Al-Jabeer does not take sides in politics, and merely serves whichever Sultan reigns without question, as his laboratory is his one true treasure, and to be denied the use of it would drive him mad.

Hostage Tower

This tower serves as prison to Ashazarade (**hawanari**[1]), the only surviving daughter of the Sultana Cirrishade and Sultan Ashur Ban. She is the only known surviving heir to the Throne of Brass. The entrance to her tower is guarded by 12 **brass men**[1], and only the Sultan of Efreet[1] has the key that unlocks her tower. Ashazarade is surprisingly well treated, yet extremely lonely. She was a young girl when her parents were defeated, and years of lies told her by the Sultan have led her to call him "uncle." She knows little of life beyond her own sumptuous tower and bides her time-consuming fairy tales and stories that have filled her head with childish notions.

Ashazarade would never do anything to displease her "uncle" who has been so kind to her and brings her books of stories and fairy tales. However, should a charismatic hero find themselves in her lonely tower, she may "pretend" that they are there to rescue her, until such time as the displeasure of the Sultan in this "game" is discovered, of course.

The Sultan intends to slay Ashazarade during a great planar conjunction, sacrificing her to his co-conspirators as he in turn devours the spirit of Sulymon. In this fashion, he means to cast down Anumon and throw open the planar gates, placing himself among the thrones of the true greater powers of the universe.

Sultan's Quarters

The Sultan's personal chambers are separated from the vast majority of the palace. This area of the palace is where the Sultan takes his rest from the pleading throngs who seek his wisdom and judgment on a daily basis. Extensive indoor gardens similar to the garden of fire, lava spas, and fountains of fire occupy many of the chambers. From this chamber the Sultan has access to **Al-Batani's Wondrous Machine**, the **Sultan's Library**, and secret passages to the **Palace of Concubines** and the dungeons beneath the **Palace of Blissful Acquiescence**. These passages may only be opened with a magical key possessed by the Sultan himself, and are undetectable by any means, including the use of a *true seeing* spell.

Objects of art, both beautiful and magical, valued in the millions of gold pieces, line the walls and stand atop ornate pedestals of the Sultan's quarters. Enough treasure to be sure to make an emperor's ransom one hundred times over. Five **efreeti** elite guards and 3 **fiendish dire lions**[1] patrol the halls and are never more than 1d4 rounds away from the Sultan no matter where he may be found.

Sultan's Library

A magically sealed door that opens only at the handprint of the sultan of efreet reveals the hidden receptacle of lore known as the Sultan's Library.

Although nothing in comparison to the Great Repository or even the Repository Annex, the Sultan possesses an extensive collection of tomes, scrolls, and ancient tablets dating back to the birth of creation. Many of these tomes are given over to dark rites and astronomical phenomena that the Sultan uses in conjunction with Al-Batani's Wondrous Machine to plot his rise as a major power of the cosmos.

Spiraling from floor to ceiling with a golden staircase following the length of the collection, the Sultan has amassed this private collection of lore consisting of several hundred copies of materials found in the Repository Annex and the Great Repository. Other works are musings known only to himself, as well as his personal spellbooks, diaries, and journals. The spellbooks contain all arcane spells found in of levels 1st through 9th.

The pages of the Sultan's private journals are written in Ignan, and each page is covered with an *illusory script* spell. Should the *illusory script* be broken, they reveal the Sultan's plans to sacrifice the royal hostage on the night of the great alignment in the presence of Set and Lucifer, if only he can find the damnable flask containing the spirit of Sulymon, his nemesis and light half.

Al-Batani's Wondrous Machine

This high-domed chamber atop one of the many spires rising from the palace contains the mechanisms and workings of Al-Batani's Wondrous Machine. The Machine emits an electrical buzz and fills the air with the scent of ozone. Made up of many huge and many more fine armatures of gold, brass, copper, mithral, adamantine, polished darkwood, and multi-colored crystalline globes, the Machine is constantly spinning and whirling. The Machine is a precise model of the planes of existence and known universes set to a one-billionth scale. The machinery is very delicate and, for that reason, only the Sultan and Grand Vizier may access the machine.

Created in ages past by the great sage Al-Batani, the Machine is a sentient and alert model of the known universes and planes of existence. Al-Batani was always concerned with the nature and workings of the universe as it evolved, and how it was in turn changed by the introduction of time, magic, and the drives and ambitions of those who dwelt within.

To this end, Al-Batani began the construction of his model, giving it awareness and consciousness to change and rebuild itself as the universe grew and changed. The Machine was to be Al-Batani's gift to his Sultan, and he spared no expense in its construction. Upon operation, the Machine was to give an extensive report of any area of the cosmos that the viewer of the Machine desired, up to the number of rabbit holes in a field or the

Al-Batani the Machine

Al-Batani is a giant machine that rests in the center of a domed chamber high atop a spire in the City of Brass. It emits an electrical buzz and fills the air with the scent of ozone. Comprising many huge and many more fine armatures of gold, brass, copper, mithral, adamantine, polished darkwood, and multi-colored crystalline globes, this machine is constantly spinning and whirring. It is a precise model of the planes of existence and known universes set to a one billionth scale. It holds the soul and consciousness of its original creator, which allows it to interact with creatures verbally. Al-Batani knows all languages but it can't read the minds of creatures. Its purposes are to document living history and to use this information to serve the Grand Sultan. Any creatures that wish to learn from Al-Batani must convince it to part with its knowledge. Failure to do so activates Al-Batani's security measures.

A non-efreeti creature attempting to gain information from Al-Batani must succeed on a DC 20 Charisma (Deception or Persuasion) check. The trap triggers on a failed check. On a successful check, the creature can ask Al-Batani up to four questions about things currently occurring in the multiverse or things that have occurred in the past. The machine has no knowledge of future events. After asking four questions, a creature must succeed on another Charisma check to continue asking questions. The answers Al-Batani gives are accurate, though vague and sometimes even cryptic answers are common. Efreeti can operate the machine but are limited to only four questions each week. The Grand Sultan has advantage on Charisma checks against the machine and is not limited in the number of questions it can ask.

Al-Batani remembers those who have wronged it. A creature has disadvantage on its Charisma check if it triggered the trap within the past 24 hours.

This trap activates when a non-efreeti fails a Charisma check against the machine. It also triggers if a creature attempts to move, dismantle, damage, or attack the machine or if an efreeti attempts to ask more than four questions in one week. The presence of the Grand Sultan prevents the trap from triggering or stops the trap immediately if it has already triggered.

When activated, Al-Batani fills the expansive chamber with its whirring armatures and arcing adamantine fixtures. It makes and unmakes arms along these fixtures. Its Large, heated core is located in the center of the room.

Heated Core. After the first round, any creature that ends its turn within 15 feet of the core takes 22 (4d10) fire damage and must succeed on a DC 20 Constitution saving throw or have disadvantage on its next saving throw against the machine's disintegrating beam. Each round, the core's heat expands 5 feet further outward, to a maximum of affecting all creatures within 40 feet of the core.

Actions

Locked Doors (Initiative Count 20). The doors to the room slam shut and magically lock. This effect activates the first time the trap is triggered and doesn't activate again.

Arm (Initiative Count 20). Mechanical arms attack creatures within 40 feet of the machine's core. Each arm makes one attack against a random creature in range with a +8 bonus to the attack roll and dealing 22 (4d10) bludgeoning damage on a hit. The machine has two arms the first time the trap is triggered. Each round, the machine creates one additional arm to attack intruders.

Disintegrating Beam (Initiative Count 10). The machine's core emits a bluish beam of energy in a 120-foot line that is 10 feet wide. Each creature in that area must make a DC 20 Dexterity saving throw, taking 44 (8d10) force damage on a failed save, or half as much damage on a successful one. The damage from the disintegrating beam increases by 11 (2d10) each round after it activates, to a maximum of 99 (18d10). A creature killed by this ray can only be restored to life with *true resurrection* or a *wish*.

The machine is immune to its own disintegrating beam.

Foiling the Trap.

There are a variety of ways to temporarily disable the machine or its active parts.

Arms. Creatures can attack the arms to destroy them or disable their components, making them useless.

Attack. A creature within 40 feet of the machine's core can ready an attack to strike at one of the arms. The arm has advantage on its attack against the creature. After the arm attacks, the creature can attack. The arm has AC 19 and 25 hit points. Destroying the arm reduces the number of arms available for the trap to use.

DC 20 Dexterity check using thieves' tools. A creature within 40 feet of the machine's core can temporarily disable the arm, preventing the machine from using it for 1 round.

Disintegrating Beam. A successful DC 20 Intelligence (Arcana) check disables the disintegrating beam for 1 round. The creature must be within 15 feet of the core to attempt the check, and only one creature can attempt this check each round.

Escape the Room. Leaving the room is the easiest and fastest way to avoid the trap, however, the doors are locked with a hidden mechanism. A successful DC 20 Intelligence (Investigation) check finds the hidden lock. A successful DC 20 Dexterity check using thieves' tool is then required to pick the lock. Finally, a successful DC 20 Strength (Athletics) check is required to force the doors open. Each check requires an action. If the trap has no targets within 40 feet of its core for 1 minute, it deactivates.

Subdue the Core. The trap can be disabled with three successful castings of *dispel magic* (DC 19) targeting the core. Doing so subdues the consciousness inhabiting the machine for the next 24 hours. During this time, the trap can't be triggered, and Al-Batani can't be activated to answer questions.

The Sultan Arrives. If the Grand Sultan of the City of Brass ends its turn within 60 feet of Al-Batani, the trap immediately deactivates, reabsorbs the parts that made up its arms, and cools its core.

age of a king who ruled a land. Such a machine, Al-Batani promised, could give up-to-the-second data on the Sultan's foes and ensure the prosperity of his rule.

Sadly, the Machine failed to impress the Sultan, who although impressed with the whirling dials and minute details, could never get the Machine to answer the specific questions he posed. Perhaps a glitch in Al-Batani's calculations caused the machine to come to a screeching halt whenever the Sultan addressed it; perhaps the personality of the Machine simply clashed with that of the Sultan, causing it to ignore his questions. Whatever the reason, the Sultan gave Al-Batani one day to make the Machine work as he had been promised or find his head separated from his shoulders. Al-Batani, frustrated and defamed, finally did the only thing that a sage could do — he became one with the Machine whose construction had dominated such a great portion of his life, placing his own consciousness, spirit, and soul into the device. Servant of his Sultan and every Sultan thereafter, Al-Batani the Machine (see Sidebar) sees all and knows all, recording and documenting the tragedies and triumphs of living history until the end of time.

Chamber of Bottles

A dazzling maze of hallways and dead-ends eventually leads to an illusionary wall. Behind the illusionary wall is a completely blank wall that is actually a locked, trapped secret door made of solid, perfectly fitted, igneous rock. The illusion may be detected only through trial and error (and a successful DC 24 Intelligence (Investigation) check) or judicious use of a *detect magic* spell. The secret door is trapped with a *wail of the banshee* trap. Noting this trap requires a successful DC 22 Intelligence (Investigation) check. If triggered, the trap releases a keening wail. The wail does 300 psychic damage total to up to 20 targets that can hear it within 40 feet. Starting with the closest creature, each creature within the area that can hear must succeed on a DC 22 Constitution saving throw or take the lesser of their current hit points or the amount of damage remaining to the effect (starting with 300 for the first affected creature). Unlocking the secret door requires a successful DC 25 Dexterity check with thieves' tools, or it can be smashed with a successful DC 30 Strength check.

Triggering the trap also summons 1d4 + 2 **efreeti** elite guards to the Chamber of Bottles every 1d6 + 2 rounds.

The chamber beyond is filled with lead-stopped brass bottles, crystal urns, iron flasks, and golden jars.

If unstopped, a bottle functions like an *iron flask*. Use the table on the following page to determine the contents of each bottle.

The Sultan's Sanctum

This chamber is where the Sultan meditates and takes what little rest he requires. The Sultan's Sanctum is also the hiding place of the *Codex of Infinite Planes*[2]. The door to the chamber is locked with a *greater arcane lock*[4] spell cast with a 9th level spell slot, a superior lock, and is trapped with a *cone of cold* trap. The trap can be detected with a successful DC 20 Intelligence (Investigation) check. If triggered, all creatures within a 60-foot cone must make a DC 20 Constitution saving throw. A creature that fails takes 54 (12d8) cold damage while a creature that succeeds takes half this amount. The trap can be temporarily dispelled with *dispel magic* cast against a 9th level spell slot. The door can be unclocked after the magical lock is removed with a successful DC 25 Dexterity check with thieves' tools or a DC 30 Strength check.

The door opens into a chamber whose entire center is shrouded in a pillar of fire. A small landing upon which stands an altar leads to the pillar of fire. The Vortex of Fire is a direct conduit to the very center of the Eye of Fire in the Elemental Plane of Fire. Inscribed upon the floor of the landing are the following words and symbols in Ignan, Aquan, Terran, and Auran:

Through the Majesty of Wind and the Purity of Fire, Through the Placidity of Water and the Might of Earth, May each of the Elders of Creation Reveal its Worth, From each must be given its right and due. All things of life are made from these, gather all before and make the path for thee. Beyond the path unseen lies the beast of nightmare gleaned, upon its back there fixed and bound, the Codex of Infinite Planes is thus found.

In order to reveal the path that leads to the *Codex* and its guardian, one must summon and then sacrifice an elder elemental of air, fire, water and earth in that exact order. Once summoned and then slain, a crystalline pathway appears that leads through the Vortex of Flames to an island whose surface is a mass of glittering jewels. Lying in the center of the island is a gigantic beast, horrific and beautiful in appearance. Bolted to the back of the beast with adamantine screws is a huge book. The book is easily the size of the thatched roof of a small cottage. Its pages are made of glittering gold leaf. The covers appear to be sewn together over a binding of cold-wrought iron, stitched from the skins of dragons and other strange creatures.

If the puzzle seems too tough for the characters, remind them that divine answers to questions may be gleaned through use of *commune* and other such spells.

The *Codex* is bolted and chained to the back of a Gargantuan **thessaltitan**[1], a debased creature with seven heads atop long snake-like necks and

d100	Contents
01–50	Empty
51–54	Air elemental
55–58	Marid
59–62	Earth elemental
63–66	Xorn
67–70	Fire elemental
71–74	Salamander
75–78	Water elemental
79–82	Efreeti
83–86	Efreeti amir[1]
87	Demon (vrock)
88	Demon (hezrou)
89	Demon (glabrezu)
90	Demon (succubus)
91	Devil (bone)
92	Devil (bearded)
93	Devil (erinyes)
94	Devil (horned)
95	Celestial (avoral [1])
96–97	Djinni
98	Rakshasa
99	Balor or pit fiend (50% chance for either)
100	Special: See below

If a "Special" result is indicated on the Chamber of Bottles Table above, roll 1d6 and consult the table below.

1d6	Contents
1	**Prepared Bottle:** Prepared bottles are ready to trigger once unstopped. The opener must succeed on a DC 17 Wisdom saving throw or be forced into the bottle.

1d6	Contents
2	**Haakan the Marid Prince:** Haakan was a marid[1] prince who allied himself with the Sultana Cirrishade. Unable to destroy him fully, the Usurper imprisoned Haakan in this bottle, where he has sat in torment for centuries. He grants the characters who free him a single *wish* and offers to serve them for one year and one day. If Haakan is slain in the service of the characters, they automatically receive an unfriendly reaction to any other marid they meet.
3	**Ponjo Tombo:** The twin of the evil **demon ape**[1] Bonjo Tombo, this beast was brought to the Sultan of Efreet[1] as a gift. Soon growing uncontrollable, Ponjo was immersed in magic-laced water and placed within this bottle. Because of the magic that contaminated his body when he shrunk, he grows one size category per round once released from the bottle. He attacks upon attaining Medium size.
4	**The Black Satin:** The (CN human) **master thief**[1] known only as "Black Satin" managed to successfully pierce the traps and travails of the Palace of the Great Sultan nearly 100 years ago, only to succumb to a prepared bottle in the Chamber of Bottles. She thanks the characters profusely for freeing her from her bottled prison and offers to join the characters in plundering the remainder of the palace. She of course attempts to rob the characters blind at the earliest opportunity and return to her home world where things are no doubt much different than they were when she was guild-mistress.
5	**The Cryohydra:** Inside this bottle is a massive **elder cryohydra**[1] that the Sultan intends to give away to one of his many enemies as a "gift" of good faith.
6	**Bottle o' Spiders:** This bottle is filled with hundreds of **red-banded line spiders**. The being opening the bottle is literally buried in spiders

Codex of Infinite Planes

Wondrous item, legendary

The *Codex of Infinite Planes* is an ancient text said to have been penned by the lords of creation at the beginning of time and recounts histories lost to the minds of mortals.

The *Codex* is massive in size and scope, and no mortal can ever hope to read it in its entirety. No matter how many pages are turned, another always remains. Anyone opening the *Codex* for the first time must make a DC 20 Constitution saving throw, being utterly annihilated on a failure and taking 35 (10d6) force damage on a sucess. Those who survive can peruse its pages and learn its powers, though not without risk. Each day spent studying the *Codex* allows the reader to make a DC 23 Intelligence (Arcana) check to learn one of its powers (choose the power learned randomly; lower the DC by 1 per additional day spent reading until a power is learned). However, each day of study also forces the reader to make a Wisdom saving throw with a DC of 20 + 1 per day of study to avoid being driven insane (as the *confusion* spell, but permanent).

The powers of the Codex of the Infinite Planes are as follows: *astral projection*, *banishment*, *elemental swarm*[4], *gate*, *planar ally*, *planar binding*, and *plane shift*. Each is usable at will by the owner of the Codex (assuming that he or she has learned how to access the power). The Codex of the Infinite Planes has spell save DCs of 25 and a spell attack bonus of +17. Activating any power requires both a Concentration check and a DC 20 Intelligence (Arcana) check. Any failure on either check indicates a catastrophe befalls the user (roll on the table below for the effect). A character can incur only one catastrophe per power use, even if he or she fails both checks.

A character who reads from the *Codex* for more than 99 weeks is automatically consumed by the power of the book and dies instantly. Such a character cannot be raised or returned to life, even by a *wish*; only a god's magic can restore such a creature to life.

1d4	Catastrophe
1	**Natural Fury:** An *earthquake* spell centered on the reader strikes every round for 1 minute, and an intensified *storm of vengeance* spell is centered and targeted on the reader.
2	**Fiendish Vengeance:** A *gate* opens and 1d3 + 1 balor demons, pit fiends, or similar evil outsiders immediately step through and attempt to destroy the owner of the Codex.
3	**Ultimate Imprisonment:** Reader's soul is captured in a random gem somewhere on the plane while his or her body is entombed beneath the earth (as *imprisonment*).
4	**Death:** The reader is subject to a *disintegration* spell. This repeats every round for 10 rounds or until the reader is dead

four pairs of arms. The beast is hugely obese, having faces in the palms of its four hands that devour the gemstones of the island. The creature is chained in the center of the island. Its chain gives it just enough slack to reach any point on the island without falling into the Vortex of Fire. Only one who subdues the beast may command it, and in turn gain access to the *Codex of Infinite Planes*[2].

Should the characters retrieve the *Codex of Infinite Planes*[2], the Sultan appears instantly (providing he hasn't been slain), bringing with him all of the wrath and fury of his domain.

Doing Battle with the Sultan of Efreet

To battle the Sultan of Efreet[1] is a challenge far beyond that of most normal characters. To even have a chance of defeating him, it is likely that the characters have gathered many of the artifacts within the City of Brass and the Plane of Molten Skies. Many of these artifacts may weaken the Sultan. Completing tasks such as the destruction of the Great Ziggurat, for example, would deny the Sultan access to his divine spells. Uncovering the flask containing the spirit of Sulymon[1] may offer great defensive aid to the characters versus some of the Sultan's more devastating powers. Tier 3 and 4 characters using many of the relics plundered from the palaces and fortresses of the City of Brass may very well be able to put up a good fight. Evil allies of the Sultan may be turned against him should he show weakness in battle. Exactly how encounters with the Sultan are played out ultimately depends on how you choose to run your campaign. Play up the intensity of any encounter with the Sultan. Understand that the characters are dealing with a planar power of great might and cunning.

Should the *flask of Sulymon*[2] be opened in the presence of the Sultan, the Sultan stops all actions and concentrates his efforts on subduing Sulymon[1] in order to capture him and then sacrifice him in a ritual designed to make himself a greater god. Because the Sultan wants to keep his other half alive, he avoids area-effect spells that would slay Sulymon.

Sulymon[1] for his part pulls no punches. He challenges his dark half in the name of Anumon and attempts to use his most withering spells and abilities to as great and devastating effect as his venerable body can muster.

If Sulymon is slain, the Sultan flies into a rage and attempts to kill everything in sight, as his long-laid plans are now ruined. If Sulymon lives and he and the characters defeat the Sultan, he ensures that the dark half is irrevocably destroyed, and then calls upon Anumon to lead him on to his afterlife. Anumon appears, blesses the characters for their deeds, and with a chorus of celestial beings carries his faithful servant into the afterlife, leaving the characters to deal with the aftermath of this final battle. You should feel free to assess any story awards you feel the characters' role-play merits during this confrontation and their dealings with the presence of a greater god in their midst.

What Happens Now?

Characters who defeat the Sultan of Efreet[1] need not be finished with their adventures in the City of Brass and the Plane of Molten Skies. As when any planar power is destroyed, or despot finally deposed, an inevitable power vacuum forms.

Quite possibly, the Grand Vizier assumes the Throne of Brass[2] and, due to pacts made with the characters, could be favorably inclined toward them.

In the event that both the Grand Vizier and the Sultan are defeated or destroyed, the remaining houses of noble efreet may elect one of their own.

Quite possibly, the characters may attempt to seize the Throne of Brass[2] for themselves. In so doing, it must be noted that only one being may occupy the Throne of Brass[2] at any given time. The throne attunes itself to that individual and remains so until that individual is destroyed or deposed.

Parties who tend toward sharing power could set up satrapies throughout their newly gained planar empire with different characters taking on governorship of the various areas that the characters may conquer or command.

Another possibility is that Ashazarade may assume rule under the blessings of Anumon, gaining the characters a favorable other-planar patron.

Regardless of any outcome, should Sulymon be revived, he soon passes from the Plane of Molten Skies forever; his service to Anumon complete and his dark half destroyed forever. In this case, Anumon manifests himself with a host of celestials and guides his humble servant to the afterlife he so richly deserves.

Appendix 1
Bestiary

Introduction and Organization

This appendix contains the stat blocks for the creatures (broadly defined) that appear in City of Brass that are not in the Fifth Edition SRD. Many of them are published in existing Frog God Games bestiaries with additional description and illustration, and some will be. At the end of this appendix are a couple of hazards — Brown Mold and Memory Moss. The table below lists the creatures alphabetically and tells you where they can be found within the appendix. Creatures with a — are listed as shown.

Creature	Location	Challenge
Acid Elemental	Elementals	5
Acolyte of Set	Jackalweres	7
Advanced Demilich	Demilich, Advanced	24
Advanced Gray Ooze	Oozes, Gray Ooze	5
Advanced Margoyle	Margoyle, Advanced	6
Advanced Mudman	Mudman, Advanced	3
Advanced Ochre Jelly	Oozes, Ochre Jelly	4
Advanced Specter	Specter, Advanced	7
Advanced Woods Ape	Woods Ape, Advanced	7
Aerial Servant	—	8
Afya Archmage	Afya	14
Afya Creature Template	Afya	NA
Afya Elemental Overlord	Afya	18
Afya Mus'ad Camel Face	Afya	16
Ahi Mau Haka	Giants — Individuals	24
Air Mephit	Mephits	1/2
Al Fatik	Burning Dervishes — Individuals	13
Al-Jabeer	Elementals — Individuals	17
Algoid	—	3
Alu Demon	Demons	3
Amphisbaena	—	3
Ancient Dust Dragon	Dragons, Dust Dragon	23
Animated Book	—	1/2

Creature	Location	Challenge
Animated Chains	—	1/2
Ankylosaurus	Dinosaurs	4
Ant Lion	—	4
Apalla the Blistered One	Demons — Individuals	16
Apprentice Druid	Humans and the Like	1/2
Apprentice Mage	Humans and the Like	1/4
Arcanist	Humans and the Like	8
Arcanoplasm	—	4
Archpriest	Humans and the Like	16
Ard	Named Individuals	20
Arrowhawk	—	5
Assassin Vine	—	4
Avoral	—	9
Azer Cleric	—	12
Azer Elite	—	8
Azer Skeleton	Skeletons	1
Azer Soldier	—	4
Baatina the Ghost	Efreet — Individuals	10
Babau	Demons	6
Bahija	Named Individuals	10
Bal-Shabiri	—	16
Ban Oook	—	16
Bandit Lord	Humans and the Like	4
Baracus	Named Individuals	16
Basalt Warhound	—	5
Beastshifter	Humans and the Like	6
Belker	—	3
Belker Prince	—	12
Berserk Brass Man	Brass Man, Berserk	9
Birhaakamen	—	1
Birhaakamen Chieftain	—	6
Birhaakamen Shaman	—	5
Birhaakamen Warrior	—	3
Black Skeleton	Skeletons, Black Skeleton	4
Blind Fiendish Megaraptor	Dinosaurs, Megaraptor	3
Blood Bush	—	3
Blood Orc	—	4

Creature	Location	Challenge
Blood Orc Elder Warrior	—	6
Bloodsuckle	—	3
Bodak	—	9
Bodak Priest	—	12
Bog Beast	—	3
Bog Creeper	—	9
Boss Flind	Flind, Boss	5
Brass Man	—	6
Bravlik	Named Individuals	10
Brazen Dragon Statue	Dragons	15
Brigand Leader	Humans and the Like	2
Brown Mold	Hazards	NA
Brown Pudding	Oozes	4
Burglar	Humans and the Like	5
Burning Dervish	—	3
Burning Dervish Child	—	1
Burning Dervish Feyhda	—	7
Burning Dervish Guard	—	7
Burning Dervish High Priest	—	11
Burning Dervish Master Assassin	—	11
Burning Dervish Minstrel	—	4
Burning Dervish Priest	—	8
Burning Dervish Sorcerer	—	11
Burning Dervish Wizard	—	9
Cackle Bird	—	4
Cacodemon	Demons	4
Cambion Demon	Demons	2
Captain	Humans and the Like	4
Caterprism	—	7
Catoblepas	—	12
Cauchemar	—	8
Champion Warrior	Humans and the Like	9
Charonademon	Demons	7
Cheitan	—	5
Choromos	Swarms	22
Chuadak the Knife	Cheitans — Individuals	6
Chufa um Sofanie	Cheitans — Individuals	14
Cinder Ghoul	Ghoul, Cinder	5
Circus Master	Faa'Thasht the Circus Master	25
Cobalt Viper	Snakes	1
Cobra-black	Named Individuals	3
Commander	Humans and the Like	5

Creature	Location	Challenge
Corpse Orgy	—	9
Corpulent Attendant	—	6
Croaker	—	1/8
Croaker Brute	—	1/2
Croaker Chieftain	—	1
Dagova Nix	Order of the Devil — Individuals	12
Dark Cardinal Paz Amare	Named Individuals	17
Dark Naga	Naga, Dark	9
Dawzin	—	10
Death Worm	—	3
Deinonychus	Dinosaurs	1/4
Demon Ape	Demons	14
Demon Gate	—	18
Demonic Knight	—	6
Derghodemon	Demons	9
Devil Cenobite	Order of the Devil	11
Devil Initiate	Order of the Devil	4
Devil Mendicant	Order of the Devil	6
Devil Monk	Order of the Devil	9
Devra	—	15
Diplodocus	Dinosaurs	10
Dire Lion	Lion, Dire	1
Dire Tiger	Tiger, Dire	8
Draninko	Named Individuals	10
Drider-Goblin	—	4
Drider-Goblin Spellcaster	—	5
Dun Pudding	Oozes	4
Dust Ghoul	Ghoul, Dust	7
Earth Mephit	Mephits	1/2
Efreeti Alchemist	—	13
Efreeti Amir	—	15
Efreeti Amir Al-umara	—	20
Efreeti Cleric	—	13
Efreeti Loremaster	—	15
Efreeti Malik	—	13
Efreeti Sardar	—	18
Efreeti Skeleton	Skeletons	7
Efreeti Sorcerer	—	13
Elder Air Elemental	Elementals, Air	13
Elder Arrowhawk	Arrowhawk, Elder	11
Elder Black Pudding	Oozes, Black Pudding	9
Elder Cryohydra	Hydras, Cryohydra	20
Elder Earth Elemental	Elementals, Earth Elemental	13

Creature	Location	Challenge
Elder Fire Elemental	Elementals, Fire Elemental	13
Elder Water Elemental	Elementals, Water	13
Elder Xorn	Xorn, Elder	9
Eldritch Archer	Humans and the Like	7
Elemental Air Dragon	Elementals	17
Elemental Fire Dragon	Elementals	21
Elemental Overlord	Humans and the Like	14
Emeritus Chaplain	Humans and the Like	12
Entertainer	Humans and the Like	4
Ephesius	Named Individuals	1
Faakhira	Efreet — Individuals	15
Fadi Al Naifa	Named Individuals	11
Fallen Paladin	Humans and the Like	8
Faa'Thasht the Circus Master	—	25
Fas'ahad	Order of the Devils — Individuals	8
Fayyad Mazin	Named Individuals	14
Feldspar	Named Individuals	11
Fiendish Death Dog	Death Dog, Fiendish	3
Fiendish Dire Lion	Lion, Fiendish Dire	2
Fiendish Dire Tiger	Tiger, Dire Fiendish	10
Fiendish Guardian Naga	Guardian Naga, Fiendish	12
Fiendish Purple Worm	Purple Worm, Fiendish	16
Fire Drake	—	1
Fire Giant Skeleton	Skeletons	8
Fire Mephit	Mephits	1/2
Fire Nymph	Nymph, Fire	1
Fire Snake	—	1
Fire Whale	—	11
Firefiend	—	5
Flayer Devil	Devils	11
Flesh Pudding	Oozes	3
Flind	—	2
Flumph	—	1/2
Flumph Hunter	—	3
Footman	Humans and the Like	1
Forester's Bane	—	4
Formian Myrmarch	—	9
Formian Queen Dryzyxxl	—	23
Formian Taskmaster	—	6
Formian Warrior	—	3
Formian Worker	—	1/2
Frankie	—	3
Frost Man	—	1/2

Creature	Location	Challenge
Fungus Folk	—	1/4
Fungus Folk Monarch	—	3
Ghost of a Master	Order of the Devil	8
Ghoulish Merfolk	—	5
Ghul Efreeti	—	5
Ghul Noble	—	12
Giant Cobalt Viper	Snakes, Cobalt Viper	2
Giant Crayfish	Crayfish, Giant	2
Giant Fiendish Viper	Snakes, Viper	2
Giant Fiendish Yellow Cobra	Snakes, Yellow Cobra	2
Giant Gar	Gar, Giant	6
Giant Killer Frog	Frog, Giant Killer	6
Giant Leech	Leech, Giant	1
Giant Ox	Ox, Giant	6
Giant Rhinoceros Beetle	Beetle, Giant Rhinoceros	6
Glaen	Giants — Individuals	18
Glass Wyrm	Dragons	14
Gnomish Engineer	Humans and the Like	1/2
Gorgimera	—	13
Grand Master Assassin	Humans and the Like	14
Grand Sultan of the Efreet	Efreet — Individuals	29
Grand Vizier	Rahib al Tarbish Zafir	26
Grashen	Named Individuals	5
Gray Nisp	—	6
Greater Abyssal Basilisk	Basilisk, Abyssal	10
Greater Air Elemental	Elementals, Air	9
Greater Barghest	Barghest, Greater	10
Greater Commoner	Humans and the Like, Commoner	1/2
Greater Earth Elemental	Elementals, Earth Elemental	9
Greater Fire Elemental	Elementals, Fire Elemental	9
Greater Hangman Tree	Hangman Tree	9
Greater Mummy	Mummy, Greater	16
Greater Obsidian Elemental	Elementals, Obsidian	14
Greater Pyrohydra	Hydras, Pyrohydra	16
Grumby the Teddy Bear	—	1/8
Gutslug	—	2
Ha-Naga	—	14
Hadrosaur	Dinosaurs	2
Haidar	Giants	9
Half-Ogre Enforcer	—	6

Creature	Location	Challenge
Handmaiden of Kal'Ay-Mah	—	12
Hardy Commoner	Humans and the Like, Commoner	1/4
Hariph Hondu Kush	—	4
Haulman Coul	Named Individuals	9
Hawanari	—	13
Heart of Nyal'oz	—	17
Hellstoker Devil	Devils	5
Hezoid	—	24
Hierophant	Humans and the Like	12
High Priest of Set	Jackalweres	14
Hired Thug	Humans and the Like	2
Hobgoblin Captain	—	5
Hobgoblin Lieutenant	—	3
Hog Face	Named Individuals	4
Holy Knight	Named Individuals	4
Hoplite	Named Individuals	1/2
Housebreaker	Named Individuals	7
Husam al Din	Burning Dervishes — Indivuduals	23
Hydrodemon	Demons	5
Ice Elemental	Elementals	5
Ilgomaxag	Dragons — Individuals	28
Illusionist	Named Individuals	3
Imam of Fire	Named Individuals	3
Incantor	Humans and the Like	9
Infiltrator	Named Individuals	9
Iron Cobra	—	1
Jackalwere	Jackalweres	2
Jackalwere Guard	Jackalweres	7
Jade Colossus of the Sultana	—	23
Jaida Malak	Named Individuals	1
Janni	—	7
Janni Skeleton	Skeletons	5
Jhadam	—	17
Juggernaut of Kil Kath Kesh	—	24
Ka–Shareech, Air Lord of Pazuzu	Demons — Individuals	14
Kanbatsu Ieyau	Named Individuals	6
Kathlin	—	3
Khalit Jinn	Humans and the Like	2
Khalit Jinn Officer	Humans and the Like	5
Killer	Humans and the Like	5
Knave Adept	Humans and the Like	8
Kobold Assassin	—	4

Creature	Location	Challenge
Kytha	Demons	9
Lady Fatima Umau	Cheitans — Individuals	16
Lava Child	—	2
Lavawight	—	22
Lemure Mass	—	12
Lightning Elemental	Elementals	6
Lightning Mephit	Mephits	1
Lightning Weird	—	7
Livesha	—	26
Living Lake	Oozes	22
Lotus Eater	Humans and the Like	5
Macyn	Giants — Individuals	21
Madman	Humans and the Like	5
Magical Monkey	Monkey, Magical	1
Magician	Humans and the Like	5
Magmoid	—	8
Maharaja Rakshasa	Rakshasa, Maharaja	22
Mandragora	—	1/8
Mandrake	—	4
Marid	—	13
Marsh Jelly	—	3
Master Bagra	Order of the Devils — Individuals	14
Master Bard	Humans and the Like	16
Master Cael O'Day	Order of the Devils — Individuals	11
Master Dasssar	Order of the Devils — Individuals	6
Master Illusionist	Humans and the Like	17
Master Mo Zhu	Order of the Devils — Individuals	9
Master Qarid	Order of the Devils — Individuals	12
Master Spy	Humans and the Like	8
Master Thief	Humans and the Like	11
Megaloceros	Dinosaurs	1
Memory Moss	Hazards	NA
Miercoles Mason	Named Individuals	9
Mihstu	—	7
Missionary	Humans and the Like	4
Mistress Harthain Gursh	Order of the Devils — Individuals	19
Mithral Golem	Golems	18
Mohrg	—	8
Monkey	—	1/8
Morhidd	Giants — Individuals	18
Mossknee	Giants — Individuals	14
Mummy Djinn	—	14

Creature	Location	Challenge
Mus'ad Camel Face	—	14
Musa Ayoub	Named Individuals	4
Myrmidon	Humans and the Like	1/2
Nar al Nar, Fire Elemental Prince	Elementals — Individuals	17
Night Terror	—	6
Nightwalker	—	20
Niln	—	5
Noman al-Ajadi	Named Individuals	9
Norl	Giants — Individuals	15
Nyissa	Named Individuals	10
Nymph	—	1
Oblivion Wraith	Wraith, Oblivion	12
Obsidian Minotaur	Minotaur, Obsidian	8
Orator	Humans and the Like	5
Oriazier	Dragons — Individuals	25
Osawi al Mujaheba	Named Individuals	4
Pang Goy	Order of the Devils — Individuals	18
Paragon Knight	Humans and the Like	8
Performer	Humans and the Like	8
Peryton	—	3
Piranha School, Large	Swarms	4
Piranha School, Medium	Swarms	1
Pixie	—	1
Preacher	Humans and the Like	8
Pteranodon	Dinosaurs	1
Pyromancer	Humans and the Like	3
Qadir	Burning Dervishes — Individuals	14
Qalb al Nar, Sparq	Elementals — Individuals	2
Queen Widushka	—	14
Qussay al Nedjari	Named Individuals	8
Raakham al Abash	Named Individuals	11
Rahib al Tarbish Zafir	Efreet — Individuals	26
Rannyn	Giants — Individuals	18
Rast	—	5
Raziya Witch Eye	Named Individuals	5
Red Jester	—	5
Red Scorpion Assassin	Humans and the Like	5
Red Scorpion Lieutenant	Humans and the Like	8
Reliquary Guardian	—	12
Repository Scholar	Humans and the Like	20
Rewonek	Named Individuals	5
Runeskull	—	1/2
Rylon the Cruel	Devils — Individuals	16
Saaid al Djinn (living form)	—	15
Saaid al Djinn (salt lich form)	—	27
Sabina	—	20
Sabre	Humans and the Like	7
Salamander Monarch	—	18
Salamander Noble	—	10
Salt Mephit	Mephits	1/2
Sandling	—	1
Sarmad Yazdg-or	Named Individuals	10
Scorpionfolk	—	6
Seeker of the Ebony Moon	Humans and the Like	6
Senior Druid	Humans and the Like	9
Seraph Genie	—	7
Shadow Captain	—	12
Shaggy Demodand	Demodand, Shaggy	12
Shape of Fire	—	26
Shazier	Named Individuals	7
Sheriff Bolen	Named Individuals	2
Si'la Merchant	Humans and the Like	1/8
Silaal	—	10
Sim ral Marla	—	25
Sinsurab	Efreet — Individuals	18
Sir Leobilus	Named Individuals	11
Siren	—	3
Skeleton Warrior	Skeletons	14
Sleeping Willow	—	10
Smoke Elemental	Elementals	5
Smoke Mephit	Mephits	1/2
Smoke Giant	Giants	7
Smoke Merchant	Humans and the Like	1
Smoldering Judge	Humans and the Like	10
Sneakthief	Humans and the Like	1/2
Sorcerer	Humans and the Like	13
Sparque, the Qalb al Nar	Elementals — Individuals	2
Sparque, the Qalb al Nar, Huge	Elementals — Individuals	9
Sparque, the Qalb al Nar, Large	Elementals — Individuals	5
Sparque, the Qalb al Nar, Medium	Elementals — Individuals	3
Spellbinder	Humans and the Like	20
Spellgorged Zombie	Zombie, Spellgorged	1
Stone Giant Child	Giants	4
Stone Maiden	—	8

Creature	Location	Challenge
Stone Pudding	Oozes	4
Stunjelly	Oozes	3
Sultan of Efreet, Grand	Efreet — Individuals	29
Sulymon	Efreet — Individuals	28
Swarm of Eye Spiders	Swarms	3
Swarm of Hellwasps	Swarms	3
Swarm of Mechanical Birds	Swarms	2
Swarm of Mosquitoes	Swarms	5
Tarry Demodand	Demodand, Tarry	8
Tatho the Mindwrack	Named Individuals	11
Tegman Zekii	Named Individuals	5
Thane Brihnda	Giants — Individuals	17
The Builders	Named Individuals	8
The Wahid	Efreet — Individuals	18
Thessal-Titan	—	30
Theurgist	Humans and the Like	2
Thunderhead	Giants — Individuals	15
Thunderheel Anger	—	17
Tienen	Named Individuals	13
Tusk Lord	—	19
Undead Hyaenodon	Hyaenodon, Undead	5
Vampiric Treant	—	17
Vicious Warrior	Humans and the Like	13
Volcano Giant	Giants	13
Volt	—	1/4
Voltar	—	4
Wahawk Deathbear	Named Individuals	7
Wang Liang Monk	Order of the Devil	10
War Golem	Golem	Varies
Water Weird	—	4
Wind Walker	—	8
Witch Tree	—	8
Woods Ape	—	5
Woods Ape Druid	—	15
Woods Ape Warrior	—	8
Woolly Rhinoceros	—	6
Xill	—	4
Xill Leader	—	7
Xilyat Xaygon Xill	—	9
Y'Cart Chi'Namk	—	25
Yasiel	—	4
Yeti	—	4

Aerial Servant

Medium elemental, neutral
Armor Class 15
Hit Points 90 (12d10 + 24)
Speed 0 ft., fly 90 ft. (hover)

STR	DEX	CON	INT	WIS	CHA
14 (+2)	20 (+5)	14 (+2)	6 (–2)	10 (+0)	6 (–2)

Damage Resistances lightning, thunder; bludgeoning, piercing, and slashing from nonmagical attacks
Damage Immunities poison
Condition Immunities exhaustion, grappled, paralyzed, petrified, poisoned, prone, restrained, unconscious
Senses darkvision 60 ft., passive Perception 10
Languages Auran
Challenge 8 (3,900 XP)

Air Form. The elemental can enter a hostile creature's space and stop there. It can move through a space as narrow as 1 inch wide without squeezing.
Natural Invisibility. If the aerial servant is on the Elemental Plane of Air, it is invisible. If it is on another plane of existence, other creatures have disadvantage on attack rolls against the aerial servant. Truesight defeats this effect.
Spellcaster Binding. If an aerial servant is summoned by a spell, it has a telepathic link with the spellcaster that functions as long as the spellcaster and the servant are on the same plane of existence. The link ends if the servant or the spellcaster dies, or if the servant's task is complete.

ACTIONS

Multiattack. The elemental makes two Slam attacks.
Slam. *Melee Weapon Attack:* +8 to hit, reach 5 ft., one target. *Hit:* 14 (2d8 + 5) bludgeoning damage.
Wind Blast (recharge 4–6). The aerial servant releases a blast of air in an 80–foot line that is 5 feet wide. Creatures in this area must make a DC 13 Strength saving throw. On a failed saving throw, the creature takes 21 (4d8 + 2) bludgeoning damage and if the creature is Large or smaller, it is pushed 15 feet and falls prone. On a successful saving throw, the target takes half the amount of damage, and no other effects.
Whirlwind (recharge 4–6). Each creature in the elemental's space must make a DC 13 Strength saving throw. On a failure, a target takes 15 (3d8 + 2) bludgeoning damage and is flung up 20 feet away from the elemental in a random direction and is knocked prone. If a thrown target strikes an object, such as a wall or floor, the target takes 3 (1d6) bludgeoning damage for every 10 feet it was thrown. If the target is thrown at another creature, that creature must succeed on a DC 13 Dexterity saving throw or takes the same damage and be knocked prone. If the saving throw is successful, the target takes half the bludgeoning damage and isn't flung away or knocked prone.

Afya

Afya Creature Template

The Grand Vizier creates afyas out of potent spellcasters punish to those who defy him. Only a humanoid, elemental, or monstrosity with the Spellcasting trait can be turned into an afya by the Grand Vizier. A creature increases its challenge rating by 2 when it becomes an afya.

Type. The afya's type changes to undead, and it no longer requires air, food, drink, or sleep.

Senses. The afya has darkvision with a radius of 60 feet.

Resistances. The afya has resistance to acid, cold, fire, lightning, and thunder damage. It also has resistance to bludgeoning, piercing, and slashing damage from nonmagical attacks not made with silver.

Immunities. The afya is immune to necrotic and poison damage, and it is immune to exhaustion and the grappled, paralyzed, petrified, poisoned, prone, and restrained conditions.

Incorporeal Movement. The afya can move through other creatures and objects as if they were difficult terrain. It takes 5 (1d10) force damage if it ends its turn inside an object.

Magic Resistance. The afya has advantage on saving throws against spells and other magical effects.

Shadow Sight. Magical darkness doesn't impede the afya's darkvision.

Shadow Stealth. While in dim light or darkness, the afya can take the Hide action as a bonus action.

Shadow Walk (2/day). As a bonus action while in dim light or darkness, the afya can teleport to an unoccupied space it can see within 30 feet that is also in dim light or darkness.

Sunlight Sensitivity. While in sunlight, the afya has disadvantage on attack rolls, as well as on Wisdom (Perception) checks that rely on sight.

New Action: Life Drain. The afya can drain the life force of creatures it touches. A touched creature takes necrotic damage equal to double the afya's challenge rating and its hit point maximum is reduced by an amount equal to the damage taken. This reduction lasts until the target finishes a long rest. The target dies if this effect reduces its hit point maximum to 0.

Afya Archmage

Medium undead, any alignment
Armor Class 12 (15 with *mage armor*)
Hit Points 99 (18d8 + 18)
Speed 30 ft.

STR	DEX	CON	INT	WIS	CHA
10 (+0)	14 (+2)	12 (+1)	20 (+5)	15 (+2)	16 (+3)

Saving Throws Int +10, Wis +7
Skills Arcana +15, History +15
Damage Resistances acid, cold, fire, lightning, thunder; bludgeoning, piercing, and slashing from nonmagical attacks not made with silver
Damage Immunities necrotic, poison
Condition Immunities exhaustion, grappled, paralyzed, petrified, poisoned, prone, restrained
Senses darkvision 60 ft., passive Perception 12
Languages any six languages
Challenge 14 (11,500 XP)

Incorporeal Movement. The afya archmage can move through other creatures and objects as if they were difficult terrain. It takes 5 (1d10) force damage if it ends its turn inside an object.

Magic Resistance. The afya archmage has advantage on saving throws against spells and other magical effects.

Shadow Sight. Magical darkness doesn't impede the afya archmage's darkvision.

Shadow Stealth. While in dim light or darkness, the afya archmage can take the Hide action as a bonus action.

Shadow Walk (3/day). As a bonus action while in dim light or darkness, the afya archmage can teleport to an unoccupied space it can see within 30 feet that is also in dim light or darkness.

Spellcasting. The afya archmage is an 18th-level spellcaster. Its spellcasting ability is Intelligence (spell save DC 18, +10 to hit with spell attacks). The afya archmage can cast *disguise self* and *invisibility* at will and has the following spells prepared:

Cantrips (at will): *fire bolt, light, mage hand, prestidigitation, shocking grasp*
1st level (4 slots): *detect magic, identify, mage armor, magic missile*
2nd level (3 slots): *detect thoughts, mirror image, misty step*
3rd level (3 slots): *counterspell, fly, lightning bolt*
4th level (3 slots): *banishment, fire shield, stoneskin*
5th level (3 slots): *cone of cold, scrying, wall of force*
6th level (1 slot): *globe of invulnerability*
7th level (1 slot): *teleport*
8th level (1 slot): *mind blank*
9th level (1 slot): *time stop*

Sunlight Sensitivity. While in sunlight, the afya archmage has disadvantage on attack rolls, as well as on Wisdom (Perception) checks that rely on sight.

ACTIONS

Dagger. *Melee or Ranged Weapon Attack:* +7 to hit, reach 5 ft. or range 20/60 ft., one target. *Hit:* 4 (1d4 + 2) piercing damage.

Life Drain. *Melee Weapon Attack:* +7 to hit, reach 5 ft., one creature. *Hit:* 28 necrotic damage and the target's hit point maximum is reduced by an amount equal to the damage taken. This reduction lasts until the target finishes a long rest. The target dies if this effect reduces its hit point maximum to 0.

Afya Elemental Overlord

Medium undead, any alignment
Armor Class 13 (16 with *mage armor*)
Hit Points 165 (30d8 + 30)
Speed 30 ft.

STR	DEX	CON	INT	WIS	CHA
10 (+0)	16 (+3)	13 (+1)	14 (+2)	15 (+2)	21 (+5)

Saving Throws Dex +9, Con +7, Cha +11
Damage Resistances acid, cold, fire, lightning, thunder; bludgeoning, piercing, and slashing from nonmagical attacks not made with silver
Damage Immunities necrotic, poison
Condition Immunities exhaustion, grappled, paralyzed, petrified, poisoned, prone, restrained
Skills Arcana +8, Intimidation +11, Persuasion +11
Damage Immunities varies (see Elemental Flexibility)
Senses darkvision 60 ft., passive Perception 12
Languages any three languages
Challenge 18 (20,000 XP)

Elemental Flexibility. At the start of its turn, the elemental overlord must choose one damage type: acid, cold, fire, or lightning. It has immunity to its chosen damage type until the start of its next turn. It can't choose the same damage type two rounds in a row.

Elemental Shield. A creature that touches the elemental overlord or hits it with a melee attack while within 5 feet of it takes 10 (3d6) damage of the type chosen with Elemental Flexibility.

Incorporeal Movement. The elemental overlord can move through other creatures and objects as if they were difficult terrain. It takes 5 (1d10) force damage if it ends its turn inside an object.

Legendary Resistance (3/day). If the elemental overlord fails a saving throw, it can choose to succeed instead.

Magic Resistance. The elemental overlord has advantage on saving throws against spells and other magical effects.

Shadow Sight. Magical darkness doesn't impede the elemental overlord's darkvision.

Shadow Stealth. While in dim light or darkness, the elemental overlord can take the Hide action as a bonus action.

Shadow Walk (2/day). As a bonus action while in dim light or darkness, the elemental overlord can teleport to an unoccupied space it can see within 30 feet that is also in dim light or darkness.

Spellcasting. The elemental overlord is a 20th-level spellcaster. Its spellcasting ability is Charisma (spell save DC 18, +10 to hit with spell attacks). The overlord has the following wizard spells prepared:

> Cantrips (at will): *acid splash, blade ward, fire bolt, light, prestidigitation*
> 1st level (4 slots): *burning hands, detect magic, mage armor, magic missile, shield*
> 2nd level (3 slots): *blur, flaming sphere, gust of wind, misty step*
> 3rd level (3 slots): *counterspell, fly, lightning bolt*
> 4th level (3 slots): *conjure minor elementals, ice storm, stoneskin, wall of fire*
> 5th level (3 slots): *cone of cold, conjure elemental, wall of stone*
> 6th level (2 slots): *chain lightning, wall of ice*
> 7th level (2 slots): *delayed blast fireball, prismatic spray*
> 8th level (1 slot): *control weather*
> 9th level (1 slot): *meteor swarm*

Sunlight Sensitivity. While in sunlight, the elemental overlord has disadvantage on attack rolls, as well as on Wisdom (Perception) checks that rely on sight.

Undead Nature. The elemental overlord doesn't require air, food, drink, or sleep.

ACTIONS

Dagger. *Melee or Ranged Weapon Attack:* +9 to hit, reach 5 ft. or range 20/60 ft., one target. *Hit:* 5 (1d4 + 3) piercing damage.

Elemental Bolt. *Ranged Spell Attack:* +11 to hit, range 120 ft., one target. *Hit:* 28 (8d6) damage of the type chosen with Elemental Flexibility, and the target must succeed on a DC 18 Constitution saving throw or have disadvantage on its next saving throw against a spell cast by the elemental overlord.

Life Drain. *Melee Weapon Attack:* +6 to hit, reach 5 ft., one creature. *Hit:* 36 necrotic damage and the target's hit point maximum is reduced by an amount equal to the damage taken. This reduction lasts until the target finishes a long rest. The target dies if this effect reduces its hit point maximum to 0.

LEGENDARY ACTIONS

The elemental overlord can take 3 legendary actions, choosing from the options below. Only one legendary action can be used at a time and only at the end of another creature's turn. The overlord regains spent legendary actions at the start of its turn.

Cantrip. The elemental overlord casts a cantrip.

Move. The elemental overlord moves up to half its speed without provoking opportunity attacks.

Elemental Bolt (costs 2 actions). The elemental overlord makes one Elemental Bolt attack.

Power Uncontained (costs 3 actions). The elemental overlord releases a burst of elemental energy. Each creature within 20 feet of it must make a DC 18 Dexterity saving throw. On a failure, a creature takes 21 (6d6) force damage and is pushed up to 10 feet away and knocked prone. On a success, a creature takes half the damage and isn't pushed or knocked prone.

Afya Mus'ad Camel Face

Large undead, lawful good
Armor Class 16 (natural armor)
Hit Points 178 (21d10 + 63)
Speed 50 ft.

STR	DEX	CON	INT	WIS	CHA
14 (+2)	16 (+3)	16 (+3)	20 (+5)	21 (+5)	19 (+4)

Saving Throws Dex +8, Con +8, Int +10, Wis +10
Skills Arcana +10, History +10, Insight +10, Perception +10, Survival +10
Damage Resistances acid, cold, fire, , thunder; bludgeoning, piercing, and slashing from nonmagical attacks not made with silver
Damage Immunities necrotic, poison
Condition Immunities exhaustion, grappled, paralyzed, petrified, poisoned, prone, restrained
Senses darkvision 60 ft., truesight 30 ft., passive Perception 20
Languages Abyssal, Celestial, Common, Infernal, Primordial
Challenge 16 (15,000 XP)

Incorporeal Movement. Mus'ad can move through other creatures and objects as if they were difficult terrain. It takes 5 (1d10) force damage if it ends its turn inside an object.

Magic Resistance. Mus'ad has advantage on saving throws against spells and other magical effects.

Prescient Weapons. Mus'ad's weapon attacks are magical. When he hits with any weapon, the weapon deals an extra 4d8 force damage (included in the attack).

Precognition (1/turn). Mus'ad has advantage on his next attack roll, ability check, or saving throw.

Shadow Sight. Magical darkness doesn't impede Mus'ad's darkvision.

Shadow Stealth. While in dim light or darkness, Mus'ad can take the Hide action as a bonus action.

Shadow Walk (2/day). As a bonus action while in dim light or darkness, Mus'ad can teleport to an unoccupied space it can see within 30 feet that is also in dim light or darkness.

Share Intuition. As a bonus action, Mus'ad shares some of his precognition with one ally within 30 feet. The ally has advantage on its next attack roll, ability check, or saving throw.

Spellcasting. Mus'ad Camel Face is an 18th-level spellcaster. His spellcasting ability is Intelligence (spell save DC 18, +10 to hit with spell attacks). Mus'ad has the following spells prepared:

> Cantrips (at will): *light, mage hand, minor illusion, prestidigitation, ray of frost*
> 1st level (4 slots): *comprehend languages, detect magic, floating disk, magic missile, shield*
> 2nd level (3 slots): *arcanist's magic aura, detect thoughts, locate object, misty step*
> 3rd level (3 slots): *clairvoyance, counterspell, fireball, fly*
> 4th level (3 slots): *arcane eye, confusion, locate creature*
> 5th level (3 slots): *cone of cold, legend lore, scrying*
> 6th level (1 slot): *globe of invulnerability*
> 7th level (1 slot): *prismatic spray*
> 8th level (1 slot): *mind blank*
> 9th level (1 slot): *prismatic wall*

Sunlight Sensitivity. While in sunlight, Mus'ad has disadvantage on attack rolls, as well as on Wisdom (Perception) checks that rely on sight.

Undead Nature. Mus'ad doesn't require air, food, drink, or sleep.

Multiattack. The sage camel makes one Bite attack and two Hooves attacks.

Bite. *Melee Weapon Attack:* +7 to hit, reach 5 ft., one target. *Hit:* 6 (1d8 + 2) bludgeoning damage plus 18 (4d8) force damage.

Hooves. *Melee Weapon Attack:* +7 to hit, reach 5 ft., one target. *Hit:* 7 (2d4 + 2) bludgeoning damage plus 18 (4d8) force damage.

Life Drain. *Melee Weapon Attack:* +7 to hit, reach 5 ft., one creature. *Hit:* 32 necrotic damage and the target's hit point maximum is reduced by an amount equal to the damage taken. This reduction lasts until the target finishes a long rest. The target dies if this effect reduces its hit point maximum to 0.

Spit (recharge 5–6). Mus'ad spits blinding saliva in a 90-foot line that is 5 feet wide. Each creature in that line must make a DC 18 Dexterity saving throw. On a failure, a creature takes 54 (12d8) acid damage and is blinded for 1 minute. On a success, a creature takes half the damage and isn't blinded. A blinded creature can repeat the saving throw at the end of each of its turns, ending the effect on itself on a success.

Algoid

Medium plant, neutral
Armor Class 14
Hit Points 45 (6d8 + 18)
Speed 20 ft.

STR	DEX	CON	INT	WIS	CHA
19 (+4)	10 (+0)	16 (+3)	4 (–3)	10 (+0)	10 (+0)

Saving Throws CON+5
Skills Stealth +4
Damage Resistances slashing and piercing damage from nonmagical attacks
Damage Immunities lightning and fire damage
Condition Immunities prone
Senses Darkvision 60 ft., tremorsense 120 ft., passive Perception 10
Languages Common (understands but can't speak)
Challenge 3 (700 XP)

Animate Trees. An algoid can innately cast the *animate objects* spell at will, requiring no components. Each casting animates two trees, which are all the algoid can control at a time. A newly-animated tree takes one full round to uproot itself. Once free, trees act on the algoid's turn.

Vulnerability to Water Magic. *Control water* and *create or destroy water* spells deal 10 (3d6) piercing damage to an algoid.

Water Camouflage. An algoid has advantage on Stealth checks when it is in or on standing water.

ACTIONS

Multiattack. The algoid makes two Slam attacks.

Slam. *Melee Weapon Attack:* +6 to hit, reach 5 ft., one creature. *Hit:* 8 (1d8 + 4) bludgeoning damage. If an algoid scores a critical hit with this attack, the target must make a successful DC 17 Constitution saving throw or be stunned. The stunned creature can repeat the saving throw at the end of each of its turns; the condition ends on a successful save.

Mind Blast. Any creature within a 60 ft. cone must succeed on a DC 13 Intelligence saving throw or be stunned for 3d4 rounds.

Amphisbaena

Large monstrosity, unaligned
Armor Class 15 (natural armor)
Hit Points 60 (8d10 + 16)
Speed 20 ft., climb 20 ft., swim 30 ft.

STR	DEX	CON	INT	WIS	CHA
17 (+3)	15 (+2)	14 (+2)	2(–4)	12 (+1)	2(–4)

Skills Stealth +6
Senses darkvision 60 ft., passive Perception 11
Languages —
Challenge 3 (700 XP)

Split. The amphisbaena functions normally even if cut in half. If dealt a critical hit with a slashing weapon, the creature is cut in half and continues to function as two separate creatures, each with half of the original amphisbaena's current hit points. The split amphisbaena can rejoin its two halves after completing a short or long rest. If one of the split creatures is slain, the amphisbaena can regrow the lost portion over the course of 1d4 + 2 weeks.

ACTIONS

Multiattack. The amphisbaena makes one Bite attack with each of its two heads.

Bite. *Melee Weapon Attack:* +5 to hit, reach 5 ft., one target. *Hit:* 12 (2d8 + 3) piercing damage, and the target must succeed on a DC 13 Constitution saving throw or become poisoned for 1 hour.

Animated Book

Small construct, unaligned
Armor Class 14 (natural armor)
Hit Points 17 (5d6)
Speed 0 ft., fly 30 ft.

STR	DEX	CON	INT	WIS	CHA
12 (+1)	15 (+2)	11 (+0)	1 (–5)	5 (–3)	1 (–5)

Saving Throws Dex +4
Damage Immunities poison, psychic
Condition Immunities blinded, charmed, deafened, frightened, paralyzed, petrified, poisoned
Senses blindsight 30 ft. (blind beyond this radius), passive Perception 7
Languages —
Challenge 1/2 (100 XP)

Antimagic Susceptibility. The animated book is incapacitated while in the area of an *antimagic field*. If targeted by *dispel magic*, the book must succeed on a Constitution saving throw against the caster's spell save DC or fall unconscious for 1 minute.

False Appearance. While the book remains motionless and isn't flying, it is indistinguishable from a normal book.

Flyby. The book doesn't provoke opportunity attacks when it flies out of an enemy's reach.

Pack Tactics. The animated book has advantage on an attack roll against a creature if at least one of the book's allies is within 5 feet of the creature and the ally isn't incapacitated.

ACTIONS

Cut. *Melee Weapon Attack:* +4 to hit, reach 5 ft., one target. *Hit:* 4 (1d4 + 2) slashing damage.

Animated Chains

Large construct, unaligned
Armor Class 14 (natural armor)
Hit Points 19 (3d10 + 3)
Speed 30 ft.

	STR	DEX	CON	INT	WIS	CHA
	15 (+2)	14 (+2)	12 (+1)	1 (−5)	5 (−3)	1 (−5)

Damage Immunities poison, psychic
Condition Immunities blinded, charmed, deafened, frightened, paralyzed, petrified, poisoned
Senses blindsight 30 ft. (blind beyond this radius), passive Perception 7
Languages —
Challenge 1/2 (100 XP)

Antimagic Susceptibility. The animated chain is incapacitated while in the area of an *antimagic field*. If targeted by *dispel magic*, the book must succeed on a Constitution saving throw against the caster's spell save DC or fall unconscious for 1 minute.

False Appearance. While the chain remains motionless, it is indistinguishable from a normal chain.

ACTIONS

Constrict. *Melee Weapon Attack:* +4 to hit, reach 5 ft., one creature. *Hit:* 6 (1d8 + 2) bludgeoning damage, and the target is grappled (escape DC 14). Until this grapple ends, the creature is restrained, and the chain can't constrict another target.

Ant Lion

Large beast, unaligned
Armor Class 15 (natural armor)
Hit Points 93 (11d10 + 33)
Speed 30 ft., burrow 10 ft.

	STR	DEX	CON	INT	WIS	CHA
	19 (+4)	10 (+0)	16 (+3)	4 (−3)	10 (+0)	10 (+0)

Saving Throws CON+5
Skills Stealth +2
Condition Immunities Charm
Senses darkvision 60 ft., tremorsense 60 ft.
Languages —
Challenge 4 (1,100 XP)

ACTIONS

Bite. *Melee Weapon Attack:* +4 to hit, reach 5 ft., one creature. *Hit:* 18 (3d10 + 2) piercing damage, and the target is grappled (escape DC 16).

Arcanoplasm

Large monstrosity, neutral
Armor Class 12 (natural armor)
Hit Points 103 (9d10 + 54)
Speed 40 ft.

	STR	DEX	CON	INT	WIS	CHA
	15 (+2)	6 (−2)	22 (+6)	10 (+0)	14 (+2)	14 (+2)

Saving Throws CON+9
Skills Athletics +5, Stealth +1
Damage Immunities poison
Condition Immunities paralyzed, poisoned, prone, stunned, unconscious
Senses darkvision 60 ft.
Languages Common, draconic (understands but can't speak)
Challenge 4 (1,100 XP)

Immutable Form. The arcanoplasm is immune to any spell or effect that would alter its form.

Absorb Arcane Energy. Any arcane spell targeted at an arcanoplasm is automatically absorbed into its body. This cures 1 point of damage per 3 points of damage the spell would otherwise deal; nondamaging spells cure 1 point of damage per spell slot level used. Spells that affect an area are not absorbed, but neither do they affect the arcanoplasm. The arcanoplasm can't absorb magic from spells that it cast itself using arcane spell mimicry, and it can't absorb divine magic, which affects it normally.

Amorphous. An arcanoplasm can move through gaps as small as 1 square inch without squeezing.

Arcanesense. An arcanoplasm can automatically detect the location of any arcane spellcaster within 100 feet. This ability is not blocked by any material.

Arcane Spell Mimicry. As an action, an arcanoplasm can mimic any arcane spell of 4th level or lower cast within 30 feet of it on its next turn. The arcanoplasm has a DC 14 spell save and +6 to hit with spell attacks and requires no components. Because of its innately magical nature, an arcanoplasm adds both its Constitution and Charisma modifiers to concentration checks when it takes damage.

ACTIONS

Multiattack. The arcanoplasm makes one Slam attack and one Constriction attack.

Slam. *Melee Weapon Attack:* +5 to hit, reach 5 ft., one creature. *Hit:* 5 (1d6 + 2) bludgeoning damage plus 3 (1d6) acid damage, and the target is grappled (escape DC 16).

Constriction. One creature already grappled by the arcanoplasm is crushed for 5 (1d6 + 2) bludgeoning damage plus 7 (2d6) acid damage.

Arrowhawk

Medium elemental, neutral
Armor Class 15
Hit Points 78 (12d8 + 24)
Speed 5 ft., fly 60 ft. (hover)

	STR	DEX	CON	INT	WIS	CHA
	12 (+1)	20 (+5)	15 (+2)	8 (−1)	14 (+2)	6 (−2)

Saving Throws Dex +8
Skills Acrobatics +8, Perception +5, Stealth +8
Damage Resistances lightning, thunder; bludgeoning, piercing, and slashing from nonmagical attacks
Damage Immunities poison
Condition Immunities paralyzed, poisoned, prone, unconscious
Senses darkvision 60 ft., passive Perception 15
Languages Auran
Challenge 5 (1,800 XP)

Flyby. The arrowhawk doesn't provoke opportunity attacks when it flies out of an enemy's reach.

Keen Sight. The arrowhawk has advantage on Wisdom (Perception) checks that rely on sight.

Actions

Multiattack. The arrowhawk makes one Beak attack and two Wing attacks. Alternatively, it can use its Lightning Ray twice.

Beak. *Melee Weapon Attack:* +8 to hit, reach 5 ft., one target. *Hit:* 12 (2d6 + 5) piercing damage.

Wing. *Melee Weapon Attack:* +8 to hit, reach 5 ft., one target. *Hit:* 10 (2d4 + 5) bludgeoning damage.

Lightning Ray. *Ranged Spell Attack:* +5 to hit, range 120 ft., one target. *Hit:* 18 (4d8) lightning damage.

Arrowhawk, Elder

Large elemental, neutral
Armor Class 17
Hit Points 123 (13d10 + 52)
Speed 5 ft., fly 90 ft. (hover)

STR	DEX	CON	INT	WIS	CHA
12 (+1)	23 (+6)	19 (+4)	8 (−1)	18 (+4)	6 (−2)

Saving Throws Dex +10, Wis +8
Skills Acrobatics +10, Insight +8, Perception +8, Stealth +10
Damage Resistances thunder; bludgeoning, piercing, and slashing from nonmagical attacks
Damage Immunities lightning, poison
Condition Immunities paralyzed, poisoned, prone, unconscious
Senses darkvision 120 ft., passive Perception 18
Languages Auran
Challenge 11 (7,200 XP)

Flyby. The elder arrowhawk doesn't provoke opportunity attacks when it flies out of an enemy's reach.

Keen Sight. The elder arrowhawk has advantage on Wisdom (Perception) checks that rely on sight.

Static. A creature that touches the elder arrowhawk or hits it with a melee attack while within 5 feet of it takes 7 (2d6) lightning damage.

Actions

Multiattack. The arrowhawk makes one Beak attack and two Wing attacks. Alternatively, it can use its Lightning Ray twice.

Beak. *Melee Weapon Attack:* +10 to hit, reach 5 ft., one target. *Hit:* 16 (3d6 + 6) piercing damage plus 10 (3d6) lightning damage.

Wing. *Melee Weapon Attack:* +10 to hit, reach 5 ft., one target. *Hit:* 13 (3d4 + 6) bludgeoning damage.

Lightning Ray. *Ranged Spell Attack:* +8 to hit, range 120 ft., one target. *Hit:* 27 (6d8) lightning damage.

Lightning Burst (recharge 5–6). The elder arrowhawk flaps its wings ferociously, lightning sparking out from them. Each creature within 20 feet of the elder arrowhawk must make a DC 18 Dexterity saving throw, taking 44 (8d10) lightning damage on a failed save, or half as much damage on a successful one.

Assassin Vine

Large plant, unaligned
Armor Class 13 (natural armor)
Hit Points 85 (10d10 + 30)
Speed 5 ft.

STR	DEX	CON	INT	WIS	CHA
20 (+5)	10 (+0)	16 (+3)	2 (−4)	13 (+1)	9 (−1)

Damage Resistances cold, fire
Damage Immunities lightning
Senses blindsight 30 ft., passive Perception 11
Languages —
Challenge 4 (1,100 XP)

Actions

Multiattack. The assassin vine can make two melee attacks: two slams or one slam and one constrict.

Slam. *Melee Weapon Attack:* +7 to hit, reach 10 ft., one target. *Hit:* 14 (2d8 + 5) bludgeoning damage. The target is grappled (escape DC 15) if the assassin vine isn't already grappling a creature. The grappled target is restrained until the grapple ends.

Constrict. *Melee Weapon Attack:* +7 to hit, reach 5 ft., one creature grappled by the assassin vine. *Hit:* 18 (3d8 + 5) bludgeoning damage.

Avoral

Medium celestial, neutral good
Armor Class 16 (natural armor)
Hit Points 120 (16d8 + 48)
Speed 30 ft., fly 90 ft.

STR	DEX	CON	INT	WIS	CHA
14 (+2)	21 (+5)	16 (+3)	17 (+3)	18 (+4)	20 (+5)

Saving Throws Wis +8, Cha +9
Skills Insight +8, Perception +8, Stealth +9
Damage Resistances lightning, radiant; bludgeoning, piercing, and slashing from nonmagical attacks
Condition Immunities charmed, exhaustion, frightened, petrified
Senses truesight 60 ft., passive Perception 18
Languages all, telepathy 120 ft.
Challenge 9 (5,000 XP)

Angelic Weapons. The avoral's weapon attacks are magical. When the avoral hits with any weapon, the weapon deals an extra 3d8 radiant damage (included in the attack).

Flyby. The avoral doesn't provoke opportunity attacks when it flies out of an enemy's reach.

Keen Sight. The avoral has advantage on Wisdom (Perception) checks that rely on sight.

Innate Spellcasting. The avoral's spellcasting ability is Charisma (spell save DC 17, +9 to hit with spell attacks). The avoral can innately cast the following spells, requiring only verbal components:

At will: *detect evil and good*
3/day each: *blur, gust of wind, hold person*
1/day each: *aid, freedom of movement*

Actions

Multiattack. The avoral makes two Claw attacks.

Claw. *Melee Weapon Attack:* +9 to hit, reach 5 ft., one target. *Hit:* 12 (2d6 + 5) slashing damage plus 13 (3d8) radiant damage.

Wing Assault (recharge 5–6). The avoral flaps its wings, creating a 30-foot cone of violent wind. Each creature in the area must make a DC 17 Dexterity saving throw. On a failure, a creature takes 36 (8d8) bludgeoning damage and is knocked prone. On a success, a creature takes half the damage and isn't knocked prone.

Healing Touch (2/day). The avoral touches another creature. The target magically regains 20 (4d8 + 2) hit points and is freed from any curse, disease, poison, blindness, or deafness.

Azer Cleric

Medium elemental (azer), lawful neutral
Armor Class 20 (natural armor)
Hit Points 114 (12d8 + 60)
Speed 40 ft.

STR	DEX	CON	INT	WIS	CHA
22 (+6)	12 (+1)	20 (+5)	12 (+1)	20 (+5)	10 (+0)

Saving Throws Str +10, Con +9, Wis +9
Skills Arcana +5, Athletics +10, Insight +9, Perception +9, Religion +5
Damage Resistances bludgeoning, piercing, and slashing from nonmagical attacks
Damage Immunities fire, poison
Condition Immunities poisoned
Senses passive Perception 19
Languages Ignan
Challenge 12 (8,400 XP)

Elemental Nature. The azer cleric doesn't require food, drink, or sleep.

Forge Master. Once per turn, the azer cleric has advantage on one attack roll if the target is wearing armor made of metal.

Heated Body. A creature that touches the azer cleric or hits it with a melee attack while within 5 feet of it takes 5 (1d10) fire damage. In addition, the azer cleric adds its Wisdom modifier to its AC (included above).

Heated Weapons. When the azer cleric hits with a metal melee weapon, it deals an extra 10 (3d6) fire damage (included in the attack).

Illumination. The azer cleric sheds bright light in a 20-foot radius and dim light for an additional 20 feet.

Legendary Resistance (3/day). If the azer cleric fails a saving throw, it can choose to succeed instead.

Spellcasting. The azer cleric is a 15th-level spellcaster. Its spellcasting ability is Wisdom (spell save DC 17, +9 to hit with spell attacks). The azer cleric has the cleric following spells prepared:

> Cantrips (at will): *guidance, mending, resistance, sacred flame, thaumaturgy*
> 1st level (4 slots): *bless, command, cure wounds, inflict wounds, sanctuary*
> 2nd level (3 slots): *calm emotions, hold person, lesser restoration, spiritual weapon*
> 3rd level (3 slots): *dispel magic, bestow curse, spirit guardians*
> 4th level (3 slots): *freedom of movement, guardian of faith, stone shape*
> 5th level (2 slots): *flame strike, planar binding*
> 6th level (1 slot): *blade barrier*
> 7th level (1 slot): *fire storm*
> 8th level (1 slot): *earthquake*

ACTIONS

Multiattack. The azer cleric makes two Maul attacks or two Hurl Flame attacks.

Maul. *Melee Weapon Attack:* +10 to hit, reach 5 ft., one target. *Hit:* 13 (2d6 + 6) bludgeoning damage plus 10 (3d6) fire damage.

Hurl Flame. *Ranged Spell Attack:* +9 to hit, range 150 ft., one target. *Hit:* 14 (4d6) fire damage. If the target is a flammable object that isn't being worn or carried, it also catches fire.

Fire's Blessing (recharge 6). The azer cleric targets one ally that is immune to fire damage within 30 feet. The target regains 21 (6d6) hit points and has advantage on its next attack roll, saving throw, or ability check.

LEGENDARY ACTIONS

The azer cleric can take 3 legendary actions, choosing from the options below. Only one legendary action can be used at a time and only at the end of another creature's turn. The azer cleric regains spent legendary actions at the start of its turn.

Cantrip. The azer cleric casts one cantrip.

Hurl Flame. The azer cleric makes one Hurl Flame attack.

Move. The azer cleric moves up to its speed without provoking opportunity attacks.

Beard Flare (costs 3 actions). The flames in the azer cleric's beard flare brightly. Each creature within 20 feet of the azer cleric must make a DC 17 Constitution saving throw. On a failure, a creature takes 21 (6d6) fire damage and is blinded until the end of its next turn. On a success a creature takes half the damage and isn't blinded. Creatures immune to fire damage have advantage on this saving throw.

Azer Elite

Medium elemental, lawful neutral
Armor Class 18 (plate)
Hit Points 85 (10d8 + 40)
Speed 40 ft.

STR	DEX	CON	INT	WIS	CHA
22 (+6)	12 (+1)	19 (+4)	12 (+1)	15 (+2)	10 (+0)

Saving Throws Str +9, Con +7
Skills Athletics +9, Perception +5
Damage Resistances bludgeoning, piercing, and slashing from nonmagical attacks
Damage Immunities fire, poison
Condition Immunities poisoned
Senses passive Perception 15
Languages Ignan
Challenge 8 (3,900 XP)

Brute. A melee weapon deals one extra die of its damage when the azer hits with it (included in the attack).

Elemental Nature. An azer doesn't require food, drink, or sleep.

Forge Master. Once per turn, the azer has advantage on one attack roll if the target is wearing armor made of metal.

Heated Body. A creature that touches the azer or hits it with a melee attack while within 5 feet of it takes 5 (1d10) fire damage.

Heated Weapons. When the azer hits with a metal melee weapon, it deals an extra 7 (2d6) fire damage (included in the attack).

Illumination. The azer sheds bright light in a 20-foot radius and dim light for an additional 20 feet.

ACTIONS

Multiattack. The elite azer makes two Maul attacks.

Maul. *Melee Weapon Attack:* +9 to hit, reach 5 ft., one target. *Hit:* 16 (3d6 + 6) bludgeoning damage plus 7 (2d6) fire damage.

Heat Burst (recharge 6). The azer expels excess heat from its body. Each creature within 20 feet of the azer must make a DC 15 Constitution saving throw, taking 31 (9d6) fire damage on a failed save, or half as much damage on a success.

Azer Soldier

Medium elemental, lawful neutral
Armor Class 17 (natural armor, shield)
Hit Points 67 (9d8 + 27)
Speed 30 ft.

STR	DEX	CON	INT	WIS	CHA
19 (+4)	12 (+1)	17 (+3)	12 (+1)	14 (+2)	10 (+0)

Saving Throws Con +5
Skills Perception +4
Damage Immunities fire, poison
Condition Immunities poisoned
Senses passive Perception 14
Languages Ignan
Challenge 4 (1,100 XP)

Elemental Nature. An azer doesn't require food, drink, or sleep.

Forge Master. Once per turn, the azer has advantage on one attack roll against a target wearing armor made of metal.

Heated Body. A creature that touches the azer or hits it with a melee attack while within 5 feet of it takes 5 (1d10) fire damage.

Heated Weapons. When the azer hits with a metal melee weapon, it deals an extra 3 (1d6) fire damage (included in the attack).

Illumination. The azer sheds bright light in a 10-foot radius and dim light for an additional 10 feet.

Actions

Multiattack. The azer soldier makes one Warhammer attack and one Shield Bash attack.

Warhammer. *Melee Weapon Attack:* +6 to hit, reach 5 ft., one target. *Hit:* 8 (1d8 + 4) bludgeoning damage, or 9 (1d10 + 4) bludgeoning damage if used with two hands, plus 3 (1d6) fire damage.

Shield Bash. *Melee Weapon Attack:* +6 to hit, reach 5 ft., one creature. *Hit:* 9 (2d4 + 4) bludgeoning damage plus 3 (1d6) fire damage. If the target is a Large or smaller creature, it must succeed on a DC 14 Strength saving throw or be knocked prone.

Reactions

Parry. The azer adds 2 to its AC against one melee attack that would hit it. To do so, the azer must see the attacker and be wielding a melee weapon.

Bal-Shabiri

Large monstrosity, chaotic evil
Armor Class 13 (natural armor)
Hit Points 135 (18d10 + 36)
Speed 30 ft.

STR	DEX	CON	INT	WIS	CHA
16 (+3)	13 (+1)	15 (+2)	14 (+2)	15 (+2)	20 (+5)

Saving Throws Wis +7, Chr +10
Skills Arcana +7, Deception +10, Insight +7, Stealth +6
Senses darkvision 60 ft., passive Perception 12
Languages Abyssal, Common
Challenge 16 (15,000 XP)

Innate Spellcasting. Bal-Shabiri's innate spellcasting ability is Charisma (spell save DC 18). She can innately cast the following spells, requiring no material components.

At will: *disguise self* (any humanoid form), *major image*
3/day each: *charm person, mirror image, scrying, suggestion*
1/day: *geas*

Spellcasting. Bal-Shabiri is a 10th-level spellcaster. Her spellcasting ability is Charisma (spell save DC 18, +10 to hit with spell attacks). She has the following sorcerer spells prepared:

Cantrips (at will): *chill touch, fire bolt, mage hand, message, prestidigitation, shocking grasp*
1st level (4 slots): *detect magic, expeditious retreat, magic missile*
2nd level (3 slots): *darkness, hold person*
3rd level (3 slots): *dispel magic, fireball*
4th level (3 slots): *polymorph, wall of fire*
5th level (2 slots): *dominate person, seeming*

Actions

Multiattack. Bal-Shabiri makes one attack with her Claws and one with her Dagger or Intoxicating Touch.

Claws. *Melee Weapon Attack:* +8 to hit, reach 5 ft., one target. *Hit:* 14 (2d10 + 3) slashing damage.

Dagger. *Melee Weapon Attack:* +8 to hit, reach 5 ft., one target. *Hit:* 5 (1d4 + 3) piercing damage.

Intoxicating Touch. *Melee Spell Attack:* +8 to hit, reach 5 ft., one creature. *Hit:* The target is magically cursed for 1 hour. Until the curse ends, the target has disadvantage on Wisdom saving throws and all ability checks.

Ban Oook

Large giant, lawful evil
Armor Class 18 (natural armor)
Hit Points 238 (28d10 + 84)
Speed 40 ft.

STR	DEX	CON	INT	WIS	CHA
14 (+2)	18 (+4)	16 (+3)	14 (+2)	18 (+4)	15 (+2)

Saving Throws Dex +9, Con +8, Wis +9, Cha +7
Skills Acrobatics +9, Arcana +7, Deception +7, Perception +9, Stealth +7
Damage Immunities fire
Senses darkvision 60 ft., passive Perception 19
Language Common, Giant, Infernal
Challenge 16 (15,000 XP)

Fists of Dark Flame (1/day). Ban Oook wreaths his fists in flame. He deals an additional 7 (2d6) fire damage when he hits with his Unarmed Strikes for 1 minute.

Innate Spellcasting. Ban Oook's innate spellcasting ability is Wisdom (spell save DC 17, +9 to hit with spell attacks). He can cast the following spells, requiring no material components.

At will: *darkness, fire bolt* (5th level), *invisibility*
3/day: *burning hands*
1/day each: *charm person, cone of cold, gaseous form, sleep*

Magic Weapons. Ban Oook's weapon attacks are considered magical for the purposes of damage resistances and immunities.

Regeneration. Ban Oook regains 10 hit points at the start of his turn if he has at least 1 hit point.

Slow Fall. Ban Oook reduces any falling damage by 30. If he does not take damage from a fall, he does not fall prone.

ACTIONS

Multiattack. Ban Oook makes three Unarmed Strikes. He can use his Flurry of Blows or Unholy Strike ability in place of one of the Unarmed Strikes.

Unarmed Strike. *Melee Weapon Attack:* +9 to hit, reach 5 ft., one target. *Hit:* 13 (2d8 + 4) bludgeoning damage, or 8 (1d8 + 4) bludgeoning damage in Small or Medium form.

Flurry of Blows (3/day). *Melee Weapon Attack:* +9 to hit, reach 5 ft., one target. *Hit:* 31 (6d8 + 4) bludgeoning damage (or 17 [3d8 + 4] bludgeoning damage in Small or Medium form), and the target suffers one of the following effects of Ban Oook's choice:

• The target must succeed on a DC 17 Dexterity saving throw or be knocked prone.

• The target must make a DC 17 Strength saving throw or be pushed up to 15 feet away from it.

• The target can't take reactions until the end of its next turn.

Unholy Strike (3/day). *Melee Weapon Attack:* +9 to hit, reach 5 ft., one target. *Hit:* 49 (10d8 + 4) necrotic damage — 26 (5d8 + 4) necrotic damage in Small or Medium form — and the target must succeed on a DC 17 Constitution saving throw. On a failed saving throw, the target's maximum hit points are reduced by an equal amount. Lost hit points are regained when the target takes a long rest.

Change Shape. Ban Oook magically polymorphs into a Small or Medium humanoid, into a Large giant, or back into his true form. Other than his size, his statistics are the same in each form. If Ban Oook dies, he reverts to his true form.

REACTIONS

Deflect Missiles. If it has one hand free, Ban Oook can use its reaction in response to being hit with a ranged weapon attack. He reduces the damage by 19 (1d10 + 14). If he reduces the damage to 0, he can catch the missile if it is small enough for him to hold with one hand.

Barghest, Greater

Large fiend, neutral evil
Armor Class 18 (natural armor)
Hit Points 136 (16d10 + 48)
Speed 60 ft. (30 ft. in goblin form)

STR	DEX	CON	INT	WIS	CHA
20 (+5)	15 (+2)	16 (+3)	13 (+1)	12 (+1)	14 (+2)

Skills Deception +6, Intimidation +6, Perception +5, Stealth +6
Damage Resistances cold, fire, lightning; bludgeoning, piercing, and slashing from nonmagical attacks
Damage Immunities acid, poison
Condition Immunities poisoned
Senses blindsight 60 ft., darkvision 120 ft., passive Perception 15
Languages Abyssal, Common, Goblin, Infernal
Challenge 10 (5,900 XP)

Shapeshifting. The barghest can use its action to polymorph into a goblin or back into its true form. Other than its speed and size (Small), its statistics are the same in each form.

Banished by Flame. When the barghest starts it turn in a source of flame that engulfs it, it must succeed on a DC 15 Charisma saving throw or be banished to the Abyss. Bursts of flame such as a fireball or dragon's breath do not have this effect.

Keen Smell. The barghest has advantage on Wisdom (Perception) checks that rely on smell.

Innate Spellcasting. The barghest's innate spellcasting ability is Charisma (spell save DC 14). The barghest can innately cast the following spells, requiring no material components:

At will: *levitate, minor illusion, pass without trace*
1/day each: *charm person, dimension door, suggestion*

ACTIONS

Bite. *Melee Weapon Attack (true form only):* +7 to hit, reach 5 ft., one target. *Hit:* 14 (2d8 + 5) piercing damage.

Claws. *Melee Weapon Attack:* +7 to hit, reach 5 ft., one target. *Hit:* 9 (1d8 + 5) slashing damage.

Basalt Warhound

Large elemental, lawful evil
Armor Class 16 (natural armor)
Hit Points 136 (16d10 + 48)
Speed 30 ft.

STR	DEX	CON	INT	WIS	CHA
16 (+3)	16 (+3)	16 (+3)	6 (–2)	14 (+2)	10 (+0)

Saving Throws Dex +6, Wis +5
Skills Perception +5
Damage Resistances bludgeoning, piercing, and slashing from nonmagical attacks
Damage Vulnerabilities cold
Damage Immunities fire, poison
Condition Immunities poisoned
Senses darkvision 60 ft., passive Perception 15
Languages Ignan
Challenge 5 (1,800 XP)

Death Burst. When basalt warhound dies, it explodes in a burst of fire. Each creature within 5 feet of it must make a DC 15 Dexterity saving throw, taking 13 (3d8) fire damage on a failed save, or half as much damage on a successful one.

Keen Smell. The basalt warhound has advantage on Wisdom (Perception) checks that rely on smell.

Pack Tactics. The basalt warhound has advantage on an attack roll against a creature if at least one of the warhound's allies is within 5 feet of the creature and the ally isn't incapacitated.

ACTIONS

Multiattack. The basalt warhound makes two Bite attacks.

Bite. *Melee Weapon Attack:* +6 to hit, reach 5 ft., one creature. *Hit:* 12 (2d8 + 3) piercing damage and 9 (2d8) fire damage.

Basilisk, Abyssal, Greater

Large monstrosity, chaotic evil
Armor Class 17 (natural armor)
Hit Points 142 (15d10 + 60)
Speed 25 ft.

STR	DEX	CON	INT	WIS	CHA
19 (+4)	10 (+0)	18 (+4)	5 (–3)	12 (+1)	6 (–2)

Saving Throws Con +8
Skills Perception +5
Damage Resistances cold, fire

Damage Immunities poison
Condition Immunities poisoned
Senses darkvision 90 ft., passive Perception 15
Languages —
Challenge 10 (5,900 XP)

Detect Good. The Abyssal basilisk can detect fey and celestial creatures within 60 feet as an ongoing effect.

Foul Breath. The Abyssal basilisk's breath is so putrid it creates an area of foul gas in a 5-foot radius around itself. Any creature entering that area or starting its turn within that area must succeed on a DC 13 Constitution save or become poisoned until the start of its next turn.

Magic Resistance. The Abyssal basilisk has advantage on saving throws against spells and other magical effects.

ACTIONS

Multiattack. The Abyssal basilisk makes one Bite attack and two Claw attacks.

Bite. *Melee Weapon Attack:* +8 to hit, reach 5 ft., one target. *Hit:* 17 (3d8 + 4) piercing damage plus 10 (3d6) poison damage.

Claw. *Melee Weapon Attack:* +8 to hit, reach 5 ft., one target. *Hit:* 13 (2d8 + 4) slashing damage.

Petrifying Gaze. If a creature starts its turn within 30 feet of the Abyssal basilisk and the two of them can see each other, the basilisk can force the creature to make a DC 15 Constitution saving throw if the basilisk isn't incapacitated. On a failed save, the creature magically begins to turn to stone and is restrained. It must repeat the saving throw at the end of its next turn. On a success, the effect ends. On a failure, the creature is petrified until freed by the *greater restoration* spell or other magic.

A creature that isn't surprised can avert its eyes to avoid the saving throw at the start of its turn. If it does so, it can't see the Abyssal basilisk until the start of its next turn, when it can avert its eyes again. If it looks at the Abyssal basilisk in the meantime, it must immediately make the save.

If the Abyssal basilisk sees its own reflection within 30 feet of it in bright light, it must succeed on a DC 10 Wisdom save or mistake itself for a rival and target itself with its gaze. The Abyssal basilisk's magic resistance gives it advantage on any resultant Constitution save versus its own gaze.

Beetle, Giant Rhinoceros

Large beast, unaligned
Armor Class 15 (natural armor)
Hit Points 114 (12d10 + 48)
Speed 20 ft.

STR	DEX	CON	INT	WIS	CHA
23 (+6)	10 (+0)	18 (+4)	1 (–5)	10 (+0)	9 (–1)

Senses darkvision 60 ft., passive Perception 10
Languages —
Challenge 6 (2,300 XP)

Trample. If the giant rhinoceros beetle moves at least 20 feet straight toward a creature and then hits it with a gore attack on the same turn, the target must succeed on a DC 16 Strength saving throw or be knocked prone. If the target is prone, the giant rhinoceros beetle can make one slam attack against it as a bonus action.

ACTIONS

Multiattack. The giant rhinoceros beetle makes one bite attack and one gore attack.

Bite. *Melee Weapon Attack:* +9 to hit, reach 5 ft., one target. *Hit:* 10 (1d8 + 6) piercing damage.

Gore. *Melee Weapon Attack:* +9 to hit, reach 5 ft., one target. *Hit:* 17 (2d10 + 6) piercing damage.

Slam. *Melee Weapon Attack:* +9 to hit, reach 5 ft., one target. *Hit:* 17 (2d10 + 6) bludgeoning damage.

Belker

Large elemental, neutral evil
Armor Class 15 (natural armor)
Hit Points 60 (8d10 + 16)
Speed 30 ft., fly 50 ft. (hover)

STR	DEX	CON	INT	WIS	CHA
14 (+2)	19 (+4)	14 (+2)	6 (–2)	11 (+0)	9 (–1)

Saving Throws Dex +6
Skills Acrobatics +6, Perception +2, Stealth + 6
Damage Immunities fire, poison
Condition Immunities exhaustion, paralyzed, petrified, poisoned, prone, unconscious
Senses darkvision 60 ft., passive Perception 12
Languages Auran
Challenge 3 (700 XP)

ACTIONS

Multiattack (normal form only). The belker makes one Bite attack and two Claw attacks.

Bite (normal form only). *Melee Weapon Attack:* +6 to hit, reach 5 ft., one target. *Hit:* 14 (3d6 + 4) piercing damage.

Claw (normal form only). *Melee Weapon Attack:* +6 to hit, reach 5 ft., one target. *Hit:* 11 (2d6 + 4) slashing damage.

Smoke Claws (smoke form only). When the belker initiates this attack, any creatures whose space overlaps with that of the belker must succeed on a DC 13 Constitution saving throw to avoid breathing in or absorbing some of the belker. A creature that fails takes 11 (2d6 + 4) slashing damage as the belker temporarily rematerializes its claws inside it. Anytime a creature under this effect moves, the belker may choose to reposition the space it occupies (one to four adjacent 5-foot squares) to continue to overlap with the moving creature, without expending any of its own movement. Creatures are affected even if they hold their breath or don't need to breathe.

BONUS ACTIONS

Smoke Form (recharge 6). The belker can turn into a form made of pure smoke and maintain that form for up to 1 minute. While in this form, it has all the properties of a creature under the effect of a *gaseous form* spell. It can move through a space as narrow as 1 inch wide without squeezing. It can enter the space(s) occupied by hostile creature(s) and stop there. When it ends its movement, it can occupy from one to four adjacent 5-foot squares, as it wishes. It cannot attack except with its Smoke Claws. It is resistant to all nonmagical damage. It retains its flying speed of 50 ft.

Belker Prince

Huge elemental, neutral evil
Armor Class 18 (natural armor)
Hit Points 139 (14d12 + 48)
Speed 30 ft., fly 50 ft. (hover)

STR	DEX	CON	INT	WIS	CHA
20 (+5)	21 (+5)	18 (+4)	10 (+0)	13 (+1)	11 (+0)

Saving Throws Con +8, Dex + 9
Skills Acrobatics +9, Perception +5, Stealth + 9
Damage Resistances cold, lightning, necrotic, thunder; bludgeoning, piercing, and slashing from nonmagical attacks
Damage Immunities fire, poison
Condition Immunities exhaustion, paralyzed, petrified, poisoned, prone, unconscious
Senses darkvision 120 ft., passive Perception 15
Languages Auran
Challenge 12 (8,400 XP)

Magic Weapons. The belker prince's attacks are magical.

ACTIONS

Multiattack (normal form only). The belker prince makes one Bite attack and two Claw attacks.

Bite (normal form only). *Melee Weapon Attack:* +9 to hit, reach 5 ft., one target. *Hit:* 21 (3d10 + 5) piercing damage.

Claw (normal form only). *Melee Weapon Attack:* +9 to hit, reach 10 ft., one target. *Hit:* 16 (2d10 + 5) slashing damage.

Smoke Claws (smoke form only). When the belker prince initiates this attack, any creatures whose space overlaps with that of the belker prince must succeed on a DC 15 Constitution saving throw to avoid breathing in or absorbing some of the belker prince. A creature that fails takes 16 (2d10 + 5) slashing damage as the belker prince temporarily rematerializes its claws inside it. Anytime a creature under this effect moves, the belker prince may choose to reposition the space it occupies (one to nine adjacent 5-foot squares) to continue to include the moving creature, without expending any of its own movement. Creatures are affected even if they hold their breath or don't need to breathe.

Summon Belkers (3/day). The belker prince may summon 1d3 + 1 belkers who appear instantaneously in unoccupied spaces within 100 feet of the belker prince and do its bidding, acting on the prince's initiative and fighting to the death if so instructed.

BONUS ACTIONS

Smoke Form (recharge 6). The belker prince can turn into a form made of pure smoke and maintain that form for up to 1 minute. While in this form, it has all the properties of a creature under the effect of a *gaseous form* spell. It can move through a space as narrow as 1 inch wide without squeezing. It can enter the space(s) occupied by hostile creature(s) and stop there. When it ends its movement, it can occupy from one to nine adjacent 5-foot squares, as it wishes. It cannot attack except with its Smoke Claws or Cloud of Smoke special abilities. It is resistant to all nonmagical damage. It retains its flying speed of 50 ft.

LEGENDARY ACTIONS

The belker prince can take 3 legendary actions, choosing from the options below. Only one legendary action can be used at a time and only at the end of another creature's turn. The belker prince regains spent legendary actions at the start of his turn.

Claw. The belker prince makes a Claw attack.

Cloud of Smoke (costs 2 actions). The belker prince chooses a point that it can see within 100 feet of it. A cloud of thick smoke 60 feet in diameter erupts from that point and lasts for 1 minute. The area is heavily obscured, and each creature in the area is blinded and must make a DC 16 Constitution saving throw. Those who fail take 14 (4d6) poison damage and are poisoned until they leave the cloud; those who succeed take half as much damage and are not poisoned.

Wing Buffet (costs 2 actions). The belker prince beats its wings. Each creature within 10 feet must succeed on a DC 16 Dexterity save or take 11 (2d6 + 4) bludgeoning damage, be knocked prone, and be pushed 10 feet away for each size category its size is below Huge (e.g. Medium creatures are pushed 20 feet back, Small creatures 30 feet).

Birhaakamen

Medium monstrosity, neutral
Armor Class 16 (breastplate)
Hit Points 13 (3d8)
Speed 30 ft., fly 30 ft.

STR	DEX	CON	INT	WIS	CHA
14 (+2)	15 (+2)	11 (+0)	10 (+0)	12 (+1)	10 (+0)

Skills Acrobatics +4, Athletics +4, Perception +3, Survival +3
Damage Resistance poison
Senses passive Perception 13
Languages Auran, Common
Challenge 1 (200 XP)

Carrion Eaters. The birhaakamen have advantage on saving throws against diseases and being poisoned.

ACTIONS

Talons. *Melee Weapon Attack:* +4 to hit, reach 5 ft., one target. *Hit:* 5 (1d6 + 2) slashing damage.

Spear. *Melee Weapon Attack:* +4 to hit, reach 5 ft. or range 20/60 ft., one target. *Hit:* 5 (1d6 + 2) piercing damage, or 6 (1d8 + 2) piercing damage if used with two hands to make a melee attack.

Birhaakamen Chieftain

Medium monstrosity, neutral
Armor Class 16 (breastplate)
Hit Points 117 (18d8 + 36)
Speed 30 ft., fly 30 ft.

STR	DEX	CON	INT	WIS	CHA
16 (+3)	15 (+2)	15 (+2)	15 (+2)	15 (+2)	11 (+0)

Saving Throws Str +6, Dex +5, Con +5
Skills Animal Handling +5, Acrobatics +5, Athletics +6, History +5, Intimidation +3, Perception +5, Persuasion +3, Survival +5
Senses passive Perception 15
Languages Auran, Common
Challenge 6 (2,300 XP)

Brave. The birhaakamen chieftain has advantage on saving throws against being frightened.

Carrion Eaters. The birhaakamen have advantage on saving throws against diseases and being poisoned.

Improved Critical. The birhaakamen chieftain scores a critical hit with a weapon attack on a roll of 19 or 20.

Martial Advantage. Once per turn, the birhaakamen chieftain can deal an extra 13 (3d8) damage to a creature he hits with a weapon attack if that creature is within 5 feet of an ally of the birhaakamen chieftain that isn't incapacitated.

Multiattack. The birhaakamen chieftain makes three melee attacks.

Talons. *Melee Weapon Attack:* +6 to hit, reach 5 ft., one target. *Hit:* 6 (1d6 + 3) slashing damage.

Spear. *Melee Weapon Attack:* +6 to hit, reach 5 ft. or range 20/60 ft., one target. *Hit:* 6 (1d6 + 3) piercing damage, or 7 (1d8 + 3) piercing damage if used with two hands to make a melee attack.

Birhaakamen Shaman

Medium monstrosity, neutral
Armor Class 12
Hit Points 71 (13d8 + 13)
Speed 30 ft., fly 30 ft.

STR	DEX	CON	INT	WIS	CHA
13 (+1)	14 (+2)	13 (+1)	12 (+1)	16 (+3)	11 (+0)

Saving Throws Int +4, Wis +6
Skills Arcana +4, Acrobatics +4, Athletics +3, Medicine +6, Nature +4, Perception +6, Survival +6
Senses passive Perception 16
Languages Auran, Common, Druidic
Challenge 5 (1,800 XP)

Carrion Eaters. The birhaakamen have advantage on saving throws against diseases and being poisoned.

Spellcasting. The birhaakamen shaman is a 5th-level spellcaster. Its spellcasting ability is Wisdom (spell save DC 14, +6 to hit with spell attacks). It has the following druid spells prepared.

> Cantrips (at will): *guidance, mending, produce flame, shillelagh*
> 1st level (4 slots): *cure wounds, detect magic, faerie fire, thunderwave*
> 2nd level (3 slots): *barkskin, gust of wind, lesser restoration*
> 3rd level (2 slots): *call lightning, lightning bolt, meld into stone*

ACTIONS

Quarterstaff. *Melee Weapon Attack:* +3 to hit (+6 to hit with shillelagh), reach 5 ft., one target. *Hit:* 4 (1d6 + 1) bludgeoning damage, 5 (1d8 + 1) bludgeoning damage if wielded with two hands, or 7 (1d8 + 3) bludgeoning damage with shillelagh.

Birhaakamen Warrior

Medium monstrosity, neutral
Armor Class 16 (breastplate)
Hit Points 52 (8d8 + 16)
Speed 30 ft., fly 30 ft.

STR	DEX	CON	INT	WIS	CHA
16 (+3)	13 (+1)	14 (+2)	10 (+0)	11 (+0)	10 (+0)

Skills Acrobatics +4, Athletics +4, Perception +3, Survival +3
Senses passive Perception 13
Languages Auran, Common
Challenge 3 (700 XP)

Carrion Eaters. The birhaakamen have advantage on saving throws against diseases and being poisoned.

Multiattack. The birhaakamen warrior makes two Spear attacks or two Talon attacks.

Talons. *Melee Weapon Attack:* +5 to hit, reach 5 ft., one target. *Hit:* 6 (1d6 + 3) slashing damage.

Spear. *Melee Weapon Attack:* +5 to hit, reach 5 ft. or range 20/60 ft., one target. *Hit:* 6 (1d6 + 3) piercing damage, or 7 (1d8 + 3) piercing damage if used with two hands to make a melee attack.

Blood Bush

Small plant, unaligned
Armor Class 13 (natural armor)
Hit Points 59 (7d6 + 35)
Speed 0 ft.

STR	DEX	CON	INT	WIS	CHA
15 (+2)	14 (+2)	20 (+5)	2 (−4)	12 (+1)	8 (−1)

Damage Vulnerabilities thunder
Damage Resistances cold, fire
Damage Immunities lightning
Senses blindsight 30 ft., passive Perception 11
Languages —
Challenge 3 (700 XP)

Germinate. Creatures that are implanted with a blood bush seed begin to suffer the effects of it rapidly germinating inside of them. Once implanted, the seed quickly begins to grow and expand. For every 24 hours that elapse, the target must repeat the DC 14 Constitution saving throw, reducing its hit point maximum by 5 (1d10) on a failure. The germinating seed is destroyed by the immune system on a success. The target dies if this reduces its hit point maximum to 0. This reduction to the target's hit point maximum lasts until the blood bush seed is removed.

ACTIONS

Multiattack. The blood bush makes one Flower Dart attack and two Tendril attacks.

Tendril. *Melee Weapon Attack:* +4 to hit, reach 5 ft., one target. *Hit:* 4 (1d4 + 2) slashing damage. If the target is a Medium or smaller creature, it is grappled (escape DC 12) and restrained, and the blood bush cannot grapple another target.

Flower Dart. *Ranged Weapon Attack:* +4 to hit, reach 5 ft., one target. *Hit:* 5 (1d6 + 2) piercing damage, and the target must succeed on a DC 14 Constitution saving throw or be implanted with a blood bush seed (see Germinate).

Blood Orc

Medium humanoid (orc), chaotic evil
Armor Class 16 (chain mail)
Hit Points 75 (10d8 + 30)
Speed 30 ft.

STR	DEX	CON	INT	WIS	CHA
17 (+3)	14 (+2)	17 (+3)	8 (−1)	6 (−2)	8 (−1)

Skills Intimidation +1
Senses darkvision 60 ft., passive Perception 8
Languages Common, Orc
Challenge 4 (1,100 XP)

Aggressive. As a bonus action, the orc can move up to its speed toward a hostile creature that it can see.

Axe Expert. The orc deals an extra die of damage when it hits with a Greataxe attack (included in the attack).

Bloodfrenzy. When the blood orc begins its turn with half or fewer of its hit points, it can make a bite attack as a bonus action when it takes the Attack action, and it has advantage on Intelligence, Wisdom, and Charisma saving throws against spells and other effects.

ACTIONS

Multiattack. The orc makes two Greataxe attacks.

Bite. *Melee Weapon Attack:* +5 to hit, reach 5 ft., one target. *Hit:* 4 (1d4 + 3) piercing damage.

Greataxe. *Melee Weapon Attack:* +5 to hit, reach 5 ft., one target. *Hit:* 16 (2d12 + 3) slashing damage.

Shotgun. *Ranged Weapon Attack:* +4 to hit, range 60/120 ft., one target. *Hit:* 4 (1d8) piercing damage or *Hit:* 9 (2d8) piercing damage.

Blood Orc Elder Warrior

Medium humanoid (blood orc), chaotic evil
Armor Class 14 (chain shirt)
Hit Points 75 (10d8 + 30)
Speed 40 ft.

STR	DEX	CON	INT	WIS	CHA
21 (+5)	13 (+1)	16 (+3)	8 (−1)	6 (−2)	6 (−2)

Saving Throws Str +8, Con +6
Skills Intimidation +0, Perception +1, Survival +1
Senses darkvision 60 ft., passive Perception 11
Languages Common, Orc
Challenge 6 (2,300 XP)

Bloodfrenzy. When the blood orc begins its turn with half or fewer of its hit points, it can make a bite attack as a bonus action when they take the Attack action, it has advantage on Intelligence, Wisdom, and Charisma saving throws against spells and other effects, and the elder warrior has resistance to bludgeoning, piercing, and slashing damage.

Brute. A melee weapon deals one extra die of its damage when the elder warrior hits with it (included in the attack).

ACTIONS

Multiattack. The elder warrior makes two melee attacks.

Bite. *Melee Weapon Attack:* +8 to hit, reach 5 ft., one target. *Hit:* 10 (2d4 + 5) piercing damage.

Greataxe. *Melee Weapon Attack:* +8 to hit, reach 5 ft., one target. *Hit:* 18 (2d12 + 5) slashing damage.

Terrorize (1/day). The elder warrior roars and displays his trophies, which are visible to all creatures within 30 feet that can see it. Creatures of the elder warrior's choice within that area must make a DC 16 Wisdom saving throw or be frightened of the warrior for 1 minute. While frightened, they are paralyzed. A frightened creature can repeat the saving throw at the end of each of its turns, ending the effect on a success.

Bloodsuckle

Large plant, unaligned
Armor Class 14 (natural armor)
Hit Points 68 (8d10 + 24)
Speed 0 ft.

STR	DEX	CON	INT	WIS	CHA
16 (+3)	10 (+0)	17 (+3)	6 (−2)	10 (+0)	8 (−1)

Skills Perception +2, Stealth +2
Damage Resistances bludgeoning
Damage Immunities poison
Condition Immunities blinded, charmed, deafened, frightened, poisoned
Senses blindsight 50 ft. (blind beyond this radius), passive Perception 12
Languages —
Challenge 3 (700 XP)

ACTIONS

Multiattack. The bloodsuckle makes two Tendril attacks and four Raking Limb attacks.

Tendril. *Melee Weapon Attack:* +5 to hit, reach 30 ft., one target. *Hit:* The target is grappled (escape DC 13) and injected with mind-altering sap. Such targets must succeed on a DC 15 Wisdom save or become charmed. If a target or its allies are currently in combat with the bloodsuckle, the target has advantage on this saving throw. Those who fail are released immediately but compelled to remain near the bloodsuckle and submit to its Blood Drain ability. A charmed creature may make a new save each time it takes damage from a source other than Blood Drain. Grappled targets who fail to break free are pulled to within 10 feet, in range of the bloodsuckle's raking limbs.

Raking Limb. *Melee Weapon Attack:* +5 to hit, reach 10 ft., one target. *Hit:* 6 (1d6 + 3) slashing damage. The bloodsuckle only rakes targets it has failed to turn into blood hosts or who present urgent danger to its survival.

BONUS ACTIONS

Blood Drain. The bloodsuckle can drain blood from each of its charmed hosts dealing 7 (2d6) necrotic damage per round. It will stop drawing from a host when that host reaches 25% of its maximum hit points, hoping to preserve sources of food as long as possible.

Bodak

Medium undead, chaotic evil
Armor Class 16 (natural armor)
Hit Points 120 (16d8 + 48)
Speed 30 ft.

STR	DEX	CON	INT	WIS	CHA
18 (+4)	18 (+4)	16 (+3)	6 (−2)	14 (+2)	10 (+0)

Saving Throws Con +7, Wis +6
Skills Perception +6, Stealth +8
Damage Resistances acid, fire, necrotic; bludgeoning, piercing, and slashing from nonmagical attacks
Damage Immunities lightning, poison
Condition Immunities charmed, frightened, poisoned
Senses darkvision 120 ft., passive Perception 16
Languages Abyssal, Common.
Challenge 9 (5,000 XP)

Aura of Obliteration. The bodak is surrounded by an annihilating aura of obliteration. All creatures other than undead and fiends that start their turn within 30 feet of the bodak take 9 (2d8) necrotic damage. The bodak can emit or suppress this aura using a bonus action.

Gaze of Orcus. If a creature starts its turn within 30 ft. of the bodak and the two of them can see each other, the bodak can force the creature to make a DC 12 Constitution saving throw if the bodak isn't incapacitated. On a failed save, the creature drops to 0 hit points, unless it is immune to the frightened condition. On a success, the creature takes 22 (4d10) psychic damage. A creature that is slain by the bodak's Gaze rises as a bodak 24 hours later unless restored to life by magical means.

A creature that isn't surprised can avert its eyes to avoid the saving throw at the start of its turn. If it does so, it can't see the bodak until the start of its next turn, when it can avert its eyes again. If it looks at the bodak in the meantime, it must immediately make the save.

Sunlight Antipathy. The bodak takes 5 radiant damage when it starts its turn in sunlight. While in sunlight, it has disadvantage on attack rolls and ability checks.

ACTIONS

Multiattack. The bodak can use its Scornful Glare and makes two Slam attacks.

Slam. *Melee Weapon Attack:* +8 to hit, reach 5 ft., one creature. *Hit:* 8 (1d8 + 4) bludgeoning damage and 13 (3d8) necrotic damage.

Scornful Glare (recharge 4–6). The bodak targets one creature it can see within 60 feet of it. If the target can see the bodak, it must attempt a DC 12 Wisdom saving throw. The creature takes 22 (4d10) necrotic damage and is frightened for 1 minute on a failed save. On a successful save, the creature takes half as much damage and is not frightened.

Bodak Priest

Medium undead, chaotic evil
Armor Class 18 (natural armor)
Hit Points 156 (24d8 + 48)
Speed 30 ft.

STR	DEX	CON	INT	WIS	CHA
13 (+1)	18 (+4)	15 (+2)	8 (−1)	25 (+7)	20 (+5)

Saving Throws Con +6, Wis +11
Skills Perception +11, Stealth +8
Damage Resistances acid, fire, necrotic; bludgeoning, piercing, and slashing from nonmagical attacks
Damage Immunities lightning, poison
Condition Immunities charmed, frightened, poisoned
Senses darkvision 120 ft., passive Perception 21
Languages Abyssal, Common.
Challenge 12 (8,400 XP)

Abyssal Blessing of Orcus. The bodak priest gains 10 temporary hit points when it reduces a hostile creature that is not undead to 0 hit points.

Aura of Obliteration. As a minion of Orcus, the bodak is surrounded by an annihilating aura of obliteration. All creatures other than undead and fiends that start their turn within 30 feet of the bodak take 9 (2d8) necrotic damage. The bodak can emit or suppress this aura using a bonus action.

Gaze of Orcus. If a creature starts its turn within 30 ft. of the bodak and the two of them can see each other, the bodak can force the creature to make a DC 12 Constitution saving throw if the bodak isn't incapacitated. On a failed save, the creature drops to 0 hit points, unless it is immune to the frightened condition. On a success, the creature takes 22 (4d10) psychic damage. A creature that is slain by the bodak's Gaze rises as a bodak 24 hours later unless restored to life by magical means.

A creature that isn't surprised can avert its eyes to avoid the saving throw at the start of its turn. If it does so, it can't see the bodak until the start of its next turn, when it can avert its eyes again. If it looks at the bodak in the meantime, it must immediately make the save.

Sunlight Antipathy. The bodak takes 5 radiant damage when it starts its turn in sunlight. While in sunlight, it has disadvantage on attack rolls and ability checks.

Spellcasting. The bodak priest is a 6th-level spellcaster. Its spellcasting ability is Wisdom (spell save DC 19, +11 to hit with spell attacks). It has the following cleric spells prepared:

Cantrips (at will): *chill touch, guidance, resistance, thaumaturgy*
1st level (4 slots): *bane, bless, cure wounds, detect magic, inflict wounds*
2nd level (3 slots): *enhance ability, hold person, silence*
3rd level (3 slots): *animate dead, bestow curse, dispel magic*

ACTIONS

Multiattack. The bodak can use its Scornful Glare and make two Slam attacks.

Slam. *Melee Weapon Attack:* +8 to hit, reach 5 ft., one creature. *Hit:* 8 (1d8 + 4) bludgeoning damage and 13 (3d8) necrotic damage.

Caress of Orcus (recharges after a short or long rest). *Melee Weapon Attack:* +8 to hit, reach 5 ft., one target. Hit: 17 (3d8 + 4) necrotic damage, and the target's Strength score is reduced by 1d6. The target dies if this reduces its Strength to 0. Otherwise, the reduction lasts until the target finishes a short or long rest.

Scornful Glare (recharge 4–6). The bodak targets one creature it can see within 60 feet of it. If the target can see the bodak, it must attempt a DC 12 Wisdom saving throw. The creature takes 22 (4d10) necrotic damage and is frightened for 1 minute on a failed save. On a successful save, the creature takes half as much damage and is not frightened.

Bog Beast

Large monstrosity, neutral
Armor Class 13 (natural armor)
Hit Points 76 (8d10 + 32)
Speed 30 ft.

STR	DEX	CON	INT	WIS	CHA
20 (+5)	11 (+0)	18 (+4)	5 (−3)	12 (+1)	9 (−1)

Skills Perception +5, Survival +5
Senses darkvision 60 ft., passive Perception 15
Languages —
Challenge 3 (700 XP)

Keen Smell. The bog beast has advantage on Wisdom (Perception) checks that rely on smell.

ACTIONS

Multiattack. The bog beast makes two Claws attacks.

Claws. *Melee Weapon Attack:* +7 to hit, reach 10 ft., one target. *Hit:* 12 (2d6 + 5) slashing damage. If the target is a creature, it must succeed on a DC 14 Constitution saving throw against disease or become poisoned until the disease is cured. Every 24 hours that elapse, the target must repeat the saving throw, reducing its hit point maximum by 5 (1d10) on a failure. The disease is cured on a success. The target dies if the disease reduces its hit point maximum to 0. This reduction of the target's hit point maximum lasts until the disease is cured.

Bog Creeper

Medium plant, unaligned
Armor Class 12 (natural armor)
Hit Points 104 (11d8 + 55)
Speed 10 ft., swim 20 ft.

STR	DEX	CON	INT	WIS	CHA
18 (+4)	10 (+0)	20 (+5)	3 (−4)	14 (+2)	6 (−2)

Skills Perception +5
Senses tremorsense 60 ft., passive Perception 15
Languages —
Challenge 9 (5,000 XP)

False Appearance. While the bog creeper remains motionless, it is indistinguishable from normal plants.
Marsh Move. A bog creeper doesn't treat marshy, swampy terrain as difficult terrain.

Actions

Multiattack. The bog creeper makes up to one Bite, one Slam, and two Tendril attacks.
Bite. Melee *Weapon Attack:* +7 to hit, reach 5 ft., one target. *Hit:* 13 (2d8 + 4) piercing damage.
Slam. Melee *Weapon Attack:* +7 to hit, reach 5 ft., one target. *Hit:* 15 (2d10 + 4) bludgeoning damage.
Tendrils. Melee *Weapon Attack:* +7 to hit, reach 10 ft., one target. *Hit:* 11 (2d6 + 4) bludgeoning damage. The target is grappled (escape DC 14) if the bog creeper isn't already grappling a creature, and the target is restrained until the grapple ends. The bog creeper can only grapple one target.
Acid Spray (3/day). The bog creeper sprays stomach acid in a 30-foot cone. Each creature in that area must make a DC 15 Dexterity saving throw, taking 14 (3d8) acid damage on a failed save, or half as much damage on a successful one.

Brass Man

Large construct, unaligned
Armor Class 18 (natural armor)
Hit Points 95 (10d10 + 40)
Speed 30 ft.

STR	DEX	CON	INT	WIS	CHA
20 (+5)	10 (+0)	18 (+4)	3 (−4)	11 (+0)	1 (−5)

Senses darkvision 60 ft., passive Perception 10
Damage Vulnerabilities cold
Damage Resistances bludgeoning, piercing, and slashing damage from attacks not made with adamantine
Damage Immunities fire, poison
Condition Immunities paralyzed, petrified, poisoned, stunned, unconscious
Languages —
Challenge 6 (2,300 XP)

Immunity to Magic. A brass man automatically succeeds on all saving throws against spells and spell-like effects. If a successful saving throw reduces damage by half, the brass man takes no damage instead. In addition, certain spells and effects function differently against the creature, as noted below (these effects override its immunity).

• A magical attack that deals lightning damage automatically slows a brass man (as the *slow* spell) for 3 rounds.

• A magical attack that deals fire damage automatically ends any *slow* effect on the brass man and repairs 1 point of damage for each 3 points of damage the attack would normally inflict deal. If the amount of healing would cause the brass man to exceed its hit point maximum, it gains the excess as temporary hit points.

Actions

Multiattack. A brass man makes two Fist attacks.
Fist. Melee *Weapon Attack:* +8 to hit, reach 10 ft., one creature. *Hit:* 10 (1d10 + 5) bludgeoning damage plus 5 (1d10) fire damage.
Greatsword. Melee *Weapon Attack:* +8 to hit, reach 10 ft., one creature. *Hit:* 18 (2d12 + 5) slashing damage.
Molten Brass (recharge 5–6). The brass man spews forth a line of molten brass 30 feet long and 5 feet wide. Each creature in the line must make a DC 15 Dexterity saving throw, taking 27 (6d8) fire damage on a failure or half as much on a success.

Brass Man, Berserk

Large construct, neutral
Armor Class 16 (natural armor)
Hit Points 136 (16d10 + 48)
Speed 30 ft.

STR	DEX	CON	INT	WIS	CHA
22 (+6)	10 (+0)	16 (+3)	2 (−4)	9 (−1)	1 (−5)

Damage Vulnerabilities cold
Damage Immunities fire, poison, psychic; bludgeoning, piercing, and slashing from attacks not made with adamantine
Condition Immunities charmed, exhaustion, frightened, paralyzed, petrified, poisoned
Senses darkvision 60 ft., passive Perception 9
Languages Abyssal, Common.
Challenge 9 (5,000 XP)
Brutal Critical. The golem can roll one additional weapon damage die when determining the extra damage for a critical hit with a melee attack.
Fire Absorption. Whenever the golem is subjected to fire damage, it takes no damage and instead regains a number of hit points equal to the fire damage dealt.
Immutable Form. The golem is immune to any spell or effect that would alter its form.
Magic Resistance. The golem has advantage on saving throws against spells and other magical effects.
Magic Weapons. The golem's weapon attacks are magical.
Reckless. At the start of its turn, the berserk brass man can gain advantage on all melee weapon attack rolls during that turn, but attack rolls against it have advantage until the start of its next turn.

Actions

Multiattack. The brass man makes two Greatsword attack and one Slam attack.
Greatsword. Melee *Weapon Attack:* +10 to hit, reach 10 ft., one target. *Hit:* 20 (4d6 + 6) slashing damage.
Slam. Melee *Weapon Attack:* +10 to hit, reach 10 ft., one

target. *Hit:* 19 (3d8 + 6) bludgeoning damage.
Molten Breath (recharge 6). The brass man exhales molten brass in a 25-foot line. Each creature along that line must make a DC 13 Dexterity saving throw, taking 28 (8d6) fire damage on a failed save, or half as much on a successful one.

Burning Dervish

Medium fiend, lawful evil
Armor Class 14 (natural armor)
Hit Points 45 (7d8 + 14)
Speed 30 ft., fly 20 ft.

STR	DEX	CON	INT	WIS	CHA
15 (+2)	16 (+3)	14 (+2)	13 (+1)	15 (+2)	15 (+2)

Skills Perception +4, Stealth +5
Damage Vulnerabilities cold
Damage Immunities fire
Senses darkvision 60 ft., passive Perception 14
Languages Common, Ignan, Infernal
Challenge 3 (700 XP)

Elemental Endurance. Burning dervishes can survive on the Elemental Planes of Air or Earth for up to 48 hours and on the Elemental Plane of Water for up to 12 hours. Failure to return to the Elemental Plane of Fire after that time deals 1 cold damage each hour to a burning dervish until it dies or returns to the Elemental Plane of Fire.

Innate Spellcasting. The burning dervish's innate spellcasting ability is Charisma (spell save DC 12, +4 to hit with spell attacks). It can cast the following spells, requiring no material components.

At will: *fire bolt, produce flame*
3/day: *invisibility* (self only)
1/day: *enlarge/reduce, flaming sphere, plane shift* (self only, Elemental, Astral, or Material Planes only)

Actions

Multiattack. The burning dervish makes two Scimitar attacks or two Fist attacks.
Scimitar. *Melee Weapon Attack:* +5 to hit, reach 5 ft., one target. *Hit:* 6 (1d6 + 3) slashing damage.
Fist (flame form only). *Melee Spell Attack:* +4 to hit, reach 5 ft., one target. *Hit:* 7 (2d4 + 2) fire damage.
Flame Form (3/day). The burning dervish magically polymorphs into a Medium–sized column of fire for 1 minute, until the dervish ends it as a bonus action, or the dervish dies. Equipment worn or carried by the dervish are absorbed into its form. While in this form, it has resistance to bludgeoning, piercing, and slashing damage from nonmagical attacks, it is immune to being grappled or restrained, and can move through a space as narrow as 1 inch wide without squeezing. A creature that touches the burning dervish in this form or hits it with a melee attack while within 5 feet of it takes 4 (1d8) fire damage. In addition, the burning dervish can enter a hostile creature's space and stop there. The first time it enters a creature's space on a turn, that creature takes 4 (1d8) fire damage and catches fire; until someone takes an action to douse the fire, the creature takes 4 (1d8) fire damage at the start of each of its turns.

Burning Dervish Child

Small fiend, lawful evil
Armor Class 14 (natural armor)
Hit Points 33 (6d6 + 12)
Speed 30 ft., fly 20 ft.

STR	DEX	CON	INT	WIS	CHA
15 (+2)	15 (+2)	14 (+2)	13 (+1)	15 (+2)	15 (+2)

Skills Perception +4, Stealth +4
Damage Vulnerabilities cold
Damage Immunities fire
Senses darkvision 60 ft., passive Perception 14
Languages Common, Ignan, Infernal
Challenge 1 (200 XP)

Elemental Endurance. Burning dervishes can survive on the Elemental Planes of Air or Earth for up to 48 hours and on the Elemental Plane of Water for up to 12 hours. Failure to return to the Elemental Plane of Fire after that time deals 1 cold damage each hour to a burning dervish until it dies or returns to the Elemental Plane of Fire.

Innate Spellcasting. The burning dervish's innate spellcasting ability is Charisma (spell save DC 12, +4 to hit with spell attacks). It can cast the following spells, requiring no material components.

At will: *fire bolt, produce flame*
3/day: *invisibility* (self only)
1/day: *enlarge/reduce, flaming sphere, plane shift* (self only, Elemental, Astral, or Material Planes only)

Actions

Multiattack. The burning dervish child makes two Fist attacks.
Scimitar. *Melee Weapon Attack:* +4 to hit, reach 5 ft., one target. *Hit:* 5 (1d6 + 2) slashing damage.
Fist (flame form only). *Melee Spell Attack:* +4 to hit, reach 5 ft., one target. *Hit:* 7 (2d4 + 2) fire damage.
Flame Form (3/day). The burning dervish magically polymorphs into a Medium–sized column of fire for 1 minute, until the dervish ends it as a bonus action, or the dervish dies. Equipment worn or carried by the dervish are absorbed into its form. While in this form, it has resistance to bludgeoning, piercing, and slashing damage from nonmagical attacks, it is immune to being grappled or restrained, and can move through a space as narrow as 1 inch wide without squeezing. A creature that touches the burning dervish in this form or hits it with a melee attack while within 5 feet of it takes 3 (1d6) fire damage. In addition, the burning dervish can enter a hostile creature's space and stop there. The first time it enters a creature's space on a turn, that creature takes 3 (1d6) fire damage and catches fire; until someone takes an action to douse the fire, the creature takes 3 (1d6) fire damage at the start of each of its turns.

Burning Dervish Feyhda

Medium fiend, lawful evil
Armor Class 15 (natural armor)
Hit Points 65 (10d8 + 20)
Speed 30 ft., fly 20 ft.

STR	DEX	CON	INT	WIS	CHA
15 (+2)	18 (+4)	14 (+2)	13 (+1)	16 (+3)	15 (+2)

Saving Throws Int +6, Wis +8
Skills Athletics +5, Acrobatics +7, Perception +6, Religion +4,

Stealth +7
Damage Vulnerabilities cold
Damage Immunities fire
Senses darkvision 60 ft., passive Perception 16
Languages Common, Ignan, Infernal
Challenge 7 (2,900 XP)

Assassin's Blessing (3/long rest). When the dervish feyhda hits with an attack and has advantage on the attack roll, the feyhda can cause the attack to deal an additional 27 (6d8) damage. The damage is the same type as the damage of the attack.

Cunning Action. On each of its turns, the feyhda can use a bonus action to take the Dash, Disengage, or Hide action.

Elemental Endurance. Burning dervishes can survive on the Elemental Planes of Air or Earth for up to 48 hours and on the Elemental Plane of Water for up to 12 hours. Failure to return to the Elemental Plane of Fire after that time deals 1 cold damage each hour to a burning dervish until it dies or returns to the Elemental Plane of Fire.

Innate Spellcasting. The burning dervish's innate spellcasting ability is Charisma (spell save DC 12, +4 to hit with spell attacks). It can cast the following spells, requiring no material components.

> At will: *fire bolt* (5th level), *produce flame*
> 3/day: *invisibility* (self only)
> 1/day: *enlarge/reduce, flaming sphere, plane shift* (self only, Elemental, Astral, or Material Planes only)

Spellcasting. The feyhda is a 5th-level spellcaster. Its spellcasting ability is Wisdom (spell save DC 14, +6 to hit with spell attacks). It has the following cleric spells prepared.

> Cantrips (at will): *guidance, mending, resistance*
> 1st level (4 slots): *bless, detect magic, sanctuary*
> 2nd level (3 slots): *blindness/deafness, enhance ability, silence*
> 3rd level (2 slots): *bestow curse, dispel magic*

Actions

Multiattack. The burning dervish feyhda makes two Scimitar attacks or two Fist attacks.

Scimitar. *Melee Weapon Attack:* +7 to hit, reach 5 ft., one target. *Hit:* 6 (1d6 + 3) slashing damage.

Fist (flame form only). *Melee Spell Attack:* +5 to hit, reach 5 ft., one target. *Hit:* 9 (2d6 + 2) fire damage.

Flame Form (3/day). The burning dervish magically polymorphs into a Medium–sized column of fire for 1 minute, until the dervish ends it as a bonus action, or the dervish dies. Equipment worn or carried by the dervish are absorbed into its form. While in this form, it has resistance to bludgeoning, piercing, and slashing damage from nonmagical attacks, it is immune to being grappled or restrained, and can move through a space as narrow as 1 inch wide without squeezing. A creature that touches the burning dervish in this form or hits it with a melee attack while within 5 feet of it takes 4 (1d8) fire damage. In addition, the burning dervish can enter a hostile creature's space and stop there. The first time it enters a creature's space on a turn, that creature takes 4 (1d8) fire damage and catches fire; until someone takes an action to douse the fire, the creature takes 4 (1d8) fire damage at the start of each of its turns.

Burning Dervish Guard

Medium fiend, lawful evil
Armor Class 16 (natural armor)
Hit Points 84 (13d8 + 26)
Speed 30 ft., fly 20 ft.

STR	DEX	CON	INT	WIS	CHA
15 (+2)	16 (+3)	14 (+2)	13 (+1)	15 (+2)	16 (+3)

Skills Perception +5, Stealth +6
Damage Vulnerabilities cold
Damage Immunities fire
Senses darkvision 60 ft., passive Perception 15
Languages Common, Ignan, Infernal
Challenge 7 (2,900 XP)

Elemental Endurance. Burning dervishes can survive on the Elemental Planes of Air or Earth for up to 48 hours and on the Elemental Plane of Water for up to 12 hours. Failure to return to the Elemental Plane of Fire after that time deals 1 cold damage each hour to a burning dervish until it dies or returns to the Elemental Plane of Fire.

Innate Spellcasting. The burning dervish's innate spellcasting ability is Charisma (spell save DC 14, +6 to hit with spell attacks). It can cast the following spells, requiring no material components.

> At will: *fire bolt* (5th level), *produce flame*
> 3/day: *invisibility* (self only)
> 1/day: *enlarge/reduce, flaming sphere, plane shift* (self only, Elemental, Astral, or Material Planes only)

Actions

Multiattack. The burning dervish makes two Scimitar attacks or two Fist attacks.

Scimitar. *Melee Weapon Attack:* +6 to hit, reach 5 ft., one target. *Hit:* 6 (1d6 + 3) slashing damage.

Fist (flame form only). *Melee Spell Attack:* +6 to hit, reach 5 ft., one target. *Hit:* 14 (2d10 + 3) fire damage.

Flame Form (3/day). The burning dervish magically polymorphs into a Medium–sized column of fire for 1 minute, until the dervish ends it as a bonus action, or the dervish dies. Equipment worn or carried by the dervish are absorbed into its form. While in this form, it has resistance to bludgeoning, piercing, and slashing damage from nonmagical attacks, it is immune to being grappled or restrained, and can move through a space as narrow as 1 inch wide without squeezing. A creature that touches the burning dervish in this form or hits it with a melee attack while within 5 feet of it takes 5 (1d10) fire damage. In addition, the burning dervish can enter a hostile creature's space and stop there. The first time it enters a creature's space on a turn, that creature takes 5 (1d10) fire damage and catches fire; until someone takes an action to douse the fire, the creature takes 5 (1d10) fire damage at the start of each of its turns.

Burning Dervish High Priest

Medium fiend, lawful evil
Armor Class 16 (natural armor)
Hit Points 108 (16d8 + 32)
Speed 30 ft., fly 20 ft.

STR	DEX	CON	INT	WIS	CHA
15 (+2)	16 (+3)	14 (+2)	13 (+1)	18 (+4)	16 (+3)

Saving Throws Wis +8, Cha +7
Skills Perception +8, Religion +5, Stealth +7

Damage Vulnerabilities cold
Damage Immunities fire
Senses darkvision 60 ft., passive Perception 18
Languages Common, Ignan, Infernal
Challenge 11 (7,200 XP)

Divine Eminence. As a bonus action, the high priest can expend a 1st level spell slot to cause its melee weapon attacks to magically deal an extra 10 (3d6) fire damage to a target on a hit. This benefit lasts until the end of the turn. If the high priest expends a spell slot of 2nd level or higher, the extra damage increases by 1d6 for each level above 1st.

Elemental Endurance. Burning dervishes can survive on the Elemental Planes of Air or Earth for up to 48 hours and on the Elemental Plane of Water for up to 12 hours. Failure to return to the Elemental Plane of Fire after that time deals 1 cold damage each hour to a burning dervish until it dies or returns to the Elemental Plane of Fire.

Innate Spellcasting. The burning dervish's innate spellcasting ability is Charisma (spell save DC 15, +7 to hit with spell attacks). It can cast the following spells, requiring no material components.

> At will: *fire bolt, produce flame*
> 3/day: *invisibility* (self only)
> 1/day: *enlarge/reduce, flaming sphere, plane shift* (self only, Elemental, Astral, or Material Planes only)

Spellcasting. The high priest is a 9th-level spellcaster. Its spellcasting ability is Wisdom (spell save DC 16, +8 to hit with spell attacks). The high priest has the following cleric spells prepared:

> Cantrips (at will): *guidance, light, resistance, thaumaturgy*
> 1st level (4 slots): *bless, burning hand, cure wounds, healing word, hellish rebuke, shield of faith*
> 2nd level (3 slots): *aid, continual flame, heat metal, lesser restoration, scorching ray*
> 3rd level (3 slots): *beacon of hope, fireball, magic circle, speak with dead*
> 4th level (3 slots): *death ward, fire shield, freedom of movement, guardian of faith, wall of fire*
> 5th level (1 slot): *mass cure wounds, raise dead*

Actions

Multiattack. The burning dervish makes two Scimitar attacks or two Fist attacks.

Scimitar. *Melee Weapon Attack:* +7 to hit, reach 5 ft., one target. *Hit:* 6 (1d6 + 3) slashing damage, plus 4 (1d8) fire damage.

Fist (flame form only). *Melee Spell Attack:* +7 to hit, reach 5 ft., one target. *Hit:* 11 (2d8 + 3) fire damage.

Flame Form (3/day). The burning dervish magically polymorphs into a Medium–sized column of fire for 1 minute, until the dervish ends it as a bonus action, or the dervish dies. Equipment worn or carried by the dervish are absorbed into its form. While in this form, it has resistance to bludgeoning, piercing, and slashing damage from nonmagical attacks, it is immune to being grappled or restrained, and can move through a space as narrow as 1 inch wide without squeezing. A creature that touches the burning dervish in this form or hits it with a melee attack while within 5 feet of it takes 4 (1d8) fire damage. In addition, the burning dervish can enter a hostile creature's space and stop there. The first time it enters a creature's space on a turn, that creature takes 4 (1d8) fire damage and catches fire; until someone takes an action to douse the fire, the creature takes 4 (1d8) fire damage at the start of each of its turns.

Beckon the Flames (1/long rest). The burning dervish high priest creates two columns of fire that are 10 feet across by 100 feet high at points it can see within 120 feet. The columns remain burning for 1 minute. Creatures that enter or begin their turns in the area of these flames must make a DC 16 Dexterity saving throw, taking 9 (2d8) fire damage on a failed saving throw, or half as much damage on a successful saving throw. The high priest can use its action to move each column up to 30 feet.

Burning Dervish Master Assassin

Medium fiend, lawful evil
Armor Class 17 (natural armor)
Hit Points 110 (17d8 + 34)
Speed 30 ft., fly 20 ft.

STR	DEX	CON	INT	WIS	CHA
15 (+2)	20 (+5)	14 (+2)	14 (+2)	16 (+3)	16 (+3)

Saving Throws Dex +9, Int +6, Wis +7
Skills Athletics +6, Acrobatics +9, Deception +7, Insight +7, Investigation +6, Perception +7, Sleight of Hand +9, Stealth +9
Damage Vulnerabilities cold
Damage Immunities fire
Senses darkvision 60 ft., passive Perception 17
Languages Common, Ignan, Infernal
Challenge 11 (7,200 XP)

Assassinate. During its first turn, the master assassin has advantage on attack rolls against any creature that hasn't taken a turn. Any hit the master assassin scores against a surprised creature is a critical hit.

Cunning Action. On each of its turns, the master assassin can use a bonus action to take the Dash, Disengage, or Hide action.

Elemental Endurance. Burning dervishes can survive on the Elemental Planes of Air or Earth for up to 48 hours and on the Elemental Plane of Water for up to 12 hours. Failure to return to the Elemental Plane of Fire after that time deals 1 cold damage each hour to a burning dervish until it dies or returns to the Elemental Plane of Fire.

Evasion. If the master assassin is subjected to an effect that allows it to make a Dexterity saving throw to take only half damage, the master assassin instead takes no damage if it succeeds on the saving throw, and only half damage if it fails.

Innate Spellcasting. The burning dervish's innate spellcasting ability is Charisma (spell save DC 15, +7 to hit with spell attacks). It can cast the following spells, requiring no material components.

> At will: *fire bolt, produce flame*
> 3/day: *invisibility* (self only)
> 1/day: *enlarge/reduce, flaming sphere, plane shift* (self only, Elemental, Astral, or Material Planes only)

Sneak Attack (1/turn). Once per turn, the master assassin deals an extra 31 (9d6) damage when it hits a target with a weapon attack and has advantage on the attack roll, or when the target is within 5 feet of an ally of the master assassin that isn't incapacitated and the master assassin doesn't have disadvantage on the attack roll.

Actions

Multiattack. The burning dervish makes two Scimitar attacks or two Fist attacks.

Scimitar. *Melee Weapon Attack:* +9 to hit, reach 5 ft., one target. *Hit:* 8 (1d6 + 5) slashing damage.

Fist (flame form only). *Melee Spell Attack:* +7 to hit, reach 5 ft., one target. *Hit:* 14 (2d10 + 3) fire damage.

Flame Form (3/day). The burning dervish magically polymorphs into a Medium–sized column of fire for 1 minute, until the dervish ends it as a bonus action, or the dervish dies. Equipment worn or carried by the dervish are absorbed into its form. While in this form, it has resistance to bludgeoning, piercing, and slashing damage from nonmagical attacks, it is immune to being grappled or restrained, and can move through a space as narrow as 1 inch wide without squeezing. A creature that touches the burning dervish in this form or hits it with a melee attack while within 5 feet of it takes 4 (1d8) fire damage. In addition, the burning dervish can enter a hostile creature's space and stop there. The first time it enters a creature's space on a turn, that creature takes 4 (1d8) fire damage and catches fire; until someone takes an action to douse the fire, the creature takes 4 (1d8) fire damage at the start of each of its turns.

Burning Dervish Minstrel

Medium fiend, lawful evil
Armor Class 14 (natural armor)
Hit Points 71 (11d8 + 22)
Speed 30 ft., fly 20 ft.

STR	DEX	CON	INT	WIS	CHA
15 (+2)	16 (+3)	14 (+2)	13 (+1)	15 (+2)	17 (+3)

Saving Throws Dex +5, Cha +5
Skills Perception +4, Performance +5, Persuasion +5, Stealth +5
Damage Vulnerabilities cold
Damage Immunities fire
Senses darkvision 60 ft., passive Perception 14
Languages Common, Ignan, Infernal
Challenge 4 (1,100 XP)

Elemental Endurance. Burning dervishes can survive on the Elemental Planes of Air or Earth for up to 48 hours and on the Elemental Plane of Water for up to 12 hours. Failure to return to the Elemental Plane of Fire after that time deals 1 cold damage each hour to a burning dervish until it dies or returns to the Elemental Plane of Fire.

Innate Spellcasting. The burning dervish's innate spellcasting ability is Charisma (spell save DC 13, +5 to hit with spell attacks). It can cast the following spells, requiring no material components.

At will: *fire bolt, produce flame*
3/day: *invisibility* (self only)
1/day: *enlarge/reduce, flaming sphere, plane shift* (self only, Elemental, Astral, or Material Planes only)

Spellcasting. The minstrel is a 4th-level spellcaster. Its spellcasting ability is Charisma (spell save DC 13, +5 to hit with spell attacks). It knows the following bard spells:

Cantrips (at will): *mage hand, message, vicious mockery*
1st level (4 slots): *burning hands, detect magic, healing word, thunderwave*
2nd level (3 slots): *blindness/deafness, heat metal, shatter*

Actions

Multiattack. The burning dervish makes two Scimitar attacks or two Fist attacks.

Scimitar. *Melee Weapon Attack:* +5 to hit, reach 5 ft., one target. *Hit:* 6 (1d6 + 3) slashing damage.

Fist (flame form only). *Melee Spell Attack:* +5 to hit, reach 5 ft., one target. *Hit:* 8 (2d4 + 3) fire damage.

Flame Form (3/day). The burning dervish magically polymorphs into a Medium–sized column of fire for 1 minute, until the dervish ends it as a bonus action, or the dervish dies. Equipment worn or carried by the dervish are absorbed into its form. While in this form, it has resistance to bludgeoning, piercing, and slashing damage from nonmagical attacks, it is immune to being grappled or restrained, and can move through a space as narrow as 1 inch wide without squeezing. A creature that touches the burning dervish in this form or hits it with a melee attack while within 5 feet of it takes 4 (1d8) fire damage. In addition, the burning dervish can enter a hostile creature's space and stop there. The first time it enters a creature's space on a turn, that creature takes 4 (1d8) fire damage and catches fire; until someone takes an action to douse the fire, the creature takes 4 (1d8) fire damage at the start of each of its turns.

Reactions

Inspire (3/day). The minstrel chooses one creature it can see within 30 feet who has just rolled an ability check, attack roll, or saving throw. That creature can roll 1d6 and add it to the result.

Burning Dervish Priest

Medium fiend, lawful evil
Armor Class 14 (natural armor)
Hit Points 78 (12d8 + 24)
Speed 30 ft., fly 20 ft.

STR	DEX	CON	INT	WIS	CHA
15 (+2)	16 (+3)	14 (+2)	13 (+1)	16 (+3)	15 (+2)

Skills Perception +6, Religion +4, Stealth +6
Damage Vulnerabilities cold
Damage Immunities fire
Senses darkvision 60 ft., passive Perception 16
Languages Common, Ignan, Infernal
Challenge 8 (3,900 XP)

Divine Eminence. As a bonus action, the priest can expend a spell slot to cause its melee weapon attacks to magically deal an extra 10 (3d6) radiant damage to a target on a hit. This benefit lasts until the end of the turn. If the priest expends a spell slot of 2nd level or higher, the extra damage increases by 1d6 for each level above 1st.

Elemental Endurance. Burning dervishes can survive on the Elemental Planes of Air or Earth for up to 48 hours and on the Elemental Plane of Water for up to 12 hours. Failure to return to the Elemental Plane of Fire after that time deals 1 cold damage each hour to a burning dervish until it dies or returns to the Elemental Plane of Fire.

Innate Spellcasting. The burning dervish's innate spellcasting ability is Charisma (spell save DC 13, +5 to hit with spell attacks). It can cast the following spells, requiring no material components.

At will: *fire bolt, produce flame*
3/day: *invisibility* (self only)
1/day: *enlarge/reduce, flaming sphere, plane shift* (self only, Elemental, Astral, or Material Planes only)

Spellcasting. The priest is a 5th-level spellcaster. Its spellcasting ability is Wisdom (spell save DC 14, +6 to hit with spell attacks). It has the following cleric spells prepared.

Cantrips (at will): *guidance, resistance, thaumaturgy*
1st level (4 slots): *burning hands, cure wounds, hellish rebuke*
2nd level (3 slots): *lesser restoration, spiritual weapon*
3rd level (2 slots): *dispel magic, spirit guardians*

Actions

Multiattack. The burning dervish makes two Scimitar attacks or two Fist attacks.

Scimitar. *Melee Weapon Attack:* +6 to hit, reach 5 ft., one target. *Hit:* 6 (1d6 + 3) slashing damage.

Fist (flame form only). *Melee Spell Attack:* +5 to hit, reach 5 ft., one target. *Hit:* 7 (2d4 + 2) fire damage.

Flame Form (3/day). The burning dervish magically polymorphs into a Medium–sized column of fire for 1 minute, until the dervish ends it as a bonus action, or the dervish dies. Equipment worn or carried by the dervish are absorbed into its form. While in this form, it has resistance to bludgeoning, piercing, and slashing damage from nonmagical attacks, it is immune to being grappled or restrained, and can move through a space as narrow as 1 inch wide without squeezing. A creature that touches the burning dervish in this form or hits it with a melee attack while within 5 feet of it takes 4 (1d8) fire damage. In addition, the burning dervish can enter a hostile creature's space and stop there. The first time it enters a creature's space on a turn, that creature takes 4 (1d8) fire damage and catches fire; until someone takes an action to douse the fire, the creature takes 4 (1d8) fire damage at the start of each of its turns.

Beckon the Flames (1/day). The burning dervish priest creates one column of fire that is 10 feet across by 100 feet high at a point it can see within 120 feet. The column remains burning for 1 minute. Creatures that enter or begin their turns in the area of these flames must make a DC 14 Dexterity saving throw, taking 9 (2d8) fire damage on a failed saving throw, or half as much damage on a successful saving throw. The priest can use its action to move the column up to 30 feet.

Burning Dervish Sorcerer

Medium fiend, lawful evil
Armor Class 15 (natural armor)
Hit Points 110 (17d8 + 34)
Speed 30 ft., fly 20 ft.

STR	DEX	CON	INT	WIS	CHA
15 (+2)	16 (+3)	14 (+2)	14 (+2)	15 (+2)	20 (+5)

Saving Throws Con +6, Cha +9
Skills Arcana +6, History +6, Perception +6, Stealth +7
Damage Vulnerabilities cold
Damage Immunities fire
Senses darkvision 60 ft., passive Perception 16
Languages Common, Ignan, Infernal
Challenge 11 (7,200 XP)

Elemental Endurance. Burning dervishes can survive on the Elemental Planes of Air or Earth for up to 48 hours and on the Elemental Plane of Water for up to 12 hours. Failure to return to the Elemental Plane of Fire after that time deals 1 cold damage each hour to a burning dervish until it dies or returns to the Elemental Plane of Fire.

Innate Spellcasting. The burning dervish's innate spellcasting ability is Charisma (spell save DC 17, +9 to hit with spell attacks). It can cast the following spells, requiring no material components.

At will: *fire bolt, produce flame*
3/day: *invisibility* (self only)
1/day: *enlarge/reduce, flaming sphere, plane shift* (self only, Elemental, Astral, or Material Planes only)

Spellcasting. The burning dervish sorcerer is a 10th-level spellcaster. Its spellcasting ability is Charisma (spell save DC 17, +9 to hit with spell attacks). It has the following wizard spells prepared.

Cantrips (at will): *acid splash, fire bolt, mending, shocking grasp, true strike*
1st level (4 slots): *burning hands, detect magic, magic missile, shield*

2nd level (3 slots): *blindness/deafness, blur, scorching ray*
3rd level (3 slots): *bestow curse, dispel magic, fireball*
4th level (3 slots): *fire shield, stoneskin, wall of fire*
5th level (2 slots): *burning rain*[4]

Swift Casting (3/day). Whenever the burning dervish sorcerer uses an action to cast a cantrip or a spell, it can cast a cantrip as a bonus action.

ACTIONS

Multiattack. The burning dervish makes two Scimitar attacks or two Fist attacks.

Scimitar. *Melee Weapon Attack:* +7 to hit, reach 5 ft., one target. *Hit:* 6 (1d6 + 3) slashing damage.

Fist (flame form only). *Melee Spell Attack:* +9 to hit, reach 5 ft., one target. *Hit:* 14 (2d8 + 5) fire damage.

Flame Form (3/day). The burning dervish magically polymorphs into a Medium-sized column of fire for 1 minute, until the dervish ends it as a bonus action, or the dervish dies. Equipment worn or carried by the dervish are absorbed into its form. While in this form, it has resistance to bludgeoning, piercing, and slashing damage from nonmagical attacks, it is immune to being grappled or restrained, and can move through a space as narrow as 1 inch wide without squeezing. A creature that touches the burning dervish in this form or hits it with a melee attack while within 5 feet of it takes 4 (1d8) fire damage. In addition, the burning dervish can enter a hostile creature's space and stop there. The first time it enters a creature's space on a turn, that creature takes 4 (1d8) fire damage and catches fire; until someone takes an action to douse the fire, the creature takes 4 (1d8) fire damage at the start of each of its turns.

Burning Dervish Wizard

Medium fiend, lawful evil
Armor Class 15 (natural armor)
Hit Points 91 (14d8 + 28)
Speed 30 ft., fly 20 ft.

STR	DEX	CON	INT	WIS	CHA
15 (+2)	16 (+3)	14 (+2)	20 (+5)	15 (+2)	15 (+2)

Skills Arcana +9, History +9, Perception +6, Stealth +7
Damage Vulnerabilities cold
Damage Immunities fire
Senses darkvision 60 ft., passive Perception 16
Languages Common, Ignan, Infernal
Challenge 9 (5,000 XP)

Elemental Endurance. Burning dervishes can survive on the Elemental Planes of Air or Earth for up to 48 hours and on the Elemental Plane of Water for up to 12 hours. Failure to return to the Elemental Plane of Fire after that time deals 1 cold damage each hour to a burning dervish until it dies or returns to the Elemental Plane of Fire.

Innate Spellcasting. The burning dervish's innate spellcasting ability is Charisma (spell save DC 14, +6 to hit with spell attacks). It can cast the following spells, requiring no material components.

At will: *fire bolt, produce flame*
3/day: *invisibility* (self only)
1/day: *enlarge/reduce, flaming sphere, plane shift* (self only, Elemental, Astral, or Material Planes only)

Spellcasting. The burning dervish wizard is a 7th-level spellcaster. Its spellcasting ability is Intelligence (spell save DC 17, +9 to hit with spell attacks). It has the following wizard spells prepared.

Cantrips (at will): *acid splash, mage hand, mending, shocking grasp*
1st level (4 slots): *burning hands, detect magic, magic missile, shield*
2nd level (3 slots): *blindness/deafness, blur, scorching ray*
3rd level (3 slots): *bestow curse, dispel magic, fireball*
4th level (1 slot): *fire shield*

ACTIONS

Multiattack. The burning dervish makes two Scimitar attacks or two Fist attacks.

Scimitar. *Melee Weapon Attack:* +7 to hit, reach 5 ft., one target. *Hit:* 6 (1d6 + 3) slashing damage.

Fist (flame form only). *Melee Spell Attack:* +6 to hit, reach 5 ft., one target. *Hit:* 7 (2d4 + 2) fire damage.

Flame Form (3/day). The burning dervish magically polymorphs into a Medium–sized column of fire for 1 minute, until the dervish ends it as a bonus action, or the dervish dies. Equipment worn or carried by the dervish are absorbed into its form. While in this form, it has resistance to bludgeoning, piercing, and slashing damage from nonmagical attacks, it is immune to being grappled or restrained, and can move through a space as narrow as 1 inch wide without squeezing. A creature that touches the burning dervish in this form or hits it with a melee attack while within 5 feet of it takes 4 (1d8) fire damage. In addition, the burning dervish can enter a hostile creature's space and stop there. The first time it enters a creature's space on a turn, that creature takes 4 (1d8) fire damage and catches fire; until someone takes an action to douse the fire, the creature takes 4 (1d8) fire damage at the start of each of its turns.

Burning Dervishes — Indiviudals

Al Fatik

Medium fiend, lawful evil
Armor Class 16 (natural armor)
Hit Points 149 (23d8 + 46)
Speed 30 ft., fly 20 ft.

STR	DEX	CON	INT	WIS	CHA
15 (+2)	16 (+3)	14 (+2)	20 (+5)	16 (+3)	15 (+2)

Saving Throws Int +10, Wis +8
Skills Arcana +10, Athletics +7, History +10, Perception +8, Stealth +8
Damage Vulnerabilities cold
Damage Immunities fire
Senses darkvision 60 ft., passive Perception 18
Languages Common, Ignan, Infernal
Challenge 13 (10,000 XP)

Special Equipment. Al Fatik carries with him at all times a *staff of fire*. When Al Fatik enters his Flame Form, he can still use the abilities of the *staff of fire*.

Elemental Endurance. Burning dervishes can survive on the Elemental Planes of Air or Earth for up to 48 hours and on the Elemental Plane of Water for up to 12 hours. Failure to return to the Elemental Plane of Fire after that time deals 1 cold damage each hour to a burning dervish until it dies or returns to the Elemental Plane of Fire.

Innate Spellcasting. The burning dervish's innate spellcasting ability is Charisma (spell save DC 15, +7 to hit with spell attacks). It can cast the following spells, requiring no material components.

At will: *fire bolt, produce flame*
3/day: *invisibility* (self only)
1/day: *enlarge/reduce, flaming sphere, plane shift* (self only, Elemental, Astral, or Material Planes only)

Potent Flames (3/day). When Al Fatik deals fire damage with a spell of 1st level or higher, he can choose one creature within 60 feet of him that he can see to make a DC 18 Dexterity saving throw, taking 21 (6d6) fire damage on a failed saving throw, or half as much damage on a successful saving throw.

Spellcasting. Al Fatik is a 16th-level spellcaster. His spellcasting ability is Intelligence (spell save DC 18, +10 to hit with spell attacks). He has the following wizard spells prepared.

Cantrips (at will): *acid splash, dancing lights, mending, prestidigitation, shocking grasp*
1st level (4 slots): *burning hands, detect magic, magic missile, shield*
2nd level (3 slots): *blindness/deafness, blur, magic weapon, misty step, scorching ray*
3rd level (3 slots): *bestow curse, fireball, haste, slow*
4th level (3 slots): *banishment, fire shield, wall of fire*
5th level (2 slots): *conjure elemental, hold monster*
6th level (1 slot): *true seeing*
7th level (1 slot): *delayed blast fireball*
8th level (1 slot): *incendiary cloud*

ACTIONS

Multiattack. The burning dervish makes two Fist attacks.

Fist (flame form only). *Melee Spell Attack:* +7 to hit, reach 5 ft., one target. *Hit:* 11 (2d8 + 2) fire damage.

Flame Form (3/day). The burning dervish magically polymorphs into a Medium–sized column of fire for 1 minute, until the dervish ends it as a bonus action, or the dervish dies. Equipment worn or carried by the dervish are absorbed into its form. While in this form, it has resistance to bludgeoning, piercing, and slashing damage from nonmagical attacks, it is immune to being grappled or restrained, and can move through a space as narrow as 1 inch wide without squeezing. A creature that touches the burning dervish in this form or hits it with a melee attack while within 5 feet of it takes 4 (1d8) fire damage. In addition, the burning dervish can enter a hostile creature's space and stop there. The first time it enters a creature's space on a turn, that creature takes 4 (1d8) fire damage and catches fire; until someone takes an action to douse the fire, the creature takes 4 (1d8) fire damage at the start of each of its turns.

Husam al Din

Medium fiend, lawful evil
Armor Class 17 (natural armor)
Hit Points 175 (27d8 + 54)
Speed 30 ft., fly 20 ft.

STR	DEX	CON	INT	WIS	CHA
15 (+2)	16 (+3)	14 (+2)	14 (+2)	20 (+5)	16 (+3)

Saving Throws Wis +12, Cha +10
Skills History +9, Insight +12, Perception +12, Religion +9, Stealth +10
Damage Vulnerabilities cold
Damage Immunities fire
Senses darkvision 60 ft., passive Perception 22
Languages Common, Ignan, Infernal
Challenge 23 (50,000 XP)

Elemental Endurance. Burning dervishes can survive on the Elemental Planes of Air or Earth for up to 48 hours and on the Elemental Plane of Water for up to 12 hours. Failure to return to the Elemental Plane of Fire after that time deals 1 cold damage each hour to a burning dervish until it dies or returns to the Elemental Plane of Fire.

Innate Spellcasting. The burning dervish's innate spellcasting ability is Charisma (spell save DC 18, +10 to hit with spell attacks). It can cast the following spells, requiring no material components.

At will: *fire bolt, produce flame*
3/day: *invisibility* (self only)
1/day: *enlarge/reduce, flaming sphere, plane shift* (self only, Elemental, Astral, or Material Planes only)

Spellcasting. Husam al Din is a 20th-level spellcaster. His spellcasting ability is Wisdom (spell save DC 20, +12 to hit with spell attacks). He has the following cleric spells prepared.4/25

Cantrips (at will): *guidance, mending, resistance, thaumaturgy*
1st level (4 slots): *bane, burning hands, command, cure wounds, detect magic, hellish rebuke*
2nd level (3 slots): *blindness/deafness, heat metal, hold person, scorching ray, silence, spiritual weapon*
3rd level (3 slots): *bestow curse, dispel magic, fireball, spirit guardians*
4th level (3 slots): *fire shield, freedom of movement, wall of fire*
5th level (3 slots): *commune, dispel evil and good, planar binding*
6th level (2 slots): *harm, planar ally, true seeing*
7th level (2 slots): *fire storm*
8th level (1 slot): *incendiary cloud*
9th level (1 slot): *gate*

ACTIONS

Multiattack. The burning dervish makes two Scimitar attacks or two Fist attacks.

Scimitar. *Melee Weapon Attack:* +10 to hit, reach 5 ft., one target. *Hit:* 6 (1d6 + 3) slashing damage, plus 9 (2d8) fire damage.

Fist (flame form only). *Melee Spell Attack:* +10 to hit, reach 5 ft., one target. *Hit:* 21 (4d8 + 3) fire damage.

Flame Form (3/day). The burning dervish magically polymorphs into a Medium–sized column of fire for 1 minute, until the dervish ends it as a bonus action, or the dervish dies. Equipment worn or carried by the dervish are absorbed into its form. While in this form, it has resistance to bludgeoning, piercing, and slashing damage from nonmagical attacks, it is immune to being grappled or restrained, and can move through a space as narrow as 1 inch wide without squeezing. A creature that touches the burning dervish in this form or hits it with a melee attack while within 5 feet of it takes 4 (1d8) fire damage. In addition, the burning dervish can enter a hostile creature's space and stop there. The first time it enters a creature's space on a turn, that creature takes 4 (1d8) fire damage and catches fire; until someone takes an action to douse the fire, the creature takes 4 (1d8) fire damage at the start of each of its turns.

Beckon the Flames (2/day). Husam al Din creates seven columns of fire that are 10 feet across by 100 feet high at points he can see within 120 feet. The columns remain burning for 1 minute. Creatures that enter or begin their turns in the area of these flames must make a DC 20 Dexterity saving throw, taking 18 (4d8) fire damage on a failed saving throw, or half as much damage on a successful saving throw. Husam can use his action to move each column up to 30 feet.

Divine Intervention (2/day). If Husam al Din is reduced to 10 hit points or less, he can use a reaction to enact one of the following options:

• Cause himself or another creature within 30 feet of him to regain 36 (8d8) hit points.

• Teleport to a location he is familiar with up to 1 mile away.

• Restore one dead creature back to life, as long as that creature has been dead for no more than 1 minute.

Qadir

Medium fiend, lawful evil
Armor Class 17 (natural armor)
Hit Points 149 (23d8 + 46)
Speed 30 ft., fly 20 ft.

STR	DEX	CON	INT	WIS	CHA
15 (+2)	16 (+3)	14 (+2)	20 (+5)	15 (+2)	17 (+3)

Saving Throws Int +10, Wis +7
Skills Arcana +10, History +10, Perception +7, Stealth +8
Damage Vulnerabilities cold
Damage Immunities fire
Senses darkvision 60 ft., passive Perception 17
Languages Common, Ignan, Infernal
Challenge 14 (11,500 XP)

Special Equipment. Qadir wields a *flame tongue* (scimitar).

Elemental Endurance. Burning dervishes can survive on the Elemental Planes of Air or Earth for up to 48 hours and on the Elemental Plane of Water for up to 12 hours. Failure to return to the Elemental Plane of Fire after that time deals 1 cold damage each hour to a burning dervish until it dies or returns to the Elemental Plane of Fire.

Innate Spellcasting. The burning dervish's innate spellcasting ability is Charisma (spell save DC 16, +8 to hit with spell attacks). It can cast the following spells, requiring no material components.

At will: *fire bolt, produce flame*
3/day: *invisibility* (self only)
1/day: *enlarge/reduce, flaming sphere, plane shift* (self only, Elemental, Astral, or Material Planes only)

Spellcasting. Qadir is a 16th-level spellcaster. His spellcasting ability is Intelligence (spell save DC 18, +10 to hit with spell attacks). He has the following wizard spells prepared.

Cantrips (at will): *acid splash, dancing lights, mending, prestidigitation, shocking grasp*
1st level (4 slots): *burning hands, detect magic, magic missile, shield*
2nd level (3 slots): *blindness/deafness, blur, magic weapon, misty step, scorching ray*
3rd level (3 slots): *bestow curse, fireball, haste, slow*
4th level (3 slots): *banishment, fire shield, wall of fire*
5th level (2 slots): *conjure elemental, hold monster*
6th level (1 slot): *true seeing*
7th level (1 slot): *prismatic spray*
8th level (1 slot): *incendiary cloud*

ACTIONS

Multiattack. The burning dervish makes two Scimitar attacks or two Fist attacks.

Flame Tongue Scimitar. *Melee Weapon Attack:* +8 to hit, reach 5 ft., one target. *Hit:* 8 (1d6 + 5) slashing damage, plus 7 (2d6) fire damage.

Fist (flame form only). *Melee Spell Attack:* +8 to hit, reach 5
ft., one target. *Hit:* 11 (2d8 + 2) fire damage.

Flame Form (3/day). The burning dervish magically polymorphs
into a Medium-sized column of fire for 1 minute, until the
dervish ends it as a bonus action, or the dervish dies.
Equipment worn or carried by the dervish are absorbed into
its form. While in this form, it has resistance to bludgeoning,
piercing, and slashing damage from nonmagical attacks,
it is immune to being grappled or restrained, and can
move through a space as narrow as 1 inch wide without
squeezing. A creature that touches the burning dervish in
this form or hits it with a melee attack while within 5 feet of it
takes 4 (1d8) fire damage. In addition, the burning dervish
can enter a hostile creature's space and stop there. The first
time it enters a creature's space on a turn, that creature
takes 4 (1d8) fire damage and catches fire; until someone
takes an action to douse the fire, the creature takes 4 (1d8)
fire damage at the start of each of its turns.

Cackle Bird

Medium monstrosity, unaligned
Armor Class 14 (natural armor)
Hit Points 65 (10d8 + 20)
Speed 40 ft., climb 20 ft.

STR	DEX	CON	INT	WIS	CHA
15 (+2)	17 (+3)	14 (+2)	7 (–2)	12 (+1)	6 (–2)

Skills Acrobatics +5, Perception +3, Stealth +7
Damage Resistances thunder
Senses darkvision 60 ft., passive Perception 13
Languages Auran
Challenge 4 (1,100 XP)

Ambusher. In the first round of combat, the cackle bird has
advantage on attack rolls against any creature it has
surprised.

Command Birds. The cackle bird can communicate with
other birds as if they shared a language. It can issue
simple commands to birds that have an Intelligence of 2
or lower, like the commands in the *command* spell.

Forest Camouflage. The cackle bird has advantage on
Dexterity (Stealth) checks made to hide in forest terrain.

Actions

Multiattack. The cackle bird makes one Beak attack and
two Claw attacks.

Beak. *Melee Weapon Attack:* +5 to hit, reach 5 ft., one
target. *Hit:* 10 (2d6 + 3) piercing damage.

Claw. *Melee Weapon Attack:* +5 to hit, reach 5 ft., one
target. *Hit:* 5 (1d4 + 3) slashing damage.

Cackle (recharge 5–6). The cackle bird screeches its
cackling call in a 15-foot cone. Each creature in that
area must make a DC 13 Constitution saving throw. On
a failure, a creature takes 21 (6d6) thunder damage
and is incapacitated until the end of its next turn. On
a success, a creature takes half the damage and isn't
incapacitated.

Caterprism

Large elemental, neutral
Armor Class 15 (natural armor)
Hit Points 76 (8d10 + 32)
Speed 30 ft., burrow 20 ft.

STR	DEX	CON	INT	WIS	CHA
20 (+5)	12 (+1)	18 (+4)	4 (–3)	13 (+1)	11 (+0)

Skills Perception +4
Condition Immunities prone
Senses darkvision 60 ft., tremorsense 60 ft., passive
Perception 14
Languages —
Challenge 7 (2,900 XP)

Crystalline Mandibles. The caterprism's mandibles ignore
resistance to slashing damage. In addition, when the
caterprism attacks a creature with at least one head with
its bite attack and rolls a natural 20 on the attack roll, it
cuts off one of the creature's heads. The creature dies
if it cannot survive without the lost head. A creature is
immune to this ability if it is immune to slashing damage,
doesn't have or need a head, has legendary actions, or
the GM decides that the creature is too big for the head
to be cut off with this attack. Such a creature instead
takes an extra 27 (6d8) slashing damage from the hit.

Tunneler. Caterprism can burrow through solid rock at 5 feet per
round leaving a 5 foot-wide, 8-foot-high tunnel in its wake.

Actions

Multiattack. The caterprism makes one bite and two claw
attacks.

Bite. *Melee Weapon Attack:* +8 to hit, reach 5 ft., one target.
Hit: 14 (2d8 +5) slashing damage. If the caterprism scores a
critical hit, it rolls damage dice four times, instead of twice.

Claws. *Melee Weapon Attack:* +8 to hit, reach 5 ft., one
target *Hit:* 16 (2d10 + 5) slashing damage.

Crystal Breath (recharge 5–6). The caterprism spews forth
a crystalline silk-like substance in a 30-foot cone that
instantly hardens into razor sharp crystalline spears. Each
creature in that area must make a DC 15 Dexterity saving
throw, taking 28 (8d6) piercing damage on a failed save,
or half as much damage on a successful one.

Catoblepas

Large monstrosity, neutral
Armor Class 14 (natural armor)
Hit Points 178 (17d10 + 85)
Speed 40 ft., swim 20 ft.

STR	DEX	CON	INT	WIS	CHA
20 (+5)	8 (–1)	21 (+5)	5 (–3)	15 (+2)	10 (+0)

Senses darkvision 60 ft. passive Perception 12
Languages —
Challenge 12 (8,400 XP)

Keen Smell. The catoblepas has advantage on Wisdom
(Perception) checks that rely on smell.

Stench. Any creature other than a catoblepas that starts
its turn within 10 feet of the catoblepas must succeed
on a DC 16 Constitution saving throw or be poisoned
until the start of the creature's next turn. On a successful
saving throw, the creature is immune to the stench of any
catoblepas for 1 hour.

Charge. If the catoblepas moves at least 20 feet straight

toward a target and then hits it with a gore attack on the same turn, the target takes an extra 9 (2d8) piercing damage. If the target is a creature, it must succeed on a DC 14 Strength saving throw or be pushed up to 10 feet away and knocked prone.

ACTIONS

Multiattack. The catoblepas makes one Hooves attack, one Gore attack, and one Tail attack.

Gore. *Melee Weapon Attack:* +9 to hit, reach 5 ft., one target. *Hit:* 18 (3d8 + 5) piercing damage.

Hooves. *Melee Weapon Attack:* +9 to hit, reach 10 ft., one target. *Hit:* 14 (2d8 + 5) slashing damage.

Tail. *Melee Weapon Attack:* +9 to hit, reach 15 ft., one target. *Hit:* 21 (5d6 + 4) bludgeoning damage, and the target must succeed on a DC 14 Strength saving throw or be pushed 10 feet away from the catoblepas and knocked prone.

Poison Breath (recharge 5–6). The catoblepas exhales its horrid, stinking breath in a 60-foot cone. Each creature in that area must make a DC 14 Constitution saving throw, taking 36 (8d8) poison damage on a failed save, or half as much damage on a successful one. If the saving throw fails by 5 or more, the target instead takes 63 (14d8) poison damage. The target dies if reduced to 0 hit points by this breath.

Stench. Any creature that starts its turn within 10 feet of the catoblepas must succeed on a DC 12 Constitution saving throw against poison. On a failed save, the creature spends its action that turn retching and reeling and is poisoned until the start of its next turn. Creatures that don't need to breathe or are immune to poison automatically succeed on this saving throw. On a successful saving throw, the creature is immune to the catoblepas's stench for 24 hours.

Cauchemar

Large fiend, neutral evil
Armor Class 15 (natural armor)
Hit Points 85 (10d10 + 30)
Speed 60 ft., fly 90 ft.

STR	DEX	CON	INT	WIS	CHA
21 (+5)	18 (+4)	16 (+3)	10 (+0)	15 (+2)	15 (+2)

Skills Athletics +8, Perception +5
Damage Resistances bludgeoning, piercing, and slashing from nonmagical attacks
Damage Immunities fire
Senses passive Perception 15
Languages understands Abyssal, Common, and Infernal but can't speak
Challenge 8 (3,900 XP)

Confer Fire Resistance. The cauchemar can grant resistance to fire damage to anyone riding it. As a bonus action, the cauchemar can improve this resistance to immunity to fire damage until the start of the cauchemar's next turn.

Illumination. The cauchemar sheds bright light in a 10-foot radius and dim light for an additional 10 feet.

Trampling Charge. If the cauchemar moves at least 20 feet straight toward a creature and then hits it with a bite attack on the same turn, that target must succeed on a DC 16 Strength saving throw or be knocked prone. If the target is prone, the cauchemar can make one Hooves attack against it as a bonus action.

ACTIONS

Multiattack. The cauchemar makes one Bite attack and one Hooves attack.

Bite. *Melee Weapon Attack:* +8 to hit, reach 5 ft., one target. *Hit:* 9 (1d8 + 5) piercing damage plus 7 (2d6) fire damage.

Hooves. *Melee Weapon Attack:* +8 to hit, reach 5 ft., one target. *Hit:* 14 (2d8 + 5) bludgeoning damage plus 7 (2d6) fire damage.

Smoke Breath (recharge 5–6). The cauchemar exhales a 15-foot cone of choking smoke. Each creature in that area must make a DC 15 Constitution saving throw. On a failure, a creature takes 21 (6d6) fire damage and is poisoned for 1 minute. On a success, a creature takes half the damage and isn't poisoned. A poisoned creature can repeat the saving throw at the end of each of its turns, ending the effect on itself on a success.

Ethereal Stride. The cauchemar and up to three willing creatures within 5 feet of it magically enter the Ethereal Plane from the Material Plane, or vice versa.

Cheitan

Medium monstrosity (cheitan), any evil alignment
Armor Class 15 (natural armor)
Hit Points 97 (13d8 + 39)
Speed 30 ft., fly 40 ft.

STR	DEX	CON	INT	WIS	CHA
18 (+4)	14 (+2)	16 (+3)	15 (+2)	10 (+0)	15 (+2)

Saving Throws Cha +5
Skills Athletics +7, Persuasion +5
Damage Resistances fire
Senses darkvision 60 ft., passive Perception 10
Languages Common, Ignan
Challenge 5 (1,800 XP)

Child of Fire. Once per turn, when the cheitan is subjected to fire damage, it has advantage on its next attack roll, saving throw, or ability check.

Heated Body. A creature that touches the cheitan or hits it with a melee attack while within 5 feet of it takes 5 (1d10) fire damage.

Fiery Weapons. When the cheitan hits with any weapon, the weapon deals an extra 2d6 fire damage (included in the attack).

ACTIONS

Multiattack. The cheitan makes two Scimitar attacks or uses its Hurl Flame twice.

Scimitar. *Melee Weapon Attack:* +7 to hit, reach 5 ft., one target. *Hit:* 7 (1d6 + 4) slashing damage plus 7 (2d6) fire damage.

Hurl Flame. *Ranged Spell Attack:* +5 to hit, range 120 ft., one target. *Hit:* 10 (3d6) fire damage.

Cheitans – Individuals

Chuadak the Knife

Small humanoid (kobold), lawful evil
Armor Class 17 (+2 studded leather armor)
Hit Points 66 (12d6 + 24)
Speed 30 ft.

STR	DEX	CON	INT	WIS	CHA
8 (–1)	16 (+3)	14 (+2)	11 (+0)	10 (+0)	10 (+0)

Saving Throws Dex +6, Int +3
Skills Deception +3, Perception +3, Sleight of Hand +6, Stealth +6
Senses darkvision 60 ft., passive Perception 13
Languages Common, Draconic, Thieves' Cant
Challenge 6 (2,300 XP)

Assassinate. Chuadak the Knife has advantage on attack rolls against any creature that hasn't yet acted in the combat. In addition, any hit he scores against a creature that is surprised counts as a critical hit.

Cunning Action. Chuadak the Knife can take a bonus action on each of his turns in combat. This action can be used only to take the Dash, Disengage, or Hide action.

Evasion. Chuadak the Knife can nimbly dodge out of the way of certain area effects. When he is subjected to an effect that allows him to make a Dexterity saving throw to only take half damage, he instead takes no damage if he succeeds on the saving throw, and only half damage if he fails.

Pack Tactics: Chuadak the Knife has advantage on an attack roll against a creature if at least one of his allies is within 5 feet of the creature and the ally isn't incapacitated.

Potion of Invisibility. Chuadak the Knife possesses a *potion of invisibility*.

Rope of Entanglement. Chuadak the Knife possesses a *rope of entanglement*.

Sneak Attack. Once per turn, Chuadak the Knife can deal an extra 5d6 damage to one creature he hits with a Dagger attack if he has advantage on the attack roll. He doesn't need advantage on the attack roll if another enemy of the target is within 5 feet of it and that enemy isn't incapacitated.

Sunlight Sensitivity: While in sunlight, Chuadak the Knife has disadvantage on attack rolls, as well as on Wisdom (Perception) checks that rely on sight.

Uncanny Dodge. When an attacker Chuadak the Knife can see hits him with an attack, he can use his reaction to halve the attack's damage against him.

ACTIONS

Multiattack. Chuadak the Knife makes two Dagger attacks (melee or ranged).

+2 Dagger. *Melee Weapon Attack:* +8 to hit, reach 5 ft., one target. *Hit:* 7 (1d4 + 5) piercing damage. The target must make a DC 15 Constitution saving throw. On a failed save, the target takes 14 (4d6) poison damage and is poisoned. On a successful saving throw, the target takes half as much damage and is not poisoned. A poisoned target may repeat the saving throw at the end of each of its turns, ending the condition on itself on a success.

Dagger. *Ranged Weapon Attack:* +6 to hit, range 20/60 ft., one target. *Hit:* 5 (1d4 + 3) piercing damage. The target must make a DC 15 Constitution saving throw. On a failed save, the target takes 14 (4d6) poison damage and is poisoned. On a successful saving throw, the target takes half as much damage and is not poisoned. A poisoned target may repeat the saving throw at the end of each of its turns, ending the condition on itself on a success.

Disguise (recharge 5–6). Chuadak the Knife may cast *disguise self* on himself (spell save DC 17).

Chufa um Sofanie

Medium monstrosity (cheitan), lawful good
Armor Class 18 (natural armor, shield)
Hit Points 180 (19d8 + 95)
Speed 30 ft., fly 60 ft.

STR	DEX	CON	INT	WIS	CHA
22 (+6)	16 (+3)	20 (+5)	13 (+1)	19 (+4)	19 (+4)

Saving Throws Str +11, Wis +9, Cha +9
Skills Athletics +11, Insight +9, Persuasion +9
Damage Resistances fire, poison
Condition Immunities poisoned
Senses darkvision 120 ft., passive Perception 14
Languages Common, Ignan
Challenge 14 (11,500 XP)

Aura of Fiery Inspiration. When an ally within 10 feet of Chufa um Sofanie hits with a melee weapon, the weapon deals an extra 2d6 fire damage.

Child of Fire. Once per turn, when Chufa um Sofanie is subjected to fire damage, she has advantage on her next attack roll, saving throw, or ability check.

Heated Body. A creature that touches Chufa um Sofanie or hits her with a melee attack while within 5 feet of her takes 5 (1d10) fire damage.

Fiery Weapons. When Chufa um Sofanie hits with any weapon, the weapon deals an extra 4d6 fire damage (included in the attack).

ACTIONS

Multiattack. Chufa um Sofanie makes three Longsword attacks. She can use her Hurl Flame in place of any Longsword attack.

Longsword. *Melee Weapon Attack:* +11 to hit, reach 5 ft., one target. *Hit:* 10 (1d8 + 6) slashing damage, or 11 (1d10 + 6) slashing damage if used with two hands, plus 14 (4d6) fire damage.

Hurl Flame. *Ranged Spell Attack:* +9 to hit, range 120 ft., one target. *Hit:* 21 (6d6) fire damage.

Healing Touch (3/day). Chufa um Sofanie touches another creature. The target magically regains 24 (5d8 + 2) hit points and is free from any curse, disease, poison, blindness, or deafness.

Leadership (recharges after short or long rest). For 1 minute, Chufa um Sofanie can utter a special command or warning whenever a nonhostile creature that she can see within 30 feet of her makes an attack roll or a saving throw. The creature can add a d4 to its roll provided it can hear and understand Chufa. A creature can benefit from only one Leadership die at a time. This effect ends if Chufa is incapacitated.

REACTIONS

Parry. Chufa um Sofanie adds 5 to her AC against one melee attack that would hit her. To do so, she must see the attacker and be wielding a melee weapon.

Lady Fatima Umau

Medium monstrosity (cheitan), lawful evil
Armor Class 19 (natural armor)
Hit Points 221 (26d8 + 104)
Speed 30 ft., fly 60 ft.

STR	DEX	CON	INT	WIS	CHA
14 (+2)	23 (+6)	18 (+4)	15 (+2)	20 (+5)	22 (+6)

Saving Throws Dex +11, Wis +10, Cha +11
Skills Deception +11, History +7, Insight +10, Intimidation +11, Persuasion +11
Damage Resistances fire
Condition Immunities charmed, frightened
Senses darkvision 120 ft., passive Perception 15
Languages Common, Ignan
Challenge 16 (15,000 XP)

Child of Fire. Once per turn, when Lady Fatima Umau is subjected to fire damage, she has advantage on her next attack roll, saving throw, or ability check.

Eye for Scandal. As a bonus action, Lady Fatima Umau studies a target to find its weakness. The target must succeed on a DC 19 Charisma saving throw or Lady Fatima has advantage on her next attack roll or ability check against the target.

Heated Body. A creature that touches Lady Fatima Umau or hits her with a melee attack while within 5 feet of her takes 5 (1d10) fire damage.

Fiery Weapons. When Lady Fatima Umau hits with any weapon, the weapon deals an extra 6d6 fire damage (included in the attack).

Actions

Multiattack. The Lady Fatima Umau can use her Slanderous Words. She can also makes three Rapier attacks. She can use her Hurl Flame in place of any Rapier attack.

Rapier. *Melee Weapon Attack:* +11 to hit, reach 5 ft., one target. *Hit:* 10 (1d8 + 6) piercing damage plus 21 (6d6) fire damage.

Hurl Flame. *Ranged Spell Attack:* +11 to hit, range 120 ft., one target. *Hit:* 28 (8d6) fire damage.

Slanderous Words. Lady Fatima Umau targets one creature with an Intelligence of 5 or higher she can see within 30 feet. If the target can hear Lady Fatima, it must succeed on a DC 19 Charisma saving throw or have disadvantage on its next attack roll, saving throw, or ability check.

Bow to the Sultan (recharge 5–6). Lady Fatima Umau barks out a command for those nearby to fall to their knees in supplication. Each creature within 20 feet that can hear Lady Fatima must make a DC 18 Wisdom saving throw. On a failed save, a creature takes 54 (12d8) thunder damage and falls prone. On a success, a creature takes half the damage and doesn't fall prone.

Corpse Orgy

Large monstrosity, chaotic evil
Armor Class 20 (natural armor)
Hit Points 207 (18d10 + 108)
Speed 30 ft.

STR	DEX	CON	INT	WIS	CHA
22 (+6)	10 (+0)	23 (+6)	14 (+2)	14 (+2)	16 (+3)

Saving Throws Con +10
Skills Perception +6
Damage Resistances piercing, slashing
Damage Immunities poison
Condition Immunities poisoned
Senses blindsight 60 ft., tremorsense 60 ft., passive Perception 16
Languages Alko, Common, Undercommon
Challenge 9 (5,000 XP)

Absorb Body. A corpse orgy can absorb the physical body of any incapacitated creature by moving over it and remaining in contact with it for at least one full round. An incapacitated opponent must make a DC 20 Constitution saving throw or be absorbed. A dead opponent gets no saving throw. When it absorbs a body, the target dies and the corpse orgy gains 12 temporary hit points. A creature whose body is absorbed can only be raised or resurrected if the corpse orgy that absorbed its body is slain and the corpse in question is recovered.

All-Around Vision. The corpse orgy sees in all directions at once. It cannot be flanked or surprised.

Actions

Multiattack. The corpse orgy makes two Slam attacks.

Slam. *Melee Weapon Attack:* +10 to hit, reach 5 ft., one creature. *Hit:* 21 (4d8 + 6) bludgeoning damage and the target is grappled (escape DC 16). Until this grapple ends, the creature is restrained.

Pain Shriek (recharge 6). All creatures within a 40 foot radius of the corpse orgy that can hear it must make a DC 16 Constitution savings throw, taking 35 (10d6) thunder damage on a failed save, or half as much damage on a successful one.

Corpulent Attendant

Large fiend, lawful evil
Armor Class 16 (natural armor)
Hit Points 95 (10d10 + 40)
Speed 30 ft.

STR	DEX	CON	INT	WIS	CHA
21 (+5)	10 (+0)	19 (+4)	16 (+3)	14 (+2)	18 (+4)

Skills History +6, Intimidation +7, Perception +5, Religion +6
Damage Resistances radiant; bludgeoning, piercing, and slashing from nonmagical attacks
Damage Immunities fire, lightning
Condition Immunities poisoned
Senses darkvision 60 ft., passive Perception 15
Languages Common, Infernal
Challenge 6 (2,300 XP)

Stench. An attendant's skin produces a foul-smelling, toxic liquid. Any creature that starts its turn within 10 feet of the attendant must succeed on a DC 14 Constitution saving throw or be poisoned until the start of its next turn. On a successful saving throw, the creature is immune to the attendant's stench for 24 hours.

Actions

Keen Dagger. *Melee Weapon Attack:* +8 to hit, reach 5 ft., one target. *Hit:* 14 (2d8 + 5) piercing damage. If the target is grappled, it is blinded for one minute.

Slam. *Melee Weapon Attack:* +8 to hit, reach 5 ft., one target. *Hit:* 18 (3d8 + 5) bludgeoning damage. If the target is a creature, it is grappled (escape DC 16).

Crayfish, Giant

Large beast, unaligned
Armor Class 15 (natural armor)
Hit Points 45 (6d10 + 12)
Speed 30 ft., swim 30 ft.

STR	DEX	CON	INT	WIS	CHA
16 (+3)	10 (+0)	14 (+2)	2 (–4)	10 (+0)	2 (–4)

Skills Stealth +4
Senses blindsight 30 ft., passive Perception 10
Languages —
Challenge 2 (450 XP)

Amphibious. The giant crayfish can breathe air and water.

ACTIONS

Multiattack. The giant crayfish makes two Pincers attacks.
Pincers. *Melee Weapon Attack:* +5 to hit, reach 5 ft., one target. *Hit:* 10 (2d6 + 3) slashing damage, and the target is grappled (escape DC 13). The crayfish has two claws, each of which can grapple only one target.

Croaker

Small monstrosity (aquatic), chaotic evil
Armor Class 14 (natural armor)
Hit Points 9 (2d6 + 2)
Speed 30 ft., swim 30 ft.

STR	DEX	CON	INT	WIS	CHA
12 (+1)	16 (+3)	12 (+1)	12 (+1)	12 (+1)	10 (+0)

Skills Stealth +5
Senses darkvision 60 ft., passive Perception 11
Languages Abyssal, Tsathar
Challenge 1/8 (25 XP)

Amphibious. The croaker can breathe air and water.
Keen Smell. The croaker has advantage on Wisdom (Perception) checks that rely on smell.
Slimy. Croakers continuously cover themselves with muck and slime. Creatures attempting to grapple a croaker do so with disadvantage.
Standing Leap. The croaker's long jump is up to 20 feet and its high jump is up to 10 feet, with or without a running start.

ACTIONS

Multiattack. The croaker makes one Bite attack and one Claws attack, or one Bite attack and one Spear attack.
Bite. *Melee Weapon Attack:* +3 to hit, reach 5 ft., one target. *Hit:* 3 (1d3 + 1) piercing damage.
Claws. *Melee Weapon Attack:* +3 to hit, reach 5 ft., one target. *Hit:* 3 (1d3 + 1) slashing damage, and the target must succeed on a DC 12 Constitution saving throw or become the living host to a croaker egg, which over the course of the egg maturing, migrates to the chest cavity of the host. The host creature must make another DC 12 Constitution saving throw 24 hours after the egg is implanted. A failed saving throw results in the host becoming violently ill, followed by a deep coma-like state that lasts 2d6 + 2 days. At the end of each day, the host can attempt another saving throw with a success indicating that its body has managed to destroy the egg through normal immune response. At the end of the incubation period, the host awakes to excruciating pain as the young croaker, freed from its egg, tears its way out of the host, who is reduced to 0 hit points in the process.
A DC 15 Wisdom (Medicine) check can be attempted to surgically extract an egg from the host. A *lesser restoration* spell will also cure the condition and purge the host of the egg.
Spear. *Melee Weapon Attack:* +3 to hit, reach 5 ft. or 20/60 ft., one target. *Hit:* 4 (1d6 + 1) piercing damage, or 5 (1d8 +1) piercing damage if used with two hands to make a melee attack.

Croaker Brute

Small monstrosity (aquatic), chaotic evil
Armor Class 14 (natural armor)
Hit Points 16 (3d6 + 6)
Speed 30 ft., swim 30 ft.

STR	DEX	CON	INT	WIS	CHA
14 (+2)	16 (+3)	13 (+1)	10 (+0)	12 (+1)	11 (+1)

Skills Stealth +5
Senses darkvision 60 ft., passive Perception 11
Languages Abyssal, Tsathar
Challenge 1/2 (100 XP)

Amphibious. The croaker can breathe air and water.
Brute. A melee weapon deals one extra die of its damage when the croaker hits with it (included in the attack.
Keen Smell. The croaker has advantage on Wisdom (Perception) checks that rely on smell.
Slimy. Croakers continuously cover themselves with muck and slime. Creatures attempting to grapple a croaker do so with disadvantage.
Standing Leap. The croaker's long jump is up to 20 feet and its high jump is up to 10 feet, with or without a running start.

ACTIONS

Multiattack. The Croaker brute makes one Bite and one Claws attack or one Bite and one Morningstar attack.
Bite. *Melee Weapon Attack:* +4 to hit, reach 5 ft., one target. *Hit:* 4 (1d4 + 2) piercing damage.
Claws. *Melee Weapon Attack:* +4 to hit, reach 5 ft., one target. *Hit:* 4 (1d4 + 2) slashing damage, and the target must succeed on a DC 13 Constitution saving throw or become the living host to a croaker egg, which over the course of the egg maturing, migrates to the chest cavity of the host. The host creature must make another DC 13 Constitution saving throw 24 hours after the egg is implanted. A failed saving throw results in the host becoming violently ill, followed by a deep coma-like state that lasts 2d6 + 2 days. At the end of each day, the host can attempt another saving throw with a success indicating that its body has managed to destroy the egg through normal immune response. At the end of the incubation period, the host awakes to excruciating pain as the young croaker, freed from its egg, tears its way out of the host, who is reduced to 0 hit points in the process.
A DC 16 Wisdom (Medicine) check can be attempted to surgically extract an egg from the host. A *lesser restoration* spell will also cure the condition and purge the host of the egg.
Morningstar. *Melee Weapon Attack:* +4 to hit, reach 5 ft. one target. *Hit:* 11 (2d8 + 2) piercing damage.

Croaker Chieftain

Medium monstrosity (aquatic), chaotic evil
Armor Class 16 (natural armor)
Hit Points 39 (6d8 +12)
Speed 30 ft., swim 30 ft.

STR	DEX	CON	INT	WIS	CHA
14 (+2)	16 (+3)	14 (+2)	12 (+1)	12 (+1)	13 (+2)

Skills Stealth (+5)
Senses darkvision 60 ft., passive Perception 11
Languages Abyssal, Tsathar
Challenge 1 (200 XP)

Amphibious. The croaker can breathe air and water.
Fetid Strike. Once on each of the chieftain's turns when it hits a creature with a weapon attack, it can cause the attack to deal an extra 9 (2d8) poison damage to the target.
Keen Smell. The croaker has advantage on Wisdom (Perception) checks that rely on smell.
Leadership (recharges after a short or long rest). For 1 minute, the chieftain can utter a special command or warning whenever a nonhostile creature that it can see within 30 feet of it makes an attack roll or a saving throw. The creature can add a d4 to its roll provided it can hear and understand the chieftain. A creature can benefit from only one Leadership die at a time. This effect ends if the chieftain is incapacitated.
Slimy. Croakers continuously cover themselves with muck and slime. Creatures attempting to grapple a croaker do so with disadvantage.
Standing Leap. The croaker's long jump is up to 20 feet and its high jump is up to 10 feet, with or without a running start.

Actions

Multiattack. The croaker chieftain makes one Bite and one Claws attack or one Bite and one Maquahuitl attack.
Bite. *Melee Weapon Attack:* +4 to hit, reach 5 ft., one target. *Hit:* 4 (1d4 + 2) piercing damage.
Claws. *Melee Weapon Attack:* +4 to hit, reach 5 ft., one target. *Hit:* 4 (1d4 + 2) slashing damage, and the target must succeed on a DC 13 Constitution saving throw or become the living host to a croaker egg, which over the course of the egg maturing, migrates to the chest cavity of the host. The host creature must make another DC 13 Constitution saving throw 24 hours after the egg is implanted. A failed saving throw results in the host becoming violently ill, followed by a deep coma-like state that lasts 2d6 + 2 days. At the end of each day, the host can attempt another saving throw with a success indicating that its body has managed to destroy the egg through normal immune response. At the end of the incubation period, the host awakes to excruciating pain as the young croaker, freed from its egg, tears its way out of the host, who is reduced to 0 hit points in the process. A DC 16 Wisdom (Medicine) check can be attempted to surgically extract an egg from the host. A *lesser restoration* spell will also cure the condition and purge the host of the egg.
Maquahuitl. *Melee Weapon Attack:* +4 to hit, reach 5 ft., one target. *Hit:* 6 (1d8 + 2) slashing damage, or 7 (1d10 + 2) slashing damage if used with two hands.

Dawzin

Small humanoid (goblinoid), lawful evil
Armor Class 19 (*ring of greater protection*[2], *bracers of defense, cloak of greater protection*[2])
Hit Points 52 (15d6)
Speed 30 ft, fly 40 ft.

STR	DEX	CON	INT	WIS	CHA
8 (−1)	16 (+3)	10 (+0)	20 (+5)	8 (−1)	13 (+1)

Saving Throws Dex +7, Int +9, Wis +3
Skills Arcana +9, Stealth +7
Senses darkvision 60 ft., passive Perception 9
Languages Common, Goblin
Challenge 10 (5,900 XP)

Spellcasting. Dawzin is a 13th-level spellcaster. His spellcasting ability is Intelligence (spell save DC 17, +9 to hit with spell attacks). He has the following wizard spells prepared:

Cantrips (at will): *acid splash, fire bolt, mage hand, message, prestidigitation*
1st level (4 slots): *detect magic, magic missile, shield, silent image*
2nd level (3 slots): *darkness, detect thoughts, invisibility, ray of enfeeblement*
3rd level (3 slots): *dispel magic, fireball, sending*
4th level (3 slots): *arcane eye, dimension door, greater invisibility*
5th level (3 slots): *cloudkill, telepathic bond*
6th level (1 slot): *true seeing*
7th level (1 slot): *finger of death*

Nimble Escape. Dawzin can take the Disengage or Hide action as a bonus action on each of his turns.

Actions

Dagger. *Melee or Ranged Weapon Attack:* **+7 to hit, reach 5 ft. or range 20/60 ft., one creature. Hit: 5 (1d4 + 3) piercing damage.**

Death Dog, Fiendish

Medium monstrosity, neutral evil
Armor Class 14 (natural armor)
Hit Points 58 (9d8 + 18)
Speed 60 ft.

STR	DEX	CON	INT	WIS	CHA
16 (+3)	15 (+2)	14 (+2)	3 (−4)	13 (+1)	6 (−2)

Skills Perception +5, Stealth +4
Damage Resistances cold; bludgeoning, piercing, and slashing from nonmagical attacks not made with silver
Damage Immunities fire, poison
Condition Immunities poisoned
Senses darkvision 120 ft., passive Perception 15
Languages —
Challenge 3 (700 XP)

Dreadful. The dog can use a bonus action to appear dreadful until the start of its next turn. Each creature, other than a devil or death dog, that starts its turn within 10 feet of the dog must succeed on a DC 12 Wisdom saving throw or be frightened until the start of the creature's next turn.
Two-Headed. The dog has advantage on Wisdom (Perception) checks and on saving throws against being

blinded, charmed, deafened, frightened, stunned, or knocked unconscious

ACTIONS

Multiattack. The dog makes two Bite attacks
Bite. *Melee Weapon Attack:* +5 to hit, reach 5 ft., one target. *Hit:* 6 (1d6 + 3) piercing damage. If the target is a creature, it must succeed on a DC 13 Constitution saving throw against disease or become poisoned until the disease is cured. Every 24 hours that elapse, the creature must repeat the saving throw, reducing its hit point maximum by 5 (1d10) on a failure. This reduction lasts until the disease is cured. The creature dies if the disease reduces its hit point maximum to 0.

Death Worm

Large monstrosity, unaligned
Armor Class 15 (natural armor)
Hit Points 59 (7d10 + 21)
Speed 20 ft., burrow 10 ft.

STR	DEX	CON	INT	WIS	CHA
18 (+4)	13 (+1)	16 (+3)	3 (–4)	11 (+0)	5 (–3)

Saving Throws Wis +3
Condition Immunities blindness, prone
Senses tremorsense 60 ft.
Languages —
Challenge 3 (700 XP)
Bite. *Melee Weapon Attack:* +6 to hit, reach 5 ft., one creature. *Hit:* 9 (1d10 + 4) piercing damage plus 4 (1d8) acid damage.
Acid Spit (recharge 5–6). All creatures along a 5-foot-wide, 30-foot-long line extending from the death worm must succeed on a DC 11 Dexterity saving throw or take 14 (4d6) acid damage.
Lightning (recharge 6). All creatures along a 5-foot-wide, 20-foot-long line extending from the death worm must make a DC 11 Dexterity saving throw, taking 18 (4d8) lightning damage on a failure, or half as much on a success.

Demilich, Advanced

Tiny undead, neutral evil
Armor Class 21 (natural armor)
Hit Points 172 (23d4 + 115)
Speed 0 ft., fly 30 ft. (hover)

STR	DEX	CON	INT	WIS	CHA
10 (+0)	10 (+0)	20 (+5)	23 (+6)	20 (+5)	23 (+6)

Saving Throws Con +12, Int +13, Wis +12
Skills Arcana +13, History +13, Perception +12, Religion +13
Damage Resistances bludgeoning, piercing, and slashing from magic weapons
Damage Immunities necrotic, poison, psychic; bludgeoning, piercing, and slashing from nonmagical attacks
Condition Immunities charmed, deafened, exhaustion, frightened, paralyzed, petrified, poisoned, prone, stunned
Senses truesight 120 ft., passive Perception 22
Languages All, telepathy 120 ft.
Challenge 24 (62,000 XP)

Annulment. If the demilich is subjected to an effect that allows it to make a saving throw to take only half damage, it instead takes no damage if it succeeds on the saving throw, and only half damage if it fails.
Legendary Resistance (3/day). If the demilich fails a saving throw, it can choose to succeed instead.

Turn Immunity. The demilich is immune to effects that turn undead.
Spellcasting. The demilich is an 18th-level spellcaster. Its spellcasting ability is Intelligence (spell save DC 28, +20 to hit with spell attacks). It has the following spells prepared:

Cantrips (at will): *mage hand, prestidigitation, ray of frost*
1st level (4 slots): *detect magic, magic missile, shield, thunderwave*
2nd level (3 slots): *acid arrow, detect thoughts, invisibility, mirror image*
3rd level (3 slots): *animate dead, counterspell, dispel magic, fireball*
4th level (3 slots): *blight, dimension door*
5th level (3 slots): *cloudkill, scrying*
6th level (1 slot): *disintegrate, globe of invulnerability*
7th level (1 slot): *finger of death, plane shift*
8th level (1 slot): *dominate monster, power word stun*
9th level (1 slot): *power word kill*

ACTIONS

Drain Life. Each non-undead creature within 10 feet of the demilich must make a DC 17 Constitution saving throw against this magic, taking 21 (6d6) necrotic damage on a failure, and the demilich regains hit points equal to the total dealt to all targets.
Soul Shatter (recharge 6). The demilich emits a string of vile words of power. All creatures within 30 feet of the demilich that it can see must succeed on a DC 17 Constitution saving throw or drop to 0 hit points. On a successful save, the creature takes 22 (4d10) psychic damage and is frightened until the end of its next turn.

LEGENDARY ACTIONS

The demilich can take 3 legendary actions, choosing from the options below. Only one legendary action option can be used at a time and only at the end of another creature's turn. The demilich regains spent legendary actions at the start of its turn.
Flight. The demilich can move up to its full movement speed and does not invoke opportunity attacks while doing so.
Bone Dust. Blinding bone dust swirls magically around the demilich. Each creature within 5 feet of the demilich must succeed on a DC 17 Constitution saving throw or be blinded until the end of the creature's next turn.
Frightening Glare (costs 2 actions). The demilich targets one creature it can see within 60 feet of it. If the target can see the demilich, it must succeed on a DC 17 Wisdom saving throw against this magic or become frightened until the end of the the demilich's next turn. If the target fails the saving throw by 5 or more, it is also paralyzed for the same duration. A target that succeeds on the saving throw is immune to the Dreadful Glare effect for the next 24 hours.
Profane Curse (costs 3 actions). The demilich targets one creature it can see within 30 feet of it. The target must succeed on a DC 17 Wisdom saving throw or be magically cursed. Until the curse ends, the target has disadvantage on ability checks, attack rolls, and saving throws. The target can repeat the saving throw at the end of each of its turns, ending the curse on a success.

Demodand, Shaggy

Large fiend (demodand), neutral evil
Armor Class 19 (natural armor)
Hit Points 210 (20d10 + 100)
Speed 30 ft., fly 60 ft.

STR	DEX	CON	INT	WIS	CHA
22 (+6)	14(+2)	20 (+5)	15 (+2)	15 (+2)	20 (+5)

Saving Throws Con +9, Dex +6
Skills Intimidation +9, Perception +6
Damage Resistances cold, fire
Damage Immunities acid, poison
Condition Immunities poisoned
Senses truesight 120 ft., passive Perception 16
Languages Abyssal, Common, Infernal
Challenge 12 (8,400 XP)

Improved Sense of Smell. The shaggy demodand has advantage on Perception checks that rely on scent.
Innate Spellcasting. The shaggy demodand's innate spellcasting is Charisma (spell save DC 17, +9 to hit with spell attacks). It can cast the following spells, requiring no material components:
> At will: *detect magic, detect thoughts, invisibility* (self only), *fear, ray of enfeeblement, spider climb*
> 3/day: *cloudkill, stinking cloud*
> 2/day: *dispel magic, black tentacles*
> 1/day: *mass suggestion*

Magic Resistance. The shaggy demodand has advantage on saving throws against spells and other magical effects.
Spellcasting. The shaggy demodand is an 8th-level spellcaster. Its spellcasting ability is Charisma (save DC 17, +9 to hit with spell attacks). The shaggy demodand has the following spells prepared:
> 1st level (4 slots): *enlarge/reduce, fog cloud, magic missile, hideous laughter*
> 2nd level (3 slots): *blur, hold person*
> 3rd level (3 slots): *blink, fireball*
> 4th level (2 slots): *confusion*

Actions

Multiattack. The shaggy demodand makes two Halberd attacks and one Bite attack.
Bite. *Melee Weapon Attack:* +10 to hit, reach 5 ft., one target. *Hit:* 19 (3d8 + 6) piercing damage. Creatures bitten by the shaggy demodand must succeed on a DC 17 Constitution saving throw or be paralyzed for 1 minute. The target can repeat the saving throw at the end of each of its turns, ending the effect on itself on a success.
+1 Halberd. *Melee Weapon Attack:* +11 to hit, reach 15 ft., one target. *Hit:* 18 (2d10 + 7) slashing damage.
Paralyzing Spittle. The shaggy demodand launches a globule of paralyzing spittle at a single target within 30 feet. The target must succeed on a DC 17 Constitution saving throw or be paralyzed for 1 minute. The target can repeat the saving throw at the end of each of its turns, ending the effect on itself on a success.
Summon Demodand (1/day). The shaggy demodand has a 50% chance of summoning 1d4 tarry demodands or one shaggy demodand to aid it for up to 1 minute. Any summoned demodands appear in unoccupied spaces within 60 feet of the summoning demodand and act on the summoner's initiative.

Bonus Actions

Halberd Shove. *Melee Weapon Attack:* +11 to hit, reach 20 ft., one target. *Hit:* 10 (1d6 + 7) bludgeoning damage and target must succeed on a DC 15 Strength (Athletics) or Dexterity (Acrobatics) check or be knocked prone. May only be used when the shaggy demodand has attacked at least once with its Halberd.

Reactions

Preemptive Strike. When a creature enters the shaggy demodand's reach (15 feet), the demodand makes a +1 Halberd attack against that creature.

Demodand, Tarry

Medium fiend (demodand), neutral evil
Armor Class 17 (natural armor)
Hit Points 127 (15d8 + 60)
Speed 40 ft., fly 40 ft.

STR	DEX	CON	INT	WIS	CHA
20 (+5)	15 (+2)	18 (+4)	11 (+0)	13 (+1)	15 (+2)

Saving Throws Constitution +7, Dexterity +5
Skills Athletics +8, Intimidation +5, Perception +4
Damage Resistances cold, fire
Damage Immunities acid, poison
Condition Immunities poisoned
Senses darkvision 60 ft., passive Perception 14
Languages Abyssal, Common?TBD
Challenge 8 (3,900 XP)

Adhesive Flesh. Any time a creature strikes the tarry demodand with a non-natural melee weapon, the attacker must succeed on a DC 16 Strength saving throw or the weapon becomes stuck to the demodand's body. If the weapon's wielder can't or won't let go of the weapon, the wielder is grappled while the weapon is stuck. While stuck, the weapon can't be used. A creature can pull the weapon free by taking an action to make a DC 16 Strength check and succeeding. Doing so, however, subjects it to an opportunity attack by the tarry demodand.
Improved Sense of Smell. The tarry demodand has advantage on Perception checks that rely on scent.
Innate Spellcasting. The tarry demodand's innate spellcasting is Charisma (spell save DC 13, +5 to hit with spell attacks). It can cast the following spells, requiring no material components:
> At will: *detect magic, invisibility* (self only), *fear, ray of enfeeblement*
> 2/day: *dispel magic, black tentacles*

Magic Resistance. The tarry demodand has advantage on saving throws against spells and other magical effects.
Reckless Attack. Each round on its turn, the tarry demodand can choose to attack recklessly, gaining advantage on all melee attack rolls during the round. However, attack rolls against the demodand then have advantage until the start of its next turn.

Actions

Multiattack. The tarry demodand makes one Bite attack and two Claw attacks.
Bite. *Melee Weapon Attack:* +8 to hit, reach 5 ft., one target. *Hit:* 15 (3d6 + 5) piercing damage.
Claw. *Melee Weapon Attack:* +8 to hit, reach 5 ft., one target. *Hit:* 14 (2d8 + 5) slashing damage and automatically initiates a grapple if the tarry demodand

wishes. Grappled creatures must succeed at a Strength (Athletics) or Dexterity (Acrobatics) check contested by the tarry demodand's Strength (Athletics) check. For each such grappled opponent, the tarry demodand must forgo one of its Claw attacks while the grapple is in effect. However, it has advantage on melee attacks conducted against grappled creatures.

Summon Demodand (1/day). The tarry demodand has a 30% chance of summoning one tarry demodand to aid it for up to 1 minute. The summoned demodand appears in an unoccupied space within 60 feet of the summoning demodand and acts on the summoner's initiative.

Bonus Actions

Rage (3/day). The tarry demodand may enter a rage. While enraged it gains advantage on Strength checks and saving throws, inflicts +3 additional damage each time it hits with a melee attack, and gains resistance to bludgeoning, piercing, and slashing damage. The rage lasts for 1 minute or until the tarry demodand chooses to end it (as a bonus action). While enraged, the tarry demodand may not use its Innate Spellcasting abilities or Summon Demodand.

Demon Gate

Large construct, chaotic evil
Armor Class 20 (natural armor)
Hit Points 253 (22d10 + 132)
Speed 0 ft.

STR	DEX	CON	INT	WIS	CHA
26 (+8)	1 (–5)	22 (+6)	20 (+5)	16 (+3)	22 (+6)

Saving Throws Str +14, Con +12, Wis +9, Cha +12
Skills Insight +9, Perception +9
Damage Resistances acid, cold
Damage Immunities fire, lightning, poison; bludgeoning, piercing, and slashing damage from nonmagical attacks
Condition Immunities poisoned
Senses truesight 120 ft., passive Perception 19
Languages Abyssal, telepathy 120 ft.
Challenge 18 (20,000 XP)

Burn. As a bonus action, the demon gate causes its body to be wreathed in flame. At the start of each of the demon gate's turns, each creature within 5 feet of it takes 10 (3d6) fire damage, and flammable objects in the aura that aren't being worn or carried ignite. A creature that touches the demon gate or hits it with a melee attack while within 5 feet of it takes 10 (3d6) fire damage.

Death Throes. When the demon gate dies, it explodes, and each creature within 30 feet of it must make a DC 20 Dexterity saving throw, taking 70 (20d6) fire damage on a failed saving throw, or half as much damage on a successful saving throw. The explosion ignites flammable objects in that area that aren't being worn or carried.

Innate Spellcasting. The demon gate's innate spellcasting ability is Charisma (spell save DC 20). It can cast the following spells, requiring no verbal or material components.

At will: *bane*
3/day each: *dispel magic, fireball, telekinesis, wall of fire*
1/day: *fire storm*

Magic Resistance. The demon gate has advantage on saving throws against spells and other magical effects.

Magic Weapons. The demon gate's weapon attacks are magical.

Rejuvenation. If a demon gate is destroyed, it gains a new body in 24 hours, regaining all its hit points and becoming active again.

Actions

Bite. *Melee Weapon Attack:* +14 to hit, reach 10 ft., one target. *Hit:* 30 (4d10 + 8) piercing damage plus 18 (4d8) fire damage and the target is grappled (escape DC 22). Until this grapple ends, the target is restrained, and the demon gate can't grapple another target. At the start of each of the demon gate's turns, the target takes 30 (4d10 + 8) bludgeoning damage plus 18 (4d8) fire damage.

Tongue. *Melee Weapon Attack:* +14 to hit, reach 15 ft., one target. *Hit:* 26 (4d8 + 8) slashing damage plus 14 (4d6) fire damage.

Demonic Knight

Medium fiend (demon), chaotic evil
Armor Class 17 (half plate)
Hit Points 85 (10d8 + 40)
Speed 30 ft.

STR	DEX	CON	INT	WIS	CHA
20 (+5)	13 (+1)	18 (+4)	17 (+3)	18 (+4)	18 (+4)

Skills Arcana +6, Athletics +8, Perception +7, Stealth +4
Damage Resistances acid, cold, fire; bludgeoning, piercing, and slashing damage from nonmagical attacks
Condition Immunities charmed, frightened
Senses truesight 60 ft., passive Perception 17
Languages Abyssal, Common
Challenge 6 (2,300 XP)

Innate Spellcasting. The demonic knight's innate spellcasting ability is Charisma (spell save DC 15, +7 to hit with spell attacks). It can cast the following spells without requiring material components:

At will: *detect magic, wall of ice*
2/day: *dispel magic*
1/day each: *bestow curse, fireball*

Magic Weapon. The demonic knight's weapon attacks are considered magical for the purposes of damage resistance.

Actions

Multiattack. The demonic knight makes two longsword attacks, or one one-handed longsword attack and one mailed fist attack.

Longsword. *Melee Weapon Attack:* +8 to hit, reach 5 ft., one target. *Hit:* 9 (1d8 + 5) slashing damage, or 10 (1d10 + 5) slashing damage if used with two hands.

Mailed Fist. *Melee Weapon Attack:* +8 to hit, reach 5 ft., one target. *Hit:* 9 (1d8 + 5) bludgeoning damage.

Breath of Unlife (recharge 5–6). The demonic knight releases a 10-foot cone of necrotic breath. Creatures in the area must make a DC 15 Constitution saving throw. On a failed save, a creature takes 28 (8d6) necrotic damage. If a humanoid creature is slain by this damage, it rises as a shadow demon under the command of the demonic knight that created it. The new shadow demon remains enslaved to the demonic knight until the knight's death and cannot summon demons of its own. A demonic knight can only have two such shadow demons under its command.

Summon Demon (1/day). A demonic knight has a 50 percent chance of summoning 1d4 shadow demons, 2 hezrous, 1 glabrezu, 1 vrock, or 1 marilith. The summoned demon appears in an unoccupied space within 60 feet.

It cannot summon further demons and remains only for 1 minute before vanishing. It disappears early if it or the demonic knight is slain.

Demons

Alu Demon

Medium fiend (demon), chaotic evil
Armor Class 14 (natural armor)
Hit Points 55 (10d8 + 10)
Speed 30 ft., fly 50 ft.

STR	DEX	CON	INT	WIS	CHA
16 (+3)	15 (+2)	13 (+1)	15 (+2)	12 (+1)	16 (+3)

Skills Acrobatics +5, Arcana +5, Deception +9, Perception +7, Persuasion +9, Stealth +5
Damage Resistances acid, cold, fire; bludgeoning, piercing, and slashing from nonmagical attacks
Damage Immunities lightning, poison
Senses darkvision 60 ft., passive Perception 17
Languages Abyssal, Common, Infernal, telepathy 60 ft.
Challenge 3 (700 XP)

Innate Spellcasting. The alu demon's innate spellcasting ability is Charisma (spell save DC 14). It can cast the following spells, requiring no material components.
    3/day each: *charm person, detect thoughts, disguise self*
    1/day: *suggestion*

ACTIONS

Multiattack. The alu demon makes two melee attacks.
Claw. Melee Weapon Attack: +6 to hit, reach 5 ft., one target. *Hit:* 10 (2d6 + 3) slashing damage, and the alu demon gains temporary hit points equal to the damage dealt by her claw attack.
Longsword. Melee Weapon Attack: +6 to hit, reach 5 ft., one target. *Hit:* 7 (1d8 + 3) slashing damage, or 8 (1d10 + 3) slashing damage if used with two hands to make a melee attack.

Babau

Medium fiend (demon), chaotic evil
Armor Class 15 (natural armor)
Hit Points 67 (9d8 + 27)
Speed 40 ft.

STR	DEX	CON	INT	WIS	CHA
15 (+2)	21 (+5)	17 (+3)	14 (+2)	13 (+1)	16 (+3)

Saving Throws Str +5, Con +8, Wis +4
Skills Acrobatics +8, Athletics +5, Insight +4, Perception +4, Sleight of Hand +11, Stealth +11, Survival +7
Damage Resistances acid, cold, fire; bludgeoning, piercing, and slashing from nonmagical attacks
Damage Immunities lightning, poison
Condition Immunities poisoned
Senses darkvision 60 ft., passive Perception 14
Languages Abyssal, Celestial, Draconic, telepathy 120 ft.
Challenge 6 (2,300 XP)

Innate Spellcasting. The babau's innate spellcasting ability is Charisma (spell save DC 14). It can cast the following spells without requiring material components.
    At will: *darkness, see invisibility*
    3/day: *dispel magic*

Protective Slime. Any creature that touches the babau, or hits it with a melee attack while within 5 feet takes 4 (1d8) acid damage. Any nonmagical weapon made of metal or wood that hits the babau corrodes. After dealing damage, the weapon takes a permanent and cumulative −1 penalty to damage rolls. If its penalty drops to −5, the weapon is destroyed. Nonmagical ammunition made of metal or wood that hits the babau is destroyed after dealing damage.

ACTIONS

Multiattack. The babau makes one Bite attack and two Claw attacks.
Bite. Melee Weapon Attack: +8 to hit, reach 5 ft., one creature. *Hit:* 10 (2d4 + 5) piercing damage.
Claw. Melee Weapon Attack: +8 to hit, reach 5 ft., one target. *Hit:* 8 (1d6 + 5) slashing damage plus 4 (1d8) acid damage.
Summon (1/day). The babau has a 40% chance to summon 1 **babau**. The summoned demon appears in an unoccupied space within 60 feet of the babau, but can't summon other demons. It remains for 1 minute, until it or the first babau is slain, or until the first babau takes an action to dismiss it.

Cacodemon

Medium fiend (demon), neutral evil
Armor Class 14 (natural armor)
Hit Points 71 (11d8 + 22)
Speed 30 ft.

STR	DEX	CON	INT	WIS	CHA
16 (+3)	13 (+1)	15 (+2)	14 (+2)	14 (+2)	15 (+2)

Skills Athletics +5, Deception +4, Intimidation +4, Perception +4, Stealth +3
Damage Resistances cold, fire, lightning; bludgeoning, piercing, and slashing from nonmagical attacks
Damage Immunities poison
Condition Immunities poisoned
Senses darkvision 60 ft., passive Perception 14
Languages Abyssal, Common, Daemonic, Infernal, telepathy 120 ft.
Challenge 4 (1,100 XP)

Innate Spellcasting. The cacodemon's innate spellcasting ability is Charisma (spell save DC 12). It can cast the following spells, requiring no material components.
    3/day each: *darkness, detect magic, detect thoughts, see invisibility*
    1/day: *hold person*
Magic Resistance. The cacodemon has advantage on saving throws against spells and other magical effects.
Magic Weapons. The cacodemon's weapon attacks are considered magical for the purposes of damage resistances.

ACTIONS

Multiattack. The cacodemon makes two Longsword and one Claw attack, or two Claw attacks.
Claws. Melee Weapon Attack: +5 to hit, reach 5 ft., one target. *Hit:* 6 (1d6 + 3) slashing damage.
Longsword. Melee Weapon Attack: +5 to hit, reach 5 ft., one target. *Hit:* 7 (1d8 + 3) slashing damage, or 8 (1d10 + 3) slashing damage if used with two hands to make a melee attack.
Change Shape. The cacodemon magically polymorphs into a humanoid who's challenge rating is equal to or

lower than its own, or back into its true form. It reverts to its true form if it dies. Any equipment it is wearing or carrying is absorbed or borne by the new form (the cacodemon's choice). In a new form, the cacodemon retains its game statistics and ability to speak, but its AC, movement modes, Strength, Dexterity, and special senses are replaced by those of the new form, and it gains any statistics and capabilities (except class features, legendary actions, and lair actions) that the new form has but that it lacks.

Summon (1/day). The cacodemon has a 35% chance to summon 1d3 **derghodemons** or 1 **cacodemon**. The summoned demon appears in an unoccupied space within 60 feet of the cacodemon, but can't summon other demons. It remains for 1 minute, until it or the first cacodemon is slain, or until the first cacodemon takes an action to dismiss it.

Cambion Demon

Medium fiend (demon), chaotic evil
Armor Class 14 (natural armor)
Hit Points 45 (7d8 + 14)
Speed 30 ft.

STR	DEX	CON	INT	WIS	CHA
15 (+2)	13 (+1)	14 (+2)	13 (+1)	12 (+1)	14 (+2)

Damage Resistances acid, cold, fire
Damage Immunities lightning, poison
Condition Immunities poisoned
Senses darkvision 60 ft., passive Perception
Languages Abyssal, Common, telepathy 30 ft.
Challenge 2 (450 XP)

Innate Spellcasting. The cambion's innate spellcasting ability is Charisma (spell save DC 12). It can cast the following spells, requiring no material components.

3/day: *command*
1/day each: *charm person, enthrall*

ACTIONS

Multiattack. The cambion makes two weapon attacks.
Claw. *Melee Weapon Attack:* +4 to hit, reach 5 ft., one target. *Hit:* 4 (1d4 + 2) slashing damage.
Scimitar. *Melee Weapon Attack:* +4 to hit, reach 5 ft., one target. *Hit:* 5 (1d6 + 2) slashing damage.
Longbow. *Melee Weapon Attack:* +3 to hit, range 150/600 ft., one target. *Hit:* 5 (1d8 + 1) piercing damage.

Charonademon

Medium fiend (demon), neutral evil
Armor Class 16 (natural armor)
Hit Points 75 (10d8 + 30)
Speed 40 ft.

STR	DEX	CON	INT	WIS	CHA
18 (+4)	16 (+3)	16 (+3)	15 (+2)	14 (+2)	18 (+4)

Saving Throws Con +6, Wis +5
Skills Arcana +6, Deception +8, Intimidation +8, Perception +6, Stealth +7, Survival +6
Damage Resistances cold, fire, lightning; bludgeoning, piercing, and slashing from nonmagical attacks
Damage Immunities acid, poison
Condition Immunities poisoned
Senses darkvision 60 ft., passive Perception 16
Languages Abyssal, Common, Daemonic, Infernal, telepathy 120 ft.

Challenge 7 (2,900 XP)

Innate Spellcasting. The charonademon's innate spellcasting ability is Charisma (spell save DC 16). It can cast the following spells, requiring no material components.

At will: *detect magic, darkness, see invisibility*
1/day: *plane shift* (skiff and self only)

Magic Resistance. The charonademon has advantage on saving throws against spells and other magical effects.

Magic Weapons. The charonademon's weapon attacks are considered magical for the purposes of damage resistances.

ACTIONS

Multiattack. The charonademon uses its Fear Gaze and makes two Quarterstaff attacks.
Quarterstaff. *Melee Weapon Attack:* +7 to hit, reach 5 ft., one target. *Hit:* 11 (2d6 + 4) bludgeoning damage, or 13 (2d8 + 4) bludgeoning damage if used with two hands to make a melee attack.
Fear Gaze. Creatures within 30 feet of the charonademon who can see it must make a DC 16 Wisdom saving throw. On a failed saving throw, the creature takes 10 (3d6) psychic damage and is frightened for 1 minute. On a successful saving throw, the creature takes half damage and is not frightened.

While frightened, the target must take the Dash action and move away from the charonademon by the safest available route on each of its turns, unless there is nowhere to move. The creature can repeat the saving throw if it ends its turn out of line of sight with the charonademon, ending the effect on a success. If the creature's saving throw succeeds, or the effect ends for it, the target is immune to a charonademon's fear gaze for 24 hours.

Summon (1/day). The charonademon has a 35% chance to summon 1d4 **hydrodemons**[1] or 1 **charonademon**[1]. The summoned demon appears in an unoccupied space within 60 feet of the charonademon, but can't summon other demons. It remains for 1 minute, until it or the first charonademon is slain, or until the first charonademon takes an action to dismiss it.

Demon Ape

Gargantuan fiend (demon), chaotic evil
Armor Class 18 (natural armor)
Hit Points 201 (13d20 + 65)
Speed 50 ft.

STR	DEX	CON	INT	WIS	CHA
25 (+7)	13 (+1)	20 (+5)	8 (−1)	8 (−1)	12 (+1)

Saving Throws Dex +6, Con +10, Wis +4
Skills Athletics +12, Perception +4, Stealth +6
Damage Resistances acid, cold, fire
Damage Immunities lightning, poison
Condition Immunities poisoned
Senses darkvision 60 ft., passive Perception 14
Languages Common
Challenge 14 (11,500 XP)

Water Vulnerability. If the demon ape begins its turn with at least half its body submerged in a body of water must make a DC 20 Constitution saving throw. On a failed saving throw, the demon ape's size is reduced by one step, from Gargantuan to Huge, or Huge to Large, to a minimum of Tiny. When this occurs, the demon ape deals half damage with all of its abilities, its maximum hit points are reduced by 20 for each reduction, and the size which the demon ape can grapple with its Claw attack is reduced by 1 step as well. The demon ape's size returns to normal over the course of 1 month.

ACTIONS

Multiattack. The demon ape makes one Bite attack and two Claw attacks.

Bite. *Melee Weapon Attack:* +12 to hit, reach 5 ft., one target. *Hit:* 17 (2d10 + 7) piercing damage.

Claw. *Melee Weapon Attack:* +12 to hit, reach 20 ft., one target. *Hit:* 20 (2d12 + 7) slashing damage, and the target is grappled (escape DC 20). The demon ape can grapple 1 Large or smaller creature in each claw.

Deafening Roar (3/day). Creatures that can hear the demon ape within 120 feet of it must make a DC 18 Constitution saving throw. On a failed saving throw, the creature takes 4d10 + 5 thunder damage and is deafened for 1 minute. On a successful saving throw, the creature takes half damage and is not deafened.

Fling. One Large or smaller object or creature grappled by the demon ape is thrown up to 60 feet in a random direction and knocked prone. If a thrown target strikes a solid surface, the target takes 3 (1d6) bludgeoning damage for every 10 feet it was thrown. If the target is thrown at another creature, that creature must succeed on a DC 20 Dexterity saving throw or take the same damage and be knocked prone.

Derghodemon

Large fiend (demon), neutral evil
Armor Class 18 (natural armor)
Hit Points 147 (14d10 + 70)
Speed 40 ft.

STR	DEX	CON	INT	WIS	CHA
25 (+7)	16 (+3)	21 (+5)	7 (−2)	14 (+2)	16 (+3)

Saving Throws Dex +7, Con +9, Wis +6, Cha +7
Skills Intimidation +7, Perception +6, Stealth +7
Damage Resistances cold, fire, lightning
Damage Immunities poison
Condition Immunities poisoned
Senses truesight 120 ft., passive Perception 20
Languages Abyssal, telepathy 120 ft.
Challenge 9 (5,000 XP)

Magic Resistance. The demon has advantage on saving throws against spells and other magical effects.

Magic Weapons. The demon's weapon attacks are magical.

Innate Spellcasting. The demon's spellcasting ability is Charisma (spell save DC 15, +7 to hit with spell attacks). The demon can innately cast the following spells, requiring no material components:

    At will: *darkness, fear, detect magic*
    1/day each: *confusion, sleep*

Rend and Tear. The demon has advantage on all melee weapon attacks against a creature it is grappling.

ACTIONS

Multiattack. The demon makes one Bite and two Claws attacks.

Bite. *Melee Weapon Attack:* +11 to hit, reach 5 ft., one target. *Hit:* 16 (2d8 + 7) piercing damage, and the target is grappled (escape DC 17). Until this grapple ends, the demon can bite only the grappled creature and has

advantage on attack rolls to do so.

Claws. *Melee Weapon Attack:* +11 to hit, reach 10 ft., one target. *Hit:* 21 (4d6 + 7) slashing damage.

Hydrodemon

Large fiend (demon), neutral evil
Armor Class 15 (natural armor)
Hit Points 85 (9d10 + 36)
Speed 30 ft., fly 40 ft., swim 60 ft.

STR	DEX	CON	INT	WIS	CHA
18 (+4)	14 (+2)	18 (+4)	8 (−1)	11 (+0)	14 (+2)

Saving Throws Dex +5, Con +7
Skills Perception +6
Damage Resistances cold, fire, lightning
Damage Immunities poison
Condition Immunities poisoned
Senses darkvision 60 ft., passive Perception 16
Languages Abyssal
Challenge 5 (1,800 XP)

Amphibious. The hydrodemon can breathe air and water.

Magic Resistance. The hydrodemon has advantage on saving throws against spells and other magical effects.

Magic Weapons. The hydrodemon's weapon attacks are magical.

Innate Spellcasting. The hydrodemon's spellcasting ability is Charisma (spell save DC 13, +5 to hit with spell attacks). It can innately cast the following spells, requiring no material components:

    At will: *darkness, detect magic, water walk*
    2/day each: *dimension door, teleport*
    1/day: *hallow*

ACTIONS

Multiattack. The hydrodemon makes one Bite attack and two Claws attacks. The demon can use its Sleep Spittle instead of using its Bite.

Bite. *Melee Weapon Attack:* +7 to hit, reach 5 ft., one target. *Hit:* 13 (2d8 + 4) piercing damage, and the target is grappled (escape DC 14). Until this grapple ends, the target is restrained and the demon can't bite another target.

Claws. *Melee Weapon Attack:* +7 to hit, reach 10 ft., one target. *Hit:* 11 (2d6 + 4) slashing damage.

Sleep Spittle. One target within 60 ft. must succeed on a DC 15 Wisdom saving throw or fall unconscious for 1 minute. The sleeping target can be awakened if someone uses an action to shake or slap the sleeper awake, and the target will wake if it takes damage.

Summon (1/day). The demon chooses what to summon and attempts a magical summoning.

A hydrodemon has a 30% chance of summoning one hydrodemon.

A summoned demon appears in an unoccupied space within 60 feet of its summoner, acts as an ally of its summoner, and can't summon other demons. It remains for 1 minute, until it or its summoner dies, or until its summoner dismisses it as an action.

Kytha

Medium fiend (demon), chaotic evil
Armor Class 16 (natural armor)
Hit Points 90 (12d8 + 36)
Speed 40 ft.

STR	DEX	CON	INT	WIS	CHA
20 (+5)	16 (+3)	17 (+3)	11 (+0)	13 (+1)	16 (+3)

Saving Throws Str +9, Con +7, Wis +5
Skills Athletics +9, Intimidation +7, Perception +9, Stealth +7
Damage Resistances acid, cold, fire; bludgeoning, piercing, and slashing from nonmagical attacks
Damage Immunities lightning, poison
Condition Immunities poisoned
Senses darkvision 60 ft., passive Perception 19
Languages Abyssal, Celestial, Draconic, telepathy 120 ft.
Challenge 9 (5,000 XP)

Innate Spellcasting. The kytha's innate spellcasting ability is Charisma (spell save DC 15). It can cast the following spells, requiring no material components.

> At will: *darkness*
> 1/day each: *hold person* (3rd level), *silence*

Magic Resistance. The kytha has advantage on saving throws against spells and other magical effects.

Magic Weapons. The kytha's weapon attacks are considered magical for the purpose of damage resistance.

ACTIONS

Multiattack. The kytha attacks twice with its Claws, and once with either its Bite or Tongue.

Tongue. *Melee Weapon Attack:* +9 to hit, reach 15 ft., one creature. *Hit:* 8 (1d6 + 5) bludgeoning damage plus 10 (3d6) poison damage.

Bite. *Melee Weapon Attack:* +9 to hit, reach 5 ft., one creature. *Hit:* 14 (2d8 + 5) piercing damage.

Claws. *Melee Weapon Attack:* +9 to hit, reach 5 ft., one target. *Hit:* 12 (2d6 + 5) slashing damage.

Summon (1/day). The kytha has a 35% chance to summon 1d2 **babau** or 1 **kytha**. The summoned demon appears in an unoccupied space within 60 feet of the kytha, but can't summon other demons. It remains for 1 minute, until it or the first kytha is slain, or until the first kytha takes an action to dismiss it.

Demons – Individuals

Apalla the Blistered One

Large fiend (demon), chaotic evil
Armor Class 17 (natural armor)
Hit Points 149 (13d10 + 78)
Speed 30 ft., fly 60 ft.

STR	DEX	CON	INT	WIS	CHA
22 (+6)	22 (+6)	23 (+6)	21 (+5)	21 (+5)	25 (+7)

Saving Throws Str +11, Dex +11, Con +11, Wis +10
Skills Acrobatics +11, Arcana +10, Deception +17, Insight +15, Perception +15, Persuasion +17, Stealth +12, Survival +12
Damage Resistances cold, fire
Damage Immunities acid, lightning, poison; bludgeoning, piercing, and slashing from nonmagical attacks
Condition Immunities charmed, exhaustion, frightened, poisoned
Senses truesight 120 ft., passive Perception 25
Languages Abyssal, Common, Ignan, Infernal, telepathy 120 ft.
Challenge 16 (15,000 XP)

Acidic Pustules. A creature that touches or hits Apalla with a melee attack while within 5 feet of it takes 10 (3d6) acid damage. Any nonmagical weapon made of metal or wood that hits Apalla corrodes and is destroyed.

Innate Spellcasting. Apalla's innate spellcasting ability is Charisma (spell save DC 20, +12 to hit with spell attacks). She can cast the following spells, requiring no material components.

> At will: *acid arrow* (4th level spell), *charm person*
> 3/day each: *bestow curse*, *blight*, *confusion*, *dispel magic*
> 1/day each: *contagion*, *dominate person*, *harm*

Legendary Resistance (3/day). If Apalla fails a saving throw, she can choose to succeed instead.

Magic Resistance. Apalla has advantage on saving throws against spells and other magical effects.

Magic Weapons. Apalla's weapon attacks are magical.

Unholy Aura. An unholy aura surrounds Apalla out to a radius of 20 feet. A creature who enters or begins their turn in the area must make a DC 20 Wisdom saving throw. On a failed saving throw, the target is frightened for 1 minute. While frightened, it is paralyzed. A frightened target can repeat the saving throw at the end of each of its turns, ending the effect on a success.

ACTIONS

Multiattack. Apalla makes one Bite attack and two Claw attacks.

Bite. *Melee Weapon Attack:* +11 to hit, reach 5 ft., one creature. *Hit:* 15 (2d8 + 6) piercing damage, and the target must make a DC 21 Constitution saving throw or contract demon fever.

Claw. *Melee Weapon Attack:* +11 to hit, reach 5 ft., one target. *Hit:* 13 (2d6 + 6) slashing damage plus 10 (3d6) acid damage.

Summon (1/day). Apalla can summon 1d4 **vrocks** or **hezrous**, 1d3 **glabrezus** or **nalfeshnees**, or 1 **balor**. The summoned demons appear in an unoccupied space within 60 feet of Apalla, but can't summon other demons. It remains for 1 minute, until it or Apalla is slain, or until Apalla takes an action to dismiss it.

LEGENDARY ACTIONS

Apalla can take 3 legendary actions, choosing from the options below. Only one legendary action can be used at a time and only at the end of another creature's turn. Apalla regains spent legendary actions at the start of her turn.

Boils. Apalla chooses one creature she can see within 60 feet of her to make a DC 20 Constitution saving throw. On a failed saving throw, acidic pustules explode from the target's skin and the creature takes 14 (4d6) acid damage, and the creature is poisoned for 1 minute. On a successful saving throw, the creature takes half the amount of damage and no further effects.

A poisoned creature repeats the saving throw at the beginning of each of their turns, ending the poisoned effect on a success. They take an additional 14 (4d6) acid damage each time they fail the saving throw against ending the poisoned condition.

Pool of Acid (costs 2 actions). Apalla conjures a pool of acid in a 20–foot radius at a point of her choice within 60 feet. Creatures that enter the area or begin their turn in the area must make a DC 20 Dexterity saving throw, taking 17 (5d6) acid damage on a failed saving throw, or half as much damage on a successful saving throw. The pool remains until the beginning of Apalla's next turn.

Miasma of Contagion (costs 3 actions). Apalla releases a miasma of disease in a 20–foot radius sphere. Creatures that enter the area or begin their turn there must make a DC 20 Constitution saving throw. On a failed saving throw, the creature suffers the effects of the *contagion* spell, as if Apalla had hit the target with a melee spell attack. This does not count as a use of Apalla's innate spellcasting ability.

Ka-Shareech, Air Lord of Pazuzu

Large fiend (demon), chaotic evil
Armor Class 15 (natural armor)
Hit Points 199 (21d10 + 84)
Speed 40 ft., fly 60 ft.

STR	DEX	CON	INT	WIS	CHA
17 (+3)	15 (+2)	18 (+4)	12 (+1)	18 (+4)	13 (+1)

Saving Throws Dex +7, Wis +9, Cha +6
Skills Insight +9, Perception +9, Religion +6
Damage Resistances cold, fire, lightning; bludgeoning, piercing, and slashing from nonmagical attacks
Damage Immunities poison
Condition Immunities poisoned
Senses darkvision 120 ft., passive Perception 19
Languages Abyssal, Auran, Ignan, Infernal, telepathy 120 ft.
Challenge 14 (11,500 XP)

Magic Resistance. Ka–Shareech has advantage on saving throws on spells and magical effects.

Spellcasting. Ka–Shareech is a 10th-level spellcaster. His spellcasting ability is Wisdom (spell save DC 17, +9 to hit with spell attacks). He has the following cleric spells prepared.

Cantrips (at will): *guidance, resistance, thaumaturgy*
1st level (4 slots): *bane, command, detect magic, inflict wounds*
2nd level (3 slots): *augury, blindness/deafness, gust of wind, hold person, silence*
3rd level (3 slots): *bestow curse, conjure animals (2 giant vultures), dispel magic, spirit guardians*
4th level (3 slots): *banishment, freedom of movement*
5th level (2 slots): *insect plague*

ACTIONS

Multiattack. Ka–Shareech makes one attack with its Beak and one with its Talons.

Beak. *Melee Weapon Attack:* +6 to hit, reach 5 ft., one target. *Hit:* 10 (2d6 + 3) piercing damage plus 4 (1d8) necrotic damage.

Talons. *Melee Weapon Attack:* +6 to hit, reach 5 ft., one target. *Hit:* 14 (2d10 + 3) slashing damage plus 4 (1d8) necrotic damage.

Spores (recharge 6). A 15-foot-radius cloud of toxic spores extends out from the vrock. The spores spread around corners. Each creature in that area must succeed on a DC 17 Constitution saving throw or become poisoned. While poisoned in this way, a target takes 5 (1d10) poison damage at the start of each of its turns. A target can repeat the saving throw at the end of each of its turns, ending the effect on itself on a success. Emptying a vial of holy water on the target also ends the effect on it.

Stunning Screech (1/day). The vrock emits a horrific screech. Each creature within 20 feet of it that can hear it and that isn't a demon must succeed on a DC 17 Constitution saving throw or be stunned until the end of the vrock's next turn.

Beckon the Flock (recharge 6). Ka–Shareech summons 1d4 + 1 **raven swarms** that appear in an unoccupied space within 5 feet of him. The raven swarms have resistance to acid, cold, and fire damage, and immunity to poison damage and the poisoned condition, as a blessing of Pazuzu. The summoned swarms appear in unoccupied spaces within 60 feet of Ka–Shareech, and remain for 1 minute, until they or Ka–Shareech are slain, or until Ka–Shareech takes an action to dismiss them. Ka–Shareech cannot use this ability again until all the swarms have been slain.

REACTIONS

Divine Intervention (1/day). If Ka–Shareech is reduced to 10 hit points or less, he can use a reaction to enact one of the following options:

- Cause himself or another creature within 30 feet of him to regain 36 (8d8) hit points.

- Teleport to a location he is familiar with up to 1 mile away.

- Restore one dead creature back to life, as long as that creature has been dead for no more than 1 minute.

Devils

Flayer Devil

Large fiend (devil), lawful evil
Armor Class 18 (natural armor)
Hit Points 142 (15d10 + 60)
Speed 40 ft.

STR	DEX	CON	INT	WIS	CHA
22 (+6)	17 (+3)	19 (+4)	15 (+2)	16 (+3)	19 (+4)

Saving Throws Str +11, Dex +8, Wis +8, Cha +9
Skills Athletics +11, Perception +8, Survival +13
Damage Resistances acid, cold; bludgeoning, piercing, and slashing from nonmagical attacks
Damage Immunities fire, poison
Condition Immunities poisoned
Senses darkvision 60 ft., passive Perception 18
Languages Common, Ignan, Infernal, telepathy 120 ft.
Challenge 11 (7,200 XP)

Devil's Sight. Magical darkness doesn't impede the devil's darkvision.

Innate Spellcasting. The flayer devil's innate spellcasting ability is Charisma (spell save DC 17, +9 to hit with spell attacks). He can cast the following spells, requiring no material components.

> At will: *detect evil and good, detect magic, scorching ray, vampiric touch*
> 1/day: *wall of fire*

Magic Resistance. The devil has advantage on saving throws against spells and other magical effects.

Regeneration. The flayer devil regains 10 hit points at the start of each of its turns. If the flayer devil takes radiant damage, or damage from a silvered weapon, this trait doesn't function at the start of the devil's next turn. The devil dies only if it starts its turn with 0 hit points and doesn't regenerate.

ACTIONS

Multiattack. The devil makes two Claw attacks and one Bite attack.

Bite. *Melee Weapon Attack:* +11 to hit, reach 5 ft., one creature. *Hit:* 15 (2d8 + 6) piercing damage.

Claw. *Melee Weapon Attack:* +11 to hit, reach 5 ft., one target. *Hit:* 13 (2d6 + 6) slashing damage.

Hellstoker Devil

Medium fiend (devil), lawful evil
Armor Class 15 (natural armor)
Hit Points 58 (9d8 + 18)
Speed 30 ft.

STR	DEX	CON	INT	WIS	CHA
15 (+2)	13 (+1)	15 (+2)	6 (−3)	10 (+0)	10 (+0)

Saving Throws Str +5, Con +5, Wis +2, Cha +2
Skills Athletics +5, Perception +2
Damage Resistances acid, cold; bludgeoning, piercing, and slashing from nonmagical attacks
Damage Immunities poison
Condition Immunities poisoned
Senses darkvision 60 ft., passive Perception 12
Languages Infernal, telepathy 120 ft.
Challenge 5 (1,800 XP)

Devil's Sight. Magical darkness doesn't impede the devil's darkvision.

Innate Spellcasting. The hellstoker's innate spellcasting ability is Charisma (spell save DC 11). It can cast the following spells, requiring no material components.

> At will: *protection from evil and good*
> 1/day: *plane shift* (self only)

Magic Resistance. The devil has advantage on saving throws against spells and other magical effects.

Oily Hide. A hellstoker has advantage on ability checks and saving throws to resist being grappled or restrained. In addition, if a hellstoker takes fire damage, it bursts into flame for 1 minute. During this time, a creature who enters the area or begins their turn in the area must make a DC 13 Dexterity saving throw, taking 4 (1d8) fire damage on a failed saving throw, or half as much damage on a successful saving throw.

ACTIONS

Multiattack. The hellstoker makes two Spear attacks.

Spear. *Melee Weapon Attack:* +5 to hit, reach 5 ft., or range 20/60 ft., one target. *Hit:* 5 (1d6 + 2) piercing damage or 6 (1d8 + 2) piercing damage if used with two hands to make a melee attack.

Bellows. The hellstoker releases a blast of fire from its bellows in a 15–foot cone. Creatures in the area must make a DC 13 Dexterity saving throw, taking 14 (4d6) fire damage on a failed saving throw, or half as much damage on a successful saving throw.

Summon (1/day). The hellstoker has a 35% chance to summon 2d8 **lemures** or 1 **hellstoker**. The summoned demon appears in an unoccupied space within 60 feet of the hellstoker, but can't summon other demons. It remains for 1 minute, until it or the first hellstoker is slain, or until the first hellstoker takes an action to dismiss it.

Devils — Individuals

Rylon the Cruel

Large fiend (devil), lawful evil
Armor Class 18 (natural armor)
Hit Points 180 (19d10 + 76)
Speed 40 ft.

STR	DEX	CON	INT	WIS	CHA
22 (+6)	17 (+3)	19 (+4)	15 (+2)	16 (+3)	19 (+4)

Saving Throws Str +11, Dex +8, Wis +8, Cha +9
Skills Athletics +11, Perception +8, Survival +13
Damage Resistances acid, cold; bludgeoning, piercing, and slashing from nonmagical attacks
Damage Immunities fire, poison
Condition Immunities poisoned
Senses darkvision 60 ft., passive Perception 18
Languages Common, Ignan, Infernal, telepathy 100 ft.
Challenge 16 (15,000 XP)

Special Equipment. Rylon carries his magical longsword *Cruelty*[2].

Devil's Sight. Magical darkness doesn't impede the devil's darkvision.

Innate Spellcasting. Rylon's innate spellcasting ability is Charisma (spell save DC 17, +9 to hit with spell attacks). He can cast the following spells, requiring no material components.

> At will: *detect evil and good, detect magic, scorching ray, vampiric touch*
> 1/day: *wall of fire*

Magic Resistance. The devil has advantage on saving throws against spells and other magical effects.

Regeneration. Rylon regains 10 hit points at the start of each of his turns. If Rylon takes radiant damage, or damage from a silvered weapon, this trait doesn't function at the start of Rylon's next turn. Rylon dies only if he starts his turn with 0 hit points and doesn't regenerate.

ACTIONS

Multiattack. Rylon makes two attacks with his magical longsword *Cruelty* and one Bite attack, or two Claw attacks and one Bite attack.

Cruelty. *Melee Weapon Attack:* +13 to hit, reach 5 ft., one target. *Hit:* 17 (2d8 + 8) slashing damage, or 19 (2d10 + 8) slashing damage if used with two hands to make a melee attack.

Bite. *Melee Weapon Attack:* +11 to hit, reach 5 ft., one creature. *Hit:* 15 (2d8 + 6) piercing damage.

Claw. *Melee Weapon Attack:* +11 to hit, reach 5 ft., one target. *Hit:* 13 (2d6 + 6) slashing damage.

Unholy Burst (3/day). The flayer devil releases a burst of hellish black vapor in a 30–foot radius. Creatures in the area must make a DC 17 Constitution saving throw. On a failed saving throw, the creature takes 10 (3d6) necrotic damage and is poisoned for 1 minute. A poisoned creature can repeat the saving throw at the end of each of its turns, ending the effect on a success.

Devra

Medium fiend (shapechanger), chaotic evil
Armor Class 17 (natural armor, *ring of protection, ioun stone*)
Hit Points 121 (22d8 + 22)
Speed 30 ft., fly 60 ft.

STR	DEX	CON	INT	WIS	CHA
8 (−1)	17 (+3)	13 (+1)	18 (+4)	12 (+1)	20 (+5)

Saving Throws Int +8, Wis +5, Cha +9
Skills Arcana +8, Deception +13, Insight +9, Perception +9, Persuasion +13
Damage Resistances cold, fire, lightning, poison; bludgeoning, piercing, and slashing from nonmagical attacks
Senses darkvision 60 ft., passive Perception 19
Languages Abyssal, Common, Infernal, telepathy 60 ft.
Challenge 15 (13,000 XP)

Dual Enchantment. If Devra casts an enchantment spell that would normally target one creature, she can have it target two.

Redirect (recharge 4–6). When a creature within 40 feet of Devra attacks her, she can use her reaction to redirect the attack. The attacking creature must succeed on a DC 17 Wisdom saving throw or target another creature of Devra's choice within range of the attack. Creatures that can't be charmed are immune to this effect.

Shapechanger. Devra can use her action to polymorph into a Small or Medium humanoid, or back into her true form. Without wings, Devra loses her flying speed. Other than her size and speed, her statistics are the same in each form. Any equipment she is wearing or carrying isn't transformed. She reverts to her true form if she dies.

Special Equipment. Devra possesses a *ring of protection* and an *ioun stone of protection*

Spellcasting. Devra is a 10th level spellcaster. Her spellcasting ability is Intelligence (spell save DC 16, +8 to hit with spell attacks). She has the following spells prepared:

> Cantrips (at will): *dancing lights, light, mage hand, minor illusion, prestidigitation*
> 1st level (4 slots): *charm person, false life, hideous laughter, magic missile, unseen servant*
> 2nd level (3 slots): *blur, detect thoughts, hold person, mirror image*
> 3rd level (3 slots): *counterspell, dispel magic, fireball*
> 4th level (3 slots): *black tentacles, confusion, greater invisibility*
> 5th level (2 slots): *dominate person, wall of force*

Telepathic Bond. Devra ignores the range restriction on her telepathy when communicating with a creature she has charmed. The two don't even need to be on the same plane of existence.

Actions

Claw (fiend form only). *Melee Weapon Attack:* +7 to hit, reach 5 ft., one target. *Hit:* 6 (1d6 + 3) slashing damage.

+1 Dagger. *Melee Weapon Attack:* +8 to hit, reach 5 ft., one target. *Hit:* 6 (1d4 + 4) piercing damage.

Charm. One humanoid Devra can see within 30 feet of her must succeed on a DC 16 Wisdom saving throw or be magically charmed for 1 day. The charmed target obeys Devra's verbal or telepathic commands. If the target suffers any harm or receives a suicidal command, it can repeat the saving throw, ending the effect on a success. If the target successfully saves against the effect, or if the effect on it ends, the target is immune to Devra's Charm for the next 24 hours. Devra can have only one target charmed at a time. If she charms another, the effect on the previous target ends.

Draining Kiss. Devra kisses a creature charmed by her or a willing creature. The target must make a DC 16 Constitution saving throw against this magic, taking 32 (5d10 + 5) psychic damage on a failed save, or half as much damage on a successful one. The target's hit point maximum is reduced by an amount equal to the damage taken. This reduction lasts until the target finishes a long rest. The target dies if this effect reduces its hit point maximum to 0.

Etherealness. Devra magically enters the Ethereal Plane from the Material Plane, or vice versa.

Bonus Actions

Hypnosis. Devra uses her charming voice to hypnotize one creature within 15 feet of her who can hear and understand her. The creature must succeed on a DC 17 Wisdom saving throw or be charmed until the end of her next turn. A hypnotized creature is incapacitated and does nothing but gaze at Devra. The effect ends for a hypnotized creature if that creature takes damage or is more than 15 feet from Devra.

Dinosaurs

Ankylosaurus

Huge beast, unaligned
Armor Class 16 (natural armor)
Hit Points 95 (10d12 + 30)
Speed 30 ft.

STR	DEX	CON	INT	WIS	CHA
21 (+5)	11 (+0)	16 (+3)	2 (−4)	10 (+0)	6 (−2)

Senses passive Perception 10
Languages —
Challenge 4 (1,100 XP)

Actions

Tail. *Melee Weapon Attack:* +7 to hit, reach 10 ft., one target. *Hit:* 23 (4d8 + 5) bludgeoning damage and Large or smaller targets must succeed on a DC 16 Strength check or be knocked prone and stunned until the end of their next turn.

Deinonychus

Medium beast, unaligned
Armor Class 12
Hit Points 9 (2d8)
Speed 40 ft.

STR	DEX	CON	INT	WIS	CHA
11 (+0)	15 (+2)	10 (+0)	2 (−4)	12 (+1)	5 (−3)

Skills Acrobatics +4, Perception +3, Stealth +4
Senses passive Perception 13
Languages —
Challenge 1/4 (50 XP)

Keen Smell. The deinonychus has advantage on Wisdom (Perception) checks that rely on smell.

Pack Tactics. The deinonychus has advantage on an attack roll against a creature if at least one of the deinonychus' allies is within 5 feet of the creature and the ally isn't incapacitated.

Rush (3/day). As a bonus action, the deinonychus can take the Dash action.

ACTIONS

Multiattack. The deinonychus makes one Bite attack and one Claw attack.

Bite. Melee Weapon Attack: +4 to hit, reach 5 ft., one target. *Hit:* 4 (1d4 + 2) piercing damage.

Claws. Melee Weapon Attack: +4 to hit, reach 5 ft., one target. *Hit:* 4 (1d4 + 2) slashing damage.

Diplodocus

Gargantuan beast, unaligned
Armor Class 16 (natural armor)
Hit Points 198 (12d20 + 72)
Speed 30 ft.

STR	DEX	CON	INT	WIS	CHA
21 (+5)	10 (+0)	23 (+6)	2 (−4)	14 (+2)	5 (−3)

Skills Athletics +9
Damage Resistances bludgeoning
Senses passive Perception 12
Languages —
Challenge 10 (5,900 XP)

Trampling Charge. If the diplodocus moves at least 20 feet straight toward a creature and then hits it with a tail attack on the same turn, that target must succeed on a DC 17 Strength saving throw or be knocked prone. If the target is prone, the diplodocus can make one stomp attack against it as a bonus action.

Unstoppable. The diplodocus has advantage on ability checks and saving throws against effects that would restrain it or knock it prone.

ACTIONS

Multiattack. The diplodocus makes two Tail Whip attacks.

Tail Whip. Melee Weapon Attack: +9 to hit, reach 20 ft., one target. *Hit:* 18 (3d8 + 5) slashing damage. If the target is a Large or smaller creature, it must succeed on a DC 17 Strength check or be knocked prone.

Stomp. Melee Weapon Attack: +9 to hit, reach 5 ft., one prone creature. *Hit:* 21 (3d10 + 5) bludgeoning damage.

LEGENDARY ACTIONS

The diplodocus can take 3 legendary actions, choosing from the options below. Only one legendary action can be used at a time and only at the end of another creature's turn. The diplodocus regains spent legendary actions at the start of its turn.

Move. The diplodocus moves up to half its speed.

Stomp (costs 2 actions). The diplodocus makes one stomp attack.

Whip Crack (costs 3 actions). The diplodocus whips its tail in the air, creating a thunderous crack. Each creature within 20 feet of it must succeed on a DC 17 Wisdom saving throw or take 14 (4d6) thunder damage and become frightened until the end of its next turn.

Hadrosaur

Huge beast, unaligned
Armor Class 14 (natural armor)
Hit Points 76 (8d12 + 24)
Speed 30 ft.

STR	DEX	CON	INT	WIS	CHA
19 (+4)	11 (+0)	17 (+3)	2 (−4)	10 (+0)	6 (−2)

Senses passive Perception 10
Languages —
Challenge 2 (450 XP)

Trampling Charge. If the Hadrosaur moves at least 20 feet straight toward a creature and hits that creature with a Ram attack on the same turn, that target must succeed on a DC 13 Strength check or be knocked prone. If the target is knocked prone, the hadrosaur may make one Stomp attack against it as a bonus action.

ACTIONS

Ram. Melee Weapon Attack: +6 to hit, reach 5 ft., one target. *Hit:* 9 (1d10 + 4) bludgeoning damage.

Stomp. Melee Weapon Attack: +6 to hit, reach 5 ft., one prone creature. *Hit:* 17 (3d8 + 4) bludgeoning damage.

Megaloceros

Large beast, unaligned
Armor Class 13 (natural armor)
Hit Points 37 (5d10 + 10)
Speed 50 ft.

STR	DEX	CON	INT	WIS	CHA
18 (+4)	13 (+1)	14 (+2)	3 (−4)	10 (+0)	7 (−2)

Senses passive Perception 10
Languages —
Challenge 1 (200 XP)

Charge. If the megaloceros moves at least 20 feet straight toward a target and then hits it with a Ram attack on the same turn, it takes an additional 9 (2d8) bludgeoning damage. If the target is a creature, it must succeed on a DC 14 Strength saving throw or be knocked prone.

ACTIONS

Ram. Melee Weapon Attack: +6 to hit, reach 5 ft., one target. *Hit:* 8 (1d8 + 4) bludgeoning damage.

Hooves. Melee Weapon Attack: +6 to hit, reach 5 ft., one prone creature. *Hit:* 11 (2d6 + 4) bludgeoning damage.

Megaraptor, Blind Fiendish

Large beast, lawful evil
Armor Class 15 (natural armor)
Hit Points 60 (8d10 + 16)
Speed 30 ft.

STR	DEX	CON	INT	WIS	CHA
18 (+4)	15 (+2)	14 (+2)	3 (−4)	12 (+1)	8 (−1)

Skills Perception +3, Stealth +6
Damage Resistances cold; bludgeoning, piercing, and slashing from nonmagical attacks not made with silver
Damage Immunities fire, poison

Condition Immunities poisoned
Senses the megaraptor is blind, passive Perception 13
Languages —
Challenge 3 (700 XP)

Blind. The megaraptor has disadvantage on all attacks, cannot see, and has advantage on perception checks that rely on hearing or scent.

Pack Tactics: The megaraptor has advantage on an attack roll against a creature if at least one of the megaraptor's allies is within 5 feet of the creature and the ally isn't incapacitated.

ACTIONS

Multiattack. The megaraptor makes one Bite attack and one Claws attack.

Bite. *Melee Weapon Attack:* +6 to hit, reach 5 ft., one target. *Hit:* 13 (2d8 + 4) piercing damage.

Claws. *Melee Weapon Attack:* +6 to hit, reach 5 ft., one target. *Hit:* 7 (1d6 + 4) slashing damage.

Pteranodon

Medium beast, unaligned
Armor Class 13 (natural armor)
Hit Points 22 (4d8 + 4)
Speed 10 ft., fly 60 ft.

STR	DEX	CON	INT	WIS	CHA
13 (+1)	17 (+3)	12 (+1)	2 (−4)	8 (−1)	7 (−2)

Skills Perception +1
Senses passive Perception 11
Languages —
Challenge 1 (200 XP)

Dive. If the pteranodon dives at least 30 feet straight toward a target and then hits it with a Bite attack on the same turn, the target takes an additional 7 (2d6) piercing damage.

Flyby. The pteranodon doesn't provoke an opportunity attack when it flies out of an enemy's reach.

ACTIONS

Bite. *Melee Weapon Attack:* +5 to hit, reach 5 ft., one target. *Hit:* 6 (1d6 + 3) piercing damage.

Dragons

Brazen Dragon Statue

Huge construct, neutral
Armor Class 18 (natural armor)
Hit Points 276 (24d12 + 120)
Speed 30 ft., fly 60 ft.

STR	DEX	CON	INT	WIS	CHA
25 (+7)	10 (+0)	20 (+5)	2 (−4)	9 (−1)	1 (−5)

Damage Vulnerabilities cold
Damage Immunities fire, poison, psychic; bludgeoning, piercing, and slashing from attacks not made with adamantine
Condition Immunities charmed, exhaustion, frightened, paralyzed, petrified, poisoned
Senses darkvision 60 ft., passive Perception 9
Languages Abyssal, Common.

Challenge 15 (13,000 XP)

Fire Absorption. Whenever the dragon is subjected to fire damage, it takes no damage and instead regains a number of hit points equal to the fire damage dealt.

Heated Body. A creature that touches the dragon or hits it with a melee attack while within 5 feet of it takes 10 (3d6) fire damage

Immutable Form. The dragon is immune to any spell or effect that would alter its form.

Magic Resistance. The dragon has advantage on saving throws against spells and other magical effects.

Magic Weapons. The dragon's weapon attacks are magical.

ACTIONS

Multiattack. The dragon makes one Bite attack and two Claw attacks.

Bite. *Melee Weapon Attack:* +12 to hit, reach 15 ft., one target. *Hit:* 18 (2d10 + 7) piercing damage plus 11 (2d10) fire damage.

Claw. *Melee Weapon Attack:* +12 to hit, reach 10 ft., one target. *Hit:* 14 (2d6 + 7) slashing damage plus 3 (1d6) fire damage.

Antimagic Breath (recharge 5–6). The dragon exhales antimagic energy in a 50-foot cone. Each creature inside the cone must make a successful DC 18 Dexterity saving throw or be affected as if it were inside an *antimagic field* (as per the spell) for 1 minute.

Dust Dragon, Ancient

Gargantuan dragon, neutral evil
Armor Class 22 (natural armor)
Hit Points 487 (25d20 + 225)
Speed 40 ft., burrow 30 ft., fly 80 ft.

STR	DEX	CON	INT	WIS	CHA
30 (+10)	10 (+0)	29 (+9)	18 (+4)	15 (+2)	23 (+6)

Saving Throws Dex +7, Con +16, Wis +9, Cha +13
Skills Perception +16, Stealth +7
Damage Immunities acid
Senses blindsight 60 ft., darkvision 120 ft., tremorsense 60 ft., passive Perception 26
Languages Common, Dragonic, Terran
Challenge 23 (50,000 XP)

Innate Spellcasting. The ancient dust dragon's innate spellcasting ability is Constitution (spell save DC 24). It can cast the following spells, requiring no material components.

> 3/day: *create or destroy water* (destroy only)
> 2/day: *stone shape*
> 1/day: *wall of stone*

Earthglide. The dragon can burrow through nonmagical, unworked earth and stone. While doing so, the dragon doesn't disturb the material it moves through.

Legendary Resistance (3/day). If the dragon fails a saving throw, it can choose to succeed instead.

ACTIONS

Multiattack. The dragon can use its Frightful Presence and make one Bite attack and two Claw attacks.

Bite. *Melee Weapon Attack:* +17 to hit, reach 15 ft., one target. *Hit:* 21 (2d10 + 10) piercing damage plus 14 (4d6) acid damage.

Claw. *Melee Weapon Attack:* +17 to hit, reach 10 ft., one target. *Hit:* 17 (2d6 + 10) slashing damage.

Tail. Melee Weapon Attack: +17 to hit, reach 20 ft., one
target. *Hit:* 19 (2d8 + 10) bludgeoning damage.

Frightful Presence. Each creature of the dragon's choice
that is within 120 feet of the dragon and aware of it must
succeed on a DC 21 Wisdom saving throw or become
frightened for 1 minute. A creature can repeat the saving
throw at the end of each of its turns, ending the effect on
itself on a success. If a creature's saving throw is successful
or the effect ends for it, the creature is immune to the
dragon's Frightful Presence for the next 24 hours.

Sand Breath (recharge 5–6). The dragon exhales shards of
stone and dust in a 90-foot cone. Each creature in that
area must succeed on a DC 24 Dexterity saving throw,
taking 85 (19d8) slashing damage on a failed saving
throw, or half as much damage on a successful one.

LEGENDARY ACTIONS

The dragon can take 3 legendary actions, choosing from
the options below. Only one legendary action can be
used as a time and only at the end of another creature's
turn. The dragon regains spent legendary actions at the
start of its turn.

Detect. The dragon makes a Wisdom (Perception) check.

Tail Attack. The dragon makes a Tail attack.

Sandstorm (costs 2 actions). The ancient dust dragon
creates a swirling maelstrom of sand and dust in a 120-
foot radius centered on itself, which swirls until the end of
the ancient dust dragon's next turn. Creatures in the area
must succeed on a DC 26 Constitution saving throw or
be blinded for 1 minute. Creatures can repeat the saving
throw at the end of each of its turns, ending the effect
on a success. The ancient dust dragon is immune to the
effects of its Sandstorm.

Wing Attack (costs 2 actions). The dragon beats its wings.
Each creature within 15 feet of the dragon must succeed
on a DC 25 Dexterity saving throw or take 17 (2d6 +
10) bludgeoning damage and be knocked prone. The
dragon can then fly up to half its flying speed.

LAIR ACTIONS

On initiative count 20 (losing initiative ties), the dragon takes
a lair action to cause one of the following effects; the
dragon can't use the same effect two rounds in a row:

• The solid stone surrounding a point on the ground
that the dragon can see within 120 feet of it turns into
dust and sand in a 20-foot radius. The area is considered
difficult terrain, and if a creature enters or begins their
turn in the area it must make a DC 18 Strength saving
throw or become restrained by the sudden quicksand.
A restrained creature can use its action to attempt to
free itself by making a DC 18 Strength check.

• The dust dragon chooses one creature it can see
within 60 feet of it to begin to petrify, as if the dust
dragon had cast the *flesh to stone* spell. The DC for this
effect is 22.

• The dust dragon creates a column of swirling
sand that is 10 feet in diameter and 40 feet high that
continues churning until the start of the next initiative
count 20. Creatures that enter or begin their turn in the
area must make a DC 18 Dexterity saving throw, taking
17 (5d6) slashing damage on a failed saving throw, or
half as much damage on a successful one.

REGIONAL EFFECTS

The region containing a legendary dust dragon's lair is
warped by the dragon's presence, which creates one or

more of the following effects:

• Creatures who succumb to the environment within 6
miles of the dust dragon's lair often rise as **dust ghouls**[1]
under the dust dragon's command.

• Oasis and water sources within 1 mile of the lair dry
up and become sand and dust quickly.

• Dust mephits and other similar creatures find
themselves at home within the area, and often attack
intruders on sight.

Glass Wyrm

Large dragon, neutral
Armor Class 19 (natural armor)
Hit Points 157 (15d10 + 75)
Speed 40 ft., fly 80 ft.

STR	DEX	CON	INT	WIS	CHA
22 (+6)	10 (+0)	21 (+5)	10 (+0)	12 (+1)	12 (+1)

Saving Throws Dex +5, Con +11, Wis +6, Cha +6
Skills Perception +11, Stealth +5
Damage Vulnerabilities thunder
Damage Resistances bludgeoning, piercing, and slashing
from nonmagical attacks
Senses blindsight 60 ft., darkvision 120 ft., passive Perception 21
Languages Draconic, Undercommon
Challenge 14 (11,500 XP)

Dazzling Brightness. If the glass wyrm starts its turn in an
area of bright light, any creature that can see the glass
wyrm must make a DC 19 Constitution saving throw or be
blinded until the end of their next turn. This feature does
not function in areas of dim light or darkness.

Legendary Resistance (3/day). If the glass wyrm fails a
saving throw against a spell or other effect, it can choose
to succeed instead.

ACTIONS

Multiattack. The wyrm can use its Frightful Presence and
make one Bite attack and two Claw attacks.

Bite. Melee Weapon Attack: +11 to hit, reach 10 ft., one
target. *Hit:* 17 (2d10 + 6) piercing damage.

Claw. Melee Weapon Attack: +11 to hit, reach 5 ft., one
target. *Hit:* 13 (2d6 + 6) slashing damage.

Tail. Melee Weapon Attack: +11 to hit, reach 15 ft., one
target. *Hit:* 15 (2d8 + 6) bludgeoning damage.

Frightful Presence. Each creature of the wyrm's choice
that is within 120 feet of the wyrm and aware of it must
succeed on a DC 14 Wisdom saving throw or become
frightened for 1 minute. A creature can repeat the saving
throw at the end of each of its turns, ending the effect on
itself on a success. If a creature's saving throw is successful
or the effect ends for it, the creature is immune to the
wyrm's Frightful Presence for the next 24 hours.

Glass Breath (recharge 5–6). The glass wyrm exhales a blast
of razor–sharp shards of glass in a 60–foot cone. Each
creature in that area must make a DC 19 Dexterity saving
throw, taking 54 (12d8) slashing damage on a failed
saving throw, or half as much damage on a successful
one.

REACTIONS

Reflect Spells (recharge 5–6). If the glass wyrm is the target
of a line spell, a *magic missile* spell, or a spell that requires
a ranged attack roll, the glass wyrm can reflect the spell

back at the caster. The caster becomes the target of the spell, using their spell save DC and spell attack modifier.

LEGENDARY ACTIONS

The glass wyrm can take 3 legendary actions, choosing from the options below. Only one legendary action option can be used at a time and only at the end of another creature's turn. The wyrm regains spent legendary actions at the start of its turn.

Detect. The wyrm makes a Wisdom (Perception) check.

Tail Attack. The wyrm makes a tail attack.

Wing Attack (costs 2 actions). The wyrm beats its wings. Each creature within 10 feet of the wyrm must succeed on a DC 19 Dexterity saving throw or take 13 (2d6 + 6) bludgeoning damage and be knocked prone. The wyrm can then fly up to half its flying speed.

Dragons – Individuals

Ilgomaxag

Gagantuan dragon (dust), neutral evil
Armor Class 22 (natural armor)
Hit Points 780 (40d20 + 360)
Speed 40 ft., burrow 30 ft., fly 80 ft.

STR	DEX	CON	INT	WIS	CHA
30 (+10)	10 (+0)	29 (+9)	18 (+4)	15 (+2)	23 (+6)

Saving Throws Dex +8, Con +17, Wis +10, Cha +14
Skills Perception +18, Stealth +8
Damage Immunities acid
Senses blindsight 60 ft., darkvision 120 ft., tremorsense 60 ft., passive Perception 28
Languages Common, Dragonic, Terran
Challenge 28 (120,000 XP)

Innate Spellcasting. The ancient dust dragon's innate spellcasting ability is Constitution (spell save DC 25). It can cast the following spells, requiring no material components.

    3/day: *create or destroy water* (destroy only)
    2/day: *stone shape*
    1/day: *wall of stone*

Earthglide. The dragon can burrow through nonmagical, unworked earth and stone. While doing so, the dragon doesn't disturb the material it moves through.

Legendary Resistance (3/day). If the dragon fails a saving throw, it can choose to succeed instead.

Spellcasting. Ilgomaxag is a 15th-level spellcaster. His spellcasting ability is Charisma (spell save DC 22, +14 to hit with spell attacks). He knows the following sorcerer spells.

    Cantrips (at will): *acid splash, dancing lights, mending, message*
    1st level (4 slots): *charm person, comprehend languages, magic missile*
    2nd level (3 slots): *fog cloud, scorching ray, see invisibility*
    3rd level (3 slots): *dispel magic, fireball*
    4th level (3 slots): *bestow curse, stoneskin*
    5th level (2 slots): *cloudkill, dominate person*
    6th level (1 slot): *chain lightning*
    7th level (1 slot): *fire storm*
    8th level (1 slot): *earthquake*

ACTIONS

Multiattack. The dragon can use its Frightful Presence and make one Bite attack and two Claw attacks.

Bite. *Melee Weapon Attack:* +18 to hit, reach 15 ft., one target. *Hit:* 21 (2d10 + 10) piercing damage plus 14 (4d6) acid damage.

Claw. *Melee Weapon Attack:* +18 to hit, reach 10 ft., one target. *Hit:* 17 (2d6 + 10) slashing damage.

Tail. *Melee Weapon Attack:* +18 to hit, reach 20 ft., one target. *Hit:* 19 (2d8 + 10) bludgeoning damage.

Frightful Presence. Each creature of the dragon's choice that is within 120 feet of the dragon and aware of it must succeed on a DC 22 Wisdom saving throw or become frightened for 1 minute. A creature can repeat the saving throw at the end of each of its turns, ending the effect on itself on a success. If a creature's saving throw is successful or the effect ends for it, the creature is immune to the dragon's Frightful Presence for the next 24 hours.

Sand Breath (recharge 5–6). The dragon exhales shards of stone and dust in a 90–foot cone. Each creature in that area must succeed on a DC 25 Dexterity saving throw, taking 85 (19d8) slashing damage on a failed saving throw, or half as much damage on a successful one.

LEGENDARY ACTIONS

The dragon can take 3 legendary actions, choosing from the options below. Only one legendary action can be used as a time and only at the end of another creature's turn. The dragon regains spent legendary actions at the start of its turn.

Detect. The dragon makes a Wisdom (Perception) check.

Tail Attack. The dragon makes a Tail attack.

Sandstorm (costs 2 actions). The ancient dust dragon creates a swirling maelstrom of sand and dust in a 120–foot radius centered on itself, which swirls until the end of the ancient dust dragon's next turn. Creatures in the area must succeed on a DC 26 Constitution saving throw or be blinded for 1 minute. Creatures can repeat the saving throw at the end of each of its turns, ending the effect on a success. The ancient dust dragon is immune to the effects of its Sandstorm.

Wing Attack (costs 2 actions). The dragon beats its wings. Each creature within 15 feet of the dragon must succeed on a DC 26 Dexterity saving throw or take 17 (2d6 + 10) bludgeoning damage and be knocked prone. The dragon can then fly up to half its flying speed.

LAIR ACTIONS

On initiative count 20 (losing initiative ties), the dragon takes a lair action to cause one of the following effects; the dragon can't use the same effect two rounds in a row:

- The solid stone surrounding a point on the ground that the dragon can see within 120 feet of it turns into dust and sand in a 20–foot radius. The area is considered difficult terrain, and if a creature enters or begins their turn in the area it must make a DC 18 Strength saving throw or become restrained by the sudden quicksand. A restrained creature can use its action to attempt to free itself by making a DC 18 Strength check.

- The dust dragon chooses one creature it can see within 60 feet of it to begin to petrify, as if the dust dragon had cast the *flesh to stone* spell. The DC for this effect is 22.

- The dust dragon creates a column of swirling sand that is 10 feet in diameter and 40 feet high that continues churning until the start of the next initiative count 20. Creatures that enter or begin their turn in the area must make a DC 18 Dexterity saving throw, taking 17 (5d6) slashing damage on a failed saving throw, or half as much damage on a successful one.

REGIONAL EFFECTS

The region containing a legendary dust dragon's lair is warped by the dragon's presence, which creates one or more of the following effects:

- Creatures who succumb to the environment within 6 miles of the dust dragon's lair often rise as **dust ghouls**[1] under the dust dragon's command.

- Oasis and water sources within 1 mile of the lair dry up and become sand and dust quickly.

- Dust mephits and other similar creatures find themselves at home within the area, and often attack intruders on sight.

Oriazier

Gargantuan dragon (solar), chaotic good
Armor Class 19 (natural armor)
Hit Points 595 (34d20 + 238)
Speed 40 ft., fly 120 ft.

STR	DEX	CON	INT	WIS	CHA
27 (+8)	10 (+0)	25 (+7)	16 (+3)	15(+2)	19 (+4)

Saving Throws Dex +8, Con +15, Wis +10, Cha +12
Skills Arcana +11, History +11, Perception +17, Persuasion +12, Stealth +8
Damage Immunities radiant
Condition Immunities blinded, paralyzed
Senses blindsight 60 ft., darkvision 120 ft., passive Perception 27
Languages Common, Draconic
Challenge 25 (75,000 XP)

Innate Spellcasting. The solar dragon's innate spellcasting ability is Charisma (spell save DC 20, +12 to hit with spell attacks). It can cast the following spells, requiring no material components.

At will: *daylight, guiding bolt*
1/day each: *flame strike, sunbeam, sunburst*

Legendary Resistance (3/day). If the solar dragon fails a saving throw against a spell or other effect, it can choose to succeed instead.

Spellcasting. Oriazier is a 17th-level spellcaster. His spellcasting ability is Charisma (spell save DC 20, +12 to hit with spell attacks). He knows the following sorcerer spells.

Cantrips (at will): *acid splash, mage hand, mending, message, ray of frost, prestidigitation*
1st level (4 slots): *detect magic, magic missile*
2nd level (3 slots): *blindness/deafness, detect thoughts, suggestion*
3rd level (3 slots): *dispel magic, fireball, slow*
4th level (3 slots): *banishment, dominate beast, wall of fire*
5th level (2 slots): *dominate person, hold monster*
6th level (1 slot): *true seeing*
7th level (1 slot): *reverse gravity*
8th level (1 slot): *power word stun*
9th level (1 slot): *time stop*

ACTIONS

Multiattack. The dragon can use its Frightful Presence and make one Bite attack and two Claw attacks.
Bite. *Melee Weapon Attack:* +16 to hit, reach 15 ft., one target. *Hit:* 19 (2d10 + 8) piercing damage.
Claw. *Melee Weapon Attack:* +16 to hit, reach 10 ft., one target. *Hit:* 15 (2d6 + 8) slashing damage.
Tail. *Melee Weapon Attack:* +16 to hit, reach 20 ft., one target. *Hit:* 17 (2d8 + 8) bludgeoning damage.
Frightful Presence. Each creature of the dragon's choice that is within 120 feet of the dragon and aware of it must succeed on a DC 20 Wisdom saving throw or become frightened for 1 minute. A creature can repeat the saving throw at the end of each of its turns, ending the effect on itself on a success. If a creature's saving throw is successful or the effect ends for it, the creature is immune to the dragon's Frightful Presence for the next 24 hours.
Breath Weapon (recharge 5–6). The dragon uses one of the following breath weapons:
Heat Breath. The dragon exhales a line of scalding heat that is 90 feet long and 10 feet wide. Creatures in the area must succeed on a DC 23 Constitution saving throw, taking 56 (16d6) fire damage on a failed saving throw, or half as much damage on a successful one.
Blinding Breath. The dragon releases a burst of blinding light in a 90–foot cone. Creature in the area must succeed on a DC 23 Constitution saving throw. On a failed saving throw, the creature takes 42 (12d6) radiant damage and is blinded for 1 minute. On a successful saving throw, the creature takes half damage and is not blinded.

LEGENDARY ACTIONS

The solar dragon can take 3 legendary actions, choosing from the options below. Only one legendary action option can be used at a time and only at the end of another creature's turn. The dragon regains spent legendary actions at the start of its turn.
Detect. The dragon makes a Wisdom (Perception) check.
Tail Attack. The dragon makes a Tail attack.
Wing Attack (costs 2 actions). The dragon beats its wings. Each creature within 10 feet of the dragon must succeed on a DC 20 Dexterity saving throw or take 13 (2d6 + 6) bludgeoning damage and be knocked prone. The dragon can then fly up to half its flying speed.

LAIR ACTIONS

On initiative count 20 (losing initiative ties), the dragon takes a lair action to cause one of the following effects; the dragon can't use the same effect two rounds in a row:

- The solar dragon causes up to 3 creatures that are not constructs or undead it can see within 60 feet of it to regain 20 (3d6 + 10) hit points.

- The solar dragon causes any magical darkness within 120 feet of it created by a spell of 8th level or lower to be dispelled.

- The solar dragon causes cylinders of pale light to shine down at four points within 120 feet of it. Each cylinder functions as if the solar dragon had cast the *moonbeam* spell with a spell save DC of 20, and remains shining until the next initiative 20.

REGIONAL EFFECTS

The region containing a legendary solar dragon's lair is warped by the dragon's presence, which creates one or more of the following effects:

- Darkness never settles within 6 miles of the solar dragon's lair, which remains at twilight even if there is no moon or other light source.

- Once per long rest, a good aligned creature who takes a short rest within 1 mile of the solar dragon's lair and spends hit dice regains an additional 10 hit points.

- Evil aligned creatures cannot take a long rest within 1 mile of a solar dragon's lair.

Drider-Goblin

Medium monstrosity, chaotic evil
Armor Class 14 (natural armor)
Hit Points 67 (9d8 + 27)
Speed 30 ft., climb 30 ft.

STR	DEX	CON	INT	WIS	CHA
14 (+2)	15 (+2)	16 (+3)	12 (+1)	13 (+1)	12 (+1)

Skills Perception +3, Stealth +4
Senses darkvision 60 ft., passive Perception 13
Languages Goblin, Undercommon
Challenge 4 (1,100 XP)

Nimble Escape. The drider-goblin can take the Disengage or Hide action as a bonus action on each of its turns.
Spider Climb. The drider-goblin can climb difficult surfaces, including upside down on ceilings, without needing to make an ability check.
Sunlight Sensitivity. While in sunlight, the drider-goblin has disadvantage on attack rolls, as well as on Wisdom (Perception) checks that rely on sight.
Web Walker. The drider-goblin ignores movement restrictions caused by webbing.

Actions

Multiattack. The drider-goblin makes one Bite attack and one Mace attack.
Bite. *Melee Weapon Attack:* +4 to hit, reach 5 ft., one target. *Hit:* 5 (1d6 + 2) piercing damage, plus 9 (2d8) poison damage.
Mace. *Melee Weapon Attack:* +4 to hit, reach 5 ft., one target. *Hit:* 5 (1d6 + 2) bludgeoning damage.
Javelin. *Melee or Ranged Weapon Attack:* +4 to hi, reach 5 ft. or range 30/120 ft., one target. *Hit:* 5 (1d6 + 2) piercing damage, or 6 (1d8 + 2) piercing damage if used with two hands to make a melee attack.

Drider-Goblin Spellcaster

Medium monstrosity, chaotic evil
Armor Class 14 (natural armor)
Hit Points 97 (13d8 + 39)
Speed 30 ft., climb 30 ft.

STR	DEX	CON	INT	WIS	CHA
14 (+2)	15 (+2)	16 (+3)	12 (+1)	13 (+1)	17 (+3)

Skills Perception +4, Stealth +5
Senses darkvision 60 ft., passive Perception 14
Languages Goblin, Undercommon
Challenge 5 (1,800 XP)

Nimble Escape. The drider-goblin can take the Disengage or Hide action as a bonus action on each of its turns.
Spellcasting. The drider-goblin spellcaster is a 4th-level spellcaster. Its spellcasting ability is Charisma (spell save DC 14, +6 to hit with spell attacks). It has the following sorcerer spells prepared.

    Cantrips (at will): *acid splash, chill touch, mending, prestidigitation, shocking grasp*
    1st level (4 slots): *detect magic, false life, magic missile*
    2nd level (3 slots): *blindness/deafness, web*
    3rd level (2 slots): *dispel magic*

Spider Climb. The drider-goblin can climb difficult surfaces, including upside down on ceilings, without needing to make an ability check.

Sunlight Sensitivity. While in sunlight, the drider-goblin has disadvantage on attack rolls, as well as on Wisdom (Perception) checks that rely on sight.
Web Walker. The drider-goblin ignores movement restrictions caused by webbing.

Actions

Multiattack. The drider-goblin makes one Bite attack and one Mace attack.
Bite. *Melee Weapon Attack:* +5 to hit, reach 5 ft., one target. *Hit:* 5 (1d6 + 2) piercing damage, plus 9 (2d8) poison damage.
Mace. *Melee Weapon Attack:* +5 to hit, reach 5 ft., one target. *Hit:* 5 (1d6 + 2) bludgeoning damage.
Javelin. *Melee or Ranged Weapon Attack:* +5 to hi, reach 5 ft. or range 30/120 ft., one target. *Hit:* 5 (1d6 + 2) piercing damage, or 6 (1d8 + 2) piercing damage if used with two hands to make a melee attack.

Efreeti Alchemist

Large elemental, lawful evil
Armor Class 17 (natural armor)
Hit Points 184 (16d10 + 96)
Speed 40 ft., fly 60 ft.

STR	DEX	CON	INT	WIS	CHA
19 (+4)	12 (+1)	22 (+6)	20 (+5)	15 (+2)	16 (+3)

Saving Throws Int +10, Wis +7, Cha +8
Skills Arcana +10
Damage Resistances poison
Damage Immunities fire
Senses darkvision 120 ft., passive Perception 12
Languages Ignan, telepathy 120 ft.
Challenge 13 (10,000 XP)

Alchemical Bandolier. The efreeti may locate and extract one alchemical substance from its well-organized bandolier of bottles and vials as a free action on each of its turns.
Alchemical Substances. The efreeti may imbibe or throw an alchemical substance to create a spell-like effect as a Use an Object action. For this purpose, the efreeti is a 10th level spellcaster. The efreeti's spellcasting ability is Intelligence (spell save DC 18). Spell-like effects created by alchemical substances do not require concentration, even if their corresponding spell does, and instead last for the maximum possible duration. These substances are completely inert in the hands of anyone but the efreeti.
The efreeti has the following substances prepared:
2/day each: *spell potion[2] of false life* (as a fourth level spell slot), *potion of fire giant strength, potion of greater healing, potion of growth, potion of invisibility, potion of speed*
1/day each: *dragon breath bomb* (all targets in a 30-foot cone must make a DC 18 Dexterity check, taking 6d6 fire damage on a failed save, or half as much damage on a successful one), *fire bomb* (as *fireball* spell with an 80-foot range), *glue bomb* (fills a 10-foot radius within 80 feet with powerful adhesive for 1 minute, so that a creature in that area must succeed on a DC 18 Dexterity saving throw or be restrained — at the beginning of each of the creature's turns, it may attempt a DC 18 Strength saving throw, escaping the area and ceasing to be restrained on a success), *spell potion[2] of fire shield, spell potion[2] of greater invisibility, potion of magic weapon* (as *magic weapon* spell), *spell potion[2] of regenerate, potion of superior healing*

Elemental Demise. If the efreeti dies, its body disintegrates in a flash of fire and puff of smoke, leaving behind only equipment the efreeti was wearing or carrying.

Innate Spellcasting. The efreeti's innate spellcasting ability is Charisma (spell save DC 16, +8 to hit with spell attacks). It can innately cast the following spells, with no need for material components:

At will: *detect magic*

3/day each: *enlarge/reduce, tongues*

1/day each: *conjure elemental* (fire elemental only), *gaseous form, invisibility, major image, plane shift, wall of fire*

Actions

Multiattack. The efreeti makes two Scimitar attacks or uses its Hurl Flame twice.

Scimitar. *Melee Weapon Attack:* +9 to hit, reach 5 ft., one target. *Hit:* 11 (2d6 + 4) slashing damage plus 7 (2d6) fire damage.

Hurl Flame. *Ranged Spell Attack:* +10 to hit, range 120 ft., one target. *Hit:* 17 (5d6) fire damage.

Bonus Actions

Two-fisted Drinking (recharge 5–6). If the efreeti has spent an action to use an Alchemical Substance, it may use another Alchemical Substance.

Efreeti Amir

Large elemental, lawful evil
Armor Class 18 (natural armor)
Hit Points 275 (22d10 + 154)
Speed 40 ft., fly 60 ft.

STR	DEX	CON	INT	WIS	CHA
24 (+7)	14 (+2)	24 (+7)	16 (+3)	15 (+2)	18 (+4)

Saving Throws Int +8, Wis +7, Cha +8
Damage Immunities fire
Senses darkvision 120 ft., passive Perception 12
Languages Ignan, telepathy 120 ft.
Challenge 15 (13,000 XP)

Action Surge (recharges after a short or long rest). The efreeti may make one additional action on its turn on top of its normal action (and possible bonus action).

Elemental Demise. If the efreeti dies, its body disintegrates in a flash of fire and puff of smoke, leaving behind only equipment the efreeti was wearing or carrying.

Improved Critical. The efreeti's weapon attacks score a critical hit on a roll of 19 or 20.

Innate Spellcasting. The efreeti's innate spellcasting ability is Charisma (spell save DC 17, +9 to hit with spell attacks). It can innately cast the following spells, with no need for material components:

At will: *detect magic*

3/day each: *enlarge/reduce, tongues*

2/day each: *conjure elemental* (fire elemental only), *gaseous form, invisibility, major image, plane shift, wall of fire*

1/day each: *flame strike, greater invisibility*

Actions

Multiattack. The efreeti makes three Scimitar attacks or uses its Hurl Flame three times.

+2 Scimitar. *Melee Weapon Attack:* +14 to hit, reach 5 ft., one target. *Hit:* 19 (3d6 + 9) slashing damage plus 7 (2d6) fire damage.

Hurl Flame. *Ranged Spell Attack:* +9 to hit, range 120 ft., one target. *Hit:* 21 (6d6) fire damage.

Bonus Actions

Second Wind (recharges after a short or long rest). The efreeti may regain 1d10 + 15 hit points.

Efreeti Amir Al-umara

Large elemental, lawful evil
Armor Class 20 (natural armor)
Hit Points 324 (24d10 + 192)
Speed 40 ft., fly 60 ft.

STR	DEX	CON	INT	WIS	CHA
24 (+7)	14 (+2)	26 (+8)	18 (+4)	16 (+3)	20 (+5)

Saving Throws Int +10, Wis +9, Cha +11
Skills Perception +9
Damage Immunities fire
Senses darkvision 120 ft., passive Perception 19
Languages Ignan, telepathy 120 ft.
Challenge 20 (25,000 XP)

Action Surge (recharges after a short or long rest). The efreeti may make one additional action on its turn on top of its normal action (and possible bonus action).

Duelist. The efreeti adds +2 to damage rolls while using a single one-handed weapon (included below).

Elemental Demise. If the efreeti dies, its body disintegrates in a flash of fire and puff of smoke, leaving behind only equipment the efreeti was wearing or carrying.

Improved Critical. The efreeti's weapon attacks score a critical hit on a roll of 18, 19, or 20.

Indomitable (1/day). The efreeti may reroll an unsuccessful saving throw. It must use the second roll.

Innate Spellcasting. The efreeti's innate spellcasting ability is Charisma (spell save DC 19, +11 to hit with spell attacks). It can innately cast the following spells, with no need for material components:

At will: *detect magic*

3/day each: *enlarge/reduce, tongues*

2/day each: *conjure elemental* (fire elemental only), *gaseous form, invisibility, major image, plane shift, wall of fire*

2/day each: *flame strike, greater invisibility*

Remarkable Athlete. The efreeti may add +2 to any Strength, Dexterity, or Constitution check that doesn't already incorporate his proficiency bonus.

Actions

Multiattack. The efreeti makes four Scimitar attacks or uses its Hurl Flame four times.

+3 Scimitar. *Melee Weapon Attack:* +16 to hit, reach 5 ft., one target. *Hit:* 25 (3d8 + 12) slashing damage plus 7 (2d6) fire damage.

Hurl Flame. *Ranged Spell Attack:* +11 to hit, range 120 ft., one target. *Hit:* 21 (6d6) fire damage.

Bonus Actions

Second Wind (recharges after a short or long rest). The efreeti may regain 1d10 + 25 hit points.

Efreeti Cleric

Large elemental, lawful evil
Armor Class 17 (natural armor)
Hit Points 184 (16d10 + 96)
Speed 40 ft., fly 60 ft.

STR	DEX	CON	INT	WIS	CHA
22 (+6)	12 (+1)	22 (+6)	16 (+3)	20 (+5)	16 (+3)

Saving Throws Int +8, Wis +10, Cha +8
Skills Religion +10
Damage Immunities fire
Senses darkvision 120 ft., passive Perception 15
Languages Ignan, telepathy 120 ft.
Challenge 13 (10,000 XP)

Channel the Sultan: Directed Strike (2/day). The efreeti gains +10 on one attack roll.

Channel the Sultan: Cooperative Strike (2/day). When a creature within 30 feet makes an attack roll, the efreeti may use its reaction to grant that creature +10 to the roll.

Holy Strike. On each of its turns, when the efreeti hits a creature with a weapon attack, it can cause the attack to deal an extra 1d8 damage of the same type normally dealt by the weapon.

Elemental Demise. If the efreeti dies, its body disintegrates in a flash of fire and puff of smoke, leaving behind only equipment the efreeti was wearing or carrying.

Innate Spellcasting. The efreeti's innate spellcasting ability is Charisma (spell save DC 16, +8 to hit with spell attacks). It can innately cast the following spells, with no need for material components:

    At will: *detect magic*
    3/day each: *enlarge/reduce, tongues*
    1/day each: *conjure elemental* (fire elemental only), *gaseous form, invisibility, major image, plane shift, wall of fire*

Spellcasting. The efreeti is a 10th level spellcaster. The efreeti's spellcasting ability is Wisdom (spell save DC 18, +10 to hit with spell attacks). It has the following spells prepared:

    Cantrips (at will): *light, mending, sacred flame, spare the dying, thaumaturgy*
    1st level (4 slots): *bane, bless, cure wounds, divine favor, healing word, shield of faith*
    2nd level (3 slots): *aid, enhance ability, lesser restoration, magic weapon, silence, spiritual weapon*
    3rd level (3 slots): *bestow curse, crusader's mantle, dispel magic, glyph of warding, mass healing word, spirit guardians*
    4th level (3 slots): *banishment, death ward, freedom of movement, stone shape, stoneskin*
    5th level (2 slots): *flame strike, greater restoration, hold monster, mass cure wounds*

ACTIONS

Multiattack. The efreeti makes two Scimitar attacks or uses its Hurl Flame twice.

Scimitar. *Melee Weapon Attack:* +11 to hit, reach 5 ft., one target. *Hit:* 13 (2d6 + 6) slashing damage plus 7 (2d6) fire damage.

Hurl Flame. *Ranged Spell Attack:* +8 to hit, range 120 ft., one target. *Hit:* 17 (5d6) fire damage.

BONUS ACTIONS

Warrior Priest (5/day). The efreeti cleric makes one weapon attack.

Efreeti Loremaster

Large elemental, lawful evil
Armor Class 17 (natural armor)
Hit Points 210g (20d10 + 100)
Speed 40 ft., fly 60 ft.

STR	DEX	CON	INT	WIS	CHA
19 (+4)	12 (+1)	21 (+5)	22 (+6)	15 (+2)	16 (+3)

Saving Throws Int +11, Wis +7, Cha +8
Skills Arcana +16, History +16, Nature +11, Perception +7
Damage Immunities fire
Senses darkvision 120 ft., passive Perception 17
Languages Abyssal, Aquan, Auran, Common, Ignan, Infernal, Terran, telepathy 120 ft.
Challenge 15 (13,000 XP)

Divination Renewal. When the efreeti casts a divination spell, it regains an expended spell slot of a level lower than the spell it cast.

Foresight. The efreeti rolls three d20s at the beginning of each day. It can use up to one of its foresight rolls to replace any attack roll, saving throw, or ability check made by it or any creature it can see within 50 feet of it. This ability can only be used once per turn.

Girded Sanity. The efreeti receives a +6 on any skill check or saving throw against illusions or becoming charmed, confused, frightened, or insane.

Innate Spellcasting. The efreeti's innate spellcasting ability is Charisma (spell save DC 16, +8 to hit with spell attacks). It can innately cast the following spells, with no need for material components:

    At will: *comprehend languages, detect magic, tongues*
    3/day: *enlarge/reduce*
    2/day each: *conjure elemental* (greater fire elemental only), *gaseous form, invisibility, major image, plane shift, wall of fire*
    1/day: *greater invisibility*

See Invisible. The efreeti can see invisible creatures and objects within 10 feet.

Spellcasting. The efreeti is a 15th level spellcaster. The efreeti's spellcasting ability is Intelligence (spell save DC 19, +11 to hit with spell attacks). It has the following spells prepared:

    Cantrips (at will): *dancing lights, light, mage hand, mending, minor illusion*
    1st level (4 slots): *charm person, false life, identify, magic missile, shield, unseen servant*
    2nd level (3 slots): *arcanist's magic aura, blur, detect thoughts, mirror image*
    3rd level (3 slots): *clairvoyance, fireball, sending, slow*
    4th level (3 slots): *arcane eye, locate creature, stoneskin*
    5th level (2 slots): *contact other plane, legend lore, scrying*
    6th level (1 slot): *globe of invulnerability*
    7th level (1 slot): *delayed blast fireball*
    8th level (1 slot): *feeblemind*

ACTIONS

Multiattack. The efreeti makes two Scimitar attacks or uses its Hurl Flame twice.

Scimitar. *Melee Weapon Attack:* +9 to hit, reach 5 ft., one target. *Hit:* 11 (2d6 + 4) slashing damage plus 7 (2d6) fire damage.

Hurl Flame. *Ranged Spell Attack:* +11 to hit, range 120 ft., one target. *Hit:* 17 (5d6) fire damage.

Efreeti Malik

Large elemental, lawful evil
Armor Class 18 (natural armor)
Hit Points 250 (20d10 + 140)
Speed 40 ft., fly 60 ft.

STR	DEX	CON	INT	WIS	CHA
23 (+6)	14 (+2)	24 (+7)	16 (+3)	15 (+2)	17 (+3)

Saving Throws Int +8, Wis +7, Cha +8
Damage Immunities fire
Senses darkvision 120 ft., passive Perception 12
Languages Ignan, telepathy 120 ft.
Challenge 13 (10,000 XP)

Action Surge (recharges after a short or long rest). The efreeti may make one additional action on its turn on top of its normal action (and possible bonus action).
Elemental Demise. If the efreeti dies, its body disintegrates in a flash of fire and puff of smoke, leaving behind only equipment the efreeti was wearing or carrying.
Improved Critical. The efreeti's weapon attacks score a critical hit on a roll of 19 or 20.
Innate Spellcasting. The efreeti's innate spellcasting ability is Charisma (spell save DC 17, +9 to hit with spell attacks). It can innately cast the following spells, with no need for material components:

> At will: *detect magic*
> 3/day each: *enlarge/reduce, tongues*
> 1/day each: *conjure elemental* (fire elemental only), *gaseous form, invisibility, major image, plane shift, wall of fire*

ACTIONS

Multiattack. The efreeti makes three Scimitar attacks or uses its Hurl Flame three times.
+1 Scimitar. *Melee Weapon Attack:* +12 to hit, reach 5 ft., one target. *Hit:* 16 (2d8 + 7) slashing damage plus 7 (2d6) fire damage.
Hurl Flame. *Ranged Spell Attack:* +8 to hit, range 120 ft., one target. *Hit:* 17 (5d6) fire damage.

BONUS ACTIONS

Second Wind (recharges after a short or long rest). The efreeti may regain 1d10 + 15 hit points.

Efreeti Sardar

Large elemental, lawful evil
Armor Class 19 (natural armor)
Hit Points 300 (24d10 + 168)
Speed 40 ft., fly 60 ft.

STR	DEX	CON	INT	WIS	CHA
24 (+7)	14 (+2)	24 (+7)	18 (+4)	16 (+3)	18 (+4)

Saving Throws Int +10, Wis +9, Cha +10
Damage Immunities fire
Senses darkvision 120 ft., passive Perception 13
Languages Ignan, telepathy 120 ft.
Challenge 18 (20,000 XP)

Action Surge (recharges after a short or long rest). The efreeti may make one additional action on its turn on top of its normal action (and possible bonus action).
Duelist. The efreeti adds +2 to damage rolls while using a single one-handed weapon (included below).
Elemental Demise. If the efreeti dies, its body disintegrates in a flash of fire and puff of smoke, leaving behind only equipment the efreeti was wearing or carrying.
Improved Critical. The efreeti's weapon attacks score a critical hit on a roll of 19 or 20.
Innate Spellcasting. The efreeti's innate spellcasting ability is Charisma (spell save DC 18, +10 to hit with spell attacks). It can innately cast the following spells, with no need for material components:

> At will: *detect magic*
> 3/day each: *enlarge/reduce, tongues*
> 2/day each: *conjure elemental* (fire elemental only), *gaseous form, invisibility, major image, plane shift, wall of fire*
> 1/day each: *flame strike, greater invisibility*

Remarkable Athlete. The efreeti may add +2 to any Strength, Dexterity, or Constitution check that doesn't already incorporate its proficiency bonus.

ACTIONS

Multiattack. The efreeti makes three Scimitar attacks or uses its Hurl Flame three times.
+3 Scimitar. *Melee Weapon Attack:* +16 to hit, reach 5 ft., one target. *Hit:* 25 (3d8 + 12) slashing damage plus 7 (2d6) fire damage.
Hurl Flame. *Ranged Spell Attack:* +10 to hit, range 120 ft., one target. *Hit:* 21 (6d6) fire damage.

BONUS ACTIONS

Second Wind (recharges after a short or long rest). The efreeti may regain 1d10 + 25 hit points.

Efreeti Sorcerer

Large elemental, lawful evil
Armor Class 17 (natural armor)
Hit Points 184 (16d10 + 96)
Speed 40 ft., fly 60 ft.

STR	DEX	CON	INT	WIS	CHA
19 (+4)	12 (+1)	22 (+6)	16 (+3)	15 (+2)	20 (+5)

Saving Throws Int +8, Wis +7, Cha +10
Skills Arcana +8
Damage Immunities fire
Senses darkvision 120 ft., passive Perception 12
Languages Ignan, telepathy 120 ft.
Challenge 13 (10,000 XP)

Elemental Demise. If the efreeti dies, its body disintegrates in a flash of fire and puff of smoke, leaving behind only equipment the efreeti was wearing or carrying.
Empowered Spells (3/day). When it rolls for spell damage, the efreeti may reroll up to five dice. It must use the new roll.
Fire Affinity. When the efreeti casts a spell that deals fire damage, it may add its Charisma modifier to that damage (included in Hurl Flame below).
Heightened Spells (2/day). When a spell cast by the efreeti forces a target to make a saving throw to resist its effects, the efreeti may cause one target to have disadvantage on its first saving throw made against the spell.
Innate Spellcasting. The efreeti's innate spellcasting ability is Charisma (spell save DC 18, +10 to hit with spell attacks). It can innately cast the following spells, with no need for material components:

> At will: *detect magic*

3/day each: *enlarge/reduce, tongues*
1/day each: *conjure elemental* (fire elemental only),
    *gaseous form, invisibility, major image, plane shift,
    wall of fire*

Quickened Spells (2/day). When it casts a spell that has
a casting time of 1 action, the efreeti can change the
casting time to 1 bonus action for this casting.

Spellcasting. The efreeti is a 10th level spellcaster. The
efreeti's spellcasting ability is Charisma (spell save DC
18, +10 to hit with spell attacks). It has the following spells
prepared:

Cantrips (at will): *blade ward, dancing lights, light,
    mage hand, minor illusion*
1st level (4 slots): *charm person, magic missile, shield*
2nd level (3 slots): *enlarge/reduce, invisibility, mirror
    image*
3rd level (3 slots): *fireball, haste, stinking cloud*
4th level (3 slots): *greater invisibility, wall of fire*
5th level (2 slots): *animate objects, cloudkill*

Actions

Multiattack. The efreeti makes two Scimitar attacks or uses its
Hurl Flame twice.

Scimitar. *Melee Weapon Attack:* +9 to hit, reach 5 ft., one
target. *Hit:* 11 (2d6 + 4) slashing damage plus 7 (2d6) fire
damage.

Hurl Flame. *Ranged Spell Attack:* +10 to hit, range 120 ft.,
one target. *Hit:* 22 (5d6 + 5) fire damage.

Efreet – Individuals

Al-Jabeer

Large elemental, lawful evil
Armor Class 17 (natural armor)
Hit Points 250 (20d10 + 140)
Speed 40 ft., fly 60 ft.

STR	DEX	CON	INT	WIS	CHA
20 (+5)	12 (+1)	24 (+7)	23 (+6)	15 (+2)	18 (+4)

Saving Throws Int +12, Wis +8, Cha +10
Skills Arcana +12
Damage Resistances poison
Damage Immunities fire
Senses darkvision 120 ft., passive Perception 12
Languages Ignan, telepathy 120 ft.
Challenge 17 (18,000 XP)

Alchemical Bandolier. Al-Jabeer may locate and extract
one alchemical substance from its well-organized
bandolier of bottles and vials as a free action on each of
its turns.

Alchemical Substances. Al-Jabeer may imbibe or throw
an alchemical substance to create a spell-like effect as
a Use an Object action. For this purpose, the Al-Jabeer
is a 20th level spellcaster. Al-Jabeer's spellcasting ability
is Intelligence (spell save DC 20). Spell-like effects
created by alchemical substances do not require
concentration, even if their corresponding spell does,
and instead last for the maximum possible duration.
These substances are completely inert in the hands of
anyone but Al-Jabeer.
Al-Jabeer has the following substances prepared:
2 each/day: *confusion bomb* (as *confusion* spell using a
    6th level spell slot), *dragon breath bomb* (all targets in
    a 40-foot cone must make a DC 20 Dexterity check,
    taking 8d6 fire damage on a failed save, or half as much

damage on a successful one), *fire bomb* (as *fireball*
spell cast using a 5th level spell slot, with an 80-foot
range), *glue bomb* (fills a 10-foot radius within 80 feet
with powerful adhesive for 1 minute, so that a creature
in that area must succeed on a DC 20 Dexterity saving
throw or be restrained — at the beginning of each of the
creature's turns, it may attempt a DC 20 Strength saving
throw, escaping the area and ceasing to be restrained
on a success), *spell potion*[2] *of false life* (as a fourth level
spell slot), *spell potion*[2] *of fire shield, potion of growth,
potion of invisibility, potion of magic weapon* (as *magic
weapon* spell but granting a +2 bonus to attack and
damage rolls), *potion of speed, potion of storm giant
strength, potion of superior healing*
1 each/day: *gravity bomb* (as *reverse gravity* spell), *spell
    potion*[2] *of greater invisibility, potion of invulnerability, spell
    potion*[2] *of regenerate, potion of supreme healing*

Elemental Demise. If Al-Jabeer dies, his body disintegrates
in a flash of fire and puff of smoke, leaving behind only
equipment he was wearing or carrying.

Innate Spellcasting. Al-Jabeer's innate spellcasting ability is
Charisma (spell save DC 18, +10 to hit with spell attacks).
He can innately cast the following spells, with no need for
material components:

At will: *detect magic*
3/day each: *enlarge/reduce, tongues*
2/day each: *conjure elemental* (fire elemental only),
    *gaseous form, invisibility, major image, plane shift,
    wall of fire*
1/day each: *flame strike, greater invisibility*

Iron Flask. Al-Jabeer possesses an empty alchemical
container which behaves as a standard magical *iron flask*,
except that it does not grant Al-Jabeer any control over
creatures released from the flask or affect those creatures'
disposition in any way.

Actions

Multiattack. Al-Jabeer makes two Scimitar attacks or uses his
Hurl Flame twice.

Scimitar. *Melee Weapon Attack:* +10 to hit, reach 5 ft., one
target. *Hit:* 12 (2d6 + 5) slashing damage plus 7 (2d6) fire
damage.

Hurl Flame. *Ranged Spell Attack:* +9 to hit, range 120 ft., one
target. *Hit:* 17 (5d6) fire damage.

Bonus Actions

Two-fisted Drinking (recharge 4–6). If Al-Jabeer has spent
an action to use an Alchemical Substance, he may use
another Alchemical Substance.

Baatina the Ghost

Large elemental, lawful evil
Armor Class 13 (natural armor)
Hit Points 158 (20d10 + 48)
Speed 0 ft., fly 60 ft.

STR	DEX	CON	INT	WIS	CHA
9 (−1)	16 (+3)	16 (+3)	22 (+6)	15 (+2)	18 (+4)

Saving Throws Int +10, Wis +7, Cha +9
Skills Arcana +11, History +11, Religion +11
Damage Resistances acid, lightning, thunder; bludgeoning,
    piercing, and slashing from nonmagical attacks
Damage Immunities cold, fire, necrotic, poison
Condition Immunities charmed, exhaustion, frightened,
    grappled, paralyzed, petrified, poisoned, prone, restrained
Senses darkvision 120 ft., passive Perception 12

Languages Common, Ignan, telepathy 120 ft.
Challenge 10 (5,900 XP)

Ethereal Sight. Baatina can see 60 feet into the Ethereal Plane when she is on the Prime Material (or in the City of Brass), and vice versa.

Incorporeal Movement. Baatina can move through other creatures and objects as if they were difficult terrain. She takes 5 (1d10) force damage if she ends her turn inside an object.

Innate Spellcasting. Baatina's innate spellcasting ability is Charisma (spell save DC 17, +9 to hit with spell attacks). She can innately cast the following spells, with no need for material components:

> At will: *detect magic*
> 3/day each: *enlarge/reduce, tongues*
> 1/day each: *conjure elemental* (fire elemental only), *invisibility, major image, plane shift, wall of fire*

ACTIONS

Multiattack. Baatina makes two Withering Touch attacks or uses her Ghostly Flame twice.

Withering Touch. *Melee Weapon Attack:* +7 to hit, reach 5 ft., one target. *Hit:* 21 (5d6 + 4) necrotic damage.

Ghostly Flame. *Ranged Spell Attack:* +8 to hit, range 120 ft., one target. *Hit:* 21 (5d6 + 4) necrotic damage.

Etherealness. Baatina enters the Ethereal Plane from the Material Plane (or City of Brass), or vice versa. She is visible on the Material (or in the City of Brass) while she is in the Border Ethereal, and vice versa, yet she can't affect or be affected by anything on the other plane.

Horrifying Visage. Each non-undead creature within 60 feet of Baatina that can see her must succeed on a DC 16 Wisdom saving throw or be frightened for 1 minute. If the save fails by 5 or more, the target also ages 1d4 x 10 years. A frightened target can repeat the saving throw at the end of each of its turns, ending the frightegned condition on itself on a success. If a target's saving throw is successful or the effect ends for it, the target is immune to Baatina's Horrifying Visage for the next 24 hours. The aging effect can be reversed with a *greater restoration* spell, but only within 24 hours of it occurring.

Possession (recharge 5–6). One humanoid that Baatina can see within 5 feet of her must succeed on a DC 17 Charisma saving throw or be possessed by Baatina; Baatina then disappears, and the target is incapacitated and loses control of its body. Baatina now controls the gbody but doesn't deprive the target of awareness. Baatina can't be targeted by any attack, spell, or other effect, except ones that turn undead, and she retains her alignment, Intelligence, Wisdom, Charisma, and immunity to being charmed and frightened. She otherwise uses the possessed target's statistics but doesn't gain access to the target's knowledge, class features, or proficiencies.

Faakhira

Large elemental, lawful neutral
Armor Class 17 (natural armor)
Hit Points 230 (20d10 + 120)
Speed 40 ft., fly 60 ft.

STR	DEX	CON	INT	WIS	CHA
20 (+5)	16 (+3)	22 (+6)	16 (+3)	15 (+2)	22 (+6)

Saving Throws Int +8, Wis +7, Cha +11
Skills Acrobatics +13, History +8, Intimidation +16, Nature +8, Perception +12, Performance +16
Damage Resistances poison

Damage Immunities fire
Senses darkvision 120 ft., passive Perception 22
Languages Ignan, telepathy 120 ft.
Challenge 15 (13,000 XP)

Elemental Demise. If Faakhira dies, her body disintegrates in a flash of fire and puff of smoke, leaving behind only equipment she was wearing or carrying.

Innate Spellcasting. Faakhira's innate spellcasting ability is Charisma (spell save DC 20, +12 to hit with spell attacks). She can innately cast the following spells, with no need for material components:

> At will: *detect magic*
> 3/day each: *enlarge/reduce, tongues*
> 2/day each: *conjure elemental* (fire elemental only), *gaseous form, invisibility, major image, plane shift, wall of fire*
> 1/day each: *flame strike, greater invisibility*

Spellcasting. Faakhira is a 16th level spellcaster. Her spellcasting ability is Charisma (spell save DC 20, +12 to hit with spell attacks). She has the following spells prepared:

> Cantrips (at will): *blade ward, dancing lights, mage hand, minor illusion*
> 1st level (4 slots): *charm person, cure wounds, hideous laughter, thunderwave*
> 2nd level (3 slots): *blindness/deafness, blur, silence, suggestion*
> 3rd level (3 slots): *dispel magic, fear, hypnotic pattern*
> 4th level (3 slots): *confusion, freedom of movement, polymorph*
> 5th level (2 slots): *animate objects, dominate person, modify memory*
> 6th level (1 slot): *irresistible dance*
> 7th level (1 slot): *fire storm, teleport*
> 8th level (1 slot): *feeblemind*

ACTIONS

Multiattack. Faakhira makes two Scimitar attacks or uses her Hurl Flame twice.

Scimitar. *Melee Weapon Attack:* +11 to hit, reach 5 ft., one target. *Hit:* 12 (2d6 + 5) slashing damage plus 7 (2d6) fire damage.

Hurl Flame. *Ranged Spell Attack:* +12 to hit, range 120 ft., one target. *Hit:* 17 (5d6) fire damage.

Countercharm. Faakhira uses words of power to disrupt mind-influencing effects. She begins a performance that lasts until the end of her next turn. During that time, she and any friendly creatures within 30 feet of her have advantage on saving throws against being frightened or charmed. Creatures must be able to hear her to gain this benefit.

BONUS ACTIONS

Cutting Words (recharge 4–6). Faakhira uses her wit to distract, confuse, and otherwise sap the confidence and competence of others. When a creatures she can see within 60 feet of her makes an attack roll, an ability check, or a damage roll, Faakhira can roll a d12, subtracting the number rolled from the creature's roll. The target must be able to hear and understand Faakhira.

The Great Sultan

Huge elemental, lawful evil
Armor Class 19 (natural armor)
Hit Points 580 (40d12 + 320)
Speed 40 ft., fly 60 ft.

STR	DEX	CON	INT	WIS	CHA
28 (+9)	16 (+3)	26 (+8)	22 (+6)	15 (+2)	18 (+4)

Saving Throws Con +17, Int +15, Wis +11, Cha +13
Skills Arcana +15, History +15, Insight +11, Perception +11, Persuasion +13
Damage Immunities acid, fire, poison; bludgeoning, piercing, and slashing from nonmagical attacks
Condition Immunities charmed, exhaustion, frightened, paralyzed, poisoned
Senses darkvision 120 ft., passive Perception 21
Languages Common, Primordial, telepathy 120 ft.
Challenge 29 (135,000 XP)

Elemental Demise. If the Great Sultan dies, his body disintegrates in a flash of fire and puff of smoke, leaving behind only equipment he is wearing or carrying.

Innate Spellcasting. The Great Sultan's innate spellcasting ability is Charisma (spell save DC 21, +13 to hit with spell attacks). He can innately cast the following spells, requiring no material components:

At will: *detect magic*
3/day each: *enlarge/reduce, tongues*
1/day each: *conjure elemental (fire elemental only), gaseous form, invisibility, major image, plane shift, wall of fire*

Legendary Resistance (3/day). If the Great Sultan fails a saving throw, he can choose to succeed instead.

Living Flame. A creature that touches the Great Sultan or hits him with a melee attack while within 5 feet of him takes 11 (2d10) fire damage. The creature must succeed on a DC 21 Dexterity saving throw or catch fire; until someone takes an action to douse the fire, the creature takes 5 (1d10) fire damage at the start of each of its turns.

Lord of Fire. The Great Sultan's weapon attacks are magical. When the Great Sultan hits a creature with an attack or spell that deals fire damage, the target's fire resistance is ignored by the Great Sultan's fire damage. If the target has immunity to fire damage, it instead has resistance to the Great Sultan's fire damage.

Magic Resistance. The Great Sultan has advantage on saving throws against spells and other magical effects.

Spellcasting. The Great Sultan is a 20th-level spellcaster. His spellcasting ability is Intelligence (spell save DC 23, +15 to hit with spell attacks). The Great Sultan has the following wizard spells prepared:

Cantrips (at will): *fire bolt, friends, mage hand, prestidigitation, true strike*
1st level (4 slots): *burning hands, charm person, protection from evil and good, shield, thunderwave*
2nd level (3 slots): *arcane lock, hold person, suggestion, web*
3rd level (3 slots): *counterspell, dispel magic, fireball*
4th level (3 slots): *banishment, confusion, wall of fire*
5th level (3 slots): *dominate person, geas, hold monster*
6th level (2 slots): *chain lightning, mass suggestions*
7th level (2 slots): *delayed blast fireball, forcecage*
8th level (1 slot): *dominate monster, incendiary cloud*
9th level (1 slot): *imprisonment, prismatic wall*

Wish Granting. At his discretion, Sulymon may grant the wish of another creature (as the *wish* spell). This is an innate power and does not use any spell slots. He may only grant three wishes per creature.

Actions

Multiattack. The Great Sultan makes four *Brazen Scimitar* attacks. He can use his Hurl Flame in place of any *Brazen Scimitar* attack.

Brazen Scimitar. *Melee Weapon Attack:* +21 to hit, reach 10 ft., one target. *Hit:* 22 (3d6 + 12) slashing damage plus 14 (4d6) fire damage.

Hurl Flame. *Ranged Spell Attack:* +13 to hit, range 120 ft., one target. *Hit:* 35 (10d6) fire damage.

Fire Tornado (recharge 6). The Great Sultan transforms into a roaring, fiery tornado and moves up to his speed in a straight line. Each creature in the path where the Great Sultan moves must make a DC 21 Dexterity saving throw. On a failure, a creature takes 98 (28d6) fire damage and is carried with the Great Sultan to the end of his path. On a success, a creature takes half the damage and isn't carried. When the Great Sultan reaches the end of his path, each creature he carries must make a DC 21 Dexterity saving throw. On a failure, a creature is thrown up to 10 feet away from the Great Sultan and knocked prone. On a success, a creature is deposited in a space within 5 feet of the Great Sultan, but isn't knocked prone. When the Great Sultan reaches the end of his path, he returns back to his true form.

Legendary Actions

The Great Sultan can take 3 legendary actions, choosing from the options below. Only one legendary action can be used at a time and only at the end of another creature's turn. The Great Sultan regains spent legendary actions at the start of its turn.

Cantrip. The Great Sultan casts a cantrip.

Move. The Great Sultan moves up to his speed without provoking opportunity attacks.

Scimitar. The Great Sultan makes one *Brazen Scimitar*[2] attack.

Heat of the Molten Skies (costs 2 actions). The Great Sultan's body temperature rises, sending waves of heat outward. Each creature within 20 feet of the Great Sultan must succeed on a DC 21 Constitution saving throw or be incapacitated by the heat until the end of its next turn.

Cast a Spell (costs 3 actions). The Great Sultan casts a spell from his list of prepared spells, using a spell slot as normal.

Rahib al Tarbish Zafir

Large elemental, lawful evil

Armor Class 21 (natural armor, *bracers of defense*, *ring of protection*)
Hit Points 400 (32d10 + 224)
Speed 40 ft., fly 60 ft.

STR	DEX	CON	INT	WIS	CHA
24 (+7)	14 (+2)	24 (+7)	20 (+5)	16 (+3)	25 (+7)

Saving Throws Int +13, Wis +11, Cha +15
Skills Arcana +13, History +13, Nature +13, Perception +11, Persuasion +15
Damage Resistances bludgeoning, piercing, and slashing from nonmagical attacks
Damage Immunities fire
Senses truesight 120 ft., passive Perception 21
Languages Common, Ignan, telepathy 120 ft.
Challenge 26 (90,000 XP), 27 in lair (105,000 XP)

Dual Concentration. Rahib al Tarbish Zafir may maintain two spells simultaneously, each of which requires concentration.

Elemental Demise. If Rahib al Tarbish Zafir dies, his body disintegrates in a flash of fire and puff of smoke, leaving behind only equipment he was wearing or carrying.

Empowered Spells (5/day). When he rolls for spell damage, Rahib al Tarbish Zafir may reroll up to seven dice.

Fire Affinity. When Rahib al Tarbish Zafir casts a spell that deals fire damage, he may add his Charisma modifier to that damage (included in Hurl Flame below).

Heightened Spells (3/day). When a spell cast by the efreeti forces a target to make a saving throw to resist its effects, the efreeti may cause one target to have disadvantage on its first saving throw made against the spell.

Innate Spellcasting. Rahib al Tarbish Zafir's innate spellcasting ability is Charisma (spell save DC 21, +13 to hit with spell attacks). He can innately cast the following spells, with no need for material components:

At will: *detect magic, dimension door, enlarge/ reduce, invisibility, tongues*

4/day each: *conjure elemental* (greater fire elemental only), *gaseous form, major image, plane shift, wall of fire*

3/day each: *flame strike, greater invisibility*

Munir Seif al Shihab. Rahib al Tarbish Zafir wields an oversized magical *+3 scimitar* named Munir Seif al Shihab. Attacks rolls made with this weapon score a critical hit on a roll of 18, 19, or 20. Only an efreeti may wield Munir Seif al Shihab.

Quickened Spells (4/day). When he casts a spell that has a casting time of 1 action, Rahib al Tarbish Zafir can change the casting time to 1 bonus action for this casting.

Spellcasting. Rahib al Tarbish Zafir is a 20th level spellcaster. His spellcasting ability is Charisma (spell save DC 21, +13 to hit with spell attacks). He has the following spells prepared:

Cantrips (at will): *blade ward, dancing lights, light, mage hand, minor illusion*

1st level (4 slots): *charm person, magic missile, shield*

2nd level (3 slots): *blur, hold person, mirror image*

3rd level (3 slots): *fireball, haste, stinking cloud*

4th level (3 slots): *black tentacles, greater invisibility, wall of fire*

5th level (3 slots): *animate objects, cloudkill, insect plague*

6th level (2 slots): *chain lightning, globe of invulnerability*

7th level (2 slots): *firestorm, spell siphon[4]*

8th level (1 slot): *incendiary cloud*

9th level (1 slot): *time stop, wish*

Tower Defenses. Rahib al Tarbish Zafir uses the magic of the Tower of the Grand Vizier to cast *animate objects, black tentacles, conjure elemental* (greater fire elemental only), or *insect plague*. Instead of their normal range, each of these spells may be centered anywhere within the Tower of the Grand Vizier.

Wish Granting. At his discretion, or if forced, Rahib al Tarbish Zafir may grant the wish of another creature (as the *wish* spell). This is an innate power and does not use any spell slots. Rahib al Tarbish Zafir retains his fundamental nature and would find a way to subvert any wish that went against his agenda. He may only grant three wishes per creature.

ACTIONS

Multiattack. Rahib al Tarbish Zafir makes two Munir Seif al Shihab attacks or uses his Hurl Flame twice.

Munir Seif al Shihab. *Melee Weapon Attack:* +18 to hit, reach 10 ft., one target. *Hit:* 26 (3d10 + 10) slashing damage plus 17 (5d6) fire damage plus 10 (3d6) radiant damage.

Hurl Flame. *Ranged Spell Attack:* +13 to hit, range 120 ft., one target. *Hit:* 35 (8d6 + 7) fire damage.

LEGENDARY ACTIONS

Rahib al Tarbish Zafir can take 3 legendary actions, choosing from the options below. Only one legendary action can be used at a time and only at the end of another creature's turn. Rahib al Tarbish Zafir regains spent legendary actions at the start of his turn.

Dimension Door. Rahib al Tarbish Zafir uses his innate spellcasting ability to cast *dimension door*.

Hurl Flame. Rahib al Tarbish Zafir makes one Hurl Flame attack.

Scimitar. Rahib al Tarbish Zafir makes one Scimitar attack.

Staff of Conjuration. Rahib al Tarbish Zafir uses one of the powers of his *staff of conjuration[2]*.

Summon Efreet (recharge 5–6). Rahib al Tarbish Zafir causes 1d6 efreet, 1d4 efreeti maliks, 1d2 efreeti amirs, or 1 efreeti amir al-umara to appear in an unoccupied space within 100 feet of him. Summoned creatures obey Rahib al Tarbish Zafir's commands and act on their own initiative.

Sinsurab

Large elemental, lawful evil

Armor Class 20 (*+1 brass chain shirt*)
Hit Points 300 (24d10 + 168)
Speed 40 ft., fly 60 ft.

STR	DEX	CON	INT	WIS	CHA
24 (+7)	14 (+2)	24 (+7)	18 (+4)	16 (+3)	18 (+4)

Saving Throws Int +10, Wis +9, Cha +10
Damage Immunities fire
Senses darkvision 120 ft., passive Perception 13
Languages Ignan, telepathy 120 ft.
Challenge 18 (20,000 XP)

Action Surge (recharges after a short or long rest). Sinsurab may make one additional action on his turn on top of his normal action (and possible bonus action).

Duelist. Sinsurab adds +2 to damage rolls while using a single one-handed weapon (included below).

Elemental Demise. If Sinsurab dies, his body disintegrates in a flash of fire and puff of smoke, leaving behind only equipment he was wearing or carrying.

Improved Critical. Sinsurab's weapon attacks score a critical hit on a roll of 19 or 20.

Indomitable (1/day). Sinsurab may reroll an unsuccessful saving throw. He must use the second roll.

Innate Spellcasting. Sinsurab's innate spellcasting ability is Charisma (spell save DC 18, +10 to hit with spell attacks). He can innately cast the following spells, with no need for material components:

At will: *detect magic*
3/day each: *enlarge/reduce*, *tongues*
2/day each: *conjure elemental* (fire elemental only), *gaseous form*, *invisibility*, *major image*, *plane shift*, *wall of fire*
1/day each: *flame strike*, *greater invisibility*

Remarkable Athlete. Sinsurab may add +2 to any Strength, Dexterity, or Constitution check that doesn't already incorporate his proficiency bonus.

Special Equipment. Sinsurab has three *potions of supreme healing*, a *horn of alarm*[2], and a *rod of alertness*.

ACTIONS

Multiattack. Sinsurab makes three Scimitar attacks or uses his Hurl Flame three times.

+2 Scimitar. *Melee Weapon Attack:* +15 to hit, reach 5 ft., one target. *Hit:* 24 (3d8 + 11) slashing damage plus 7 (2d6) fire damage.

Hurl Flame. *Ranged Spell Attack:* +10 to hit, range 120 ft., one target. *Hit:* 21 (6d6) fire damage.

BONUS ACTIONS

Second Wind (recharges after a short or long rest). Sinsurab may regain 1d10 + 25 hit points.

Sulymon

Huge elemental, lawful good
Armor Class 20 (natural armor)
Hit Points 375 (30d12 + 180)
Speed 40 ft., fly 60 ft.

STR	DEX	CON	INT	WIS	CHA
30(+10)	17 (+3)	22 (+6)	24 (+7)	22 (+6)	20 (+5)

Saving Throws Wis +14, Cha +13
Skills Arcana +15, History + 14, Insight +15, Perception +14, Persuasion +13, Religion +23
Damage Immunities acid, fire, poison; bludgeoning, piercing, and slashing from nonmagical attacks
Condition Immunities charmed, exhaustion, frightened, paralyzed, poisoned
Senses darkvision 120 ft., passive Perception 24
Languages Aquan, Auran, Common, Ignan, Terran, telepathy 120 ft.
Challenge 28 (120,000 XP)

Channel Divinity: Turn Undead (3/day). Sulymon uses an action to present his holy symbol and speak a prayer censuring the undead. Each undead that can see or hear him within 30 feet of him must make a Wisdom saving throw. If the creature fails its saving throw, if it is Challenge 2 or less it is destroyed instantly, otherwise it is turned for 1 minute or until it takes any damage.

A turned creature must spend its turns trying to move as far away from Sulymon as it can, and it can't willingly move to a space within 30 feet of him. It also can't take reactions. For its action, it can use only the Dash action or try to escape from an effect that prevents it from moving. If there's nowhere to move, the creature can use the Dodge action.

Divine Intervention (1/day). Sulymon calls upon Anumon for assistance. The DM decides the nature of the assistance provided.

Dual Concentration. Sulymon may maintain two spells simultaneously, each of which requires concentration.

Elemental Demise. If Sulymon dies, his body disintegrates in a puff of blue smoke, leaving behind only equipment he is wearing or carrying.

Expert Transmutation. When he uses a transmutation spell, Sulymon can create or affect twice as much material. For spells that affect a single creature, the duration is doubled instead.

Legendary Resistance (3/day). If Sulymon fails a saving throw, he can choose to succeed instead.

Longevity. Sulymon is immune to magical aging effects.

Magic Resistance. Sulymon has advantage on saving throws against spells and other magical effects.

Spellcasting. Sulymon is a 20th level spellcaster. His spellcasting ability is Wisdom (spell save DC 23, +15 to hit with spell attacks). He has the following spells prepared:

Cantrips (at will): *light*, *mending*, *sacred flame*, *spare the dying*, *thaumaturgy*
1st level (4 slots): *bless*, *cure wounds*, *false life*, *fog cloud*, *healing word*, *sanctuary*
2nd level (3 slots): *alter self*, *enhance ability*, *enlarge/reduce*, *lesser restoration*, *silence*, *spiritual weapon*
3rd level (3 slots): *bestow curse*, *blink*, *dispel magic*, *mass healing word*, *meld into stone*, *spirit guardians*, *water walk*
4th level (3 slots): *banishment*, *death ward*, *freedom of movement*, *polymorph*, *stone shape*
5th level (3 slots): *flame strike*, *greater restoration*, *mass cure wounds*, *passwall*, *raise dead*, *wall of stone*
6th level (2 slots): *blade barrier*, *heal*, *planar ally* (Sulymon knows the name of celestials in the service of Anumon)
7th level (2 slots): *fire storm*, *regenerate*
8th level (1 slots): *earthquake*
9th level (1 slots): *gate* (Sulymon knows the true name of a solar in service of Anumon)

Wish Granting. At his discretion, Sulymon may grant the wish of another creature (as the *wish* spell). This is an innate power and does not use any spell slots. He may only grant three wishes per creature.

ACTIONS

Multiattack. Sulymon makes two Staff of the Prophet attacks.

Staff of the Prophet. *Melee Weapon Attack:* +21 to hit, reach 5 ft., one target. *Hit:* 17 (2d6 + 13) bludgeoning damage plus 17 (5d6) force damage.

Tornado (recharge 6). Sulymon transforms into a roaring tornado and moves up to his speed in a straight line. Each creature in the path where Sulymon moves must make a DC 21 Dexterity saving throw. On a failure, a creature takes 98 (28d6) force damage and is carried with Sulymon to the end of his path. On a success, a creature takes half the damage and isn't carried. When Sulymon reaches the end of his path, each creature he carries must make a DC 21 Dexterity saving throw. On a failure, a creature is thrown up to 10 feet away from Sulymon and knocked prone. On a success, a creature is deposited in a space within 5 feet of Sulymon, but isn't knocked prone. When Sulymon reaches the end of his path, he returns back to his true form.

BONUS ACTIONS

Echoes of Creation. Sulymon makes a verbal attack against a single creature within 50 feet of him using his spell attack modifier. If the attack succeeds, the creature takes 2d8 force damage and must succeed on a DC 23 Strength saving throw or be pushed 5 feet.

LEGENDARY ACTIONS

Sulymon can take 3 legendary actions, choosing from the options below. Only one legendary action can be used at a time and only at the end of another creature's turn. Sulymon regains spent legendary actions at the start of his turn.

Staff of the Prophet. Sulymon makes one Staff of the Prophet attack or invokes one of the abilities of his *staff of the prophet*[2].

Unmaking (2 Actions). Sulymon casts *disintegrate* (as an 8th level slot) with a range of 120 feet and no need for material components. This does not use one of his spell slots.

Echoes of Creation. Sulymon makes an Echoes of Creation attack.

The Wahid

Large elemental, lawful evil
Armor Class 19 (natural armor)
Hit Points 300 (24d10 + 168)
Speed 40 ft., fly 60 ft.

STR	DEX	CON	INT	WIS	CHA
23 (+6)	19 (+4)	24 (+7)	18 (+4)	16 (+3)	17 (+3)

Saving Throws Dex +10, Int +10, Wis +9, Cha +9
Skills Acrobatics +15, Deception +9, Perception +9, Sleight of Hand +15, Stealth +15
Damage Immunities fire
Senses darkvision 120 ft., passive Perception 19
Languages Common, Ignan, Thieves' Cant, telepathy 120 ft.
Challenge 18 (20,000 XP)

Action Surge (recharges after a short or long rest). The Wahid may make one additional action on his turn on top of his normal action (and possible bonus action).

Cunning Action. The Wahid can take a bonus action on each of his turns in combat. This action can be used only to disarm a trap or open a lock, or to take the Dash, Dexterity (Sleight of Hand), Disengage, Hide, or Use an Object action.

Elemental Demise. If the Wahid dies, his body disintegrates in a flash of fire and puff of smoke, leaving behind only equipment he was wearing or carrying.

Evasion. The Wahid can nimbly dodge out of the way of certain area effects. When he is subjected to an effect that allows him to make a Dexterity saving throw to only take half damage, he instead takes no damage if he succeeds on the saving throw, and only half damage if he fails.

Innate Spellcasting. The Wahid's innate spellcasting ability is Charisma (spell save DC 17, +9 to hit with spell attacks). He can innately cast the following spells, with no need for material components:

At will: *detect magic*
3/day each: *enlarge/reduce, tongues*
1/day each: *conjure elemental* (fire elemental only), *gaseous form, invisibility, major image, plane shift, wall of fire*

Maneuvers (5/day). The Wahid may use any one of the following maneuvers, once per turn:

Counterstrike. When a creature misses the Wahid with a melee attack, he may use his reaction to make a melee weapon attack against that creature. If he hits, he rolls 1d8 and adds the result to his damage roll.

Disarming Strike. When the Wahid hits a creature with a weapon attack, he rolls 1d8 and adds the result to his damage roll. The target must succeed on a DC 20 Strength saving throw, or it drops an object of the Wahid's choice that it was holding.

False Strike. The Wahid uses his bonus action to feint at one creature within 5 feet of him. He then has advantage on his next attack roll against that creature. If the attack hits, he rolls 1d8 and adds the result to his damage roll.

Terrorizing Strike. When the Wahid hits a creature with a weapon attack, he rolls 1d8 and adds the result to his damage roll. The target must succeed on a DC 20 Wisdom saving throw or be frightened until the end of the Wahid's next turn.

Tripping Strike. When the Wahid hits a creature with a weapon attack, he rolls 1d8 and adds the result to his damage roll. If the creature is Huge or smaller, it must succeed on a DC 20 Strength saving throw or be knocked prone.

Sneak Attack. Once per turn, the Wahid can deal an extra 4d6 damage to one creature he hits with a Dagger attack if he has advantage on the attack roll. He doesn't need advantage on the attack roll if another enemy of the target is within 5 feet of it and that enemy isn't incapacitated.

Thieves' Tools. The Wahid adds his proficiency bonus to any ability checks he makes to disarm traps or open locks.

Uncanny Dodge. When an attacker the Wahid can see hits him with an attack, he can use his reaction to halve the attack's damage against him.

ACTIONS

Multiattack. The Wahid makes two Scimitar and two Dagger attacks or uses its Hurl Flame three times.

+1 Scimitar. *Melee Weapon Attack*: +13 to hit, reach 5 ft., one target. *Hit*: 16 (2d8 + 7) slashing damage plus 7 (2d6) fire damage.

+2 Dagger. *Melee Weapon Attack*: +14 to hit, reach 5 ft., one target. *Hit*: 13 (2d4 + 8) slashing damage plus 7 (2d6) fire damage.

Hurl Flame. *Ranged Spell Attack*: +9 to hit, range 120 ft., one target. *Hit*: 17 (5d6) fire damage.

BONUS ACTIONS

Amulet of Shapechange (1/day). The Wahid uses his *amulet of shapechange*[2].

Second Wind (recharges after a short or long rest). The Wahid may regain 1d10 + 20 hit points.

Elementals

Acid Elemental

Medium elemental, neutral
Armor Class 13
Hit Points 68 (8d8 + 32)
Speed 20 ft., swim 80 ft.

STR	DEX	CON	INT	WIS	CHA
21 (+5)	16 (+3)	19 (+4)	6 (–2)	11 (+0)	11 (+0)

Skills Stealth +6
Damage Resistances bludgeoning, piercing, and slashing from nonmagical weapons

Damage Immunities acid, poison
Condition Immunities exhaustion, grappled, paralyzed, petrified, poisoned, prone, restrained, unconscious
Senses darkvision 60 ft., passive Perception 10
Languages —
Challenge 5 (1,800 XP)

Acid. A creature that touches the acid elemental or hits it with a melee attack while within 5 feet of it takes 5 (2d4) acid damage. Any nonmagical weapon made of metal or wood that hits the pudding corrodes. After dealing damage, the weapon takes a permanent and cumulative –1 penalty to damage rolls. If its penalty drops to –5, the weapon is destroyed. Nonmagical ammunition made of metal or wood that hits the acid elemental is destroyed after dealing damage. The acid elemental can eat through 2-inch-thick, nonmagical wood or metal in 1 round.

Fumes. Creatures who begin their turn within 5 feet of the acid elemental must succeed on a DC 15 Constitution saving throw or be poisoned until the start of its next turn. On a successful saving throw, the creature is immune to the elemental's fumes for 24 hours.

Vulnerability to Water. For every 5 feet that the elemental moves in water, or for every gallon of water splashed on it, it takes 1 fire damage.

ACTIONS

Slam. *Melee Weapon Attack:* +8 to hit, reach 5 ft., one target. *Hit:* 9 (1d8 + 5) bludgeoning damage plus 14 (4d6) acid damage. In addition, nonmagical armor worn by the target is partly dissolved and takes a permanent and cumulative –1 penalty to the AC it offers. The armor is destroyed if the penalty reduces its AC to 10.

Air Elemental, Elder

Huge elemental, neutral
Armor Class 17
Hit Points 189 (18d12 + 72)
Speed 0 ft., fly 90 ft. (hover)

STR	DEX	CON	INT	WIS	CHA
20 (+5)	24 (+7)	18 (+4)	10 (+0)	14 (+2)	6 (–2)

Damage Resistances bludgeoning, piercing, and slashing from nonmagical attacks
Damage Immunities lightning, poison, thunder
Condition Immunities exhaustion, grappled, paralyzed, petrified, poisoned, prone, restrained, unconscious
Senses darkvision 60 ft., passive Perception 12
Languages Auran
Challenge 13 (10,000 XP)

Air Form. The elemental can enter a hostile creature's space and stop there. It can move through a space as narrow as 1 inch wide without squeezing.

Air Mastery. Creatures of size Large or smaller have disadvantage on attacks made against the elemental while flying.

ACTIONS

Multiattack. The elemental makes two Slam attacks.

Slam. *Melee Weapon Attack:* +12 to hit, reach 10 ft., one target. *Hit:* 23 (3d10 + 7) bludgeoning damage. If the target is a creature, it must succeed on a DC 17 Strength saving throw or be knocked prone.

Whirlwind (recharge 4–6): Each creature in the elemental's space must make a DC 17 Strength saving throw. On a failure, a target takes 27 (4d10 + 5) bludgeoning damage and is flung up to 40 feet away from the elemental in a random direction and knocked prone. If a thrown target strikes an object, such as a wall or floor, the target takes 3 (1d6) bludgeoning damage for every 10 feet it was thrown. If the target is thrown at another creature, that creature must succeed on a DC 17 Dexterity saving throw or take the same damage (1d6 per 10 feet target was thrown) and be knocked prone.

If the saving throw is successful, the target takes half the bludgeoning damage and isn't flung away or knocked prone.

Air Elemental, Greater

Huge elemental, neutral
Armor Class 16
Hit Points 142 (15d12 + 45)
Speed 0 ft., fly 90 ft. (hover)

STR	DEX	CON	INT	WIS	CHA
18 (+4)	22 (+6)	16 (+3)	8 (–1)	12 (+1)	6 (–2)

Damage Resistances lightning, thunder; bludgeoning, piercing, and slashing from nonmagical attacks
Damage Immunities poison
Condition Immunities exhaustion, grappled, paralyzed, petrified, poisoned, prone, restrained, unconscious
Senses darkvision 60 ft., passive Perception 11
Languages Auran
Challenge 9 (5,000 XP)

Air Form. The elemental can enter a hostile creature's space and stop there. It can move through a space as narrow as 1 inch wide without squeezing.

Air Mastery. Creatures of size Large or smaller have disadvantage on attacks made against the elemental while flying.

ACTIONS

Multiattack. The elemental makes two Slam attacks.

Slam. *Melee Weapon Attack:* +9 to hit, reach 10 ft., one target. *Hit:* 19 (3d8 + 6) bludgeoning damage. If the target is a creature, it must succeed on a DC 15 Strength saving throw or be knocked prone.

Whirlwind (recharge 4–6): Each creature in the elemental's space must make a DC 15 Strength saving throw. On a failure, the creature takes 21 (4d8 + 3) bludgeoning damage and is flung up to 30 feet away from the elemental in a random direction and knocked prone. If a thrown target strikes an object, such as a wall or floor, the target takes 3 (1d6) bludgeoning damage for every 10 feet it was thrown. If the target is thrown at another creature, that creature must succeed on a DC 15 Dexterity saving throw or take the same damage (1d6 per 10 feet target was thrown) and be knocked prone.

If the saving throw is successful, the target takes half the bludgeoning damage and isn't flung away or knocked prone.

Earth Elemental, Elder

Huge elemental, neutral
Armor Class 19 (natural armor)
Hit Points 207 (18d12 + 90)
Speed 30 ft., burrow 30 ft.

STR	DEX	CON	INT	WIS	CHA
24 (+7)	8 (–1)	21 (+5)	8 (–1)	14 (+2)	5 (–3)

Damage Vulnerabilities thunder
Damage Resistances bludgeoning, piercing, and slashing

from nonmagical attacks
Damage Immunities poison
Condition Immunities exhaustion, paralyzed, petrified,
poisoned, unconscious
Senses darkvision 60 ft., tremorsense 60 ft., passive
Perception 12
Languages Terran
Challenge 13 (10,000 XP)

Earth Glide. The elemental can burrow through nonmagical,
unworked earth and stone. While doing so, the elemental
doesn't disturb the material it moves through.
Siege Monster. The elemental deals double damage to
objects and structures.

ACTIONS

Multiattack. The elemental makes two Slam attacks.
Slam. *Melee Weapon Attack:* +12 to hit, reach 10 ft., one
target. *Hit:* 23 (3d10 + 7) bludgeoning damage. If the
target is a creature, it must succeed on a DC 17 Strength
saving throw or be knocked prone.
Earth Tremor (recharge 4–6). The elemental causes intense
tremors to rip through the ground within 60 feet of itself.
Any creature on the ground in this area must succeed
on a DC 17 Dexterity saving throw or take 10 (1d6 + 7)
bludgeoning damage and be knocked prone.

Earth Elemental, Greater

Huge elemental, neutral
Armor Class 18 (natural armor)
Hit Points 172 (15d12 + 75)
Speed 30 ft., burrow 30 ft.

STR	DEX	CON	INT	WIS	CHA
22 (+6)	8 (−1)	20 (+5)	6 (−2)	12 (+1)	5 (−3)

Damage Vulnerabilities thunder
Damage Resistances bludgeoning, piercing, and slashing
from nonmagical attacks
Damage Immunities poison
Condition Immunities exhaustion, paralyzed, petrified,
poisoned, unconscious
Senses darkvision 60 ft., tremorsense 60 ft., passive
Perception 11
Languages Terran
Challenge 9 (5,000 XP)

Earth Glide. The elemental can burrow through nonmagical,
unworked earth and stone. While doing so, the elemental
doesn't disturb the material it moves through.
Siege Monster. The elemental deals double damage to
objects and structures.

ACTIONS

Multiattack. The elemental makes two Slam attacks.
Slam. *Melee Weapon Attack:* +10 to hit, reach 10 ft., one
target. *Hit:* 19 (3d8 + 6) bludgeoning damage. If the target
is a creature, it must succeed on a DC 15 Strength saving
throw or be knocked prone.
Earth Tremor (recharge 5–6). The elemental causes intense
tremors to rip through the ground within 60 feet of itself.
Any creature on the ground in this area must succeed
on a DC 15 Dexterity saving throw or take 9 (1d6 + 6)
bludgeoning damage and be knocked prone.

Elemental Air Dragon

Huge elemental, neutral evil
Armor Class 15
Hit Points 312 (25d12 + 150)
Speed 40 ft., fly 80 ft.

STR	DEX	CON	INT	WIS	CHA
27 (+7)	20 (+5)	23 (+6)	16 (+3)	15 (+2)	19 (+4)

Saving Throws Dex +11, Con +12, Wis +8, Cha +10
Skills Arcana +9, Nature +9, Perception +14, Stealth +11
Damage Resistances lightning, thunder; bludgeoning,
piercing, and slashing from nonmagical weapons
Damage Immunities poison
Condition Immunities exhaustion, grappled, paralyzed,
petrified, poisoned, prone, restrained, unconscious
Senses blindsight 60 ft., darkvision 120 ft., passive Perception 24
Languages Auran, Common
Challenge 17 (18,000 XP)

Innate Spellcasting. The elemental dragon's innate
spellcasting is Charisma (spell save DC 18). It can cast the
following spell requiring no material components.
At will: *gust of wind*
3/day each: *call lightning, wind wall*
1/day each: *control weather, plane shift*
Legendary Resistance (3/day). If the dragon fails a saving
throw, it can choose to succeed instead.

ACTIONS

Multiattack. The dragon can make one Bite attack and two
Claw attacks.
Bite. *Melee Weapon Attack:* +13 to hit, reach 10 ft., one
target. *Hit:* 18 (2d10 + 7) piercing damage plus 10 (3d6)
fire damage.
Claw. *Melee Weapon Attack:* +13 to hit, reach 5 ft., one
target. *Hit:* 14 (2d6 + 7) slashing damage.
Tail. *Melee Weapon Attack:* +13 to hit, reach 15 ft., one
target. *Hit:* 16 (2d8 + 7) bludgeoning damage.
Scalding Breath (recharge 5–6). The dragon releases a
60-foot cone of superheated air that wraps around
corners. Creatures within the area must make a DC 21
Constitution saving throw, taking 63 (18d6) fire damage
on a failed saving throw, or half as much damage on a
successful one.
Whirlwind (recharge 5–6). The dragon creates a cyclone
in a 30-foot radius centered on itself. Creatures, other
than the dragon, within the area can only move half
their normal movement, nonmagical ranged attacks
automatically fail, and all nonmagical unprotected flames
are automatically extinguished. Large or smaller creatures
within the area must also succeed on a DC 21 Strength
saving throw. On a failed saving throw, the creature takes
20 (3d8 + 7) bludgeoning damage and is knocked prone
and pushed 30 in a random direction. On a successful
saving throw, the creature takes half damage and is not
affected further.

LEGENDARY ACTIONS

The dragon can take 3 legendary actions, choosing from
the options below. Only one legendary action option
can be used at a time and only at the end of another
creature's turn. The dragon regains spent legendary
actions at the start of its turn.
Detect. The dragon makes a Wisdom (Perception) check.
Tail Attack. The dragon makes a tail attack.

Wing Attack (costs 2 actions). The dragon beats its wings. Each creature within 15 feet of the dragon must succeed on a DC 21 Dexterity saving throw or take 14 (2d6 + 7) bludgeoning damage and be knocked prone. The dragon can then fly up to half its flying speed.

Elemental Fire Dragon

Huge elemental, neutral evil
Armor Class 15
Hit Points 445 (33d12 + 231)
Speed 40 ft., fly 80 ft.

STR	DEX	CON	INT	WIS	CHA
27 (+8)	20 (+5)	25 (+7)	16 (+3)	13 (+1)	21 (+5)

Saving Throws Dex +7, Con +14, Wis +8, Cha +12
Skills Arcana +10, Nature +10, Perception +15, Stealth +7
Damage Vulnerabilities cold
Damage Resistances bludgeoning, piercing, and slashing from nonmagical weapons
Damage Immunities fire, poison
Condition Immunities exhaustion, grappled, paralyzed, petrified, poisoned, prone, restrained, unconscious
Senses blindsight 60 ft., darkvision 120 ft., passive Perception 25
Languages Common, Ignan
Challenge 21 (33,000 XP)

Fiery Aura. At the start of each of the dragon's turns, each creature within 15 feet of it takes 14 (4d6) fire damage, and flammable objects in the aura that aren't being worn or carried ignite. A creature that touches the dragon or hits it with a melee attack while within 5 feet of it takes 14 (4d6) fire damage.
Illumination. The dragon sheds bright light in a 30-foot radius and dim light in an additional 30 feet.
Innate Spellcasting. The dragon's innate spellcasting ability is Charisma (spell save DC 20). It can cast the following spells, requiring no material components:
At will: *fireball, heat metal*
3/day: *fire storm*
1/day each: *incendiary cloud, plane shift*
Legendary Resistance (3/day). If the dragon fails a saving throw, it can choose to succeed instead.
Water Susceptibility. For every 5 feet that the dragon moves in water, or for every gallon of water splashed on it, it takes 1 cold damage.

ACTIONS

Multiattack. The dragon can make three attacks: one with its bite and two with its claws.
Bite. Melee Weapon Attack: +15 to hit, reach 10 ft., one target. *Hit:* 19 (2d10 + 8) piercing damage plus 14 (4d6) fire damage.
Claw. Melee Weapon Attack: +15 to hit, reach 5 ft., one target. *Hit:* 15 (2d6 + 8) slashing damage.
Tail. Melee Weapon Attack: +15 to hit, reach 15 ft., one target. *Hit:* 17 (2d8 + 8) bludgeoning damage.
Elemental Fire Breath (recharge 5–6). The dragon breathes a 60-foot cone of elemental fire. Creatures in the area must make a DC 22 Dexterity saving throw, taking 77 (22d6) fire damage on a failed saving throw, or half as much damage on a successful one.

LEGENDARY ACTIONS

The dragon can take 3 legendary actions, choosing from the options below. Only one legendary action option can be used at a time and only at the end of another creature's turn. The dragon regains spent legendary actions at the start of its turn.
Detect. The dragon makes a Wisdom (Perception) check.
Tail Attack. The dragon makes a tail attack.
Wing Attack (costs 2 actions). The dragon beats its wings. Each creature within 15 feet of the dragon must succeed on a DC 23 Dexterity saving throw or take 15 (2d6 + 8) bludgeoning damage and be knocked prone. The dragon can then fly up to half its flying speed.
Rain of Fire (costs 3 actions). The elemental fire dragon beats its wings, casting fire out in a 100-foot sphere around itself. All creatures within the area must make a DC 22 Dexterity saving throw, taking 14 (4d6) fire damage on a failed saving throw, or half as much damage on a successful one. Objects not held or worn are set alight and continue burning until extinguished.

Fire Elemental, Elder

Huge elemental, neutral
Armor Class 15
Hit Points 207 (18d12 + 90)
Speed 50 ft.

STR	DEX	CON	INT	WIS	CHA
14 (+2)	21 (+5)	20 (+5)	10 (+0)	14 (+2)	7 (−2)

Damage Resistances bludgeoning, piercing, and slashing from nonmagical attacks
Damage Immunities fire, poison
Condition Immunities exhaustion, grappled, paralyzed, petrified, poisoned, prone, restrained, unconscious
Senses darkvision 60 ft., passive Perception 12
Languages Ignan
Challenge 13 (10,000 XP)

Fire Form. The elemental can move through a space as narrow as 1 inch wide without squeezing. A creature that touches the elemental or hits it with a melee attack while within 5 feet of it takes 5 (1d10) fire damage. In addition, the elemental can enter a hostile creature's space and stop there. The first time it enters a creature's space on a turn, that creature takes 5 (1d10) fire damage and ignites. A burning creature takes 5 (1d10) fire damage at the start of each of its turns. A creature can use an action to douse the fire, ending the effect.
Illumination. The elemental sheds bright light in a 40-foot radius and dim light for an additional 40 feet.
Water Susceptibility. For every 5 feet the elemental moves in water, or for every gallon of water splashed on it, it takes 1 cold damage.

ACTIONS

Multiattack. The elemental makes two Touch attacks.
Touch. Melee Weapon Attack: +10 to hit, reach 10 ft., one target. *Hit:* 19 (4d6 + 5) fire damage. If the target is a creature or flammable object, it ignites. A burning creature takes 5 (1d10) fire damage at the start of each of its turns. A creature can use an action to douse the fire, ending the effect.
Firestorm (recharge 4–6): The elemental emits a fan of flame all around it. Any target within 15 feet must make a DC 17 Dexterity saving throw. On a failure, a target takes 11 (2d10) fire damage and ignites. If the saving throw is successful, the target takes half the fire damage and is still ignited (as above). A burning creature takes 5 (1d10) fire damage at the start of each of its turns. A creature can use an action to douse the fire, ending the effect.

Fire Elemental, Greater

Huge elemental, neutral
Armor Class 14
Hit Points 157 (15d12 + 60)
Speed 50 ft.

STR	DEX	CON	INT	WIS	CHA
12 (+1)	19 (+4)	18 (+4)	8 (–1)	12(+1)	7 (–2)

Damage Resistances bludgeoning, piercing, and slashing from nonmagical attacks
Damage Immunities fire, poison
Condition Immunities exhaustion, grappled, paralyzed, petrified, poisoned, prone, restrained, unconscious
Senses darkvision 60 ft., passive Perception 11
Languages Ignan
Challenge 9 (5,000 XP)

Fire Form. The elemental can move through a space as narrow as 1 inch wide without squeezing. A creature that touches the elemental or hits it with a melee attack while within 5 feet of it takes 5 (1d10) fire damage. In addition, the elemental can enter a hostile creature's space and stop there. The first time it enters a creature's space on a turn, that creature takes 5 (1d10) fire damage and ignites. A burning creature takes 5 (1d10) fire damage at the start of each of its turns. A creature can use an action to douse the fire, ending the effect.
Illumination. The elemental sheds bright light in a 40-foot radius and dim light in an additional 40 feet.
Water Susceptibility. For every 5 feet the elemental moves in water, or for every gallon of water splashed on it, it takes 1 cold damage.

Actions

Multiattack. The elemental makes two Slam attacks.
Touch. *Melee Weapon Attack:* +8 to hit, reach 10 ft., one target. *Hit:* 14 (3d6 + 4) fire damage. If the target is a creature or flammable object, it ignites. A burning creature takes 5 (1d10) fire damage at the start of each of its turns. A creature can use an action to douse the fire, ending the effect.
Firestorm (recharge 4–6): The elemental emits a fan of flame all around it. Any target within 15 feet must make a DC 15 Dexterity saving throw. On a failure, a target takes 11 (2d10) fire damage and ignites. A burning creature takes 5 (1d10) fire damage at the start of each of its turns. A creature can use an action to douse the fire, ending the effect.

Ice Elemental

Large elemental, neutral
Armor Class 16 (natural armor)
Hit Points 114 (12d10 + 48)
Speed 30 ft., burrow 30 ft.

STR	DEX	CON	INT	WIS	CHA
18 (+4)	15 (+2)	18 (+4)	6 (–2)	10 (+0)	7 (–2)

Damage Vulnerabilities fire, thunder
Damage Resistances acid, bludgeoning; piercing, and slashing from nonmagical attacks
Damage Immunities cold, poison
Condition Immunities exhaustion, paralyzed, petrified, poisoned, unconscious
Senses darkvision 60 ft., passive Perception 10
Languages Aquan, Auran
Challenge 5 (1,800 XP)

Ice Form. A creature that touches the elemental or hits it with a melee attack while within 5 feet of it takes 5 (1d10) cold damage and has disadvantage on Dexterity checks and saving throws until the end of its next turn.
Ice Glide. The elemental can burrow through nonmagical ice. While doing so, the elemental doesn't disturb the material it is moving through.
Slippery. Creatures attempting to grapple the elemental have disadvantage on their checks to grapple.
Thaw. If the elemental takes fire damage, it becomes partially thawed until the end of its next turn; while partially thawed, its speed is reduced by 20 feet.

Actions

Multiattack. The elemental makes two Slam attacks or two Ice Shards attacks.
Slam. *Melee Weapon Attack:* +7 to hit, reach 10 ft., one target. *Hit:* 13 (2d8 + 4) bludgeoning damage. If the target is a creature, it has disadvantage on Dexterity checks and saving throws until the end of its next turn.
Ice Shards. *Ranged Weapon Attack:* +7 to hit, range 60 ft., one target. *Hit:* 11 (2d6 + 4) piercing damage.

Lightning Elemental

Medium elemental, neutral
Armor Class 15
Hit Points 67 (9d8 + 27)
Speed 0 ft., fly 50 ft.

STR	DEX	CON	INT	WIS	CHA
14 (+2)	20 (+5)	16 (+3)	4 (–3)	11 (+0)	11 (+0)

Damage Resistances acid, fire; bludgeoning, piercing, and slashing damage from nonmagical weapons
Damage Immunities lightning, poison
Condition Immunities exhaustion, grappled, paralyzed, petrified, poisoned, prone, restrained, unconscious
Senses darkvision 60 ft., passive Perception 10
Languages Auran
Challenge 6 (2,300 XP)

Lightning. A creature that touches the lightning elemental or hits it with a melee attack while within 5 feet of it takes 7 (2d6) lightning damage.
Water Susceptibility. For every 5 feet that the lightning elemental moves in water, or for every gallon of water splashed on it, it takes 1 cold damage.

Actions

Multiattack. The lightning elemental makes two slam attacks.
Slam. *Melee Weapon Attack:* +8 to hit, reach 5 ft., one target. *Hit:* 14 (2d8 + 5) lightning damage.
Lightning Bolt. *Ranged Spell Attack:* +8 to hit, range 20/60 ft., one target. *Hit:* 36 (7d8 + 5) lightning damage.
Globe Lightning (1/short or long rest). The lightning elemental discharges 3 globes of electricity that hover in its space for 1 minute. Whenever a creature enters or starts its turn within 5 feet of the elemental, one of the globes discharges. The target must make a DC 15 Dexterity saving throw, taking 9 (1d8 + 5) lightning damage on a failed saving throw, or half as much damage on a successful one. As each globe discharges, it disappears.

Obsidian Elemental, Greater

Huge elemental, neutral
Armor Class 18 (natural armor)
Hit Points 175 (14d12 + 84)
Speed 20 ft.

STR	DEX	CON	INT	WIS	CHA
20 (+5)	8 (−1)	22 (+6)	4 (−3)	11 (+0)	11 (+0)

Damage Resistances cold, fire; bludgeoning, piercing, and slashing damage from nonmagical attacks
Damage Immunities poison
Condition Immunities exhaustion, paralyzed, petrified, poisoned, unconscious
Senses darkvision 60 ft., passive Perception 10
Languages Terran
Challenge 14 (11,500 XP)

Brute. A melee weapon attack deals one extra die of its damage when the obsidian elemental hits with it (included in the attack).
Death Throes. When the obsidian elemental dies, it explodes, and each creature within 30 feet of it must make a DC 19 Dexterity saving throw, taking 42 (12d6) slashing damage and 42 (12d6) fire damage on a failed saving throw, or half as much damage on a successful one.
Molten Glass. A creature that hits the obsidian elemental with a melee attack while within 5 feet of it takes 7 (2d6) fire damage.

Actions

Multiattack. The obsidian elemental makes two claw attacks.
Claw. *Melee Weapon Attack:* +10 to hit, reach 5 ft., one target. *Hit:* 23 (4d8 + 5) slashing damage plus 13 (3d8) fire damage.

Smoke Elemental

Large elemental, neutral
Armor Class 15
Hit Points 90 (12d10 + 24)
Speed 0 ft., fly 60 ft. (hover)

STR	DEX	CON	INT	WIS	CHA
14 (+2)	20 (+5)	15 (+2)	6 (−2)	10 (+0)	6 (−2)

Skills Stealth +8
Damage Resistances thunder; bludgeoning, piercing, and slashing from nonmagical attacks
Damage Immunities fire, poison
Condition Immunities exhaustion, grappled, paralyzed, petrified, poisoned, prone, restrained, unconscious
Senses darkvision 60 ft., passive Perception 10
Languages Auran, Ignan
Challenge 5 (1,800 XP)

Smoke Form. The elemental can enter a hostile creature's space and stop there. It can move through a space as narrow as 1 inch wide without squeezing. A creature that touches the elemental or hits it with a melee attack while within 5 feet of it must succeed on a DC 15 Constitution saving throw or be blinded until the end of its next turn. If a creature starts its turn in the elemental's space or enters it on its turn, that creature must succeed on a DC 15 Constitution saving throw or be blinded until the end of its next turn.

Actions

Multiattack. The elemental makes two Slam attacks.
Slam. *Melee Weapon Attack:* +8 to hit, reach 10 ft., one target. *Hit:* 14 (2d8 + 5) bludgeoning damage. If the target is a creature, it must succeed on a DC 15 Constitution saving throw or be blinded until the end of its next turn.
Stoke. Each creature in the elemental's space must succeed on a DC 15 Constitution saving throw or be incapacitated until it is no longer in the elemental's space.

Water Elemental, Elder

Huge elemental, neutral
Armor Class 16
Hit Points 225 (18d12 + 108)
Speed 30 ft., swim 90 ft.

STR	DEX	CON	INT	WIS	CHA
22 (+6)	16 (+3)	22 (+6)	9 (−1)	14 (+2)	8 (−1)

Damage Resistances bludgeoning, piercing, and slashing from nonmagical attacks
Damage Immunities acid, poison
Condition Immunities exhaustion, grappled, paralyzed, petrified, poisoned, prone, restrained, unconscious
Senses darkvision 60 ft., passive Perception 12
Languages Aquan
Challenge 13 (10,000 XP)

Water Form. The elemental can enter a hostile creature's space and stop there. It can move through a space as narrow as 1 inch wide without squeezing.
Freeze. If the elemental takes cold damage, it becomes partially frozen until the end of its next turn; while partially frozen, its speed is reduced by 20 feet.

Actions

Multiattack. The elemental makes two Slam attacks.
Slam. *Melee Weapon Attack:* +11 to hit, reach 10 ft., one target. *Hit:* 22 (3d10 + 6) bludgeoning damage. If the target is a creature, it must succeed on a DC 17 Strength saving throw or be knocked prone.
Whelm (recharge 4–6). Each creature in the elemental's space must make a DC 17 Strength saving throw. On a failure, a target takes 22 (3d10 + 6) bludgeoning damage. If it is Huge or smaller, it is also grappled (escape DC 16). Until this grapple ends, the target is restrained and unable to breathe unless it can breathe water. If the saving throw is successful, the target is pushed out of the elemental's space.
The elemental can grapple one Huge, up to two Large, or up to four Medium or smaller creatures at one time. At the start of each of the elemental's turns, each creature grappled by it takes 22 (3d10 +6) bludgeoning damage. A creature within 5 feet of the elemental can pull a creature or object out of it by taking an action to make a DC 16 Strength check and succeeding.

Elementals — Individuals

Nar al Nar, Fire Elemental Prince

Huge elemental, neutral
Armor Class 17
Hit Points 351 (26d12 + 182)
Speed 50 ft.

STR	DEX	CON	INT	WIS	CHA
19 (+4)	23 (+6)	25 (+7)	13 (+1)	14 (+2)	10 (+0)

Damage Resistances bludgeoning, piercing, and slashing from nonmagical attacks
Damage Immunities fire, poison
Condition Immunities exhaustion, grappled, paralyzed, petrified, poisoned, prone, restrained, unconscious
Senses darkvision 60 ft., passive Perception 12
Languages Aquan, Common, Ignan
Challenge 17 (18,000 XP)

Fire Form. Nar al Nar can move through a space as narrow as 1 inch wide without squeezing. A creature that touches Nar al Nar or hits him with a melee attack while within 5 feet of him takes 11 (2d10) fire damage. In addition, Nar al Nar can enter a hostile creature's space and stop there. The first time he enters a creature's space on a turn, that creature takes 11 (2d10) fire damage and ignites. A burning creature takes 11 (2d10) fire damage at the start of each of its turns. A creature can use an action to douse the fire, ending the effect.
Illumination. Nar al Nar sheds bright light in a 50-foot radius and dim light in an additional 50 feet.
Magic Resistance. Nar al Nar has advantage on saving throws versus spells and other magical effects.
Magic Weapons. Nar al Nar's attacks are magical.
Water Susceptibility. For every 5 feet Nar al Nar moves in water, or for every gallon of water splashed on him, he takes 1 cold damage.

ACTIONS

Multiattack. Nar al Nar makes two Touch attacks.
Touch. *Melee Weapon Attack:* +12 to hit, reach 10 ft., one target. *Hit:* 24 (4d8 + 6) fire damage. If the target is a creature or flammable object, it ignites. A burning creature takes 11 (2d10) fire damage at the start of each of its turns. A creature can use an action to douse the fire, ending the effect.
Firestorm (recharge 5–6): Nar al Nar emits a fan of flame all around him. Any target within 20 feet must make a DC 18 Dexterity saving throw. On a failure, a target takes 16 (3d10) fire damage and ignites. A burning creature takes 11 (2d10) fire damage at the start of each of its turns. A creature can use an action to douse the fire, ending the effect.
Summon Fire Elementals (2/day). Nar al Nar may summon 1d4 Large fire elementals. They appear in unoccupied spaces of Nar al Nar's choice within 100 feet of Nar al Nar, act on their own initiative, and obey Nar al Nar unquestioningly.

Sparque, the Qalb al Nar

Small elemental, neutral
Armor Class 13
Hit Points 33 (6d6 + 12)
Speed 30 ft.

STR	DEX	CON	INT	WIS	CHA
10 (+0)	17 (+3)	15 (+2)	10 (+0)	10 (+0)	9 (−1)

Damage Resistances bludgeoning, piercing, and slashing from nonmagical attacks
Damage Immunities fire, poison
Condition Immunities exhaustion, grappled, paralyzed, petrified, poisoned, prone, restrained, unconscious
Senses darkvision 60 ft., passive Perception 12
Languages Common, Ignan
Challenge 2 (450 XP)

Fire Form. Sparque can move through a space as narrow as 1 inch wide without squeezing. A creature that touches Sparque or hits him with a melee attack while within 5 feet of him takes 5 (1d10) fire damage. In addition, Sparque can enter a hostile creature's space and stop there. The first time he enters a creature's space on a turn, that creature takes 5 (1d10) fire damage and ignites. A burning creature takes 5 (1d10) fire damage at the start of each of its turns. A creature can use an action to douse the fire, ending the effect.
Growth Potential. Sparque grows in size and power as his companions do. For each increase in average party level, Sparque gains one hit die. When he reaches 9 hit dice, he becomes Medium size. At 12 hit dice, he becomes Large. At 15 hit dice, he becomes Huge. (See below for statistics.)
Illumination. Sparque sheds bright light in a 30-foot radius and dim light in an additional 30 feet.
Soul Phylactery. Sparque's soul is trapped in the Ring of Qalb. Each time he is killed, he comes back to life one day later with one fewer hit dice. If his new form has 14 hit dice, he has shrunk to Large size. If his new form has 11 hit dice, he has shrunk to Medium size. If his new form has 8 hit dice, he has shrunk to Small size. If he is killed when he has 1 hit die, he is irrevocably destroyed.
Water Susceptibility. For every 5 feet Sparque moves in water, or for every gallon of water splashed on him, it takes 1 cold damage.

ACTIONS

Multiattack. Sparque makes two Touch attacks.
Touch. *Melee Weapon Attack:* +5 to hit, reach 5 ft., one target. *Hit:* 6 (1d6 + 3) fire damage. If the target is a creature or flammable object, it ignites. A burning creature takes 5 (1d10) fire damage at the start of each of its turns. A creature can use an action to douse the fire, ending the effect.

Sparque, the Qalb al Nar, Huge

Huge elemental, neutral
As a Greater Fire Elemental with Growth Potential and Soul Phylactery that speaks Common

Sparque, the Qalb al Nar, Large

Large elemental, neutral
As a Fire Elemental with Growth Potential and Soul Phylactery that speaks Common

Sparque, the Qalb al Nar, Medium

Medium elemental, neutral
Armor Class 13
Hit Points 67 (9d8 + 27)
Speed 40 ft.

STR	DEX	CON	INT	WIS	CHA
10 (+0)	17 (+3)	16 (+3)	11 (+0)	10 (+0)	9 (−1)

Damage Resistances bludgeoning, piercing, and slashing from nonmagical attacks
Damage Immunities fire, poison
Condition Immunities exhaustion, grappled, paralyzed, petrified, poisoned, prone, restrained, unconscious
Senses darkvision 60 ft., passive Perception 12
Languages Common, Ignan
Challenge 3 (700 XP)

Fire Form. Sparque can move through a space as narrow as 1 inch wide without squeezing. A creature that touches Sparque or hits him with a melee attack while within 5 feet of him takes 5 (1d10) fire damage. In addition, Sparque can enter a hostile creature's space and stop there. The first time he enters a creature's space on a turn, that creature takes 5 (1d10) fire damage and ignites. A burning creature takes 5 (1d10) fire damage at the start of each of its turns. A creature can use an action to douse the fire, ending the effect.

Growth Potential. Sparque grows in size and power as his companions do. For each level the majority of his companions gain, Sparque gains one hit die. When he reaches 9 hit dice, he becomes Medium size. At 12 hit dice, he becomes Large. At 15 hit dice, he becomes Huge. (See below for statistics.)

Illumination. Sparque sheds bright light in a 30-foot radius and dim light in an additional 30 feet.

Soul Phylactery. Sparque's soul is trapped in the Ring of Qalb. Each time he is killed, he comes back to life one day later with one fewer hit dice. If his new form has 12 hit dice, he has shrunk to Large size. If his new form has 9 hit dice, he has shrunk to Medium size. If his new form has 6 hit dice, he has shrunk to Small size. If he is killed when he has 1 hit die, he is irrevocably destroyed.

Water Susceptibility. For every 5 feet Sparque moves in water, or for every gallon of water splashed on him, it takes 1 cold damage.

Actions

Multiattack. Sparque makes two Touch attacks.
Touch. *Melee Weapon Attack:* +5 to hit, reach 5 ft., one target. *Hit:* 8 (1d10 + 3) fire damage. If the target is a creature or flammable object, it ignites. A burning creature takes 5 (1d10) fire damage at the start of each of its turns. A creature can use an action to douse the fire, ending the effect.

Faa'Thasht the Circus Master

Medium humanoid (n'gathau), chaotic evil
Armor Class 23 (*bracers of superior defense*[2])
Hit Points 362 (25d8 + 250)
Speed 40 ft.

STR	DEX	CON	INT	WIS	CHA
33 (+11)	24 (+7)	31 (+10)	26 (+8)	23 (+6)	25 (+7)

Saving Throws Dex +15, Con +18, Int +16, Wis +14
Skills Acrobatics +15, Arcana +16, Intimidation +15, Investigation +16, Perception +14, Persuasion +15, Stealth +15, Survival +14
Damage Resistances cold, fire; bludgeoning, piercing, and slashing from nonmagical attacks
Damage Immunities acid, poison
Condition Immunities poisoned
Senses darkvision 60 ft., passive Perception 24
Languages Common, N'gathian
Challenge 25 (75,000 XP)

Legendary Resistance (3/day). If Faa'Thasht fails a saving throw, it can choose to succeed instead.

Cruelty's Bliss. If Faa'Thasht scores a critical hit, it rolls damage dice three times, instead of twice.

Spellcasting. Faa'Thasht is a 20th-level spellcaster. Its spellcasting ability is Intelligence (spell save DC 22, +14 to hit with spell attacks). It has the following wizard spells prepared:

Cantrips (at will): *fire bolt, mage hand, minor illusion, prestidigitation, ray of frost*
1st level (4 slots): *charm person, detect magic, hideous laughter, magic missile*
2nd level (3 slots): *detect thoughts, invisibility, mirror image, suggestion*
3rd level (3 slots): *blink, dispel magic, lightning bolt, slow*
4th level (3 slots): *banishment, dimension door, phantasmal killer*
5th level (3 slots): *dominate person, scrying, wall of force*
6th level (2 slots): *disintegrate, globe of invulnerability, true seeing*
7th level (2 slots): *delayed blast fireball, reverse gravity, teleport*
8th level (1 slot): *maze, mind blank*
9th level (1 slot): *astral projection, shapechange*

Actions

Multiattack. Faa'Thasht makes two Greatsword attacks or two Harmonious Lash attacks.

+2 Corrosive Greatsword. *Melee Weapon Attack:* +21 to hit, reach 5 ft., one target. *Hit:* 20 (2d6 + 13) slashing damage plus 21 (6d6) acid damage.

Harmonious Lash. *Melee Weapon Attack:* +25 to hit, reach 10 ft., one target. *Hit:* 19 (1d4 + 17) slashing damage, and the target must succeed on a DC 18 Constitution saving throw or take 55 (10d10) poison damage. One minute later, a new save must be made (same DC) to avoid another 55 (10d10) poison damage. Damage from the lash does not heal normally. Wounds can be healed magically but only by a *wish* or a *heal* spell. No other form of magical healing (*cure* spells, *potions*, and so on) works. A creature hit by the whip must succeed on a DC 16 Dexterity saving throw or be grappled by it. The creature must use an action and succeed on a DC 18 Strength (Athletics) or Dexterity (Acrobatics) check to escape.

Delicious Agony. *Melee Weapon Attack:* +19 to hit, reach 5 ft., one target. *Hit:* The target is grappled (escape DC 21), and Faa'Thasht claws away a portion of the target's flesh and devours it, dealing 15 (1d8 + 11) points of slashing damage plus 21 (6d6) necrotic damage. The target's hit point maximum is reduced by an amount equal to the necrotic damage taken, and Faa'Thasht regains hit points equal to that amount. The reduction lasts until the target finishes a long rest. The target dies if this effect reduces its hit point maximum to 0.

Wave of Pain. Faa'Thasht magically emits a blast of agonizing pain in a 40-foot cone. Each creature in that area must succeed on a DC 21 Constitution saving throw or be stunned for 1 minute. A creature can repeat the saving throw at the end of each of its turns, ending the effect on itself on a success.

Horrifying Appearance. Each creature of Faa'Thasht 's choice that is within 60 feet of it and aware of it must succeed on a DC 21 Wisdom saving throw or become frightened for 1 minute. A creature can repeat the saving throw at the end of each of its turns, ending the effect on itself on a success. If a creature's saving throw is successful or the effect ends for it, the creature is immune to the Faa'Thasht 's Horrifying Appearance for the next 24 hours.

LEGENDARY ACTIONS

Faa'Thasht can take 3 legendary actions, choosing from the options below. Only one legendary action can be used at a time and only at the end of another creature's turn. Faa'Thasht regains spent legendary actions at the start of his/her turn.

+2 Corrosive Greatsword. Faa'Thasht makes one Corrosive Greatsword +2 attack.

Harmonious Lash. Faa'Thasht makes one Harmonious Lash attack.

Delicious Agony (costs 2 actions). Faa'Thasht makes one Delicious Agony attack.

Fire Drake

Small dragon, chaotic evil
Armor Class 13 (natural armor)
Hit Points 27 (6d6 + 6)
Speed 20 ft., fly 60 ft.

STR	DEX	CON	INT	WIS	CHA
13 (+1)	13 (+1)	13 (+1)	4 (−3)	11 (+0)	10 (+0)

Skills Perception +4, Stealth +3
Damage Immunities fire
Condition Immunities paralyzed
Senses darkvision 60 ft., passive Perception 14
Languages Draconic
Challenge 1 (200 XP)

Pyrophoric Blood. A creature that hits the fire drake with a weapon attack from within 5 feet of the fire drake must make a DC 11 Dexterity saving throw or take 3 (1d6) fire damage.

ACTIONS

Multiattack. The fire drake makes one Bite attack and one attack with its Claws.

Bite. *Melee Weapon Attack:* +3 to hit, reach 5 ft., one target. *Hit:* 5 (1d8 + 1) piercing damage.

Claws. *Melee Weapon Attack:* +3 to hit, reach 5 ft., one target. *Hit:* 8 (2d6 + 1) slashing damage.

Fire Breath (recharge 6). The fire drake exhales fire in a 15-foot cone. Creatures in the area must make a DC 11 Dexterity saving throw, taking 10 (3d6) fire damage on a failed saving throw, or half a much damage on a successful saving throw.

Fire Snake

Small elemental, neutral evil
Armor Class 14 (natural armor)
Hit Points 18 (4d6 + 4)
Speed 30 ft.

STR	DEX	CON	INT	WIS	CHA
7 (−2)	16 (+3)	13 (+1)	6 (−2)	12 (+1)	3 (−4)

Skills Stealth +5
Damage Vulnerabilities cold
Damage Immunities fire, poison
Condition Immunities poisoned
Senses blindsight 10 ft., darkvision 60 ft., passive Perception 11
Languages understands Ignan but can't speak
Challenge 1 (200 XP)

Heated Body. Any creature that touches the fire snake or hits it with a melee attack while within 5 feet of it takes 3 (1d6) fire damage.

Fire Stealth. When the fire snake is within 5 feet of an open flame larger than a torch, it may take the Hide action as a bonus action.

ACTIONS

Bite. *Melee Weapon Attack:* +5 to hit, reach 5 ft., one target. *Hit:* 4 (1d3 + 3) piercing damage plus 3 (1d6) fire damage, and the target must make a DC 12 Constitution saving throw or be paralyzed for 1d6 rounds.

Fire Whale

Huge elemental, unaligned
Armor Class 14 (natural armor)
Hit Points 175 (14d12 + 84)
Speed swim 40 ft.

STR	DEX	CON	INT	WIS	CHA
30 (+10)	13 (+1)	22 (+6)	2 (−4)	12 (+1)	6 (−2)

Skills Perception +5
Damage Immunities fire
Senses blindsight 120 ft., passive Perception 15
Languages —
Challenge 11 (7,200 XP)

Echolocation. The whale can't use its blindsight while deafened.

Hold Breath. The whale can hold its breath for 30 minutes.

Keen Hearing. The whale has advantage on Wisdom (Perception) checks that rely on hearing.

ACTIONS

Multiattack. The fire whale one Bite attack and one Tail Slap.

Bite. *Melee Weapon Attack:* +14 to hit, reach 5 ft., one target. *Hit:* 34 (7d6 + 10) piercing damage.

Tail Slap. *Melee Weapon Attack:* +14 to hit, reach 15 ft., one target. *Hit:* 23 (2d12 + 10) bludgeoning damage.

Scalding Blast (recharge 5–6). A fire whale can release a blast of superheated air in a 60-foot cone from its blowhole that scalds or burns those contacting it. Each creature in that area must make a DC 16 Dexterity saving throw, taking 49 (14d6) fire damage on a failed save, or half as much on a successful one.

Firefiend

Medium elemental, chaotic evil
Armor Class 15 (natural armor)
Hit Points 61 (10d8 + 16)
Speed 30 ft., fly 30 ft. (hover)

STR	DEX	CON	INT	WIS	CHA
13 (+1)	18 (+4)	15 (+2)	6 (–2)	12 (+1)	7 (–2)

Skills Perception +7
Damage Resistances bludgeoning, piercing, and slashing
from nonmagical attacks
Damage Immunities fire, poison
Condition Immunities poisoned
Senses darkvision 60 ft., passive Perception 17
Languages Ignan
Challenge 5 (1,800 XP)

Adamantine Weapons. The firefiend's weapons are forged
with adamantine, nearly indestructible, and do an
additional 2 points of the weapon's damage type with
each hit (included below).
Fire Body. Any creature that touches the firefiend or hits it
with a melee attack while within 5 feet of it takes 5 (1d10)
fire damage and ignites. A burning creature takes 5 (1d10)
fire damage at the start of each of its turns. A creature
can use an action to douse the fire, ending the effect.
Weapon Recall. If the firefiend is disarmed, it may cause any
of its lost weapons within 50 feet to fly back to its hands as
a bonus action, even if another creature was holding the
weapon.

ACTIONS

Multiattack. The firefiend makes one Flail attack, one
Longsword attack, and one Morningstar attack. It may
substitute a Touch attack for any or all of these.
Flail. *Melee Weapon Attack:* +6 to hit, reach 5 ft., one
target. *Hit:* 10 (1d8 + 6) bludgeoning damage plus 3 (1d6)
fire damage.
Longsword. *Melee Weapon Attack:* +6 to hit, reach 5 ft., one
target. *Hit:* 10 (1d8 + 6) slashing damage plus 3 (1d6) fire
damage.
Morningstar. *Melee Weapon Attack:* +6 to hit, reach 5 ft.,
one target. *Hit:* 10 (1d8 + 6) piercing damage plus 3 (1d6)
fire damage.
Touch. *Melee Weapon Attack:* +6 to hit, reach 5 ft., one target.
Hit: 6 (1d4 + 4) fire damage. If the target is a creature or
flammable object, it ignites. A burning creature takes 5 (1d10)
fire damage at the start of each of its turns. A creature can
use an action to douse the fire, ending the effect.

Flind

Medium humanoid (flind), lawful evil
Armor Class 16 (scale mail)
Hit Points 45 (7d8 + 14)
Speed 30 ft.

STR	DEX	CON	INT	WIS	CHA
16 (+3)	14 (+2)	15 (+2)	12 (+1)	13 (+1)	9 (–1)

Skills Stealth +4
Senses darkvision 60 ft., passive Perception
Languages Common, Gnoll
Challenge 2 (450 XP)

Ambusher. The flind has advantage on attack rolls against
any creature it has surprised.

Surprise Attack. If the flind surprises a creature and hits it
with an attack during the first round of combat, the target
takes an extra 10 (3d6) damage from the attack.

ACTIONS

Club. *Melee Weapon Attack:* +5 to hit, reach 5 ft., one
target. *Hit:* 5 (1d4 + 3) bludgeoning damage.
Longbow. *Ranged Weapon Attack:* +4 to hit, range 150/600
ft., one target. *Hit:* 6 (1d8 + 2) piercing damage.
Automatic Pistol (single shot). *Ranged Weapon Attack:* +4
to hit, range 50/100 ft., one target. *Hit:* 6 (1d8 + 2) piercing
damage.
Automatic Pistol (burst). The flind fires a burst of bullets in
a 20-foot cone. Creatures in the area must make a DC
15 Dexterity saving throw or take 6 (1d8 + 2) piercing
damage.

Flind, Boss

Medium humanoid (flind), lawful evil
Armor Class 16 (scale mail)
Hit Points 97 (13d8 + 39)
Speed 30 ft.

STR	DEX	CON	INT	WIS	CHA
20 (+5)	14 (+2)	16 (+3)	10 (+0)	12 (+1)	11 (+0)

Saving Throws Str +8, Con +5
Skills Animal Handling +4, Perception +4, Stealth +5
Senses darkvision 60 ft., passive Perception 14
Languages Common, Gnoll
Challenge 5 (1,800 XP)
Ambusher. The flind has advantage on attack rolls against
any creature it has surprised.
Surprise Attack. If the flind surprises a creature and hits it
with an attack during the first round of combat, the target
takes an extra 10 (3d6) damage from the attack.

ACTIONS

Multiattack. The boss flind makes two Greatclub attacks.
Greatclub. *Melee Weapon Attack:* +8 to hit, reach 5 ft., one
target. *Hit:* 14 (2d8 + 5) bludgeoning damage.

Flumph

Small aberration, lawful good
Armor Class 12
Hit Points 10 (3d6)
Speed 5 ft., fly 20 ft.

STR	DEX	CON	INT	WIS	CHA
7 (–2)	15 (+2)	11 (+0)	14 (+2)	15 (+2)	10 (+0)

Skills Arcana +4, Persuasion +2
Senses darkvision 60 ft., passive Perception 12
Languages understands but can't speak Common and
Undercommon, telepathy 60 ft.
Challenge 1/2 (100 XP)

ACTIONS

Multiattack. The flumph makes two Tentacle attacks or uses
its Stench Spray and makes one Tentacle attack.
Stench Spray (recharge 5–6). The flumph expels a 20-foot
cone of foul-smelling liquid. Any creature in the area must
succeed on a DC 13 Dexterity saving throw or become
coated in the liquid and poisoned. A coated creature
has disadvantage on Charisma and Stealth checks. The

stench lasts for 1 day or until thorough bathing or magic are employed to remove the odor.

Tentacle. *Melee Weapon Attack:* +4 to hit, reach 5 ft., one target. *Hit:* 2 (1d4) bludgeoning damage and the target is smeared with acid. It takes 5 (2d4) acid damage immediately and 2 (1d4) acid damage at the end of its next turn.

Flumph Hunter

Small aberration, lawful good

Armor Class 17 (natural armor)
Hit Points 60 (11d6 + 22)
Speed 5 ft., fly 20 ft.

STR	DEX	CON	INT	WIS	CHA
12 (+1)	20 (+5)	15 (+2)	12 (+1)	14 (+2)	8 (−1)

Skills Perception +6, Stealth +7
Damage Resistances acid
Senses darkvision 60 ft., passive Perception 16
Languages —
Challenge 3 (700 XP)

Keen Hearing and Sight. The flumph has advantage on Wisdom (Perception) checks that rely on hearing or sight.

ACTIONS

Multiattack. The flumph makes two stinging dart attacks.

Stinging Dart. *Melee or Ranged Weapon Attack:* +7 to hit, reach 5 ft., or range 60 ft., one target. *Hit:* 8 (1d6 + 5) piercing damage and 3 (1d6) acid damage.

Stench Spray (recharge 5–6). When the flumph unleashes its stench spray, all creatures within a 20-foot radius of it must succeed on a DC 11 Dexterity saving throw or be covered in a disgusting, oily fluid. A covered creature is poisoned for 1d4 hours, and any creature within 5 feet of it is also poisoned. Creatures poisoned in this manner also have disadvantage on Dexterity (Stealth) checks. The fetid flumph musk can only be removed by vigorously bathing in lamp oil or kerosene. The smell wears off once the creature is no longer poisoned.

Forester's Bane

Large plant, unaligned

Armor Class 14 (natural armor)
Hit Points 60 (8d10 + 16)
Speed 0 ft.

STR	DEX	CON	INT	WIS	CHA
17 (+3)	10 (+0)	15 (+2)	1 (−5)	11 (+0)	7 (−2)

Damage Immunities poison
Condition Immunities blinded, charmed, deafened, frightened, paralyzed, poisoned, prone, stunned, unconscious
Senses blindsight 30 ft. (blind beyond this radius), passive Perception 10
Languages —
Challenge 4 (1,100 XP)

ACTIONS

Multiattack. The forester's bane makes up to four Leaf attacks and six Stalk attacks.

Leaf. *Melee Weapon Attack:* +5 to hit, reach 10 ft., one target. *Hit:* If the target is Medium or smaller, it is grappled (escape DC 14). If the target was already grappled by a different Leaf, the escape DC increases by 2. Until this grapple ends, the target is restrained, and the forester's bane has one fewer Leaf attack.

Stalk. *Melee Weapon Attack:* +5 to hit, reach 10 ft., one target. *Hit:* 6 (1d6 + 3) slashing damage.

Formian Myrmarch

Large aberration, lawful neutral

Armor Class 18 (natural armor)
Hit Points 152 (16d10 +64)
Speed 50 ft., burrow 15 ft.

STR	DEX	CON	INT	WIS	CHA
18 (+4)	16 (+3)	18 (+4)	16 (+3)	16 (+3)	17 (+3)

Skills Athletics +8, Insight +7, Perception +7, Persuasion +7
Damage Immunities acid, poison
Condition Immunities poisoned
Senses blindsight 30 ft., darkvision 60 ft., passive Perception 17
Languages Common, pheromone telepathy 120 ft.
Challenge 9 (5,000 XP)

Innate Spellcasting. The formian's spellcasting ability is Intelligence (spell save DC 15, +7 to hit with spell attacks). The formian can innately cast the following spells, requiring no material components:

At will: *clairvoyance, comprehend languages, detect magic, detect thoughts*
3/day each: *charm monster, hold monster, suggestion*
1/day: *feeblemind*

Swarm Tactics. The formian has advantage on an attack roll against a creature if at least one other formian ally is within 5 feet of the creature and the ally is not incapacitated. If a formian makes an attack with advantage and hits, the target must succgeed on a DC 15 Strength saving throw or be knocked prone.

Surefooted. The formian has advantage on saving throws versus being knocked prone.

ACTIONS

Multiattack. The formian makes one Bite attack, two Claw attacks, and one Sting attack, or it makes two Javelin attacks.

Bite. *Melee Weapon Attack:* +8 to hit, reach 5 ft., one target. *Hit:* 13 (2d8 + 4) piercing damage.

Claw. *Melee Weapon Attack:* +8 to hit, reach 5 ft., one target. *Hit:* 11 (2d6 + 4) slashing damage.

Sting. *Melee Weapon Attack:* +8 to hit, reach 5 ft., one target. *Hit:* 9 (1d10 + 4) piercing damage. If the target is a creature, it must make a DC 17 Constitution saving throw. On a failure, the target takes 13 (3d8) acid damage and becomes poisoned until the end of its next turn. If the saving throw is successful, the target takes half as much damage and is not poisoned.

Javelin. *Ranged Weapon Attack:* +8 to hit, range 30/120, one target. *Hit:* 6 (1d6 + 4) piercing damage. If the target is a creature, it must make a DC 17 Constitution saving throw. On a failure, the target takes 9 (2d8) acid damage and becomes poisoned until the end of its next turn. If the saving throw is successful, the target takes half as much damage and is not poisoned.

BONUS ACTIONS

Inspire Hive (1/day). The formian can inspire all other formians within 120 feet, granting each of them 12 temporary hit points, +2 on attack rolls, and immunity

to being frightened. The effect lasts for 1 minute. Note,
the effects of multiple Inspire Hive actions do not stack;
recipients may choose which effect to accept.

Formian Queen Dryzyxxl

Huge aberration, lawful neutral
Armor Class 18 (natural armor)
Hit Points 432 (32d12 + 224)
Speed 10 ft., burrow 5 ft.

STR	DEX	CON	INT	WIS	CHA
15 (+2)	8 (–1)	24 (+7)	19 (+4)	19 (+4)	20 (+5)

Skills Arcana +11, History +11, Insight + 11, Intimidate + 12,
Perception +11, Persuasion +12
Damage Immunities poison
Condition Immunities poisoned
Senses blindsight 30 ft., darkvision 60 ft., passive Perception 21
Languages Common, telepathy 240 ft.
Challenge 23 (50,000 XP)

Call of the Queen. All other formians within 1 mile obey the
queen's commands and prioritize her safety above all else.
Innate Spellcasting. The formian's spellcasting ability is
Intelligence (spell save DC 19, +11 to hit with spell attacks).
The formian can innately cast the following spells,
requiring no material components:
> At will: *clairvoyance, comprehend languages, detect
> magic, detect thoughts*
> 3/day each: *charm monster, hold monster, suggestion*
> 2/day each: *dominate monster, feeblemind, mass
> suggestion*
Swarm Tactics. The formian has advantage on an attack
roll against a creature if at least one other formian
ally is within 5 feet of the creature and the ally is not
incapacitated. If a formian makes an attack with
advantage and hits, the target must succeed on a DC 16
Strength saving throw or be knocked prone.
Surefooted. The formian has advantage on saving throws
versus being knocked prone.

ACTIONS

Multiattack. The formian makes one Bite attack, two Claw
attacks, and one Sting attack.
Bite. Melee Weapon Attack: +8 to hit, reach 10 ft., one
target. *Hit:* 13 (2d10 + 2) piercing damage.
Claw. Melee Weapon Attack: +8 to hit, reach 10 ft., one
target. *Hit:* 11 (2d8 + 2) slashing damage.
Sting. Melee Weapon Attack: +8 to hit, reach 10 ft., one
target. *Hit:* 8 (1d12 + 2) piercing damage. The target must
make a DC 17 Constitution saving throw. On a failure,
the target takes 21 (6d6) acid damage and becomes
poisoned until the end of its next turn. If the saving throw is
successful, the target takes half as much damage and is
not poisoned.
Mental Blast (recharge 5–6). The formian sends out a wave
of psychic energy in a 60-foot radius. Each enemy in that
area must succeed on a DC 20 Intelligence saving throw
or take 26 (4d10 + 4) psychic damage and be stunned for
1 minute. A creature can repeat the saving throw at the
end of each of its turns, ending the effect on itself on a
success.

BONUS ACTIONS

Hive Frenzy (2/day). The formian can whip all other formians
within 120 feet into a frenzy, granting them the benefits of
a *haste* spell. Each target's speed is doubled, it gains +2 to

its AC, it gains advantage on any Dexterity saving throws,
and it may take an additional action each round. That
action is limited to a single Attack (no multiattack), Dash,
Disengage, Hide, or Use an Object action. The effect lasts
for 1 minute.
Inspire Hive (2/day). The formian can inspire all other
formians within 120 feet, granting each of them 18
temporary hit points, +2 on attack rolls, and immunity
to being frightened. The effect lasts for 1 minute. Note,
the effects of multiple Inspire Hive actions do not stack;
recipients may choose which effect to accept.

Formian Taskmaster

Medium aberration, lawful neutral
Armor Class 16 (natural armor)
Hit Points 90 (12d8 + 36)
Speed 40 ft., burrow 10 ft.

STR	DEX	CON	INT	WIS	CHA
17 (+3)	15 (+2)	16 (+3)	14 (+2)	14 (+2)	15 (+2)

Skills Athletics +6, Intimidation +5, Perception +5
Damage Immunities acid, poison
Condition Immunities poisoned
Senses blindsight 30 ft., darkvision 60 ft., passive Perception 15
Languages Common, telepathy 120 ft.
Challenge 6 (2,300 XP)

Innate Spellcasting. The formian's spellcasting ability is
Intelligence (spell save DC 13, +5 to hit with spell attacks).
The formian can innately cast the following spells,
requiring no material components:
> At will: *comprehend languages, detect magic,
> mending*
> 3/day each: *detect thoughts, charm person*
> 2/day: *suggestion*
Swarm Tactics. The formian has advantage on an attack
roll against a creature if at least one other formian
ally is within 5 feet of the creature and the ally is not
incapacitated. If a formian makes an attack with
advantage and hits, the target must succeed on a DC 14
Strength saving throw or be knocked prone.
Surefooted. The formian has advantage on saving throws
versus being knocked prone.

ACTIONS

Multiattack. The formian makes one Bite attack, two Claw
attacks, and one Sting attack, or it makes two Javelin
attacks.
Bite. Melee Weapon Attack: +6 to hit, reach 5 ft., one target.
Hit: 10 (2d6 + 3) slashing damage.
Claw. Melee Weapon Attack: +6 to hit, reach 5 ft., one
target. *Hit:* 8 (2d4 + 3) slashing damage.
Sting. Melee Weapon Attack: +6 to hit, reach 5 ft., one
target. *Hit:* 7 (1d8 + 3) piercing damage. The target must
make a DC 15 Constitution saving throw. On a failure,
the target takes 10 (3d6) acid damage and becomes
poisoned until the end of its next turn. If the saving throw is
successful, the target takes half as much damage and is
not poisoned.
Javelin. Ranged Weapon Attack: +6 to hit, range 30/120 ft.,
one target. *Hit:* 5 (1d6 + 2) piercing damage. If the target
is a creature, it must make a DC 15 Constitution saving
throw. On a failure, the target takes 9 (2d8) acid damage
and becomes poisoned until the end of its next turn. If the
saving throw is successful, the target takes half as much
damage and is not poisoned.

Inspire Hive (1/day). The formian can inspire all other formians within 120 feet, granting each of them 8 temporary hit points, +1 on attack rolls, and immunity to being frightened. The effect lasts for 1 minute. Note, the effects of multiple Inspire Hive actions do not stack; recipients may choose which effect to accept.

Formian Warrior

Medium aberration, lawful neutral
Armor Class 15 (natural armor)
Hit Points 58 (9d8 + 18)
Speed 40 ft., burrow 10 ft.

STR	DEX	CON	INT	WIS	CHA
16 (+3)	14 (+2)	14 (+2)	10 (+0)	12 (+1)	10 (+0)

Skills Athletics +4, Perception +3
Damage Immunities poison
Condition Immunities poisoned
Senses blindsight 30 ft., darkvision 60 ft., passive Perception 13
Languages Common, telepathy 60 ft.
Challenge 3 (700 XP)

Swarm Tactics. The formian has advantage on an attack roll against a creature if at least one other formian ally is within 5 feet of the creature and the ally is not incapacitated. If a formian makes an attack with advantage and hits, the target must succeed on a DC 13 Strength saving throw or be knocked prone.
Surefooted. The formian has advantage on saving throws versus being knocked prone.

ACTIONS

Multiattack. The formian makes one Bite attack, one Claw attack, and one Sting attack, or it makes two Javelin attacks.
Bite. *Melee Weapon Attack:* +5 to hit, reach 5 ft., one target. *Hit:* 10 (2d6 + 3) slashing damage.
Claw. *Melee Weapon Attack:* +5 to hit, reach 5 ft., one target. *Hit:* 8 (2d4 + 3) slashing damage.
Sting. *Melee Weapon Attack:* +5 to hit, reach 5 ft., one target. *Hit:* 7 (1d8 + 3) piercing damage. The target must make a DC 13 Constitution saving throw. On a failure, the target takes 7 (2d6) acid damage and becomes poisoned until the end of its next turn. If the saving throw is successful, the target takes half as much damage and is not poisoned.
Javelin. *Ranged Weapon Attack:* +5 to hit, range 30/120 ft., one target. *Hit:* 6 (1d6 + 3) piercing damage. If the target is a creature, it must make a DC 13 Constitution saving throw. On a failure, the target takes 7 (2d6) acid damage and becomes poisoned until the end of its next turn. If the saving throw is successful, the target takes half as much damage and is not poisoned.

Formian Worker

Medium aberration, lawful neutral
Armor Class 14 (natural armor)
Hit Points 21 (4d8 + 3)
Speed 40 ft., burrow 10 ft.

STR	DEX	CON	INT	WIS	CHA
14 (+2)	12 (+1)	13 (+1)	8 (−1)	10 (+0)	10 (+0)

Skills Perception +2
Damage Immunities poison
Condition Immunities poisoned
Senses blindsight 30 ft., darkvision 60 ft., passive Perception 12
Languages Common, telepathy 60 ft.
Challenge 1/2 (100 XP)

Swarm Tactics. The formian has advantage on an attack roll against a creature if at least one other formian ally is within 5 feet of the creature and the ally is not incapacitated. If a formian makes an attack with advantage and hits, the target must succeed on a DC 12 Strength saving throw or be knocked prone.
Surefooted. The formian has advantage on saving throws versus being knocked prone.
Loadbearer. The formian can carry up to 400 pounds without being encumbered. It can push or drag up to 800 pounds, but its speed drops to 20 ft. When moving with a grappled creature, the formian's speed is not halved.

ACTIONS

Multiattack. The formian makes one Bite attack and one Sting attack.
Bite. *Melee Weapon Attack:* +4 to hit, reach 5 ft., one target. *Hit:* 5 (1d6 + 2) slashing damage.
Sting. *Melee Weapon Attack:* +4 to hit, reach 5 ft., one target. *Hit:* 5 (1d6 + 2) piercing damage and the target must make a DC 12 Constitution saving throw. On a failure, the target takes 4 (1d8) acid damage and becomes poisoned until the end of its next turn. If the saving throw is successful, the target takes half as much damage and is not poisoned.

Frankie

Tiny beast, lawful evil
Armor Class 13
Hit Points 28 (8d4 + 8)
Speed 30 ft., climb 20 ft.

STR	DEX	CON	INT	WIS	CHA
8 (−1)	16 (+3)	12 (+1)	10 (+0)	14 (+2)	14 (+2)

Saving Throws Dex +5
Skills Acrobatics +5, Perception +4
Senses darkvision 60 ft., passive Perception 14
Languages understands Common but can't speak
Challenge 3 (700 XP)

Keen Smell. Frankie has advantage on Wisdom (Perception) checks that rely on smell.
Drain Life. Each hour that Frankie remains within 20 feet of a creature under the effects of its Fascinate ability, Frankie deals 4 (1d8) necrotic damage to the creature, and the creature's hit point maximum is reduced by an amount equal to the damage taken. The reduction lasts until the target finishes a long rest. The target dies if this effect reduces its hit point maximum to 0.

ACTIONS

Claws. *Melee Weapon Attack:* +5 to hit, reach 5 ft., one target. *Hit:* 1 slashing damage.
Fascinate. Frankie targets one creature it can see within 30 feet of it. The target must succeed on a DC 13 Wisdom saving throw or be charmed by Frankie. The charmed target regards Frankie as a treasured companion that must be protected. The target can repeat the saving throw every 24 hours or each time Frankie or Frankie's companions do anything harmful to the target (including Frankie's Drain Life ability), ending the effect on itself on a success.

Frog, Giant Killer

Large beast, unaligned
Armor Class 16 (natural armor)
Hit Points 105 (10d10 + 50)
Speed 30 ft., swim 30 ft.

STR	DEX	CON	INT	WIS	CHA
20 (+5)	18 (+4)	20 (+5)	5 (–3)	10 (+0)	10 (+0)

Senses passive Perception 10
Languages —
Challenge 6 (2,300 XP)

Amphibious. The giant killer frog can breathe air and water.
Keen Smell. The giant killer frog has advantage on Wisdom (Perception) checks that rely on smell.
Standing Leap. The giant killer frog's long jump is up to 30 feet and its high jump is up to 20 feet, with or without a running start.

ACTIONS

Multiattack. The giant killer frog one Bite attack and two Claws attacks.
Bite. *Melee Weapon Attack:* +8 to hit, reach 5 ft., one target. *Hit:* 12 (2d6 + 5) piercing damage.
Claws. *Melee Weapon Attack:* +8 to hit, reach 10 ft., one target. *Hit:* 14 (2d8 + 5) slashing damage.

Frost Man

Medium elemental, lawful evil
Armor Class 13 (studded leather)
Hit Points 27 (5d8 + 5)
Speed 30 ft.

STR	DEX	CON	INT	WIS	CHA
10 (+0)	12 (+1)	12 (+1)	10 (+0)	11 (+0)	11 (+0)

Skills Survival +2
Damage Vulnerabilities fire
Damage Immunities cold
Senses darkvision 60 ft., passive Perception 10
Languages Common, Nørsk
Challenge 1/2 (100 XP)

ACTIONS

Morningstar. *Melee Weapon Attack:* +2 to hit, reach 5 ft., one target. *Hit:* 4 (1d8) piercing damage.
Longbow. *Ranged Weapon Attack:* +3 to hit, range 150/600 ft., one target. *Hit:* 5 (1d8 + 1) piercing damage.
Ice Blast (3/day). As a bonus action, the frost man can use its action to remove his eye patch, blasting everything in a 30-foot cone with a freezing mist. All creatures in the area of the cone must make a DC 13 Dexterity saving throw, taking 14 (4d6) cold damage on a failed save, or half as much on a successful save.

Fungus Folk

Small plant, unaligned
Armor Class 13 (natural armor)
Hit Points 18 (4d6 + 4)
Speed 20 ft.

STR	DEX	CON	INT	WIS	CHA
10 (+0)	13 (+1)	13(+1)	9 (–1)	12 (+1)	10 (+0)

Skills Perception +3
Damage Vulnerabilities fire
Damage Immunities poison
Condition Immunities blinded, deafened, exhaustion
Senses darkvision 60 ft., passive Perception 13
Languages —
Challenge 1/4 (50 XP)

ACTIONS

Slam. *Melee Weapon Attack:* +2 to hit, reach 5 ft., one target. *Hit:* 5 (2d4) bludgeoning damage.
Spore Cloud. The fungus folk releases a cloud of spores in a 10-foot radius. All creatures in this area must succeed on a DC 11 Constitution saving throw or be poisoned for 1 minute. The target can repeat the saving throw at the end of each of its turns, ending the effect on itself on a success.

Fungus Folk Monarch

Medium plant, unaligned
Armor Class 14 (natural armor)
Hit Points 82 (11d8 + 33)
Speed 30 ft.

STR	DEX	CON	INT	WIS	CHA
14 (+2)	15 (+2)	17 (+3)	9 (–1)	12 (+1)	10 (+0)

Damage Vulnerabilities fire
Damage Immunities poison
Condition Immunities blinded, deafened, exhaustion
Senses darkvision 60 ft., passive Perception 11
Languages —
Challenge 3 (700 XP)

ACTIONS

Slam. *Melee Weapon Attack:* +4 to hit, reach 5 ft., one target. *Hit:* 12 (3d6 + 2) bludgeoning damage.
Spore Cloud. The fungus folk monarch releases a cloud of spores in a 10-foot radius. All creatures in this area must succeed on a DC 13 Constitution saving throw or be poisoned for 1 minute. The target can repeat the saving throw at the end of each of its turns, ending the effect on itself on a success.

Gar, Giant

Huge beast, unaligned
Armor Class 14 (natural armor)
Hit Points 112 (9d12 + 54)
Speed swim 60 ft.

STR	DEX	CON	INT	WIS	CHA
29 (+9)	10 (+0)	22 (+6)	2 (–4)	13 (+1)	2 (–4)

Skills Athletics +12, Perception +7
Senses passive Perception 17

Languages —
Challenge 6 (2,300 XP)

Water Breathing. The giant gar can only breathe underwater.

ACTIONS

Bite. *Melee Weapon Attack:* +12 to hit, reach 5 ft., one target. *Hit:* 30 (6d6 + 9) piercing damage, and the target is grappled (escape DC 20). Until this grapple ends, the target is restrained, and the gar can't bite another target.

Swallow. The gar makes one bite attack against a Large or smaller target it is grappling. If the attack hits, the target is swallowed, and the grapple ends. The swallowed target is blinded and restrained, it has total cover against attacks and other effects outside the gar, and it takes 21 (6d6) acid damage at the start of each of the gar's turns. The gar can have only one target swallowed at a time.

If the gar dies, a swallowed creature is no longer restrained by it and can escape from the corpse using 5 feet of movement, exiting prone.

Ghoul, Cinder

Large undead, chaotic evil
Armor Class 18 (natural armor)
Hit Points 90 (12d10 + 24)
Speed fly 40 ft. (hover)

STR	DEX	CON	INT	WIS	CHA
16 (+3)	20 (+5)	15 (+2)	4 (−3)	12 (+1)	19 (+4)

Damage Resistances cold; bludgeoning, piercing, and slashing from nonmagical attacks
Damage Immunities fire
Condition Immunities charmed, exhaustion, paralyzed, poisoned, unconscious
Senses darkvision 60 ft., passive Perception 11
Languages —
Challenge 5 (1,800 XP)

Gaseous Form. While in this form, the cinder ghoul can't take any actions, speak, or manipulate objects. It is weightless, has a flying speed of 40 feet, can hover, and can enter a hostile creature's space and stop there. In addition, if air can pass through a space, the mist can do so without squeezing. It cannot pass through water. It has advantage on Strength, Dexterity, and Constitution saving throws, and it is immune to all nonmagical damage.

Magic Resistance. The cinder ghoul has advantage on saving throws against spells and other magical effects.

ACTIONS

Slam. *Melee Weapon Attack:* +8 to hit, reach 5 ft., one target. *Hit:* 14 (2d8 + 5) bludgeoning damage plus 7 (2d6) fire damage.

Smoke Inhalation. One creature that isn't a construct or undead and is in the cinder ghoul's space must make a DC 15 Constitution saving throw. On a failed save, the target takes 10 (3d6) fire damage and its hit point maximum is reduced by an amount equal to the fire damage taken. The target dies if this reduces its hit point maximum to 0. This reduction of the target's hit point maximum lasts until the target finishes a long rest.

Ghoul, Dust

Medium undead, chaotic evil
Armor Class 16 (natural armor)
Hit Points 104 (16d8 + 32)
Speed 40 ft., fly 40 ft., burrow 20 ft.

STR	DEX	CON	INT	WIS	CHA
21 (+5)	16 (+3)	15 (+2)	14 (+2)	14 (+2)	16 (+3)

Damage Immunities poison
Condition Immunities charmed, exhaustion, frightened, paralyzed, poisoned
Senses darkvision 60 ft., passive Perception 18
Languages Common
Challenge 7 (2,900 XP)

Improved Critical. The ghoul's attacks score a critical hit on a roll of 19 or 20.

ACTIONS

Multiattack. The dust ghoul makes one Bite and two Claws attacks.

Bite. *Melee Weapon Attack:* +8 to hit, reach 5 ft., one target. *Hit:* 14 (2d8 + 5) piercing damage.

Claws. *Melee Weapon Attack:* +8 to hit, reach 5 ft., one target. *Hit:* 15 (3d6 + 5) slashing damage.

Blinding Dust (1/day). Blinding dust and sand swirls magically around the ghoul. Each creature within 5 feet of the ghoul must succeed on a DC 15 Constitution saving throw or be blinded until the end of the creature's next turn.

Paralyzing Shriek (recharge 5–6). The dust ghoul unleashes a hellish shriek. Each creature that is within 60 feet of the ghoul and can hear it must succeed on a DC 13 Constitution saving throw or be paralyzed for 1 minute. The target can repeat the saving throw at the end of each of its turns, ending the effect on itself on a success.

Ghoulish Merfolk

Medium undead, chaotic evil
Armor Class 16 (natural armor)
Hit Points 93 (11d8 + 44)
Speed 10 ft., swim 40 ft.

STR	DEX	CON	INT	WIS	CHA
16 (+3)	18 (+4)	12 (+1)	10 (+0)	13 (+1)	11 (+0)

Saving Throws Wis +4
Skills Athletics +6, Perception +4, Stealth +7
Damage Immunities poison
Condition Immunities charmed, exhaustion, poisoned
Senses darkvision 60 ft., passive Perception 14
Languages understands Aquan and Common but can't speak
Challenge 5 (1,800 XP)

Aura of Rotting Fish. Any creature that starts its turn within 5 feet of the ghoulish merfolk must succeed on a DC 12 Constitution saving throw or take 2 (1d4) poison damage and be poisoned until the start of its next turn.

Turn Resistance. The ghoulish merfolk has advantage on saving throws against any effect that turns undead.

Undead Nature. The ghoulish merfolk doesn't require air, food, drink, or sleep.

ACTIONS

Multiattack. The ghoulish merfolk makes one Bite attack and two Spear attacks. It can make one Claw attack in place of its two Spear attacks.

Bite. *Melee Weapon Attack:* +7 to hit, reach 5 ft., one target. *Hit:* 13 (2d8 + 4) piercing damage.

Claw. *Melee Weapon Attack:* +7 to hit, reach 5 ft., one target. *Hit:* 11 (2d6 + 4) slashing damage. If the target is a creature other than an undead, it must succeed on a DC 12 Constitution saving throw or be paralyzed for 1 minute. The target can repeat the saving throw at the end of each of its turns, ending the effect on itself on a success.

Spear. *Melee or Ranged Weapon Attack:* +6 to hit, reach 5 ft. or range 20/60 ft., one target. *Hit:* 6 (1d6 + 3) piercing damage, or 7 (1d8 + 3) piercing damage if used with two hands to make a melee attack.

Ghul Efreeti

Large undead, chaotic evil
Armor Class 15 (natural armor)
Hit Points 68 (8d10 + 24)
Speed 30 ft., fly 30 ft.

STR	DEX	CON	INT	WIS	CHA
18 (+4)	15 (+2)	16 (+3)	15 (+2)	16 (+3)	18 (+4)

Skills Perception +6, Stealth +5
Damage Resistances necrotic; bludgeoning, piercing, and slashing from nonmagical attacks not made with silver
Damage Immunities acid, poison
Condition Immunities charmed, exhaustion, poisoned
Senses darkvision 60 ft., passive Perception 16
Languages Common, Infernal, Primordial
Challenge 5 (1,800 XP)

Elemental Demise. If the ghul dies, its body disintegrates into a warm, putrid breeze, leaving behind only the equipment the ghul was wearing or carrying.

Genie-kin. Ghuls are undead djinn and are considered genies even though their type is undead.

Magic Weapons. The ghul's weapon attacks are magical.

Undead Nature. A ghul doesn't require air, food, drink, or sleep.

ACTIONS

Multiattack. The ghul makes one Bite attack and one Claws attack.

Bite. *Melee Weapon Attack:* +7 to hit, reach 5 ft., one target. *Hit:* 17 (3d8 + 4) piercing damage.

Claws. *Melee Weapon Attack:* +7 to hit, reach 5 ft., one target. *Hit:* 14 (3d6 + 4) slashing damage. If the target is a creature other than an undead, it must succeed on a DC 14 Constitution saving throw or be paralyzed for 1 minute. The target can repeat the saving throw at the end of each of its turns, ending the effect on itself on a success.

Ghul Noble

Large undead, chaotic evil
Armor Class 16 (natural armor)
Hit Points 187 (22d10 + 66)
Speed 30 ft., fly 30 ft.

STR	DEX	CON	INT	WIS	CHA
20 (+5)	17 (+3)	16 (+3)	15 (+2)	16 (+3)	20 (+5)

Saving Throws Wis +7, Cha +9
Skills History +6, Intimidation +9, Perception +7, Stealth +7
Damage Resistances necrotic; bludgeoning, piercing, and slashing from nonmagical attacks not made with silver
Damage Immunities acid, poison
Condition Immunities charmed, exhaustion, poisoned
Senses darkvision 60 ft., passive Perception 17
Languages Common, Infernal, Primordial, telepathy 120 ft.
Challenge 12 (8,400 XP)

Elemental Demise. If the ghul noble dies, its body disintegrates into a warm, putrid breeze, leaving behind only the equipment it was wearing or carrying.

Genie-kin. Ghul nobles are undead djinn and are considered genies even though their type is undead.

Magic Weapons. The ghul noble's weapon attacks are magical.

Turning Defiance. The ghul noble and any ghuls within 30 feet of it have advantage on saving throws against effects that turn undead.

Wrongful Demise. As a bonus action, the ghul noble can force its anger and resentment at its wrongful demise into a creature within 30 feet. The target must succeed on a DC 17 Charisma saving throw or use its reaction to make one attack against a creature of the ghul noble's choice within 5 feet of the target.

Undead Nature. A ghul doesn't require air, food, drink, or sleep.

ACTIONS

Multiattack. The ghul noble makes three melee attacks, but can use its Bite and Claws attacks only once each.

Bite. *Melee Weapon Attack:* +9 to hit, reach 5 ft., one target. *Hit:* 18 (3d8 + 5) piercing damage. A genie slain by this attack rises 24 hours later as a ghul under the ghul noble's control, unless the genie is restored to life or its body is destroyed. The ghul noble can have no more than four ghuls under its control at one time.

Claws. *Melee Weapon Attack:* +9 to hit, reach 5 ft., one target. *Hit:* 15 (3d6 + 5) slashing damage. If the target is a creature other than an undead, it must succeed on a DC 15 Constitution saving throw or be paralyzed for 1 minute. The target can repeat the saving throw at the end of each of its turns, ending the effect on itself on a success.

Scimitar. *Melee Weapon Attack:* +9 to hit, reach 5 ft., one target. *Hit:* 12 (2d6 + 5) slashing damage.

Paralyzing Spit (recharge 5–6). The ghul noble spits paralyzing saliva in a 60-foot line that is 5 feet wide. Each creature in that line must make a DC 15 Dexterity saving throw. On a failure, a creature takes 45 (10d8) acid damage and is paralyzed for 1 minute. On a success, a creature takes half the damage and isn't paralyzed. A paralyzed creature can repeat the saving throw at the end of each of its turns, ending the effect on itself on a success.

Invisibility. The ghul noble magically turns invisible until it attacks or uses its Paralyzing Spit, or until its concentration ends (as if concentrating on a spell). Any equipment the ghul noble wears or carries is invisible with it.

REACTIONS

Parry. The ghul noble adds 3 to its AC against one melee attack that would hit it. To do so, the ghul noble must see the attacker and be wielding a melee weapon.

Giants

Haidar

Huge giant, neutral evil
Armor Class 16 (natural armor)
Hit Points 200 (16d12 + 96)
Speed 40 ft., burrow 20 ft.

STR	DEX	CON	INT	WIS	CHA
27 (+8)	14 (+2)	22 (+6)	12 (+1)	14 (+2)	12 (+1)

Saving Throws Con +10, Wis +6
Skills Perception +6
Senses passive Perception 16
Languages Common, Giant
Challenge 9 (5,000 XP)

Sand Sculptor. The Haidar can manipulate the terrain around it. This trait works like the *move earth* spell except it has no duration, the Haidar can only affect sand and loose soil, and the Haidar can affect an area of terrain no larger than 60 feet on a side.

Siege Monster. The Haidar deals triple damage to objects and structures with its melee and ranged weapon attacks.

Actions

Multiattack. The Haidar makes two Greatsword attacks.

Greatsword. *Melee Weapon Attack:* +12 to hit, reach 10 ft., one target. *Hit:* 29 (6d6 + 8) slashing damage.

Rock. *Ranged Weapon Attack:* +12 to hit, range 60/240 ft., one target. *Hit:* 30 (4d10 + 8) bludgeoning damage.

Fist of Sand (recharge 5–6). The giant slams its fist violently into the ground. Each creature within 10 feet of a point the Haidar can see within 120 feet of it must make a DC 16 Dexterity saving throw as a fist of sand bursts up from the earth beneath it. On a failure, a creature takes 21 (6d6) bludgeoning damage and is knocked prone. On a success, a creature takes half the damage and isn't knocked prone.

Smoke Giant

Large giant, neutral evil
Armor Class 16 (natural armor)
Hit Points 76 (8d10 + 32)
Speed 40 ft.

STR	DEX	CON	INT	WIS	CHA
21 (+5)	16 (+3)	19 (+4)	8 (−1)	11 (+0)	12 (+1)

Skills Acrobatics +6, Perception +3, Stealth +6
Damage Vulnerabilities cold
Damage Immunities fire
Senses darkvision 60 ft., passive Perception 13
Languages Giant
Challenge 7 (2,900 XP)

Gaseous Form. The smoke giant can use its action to polymorph into a Large cloud of smoke, or back into its true form. It reverts to its true form if it dies. While in this form, the smoke giant can't take any actions, speak, or manipulate objects. It is weightless, has a flying speed of 40 feet, can hover, and can enter a hostile creature's space and stop there. In addition, if air can pass through a space, the smoke giant can do so without squeezing. It cannot pass through water. It has advantage on Strength, Dexterity, and Constitution saving throws, and it is immune to all nonmagical damage.

Heated Weapons. Smoke giants transfer the heat of their bodies to their weapons, dealing an additional 10 (3d6) fire damage on a hit (included below).

Innate Spellcasting. The giant's innate spellcasting ability is Constitution (spell save DC 15, +7 to hit with spell attacks). It can innately cast *fog cloud* and *heat metal* 3/day, requiring no material components.

Actions

Multiattack. The smoke giant makes one Mace attack and one Slam attack.

Mace. *Melee Weapon Attack:* +8 to hit, reach 10 ft., one target. *Hit:* 12 (2d6 + 5) bludgeoning damage plus 10 (3d6) fire damage.

Slam. *Melee Weapon Attack:* +8 to hit, reach 10 ft., one target. *Hit:* 14 (2d8 + 5) bludgeoning damage plus 10 (3d6) fire damage.

Rock. *Ranged Weapon Attack:* +8 to hit, range 60/240 ft., one target. *Hit:* 23 (4d8 + 5) bludgeoning damage plus 10 (3d6) fire damage.

Stone Giant Child

Large giant, neutral
Armor Class 16 (natural armor)
Hit Points 66 (7d10 + 28)
Speed 40 ft.

STR	DEX	CON	INT	WIS	CHA
19 (+4)	13 (+1)	18 (+4)	10 (+0)	11 (+0)	9 (−1)

Saving Throws Dex +3, Con +6, Wis +2
Skills Athletics +6, Perception +2
Senses darkvision 60 ft., passive Perception 12
Languages Giant
Challenge 4 (1,100 XP)

Stone Camouflage. The giant has advantage on Dexterity (Stealth) checks made to hide in rocky terrain.

Actions

Multiattack. The giant makes two Slam attacks.

Slam. *Melee Weapon Attack:* +6 to hit, reach 10ft., one target. Hit: 14 (3d6 + 4) bludgeoning damage.

Rock. *Ranged Weapon Attack:* +6 to hit, range 40/160 ft., one target. Hit: 17 (3d8 + 4) bludgeoning damage. If the target is a creature, it must succeed on a DC 14 Strength saving throw or be knocked prone.

Reactions

Rock Catching. If a rock or similar object is hurled at the giant, it can, with a successful DC 12 Dexterity saving throw, catch the missile and take no bludgeoning damage from it.

Volcano Giant

Huge giant, chaotic neutral
Armor Class 19 (natural armor)
Hit Points 187 (15d12 + 90)
Speed 40 ft.

STR	DEX	CON	INT	WIS	CHA
29 (+9)	15 (+2)	22 (+6)	16 (+3)	18 (+4)	18 (+4)

Saving Throws Con +11
Skills Acrobatics +7, Intimidation +9, Nature +8, Perception +9
Damage Vulnerabilities cold
Damage Immunities fire
Senses passive Perception 19
Languages Giant, Ignan
Challenge 13 (10,000 XP)

Heated Body. The volcano giant's attacks deal an additional 7 (2d6) fire damage (included in the attacks below).

ACTIONS

Multiattack. The volcano giant makes one one-handed spear attack and one slam attack, or two slam attacks.

Spear. *Melee or Ranged Weapon Attack:* +14 to hit, reach 10 ft. or range 40/120 ft., one target. *Hit:* 23 (4d6 + 9) piercing damage plus 7 (2d6) fire damage, or 27 (4d8 + 9) piercing damage plus 7 (2d6) fire damage if used with two hands to make a melee attack.

Slam. *Melee Weapon Attack:* +14 to hit, reach 15 ft., one target. *Hit:* 19 (3d6 + 9) bludgeoning damage plus 7 (2d6) fire damage.

Rock. *Ranged Weapon Attack:* +14 to hit, range 60/240 ft., one target. *Hit:* 27 (4d8 + 9) bludgeoning damage plus 7 (2d6) fire damage.

Sulfuric Breath (recharge 5–6). A volcano giant can exhale a cloud of warm and sulfuric gas in a 30-foot cone. All creatures in the area must succeed on a DC 19 Constitution saving throw or take 35 (10d6) acid damage and be poisoned for 1 minute.

Giants – Individuals

Ahi Mau Haka

Huge giant, chaotic neutral
Armor Class 19 (natural armor)
Hit Points 324 (24d12 + 168)
Speed 40 ft.

STR	DEX	CON	INT	WIS	CHA
35 (+12)	15 (+2)	25 (+7)	17 (+3)	18 (+4)	18 (+4)

Saving Throws Con +14
Skills Acrobatics +9, Athletics +19, Intimidation +11, Nature +11, Perception +11
Damage Vulnerabilities cold
Damage Immunities fire
Senses passive Perception 21
Languages Giant, Ignan
Challenge 24 (62,000 XP)

Heated Body. Ahi Mau Haka's attacks deal an additional 10 (3d6) fire damage (included in the attacks below).

Legendary Resistance (3/day). If Ahi Mau Haka fails a saving throw, he can choose to succeed instead.

Second Wind (recharges after a short or long rest). As a bonus action, Ahi Mau Haka can regain 29 hit points.

ACTIONS

Multiattack. Ahi Mau Haka makes one Slam attack and two one-handed Greatspear attacks, or three Greatspear attacks.

Greatspear. *Melee or Ranged Weapon Attack:* +19 to hit, reach 15 ft. or range 40/120 ft., one target. *Hit:* 30 (4d8 + 12) piercing damage plus 10 (3d6) fire damage, or 34 (4d10 + 12) piercing damage plus 10 (3d6) fire damage if used with two hands to make a melee attack.

Slam. *Melee Weapon Attack:* +19 to hit, reach 10 ft., one creature. *Hit:* 25 (3d8 + 12) bludgeoning damage plus 10 (3d6) fire damage. If the target is a Huge or smaller creature, it must succeed on a DC 21 Strength saving throw or be knocked prone.

Rock. *Ranged Weapon Attack:* +19 to hit, range 60/240 ft., one target. *Hit:* 38 (4d12 +12) bludgeoning damage plus 10 (3d6) fire damage.

Sulfuric Breath (recharge 5–6). Ahi Mau Haka can exhale a cloud of warm and sulfuric gas in a 30-foot cone. All creatures in the area must succeed on a DC 21 Constitution saving throw or take 52 (15d6) acid damage and be poisoned for 1 minute.

REACTIONS

Parry. Ahi Mau Haka adds 5 to his AC against one melee attack that would hit him. To do so, Ahi Mau Haka must see the attacker and be wielding a melee weapon.

LEGENDARY ACTIONS

Ahi Mau Haka can take 3 legendary actions, choosing from the options below. Only one legendary action can be used at a time and only at the end of another creature's turn. Ahi Mau Haka regains spent legendary actions at the start of his turn.

Greatspear. Ahi Mau Haka makes one Greatspear attack.

Slam. Ahi Mau Haka makes one Slam attack.

Quake. Ahi Mau Haka stomps his foot on the ground, and each **creature on the ground within 30 feet of** him must succeed on a DC 21 Dexterity saving throw or be knocked prone.

Glaen

Huge giant, neutral evil
Armor Class 18 (plate)
Hit Points 253 (22d12 + 110)
Speed 40 ft., burrow 20 ft.

STR	DEX	CON	INT	WIS	CHA
27 (+8)	14 (+2)	20 (+5)	15 (+2)	21 (+5)	19 (+4)

Saving Throws Con +11, Wis +11
Skills Insight +11, Perception +11, Persuasion +10, Religion +8
Condition Immunities charmed
Senses passive Perception 21
Languages Common, Giant
Challenge 18 (20,000 XP)

Eyes of the Trickster God. When a creature that can see Glaen's eyes starts its turn within 30 feet of Glaen, Glaen can force it to make a DC 18 Charisma saving throw if Glaen isn't incapacitated and can see the creature. On a failed saving throw, the creature is charmed for 1 minute. A creature can repeat the saving throw at the end of each of its turns, with disadvantage if Glaen is within line of sight, ending the effect on itself on a success. If a creature's saving throw is successful or the effect ends for it, the creature is immune to Glaen's Eyes of the Trickster God for the next 24 hours.

Unless surprised, a creature can avert its eyes to avoid the saving throw at the start of its turn. If the creature does so, it can't see Glaen until the start of its next turn, when it can avert its eyes again. If the creature looks at Glaen in the meantime, it must immediately make the save.

Loki's Blessing. As a bonus action, Glaen calls on Loki for a blessing. Roll a die. On an even number, one random ally of Glaen within 30 feet has advantage on its next attack roll. On an odd number, one random enemy of Glaen within 30 feet has disadvantage on its next attack roll. The target can resist this blessing by succeeding on a DC 18 Charisma saving throw.

Sand Sculptor. Glaen can manipulate the terrain around her. This trait works like the *move earth* spell except it has no duration, Glaen can only affect sand and loose soil, and she can affect an area of terrain no larger than 60 feet on a side.

Siege Monster. Glaen deals triple damage to objects and structures with her melee and ranged weapon attacks.

Spellcasting. Glaen is a 13th-level spellcaster. Her spellcasting ability is Wisdom (spell save DC 19, +11 to hit with spell attacks). Glaen has the following cleric spells prepared:

Cantrips (at will): *guidance, light, mending, sacred flame, thaumaturgy*
1st level (4 slots): *command, cure wounds, inflict wounds, sanctuary*
2nd level (3 slots): *aid, lesser restoration, warding bond*
3rd level (3 slots): *clairvoyance, daylight, protection from energy*
4th level (3 slots): *divination, freedom of movement, stone shape*
5th level (2 slots): *insect plague, mass cure wounds*
6th level (1 slot): *harm, heal*
7th level (1 slot): *divine word*

Actions

Multiattack. Glaen makes three Maul attacks.

Maul. *Melee Weapon Attack:* +14 to hit, reach 10 ft., one target. *Hit:* 29 (6d6 + 8) slashing damage.

Rock. *Ranged Weapon Attack:* +14 to hit, range 60/240 ft., one target. *Hit:* 34 (4d12 + 8) bludgeoning damage.

Fist of Sand (recharge 5–6). Glaen slams her fist violently into the ground. Each creature within 10 feet of a point Glaen can see within 120 feet of her must make a DC 19 Dexterity saving throw as a fist of sand bursts up from the earth beneath it. On a failure, a creature takes 56 (16d6) bludgeoning damage and is knocked prone. On a success, a creature takes half the damage and isn't knocked prone.

Macyn

Huge giant, neutral evil
Armor Class 18 (plate)
Hit Points 300 (24d12 + Con modifier times 144)
Speed 40 ft., burrow 20 ft.

STR	DEX	CON	INT	WIS	CHA
30 (+10)	14 (+2)	23 (+6)	12 (+1)	15 (+2)	17 (+3)

Saving Throws Con +13, Wis +9
Skills Athletics +17, Intimidation +10, Perception +9
Damage Resistances bludgeoning, piercing, and slashing from nonmagical attacks
Damage Immunities fire
Condition Immunities frightened
Senses passive Perception 19
Languages Common, Giant
Challenge 21 (33,000 XP)

Indomitable Leader. If a Haidar is within 20 feet of Macyn and he can see or hear it, Macyn has advantage on Charisma (Intimidation) checks and on saving throws against effects that cause the charmed, incapacitated, paralyzed, restrained, stunned, and unconscious conditions.

Legendary Resistance (3/day). If Macyn fails a saving throw, he can choose to succeed instead.

Reckless. At the start of his turn, Macy can gain advantage on all melee weapon attack rolls he makes during that turn, but attack rolls against him have advantage until the start of his next turn.

Sand Sculptor. Macyn can manipulate the terrain around it. This trait works like the *move earth* spell except it has no duration, Macyn can only affect sand and loose soil, and he can affect an area of terrain no larger than 60 feet on a side.

Siege Monster. Macyn deals triple damage to objects and structures with his melee and ranged weapon attacks.

Sirocco Aura. At the start of each of Macyn's turns, each creature within 5 feet of him takes 7 (2d6) fire damage and must succeed on a DC 21 Constitution saving throw or be blinded until the start of Macyn's next turn. The Haidar are immune to Macyn's Sirocco Aura.

Actions

Multiattack. Macyn makes two Greatsword attacks.

Greataxe. *Melee Weapon Attack:* +17 to hit, reach 10 ft., one target. *Hit:* 29 (3d12 + 10) slashing damage.

Rock. *Ranged Weapon Attack:* +17 to hit, range 60/240 ft., one target. *Hit:* 36 (4d12 + 10) bludgeoning damage.

Fist of Sand (recharge 5–6). Macyn slams his fist violently into the ground. Each creature within 10 feet of a point Macyn can see within 120 feet of him must make a DC 20 Dexterity saving throw as a fist of sand bursts up from the earth beneath it. On a failure, a creature takes 70 (20d6) bludgeoning damage and is knocked prone. On a success, a creature takes half the damage and isn't knocked prone.

Legendary Actions

Macyn can take 3 legendary actions, choosing from the options below. Only one legendary action can be used at a time and only at the end of another creature's turn. Macyn regains spent legendary actions at the start of his turn.

Greataxe. Macyn makes one Greataxe attack.

Move. Macyn moves up to his speed without provoking opportunity attacks.

Chieftain's Roar (costs 2 actions). Macyn releases a mighty roar. Each creature within 30 feet of Macyn that can hear him must succeed on a DC 20 Wisdom saving throw or become frightened for 1 minute. A creature can repeat the saving throw at the end of each of its turns, ending the effect on itself on a success. If a creature's saving throw is successful or the effect ends for it, the creature is immune to Macyn's Chieftain's Roar for the next 24 hours.

Rally Tribe (costs 3 actions). Macyn calls out to his tribe, bolstering them. Each member of the Haidar tribe that is within 15 feet of Macyn and that can hear Macyn has advantage on its next melee attack roll.

Morhidd

Large giant, neutral evil
Armor Class 18 (natural armor)
Hit Points 237 (25d10 + 100)
Speed 40 ft.

STR	DEX	CON	INT	WIS	CHA
21 (+5)	18 (+4)	19 (+4)	10 (+0)	11 (+0)	14 (+2)

Saving Throws Dex +10, Con +10, Wis +6
Skills Athletics +11, Intimidation +8, Perception +6, Sleight of Hand +10, Stealth +10
Damage Immunities bludgeoning
Senses passive Perception 16
Languages Common, Giant
Challenge 18 (20,000 XP)

Brave. Morhidd has advantage on saving throws against being frightened.

Evasion. If Morhidd is subjected to an effect that allows him to make a Dexterity saving throw to take only half damage, Morhidd instead takes no damage if he succeeds on the saving throw, and only half damage if he fails.

House Always Wins. Morhidd has advantage on Dexterity (Sleight of Hand) checks.

Sneak Attack (1/turn). Morhidd deals an extra 7 (2d6) damage when he hits a target with a weapon attack and has advantage on the attack roll, or when the target is within 5 feet of an ally of Morhidd that isn't incapacitated and Morhidd doesn't have disadvantage on the attack roll.

The Boss' Orders. As a bonus action, Morhidd gives one ally within 30 feet advantage on its next attack roll against a creature Morhidd attacked this round.

The One-Eyed Jack. Morhidd has advantage on Charisma (Intimidation) checks while wearing an eye patch.

ACTIONS

Multiattack. Morhidd makes four attacks, only one of which can be a Crushing Hug attack.

Headbutt. *Melee Weapon Attack:* +11 to hit, reach 5 ft., one target. *Hit:* 27 (4d10 + 5) bludgeoning damage.

Crushing Hug. *Melee Weapon Attack:* +11 to hit, reach 5 ft., one Large or smaller creature. *Hit:* 27 (4d10 + 5) bludgeoning damage. The target is grappled (escape DC 19) if Morhidd isn't already grappling a creature, and the target is restrained until this grapple ends.

Darts. *Ranged Weapon Attack:* +10 to hit, range 20/60 ft., one target. *Hit:* 10 (2d4 + 5) piercing damage, and the target must make a DC 18 Constitution saving throw, taking 14 (4d6) poison damage on a failed save, or half as much damage on a successful one.

REACTIONS

Roll With The Punches. When a creature Morhidd can see hits him with a melee attack, he halves the damage.

Mossknee

Huge giant, neutral
Armor Class 17 (natural armor)
Hit Points 149 (13d12 + 65)
Speed 40 ft.

STR	DEX	CON	INT	WIS	CHA
23 (+6)	15 (+2)	20 (+5)	10 (+0)	12 (+1)	17 (+3)

Saving Throws Dex +7, Con +10, Wis +6
Skills Athletics +11, Perception +6, Persuasion +8
Senses darkvision 60 ft., passive Perception 16
Languages Giant
Challenge 14 (11,500 XP)

Spellcasting. Mossknee is a 5th-level spellcaster. His spellcasting ability is Charisma (spell save DC 16, +8 to hit with spell attacks). He has the following sorcerer spells prepared:

Cantrips (at will): *chill touch, dancing lights, message, minor illusion, prestidigitation*
1st level (4 slots): *detect magic, shield*
2nd level (3 slots): *detect thoughts, mirror image*
3rd level (2 slots): *dispel magic, lightning bolt*

Stone Camouflage. Mossknee has advantage on Dexterity (Stealth) checks made to hide in rocky terrain.

ACTIONS

Multiattack. Mossknee makes two Greatclub attacks.

Greatclub. *Melee Weapon Attack:* +11 to hit, reach 15ft., one target. *Hit:* 19 (3d8 + 6) bludgeoning damage.

Rock. *Ranged Weapon Attack:* +11 to hit, range 60/240 ft., one target. *Hit:* 28 (4d10 + 6) bludgeoning damage. If the target is a creature, it must succeed on a DC 19 Strength saving throw or be knocked prone.

REACTIONS

Rock Catching. If a rock or similar object is hurled at Thunderhead, he can, with a successful DC 10 Dexterity saving throw, catch the missile and take no bludgeoning damage from it.

Norl

Huge giant, neutral evil
Armor Class 17 (natural armor)
Hit Points 200 (16d12 + 96)
Speed 40 ft.

STR	DEX	CON	INT	WIS	CHA
27 (+8)	17 (+3)	22 (+6)	12 (+1)	23 (+6)	16 (+3)

Saving Throws Con +11, Wis +11, Cha +8
Skills Athletics +13, Insight +11, Perception +11, Religion +6
Senses passive Perception 21
Languages Common, Giant
Challenge 15 (13,000 XP)

Chosen of Pazuzu. Norl has advantage on attack rolls against creatures that are flying. In addition, winged creatures with an Intelligence of 3 or lower have disadvantage on attack rolls and ability checks against Norl.

Keen Smell. Norl has advantage on Wisdom (Perception) checks that rely on spell.

Innate Spellcasting. Norl's innate spellcasting ability is

Charisma. He can innately cast the following spells, requiring no material components:

At will: *detect magic, fog cloud, light*
3/day each: *feather fall, fly, misty step, telekinesis*
1/day each: *control weather, gaseous form*

Legendary Resistance (3/day). If Norl fails a saving throw, he can choose to succeed instead.

Lover of the Arts. Creatures with proficiency in Charisma (Performance) have advantage on Charisma checks against Norl.

Spellcasting. Norl is a 10th-level spellcaster. His spellcasting ability is Wisdom (spell save DC 19, +11 to hit with spell attacks). Norl has the following cleric spells prepared:

Cantrips (at will): *guidance, light, mending, resistance, sacred flame*
1st level (4 slots): *command, cure wounds, detect magic, inflict wounds, protection from evil and good*
2nd level (3 slots): *augury, blindness/deafness, spiritual weapon*
3rd level (3 slots): *bestow curse, dispel magic, spirit guardians*
4th level (3 slots): *divination, freedom of movement*
5th level (2 slots): *contagion, insect plague*

ACTIONS

Multiattack. Norl makes two Morningstar attacks.

Morningstar. *Melee Weapon Attack:* +13 to hit, reach 10 ft., one target. *Hit:* 21 (3d8 + 8) piercing damage.

Rock. *Ranged Weapon Attack:* +13 to hit, range 60/240 ft., one target. *Hit:* 30 (4d10 + 8) bludgeoning damage.

Rotten Wind (recharge 5–6). Norl unleashes a foul, rotten wind in a 60-foot cone. Each creature in that area must make a DC 19 Constitution saving throw, taking 54 (12d8) poison damage on a failed save, or half as much damage on a successful one.

LEGENDARY ACTIONS

Norl can take 3 legendary actions, choosing from the options below. Only one legendary action can be used at a time and only at the end of another creature's turn. Norl regains spent legendary actions at the start of his turn.

Blessed Jump. Four spectral wings appear on Norl's back and he flies up to his speed without provoking opportunity attacks. Norl's movement must end on a solid surface or he falls, taking falling damage.

Gaze of Pazuzu (costs 2 actions). The spectral face of Pazuzu appears over Norl's face, and its eyes flash at one creature Norl can see within 20 feet of him. The target must succeed on a DC 19 Wisdom saving throw or be frightened for 1 minute. The target can repeat the saving throw at the end of each of its turns, ending the effect on itself on a success. If a target's saving throw is successful or the effect ends for it, the target is immune to Norl's Gaze of Pazuzu for the next 24 hours.

Sweep (costs 3 actions). Norl swings his morningstar in a wide arc around him. Each creature within 15 feet of Norl must make a DC 16 Dexterity saving throw. On a failure, a creature takes 13 (3d8) bludgeoning damage and is knocked prone. On a success, a creature takes half the damage and isn't knocked prone.

Rannyn

Huge giant, neutral evil
Armor Class 18 (natural armor)
Hit Points 253 (22d12 + 110)
Speed 40 ft., burrow 20 ft.

STR	DEX	CON	INT	WIS	CHA
20 (+5)	18 (+4)	20 (+5)	15 (+2)	19 (+4)	21 (+5)

Saving Throws Con +11, Wis +10
Skills Arcana +8, Deception +11, Perception +10, Persuasion +11
Senses passive Perception 20
Languages Common, Giant
Challenge 18 (20,000 XP)

Desert's Heat. A creature that touches Rannyn or hits him with a melee attack while within 5 feet of him takes 7 (2d6) fire damage.

Sand Sculptor. Rannyn can manipulate the terrain around him. This trait works like the *move earth* spell except it has no duration, Rannyn can only affect sand and loose soil, and he can affect an area of terrain no larger than 60 feet on a side.

Siege Monster. Rannyn deals triple damage to objects and structures with his melee and ranged weapon attacks.

Spellcasting. Rannyn is a 13th-level spellcaster. His spellcasting ability is Charisma (spell save DC 19, +11 to hit with spell attacks). Rannyn has the following wizard spells prepared:

Cantrips (at will): *acid splash, fire bolt, light, mage hand, prestidigitation*
1st level (4 slots): *burning hands, detect magic, shield, thunderwave*
2nd level (3 slots): *flaming sphere, gust of wind, misty step, scorching ray*
3rd level (3 slots): *fireball, gaseous form, haste*
4th level (3 slots): *arcane eye, stoneskin, wall of fire*
5th level (2 slots): *conjure elemental, teleportation circle*
6th level (1 slot): *sunbeam*
7th level (1 slot): *delayed blast fireball*

ACTIONS

Multiattack. Rannyn makes four Quarterstaff attacks.

Quarterstaff. *Melee Weapon Attack:* +11 to hit, reach 10 ft., one target. *Hit:* 15 (3d6 + 5) bludgeoning damage, or 18 (3d8 + 5) bludgeoning damage if used with two hands.

Rock. *Ranged Weapon Attack:* +11 to hit, range 60/240 ft., one target. *Hit:* 34 (4d12 + 8) bludgeoning damage.

Fist of Sand (recharge 5–6). Rannyn slams his fist violently into the ground. Each creature within 10 feet of a point Rannyn can see within 120 feet of him must make a DC 18 Dexterity saving throw as a fist of sand bursts up from the earth beneath it. On a failure, a creature takes 56 (16d6) bludgeoning damage and is knocked prone. On a success, a creature takes half the damage and isn't knocked prone.

Quicksand. Rannyn creates a pool of quicksand on a point he can see within 60 feet of him. The pool can form only on areas of dirt, sand, or clay. It has a 10-foot radius, is 10 feet deep, and lasts for 1 minute or until Rannyn uses this action to create another pool of quicksand. A creature in the area when the quicksand appears or that enters the area of quicksand must succeed on a DC 18 Dexterity saving throw or be restrained by the quicksand. At the start of each of its turns, a creature restrained by quicksand must succeed on a DC 18 Dexterity saving throw or sink 2 feet deeper into the quicksand. A creature submerged in quicksand can't breathe and begins to suffocate. A creature, including the restrained target, can take its action to escape the quicksand by succeeding on a DC 19 Strength check. This DC increases by 1 for each foot the creature has sunk in the quicksand.

- A Haidar can't be restrained by Rannyn's Quicksand, but the quicksand is difficult terrain for a Haidar walking through it.

Thane Brihnda

Huge giant, lawful evil
Armor Class 18 (plate)
Hit Points 337 (27d12 + 162)
Speed 30 ft.

STR	DEX	CON	INT	WIS	CHA
25 (+7)	9 (−1)	23 (+6)	16 (+3)	14 (+2)	22 (+6)

Saving Throws Dex +5, Con +12, Cha +12
Skills Arcana +9, Athletics +13, Perception +8, Religion +9
Damage Resistances cold
Damage Immunities fire
Senses passive Perception 18
Languages Common, Giant, Ignan
Challenge 17 (18,000 XP)

Special Equipment. Brihnda wears a *ring of resistance* (cold) and wields a weapon she is most proud of, her *flame tongue* (greatsword).
Innate Spellcasting. Brihnda's innate spellcasting ability is Charisma (spell save DC 20, +12 to hit with spell attacks). She can cast the following spells, requiring no material components.

 At will: *fire bolt* (17th level)

Spellcasting. Thane Brihnda is a 14th-level spellcaster. Her spellcasting ability is Charisma (spell save DC 20, +12 to hit with spell attacks). She knows the following sorcerer spells.

 Cantrips (at will): *acid splash, chill touch, light, mage hand, ray of frost*
 1st level (4 slots): *burning hands, detect magic, identify, magic missile*
 2nd level (3 slots): *blur, enhance ability, misty step, scorching ray, suggestion*
 3rd level (3 slots): *dispel magic, fireball, haste*
 4th level (3 slots): *banishment, fire shield*
 5th level (2 slots): *burning rain[4], conjure elemental* (fire elemental only), *dominate person*
 6th level (1 slot): *disintegrate, true seeing*
 7th level (1 slot): *fire storm, plane shift*

ACTIONS

Multiattack. Thane Brihnda makes two Greatsword attacks.
Greatsword. *Melee Weapon Attack:* +13 to hit, reach 10 ft., one target. *Hit:* 28 (6d6 + 7) slashing damage, plus 7 (2d6) fire damage.
Rock. *Ranged Weapon Attack:* +13 to hit, range 60/240 ft., one target. *Hit:* 29 (4d10 + 7) bludgeoning damage.
Blessings of Surtur (1/day). Thane Brihnda gains resistance to bludgeoning, piercing, and slashing damage, and deals an additional 4 (1d8) damage with each of her attacks. The damage type of the extra damage is the same as the weapon's damage. These benefits last for 1 minute.

REACTIONS

Rock Catching. If a rock or similar object is hurled at **Thane Brihnda**, she can, with a successful DC 10 Dexterity saving throw, catch the missile and take no bludgeoning damage from it.

Thunderhead

Huge giant, neutral
Armor Class 17 (natural armor)
Hit Points 172 (15d12 + 75)
Speed 40 ft.

STR	DEX	CON	INT	WIS	CHA
25 (+7)	15 (+2)	20 (+5)	12 (+1)	18 (+4)	13 (+1)

Saving Throws Dex +7, Con +10, Wis +9
Skills Athletics +12, Nature +6, Perception +9
Senses darkvision 60 ft., passive Perception 19
Languages Giant
Challenge 15 (13,000 XP)

Spellcasting. Thunderhead is a 6th-level spellcaster. His spellcasting ability is Wisdom (spell save DC 17, +9 to hit with spell attacks). He has the following druid spells prepared:

 Cantrips (at will): *druidcraft, mending, produce flame*
 1st level (4 slots): *cure wounds, entangle, fog cloud, speak with animals*
 2nd level (3 slots): *animal messenger, gust of wind, spike growth*
 3rd level (3 slots): *call lightning, meld into stone, plant growth*

Stone Camouflage. Thunderhead has advantage on Dexterity (Stealth) checks made to hide in rocky terrain.

ACTIONS

Multiattack. Thunderhead makes two Greatclub attacks.
Greatclub. Melee Weapon Attack: +12 to hit, reach 15ft., one target. Hit: 23 (3d10 + 7) bludgeoning damage.
Rock. Ranged Weapon Attack: +12 to hit, range 60/240 ft., one target. Hit: 39 (5d12 + 7) bludgeoning damage. If the target is a creature, it must succeed on a DC 20 Strength saving throw or be knocked prone.

REACTIONS

Rock Catching. If a rock or similar object is hurled at Thunderhead, he can, with a successful DC 10 Dexterity saving throw, catch the missile and take no bludgeoning damage from it.

Golems

Mithral Golem

Huge construct, unaligned
Armor Class 26 (natural armor)
Hit Points 276 (24d12 + 120)
Speed 60 ft.

STR	DEX	CON	INT	WIS	CHA
28 (+9)	20 (+5)	20 (+5)	3 (−4)	11 (+0)	1 (−5)

Damage Resistances acid
Damage Immunities poison, psychic; bludgeoning, piercing, and slashing from attacks not made with adamantine
Condition Immunities charmed, exhaustion, frightened,

paralyzed, petrified, poisoned
Senses darkvision 120 ft., passive Perception 10
Languages understands the languages of its creator but can't speak
Challenge 18 (20,000 XP)

Immutable Form. The golem is immune to any spell or effect that would alter its form.

Magic Resistance. The golem has advantage on saving throws against spells and other magical effects.

Magic Weapons. The golem's weapon attacks are magical.

Fluid Form. The golem can use a bonus action to take on a form like liquid silver. When in this form, the golem's reach becomes 30 ft. and it gains resistance to magical bludgeoning damage and vulnerability to cold damage. When in this form, the golem can move through a space as narrow as 1 inch wide without squeezing. The golem may return to its original form as a bonus action.

Evasion. If the golem is subjected to an effect that allows it to make a Dexterity saving throw to take only half damage, the golem instead takes no damage if it succeeds on the saving throw, and only half damage if it fails.

Actions

Multiattack. The golem makes three Slam attacks.

Slam. Melee Weapon Attack: +15 to hit, reach 15 ft., one target. Hit: 31 (4d10 + 9) bludgeoning damage.

War Golem

Large construct, unaligned

The war golem uses the statistics of either the stone golem or the iron golem but has a magical weapon strapped it, giving it one of the following additional action options:

Lightning Blaster. The golem fires a bolt of lightning in a 60-foot line that is 5 feet wide. Each creature in that line must make a DC 17 Dexterity saving throw, taking 17 (5d6) points of lightning damage on a failure, or half as much damage on a successful one.

Fireball Cannon (recharge 4–6). The golem fires its cannon and chooses a point within 150 feet of it that the golem can see. Flames erupt from that point in a 20-foot radius sphere, and each creature within that area must make a DC 17 Dexterity saving throw, taking 28 (8d6) fire damage on a failure, or half as much damage on a successful one.

Cold Cannon (recharge 4–6). The golem fires an icy blast in a 60-foot cone. Each creature in that area must make a DC 17 Constitution saving throw, taking 36 (8d8) points of cold damage on a failure, or half as much damage on a successful one.

Gorgimera

Large monstrosity, neutral
Armor Class 14 (natural armor)
Hit Points 114 (12d10 + 48)
Speed 40 ft., fly 50 ft.

STR	DEX	CON	INT	WIS	CHA
19 (+4)	13 (+1)	19 (+4)	4 (−3)	13 (+1)	10 (+0)

Saving Throws Dex +6, Con +9
Skills Perception +11
Senses darkvision 60 ft., passive Perception 21
Languages Draconic
Challenge 13 (10,000 XP)

Roll a d10 and refer to the table below for the color of the gorgimera's dragon head.

d10	Head Color	Breath Weapon
1–2	Black	40-foot long, 5-foot wide line of acid
3–4	Blue	40-foot long, 5-foot wide line of lightning
5–6	Green	20-foot cone of poisonous gas
7–8	Red	20-foot cone of fire
9–10	White	20-foot cone of cold

Flyby. The gorgimera doesn't provoke an opportunity attack when it flies out of an enemy's reach.

Keen Smell. The gorgimera has advantage on Wisdom (Perception) checks that rely on smell.

Charge. If the gorgimera moves at least 20 feet straight towards a creature and then hits with a gore attack on the same turn, the target takes an extra 9 (2d8) piercing damage. If the target is a creature, it must succeed on a DC 14 Strength saving throw or be pushed up to 10 feet away and knocked prone.

Actions

Multiattack. The gorgimera makes two Claws, two Bites and one Gore attack. It can use its two breath weapons in place of the bite attacks.

Bite. Melee Weapon Attack: +9 to hit, reach 5 ft., one target. Hit: 17 (3d8 + 4) piercing damage.

Claws. Melee Weapon Attack: +9 to hit, reach 5 ft., one target. Hit: 11 (2d6 + 4) slashing damage.

Gore. Melee Weapon Attack: +9 to hit, reach 5 ft., one target. Hit: 13 (2d8 + 4) piercing damage.

Dragon Breath (recharge 5–6). The dragon head exhales its breath based on the results from the table above. Each creature in the area affected must make a DC 18 Dexterity saving throw, taking 31 (7d8) damage on a failed save, of half as much on a successful one. Damage type determined by the table above.

Gorgon Breath. (recharge 5–6). The gorgon head exhales petrifying gas in a 30-foot cone. Each creature in that area must succeed on a DC 18 Constitution saving throw. On a failed save, a target begins to turn to stone and is restrained. The restrained target must repeat the saving throw at the end of its next turn. On a success, the effect ends on the target. On a failure, the target is petrified until freed by the *greater restoration* spell or other magic.

Gray Nisp

Large fey, chaotic neutral
Armor Class 15 (natural armor)
Hit Points 85 (9d10 + 36)
Speed 10 ft., swim 40 ft.

STR	DEX	CON	INT	WIS	CHA
17 (+3)	17 (+3)	19 (+4)	5 (−3)	12 (+1)	7 (−2)

Senses darkvision 60 ft., tremorsense 180 ft.
Languages Gray Nisp
Challenge 6 (2,300 XP)

Keen Scent. A gray nisp can taste blood in the surrounding water from a distance of up to 1 mile.

Innate Spellcasting. A gray nisp can use the following spell-like abilities, using Wisdom as its casting ability (spell save DC 12, +4 to hit with spell attacks). The gray nisp doesn't need material components to use these abilities.

At will: *confusion, detect thoughts, minor illusion* (auditory only), *hold monster, slow*

Water Dependent. A gray nisp can survive out of water for only 10 minutes. After that, it begins suffocating.

ACTIONS

Multiattack. A gray nisp makes one Bite attack and two Claw attacks.

Bite. *Melee Weapon Attack:* +6 to hit, reach 5 ft., one creature. *Hit:* 9 (1d12 + 3) piercing damage.

Claw. *Melee Weapon Attack:* +6 to hit, reach 5 ft., one creature. *Hit:* 8 (1d10 + 3) slashing damage. If both claws hit the same target, it takes an additional 8 (1d10 + 3) slashing damage.

Grumby the Teddy Bear

Tiny construct, lawful evil
Armor Class 6
Hit Points 1 (1d4 − 1)
Speed 10 ft.

STR	DEX	CON	INT	WIS	CHA
3 (−4)	3 (−4)	8 (−1)	18 (+4)	18 (+4)	18 (+4)

Skills Deception +8, Persuasion +8, Stealth +0
Damage Immunities cold, poison, psychic, thunder; bludgeoning, piercing, and slashing from nonmagical attacks
Condition Immunities charmed, exhaustion, frightened, paralyzed, petrified, poisoned
Senses passive Perception 14
Languages understands Common and Infernal but can't speak, telepathy 30 ft.
Challenge 1/8 (25 XP)

True Name Tag. Sewn on a small tag inside Grumby the Teddy Bear is the true name of Lucifer (or another powerful devil, at the DM's discretion), which could give the possessor great power over such a creature.

ACTIONS

Bite. *Melee Weapon Attack:* −2 to hit, reach 5 ft., one target. *Hit:* 1 piercing damage.

Charming Gaze. Grumby the Teddy Bear fixes his adorable gaze on one creature within 30 feet of him. If that creature can see him, it must succeed on a DC 16 Wisdom saving throw or be charmed by Grumby the Teddy Bear, who then uses his telepathy to persuade the charmed creature to help him return to his dark master Lucifer in the Nine Hells. A charmed creature may repeat its saving throw at the end of each of its turns, ending the condition on itself on a success.

Mark of Lucifer. Grumby the Teddy Bear focuses on a creature within 5 feet of him. The target must make a DC 16 Wisdom saving throw. On a failed save, the creature is marked with an invisible sign of Lucifer. Even those with truesight or similar ability to see invisible things must succeed on a DC 18 Intelligence check in order to notice the mark, but it is visible and obvious to any devil. Devils will be instinctively hostile to the creature and receive a +1 on their attack rolls versus the creature. Lucifer himself might take great interest in those so marked. The mark may only be removed by a creature aware of its existence casting a *remove curse*, *greater restoration*, or *wish* spell.

Guardian Naga, Fiendish

Large monstrosity, lawful evil
Armor Class 18 (natural armor)
Hit Points 170 (20d10 + 60)
Speed 40 ft.

STR	DEX	CON	INT	WIS	CHA
19 (+4)	18 (+4)	16 (+3)	16 (+3)	19 (+4)	18 (+2)

Saving Throws DEX +8, CON +7, INT +7, WIS +8, CHA +8
Damage Resistances cold; bludgeoning, piercing, and slashing from nonmagical attacks not made with silver
Damage Immunities fire, poison
Condition Immunities charmed, poisoned
Senses darkvision 120 ft., passive Perception 15
Languages Common, Infernal
Challenge 12 (8,400 XP)

Rejuvenation. If it dies, the naga returns to life in 1d6 days and regains all its hit points. Only a *wish* spell can prevent this trait from functioning.

Spellcasting. The naga is an 11th-level spellcaster. Its spellcasting ability is Wisdom (spell save DC 16, +8 to hit with spell attacks), and it needs only verbal components to cast its spells. It has the following cleric spells prepared:

Cantrips (at will): *mending, sacred flame, thaumaturgy*
1st level (4 slots): *command, inflict wounds, shield of faith*
2nd level (3 slots): *calm emotions, hold person*
3rd level (3 slots): *bestow curse, clairvoyance*
4th level (3 slots): *banishment, freedom of movement*
5th level (2 slots): *flame strike, geas*
6th level (1 slot): *true seeing*

ACTIONS

Bite. *Melee Weapon Attack:* +8 to hit, reach 10 ft., one creature. *Hit:* 9 (1d10 + 4) piercing damage, and the target must make a DC 17 Constitution saving throw, taking 55 (10d10) poison damage on a failed save, or half as much damage on a successful one.

Spit Poison. *Ranged Weapon Attack:* +8 to hit, range 15/30 ft., one creature. *Hit:* The target must make a DC 17 Constitution saving throw, taking 55 (10d10) poison damage on a failed save, or half as much damage on a successful one.

Gutslug

Medium beast, unaligned
Armor Class 15 (natural armor)
Hit Points 52 (8d8 + 16)
Speed 20 ft., fly 50 ft.

STR	DEX	CON	INT	WIS	CHA
14 (+2)	16 (+3)	15 (+2)	2 (−4)	10 (+0)	3 (−4)

Skills Stealth +3
Damage Immunities poison
Condition Immunities blinded, charmed, deafened, frightened, poisoned
Senses blindsight 50 ft. (blind beyond this radius), passive Perception 10
Languages —
Challenge 2 (450 XP)

Salt Vulnerability. The gutslug's slimy skin makes it vulnerable to contact with salt. It takes 9 (2d8) necrotic damage each time it is hit with a cup or more of salt.

Actions

Bite. *Melee Weapon Attack:* +5 to hit, reach 5 ft., one target. *Hit:* 7 (1d8 + 3) piercing damage, and the target is grappled (escape DC 15). Until the grapple ends, the target is restrained.

Bonus Actions

Blood Drain. The gutslug can drain blood from any creature it has grappled, dealing 7 (3d4) necrotic damage.

Ha-Naga

Gargantuan aberration, chaotic evil
Armor Class 19 (natural armor)
Hit Points 350 (20d20 + 140)
Speed 60 ft., fly 120 ft.

STR	DEX	CON	INT	WIS	CHA
27 (+8)	22 (+6)	25 (+7)	25 (+7)	21 (+5)	27 (+8)

Saving Throws Dex +13, Con +14, Int +14, Wis +12, Cha +15
Skills Arcana +14, Deception +15, History +14, Insight +12, Perception +12, Religion +14, Stealth +13
Damage Immunities poison
Condition Immunities charmed, poisoned
Senses darkvision 60 ft., passive Perception 22
Languages Abyssal, Common
Challenge 22 (41,000 XP)

Rejuvenation. If it dies, the ha-naga returns to life in 1d6 days and regains all its hit points. Only a wish spell can prevent this trait from functioning.
Legendary Resistance (3/day). If the ha-naga fails a saving throw, it can choose to succeed instead.
Chameleon Skin. The ha-naga has advantage on Dexterity (Stealth) checks made to hide.
Innate Spellcasting. The ha-naga's innate spellcasting ability is Charisma (spell save DC 23). It can innately cast the following spells, and it needs only verbal components to cast its spells.
  At will: *charm person, detect thoughts, suggestion*
  3/day each: *dominate person, mass suggestion*
Spellcasting. The ha-naga is a 20th-level spellcaster. Its spellcasting ability is Charisma (spell save DC 23, +15 to hit with spell attacks), and it needs only verbal components to cast its spells. It has the following sorcerer spells prepared:
  Cantrips (at will): *acid splash, fire bolt, mage hand, minor illusion, prestidigitation, ray of frost*
  1st level (4 slots): *detect magic, fog cloud, magic missile*
  2nd level (3 slots): *darkness, hold person*
  3rd level (3 slots): *lightning bolt, stinking cloud*
  4th level (3 slots): *confusion, polymorph*
  5th level (3 slots): *cloudkill, telekinesis*
  6th level (2 slots): *circle of death*
  7th level (2 slots): *teleport*
  8th level (1 slot): *power word stun*
  9th level (1 slot): *meteor swarm*

Actions

Multiattack. The ha-naga makes one Constrict attack and one Sting attack.
Constrict. *Melee Weapon Attack:* +15 to hit, reach 10 ft., one target. *Hit:* 22 (4d6 + 8) bludgeoning damage and the target is grappled (escape DC 23). Until this grapple ends, the creature is restrained, and the ha-naga can't constrict another target.
Sting. *Melee Weapon Attack:* +15 to hit, reach 15 ft., one target. *Hit:* 20 (3d8 + 8) piercing damage, and the target must make a DC 23 Constitution saving throw, taking 55 (10d10) poison damage on a failed save, or half as much damage on a successful one.

Legendary Actions

The ha-naga can take 3 legendary actions, choosing from the options below. Only one legendary action can be used at a time and only at the end of another creature's turn. The ha-naga regains spent legendary actions at the start of his turn.
Constrict. The ha-naga makes one Constrict attack.
Sting. The ha-naga makes one Sting attack.
Move. The ha-naga moves up to its speed without provoking attacks of opportunity.

Half-Ogre Enforcer

Large giant (half-ogre), neutral evil
Armor Class 18 (+1 chain mail armor)
Hit Points 102 (12d10 + 36)
Speed 30 ft.

STR	DEX	CON	INT	WIS	CHA
17 (+3)	13 (+1)	16 (+3)	8 (−1)	10 (+0)	10 (+0)

Saving Throws Str +6, Con +6
Skills Intimidation +3, Perception +3, Survival +2
Senses darkvision 60 ft., passive Perception 10
Languages Common, Giant
Challenge 6 (2,300 XP)

Action Surge (recharges after a short or long rest). The half-ogre enforcer may make one additional action on its turn on top of its normal action (and possible bonus action).
Defense. The half-ogre enforcer gains +1 to its AC while wearing armor (included above)
Great Weapon Fighting When the half-ogre enforcer rolls a 1 or a 2 on a damage die for an attack it makes with a melee weapon that it is wielding with two hands, it may reroll the die and must use the new roll.
Improved Critical. The half-ogre enforcer's weapon attacks score a critical hit on a roll of 19 or 20.
Special Equipment. The half-ogre enforcer possesses a *lesser brazen amulet* and a *potion of superior healing*.

Actions

Multiattack. The half-ogre enforcer may make two melee or two ranged weapon attacks.
+1 Great Sword. *Melee Weapon Attack:* +7 to hit, reach 5 ft., one target. *Hit:* 14 (3d6 + 4) slashing damage.
Javelin. *Melee or Ranged Weapon Attack:* +6 to hit, reach 5 ft. or range 30/120 ft., one target. *Hit:* 10 (2d6 + 3) piercing damage.

Bonus Actions

Second Wind (recharges after a short or long rest). The half-ogre enforcer may regain 1d10 + 8 hit points.

Handmaiden of Kal'Ay-Mah

Large aberration, lawful evil
Armor Class 18 (natural armor)
Hit Points 161 (14d10 + 84)
Speed 40 ft.

STR	DEX	CON	INT	WIS	CHA
22(+6)	17 (+3)	22 (+6)	16 (+3)	16 (+3)	19 (+4)

Saving Throws Dex +7, Wis +7, Cha +8
Skills Intimidation +9, Perception +7, Stealth +7
Damage Resistances bludgeoning, piercing and slashing from nonmagical attacks
Damage Immunities poison
Condition Immunities frightened
Senses darkvision 60 ft., passive Perception 17
Languages telepathy 100 ft.
Challenge 12 (8,400 XP)

Innate Spellcasting. The handmaiden of Kal'Ay-Mah's innate spellcasting ability is Charisma (spell save DC 17, +9 to hit with spell attacks). It can innately cast the following spells, with no need for material components:

> At will: *fear*, *inflict wounds* (3rd level spell slot), *see invisibility*, *teleport* (self only)
> 3/day each: *harm*, *shatter*
> 1/day each: *circle of death*, *disintegrate*

Magic Resistance. The handmaiden of Kal'Ay-Mah has advantage on saving throws versus spells and other magical effects.

Actions

Multiattack. The handmaiden of Kal'Ay-Mah makes four Longsword attacks and one Bite attack.
Longsword. *Melee Weapon Attack:* +11 to hit, reach 5 ft., one target. *Hit:* 13 (2d6 + 6) slashing damage.
Bite. *Melee Weapon Attack:* +11 to hit, reach 5 ft., one target. *Hit:* (1d8 + 6) piercing damage. The target must make a DC 17 Constitution saving throw. On a failed save, the target takes 14 (4d6) poison damage and is poisoned until the end of the handmaiden of Kal'Ay-Mah's next turn. A target that successfully saves takes half as much poison damage and is not poisoned.

Hangman Tree, Greater

Gargantuan plant, neutral evil
Armor Class 20 (natural armor)
Hit Points 248 (16d20 + 80)
Speed 10 ft.

STR	DEX	CON	INT	WIS	CHA
24 (+7)	7 (–2)	20 (+5)	8 (–1)	14 (+2)	10 (+0)

Damage Vulnerabilities lightning
Damage Resistances bludgeoning and piercing
Damage Immunities psychic
Condition Immunities charmed, frightened, prone, stunned, unconscious
Senses darkvision 60 ft., passive Perception 12
Languages Common
Challenge 9 (5,000 XP)

Paralyzed by Cold. A hangman tree is paralyzed for 1 round if it fails a Constitution saving throw after taking cold damage. The DC of the saving throw equals 10 or half the damage it takes, whichever is greater.

Slowed by Darkness. Spells that engulf the hangman tree in darkness affect it as the *slow* spell for 1d4 rounds.
Vines. The vines of a hangman tree have AC 15 and 10 hit points. Only slashing damage affects them. Damage done to a vine is not subtracted from the hangman tree's overall total and does not reduce its number of vine attacks (the tree has plenty of vines to replace any that are severed).

Actions

Multiattack. A hangman tree makes four Vine attacks.
Vine. *Melee Weapon Attack:* +11 to hit, reach 15 ft., one creature. *Hit:* 13 (1d12 + 7) bludgeoning damage and the target must make a successful DC 16 Dexterity saving throw or be grappled (escape DC 16). While the creature is grappled, it is restrained, can't speak or cast spells with verbal components, and must succeed on a DC 16 Strength saving throw at the beginning of its turn or be hung by its neck, take 13 (1d12 + 7) bludgeoning damage, and be unable to breathe.
Hallucinatory Spores (recharge 4–6). Each creature within a 50 ft. sphere centered on the tree must make a successful DC 16 Wisdom saving throw or be charmed by the tree for 2d6 minutes. A charmed creature believes the tree to be of some ordinary sort (or to be a treant or other friendly tree creature). An affected creature won't attack the hangman tree for any reason while charmed. A successful saving throw renders a creature immune to this tree's hallucinatory spores for 24 hours.

Hariph Hondu Kush

Medium humanoid (hobgoblin), lawful evil
Armor Class 20 (+1 breastplate of fire resistance[2], shield)
Hit Points 90 (12d8 + 36)
Speed 30 ft.

STR	DEX	CON	INT	WIS	CHA
16 (+3)	15 (+2)	16 (+3)	10 (+0)	14 (+2)	10 (+0)

Saving Throws Con +5, Wis +5
Senses darkvision 60 ft., passive Perception 12
Languages Common, Goblin
Challenge 4 (1,100 XP)

Unholy Strike. Once on each of Hondu Kush's turns when he hits a creature with a weapon attack, he can cause the attack to deal an extra 4 (1d8) necrotic damage to the target.
Spellcasting. Hondu Kush is a 3rd-level spellcaster. His spellcasting ability is Wisdom (spell save DC 12, +4 to hit with spell attacks). He has the following cleric spells prepared:

> Cantrips (at will): *guidance, resistance, thaumaturgy*
> 1st level (4 slots): *bane, cure wounds, protection from evil and good*
> 2nd level (2 slots): *blindness/deafness, enhance ability*

Actions

Multiattack. Hondu Kush makes two attacks with his *flaming longsword*[2].
Flaming Longsword. *Melee Weapon Attack:* +6 to hit, reach 5 ft., one target. *Hit:* 7 (1d8 + 4) slashing damage and 3 (1d6) fire damage.

Hawanari

Large elemental, lawful evil
Armor Class 17 (natural armor)
Hit Points 230 (20d10 + 120)
Speed 40 ft., fly 90 ft.

STR	DEX	CON	INT	WIS	CHA
22(+6)	14 (+2)	23 (+6)	16 (+3)	16 (+3)	18 (+4)

Saving Throws Dex +7, Int +8, Wis +8, Cha +9
Damage Resistances fire, lightning, thunder
Senses darkvision 120 ft., passive Perception 13
Languages Auran, Ignan, telepathy 120 ft.
Challenge 13 (10,000 XP)

Action Surge (recharges after a short or long rest). The hawanari may make one additional action on its turn on top of its normal action (and possible bonus action).

Elemental Demise. If the hawanari dies, its body disintegrates in a flash of fire and gust of hot wind, leaving behind only equipment the hawanari was wearing or carrying.

Improved Critical. The hawanari's weapon attacks score a critical hit on a roll of 19 or 20.

Innate Spellcasting. The hawanari's innate spellcasting ability is Charisma (spell save DC 17, +9 to hit with spell attacks). It can innately cast the following spells, with no need for material components:

At will: *detect evil and good, detect magic, thunderwave*

3/day each: *create food and water* (can create wine instead of water), *enlarge/reduce, tongues, wind walk*

1/day each: *conjure elemental* (air or fire elemental only), *creation, gaseous form, invisibility, major image, plane shift, wall of fire*

ACTIONS

Multiattack. The hawanari makes three Scimitar attacks or uses its Hurl Flame twice.

+1 Scimitar. *Melee Weapon Attack:* +12 to hit, reach 5 ft., one target. *Hit:* 14 (2d6 + 7) slashing damage plus 5 (1d6 + 2) fire, lightning, or thunder damage (hawanari's choice).

Hurl Flame. *Ranged Spell Attack:* +9 to hit, range 120 ft., one target. *Hit:* 17 (5d6) fire damage.

***Create Whirlwind*:** A 5-foot-radius, 30-foot-tall cylinder of swirling air magically forms on a point the hawanari can see within 120 feet of it. The whirlwind lasts as long as the hawanari maintains concentration (as if concentrating on a spell). Any creature but the hawanari that enters the whirlwind must succeed on a DC 18 Strength saving throw or be restrained by it. The hawanari can move the whirlwind up to 60 feet as an action, and creatures restrained by the whirlwind move with it. The whirlwind ends if the hawanari loses sight of it.

A creature can use its action to free a creature restrained by the whirlwind, including itself, by succeeding on a DC 18 Strength check. If the check succeeds, the creature is no longer restrained and moves to the nearest space outside the whirlwind.

BONUS ACTIONS

Second Wind (recharges after a short or long rest). The hawanari may regain 1d10 + 15 hit points.

Heart of Nyal'oz

Huge monstrosity, chaotic evil
Armor Class 21 (natural armor)
Hit Points 312 (25d12 + 150)
Speed 0 ft.

STR	DEX	CON	INT	WIS	CHA
18 (+4)	17 (+3)	22 (+6)	24 (+7)	24 (+7)	24 (+7)

Saving Throws Con +12, Wis +13, Int +13, Chr +13
Damage Resistances cold, fire; bludgeoning, piercing, and slashing from nonmagical attacks not made with silver
Damage Immunities acid, lightning
Condition Immunities blinded, prone
Skills Arcana +13, Deception +13, History +13, Insight +13, Perception +13, Persuasion +13, Survival +13
Senses darkvision 60 ft., tremorsense 120 ft., passive Perception 23
Languages telepathy 120 ft.
Challenge 17 (18,000 XP)

Legendary Resistance (3/day). If Heart of Nyal'oz fails a saving throw, it can choose to succeed instead.

Innate Spellcasting. Heart of Nyal'oz's innate spellcasting ability is Intelligence (spell save DC 21). It can innately cast the following spells, requiring no material components.

At will: *detect thoughts*

3/day each: *hold person, confusion*

1/day: *mind blank*

ACTIONS

Multiattack. Heart of Nyal'oz makes six Tendril attacks.

Tendril. *Melee Weapon Attack:* +10 to hit, reach 20 ft., one target. *Hit:* 11 (2d6 + 4) bludgeoning damage. If the target is Large or smaller, it is grappled (escape DC 18) and restrained until the grapple ends.

Mind Thrust. Heart of Nyal'oz targets one creature it can see within 60 feet of it. The target must succeed on a DC 19 Intelligence saving throw or take 55 (10d10) psychic damage.

LEGENDARY ACTIONS

Heart of Nyal'oz can take 3 legendary actions, choosing from the options below. Only one legendary action can be used at a time and only at the end of another creature's turn. Heart of Nyal'oz regains spent legendary actions at the start of its turn.

Tendrils. Heart of Nyal'oz makes two Tendril attacks.

Mind Thrust (costs 2 actions). Heart of Nyal'oz targets one creature with Mind Thrust.

Psychic Storm (costs 3 actions). Heart of Nyal'oz emits psychic energy in a 30-foot radius centered on it. Each creature in that area must succeed on a DC 19 Intelligence saving throw or take 27 (5d10) psychic damage and be stunned for 1 minute. A creature can repeat the saving throw at the end of each of its turns, ending the effect on itself on a success.

Hezoid

Gargantuan celestial (titan), chaotic good
Armor Class 23 (natural armor, +2 breastplate)
Hit Points 656 (32d20 + 320)
Speed 80 ft.

STR	DEX	CON	INT	WIS	CHA
30 (+10)	10 (+0)	30 (+10)	15 (+2)	27 (+8)	23 (+6)

Saving Throws Str +17, Int +9, Wis +15, Cha +13
Skills Athletics +17, Insight +15, Intimidation +13, Persuasion +13
Damage Resistances fire
Damage Immunities poison; bludgeoning, piercing, and slashing from nonmagical attacks
Condition Immunities frightened, poisoned
Senses truesight 120 ft., passive Perception 18
Languages all, telepathy 300 ft.
Challenge 24 (62,000 XP)

Action Surge (recharges after a short or long rest). Hezoid may make one additional action on his turn on top of his normal action (and possible bonus action).

Great Weapon Fighting. When Hezoid rolls a 1 or a 2 on a damage die for an attack he made with a melee weapon that he is wielding with two hands, he may reroll the die and must use the new roll.

Improved Critical. Hezoid's weapon attacks score a critical hit on a roll of 19 or 20.

Innate Spellcasting. Hezoid's spellcasting ability is Wisdom (spell save DC 23, +15 to hit with spell attacks). He can innately cast the following spells, requiring no material components:

At will: *divination, dispel magic, dominate person, levitate, mind blank, sending*
3/day: *bestow curse, chain lightning, scrying, heal, mass suggestion*
1/day: *freedom of movement, planar ally, meteor swarm*

Magic Resistance. Hezoid has advantage on saving throws against spells and other magical effects.

Memory Loss. Hezoid has had all memories of his life before coming to the City of Brass erased. If his brass slave collar is removed and those memories are restored, his Intelligence becomes 20.

Ring of Fire Resistance. Hezoid possesses a *ring of resistance* (fire).

Trampling Charge. If Hezoid moves at least 40 feet straight toward a target and then hits it with a melee attack on the same turn, that target must succeed on a DC 24 Strength saving throw or be knocked prone. If the target is prone, Hezoid can make one Stomp attack against it as a bonus action.

Actions

Multiattack. Hezoid makes two weapon attacks.

Maul of Hezoid[2]. *Melee or Ranged Weapon Attack:* +20 to hit, reach 30 ft. or range 60/180 ft., one target. *Hit:* 44 (7d8 + 13) bludgeoning damage. Critical hits inflict 4 (1d8) additional thunder damage.

Slam. *Melee Weapon Attack:* +17 to hit, reach 15 ft., one target. *Hit:* 23 (3d8 + 10) bludgeoning damage.

Stomp. *Melee Weapon Attack:* +17 to hit, reach 10 ft., one target. *Hit:* 32 (4d10 + 10) bludgeoning damage, and all creatures within 20 feet of Hezoid must succeed on a DC 20 Dexterity saving throw or be knocked prone as Hezoid causes the ground to heave.

Bonus Actions

Second Wind (recharges after a short or long rest). Hezoid may regain 1d10 + 15 hit points.

Hobgoblin Captain

Medium humanoid (hobgoblin), lawful evil
Armor Class 19 (half plate, shield)
Hit Points 82 (11d8 + 33)
Speed 30 ft.

STR	DEX	CON	INT	WIS	CHA
16 (+3)	14 (+2)	16 (+3)	12 (+1)	13 (+1)	13 (+1)

Saving Throws Int +4, Wis +4, Cha +4
Senses darkvision 60 ft., passive Perception 11
Languages Common, Goblin
Challenge 5 (1,800 XP)

Martial Advantage. Once per turn, the hobgoblin captain can deal an extra 14 (4d6) damage to a creature it hits with a weapon attack if that creature is within 5 feet of an ally of the hobgoblin that isn't incapacitated.

Actions

Multiattack. The hobgoblin captain makes three melee attacks or two ranged attacks.

Longsword. *Melee Weapon Attack:* +6 to hit, reach 5 ft., one target. *Hit:* 7 (1d8 + 3) slashing damage, or 8 (1d10 + 3) slashing damage if used with two hands.

Shield Bash. *Melee Weapon Attack:* +6 to hit, reach 5 ft., one target. *Hit:* 8 (2d4 + 3) bludgeoning damage and the target must succeed on a DC 14 Strength saving throw or be knocked prone.

Javelin. *Melee or Ranged Weapon Attack:* +6 to hit, range 30/120 ft., one target. *Hit:* 6 (1d6 + 3) piercing damage.

Reactions

Parry. The hobgoblin captain adds 3 to its AC against one melee attack that would hit it. To do so, it must see the attacker and be wielding a melee weapon.

Hobgoblin Lieutenant

Medium humanoid (hobgoblin), lawful evil
Armor Class 17 (scale mail, shield)
Hit Points 39 (6d8 + 12)
Speed 30 ft.

STR	DEX	CON	INT	WIS	CHA
16 (+3)	14 (+2)	15 (+2)	10 (+0)	11 (+0)	13 (+1)

Senses darkvision 60 ft., passive Perception 10
Languages Common, Goblin
Challenge 3 (700 XP)

Martial Advantage. Once per turn, the hobgoblin lieutenant can deal an extra 10 (3d6) damage to a creature it hits with a weapon attack if that creature is within 5 feet of an ally of the hobgoblin that isn't incapacitated.

Actions

Multiattack. The hobgoblin lieutenant makes two melee attacks.

Longsword. *Melee Weapon Attack:* +5 to hit, reach 5 ft., one target. *Hit:* 7 (1d8 + 3) slashing damage, or 8 (1d10 + 3) slashing damage if used with two hands.

Shield Bash. *Melee Weapon Attack:* +5 to hit, reach 5 ft., one target. *Hit:* 5 (1d4 + 3) bludgeoning damage.

Javelin. *Melee or Ranged Weapon Attack:* +5 to hit, range 30/120 ft., one target. *Hit:* 6 (1d6 + 3) piercing damage.

Humans and the Like

Apprentice Druid

Medium humanoid (any race), any neutral alignment
Armor Class 11
Hit Points 16 (3d8 + 3)
Speed 30 ft.

STR	DEX	CON	INT	WIS	CHA
10 (+0)	12 (+1)	13 (+1)	12 (+1)	15 (+2)	11 (+0)

Skills Medicine +4, Nature +3, Perception +4
Senses passive Perception 14
Languages Druidic plus any two languages
Challenge 1/2 (100 XP)

Spellcasting. The apprentice druid is a 2nd-level spellcaster. Its spellcasting ability is Wisdom (spell save DC 12, +4 to hit with spell attacks). It has the following druid spells prepared.

Cantrips (at will): *druidcraft, produce flame, shillelagh*
1st level (3 slots): *entangle, longstrider, speak with animals, thunderwave*

ACTIONS

Quarterstaff. *Melee Weapon Attack:* +2 to hit (+4 to hit with *shillelagh*), reach 5 ft., one target. *Hit:* 3 (1d6) bludgeoning damage, 4 (1d8) bludgeoning damage if wielded with two hands, or 6 (1d8 + 2) bludgeoning damage with *shillelagh*.

Apprentice Mage

Medium humanoid (any), any alignment
Armor Class 10 (13 with *mage armor*)
Hit Points 9 (2d8)
Speed 30 ft.

STR	DEX	CON	INT	WIS	CHA
10 (+0)	10 (+0)	10 (+0)	14 (+2)	10 (+0)	11 (+0)

Skills Arcana +4, History +4
Senses passive Perception 10
Languages any one language (usually Common)
Challenge 1/4 (50 XP)

Spellcasting. The apprentice mage is a 1st-level spellcaster. Its spellcasting ability is Intelligence (spell save DC 12, +4 to hit with spell attacks). It has the following wizard spells prepared:

Cantrips (at will): *fire bolt, mending, prestidigitation*
1st level (2 slots): *burning hands, mage armor, shield*

ACTIONS

Dagger. *Melee or Ranged Weapon Attack:* +2 to hit, reach 5 ft. or range 20/60 ft., one target. *Hit:* 2 (1d4) piercing damage.

Arcanist

Medium humanoid (any), any alignment
Armor Class 13
Hit Points 66 (12d8 + 12)
Speed 30 ft.

STR	DEX	CON	INT	WIS	CHA
10 (+0)	16 (+3)	12 (+1)	19 (+4)	15 (+2)	14 (+2)

Saving Throws Int +7, Wis +5
Skills Arcana +10, History +7, Perception +5
Senses darkvision 60 ft., passive Perception 15
Languages Common, Elvish, Ignan
Challenge 8 (3,900 XP)

Changeable Illusions. When the arcanist casts an illusion spell with a duration greater than 1 round, it can use an action to modify the form of that illusion.

Illusory Double (recharge 6). When the arcanist is targeted by an attack, it creates a temporary illusionary copy of itself. The illusion is hit by the attack instead of the arcanist.

Persistent Illusions. When the arcanist casts an illusion spell with a duration greater than 1 round which requires concentration, the spell will continue for 1 round for every four caster levels of the arcanist, even after concentration ends. This ability can extend the duration of an illusion beyond its normal limit but does not function if the arcanist is unconscious or dead.

Spellcasting. The arcanist is a 12th level spellcaster. The arcanist's spellcasting ability is Intelligence (spell save DC 15, +7 to hit with spell attacks). It has the following spells prepared:

Cantrips (at will): *dancing lights, fire bolt, light, mage hand, minor illusion, prestidigitation*
1st level (4 slots): *charm person, disguise self, fog cloud, silent image, unseen servant*
2nd level (3 slots): *blur, invisibility, mirror image, misty step, suggestion*
3rd level (3 slots): *counterspell, hypnotic pattern, lightning bolt, major image*
4th level (3 slots): *greater invisibility, phantasmal killer, resilient sphere, stoneskin*
5th level (2 slots): *cone of cold, creation, seeming*
6th level (1 slot): *programmed illusion*

ACTIONS

Quarterstaff. *Melee Weapon Attack:* +3 to hit, reach 5 ft., one target. *Hit:* 4 (1d6) bludgeoning damage or 5 (1d8) bludgeoning damage if used with two hands.

Archpriest

Medium humanoid (any race), any alignment
Armor Class 18 (breastplate, shield)
Hit Points 180 (24d8 + 72)
Speed 30 ft.

STR	DEX	CON	INT	WIS	CHA
13 (+1)	14 (+2)	17 (+3)	18 (+4)	21 (+5)	18 (+4)

Saving Throws Con +8, Wis +10, Cha +9
Skills Insight +10, Medicine +10, Persuasion +9, Religion +9
Senses passive Perception 15
Languages any four languages
Challenge 16 (15,000 XP)

Command the Faithful. As a bonus action, the archpriest commands an ally within 30 feet to use its reaction to make one attack against a creature within 15 feet of the archpriest.

Spellcasting. The archpriest is a 14th-level spellcaster. Its spellcasting ability is Wisdom (spell save DC 18, +10 to hit with spell attacks). The archpriest has the following cleric spells prepared:

Cantrips (at will): *guidance, light, resistance, sacred flame, thaumaturgy*
1st level (4 slots): *command, cure wounds, inflict wounds, shield of faith*
2nd level (3 slots): *blindness/deafness, hold person, spiritual weapon*
3rd level (3 slots): *beacon of hope, bestow curse, dispel magic, mass healing word*
4th level (3 slots): *banishment, freedom of movement, guardian of faith*
5th level (2 slots): *flame strike, insect plague, mass cure wounds*
6th level (1 slot): *harm, heal*
7th level (1 slot): *fire storm*

Multiattack. The archpriest makes three Divine Bolt attacks.
Dagger. *Melee or Ranged Weapon Attack:* +4 to hit, reach 5 ft. or range 20/60 ft., one target. *Hit:* 4 (1d4 + 2) piercing damage.
Divine Bolt. *Ranged Spell Attack:* +10 to hit, range 120 ft., one target. *Hit:* 28 (8d6) radiant (good or neutral archpriests) or necrotic (evil archpriests) damage.
Deific Wrath (recharge 5–6). The archpriest calls on its deity to smite up to three creatures it can see within 60 feet of it. Each target must make a DC 18 Wisdom saving throw. On a failure, a target takes 42 (12d6) radiant (good or neutral archpriests) or necrotic (evil archpriests) damage and is paralyzed until the start of its next turn as it becomes overwhelmed with divine might. On a success, a target takes half the damage and isn't paralyzed.

Rebuke the Unfaithful. When a creature hits the archpriest with a melee attack, it must succeed on a DC 18 Wisdom saving throw or take 14 (4d6) radiant (good or neutral archpriests) or necrotic (evil archpriests) damage and be pushed up to 10 feet away from the archpriest.

Bandit Lord

Medium humanoid (any race), any non-lawful alignment
Armor Class 16 (breastplate)
Hit Points 91 (14d8 + 28)
Speed 30 ft.

STR	DEX	CON	INT	WIS	CHA
16 (+3)	15 (+2)	14 (+2)	14 (+2)	11 (+0)	14 (+2)

Saving Throws Str +5, Dex +4, Wis +2
Skills Athletics +5, Deception +4, Intimidation +4
Senses passive Perception 10
Language Any two languages
Challenge 4 (1,100 XP)

Pack Tactics. The bandit lord has advantage on attack rolls against a creature if at least one of the bandit lord's allies is within 5 feet of the creature and the ally isn't incapacitated.

Multiattack. A bandit lord makes three melee or ranged attacks.
Greatsword. *Melee Weapon Attack:* +5 to hit, reach 5 ft., one target. *Hit:* 10 (2d6 + 3) slashing damage.
Dagger. *Melee or Ranged Weapon Attack:* +5 to hit, reach 5 ft. or range 20/60 ft., one target. *Hit:* 5 (1d4 + 3) piercing damage.
Leadership (recharges after a short or long rest). For 1 minute, the bandit lord can utter a special command or warning whenever a nonhostile creature that it can see within 30 feet of it makes an attack roll or a saving throw. The creature can add a d4 to its roll provided it can hear and understand the bandit lord. A creature can benefit from only one Leadership die at a time. This effect ends if the bandit lord is incapacitated.

The bandit lord can be found in ***Tome of Beasts*** by **Kobold Press**.

Beastshifter

Medium humanoid (any race), any alignment
Armor Class 17 (studded leather)
Hit Points 58 (9d8 + 18)
Speed 30 ft.

STR	DEX	CON	INT	WIS	CHA
11 (+0)	16 (+3)	14 (+2)	10 (+0)	18 (+4)	14 (+2)

Skills Animal Handling +7, Medicine +7, Nature +6, Perception +7, Survival +7
Senses darkvision 60 ft., passive Perception 17
Languages Common, Druidic, Goblin
Challenge 6 (2,300 XP)

Spellcasting. The beastshifter's spellcasting ability is Wisdom (spell save DC 15, +7 to hit with spell attacks). It can cast the following spells:

Cantrips (at will): *bramble whip[4,] druidcraft, poison spray, produce flame*
1st level (4 slots): *cure wounds, faerie fire, fog cloud, longstrider, thunderwave*
2nd level (3 slots): *barkskin, enhance ability, flame blade, heat metal*
3rd level (3 slots): *call lightning, conjure animals, sleet storm, wind wall*
4th level (2 slots): *blight, conjure minor elementals, stoneskin*

Primal Strike. While in beast form, the beastshifter's attacks are considered magical.

Club. *Melee Weapon Attack:* +6 to hit, reach 5 ft., one target. *Hit:* 5 (1d6 + 2) bludgeoning damage.
Wild Shape (2/day). The beastshifter can take a bonus action to magically assume the shape of a beast that it has seen before, provided that the beast has a challenge rating of 2 or lower, and has no flying speed. It can use this feature twice per day.

While in a new form, the beastshifter retains its ability to speak, and its Intelligence, Wisdom, and Charisma scores. It also retains all of its skill and saving throw proficiencies in addition to gaining those of the creature whose form it assumes. It assumes the Hit Dice, hit points, AC, movement modes, Strength, Dexterity, and Constitution scores, and the attack and damage statistics of the beast.

Brigand Leader

Medium humanoid (any race), neutral evil
Armor Class 16 (studded leather, shield)
Hit Points 71 (11d8 + 22)
Speed 30 ft.

STR	DEX	CON	INT	WIS	CHA
10 (+0)	15 (+2)	14 (+2)	11 (+0)	14 (+2)	10 (+0)

Saving Throws Dex +4, Wis +4
Skills Deception +4, Intimidation +4, Perception +4, Stealth +4
Senses passive Perception 14
Language Common, Goblin
Challenge 2 (450 XP)

Pack Tactics. The brigand leader has advantage on attack rolls against a creature if at least one of the brigand leader's allies is within 5 feet of the creature and the ally isn't incapacitated.

ACTIONS

Multiattack. A brigand leader makes three melee attacks: two with its rapier and one with its dagger.
Rapier. *Melee Weapon Attack:* +4 to hit, reach 5 ft., one target. *Hit:* 6 (1d8 + 2) piercing damage.
Dagger. *Melee or Ranged Weapon Attack:* +4 to hit, reach 5 ft. or range 20/60 ft., one target. *Hit:* 4 (1d4 + 2) piercing damage.
Shortbow. *Ranged Weapon Attack:* +4 to hit, range 80/320 ft., one target. *Hit:* 5 (1d6 + 2) piercing damage.

REACTIONS

Parry. The brigand leader adds 3 to its AC against one melee attack that would hit it. To do so, the brigand leader must see the attacker and be wielding a melee weapon.

Burglar

Medium humanoid (any), any alignment
Armor Class 15 (leather armor)
Hit Points 52 (8d8 + 16)
Speed 30 ft.

STR	DEX	CON	INT	WIS	CHA
13 (+1)	18 (+4)	15 (+2)	12 (+1)	14 (+2)	10 (+0)

Saving Throws Dex +7, Int +4
Skills Acrobatic +7, Athletics +4, Perception +5, Sleight of Hand +7, Stealth +7
Senses passive Perception 15
Languages Thieves' cant plus any two languages
Challenge 5 (1,800 XP)

Cunning Action. The burglar can use a bonus action on its turn to take the Dash, Disengage, Hide, or Use an Object action.
Evasion. When the burglar is subjected to an effect that allows it to make a Dexterity saving throw to take only half damage, it instead takes no damage if the saving throw is successful, and only half damage if the roll is a failure.
Sneak Attack. Once per turn, the burglar can deal an extra 14 (4d6) damage to one creature it hits with an attack if it has advantage on the attack roll. The attack must use a finesse or ranged weapon. The burglar doesn't need advantage on the attack roll if another enemy of the target is within 5 feet of it, that enemy isn't incapacitated, and the burglar doesn't have disadvantage on the attack roll.

ACTIONS

Multiattack. The burglar can make two attacks with either its Shortsword, its Dagger, or its Light Crossbow.
Shortsword. *Melee Weapon Attack:* +7 to hit, reach 5 ft., one target. *Hit:* 7 (1d6 + 4) piercing damage.
Dagger. *Melee or Ranged Weapon Attack:* +7 to hit, reach 5 ft. or range 20/60 ft., one target. *Hit:* 6 (1d4 + 4) piercing damage.
Light Crossbow. *Ranged Weapon Attack:* +7 to hit, range 80/320 ft., one target. *Hit:* 8 (1d8 + 4) piercing damage.

Captain

Medium humanoid (any race), any alignment
Armor Class 18 (chain mail and shield)
Hit Points 65 (10d8+20)
Speed 30 ft.

STR	DEX	CON	INT	WIS	CHA
18 (+4)	10 (+0)	15 (+2)	12 (+1)	12 (+1)	16 (+3)

Saving Throws Str +6, Con +4
Skills Athletics +6, Perception +5, Intimidation +7
Senses passive Perception 15
Languages Common, Dwarven
Challenge 4 (1,100 XP)

Brave. The captain has advantage on all saving throws against fear.
Leadership (recharges after a short or long rest). For 1 minute, the captain can utter a special command or warning whenever a nonhostile creature that it can see within 30 feet of it makes an attack roll or a saving throw. The creature can add a d4 to its roll provided it can hear and understand the captain. A creature can benefit from only one Leadership die at a time. This effect ends if the captain is incapacitated.

ACTIONS

Multiattack. The captain makes three melee attacks.
Longsword. *Melee Weapon Attack:* +6 to hit, reach 5 ft., one target. *Hit:* 8 (1d8 + 4) slashing damage, or 9 (1d10 + 4) if used with two hands.
Heavy Crossbow. *Ranged Weapon Attack:* +2 to hit, range 100/400, one target. *Hit:* 5 (1d10) piercing damage.

Champion Warrior

Medium humanoid (any race), any alignment
Armor Class 20 (plate, shield)
Hit Points 135 (18d8 + 54)
Speed 30 ft.

STR	DEX	CON	INT	WIS	CHA
18 (+4)	14 (+2)	16 (+3)	10 (+0)	12 (+1)	10 (+0)

Saving Throws Str +8, Con +7, Wis +5
Skills Animal Handling +5, Athletics +8, History +4, Insight +5, Intimidation +4, Perception +5
Senses passive Perception 15
Languages Common plus one other language
Challenge 9 (5,000 XP)

Brave. The warrior has advantage on saving throws against being frightened.

Improved Critical. The warrior scores a critical hit with a weapon attack on a roll of 19 or 20.

Martial Advantage. Once per turn, the warrior can deal an extra 18 (4d8) damage to a creature it hits with a weapon attack if that creature is within 5 feet of an ally of the warrior's that isn't incapacitated.

ACTIONS

Multiattack. The warrior can make three longsword attacks.

Longsword. *Melee Weapon Attack:* +8 to hit, reach 5 ft., one target. *Hit:* 8 (1d8 + 4) slashing damage, or 9 (1d10 + 4) slashing damage if used with two hands to make a melee attack.

Light Crossbow. *Ranged Weapon Attack:* +6 to hit, range 80/320 ft., one target. *Hit:* 6 (1d8 + 2) piercing damage.

Leadership (recharges after a short or long rest). For 1 minute, the warrior can utter a special command or warning whenever a nonhostile creature that it can see within 30 feet of him makes an attack roll or a saving throw. The creature can add a d4 to its roll provided it can hear and understand the warrior. A creature can benefit from only one Leadership die at a time. This effect ends if the warrior is incapacitated.

REACTIONS

Parry. The warrior adds 4 to his AC against one melee attack that would hit him. To do so, he must see the attacker and be wielding a melee weapon.

Commander

Medium humanoid (any race), any alignment
Armor Class 19 (splint, shield)
Hit Points 110 (17d8+34)
Speed 30 ft.

STR	DEX	CON	INT	WIS	CHA
19 (+4)	12 (+1)	14 (+2)	13 (+1)	14 (+2)	12 (+1)

Saving Throws Str +7, Con +5
Skills Animal Handling +5, Athletics +7, Insight +5, Perception +5
Senses passive Perception 15
Languages Common, Dwarven
Challenge 5 (1,800 XP)

Indomitable (1/day). The commander rerolls a failed saving throw.

Second Wind (recharges after a short or long rest). As a bonus action, the commander can regain 10 hit points.

Leadership (recharges after a short or long rest). For 1 minute, the commander can utter a special command or warning whenever a nonhostile creature that it can see within 30 feet of it makes an attack roll or a saving throw. The creature can add a d4 to its roll provided it can hear and understand the commander. A creature can benefit from only one Leadership die at a time. This effect ends if the commander is incapacitated.

ACTIONS

Multiattack. The commander makes three melee attacks.

Longsword. *Melee Weapon Attack:* +7 to hit, reach 5 ft., one target. *Hit:* 8 (1d8 + 4) slashing damage, or 9 (1d10 + 4) slashing damage if used with two hands.

Heavy Crossbow. *Ranged Weapon Attack:* +4 to hit, range 100/400, one target. *Hit:* 6 (1d10 + 1) piercing damage.

Commoner, Greater

Medium humanoid (any), any
Armor Class 12
Hit Points 39 (6d8 + 12)
Speed 30 ft.

STR	DEX	CON	INT	WIS	CHA
16 (+3)	16 (+3)	14 (+2)	10 (+0)	12 (+1)	10 (+0)

Skills Athletics +5, Survival +3
Senses passive Perception 11
Languages Common
Challenge 1/2 (100 XP)

ACTIONS

Multiattack. The greater commoner makes two Improvised Weapon attacks (either melee or ranged).

Improvised Melee Weapon. *Melee Weapon Attack:* +5 to hit, reach 5 ft., one target. *Hit:* 6 (1d6 + 3) bludgeoning, piercing, or slashing damage.

Improvised Ranged Weapon. *Ranged Weapon Attack:* +5 to hit, range 20 ft., one target. *Hit:* 5 (1d4 + 3) bludgeoning, piercing, or slashing damage.

Commoner, Hardy

Medium humanoid (any), any
Armor Class 12
Hit Points 22 (4d8 + 4)
Speed 30 ft.

STR	DEX	CON	INT	WIS	CHA
14 (+2)	14 (+2)	12 (+1)	10 (+0)	12 (+1)	10 (+0)

Skills Athletics +4, Survival +2
Senses passive Perception 11
Languages Common
Challenge 1/4 (50 XP)

ACTIONS

Improvised Melee Weapon. *Melee Weapon Attack:* +4 to hit, reach 5 ft., one target. *Hit:* 5 (1d6 + 2) bludgeoning, piercing, or slashing damage.

Improvised Ranged Weapon. *Ranged Weapon Attack:* +4 to hit, range 20 ft., one target. *Hit:* 4 (1d4 + 2) bludgeoning, piercing, or slashing damage.

Eldritch Archer

Medium humanoid (elf), neutral
Armor Class 16 (chain mail)
Hit Points 88 (16d8 + 16)
Speed 30 ft.

STR	DEX	CON	INT	WIS	CHA
12 (+1)	20 (+5)	13 (+1)	16 (+3)	16 (+3)	12 (+1)

Saving Throws Dex +8, Int +6
Skills Perception +6, Stealth +8, Survival +6
Senses darkvision 60 ft., passive Perception 16
Languages Common, Elven
Challenge 7 (2,900 XP)

Eldritch Arrow. Once per turn, the eldritch archer can apply an eldritch effect to an arrow fired from its longbow. The eldritch effect does 4 (1d8) damage. The damage type can be either acid, cold, fire, lightning, or poison.

Fey Ancestry. The elf has advantage on saving throws against being charmed, and magic can't put the elf to sleep.

Keen Hearing and Sight. The elf has advantage on Wisdom (Perception) checks related to hearing or sight.

Spellcasting. The eldritch archer is a 5th-level spellcaster. Its spellcasting ability is Intelligence (spell save DC 14, +6 to hit with spell attacks). It can cast the following spells:

> Cantrips (at will): *fire bolt, mage hand, mending, prestidigitation*
> 1st level (4 slots): *burning hands, expeditious retreat, shield*
> 2nd level (3 slots): *darkness, enhance ability, silence*
> 3rd level (2 slots): *blink, gaseous form*

ACTIONS

Multiattack. The eldritch archer makes two melee or three ranged weapon attacks.

Rapier. *Melee Weapon Attack:* +8 to hit, reach 5 ft., one target. *Hit:* 9 (1d8 + 5) piercing damage.

+2 Longbow. *Ranged Weapon Attack:* +10 to hit, range 150/600 ft., one target. *Hit:* 11 (1d8 + 7) piercing damage.

Elemental Overlord

Medium humanoid (any race), any alignment
Armor Class 13 (16 with *mage armor*)
Hit Points 165 (30d8 + 30)
Speed 30 ft.

STR	DEX	CON	INT	WIS	CHA
10 (+0)	16 (+3)	13 (+1)	14 (+2)	15 (+2)	21 (+5)

Saving Throws Dex +8, Con +6, Cha +10
Skills Arcana +7, Intimidation +10, Persuasion +10
Damage Immunities varies (see Elemental Flexibility)
Senses passive Perception 12
Languages any three languages
Challenge 14 (11,500 XP)

Elemental Flexibility. At the start of its turn, the elemental overlord must choose one damage type: acid, cold, fire, or lightning. It has immunity to its chosen damage type until the start of its next turn. It can't choose the same damage type two rounds in a row.

Elemental Shield. A creature that touches the elemental overlord or hits it with a melee attack while within 5 feet of it takes 10 (3d6) damage of the type chosen with Elemental Flexibility.

Legendary Resistance (3/day). If the elemental overlord fails a saving throw, it can choose to succeed instead.

Spellcasting. The elemental overlord is a 20th-level spellcaster. Its spellcasting ability is Charisma (spell save DC 18, +10 to hit with spell attacks). The overlord has the following wizard spells prepared:

> Cantrips (at will): *acid splash, blade ward, fire bolt, light, prestidigitation*
> 1st level (4 slots): *burning hands, detect magic, mage armor, magic missile, shield*
> 2nd level (3 slots): *blur, flaming sphere, gust of wind, misty step*
> 3rd level (3 slots): *counterspell, fly, lightning bolt*
> 4th level (3 slots): *conjure minor elementals, ice storm, stoneskin, wall of fire*
> 5th level (3 slots): *cone of cold, conjure elemental, wall of stone*
> 6th level (2 slots): *chain lightning, wall of ice*
> 7th level (2 slots): *delayed blast fireball, prismatic spray*
> 8th level (1 slot): *control weather*
> 9th level (1 slot): *meteor swarm*

ACTIONS

Dagger. *Melee or Ranged Weapon Attack:* +8 to hit, reach 5 ft. or range 20/60 ft., one target. *Hit:* 5 (1d4 + 3) piercing damage.

Elemental Bolt. *Ranged Spell Attack:* +10 to hit, range 120 ft., one target. *Hit:* 28 (8d6) damage of the type chosen with Elemental Flexibility, and the target must succeed on a DC 18 Constitution saving throw or have disadvantage on its next saving throw against a spell cast by the elemental overlord.

LEGENDARY ACTIONS

The elemental overlord can take 3 legendary actions, choosing from the options below. Only one legendary action can be used at a time and only at the end of another creature's turn. The overlord regains spent legendary actions at the start of its turn.

Cantrip. The elemental overlord casts a cantrip.

Move. The elemental overlord moves up to half its speed without provoking opportunity attacks.

Elemental Bolt (costs 2 actions). The elemental overlord makes one Elemental Bolt attack.

Power Uncontained (costs 3 actions). The elemental overlord releases a burst of elemental energy. Each creature within 20 feet of it must make a DC 18 Dexterity saving throw. On a failure, a creature takes 21 (6d6) force damage and is pushed up to 10 feet away and knocked prone. On a success, a creature takes half the damage and isn't pushed or knocked prone.

Emeritus Chaplain

Medium humanoid (any race), any alignment
Armor Class 17 (breastplate, shield)
Hit Points 135 (18d8 + 54)
Speed 30 ft.

STR	DEX	CON	INT	WIS	CHA
18 (+4)	12 (+1)	16 (+3)	14 (+2)	21 (+5)	15 (+2)

Saving Throws Con +7, Wis +9, Cha +6
Skills History +6, Insight +9, Medicine +9, Religion +6
Senses passive Perception 15
Languages any four languages
Challenge 12 (8,400 XP)

Aura of Mettle. At the start of each of the emeritus chaplain's turns, each ally within 10 feet of it, including the emeritus chaplain, that has less than half its maximum hit points regains 5 (2d4) hit points. In addition, each ally within 10 feet of the emeritus chaplain has advantage on saving throws against effects that cause the charmed or frightened conditions.

Divine Weapons. The emeritus chaplain's weapon attacks are magical. When the emeritus chaplain hits with any weapon, the weapon deals an extra 4d8 radiant (good or neutral chaplains) or necrotic (evil chaplains) damage.

Spellcasting. The emeritus chaplain is a 10th-level spellcaster. Its spellcasting ability is Wisdom (spell save DC 17, +9 to hit with spell attacks). The emeritus chaplain has the following cleric spells prepared:

> Cantrips (at will): *guidance, light, resistance, sacred flame, thaumaturgy*
> 1st level (4 slots): *bless, detect evil and good, cure wounds, healing word, inflict wounds*
> 2nd level (3 slots): *aid, silence, spiritual weapon*

3rd level (3 slots): *dispel magic, mass healing word, spirit guardians*
4th level (3 slots): *freedom of movement, guardian of faith*
5th level (2 slots): *dispel evil and good, mass cure wounds*

ACTIONS

Multiattack. The emeritus chaplain makes three Shortsword attacks.

Shortsword. *Melee Weapon Attack:* +8 to hit, reach 5 ft., one target. *Hit:* 7 (1d6 + 4) piercing damage plus 18 (4d8) radiant (good or neutral chaplains) or necrotic (evil chaplains) damage.

Entertainer

Medium humanoid (any race), any alignment
Armor Class 15 (studded leather)
Hit Points 65 (10d8 + 20)
Speed 30 ft.

STR	DEX	CON	INT	WIS	CHA
12 (+1)	16 (+3)	15 (+2)	11 (+0)	14 (+2)	17 (+3)

Saving Throws Dex +5
Skills Acrobatics +5, Performance +7, Sleight of Hand +5
Damage Resistances fire
Senses passive Perception 12
Languages any two languages
Challenge 4 (1,100 XP)

Spellcasting. The entertainer is a 6th-level spellcaster. Its spellcasting ability is Charisma (spell save DC 13, +5 to hit with spell attacks). It has the following bard spells prepared:
Cantrips (at will): *light, prestidigitation, vicious mockery*
1st level (4 slots): *disguise self, dissonant whispers, faerie fire, hideous laughter*
2nd level (3 slots): *invisibility, shatter, silence*
3rd level (3 slots): *bestow curse, stinking cloud*

What's Over There? (3/day). As a bonus action, the entertainer distracts creatures within 10 feet of it. Each creature in the area must make a DC 13 Charisma saving throw. If each creature fails the save, the entertainer can move up to its speed without provoking opportunity attacks.

ACTIONS

Multiattack. The entertainer makes two Juggling Dagger attacks.

Juggling Dagger. *Melee or Ranged Weapon Attack:* +5 to hit, reach 5 ft. or range 30/120 ft., one target. *Hit:* 5 (1d4 + 3) piercing damage plus 3 (1d6) poison damage.

Fire Eater (recharge 5–6). The entertainer mixes flammable oils in its mouth and spits the concoction in a 15-foot cone. Each creature in the area must make a DC 13 Dexterity saving throw, taking 21 (6d6) fire damage on a failed save, or half as much damage on a successful one. Flammable objects that aren't being worn or carried in that area are ignited.

REACTIONS

Tumble. When a creature the entertainer can see targets it with a melee attack, the entertainer can tumble to an unoccupied space within 5 feet of the attacker, halving the damage.

Fallen Paladin

Medium humanoid (any), any evil alignment
Armor Class 20 (plate armor, shield)
Hit Points 100 (12d8 + 24)
Speed 30 ft.

STR	DEX	CON	INT	WIS	CHA
18 (+4)	12 (+1)	14 (+2)	12 (+1)	16 (+3)	18 (+4)

Saving Throws Wis +6, Cha +7
Skills Athletics +7, Medicine +4, Persuasion +7, Religion +4
Senses passive Perception 13
Languages Common, plus one other language
Challenge 8 (3,900 XP)

Unholy Smite. When the fallen paladin hits with a melee weapon attack, it can expend a spell slot to deal additional necrotic damage to the target, in addition to the weapon's damage. The extra damage is 9 (2d8) for a 1st-level spell slot, plus 4 (1d8) for each spell level higher than 1st, to a maximum of 21 (5d8). The damage increases by 4 (1d8) if the target is a celestial.

Unholy Resilience. The fallen paladin is immune to disease, and cannot be charmed or frightened. It has a +4 bonus to any saving throw it makes. These benefits cease to function if the fallen paladin is unconscious or slain.

Spellcasting. The fallen paladin is a 12th-level spellcaster. Its spellcasting ability is Charisma (spell save DC 15). It has the following paladin spells prepared.
1st level (4 slots): *bane, divine favor, protection from evil and good, sanctuary, shield of faith*
2nd level (3 slots): *aid, lesser restoration, hold person, silence*
3rd level (3 slots): *bestow curse, dispel magic, protection from energy*

ACTIONS

Multiattack. The fallen paladin makes two Longsword attacks.

Longsword. *Melee Weapon Attack:* +7 to hit, reach 5 ft., one target. *Hit:* 8 (1d8 + 4) slashing damage, or 9 (1d10 + 4) slashing damage if wielded with two hands, plus 4 (1d8) necrotic damage.

Lay of Hands. The fallen paladin has a pool of 60 hit points to use with its Lay on Hands ability. It regains spent hit points from this pool when it takes a long rest. It can use this ability to cause a creature within 5 feet of it or itself to regain any number of hit points, up to its hit point maximum or the fallen paladin's pool of hit points is reduced to 0.

Unholy Weapon (1/short or long rest). The fallen paladin adds +4 to its attack and damage rolls for 1 minute, and its weapon is considered magical for the purposes of damage resistances.

Footman

Medium humanoid (any race), any alignment
Armor Class 15 (studded leather, shield)
Hit Points 38 (7d8 + 7)
Speed 30 ft.

STR	DEX	CON	INT	WIS	CHA
14 (+2)	12 (+1)	12 (+1)	10 (+0)	10 (+0)	10 (+0)

Senses passive Perception 10
Languages Common
Challenge 1 (200 XP)

Multiattack. The footman makes two Spear attacks or two Longsword attacks.

Spear. *Melee or Ranged Weapon Attack:* +4 to hit, reach 5 ft. or range 20/60 ft., one target. *Hit:* 5 (1d6 + 2) piercing damage, or 6 (1d8 + 2) piercing damage if used with two hands.

Longsword. *Melee Weapon Attack:* +4 to hit, reach 5 ft., one target. *Hit:* 6 (1d8 + 2) slashing damage, or 7 (1d10 + 2) piercing damage if used with two hands.

Light Crossbow. *Ranged Weapon Attack:* +3 to hit, range 80/320 ft., one target. *Hit:* 5 (1d8 + 1) piercing damage.

Gnomish Engineer

Small humanoid (gnome), neutral
Armor Class 12 (leather)
Hit Points 16 (3d8 + 3)
Speed 25 ft.

STR	DEX	CON	INT	WIS	CHA
9 (–1)	13 (+1)	12 (+1)	15 (+2)	12 (+1)	10 (+0)

Saving Throws Int +4, Wis +3
Skills Arcana +6, Nature +4, Survival +3
Senses darkvision 60 ft., passive Perception 11
Languages Common, Gnomish, Ignan
Challenge 1/2 (100 XP)

Gnome Cunning. The gnomish engineer has advantage on Intelligence, Wisdom, and Charisma saving throws against magic.

Spellcasting. The gnomish engineer is a 2nd-level spellcaster. Its spellcasting ability is Intelligence (spell save DC 12, +4 to hit with spell attacks). It has the following wizard spells prepared.

> Cantrips (at will): *fire bolt, mending, prestidigitation*
> 1st level (3 slots): *burning hands, detect magic, identify, magic missile*

Tinker. The gnomish engineers add twice their proficiency bonus to any ability check made with tinker's tools.

ACTIONS

Light Hammer. *Melee or Ranged Weapon Attack:* +1 to hit, reach 5 ft. or range 20/60 ft., one target. *Hit:* 1 (1d4 – 1) bludgeoning damage.

Grand Master Assassin

Medium humanoid (any race), any alignment
Armor Class 17 (studded leather)
Hit Points 104 (16d8 + 32)
Speed 35 ft.

STR	DEX	CON	INT	WIS	CHA
13 (+1)	20 (+5)	15 (+2)	15 (+2)	16 (+3)	16 (+3)

Saving Throws Dex +9, Int +6, Wis +7
Skills Athletics +5, Acrobatics +10, Deception +7, Insight +7, Investigation +6, Perception +11, Sleight of Hand +9, Stealth +13
Senses blindsight 10 ft., passive Perception 21
Languages Thieves' Cant plus any three languages
Challenge 14 (11,500 XP)

Assassinate. During its first turn, the grand master assassin has advantage on attack rolls against any creature that hasn't yet acted in the combat. Any hit the grand master assassin scores against a surprised creature counts as a critical hit.

Cunning Action. On each of its turns, the grand master assassin can use a bonus action to take the Dash, Disengage, or Hide action.

Evasion. If the grand master assassin is subjected to an effect that allows it to make a Dexterity saving throw to take only half damage, the grand master assassin instead takes no damage if it succeeds on the saving throw, and only half damage if it fails.

Practiced Impersonator. The grand master assassin has advantage on any Intelligence ability check to disguise themselves.

Sneak Attack (1/turn). Once per turn, the grand master assassin deals an extra 31 (9d6) damage when it hits a target with a weapon attack and has advantage on the attack roll, or when the target is within 5 feet of an ally of the grand master assassin that isn't incapacitated and the grand master assassin doesn't have disadvantage on the attack roll.

ACTIONS

Multiattack. The grand master assassin makes two Rapier attacks or two Dagger attacks.

Dagger. *Melee or Ranged Weapon Attack:* +9 to hit, reach 5 ft. or range 20/60 ft., one target. *Hit:* 7 (1d4 + 5) piercing damage.

Shortsword. *Melee Weapon Attack:* +9 to hit, reach 5 ft., one target. *Hit:* 8 (1d6 + 5) piercing damage.

Light Crossbow. *Ranged Weapon Attack:* +9 to hit, range 80/320 ft., one target. *Hit:* 9 (1d8 + 5) piercing damage.

LEGENDARY ACTIONS

The grand master assassin can take 3 legendary actions, choosing from the options below. Only one legendary action option can be used at a time and only at the end of another creature's turn. The grand master assassin regains spent legendary actions at the start of its turn.

Grasp the Advantage. The grand master assassin makes one rapier or dagger attack on a creature within range that has made an attack this round.

Poison Weapon (costs 2 actions). The next melee or ranged weapon attack the grand master assassin makes is poisoned, and the target that takes damage from it must make a DC 15 Constitution saving throw. On a failed saving throw, the target takes 24 (7d6) poison damage, or half as much damage on a successful saving throw.

Hired Thug

Medium humanoid (any race), any alignment
Armor Class 13 (leather)
Hit Points 18 (4d8)
Speed 30 ft.

STR	DEX	CON	INT	WIS	CHA
12 (+1)	14 (+2)	11 (+0)	10 (+0)	13 (+1)	13 (+1)

Skills Deception +3, Perception +3, Stealth +6
Senses passive Perception 13
Languages Thieves' cant plus any one language
Challenge 2 (450 XP)

Cunning Action. On each of its turns, the hired thug can use a bonus action to take the Dash, Disengage, or Hide action.

Sneak Attack (1/turn). Once per turn, the hired thug deals an extra 7 (2d6) damage when it hits a target with a weapon attack and has advantage on the attack roll, or when the target is within 5 feet of an ally of the hired thug that isn't incapacitated and the hired thug doesn't have disadvantage on the attack roll.

ACTIONS

Dagger. *Melee or Ranged Weapon Attack:* +4 to hit, reach 5 ft. or range 20/60 ft., one target. *Hit:* 1d4 + 2 piercing damage.

Shortsword. *Melee Weapon Attack:* +4 to hit, reach 5 ft., one target. *Hit:* 5 (1d6 + 2) piercing damage.

Hoplite

Medium humanoid (human), any lawful alignment

The hoplite uses the statistics of the **scout** except that it has AC 18 (breastplate and shield), STR 14, and has a spear or javelin instead of a longbow. Its Spear or Javelin attack is as below:

Spear. *Melee or Ranged Weapon Attack:* +4 to hit, reach 5 ft. and range 20/60 ft., one target. *Hit:* 7 (1d6 + 4) piercing damage, or 8 (1d8 + 4) piercing damage if used with two hands to make a melee attack.

Javelin. *Melee or Ranged Weapon Attack:* +4 to hit, reach 5 ft. and range 30/120 ft., one target. *Hit:* 7 (1d6 + 4) piercing damage.

Hierophant

Medium humanoid (any race), any alignment
Armor Class 16 (hide armour, shield)
Hit Points 132 (24d8 + 24)
Speed 30 ft.

STR	DEX	CON	INT	WIS	CHA
10 (+4)	14 (+2)	12 (+1)	12 (+1)	20 (+5)	11 (+0)

Saving Throws Int +5, Wis +9
Skills Medicine +9, Nature +5, Perception +9
Senses passive Perception 19
Languages Druidic plus any two languages
Challenge 12 (8,400 XP)

Spellcasting. The hierophant is an 18th-level spellcaster. Its spellcasting ability is Wisdom (spell save DC 17, +9 to hit with spell attacks). It has the following druid spells prepared:

Cantrips (at will): *druidcraft, mending, poison spray, produce flame*
1st level (4 slots): *cure wounds, entangle. faerie fire, speak with animals*
2nd level (3 slots): *animal messenger, beast sense, hold person*
3rd level (3 slots): *conjure animals, meld into stone, water breathing*
4th level (3 slots): *dominate beast, locate creature, stoneskin, wall of fire*
5th level (3 slots): *commune with nature, mass cure wounds, tree stride*
6th level (1 slot): *heal, heroes' feast, sunbeam*
7th level (1 slot): *fire storm*
8th level (1 slot): *animal shapes*

ACTIONS

Scimitar. *Melee Weapon Attack:* +6 to hit, reach 5 ft., one target. *Hit:* 5 (1d6 + 2) slashing damage.

Change Shape (2/day). The hierophant magically polymorphs into a beast or elemental with a challenge rating of 6 or less, and can remain in this form for up to 9 hours. The hierophant can choose whether its equipment falls to the ground, melds with its new form, or is worn by the new form. The hierophant reverts to its true form if it dies or falls unconscious. The hierophant can revert to its true form using a bonus action on its turn.

While in a new form, the hierophant retains its game statistics and ability to speak, but its AC, movement modes, Strength, and Dexterity are replaced by those of the new form, and it gains any special senses, proficiencies, traits, actions, and reactions (except class features, legendary actions, and lair actions) that the new form has but that it lacks. It can cast its spells with verbal or somatic components in its new form. The new form's attacks count as magical for the purpose of overcoming resistances and immunity to nonmagical attacks.

Holy Knight

Medium humanoid (any), any alignment
Armor Class 20 (plate, shield)
Hit Points 65 (10d8 + 20)
Speed 30 ft.

STR	DEX	CON	INT	WIS	CHA
16 (+3)	11 (+0)	14 (+2)	11 (+0)	11 (+0)	15 (+2)

Saving Throws Wis +2, Cha +4
Skills Insight +2, Religion +2
Senses passive Perception 10
Languages Common, plus one other language
Challenge 4 (1,100 XP)

Divine Blessings. The holy knight has advantage on saving throws against being frightened, and is immune to disease.

Divine Smite. When the holy knight hits with a melee weapon attack, it can expend a spell slot to deal additional radiant damage to the target, in addition to the weapon's damage. The extra damage is 9 (2d8) for a 1st-level spell slot, plus 4 (1d8) for each spell level higher than 1st, to a maximum of 21 (5d8). The damage increases by 4 (1d8) if the target is a fiend or undead.

Spellcasting. The holy knight is a 5th-level spellcaster. Its spellcasting ability is Charisma (spell save DC 12). It has the following paladin spells.

1st level (4 slots): *bless, divine favor, protection from evil and good, sanctuary, shield of faith*
2nd level (2 slots): *aid, lesser restoration, protection from poison, zone of truth*

ACTIONS

Multiattack. The holy knight makes two Longsword attacks.

Longsword. *Melee Weapon Attack:* +5 to hit, reach 5 ft., one target. *Hit:* 7 (1d8 + 3) slashing damage, or 8 (1d10 + 3) slashing damage if used with two hands to make a melee attack.

Lay on Hands. The holy knight has a pool of 25 hit points to use with its Lay on Hands ability. It regains spent hit points from this pool when it takes a long rest. It can use this ability to cause a creature within 5 feet of it or itself to regain any number of hit points, up to its hit point maximum or its pool of hit points is reduced to 0.

Housebreaker

Medium humanoid (any), any alignment
Armor Class 16 (studded leather)
Hit Points 66 (12d8 + 12)
Speed 30 ft., climb 30 ft.

STR	DEX	CON	INT	WIS	CHA
11 (+0)	18 (+4)	13 (+1)	15 (+2)	16 (+3)	15 (+2)

Saving Throws Dex +7, Int +5
Skills Acrobatics +7, Athletics +3, Deception +6, Perception +6, Sleight of Hand +10, Stealth +10
Senses passive Perception 16
Languages Thieves' cant, plus any two languages
Challenge 7 (2,900 XP)

Cunning Action. The housebreaker can use a bonus action on its turn to take the Dash, Disengage, Hide action, or Use an Object action.

Daggermaster. The housebreaker deals an additional die of damage when attacking with daggers, and doubles both the short and long ranges of a thrown dagger (included in the attack).

Evasion. When the housebreaker is subjected to an effect that allows it to make a Dexterity saving throw to take only half damage, it instead takes no damage if the saving throw is successful, and only half damage if the roll is a failure.

Sneak Attack. Once per turn, the housebreaker can deal an extra 21 (6d6) damage to one creature it hits with an attack if it has advantage on the attack roll. The attack must use a finesse or ranged weapon. The housebreaker doesn't need advantage on the attack roll if another enemy of the target is within 5 feet of it, that enemy isn't incapacitated, and the housebreaker doesn't have disadvantage on the attack roll.

Actions

Multiattack. The housebreaker uses its Dagger Flourish and makes three Dagger attacks, or makes two Shortsword attacks.

Dagger. *Melee or Ranged Weapon Attack:* +7 to hit, reach 5 ft. or range 60/120 ft., one target. *Hit:* 9 (2d4 + 4) piercing damage.

Shortsword. *Melee Weapon Attack:* +7 to hit, reach 5 ft., one target. *Hit:* 7 (1d6 + 4) piercing damage.

Dagger Flourish. One creature that is wielding a weapon within 5 feet of the housebreaker must make a DC 15 Strength saving throw. On a failed saving throw, all the attacks the housebreaker makes against the target until the end of its turn have advantage. In addition, the housebreaker can choose to apply one of the following effects to the target:

Blinding Strike. The target has disadvantage on attack rolls it makes until the end of its next turn.

Confounding Blades. The target can't take reactions until the start of the target's next turn.

Sneaky Maneuver. The target is pushed 5 feet away from the housebreaker.

Reactions

Uncanny Dodge. The housebreaker halves the damage that it takes from one attack that hits it. The housebreaker must be able to see the attacker to use this ability.

Illusionist

Medium humanoid (any), any
Armor Class 12
Hit Points 22 (5d8)
Speed 30 ft.

STR	DEX	CON	INT	WIS	CHA
14 (+2)	15 (+2)	11 (+0)	17 (+3)	13 (+1)	15 (+2)

Saving Throws Int +5, Wis +3
Skills History +5, Performance +4, Persuasion +4
Senses passive Perception 11
Languages Common
Challenge 3 (700 XP)

Spellcasting. The illusionist is a 5th-level spellcaster. Its spellcasting ability is Intelligence (spell save DC 13, +5 to hit with spell attacks). It has the following wizard spells prepared:

Cantrips (at will): *chill touch, dancing lights, minor illusion, prestidigitation*
1st level (4 slots): *disguise self, silent image, sleep*
2nd level (3 slots): *invisibility, mirror image, phantasmal force*
3rd level (2 slots): *hypnotic pattern, major image*

Actions

Dagger. *Melee Weapon Attack:* +4 to hit, reach 5 ft., one target. *Hit:* 4 (1d4 + 2) piercing damage.

Imam of Fire

Medium humanoid (human), chaotic neutral
Armor Class 14 (leather armor)
Hit Points 26 (4d8+8)
Speed 30 ft.

STR	DEX	CON	INT	WIS	CHA
12 (+1)	15 (+2)	14 (+2)	10 (+0)	16 (+3)	13 (+1)

Damage Resistances fire
Saving Throws Int +2, Wis +5
Skills Deception +3, Persuasion +3, Religion +5
Senses passive Perception 13
Languages Common
Challenge 3 (700 XP)

Spellcasting. The imam is a 3rd-level spellcaster. Its spellcasting ability is Wisdom (spell save DC 13, +5 to hit with spell attacks). It has the following cleric spells prepared:

Cantrips (at will): *fire bolt, light, thaumaturgy*
1st level (4 slots): *burning hands, command, cure wounds, shield of faith*
2nd level (2 slots): *hold person, scorching ray*

Actions

Quarterstaff. *Melee Weapon Attack:* +3 to hit, reach 5 ft., one target. *Hit:* 4 (1d6 + 1) bludgeoning damage.

Incantor

Medium humanoid (any), any alignment
Armor Class 13 (16 with *mage armor*)
Hit Points 91 (14d8 + 28)
Speed 30 ft.

STR	DEX	CON	INT	WIS	CHA
10 (+0)	16 (+3)	14 (+2)	20 (+5)	15 (+2)	14 (+2)

Saving Throws Int +9, Wis +6
Skills Arcana +13, Nature +9, Perception +6
Senses darkvision 120 ft., passive Perception 16
Languages Common, Elvish, Ignan, Undercommon
Challenge 9 (5,900 XP)

Dual Enchantment. If the incantor casts an enchantment spell that would normally target one creature, it can have it target two.

Redirect (recharge 4–6). When a creature within 40 feet of the incantor attacks it, it can use its reaction to redirect the attack. The attacking creature must succeed on a DC 17 Wisdom saving throw or target another creature of the incantor's choice within range of the attack. Creatures that can't be charmed are immune to this effect.

Spellcasting. The incantor is a 14th level spellcaster. The incantor's spellcasting ability is Intelligence (spell save DC 17, +9 to hit with spell attacks). It has the following spells prepared:

Cantrips (at will): *dancing lights, fire bolt, mage hand, poison spray, prestidigitation*
1st level (4 slots): *mage armor, enlarge/reduce, hideous laughter, magic missile, sleep*
2nd level (3 slots): *arcane lock, hold person, mirror image, suggestion*
3rd level (3 slots): *counterspell, glyph of warding, sleet storm*
4th level (3 slots): *confusion, fire shield, greater invisibility*
5th level (2 slots): *dispel evil and good, dominate person, flame strike, passwall*
6th level (1 slot): *disintegrate, mass suggestion*
7th level (1 slot): *forcecage*

Sunlight Sensitivity. While in sunlight, the incantor has disadvantage on attack rolls, as well as on Wisdom (Perception) checks that rely on sight.

Actions

Dagger. *Melee Weapon Attack:* +7 to hit, reach 5 ft., one target. *Hit:* 6 (1d4 + 3) piercing damage.

Hand Crossbow. *Ranged Weapon Attack* +7 to hit, range 30/120 ft., one target. *Hit:* 6 (1d6 + 3) piercing damage, and the target must succeed on a DC 13 Constitution saving throw or be poisoned for 1 hour. If the saving throw fails by 5 or more, the target is also unconscious while poisoned in this way. The target wakes up if it takes damage or if another creature takes an action to shake it awake.

Bonus Actions

Hypnosis. The incantor uses its charming voice to hypnotize one creature within 15 feet of it who can hear and understand it. The creature must succeed on a DC 17 Wisdom saving throw or be charmed until the end of the incantor's next turn. A hypnotized creature is incapacitated and does nothing but gaze at the incantor. The effect ends for a hypnotized creature if that creature takes damage or is more than 15 feet from the incantor.

Infiltrator

Medium humanoid (any), any alignment
Armor Class 17 (studded leather)
Hit Points 82 (15d8 + 15)
Speed 30 ft., climb 30 ft.

STR	DEX	CON	INT	WIS	CHA
11 (+0)	20 (+5)	13 (+1)	15 (+2)	16 (+3)	15 (+2)

Saving Throws Dex +9, Int +7, Wis +8
Skills Acrobatics +9, Athletics +4, Deception +6, Perception +7, Sleight of Hand +13, Stealth +13
Senses blindsight 10 ft., passive Perception 17
Languages Thieves' cant, plus any two languages
Challenge 9 (5,000 XP)

Cunning Action. The infiltrator can use a bonus action on its turn to take the Dash, Disengage, Hide, or Use an Object action.

Daggermaster. The infiltrator deals an additional die of damage when attacking with daggers, and doubles both the short and long ranges of a thrown dagger (included in the attack).

Evasion. When the infiltrator is subjected to an effect that allows it to make a Dexterity saving throw to take only half damage, it instead takes no damage if the saving throw is successful, and only half damage if the roll is a failure.

Sneak Attack. Once per turn, the infiltrator can deal an extra 28 (8d6) damage to one creature it hits with an attack if it has advantage on the attack roll. The attack must use a finesse or ranged weapon. The infiltrator doesn't need advantage on the attack roll if another enemy of the target is within 5 feet of it, that enemy isn't incapacitated, and the infiltrator doesn't have disadvantage on the attack roll.

Actions

Multiattack. The infiltrator uses its Dagger Flourish and makes three Dagger attacks, or two Shortsword attacks.

Dagger. *Melee or Ranged Weapon Attack:* +9 to hit, reach 5 ft. or range 60/120 ft., one target. *Hit:* 10 (2d4 + 5) piercing damage.

Shortsword. *Melee Weapon Attack:* +9 to hit, reach 5 ft., one target. *Hit:* 8 (1d6 + 5) piercing damage.

Dagger Flourish. One creature that is wielding a weapon within 5 feet of the infiltrator must make a DC 17 Strength saving throw. On a failed saving throw, all the attacks the infiltrator makes against the target until the end of its turn have advantage. In addition, the infiltrator can choose to apply one of the following effects to the target:

Blinding Strike. The target has disadvantage on attack rolls it makes until the end of its next turn.

Confounding Blades. The target can't take reactions until the start of the target's next turn.

Sneaky Maneuver. The target is pushed 5 feet away from the infiltrator.

Reactions

Uncanny Dodge. The infiltrator halves the damage that it takes from one attack that hits it. The infiltrator must be able to see the attacker to use this ability.

Khalit Jinn

Medium humanoid (khalit jinn), lawful evil
Armor Class 16 (breastplate)
Hit Points 33 (6d8 + 6)

Speed 30 ft.

STR	DEX	CON	INT	WIS	CHA
13 (+1)	14 (+2)	12 (+1)	10 (+0)	13 (+1)	14 (+2)

Skills Deception +4, Persuasion +4, Religion +3, Survival +3
Damage Resistances fire
Senses passive Perception 11
Languages Common, Ignan
Challenge 2 (450 XP)

Special Equipment. The khalit jinn that serve within the Brazen Spire carry a *+1 scimitar*, a *potion of healing*, and wear a *lesser brazen amulet*[2].
Dark Devotion. The khalit jinn has advantage on saving throws against being charmed or frightened.
Spellcasting. The khalit jinn is a 4th-level spellcaster. Its spellcasting ability is Wisdom (spell save DC 11, +3 to hit with spell attacks). The khalit jinn has the following cleric spells prepared:

> Cantrips (at will): *light, fire bolt, thaumaturgy*
> 1st level (4 slots): *burning hands, command, shield of faith*
> 2nd level (3 slots): *hold person, spiritual weapon*

ACTIONS

Multiattack. The khalit jinn makes two Scimitar attacks.
Scimitar. *Melee Weapon Attack:* +5 to hit, reach 5 ft., one target. *Hit:* 6 (1d6 + 3) slashing damage.

Khalit Jinn Officer

Medium humanoid (khalit jinn), lawful evil
Armor Class 16 (breastplate)
Hit Points 58 (9d8 + 18)
Speed 30 ft.

STR	DEX	CON	INT	WIS	CHA
13 (+1)	14 (+2)	14 (+2)	10 (+0)	13 (+1)	14 (+2)

Skills Deception +5, Persuasion +5, Religion +4, Survival +4
Damage Resistances fire
Senses passive Perception 11
Languages Common, Ignan
Challenge 5 (1,800 XP)

Special Equipment. The khalit jinn officer that serve within the Brazen Spire carry a *+1 scimitar*, a *potion of healing*, and wear a *lesser brazen amulet*[2].
Dark Devotion. The khalit jinn officer has advantage on saving throws against being charmed or frightened.
Spellcasting. The khalit jinn officer is a 6th-level spellcaster. Its spellcasting ability is Wisdom (spell save DC 12, +4 to hit with spell attacks). The khalit jinn officer has the following cleric spells prepared:

> Cantrips (at will): *light, fire bolt, thaumaturgy*
> 1st level (4 slots): *burning hands, command, shield of faith*
> 2nd level (3 slots): *hold person, spiritual weapon*
> 3rd level (3 slots): *dispel magic, fireball, spirit guardians*

ACTIONS

Multiattack. The khalit jinn officer makes two Scimitar attacks.
Scimitar. *Melee Weapon Attack:* +6 to hit, reach 5 ft., one target. *Hit:* 6 (1d6 + 3) slashing damage.
Longbow. *Ranged Weapon Attack:* +5 to hit, range 150/600 ft., one target. *Hit:* 6 (1d8 + 2) piercing damage.

Killer

Medium humanoid (any race), any alignment
Armor Class 15 (studded leather)
Hit Points 38 (7d8 + 7)
Speed 30 ft.

STR	DEX	CON	INT	WIS	CHA
12 (+1)	16 (+3)	12 (+1)	13 (+1)	14 (+2)	13 (+1)

Saving Throws Dex +6, Int +4
Skills Athletics +4, Acrobatics +9, Deception +4, Perception +4, Stealth +9
Senses passive Perception 14
Languages Thieves' cant plus any two languages
Challenge 5 (1,800 XP)

Assassinate. During its first turn, the killer has advantage on attack rolls against any creature that hasn't yet acted in the combat. Any hit the killer scores against a surprised creature counts as a critical hit.
Cunning Action. On each of its turns, the killer can use a bonus action to take the Dash, Disengage, or Hide action.
Sneak Attack (1/turn). Once per turn, the killer deals an extra 17 (5d6) damage when it hits a target with a weapon attack and has advantage on the attack roll, or when the target is within 5 feet of an ally of the killer that isn't incapacitated and the killer doesn't have disadvantage on the attack roll.

ACTIONS

Multiattack. The killer makes two Dagger or two Shortsword attacks.
Dagger. *Melee or Ranged Weapon Attack:* +6 to hit, reach 5 ft. or range 20/60 ft., one target. *Hit:* 5 (1d4 + 3) piercing damage.
Shortsword. *Melee Weapon Attack:* +6 to hit, reach 5 ft., one target. *Hit:* 6 (1d6 + 3) piercing damage.

Knave Adept

Medium humanoid (any), any alignment
Armor Class 16 (studded leather)
Hit Points 66 (12d8 + 12)
Speed 30 ft.

STR	DEX	CON	INT	WIS	CHA
11 (+0)	18 (+4)	13 (+1)	18 (+4)	16 (+3)	15 (+2)

Saving Throws Dex +7, Int +7
Skills Acrobatics +7, Arcana +7, Athletics +3, Perception +6, Sleight of Hand +10, Stealth +10
Senses passive Perception 16
Languages Thieves' cant, plus any two languages
Challenge 8 (3,900 XP)

Adept's Legerdemain. The knave adept can summon a magical dagger, rapier, or shortsword, or a set of thieves' tools, as a bonus action on its turn. They count as magical for the purposes of damage resistances and immunities. The items disappear after 1 minute. In addition, the knave adept can expend a spell slot when conjuring a weapon. When it does so, the weapon deals an additional 3 (1d6) damage for a 1st level spell slot, plus 3 (1d6) for each additional spell slot level above 1st, until the weapon is dismissed.
Cunning Action. The knave adept can use a bonus action on its turn to take the Dash, Disengage, or Hide action.

Evasion. When the knave adept is subjected to an effect that allows it to make a Dexterity saving throw to take only half damage, it instead takes no damage if the saving throw is successful, and only half damage if the roll is a failure.

Sneak Attack. Once per turn, the knave adept can deal an extra 21 (6d6) damage to one creature it hits with an attack if it has advantage on the attack roll. The attack must use a finesse or ranged weapon. The knave adept doesn't need advantage on the attack roll if another enemy of the target is within 5 feet of it, that enemy isn't incapacitated, and the knave adept doesn't have disadvantage on the attack roll.

Spellcasting. The knave adept is a 12th-level spellcaster. Its spellcasting ability is Intelligence (spell save DC 15, +7 to hit with spell attacks). It knows the following wizard spells.

Cantrips (at will): *acid splash, mage hand, minor illusion, prestidigitation*
1st level (4 slots): *color spray, detect magic, feather fall, identify*
2nd level (3 slots): *blur, knock, invisibility*

ACTIONS

Multiattack. The knave adept makes two Dagger, Rapier, or Shortsword attacks.

Dagger. +7 to hit, reach 5 ft. or range 20/60 ft., one target. *Hit:* 6 (1d4 + 4) piercing damage.

Rapier. +7 to hit, reach 5 ft., one target. *Hit:* 8 (1d8 + 4) piercing damage.

Shortsword. +7 to hit, reach 5 ft., one target. *Hit:* 7 (1d6 + 4) piercing damage.

REACTIONS

Uncanny Dodge. The knave adept halves the damage that it takes from one attack that hits it. The knave adept must be able to see the attacker to use this ability.

Lotus Eater

Medium humanoid (human) chaotic evil
Armor Class 16 (studded leather, shield)
Hit Points 112 (15d8 + 45)
Speed 30 ft.

STR	DEX	CON	INT	WIS	CHA
18 (+4)	15 (+2)	16 (+3)	10 (+0)	12 (+1)	15 (+2)

Condition Immunities frightened
Saving Throws Str +7, Dex +5, Con +6
Skills Athletics +10, Intimidation +5
Senses passive Perception 11
Languages any one language (usually Common)
Challenge 5 (1,800 XP)

Hard to Kill (recharges on a long rest). If damage reduces the lotus eater to 0 hit points, the lotus eater drops to 1 hit point instead.

ACTIONS

Multiattack. The Lotus Eater makes three melee attacks or two ranged attacks.

Spear. Melee or Ranged Weapon Attack: +7 to hit, reach 5 ft. and range 20/60 ft., one target. *Hit:* 11 (2d6 + 4) piercing damage, or 13 (2d8 + 4) piercing damage if used with two hands to make a melee attack.

Longsword. Melee Weapon Attack: +7 to hit, reach 5 ft., one creature. *Hit:* 8 (1d8 + 4) slsahing damage.

Madman

Medium humanoid (any race), chaotic evil
Armor Class 14 (hide)
Hit Points 95 (10d8 + 50)
Speed 40 ft.

STR	DEX	CON	INT	WIS	CHA
26 (+8)	16 (+3)	20 (+5)	5 (–3)	5 (–3)	10 (+0)

Skills Athletics +11
Damage Immunities psychic
Condition Immunities charmed, frightened
Senses passive Perception 7
Languages Common
Challenge 5 (1,800 XP)

Brute. A melee weapon deals one extra die of its damage when A madman hits with it (included in the attack).

Insane. A madman is immune to all spells and magical effects that impact the mind.

Reckless. At the start of his turn, A madman can gain advantage on all melee weapon attack rolls during that turn, but attack rolls against him have advantage until the start of his next turn.

ACTIONS

Multiattack. A madman makes two melee attacks.

Greatclub. Melee Weapon Attack: +11 to hit, reach 5 ft., one target. *Hit:* 17 (2d8 + 8) bludgeoning damage.

Magician

Medium humanoid (any), any alignment
Armor Class 13 (16 with *mage armor*)
Hit Points 32 (5d8 + 10)
Speed 30 ft.

STR	DEX	CON	INT	WIS	CHA
10 (+0)	16 (+3)	14 (+2)	19 (+4)	15 (+2)	11 (+0)

Saving Throws Int +7, Wis +5
Skills Arcana +7, History +7
Senses passive Perception 12
Languages Common
Challenge 5 (1,800 XP)

Spellcasting. The theurgist is a 3rd level spellcaster. The theurgist's spellcasting ability is Intelligence (spell save DC 14, +6 to hit with spell attacks). It has the following spells prepared:

Cantrips (at will): *fire bolt, light, mage hand, prestidigitation*
1st level (4 slots): *burning hands, false life, mage armor, magic missile*
2nd level (3 slots): *acid arrow, mirror image, scorching ray*
3rd level (2 slots): *fireball, lightning bolt*

ACTIONS

Dagger. Melee Weapon Attack: +6 to hit, reach 5 ft., one target. *Hit:* 5 (1d4 + 3) piercing damage.

Sling. Ranged Weapon Attack: +6 to hit, range 30/120 ft., one target. *Hit:* 5 (1d4 + 3) bludgeoning damage.

Master Bard

Medium humanoid (any race), any alignment
Armor Class 18 (studded leather)
Hit Points 195 (26d8 + 78)
Speed 30 ft.

STR	DEX	CON	INT	WIS	CHA
13 (+1)	22 (+6)	17 (+3)	15 (+2)	14 (+2)	23 (+6)

Saving Throws Dex +11, Con +8, Cha +11
Skills Acrobatics +11, Arcana +7, Perception +7, Performance +16
Condition Immunities deafened
Senses passive Perception 17
Languages any three languages
Challenge 16 (15,000 XP)

Legendary Resistance (3/day). If the master bard fails a saving throw, it can choose to succeed instead.

Spellcasting. The master bard is an 18th-level spellcaster. Its spellcasting ability is Charisma (spell save DC 19, +11 to hit with spell attacks). It has the following bard spells prepared:

> Cantrips (at will): blade ward, light, prestidigitation, vicious mockery
> 1st level (4 slots): dissonant whispers, faerie fire, heroism, hideous laughter, sleep
> 2nd level (3 slots): detect thoughts, enthrall, hold person, shatter, suggestion
> 3rd level (3 slots): bestow curse, clairvoyance, dispel magic, sending
> 4th level (3 slots): compulsion, confusion, freedom of movement, greater invisibility
> 5th level (3 slots): dominate person, hold monster, seeming
> 6th level (1 slot): irresistible dance
> 7th level (1 slot): teleport
> 8th level (1 slot): power word stun
> 9th level (1 slot): foresight

ACTIONS

Multiattack. The master bard makes two Bow Strike attacks or two Prestissimo attacks.

Bow Strike. *Melee Weapon Attack:* +11 to hit, reach 5 ft., one target. *Hit:* 9 (1d6 + 6) slashing damage plus 21 (6d6) force damage.

Prestissimo. *Ranged Spell Attack:* +11 to hit, range 120 ft., one target. *Hit:* 31 (7d8) psychic damage.

Adagio (recharge 6). The master bard launches a slow, expressive refrain at one target within 30 feet. The target regains 18 (4d8) hit points and is cured of the charmed, deafened, and frightened conditions.

REACTIONS

Discordant Note. When a spell with a verbal component is cast within 30 feet of the master bard, the master bard unleashes a single, unnerving note to counter the spell. This works like the *counterspell* spell with a +6 spellcasting ability check.

LEGENDARY ACTIONS

The master bard can take 3 legendary actions, choosing from the options below. Only one legendary action can be used at a time and only at the end of another creature's turn. The master bard regains spent legendary actions at the start of its turn.

Cantrip. The master bard casts one cantrip.

Move. The master bard moves up to its speed without provoking opportunity attacks.

Jubilant Aria (costs 2 actions). The master bard sings a joyful tune. Each of the master bard's allies within 15 feet of it that can hear it has advantage on its next attack roll, saving throw, or ability check.

Melancholic Aria (costs 2 actions). The master bard sings a solemn melody. Each creature of the master bard's choice within 30 feet of it that can hear it must make a DC 19 Charisma saving throw. On a failure, a creature takes 14 (4d6) psychic damage and falls prone as it weeps with overwhelming despair. On a success, a creature takes half the damage and doesn't fall prone.

Master Illusionist

Medium humanoid (any), any alignment
Armor Class 16 (bracers of greater defense[2])
Hit Points 93 (17d8 + 17)
Speed 30 ft.

STR	DEX	CON	INT	WIS	CHA
12 (+1)	15 (+2)	13 (+1)	20 (+5)	18 (+4)	18 (+4)

Saving Throws Int +11, Wis +10
Skills Arcana +11, Deception +10, History +11, Persuasion +10
Senses darkvision 60 ft., passive Perception 14
Languages Common, Elven
Challenge 17 (18,000 XP)

Spellcasting. The master illusionist is a 17th-level spellcaster. Its spellcasting ability is Intelligence (spell save DC 19, +11 to hit with spell attacks). It has the following wizard spells prepared:

> Cantrips (at will): *dancing lights, fire bolt, mage hand, minor illusion, prestidigitation*
> 1st level (4 slots): *disguise self, illusory script, magic missile, silent image*
> 2nd level (3 slots): *invisibility, mirror image, phantasmal force*
> 3rd level (3 slots): *hypnotic pattern, major image, phantom steed*
> 4th level (3 slots): *dimension door, greater invisibility, phantasmal killer*
> 5th level (2 slots): *dominate person, mislead, seeming*
> 6th level (1 slot): *mass suggestion, programmed illusion*
> 7th level (1 slot): *prismatic spray, project image*
> 8th level (1 slot): *maze*
> 9th level (1 slot): *weird*

Displacement (recharges after the master illusionist casts an illusion spell of 1st level or higher). As a bonus action, the master illusionist projects an illusion that makes it appear to be standing in a place a few inches from its actual location, causing any creature to have disadvantage on attack rolls against it. The effect ends if the master illusionist takes damage, is incapacitated, or its speed becomes 0.

Shadow Magic. The master illusionist can weave shadow magic into its illusions to give them a semi-reality. When the master illusionist casts an illusion spell of 1st level or higher, it can choose one inanimate, nonmagical object that is part of the illusion and make that object real. The master illusionist can do this on its turn as a bonus action while the spell is ongoing. The object remains real for 1 minute. The object can't deal damage or otherwise directly harm anyone.

Quarterstaff +3*. Melee Weapon Attack:* +10 to hit, reach 5 ft., one target. *Hit:* 7 (1d6 + 4) bludgeoning damage.

Master Spy

Medium humanoid (any), any alignment
Armor Class 16 (studded leather)
Hit Points 84 (13d8 + 26)
Speed 30 ft.

STR	DEX	CON	INT	WIS	CHA
11 (+0)	18 (+4)	15 (+2)	15 (+2)	13 (+1)	10 (+0)

Saving Throws Dex +7, Int +5
Skills Insight +4, Investigation +5, Perception +4, Sleight of Hand +10, Stealth +10
Senses passive Perception 14
Languages Common, thieves' cant
Challenge 8 (3,900 XP)

Cunning Action. On each of its turns, the master spy can use a bonus action to take the Dash, Disengage, or Hide action.

Evasion. When the master spy is subjected to an effect that allows it to make a Dexterity saving throw to take only half damage, the it instead takes no damage if the save is successful, and only half damage if the roll is a failure.

Martial Advantage. Once per turn, the master spy can deal an extra 10 (3d6) damage to a creature it hits with a weapon attack if that creature is within 5 feet of an ally of the master spy that isn't incapacitated.

ACTIONS

Multiattack. The master spy can make three attacks with either its rapier or its hand crossbow.

Rapier. *Melee Weapon Attack:* +7 to hit, reach 5 ft.; one creature. *Hit:* 8 (1d8 + 4) piercing damage.

Hand Crossbow. *Ranged Weapon Attack:* +7 to hit, range 30/120 ft., one target. *Hit:* 7 (1d6 + 4) piercing damage.

REACTIONS

Parry. The master spy adds 3 to its AC against one melee attack that would hit it. To do so, the master spy must see the attacker and be wielding a melee weapon.

Master Thief

Medium humanoid (any), any alignment
Armor Class 17 (studded leather)
Hit Points 117 (18d8 + 36)
Speed 30 ft., climb 30 ft.

STR	DEX	CON	INT	WIS	CHA
12 (+1)	20 (+5)	14 (+2)	16 (+3)	17 (+3)	15 (+2)

Saving Throws Dex +9, Int +7, Wis +7
Skills Acrobatics +9, Athletics +5, Deception +6, Perception +7, Sleight of Hand +13, Stealth +13
Senses blindsight 10 ft., passive Perception 17
Languages Thieves' cant, plus any two languages
Challenge 11 (7,200 XP)

Cunning Action. The master thief can use a bonus action on its turn to take the Dash, Disengage, Hide, or Use an Object action.

Daggermaster. The master thief deals an additional die of damage when attacking with daggers, and doubles both the short and long ranges of a thrown dagger (included in the attack).

Evasion. When the master thief is subjected to an effect that allows it to make a Dexterity saving throw to take only half damage, it instead takes no damage if the saving throw is successful, and only half damage if the roll is a failure.

Sneak Attack. Once per turn, the master thief can deal an extra 31 (9d6) damage to one creature it hits with an attack if it has advantage on the attack roll. The attack must use a finesse or ranged weapon. The master thief doesn't need advantage on the attack roll if another enemy of the target is within 5 feet of it, that enemy isn't incapacitated, and the master thief doesn't have disadvantage on the attack roll.

ACTIONS

Multiattack. The master thief uses its Dagger Flourish and makes three Dagger attacks, or two Shortsword attacks.

Dagger. *Melee or Ranged Weapon Attack:* +9 to hit, reach 5 ft. or range 60/120 ft., one target. *Hit:* 10 (2d4 + 5) piercing damage.

Shortsword. *Melee Weapon Attack:* +9 to hit, reach 5 ft., one target. *Hit:* 8 (1d6 + 5) piercing damage.

Dagger Flourish. One creature that is wielding a weapon within 5 feet of the master thief must make a DC 17 Strength saving throw. On a failed saving throw, all the attacks the master thief makes against the target until the end of its turn have advantage. In addition, the master thief can choose to apply one of the following effects to the target:

Blinding Strike. The target has disadvantage on attack rolls it makes until the end of its next turn.

Confounding Blades. The target can't take reactions until the start of the target's next turn.

Sneaky Maneuver. The target is pushed 5 feet away from the infiltrator.

REACTIONS

Uncanny Dodge. The master thief halves the damage that it takes from one attack that hits it. The infiltrator must be able to see the attacker to use this ability.

Missionary

Medium humanoid (any race), any alignment
Armor Class 15 (chain shirt)
Hit Points 55 (10d8 + 10)
Speed 30 ft.

STR	DEX	CON	INT	WIS	CHA
10 (+0)	15 (+2)	13 (+1)	10 (+0)	18 (+4)	14 (+2)

Saving Throws Con +3
Skills Medicine +6, Persuasion +6, Religion +2
Senses passive Perception 14
Languages any two languages
Challenge 4 (1,100 XP)

Spellcasting. The missionary is a 6th-level spellcaster. Its spellcasting ability is Wisdom (spell save DC 14, +6 to hit with spell attacks). The missionary has the following cleric spells prepared:

Cantrips (at will): *guidance, light, sacred flame, thaumaturgy*
1st level (4 slots): *bane, bless, command, cure wounds, inflict wounds*

2nd level (3 slots): *calm emotions, hold person*
3rd level (3 slots): *bestow curse, tongues*

Unpopular Words. As a bonus action, the missionary sermonizes. Each creature within 60 feet that can hear the missionary has advantage on attack rolls against the missionary and disadvantage on saving throws against the missionary's enchantment spells until the start of the missionary's next turn.

Worldly Traveler. Difficult terrain made of natural terrain, such as forest or snow, doesn't cost the missionary extra movement.

ACTIONS

Multiattack. The missionary makes three attacks.

Dagger. *Melee or Ranged Weapon Attack:* +4 to hit, reach 5 ft. or range 20/60 ft., one target. *Hit:* 4 (1d4 + 2) piercing damage.

Shortbow. *Ranged Weapon Attack:* +4 to hit, range 80/320 ft., one target. *Hit:* 5 (1d6 + 2) piercing damage.

Convert or Suffer (recharge 5–6). The missionary calls upon its deity's power and commands creatures in a 30-foot cone to convert or suffer the consequences. Each creature in that area must make a DC 14 Wisdom saving throw. On a failure, a creature takes 14 (4d6) thunder damage and is charmed for 1 minute. On a success, a creature takes twice as much damage but is not charmed. A charmed creature can repeat the saving throw at the end of each of its turns, ending the effect on itself on a success.

Myrmidon

Medium humanoid (any race), any alignment
Armor Class 14 (chain shirt)
Hit Points 22 (4d8 + 4)
Speed 30 ft.

STR	DEX	CON	INT	WIS	CHA
13 (+1)	12 (+1)	12 (+1)	14 (+2)	11 (+0)	10 (+0)

Skills Arcana +4, Perception +2
Senses passive Perception 12
Languages Common, plus one other language
Challenge 1/2 (100 XP)

Arcane Strike. When the myrmidon hits with a weapon attack, it can expend a spell slot to cause the weapon attack to deal an additional 11 (2d10) force damage.

Spellcasting. The myrmidon is a 2nd-level spellcaster. Its spellcasting ability is Intelligence (spell save DC 12, +4 to hit with spell attacks). It has the following wizard spells prepared.

Cantrips (at will): *fire bolt, light, ray of frost, shocking grasp*
1st level (3 slots): *burning hands, longstrider, magic missile, shield*

ACTIONS

Longsword. *Melee Weapon Attack:* +3 to hit, reach 5 ft., one target. *Hit:* 5 (1d8 + 1) slashing damage, or 6 (1d10 + 1) slashing damage if used with two hands to make a melee attack.

Orator

Medium humanoid (any), any alignment
Armor Class 13 (leather)
Hit Points 38 (7d8 + 7)
Speed 30 ft.

STR	DEX	CON	INT	WIS	CHA
15 (+2)	14 (+2)	12 (+1)	10 (+0)	14 (+2)	18 (+4)

Saving Throws Dex +5, Cha +7
Skills Acrobatics +5, Perception +5, Performance +10, Persuasion +10
Senses passive Perception 15
Languages Common, plus two more languages
Challenge 5 (1,800 XP)

Spellcasting. The orator is a 7th-level spellcaster. Its spellcasting ability is Charisma (spell save DC 15, +7 to hit with spell attacks). It knows the following bard spells:

Cantrips (at will): *mage hand, message, vicious mockery*
1st level (4 slots): *detect magic, healing word, sleep, thunderwave*
2nd level (3 slots): *blindness/deafness, detect thoughts, heat metal, shatter*
3rd level (3 slots): *dispel magic, hypnotic pattern, lightning bolt, tongues*
4th level (1 slot): *confusion*

ACTIONS

Rapier. *Melee Weapon Attack:* +5 to hit, reach 5 ft., one target. *Hit:* 6 (1d8 + 2) piercing damage.

Hand Crossbow. *Ranged Weapon Attack:* +5 to hit, range 30/120 ft., one target. *Hit:* 5 (1d6 + 2) piercing damage.

REACTIONS

Countercharm. Whenever a creature within 60 feet of the orator fails a saving throw, the orator can use its reaction to allow the creature to reroll that saving throw and add +4 to the new result.

Cutting Words (5/day). The orator chooses one creature it can see within 30 feet who has just rolled an ability check or an attack roll. That creature rolls 1d8 and the orator chooses whether it is added to the result or subtracted from the result.

Paragon Knight

Medium humanoid (human), lawful good
Armor Class 20 (plate armor, shield)
Hit Points 100 (12d8 + 24)
Speed 30 ft.

STR	DEX	CON	INT	WIS	CHA
18 (+4)	12 (+1)	14 (+2)	12 (+1)	16 (+3)	18 (+4)

Saving Throws Wis +6, Cha +7
Skills Athletics +7, Medicine +4, Persuasion +7, Religion +4
Senses passive Perception 13
Languages Common, Celestial
Challenge 8 (3,900 XP)

Divine Aura. The paragon knight or a friendly creature within 10 feet of it cannot be charmed or frightened, and has a +4 bonus to any saving throw it makes. These benefits cease to function is paragon knight is unconscious or slain.

Divine Blessings. The paragon knight is immune to disease.

Divine Smite. When the paragon knight hits with a melee weapon attack, it can expend a spell slot to deal additional radiant damage to the target, in addition to the weapon's damage. The extra damage is 9 (2d8) for a 1st-level spell slot, plus 4 (1d8) for each spell level higher than 1st, to a maximum of 21 (5d8). The damage increases by 4 (1d8) if the target is a fiend or undead.

Spellcasting. The paragon knight is a 12th-level spellcaster. Its spellcasting ability is Charisma (spell save DC 15). It has the following paladin spells prepared.

> 1st level (4 slots): *bless, divine favor, protection from evil and good, sanctuary, shield of faith*
> 2nd level (3 slots): *aid, lesser restoration, magic weapon, zone of truth*
> 3rd level (3 slots): *beacon of hope, daylight, dispel magic, remove curse, revivify*

ACTIONS

Multiattack. The paragon knight makes two Longsword attacks.

Longsword. *Melee Weapon Attack:* +7 to hit, reach 5 ft., one target. *Hit:* 8 (1d8 + 4) slashing damage, or 9 (1d10 + 4) slashing damage if used with two hands to make a melee attack, plus 4 (1d8) radiant damage.

Lay on Hands. The paragon knight has a pool of 60 hit points to use with its lay on hands ability. It regains spent hit points from this pool when it takes a long rest. It can use this ability to cause a creature within 5 feet of it or itself to regain any number of hit points, up to its hit point maximum or the paragon knight's pool of hit points is reduced to 0.

Sacred Weapon (1/short or long rest). The paragon knight adds +4 to hit attack and damage rolls for 1 minute, and its weapon is considered magical for the purposes of damage resistances.

Turn the Unholy (1/short or long rest). Each fiend or undead that can see or hear the paragon knight within 30 feet of the knight must make a DC 15 Wisdom saving throw. On a failed saving throw, it is turned for 1 minute. While turned, the creature must use its turns trying to move as far away from the paragon knight as it can, and it can't willingly move into a space within 30 feet of the knight. It cannot take reactions, and can only take the Dash action, or try to escape from an effect that prevents it from moving.

Performer

Medium humanoid (any race), any alignment
Armor Class 16 (studded leather)
Hit Points 78 (12d8 + 24)
Speed 30 ft.

STR	DEX	CON	INT	WIS	CHA
12 (+1)	19 (+4)	15 (+2)	11 (+0)	14 (+2)	20 (+5)

Saving Throws Dex +7, Cha +8
Skills Deception +8, Performance +11, Persuasion +8
Condition Immunities charmed
Senses passive Perception 12
Languages any two languages
Challenge 8 (3,900 XP)

Martial Dancer. Once per turn, when the performer makes an attack with its Runed Scarf and hits, it can attempt to trip its target. The target must succeed on a DC 15 Dexterity saving throw or be knocked prone.

Soothing Song (2/day). As a bonus action, the performer sings a soft, soothing melody. Each of the performer's allies within 15 feet of the performer regains 5 (2d4) hit points and is cured of the charmed and frightened conditions.

Spellcasting. The performer is a 10th-level spellcaster. Its spellcasting ability is Charisma (spell save DC 16, +8 to hit with spell attacks). It has the following bard spells prepared:

> Cantrips (at will): *friends, light, minor illusion, prestidigitation*
> 1st level (4 slots): *disguise self, heroism, hideous laughter, silent image*
> 2nd level (3 slots): *calm emotions, detect thoughts, silence*
> 3rd level (3 slots): *hypnotic pattern, major image, tongues*
> 4th level (3 slots): *compulsion, dimension door, freedom of movement*
> 5th level (2 slots): *dominate person, mislead*

ACTIONS

Multiattack. The performer makes three Runed Scarf attacks.

Runed Scarf. *Melee Weapon Attack:* +7 to hit, reach 10 ft., one target. *Hit:* 7 (1d6 + 4) slashing damage plus 10 (3d6) fire damage.

Dazzling Dance (recharge 5–6). The performer dances hypnotically, enchanting creatures within 30 feet. Each creature in that area must succeed on a DC 16 Charisma saving throw or be charmed for 1 minute. While charmed, a creature is restrained and must continue watching the performer. A creature can repeat the saving throw at the end of each of its turns, ending the effect on itself on a success. If the charmed creature takes damage from one of the performer's allies, it has advantage on the next saving throw. The effect also ends if the charmed creature can't see the performer.

Preacher

Medium humanoid (any race), any alignment
Armor Class 16 (chain shirt, shield)
Hit Points 78 (12d8 + 24)
Speed 30 ft.

STR	DEX	CON	INT	WIS	CHA
16 (+3)	12 (+1)	14 (+2)	13 (+1)	20 (+5)	17 (+3)

Saving Throws Con +5, Wis +8
Skills History +4, Performance +6, Persuasion +9, Religion +4
Senses passive Perception 15
Languages any three languages
Challenge 8 (3,900 XP)

Spellcasting. The preacher is a 10th-level spellcaster. Its spellcasting ability is Wisdom (spell save DC 16, +8 to hit with spell attacks). The preacher has the following cleric spells prepared:

> Cantrips (at will): *guidance, light, resistance, sacred flame, thaumaturgy*
> 1st level (4 slots): *bane, bless, command, cure wounds, inflict wounds*
> 2nd level (3 slots): *aid, hold person, spiritual weapon*
> 3rd level (3 slots): *beacon of hope, mass healing word, tongues*
> 4th level (3 slots): *freedom of movement, locate creature*
> 5th level (2 slots): *flame strike, geas*

Unshakeable Faith. The preacher has advantage on Wisdom and Charisma saving throws.

ACTIONS

Multiattack. The preacher uses its Speech and makes three melee attacks.

Morningstar. *Melee Weapon Attack:* +6 to hit, reach 5 ft., one target. *Hit:* 7 (1d8 + 3) piercing damage.

Speech. The preacher makes one of the following speeches; it can't use the same speech two rounds in a row:

Condemning Speech. The preacher speaks words of condemnation at one target within 30 feet of it. The target must make a DC 16 Wisdom saving throw. On a failure, the target takes 28 (8d6) thunder damage and is frightened for 1 minute. On a success, the target takes half the damage and isn't frightened. A frightened creature can repeat the saving throw at the end of each of its turns, ending the effect on itself on a success. If the creature's saving throw is successful or the effect ends for it, the creature is immune to the preacher's Condemning Speech for the next 24 hours.

Inspiring Speech. The preacher targets up to three creatures it can see within 30 feet of it and speaks words of inspiration. Each target has advantage on its next attack roll, saving throw, or ability check.

Swaying Speech. The preacher speaks persuasively to one target within 30 feet of it. The target must make a DC 16 Wisdom saving throw. On a failure, the target takes 28 (8d6) psychic damage and is charmed for 1 minute. On a success, the target takes half the damage and isn't charmed. A charmed creature can repeat the saving throw at the end of each of its turns, ending the effect on itself on a success. If a creature's saving throw is successful or the effect ends for it, the creature is immune to the preacher's Swaying Speech for the next 24 hours.

Pyromancer

Medium humanoid (any), any chaotic alignment
Armor Class 11 (14 with *mage armor*)
Hit Points 38 (7d8 + 7)
Speed 30ft

STR	DEX	CON	INT	WIS	CHA
10 (+0)	12 (+1)	12 (+1)	10 (+0)	10 (+0)	18 (+4)

Saving Throws Con +3, Cha +6
Skills Deception +6, Insight +2
Senses passive Perception 10
Languages Common
Challenge 3 (700 XP)

Fire Adept. Whenever the pyromancer takes any fire damage, it gains a 1st-level spell slot. This can increase the number of available slots that the pyromancer has to cast 1st-level spells above 4. The extra slots disappear if the pyromancer takes a long rest.

Spellcasting. The pyromancer is a 6th-level spellcaster. Its spellcasting ability is Charisma (spell save DC 14, +6 to hit with spell attacks). It knows the following sorcerer spells.

> Cantrips (at will): *dancing lights, fire bolt, light, shocking grasp, true strike*
> 1st level (4 slots): *burning hands, mage armor, magic missile*
> 2nd level (3 slots): *flaming sphere, scorching ray*
> 3rd level (2 slots): *fireball, protection from energy*

Swift Casting (3/day). Whenever the pyromancer uses an action to cast a cantrip or a spell, it can cast a cantrip as a bonus action.

ACTIONS

Dagger. *Melee or Ranged Weapon Attack:* +3 to hit, reach 5ft. or range 20/60 ft., one target. *Hit:* 3 (1d4 + 1) piercing

Red Scorpion Assassin

Medium humanoid (any), any alignment
Armor Class 15 (studded leather)
Hit Points 38 (7d8 + 7)
Speed 30 ft.

STR	DEX	CON	INT	WIS	CHA
12 (+1)	16 (+3)	12 (+1)	13 (+1)	14 (+2)	13 (+1)

Saving Throws Dex +6, Int +4
Skills Athletics +4, Acrobatics +9, Deception +4, Perception +4, Stealth +9
Senses passive Perception 14
Languages Thieves' cant plus any two languages
Challenge 5 (1,800 XP)

Assassinate. During its first turn, the Red Scorpion assassin has advantage on attack rolls against any creature that hasn't yet acted in the combat. Any hit the Red Scorpion assassin scores against a surprised creature counts as a critical hit.

Cunning Action. On each of its turns, the Red Scorpion assassin can use a bonus action to take the Dash, Disengage, or Hide action.

Sneak Attack. Once per turn, the Red Scorpion assassin deals an extra 17 (5d6) damage when it hits a target with a weapon attack and has advantage on the attack roll, or when the target is within 5 feet of an ally of the Red Scorpion assassin that isn't incapacitated and the Red Scorpion assassin doesn't have disadvantage on the attack roll.

ACTIONS

Multiattack. The Red Scorpion assassin makes two Dagger or two Shortsword attacks.

Dagger. *Melee or Ranged Weapon Attack:* +6 to hit, reach 5 ft. or range 20/60 ft., one target. *Hit:* 5 (1d4 + 3) piercing damage.

Shortsword. *Melee Weapon Attack:* +6 to hit, reach 5 ft., one target. *Hit:* 6 (1d6 + 3) piercing damage.

Red Scorpion Lieutenant

Medium humanoid (any), any alignment
Armor Class 15 (leather)
Hit Points 91 (14d8 + 28)
Speed 30 ft.

STR	DEX	CON	INT	WIS	CHA
14 (+2)	18 (+4)	14 (+2)	14 (+2)	16 (+3)	10 (+0)

Saving Throws Dex +7, Int +5
Skills Athletics +8, Acrobatics +10, Investigation +5, Perception +10, Stealth +10, Survival +6
Senses passive Perception 20
Languages Thieves' cant plus any two languages
Challenge 8 (3,900 XP)

Assassinate. During its first turn, the Red Scorpion lieutenant has advantage on attack rolls against any creature that hasn't yet acted in the combat. Any hit the Red Scorpion lieutenant scores against a surprised creature counts as a critical hit.

Cunning Action. On each of its turns, the Red Scorpion lieutenant can use a bonus action to take the Dash, Disengage, or Hide action.

Sneak Attack. Once per turn, the Red Scorpion lieutenant deals an extra 28 (8d6) damage when it hits a target with a weapon attack and has advantage on the attack roll, or when the target is within 5 feet of an ally of the Red Scorpion lieutenant that isn't incapacitated and the misericorde doesn't have disadvantage on the attack roll.

Sniper. The Red Scorpion lieutenant ignores disadvantage from attacking beyond a weapon's normal range. In addition, the Red Scorpion lieutenant deals an additional die of damage on a ranged weapon attack (included in the attacks).

ACTIONS

Multiattack. The Red Scorpion lieutenant makes two Dagger or two Shortsword attacks.

Dagger. *Melee or Ranged Weapon Attack:* +7 to hit, reach 5 ft. or range 20/60 ft., one target. *Hit:* 6 (1d4 + 4) piercing damage, or 9 (2d4 + 4) piercing damage if used to make a ranged attack.

Shortsword. *Melee Weapon Attack:* +7 to hit, reach 5 ft., one target. *Hit:* 7 (1d6 + 4) piercing damage.

Heavy Crossbow. *Ranged Weapon Attack:* +7 to hit, range 100/400 ft., one target. *Hit:* 15 (2d10 + 4) piercing damage.

Repository Scholar

Medium humanoid (any race), any alignment
Armor Class 17 (chain shirt, shield)
Hit Points 225 (30d8 + 90)
Speed 30 ft.

STR	DEX	CON	INT	WIS	CHA
16 (+3)	14 (+2)	17 (+3)	20 (+5)	23 (+6)	16 (+3)

Saving Throws Con +9, Int +11, Wis +12
Skills History +11, Insight +12, Persuasion +9, Religion +11
Senses passive Perception 16
Languages any six languages
Challenge 20 (25,000 XP)

Legendary Resistance (3/day). If the repository scholar fails a saving throw, it can choose to succeed instead.

Magic Resistance. The repository scholar has advantage on saving throws against spells and other magical effects.

Magic Weapons. The repository scholar's weapon attacks are magical.

Professor of the Arts. The repository scholar has advantage on ability checks based on Intelligence or Charisma when interacting with other spellcasters.

Spellcasting. The repository scholar is an 18th-level spellcaster. Its spellcasting ability is Wisdom (spell save DC 20, +12 to hit with spell attacks). The repository scholar has the following cleric spells prepared:

Cantrips (at will): *guidance, light, mending, sacred flame, thaumaturgy*
1st level (4 slots): *command, cure wounds, inflict wounds, sanctuary*
2nd level (3 slots): *calm emotions, hold person, silence, zone of truth*
3rd level (3 slots): *clairvoyance, dispel magic, glyph of warding, tongues*
4th level (3 slots): *banishment, freedom of movement, locate creature*
5th level (3 slots): *dispel evil and good, mass cure wounds, scrying*
6th level (1 slot): *harm, heal*
7th level (1 slot): *divine word, symbol*
8th level (1 slot): *holy aura*
9th level (1 slot): *astral projection*

ACTIONS

Multiattack. The repository scholar makes two Holy Text attacks or two Inked Quill attacks.

Holy Text. *Melee Weapon Attack:* +9 to hit, reach 5 ft., one target. *Hit:* 6 (1d6 + 3) bludgeoning damage plus 28 (8d6) radiant (good or neutral rectors) or necrotic (evil rectors) damage.

Inked Quill. *Ranged Weapon Attack:* +8 to hit, range 20/60 ft., one target. *Hit:* 4 (1d4 + 2) piercing damage, and the target must make a DC 20 Constitution saving throw, taking 21 (6d6) poison damage on a failed save, or half as much damage on a successful one.

Lecture (recharge 5–6). The repository scholar speaks a long, droning lecture in a 60-foot cone. Each creature in that area must make a DC 19 Intelligence saving throw. On a failure, a creature takes 54 (12d8) psychic damage and falls unconscious for 10 minutes. On a success, a creature takes half the damage and doesn't fall unconscious. An unconscious creature awakens if it takes damage or another creature takes an action to wake it. This lecture has no effect on creatures with an Intelligence of 5 or lower.

REACTIONS

Paper Shield. When a creature the repository scholar can see targets it with a weapon attack, nearby scrolls and books fly up to protect it. The repository scholar has resistance to bludgeoning, piercing, and slashing damage until the end of its next turn.

LEGENDARY ACTIONS

The repository scholar can take 3 legendary actions, choosing from the options below. Only one legendary action can be used at a time and only at the end of another creature's turn. The repository scholar regains spent legendary actions at the start of its turn.

Inked Quill. The repository scholar makes one Inked Quill attack.

Move. The repository scholar moves up to its speed without provoking opportunity attacks.

Cast a Spell (costs 3 actions). The repository scholar casts a spell from its list of prepared spells, using a spell slot as normal.

Sabre

Medium humanoid (any race), any alignment
Armor Class 16 (studded leather)
Hit Points 78 (12d8 + 24)
Speed 30 ft.

STR	DEX	CON	INT	WIS	CHA
13 (+1)	18 (+4)	14 (+2)	12 (+1)	14 (+2)	10 (+0)

Saving Throws Dex +7, Int +4
Skills Athletics +4, Acrobatics +7, Perception +8, Stealth +10
Senses passive Perception 18
Languages Thieves' cant plus any two languages
Challenge 7 (2,900 XP)

Cunning Action. On each of its turns, the sabre can use a bonus action to take the Dash, Disengage, or Hide action.

Sneak Attack (1/turn). Once per turn, the sabre deals an extra 24 (7d6) damage when it hits a target with a weapon attack and has advantage on the attack roll, or when the target is within 5 feet of an ally of the sabre that isn't incapacitated and the sabre doesn't have disadvantage on the attack roll.

ACTIONS

Multiattack. The sabre makes one Dagger attack or uses its Dagger Flourish ability, and makes two Rapier attacks.

Rapier. *Melee Weapon Attack:* +7 to hit, reach 5 ft., one target. *Hit:* 8 (1d8 + 4) piercing damage.

Dagger. *Melee or Ranged Weapon Attack:* +7 to hit, reach 5 ft. or range 20/60 ft., one target. *Hit:* 6 (1d4 + 4) piercing damage.

Dagger Flourish. One creature that is wielding a weapon within 5 feet of the sabre must make a DC 15 Strength saving throw. On a failed saving throw, all the attacks the sabre makes against the target until the end of its turn have advantage.

REACTIONS

Parry. The sabre adds 3 to its AC against one melee attack that would hit it. To do so, the sabre must see the attacker and be wielding a melee weapon.

Seeker of the Ebony Moon

Medium humanoid (any race), lawful evil
Armor Class 15 (chain shirt)
Hit Points 91 (14d8 + 28)
Speed 30 ft.

STR	DEX	CON	INT	WIS	CHA
16 (+3)	15 (+2)	14 (+2)	17 (+3)	18 (+4)	14 (+2)

Saving Throws Int +6, Wis +7
Skills Arcana +6, Nature +6, Perception +7, Religion +6, Stealth +6
Damage Resistances varies (see Lunar Empowerment)
Condition Immunities varies (see Lunar Empowerment)
Senses darkvision 60 ft., passive Perception 17
Languages any three languages
Challenge 6 (2,300 XP)

Blessing of the Moon. The seeker of the ebony moon has darkvision and magical darkness doesn't impede its darkvision.

Lunar Empowerment. The seeker of the ebony moon's power is tied to the moon. Its resistances, immunities, and Lunar Bolt action are affected by the current phase of the moon:

New Moon: The seeker has resistance to necrotic damage and its Lunar Bolt deals an extra 3 (1d6) necrotic damage.

Crescent Moon: A target hit by the seeker's Lunar Bolt must succeed on a DC 15 Wisdom saving throw or be frightened until the end of its next turn.

Gibbous Moon: A target hit by the seeker's Lunar Bolt must succeed on a DC 15 Wisdom saving throw or be blinded until the end of its next turn.

Full Moon: The seeker is immune to the blinded condition and has resistance to radiant damage. Its Lunar Bolt deals an extra 3 (1d6) radiant damage.

Moon-Touched Weapons. When the seeker of the ebony moon hits with any weapon, the weapon deals an extra 4d6 radiant (if in bright or dim light) or necrotic (if in darkness) damage (included in the attack).

Shadow Stealth. While in dim light or darkness, the seeker of the ebony moon can take the Hide action as a bonus action.

Spellcasting. The seeker of the ebony moon is a 5th-level spellcaster. Its spellcasting ability is Wisdom (spell save DC 15, +7 to hit with spell attacks). The seeker has the following cleric spells prepared:

Cantrips (at will): *guidance, light, resistance, thaumaturgy*
1st level (4 slots): *command, cure wounds, inflict wounds, protection from evil and good*
2nd level (3 slots): *hold person, silence, spiritual weapon*
3rd level (2 slots): *animate dead, bestow curse*

ACTIONS

Multiattack. The seeker of the ebony moon makes two Mace attacks or uses its Lunar Bolt twice.

Mace. *Melee Weapon Attack:* +6 to hit, reach 5 ft., one target. *Hit:* 6 (1d6 + 3) bludgeoning damage plus 14 (4d6) radiant or necrotic damage (see Moon-Touched Weapons).

Lunar Bolt. *Ranged Spell Attack:* +7 to hit, range 120 ft., one target. *Hit:* 18 (4d8) radiant (if the target is in bright or dim light) or necrotic (if the target is in darkness) damage.

Senior Druid

Medium humanoid (human), neutral evil
Armor Class 13 (16 with *barkskin*)
Hit Points 120 (16d8 + 48)
Speed 30 ft.

STR	DEX	CON	INT	WIS	CHA
16 (+3)	16 (+3)	16 (+3)	14 (+2)	20 (+5)	15 (+2)

Saving Throws Int +6, Wis +9
Skills Animal Handling +9, Medicine +9, Nature +6, Perception +9
Senses passive Perception 19
Languages Common, Druidic, Ignan
Challenge 9 (5,000 XP)

Special Equipment. The senior druid carries a *staff of the woodlands.* Its bonuses are included in the statistics below.

Spellcasting. Senior druid is a 16th-level spellcaster. Its spellcasting ability is Wisdom (spell save DC 17, +11 to hit with spell attacks). It has the following druid spells prepared.

Cantrips (at will): *guidance, mending, resistance, shillelagh*
1st level (4 slots): *cure wounds, detect magic, entangle, thunderwave*
2nd level (3 slots): *barkskin, blur, heat metal, lesser restoration, silence*
3rd level (3 slots): *conjure animals, create food and water, dispel magic, protection from energy*
4th level (3 slots): *blight, dominate beast, hallucinatory terrain, locate creature*
5th level (2 slots): *conjure elemental, greater restoration, insect plague, wall of stone*
6th level (1 slot): *sunbeam*
7th level (1 slot): *fire storm*
8th level (1 slot): *animal shapes*

ACTIONS

Staff of the Woodlands. +5 to hit (+11 to hit with *shillelagh*), reach 5 ft., one target. *Hit:* 8 (1d6 + 5) bludgeoning damage, 8 (1d8 + 5) bludgeoning damage if wielded with two hands, or 11 (1d8 + 7) bludgeoning damage with *shillelagh*.

Change Shape (2/short or long rest). The senior druid magically polymorphs into a beast or elemental with a challenge rating of 6 or less and can remain in this form for up to 9 hours. The druid can choose whether its equipment falls to the ground, melds with its new form, or is worn by the new form. The druid reverts to its true form if it dies or falls unconscious, or if it uses a bonus action on his turn to end the effect.

While in a new form, the senior druid retains its game statistics and ability to speak, but its AC, movement modes, Strength, and Dexterity are replaced by those of the new form, and the druid gains any special senses, proficiencies, traits, actions, and reactions (except class features, legendary actions, and lair actions) that the new form has but that the druid lacks. The druid can cast spells with verbal or somatic components in the new form. The new form's attacks count as magical for the purposes of overcoming damage resistances and immunities to nonmagical attacks.

Si'la Merchant

Medium humanoid (any), any alignment
Armor Class 11
Hit Points 13 (3d8)
Speed 30 ft.

STR	DEX	CON	INT	WIS	CHA
11 (+0)	12 (+1)	11 (+0)	12 (+1)	14 (+2)	16 (+3)

Skills Deception +5, Insight +4, Persuasion +5
Senses passive Perception 12
Languages Common, Ignan
Challenge 1/8 (25 XP)

ACTIONS

Dagger. *Melee or Ranged Weapon Attack:* +3 to hit, reach 5 ft. or range 20/60 ft., one target. *Hit:* 3 (1d4 + 1) piercing damage.

Smoke Merchant

Medium humanoid (any), neutral
Armor Class 11
Hit Points 45 (10d8)
Speed 30 ft.

STR	DEX	CON	INT	WIS	CHA
11 (+0)	12 (+1)	10 (+0)	14 (+2)	14 (+2)	15 (+2)

Skills Deception +4, Insight +4, Persuasion +4
Senses passive Perception 12
Languages Common, Ignan
Challenge 1 (200 XP)

Martial Advantage. Once per turn, the smoke merchant can deal an extra 13 (3d8) damage to a creature he hits with a weapon attack if that creature is within 5 feet of an ally of his that isn't incapacitated.

ACTIONS

Multiattack. The smoke merchant makes two Dagger attacks.
Dagger. *Melee or Ranged Weapon Attack:* +3 to hit, reach 5 ft. or range 20/60 ft., one target. *Hit:* 3 (1d4 + 1) piercing damage.

Smoldering Judge

Medium humanoid, lawful evil
Armor Class 17 (+2 chain shirt)
Hit Points 85 (10d8 + 40)
Speed 30 ft.

STR	DEX	CON	INT	WIS	CHA
25 (+7)	15 (+2)	19 (+4)	11 (+0)	20 (+5)	13 (+1)

Skills Perception +8, Religion +8
Damage Resistances fire or cold (*halberd of flame/frost*[2])
Senses passive Perception 18
Languages Common, Ignan
Challenge 10 (5,900 XP)

Channel Divinity: Directed Strike (2/day). The smoldering judge gains a +10 on one attack roll.
Special Equipment. The smoldering judge possesses a *belt of giant strength* (fire, included above), a *spell wand*[2] of *forcecage*, a *spell wand*[2] of *hold person*, a *spell wand*[2] of *power word stun*, a *spell wand*[2] of *sleep*.
Spellcasting. The smoldering judge is a 10th level spellcaster. Its spellcasting ability is Wisdom (save DC 17, +9 to hit with spell attacks). The smoldering judge has the following spells prepared:

    Cantrips (at will): *light, mending, sacred flame, spare the dying, thaumaturgy*
    1st level (4 slots): *cure wounds, detect evil and good, divine favor, healing word, shield of faith*
    2nd level (3 slots): *hold person, magic weapon, silence, spiritual weapon*
    3rd level (3 slots): *bestow curse, dispel magic, mass healing word, spirit guardians*
    4th level (3 slots): *banishment, freedom of movement, locate person, stoneskin*
    5th level (2 slots): *flame strike, hold monster, mass cure wounds*

ACTIONS

Halberd of Flame/Frost. *Melee Weapon Attack:* +11 to hit, reach 5 ft., one target. *Hit:* 12 (1d10 + 7) slashing damage plus 7 (2d6) fire or cold damage (judge's choice).

Bonus Actions

Warrior Priest (5/day). The smoldering judge makes one weapon attack.

Sneakthief

Medium humanoid (any), any alignment
Armor Class 14 (leather)
Hit Points 18 (4d8)
Speed 30 ft.

STR	DEX	CON	INT	WIS	CHA
12 (+1)	15 (+2)	11 (+0)	10 (+0)	14 (+2)	10 (+0)

Saving Throws Dex +4, Int +2
Skills Acrobatics +4, Athletics +3, Deception +2, Perception +4, Sleight of Hand +6, Stealth +6
Senses passive Perception 14
Languages Thieves' cant plus any one language
Challenge 1/2 (100 XP)

Sneak Attack. Once per turn, the sneakthief can deal an extra 7 (2d6) damage to one creature it hits with an attack if it has advantage on the attack roll. The attack must use a finesse or a ranged weapon. The sneakthief doesn't need advantage on the attack roll if another enemy of the target is within 5 feet of it, that enemy isn't incapacitated, and the sneakthief doesn't have disadvantage on the attack roll.

ACTIONS

Rapier. *Melee Weapon Attack:* +4 to hit, reach 5 ft., one target. *Hit:* 6 (1d8 + 2) piercing damage.

Shortbow. *Ranged Weapon Attack:* +4 to hit, range 80/320 ft., one target. *Hit:* 5 (1d6 + 2) piercing damage.

Sorcerer

Medium humanoid (any race), any alignment
Armor Class 18 (natural armor, *bracers of defense*)
Hit Points 91 (14d8 + 14 + Draconic Resilience)
Speed 30 ft.

STR	DEX	CON	INT	WIS	CHA
12 (+1)	17 (+3)	13 (+1)	11 (+0)	12 (+1)	19 (+4)

Saving Throws Con +6, Cha +9
Skills Arcana +5, Deception +9
Damage Resistances fire
Senses passive Perception 11
Languages Common, Draconic, other languages by race
Challenge 13 (10,000 XP)

Draconic Resilience. The sorcerer has one extra maximum hit point for each spellcaster level (included above)

Empowered Spells (2/day). When it rolls for spell damage, the sorcerer may reroll up to four dice. It must use the new roll.

Fire Affinity. When the sorcerer casts a spell that deals fire damage, it may add its Charisma modifier to that damage.

Heightened Spells (2/day). When a spell cast by the sorcerer forces a target to make a saving throw to resist its effects, the sorcerer may cause one target to have disadvantage on its first saving throw made against the spell.

Quickened Spells (4/day). When it casts a spell that has a casting time of 1 action, the sorcerer can change the casting time to 1 bonus action for this casting.

Special Equipment. The sorcerer possesses a *cloak of displacement* and two *potions of superior healing.*

Spellcasting. The sorcerer is a 14th level spellcaster. Its spellcasting ability is Charisma (spell save DC 17, +9 to hit with spell attacks). It has the following spells prepared:

> Cantrips (at will): *blade ward, dancing lights, fire bolt, light, mage hand, minor illusion*
> 1st level (4 slots): *burning hands, charm person*
> 2nd level (2 slots): *mirror image, scorching ray, suggestion*
> 3rd level (3 slots): *counterspell, fireball, haste*
> 4th level (3 slots): *greater invisibility, wall of fire*
> 5th level (2 slots): *dominate person*
> 6th level (1 slot): *mass suggestion*
> 7th level (1 slot): *fire storm*

ACTIONS

Staff of Striking. *Melee Weapon Attack:* +9 to hit, reach 5 ft., one target. *Hit:* 6 (1d6 + 4) bludgeoning damage, and the sorcerer can expend up to three charges; for each charge expended, the target takes an extra 1d6 force damage.

+2 Dart. *Ranged Weapon Attack:* +10 to hit, range 20/60 ft., one target. *Hit:* 7 (1d4 + 5) piercing damage.

BONUS ACTIONS

Dragon Wings. The sorcerer sprouts a pair of dragon wings and gains a fly speed of 30 ft or retracts those wings back into its body if already out.

Spellbinder

Medium humanoid (any), any alignment
Armor Class 13 (16 with *mage armor*)
Hit Points 170 (20d8 + 80)
Speed 30 ft.

STR	DEX	CON	INT	WIS	CHA
14 (+2)	17 (+3)	19 (+4)	21 (+5)	16 (+3)	17 (+3)

Saving Throws Int +11, Wis +9
Skills Arcana +17, Nature +17, Perception +9, Persuasion +9
Senses passive Perception 19
Languages Common, Ignan
Challenge 20 (25,000 XP)

Empowered Evocation. The spellbinder can add its Intelligence modifier (+5) to the damage roll of any wizard evocation spell it casts.

Overchannel (3/day). When the spellbinder casts a wizard spell of 1st through 5th level that deals damage, it can deal maximum damage with that spell.

Sculpt Spells. When the spellbinder casts an evocation spell that affects other creatures that it can see, it can choose a number of them equal to 1 + the spell's level. The chosen creatures automatically succeed on their saving throws against the spell, and they take no damage if they would normally take half damage on a successful save.

Signature Spells (1/day each). The spellbinder can cast *fireball* and *lightning bolt* at 3rd level without expending a spell slot.

Special Equipment. The spellbinder possesses an *amulet of health*, a *potion of invulnerability*, two *potions of supreme healing.*

Spell Mastery. The spellbinder may cast *magic missile* or *mirror image* at their lowest possible level without expending a spell slot.

Spellcasting. The spellbinder is a 20th level spellcaster. The spellbinder's spellcasting ability is Intelligence (spell save DC 19, +11 to hit with spell attacks). It has the following spells prepared:

> Cantrips (at will): *dancing lights, fire bolt, mage hand, prestidigitation, ray of frost*
> 1st level (4 slots): *mage armor, charm person, magic missile, thunderwave*
> 2nd level (3 slots): *darkness, flaming sphere, levitate, mirror image*
> 3rd level (3 slots): *counterspell, fireball, fly, lightning bolt*
> 4th level (3 slots): *banishment, fire shield, greater invisibility*
> 5th level (3 slots): *cone of cold, telekinesis, wall of force*
> 6th level (2 slots): *chain lightning, freezing sphere, move earth*
> 7th level (2 slots): *reverse gravity, teleport*
> 8th level (1 slot): *control weather, sunburst*
> 9th level (1 slot): *wish*

ACTIONS

Quarterstaff. *Melee Weapon Attack:* +8 to hit, reach 5 ft., one target. *Hit:* 6 (1d6 + 2) bludgeoning damage or 8 (1d8 + 4) bludgeoning damage if used with two hands.

Theurgist

Medium humanoid (any), any alignment
Armor Class 13 (16 with *mage armor*)
Hit Points 19 (3d8 + 6)
Speed 30 ft.

STR	DEX	CON	INT	WIS	CHA
10 (+0)	16 (+3)	14 (+2)	18 (+4)	15 (+2)	11 (+0)

Saving Throws Int +6, Wis +4
Skills Arcana +6, History +6
Senses passive Perception 12
Languages Common
Challenge 2 (450 XP)

Spellcasting. The theurgist is a 3rd level spellcaster. The theurgist's spellcasting ability is Intelligence (spell save DC 14, +6 to hit with spell attacks). It has the following spells prepared:

> Cantrips (at will): *fire bolt, light, mage hand*
> 1st level (4 slots): *burning hands, false life, mage armor, magic missile*
> 2nd level (2 slots): *acid arrow, mirror image, scorching ray*

ACTIONS

Dagger. *Melee Weapon Attack:* +5 to hit, reach 5 ft., one target. *Hit:* 5 (1d4 + 3) piercing damage.
Sling. *Ranged Weapon Attack:* +5 to hit, range 30/120 ft., one target. *Hit:* 5 (1d4 + 3) bludgeoning damage.

Vicious Warrior

Medium humanoid (any race), any chaotic alignment
Armor Class 17 (half plate)
Hit Points 190 (20d8 + 100)
Speed 40 ft.

STR	DEX	CON	INT	WIS	CHA
21 (+5)	15 (+2)	20 (+5)	10 (+0)	12 (+1)	14 (+2)

Saving Throws Str +10, Dex +7, Con +10
Skills Athletics +10, Intimidation +7, Perception +6
Condition Immunities frightened
Senses passive Perception 16
Languages any one language
Challenge 13 (10,000 XP)

Brute. A melee weapon deals one extra die of its damage when the vicious warrior hits with it (included in the attack).
Reckless. At the start of its turn, the vicious warrior can gain advantage on all melee weapon attack rolls it makes during that turn, but attack rolls against it have advantage until the start of its next turn.

ACTIONS

Multiattack. The vicious warrior makes four Serrated Greatsword attacks. Alternatively, it can make three ranged attacks with its Javelins.
Serrated Greatsword. *Melee Weapon Attack:* +10 to hit, reach 5 ft., one target. *Hit:* 15 (3d6 + 5) slashing damage. If the target is a creature other than an undead or construct, it must succeed on a DC 18 Constitution saving throw or suffer a deep laceration. At the start of each of its turns it loses 10 (3d6) hit points as its laceration continues to bleed. Any creature can take an action to stanch the bleeding with a successful DC 14 Wisdom (Medicine) check. The bleeding also stops if the target receives magical healing.
Javelin. *Melee or Ranged Weapon Attack:* +10 to hit, reach 5 ft. or range 30/120 ft., one target. *Hit:* 8 (1d6 + 5) piercing damage, or 12 (2d6 + 5) piercing damage if used to make a melee attack.
Swirling Slash (recharge 5–6). The vicious warrior spins its sword in a wide arc. Each creature within 10 feet of the vicious warrior must make a DC 18 Dexterity saving throw, taking 42 (12d6) slashing damage on a failed save, or half as much damage on a successful one.

Named Individuals

Ard

Medium humanoid (human), lawful evil
Armor Class 20 (*robe of the archmagi, staff of power*)
Hit Points 161 (19d8 + 76)
Speed 30 ft.

STR	DEX	CON	INT	WIS	CHA
14 (+2)	17 (+3)	19 (+4)	21 (+5)	16 (+3)	17 (+3)

Saving Throws Int +11, Wis +9
Skills Arcana +11, Deception +17, Perception +9, Persuasion +9
Senses darkvision 120 ft., passive Perception 19
Languages Abyssal, Common, Ignan, Infernal
Challenge 20 (25,000 XP)

Intense Concentration. While he is concentrating on a conjuration spell, Ard's concentration cannot be broken by taking damage.
Death Contingency. Ard has used magic similar to the *contingency* spell on himself. When he is first reduced to 0 hit points, he is teleported to his summoning chamber and revived with 1 hit point.
Robe of the Archmagi. Ard has advantage on saving throws against spells and other magical effects. AC and spell attack bonus are included above and below.
Special Equipment. Ard possesses an *amulet of health*, a *candle of invocation* (Lightbringer — lawful evil), an *iron flask* (with horned devil inside), a *potion of invulnerability*, and two *potions of supreme healing*.
Spell Mastery. Ard may cast *fog cloud* or *flaming sphere* at their lowest level without expending a spell slot.
Spellcasting. Ard is a 19th level spellcaster. His spellcasting ability is Intelligence (spell save DC 23, +15 to hit with spell attacks, including bonuses from magic items). He has the following spells prepared:

> Cantrips (at will): *dancing lights, fire bolt, mage hand, mending, prestidigitation*
> 1st level (4 slots): *charm person, magic missile, unseen servant*
> 2nd level (3 slots): *flaming sphere, mirror image, suggestion, web*
> 3rd level (3 slots): *counterspell, fireball, sleet storm, stinking cloud*
> 4th level (3 slots): *black tentacles, conjure minor elementals, faithful hound, greater invisibility*
> 5th level (3 slots): *cloudkill, conjure elemental, dominate person*
> 6th level (2 slots): *chain lightning, instant summons*
> 7th level (1 slot): *teleport*
> 8th level (1 slot): *incendiary cloud, maze*

9th level (1 slot): *gate* (Ard knows the true name of a pit fiend with whom he is allied)

Staff of Power. While holding this staff, Ard has a +2 bonus to AC (included above), saving throws, and spell attack rolls; he can use an action to expend 1 or more of its charges to cast one of the following spells from it, using his spell save DC and spell attack bonus: *cone of cold* (5 charges), *fireball* (5th-level version, 5 charges), *globe of invulnerability* (6 charges), *hold monster* (5 charges), *levitate* (2 charges), *lightning bolt* (5th-level version, 5 charges), *magic missile* (1 charge), *ray of enfeeblement* (1 charge), or *wall of force* (5 charges).

Sturdy Conjuration. Any creature Ard summons with a conjuration spell appears with 35 temporary hit points.

ACTIONS

Staff of Power. *Melee Weapon Attack:* +10 to hit, reach 5 ft., one target. *Hit:* 6 (1d6 + 4) bludgeoning damage or 8 (1d8 + 4) bludgeoning damage if used with two hands. Ard may expend 1 charge to inflict an additional 1d6 force damage.

BONUS ACTIONS

Supplant the Summoned. Ard can teleport up to 50 feet, exchanging places with a creature he can see which he has summoned with a conjuration spell.

Bahija

Medium humanoid (human), neutral evil
Armor Class 13 (16 with *mage armor*)
Hit Points 104 (16d8 + 32)
Speed 30 ft.

STR	DEX	CON	INT	WIS	CHA
12 (+1)	16 (+3)	14 (+2)	20 (+5)	15 (+2)	13 (+1)

Saving Throws Int +9, Wis +6
Skills Arcana +9, History +9, Medicine +9
Damage Resistances fire; bludgeoning, piercing, and slashing from nonmagical attacks (from *stoneskin*)
Senses blindsight 10 ft., darkvision 60 ft., passive Perception 12
Languages Common, Draconic
Challenge 10 (5,900 XP)

Savant Necromancer. Whenever the necromancer creates an undead with a spell, that undead has advantage on saving throws against spells and other magical effects and 16 additional hit points.

Spellcasting. Bahija is a 16th-level spellcaster. Her spellcasting ability is Intelligence (spell save DC 17, +9 to hit with spell attacks). She has the following wizard spells prepared.

Cantrips (at will): *chill touch, mage hand, mending, prestidigitation, shocking grasp*
1st level (4 slots): *detect magic, false life, mage armor, magic missile, shield*
2nd level (3 slots): *blur, mirror image, ray of enfeeblement*
3rd level (3 slots): *animate dead, bestow curse, dispel magic*
4th level (3 slots): *banishment, stoneskin*
5th level (2 slots): *cloudkill, hold monster*
6th level (1 slot): *create undead*
7th level (1 slot): *finger of death*
8th level (1 slot): *power word stun*

ACTIONS

Dagger. *Melee or Ranged Weapon Attack:* +9 to hit, reach 5 ft. or range 20/60 ft., one target. *Hit:* 5 (1d4 + 3) piercing damage.

Fire Breath (recharge 5–6). Bahija exhales fire in a 15-foot cone. Each creature in that area must make a DC 16 Dexterity saving throw, taking 24 (7d6) fire damage on a failed saving throw, or half as much damage on a successful one.

Baracus

Medium humanoid (human), chaotic good
Armor Class 17 (splint)
Hit Points 209 (22d8 + 110)
Speed 40 ft.

STR	DEX	CON	INT	WIS	CHA
23 (+6)	16 (+3)	21 (+5)	12 (+1)	14 (+2)	19 (+4)

Saving Throws Str +11, Con +10, Cha +9
Skills Arcana +6, Athletics +11, Intimidation +9, Perception +7
Condition Immunities frightened
Senses passive Perception 17
Languages Common, Ignan
Challenge 16 (15,000 XP)

Infuse Weapons. As a bonus action, Baracus can infuse one of his weapons with a measure of his magical power before attacking with it. On a successful hit, the weapon releases its power, causing one of the following effects (only one effect can be used at a time):

- *Cold Infusion.* The target takes an extra 22 (4d10) cold damage and must succeed on a DC 18 Dexterity saving throw or be restrained until the end of its next turn.

- *Lightning Infusion.* The target takes an extra 22 (4d10) lightning damage and must succeed on a DC 18 Constitution saving throw or be incapacitated until the end of its next turn.

- *Poison Infusion.* The target takes an extra 22 (4d10) poison damage and must succeed on a DC 18 Constitution saving throw or be poisoned for 1 minute. The target can repeat the saving throw at the end of each of its turns, ending the effect on itself on a success.

Innate Spellcasting. Baracus' innate spellcasting ability is Charisma (spell save DC 17, +9 to hit with spell attacks). He can innately cast the following spells, requiring no material components.

At will: *blade ward, fire bolt* (2d10), *poison spray* (2d12), *mending, ray of frost* (2d8), *shocking grasp* (2d8)
3/day each: *fabricate, fire shield, fly, stone shape*
1/day each: *animate objects, conjure elemental, wall of fire*

Legendary Resistance (3/day). If Baracus fails a saving throw, he can choose to succeed instead.

Magic Weapons. Baracus' weapon attacks are magical.

Reckless. At the start of its turn, Baracus can gain advantage on all melee weapon attack rolls it makes during that turn, but attack rolls against it have advantage until the start of its next turn.

ACTIONS

Multiattack. Baracus makes three Greatsword attacks or three Longbow attacks.

Greatsword. *Melee Weapon Attack:* +11 to hit, reach 5 ft., one target. *Hit:* 13 (2d6 + 6) slashing damage.

Longbow. *Ranged Weapon Attack:* +8 to hit, range 150/600 ft., one target. *Hit:* 7 (1d8 + 3) piercing damage.

Baracus can take 3 legendary actions, choosing from the options below. Only one legendary action can be used at a time and only at the end of another creature's turn. Baracus regains spent legendary actions at the start of its turn.

At Will Spell. Baracus casts one at will spell from his list.

Greatsword. Baracus makes one Greatsword attack.

Move. Baracus moves up to his speed without provoking opportunity attacks.

Thunderous Roar (costs 3 actions). Baracus infuses his voice with magical energy and releases a cacophonous roar in a 30-foot cone. Each creature in that area must make a DC 18 Constitution saving throw. On a failure, a creature takes 21 (6d6) thunder damage and is knocked prone. On a success, a creature takes half the damage and isn't knocked prone.

Bravlik

Bravlik uses the statistics of a **sabre**[1], except for the following:

• His Challenge Rating is 10 (5,900 XP).

• He wears a set of studded leather *fire armor*[2], which gives him resistance to fire damage and 18 Armor Class.

• He carries a *+3 rapier* and an automatic pistol[3]:

> *Automatic Pistol* **(single shot).** *Ranged Weapon Attack:* +7 to hit, range 50/100 ft., one target. *Hit:* 8 (1d8 + 4) piercing damage.
> *Automatic Pistol* **(burst).** Bravlik fires a burst of bullets in a 20-foot cone. Creatures in the area must make a DC 15 Dexterity saving throw or take 8 (1d8 + 4) piercing damage.

He can make a single shot with the Automatic Pistol in place of making a Dagger attack or using his Dagger Flourish ability.

Cobra-black

Medium humanoid (inphidian), neutral evil
Armor Class 16 (natural armor)
Hit Points 39 (6d8 + 12)
Speed 30 ft.

STR	DEX	CON	INT	WIS	CHA
16 (+3)	17 (+3)	15 (+2)	12 (+1)	13 (+1)	12 (+1)

Saving Throws Dex +5, Con +4, Wis +3
Skills Acrobatics +5, Insight +3, Perception +3, Stealth +5
Senses darkvision 60 ft., passive Perception 13
Languages Common, Inphidian
Challenge 3 (700 XP)

ACTIONS

Multiattack. Cobra-black makes two Snake-hand Bite attacks.

Snake-hand Bite. Melee Weapon Attack: +5 to hit, reach 5 ft., one target. Hit: 5 (1d4 + 3) piercing damage plus 10 (3d6) poison damage.

Spit Poison (recharge 5–6). Cobra-black spits poison at one target within 20 ft. of it. A target creature must succeed on a DC 13 Constitution saving throw or be blinded for 1 minute. A creature can repeat the saving throw at the end of each of its turns, ending the effect on itself on a success.

Dark Cardinal Paz Amare

Medium humanoid (human, shapechanger), lawful evil
Armor Class 18 (*robe of armor*[2] *ring of superior protection*[2]) in human form, 21 (natural armor) in hybrid form
Hit Points 180 (24d8 + 72)
Speed 30 ft.

STR	DEX	CON	INT	WIS	CHA
17 (+3)	14 (+2)	17 (+3)	18 (+4)	21 (+5)	18 (+4)

Saving Throws Con +9, Wis +11, Cha +10
Skills Deception +10, Insight +10, Intimidation +10, Medicine +11, Persuasion +10, Religion +10
Damage Immunities fire, radiant
Condition Immunities charmed, frightened
Senses darkvision 60 ft., passive Perception 15
Languages Abyssal, Common, Ignan, Infernal
Challenge 17 (18,000 XP)

Special Equipment. Paz Amare wields a *+3 trident*, and wears a *robe of armor*[2] as well as a *ring of superior protection*[2].

Command the Faithful. As a bonus action, Amare can command an ally within 30 feet of him to use its reaction to make one attack against a creature within 15 feet of him.

Devilish Aspect. Paz Amare can use his action to magically polymorph into a human-devil hybrid, or back into his true form, which is humanoid. While in hybrid form, any equipment he is wearing or carrying isn't transformed, and his statistics are the same, other than his AC and the following benefits:

• His darkvision functions normally in magical and nonmagical darkness.

• He has a flying speed of 30.

• He has resistance to acid and cold damage, as well as bludgeoning, piercing, and slashing damage from nonmagical attacks.

• He has advantage on saving throws against magic.

Spellcasting. Paz Amare is a 14th-level spellcaster. His spellcasting ability is Wisdom (spell save DC 19, +11 to hit with spell attacks). Amare has the following cleric spells prepared.

> Cantrips (at will): *guidance, light, resistance, sacred flame, thaumaturgy*
> 1st level (4 slots): *command, cure wounds, inflict wounds, shield of faith*
> 2nd level (3 slots): *blindness/deafness, hold person, spiritual weapon*
> 3rd level (3 slots): *beacon of hope, bestow curse, dispel magic, mass healing word*
> 4th level (3 slots): *banishment, freedom of movement, guardian of faith*
> 5th level (2 slots): *flame strike, insect plague, mass cure wounds*
> 6th level (1 slot): *harm, heal*
> 7th level (1 slot): *fire storm*

ACTIONS

Multiattack. Paz Amare makes two Trident attacks or three Divine Bolt attacks.

Trident. Melee or Ranged Weapon Attack: +12 to hit, reach 5 ft. or range 20/60 ft., one target. *Hit:* 9 (1d6 + 6) piercing damage, or 10 (1d8 + 6) piercing damage if used with two hands to make a melee attack, plus 9 (2d8) radiant or necrotic damage (Amare's choice).

Divine Bolt. *Ranged Spell Attack:* +11 to hit, range 120 ft., one target. *Hit:* 28 (8d6) radiant damage or 28 (8d6) necrotic damage, Amare's choice.

Deific Wrath (recharge 5–6). Paz Amare calls on Lucifer to smite up to three creatures Amare can see within 60 feet of him. Each target must make a DC 19 Wisdom saving throw. On a failure, a target takes 42 (12d6) radiant or necrotic damage (Amare's choice) and is paralyzed until the start of its next turn as it becomes overwhelmed with divine might. On a success, a target takes half the damage and isn't paralyzed.

Prince of Lies (1/long rest). Paz Amare calls on the blessings of the Prince of Lies. For 1 hour, he is considered to be under the effects of the *glibness* spell.

REACTIONS

Rebuke the Unfaithful. When a creature hits Amare with a melee attack, it must succeed on a DC 19 Wisdom saving throw or take 14 (4d6) radiant or necrotic damage (Amare's choice) and be pushed up to 10 feet away from Amare.

Draninko

Draninko uses the statistics of the **sabre**[1], but has several changes:

- His Challenge Rating is 10 (5,900 XP).

- He has 91 (14d8 + 28) hit points.

- He has the following new trait:

> **Evasion.** If Draninko is subjected to an effect that allows him to make a Dexterity saving throw to take only half damage, he instead takes no damage if he succeeds on the saving throw, and only half damage if he fails.

- He wears a set of *studded leather* that grants resistance to poison damage and carries a *sword of speed* (scimitar).

> **Scimitar.** *Melee Weapon Attack:* +9 to hit, reach 5 ft., one target. *Hit:* 9 (1d6 + 6) slashing damage.

- He has several enhancements, which provide him with the following features:

> **Enhancements.** Draninko has both a cybernetic eye and hand, which allow him to innately cast the *fire bolt* spell at will. In addition, he can cast the *burning hands* or *detect magic* spell. Once he has cast one of these spells, he cannot do so again until he takes a long rest. His cybernetic hand allows him to cast the *shocking grasp* spell at will. He can also use a bonus action on his turn to create a semi-ethereal *+1 dagger* or *+1 shortsword*. The weapon vanishes if it is more than 30 feet from Draninko for more than a minute, but he can use a bonus action to dismiss it and resummons it if it is not in his hand. Constitution is his spellcasting ability for the spells granted by his enhancements (spell save DC 13, +5 to hit with spell attacks).

Ephesius

Medium humanoid (human), lawful neutral
Armor Class 11
Hit Points 75 (12d8 + 12)
Speed 25 ft.

STR	DEX	CON	INT	WIS	CHA
11 (+0)	13 (+1)	13 (+1)	14 (+2)	15 (+2)	12 (+1)

Skills History +4, Insight +4, Persuasion +5, Religion +4
Senses darkvision 60 ft., passive Perception 12
Languages Common, Ignan
Challenge 1 (200 XP)

Martial Advantage. Once per turn, Ephesius can deal an extra 13 (3d8) damage to a creature he hits with a weapon attack if that creature is within 5 feet of an ally of his that isn't incapacitated.

ACTIONS

Multiattack. Ephesius makes two Dagger attacks.
Dagger. *Melee or Ranged Weapon Attack:* +3 to hit, reach 5 ft. or range 20/60 ft., one target. *Hit:* 3 (1d4 + 1) bludgeoning damage.

Fadi Al Naifa

Medium humanoid (human), lawful evil
Armor Class 17 (studded leather)
Hit Points 117 (18d8 + 36)
Speed 30 ft.

STR	DEX	CON	INT	WIS	CHA
12 (+1)	20 (+5)	14 (+2)	14 (+2)	14 (+2)	16 (+3)

Saving Throws Dex +8, Int +6
Skills Athletics +5, Acrobatics +9, Deception +7, Perception +10, Stealth +9
Damage Resistances fire, poison
Senses passive Perception 20
Languages Common, Thieves' Cant
Challenge 11 (7,200 XP)

Special Equipment. Fadi Al Naifa wears a *ring of resistance* (fire).
Assassinate. During its first turn, Fadi Al Naifa has advantage on attack rolls against any creature that hasn't yet acted in the combat. Any hit she scores against a surprised creature counts as a critical hit.
Cunning Action. On each of its turns, Fadi Al Naifa can use a bonus action to take the Dash, Disengage, or Hide action.
Evasion. If Fadi Al Naifa is subjected to an effect that allows her to make a Dexterity saving throw to take only half damage, she instead takes no damage if she succeeds on the saving throw, and only half damage if she fails.
Sneak Attack (1/turn). Once per turn, Fadi Al Naifa deals an extra 21 (6d6) damage when she hits a target with a weapon attack and has advantage on the attack roll, or when the target is within 5 feet of an ally of her that isn't incapacitated and she doesn't have disadvantage on the attack roll.
Spellcasting. Fadi Al Naifa is a 6th-level spellcaster. Her spellcasting ability is Charisma (spell save DC 15, +7 to hit with spell attacks). She knows the following sorcerer spells.
> Cantrips (at will): *acid splash, light, mage hand, minor illusion, shocking grasp*
> 1st level (4 slots): *charm person, detect magic, disguise self*
> 2nd level (3 slots): *invisibility*
> 3rd level (3 slots): *dispel magic*

Subtle Casting (3/day). Whenever Fadi Al Naifa casts a spell, she can do so without any somatic or verbal components.

ACTIONS

Multiattack. Fadi Al Naifa makes two Dagger or two Shortsword attacks.
Dagger. *Melee or Ranged Weapon Attack:* +9 to hit, reach 5 ft. or range 20/60 ft., one target. *Hit:* 6 (1d4 + 5) piercing damage, and the target must make a DC 15 Constitution saving throw, taking 24 (7d6) poison damage on a failed save, or half as much damage on a successful one.
Shortsword. *Melee Weapon Attack:* +9 to hit, reach 5 ft., one target. *Hit:* 6 (1d6 + 5) piercing damage, and the target must make a DC 15 Constitution saving throw, taking 24 (7d6) poison damage on a failed save, or half as much damage on a successful one.

Fayyad Mazin

Medium humanoid (human), neutral good
Armor Class 18 (half plate, shield)
Hit Points 165 (22d8 + 66)
Speed 30 ft.

STR	DEX	CON	INT	WIS	CHA
20 (+5)	14 (+2)	17 (+3)	13 (+1)	18 (+4)	15 (+2)

Saving Throws Con +8, Int, +6, Wis +9
Skills Insight +9, Medicine +9, Religion +6
Damage Resistances fire
Condition Immunities blinded
Senses passive Perception 14
Languages capitalized; lowercase telepathy always at end, "all" lowercase
Challenge 14 (11,500 XP)

Beacon of Divine Light. Fayyad Mazin sheds bright light in a 15-foot radius and dim light for an additional 15 feet. At the start of each of his turns, Fayyad chooses whether this light is active or suppressed.

Divine Flames. As a bonus action, Fayyad Mazin imbues his weapons with the divine might of the sun. When he hits with any weapon, it deals an extra 2d6 fire damage and 2d6 radiant damage.

Spellcasting. Fayyad Mazin is a 12th-level spellcaster. His spellcasting ability is Wisdom (spell save DC 17, +9 to hit with spell attacks). Fayyad Mazin has the following cleric spells prepared:

> Cantrips (at will): *guidance, mending, resistance, sacred flame, thaumaturgy*
> 1st level (4 slots): *bless, detect evil and good, cure wounds, healing word*
> 2nd level (3 slots): *aid, hold person, silence*
> 3rd level (3 slots): *daylight, mass healing word, spirit guardians*
> 4th level (3 slots): *divination, freedom of movement*
> 5th level (2 slots): *dispel evil and good, flame strike*
> 6th level (1 slot): *blade barrier, heal*

ACTIONS

Multiattack. Fayyad Mazin makes three melee attacks. He can use Hurl Flame in place of any melee attack.

Longsword. *Melee Weapon Attack:* +10 to hit, reach 5 ft., one target. *Hit:* 9 (1d8 + 5) slashing damage, or 10 (1d10 + 5) slashing damage if used with two hands.

Shield Bash. *Melee Weapon Attack:* +10 to hit, reach 5 ft., one target. *Hit:* 10 (2d4 + 5) bludgeoning damage. If the target is a Medium or smaller creature, it must succeed on a DC 18 Strength saving throw or be knocked prone.

Hurl Flame. *Ranged Spell Attack:* +9 to hit, range 120 ft., one target. *Hit:* 21 (6d6) fire damage.

REACTIONS

Retributive Fire. When Fayyad Mazin is hit with a melee weapon attack, the attacker must succeed on a DC 18 Dexterity saving throw or take 9 (2d8) fire damage.

Feldspar

Medium humanoid (dwarf), chaotic good
Armor Class 16 (breastplate)
Hit Points 170 (20d8 + 80)
Speed 25 ft.

STR	DEX	CON	INT	WIS	CHA
18 (+4)	15 (+2)	18 (+4)	20 (+5)	13 (+1)	16 (+3)

Saving Throws Int +9, Wis +5
Skills Arcana +9, Athletics +8, History +9, Perception +5
Damage Resistances poison
Senses darkvision 60 ft., passive Perception 15
Languages Common, Dwarvish, Ignan, Terran
Challenge 11 (7,200 XP)

Arcane Strike. When Feldspar hits with a weapon attack, he can expend a spell slot to cause the weapon attack to deal an additional 22 (4d10) force damage. If Feldspar expends a spell slot of 2nd level or higher, the extra damage increases by 1d10 for each level above 1st.

Dwarven Resistance. Feldspar has advantage on saving throws against poison.

Spellcasting. Feldspar is a 10th-level spellcaster. His spellcasting ability is Intelligence (spell save DC 17, +9 to hit with spell attacks). He has the following wizard spells prepared.

> Cantrips (at will): *fire bolt, mage hand, ray of frost, prestidigitation, shocking grasp*
> 1st level (4 slots): *burning hands, magic missile, shield, thunderwave*
> 2nd level (3 slots): *blur, magic weapon, mirror image*
> 3rd level (3 slots): *counterspell, fireball, haste*
> 4th level (3 slots): *fire shield, stoneskin*
> 5th level (2 slots): *hold monster, wall of force*

ACTIONS

Multiattack. Feldspar makes two melee attacks.

Longsword. *Melee Weapon Attack:* +8 to hit, reach 5 ft., one target. *Hit:* 8 (1d8 + 4) slashing damage, or 9 (1d10 + 4) slashing damage if used with two hands to make a melee attack.

Grashen

Grashen uses the statistics of a **boss flind**[1], but he carries a *+3 morningstar* and an automatic rifle:

> ***Morningstar.*** *Melee Weapon Attack:* +11 to hit, reach 5 ft., one target. *Hit:* 17 (2d8 + 8) bludgeoning damage.
>
> ***Automatic Rifle (single shot).*** *Ranged Weapon Attack:* +5 to hit, range 50/100 ft., one target. *Hit:* 7 (1d10 + 2) piercing damage.
>
> ***Automatic Rifle (burst).*** The flind fires a burst of bullets in a 20-foot cone. Creatures in the area must make a DC 15 Dexterity saving throw or take 7 (1d10 + 2) piercing damage.

Haulman Coul

Haulman Coul uses the statistics of a **sabre**[Isch], save for the changes below:

- His Challenge Rating is 9 (5,000 XP).

- Haulmon is a dark elf, and has the following additional traits:

> ***Fey Ancestry.*** Coul has advantage on saving throws against being charmed, and magic can't put the drow to sleep.
>
> ***Innate Spellcasting.*** The drow's spellcasting ability is Charisma (spell save DC 11). It can innately cast the following spells, requiring no material components:
>
> > At will: *dancing lights*
> > 1/day each: *darkness, faerie fire*

Sunlight Sensitivity. While in sunlight, the drow has disadvantage on attack rolls, as well as on Wisdom (Perception) checks that rely on sight.

He also carries several magic items:

• He does not wear studded leather armor, but wears both a *ring of greater protection*[2] and a pair of *bracers of greater defense*[2] instead, making his Armor Class 20, and granting him a +2 bonus to all saving throws.

• He wields a *+2 rapier* as well as a *+2 hand crossbow*.

Hand Crossbow. *Ranged Weapon Attack:* +9 to hit, range 30/120 ft., one target. *Hit:* 9 (1d6 + 6) piercing damage.

Haulman Coul can make two attacks with the Hand Crossbow as long as he has a hand free.

Hog Face

Medium humanoid (orc), chaotic evil
Armor Class 16 (chain mail)
Hit Points 75 (10d8 + 30)
Speed 30 ft.

STR	DEX	CON	INT	WIS	CHA
17 (+3)	14 (+2)	17 (+3)	10 (+0)	12 (+1)	14 (+2)

Skills Intimidation +4, Perception +3
Senses darkvision 60 ft., passive Perception 13
Languages Common, Orc
Challenge 4 (1,100 XP)

Aggressive. As a bonus action, Hog Face can move up to his speed toward a hostile creature that he can see.
Axe Expert. Hog Face deals an extra die of damage when he hits with a Battleaxe attack (included in the attack).

Actions

Multiattack. Hog Face makes two Battleaxe attacks or two Rifle attacks.
Battleaxe. *Melee Weapon Attack:* +5 to hit, reach 5 ft., one target. *Hit:* 12 (2d8 + 3) slashing damage, or 14 (2d10 + 3) slashing damage when used with two hands.
Rifle. *Ranged Weapon Attack:* +4 to hit, range 90/270 ft., one target. *Hit:* 5 (1d10) piercing damage. Critical hit on a 19 or 20.
Rifle Burst. Hog Face fires a burst from its rifle in a 30-foot cone. Each creature in that area must succeed on a DC 12 Dexterity saving throw, taking 5 (1d10) piercing damage.

Jaida Malak

Medium humanoid (elf), neutral
Armor Class 13 (padded armor)
Hit Points 49 (9d8 + 9)
Speed 30 ft.

STR	DEX	CON	INT	WIS	CHA
10 (+0)	14 (+2)	12 (+1)	15 (+2)	13 (+1)	12 (+1)

Skills Nature +6, Perception +3, Stealth +4
Senses darkvision 120 ft., passive Perception 13
Languages Common, Elvish, Undercommon
Challenge 1 (200 XP)

Fey Ancestry. Jaida Malak has advantage on saving throws against being charmed, and magic can't put her to sleep.
Innate Spellcasting. Jaida Malak's innate spellcasting ability is Charisma (spell save DC 11, +3 to hit with spell attacks). She can innately cast the following spells, with no need for material components:

At will: *dancing lights, poison spray*
1/day each: *darkness, entangle, faerie fire, plant growth*
Sunlight Sensitivity. While in sunlight, Jaida Malak has disadvantage on attack rolls, as well as on Wisdom (Perception) checks that rely on sight.

Actions

Dagger. *Melee Weapon Attack:* +4 to hit, reach 5 ft., one target. *Hit:* 4 (1d4 + 2) piercing damage.

Bonus Actions

Opium Powder. *Ranged Weapon Attack:* +4 to hit, range 10 ft., one target. *Hit:* Jaida Malak hurls a fistful of opium powder into a creature's face. The creature must make a DC 12 Constitution saving throw. On a failed save, it takes 5 (1d8 + 1) poison damage and is blinded and poisoned for 1 minute. A creature can repeat the saving throw at the end of each of its turns, ending the effects on itself on a success.

Kanbatsu Ieyau

Medium humanoid (human), neutral good
Armor Class 12 (15 with *mage armor*)
Hit Points 110 (17d8 + 34)
Speed 30 ft.

STR	DEX	CON	INT	WIS	CHA
17 (+3)	14 (+2)	14 (+2)	15 (+2)	12 (+1)	18 (+4)

Saving Throws Con +5, Cha +7
Skills Arcana +5, Deception +7, Persuasion +7
Senses passive Perception 11
Languages Common, Ignan
Challenge 6 (2,300 XP)

Magic Tattoos. Kanbatsu can cast the following spells from his tattoos: *mage armor, magic missile,* and *hold person.* Once he has done so, he cannot do so again for one week.
Spellcasting. Kanbatsu is an 11th-level spellcaster. His spellcasting ability is Charisma (spell save DC 15, +7 to hit with spell attacks). He knows the following sorcerer spells.

Cantrips (at will): *acid splash, dancing lights, mending, ray of frost, shocking grasp*
1st level (4 slots): *detect magic, mage armor, magic missile, shield*
2nd level (3 slots): *darkvision, hold person, mirror image*
3rd level (3 slots): *dispel magic, haste*
4th level (3 slots): *blight, magic tattoo*[4]
5th level (2 slots): *cone of cold*
6th level (1 slot): *disintegrate*
Twinned Spell (3/day). When Kanbatsu casts a spell that targets only one creature and doesn't have a range of self, he can target a second creature in range with the same spell.

Actions

Multiattack. Kanbatsu makes two melee attacks.
Longsword. *Melee Weapon Attack:* +6 to hit, reach 5 ft., one target. *Hit:* 7 (1d8 + 3) slashing damage, or 8 (1d10 + 3) slashing damage if used with two hands to make a melee attack.

Miercoles Mason

Miercoles Mason uses the statistics of a **housebreaker**, except for the following changes:

- Her Challenge Rating is 9 (5,000 XP).
- She has an Armor Class of 23 from *bracers of greater defense[2]* and a *ring of greater protection[2]*, and she wears *boots of flying[2]*, and *gauntlets of dexterity[2]*. She carries a *+2 rapier* giving her +10 to hit, for 10 (1d8 + 6) piercing damage, in place of a shortsword, a *+1 shortbow* giving her +9 to hit, range 80/320 ft., for 8 (1d6 + 5) piercing damage, 20 *+1 arrows*, and a *bag of holding*.

Musa Ayoub

Medium humanoid (dwarf), lawful neutral
Armor Class 11
Hit Points 75 (10d8 + 30)
Speed 25 ft.

STR	DEX	CON	INT	WIS	CHA
16 (+3)	13 (+1)	16 (+3)	14 (+2)	15 (+2)	11 (+0)

Skills History +4, Insight +4, Nature +4, Persuasion +2, Religion +4
Damage Resistances poison
Senses darkvision 60 ft., passive Perception 12
Languages Common, Dwarven, Ignan
Challenge 4 (1,100 XP)

Dwarven Resilience. Musa has advantage on saving throws against poison.
Martial Advantage. Once per turn, Musa Ayoub can deal an extra 13 (3d8) damage to a creature he hits with a weapon attack if that creature is within 5 feet of an ally of his that isn't incapacitated.

ACTIONS

Multiattack. Musa makes two Club attacks.
Club. *Melee Weapon Attack:* +6 to hit, reach 5 ft., one target. *Hit:* 5 (1d4 + 3) bludgeoning damage.

Noman al-Ajadi

Medium humanoid (human), lawful neutral
Armor Class 16 (breastplate)
Hit Points 91 (14d8 + 28)
Speed 30 ft.

STR	DEX	CON	INT	WIS	CHA
16 (+3)	16 (+3)	14 (+2)	15 (+2)	15 (+2)	16 (+3)

Skills Deception +7, History +6, Insight +6, Perception +6, Persuasion +7
Damage Immunities fire
Senses passive Perception 16
Languages Common, Ignan
Challenge 9 (5,000 XP)

Special Equipment. Noman al-Ajadi wields a *+3 longsword* and wears a *ring of immunity* (fire).
Martial Advantage. Once per turn, Noman al-Ajadi can deal an extra 13 (3d8) damage to a creature he hits with a weapon attack if that creature is within 5 feet of an ally of his that isn't incapacitated.

ACTIONS

Multiattack. Noman makes three Longsword attacks.
Longsword. *Melee Weapon Attack:* +10 to hit, reach 5 ft., one target. *Hit:* 10 (1d8 + 6) slashing damage, or 11 (1d10 + 6) slashing damage if wielded with two hands.

REACTIONS

Parry. Noman adds 4 to his AC against one melee attack that would hit him. To do so, he must see the attacker and be wielding a melee weapon.

Nyissa

Medium humanoid (elf), chaotic evil
Armor Class 16 (studded leather)
Hit Points 117 (18d8 + 36)
Speed 30 ft., climb 15 ft.

STR	DEX	CON	INT	WIS	CHA
11 (+0)	18 (+4)	15 (+2)	10 (+0)	16 (+3)	14 (+2)

Saving Throws Dex +8, Wis +7
Skills Acrobatics +8, Medicine +7, Perception +7, Stealth +8
Damage Immunities poison
Condition Immunities poisoned
Senses darkvision 60 ft., passive Perception 17
Languages Common, Elvish
Challenge 10 (5,900 XP)

Fey Ancestry. Nyissa has advantage on saving throws against being charmed, and magic can't put her to sleep.
Poison Prophet (3/day). As a bonus action, Nyissa ingests some of her homemade poison and gains limited vision of the near future. She has advantage on all attack rolls, ability checks, and saving throws until the start of her next turn.
Speak with Spiders. Nyissa can communicate with spiders as if they shared a language.
Spellcasting. Nyissa is a 4th-level spellcaster. Its spellcasting ability is Wisdom (spell save DC 15, +7 to hit with spell attacks). Nyissa has the following cleric spells prepared:
Cantrips (at will): *guidance, resistance, sacred flame, thaumaturgy*
1st level (4 slots): *command, inflict wounds, sanctuary, shield of faith*
2nd level (3 slots): *bestow curse, clairvoyance, dispel magic*
Spider Friend. Spiders see Nyissa as an ally and don't willingly attack her. They can be forced to do so through magical means.
Web Walker. Nyissa ignores movement restrictions caused by webbing.

ACTIONS

Multiattack. Nyissa makes two Shortsword attacks.
Shortsword. *Melee Weapon Attack:* +8 to hit, reach 5 ft., one target. *Hit:* 7 (1d6 + 4) piercing damage, and the target must make a DC 16 Constitution saving throw, taking 21 (6d6) poison damage on a failed save, or half as much damage on a successful one.
Light Crossbow. *Ranged Weapon Attack:* +8 to hit, range 80/320 ft., one target. *Hit:* 8 (1d8 + 4) piercing damage, and the target must make a DC 16 Constitution saving throw, taking 21 (6d6) poison damage on a failed save, or half as much damage on a successful one.
Shadow Bites (recharge 5–6). Nyissa creates a wave of shadowy spiders that unfurls from her and washes over nearby creatures. Each creature within 20 feet of Nyissa must make a DC 16 Constitution saving throw. On a failure, a creature takes 36 (8d8) necrotic damage and is poisoned for 1 minute. On a success, a creature takes half the damage and isn't poisoned.

Osawi al Mujaheba

Medium humanoid (human), neutral
Armor Class 12
Hit Points 75 (10d8 + 30)
Speed 30 ft.

STR	DEX	CON	INT	WIS	CHA
16 (+3)	15 (+2)	16 (+3)	10 (+0)	12 (+1)	12 (+1)

Skills Athletics +5, Insight +3, Perception +3
Senses passive Perception 13
Languages Common, Ignan
Challenge 4 (1,100 XP)

Martial Advantage. Once per turn, Osawi can deal an extra 13 (3d8) damage to a creature he hits with a weapon attack if that creature is within 5 feet of an ally of his that isn't incapacitated.

ACTIONS

Multiattack. Osawi makes two Dagger attacks.
Dagger. Melee or Ranged Weapon Attack: +5 to hit, reach 5 ft. or range 20/60 ft., one target. *Hit:* 5 (1d4 + 3) piercing damage.

Qussay al Nedjari

Medium humanoid (human), neutral
Armor Class 12 (15 with *mage armor*)
Hit Points 104 (16d8 + 32)
Speed 30 ft.

STR	DEX	CON	INT	WIS	CHA
16 (+3)	14 (+2)	14 (+2)	20 (+5)	15 (+2)	13 (+1)

Saving Throws Int +8, Wis +5
Skills Arcana +8, Nature +8, Religion +8
Senses passive Perception 12
Languages Common, Ignan
Challenge 8 (3,900 XP)

Special Equipment. Qussay wears a *robe of fire* and carries a *flaming weapon (light hammer)*[2].
Unaging. Qussay does not age, and cannot be aged by magic.
Spellcasting. Qussay is a 16th-level spellcaster. His spellcasting ability is Intelligence (spell save DC 16, +8 to hit with spell attacks). He has the following wizard spells prepared.

    Cantrips (at will): *acid splash, fire bolt, mage hand, mending, prestidigitation*
    1st level (4 slots): *burning hands, detect magic, mage armor, magic missile*
    2nd level (3 slots): *blindness/deafness, blur, hold person, scorching ray*
    3rd level (3 slots): *dispel magic, fireball, fly*
    4th level (3 slots): *fabricate, fire shield, wall of fire*
    5th level (2 slots): *conjure elemental*
    6th level (1 slot): *disintegrate*
    7th level (1 slot): *prismatic spray*
    8th level (1 slot): *incendiary cloud*

ACTIONS

Flaming Light Hammer. Melee or Ranged Weapon Attack: +7 to hit, reach 5 ft. or range 20/60 ft., one target. *Hit:* 5 (1d4 + 4) bludgeoning damage plus 3 (1d6) fire damage.

Raakham al Abash

Medium humanoid (human), neutral evil
Armor Class 13
Hit Points 88 (16d8 + 16)
Speed 30 ft.

STR	DEX	CON	INT	WIS	CHA
10 (+0)	16 (+3)	13 (+1)	20 (+5)	17 (+3)	11 (+0)

Skills Arcana + 9, Nature +13, Stealth +7
Senses passive Perception 13
Languages Common, Ignan
Challenge 11 (7,200 XP)

Alchemical Substances. Raakham al Abash may imbibe or throw an alchemical substance to create a spell-like effect as a Use an Object action. For this purpose, he is a 16th level spellcaster. Raakham al Abash's spellcasting ability is Intelligence (spell save DC 16). Spell-like effects created by alchemical substances do not require concentration, even if their corresponding spell does, and instead last for the maximum possible duration. These substances are completely inert in the hands of anyone but Raakham al Abash.
Raakham al Abash has the following substances prepared:
3 each/day: *spell potion*[2] *of false life* (as fourth level spell slot), *potion of growth, potion of greater healing, potion of invisibility, stink bomb* (as *stinking cloud* spell)
2 each/day: *fire bomb* (as *fireball* spell with an 80-foot range), *glue bomb* (fills a 10-foot radius within 80 feet with powerful adhesive for 1 minute, so that a creature in that area must succeed on a DC 16 Dexterity saving throw or be restrained — at the beginning of each of the creature's turns, it may attempt a DC 16 Strength saving throw, escaping the area and ceasing to be restrained on a success), *poison bomb* (as *cloudkill* spell with an 80-foot range), *spell potion*[2] *of barkskin*
1 each/day: *confusion bomb* (as *confusion* spell), *potion of flying, spell potion*[2] *of greater invisibility, potion of invulnerability, spell potion*[2] *of regenerate, potion of speed, potion of giant strength (stone), potion of superior healing*
Oil of Sharpness. Raakham al Abash has applied *oil of sharpness* to his dagger, making it magical and granting it a +3 bonus to hit and damage (included below).

Raziya Witch Eye

Medium humanoid (human), lawful evil
Armor Class 15 (*bracers of defense*, 18 with *mage armor*)
Hit Points 32 (5d8 + 10)
Speed 30 ft.

STR	DEX	CON	INT	WIS	CHA
10 (+0)	16 (+3)	14 (+2)	12 (+1)	14 (+2)	18 (+4)

Damage Immunities fire (*Hariph's Amulet*)
Saving Throws Wis +5, Cha +7
Skills Arcana +4, Deception +7
Senses passive Perception 12
Languages Common, Ignan
Challenge 5 (1,800 XP)

Agonizing Blast. When Raziya Witch Eye casts *eldritch blast*, she adds her Charisma modifier to the damage it deals on a hit.
Armor of Shadows. Raziya Witch eye can cast *mage armor* on herself at will, without expending a spell slot or material components.

Dark One's Blessing. When she reduces a hostile creature to 0 hit points, Raziya Witch Eye gains 9 temporary hit points.

Fiendish Vigor. Raziya Witch Eye can cast *false life* on herself at will as a 1st-level spell, without expending a spell slot or material components.

Pact of the Chain. Raziya Witch Eye's fiendish patron has enabled her to summon a quasit to serve as her familiar. It obeys her commands and acts on its own initiative.

Special Equipment. Raziya Witch Eye possesses a *hariph's amulet*[2], a *potion of flying*, a *potion of greater healing*, and a *wand of fireballs*.

Innate Spellcasting. Raziya Witch Eye's spellcasting ability is Charisma (spell save DC 15, +7 to hit with spell attacks). She can cast the following spells without components:

> At will: *eldritch blast, mage hand, poison spray*
> 1/day each: *hellish rebuke, protection from evil and good, enthrall, invisibility, hypnotic pattern, vampiric touch*

ACTIONS

Dagger. *Melee Weapon Attack:* +6 to hit, reach 5 ft., one target. *Hit:* 5 (1d4 + 3) piercing damage.

Crossbow. *Ranged Weapon Attack:* +6 to hit, range 80/320 ft., one target. *Hit:* 7 (1d8 + 3) piercing damage.

Rewonek

Medium humanoid (elf), neutral
Armor Class 14 (studded leather)
Hit Points 66 (12d8 + 12)
Speed 30 ft.

STR	DEX	CON	INT	WIS	CHA
10 (+0)	14 (+2)	12 (+1)	18 (+4)	13 (+1)	12 (+1)

Saving Throws Int +7, Wis +4
Skills Animal Handling +4, Nature +7, Perception +4, Stealth +5, Survival +4
Senses darkvision 120 ft., passive Perception 14
Languages Common, Elvish, Ignan, Undercommon
Challenge 5 (1,800 XP)

Fey Ancestry. Rewonek has advantage on saving throws against being charmed, and magic can't put him to sleep.

Innate Spellcasting. Rewonek's spellcasting ability is Charisma (spell save DC 12). It can innately cast the following spells, requiring no material components:

> At will: *dancing lights*
> 1/day each: *darkness, faerie fire*

Spellcasting. Rewonek is a 9th-level spellcaster. His spellcasting ability is Intelligence (spell save DC 15, +7 to hit with spell attacks). He has the following wizard spells prepared.

> Cantrips (at will): *acid splash, mage hand, mending, ray of frost*
> 1st level (4 slots): *charm person, detect magic, magic missile, shield*
> 2nd level (3 slots): *blur, hold person, shatter*
> 3rd level (3 slots): *dispel magic, fly, lightning bolt*
> 4th level (3 slots): *banishment, black tentacles*
> 5th level (1 slot): *wall of force*

Sunlight Sensitivity. While in sunlight, Rewonek has disadvantage on attack rolls, as well as on Wisdom (Perception) checks that rely on sight.

ACTIONS

Multiattack. Rewonek makes two Shortsword attacks.

Shortsword. *Melee Weapon Attack:* +5 to hit, reach 5 ft., one target. *Hit:* 5 (1d6 + 2) piercing damage.

Hand Crossbow. *Ranged Weapon Attack:* +5 to hit, range 30/120 feet, one target. *Hit:* 5 (1d6 + 2) piercing damage, and the target must succeed on a DC 13 Constitution saving throw or be poisoned for 1 hour. If the saving throw fails by 5 or more, the target is also unconscious while poisoned in this way. The target wakes up if it takes damage or if another creature takes an action to shake it awake.

Sarmad Yazdg-or

Medium humanoid (human), lawful evil
Armor Class 18 (robe of armor, ring of superior protection)
Hit Points 91 (14d8 + 28)
Speed 30 ft.

STR	DEX	CON	INT	WIS	CHA
12 (+1)	14 (+2)	14 (+2)	13 (+1)	18 (+4)	13 (+1)

Saving Throws Wis +8, Cha +5
Skills Arcana +5, History +5, Medicine +8, Persuasion +5, Religion +5
Damage Resistances lightning, thunder
Senses passive Perception 14
Languages Auran, Common, Celestial, Infernal
Challenge 10 (5,900 XP)

Special Equipment. Sarmad wears a *circlet of telepathy* (as the helm), a *ring of superior protection*[2], a *robe of armor*[2], and carries *spell scrolls of planar ally, dispel evil and good,* and *harm.*

Potent Cantrip. Whenever Sarmad casts a cantrip that deals damage, he deals an additional 4 damage of the same type as the cantrip.

Spellcasting. Sarmad is a 14th-level spellcaster. His spellcasting ability is Wisdom (spell save DC 16, +8 to hit with spell attacks). Sarmad has the following cleric spells prepared.

> Cantrips (at will): *guidance, light, lightning spike*[4], *resistance, shocking grasp*
> 1st level (4 slots): *bane, cure wounds, detect magic, identify, inflict wounds, magic missile*
> 2nd level (3 slots): *aid, arcane lock, blindness/deafness, lesser restoration, mirror image, silence, spiritual weapon*
> 3rd level (3 slots): *dispel magic, gaseous form, lightning bolt, spirit guardians*
> 4th level (3 slots): *arcane eye, banishment, dimension door*
> 5th level (2 slots): *conjure elemental, insect plague, legend lore*
> 6th level (2 slots): *blade barrier, true seeing*
> 7th level (1 slot): *divine word*

ACTIONS

Dagger. *Melee or Ranged Weapon Attack:* +5 to hit, reach 5 ft. or range 20/60 ft., one target. *Hit:* 1d4 + 2 piercing damage.

Beckon Hellhound (1/long rest). Sarmad calls to Hecate and summons 1d4 **hellhounds**, which appears in an unoccupied space within 5 feet of him. A summoned hellhound remains for 1 minute, until it or Sarmad is slain, or until Sarmad takes an action to dismiss it.

Turn Undead (1/short or long rest). Each undead that can see or hear Sarmad within 30 feet of him must make a DC 16 Wisdom saving throw. On a failed saving throw, if the undead's Challenge Rating is 2 or lower, it is instantly destroyed. If the undead's Challenge Rating is 3 or higher, it is turned for 1 minute. While turned, the undead must use its turns trying to move as far away from Sarmad as it can, and it can't willingly move into a space within 30 feet of him. It cannot take reactions, and can only take the Dash action, or try to escape from an effect that prevents it from moving.

REACTIONS

Divine Intervention (1/long rest). If Sarmad is reduced to 10 hit points or less, he can use a reaction to enact one of the following options:
Cause himself or another creature within 30 feet of him to regain 36 (8d8) hit points.
Teleport to a location he is familiar with up to 1 mile away.
Restore one dead creature back to life, as long as that creature has been dead for no more than 1 minute.

Shazier

Medium humanoid (dwarf), neutral evil
Armor Class 19 (+3 *studded leather*)
Hit Points 97 (15d8 + 30)
Speed 25 ft., climb 25 ft.

STR	DEX	CON	INT	WIS	CHA
17 (+3)	18 (+4)	15 (+2)	14 (+2)	16 (+3)	12 (+1)

Saving Throws Str +6, Dex +7
Skills Nature +5, Perception +6, Stealth +7, Survival +6
Damage Resistances poison
Senses darkvision 60 ft., passive Perception 16
Languages Common, Dwarven, Ignan
Challenge 7 (2,900 XP)

Special Equipment. Shazier wears a set of *+3 studded leather armor* and a pair of *slippers of spider climbing*. The dwarf's favored weapon is a *+3 warhammer*.
Dwarven Resilience. Shazier has advantage on saving throws to resist poison.
Favored Enemy. Shazier treats fiends and giants as his favored enemy. He has advantage on Wisdom (Survival) checks to track its favored enemies as well as on Intelligence checks to recall information about them. In addition, when Shazier hits with a weapon attack on a fiend or giant, he can deal an additional 10 (3d6) damage to the target of the attack.
Keen Hearing and Sight. Shazier has advantage on Wisdom (Perception) checks related to hearing or sight.

ACTIONS

Multiattack. Shazier can make two Warhammer attacks, or one Heavy Crossbow attack.
Warhammer. *Melee Weapon Attack:* +9 to hit, reach 5 ft., one target. *Hit:* 10 (1d8 + 6) bludgeoning damage, or 11 (1d10 + 6) bludgeoning damage if wielded with two hands.
Heavy Crossbow. *Ranged Weapon Attack:* +7 to hit, range 100/400 ft., one target. *Hit:* 9 (1d10 + 4) piercing damage.

Sheriff Bolen

Medium humanoid (human), lawful evil
Armor Class 18 (chain mail and shield)
Hit Points 52 (8d8 + 16)
Speed 30 ft.

STR	DEX	CON	INT	WIS	CHA
12 (+1)	14 (+2)	15 (+2)	12 (+1)	12 (+1)	16 (+3)

Skills Insight +5, Perception +5, Persuasion +5
Senses passive Perception 15
Languages Common, Elven, Giant, Goblin
Challenge 2 (450 XP)

Leadership (recharges after a short or long rest). For 1 minute, Sheriff Bolen can utter a special command or warning whenever a nonhostile creature that it can see within 30 feet of it makes an attack roll or a saving throw. The creature can add a d4 to its roll provided it can hear and understand Sheriff Bolen. A creature can benefit from only one Leadership die at a time. This effect ends if Sheriff Bolen is incapacitated.

ACTIONS

Longsword. *Melee Weapon Attack:* +3 to hit, reach 5 ft., one target. *Hit:* 5 (1d8 + 1) slashing damage, or 6 (1d10 + 1) if used with two hands.
Heavy Crossbow. *Ranged Weapon Attack:* +4 to hit, range 100/400, one target. *Hit:* 7 (1d10 + 2) piercing damage.

Sir Leobilus

Medium humanoid (human), lawful good
Armor Class 11
Hit Points 135 (18d8 + 54)
Speed 30 ft.

STR	DEX	CON	INT	WIS	CHA
16 (+3)	12 (+1)	16 (+3)	9 (−1)	17 (+3)	18 (+4)

Saving Throws Con +7, Wis +7, Cha +8
Skills Medicine +7, Perception +7
Senses passive Perception 17
Languages Common
Challenge 11 (7,200 XP)

Aura of Protection. An aura of protection surrounds Sir Leobilus. Sir Leobilus and his allies within 10 feet of him can add his Charisma bonus to saving throws.
Aura of Courage. Sir Leobilus and his allies that are within 10 feet of him cannot be frightened.
Divine Health. Sir Leobilus is immune to disease.
Divine Sense. Sir Leobilus is aware of the location of any celestial, fiend, or undead within 60 feet. Within the same radius he can also detect the presence of any place or object that has been consecrated or desecrated.
Divine Strike. Whenever Sir Leobilus hits a creature with a melee attack, the creature takes an extra 1d8 radiant damage (included in below).
Lay on Hands. As an action, Sir Leobilus can touch a creature, healing it for a maximum of 60 hit points. After he has healed a total of 60 hit points, he can't use this ability again until after a short or long rest.
Spellcasting. Sir Leobilus is a 12th-level spellcaster. His spellcasting ability is Charisma (spell save DC 15, +7 to hit with spell attacks). He can cast the following spells:
    1st level (4 slots): *bless, cure wounds, divine favor, shield of faith*
    2nd level (3 slots): *aid, branding smite, lesser restoration*
    3rd level (3 slots): *create food and water, remove curse, revivify*

ACTIONS

Multiattack. Sir Leobilus makes three melee attacks.
Unarmed Strike. *Melee Weapon Attack:* +7 to hit, reach 5 ft., one target. *Hit:* 4 (1d2 + 3) bludgeoning damage and 4 (1d8) radiant damage.
Longsword. *Melee Weapon Attack:* +7 to hit, reach 5 ft., one target. *Hit:* 7 (1d8 + 3) slashing damage, or 8 (1d10 +

3) slashing damage if used with two hands, and 4 (1d8) radiant damage.

Shield Bash. *Melee Weapon Attack:* +7 to hit, reach 5 ft., one target. *Hit:* 8 (2d4 + 3) bludgeoning damage and 4 (1d8) radiant damage, and the target must succeed on a DC 15 Strength saving throw or be knocked prone.

Tatho the Mindwrack

Medium humanoid (human), lawful evil
Armor Class 19 (robe of armor, bracers of greater defense)
Hit Points 99 (18d8 + 18)
Speed 30 ft.

STR	DEX	CON	INT	WIS	CHA
13 (+1)	15 (+2)	12 (+1)	20 (+5)	16 (+3)	16 (+3)

Saving Throws Int +9, Wis +7
Skills Arcana +9, Deception +7, History +9, Insight +7, Medicine +7, Perception +7
Damage Immunities fire, psychic
Senses passive Perception 17
Languages Aklo, Common, Ignan; telepathy 120 ft.
Challenge 11 (7,200 XP)

Special Equipment. Tatho wears a pair of *bracers of greater defense*[2], a *ring of immunity* (fire)[2], a *robe of armor*[2], and wields a *staff of illusion*[2].

Magic Resistance. Tatho has advantage on saving throws against spells and other magical effects.

Master of the Mind. Tatho always succeeds on Constitution saving throws to maintain concentration on enchantment and illusion spells. Whenever Tatho casts an enchantment or illusion spell, Tatho can use his reaction to force a target to reroll their saving throw, taking the lower of the two results.

Spellcasting. Tatho is an 18th-level spellcaster. His spellcasting ability is Intelligence (spell save DC 17, +9 to hit with spell attacks). He can cast the *charm person* and *suggestion* spells at will. He has the following wizard spells prepared.

> Cantrips (at will): *chill touch, dancing lights, fire bolt, minor illusion, shocking grasp*
> 1st level (4 slots): *detect magic, hideous laughter, magic missile, shield*
> 2nd level (3 slots): *blindness/deafness, detect thoughts, mirror image, alter self*
> 3rd level (3 slots): *bestow curse, dispel magic, hypnotic pattern, slow*
> 4th level (3 slots): *greater invisibility, hallucinatory terrain, phantasmal killer*
> 5th level (3 slots): *dominate person, modify memory, seeming*
> 6th level (1 slot): *mass suggestion*
> 7th level (1 slot): *forcecage*
> 8th level (1 slot): *feeblemind*
> 9th level (1 slot): *weird*

ACTIONS

Psychic Blast. Tatho releases a psychic blast in a 30-foot cone. Creatures in the area must make a DC 17 Intelligence saving throw. On a failed saving throw, the target takes 27 (4d10 + 5) psychic damage and is stunned until the end of the target's next turn. On a successful saving throw, the target takes half damage and is not stunned.

Dagger. *Melee or Ranged Weapon Attack:* +6 to hit, reach 5 ft. or range 20/60 ft., one target. *Hit:* 4 (1d4 + 2) piercing damage.

Tegman Zekii

Medium humanoid (human), lawful evil
Armor Class 16 (studded leather armor)
Hit Points 39 (6d8 + 12)
Speed 30 ft.

STR	DEX	CON	INT	WIS	CHA
14 (+2)	18 (+4)	14 (+2)	16 (+3)	13 (+1)	9 (−1)

Saving Throws Dex +7, Int +6, Wis +4
Skills Acrobatics +7, Arcana +6, Insight +4, Perception +4, Sleight of Hand +7, Stealth +7
Senses passive Perception 14
Languages Common
Challenge 5 (1,800 XP)

Assassinate. Tegman Zekii has advantage on attack rolls against any creature that hasn't yet acted in the combat, and any hit he scores against a surprised creature counts as a critical hit.

Cunning Action. Tegman Zekii can take a bonus action on each of his turns in combat. This action can be used only to take the Dash, Disengage, or Hide action.

Sneak Attack. Once per turn, Tegman Zekii can deal an extra 2d6 damage to one creature he hits with a Dagger attack if he has advantage on the attack roll. He doesn't need advantage on the attack roll if another enemy of the target is within 5 feet of it and that enemy isn't incapacitated.

Special Equipment. Tegman Zekii possesses *dust of disappearance* and a *potion of greater healing*.

Spellcasting. Tegman Zekii is a 3rd level spellcaster. His spellcasting ability is Intelligence (spell save DC 14, +6 to hit with spell attacks). He has the following spells prepared:

> Cantrips (at will): *dancing lights, poison spray, prestidigitation*
> 1st level (4 slots): *burning hands, charm person, fog cloud*
> 2nd level (2 slots): *invisibility, mirror image, misty step*

ACTIONS

+1 Dagger. *Melee or Ranged Weapon Attack:* +8 to hit, reach 5 ft. or range 20/60 ft., one target. *Hit:* 7 (1d4 + 5) piercing damage plus 9 (2d8) poison damage.

BONUS ACTIONS

Hypnosis. Tegman Zekii uses his charming voice to hypnotize one creature within 15 feet of him who can hear and understand him. The creature must succeed on a DC 14 Wisdom saving throw or be charmed until the end of his next turn. A hypnotized creature is incapacitated and does nothing but gaze at Tegman Zekii. The effect ends for a hypnotized creature if that creature takes damage or is more than 15 feet from Tegman Zekii.

The Builders

Medium humanoid (human), neutral
Armor Class 12
Hit Points 91 (14d8 + 28)
Speed 30 ft.

STR	DEX	CON	INT	WIS	CHA
12 (+1)	14 (+2)	14 (+2)	13 (+1)	18 (+4)	13 (+1)

Saving Throws Wis +8, Cha +5
Skills Arcana +5, History +5, Medicine +8, Persuasion +5, Religion +5
Damage Immunities fire
Senses passive Perception 14
Languages Common, Ignan
Challenge 8 (3,900 XP)

Potent Cantrip. Whenever the builder casts a cantrip that deals damage, it deals an additional 4 damage of the same type as the cantrip.

Unaging. The builders do not age, and cannot be aged by magic.

Spellcasting. The builders are 14th-level spellcasters. Their spellcasting ability is Wisdom (spell save DC 16, +8 to hit with spell attacks). They have the following cleric spells prepared.

> Cantrips (at will): *guidance, light, resistance, sacred flame, shocking grasp*
> 1st level (4 slots): *bless, create or destroy water, cure wounds, detect magic, guiding bolt*
> 2nd level (3 slots): *aid, blindness/deafness, lesser restoration, shatter, silence, spiritual weapon*
> 3rd level (3 slots): *dispel magic, protection from energy, spirit guardians*
> 4th level (3 slots): *banishment, dimension door, stone shape*
> 5th level (2 slots): *commune, greater restoration*
> 6th level (2 slots): *blade barrier, true seeing*
> 7th level (1 slot): *divine word*

ACTIONS

Turn Undead (1/short or long rest). Each undead that can see or hear the builder within 30 feet of it must make a DC 16 Wisdom saving throw. On a failed saving throw, if the undead's Challenge Rating is 2 or lower, it is instantly destroyed. If the undead's Challenge Rating is 3 or higher, it is turned for 1 minute. While turned, the undead must use its turns trying to move as far away from the builder as it can, and it can't willingly move into a space within 30 feet of him. It cannot take reactions, and can only take the Dash action, or try to escape from an effect that prevents it from moving.

REACTIONS

Divine Intervention (1/long rest). If the builder is reduced to 10 hit points or less, it can use a reaction to enact one of the following options:

- Cause itself or another creature within 30 feet of it to regain 36 (8d8) hit points.
- Teleport to a location it is familiar with up to 1 mile away.
- Restore one dead creature back to life, as long as that creature has been dead for no more than 1 minute.

Tienen

Medium humanoid (human), chaotic neutral
Armor Class 18 (*glamoured studded leather*)
Hit Points 123 (19d8 + 38)
Speed 30 ft.

STR	DEX	CON	INT	WIS	CHA
11 (+0)	20 (+5)	14 (+2)	20 (+5)	17 (+3)	16 (+3)

Saving Throws Dex +10, Int +10, Wis +8
Skills Acrobatics +15, Arcana +10, Athletics +5, Deception +8, Insight +8, Perception +13, Sleight of Hand +15, Stealth +15
Damage Immunities fire
Senses blindsight 10 ft., passive Perception 23
Languages Common, Ignan, Thieves' cant
Challenge 13 (10,000 XP)

Special Equipment. Tienen wears a set of *glamoured studded leather*, as well as a *ring of immunity* (fire) and a *cloak of etherealness*. His most prized possession, however, is his *amulet of the planes*.

Adept's Legerdemain. Tienen can summon a magical dagger, rapier, or shortsword, or a set of thieves' tools, as a bonus action on his turn. The objects count as magical for the purposes of damage resistances and immunities and disappear after 1 minute. In addition, Tienen can expend a spell slot when conjuring a weapon. When he does so, the weapon deals an additional 3 (1d6) damage for a 1st level spell slot, plus 3 (1d6) for each additional spell slot level above 1st, until the weapon is dismissed.

Cunning Action. Tienen can use a bonus action on his turn to take the Dash, Disengage, or Hide action.

Evasion. When Tienen is subjected to an effect that allows him to make a Dexterity saving throw to take only half damage, he instead takes no damage if the saving throw is successful, and only half damage if the roll is a failure.

Sneak Attack. Once per turn, Tienen can deal an extra 31 (9d6) damage to one creature he hits with an attack if he has advantage on the attack roll. The attack must use a finesse or ranged weapon. Tienen doesn't need advantage on the attack roll if another enemy of the target is within 5 feet of it, that enemy isn't incapacitated, and Tienen doesn't have disadvantage on the attack roll.

Spellcasting. Tienen is a 19th-level spellcaster. His spellcasting ability is Intelligence (spell save DC 18, +10 to hit with spell attacks). He knows the following wizard spells.

> Cantrips (at will): *acid splash, mage hand, minor illusion, prestidigitation*
> 1st level (4 slots): *color spray, detect magic, feather fall, identify*
> 2nd level (3 slots): *blur, detect thoughts, knock, invisibility*
> 3rd level (3 slots): *dispel magic, fly, haste, nondetection*
> 4th level (1 slot): *greater invisibility*

ACTIONS

Multiattack. Tienen makes two Dagger, Rapier, or Shortsword attacks.

Dagger. +10 to hit, reach 5 ft. or range 20/60 ft., one target. *Hit:* 7 (1d4 + 5) piercing damage.

Rapier. +10 to hit, reach 5 ft., one target. *Hit:* 9 (1d8 + 5) piercing damage.

Shortsword. +10 to hit, reach 5 ft., one target. *Hit:* 8 (1d6 + 5) piercing damage.

Uncanny Dodge. Tienen halves the damage that he takes from one attack that hits him. Tienen must be able to see the attacker to use this ability.

Wahawk Deathbear

Medium humanoid (bugbear), chaotic evil
Armor Class 19 (+2 breastplate)
Hit Points 105 (14d8 + 42)
Speed 30 ft.

STR	DEX	CON	INT	WIS	CHA
18 (+4)	14 (+2)	16 (+3)	11 (+0)	12 (+1)	13(+1)

Saving Throws Str +7, Con +6
Skills Intimidation +4, Stealth +5, Survival +4
Senses darkvision 60 ft., passive Perception 11
Languages Common, Goblin
Challenge 7 (2,900 XP)

Action Surge (recharges After a short or long rest). Wahawk Deathbear may make one additional action on his turn on top of his normal action (and possible bonus action).
Boots of Haste. Wahawk Deathbear possesses a pair of *boots of haste*[2].
Brute. A melee weapon deals one extra die of its damage when Wahawk Deathbear hits with it (included in the attack).
Defense. Wahawk Deathbear gains +1 to his AC while wearing armor (included above)
Heart of the Tiger. Wahawk Deathbear has advantage on saving throws against being charmed, frightened, paralyzed, poisoned, stunned, or put to sleep.
Improved Critical. Wahawk Deathbear's weapon attacks score a critical hit on a roll of 19 or 20.
Indomitable (1/day). Wahawk Deathbear may reroll an unsuccessful saving throw. He must use the second roll.
Remarkable Athlete. Wahawk Deathbear may add +2 to any Strength, Dexterity, or Constitution check that doesn't already incorporate his proficiency bonus.
Surprise Attack. If Wahawk Deathbear surprises a creature and hits it with an attack during the first round of combat, the target takes an extra 7 (2d6) damage from the attack.

ACTIONS

Multiattack. Wahawk Deathbear may make two melee attacks.
+2 Great Mace. *Melee Weapon Attack:* +9 to hit, reach 5 ft., one target. *Hit:* 16 (3d6 + 6) bludgeoning damage.

BONUS ACTIONS

Second Wind (recharges after a short or long rest). As a bonus action, Wahawk Deathbear may regain 1d10 + 10 hit points.

Hydras

Cryohydra, Elder

Huge monstrosity, unaligned
Armor Class 18 (natural armor)
Hit Points 275 (22d12 + 132)
Speed 30 ft., swim 30 ft.

STR	DEX	CON	INT	WIS	CHA
22 (+6)	12 (+1)	22 (+6)	2 (–4)	10 (+0)	7 (–2)

Skills Perception +12
Damage Immunities cold
Senses darkvision 60 ft., passive Perception 22
Languages —
Challenge 20 (25,000 XP)

Hold Breath. The elder cryohydra can hold its breath for 1 hour.
Multiple Heads. The elder cryohydra has twelve heads. While it has more than one head, the elder cryohydra has advantage on saving throws against being blinded, charmed, deafened, frightened, stunned, and knocked unconscious.
Whenever the elder cryohydra takes 25 or more damage in a single turn, one of its heads dies. If all its heads die, the elder cryohydra dies.
At the end of its turn, it grows two heads (up to a maximum of twenty-four heads) for each of its heads that died since its last turn, unless it has taken fire damage since its last turn. The elder cryohydra regains 10 hit points for each head regrown in this way.
If the cryophydra has more than twelve heads, it loses one of its heads when it takes a long rest.
Reactive Heads. For each head the elder cryohydra has beyond one, it gets an extra reaction that can be used only for opportunity attacks.
Wakeful. While the elder cryohydra sleeps, at least one of its heads is awake.

ACTIONS

Multiattack. The elder cryohydra makes one Bite attack with each head.
Bite. *Melee Weapon Attack:* +11 to hit, reach 10 ft., one target. *Hit:* 11 (1d10 + 6) piercing damage plus 5 (2d4) cold damage.
Cold Breath (recharge 5–6). The elder cryohydra uses all its heads to exhale frost which fills a 30-foot radius sphere centered on a point it chooses within 60 feet of it. Each creature in that area must make a DC 19 Dexterity saving throw, taking 84 (24d6) cold damage on a failed save or half as much on a successful one.

Pyrohydra, Greater

Huge monstrosity, unaligned
Armor Class 17 (natural armor)
Hit Points 218 (19d12 + 95)
Speed 30 ft., swim 30 ft.

STR	DEX	CON	INT	WIS	CHA
21 (+5)	12 (+1)	21 (+5)	2 (–4)	10 (+0)	7 (–2)

Skills Perception +10
Damage Immunities fire
Senses darkvision 60 ft., passive Perception 20
Languages —
Challenge 16 (15,000 XP)

Hold Breath. The greater pyrohydra can hold its breath for 1 hour.

Multiple Heads. The greater pyrohydra has nine heads. While it has more than one head, the greater pyrohydra has advantage on saving throws against being blinded, charmed, deafened, frightened, stunned, and knocked unconscious.

Whenever the greater pyrohydra takes 25 or more damage in a single turn, one of its heads dies. If all its heads die, the greater pyrohydra dies.

At the end of its turn, it grows two heads (up to a maximum of eighteen heads) for each of its heads that died since its last turn, unless it has taken acid or cold damage since its last turn. The greater pyrohydra regains 10 hit points for each head regrown in this way.

If the pyophydra has more than nine heads, it loses one of its heads when it takes a long rest.

Reactive Heads. For each head the elder pyrohydra has beyond one, it gets an extra reaction that can be used only for opportunity attacks.

Wakeful. While the greater pyrohydra sleeps, at least one of its heads is awake.

Actions

Multiattack. The greater pyrohydra makes one Bite attack with each head.

Bite. *Melee Weapon Attack:* +10 to hit, reach 10 ft., one target. *Hit:* 10 (1d10 + 5) piercing damage plus 5 (2d4) cold damage.

Fire Breath (recharge 5–6). The greater pyrohydra uses all its heads to exhale flame which fills a 25-foot radius sphere centered on a point it chooses within 50 feet of it. Each creature in that area must make a DC 18 Dexterity saving throw, taking 63 (18d6) fire damage on a failed save or half as much on a successful one.

Hyaenodon, Undead

Large undead, neutral evil
Armor Class 15 (natural armor)
Hit Points 75 (10d10 + 20)
Speed 30 ft.

STR	DEX	CON	INT	WIS	CHA
19 (+4)	16 (+3)	14 (+2)	7 (–2)	13 (+1)	6 (–2)

Skills Perception +7, Stealth +6, Survival +7
Damage Resistances necrotic
Damage Immunities poison
Condition Immunities charmed, exhaustion, poisoned
Senses darkvision 60 ft., passive Perception 17
Languages —
Challenge 5 (1,800 XP)

Improved Sense of Smell. The undead hyaenodon has advantage on Perception checks that rely on scent.

Actions

Multiattack. The undead hyaenodon makes one Bite attack and one Claws attack.

Bite. *Melee Weapon Attack:* +7 to hit, reach 5 ft., one creature. *Hit:* 15 (2d10 + 4) piercing damage. If the target is a creature other than an elf or an undead, it must succeed on a DC 13 Constitution saving throw or contract ghoul fever. A creature affected by this disease shows symptoms including fatigue, strange cravings, and muscle aches after 1d4 hours and gains one level of exhaustion. An infected creature regains no hit points from short or long rests and must make a DC 13 Constitution saving throw at the completion of each long rest. On a failed save, the creature gains one level of exhaustion. On a successful save, the creature loses one level of exhaustion. If a successful saving throw reduces a creature's exhaustion level to 0, the creature is cured. If a creature dies of this disease, it rises as a ghoul at the next midnight.

Claws. *Melee Weapon Attack:* +7 to hit, reach 5 ft., one target. *Hit:* 13 (2d8 + 4) slashing damage. If the target is a creature other than an elf or an undead, it must succeed on a DC 13 Constitution saving throw or be paralyzed for 1 minute. The target can repeat the saving throw at the end of each of its turns, ending the effect on itself on a success.

Iron Cobra

Small construct, neutral
Armor Class 13 (natural armor)
Hit Points 27 (6d6 + 6)
Speed 40 ft.

STR	DEX	CON	INT	WIS	CHA
12 (+1)	15 (+2)	13 (+1)	5 (–3)	12 (+1)	1 (–5)

Skills Perception +3, Stealth +4
Damage Immunities poison, psychic; bludgeoning, piercing, and slashing from nonmagical attacks not made with adamantine
Condition Immunities charmed, exhaustion, frightened, paralyzed, petrified, poisoned
Senses darkvision 60 ft., passive Perception 13
Languages understands the languages of its creator but can't speak
Challenge 1 (200 XP)

Find Target. The iron cobra knows the location of a specific target creature as long as that creature is within 1 mile of it. If the creature is moving, it knows the direction if that creature's movement. If the target is beyond this distance, the iron cobra can't locate the target creature.

Immutable Form. The iron cobra is immune to any spell or effect that would alter its form.

Magic Resistance. The iron cobra has advantage on saving throws against spells and other magical effects.

Magic Weapon. The iron cobra's weapon attacks are magical.

Poison. The iron cobra contains enough venom for three attacks. After that, it does not deal the poison damage listed in its bite attack.

Actions

Bite. *Melee Weapon Attack:* +4 to hit, reach 5 ft., one target. *Hit:* 7 (2d4 + 2) piercing damage, and the target must make a DC 11 Constitution saving throw, taking 10 (3d6) poison damage on a failed saving throw, or half as much damage on a successful one.

Jackalweres

Acolyte of Set

Medium humanoid (shapechanger), chaotic evil
Armor Class 16 (breastplate)
Hit Points 91 (14d8 + 28)
Speed 30 ft.

STR	DEX	CON	INT	WIS	CHA
15 (+2)	16 (+3)	15 (+2)	12 (+1)	19 (+4)	14 (+2)

Skills Deception +5, Insight +7, Perception +7, Religion +7
Damage Immunities bludgeoning, piercing, and slashing

from nonmagical attacks not made with silver

Senses passive Perception 17
Languages Common (can't speak in jackal form)
Challenge 7 (2,900 XP)

Blessing of Set. As a bonus action, the acolyte of Set targets one ally it can see within 30 feet of it. The next time the target hits with any weapon, the weapon deals an extra 7 (2d6) poison damage.

Keen Smell. The acolyte of Set has advantage on Wisdom (Perception) checks that rely on smell.

Rampage (jackal or hybrid form only). When the acolyte of Set reduces a creature to 0 hit points with a melee attack on its turn, the acolyte can take a bonus action to move up to half its speed and make a bite attack.

Shapechanger. The acolyte of Set can use its action to polymorph into a specific Medium human or a jackal-humanoid hybrid, or back into its true form, which is a Small jackal. Any equipment it is wearing or carrying isn't transformed. It reverts to its true form if it dies.

Spellcasting. The acolyte of Set is a 10th-level spellcaster. Its spellcasting ability is Intelligence (spells save DC 15, +7 to hit with spell attacks). The acolyte has the following cleric spells prepared:

Cantrips (at will): *guidance, light, mending, sacred flame, thaumaturgy*
1st level (4 slots): *command, cure wounds, inflict wounds, protection from evil and good*
2nd level (3 slots): *blindness/deafness, hold person, silence*
3rd level (3 slots): *animate dead, bestow curse, speak with dead*
4th level (3 slots): *freedom of movement, locate creature*
5th level (2 slots): *contagion, insect plague*

ACTIONS

Multiattack (humanoid or hybrid form only). The acolyte of Set uses its Sleep Gaze and makes three attacks, only one of which can be a Bite.

Bite (jackal or hybrid form only). *Melee Weapon Attack:* +6 to hit, reach 5 ft., one target. *Hit:* 7 (1d8 + 3) piercing damage plus 10 (3d6) poison damage, and the target must succeed on a DC 14 Constitution saving throw or be poisoned until the end of its next turn.

Pike (humanoid or hybrid form only). *Melee Weapon Attack:* +5 to hit, reach 10 ft., one target. *Hit:* 7 (1d10 + 2) piercing damage.

Sleep Gaze. The acolyte of Set gazes at one creature it can see within 30 feet of it. The target must make a DC 15 Wisdom saving throw. On a failed save, the target succumbs to a magical slumber, falling unconscious for 10 minutes or until someone uses an action to shake the target awake. A creature that successfully saves against the effect is immune to this acolyte's gaze for the next 24 hours. Undead and creatures immune to being charmed aren't affected by it.

High Priest of Set

Medium humanoid (shapechanger), chaotic evil
Armor Class 17 (half plate)
Hit Points 169 (26d8 + 52)
Speed 30 ft.

STR	DEX	CON	INT	WIS	CHA
18 (+4)	16 (+3)	15 (+2)	12 (+1)	21 (+5)	16 (+3)

Skills Deception +8, Insight +10, Perception +10, Persuasion +8, Religion +11

Damage Immunities bludgeoning, piercing, and slashing from nonmagical attacks not made with silver
Senses passive Perception 20
Languages Common (can't speak in jackal form)
Challenge 14 (11,500 XP)

Keen Smell. The high priest of Set has advantage on Wisdom (Perception) checks that rely on smell.

My Brother's Killer. As a bonus action, the high priest of Set targets one creature it can see within 30 feet of it. The target must succeed on a DC 18 Charisma saving throw or use its reaction to make one attack roll against its nearest ally.

Rampage (jackal or hybrid form only). When the high priest of Set reduces a creature to 0 hit points with a melee attack on its turn, the high priest can take a bonus action to move up to half its speed and make a bite attack.

Shapechanger. The high priest of Set can use its action to polymorph into a specific Medium human or a jackal-humanoid hybrid, or back into its true form, which is a Small jackal. Any equipment it is wearing or carrying isn't transformed. It reverts to its true form if it dies.

Spellcasting. The high priest of Set is a 16th-level spellcaster. Its spellcasting ability is Intelligence (spells save DC 18, +10 to hit with spell attacks). The high priest has the following cleric spells prepared:

Cantrips (at will): *guidance, light, mending, sacred flame, thaumaturgy*
1st level (4 slots): *command, cure wounds, inflict wounds, protection from evil and good*
2nd level (3 slots): *blindness/deafness, hold person, silence*
3rd level (3 slots): *animate dead, bestow curse, speak with dead*
4th level (3 slots): *divination, freedom of movement, locate creature*
5th level (2 slots): *contagion, flame strike, insect plague*
6th level (1 slot): *create undead, harm*
7th level (1 slot): *divine word, symbol*
8th level (1 slot): *antimagic field*

ACTIONS

Multiattack (humanoid or hybrid form only). The high priest of Set uses its Eyes of Set and makes four attacks, only one of which can be a Bite.

Bite (jackal or hybrid form only). *Melee Weapon Attack:* +9 to hit, reach 5 ft., one target. *Hit:* 8 (1d8 + 4) piercing damage plus 21 (6d6) poison damage, and the target must succeed on a DC 18 Constitution saving throw or be poisoned for 1 minute.

Pike (humanoid or hybrid form only). *Melee Weapon Attack:* +9 to hit, reach 10 ft., one target. *Hit:* 9 (1d10 + 4) piercing damage.

Eyes of Set. The high priest of Set gazes at one creature it can see within 30 feet of it. The target must make a DC 18 Wisdom saving throw or be affected by one of the below gazes. The high priest can't use the same gaze two rounds in a row. Undead and creatures immune to being charmed aren't affected by the high priest's Eyes of Set.

Conversion Gaze. On a failed save, the target is charmed for 1 minute. The charmed target obeys the high priest's verbal commands. If the target suffers any harm or receives a suicidal command, it can repeat the saving throw, ending the effect on a success. If the target successfully saves against the effect, or if the effect ends on it, the target is immune to this high priest's Conversion Gaze for the next 24 hours. The high priest can have only one target charmed at a time. If it uses its Conversion Gaze on another target, the effect on the previous target ends.

Frightful Gaze. On a failed save, the target is frightened for 1 minute. The frightened target can repeat the saving throw at the end of each of its turns, ending the effect on itself on a success. If a creature's saving throw is successful or the effect ends for it, the creature is immune to the high priest's Frightful Gaze for the next 24 hours.

Sleep Gaze. On a failed save, the target succumbs to a magical slumber, falling unconscious for 10 minutes or until someone uses an action to shake the target awake. A creature that successfully saves against the effect is immune to this high priest's Sleep Gaze for the next 24 hours.

Jackalwere

Medium humanoid (shapechanger), chaotic evil
Armor Class 14
Hit Points 26 (4d8 + 8)
Speed 30 ft.qa34

STR	DEX	CON	INT	WIS	CHA
15 (+2)	18 (+4)	15 (+2)	12 (+1)	12 (+1)	10 (+0)

Skills Deception +4, Perception +5, Stealth +6
Damage Immunities bludgeoning, piercing, and slashing from nonmagical attacks not made with silver
Senses passive Perception 15
Languages Common (can't speak in jackal form)
Challenge 2 (450 XP)

Keen Smell. The jackalwere has advantage on Wisdom (Perception) checks that rely on smell.

Pack Tactics. The jackalwere has advantage on an attack roll against a creature if at least one of the jackalwere's allies is within 5 ft. of the creature and the ally isn't incapacitated.

Rampage (jackal or hybrid form only). When the jackalwere reduces a creature to 0 hit points with a melee attack on its turn, the jackalwere can take a bonus action to move up to half its speed and make a bite attack.

Shapechanger. The jackalwere can use its action to polymorph into a specific Medium human or a jackal-humanoid hybrid, or back into its true form, which is a Small jackal. Its statistics, other than its size, are the same in each form. Any equipment it is wearing or carrying isn't transformed. It reverts to its true form if it dies.

Actions

Multiattack (jackal or hybrid form only). The jackalwere makes two melee weapon attacks.

Bite (jackal or hybrid form only). *Melee Weapon Attack:* +6 to hit, reach 5 ft., one target. *Hit:* 8 (1d8 + 4) piercing damage.

Battleaxe (humanoid or hybrid form only). *Melee Weapon Attack:* +4 to hit, reach 5 ft., one target. *Hit:* 6 (1d8 + 2) slashing damage, or 7 (1d10 + 2) slashing damage if used with two hands.

Sleep Gaze. The jackalwere gazes at one creature it can see within 30 feet of it. The target must make a DC 13 Wisdom saving throw. On a failed save, the target succumbs to a magical slumber, falling unconscious for 10 minutes or until someone uses an action to shake the target awake. A creature that successfully saves against the effect is immune to this jackalwere's gaze for the next 24 hours. Undead and creatures immune to being charmed aren't affected by it.

Jackalwere Guard

Medium humanoid (shapechanger), chaotic evil
Armor Class 16 (hide, shield)
Hit Points 102 (12d8 + 48)
Speed 30 ft.

STR	DEX	CON	INT	WIS	CHA
15 (+2)	20 (+5)	18 (+4)	12 (+1)	12 (+1)	10 (+0)

Skills Athletics +5, Deception +6, Perception +7, Stealth +8
Damage Immunities bludgeoning, piercing, and slashing from nonmagical attacks not made with silver
Senses passive Perception 17
Languages Common (can't speak in jackal form)
Challenge 7 (2,900 XP)

Brute. A melee weapon deals one extra die of its damage when the jackalwere hits with it (included in the attack).

Evasion. If the jackalwere is subjected to an effect that allows it to make a Dexterity saving throw to take only half damage, the jackalwere instead takes no damage if it succeeds on the saving throw, and only half damage if it fails.

Keen Smell. The jackalwere has advantage on Wisdom (Perception) checks that rely on smell.

Rampage (jackal or hybrid form only). When the jackalwere reduces a creature to 0 hit points with a melee attack on its turn, the jackalwere can take a bonus action to move up to half its speed and make a bite attack.

Shapechanger. The jackalwere can use its action to polymorph into a specific Medium human or a jackal-humanoid hybrid, or back into its true form, which is a Small jackal. Any equipment it is wearing or carrying isn't transformed. It reverts to its true form if it dies.

Actions

Multiattack (humanoid or hybrid form only). The jackalwere guard uses its Sleep Gaze and makes three attacks, only one of which can be a Bite.

Bite (jackal or hybrid form only). *Melee Weapon Attack:* +8 to hit, reach 5 ft., one target. *Hit:* 14 (2d8 + 5) piercing damage. If the target is a creature, it must succeed on a DC 15 Strength saving throw or be knocked prone.

Shortsword (humanoid or hybrid form only). *Melee Weapon Attack:* +8 to hit, reach 5 ft., one target. *Hit:* 12 (2d6 + 5) piercing damage.

Sleep Gaze. The jackalwere gazes at one creature it can see within 30 feet of it. The target must make a DC 15 Wisdom saving throw. On a failed save, the target succumbs to a magical slumber, falling unconscious for 10 minutes or until someone uses an action to shake the target awake. A creature that successfully saves against the effect is immune to this jackalwere's gaze for the next 24 hours. Undead and creatures immune to being charmed aren't affected by it.

Reactions

Defend. When a creature makes a melee attack against an ally of the jackalwere, the jackalwere grants a +2 bonus to the ally's AC if the ally is within 5 feet of the jackalwere.

Jade Colossus of the Sultana

Gargantuan construct, chaotic good

Armor Class 18 (natural armor)
Hit Points 333 (18d20 + 144)
Speed 40 ft.

STR	DEX	CON	INT	WIS	CHA
30 (+10)	10 (+0)	26 (+8)	18 (+4)	21 (+5)	19 (+4)

Saving Throws Dex +7, Con +15, Wis +12, Cha +11
Skills Arcana +11, History +11, Insight +12, Intimidation +11, Perception +12
Damage Immunities fire, poison, psychic; bludgeoning, piercing, and slashing from nonmagical attacks not made with adamantine
Condition Immunities charmed, exhaustion, frightened, paralyzed, petrified, poisoned, unconscious
Senses darkvision 120 ft., passive Perception 22
Languages Common, Primordial
Challenge 23 (50,000 XP)

Berserk. Whenever the jade colossus starts its turn with only the *eyes of the sultana*[2] equipped, roll a d6. On a 6, the jade colossus goes berserk. On each of its turns while berserk, the jade colossus attacks the nearest creature it can see. If no creature is near enough to move to and attack, the jade colossus attacks an object with preference for an object smaller than itself. At the start of each of its turns, roll a d6 again. If the roll is 4 or more, the jade colossus continues to berserk until the roll is less than 4 or the *eyes of the sultana*[2] are removed with a successful DC 20 Strength (Athletics) check while grappling the jade colossus.

Construct Nature. The jade colossus doesn't require air, food, drink, or sleep.

Fire Absorption. Whenever the jade colossus is subjected to fire damage, it takes no damage and instead regains a number of hit points equal to the fire damage dealt.

Immutable Form. The jade colossus is immune to any spell or effect that would alter its form.

Legendary Resistance (3/day). If the jade colossus fails a saving throw, it can choose to succeed instead.

Magic Resistance. The jade colossus has advantage on saving throws against spells and other magical effects.

Magic Weapons. The jade colossus' weapon attacks are magical.

ACTIONS

Multiattack. The jade colossus makes three Jade Fist attacks or two Jade Fist attacks and one Stomp attack.

Jade Fist. *Melee Weapon Attack:* +17 to hit, reach 15 ft., one target/creature. *Hit:* 19 (2d8 + 10) bludgeoning damage.

Stomp. *Melee Weapon Attack:* +17 to hit, reach 10 ft., one Large or smaller target. *Hit:* 26 (3d10 + 10) bludgeoning damage and the target must succeed on a DC 25 Strength saving throw or be knocked prone.

Jade Breath (recharge 5–6). The jade colossus exhales a blast of green energy in a 90-foot cone. Each creature in that area must make a DC 23 Dexterity saving throw. On a failure, a creature takes 54 (12d8) force damage and is restrained as it begins to turn to jade. On a success, a creature takes half the damage and isn't restrained. The restrained creature must repeat the saving throw at the end of its next turn, becoming petrified on a failure or ending the effect on a success. The petrified creature becomes a statue of jade until it is freed by the *greater restoration* spell or similar magic.

REACTIONS

Reflective Skin. When the jade colossus is targeted by a spell that requires an attack roll, the spellcaster must make a DC 23 spellcasting ability check or the spell is reflected back onto the spellcaster.

LEGENDARY ACTIONS

The jade colossus can take 3 legendary actions, choosing from the options below. Only one legendary action can be used at a time and only at the end of another creature's turn. The jade colossus regains spent legendary actions at the start of its turn.

Detect. The jade colossus makes a Wisdom (Perception) check.

Jade Fist. The jade colossus makes one Jade Fist attack.

Reflect Light (costs 2 actions). The jade colossus reflects light in a 90-foot line that is 5 feet wide. Each creature in that line must make a DC 20 Constitution saving throw. On a failure, a creature takes 28 (8d6) radiant damage and is blinded until the end of the jade colossus' next turn. On a success, a creature takes half the damage and isn't blinded.

Janni

Large elemental, neutral

Armor Class 15 (leather armor)
Hit Points 136 (16d10 + 48)
Speed 30 ft., fly 20 ft.

STR	DEX	CON	INT	WIS	CHA
15 (+2)	18 (+4)	17 (+3)	13 (+1)	12 (+1)	16 (+3)

Saving Throws Str +5, Cha +6
Skills Acrobatics +7, Perception +4, Persuasion +6
Damage Resistances acid, cold, fire, lightning, thunder
Senses darkvision 60 ft., passive Perception 14
Languages Common, Primordial
Challenge 7 (2,900 XP)

Elemental Demise. If the janni dies, its body disintegrates into a mixture of elements, leaving behind only equipment the janni was wearing or carrying.

Elemental Weapons. The janni's weapon attacks are magical. When the janni hits with any weapon, the weapon deals an extra 1d6 cold, fire, lightning, or thunder (the janni's choice) damage (included in the attack).

Innate Spellcasting. The janni's innate spellcasting ability is Charisma (spell save DC 14). It can innately cast the following spells, requiring no material components:

At will: *detect evil and good, detect magic*
3/day each: *continual flame, move earth, tongues, water breathing, wind walk*
1/day each: *conjure elemental, invisibility* (self only), *plane shift* (self only)

Wiry. The janni has advantage on Strength and Dexterity ability checks and saving throws against effects that would grapple or restrain it and on checks to escape a grapple.

ACTIONS

Multiattack. The janni makes two melee attacks. It can use Elemental Bolt in place of any melee attack.

Scimitar. *Melee Weapon Attack:* +7 to hit, reach 5 ft., one target. *Hit:* 11 (2d6 + 4) plus 3 (1d6) cold, fire, lightning, or thunder (the janni's choice) damage.

Elemental Bolt. *Ranged Spell Attack:* +6 to hit, range 120 ft., one target. *Hit:* 10 (3d6) cold, fire, lightning, or thunder (the janni's choice) damage.

Elemental Blood. When a creature the janni can see hits it with a melee weapon attack, the attacker must succeed on a DC 15 Dexterity saving throw or take 7 (2d6) cold, fire, lightning, or thunder (the janni's choice) damage.

Jhadam

Medium humanoid (n'gathau), neutral evil
Armor Class 17 (natural armor)
Hit Points 250 (20d8 + 160)
Speed 30 ft.

STR	DEX	CON	INT	WIS	CHA
29 (+9)	15 (+2)	27 (+8)	13 (+1)	15 (+2)	10 (+0)

Saving Throws Str +15, Dex +8, Con +14, Wis +8
Skills Athletics +15, Intimidation +6, Perception +8
Damage Resistances cold, fire; bludgeoning, piercing, and slashing from nonmagical attacks
Damage Immunities acid, poison
Condition Immunities poisoned
Senses darkvision 60 ft., passive Perception 18
Languages Common, Dwarvish, N'gathian
Challenge 17 (18,000 XP)

Indomitable (2/day). Jhadam rerolls a failed saving throw.
Second Wind (recharges after a short or long rest). As a bonus action, Jhadam can regain 28 hit points.
Magic Weapons. Jhadam's weapon attacks are magical.
Superior Critical. Jhadam's weapon attacks score a critical hit on a roll of 18–20.
Aura of Pain. Any creature within 15 feet of Jhadam that isn't protected by a mind blank spell hears in its mind the tortured screams that emanate from Jhadam's broken psyche. As a bonus action, Jhadam can force all creatures that can hear the screams to make a DC 19 Wisdom saving throw. Each creature takes 22 (4d10) psychic damage on a failed save, or half as much damage on a successful one

ACTIONS

Multiattack. Jhadam makes four melee attacks.
Chain Whip. Melee Weapon Attack: +15 to hit, reach 20 ft., one target. *Hit:* 18 (2d8 + 9) slashing damage and the target is pulled up to 15 feet straight toward Jhadam.
Blade. Melee Weapon Attack: +15 to hit, reach 5 ft., one target. *Hit:* 23 (4d6 + 9) slashing damage.

REACTIONS

Parry. Jhadam adds 5 to his AC against one melee attack that would hit him.

Juggernaut of Kil Kath Kesh

Huge construct, unaligned
Armor Class 21 (natural armor)
Hit Points 270 (20d12 + 140)
Speed 20 ft., fly 60 ft.

STR	DEX	CON	INT	WIS	CHA
27 (+8)	11 (+0)	24 (+7)	3 (–4)	11 (+0)	7 (–2)

Damage Resistances cold, necrotic
Damage Immunities fire, poison, psychic; bludgeoning, piercing, and slashing from nonmagical attacks

Condition Immunities charmed, exhaustion, frightened, paralyzed, petrified, poisoned
Senses darkvision 120 ft., passive Perception 10
Languages understands Common and Ignan but can't speak
Challenge 24 (62,000 XP)

Construct. The juggernaut of Kil Kath Kesh obeys the simple commands of whoever activated it by placing a brain gem in its arm. It becomes inanimate if the brain gem is removed.
Fire Absorption. Whenever the juggernaut of Kil Kath Kesh is subjected to fire damage, it takes no damage and instead regains a number of hit points equal to the fire damage dealt.
Immutable Form. The juggernaut of Kil Kath Kesh is immune to any spell or effect that would alter its form.
Insanity. If an inauthentic brain gem was used to activate the juggernaut of Kil Kath Kesh artifact, it goes insane after 1d4 + 1 rounds, attacking all creatures in its vicinity and refusing to obey commands.
Magic Resistance. The juggernaut of Kil Kath Kesh has advantage on saving throws against spells and other magical effects.
Magic Weapons. The juggernaut of Kil Kath Kesh's attacks are magical.
Secret Compartment. A secret compartment exists inside the back of the juggernaut of Kil Kath Kesh, big enough for four Medium humanoids.
Vorpal Pincer. When it rolls a 20 on a Pincer attack roll against a creature of size Huge or less which has at least one head, the juggernaut of Kil Kath Kesh has cut off one of the creature's heads. The creature dies if it cannot survive without the lost head. Creatures who do not have a head cut off instead suffer an extra 6d8 slashing damage from the hit.

ACTIONS

Multiattack. The juggernaut of Kil Kath Kesh makes eight Flail attacks, one Pincer attack, and one Prismatic Spray Cannon attack.
Flail. Melee Weapon Attack: +15 to hit, reach 10 ft., one target. *Hit:* 22 (4d6 + 8) bludgeoning damage.
Pincer. Melee Weapon Attack: +15 to hit, reach 10 ft., one target. *Hit:* 29 (6d6 + 8) slashing damage.
Prismatic Spray Cannon. The juggernaut of Kil Kath Kesh uses its bejeweled arm to cast *prismatic spray* (spell save DC 20) in a 100-foot cone.

Kathlin

Large monstrosity, neutral good
Armor Class 14 (natural armor)
Hit Points 51 (6d10 + 18)
Speed 50 ft.

STR	DEX	CON	INT	WIS	CHA
18 (+4)	15 (+2)	17 (+3)	5 (–3)	13 (+1)	8 (–1)

Saving Throws Dex +4, Con +5
Skills Perception +3
Senses darkvision 60 ft., passive Perception 13
Languages understands Common and Sylvan but can't speak
Challenge 3 (700 XP)

ACTIONS

Multiattack. The kathlin makes four Hoof attacks.
Hoof. Melee Weapon Attack: +6 to hit, reach 5ft., one target. Hit: 7 (1d6 + 4) bludgeoning damage.

Kobold Assassin

Small humanoid (kobold), lawful evil
Armor Class 16 (+1 *studded leather armor*)
Hit Points 49 (9d6 + 18)
Speed 30 ft.

STR	DEX	CON	INT	WIS	CHA
8 (−1)	15 (+2)	14 (+2)	11 (+0)	10 (+0)	10 (+0)

Saving Throws Dex +4, Int +2
Skills Deception +2, Perception +2, Sleight of Hand +4, Stealth +4
Senses darkvision 60 ft., passive Perception 12
Languages Common, Draconic, Thieves' Cant
Challenge 4 (1,100 XP)

Assassinate. The kobold assassin has advantage on attack rolls against any creature that hasn't yet acted in the combat. In addition, any hit it scores against a creature that is surprised counts as a critical hit.

Cunning Action. The kobold assassin can take a bonus action on each of its turns in combat. This action can be used only to take the Dash, Disengage, or Hide action.

Evasion. The kobold assassin can nimbly dodge out of the way of certain area effects. When it is subjected to an effect that allows it to make a Dexterity saving throw to only take half damage, it instead takes no damage if it succeeds on the saving throw, and only half damage if it fails.

Innate Spellcasting. The kobold assassin may cast *disguise self* on itself (spell save DC 15) 3/day with no material components.

Pack Tactics: The kobold assassin has advantage on an attack roll against a creature if at least one of its allies is within 5 feet of the creature and the ally isn't incapacitated.

Sneak Attack. Once per turn, the kobold assassin can deal an extra 4d6 damage to one creature it hits with a Dagger attack if it has advantage on the attack roll. It doesn't need advantage on the attack roll if another enemy of the target is within 5 feet of the target and that enemy isn't incapacitated.

Sunlight Sensitivity: While in sunlight, the kobold assassin has disadvantage on attack rolls, as well as on Wisdom (Perception) checks that rely on sight.

Uncanny Dodge. When an attacker the kobold assassin can see hits it with an attack, it can use its reaction to halve the attack's damage against it.

Actions

Multiattack. The kobold assassin makes two Dagger attacks (melee or ranged).

+1 Dagger. *Melee Weapon Attack:* +5 to hit, reach 5 ft., one target. *Hit:* 5 (1d4 + 3) piercing damage. The target must make a DC 15 Constitution saving throw. On a failed save, the target takes 10 (3d6) poison damage and is poisoned. On a successful saving throw, the target takes half as much damage and is not poisoned. A poisoned target may repeat the saving throw at the end of each of its turns, ending the condition on itself on a success.

Dagger. *Ranged Weapon Attack:* +4 to hit, range 20/60 ft., one target. *Hit:* 4 (1d4 + 2) piercing damage. The target must make a DC 15 Constitution saving throw. On a failed save, the target takes 10 (3d6) poison damage and is poisoned. On a successful saving throw, the target takes half as much damage and is not poisoned. A poisoned target may repeat the saving throw at the end of each of its turns, ending the condition on itself on a success.

Lava Child

Medium humanoid (elemental), neutral
Armor Class 13 (natural armor)
Hit Points 27 (5d8 + 5)
Speed 30 ft.

STR	DEX	CON	INT	WIS	CHA
13 (+1)	11 (+0)	13 (+1)	10 (+0)	11 (+0)	11 (+0)

Skills Perception +4
Damage Vulnerability cold
Damage Resistances force
Damage Immunities fire; bludgeoning, piercing, and slashing from metal weapons
Senses darkvision 60 ft., passive Perception 14
Languages Ignan, Lava Child
Challenge 2 (450 XP)

Heated Body. A creature that touches the lava child or hits it with a melee attack while within 5 ft. of it takes 7 (2d6) fire damage.

Metal Immunity. Lava children are unaffected by metal. They can walk through solid metal doors as if the door wasn't there. Metal weapons, even magical, have no effect on lava children. Lava children makes all attacks with advantage against foes wearing metal armor.

Water Vulnerability. For every 1 gallon of water splashed on a lava child, it takes 3 cold damage.

Actions

Multiattack. The lava child makes one bite attack and one attack with its claws.

Bite. *Melee Weapon Attack:* +3 to hit, reach 5 ft., one target. *Hit:* 4 (1d6 + 1) piercing damage.

Claws. *Melee Weapon Attack:* +3 to hit, reach 5 ft., one target. *Hit:* 5 (1d8 + 1) slashing damage.

Lavawight

Medium undead, chaotic evil
Armor Class 22 (natural armor)
Hit Points 304 (32d8 + 160)
Speed 60 ft.

STR	DEX	CON	INT	WIS	CHA
25 (+7)	18 (+4)	21 (+5)	10 (+0)	18 (+4)	21 (+5)

Damage Immunities fire, necrotic, poison; bludgeoning, piercing, and slashing from nonmagical attacks
Damage Vulnerabilities cold
Condition Immunities charmed, exhaustion, frightened, paralyzed, petrified, poisoned
Senses darkvision 60 ft., passive Perception 14
Languages Common, Infernal
Challenge 22 (41,000 XP)

Heat Aura. Creatures which begin their turn within 10 feet of the lavawight take 11 (2d10) fire damage.

Innate Spellcasting. The lavawight's innate spellcasting ability is Charisma (spell save DC 20, +12 to hit with spell attacks). It can innately cast the following spells, with no need for material components:

At will: *dimension door, fireball, flame arrow, wall of fire*
3/day: *counterspell*

Life Drain. If the lavawight hits a creature with a Claw or Skull Butt attack, that creature must succeed on a DC 20 Constitution saving throw or its hit point maximum is reduced by an amount equal to the fire damage taken, and the lavawight regains hit points equal to that amount. This reduction lasts until the target finishes a long rest. The target dies if this effect reduces its hit point maximum to 0. A creature killed by this reduction is turned into a pile of ash and may only be restored to life with a *resurrection*, *true resurrection*, or *wish* spell.

Molten Healing. All fire-based creatures (such as fire elementals and magma mephits), including the lavawight itself, which begin their turn within 10 feet of the lavawight regain 10 hit points. The lavawight dies if it is reduced to 0 hit points, and this ability does not function.

Rend. If the lavawight hits the same target with two Claw attacks in the same turn, it deals an additional 34 (6d8 + 7) slashing damage to that target.

Turn Resistance. The lavawight has advantage on saving throws against any effect that turns undead.

ACTIONS

Multiattack. The lavawight makes two Claw attacks and one Skull Butt attack.

Claw. *Melee Weapon Attack:* +14 to hit, reach 5 ft., one target. *Hit:* 25 (4d8 + 7) slashing damage plus 11 (2d10) fire damage. If the target is a creature, see Life Drain above.

Skull Butt. *Melee Weapon Attack:* +14 to hit, reach 5 ft., one target. *Hit:* 17 (3d6 + 7) bludgeoning damage plus 16 (3d10) fire damage. If the target is a creature, see Life Drain above.

Leech, Giant

Medium beast (aquatic), unaligned
Armor Class 11
Hit Points 26 (4d8 + 8)
Speed 5 ft., swim 20 ft.

STR	DEX	CON	INT	WIS	CHA
11 (+0)	12 (+1)	14 (+2)	2 (−4)	10 (+0)	1 (−5)

Senses blindsight 30 ft., passive Perception 10
Languages —
Challenge 1 (200 XP)

Vulnerability to Salt. A handful of salt burns a giant leech as if it were a flask of acid, causing 1d6 acid damage per use.

ACTIONS

Blood Drain. *Melee Weapon Attack:* +3 to hit, reach 5 ft. one creature. Hit: 4 (1d6 + 1) piercing damage, and the leech attaches to the target. While attached, the leech doesn't attack. Instead, at the start of the leech's turns, the target loses 5 (1d8 + 1) hit points due to blood loss.

The leech can detach itself by spending 5 feet of its movement. It does so after it drains 25 hit points of blood from the target or the target dies. A creature, including the target, can use its action to make a DC 10 Strength check to rip the leech off and make it detach.

Lemure Mass

Huge fiend (devil), lawful evil
Armor Class 13
Hit Points 150 (20d12 + 20)
Speed 15 ft.

STR	DEX	CON	INT	WIS	CHA
20 (+5)	5 (+2)	12 (+1)	1 (−5)	8 (−1)	3 (−4)

Damage Resistances bludgeoning, cold, piercing, and slashing
Damage Immunities fire, poison
Condition Immunities charmed, frightened, poisoned
Senses darkvision 120 ft., passive Perception 9
Languages understands Infernal but can't speak
Challenge 12 (8,400 XP)

Devil's Sight. Magical darkness does not impede the lemure mass's darkvision.

Hellish Rejuvenation. If the lemure mass dies in the Nine Hells, it comes back to life with all its hit points in 1d10 days unless it is killed by a good-aligned creature with a *bless* spell cast on that creature or its remains are sprinkled with holy water.

Spawn. When the lemure mass reduces a creature to 0 hit poins, that creature immediately turns into a lemure and is absorbed into the lemure mass. The lemure mass regains 13 hit points for each lemure it absorbs, and its maximum hit points are increased by 13.

ACTIONS

Multiattack. The lemure mass makes five Fist attacks.

Fist. *Melee Weapon Attack:* +9 to hit, reach 5 ft., one target. *Hit:* 19 (4d6 + 5) bludgeoning damage.

Lightning Weird

Large elemental, chaotic evil
Armor Class 18 (natural armor)
Hit Points 90 (12d10 + 24)
Speed 50 ft.

STR	DEX	CON	INT	WIS	CHA
17 (+3)	20 (+5)	15 (+2)	10 (+0)	12 (+1)	14 (+2)

Damage Resistances bludgeoning, piercing, and slashing from nonmagical weapons
Damage Immunities acid, lightning, poison, thunder
Condition Immunities exhaustion, grappled, paralyzed, petrified, poisoned, prone, restrained, unconscious
Senses blindsight 30 ft., passive Perception 11
Languages Auran, Common, Weirdling
Challenge 7 (2,900 XP)

Electricity. If a creature attacks the lighting weird with a melee weapon, that creature takes 9 (2d8) lightning damage.

Lightning Mote. A lightning weird's mote is a crackling, dancing, arcing, ball of electricity that occupies a 5-foot space. Creatures that start their turn within 5 feet of the lightning mote take 13 (3d8) lightning damage; creatures wearing metal armor must make a successful DC 15 Constitution saving throw if they take lightning damage from being near the mote. On a failed saving throw, the target is stunned until the end of its next turn. The lightning can move its mote up to 30 ft. as a bonus action. The mote must remain within 90 ft.

Reform. When reduced to 0 hit points, a lightning weird collapses back into its pool. Four rounds later, it reforms at full strength minus any damage taken from fire-based attacks and effects (including attacks by earth or fire elemental creatures).

Transparent. Even when the lightning weird is in plain sight, it takes a successful DC 15 Wisdom (Perception) check to spot a lightning weird that has neither moved nor attacked. A creature that tries to enter the lightning weird's space while unaware of the lightning weird is surprised by the lightning weird.

ACTIONS

Bite. *Melee Weapon Attack:* +8 to hit, reach 5 ft., one target. *Hit:* 14 (2d8 + 5) piercing damage plus 9 (2d8) lightning damage.

Command Elemental. One air elemental that the lightning weird can see within 60 feet of it must make a DC 13 Wisdom saving throw. On a failed saving throw, the air elemental is charmed for 1 minute. While charmed, the air elemental follows the lightning weird's commands.

Lion, Dire

Large beast unaligned
Armor Class 14 (natural armor)
Hit Points 60 (8d10 + 16)
Speed 30 ft.

STR	DEX	CON	INT	WIS	CHA
17 (+3)	15 (+2)	14 (+2)	3 (−4)	12 (+1)	8 (−1)

Skills Perception +3, Stealth +6
Senses passive Perception 13
Languages —
Challenge 1 (200 XP)

Keen Smell. The lion has advantage on Wisdom (Perception) checks that rely on smell.

Pack Tactics: The lion has advantage on an attack roll against a creature if at least one of the lion's allies is within 5 feet of the creature and the ally isn't incapacitated.

Pounce. If the lion moves at least 20 feet straight toward a creature and then hits it with a claw attack on the same turn, that target must succeed on a DC 14 Strength saving throw or be knocked prone. If the target is prone, the lion can make one bite attack against it as a bonus action.

Running Leap. With a 10-foot running start, the lion can long jump up to 25 feet.

ACTIONS

Bite. *Melee Weapon Attack:* +5 to hit, reach 5 ft., one target. *Hit:* 7 (1d8 + 3) piercing damage.

Claw. *Melee Weapon Attack:* +5 to hit, reach 5 ft., one target. *Hit:* 6 (1d6 + 3) slashing damage.

Lion, Fiendish Dire

Large beast, lawful evil
Armor Class 14 (natural armor)
Hit Points 60 (8d10 + 16)
Speed 30 ft.

STR	DEX	CON	INT	WIS	CHA
18 (+4)	15 (+2)	14 (+2)	3 (−4)	12 (+1)	8 (−1)

Skills Perception +3, Stealth +6
Damage Resistances cold; bludgeoning, piercing, and slashing from nonmagical attacks not made with silver

Damage Immunities fire, poison
Condition Immunities poisoned
Senses passive Perception 13
Languages —
Challenge 2 (450 XP)

Keen Smell. The lion has advantage on Wisdom (Perception) checks that rely on smell.

Pack Tactics: The lion has advantage on an attack roll against a creature if at least one of the lion's allies is within 5 feet of the creature and the ally isn't incapacitated.

Pounce. If the lion moves at least 20 feet straight toward a creature and then hits it with a claw attack on the same turn, that target must succeed on a DC 14 Strength saving throw or be knocked prone. If the target is prone, the lion can make one bite attack against it as a bonus action.

Rampage. When it reduces a creature to 0 hit points with a melee attack on its turn, the lion can take a bonus action to move up to half its speed and make a Bite attack.

Running Leap. With a 10-foot running start, the lion can long jump up to 25 feet.

ACTIONS

Bite. *Melee Weapon Attack:* +6 to hit, reach 5 ft., one target. *Hit:* 8 (1d8 + 4) piercing damage.

Claw. *Melee Weapon Attack:* +6 to hit, reach 5 ft., one target. *Hit:* 7 (1d6 + 4) slashing damage.

Livesha

Large undead, neutral
Armor Class 19 (natural armor, *bracers of defense, ring of protection*)
Hit Points 322 (28d10 + 168)
Speed 30 ft., fly 90 ft.

STR	DEX	CON	INT	WIS	CHA
21 (+5)	16 (+3)	22 (+6)	16 (+3)	20 (+5)	20 (+5)

Saving Throws Dex +11, Con +14, Int +11, Wis +13, Cha +13
Skills Arcana +11, History +11, Insight +13, Perception +13, Religion +19
Damage Resistances cold, necrotic
Damage Immunities lightning, poison, thunder; bludgeoning, piercing, and slashing from nonmagical attacks
Condition Immunities charmed, exhaustion, frightened, paralyzed, poisoned
Senses truesight 120 ft., passive Perception 23
Languages Abyssal, Auran, Common, telepathy 120 ft.
Challenge 26 (90,000 XP), 27 in lair (105,000 XP)

Channel Orcus: Storm Wrath (3/day). When she deals lightning or thunder damage, Livesha deals maximum damage (no roll required).

Elemental Demise. If Livesha dies, her body disintegrates into a warm breeze, leaving behind only equipment she was wearing or carrying.

Innate Spellcasting. Livesha's innate spellcasting ability is Charisma (spell save DC 21, +13 to hit with spell attacks). She can innately cast the following spells, with no need for material components:

At will: *detect evil and good, detect magic, thunderwave*
3/day each: *create food and water* (can create wine instead of water), *tongues, wind walk*
2/day each: *conjure elemental* (air elemental only), *creation, gaseous form, greater invisibility, lightning bolt, major image, plane shift*

Legendary Resistances (3/day). If Livesha fails a saving throw, she can choose to succeed instead.

Rejuvenation: If she has a phylactery and is destroyed, Livesha gains a new body in 1d10 days, regaining all her hit points and becoming active again. The new body appears within 5 feet of the phylactery.

Ring of Protection. Livesha has +1 on all saving throws while wearing this ring.

Spellcasting. Livesha is a 20th level spellcaster. Her spellcasting ability is Wisdom (spell save DC 21, +13 to hit with spell attacks). She has the following spells prepared:

> Cantrips (at will): *eldritch blast, mending, sacred flame, spare the dying, thaumaturgy*
> 1st level (4 slots): *bane, fog cloud, inflict wounds* (cumulative with Paralyzing Touch attack), *shield of faith*
> 2nd level (3 slots): *blindness/deafness, enhance ability, gust of wind, hold person, shatter, silence*
> 3rd level (3 slots): *animate dead, bestow curse, call lightning, dispel magic, sleet storm, spirit guardians*
> 4th level (3 slots): *banishment, control water, death ward, freedom of movement, guardian of faith, ice storm, stone shape*
> 5th level (3 slots): *contagion, destructive wave, flame strike, insect plague*
> 6th level (2 slots): *blade barrier, harm, word of recall*
> 7th level (2 slots): *divine word, fire storm*
> 8th level (1 slot): *earthquake*
> 9th level (1 slot): *gate* (Livesha knows the true name of a balor in the service of Orcus)

Thunderbolt Strike. When Livesha deals lightning damage to a target that is Huge or smaller, she can push it up to 10 feet away from her.

Touch Spells. When Livesha successfully hits with a melee spell attack, she also causes the effects of a Paralyzing Touch action.

Turn Resistance. Livesha has advantage on saving throws against any effect that turns undead.

ACTIONS

Multiattack. Livesha makes three melee weapon attacks or two Paralyzing Touch attacks.

+2 Sword of Life Stealing. *Melee Weapon Attack:* +15 to hit, reach 5 ft., one target. *Hit:* 16 (2d8 + 7) slashing damage plus 9 (2d8) lightning or thunder damage (Livesha's choice). When Livesha attacks a creature with this magic weapon and rolls a 20 on the attack roll, that target takes an extra 10 (3d6) necrotic damage, provided that the target isn't a construct or an undead. She gains temporary hit points equal to the extra damage dealt.

Paralyzing Touch: *Melee Spell Attack:* +13 to hit, reach 5 ft., one creature. *Hit:* 10 (3d6) cold damage. The target must succeed on a DC 19 Constitution saving throw or be paralyzed for 1 minute. The target can repeat the saving throw at the end of each of its turns, ending the effect on itself on a success.

Create Whirlwind: A 5-foot-radius, 30-foot-tall cylinder of swirling air magically forms on a point Livesha can see within 120 feet of her. The whirlwind lasts as long as Livesha maintains concentration (as if concentrating on a spell). Any creature but Livesha that enters the whirlwind must succeed on a DC 19 Strength saving throw or be restrained by it. Livesha can move the whirlwind up to 60 feet as an action, and creatures restrained by the whirlwind move with it. The whirlwind ends if Livesha loses sight of it.

A creature can use its action to free a creature restrained by the whirlwind, including itself, by succeeding on a DC 19 Strength check. If the check succeeds, the creature is no longer restrained and moves to the nearest space outside the whirlwind.

LEGENDARY ACTIONS

Livesha can take 3 legendary actions, choosing from the options below. Only one legendary action option can be used at a time and only at the end of another creature's turn. Livesha regains spent legendary actions at the start of her turn.

Cantrip: Livesha casts a cantrip.

Paralyzing Touch (costs 2 actions): Livesha uses her Paralyzing Touch.

Frightening Gaze (costs 2 actions): Livesha fixes her gaze on one creature she can see within 10 feet of her. The target must succeed on a DC 19 Wisdom saving throw against this magic or become frightened for 1 minute. The frightened target can repeat the saving throw at the end of each of its turns, ending the effect on itself on a success. If a target's saving throw is successful or the effect ends for it, the target is immune to the Livesha's gaze for the next 24 hours.

Disrupt Life (costs 3 actions): Each non-undead creature within 20 feet of Livesha must make a DC 19 Constitution saving throw against this magic, taking 21 (6d6) necrotic damage on a failed save, or half as much damage on a successful one.

LAIR ACTIONS

On initiative count 20 (losing initiative ties), Livesha can take a lair action to cause one of the following magical effects; she can't use the same effect two rounds in a row:

Spell Recall. Livesha rolls 2d4 and regains an expended spell slot of that level or lower.

Life Bond. Livesha creates a negative energy bond with one creature she can see within 30 feet. Whenever Livesha takes damage, the creature must make a DC 19 Constitution saving throw. On a failed save, Livesha takes half of the damage (rounded down), and the target takes the remainder of the damage. This bond lasts until initiative count 20 on the next round or until either Livesha or the creature leaves her lair.

Teleport. Livesha can teleport anywhere in her lair any time a creature in that tomb interferes with the City of Brass model.

Vengeful Spirits. Livesha calls vengeful spirits of the dead who materialize just long enough to attack one creature she can see within 60 feet of her. The target must succeed on a DC 19 Constitution saving throw, taking 52 (15d6) necrotic damage on a failed save, or half as much damage on a success.

Magmoid

Large elemental, neutral
Armor Class 14 (natural armor)
Hit Points 120 (16d10 + 32)
Speed 40 ft.

STR	DEX	CON	INT	WIS	CHA
14 (+2)	17 (+3)	15 (+2)	4 (–3)	10 (+0)	5 (–3)

Damage Vulnerabilities cold
Damage Resistances bludgeoning, piercing, and slashing from nonmagical attacks
Damage Immunities fire, lightning, poison
Condition Immunities exhaustion, paralyzed, petrified, poisoned, prone, restrained, unconscious
Senses blindsight 60 ft., passive Perception 10
Languages Ignan, Terran
Challenge 8 (3,900 XP)

Illumination. The elemental sheds bright light in a 30-foot radius and dim light in an additional 30 feet.

Magma Form. The magmoid can move through a space as narrow as 1 inch wide without squeezing. A creature that touches the magmoid or hits it with a melee attack while within 5 feet of it takes 9 (2d8) fire damage. In addition, the magmoid can flow into a hostile creature's space and stop there. The first time it enters a hostile creature's space on a turn, that creature takes 9 (2d8) fire damage and catches fire; until someone takes an action to douse the flames, the creature takes 4 (1d8) fire damage at the start of each of its turns.

Melt Weapons. Any nonmagical weapon made of metal that hits the magmoid melts. After dealing damage, the weapon takes a permanent and cumulative –1 penalty to damage rolls. If its penalty drops to –5, the weapon is destroyed. Nonmagical ammunition made of metal or other flammable material is melted or burned and is destroyed after dealing damage.

Siege Monster. The magmoid deals double damage to objects and structures.

ACTIONS

Multiattack. The magmoid makes two Slam attacks.

Slam. *Melee Weapon Attack:* +6 to hit, reach 5 ft., one target. *Hit:* 10 (2d6 + 3) bludgeoning damage and 9 (2d8) fire damage. If the target is a creature or a flammable object, it ignites. Until a creature takes an action to douse the fire, the target takes 4 (1d8) fire damage at the start of each of its turns.

Magma Blast (recharge 6). The magmoid hurls a blast of magma in a 60-foot line that is 5-foot-wide. Each creature in the line must make a DC 15 Dexterity saving throw, taking 18 (4d8) fire damage on a failure and half as much damage on a success. In addition, any creature or a flammable object in the line ignites. Until a creature takes an action to douse the fire, the target takes 4 (1d8) fire damage at the start of each of its turns.

Mandragora

Small plant, neutral evil
Armor Class 11
Hit Points 4 (1d6 + 1)
Speed 30 ft., burrow 15 ft.

STR	DEX	CON	INT	WIS	CHA
11 (+0)	13 (+1)	13 (+1)	8 (–1)	10 (+0)	9 (–1)

Damage Resistances fire
Damage Immunities psychic
Condition Immunities charmed, frightened, stunned, unconscious
Senses darkvision 60 ft., tremorsense 60 ft. passive Perception 10
Languages —
Challenge 1/8 (25 XP)

ACTIONS

Tentacles. *Melee Weapon Attack:* +3 to hit, reach 5 ft., one creature. *Hit:* 3 (1d4 + 1) bludgeoning damage and the target must make a successful DC 11 Dexterity saving throw or be grappled (escape DC 11).

Strangulation. one creature already grappled by the mandragora takes 4 (1d6 + 1) bludgeoning damage.

Mandrake

Small plant, chaotic evil
Armor Class 16 (natural armor)
Hit Points 32 (5d6 + 15)
Speed 40 ft., burrow 10 ft., climb 40 ft.

STR	DEX	CON	INT	WIS	CHA
15 (+2)	18 (+4)	17 (+3)	8 (–1)	13 (+1)	10 (+0)

Saving Throws Dex +6, Con +5
Skills Athletics +4, Perception +3, Stealth +6
Damage Resistances acid, cold, electricity
Damage Immunities poison
Condition Immunities charmed, exhaustion, frightened, poisoned
Senses darkvision 120 ft., passive Perception 13
Languages Abyssal, Common
Challenge 4 (1,100 XP)

ACTIONS

Multiattack. The mandrake makes one Bite attack and two Vine attacks.

Vine. *Melee Weapon Attack:* +6 to hit, reach 10 ft., one target. *Hit:* 6 (1d4 + 4) bludgeoning damage, and target must make a DC 15 Constitution saving throw, taking 10 (3d6) poison damage on a failure, or half as much damage on a success.

Bite. *Melee Weapon Attack:* +6 to hit, reach 5 ft., one target. *Hit:* 7 (1d6 + 4) piercing damage, and target must succeed on a DC 15 Constitution saving throw or the target's Constitution score is reduced by 1d4. The target dies if this reduces its Constitution to 0. Otherwise, the reduction lasts until the target finishes a short or long rest.

Shriek (1/day). The mandrake gives voice to an unsettling shriek. All creatures within a 30-foot radius of a shrieking mandrake must succeed on a DC 15 Wisdom saving throw or become poisoned. A target can repeat the saving throw at the end of each of its turns, ending the effect on itself on a success.

Margoyle, Advanced

Medium elemental, chaotic evil
Armor Class 18 (natural armor)
Hit Points 95 (10d8 + 50)
Speed 30 ft., fly 60 ft.

STR	DEX	CON	INT	WIS	CHA
19 (+4)	15 (+2)	21 (+5)	8 (–1)	12 (+1)	8 (–1)

Damage Resistances bludgeoning, piercing, and slashing from nonmagical attacks not made with adamantine
Damage Immunities poison
Condition Immunities exhaustion, petrified, poisoned
Senses darkvision 120 ft., passive Perception 11
Languages Terran
Challenge 6 (2,300 XP)

False Appearance. When the margoyle remains motionless, it is indistinguishable from an inanimate statue.

ACTIONS

Multiattack. The margoyle makes one Bite attack and one Claws attack.
Bite. *Melee Weapon Attack:* +7 to hit, reach 5 ft., one target. *Hit:* 24 (2d6 + 4) piercing damage.
Claws. *Melee Weapon Attack:* +7 to hit, reach 5 ft., one target. *Hit:* 24 (2d6 + 4) slashing damage.

Marid

Large elemental, chaotic neutral
Armor Class 18 (natural armor)
Hit Points 230 (20d10 + 120)
Speed 30 ft., fly 40 ft., swim 90 ft.

STR	DEX	CON	INT	WIS	CHA
16 (+3)	24 (+7)	22 (+6)	15 (+2)	13 (+1)	19 (+4)

Saving Throws Str +8, Wis +6, Cha +9
Skills Deception +9, History +9, Performance +9, Persuasion +9
Damage Immunities cold, lightning
Senses darkvision 120 ft., passive Perception 11
Languages Aquan
Challenge 13 (10,000 XP)

Amphibious. The marid can breathe air and water.
Elemental Demise. If the marid dies, it disintegrates into a spray of bubbles and water, leaving behind only equipment the marid was wearing or carrying.
Frigid Aura. At the start of each of the marid's turns, each creature within 10 feet of it takes 7 (2d6) cold damage. A creature that touches the marid or hits it with a melee attack while within 10 feet of it takes 7 (2d6) cold damage. A creature must succeed on a DC 17 Constitution saving throw each minute it spends in the aura or gain one level of exhaustion.
Innate Spellcasting. The marid's innate spellcasting ability is Charisma (spell save DC 17, +9 to hit with spell attacks). It can innately cast the following spells, requiring no material components:

At will: *create or destroy water, detect evil and good, detect magic, speak with animals* (water-based creatures only)
3/day each: *control water, tongues, water walk, water breathing*
1/day each: *conjure elemental* (water elemental only), *gaseous form, invisibility, major image, plane shift*

Riptide. If a creature is more than 10 feet away from the marid and it hits the marid with an attack, it must succeed on a DC 17 Strength saving throw or be pulled up to 10 feet closer to the marid.

ACTIONS

Multiattack. The marid makes one Scimitar attack and one Water Whip attack.
Scimitar. *Melee Weapon Attack:* +12 to hit, reach 5 ft., one target. *Hit:* 14 (2d6 + 7) slashing damage plus 10 (3d6) cold damage.
Water Whip. *Melee Weapon Attack:* +12 to hit, reach 25 ft., one target. *Hit:* 12 (2d4 + 7) slashing damage plus 10 (3d6) cold damage, and the target must succeed on a DC 17 Strength saving throw or be pulled up to 20 feet toward the marid.
Whirlpool (recharge 5–6). Water swirls rapidly around the marid. Each creature within 20 feet of the marid must make a DC 17 Dexterity saving throw. On a failure, a creature takes 56 (16d6) cold damage and is knocked prone. On a success, a creature takes half the damage and isn't knocked prone.

Marsh Jelly

Medium aberration, unaligned
Armor Class 13
Hit Points 58 (9d8 + 18)
Speed 5 ft., fly 30 ft. (hover)

STR	DEX	CON	INT	WIS	CHA
10 (+0)	17 (+3)	14 (+2)	3 (–4)	12 (+1)	11 (+0)

Skills Perception +3, Stealth +5
Condition Immunities blinded, prone
Senses darkvision 60 ft., passive Perception 13
Languages —
Challenge 3 (700 XP)

Death Burst. When the marsh jelly dies, its body bursts in a spray of acid and protoplasm. Each creature within 10 feet of it must make a DC 13 Dexterity saving throw, taking 10 (3d6) acid damage on a failed save, or half as much damage on a successful one.
Keen Smell. The marsh jelly has advantage on Wisdom (Perception) checks that rely on smell.

ACTIONS

Multiattack. The marsh jelly makes two Tentacle attacks.
Tentacle. *Melee Weapon Attack:* +5 to hit, reach 5 ft., one target. *Hit:* 6 (1d6 + 3) bludgeoning damage plus 3 (1d6) poison damage.
Paralyzing Sting (recharge 5–6). The marsh jelly makes a tentacle attack. If the attack hits, the target takes an extra 7 (2d6) poison damage and must succeed on a DC 12 Constitution saving throw or be paralyzed for 1 minute. The target can repeat the saving throw at the end of each of its turns, ending the effect on itself on a success.

REACTIONS

Disorienting Glow. When a creature the marsh jelly can see hits it with an attack, the marsh jelly's body glows and dims rapidly, disorienting creatures within 5 feet of the marsh jelly. Each creature in that area must succeed on a DC 12 Constitution saving throw or be blinded until the end of its next turn.

Mephits

Air Mephit

Small elemental, neutral evil
Armor Class 13
Hit Points 21 (6d6)
Speed 30 ft., fly 60 ft.

STR	DEX	CON	INT	WIS	CHA
11 (+0)	17 (+3)	10 (+0)	6 (−2)	11 (+0)	14 (+2)

Skills Perception +2, Stealth +5
Damage Immunities poison
Condition Immunities poisoned
Senses darkvision 60 ft., passive Perception 12
Languages Auran
Challenge 1/2 (100 XP)

Death Burst. When the mephit dies, it explodes in a burst of wind. Each creature within 5 feet of the mephit must succeed on a DC 11 Dexterity saving throw or take 2 (1d4) bludgeoning damage and be knocked prone.

Innate Spellcasting (1/day). The mephit's innate spellcasting ability is Charisma *(spell save DC 12)*. The mephit can innately cast *blur*, requiring no material components.

Actions

Claws. *Melee Weapon Attack:* +5 to hit, reach 5 ft., one target. *Hit:* 5 (1d4 + 3) slashing damage.

Wind Breath (recharge 6). The mephit exhales air in a 15-foot cone. Each creature in the area must succeed on a DC 11 Strength saving throw or be pushed up to 5 feet away and knocked prone.

Earth Mephit

Small elemental, neutral evil
Armor Class 12 (natural armor)
Hit Points 33 (6d6 + 12)
Speed 30 ft., fly 30 ft.

STR	DEX	CON	INT	WIS	CHA
11 (+0)	13 (+1)	14 (+2)	6 (−2)	11 (+0)	14 (+2)

Skills Perception +2, Stealth +3
Damage Immunities poison
Condition Immunities poisoned
Senses darkvision 60 ft., passive Perception 12
Languages Terran
Challenge 1/2 (100 XP)

Death Burst. When the mephit dies, it explodes in a burst of earthen fragments. Each creature within 5 feet of the mephit must succeed on a DC 11 Dexterity saving throw or take 7 (2d6) bludgeoning damage.

Innate Spellcasting (1/day). The mephit's innate spellcasting ability is Charisma. It can innately cast enlarge/reduce (self only, enlarge only), requiring no material components.

Actions

Fists. *Melee Weapon Attack:* +3 to hit, reach 5 ft., one target. *Hit:* 4 (1d6 + 1) bludgeoning damage.

Earthen Breath (recharge 6). The mephit belches chunks of earth in a 15-foot cone, and the ground in that area becomes difficult terrain until cleared away. Each 5-foot-square portion of the area requires at least 1 minute to clear by hand.

Fire Mephit

Small elemental, neutral evil
Armor Class 12
Hit Points 27 (6d6 + 6)
Speed 30 ft., fly 40 ft.

STR	DEX	CON	INT	WIS	CHA
13 (+1)	15 (+2)	12 (+1)	6 (−2)	11 (+0)	14 (+2)

Skills Perception +2, Stealth +4
Damage Vulnerabilities cold
Damage Immunities fire, poison
Condition Immunities poisoned
Senses darkvision 60 ft., passive Perception 12
Languages Ignan
Challenge 1/2 (100 XP)

Death Burst. When the mephit dies, it explodes in a burst of flame. Each creature within 5 feet of the mephit must succeed on a DC 11 Dexterity saving throw or take 5 (1d10) fire damage.

Innate Spellcasting (1/day). The mephit's innate spellcasting ability is Charisma (spell save DC 12). It can innately cast *heat metal*, requiring no material components.

Actions

Claws. *Melee Weapon Attack:* +4 to hit, reach 5 ft., one target. *Hit:* 4 (1d4 + 2) slashing damage plus 3 (1d6) fire damage.

Fire Breath (recharge 6). The mephit exhales fire in a 30-foot line that is 5 feet wide. Each creature in the area must make a DC 11 Dexterity saving throw, taking 10 (3d6) fire damage on a failed save, or half as much damage on a successful one.

Lightning Mephit

Small elemental, neutral evil
Armor Class 13
Hit Points 21 (6d6)
Speed 30 ft., fly 30 ft.

STR	DEX	CON	INT	WIS	CHA
10 (+0)	17 (+3)	10 (+0)	6 (−2)	11 (+0)	15 (+2)

Skills Perception +4, Stealth +5
Damage Immunities lightning, poison
Condition Immunities poisoned
Senses darkvision 60 ft., passive Perception 14
Languages Auran
Challenge 1 (200 XP)

Death Burst. When the mephit dies, it explodes in a flare of lightning in a 15-foot radius. Creatures in the area must make a DC 12 Dexterity saving throw, taking 9 (2d8) lightning damage on a successful saving throw, or half as much damage on a failed one.

Innate Spellcasting. The mephit's spellcasting ability is Charisma (spell save DC 12, +4 to hit with spell attacks). It can innately cast *shocking grasp* at will requiring no material components.

Actions

Claws. *Melee Weapon Attack:* +5 to hit, reach 5 ft., one
target. *Hit:* 5 (1d4 + 3) piercing damage plus 2 (1d4)
lightning damage.

Lightning Breath (recharge 6). The mephit exhales lightning
in a 15-foot line that is 1-foot wide. All creatures within that
area must make a DC 12 Dexterity saving throw, taking 9
(2d8) lightning damage on a failed save, or half as much
damage on a successful one.

Salt Mephit

Small elemental, neutral evil
Armor Class 12
Hit Points 27 (6d6 + 6)
Speed 30 ft., fly 30 ft.

STR	DEX	CON	INT	WIS	CHA
13 (+1)	15 (+2)	12 (+1)	6 (−2)	11 (+0)	14 (+2)

Skills Perception +2, Stealth +4
Damage Immunities poison
Condition Immunities poisoned
Senses darkvision 60 ft., passive Perception 12
Languages Terran
Challenge 1/2 (100 XP)

Death Burst. When the mephit dies, it explodes in a burst
of salt crystals. Each creature within 5 feet of the mephit
must succeed on a DC 11 Dexterity saving throw or take
2 (1d4) slashing damage and be poisoned for 1 minute. A
creature can repeat the saving throw at the end of each
of its turns, ending the effect on itself on a success.

Dehydrate (1/day). The mephit draws moisture from an area
centered on itself. Living creatures within a 20-foot radius
of the mephit must succeed on a DC 11 Constitution
saving throw or take 9 (2d8) necrotic damage. Plant
creatures and magical plants make the saving throw with
disadvantage, and the effect does maximum damage to
them if they fail. Nonmagical plants within the area simply
wither and die.

Actions

Claws. *Melee Weapon Attack:* +4 to hit, reach 5 ft., one
target. *Hit:* 4 (1d4 + 2) slashing damage plus 2 (1d4)
necrotic damage.

Salt Breath (recharge 6). The mephit exhales a spray of
salt crystals in a 15-foot cone. Each creature in the area
must succeed on a DC 11 Constitution saving throw or be
poisoned for 1 minute. A creature can repeat the saving
throw at the end of each of its turns, ending the effect on
itself on a success.

Smoke Mephit

Small elemental, neutral evil
Armor Class 12
Hit Points 21 (6d6)
Speed 30 ft., fly 30 ft.

STR	DEX	CON	INT	WIS	CHA
10 (+0)	14 (+2)	10 (+0)	6 (−2)	11 (+0)	15 (+2)

Skills Perception +4, Stealth +4
Damage Vulnerabilities cold
Damage Immunities fire, poison
Condition Immunities poisoned
Senses darkvision 60 ft., passive Perception 14
Languages Ignan

Challenge 1/2 (100 XP)

Death Burst. When the mephit dies, it explodes in a cloud
of smoke. Each creature within 5 feet of the mephit must
make a successful DC 10 Constitution saving throw or
take 1d4 fire damage and be poisoned for 1 minute. A
poisoned creature can repeat the saving throw at the
end of each of its turns, ending the effect on a success.

Innate Spellcasting. The mephit can innately cast *blur* 1/day,
requiring no material components. Its innate spellcasting
ability is Charisma (spell save DC 12, +4 to hit with spell
attacks).

Actions

Claw. *Melee Weapon Attack:* +4 to hit, reach 5 ft., one
target. *Hit:* 4 (1d4 + 2) slashing damage plus 2 (1d4) fire
damage.

Sooty Breath (recharge 5–6). The mephit exhales black soot
in a 15-foot cone. All creatures within that area must make
a DC 12 Dexterity saving throw, taking 9 (2d8) fire damage
on a failed save, or half as much damage on a successful
one.

Ember Storm (1/day). A smoke mephit can create a
downpour of white-hot embers that affects a 20-foot
radius sphere centered on itself. All creatures caught
in the storm must make a DC 12 Dexterity saving throw,
taking 10 (3d6) fire damage on a failed save, or half as
much damage on a successful one.

Mihstu

Medium elemental, neutral evil
Armor Class 15
Hit Points 112 (15d8 + 45)
Speed fly 90 ft. (hover)

STR	DEX	CON	INT	WIS	CHA
14 (+2)	20 (+5)	16 (+3)	8 (−1)	10 (+0)	6 (−2)

Skills Perception +3, Stealth +8
Damage Resistances cold, thunder; bludgeoning, piercing,
and slashing from nonmagical attacks
Damage Immunities lightning, poison
Condition Immunities exhaustion, paralyzed, petrified,
poisoned, prone, restrained, unconscious
Senses darkvision 60 ft., passive Perception 13
Languages Auran
Challenge 7 (2,900 XP)

Air Form. The mihstu can enter a hostile creature's space
and stop there. It can move through a space as narrow as
1 inch wide without squeezing.

Aura of Wind. Ranged attacks against the mihstu have
disadvantage. When a creature within 10 feet of the
mihstu casts a spell with a material component, it must
succeed on a DC 14 Dexterity saving throw or fail to cast
the spell as the material component is blown out of the
creature's hand into a space within 5 feet of it.

Elemental Nature. The mihstu doesn't require air, food, drink,
or sleep.

Actions

Multiattack. The mihstu makes two Lightning Tentacle
attacks.

Lightning Tentacle. *Melee Weapon Attack:* +8 to hit, reach 5
ft., one target. *Hit:* 12 (2d6 + 5) bludgeoning damage plus
7 (2d6) lightning damage.

Draining Presence (recharge 5–6). The mihstu's cold, windy embrace drains vital fluids from a creature in the mihstu's space. The creature must make a DC 14 Constitution saving throw, taking 27 (6d8) cold damage on a failed save, or half as much damage on a successful one. The mihstu regains hit points equal to the damage dealt.

REACTIONS

Static Discharge. When a creature that is wearing metal armor or that is attacking with a weapon made of metal hits the mihstu, the creature must succeed on a DC 14 Dexterity saving throw or take 3 (1d6) lightning damage.

Minotaur, Obsidian

Large construct, neutral
Armor Class 16 (natural armor)
Hit Points 76 (8d10 + 32)
Speed 30 ft.

STR	DEX	CON	INT	WIS	CHA
21 (+5)	10 (+0)	18 (+4)	3 (−4)	11 (+0)	1 (−5)

Damage Immunities acid, fire, poison, psychic; bludgeoning, piercing, and slashing from nonmagical attacks not made with adamantine
Condition Immunities charmed, exhaustion, frightened, paralyzed, petrified, poisoned
Senses darkvision 60 ft., passive Perception 10
Languages understands the languages of its creator but can't speak
Challenge 8 (3,900 XP)

Charge. If the obsidian minotaur moves at least 10 feet straight toward a target and then hits it with a gore attack on the same turn, the target takes an extra 9 (2d8) piercing damage. If the target is a creature, it must succeed on a DC 16 Strength saving throw or be pushed up to 10 feet away and knocked prone.
Immutable Form. The minotaur is immune to any spell or effect that would alter its form.
Magic Resistance. The minotaur has advantage on saving throws against spells and other magic effects.
Magic Weapons. The minotaur's weapon attacks are magical.

ACTIONS

Multiattack. The obsidian minotaur makes one gore attack and two claw attacks.
Gore. Melee Weapon Attack: +8 to hit, reach 5 ft., one target. *Hit:* 14 (2d8 + 5) piercing damage plus 7 (2d6) fire damage.
Claw. Melee Weapon Attack: +8 to hit, reach 10 ft., one target. *Hit:* 12 (2d6 + 5) slashing damage plus 7 (2d6) fire damage.
Burning Breath (recharge 5–6). An obsidian minotaur expels a cloud of superheated gas that fills a 10-foot cube adjacent to it. The gas fades after the end of the minotaur's next turn. Creatures who enter the area or start their turn there must make a DC 16 Constitution saving throw. On a failed saving throw, the target takes 31 (9d6) fire damage and it is poisoned for 1 minute. On a successful saving throw, the target takes half the damage and is not poisoned.

Mohrg

Medium undead, chaotic evil
Armor Class 12
Hit Points 112 (15d8 + 45)
Speed 30 ft.

STR	DEX	CON	INT	WIS	CHA
18 (+4)	14 (+2)	17 (+3)	11 (+0)	10 (+0)	8 (−1)

Damage Immunities poison
Condition Immunities charmed, exhaustion, frightened, paralyzed, petrified, poisoned, stunned
Senses darkvision 60ft., passive Perception 10
Languages —
Challenge 8 (3,900 XP)
Create Spawn. Any humanoid creature slain by the mohrg rises as a zombie at the beginning of the mohrg's next turn. If this occurs, the mohrg regains 10 hit points, and the morhg can immediately make one slam attack as a reaction.

ACTIONS

Multiattack. The mohrg makes two slam attacks, and one attack with its tongue.
Slam. Melee Weapon Attack: +7 to hit, reach 5 ft., one target. *Hit:* 13 (2d8 + 4) bludgeoning damage, and the target is grappled and restrained (escape DC15), and the morhg can't grapple another creature or use its slam attack.
Tongue. Melee Weapon Attack: +7 to hit, reach 5 ft., one target. *Hit:* The target must make a DC 16 Constitution saving throw. On a failed save, the target takes 21 (6d6) necrotic damage, and is paralyzed for 1 minute. The creature can repeat the saving throw at the end of each of its turns, ending the effect on a success.

Monkey

Tiny beast, unaligned
Armor Class 12
Hit Points 5 (2d4)
Speed 30 ft., climb 30 ft.

STR	DEX	CON	INT	WIS	CHA
4 (−3)	15 (+2)	10 (+0)	3 (−4)	12 (+1)	5 (−3)

Skills Acrobatics +4, Perception +3
Senses passive Perception 13
Languages —
Challenge 1/8 (25 XP)

ACTIONS

Bite. Melee Weapon Attack: +4 to hit, reach 5 ft., one target. *Hit:* 1 piercing damage.

Monkey, Magical

Tiny beast, unaligned
Armor Class 13
Hit Points 14 (4d4 + 4)
Speed 30 ft., climb 30 ft.

STR	DEX	CON	INT	WIS	CHA
6 (−2)	17 (+3)	13 (+1)	3 (−4)	12 (+1)	5 (−3)

Skills Acrobatics +5, Perception +3, Stealth +7
Senses darkvision 60 ft., passive Perception 13

Languages —
Challenge 1 (200 XP)

ACTIONS

Bite. *Melee Weapon Attack:* +5 to hit, reach 5 ft., one target. *Hit:* 1 piercing damage.

Exploding Fruit. The magical monkey lobs a gem-like fruit at a point within 30 ft. of it. The fruit explodes on impact, and all creatures within a 20 ft. radius of the impact point must succeed on a DC 13 Dexterity saving throw or take 9 (2d8) bludgeoning damage.

Mudman, Advanced

Medium elemental, neutral
Armor Class 13 (natural armor)
Hit Points 51 (6d8 + 24)
Speed 15 ft.

STR	DEX	CON	INT	WIS	CHA
17 (+3)	10 (+0)	19 (+4)	3 (−4)	10 (+0)	10 (+0)

Saving Throws Con +6
Skills Stealth +2
Damage Resistances **bludgeoning, piercing, and slashing from nonmagical attacks**
Damage Immunities poison
Condition Immunities charmed, exhaustion, frightened, grappled, paralyzed, poisoned, restrained, unconscious
Senses tremorsense 60 ft., passive Perception 10
Languages —
Challenge 3 (700 XP)

Mud Pool. If the mudman leaves the mud pool it dwells in, it has disadvantage of all attack rolls, ability checks, and saving throws while outside the pool.

False Appearance. While the mudman remains motionless, it is indistinguishable from an ordinary mound of mud.

ACTIONS

Multiattack. The mudman makes two Slam attacks.

Slam. *Melee Weapon Attack:* +5 to hit, reach 5 ft., one target. *Hit:* 6 (1d6 + 3) bludgeoning damage.

Mud Bomb. *Ranged Weapon Attack:* +5 to hit, range 10 ft., one target. *Hit:* The target is blinded and restrained. A creature restrained by a mud bomb can use its action to make a DC 13 Strength check. On a success, it frees itself, ending the restrained and blinded conditions.

Engulf (recharge 5–6). The mudman moves up to its speed. While doing so, it can enter a Medium or smaller creature's space. Whenever the mudman enters a creature's space, the creature must make a DC 13 Dexterity saving throw. On a successful save, the mudman is pushed 5 feet back and knocked prone. On a failed save, the mudman enters the creature's space. The engulfed creature can't breathe, is restrained and blinded, and takes 6 (1d6 + 3) bludgeoning damage at the start of each of the mudman's turns. An engulfed creature can try to escape by taking an action to make a DC 13 Strength check. On a success, the creature escapes and enters a space of its choice within 5 feet of the mudman, ending the restrained and blinded conditions.

Mummy, Greater

Medium undead, lawful evil
Armor Class 17 (natural armor)
Hit Points 156 (24d8 + 48)
Speed 20 ft.

STR	DEX	CON	INT	WIS	CHA
15 (+2)	16 (+3)	15 (+2)	10 (+0)	15 (+2)	20 (+5)

Saving Throws Con +7, Wis +7, Cha +10
Skills Perception +7
Damage Vulnerabilities fire
Damage Resistances acid, cold, lightning
Damage Immunities necrotic, poison; bludgeoning, piercing, and slashing from nonmagical attacks
Condition Immunities charmed, exhaustion, frightened, paralyzed, poisoned
Senses darkvision 60 ft., passive Perception 17
Languages Common
Challenge 16 (15,000 XP)

Magic Resistance. The greater mummy has advantage on saving throws against spells and other magical effects.

Rejuvenation. The greater mummy gains a new body in 24 hours if its heart is intact, regaining all its hit points and becoming active again. The new body appears within 5 feet of the mummy's heart.

Turn Resistance. The greater mummy has advantage on saving throws against any effect that turns undead.

Spellcasting. The greater mummy is a 10th-level spellcaster. Its spellcasting ability is Charisma (spell save DC 18, +10 to hit with spell attacks). It can cast the following spells:
> Cantrips (at will): *dancing lights, message, poison spray, ray of frost, true strike*
> 1st level (4 slots): *burning hands, detect magic, fog cloud, magic missile*
> 2nd level (3 slots): *arcane lock, ray of enfeeblement, scorching ray, web*
> 3rd level (3 slots): *counterspell, lightning bolt, stinking cloud*
> 4th level (3 slots): *confusion, ice storm, wall of fire*
> 5th level (1 slot): *arcane hand, cone of cold*

ACTIONS

Multiattack. The greater mummy can use its Dreadful Glare and make one attack with its Rotting Fist.

Rotting Fist. *Melee Weapon Attack:* +8 to hit, reach 5 ft., one target. *Hit:* 13 (3d6 + 3) bludgeoning damage plus 21 (6d6) necrotic damage. If the target is a creature, it must succeed on a DC 18 Constitution saving throw or be cursed with mummy rot[3].

Dreadful Glare. The greater mummy targets one creature it can see within 60 feet of it. If the target can see the mummy, it must succeed on a DC 19 Wisdom saving throw against this magic or become frightened until the end of the mummy's next turn. If the target fails the saving throw by 5 or more, it is also paralyzed for the same duration. A target that succeeds on the saving throw is immune to the Dreadful Glare from mummies of all types for the next 24 hours.

LEGENDARY ACTIONS

The greater mummy can take 3 legendary actions, choosing from the options below. Only one legendary action option can be used at a time and only at the end of another creature's turn. The mummy regains spent legendary actions at the start of its turn.

Attack. The greater mummy makes one melee attack or uses its Dreadful Glare.

Blinding Dust. Blinding dust and sand swirls magically around the greater mummy. Each creature within 5 feet of the mummy must succeed on a DC 19 Constitution saving throw or be blinded until the end of the creature's next turn.

Blasphemous Word (costs 2 actions). The greater mummy utters a blasphemous word. Each non-undead creature within 10 feet of the mummy that can hear the magical utterance must succeed on a DC 19 Constitution saving throw or be stunned until the end of the mummy's next turn.

Channel Negative Energy (costs 2 actions). The greater mummy magically unleashes negative energy. Creatures within 60 feet of the mummy, including ones behind barriers and around corners, can't regain hit points until the end of the mummy's next turn.

Whirlwind of Sand (costs 2 actions). The greater mummy magically transforms into a whirlwind of sand, moves up to 60 feet, and reverts to its normal form. While in whirlwind form, the mummy is immune to all damage, and it can't be grappled, petrified, knocked prone, restrained, or stunned. Equipment worn or carried by the mummy remains in its possession.

Mummy Djinn

Huge undead, lawful evil
Armor Class 23 (natural armor)
Hit Points 142 (15d12 + 45)
Speed 20 ft., fly 60 ft.

STR	DEX	CON	INT	WIS	CHA
31 (+10)	17 (+3)	16 (+3)	14 (+2)	20 (+5)	17 (+3)

Saving Throws Con +8, Int +7, Wis +10, Cha +8
Skills Arcana +7, Insight +10, Perception +10, Persuasion +8, Religion +7, Stealth +8
Damage Vulnerabilities fire
Damage Resistances lightning, thunder
Damage Immunities acid, necrotic, poison; bludgeoning, piercing, and slashing from nonmagical attacks
Condition Immunities charmed, exhaustion, frightened, paralyzed, poisoned
Senses darkvision 60 ft., passive Perception 20
Languages Auran, Common, telepathy 120 ft.
Challenge 14 (11,500 XP)

Magic Resistance. The mummy djinn has advantage on saving throws against spells and other magical effects.

Spellcasting. The mummy djinn is a 10th-level spellcaster. Its spellcasting ability is Wisdom (spell save DC 18, +10 to hit with spell attacks). It has the following cleric spells prepared:

Cantrips (at will): *guidance, mending, sacred flame, thaumaturgy*
1st level (4 slots): *bane, command, inflict wounds, shield of faith*
2nd level (3 slots): *blindness/deafness, hold person, spiritual weapon*
3rd level (3 slots): *animate dead, dispel magic, spirit guardians*
4th level (3 slots): *divination, banishment, guardian of faith*
5th level (2 slots): *contagion, insect plague*

ACTIONS

Multiattack. The mummy djinn makes 2 Falchion attacks and one Rotting Fist attack.

Falchion of Law. Melee Weapon Attack: +17 to hit, reach 10 ft., one target. *Hit:* 23 (3d8 + 12) slashing damage. When it attacks a creature that has at least one head with this weapon and rolls a 20 on the attack roll, it cuts off one of the creature's heads. The creature dies if it can't survive without the lost head.

Rotting Fist. Melee Weapon Attack: +15 to hit, reach 10 ft., one target. *Hit:* 17 (2d6 + 10) bludgeoning damage plus 21 (6d6) necrotic damage. If the target is a creature, it must succeed on a DC 18 Constitution saving throw or be cursed with mummy rot. The cursed target can't regain hit points, and its hit point maximum decreases by 10 (3d6) for every 24 hours that elapse. If the curse reduces the target's hit point maximum to 0, the target dies, and its body turns to dust. The curse lasts until removed by the *remove curse* spell or other magic.

Swirling Sandstorm. A 10-foot-radius, 30-foot-tall cylinder of swirling air and sand magically forms at a point the mummy djinn can see within 120 feet of it. The sandstorm lasts as long as the mummy djinn maintains concentration (as if concentrating on a spell) and its area is heavily obscured. Any creature but the mummy djinni that enters the sandstorm must succeed on a DC 18 Strength saving throw or be restrained by it. The mummy djinn can move the sandstorm up to 60 feet as an action, and creatures restrained by the sandstorm move with it. The sandstorm ends if the mummy djinn loses sight of it. A creature can use its action to free a creature restrained by the sandstorm, including itself, by succeeding on a DC 18 Strength check. If the check succeeds, the creature is no longer restrained and moves to the nearest unoccupied space outside the sandstorm.

Mus'ad Camel Face

Large monstrosity, lawful good
Armor Class 16 (natural armor)
Hit Points 178 (21d10 + 63)
Speed 50 ft.

STR	DEX	CON	INT	WIS	CHA
14 (+2)	16 (+3)	16 (+3)	20 (+5)	21 (+5)	19 (+4)

Saving Throws Dex +8, Con +8, Int +10, Wis +10
Skills Arcana +10, History +10, Insight +10, Perception +10, Survival +10
Condition Immunities frightened
Senses truesight 30 ft., passive Perception 20
Languages Abyssal, Celestial, Common, Infernal, Primordial
Challenge 14 (11,500 XP)

Prescient Weapons. Mus'ad's weapon attacks are magical. When he hits with any weapon, the weapon deals an extra 4d8 force damage (included in the attack).

Precognition (1/turn). Mus'ad has advantage on his next attack roll, ability check, or saving throw.

Share Intuition. As a bonus action, Mus'ad shares some of his precognition with one ally within 30 feet. The ally has advantage on its next attack roll, ability check, or saving throw.

Spellcasting. Mus'ad Camel Face is an 18th-level spellcaster. His spellcasting ability is Intelligence (spell save DC 18, +10 to hit with spell attacks). Mus'ad has the following spells prepared:

Cantrips (at will): *light, mage hand, minor illusion, prestidigitation, ray of frost*
1st level (4 slots): *comprehend languages, detect magic, floating disk, magic missile, shield*

2nd level (3 slots): *arcanist's magic aura, detect thoughts, locate object, misty step*
3rd level (3 slots): *clairvoyance, counterspell, fireball, fly*
4th level (3 slots): *arcane eye, confusion, locate creature*
5th level (3 slots): *cone of cold, legend lore, scrying*
6th level (1 slot): *globe of invulnerability*
7th level (1 slot): *prismatic spray*
8th level (1 slot): *mind blank*
9th level (1 slot): *prismatic wall*

ACTIONS

Multiattack. The sage camel makes one Bite attack and two Hooves attacks.

Bite. *Melee Weapon Attack:* +7 to hit, reach 5 ft., one target. *Hit:* 6 (1d8 + 2) bludgeoning damage plus 18 (4d8) force damage.

Hooves. *Melee Weapon Attack:* +7 to hit, reach 5 ft., one target. *Hit:* 7 (2d4 + 2) bludgeoning damage plus 18 (4d8) force damage.

Spit (recharge 5–6). Mus'ad spits blinding saliva in a 90-foot line that is 5 feet wide. Each creature in that line must make a DC 18 Dexterity saving throw. On a failure, a creature takes 54 (12d8) acid damage and is blinded for 1 minute. On a success, a creature takes half the damage and isn't blinded. A blinded creature can repeat the saving throw at the end of each of its turns, ending the effect on itself on a success.

Naga, Dark

Large aberration, lawful evil
Armor Class 17 (natural armor)
Hit Points 102 (12d10 + 36)
Speed 40 ft.

STR	DEX	CON	INT	WIS	CHA
14 (+2)	18 (+4)	17 (+3)	16 (+3)	15 (+2)	17 (+3)

Saving Throws Dex +8, Con +7, Int +7, Wis +6, Cha +7
Skills Arcana +7, Deception +7, Insight +6, Perception +6, Stealth +8
Damage Immunities poison, psychic
Condition Immunities charmed, poisoned
Senses darkvision 60 ft., passive Perception 16
Languages Common, Infernal
Challenge 9 (5,000 XP)

Rejuvenation. If it dies, the naga returns to life in 1d6 days and regains all its hit points. Only a *wish* spell can prevent this trait from functioning.

Guarded Thoughts. The naga's thoughts may not be read.

Innate Spellcasting. The naga can innately cast *detect thoughts* (spell save DC 15) at will, and it needs only verbal components to cast this spell. Its innate spellcasting ability is Charisma.

Spellcasting. The naga is a 7th-level spellcaster. Its spellcasting ability is Charisma (spell save DC 15, +7 to hit with spell attacks), and it needs only verbal components to cast its spells. It has the following sorcerer spells prepared:

Cantrips (at will): *acid splash, fire bolt, mage hand, minor illusion, ray of frost*
1st level (4 slots): *charm person, expeditious retreat, magic missile*
2nd level (3 slots): *misty step, scorching ray*
3rd level (3 slots): *fireball, major image*
4th level (1 slot): *confusion*

ACTIONS

Multiattack. The naga makes one Bite attack and one Sting attack. It can't make both attacks against the same target.

Bite. *Melee Weapon Attack:* +8 to hit, reach 10 ft., one target. *Hit:* 7 (1d6 + 4) piercing damage, and the target must make a DC 14 Constitution saving throw, taking 40 (9d8) poison damage on a failed save, or half as much damage on a successful one.

Sting. *Melee Weapon Attack:* +8 to hit, reach 10 ft., one target. *Hit:* 9 (2d4 + 4) piercing damage, and the target must succeed on a DC 14 Constitution saving throw or be poisoned for 24 hours. Until this poison ends, the target is unconscious. Another creature can use an action to shake the target awake.

Night Terror

Small aberration, chaotic evil
Armor Class 19
Hit Points 35 (10d6)
Speed 0 ft., fly 50 ft.

STR	DEX	CON	INT	WIS	CHA
1 (−5)	28 (+9)	10 (+0)	15 (+2)	16 (+3)	14 (+2)

Skills Perception +6, Stealth +12
Damage Immunities fire, lightning
Condition Immunities poisoned
Senses blindsight 30 ft., darkvision 60 ft., passive Perception 16
Languages Common, Deep Speech
Challenge 6 (2,300 XP)

Feed on Fear. The night terror regains 10 hit points at the start of its turn if it has at least 1 hit point and a creature within 30 feet of it has the fear condition.

Incorporeal Movement. The night terror can move through other creatures and objects as if they were difficult terrain. It takes 5 (1d10) force damage if it ends its turn inside an object.

Illumination. The night terror sheds dim light in a 5- to 20foot radius. The night terror can alter the radius as a bonus action.

Light Sensitivity. While in bright light, the night terror has disadvantage on attack rolls, as well as on Wisdom (Perception) checks that rely on sight.

Limited Magic Immunity. The night terror can't be affected or detected by spells of 4th level or lower unless it wishes to be. It has advantage on saving throws against all other spells and magical effects.

ACTIONS

Chill. *Melee Weapon Attack:* +12 to hit, reach 5 ft., one target. *Hit:* 19 (3d6 + 9) cold damage, and the target must succeed on a DC 15 Wisdom saving throw or be frightened for 1 minute. A creature can repeat the saving throw at the end of each of its turns, ending the effect on itself on a success.

Invisibility. The night terror and its light magically become invisible until it attacks or until its concentration ends (as if concentrating on a spell).

Nightwalker

Huge undead, chaotic evil
Armor Class 19 (natural armor)
Hit Points 345 (30d12 + 150)
Speed 40 ft.

STR	DEX	CON	INT	WIS	CHA
35 (+12)	14 (+2)	21 (+5)	20 (+5)	21 (+5)	19 (+4)

Saving Throws Str +18, Dex +8, Con +11, Wis +11
Skills Arcana +11, Insight +11, Perception +11, Stealth +8
Damage Resistances necrotic; bludgeoning, piercing, and slashing from nonmagical attacks
Damage Immunities poison
Condition Immunities charmed, exhaustion, frightened, paralyzed, poisoned
Senses darkvision 120 ft., passive Perception 21
Languages Abyssal, Common, Infernal, telepathy 120 ft.
Challenge 20 (25,000 XP)

Siege Monster. The nightwalker deals double damage to objects and structures.
Desecrating Aura. Undead within a 30-foot radius of the nightwalker have advantage on attack rolls and saving throws.
Eyes of Night. Magical darkness doesn't impede the nightwalker's darkvision.
Sunlight Weakness. While in sunlight, the nightwalker has disadvantage on attack rolls, ability checks, and saving throws.
Innate Spellcasting. The nightwalker's innate spellcasting ability is Intelligence (spell save DC 19). It can innately cast the following spells, requiring no material components.
At will: *contagion, darkness, dispel magic, blight*
3/day each: *confusion, haste, hold monster, invisibility*
1/day each: *cone of cold, finger of death, plane shift*

ACTIONS

Multiattack. The nightwalker makes two Claw attacks.
Claw. *Melee Weapon Attack:* +18 to hit, reach 15 ft., one target. *Hit:* 25 (3d8 + 12) slashing damage plus 14 (4d6) cold damage.
Army of Shadows (1/day). The nightwalker magically calls 2d4 shadows, provided that the nightwalker is not in bright light. The shadows arrive in one round, acting as allies of the nightwalker and obeying its commands. The shadows remain for 1 hour, until the nightwalker dies, or until the nightwalker dismisses them as a bonus action.

Niln

Medium elemental, neutral
Armor Class 14
Hit Points 61 (10d8 + 16)
Speed 0 ft., fly 60 ft. (hover)

STR	DEX	CON	INT	WIS	CHA
12 (+1)	19 (+4)	14 (+2)	6 (−2)	13 (+1)	11 (+0)

Saving Throws Dex +7
Skills Perception +4, Stealth +7
Damage Resistances cold, lightning, thunder; bludgeoning, piercing, and slashing from nonmagical attacks
Damage Immunities poison
Condition Immunities exhaustion, grappled, paralyzed, petrified, poisoned, prone, restrained, unconscious
Senses darkvision 60 ft., passive Perception 14
Languages Niln
Challenge 5 (1,800 XP)

Gaseous Form. The niln can enter a hostile creature's space and stop there. It can move through a space as narrow as 1 inch wide without squeezing.
Drowning Fog. As a bonus action, the niln can fill the area within a 30 ft. radius of it with a cold, semi-solid fog. This area is difficult terrain and heavily obscured for all creatures except nilns until the start of the niln's next turn, and any creature in the affected area is unable to breathe unless it can breathe water.

ACTIONS

Multiattack. The niln makes two Slam attacks.
Slam. *Melee Weapon Attack:* +7 to hit, reach 5 ft., one target. *Hit:* 11 (2d6 + 4) bludgeoning damage.
Drench. All nonmagical, open flames within a 30 ft. radius of the niln are extinguished.

Nymph

Medium fey, chaotic good
Armor Class 11 (16 with barkskin)
Hit Points 22 (5d8)
Speed 30 ft.

STR	DEX	CON	INT	WIS	CHA
10 (+0)	12 (+1)	11 (+0)	14 (+2)	15 (+2)	18 (+4)

Skills Perception +4, Stealth +5
Senses darkvision 60 ft., passive Perception 14
Languages Elvish, Syvan
Challenge 1 (200 XP)

Innate Spellcasting. The nymph's innate spellcasting ability is Charisma (spell save DC 14). The nymph can innately cast the following spells, requiring no material components:
At will: *druidcraft, misty step*
3/day each: *conjure woodland beings, entangle, goodberry*
1/day each: *barkskin, geas, shillelagh*
Magic Resistance. The nymph has advantage on saving throws against spells and other magical effects.
Speak with Beasts and Plants. The nymph can communicate with beasts and plants as if they shared a language.

ACTIONS

Club. *Melee Weapon Attack:* +2 to hit (+6 to hit with shillelagh), reach 5 ft., one target. *Hit:* 2 (1d4) bludgeoning damage, or 8 (1d8 + 4) bludgeoning damage with shillelagh.
Fey Charm. The nymph targets one humanoid or beast that she can see within 30 feet of her. If the target can see the nymph, it must succeed on a DC 14 Wisdom saving throw or be magically charmed. The charmed creature regards the nymph as a trusted friend to be heeded and protected. Although the target isn't under the nymph's control, it takes the nymph's requests or actions in the most favorable way it can.
Each time the nymph or its allies do anything harmful to the target, the target can repeat the saving throw, ending the effect on itself on a success. Otherwise, the effect lasts 24 hours or until the nymph dies, is on a different plane of existence from the target, or ends the effect as a bonus action. If a target's saving throw is successful, the target is immune to the nymph's Fey Charm for the next 24 hours.
The nymph can have no more than one humanoid and up to three beasts charmed at a time.

Nymph, Fire

Medium fey, neutral
Armor Class 11 (16 with barkskin)
Hit Points 22 (5d8)
Speed 30 ft.

STR	DEX	CON	INT	WIS	CHA
10 (+0)	12 (+1)	11 (+0)	14 (+2)	15 (+2)	18 (+4)

Skills Perception +4, Stealth +5
Damage Immunities fire
Senses darkvision 60 ft., passive Perception 14
Languages Elvish, Syvan
Challenge 1 (200 XP)

Innate Spellcasting. The nymph's innate spellcasting ability is Charisma (spell save DC 14). The nymph can innately cast the following spells, requiring no material components:

> At will: druidcraft, produce flame, misty step
> 3/day each: conjure minor elementals, flaming sphere, goodberry
> 1/day each: barkskin, shillelagh, wall of fire

Magic Resistance. The nymph has advantage on saving throws against spells and other magical effects.
Speak with Beasts and Plants. The nymph can communicate with beasts and plants as if they shared a language.

ACTIONS

Club. *Melee Weapon Attack:* +2 to hit (+6 to hit with *shillelagh*), reach 5 ft., one target. *Hit:* 2 (1d4) bludgeoning damage plus 2 (1d4) fire damage, or 8 (1d8 + 4) bludgeoning damage with *shillelagh* plus 2 (1d4) fire damage.
Fey Charm. The nymph targets one humanoid or beast that she can see within 30 feet of her. If the target can see the nymph, it must succeed on a DC 14 Wisdom saving throw or be magically charmed. The charmed creature regards the nymph as a trusted friend to be heeded and protected. Although the target isn't under the nymph's control, it takes the nymph's requests or actions in the most favorable way it can.

Each time the nymph or its allies do anything harmful to the target, the target can repeat the saving throw, ending the effect on itself on a success. Otherwise, the effect lasts 24 hours or until the nymph dies, is on a different plane of existence from the target, or ends the effect as a bonus action. If a target's saving throw is successful, the target is immune to the nymph's Fey Charm for the next 24 hours.

The nymph can have no more than one humanoid and up to three beasts charmed at a time.

Order of the Devil

Devil Cenobite

Medium humanoid (any), any evil alignment
Armor Class 19 (natural armor)
Hit Points 135 (18d8 + 54)
Speed 50 ft.

STR	DEX	CON	INT	WIS	CHA
10 (+0)	20 (+5)	16 (+3)	11 (+0)	18 (+4)	12 (+1)

Saving Throws Dex +9, Wis +9
Skills Acrobatics +9, Stealth +9
Damage Immunities fire, poison
Condition Immunites poisoned
Senses passive Perception 14
Language Common, Infernal
Challenge 11 (7,200 XP)

Fists of Dark Flame (1/day). The devil cenobite wreaths its fists in flame. It deals an additional 7 (2d6) fire damage when it hits with its Unarmed Strikes for 1 minute.
Innate Spellcasting. The devil cenobite's innate spellcasting ability is Wisdom (spell save DC 17, +9 to hit with spell attacks). It can cast the following spells, requiring no material components.

> At will: *fire bolt* (5th level)
> 3/day: *burning hands* (3rd-level, 5d6 fire damage)
> 1/day: *misty step*

Magic Weapons. The devil cenobite's weapon attacks are considered magical for the purposes of damage resistances and immunities.
Slow Fall. The devil cenobite reduces any falling damage by 30. If it does not take damage from a fall, it does not fall prone.

ACTIONS

Multiattack. The devil cenobite makes three Unarmed Strikes. It can use its Flurry of Blows or Unholy Strike ability in place of one of the Unarmed Strikes.
Unarmed Strike. *Melee Weapon Attack:* +9 to hit, reach 5 ft., one target. *Hit:* 10 (1d10 + 5) bludgeoning damage.
Flurry of Blows (3/day). *Melee Weapon Attack:* +9 to hit, reach 5 ft., one target. *Hit:* 18 (3d10 + 5) bludgeoning damage, and the target suffers one of the following effects of the devil cenobite's choice:

- The target must succeed on a DC 16 Dexterity saving throw or be knocked prone.
- The target must make a DC 16 Strength saving throw or be pushed up to 15 feet away from it.
- The target can't take reactions until the end of its next turn.

Unholy Strike (3/day). *Melee Weapon Attack:* +9 to hit, reach 5 ft., one target. *Hit:* 32 (5d10 + 5) necrotic damage, and the target must succeed on a DC 16 Constitution saving throw. On a failed saving throw, the target's maximum hit points are reduced by an equal amount. Lost hit points are regained when the target takes a long rest.

REACTIONS

Deflect Missiles. If it has one hand free, the devil cenobite can use its reaction in response to being hit with a ranged weapon attack. It reduces the damage by 22 (1d10 + 17). If it reduces the damage to 0, it can catch the missile if it is small enough for it to hold with one hand.

Devil Initiate

Medium humanoid (any), any evil alignment
Armor Class 16 (natural armor)
Hit Points 49 (9d8 + 9)
Speed 40 ft.

STR	DEX	CON	INT	WIS	CHA
10 (+0)	16 (+3)	13 (+1)	11 (+0)	16 (+3)	10 (+0)

Saving Throws Dex +5, Wis +5
Skills Acrobatics +5, Stealth +5
Damage Resistance fire
Senses passive Perception 13
Language Common, Infernal

Challenge 4 (1,100 XP)

Fists of Dark Flame (1/day). The devil initiate wreaths its fists in flame. It deals an additional 7 (2d6) fire damage when it hits with its Unarmed Strikes for 1 minute.

Slow Fall. The devil initiate reduces any falling damage by 30. If it does not take damage from a fall, it does not fall prone.

ACTIONS

Multiattack. The devil initiate makes two Unarmed Strikes. It can use its Flurry of Blows ability in place of one of the Unarmed Strikes.

Unarmed Strike. *Melee Weapon Attack:* +5 to hit, reach 5 ft., one target. *Hit:* 6 (1d6 + 3) bludgeoning damage.

Flurry of Blows (3/day). *Melee Weapon Attack:* +5 to hit, reach 5 ft., one target. *Hit:* 13 (3d6 + 3) bludgeoning damage, and the target suffers one of the following effects of the devil initiate's choice:

- The target must succeed on a DC 14 Dexterity saving throw or be knocked prone.
- The target must make a DC 14 Strength saving throw or be pushed up to 15 feet away from it.
- The target can't take reactions until the end of its next turn.

REACTIONS

Deflect Missiles. If it has one hand free, the devil initiate can use its reaction in response to being hit with a ranged weapon attack. It reduces the damage by 11 (1d10 + 6). If it reduces the damage to 0, it can catch the missile if it is small enough for it to hold with one hand.

Devil Mendicant

Medium humanoid (any), any evil alignment
Armor Class 18 (natural armor)
Hit Points 66 (12d8 + 12)
Speed 40 ft.

STR	DEX	CON	INT	WIS	CHA
10 (+0)	18 (+4)	13 (+1)	11 (+0)	18 (+4)	12 (+1)

Saving Throws Dex +7, Wis +7
Skills Acrobatics +7, Stealth +7
Damage Resistance fire
Senses passive Perception 14
Language Common, Infernal
Challenge 6 (2,300 XP)

Fists of Dark Flame (1/day). The devil mendicant wreaths its fists in flame. It deals an additional 7 (2d6) fire damage when it hits with its Unarmed Strikes for 1 minute.

Slow Fall. The devil mendicant reduces any falling damage by 30. If it does not take damage from a fall, it does not fall prone.

ACTIONS

Multiattack. The devil mendicant makes three Unarmed Strikes. It can use its Flurry of Blows ability in place of one of the Unarmed Strikes.

Unarmed Strike. *Melee Weapon Attack:* +7 to hit, reach 5 ft., one target. *Hit:* 7 (1d6 + 4) bludgeoning damage.

Flurry of Blows (3/day). *Melee Weapon Attack:* +7 to hit, reach 5 ft., one target. *Hit:* 14 (3d6 + 4) bludgeoning

damage, and the target suffers one of the following effects of the devil mendicant's choice:

- The target must succeed on a DC 15 Dexterity saving throw or be knocked prone.
- The target must make a DC 15 Strength saving throw or be pushed up to 15 feet away from it.
- The target can't take reactions until the end of its next turn.

REACTIONS

Deflect Missiles. If it has one hand free, the devil mendicant can use its reaction in response to being hit with a ranged weapon attack. It reduces the damage by 16 (1d10 + 11). If it reduces the damage to 0, it can catch the missile if it is small enough for it to hold with one hand.

Devil Monk

Medium humanoid (any), any evil alignment
Armor Class 18 (natural armor)
Hit Points 97 (15d8 + 30)
Speed 40 ft.

STR	DEX	CON	INT	WIS	CHA
10 (+0)	18 (+4)	14 (+2)	11 (+0)	18 (+4)	12 (+1)

Saving Throws Dex +8, Wis +8
Skills Acrobatics +8, Stealth +8
Damage Immunities fire
Senses passive Perception 14
Language Common, Infernal
Challenge 9 (5,000 XP)

Fists of Dark Flame (1/day). The devil monk wreaths its fists in flame. It deals an additional 7 (2d6) fire damage when it hits with its Unarmed Strikes for 1 minute.

Innate Spellcasting. The devil monk's innate spellcasting ability is Wisdom (spell save DC 16, +8 to hit with spell attacks). It can cast the following spells, requiring no material components.

At will: *fire bolt* (5th level)
3/day: *burning hands*

Magic Weapons. The devil monk's weapon attacks are considered magical for the purposes of damage resistances and immunities.

Slow Fall. The devil monk reduces any falling damage by 30. If it does not take damage from a fall, it does not fall prone.

ACTIONS

Multiattack. The devil monk makes three Unarmed Strikes. It can use its Flurry of Blows or Unholy Strike ability in place of one of the Unarmed Strikes.

Unarmed Strike. *Melee Weapon Attack:* +8 to hit, reach 5 ft., one target. *Hit:* 8 (1d8 + 4) bludgeoning damage.

Flurry of Blows (3/day). *Melee Weapon Attack:* +8 to hit, reach 5 ft., one target. *Hit:* 17 (3d8 + 4) bludgeoning damage, and the target suffers one of the following effects of the devil monk's choice:

- The target must succeed on a DC 16 Dexterity saving throw or be knocked prone.
- The target must make a DC 16 Strength saving throw or be pushed up to 15 feet away from it.
- The target can't take reactions until the end of its next turn.

Unholy Strike (3/day). Melee Weapon Attack: +8 to hit, reach 5 ft., one target. *Hit:* 26 (5d8 + 4) necrotic damage, and the target must succeed on a DC 15 Constitution saving throw. On a failed saving throw, the target's maximum hit points are reduced by an equal amount. Lost hit points are regained when the target takes a long rest.

REACTIONS

Deflect Missiles. If it has one hand free, the devil monk can use its reaction in response to being hit with a ranged weapon attack. It reduces the damage by 19 (1d10 + 14). If it reduces the damage to 0, it can catch the missile if it is small enough for it to hold with one hand.

Ghost of a Master

Medium undead, lawful evil
Armor Class 18 (natural armor)
Hit Points 66 (12d8 + 12)
Speed 40 ft.

STR	DEX	CON	INT	WIS	CHA
10 (+0)	18 (+4)	13 (+1)	11 (+0)	18 (+4)	14 (+2)

Saving Throws Dex +7, Wis +7
Skills Acrobatics +7, Stealth +7
Damage Resistance acid, fire, lightning, thunder; bludgeoning, piercing, and slashing from nonmagical attacks
Damage Immunities cold, necrotic, poison
Condition Immunities charmed, exhaustion, frightened, grappled, paralyzed, petrified, poisoned, prone, restrained
Senses darkvision 60 ft., passive Perception 14
Language Common, Infernal
Challenge 8 (3,900 XP)

Fists of Dark Flame (1/day). The ghost of a master wreaths its fists in flame. It deals an additional 7 (2d6) fire damage when it hits with its Unarmed Strikes for 1 minute.
Ethereal Sight. The ghost of the master can see 60 feet into the Ethereal Plane when it is on the Material Plane, and vice versa.
Incorporeal Movement. The ghost of a master can move through other creatures and objects as if they were difficult terrain. It takes 5 (1d10) force damage if it ends its turn inside an object.

ACTIONS

Multiattack. The ghost of a master makes three Unarmed Strikes. It can use its Flurry of Blows ability in place of one of the Unarmed Strikes.
Unarmed Strike. Melee Weapon Attack: +7 to hit, reach 5 ft., one target. *Hit:* 7 (1d6 + 4) necrotic damage.
Flurry of Blows (3/day). Melee Weapon Attack: +7 to hit, reach 5 ft., one target. *Hit:* 14 (3d6 + 4) necrotic damage, and the target suffers one of the following effects of the ghost of a master's choice:

- The target must succeed on a DC 15 Dexterity saving throw or be knocked prone.

- The target must make a DC 15 Strength saving throw or be pushed up to 15 feet away from it.

- The target can't take reactions until the end of its next turn.

Etherealness. The ghost of a master enters the Ethereal Plane from the Material Plane, or vice versa. It is visible on the Material Plane while it is in the Border Ethereal, and vice versa, yet it can't affect or be affected by anything on the other plane.
Horrifying Visage. Each non-undead creature within 60 feet of the ghost that can see it must succeed on a DC 13 Wisdom saving throw or be frightened for 1 minute. If the save fails by 5 or more, the target also ages 1d4 x 10 years. A frightened target can repeat the saving throw at the end of each of its turns, ending the frightened condition on itself on a success. If a target's saving throw is successful or the effect ends for it, the target is immune to this ghost's Horrifying Visage for the next 24 hours. The aging effect can be reversed with a *greater restoration* spell, but only within 24 hours of it occurring.
Possession (recharge 6). One humanoid that the ghost can see within 5 feet of it must succeed on a DC 13 Charisma saving throw or be possessed by the ghost; the ghost then disappears, and the target is incapacitated and loses control of its body. The ghost now controls the body but doesn't deprive the target of awareness. The ghost can't be targeted by any attack, spell, or other effect, except ones that turn undead, and it retains its alignment, Intelligence, Wisdom, Charisma, and immunity to being charmed and frightened. It otherwise uses the possessed target's statistics, but doesn't gain access to the target's knowledge, class features, or proficiencies.
The possession lasts until the body drops to 0 hit points, the ghost ends it as a bonus action, or the ghost is turned or forced out by an effect like the *dispel evil and good* spell. When the possession ends, the ghost reappears in an unoccupied space within 5 feet of the body. The target is immune to this ghost's Possession for 24 hours after succeeding on the saving throw or after the possession ends.

Wang Liang Monk

Medium fiend, lawful evil
Armor Class 18 (natural armor)
Hit Points 88 (16d8 + 16)
Speed 40 ft.

STR	DEX	CON	INT	WIS	CHA
10 (+0)	18 (+4)	13 (+1)	11 (+0)	18 (+4)	12 (+1)

Saving Throws Dex +8, Wis +8
Skills Acrobatics +8, Perception +8, Stealth +8, Survival +8
Damage Resistance fire; bludgeoning, piercing, and slashing from nonmagical attacks not made with silver
Damage Immunities poison
Condition Immunities poisoned
Senses darkvision 60 ft., passive Perception 18
Language Common, Infernal
Challenge 10 (5,900 XP)

Devil's Sight. Magical darkness doesn't impede the wang liang's darkvision.
Fists of Dark Flame (1/day). The wang liang monk wreaths its fists in flame. It deals an additional 7 (2d6) fire damage when it hits with its Unarmed Strikes for 1 minute.
Poison. Whenever the wang liang hits with a Bite or Unarmed Strike attack, the target must make a DC 13 Constitution saving throw, taking 14 (4d6) poison damage on a failed saving throw, or half as much damage on a successful saving throw.
Slow Fall. The wang liang monk reduces any falling damage by 30. If it does not take damage from a fall, it does not fall prone.

ACTIONS

Multiattack. The wang liang monk makes three Unarmed Strikes. It can use its Bite attack or Flurry of Blows ability in place of one of the Unarmed Strikes.

Unarmed Strike. *Melee Weapon Attack:* +8 to hit, reach 5 ft., one target. *Hit:* 7 (1d6 + 4) bludgeoning damage.

Bite. *Melee Weapon Attack:* +8 to hit, reach 5 ft., one target. *Hit:* 7 (1d6 + 4) piercing damage.

Flurry of Blows (3/day). *Melee Weapon Attack:* +8 to hit, reach 5 ft., one target. *Hit:* 14 (3d6 + 4) bludgeoning damage, and the target suffers one of the following effects of the monk's choice:

- The target must succeed on a DC 15 Dexterity saving throw or be knocked prone.
- The target must make a DC 15 Strength saving throw or be pushed up to 15 feet away from it.
- The target can't take reactions until the end of its next turn.

REACTIONS

Deflect Missiles. If it has one hand free, the wang liang monk can use its reaction in response to being hit with a ranged weapon attack. It reduces the damage by 16 (1d10 + 11). If it reduces the damage to 0, it can catch the missile if it is small enough for it to hold with one hand.

Order of the Devil — Individuals

Dagova Nix

Large monstrosity, lawful evil

Armor Class 20 (natural armor)
Hit Points 127 (15d10 + 45)
Speed 40 ft.

STR	DEX	CON	INT	WIS	CHA
18 (+4)	16 (+3)	16 (+3)	11 (+0)	16 (+3)	9 (−1)

Saving Throws Dex +7, Wis +7
Skills Acrobatics +7, Perception +11, Stealth +7
Damage Immunities fire
Senses darkvision 60 ft., passive Perception 21
Language Abyssal, Common, Infernal
Challenge 12 (8,400 XP)

Charge. If Dagova Nix moves at least 10 feet straight toward a target and then hits it with a gore attack on the same turn, the target takes an extra 9 (2d8) piercing damage. If the target is a creature, it must succeed on a DC 16 Strength saving throw or be pushed up to 10 feet away and knocked prone.

Fists of Dark Flame (1/day). Dagova wreaths his fists in flame. He deals an additional 7 (2d6) fire damage when it hits with its Unarmed Strikes for 1 minute.

Innate Spellcasting. Dagova's innate spellcasting ability is Wisdom (spell save DC 15, +7 to hit with spell attacks). He can cast the following spells, requiring no material components.

At will: *fire bolt* (5th level)
3/day: *burning hands*

Labyrinthine Recall. Dagova Nix can perfectly recall any path he has traveled.

Magic Weapons. Dagova's weapon attacks are considered magical for the purposes of damage resistances and immunities.

Reckless. At the start of his turn, Dagova can gain advantage on all melee weapon attack rolls he makes during that turn, but attack rolls against him have advantage until the start of his next turn.

Slow Fall. Dagova reduces any falling damage by 30. If he does not take damage from a fall, he does not fall prone.

ACTIONS

Multiattack. Dagova makes three Unarmed Strikes. He can use his Gore, Flurry of Blows, or Unholy Strike ability in place of one of the Unarmed Strikes.

Unarmed Strike. *Melee Weapon Attack:* +8 to hit, reach 5 ft., one target. *Hit:* 13 (2d8 + 4) bludgeoning damage.

Gore. *Melee Weapon Attack:* +8 to hit, reach 5 ft., one target. *Hit:* 13 (2d8 + 4) piercing damage.

Flurry of Blows (3/day). *Melee Weapon Attack:* +8 to hit, reach 5 ft., one target. *Hit:* 31 (6d8 + 4) bludgeoning damage, and the target suffers one of the following effects of Dagova's choice:

- The target must succeed on a DC 15 Dexterity saving throw or be knocked prone.
- The target must make a DC 15 Strength saving throw or be pushed up to 15 feet away from it.
- The target can't take reactions until the end of its next turn.

Unholy Strike (3/day). *Melee Weapon Attack:* +8 to hit, reach 5 ft., one target. *Hit:* 49 (10d8 + 4) necrotic damage, and the target must succeed on a DC 15 Constitution saving throw. On a failed saving throw, the target's maximum hit points are reduced by an equal amount. Lost hit points are regained when the target takes a long rest.

REACTIONS

Deflect Missiles. If it has one hand free, Dagova can use his reaction in response to being hit with a ranged weapon attack. He reduces the damage by 18 (1d10 + 13). If he reduces the damage to 0, he can catch the missile if it is small enough for him to hold with one hand.

Fas'ahad

Medium humanoid (human), lawful evil

Armor Class 16 (natural armor)
Hit Points 82 (15d8 + 15)
Speed 40 ft.

STR	DEX	CON	INT	WIS	CHA
12 (+1)	18 (+4)	14 (+2)	11 (+0)	16 (+3)	15 (+2)

Saving Throws Dex +7, Int +3
Skills Acrobatics +7, Deception +8, Persuasion +5, Perception +6, Stealth +10
Damage Resistances fire
Senses passive Perception 16
Languages Common, Infernal, Thieves' cant
Challenge 8 (3,900 XP)

Special Equipment. Fas'ahad carries with him a *+1 dagger* and wears a *ring of comfort*[2].

Assassinate. During his first turn, Fas'ahad has advantage on attack rolls against any creature that hasn't taken a turn. Any hit he scores against a surprised creature is a critical hit.

Cunning Action. Once on each of his turns, Fas'ahad can use a bonus action to take the Dash, Disengage, or Hide action.

Fists of Dark Flame (1/day). Fas'ahad wreaths his fists in flame. He deals an additional 7 (2d6) fire damage when he hits with his Unarmed Strikes for 1 minute.

Slow Fall. Fas'ahad reduces any falling damage by 30. If he does not take damage from a fall, he does not fall prone.

Sneak Attack. Once per turn, Fas'ahad deals an extra 14 (4d6) damage when he hits a target with a weapon attack that isn't his Unarmed Strike and has advantage on the attack roll, or when the target is within 5 feet of an ally of Fas'ahad that isn't incapacitated and Fas'ahad doesn't have disadvantage on the attack roll.

Actions

Multiattack. Fas'ahad makes two Dagger attacks or two Unarmed Strikes. He can use his Flurry of Blows ability in place of one of the attacks.

Dagger. *Melee or Ranged Weapon Attack:* +8 to hit, reach 5 ft. or range 20/60 ft., one target. *Hit:* 7 (1d4 + 5) piercing damage.

Unarmed Strike. *Melee Weapon Attack:* +7 to hit, reach 5 ft., one target. *Hit:* 7 (1d6 + 4) bludgeoning damage.

Flurry of Blows (3/day). *Melee Weapon Attack:* +7 to hit, reach 5 ft., one target. *Hit:* 14 (3d6 + 4) bludgeoning damage, and the target suffers one of the following effects of Fas'ahad's choice:

- The target must succeed on a DC 15 Dexterity saving throw or be knocked prone.

- The target must make a DC 15 Strength saving throw or be pushed up to 15 feet away from him.

- The target can't take reactions until the end of its next turn.

Reactions

Deflect Missiles. If he has one hand free, Fas'ahad can use his reaction in response to being hit with a ranged weapon attack. He reduces the damage by 11 (1d10 + 6). If he reduces the damage to 0, he can catch the missile if it is small enough for him to hold with one hand.

Master Bagra

Medium humanoid (human, shapechanger), lawful evil
Armor Class 18 (natural armor)
Hit Points 232 (31d8 + 93)
Speed 40 ft. (50 ft. in tiger form)

STR	DEX	CON	INT	WIS	CHA
17 (+3)	18 (+4)	16 (+3)	10 (+0)	18 (+4)	11 (+0)

Saving Throws Dex +9, Wis +9
Skills Acrobatics +9, Perception +9, Stealth +9
Damage Immunities fire; bludgeoning, piercing, and slashing from nonmagical attacks not made with silver
Senses darkvision 60 ft., passive Perception 19
Languages Common, Infernal (can't speak in tiger form)
Challenge 14 (11,500 XP)

Fists of Dark Flame (1/day). Bagra wreaths his claws in flame. He deals an additional 7 (2d6) fire damage when he hits with his Unarmed Strikes for 1 minute.

Innate Spellcasting. Bagra's innate spellcasting ability is Wisdom (spell save DC 17, +9 to hit with spell attacks). He can cast the following spells, requiring no material components.

At will: *fire bolt* (5th level)
3/day: *burning hands*

Keen Hearing and Smell. The weretiger has advantage on Wisdom (Perception) checks that rely on hearing or smell.

Magic Weapons. Bagra's weapon attacks are considered magical for the purposes of damage resistances and immunities.

Pounce (tiger or hybrid form only). If the weretiger moves at least 15 feet straight toward a creature and then hits it with a claw attack on the same turn, that target must succeed on a DC 16 Strength saving throw or be knocked prone. If the target is prone, the weretiger can make one Bite attack against it as a bonus action.

Shapechanger. Bagra can use his action to polymorph into a tiger-humanoid hybrid or into a tiger, or back into its true form, which is humanoid. Its statistics, other than its size, are the same in each form. Any equipment he is wearing or carrying isn't transformed. He reverts to his true form if he dies.

Slow Fall. Bagra reduces any falling damage by 30. If he does not take damage from a fall, he does not fall prone.

Actions

Multiattack. Bagra makes three Unarmed Strikes. He can use his Bite, Flurry of Blows, or Unholy Strike ability in place of one of the Unarmed Strike.

Bite (tiger or hybrid form only). *Melee Weapon Attack:* +8 to hit, reach 5 ft., one target. *Hit:* 8 (1d10 + 3) piercing damage. If the target is a humanoid, it must succeed on a DC 16 Constitution saving throw or be cursed with weretiger lycanthropy.

Unarmed Strike. *Melee Weapon Attack:* +9 to hit, reach 5 ft., one target. *Hit:* 8 (1d8 + 4) slashing damage.

Flurry of Blows (3/day). *Melee Weapon Attack:* +9 to hit, reach 5 ft., one target. *Hit:* 17 (3d8 + 4) slashing damage, and the target suffers one of the following effects of Bagra's choice:

- The target must succeed on a DC 17 Dexterity saving throw or be knocked prone.

- The target must make a DC 17 Strength saving throw or be pushed up to 15 feet away from him.

- The target can't take reactions until the end of its next turn.

Unholy Strike (3/day). *Melee Weapon Attack:* +9 to hit, reach 5 ft., one target. *Hit:* 26 (5d8 + 4) necrotic damage, and the target must succeed on a DC 17 Constitution saving throw. On a failed saving throw, the target's maximum hit points are reduced by an equal amount. Lost hit points are regained when the target takes a long rest.

Reactions

Deflect Missiles. If Bagra has one hand free, he can use his reaction in response to being hit with a ranged weapon attack. He reduces the damage by 19 (1d10 + 14). If he reduces the damage to 0, he can catch the missile if it is small enough for him to hold with one hand.

Master Cael O'Day

Small fey, chaotic evil
Armor Class 18
Hit Points 104 (19d6 + 38)
Speed 100 ft.

STR	DEX	CON	INT	WIS	CHA
8 (−1)	18 (+4)	14 (+2)	11 (+0)	18 (+4)	12 (+1)

Saving Throws Dex +8, Wis +8
Skills Acrobatics +8, Perception +8, Stealth +8
Damage Immunities fire
Senses darkvision 60 ft., passive Perception 18
Languages Aklo, Common, Infernal
Challenge 11 (7.200 XP)

Cunning Action. Cael can take the Dash, Disengage, or Hide action as a bonus action on each of his turns.

Fists of Dark Flame (1/day). Cael wearths his fists in flame. He deals an additional 7 (2d6) fire damage when he hits with his Unarmed Strike for 1 minute.

Innate Spellcasting. Cael's innate spellcasting ability is Wisdom (spell save DC 16, +8 to hit with spell attacks). He can cast the following spells, requiring no material components.

At will: *dancing lights, fire bolt* (5th level), *minor illusion*
3/day: *burning hands*
1/day each: *levitate, shatter*

Magic Weapons. Cael's weapon attacks are considered magical for the purposes of overcoming damage resistances and immunities.

Slow Fall. Cael reduces any falling damage by 30. It he does not take damage from a fall, he does not fall prone.

Supernatural Speed. Cael's supernatural speed means that attacks have disadvantage against him as long as he is not grappled or restrained. If Cael does not move over the course of his turn, he is invisible until the end of his next turn, or until he moves or takes an action. In addition, if Cael fails his saving throw against the *slow* spell, he cannot use the benefits above, and is poisoned until the *slow* effect ends on him.

ACTIONS

Multiattack. Cael O'Day makes three Unarmed Strikes. He can use his Flurry of Blows or Unholy Strike in place of one of the Unarmed Strikes.

Unarmed Strikes. *Melee Weapon Attack:* +8 to hit, reach 5 ft., one target. *Hit:* 8 (1d8 + 4) bludgeoning damage.

Flurry of Blows (3/day). *Melee Weapon Attack:* +8 to hit, reach 5 ft., one target. *Hit:* 17 (3d8 + 4) bludgeoning damage, and the target suffers one of the following effects of Cael's choice:

- The target must succeed on a DC 16 Dexterity saving throw or be knocked prone.

- The target must make a DC 16 Strength saving throw or be pushed up to 15 feet away from him.

- The target can't take reactions until the end of its next turn.

Unholy Strike (3/day). *Melee Weapon Attack:* +8 to hit, reach 5 ft., one target. *Hit:* 26 (5d8 + 4) necrotic damage, and the target must succeed on a DC 16 Constitution saving throw. On a failed saving throw, the target's maximum hit points are reduced by an equal amount. Lost hit points are regained when the target takes a long rest.

REACTIONS

Deflect Missiles. If Cael has one hand free, he can use his reaction in response to being hit with a ranged weapon attack. He reduces the damage by 19 (1d10 + 14). It he reduces the damage to 0, he can catch the missile if it is small enough for him to hold with one hand.

Master Dasssar

Master Dasssar uses the statistics of a **devil mendicant**, except for the following:

- Dasssar speaks Draconic in addition to the languages of the **devil mendicant**. He also has proficiency in Perception (+7) and Survival (+7) checks; his passive Perception is 17.

- Dasssar's Armor Class is 21 (natural armor).

- Dasssar has a swim speed equal to his normal speed.

- Dasssar has the following additional feature:

    Hold Breath. Dasssar can hold his breath for 15 minutes.

- Dasssar has the following additional attack, which he can substitute for any of his Unarmed Strikes:

    Bite. *Melee Weapon Attack:* +3 to hit, reach 5 ft., one target. *Hit:* 3 (1d6) piercing damage.

Master Mo Zhu

Large monstrosity, chaotic evil
Armor Class 19 (natural armor)
Hit Points 190 (20d10 + 80)
Speed 45 ft., climb 45 ft.

STR	DEX	CON	INT	WIS	CHA
16 (+3)	18 (+4)	18 (+4)	13 (+1)	16 (+3)	12 (+1)

Saving Throws Dex +8, Wis +7
Skills Acrobatics +7, Insight +7, Perception +7, Stealth +12
Senses darkvision 120 ft., passive Perception 17
Languages Elvish, Undercommon
Challenge 9 (5,000 XP)

Special Equipment. Mo Zhu wields a *staff of thunder and lightning*.

Evasion. If Mo Zhu is subjected to an effect that allows it to make a Dexterity saving throw to take only half damage, Mo Zhu instead takes no damage if it succeeds on the saving throw, and only half damage if it fails.

Fey Ancestry. The drider has advantage on saving throws against being charmed, and magic can't put the drider to sleep.

Innate Spellcasting. The drider's innate spellcasting ability is Wisdom (spell save DC 15). The drider can innately cast the following spells, requiring no material components:

At will: *dancing lights*
1/day each: *darkness, faerie fire*

Magic Weapon. Mo Zhu's attacks count as magical for the purposes of damage resistances and immunities.

Slow Fall. Mo Zhu reduces all falling damage by 35. If it does not take damage from a fall, it does not drop prone.

Spider Climb. The drider can climb difficult surfaces, including upside down on ceilings, without needing to make an ability check.

Sunlight Sensitivity. While in sunlight, the drider has disadvantage on attack rolls, as well as on Wisdom (Perception) checks that rely on sight.

Web Walker. The drider ignores movement restrictions caused by webbing.

ACTIONS

Multiattack. Mo Zhu makes two Quarterstaff attacks and one Unarmed Strike, or makes three Unarmed Strikes. It can use its Bite, Flurry of Blows, or Stunning Strike attack in place of one of the unarmed strikes each round.

Bite. *Melee Weapon Attack:* +7 to hit, reach 5 ft., one creature. *Hit:* 5 (1d4 + 3) piercing damage plus 9 (2d8) poison damage.

Quarterstaff. *Melee Weapon Attack:* +10 to hit, reach 5 ft., one target. *Hit:* 9 (1d6 + 6) bludgeoning damage, or 10 (1d8 + 6) bludgeoning damage is used with two hands to make a melee attack.

Unarmed Strike. *Melee Weapon Attack:* +8 to hit, reach 5 ft., one target. *Hit:* 7 (1d6 + 4) bludgeoning damage.

Flurry of Blows (3/day). *Melee Weapon Attack:* +8 to hit, reach 5 ft., one target. *Hit:* 13 (3d6 + 4) bludgeoning damage, and the target suffers one of the following effects of Mo Zhu's choice:

- The target must succeed on a DC 16 Dexterity saving throw or be knocked prone.

- The target must make a DC 16 Strength saving throw or be pushed up to 15 feet away from Mo Zhu.

- The target can't take reactions until the end of Mo Zhu's next turn.

Stunning Strike (3/day). *Melee Weapon Attack:* +8 to hit, reach 5 ft., one target. *Hit:* 7 (1d6 + 4) bludgeoning damage, and the target must succeed on a DC 16 Constitution saving throw or be stunned until the end of Mo Zhu's next turn.

Fists of Dark Flame (1/day). Mo Zhu deals an additional 7 (2d6) fire damage when he hits with his Unarmed Strikes for 1 minute.

REACTIONS

Deflect Missiles. If Mo Zhu has one hand free, it can use its reaction in response to being hit with a ranged weapon attack. It reduces the damage by 16 (1d10 + 11). If it reduces the damage to 0, it can catch the missile if it is small enough for it to hold with one hand.

Master Qarid

Medium monstrosity (cheitan), lawful evil
Armor Class 18 (natural armor)
Hit Points 136 (16d8 + 64)
Speed 30 ft., fly 60 ft.

STR	DEX	CON	INT	WIS	CHA
16 (+3)	20 (+5)	18 (+4)	17 (+3)	17 (+3)	12 (+1)

Saving Throws Wis +7, Cha +5
Skills Acrobatics +9, Insight +7, Perception +7
Damage Resistances fire; bludgeoning, piercing, and slashing from nonmagical attacks not made with silver
Damage Immunities poison
Condition Immunities poisoned
Senses darkvision 120 ft., passive Perception 17
Languages Common, Ignan, Infernal
Challenge 12 (8,400 XP)

Child of Fire. Once per turn, when Master Qarid is subjected to fire damage, he has advantage on his next attack roll, saving throw, or ability check.

Devil's Sight. Magical darkness doesn't impede Master Qarid's darkvision.

Heated Body. A creature that touches Master Qarid or hits him with a melee attack while within 5 feet of him takes 5 (1d10) fire damage.

Fiery Weapons. When Master Qarid hits with any weapon, the weapon deals an extra 4d6 fire damage (included in the attack).

Magic Resistance. Master Qarid has advantage on saving throws against spells and other magical effects.

ACTIONS

Multiattack. Master Qarid makes three Unarmed Strikes or uses his Hurl Flame twice.

Unarmed Strike. *Melee Weapon Attack:* +9 to hit, reach 5 ft., one target. *Hit:* 9 (1d8 + 5) slashing damage plus 14 (4d6) fire damage.

Hurl Flame. *Ranged Spell Attack:* +7 to hit, range 120 ft., one target. *Hit:* 21 (6d6) fire damage.

REACTIONS

Stunning Rebuke. When a creature Master Qarid can see hits him with a melee attack while within 5 feet of Master Qarid, it must succeed on a DC 16 Constitution saving throw or be stunned until the end of its next turn.

Mistress Harthain Gursh

Huge giant, lawful evil
Armor Class 19 (natural armor)
Hit Points 250 (20d12 + 120)
Speed 40 ft.

STR	DEX	CON	INT	WIS	CHA
25 (+7)	15 (+2)	23 (+6)	10 (+0)	18 (+4)	12 (+1)

Saving Throws Dex +8, Con +12, Wis +10, Cha +7
Skills Acrobatics +8, Athletics +13, Perception +10, Stealth +8
Damage Immunities fire
Senses passive Perception 20
Languages Common, Giant, Infernal
Challenge 19 (22,000 XP)

Fists of Dark Flame (1/day). Harthain wreaths her fists in flame. She deals an additional 7 (2d6) fire damage when she hits with her Unarmed Strike for 1 minute.

Innate Spellcasting. Harthain's innate spellcasting ability is Wisdom (spell save DC 18, +10 to hit with spell attacks). She can cast the following spells, requiring no material components.

At will: *fire bolt* (5th level)
3/day: *burning hands*

Magic Weapons. Harthain's weapon attacks are considered magical for the purposes of damage resistances and immunities.

Slow Fall. Harthain reduces any falling damage by 30. It she does not take damage from a fall, she does not fall prone.

ACTIONS

Multiattack. Harthain makes three Unarmed Strikes. She can use her Flurry of Blows or Unholy Strike ability in place of one of the Unarmed Strikes.

Unarmed Strike. *Melee Weapon Attack:* +13 to hit, reach 10 ft., one target. *Hit:* 20 (3d8 + 7) bludgeoning damage.

Flurry of Blows (3/day). *Melee Weapon Attack:* +13 to hit, reach 10 ft., one target. *Hit:* 47 (9d8 + 7) bludgeoning damage, and the target suffers one of the following effects of Harthain's choice:

- The target must succeed on a DC 18 Dexterity saving throw or be knocked prone.

- The target must make a DC 18 Strength saving throw or be pushed up to 15 feet away from her.

- The target can't take reactions until the end of its next turn.

Unholy Strike (3/day). *Melee Weapon Attack:* +13 to hit, reach 10 ft., one target. *Hit:* 74 (15d8 + 7) necrotic damage, and the target must succeed on a DC 18 Constitution saving throw. On a failed saving throw, the target's maximum hit points are reduced by an equal amount. Lost hit points are regained when the target takes a long rest.

REACTIONS

Deflect Missiles. If she has one hand free, Harthain can use her reaction in response to being hit with a ranged weapon attack. She reduces the damage by 19 (1d10 + 14). If she reduces the damage to 0, she can catch the missile if it is small enough for her to hold with one hand.

Pang Goy

Medium fiend, lawful evil
Armor Class 20 (natural armor)
Hit Points 153 (18d8 + 72)
Speed 60 ft.

STR	DEX	CON	INT	WIS	CHA
20 (+5)	20 (+5)	18 (+4)	16 (+3)	20 (+5)	18 (+4)

Saving Throws Str +11, Dex +11, Con +10, Int +9, Wis +11, Cha +10
Skills Acrobatics +11, Athletics +11, History +9, Perception +11, Religion +9, Stealth +11
Damage Resistances acid, cold, lightning; bludgeoning, piercing, and slashing damage from nonmagical attacks not made with silver
Damage Immunities fire, poison
Condition Immunities charmed, frightened, poisoned
Senses darkvision 60 ft., passive Perception 21
Languages Common, Ignan, Infernal
Challenge 18 (20,000 XP)

Special Equipment. Pang Goy has replaced his hands with the *hands of Pang Goy.* The bonuses of this potent magic item are included in Pang Goy's statistics.

Evasion. If Pang Goy is subjected to an effect that allows him to make a Dexterity saving throw to take only half damage, he instead takes no damage if he succeeds on the saving throw, and only half damage if he fails.

Fists of Dark Flame (1/day). Pang Goy wreaths his fists in flame. He deals an additional 10 (3d6) fire damage when he hits with his Unarmed Strikes for 1 minute.

Innate Spellcasting. Pang Goy's innate spellcasting ability is Wisdom (spell save DC 19, +11 to hit with spell attacks). He can cast the following spells, requiring no material components.

At will: *fire bolt* (17th level)
3/day each: *blight, burning hands* (3rd-level, 5d6 fire damage), *darkness*
1/day: *misty step*

Magic Weapons. Pang Goy's weapon attacks are considered magical for the purposes of damage resistances and immunities.

Slow Fall. Pang Goy reduces any falling damage by 30. If it does not take damage from a fall, it does not fall prone.

ACTIONS

Multiattack. Pang Goy makes three Unarmed Strikes. He can use his Flurry of Blows or Unholy Strike ability in place of one of the Unarmed Strikes.

Unarmed Strike. *Melee Weapon Attack:* +14 to hit, reach 5 ft., one target. *Hit:* 19 (2d10 + 8) bludgeoning damage, plus 9 (2d8) force damage.

Flurry of Blows (3/day). *Melee Weapon Attack:* +14 to hit, reach 5 ft., one target. *Hit:* 41 (6d10 + 8) bludgeoning damage, plus 9 (2d8) force damage, and the target suffers one of the following effects of Pang Goy's choice:

- The target must succeed on a DC 19 Dexterity saving throw or be knocked prone.

- The target must make a DC 19 Strength saving throw or be pushed up to 15 feet away from it.

- The target can't take reactions until the end of its next turn.

Unholy Strike (3/day). *Melee Weapon Attack:* +14 to hit, reach 5 ft., one target. *Hit:* 63 (10d10 + 8) necrotic damage, plus 9 (2d8) force damage, and the target must succeed on a DC 19 Constitution saving throw. On a failed saving throw, the target's maximum hit points are reduced by an equal amount. Lost hit points are regained when the target takes a long rest.

Death Strike (1/day). *Melee Weapon Attack:* +14 to hit, reach 5 ft., one target that is not a construct or undead. *Hit:* The target must make a DC 19 Constitution saving throw. On a failed saving throw, the target drops to 0 hit points. On a successful saving throw, the target takes 55 (10d10) necrotic damage.

REACTIONS

Deflect Missiles. If he has one hand free, Pang Goy can use his reaction in response to being hit with a ranged weapon attack. He reduces the damage by 26 (1d10 + 21). If he reduces the damage to 0, he can catch the missile if it is small enough for him to hold with one hand.

Oozes

Black Pudding, Elder

Huge ooze, unaligned
Armor Class 8
Hit Points 147 (14d12 + 56)
Speed 20 ft., climb 20 ft.

STR	DEX	CON	INT	WIS	CHA
18 (+4)	7 (−2)	18 (+4)	3 (−4)	9 (−1)	1 (−5)

Damage Resistances bludgeoning and piercing from nonmagical attacks
Damage Immunities acid, cold, lightning, slashing
Condition Immunities blinded, charmed, deafened, exhaustion, frightened, prone
Senses blindsight 60 ft. (blind beyond this radius), passive Perception 9
Languages —
Challenge 9 (5,000 XP)

Amorphous. The pudding can move through a space as narrow as 1 inch wide without squeezing.

Corrosive Form. A creature that touches the pudding or hits it with a melee attack while within 5 feet of it takes 9 (2d8) acid damage. Any nonmagical weapon made of metal or wood (or other organic material) that hits the pudding partly dissolves.

After hitting the pudding, the weapon takes a permanent and cumulative –1 to damage rolls. If its penalty drops to –5, the weapon is destroyed. Nonmagical ammunition made of metal or wood (or other organic material) that hits the pudding is destroyed after dealing damage.

The pudding can eat through 4-inch thick, nonmagical metal or wood (or other organic material) in 1 round.

Spider Climb. The pudding can climb difficult surfaces, including upside down and ceilings, without needing to make an ability check.

ACTIONS

Multiattack. The pudding makes two Pseudopod attacks.

Pseudopod. *Melee Weapon Attack:* +7 to hit, reach 10 ft., one target. *Hit:* 9 (1d10 + 4) bludgeoning damage plus 18 (4d8) acid damage. In addition, nonmagical armor worn by the target is partly dissolved and takes a permanent and cumulative –1 to the AC it offers. The armor is destroyed if the penalty reduces its AC to 10.

REACTIONS

Split. When a pudding that is Medium or larger is exposed to lightning or slashing damage, it splits into two new puddings if it has at least 10 hit points. Each new pudding has hit points equal to half the original pudding's, rounded down. New puddings are one size smaller than the original pudding.

Brown Pudding

Large ooze, unaligned
Armor Class 12 (natural armor)
Hit Points 68 (8d10 + 24)
Speed 20 ft., climb 20 ft.

STR	DEX	CON	INT	WIS	CHA
14 (+2)	6 (–2)	16 (+3)	1 (–5)	6 (–2)	1 (–5)

Damage Resistances piercing from nonmagical attacks
Damage Immunities acid, cold, lightning, slashing
Condition Immunities blinded, charmed, deafened, exhaustion, frightened, prone
Senses blindsight 60 ft. (blind beyond this radius), passive Perception 8
Languages —
Challenge 4 (1,100 XP)

Amorphous. The pudding can move through a space as narrow as 1 inch wide without squeezing.

Corrosive Form. A creature that touches the pudding or hits it with a melee attack while within 5 feet of it takes 4 (1d8) acid damage. Any nonmagical weapon made of wood or other organic material that hits the pudding partly dissolves. After hitting the pudding, the weapon takes a permanent and cumulative –1 to damage rolls. If its penalty drops to –5, the weapon is destroyed. Nonmagical ammunition made of wood or other organic material that hits the pudding is destroyed after dealing damage.

The pudding can eat through 2-inch thick, nonmagical wood or other organic material in 1 round.

Spider Climb. The pudding can climb difficult surfaces, including upside down and ceilings, without needing to make an ability check.

ACTIONS

Pseudopod. *Melee Weapon Attack:* +4 to hit, reach 5 ft., one target. *Hit:* 5 (1d6 + 2) bludgeoning damage plus 14 (4d6) acid damage. In addition, nonmagical armor made of leather or other organic material worn by the target is partly dissolved and takes a permanent and cumulative –1 to the AC it offers. The armor is destroyed if the penalty reduces its AC to 10.

REACTIONS

Split. When a pudding that is Medium or larger is exposed to lightning or slashing damage, it splits into two new puddings if it has at least 10 hit points. Each new pudding has hit points equal to half the original pudding's, rounded down. New puddings are one size smaller than the original pudding.

Dun Pudding

Large ooze, neutral
Armor Class 9
Hit Points 68 (8d10 + 24)
Speed 30 ft., climb 30 ft.

STR	DEX	CON	INT	WIS	CHA
16 (+3)	8 (–1)	16 (+3)	1 (–5)	6 (–2)	1 (–5)

Skills Stealth +3 (+4 if not moving)
Damage Resistances piercing from nonmagical attacks
Damage Immunities acid, fire, lightning, slashing
Condition Immunities blinded, charmed, deafened, exhaustion, frightened, prone
Senses blindsight 60 ft. (blind beyond this radius), passive Perception 8
Languages —
Challenge 4 (1,100 XP)

Amorphous. The pudding can move through a space as narrow as 1 inch wide without squeezing.

Corrosive Form. A creature that touches the pudding or hits it with a melee attack while within 5 feet of it takes 4 (1d8) acid damage. Any nonmagical weapon made of metal or wood (or other organic material) that hits the pudding partly dissolves. After hitting the pudding, the weapon takes a permanent and cumulative –1 to damage rolls. If its penalty drops to –5, the weapon is destroyed. Nonmagical ammunition made of metal or wood (or other organic material) that hits the pudding is destroyed after dealing damage.

The pudding can eat through 2-inch thick, nonmagical metal or wood (or other organic material) in 1 round.

Spider Climb. The pudding can climb difficult surfaces, including upside down and ceilings, without needing to make an ability check.

ACTIONS

Pseudopod. *Melee Weapon Attack:* +5 to hit, reach 5 ft., one target. *Hit:* 6 (1d6 + 3) bludgeoning damage plus 14 (4d6) acid damage. In addition, nonmagical armor worn by the target is partly dissolved and takes a permanent and cumulative –1 to the AC it offers. The armor is destroyed if the penalty reduces its AC to 10.

REACTIONS

Split. When a pudding that is Medium or larger is exposed to lightning or slashing damage, it splits into two new puddings if it has at least 10 hit points. Each new pudding has hit points equal to half the original pudding's, rounded down. New puddings are one size smaller than the original pudding.

Flesh Pudding

Large ooze, unaligned
Armor Class 8
Hit Points 68 (8d10 + 24)
Speed 20 ft., climb 20 ft.

STR	DEX	CON	INT	WIS	CHA
14 (+2)	7 (−2)	17 (+3)	1 (−5)	6 (−2)	1 (−5)

Damage Immunities piercing, slashing
Condition Immunities blinded, charmed, deafened, exhaustion, frightened, prone
Senses blindsight 60 ft. (blind beyond this radius), passive Perception 8
Languages —
Challenge 3 (700 XP)

Amorphous. The pudding can move through a space as narrow as 1 inch wide without squeezing.
Reactive Regeneration. When the pudding is exposed to piercing or slashing damage, it regains 6 hit points.
Spider Climb. The pudding can climb difficult surfaces, including upside down and ceilings, without needing to make an ability check.
Tumorous Form. Any creature who touches the pudding or hits it with a melee attack while within 5 feet of it must succeed on a DC 15 Constitution saving throw or contract a tumorous disease which manifests immediately. The diseased creature suffers disadvantage on Charisma checks and −2 on attack rolls, and its hit point maximum is reduced by 10 for every 24 hours that elapse. Magic such as a *lesser restoration* spell cures the disease. If the disease reduces the target's hit point maximum to 0, the target dies and reanimates in 2 (1d4) hours as a flesh pudding.

Actions

Pseudopod. *Melee Weapon Attack:* +4 to hit, reach 5 ft., one target. *Hit:* 6 (1d8 + 2) bludgeoning damage. If the target is a creature, it must make a DC 14 Constitution saving throw. On a failure, the creature is afflicted with a tumorous disease. The diseased target suffers disadvantage on Charisma checks and −2 on attack rolls, and its hit point maximum is reduced by 10 for every 24 hours that elapse. Magic such as a *lesser restoration* spell will cure the disease. If the disease reduces the target's hit point maximum to 0, the target dies and reanimates in 2 (1d4) hours as a flesh pudding.
Devour Corpse. The pudding consumes the dead body of a creature at least Small in size. It gains a cumulative +1 to attack and damage rolls for 1 minute and regains 12 hit points. Any points beyond its hit point maximum are treated as temporary hit points.

Gray Ooze, Advanced

Large ooze, unaligned
Armor Class 9
Hit Points 114 (12d10 + 48)
Speed 20 ft., climb 20 ft.

STR	DEX	CON	INT	WIS	CHA
16 (+3)	8 (−1)	18 (+4)	1 (−5)	8 (−1)	2 (−4)

Damage Resistances acid, cold, fire
Condition Immunities blinded, charmed, deafened, exhaustion, frightened, prone
Senses blindsight 60 ft. (blind beyond this radius), passive
Perception 9
Languages —
Challenge 5 (1,800 XP)

Amorphous. The ooze can move through a space as narrow as 1 inch wide without squeezing.
Corrode Metal. Any nonmagical weapon made of metal that hits the ooze corrodes. After dealing damage, the weapon takes a permanent and cumulative −1 penalty to damage rolls. If its penalty drops to −5, the weapon is destroyed. Nonmagical ammunition made of metal that hits the ooze is destroyed after dealing damage.
The ooze can eat through 3-inch-thick nonmagical metal in 1 round.
False Appearance. While the ooze remains motionless, it is indistinguishable from an oily pool or wet rock.

Actions

Multiattack. The ooze makes three Pseudopod attacks.
Pseudopod. *Melee Weapon Attack:* +5 to hit, reach 5 ft., one target. *Hit:* 7 (1d8 + 3) bludgeoning damage plus 7 (2d6) acid damage, and if the target is wearing nonmagical metal armor, its armor is partly corroded and takes a permanent and cumulative −1 to the AC it offers. The armor is destroyed if the penalty reduces its AC to 10.

Living Lake

Gargantuan ooze, neutral (50%), neutral good (25%), or neutral evil (25%)
Armor Class 14 (natural armor)
Hit Points 495 (30d20 + 180)
Speed 20 ft., swim 30 ft.

STR	DEX	CON	INT	WIS	CHA
27 (+8)	10 (+0)	23 (+6)	18 (+4)	12 (+1)	14 (+2)

Saving Throws Con +13, Int +10, Wis +8
Skills History +10, Insight +8, Religion +10
Damage Immunities acid, cold, lightning
Condition Immunities blinded, charmed, deafened, exhaustion, frightened, prone
Senses blindsight 120 ft. (blind beyond this radius), passive Perception 11
Languages Aquan, Common, Sylvan
Challenge 22 (41,000 XP)

False Appearance. While the living lake remains motionless, it is indistinguishable from an ordinary lake or other large body of water.
Legendary Resistance (3/day). If the living lake fails a saving throw, it can choose to succeed instead.
Ooze Nature. The living lake doesn't require sleep.
Spellcasting. The living lake is an 18th-level spellcaster. Its spellcasting ability is Intelligence (spell save DC 19, +11 to hit with spell attacks). The living lake has the following druid spells prepared:

Cantrips (at will): *druidcraft, guidance, mending, thorn whip*
1st level (4 slots): *create or destroy water, cure wounds, entangle, fog cloud, speak with animals*
2nd level (3 slots): *animal messenger, beast sense, gust of wind, spike growth*
3rd level (3 slots): *call lightning, sleet storm, water breathing*
4th level (3 slots): *blight, control water, dominate beast*
5th level (3 slots): *conjure elemental, insect plague, scrying*
6th level (1 slot): *wall of thorns*

7th level (1 slot): *fire storm*
8th level (1 slot): *control weather*
9th level (1 slot): *storm of vengeance*

ACTIONS

Multiattack. The living lake makes two Pseudopod attacks and one Grasping Tendrils attack. It can use its Engulf in place of one Grasping Tendrils attack.

Pseudopod. *Melee Weapon Attack:* +15 to hit, reach 30 ft., one target. *Hit:* 15 (2d6 + 8) bludgeoning damage plus 10 (3d6) acid damage.

Grasping Tendrils. *Melee Weapon Attack:* +15 to hit, reach 10 ft., one Huge or smaller creature. *Hit:* 21 (6d6) acid damage, and the target is grappled (escape DC 15). Until this grapple ends, the target is restrained.

Engulf. The living lake makes one Grasping Tendrils attack against one Large or smaller target it is grappling. If the attack hits, the target is also engulfed, and the grapple ends. The engulfed target is blinded, restrained, and unable to breathe, and it must succeed on a DC 21 Constitution saving throw at the start of each of the living lake's turns or take 28 (8d6) acid damage. If the living lake moves, the engulfed target moves with it. The living lake can have only four creatures engulfed at a time.

An engulfed creature can try to escape by taking an action to make a DC 23 Strength check. On a success, the creature escapes and enters a space of its choice within 5 feet of the living lake. A creature within 5 feet of the living lake can take an action to pull a creature or object out of the living lake. Doing so requires a successful DC 23 Strength check, and the creature making the attempt takes 14 (4d6) acid damage.

LEGENDARY ACTIONS

The living lake can take 3 legendary actions, choosing from the options below. Only one legendary action can be used at a time and only at the end of another creature's turn. The living lake regains spent legendary actions at the start of its turn.

Cantrip. The living lake casts a cantrip

Pseudopod. The living lake makes a Pseudopod attack.

Protoplasm Splash (costs 2 actions). The living lake splashes bits of its protoplasm onto nearby creatures. If the living lake is good, each creature within 20 feet of it regains 14 (4d6) hit points. If the living lake is evil, each creature within 20 feet of it must make a DC 21 Dexterity saving throw, taking 21 (6d6) acid damage on a failed save, or half as much damage on a successful one. If the living lake is neutral, it chooses each day whether its Protoplasm Splash will heal nearby creatures or harm them that day.

Cast a Spell (costs 3 actions). The living lake casts a spell from its list of prepared spells, using a spell slot as normal.

Ochre Jelly, Advanced

Huge ooze, unaligned
Armor Class 8
Hit Points 126 (12d12 + 48)
Speed 15 ft., climb 15 ft.

STR	DEX	CON	INT	WIS	CHA
19 (+4)	6 (−2)	18 (+4)	4 (−3)	6 (−2)	1 (−5)

Damage Resistances acid
Damage Immunities lightning, slashing
Condition Immunities blinded, charmed, deafened, exhaustion, frightened, prone
Senses blindsight 60 ft. (blind beyond this radius), passive Perception 8

Languages —
Challenge 4 (1,100 XP)

Amorphous. The jelly can move through a space as narrow as 1 inch wide without squeezing.

Spider Climb. The jelly can climb difficult surfaces, including upside down on ceilings, without needing to make an ability check.

ACTIONS

Pseudopod. *Melee Weapon Attack:* +6 to hit, reach 5 ft., one target. *Hit:* 15 (2d10 + 4) bludgeoning damage plus 14 (4d6) acid damage.

REACTIONS

Split. When a jelly that is Medium or larger is subjected to lightning or slashing damage, it splits into two new jellies if it has at least 10 hit points. Each new jelly has hit points equal to half the original jelly's, rounded down. New jellies are one size smaller than the original jelly.

Stone Pudding

Large ooze, unaligned
Armor Class 7
Hit Points 76 (8d10 + 32)
Speed 20 ft., climb 20 ft.

STR	DEX	CON	INT	WIS	CHA
14 (+2)	5 (−3)	18 (+4)	1 (−5)	6 (−2)	1 (−5)

Damage Resistances piercing from nonmagical attacks
Damage Immunities acid, cold, lightning, slashing
Condition Immunities blinded, charmed, deafened, exhaustion, frightened, prone
Senses blindsight 60 ft. (blind beyond this radius), passive Perception 8
Languages —
Challenge 4 (1,100 XP)

Amorphous. The pudding can move through a space as narrow as 1 inch wide without squeezing.

Petrifying Form. A creature that touches the pudding or hits it with a melee attack while within 5 feet of it must make a DC 15 Constitution saving throw. On a failed save, the creature magically begins to turn to stone and is restrained. If it used a nonmagical weapon made of wood or other organic material to hit the pudding, that weapon turns to stone. The creature must repeat the saving throw at the end of its next turn. On a success, the effect ends. On a failure, the creature is petrified until freed by the *greater restoration* spell or other magic. Nonmagical ammunition made of wood or other organic material that hits the pudding is turned to stone after dealing damage. Nonmagical ammunition made of stone that hits the pudding is destroyed after dealing damage.

Corrosive Form. The pudding can eat through 2-inch thick, nonmagical stone, including petrified creatures, in 1 round.

Spider Climb. The pudding can climb difficult surfaces, including upside down and ceilings, without needing to make an ability check.

ACTIONS

Pseudopod. *Melee Weapon Attack:* +4 to hit, reach 5 ft., one target. *Hit:* 5 (1d6 + 2) bludgeoning damage. If the target is a creature, it must make a DC 15 Constitution saving throw. On a failed save, the creature magically begins to turn to stone and is restrained. If it is wearing armor made of leather or other organic material when hit by the pudding, that armor is turned to stone. The creature must repeat the saving throw at the end of its next turn. On a success, the effect ends. On a failure, the creature is petrified until freed by the *greater restoration* spell or other magic.

Eat stone. The pudding touches an object or creature made of stone and digests up to 2 inches of material over a one-foot square surface. The pudding recovers 5 (1d10) hit points.

REACTIONS

Split. When a pudding that is Medium or larger is exposed to lightning or slashing damage, it splits into two new puddings if it has at least 10 hit points. Each new pudding has hit points equal to half the original pudding's, rounded down. New puddings are one size smaller than the original pudding.

Stunjelly

Large ooze, unaligned
Armor Class 9
Hit Points 57 (6d10 + 24)
Speed 20 ft., climb 20 ft.

STR	DEX	CON	INT	WIS	CHA
14 (+2)	9 (−1)	18 (+4)	1 (−5)	6 (−2)	1 (−5)

Damage Resistances piercing
Damage Immunities acid, cold, lightning, poison
Condition Immunities blinded, charmed, deafened, exhaustion, frightened, poisoned, prone
Senses blindsight 60 ft. (blind beyond this radius), passive Perception 8
Languages —
Challenge 3 (700 XP)

Amorphous. The stunjelly can move through a space as narrow as 1 inch wide without squeezing.

Corrosive Form. A creature that touches the stunjelly or hits it with a melee attack while within 5 feet of it takes 7 (2d6) acid damage. Any nonmagical weapon made of wood or other organic material that hits the stunjelly partly dissolves. After hitting the stunjelly, the weapon takes a permanent and cumulative −1 to damage rolls. If its penalty drops to −5, the weapon is destroyed. Nonmagical ammunition made of wood (or other organic material) that hits the stunjelly is destroyed after dealing damage.

Engulfing. When the stunjelly hits a creature with a Slam attack, it may make one Engulf attack against that creature as a bonus action.

Spider Climb. The stunjelly can climb difficult surfaces, including upside down and ceilings, without needing to make an ability check.

ACTIONS

Slam. *Melee Weapon Attack:* +4 to hit, reach 5 ft., one target. *Hit:* 5 (1d6 + 2) bludgeoning damage plus 7 (2d6) acid damage. If the target is a creature, it must make a DC 14 Constitution saving throw. On a failed save, the creature is paralyzed for 1 minute. The creature may repeat this saving throw at the end of each of its turns, ending the paralysis on itself on a success.

If the creature is wearing armor made of leather or other organic material when hit by the stunjelly, that armor is partly dissolved and takes a permanent and cumulative −1 to the AC it offers. The armor is destroyed if the penalty reduces its AC to 10.

Engulf. The stunjelly attempts to engulf one creature of size Large or smaller within 5 feet of it. The creature must make a DC 15 Dexterity saving throw. On a failed save, the stunjelly enters the creature's space, and the creature takes 7 (2d6) acid damage and is engulfed. The engulfed creature can't breathe, is restrained, and must succeed on a DC 14 Constitution saving throw or be paralyzed for 1 minute. The creature may repeat this Constitution saving throw at the end of each of its turns, ending the paralysis on itself on a success.

At the start of each of the stunjelly's turns, the engulfed creature takes 14 (4d6) acid damage, and any equipment it is carrying made of leather or other organic material is partly dissolved (see Slam above). When the stunjelly moves, the engulfed creature moves with it. An engulfed creature can try to escape by taking an action to make a DC 14 Strength check. On a success, the creature escapes and enters a space of its choice within 5 feet of the stunjelly.

The stunjelly may only engulf 1 Large, 2 Medium, or 4 Small or smaller creatures at one time.

Ox, Giant

Huge beast, unaligned
Armor Class 12 (natural armor)
Hit Points 94 (9d12 + 36)
Speed 50 ft.

STR	DEX	CON	INT	WIS	CHA
25 (+7)	10 (+0)	19 (+4)	2 (−4)	12 (+1)	5 (−3)

Senses passive Perception 11
Languages —
Challenge 6 (2,300 XP)

Charge. If the ox moves at least 20 feet straight toward a target and then hits it with a Gore attack on the same turn, the target takes an extra 22 (4d10) piercing damage. If the target is a creature, it must succeed on a DC 18 Strength saving throw or be knocked prone.

ACTIONS

Gore. *Melee Weapon Attack:* +10 to hit, reach 10ft., one target. *Hit:* 29 (4d10 + 7) piercing damage.

Peryton

Medium monstrosity, chaotic evil
Armor Class 13 (natural armor)
Hit Points 39 (6d8 + 12)
Speed 15 ft., fly 60 ft.

STR	DEX	CON	INT	WIS	CHA
16 (+3)	15 (+2)	14 (+2)	8 (−1)	11 (+0)	9 (−1)

Skills Perception +2
Damage Resistances bludgeoning, piercing, and slashing from nonmagical attacks
Senses passive Perception 10
Languages —
Challenge 3 (700 XP)

Flyby. The peryton doesn't provoke an opportunity attack when it flies out of an enemy's reach.

Heart Devourer. If the peryton slays a creature which possesses a heart, it may use a bonus action to rend the creature's heart from its chest and eat it. The peryton gains 10 temporary hit points and has advantage on attack rolls for the next round. Any creatures within 30 feet who witness this devouring must succeed on a DC 13 Wisdom (fear) saving throw or become frightened until the end of their next turn.

Slash and Snatch. If the peryton dives at least 30 feet straight toward a target and then hits it with a Talon attack on the same turn, the target takes an additional 10 (3d6) slashing damage. If the target is size Small or smaller, it is grappled (escape DC 13). The peryton has picked it up and may begin flying away with it.

Actions

Multiattack. The peryton makes one Antler attack and one Talon attack

Antler. *Melee Weapon Attack:* +5 to hit, reach 5 ft., one target. *Hit:* 8 (1d8 + 3) piercing damage.

Talon. *Melee Weapon Attack:* +5 to hit, reach 5 ft., one target. *Hit:* 10 (2d6 + 3) slashing damage.

Pixie

Tiny fey, neutral good
Armor Class 15
Hit Points 17 (5d4 + 5)
Speed 20ft., fly 60ft.

STR	DEX	CON	INT	WIS	CHA
7 (−2)	20 (+5)	12 (+1)	16 (+3)	15 (+2)	16 (+3)

Skills Deception +5, Nature +5, Perception +6, Stealth +9
Senses passive Perception 16
Languages Common, Sylvan
Challenge 1 (200 XP)

Magic Resistance. The pixie has advantage on saving throws against spells and other magical effects.

Innate Spellcasting. The pixie's innate spellcasting ability is Charisma (spell save DC13, +5 to hit with spell attacks). It can cast the following spells, requiring only its pixie dust as a component:

> At will: *druidcraft, greater invisibility* (self only)
> 1/day each: *confusion, dancing lights, detect evil and good, detect thoughts, dispel magic, entangle, fly, polymorph, sleep*

Actions

Shortsword. *Melee Weapon Attack:* +7 to hit, reach 5 ft., one target. *Hit:* 8 (1d6 + 5) piercing damage.

Shortbow. *Ranged Weapon Attack:* +7 to hit, range 80/320ft., one target. *Hit:* 8 (1d6 + 5) piercing damage.

Purple Worm, Fiendish

Gargantuan monstrosity, neutral evil
Armor Class 18 (natural armor)
Hit Points 330 (20d20 + 120)
Speed 50 ft., burrow 30 ft.

STR	DEX	CON	INT	WIS	CHA
28 (+9)	7 (−2)	22 (+6)	1 (−5)	8 (−1)	4 (−3)

Saving Throws CON +11, WIS +4
Damage Resistances cold; bludgeoning, piercing, and slashing from nonmagical attacks not made with silver
Damage Immunities fire, poison
Condition Immunities poisoned
Senses Blindsight 30 ft., Tremorsense 60 ft., Passive Perception 9
Languages —
Challenge 16 (15,000 XP)

Tunneler. The worm can burrow through solid rock at half its burrow speed and leaves a 10-foot-diameter tunnel in its wake.

Actions

Multiattack. The worm makes one Bite attack and one Stinger attack.

Bite. *Melee Weapon Attack:* +9 to hit, reach 10 ft., one target. *Hit:* 22 (3d8 + 9) piercing damage. If the target is a Large or smaller creature, it must succeed on a DC 19 Dexterity saving throw or be swallowed by the worm. A swallowed creature is blinded and restrained, it has total cover against attacks and other effects outside the worm, and it takes 21 (6d6) acid damage and 10 (3d6) fire damage at the start of each of the worm's turns.

If the worm takes 30 damage or more on a single turn from a creature inside it, the worm must succeed on a DC 21 Constitution saving throw at the end of that turn or regurgitate all swallowed creatures, which fall prone in a space within 10 feet of the worm. If the worm dies, a swallowed creature is no longer restrained by it and can escape from the corpse by using 20 feet of movement, exiting prone.

Tail Stinger. *Melee Weapon Attack:* +9 to hit, reach 10 ft., one creature. *Hit:* 19 (3d6 + 9) piercing damage, and the target must make a DC 19 Constitution saving throw, taking 42 (12d6) poison damage on a failed save, or half as much damage on a successful one.

Queen Widushka

Large monstrosity, chaotic evil
Armor Class 19 (natural armor)
Hit Points 247 (26d10 + 104)
Speed 30 ft., climb 30 ft.

STR	DEX	CON	INT	WIS	CHA
16 (+3)	16 (+3)	18 (+4)	15 (+2)	18 (+4)	14 (+2)

Saving Throws Wis +9, Cha +7
Skills Perception +14, Religion +7, Stealth +8
Senses darkvision 120 ft., passive Perception 24
Languages Elvish, Undercommon
Challenge 14 (11,500 XP)

Fey Ancestry. The drider has advantage on saving throws against being charmed, and magic can't put the drider to sleep.

Innate Spellcasting. The drider's innate spellcasting ability is Wisdom (spell save DC 15). The drider can innately cast the following spells, requiring no material components:

> At will: *dancing lights*
> 1/day each: *darkness, faerie fire*

Spellcasting. Widushka is a 13th-level spellcaster. Its spellcasting ability is Wisdom (spell save DC 17, +9 to hit with spell attacks). It has the following cleric spells prepared:

> Cantrips (at will): *guidance, poison spray, resistance, spare the dying, thaumaturgy*
> 1st level (4 slots): *animal friendship, cure wounds, detect poison and disease, ray of sickness*
> 2nd level (3 slots): *lesser restoration, invisibility, protection from poison*
> 3rd level (3 slots): *conjure animals* (2 **giant spiders**),

dispel magic

4th level (3 slots): *banishment, freedom of movement*
5th level (2 slots): *insect plague, mass cure wounds*
6th level (1 slot): *harm*
7th level (1 slot): *etherealness*

Spider Climb. The drider can climb difficult surfaces, including upside down on ceilings, without needing to make an ability check.

Sunlight Sensitivity. While in sunlight, the drider has disadvantage on attack rolls, as well as on Wisdom (Perception) checks that rely on sight.

Web Walker. The drider ignores movement restrictions caused by webbing.

ACTIONS

Multiattack. The drider makes three attacks, either with its longsword or its longbow. It can replace one of those attacks with a bite attack.

Bite. *Melee Weapon Attack:* +8 to hit, reach 5 ft., one creature. *Hit:* 5 (1d4 + 3) piercing damage plus 13 (3d8) poison damage.

Longsword. *Melee Weapon Attack:* +8 to hit, reach 5 ft., one target. *Hit:* 7 (1d8 + 3) slashing damage plus 4 (1d8) poison damage, or 8 (1d10 + 3) slashing damage if used with two hands.

Longbow. *Ranged Weapon Attack:* +8 to hit, range 150/600 ft., one target. *Hit:* 7 (1d8 + 3) piercing damage plus 9 (2d8) poison damage.

Rakshasa, Maharaja

Medium fiend, lawful evil
Armor Class 24 (natural armor)
Hit Points 310 (23d8 + 207)
Speed 40 ft., fly 30 ft.

STR	DEX	CON	INT	WIS	CHA
26 (+8)	27 (+8)	29 (+9)	24 (+7)	21 (+5)	28 (+9)

Saving Throws Dex +15, Con +16, Wis +12, Cha +16
Skills Arcana +14, Deception +16, Insight +12, Perception +12, Persuasion +16, Stealth +15
Damage Resistances cold; bludgeoning and slashing from nonmagical attacks
Damage Immunities poison; piercing from nonmagical attacks
Condition Immunities frightened, poisoned
Senses darkvision 60 ft., passive Perception 22
Languages all
Challenge 22 (41,000 XP)

Be Quick or Be Dead. The maharaja rakshasa has advantage on initiative rolls.

Limited Magic Immunity. The maharaja rakshasa can't be affected or detected by spells of 6th level or lower unless it wishes to be. It has advantage on saving throws against all other spells and magical effects.

Polyglot. The maharaja rakshasa is fluent in all languages.

Innate Spellcasting. The maharaja rakshasa's innate spellcasting ability is Charisma (spell save DC 24, +16 to hit with spell attacks). The rakshasa can innately cast the following spells, requiring no material components:

At will: *detect thoughts, clairvoyance*
3/day: *charm person*
1/day: *plane shift*

Spellcasting. The maharaja rakshasa is an 18th-level spellcaster. Its spellcasting ability is Charisma (spell save DC 24, +16 to hit with spell attacks). It can cast the following spells:

Cantrips (at will): *dancing lights, mage hand, minor illusion, resistance, shocking grasp*
1st level (4 slots): *color spray, detect magic, fog cloud, magic missile*
2nd level (3 slots): *darkness, hold person, see invisibility, spider climb*
3rd level (3 slots): *bestow curse, dispel magic, nondetection, vampiric touch*
4th level (3 slots): *confusion, dimension door, greater invisibility, phantasmal killer*
5th level (3 slots): *dominate person, mislead, modify memory, scrying*
6th level (1 slot): *irresistible dance, mass suggestion, programmed illusion*
7th level (1 slot): *pristmatic spray, project image, teleport*
8th level (1 slot): *feeblemind, mind blank*
9th level (1 slot): *prismatic wall, weird*

ACTIONS

Multiattack. The rakshasa makes four Bite attacks and one Greatsword attack.

Greatsword. *Melee Weapon Attack:* +15 to hit, reach 5 ft., one target. *Hit:* 15 (2d6 + 8) slashing damage.

Bite. *Melee Weapon Attack:* +15 to hit, reach 5 ft., one target. *Hit:* 17 (2d8 + 8) piercing damage.

Rast

Medium aberration, neutral
Armor Class 15 (natural armor)
Hit Points 67 (9d8 + 27)
Speed 5 ft., fly 60 ft.

STR	DEX	CON	INT	WIS	CHA
14 (+2)	12 (+1)	17 (+3)	3 (−4)	13 (+1)	12 (+1)

Skills Perception +4, Stealth +4
Damage Vulnerabilities cold
Damage Immunities fire
Senses darkvision 60 ft., passive Perception 14
Languages understands Ignan but can't speak
Challenge 5 (1,800 XP)

ACTIONS

Multiattack. The rast uses its Paralyzing Gaze ability and makes one Bite attack and two Claw attacks.

Bite. *Melee Weapon Attack:* +5 to hit, reach 5 ft., one target. *Hit:* 9 (2d6 + 2) piercing damage plus 3 (1d6) necrotic damage.

Claw. *Melee Weapon Attack:* +5 to hit, reach 10 ft., one target. *Hit:* 6 (1d8 + 2) slashing damage.

Paralyzing Gaze. The rast chooses one creature it can see within 30 feet of it to make a DC 14 Wisdom saving throw. On a failed saving throw, the creature is paralyzed for 1 minute. A paralyzed creature can repeat the saving throw at the end of each of its turns, ending the effect on a success.

Red Jester

Medium undead, chaotic neutral
Armor Class 14 (natural armor)
Hit Points 67 (15d8)
Speed 30 ft.

STR	DEX	CON	INT	WIS	CHA
15 (+2)	17 (+3)	10 (+0)	15 (+2)	14 (+2)	16 (+3)

Saving Throws Dex +6
Skills Acrobatics +6, Deception +6, Sleight of Hand +6
Damage Resistances bludgeoning, piercing, and slashing damage from nonmagical attacks
Damage Immunities necrotic, poison
Condition Immunities exhaustion, frightened, poisoned, unconscious
Senses darkvision 60 ft., passive Perception 12
Languages Common and any two others
Challenge 5 (1,800 XP)

Unassailable Mind. The mind of a red jester is a twisted and dangerous place to peer into. If a living creature targets a red jester with an attack that normally causes psychic damage, or tries to use telepathy on a red jester, that creature must make a successful DC 13 Intelligence saving throw or be cursed, with an effect identical to a permanent *confusion* spell. The *confusion* effect can be ended only by magic that lifts the curse.

ACTIONS

Multiattack. A red jester makes two Fist attacks or Two Mace attacks.
Fist. *Melee Weapon Attack:* +6 to hit, reach 5 ft., one creature. *Hit:* 15 (1d12 + 3) bludgeoning damage.
Jester's Deck. *Ranged Weapon Attack:* +6 to hit (range 20 ft.; one creature). *Hit:* the target creature is affected as if he or she drew a random card from the *deck of many things*. In the hands of anyone but a red jester, the jester's deck acts as a normal, nonmagical deck of playing cards.
+2 Mace of Merriment. *Melee Weapon Attack:* +7 to hit. reach 5 ft., one creature) *Hit:* 14 (2d8 + 5) bludgeoning damage and the target must make a successful DC 14 Wisdom saving throw or be paralyzed with merriment for 1d3 rounds. In the hands of anyone but a red jester, the weapon acts as a *+1 mace*.
Fear Cackle (1/day). The red jester unleashes a fear-inducing cackle. All creatures within 60 feet that hear the cackle must make a successful DC 14 Wisdom saving throw or be frightened for 2d4 rounds. A frightened creature has a 50% chance of immediately dropping everything it holds in its hands.

Reliquary Guardian

Large construct, lawful evil
Armor Class 19 (natural armor)
Hit Points 170 (20d10 + 60)
Speed 30 ft., fly 60 ft.

STR	DEX	CON	INT	WIS	CHA
19 (+4)	12 (+1)	17 (+3)	10 (+0)	17 (+3)	21 (+5)

Skills Perception +7
Damage Immunities bludgeoning, piercing, and slashing from nonmagical attacks not made with adamantine
Condition Immunities charmed, exhaustion, frightened, paralyzed, petrified, poisoned
Senses darkvision 60 ft., passive Perception 17
Languages speaks and understands the languages of its creator
Challenge 12 (8,400 XP)

Divine Blessing. The reliquary guardian deals an additional 14 (4d6) damage with its weapon attacks, included below. This damage is either radiant, if lawfully aligned, or necrotic, if chaotically aligned.
Immutable Form. The reliquary guardian is immune to any spell or effect that would alter its form.
Innate Spellcasting. The reliquary guardian's innate spellcasting ability is Charisma (spell save DC 17, +9 to hit with spell attacks). It can innately cast the following spells, requiring no material components:

At will: *chill touch* (17th level, if chaotically aligned), *protection from evil and good, sacred flame* (17th level, if lawfully aligned)
3/day each: *lightning bolt, flame strike* (deals necrotic instead of radiant if chaotically aligned), *spirit guardians, spiritual weapon*
1/day each: *commune, dispel evil and good, dispel magic*

Magic Resistance. The reliquary guardian has advantage on saving throws against spells and other magical effects.
Magic Weapons. The reliquary guardian's weapon attacks are magical.

ACTIONS

Multiattack. The reliquary guardian makes two Greatsword attacks or two Slam attacks.
Greatsword. *Melee Weapon Attack:* +8 to hit, reach 10 ft., one target. *Hit:* 18 (4d6 + 4) slashing damage and 14 (4d6) necrotic or radiant damage.
Slam. *Melee Weapon Attack:* +8 to hit, reach 10 ft., one target. *Hit:* 22 (4d8 + 4) bludgeoning damage and 14 (4d6) necrotic or radiant damage.
Pronouncement (1/day). All creatures within 120 feet of the reliquary guardian that can hear it must succeed on a DC 17 Wisdom saving throw. On a failed saving throw, the target takes 66 (12d10) thunder damage and is stunned for 1 minute. On a successful saving throw, the target takes half damage and is not stunned. A stunned creature can repeat the saving throw at the end of each of its turns, ending the effect on a success.

Runeskull

Tiny undead, neutral evil
Armor Class 13
Hit Points 18 (4d4 + 8)
Speed 0 ft., fly 30 ft.

STR	DEX	CON	INT	WIS	CHA
1 (−5)	17 (+3)	14 (+2)	10 (+0)	11 (+0)	14 (+2)

Skills Perception +2
Damage Resistances lightning, necrotic, piercing
Damage Immunities poison
Condition Immunities charmed, frightened, paralyzed, poisoned, prone
Senses darkvision 60 ft., passive Perception 12
Languages Common
Challenge 1/2 (100 XP)

Spellcasting. The runeskull is a 2nd-level spell caster. Its spellcasting ability is Charisma (spell save DC 12, +4 to hit with spell attacks). It requires no somatic or material components to cast its spells. The runeskull has the following sorcerer spells prepared:

Cantrips (at will): *chill touch, mage hand*
1st level (3 slots): *shield, thunderwave*

ACTIONS

Steal Life. The runeskull targets one creature it can see within 30 feet of it. The target must succeed on a DC 12 Constitution saving throw or take 2 (1d4) necrotic damage. The runeskull regains hit points equal to that amount.

Saaid al Djinn (living form)

Large elemental, chaotic good
Armor Class 17 (natural armor)
Hit Points 207 (18d10 + 108)
Speed 30 ft., fly 90 ft.

STR	DEX	CON	INT	WIS	CHA
21 (+5)	15 (+2)	22 (+6)	20 (+5)	16 (+3)	20 (+5)

Saving Throws Dex +7, Wis +8, Cha +10
Skills Arcana +10, History +10, Nature +10, Perception +8
Damage Immunities lightning, thunder
Senses darkvision 120 ft., passive Perception 18
Languages Auran, Common, Ignan, telepathy 120 ft.
Challenge 15 (13,000 XP)

Dual Concentration. Saaid al Djinn may maintain two spells simultaneously, each of which requires concentration.

Elemental Demise. If Saaid al Djinn dies, his body disintegrates into a warm breeze, leaving behind only equipment he was wearing or carrying.

Empowered Evocation. Saaid Al Djinn can add his Intelligence modifier (+5) to the damage roll of any wizard evocation spell he casts.

Innate Spellcasting. Saaid al Djinn's innate spellcasting ability is Charisma (spell save DC 18, +10 to hit with spell attacks). He can innately cast the following spells, with no need for material components:

> At will: *detect evil and good, detect magic, thunderwave*
> 3/day each: *create food and water* (can create wine instead of water), *tongues, wind walk*
> 1/day each: *conjure elemental* (air elemental only), *creation, gaseous form, invisibility, major image, plane shift*

Sculpt Spells. When Saaid al Djinn casts an evocation spell that affects other creatures that he can see, he can choose a number of them equal to 1 + the spell's level. The chosen creatures automatically succeed on their saving throws against the spell, and they take no damage if they would normally take half damage on a successful save.

Spellcasting. Saaid al Djinn is a 10th level spellcaster. Saaid al Djinn's spellcasting ability is Intelligence (spell save DC 18, +10 to hit with spell attacks). He has the following spells prepared:

> Cantrips (at will): *chill touch, light, mage hand, ray of frost, shocking grasp*
> 1st level (4 slots): *fog cloud, magic missile, shield, thunderwave*
> 2nd level (3 slots): *blur, gust of wind, mirror image, shatter*
> 3rd level (3 slots): *fireball, lightning bolt, stinking cloud*
> 4th level (3 slots): *greater invisibility, ice storm*
> 5th level (2 slots): *cloudkill, conjure elemental* (air elemental only)

ACTIONS

Multiattack. Saaid al Djinn makes three Scimitar attacks.

Scimitar. *Melee Weapon Attack:* +10 to hit, reach 5 ft., one target. *Hit:* 12 (2d6 + 5) slashing damage plus 7 (2d6) lightning or thunder damage (Saaid al Djinn's choice).

Create Whirlwind. A 5-foot-radius, 30-foot-tall cylinder of swirling air magically forms on a point Saaid al Djinn can see within 120 feet of him. The whirlwind lasts as long as Saaid al Djinn maintains concentration (as if concentrating on a spell). Any creature but Saaid al Djinn that enters the whirlwind must succeed on a DC 18 Strength saving throw or be restrained by it. Saaid al Djinn can move the whirlwind up to 60 feet as an action, and creatures restrained by the whirlwind move with it. The whirlwind ends if Saaid al Djinn loses sight of it.

A creature can use its action to free a creature restrained by the whirlwind, including itself, by succeeding on a DC 18 Strength check. If the check succeeds, the creature is no longer restrained and moves to the nearest space outside the whirlwind.

Saaid al Djinn (salt lich form)

Large elemental, chaotic good
Armor Class 18 (natural armor)
Hit Points 322 (28d10 + 140)
Speed 30 ft., fly 90 ft.

STR	DEX	CON	INT	WIS	CHA
21 (+5)	15 (+2)	22 (+6)	24 (+7)	16 (+3)	20 (+5)

Saving Throws Dex +10, Con +14, Int +15, Wis +11, Cha +13
Skills Arcana +23, History +15, Nature +15, Perception +11
Damage Resistances acid, fire
Damage Immunities cold, lightning, necrotic, poison, thunder; bludgeoning, piercing, and slashing from nonmagical attacks
Condition Immunities charmed, exhaustion, frightened, grappled, paralyzed, petrified, poisoned, prone, restrained
Senses truesight 120 ft., passive Perception 21
Languages Auran, Common, Ignan, telepathy 120 ft.
Challenge 27 (105,000 XP), 28 in lair (120,000 XP)

Elemental Demise. If Saaid al Djinn dies, his body disintegrates into a warm breeze, leaving behind only equipment he was wearing or carrying.

Empowered Evocation. Saaid Al Djinn can add his Intelligence modifier (+7) to the damage roll of any wizard evocation spell he casts.

Innate Spellcasting. Saaid al Djinn's innate spellcasting ability is Charisma (spell save DC 21, +13 to hit with spell attacks). He can innately cast the following spells, with no need for material components:

> At will: *detect evil and good, detect magic, thunderwave*
> 3/day each: *create food and water* (can create wine instead of water), *tongues, wind walk*
> 2/day each: *conjure elemental* (air elemental only), *creation, gaseous form, greater invisibility, lightning bolt, major image, plane shift*

Legendary Resistances (3/day). If Saaid al Djinn fails a saving throw, he can choose to succeed instead.

Overchannel (3/day). When Saaid al Djinn casts a wizard spell of 1st through 5th level that deals damage, he can deal maximum damage with that spell.

Rejuvenation. If he has a phylactery and is destroyed, Saaid al Djinn gains a new body in 1d10 days, regaining all his hit points and becoming active again. The new body appears within 5 feet of the phylactery.

Sculpt Spells. When Saaid al Djinn casts an evocation spell that affects other creatures that he can see, he can choose a number of them equal to 1 + the spell's level. The chosen creatures automatically succeed on their saving throws against the spell, and they take no damage if they would normally take half damage on a successful save.

Spellcasting. Saaid al Djinn is a 20th level spellcaster. Saaid al Djinn's spellcasting ability is Intelligence (spell save DC 23, +15 to hit with spell attacks). He has the following spells prepared:

> Cantrips (at will): *chill touch, light, mage hand, ray of*

frost, shocking grasp

1st level (4 slots): *fog cloud, magic missile, shield, thunderwave*

2nd level (3 slots): *blur, gust of wind, mirror image, shatter*

3rd level (3 slots): *fireball, lightning bolt, stinking cloud*

4th level (3 slots): *banishment, blight, ice storm*

5th level (3 slots): *cloudkill, cone of cold, conjure elemental* (air elemental only), *wall of force*

6th level (2 slots): *chain lightning, disintegrate, globe of invulnerability*

7th level (2 slots): *forcecage, prismatic spray, reverse gravity*

8th level (1 slots): *antimagic field, incendiary cloud*

9th level (1 slot): *time stop, wish*

Touch Spells. When Saaid al Djinn successfully hits with a melee spell attack, he also causes the effects of a Dessicating Touch action.

Turn Resistance. Saaid al Djinn has advantage on saving throws against any effect that turns undead.

Wish Granting. At his discretion, or if forced, Saaid al Djinn may grant the wish of another creature (as the *wish* spell). Saaid al Djinn retains his devotion to the Sultana and to his duty and would find a way to subvert any wish that went against his fundamental nature. He may only grant three wishes per creature.

ACTIONS

Multiattack. Saaid al Djinn makes three Scimitar attacks or two Desiccating Touch attacks.

+1 Scimitar. *Melee Weapon Attack:* +14 to hit, reach 5 ft., one target. *Hit:* 13 (2d6 + 6) slashing damage plus 9 (2d8) lightning or thunder damage (Saaid al Djinn's choice).

Desiccating Touch. *Melee Spell Attack:* +13 to hit, reach 5 ft., one creature. *Hit:* 14 (4d6) necrotic damage. The target must succeed on a DC 19 Constitution saving throw or be paralyzed for 1 minute. The target can repeat the saving throw at the end of each of its turns, ending the effect on itself on a success.

Create Whirlwind. A 5-foot-radius, 30-foot-tall cylinder of swirling air magically forms on a point Saaid al Djinn can see within 120 feet of him. The whirlwind lasts as long as Saaid al Djinn maintains concentration (as if concentrating on a spell). Any creature but Saaid al Djinn that enters the whirlwind must succeed on a DC 18 Strength saving throw or be restrained by it. Saaid al Djinn can move the whirlwind up to 60 feet as an action, and creatures restrained by the whirlwind move with it. The whirlwind ends if Saaid al Djinn loses sight of it.

A creature can use its action to free a creature restrained by the whirlwind, including itself, by succeeding on a DC 18 Strength check. If the check succeeds, the creature is no longer restrained and moves to the nearest space outside the whirlwind.

LEGENDARY ACTIONS

Saaid al Djinn can take 3 legendary actions, choosing from the options below. Only one legendary action option can be used at a time and only at the end of another creature's turn. Saai al Djinn regains spent legendary actions at the start of his turn.

Cantrip: Saaid al Djinn casts a cantrip.

Desiccating Touch (costs 2 actions): Saaid al Djinn uses his Desiccating Touch.

Frightening Gaze (costs 2 actions): Saaid al Djinn fixes his gaze on one creature he can see within 10 feet of him. The target must succeed on a DC 19 Wisdom saving throw against this magic or become frightened for 1 minute.

The frightened target can repeat the saving throw at the end of each of its turns, ending the effect on itself on a success. If a target's saving throw is successful or the effect ends for it, the target is immune to the Saaid al Djinn's gaze for the next 24 hours.

Disrupt Life (costs 3 actions): Each non-undead creature within 20 feet of Saaid al Djinn must make a DC 19 Constitution saving throw against this magic, taking 21 (6d6) necrotic damage on a failed save, or half as much damage on a successful one.

LAIR ACTIONS

On initiative count 20 (losing initiative ties), Saaid al Djinn can take a lair action to cause one of the following magical effects; he can't use the same effect two rounds in a row:

Spell Recall. Saaid al Djinn rolls 2d4 and regains an expended spell slot of that level or lower.

Life Bond. Saaid al Djinn creates a negative energy bond with one creature he can see within 30 feet. Whenever Saaid al Djinn takes damage, the creature must make a DC 19 Constitution saving throw. On a failed save, Saaid al Djinn takes half of the damage (rounded down), and the target takes the remainder of the damage. This bond lasts until initiative count 20 on the next round or until either Saaid al Djinn or the creature leaves his lair.

Vengeful Spirits. Saaid al Djinn calls vengeful spirits of the dead who materialize just long enough to attack one creature he can see within 60 feet of him. The target must succeed on a DC 19 Constitution saving throw, taking 52 (15d6) necrotic damage on a failed save, or half as much damage on a success.

Sabina

Gargantuan celestial (titan), chaotic good

Armor Class 19 (natural armor)

Hit Points 507 (26d20 + 234)

Speed 60 ft.

STR	DEX	CON	INT	WIS	CHA
28 (+9)	10 (+0)	28 (+9)	20 (+5)	22 (+5)	28 (+9)

Saving Throws Str +15, Int +11, Wis +11, Cha +15

Skills Insight +11, Persuasion +15

Damage Immunities poison; bludgeoning, piercing, and slashing from nonmagical attacks

Condition Immunities frightened, poisoned

Senses truesight 120 ft., passive Perception 15

Languages all, telepathy 300 ft.

Challenge 20 (33,000 XP)

Innate Spellcasting. Sabina's spellcasting ability is Wisdom (spell save DC 22, +14 to hit with spell attacks). She can innately cast the following spells, requiring no material components:

At will: *divination, dispel magic, dominate person, levitate, mind blank, sending*

3/day: *bestow curse, scrying, heal, mass suggestion*

1/day: *dominate monster, freedom of movement, planar ally, meteor swarm, seeming*

Trampling Charge. If Sabina moves at least 40 feet straight toward a target and then hits it with a melee attack on the same turn, that target must succeed on a DC 24 Strength saving throw or be knocked prone. If the target is prone, Sabina can make one Stomp attack against it as a bonus action.

ACTIONS

Multiattack. Sabina makes two Slam attacks.
Slam. *Melee Weapon Attack:* +15 to hit, reach 15 ft., one target. *Hit:* 22 (3d8 + 9) bludgeoning damage.
Stomp. *Melee Weapon Attack:* +15 to hit, reach 10 ft., one target. *Hit:* 31 (4d10 + 9) bludgeoning damage, and all creatures within 20 feet of Sabina must succeed on a DC 20 Dexterity saving throw or be knocked prone as Sabina causes the ground to heave.

Salamander Monarch

Large elemental, chaotic evil
Armor Class 15 (natural armor)
Hit Points 253 (22d10 + 132)
Speed 30 ft.

STR	DEX	CON	INT	WIS	CHA
21 (+5)	12 (+1)	23 (+6)	16 (+3)	20 (+5)	18 (+4)

Saving Throws Con +12, Wis +11, Cha +10
Skills Arcana +9, Insight +11, Perception +11, Religion +9
Damage Vulnerabilities cold
Damage Resistances bludgeoning, piercing, and slashing from nonmagical attacks
Damage Immunities fire
Senses darkvision 60 ft., passive Perception 21
Languages Common, Ignan
Challenge 18 (20,000 XP)

Heated Body. A creature that touches the salamander monarch or hits it with a melee attack while within 5 feet of it takes 14 (4d6) fire damage.
Heated Weapons. Any metal melee weapon the salamander monarch wields deals an extra 14 (4d6) fire damage on a hit (included in the attack).
Innate Spellcasting. The salamander monarch's innate spellcasting ability is Charisma (spell save DC 18, +10 to hit with spell attacks). The salamander monarch can cast the following spells without requiring any material components.
    3/day each: *burning hands, fireball, flaming sphere, wall of fire*
1/day each: *dispel magic, conjure elemental*
Spellcasting. The salamander monarch is a 10th-level spellcaster. Its spellcasting ability is Wisdom (spell save DC 19, +11 to hit with spell attacks). He can cast the following spells:
    Cantrips: *guidance, sacred flame, fire bolt* (3d10 fire damage), *resistance, true strike*
    1st level (4 slots): *bless, cure wounds, detect magic, healing word, shield of faith*
    2nd level (3 slots): *aid, blindness/deafness, enhance ability, hold person, spiritual weapon*
    3rd level (3 slots): *beacon of hope, bestow curse, fireball, mass healing word*
    4th level (3 slots): *blight, death ward, fire shield, freedom of movement*
    5th level (2 slots): *flame strike, mass cure wounds*

Actions

Multiattack. The salamander monarch makes one Spear attack and one Tail attack.
+2 Spear. *Melee or Ranged Weapon Attack:* +13 to hit, reach 10 ft. or range 20 ft./60 ft., one target. *Hit:* 10 (1d6 + 7) piercing damage, or 11 (1d8 + 7) piercing damage if used with two hands to make a melee attack, plus 14 (4d6) fire damage.
Tail. *Melee Weapon Attack:* +11 to hit, reach 10 ft., one target. *Hit:* 14 (2d8 + 5) bludgeoning damage plus 14 (4d6) fire damage, and the target is grappled (escape DC 18). Until this grapple ends, the target is restrained, the salamander can automatically hit the target with its tail, and the salamander can't make tail attacks against other targets.

Salamander Noble

Large elemental, chaotic evil
Armor Class 17 (natural armor)
Hit Points 189 (18d10 + 90)
Speed 30 ft.

STR	DEX	CON	INT	WIS	CHA
23 (+6)	12 (+1)	21 (+5)	14 (+2)	15 (+2)	18 (+4)

Skills Perception +12
Damage Vulnerabilities cold
Damage Resistances bludgeoning, piercing, and slashing from nonmagical attacks
Damage Immunities fire
Senses darkvision 60 ft., passive Perception 22
Languages Common, Ignan
Challenge 10 (5,900 XP)

Heated Body. A creature that touches the noble salamander or hits it with a melee attack while within 5 feet of it takes 14 (4d6) fire damage.
Heated Weapons. Any metal melee weapon the noble salamander wields deals an extra 10 (3d6) fire damage on a hit (included in the attack).
Innate Spellcasting. The noble salamander's innate spellcasting ability is Charisma (spell save DC 16, +8 to hit with spell attacks). The salamander can cast the following spells without requiring any material components.
    3/day each: *burning hands, fireball, flaming sphere, wall of fire*
    1/day each: *dispel magic, conjure elemental*

Actions

Multiattack. The noble salamander makes one Spear attack and one Tail attack.
Spear. *Melee or Ranged Weapon Attack:* +10 to hit, reach 10 ft. or range 20 ft./60 ft., one target. *Hit:* 13 (2d6 + 6) piercing damage, or 15 (2d8 + 6) piercing damage if used with two hands to make a melee attack, plus 10 (3d6) fire damage.
Tail. *Melee Weapon Attack:* +10 to hit, reach 10 ft., one target. *Hit:* 15 (2d8 + 6) bludgeoning damage plus 10 (3d6) fire damage, and the target is grappled (escape DC 17). Until this grapple ends, the target is restrained, the salamander can automatically hit the target with its tail, and the salamander can't make tail attacks against other targets.

Sandling

Large elemental, unaligned
Armor Class 15 (natural armor)
Hit Points 26 (4d10 + 4)
Speed 30 ft., burrow 20 ft.

STR	DEX	CON	INT	WIS	CHA
17 (+3)	13 (+1)	13 (+1)	4 (−3)	11 (+0)	11 (+0)

Damage Resistances piercing and slashing damage from nonmagical attacks
Damage Immunities poison
Condition Immunities paralyzed, poisoned, prone, stunned,

unconscious
Senses darkvision 60 ft., tremorsense 60 ft., passive
Perception 10
Languages: Understands Terran but can't speak
Challenge 1 (200 XP)
Vulnerability to Water. A sandling that is hit by at least two
gallons of water has its speed halved, its AC reduced by 2,
and it can't use reactions for one round.

ACTIONS

Bite. *Melee Weapon Attack.* +5 to hit, reach 5 ft., one
creature). *Hit.* 7 (1d8 + 3) bludgeoning damage.

Scorpionfolk

Large monstrosity, lawful evil
Armor Class 15 (natural armor)
Hit Points 60 (8d8 + 24)
Speed 40 ft.

STR	DEX	CON	INT	WIS	CHA
19 (+4)	12 (+1)	16 (+3)	8 (−1)	14 (+2)	15 (+2)

Skills Athletics +7, Perception +5, Stealth +4, Survival +5
Damage Immunities poison
Condition Immunities poisoned
Senses darkvision 60 ft., tremorsense 60 ft., passive
Perception 15
Languages Common, Sadara
Challenge 6 (2,300 XP)

ACTIONS

Multiattack. The scorpionfolk makes two Claw or two
Longsword attacks, and one Stinger attack.
Longsword. *Melee Weapon Attack:* +7 to hit, reach 5 ft., one
target. *Hit:* 8 (1d8 + 4) slashing damage, or 9 (1d10 + 4)
slashing damage.
Claw. *Melee Weapon Attack:* +7 to hit, reach 5 ft., one
target. *Hit:* 7 (1d6 + 4) slashing damage.
Stinger. *Melee Weapon Attack:* +7 to hit, reach 10 ft., one
target. *Hit:* 9 (1d10 + 4) piercing damage and the target
must make a DC 14 Constitution saving throw, taking 22
(4d10) poison damage on a failed saving throw, or half as
much damage on a successful one.

Seraph Genie

Large elemental (genie), neutral good
Armor Class 15 (natural armor)
Hit Points 102 (12d10 + 36)
Speed 40 ft., fly 30 ft.

STR	DEX	CON	INT	WIS	CHA
19 (+4)	16 (+3)	17 (+3)	15 (+2)	15 (+2)	19 (+4)

Saving Throws Int +5, Wis +5
Skills Arcana +5, Deception +7, Insight +5, Perception +5
Damage Vulnerabilities cold
Damage Immunities fire
Senses darkvision 60 ft., passive Perception 15
Languages Celestial, Common, Ignan; telepathy 100 ft.
Challenge 7 (2,900 XP)

Heat. A seraph's body generates heat. Creatures who touch
the genie take 7 (2d6) fire damage. If the seraph genie
uses a metal weapon it adds this additional damage to
the weapon's attacks. A seraph genie can suppress this
effect for 1 hour as a bonus action.
Innate Spellcasting. A seraph genie's innate spellcasting
ability is charisma (spell save DC 15, +7 to hit with spell
attacks). It can cast the following spells without requiring
material components.
    At will: *detect evil and good, detect magic, flame
blade, plane shift* (self only), *produce flame*
    3/day each: *fireball, flame strike, invisibility, see
invisibility, wall of fire*
    1/day: *fire storm*

ACTIONS

Multiattack. A seraph genie makes three Scimitar attacks.
Scimitar. *Melee Weapon Attack:* +7 to hit, reach 5 ft., one
target. *Hit:* 7 (1d6 + 4) slashing damage plus 7 (2d6) fire
damage.
Fire Burst (recharge 5–6). The seraph genie emits a blast of
elemental fire in a 30 foot radius. All creatures in the area
must make a DC 15 Dexterity saving throw, taking 28 (8d6)
fire damage on a failed saving throw, or half as much on
a successful one.

Shadow Captain

Medium undead, lawful evil
Armor Class 19 (half plate, shield)
Hit Points 156 (24d8 + 48)
Speed 30 ft.

STR	DEX	CON	INT	WIS	CHA
18 (+4)	14 (+2)	14 (+2)	10 (+0)	16 (+3)	10 (+0)

Saving Throws Str +8, Wis +7
Skills Perception +11, Stealth +10
Damage Resistances lightning; bludgeoning, piercing, and
slashing from nonmagical attacks
Damage Immunities cold, necrotic, poison
Condition Immunities charmed, exhaustion, frightened,
paralyzed, poisoned, unconscious
Senses darkvision 60 ft. passive Perception 21
Languages Common
Challenge 12 (8,400 XP)

Alter Self. The shadow captain can assume a different form
at will. The magic that provides the shadow captain with
this ability is so powerful that only a *true seeing* spell can
discern what lies under the illusion.
Innate Spellcasting. The shadow captain's spellcasting
ability is Wisdom (spell save DC 15, +7 to hit with spell
attacks). The shadow captain can innately cast the
following spells, requiring no material components:
    At will: *alter self, resistance, sacred flame*
    3/day each: *bane, inflict wounds, shield of faith*
    1/day each: *animate dead, contagion*
Regeneration. The shadow captain regains 10 hit points at
the start of its turn. If the shadow captain takes acid or fire
damage, this trait doesn't function at the start of its next
turn. The shadow captain dies only if it starts its turn with 0
hit points and doesn't regenerate.

ACTIONS

Multiattack. The shadow captain makes two Longsword
attacks.
Longsword. *Melee Weapon Attack:* +8 to hit, reach 5 ft., one
target. *Hit:* 15 (2d10 + 4) slashing damage plus 22 (4d10)
cold damage.
Draining Touch. *Melee Weapon Attack:* +6 to hit, reach 5
ft., one target. *Hit:* 15 (3d8 + 2) cold damage. The target

must succeed on a DC 14 Constitution saving throw or its hit point maximum is reduced by an amount equal to the damage taken. This reduction lasts until the target finishes a long rest. The target dies if this effect reduces its hit point maximum to 0.

Shape of Fire

Large undead, lawful evil
Armor Class 19 (natural armor)
Hit Points 418 (31d10 + 248)
Speed 30 ft., fly 60 ft.

STR	DEX	CON	INT	WIS	CHA
24 (+7)	17 (+3)	26 (+8)	6 (–2)	10 (+0)	7 (–2)

Damage Vulnerabilities cold
Damage Resistances acid, lightning, thunder
Damage Immunities fire, necrotic, poison; bludgeoning, piercing, and slashing damage from nonmagical attacks
Condition Immunities charmed, exhaustion, frightened, grappled, paralyzed, petrified, poisoned, prone, restrained, unconscious
Senses blindsight 60 ft. (blind beyond this radius), passive Perception 10
Languages understands Ignan but can't speak
Challenge 26 (90,000 XP)

Immaterial Fire. The shape of fire can move through a space as narrow as 1 inch wide without squeezing. A creature that begins its turn within 10 feet of the shape of fire takes 22 (4d10) fire damage. In addition, the shape of fire can enter a hostile creature's space and stop there. The first time it enters a creature's space on a turn, that creature takes 22 (4d10) fire damage.

Innate Spellcasting. The shape of fire's innate spellcasting ability is Constitution (spell save DC 24). It can cast the following spells, requiring no material components.

At will: *fireball* (5th level, 11d6 fire damage)
3/day each: *fire storm, incendiary cloud*

Turn Resistance. The shape of fire has advantage on saving throws against any effect that turns undead.

ACTIONS

Multiattack. The shape of fire makes two Touch attacks.
Touch. *Melee Weapon Attack:* +15 to hit, reach 10 ft., one target. *Hit:* 29 (4d10 + 7) fire damage. If the target is a creature, it must make a DC 24 Constitution saving throw or be cursed for 1 minute. While cursed, at the beginning of each of the creature's turns, it must repeat the saving throw. On a successful saving throw, the creature is still cursed but suffers no other effects. On a failed saving throw, the target's maximum hit points are reduced by 22 (4d10), and the shape of fire regains an equal amount of hit points, up to its maximum. A creature whose maximum hit points are brought to zero by this curse is slain. The curse can be ended early with magic such as *remove curse*. Lost hit points can only be restored by magic such as *greater restoration, heal, regenerate,* or *wish.*

If a humanoid creature is slain by the shape of fire, it rises as a **lavawight** at the end of the shape of fire's next turn. The lavawight is under the command of the shape of fire, and the shape of fire can have no more than 12 lavawights under its command at a time.

Silaal

Large aberration, neutral evil
Armor Class 17 (natural armor)
Hit Points 112 (15d10 + 30)
Speed 30 ft.

STR	DEX	CON	INT	WIS	CHA
17 (+3)	16 (+3)	15 (+2)	18 (+4)	18 (+4)	18 (+4)

Skills Arcana +8, Deception +8, Insight +8, Intimidation +8, Investigation +8, Medicine +8, Survival +8
Damage Resistances cold, fire
Damage Immunities acid
Senses darkvision 60 ft., passive Perception 14
Languages understands Aklo, Common, but can't speak; telepathy 120 ft.
Challenge 10 (5,900 XP)

Innate Spellcasting. The silaal's innate spellcasting ability is Charisma (spell save DC 16). It can cast the following spells, requiring no material components.

At will: *cure wounds, detect thoughts, see invisibility*
3/day each: *fear, wall of fire*
1/day each: *blade barrier, dominate person, revivify*

ACTIONS

Multiattack. The silaal makes two Kukri attacks.
Kukri. *Melee or Ranged Weapon Attack:* +7 to hit, reach 5 ft. or range 20/60 ft., one target. *Hit:* 7 (2d4 + 3) piercing damage. If the target is a creature that isn't an undead or construct and it isn't already bleeding profusely, the target must make a DC 15 Constitution saving throw. On a failed saving throw, the target begins bleeding profusely. At the beginning of each of its turns, the target's maximum hit points are reduced by 18 (4d8). The target continues to bleed profusely until the target's maximum hit points reach 0 and it dies. The target can repeat the saving throw at the end of each of its turns, or the target or another creature can use their action to make a DC 15 Wisdom (Medicine) check to staunch the bleeding, ending the effect on a success. Lost hit points return when the target takes a long rest.

Sim ral Marla

Large undead, lawful evil
Armor Class 19 (natural armor, *bracers of defense*)
Hit Points 299 (26d10 + 156)
Speed 30 ft., fly 90 ft.

STR	DEX	CON	INT	WIS	CHA
20 (+5)	12 (+1)	24 (+7)	19 (+4)	15 (+2)	16 (+3)

Saving Throws Con +15, Int +12, Wis +10, Cha +11
Skills Arcana +20, History +12, Insight +10, Perception +10
Damage Resistances cold, lightning, necrotic
Damage Immunities fire, poison; bludgeoning, piercing, and slashing from nonmagical attacks
Condition Immunities charmed, exhaustion, frightened, paralyzed, poisoned
Senses truesight 120 ft., passive Perception 20
Languages Common, Ignan, telepathy 120 ft.
Challenge 25 (75,000 XP), 26 in lair (90,000 XP)

Elemental Demise. If Sim ral Marla dies, his body disintegrates in a flash of fire and puff of smoke, leaving behind only equipment he was wearing or carrying.

Deadly Harvest. Once per turn, when Sim ral Marla kills a creature (excluding constructs and undead) with a spell of 1st level or higher, he regains hit points equal to three times the spell's level.

Innate Spellcasting. Sim ral Marla's innate spellcasting ability is Charisma (spell save DC 19, +11 to hit with spell attacks). He can innately cast the following spells, with no need for material components:

At will: *detect magic*
3/day each: *enlarge/reduce, tongues*
2/day each: *conjure elemental* (fire elemental only), *gaseous form, invisibility, major image, plane shift, wall of fire*
1/day: *greater invisibility*

Legendary Resistances (3/day). If Sim ral Marla fails a saving throw, he can choose to succeed instead.

Rejuvenation. If he has a phylactery and is destroyed, Sim ral Marla gains a new body in 1d10 days, regaining all his hit points and becoming active again. The new body appears within 5 feet of the phylactery.

Signature Spells (1/day each). Sim ral Marla can cast *fireball* and *vampiric touch* at 3rd level without expending a spell slot.

Special Equipment. Sim ral Marla possesses a *brazier of controlling fire elementals*, a *spell wand*[2] of *greater invisibility*, and a *staff of necromancy*[2].

Spell Mastery. Sim ral Marla may cast *magic missile* or *mirror image* at their lowest possible level without expending a spell slot.

Spellcasting. Sim ral Marla is a 20th level spellcaster. His spellcasting ability is Intelligence (spell save DC 20, +12 to hit with spell attacks). He has the following spells prepared:

Cantrips (at will): *chill touch, light, mage hand, ray of frost, shocking grasp*
1st level (4 slots): *fog cloud, magic missile, shield*
2nd level (3 slots): *blindness/deafness, blur, hold person, mirror image*
3rd level (3 slots): *animate dead, counterspell, fireball, vampiric touch*
4th level (3 slots): *banishment, blight, wall of fire*
5th level (3 slots): *cloudkill, conjure elemental* (fire elemental only), *telekinesis*
6th level (2 slots): *chain lightning, disintegrate, globe of invulnerability*
7th level (2 slots): *finger of death, forcecage*
8th level (1 slots): *antimagic field, incendiary cloud*
9th level (1 slot): *power word kill*

Touch Spells. When Sim ral Marla successfully hits with a melee spell attack, he also causes the effects of a Paralyzing Touch action.

Turn Resistance. Sim ral Marla has advantage on saving throws against any effect that turns undead.

Undead Servants. When Sim ral Marla casts animate dead, he can create one additional undead. Whenever he uses a necromancy spell to create an undead, that undead's hit point maximum is increased by 20, and that undead adds +8 to its weapon damage rolls.

ACTIONS

Multiattack. Sim ral Marla makes two Scimitar attacks or two Paralyzing Touch attacks.

Scimitar. *Melee Weapon Attack:* +13 to hit, reach 5 ft., one target. *Hit:* 12 (2d6 + 5) slashing damage plus 7 (2d6) fire damage.

Paralyzing Touch. *Melee Spell Attack:* +13 to hit, reach 5 ft., one creature. *Hit:* 10 (3d6) cold damage. The target must succeed on a DC 19 Constitution saving throw or be paralyzed for 1 minute. The target can repeat the saving throw at the end of each of its turns, ending the effect on itself on a success.

Hurl Flame. *Ranged Spell Attack:* +11 to hit, range 120 ft., one target. *Hit:* 17 (5d6) fire damage.

Dominate Undead. Sim ral Marla chooses one undead he can see within 50 feet of him. That undead must succeed on a DC 20 Charisma saving throw or become friendly to Sim al Marla and obey his orders. If the undead succeeds on its saving throw, Sim ral Marla cannot use this feature on it again. Sim ral Marla may only dominate one undead at a time using this ability; when he uses it, an already-dominated undead is freed from his control.

LEGENDARY ACTIONS

Sim ral Marla can take 3 legendary actions, choosing from the options below. Only one legendary action option can be used at a time and only at the end of another creature's turn. Sim ral Marla regains spent legendary actions at the start of his turn.

Cantrip. Sim ral Marla casts a cantrip.

Paralyzing Touch (costs 2 actions). Sim ral Marla uses his Paralyzing Touch.

Frightening Gaze (costs 2 actions). Sim ral Marla fixes his gaze on one creature he can see within 10 feet of him. The target must succeed on a DC 19 Wisdom saving throw against this magic or become frightened for 1 minute. The frightened target can repeat the saving throw at the end of each of its turns, ending the effect on itself on a success. If a target's saving throw is successful or the effect ends for it, the target is immune to the Sim ral Marla's gaze for the next 24 hours.

Disrupt Life (costs 3 actions). Each non-undead creature within 20 feet of Sim ral Marla must make a DC 19 Constitution saving throw against this magic, taking 21 (6d6) necrotic damage on a failed save, or half as much damage on a successful one.

LAIR ACTIONS

On initiative count 20 (losing initiative ties), Sim ral Marla can take a lair action to cause one of the following magical effects; he can't use the same effect two rounds in a row:

Spell Recall. Sim ral Marla rolls 2d4 and regains an expended spell slot of that level or lower.

Life Bond. Sim ral Marla creates a negative energy bond with one creature he can see within 30 feet. Whenever Sim ral Marla takes damage, the creature must make a DC 19 Constitution saving throw. On a failed save, Sim ral Marla takes half of the damage (rounded down), and the target takes the remainder of the damage. This bond lasts until initiative count 20 on the next round or until either Sim ral Marla or the creature leaves his lair.

Vengeful Spirits. Sim ral Marla calls vengeful spirits of the dead who materialize just long enough to attack one creature he can see within 60 feet of him. The target must succeed on a DC 19 Constitution saving throw, taking 52 (15d6) necrotic damage on a failed save, or half as much damage on a success.

Siren

Medium fey, chaotic neutral

Armor Class 15 (natural armor)
Hit Points 49 (9d8 + 9)
Speed 30 ft., fly 60 ft.

STR	DEX	CON	INT	WIS	CHA
10 (+0)	18 (+4)	12 (+1)	13 (+1)	16 (+3)	19 (+4)

Skills Deception +8, Perception +8
Senses darkvision 60 ft., passive Perception 18

Languages Common, Elvish, Sylvan
Challenge 3 (700 XP)

Flyby. The siren doesn't provoke opportunity attacks when it flies out of an enemy's reach.

Innate Spellcasting. The siren 's innate spellcasting ability is Charisma (spell save DC 14, +6 to hit with spell attacks). It can innately cast the following spells 1/day each, requiring no material components: *charm person.fog cloud, greater invisibility, polymorph* (self only).

Luring Song. The siren sings a magical melody. Every humanoid and giant within 300 feet of the siren that can hear the song must succeed on a DC 12 Wisdom saving throw or be charmed until the song ends. The siren must take a bonus action on its subsequent turns to continue singing. It can stop singing at any time. The song ends if the siren is incapacitated.

While charmed by the siren, a target is incapacitated and ignores the songs of other sirens. If the charmed target is more than 5 feet away from the siren, the target must move on its turn toward the siren by the most direct route, trying to get within 5 feet. It doesn't avoid opportunity attacks, but before moving into damaging terrain, such as lava or a pit, and whenever it takes damage from a source other than the siren, the target can repeat the saving throw. A charmed target can also repeat the saving throw at the end of each of its turns. If the saving throw is successful, the effect ends on it.

A target that successfully saves is immune to this siren's song for the next 24 hours.

Magic Resistance. The siren has advantage on saving throws against spells and other magical effects.

ACTIONS

Multiattack. The siren makes two Talons attacks.

Talons. *Melee Weapon Attack:* +6 to hit, reach 5 ft., one target. *Hit:* 11 (2d6 + 4) piercing damage.

Skeletons

Azer Skeleton

Medium undead, lawful evil
Armor Class 14 (natural armor)
Hit Points 16 (3d8 + 3)
Speed 30 ft.

STR	DEX	CON	INT	WIS	CHA
15 (+2)	10 (+0)	13 (+1)	6 (−2)	8 (−1)	5 (−3)

Saving Throws Con +3
Damage Vulnerabilities bludgeoning
Damage Immunities fire, poison
Condition Immunities exhaustion, poisoned
Senses darkvision 60 ft., passive Perception 9
Languages understands Ignan but can't speak
Challenge 1 (200 XP)

Heated Body. A creature that touches the azer skeleton or hits it with a melee attack while within 5 feet of it takes 3 (1d6) fire damage.

Illumination. The azer skeleton sheds bright light in a 10-foot radius and dim light for an additional 10 feet.

Undead Nature. The azer skeleton doesn't require air, food, drink, or sleep.

ACTIONS

Magma Fist. *Melee Weapon Attack:* +4 to hit, reach 5 ft., one target. *Hit:* 5 (1d6 + 2) plus 3 (1d6) fire damage, and the target must succeed on a DC 12 Dexterity saving throw or be restrained by cooling magma. As an action the restrained target can make a DC 12 Strength check, breaking the cooled magma on a success. The magma can also be attacked and destroyed (AC 10; hp 5; vulnerability to cold damage; immunity to bludgeoning, poison, and psychic damage).

REACTIONS

Magma Body. When a creature the azer skeleton can see hits it with an attack, its magma-coated bones harden and it gains resistance to that type of damage, including the damage that triggered this reaction, until the end of its next turn.

Black Skeleton

Medium undead, chaotic evil
Armor Class 17 (chain shirt)
Hit Points 71 (13d8 + 13)
Speed 40 ft.

STR	DEX	CON	INT	WIS	CHA
11 (+0)	19 (+4)	13 (+1)	13 (+1)	10 (+0)	14 (+2)

Skills Perception +4, Stealth +6
Damage Vulnerabilities bludgeoning, radiant
Damage Resistances cold
Damage Immunities necrotic, poison
Condition Immunities exhaustion, poisoned
Senses darkvision 60 ft., passive Perception 14
Languages understands the languages it knew in life but can't speak
Challenge 4 (1,100 XP)

Shortsword Masters. Black skeletons gain defensive bonuses (+2 to AC) and bonuses to attack (+2 to hit) when wielding dual shortswords (included in the statistics).

ACTIONS

Multiattack. The black skeleton makes two claw attacks or two shortsword attacks.

Claw. *Melee Weapon Attack:* +6 to hit, reach 5 ft., one target. *Hit:* 8 (1d8 + 4) slashing damage, and the target's Strength score is reduced by 1d4. The target dies if this reduces its strength to 0. Otherwise, the reduction lasts until the target finishes a short or long rest.

Shortsword. *Melee Weapon Attack:* +8 to hit, reach 5 ft., one target. *Hit:* 11 (2d6 + 4) piercing damage, and the target's Strength score is reduced by 1d4. The target dies if this reduces its strength to 0. Otherwise, the reduction lasts until the target finishes a short or long rest

Efreeti Skeleton

Large undead, lawful evil
Armor Class 16 (natural armor)
Hit Points 95 (10d10 + 40)
Speed 30 ft., fly 30 ft.

STR	DEX	CON	INT	WIS	CHA
17 (+3)	10 (+0)	19 (+4)	8 (−1)	8 (−1)	14 (+2)

Saving Throws Wis +2, Cha +5
Damage Vulnerabilities bludgeoning

Damage Immunities fire, poison
Condition Immunities exhaustion, poisoned
Senses darkvision 120 ft., passive Perception 9
Languages understands Ignan but can't speak
Challenge 7 (2,900 XP)

Fiery Bones. The process that creates an efreet skeleton captures the creature's essence but leaves its body an unstable figure of burning bones. At the start of each of the efreet skeleton's turns, its unstable bones spark and crackle, and each creature within 5 feet of it takes 3 (1d6) fire damage.

Undead Nature. The efreet skeleton doesn't require air, food, drink, or sleep.

Actions

Multiattack. The efreet skeleton makes two Fiery Claws attacks or uses its Hurl Flame twice.

Fiery Claws. *Melee Weapon Attack:* +6 to hit, reach 5 ft., one target. *Hit:* 7 (1d6 + 4) slashing damage plus 7 (2d6) fire damage.

Hurl Flame. *Ranged Spell Attack:* +5 to hit, range 120 ft., one target. *Hit:* 14 (4d6) fire damage.

Dead, Not Fallen (recharge 5–6). The efreet skeleton raises its head haughtily, its crown of flames flaring. Each creature within 20 feet of the efreet skeleton must make a DC 15 Dexterity saving throw. On a failure, a creature takes 28 (8d6) fire damage and is knocked prone in supplication. On a success, a creature takes half the damage and isn't knocked prone.

Fire Giant Skeleton

Huge undead, lawful evil
Armor Class 16 (armor scraps)
Hit Points 136 (13d12 + 52)
Speed 30 ft.

STR	DEX	CON	INT	WIS	CHA
20 (+5)	9 (–1)	18 (+4)	6 (–2)	8 (–1)	5 (–3)

Saving Throws Dex +2, Cha +0
Skills Athletics +8, Perception +2
Damage Vulnerabilities bludgeoning
Damage Immunities fire, poison
Condition Immunities exhaustion, poisoned
Senses darkvision 60 ft., passive Perception 12
Languages understands Giant but can't speak
Challenge 8 (3,900 XP)

Reinforced Bones. A creature that damages the fire giant skeleton's metal bones with a metal weapon must succeed on a DC 15 Constitution saving throw or drop the weapon at its feet as the resulting vibration numbs the creature's limb.

Undead Nature. The fire giant skeleton doesn't require air, food, drink, or sleep.

Actions

Multiattack. The fire giant skeleton makes two Metal Claws attacks.

Metal Claws. *Melee Weapon Attack:* +8 to hit, reach 10 ft., one target. *Hit:* 15 (3d6 + 5) slashing damage plus 3 (1d6) fire damage.

Rock. *Ranged Weapon Attack:* +8 to hit, range 60/240 ft., one target. *Hit:* 21 (3d10 + 5) bludgeoning damage.

Super Heat (recharge 5–6). The forge magic powering the fire giant skeleton heats its metal bones to an orange glow. Each creature within 20 feet of the skeleton must make a DC 15 Constitution saving throw, taking 28 (8d6) fire damage on a failed save, or half as much damage on a successful one. A creature wearing heavy or medium metal armor instead takes 36 (8d8) fire damage on a failed save, or half as much damage on a successful one.

Janni Skeleton

Large undead, lawful evil
Armor Class 14
Hit Points 93 (11d10 + 33)
Speed 30 ft., fly 20 ft.

STR	DEX	CON	INT	WIS	CHA
15 (+2)	18 (+4)	17 (+3)	6 (–2)	8 (–1)	5 (–3)

Saving Throws Wis +2
Skills Perception +2
Damage Vulnerabilities bludgeoning
Damage Resistances acid, cold, fire, lightning, thunder
Damage Immunities poison
Condition Immunities exhaustion, poisoned
Senses darkvision 60 ft., passive Perception 12
Languages understands all languages in knew in life but can't speak
Challenge 5 (1,800 XP)

Elemental Instability. The process that creates a janni skeleton captures the creature's essence but leaves its body an unstable amalgam of the elements. At the start of each of the janni skeleton's turns, roll a d4. The janni skeleton's element that turn is either cold (1), fire (2), lightning (3), or thunder (4), depending on the result of the roll.

Undead Nature. The janni skeleton doesn't require air, food, drink, or sleep.

Actions

Multiattack. The janni skeleton makes two Elemental Claws attacks.

Elemental Claws. *Melee Weapon Attack:* +7 to hit, reach 5 ft., one target. *Hit:* 10 (3d6) damage of the janni skeleton's element type.

Elemental Explosion (recharge 5–6). The elemental material holding the janni's spirit in a skeletal form temporarily ruptures, sending out splinters of elemental bone. Each creature within 15 feet of the janni skeleton must make a DC 15 Dexterity saving throw, taking 9 (2d8) piercing damage and 14 (4d6) damage of the janni skeleton's element type on a failed save, or half as much damage on a successful one. The janni skeleton then disappears. It reforms at the start of its next turn in a space within 15 feet of where it exploded with 3 (1d6) fewer hit points.

Skeleton Warrior

Medium undead, neutral evil
Armor Class 19 (+2 *splint mail*)
Hit Points 97 (13d8 + 39)
Speed 30 ft.

STR	DEX	CON	INT	WIS	CHA
20 (+5)	13 (+1)	16 (+3)	10 (+0)	13 (+1)	14 (+2)

Saving Throws Con +8, Wis +6, Cha +7
Skills Insight +6, Intimidate +7, Perception +6
Damage Resistances piercing and slashing damage from nonmagical attacks

Crypt Fatigue

A creature infected with crypt fatigue gains one level of exhaustion immediately, and gains one more level every time it fails the DC 16 Constitution saving throw after taking damage from a skeleton warrior's longbow. An infected creature must make another DC 16 Constitution saving throw at the end of every long rest; with a successful save, it recovers one level of exhaustion, but with a failed save, it gains one level of exhaustion. The disease is cured when the victim no longer has any levels of exhaustion.

Skeleton Warrior's Circlet

In the process of transforming into a skeleton warrior, the dying warrior's soul is trapped in a golden circlet. Anyone possessing one of these circlets can exert control over the skeleton warrior whose soul the circlet contains. To establish control, the controller must be within 300 feet of the skeleton warrior, must wear the circlet, and must spend one full round doing nothing but concentrating on the skeleton warrior. If the controller is not interrupted during this time, resolve a Charisma (Intimidation) contest between the skeleton warrior and the creature with the circlet (note that the skeleton warrior adds its proficiency bonus to Intimidation skill checks). If the wearer of the circlet wins the contest, the skeleton warrior is charmed, views that character as an ally, and interprets any of the character's suggestions in the most positive light. It is not dominated or controlled, but it doesn't feel the urge to immediately kill the wearer of the circlet and recover its soul, either. It would like its soul back eventually, but it can wait until its new ally is slain by some other creature or dies naturally. If the skeleton warrior wins the contest, it is immune from attempts to use the circlet to charm it for 24 hours.

While within 300 feet of the charmed skeleton warrior, a person wearing the circlet can exert the following types of influence over the skeleton warrior. He or she can:

- choose to see through the skeleton warrior's eyes

- try to force the skeleton warrior to attack something by making a successful DC 15 Charisma check (failing the check means the skeleton warrior acts as it chooses)

- try to force the skeleton warrior to take some other action — search an area, move across a room, etc. — by making a successful DC 10 Charisma check (failing the check means the skeleton warrior acts as it chooses);

- try to place the skeleton warrior in "inert mode" by making a successful DC 15 Charisma check. If this check succeeds, the skeleton warrior stands motionless, effectively unconscious and paralyzed, until the wearer of the circlet wills it back into wakefulness. If this check fails, the skeletal warrior is no longer charmed.

While forcing the skeleton warrior to do anything, the circlet wearer can't move or take any other action. If the circlet wearer moves more than 300 feet away from the skeleton warrior or removes the circlet from his or her head while the skeleton warrior is active (not inert), the skeleton warrior is no longer charmed. If someone else becomes the circlet's owner, the skeleton warrior knows instantly; if it was charmed, it's not anymore, and if it was inert, it becomes active again.

If a skeleton warrior ever gains control of the circlet containing its soul, it places the circlet on its head and "dies," vanishing in a flash of light. The circlet falls to the ground and crumbles to dust.

Damage Immunities necrotic, poison
Condition Immunities exhaustion, frightened, poisoned, unconscious
Senses Truesight 60 ft., passive Perception 16
Languages Common, any other language the warrior knew in life
Challenge 14 (11,500 XP)

Legendary Resistance (3/day). If the skeleton warrior fails a saving throw, it can choose to succeed instead.
Track Circlet. A skeleton warrior can track and find its circlet unerringly. It can also find the last person who possessed the circlet.
Unholy Fortitude. Skeleton Warriors have advantage on saving throws against being turned.

Actions

Multiattack. A skeleton warrior makes two Greatsword attacks
+2 Greatsword. *Melee Weapon Attack:* +12 to hit, reach 5 ft., one creature. *Hit:* 14 (2d6 + 7) slashing damage plus 3 (1d6) necrotic damage.
Longbow. *Ranged Weapon Attack:* +6 to hit, range 150 ft./600 ft., one creature. *Hit:* 7 (1d12 + 1) piercing damage plus 7 (2d6) necrotic damage, and the target must make a successful DC 16 Constitution saving throw or be infected with crypt fatigue

Legendary Actions

The skeleton warrior can take up to three legendary actions per round. Legendary actions are taken at the end of another creature's turn, and only one can be taken after each turn.
Attack. The skeleton warrior makes a Greatsword or Longbow attack.
Drain Life. *Melee Weapon Attack:* +10 to hit, reach 5 ft.; one creature. *Hit:* the target must make a successful DC 16 Constitution saving throw or be infected with crypt fatigue. If already infected, a failed saving throw causes the creature to gain another level of exhaustion.
Instill Dread. One living creature within 50 feet of the skeleton warrior, which the skeleton warrior can see, must make a successful DC 15 Wisdom saving throw or be frightened for 2d4 rounds. A successful save renders the target immune to this skeleton warrior's dread for 24 hours.

Sleeping Willow

Huge plant, neutral evil
Armor Class 17 (natural armor)
Hit Points 114 (12d12 + 36)
Speed 10 ft.

STR	DEX	CON	INT	WIS	CHA
19 (+4)	5 (–3)	17 (+3)	6 (–2)	11 (+0)	10 (+0)

Skills Perception +4, Stealth +5 (+8 if not moving)
Damage Resistances bludgeoning, piercing
Damage Immunities poison
Damage Vulnerabilities fire
Condition Immunities blinded, charmed, deafened, frightened, paralyzed, poisoned, prone, stunned, unconscious
Senses blindsight 90 ft. (blind beyond this radius), passive Perception 14
Languages —
Challenge 10 (5,900 XP)

Health Drain. At the beginning of the sleeping willow's turn, all creatures already grappled by it are constricted and take 13 (2d8 + 4) bludgeoning damage and 5 (2d4) necrotic damage. The sleeping willow regains a number of hit points equal to the necrotic damage inflicted. The sleeping willow's number of Slam attacks in its Multiattack is reduced by one for each such grappled creature.

Sleep Spores. The sleeping willow emits a cloud of sleep-inducing spores in a 30-foot-radius, 10-foot-high cylinder around it. Each creature in this area must succeed on a DC 18 Constitution saving throw or fall asleep for 5 minutes or until the sleeper takes damage, or someone uses an action to shake or slap the sleeper awake.

ACTIONS

Multiattack. The sleeping willow makes up to four Slam attacks.

Slam. *Melee Weapon Attack:* +8 to hit, reach 15 ft., one target. *Hit:* 13 (2d8 + 4) bludgeoning damage and 5 (2d4) necrotic damage inflicted. The sleeping willow regains a number of hit points equal to the necrotic damage. If the target is Large or smaller, it is also grappled (escape DC 18).

Snakes

Cobalt Viper

Medium beast, unaligned
Armor Class 14 (natural armor)
Hit Points 32 (5d8 + 10)
Speed 20 ft., climb 20 ft.

STR	DEX	CON	INT	WIS	CHA
12 (+1)	17 (+3)	13 (+2)	3 (–4)	12 (+1)	10 (+0)

Skills Perception +3, Stealth +5
Senses darkvision 60 ft., passive Perception 13
Languages —
Challenge 1 (200 XP)

Keen Smell. The viper has advantage on Wisdom (Perception) checks that rely on smell.

Poison Aura. At the start of each of the viper's turns, if the viper is not incapacitated, each creature within 20 feet of it must succeed on a DC 12 Constitution saving throw or become poisoned for 1 minute. If a saving throw is successful, the creature is not affected by the viper's Poison Aura for 24 hours.

ACTIONS

Bite. *Melee Weapon Attack:* +5 to hit, reach 10 ft., one target. *Hit:* 6 (1d6 + 3) piercing damage, and the target must make a DC 12 Constitution saving throw, taking 10 (3d6) poison damage on a failed save, or half as much damage on a successful one.

Cobalt Viper, Giant

Large beast, unaligned
Armor Class 15 (natural armor)
Hit Points 75 (10d10 + 20)
Speed 20 ft., cllmb 20 ft.

STR	DEX	CON	INT	WIS	CHA
14 (+2)	18 (+4)	13 (+2)	3 (–4)	12 (+1)	10 (+0)

Skills Perception +3, Stealth +6
Senses darkvision 60 ft., passive Perception 13

Languages —
Challenge 2 (450 XP)

Keen Smell. The viper has advantage on Wisdom (Perception) checks that rely on smell.

Poison Aura. At the start of each of the viper's turns, if the viper is not incapacitated, each creature within 20 feet of it must make a DC 13 Constitution saving throw, taking 10 (3d6) poison damage on a failed save and becomes poisoned for 1 minute, or half as much damage on a successful one. If a saving throw is successful, the creature is not affected by the viper's Poison Aura for 24 hours.

ACTIONS

Bite. *Melee Weapon Attack:* +6 to hit, reach 10 ft., one target. *Hit:* 11 (2d6 + 4) piercing damage, and the target must make a DC 13 Constitution saving throw, taking 14 (4d6) poison damage on a failed save, or half as much damage on a successful one.

Viper, Giant Fiendish

Large beast, neutral evil
Armor Class 14
Hit Points 13 (2d10 + 2)
Speed 30 ft., swim 30 ft.

STR	DEX	CON	INT	WIS	CHA
10 (+0)	18 (+4)	13 (+1)	2 (–4)	10 (+0)	3 (–4)

Damage Resistances cold; bludgeoning, piercing, and slashing from nonmagical attacks not made with silver
Damage Immunities fire, poison
Condition Immunities poisoned

Skills Perception +2
Senses blindsight 10 ft., passive Perception 12
Languages —
Challenge 2 (450 XP)

Keen Smell. The viper has advantage on Wisdom (Perception) checks that rely on smell.

ACTIONS

Bite. *Melee Weapon Attack:* +6 to hit, reach 10 ft., one target. *Hit:* 6 (2d6 + 4) piercing damage, and the target must make a DC 13 Constitution saving throw, taking 10 (3d6) poison damage on a failed save, or half as much damage on a successful one.

Yellow Cobra, Giant Fiendish

Large beast, neutral evil
Armor Class 14 (natural armor)
Hit Points 13 (2d10 + 2)
Speed 30 ft., swim 30 ft.

STR	DEX	CON	INT	WIS	CHA
10 (+0)	18 (+4)	13 (+1)	2 (–4)	10 (+0)	3 (–4)

Damage Resistances cold; bludgeoning, piercing, and slashing from nonmagical attacks not made with silver
Damage Immunities fire, poison
Condition Immunities poisoned

Skills Perception +2
Senses blindsight 10 ft., passive Perception 12

Languages —
Challenge 2 (450 XP)

Keen Smell. The cobra has advantage on Wisdom (Perception) checks that rely on smell.

ACTIONS

Bite. *Melee Weapon Attack:* +6 to hit, reach 10 ft., one target. *Hit:* 6 (2d6 + 4) piercing damage, and the target must make a DC 13 Constitution saving throw, taking 10 (3d6) poison damage on a failed save, or half as much damage on a successful one.

Spit Poison. *Ranged Weapon Attack:* +6 to hit, range 15/30 ft., one creature. *Hit:* The target must make a DC 13 Dexterity saving throw, taking 10 (3d6) poison damage on a failed save and the target is blinded for 1 minute, or half as much damage on a successful one. If blinded, the target can repeat the save at the end of their turn, ending the condition on a successful save.

Specter, Advanced

Medium undead, chaotic evil
Armor Class 15
Hit Points 88 (16d8 + 16)
Speed 0 ft., fly 50 ft. (hover)

STR	DEX	CON	INT	WIS	CHA
1 (−5)	16 (+3)	13 (+1)	10 (+0)	10 (+0)	13 (+1)

Damage Resistances acid, cold, fire, lightning, thunder; bludgeoning, piercing, and slashing from nonmagical attacks
Damage Immunities necrotic, poison
Condition Immunities charmed, exhaustion, grappled, paralyzed, petrified, poisoned, prone, restrained, unconscious
Senses darkvision 60 ft., passive Perception 10
Languages the languages it knew in life
Challenge 7 (2,900 XP)

Incorporeal Movement. The advanced specter can move through other creatures and objects as if they were difficult terrain. It takes 5 (1d10) force damage if it ends its turn inside an object.

Sunlight Sensitivity. While in sunlight, the advanced specter has disadvantage on attack rolls as well as on Wisdom (Perception) checks that rely on sight.

ACTIONS

Multiattack. The advanced specter makes one Frightening Gaze attack and two Life Drain attacks.

Life Drain. *Melee Spell Attack:* +6 to hit, reach 5 ft., one creature. *Hit:* 24 (6d6 + 3) necrotic damage. The target must succeed on a DC 16 Constitution saving throw or its hit point maximum is reduced by an amount equal to the damage taken. This reduction lasts until the creature finishes a long rest. The target dies if this effect reduces its hit point maximum to 0.

Frightening Gaze. The advanced specter fixes its gaze on one creature it can see within 10 feet of it. The target must succeed on a DC 16 Wisdom saving throw against this magic or become frightened for 1 minute. The frightened target can repeat the saving throw at the end of each of its turns, ending the effect on itself on a success. If a target's saving throw is successful or the effect ends for it,

the target is immune to the advanced specter's gaze for the next 24 hours.

Create Specter. The advanced specter targets a humanoid within 10 feet of it that has been dead for no longer than 1 minute and died violently. The target's spirit rises as a specter in the space of its corpse or in the nearest unoccupied space. The specter is under the advanced specter's control. The advanced specter can have no more than seven specters under its control at one time.

Stone Maiden

Medium elemental, neutral
Armor Class 17
Hit Points 102 (12d8 + 48)
Speed 30 ft.

STR	DEX	CON	INT	WIS	CHA
18 (+4)	11 (+0)	18 (+4)	15 (+2)	16 (+3)	20 (+5)

Saving Throws Str +7, Con +7, Cha +8
Skills Perception +6, Persuasion +8
Damage Resistances cold, fire; bludgeoning, piercing, and slashing from nonmagical attacks
Damage Immunities necrotic, poison
Damage Vulnerabilities thunder
Condition Immunities exhaustion, paralyzed, petrified, poisoned, unconscious
Senses darkvision 60 ft., passive Perception 16
Languages Common, Terran
Challenge 8 (3,900 XP)

Earth Magic Immunity. The stone maiden is immune to any spell or magical effect that employs or manipulates earth or stone, including her own *spike growth* spell.

Earth Mastery. If both the stone maiden and a creature are standing on the ground, the creature suffers a −1 to its attack and damage rolls against the stone maiden and had disadvantage on grappling checks made against the stone maiden.

Innate Spellcasting. The stone maiden's innate spellcasting ability is Charisma (spell save DC 16, +8 to hit with spell attacks). She can innately cast the following spells, with no need for material components or concentration:

At will: *meld into stone, spike growth, stone shape*
2/day: *move earth, wall of stone*

ACTIONS

Multiattack. The stone maiden makes two Longsword or Slam attacks.

Longsword. *Melee Weapon Attack:* +7 to hit, reach 5 ft., one creature. *Hit:* 13 (2d8 + 4) slashing damage.

Slam. *Melee Weapon Attack:* +7 to hit, reach 5 ft., one creature. *Hit:* 11 (2d6 + 4) bludgeoning damage.

Animate Rocks (recharge 4–6). The stone maiden causes a pile of rocks she can see within 100 feet of her to animate into a humanoid shape. The rock form has statistics identical to the stone maiden, except it may only use Slam attacks. The rocks act under the control of the stone maiden, but do not require her concentration, and return to their lifeless state when reduced to 0 hit points or when they are more than 100 feet from the stone maiden.

Swarms

Choromos

Huge swarm of Medium fiends, neutral evil
Armor Class 18 (natural armor)
Hit Points 299 (26d12 + 130)
Speed 20 ft., fly 50 ft. (hover)

STR	DEX	CON	INT	WIS	CHA
14 (+2)	23 (+6)	20 (+5)	16 (+3)	19 (+4)	21 (+5)

Saving Throws Dex +13, Con +12, Int +10, Wis +11
Skills Perception +11, Performance +12
Damage Resistances bludgeoning, piercing, slashing
Damage Immunities poison
Condition Immunities charmed, frightened, paralyzed, petrified, poisoned, prone, restrained, stunned
Senses blindsight 60 ft. (blind beyond this radius), passive Perception 21
Languages Abyssal, Common, Infernal
Challenge 22 (41,000 XP)

Deranged Hum. At the start of each of the choromos' turns, each creature within 5 feet of it takes 10 (3d6) psychic damage. Fiends are immune to a choromos' Deranged Hum.

Magic Resistance. The choromos has advantage on saving throws against spells and other magical effects.

Magic Weapons. The choromos' weapon attacks are magical.

Swarm. The choromos can occupy another creature's space and vice versa, and the choromos can move through any opening large for a Medium fiend. The choromos can't regain hit points or gain temporary hit points.

Actions

Multiattack. The choromos makes three Poisoned Claw attacks or two Screech attacks.

Poisoned Claws. *Melee Weapon Attack:* +13 to hit, reach 0 ft., one creature in the swarm's space. *Hit:* 35 (10d6) slashing damage, or 17 (5d6) slashing damage if the swarm has half of its hit points or fewer. The target must make a DC 20 Constitution saving throw, taking 18 (4d8) poison damage on a failed save, or half as much damage on a successful one.

Screech. *Ranged Spell Attack:* +12 to hit, ranged 120 ft., one target. *Hit:* 45 (10d8) thunder damage and the target must succeed on a DC 20 Constitution saving throw or be incapacitated until the end of its next turn.

Maddening Cacophony (recharge 5–6). The choromos' many voices rumble into a maddening semblance of harmony. Each creature within 30 feet of the choromos that can hear it must make a DC 19 Wisdom saving throw. On a failure, a creature takes 70 (20d6) psychic damage and suffers one short-term madness. On a success, a creature takes half the damage and doesn't suffer a short-term madness.

Swarm of Eye Spiders

Medium swarm of Tiny constructs, unaligned
Armor Class 13
Hit Points 45 (10d8)
Speed 20 ft., climb 20 ft.

STR	DEX	CON	INT	WIS	CHA
13 (+1)	13 (+1)	10 (+0)	1 (–5)	9 (–1)	3 (–4)

Damage Resistances bludgeoning, piercing, and slashing
Damage Immunities lightning, poison; bludgeoning, piercing, and slashing from nonmagical attacks not made with adamantine
Condition Immunities charmed, exhaustion, frightened, paralyzed, petrified, poisoned, prone, restrained, stunned
Senses darkvision 60 ft., passive Perception 9
Languages understands the language of its creator but can't speak
Challenge 3 (700 XP)

Distraction. Any living creature that begins its turn with the swarm in its space must succeed on a DC 14 Constitution save or be frightened for 1 round.

Swarm. The swarm can occupy one or more other creatures' spaces and vice versa, and the swarm can move through an opening large enough for a Tiny eye spider. The swarm can't regain hit points or gain temporary hit points.

Actions

Slam. *Melee Weapon Attack:* +4 to hit, reach 0 ft., one creature in the swarm's space. *Hit:* 5 (1d8 + 1) bludgeoning damage or 3 (1d8 – 1) bludgeoning damage if the swarm has half of its hit points or fewer.

Bonus Actions

Mind Ruin. The swarm flashes and pulsates. Any creature caught within its space when it does so has its mind suddenly filled with thousands of tangled visual images composed of text, passages, and secrets that the eyes of the swarm have seen over the centuries. The creature must succeed on a DC 14 Wisdom saving throw or be confused, as if by a *confusion* spell. If the target fails three consecutive saving throws, the condition is permanent until cured by a *greater restoration* or other magic.

Swarm of Hellwasps

Large swarm of Tiny fiends, lawful evil
Armor Class 15
Hit Points 90 (12d10 + 24)
Speed 5 ft., fly 40 ft.

STR	DEX	CON	INT	WIS	CHA
12 (+1)	20 (+5)	14 (+2)	5 (–3)	11 (+0)	3 (–4)

Damage Resistances bludgeoning, piercing, and slashing
Damage Immunities fire, poison
Condition Immunities charmed, frightened, paralyzed, petrified, poisoned, prone, restrained, stunned
Senses darkvision 60 ft., passive Perception 10
Languages understands Infernal but can't speak
Challenge 3 (700 XP)

Swarm. The swarm can occupy one or more other creatures' spaces and vice versa, and the swarm can move through an opening large enough for a Tiny hellwasp. The swarm can't regain hit points or gain temporary hit points.

ACTIONS

Multiattack. The swarm makes two Stings attacks.

Stings. *Melee Weapon Attack:* +7 to hit, reach 0 ft., one creature in the swarm's space. *Hit:* 12 (2d6 + 5) piercing damage, or 6 (1d6 + 3) piercing damage if the swarm has half of its hit points or fewer. The target must make a DC 15 Constitution saving throw. On a failed save, it takes 21 (6d6) poison damage and is poisoned until the end of its next turn. On a successful saving throw, it takes half as much poison damage and is not poisoned.

Inhabit. The swarm enters the body of a dead or incapacitated creature of size Small, Medium, or Large. If the creature was dead, it becomes a zombie of the appropriate variety with full hit points under the control of the swarm. If the creature is alive, it must succeed on a DC 16 Constitution saving throw or the swarm takes complete control of its body. The swarm may cause the creature to take any of its normal actions, except spellcasting. Damage done to an inhabited creature is split evenly between the creature and the swarm. When a creature begins its turn inhabited by the swarm, it takes 7 (2d6) necrotic damage. An inhabited creature may repeat its saving throw at the end of each of its turns, expelling the swarm from its body and ending the swarm's control over it on a success. A living inhabited creature which dies from the swarm's necrotic damage becomes a zombie of the appropriate variety with full points under the control of the swarm. Casting *greater restoration* or *heal* on a living inhabited creature expels the swarm.

Swarm of Mechanical Birds

Medium swarm of Tiny constructs, unaligned
Armor Class 16 (natural armor)
Hit Points 33 (6d8 + 6)
Speed 10 ft., fly 60 ft.

STR	DEX	CON	INT	WIS	CHA
1 (−5)	21 (+5)	12 (+1)	1 (−5)	10 (+0)	6 (−2)

Skills Perception +4, Stealth +9
Damage Vulnerabilities bludgeoning
Damage Resistances piercing, slashing
Damage Immunities poison
Condition Immunities charmed, frightened, grappled, paralyzed, petrified, poisoned, prone, restrained, stunned
Senses darkvision 60 ft., passive Perception 14
Languages —
Challenge 2 (450 XP)

Swarm. The mechanical bird swarm can occupy another creature's space and vice versa, and the swarm can move through any opening large enough for a Tiny creature. The swarm can't regain hit points or gain temporary hit points.

ACTIONS

Pierce. *Melee Weapon Attack:* +7 to hit, reach 5 ft., one creature. *Hit:* 8 (1d6 + 5) piercing damage. On a critical hit, the target must succeed on a DC 14 Dexterity saving throw or lose an eye, if it has one.

Swarm of Mosquitoes

Medium swarm of Tiny insects, unaligned
Armor Class 15 (natural armor)
Hit Points 58 (13d8)
Speed 10 ft., fly 40 ft.

STR	DEX	CON	INT	WIS	CHA
3 (−4)	19 (+4)	10 (+0)	1 (−5)	12 (+1)	6 (−2)

Skills Perception +7
Damage Resistances bludgeoning, piercing, slashing
Condition Immunities charmed, frightened, grappled, paralyzed, petrified, prone, restrained, stunned
Senses darkvision 60 ft., passive Perception 17
Languages —
Challenge 5 (1,800 XP)

Swarm. The mosquito swarm can occupy another creature's space and vice versa, and the swarm can move through any opening large enough for a Tiny creature. The swarm can't regain hit points or gain temporary hit points.

ACTIONS

Blood Drain. *Melee Weapon Attack:* +7 to hit, reach 5 ft., one creature. *Hit:* 19 (6d4 + 4) piercing damage, and the some mosquitoes attache to the target. While attached, the mosquitoes don't attack. Instead, at the start of each of the mosquito's turns, the target loses 19 (6d4 + 4) hit points due to blood loss.
The mosquito swarm can detach itself by spending 5 feet of its movement. It does so after it drains 10 hit points of blood from the target or the target dies. A creature, including the target, can use its action to detach the mosquito swarm.

Piranha School, Large

Large swarm of Tiny beasts, unaligned
Armor Class 12
Hit Points 72 (16d10 − 16)
Speed 0 ft., swim 50 ft.

STR	DEX	CON	INT	WIS	CHA
11 (+0)	15 (+2)	9 (−1)	1 (−5)	8 (−1)	3 (−4)

Damage Resistances bludgeoning, piercing, and slashing
Condition Immunities charmed, frightened, paralyzed, petrified, prone, restrained, stunned
Senses darkvision 60 ft., passive Perception 9
Languages —
Challenge 4 (1,100 XP)

Feeding Frenzy. The swarm has advantage on attack rolls against creatures that do not have all their hit points as a result of having taken piercing or slashing damage (including from the swarm itself).

Swarm. The swarm can occupy one or more other creatures' spaces and vice versa, and the swarm can move through an opening large enough for a Tiny piranha. The swarm can't regain hit points or gain temporary hit points. While the swarm occupies the space of a Large or larger creature, the swarm has from cover. Weapon attacks directed at the swarm which miss, but which would have hit without the bonus from cover, instead hit the creature sharing the space.

Water Breathing. The swarm can only breathe underwater.

ACTIONS

Multiattack. The swarm makes up to three Bite attacks, each on a different target.

Bite. *Melee Weapon Attack:* +4 to hit, reach 0 ft., one creature in the swarm's space. *Hit:* 12 (4d4 + 2) piercing damage or 7 (2d4 + 2) piercing damage if the swarm has half of its hit points or fewer.

Piranha School, Medium

Medium swarm of Tiny beasts, unaligned
Armor Class 12
Hit Points 28 (8d8 – 8)
Speed 0 ft., swim 50 ft.

STR	DEX	CON	INT	WIS	CHA
11 (+0)	15 (+2)	9 (–1)	1 (–5)	8 (–1)	3 (–4)

Damage Resistances bludgeoning, piercing, and slashing
Condition Immunities charmed, frightened, paralyzed, petrified, prone, restrained, stunned
Senses darkvision 60 ft., passive Perception 9
Languages —
Challenge 1 (200 XP)

Feeding Frenzy. The swarm has advantage on attack rolls against creatures that do not have all their hit points as a result of having taken piercing or slashing damage (including from the swarm itself).

Swarm. The swarm can occupy one or more other creatures' spaces and vice versa, and the swarm can move through an opening large enough for a Tiny piranha. The swarm can't regain hit points or gain temporary hit points. While the swarm occupies the space of a Medium or larger creature, the swarm has half cover. Weapon attacks directed at the swarm which miss, but which would have hit without the bonus from cover, instead hit the creature sharing the space.

Water Breathing. The swarm can only breathe underwater.

ACTIONS

Bite. *Melee Weapon Attack:* +4 to hit, reach 0 ft., one creature in the swarm's space. *Hit:* 12 (4d4 + 2) piercing damage or 7 (2d4 + 2) piercing damage if the swarm has half of its hit points or fewer.

Thessal-Titan

Gargantuan celestial (titan), chaotic evil
Armor Class 25 (natural armor, +2 scale mail armor)
Hit Points 738 (36d20 + 360)
Speed 50 ft.

STR	DEX	CON	INT	WIS	CHA
30 (+10)	10 (+0)	30 (+10)	20 (+5)	22 (+6)	8 (–1)

Saving Throws Str +19, Con +19
Skills Perception +15
Damage Immunities acid, poison; bludgeoning, piercing, and slashing from nonmagical attacks
Condition Immunities blinded, charmed, frightened, poisoned, prone
Senses truesight 120 ft., passive Perception 25
Languages all, telepathy 300 ft.
Challenge 30 (155,000 XP)

Innate Spellcasting. The thessal-titan's spellcasting ability is Wisdom (spell save DC 23, +15 to hit with spell attacks). It can innately cast the following spells, requiring no material components:

At will: *bestow curse, dispel magic, dominate person, levitate*
3/day: *chain lightning, hold monster* (as 7th level slot)
1/day: *arcane hand* (as 7th level slot), *dominate monster, freedom of movement, planar ally, meteor swarm*

Multiple Heads. The thessal-titan has seven heads. While it has more than one head, the thessal-titan has advantage on saving throws against being blinded, charmed, deafened, frightened, stunned, and knocked unconscious.

Whenever the thessal-titan takes 90 or more damage in a single turn, one of its heads is severed and dies. When one of its heads dies, the wound heals immediately and the thessal-titan regains 40 hit points. If all its heads die, the thessal-titan dies.

Reactive Heads. For each head the thessal-titan has beyond one, it gets an extra reaction that can be used only for opportunity attacks.

Regeneration. The thessal-titan regains 10 hit points at the start of its turn. The thessal-titan dies if it is reduced to 0 hit points, and this ability does not function.

Trampling Charge. If the thessal-titan moves at least 40 feet straight toward a target and then hits it with a Slam attack on the same turn, that target must succeed on a DC 24 Strength saving throw or be knocked prone. If the target is prone, the thessal-titan can make one Stomp attack against it as a bonus action.

Wakeful. While the thessal-titan sleeps, at least one of its heads is awake.

ACTIONS

Multiattack. The thessal-titan makes one Stomp attack, four Slam attacks, and as many Bite attacks as it has heads. It may substitute one Acid Spit attack for one Bite attack.

Bite. *Melee Weapon Attack:* +19 to hit, reach 10 ft., one target. *Hit:* 15 (1d10 + 10) piercing damage plus 7 (2d6) acid damage.

Slam. *Melee Weapon Attack:* +19 to hit, reach 15 ft., one target. *Hit:* 23 (3d8 + 10) bludgeoning damage.

Acid Spit. The thessal-titan spits a stream of acid at a single target within 60 feet of it. If the target is a creature, it must make a DC 20 Dexterity saving throw, taking 35 (10d6) acid damage on a failed save or half as much on a successful one.

Stomp. *Melee Weapon Attack:* +18 to hit, reach 10 ft., one target. *Hit:* 32 (4d10 + 10) bludgeoning damage, and all creatures within 20 feet of the thessal-titan must succeed on a DC 20 Dexterity saving throw or be knocked prone as the thessal-titan causes the ground to heave.

Thunderheel Anger

Large monstrosity, lawful evil
Armor Class 18 (natural armor, *bracers of greater defense*[2])
Hit Points 212 (25d10 + 75)
Speed 40 ft.

STR	DEX	CON	INT	WIS	CHA
18 (+4)	11 (+0)	16 (+3)	14 (+2)	16 (+3)	20 (+5)

Saving Throws Con +9, Wis +9, Cha +11
Skills Arcana +8, History +8, Perception +15
Damage Immunities fire
Senses darkvision 60 ft., passive Perception 25

Languages Abyssal, Ignan, Common
Challenge 17 (18,000 XP)

Special Equipment. Thunderheel wears a *ring of immunity* (fire) as well as a set of *bracers of greater defense*[2], and carries a *staff of fire*.

Charge. If the minotaur moves at least 10 feet straight toward a target and then hits it with a gore attack on the same turn, the target takes an extra 9 (2d8) piercing damage. If the target is a creature, it must succeed on a DC 14 Strength saving throw or be pushed up to 10 feet away and knocked prone.

Distant Spell (3/day). When Thunderheel casts a spell that has a range of 5 feet or greater, he can double the range of the spell. Alternatively, if he casts a spell that has a range of touch, he can make the range of the spell 30 feet.

Heightened Spell (3/day). When Thunderheel casts a spell that forces a creature to make a saving throw to resist its effects, he can give one target of the spell disadvantage on its first saving throw made against the spell.

Labyrinthine Recall. The minotaur can perfectly recall any path it has traveled.

Reckless. At the start of its turn, the minotaur can gain advantage on all melee weapon attack rolls it makes during that turn, but attack rolls against it have advantage until the start of its next turn.

Spellcasting. Thunderheel is a 16th-level spellcaster. His spellcasting ability is Charisma (spell save DC 19, +11 to hit with spell attacks). He knows the following sorcerer spells.

Cantrips (at will): *acid splash, chill touch, mage hand, prestidigitation, ray of frost, shocking grasp*
1st level (4 slots): *detect magic, magic missile, shield, thunderwave*
2nd level (3 slots): *hold person, misty step*
3rd level (3 slots): *dispel magic, fireball*
4th level (3 slots): *stoneskin, wall of fire*
5th level (2 slots): *telekinesis*
6th level (1 slot): *chain lightning*
7th level (1 slot): *prismatic spray*
8th level (1 slot): *incendiary cloud*

Gore. *Melee Weapon Attack:* +10 to hit, reach 5 ft., one target. *Hit:* 13 (2d8 + 4) piercing damage.

Tiger, Dire

Large beast, unaligned
Armor Class 18 (natural armor)
Hit Points 135 (18d10 + 36)
Speed 40 ft.

STR	DEX	CON	INT	WIS	CHA
20 (+5)	16 (+3)	15 (+2)	3 (−4)	12 (+1)	8 (−1)

Skills Perception +4, Stealth +9
Senses passive Perception 14
Languages —
Challenge 8 (3,900 XP)

Improved Critical. The tiger's Bite attack scores a critical hit on a roll of 19 or 20.

Keen Smell. The tiger has advantage on Wisdom (Perception) checks that rely on smell.

Pounce. If the tiger moves at least 20 feet straight toward a creature and then hits it with a Claw attack on the same turn, that target must succeed on a DC 16 Strength saving throw or be knocked prone. If the target is prone, the tiger can make one Bite attack against it as a bonus

action.

ACTIONS

Multiattack. The tiger makes one Bite attack and one Claw attack.

Bite. *Melee Weapon Attack:* +8 to hit, reach 5 ft., one target. *Hit:* 21 (3d10 + 5) piercing damage.

Claw. *Melee Weapon Attack:* +8 to hit, reach 5 ft., one target. *Hit:* 15 (3d6 + 5) slashing damage.

Tiger, Dire Fiendish

Large beast, neutral evil
Armor Class 18 (natural armor)
Hit Points 120 (16d10 + 32)
Speed 40 ft.

STR	DEX	CON	INT	WIS	CHA
20 (+5)	16 (+3)	15 (+2)	3 (−4)	12 (+1)	8 (−1)

Skills Perception +5, Stealth +11
Damage Resistances cold; bludgeoning, piercing, and slashing from nonmagical attacks not made with silver
Damage Immunities fire, poison
Condition Immunities poisoned
Senses passive Perception 15
Languages —
Challenge 10 (5,900 XP)

Keen Smell. The tiger has advantage on Wisdom (Perception) checks that rely on smell.

Pounce. If the tiger moves at least 20 feet straight toward a creature or attacks a creature with advantage and then hits it with a Claw attack on the same turn or attack, that target must succeed on a DC 16 Strength saving throw or be knocked prone. If the target is prone, the tiger can make one Bite attack against it as a bonus action.

ACTIONS

Multiattack. The tiger makes one Bite attack and one Claw attack.

Bite. *Melee Weapon Attack:* +9 to hit, reach 5 ft., one target. *Hit:* 21 (3d10 + 5) piercing damage.

Claw. *Melee Weapon Attack:* +9 to hit, reach 5 ft., one target. *Hit:* 16 (3d6 + 5) slashing damage.

Tusk Lord

Gargantuan monstrosity, neutral
Armor Class 20
Hit Points 444 (24d20 + 192)
Speed 30 ft.

STR	DEX	CON	INT	WIS	CHA
30 (+10)	13 (+1)	27 (+8)	17 (+3)	22 (+6)	16 (+3)

Saving Throws Str +16, Con +14, Wis +12, Cha +9
Skills Arcana +9, History +9, Nature +9, Perception +12, Religion +9
Damage Resistances bludgeoning, piercing, and slashing from nonmagical attacks
Damage Immunities acid, cold, fire, lightning, poison, thunder
Condition Immunities charmed, frightened, poisoned
Senses darkvision 120 ft., passive Perception 22
Languages understands all but speaks only Tusk Lord
Challenge 19 (22,000 XP)

Immortal. The tusk lord does not need to breathe, eat, or sleep. It will not die of old age but may still be killed.

Improved Sense of Smell. The tusk lord has advantage on Perception checks that rely on scent.

Innate Spellcasting. The tusk lord's innate spellcasting ability is Wisdom (spell save DC 20, +12 to hit with spell attacks). It can innately cast the following spells, 2/day each, with no need for material components or concentration: *antimagic field, etherealness, globe of invulnerability*

Sealed Mind. The tusk lord is immune to mind-altering magic such as charm, compulsion, fear, illusion, or sleep.

Wish Granting. At its discretion, the tusk lord may grant the wish of a creature (as the *wish* spell). The tusk lord will only do this if presented with a pleasing whale song. Magical reproductions of such a noise automatically qualify; otherwise a creature must succeed on a DC 20 Charisma (Performance) check to create a reasonable facsimile by mundane means. The tusk lord may only grant one wish per creature.

ACTIONS

Multiattack. The tusk lord makes one Gore attack and two Stomp attacks.

Gore. *Melee Weapon Attack:* +16 to hit, reach 15 ft., one creature. *Hit:* 37 (6d8 + 10) piercing damage.

Stomp. *Melee Weapon Attack:* +16 to hit, reach 15 ft., one creature. *Hit:* 32 (4d10 + 10) bludgeoning damage, and the target must succeed on a DC 20 Strength saving throw or be knocked prone.

Vampiric Treant

Huge plant, chaotic evil
Armor Class 16 (natural armor)
Hit Points 212 (17d12 + 102)
Speed 30 ft.

STR	DEX	CON	INT	WIS	CHA
23 (+6)	12 (+1)	22 (+6)	12 (+1)	16 (+3)	14 (+2)

Saving Throws Dex +7, Wis +9, Cha +8
Skills Perception +9, Stealth +7
Damage Resistances bludgeoning, cold, lightning, necrotic, piercing; slashing from nonmagical attacks
Damage Immunities poison
Damage Vulnerabilities fire
Condition Immunities poisoned
Senses darkvision 120 ft., passive Perception 19
Languages Common, Druidic, Elvish, Sylvan
Challenge 17 (18,000 XP)

False Appearance. While the vampiric treant remains motionless, it is indistinguishable from a normal tree.

Legendary Resistance (3/day). If the vampiric treant fails a saving throw, it can choose to succeed instead.

Regeneration. The vampiric treant regains 20 hit points at the start of its turn if it has at least 1 hit point and didn't take fire damage since its last turn.

Siege Monster. The vampiric treant deals double damage to objects and structures.

ACTIONS

Multiattack. The vampiric treant makes two attacks, only one of which may be a Charm attack.

Slam. *Melee Weapon Attack:* +12 to hit, reach 5 ft., one target. *Hit:* 16 (3d6 + 6) bludgeoning damage plus 10 (3d6) necrotic damage. If the target is a creature, the target's hit point maximum is reduced by an amount equal to the necrotic damage taken, and the vampiric treant regains hit points equal to that amount. The reduction lasts until the target completes a long rest.

Rock. *Ranged Weapon Attack:* +12 to hit, range 60/180 ft., one target. *Hit:* 28 (4d10 + 6) bludgeoning damage.

Charm. The vampiric treant targets one humanoid it can see within 30 feet of it. If the target can see the vampiric treant, the target must succeed on a DC 17 Wisdom saving throw against this magic or be charmed by the vampiric treant. The charmed target regards the vampiric treant as a trusted friend to be heeded and protected. Although the target isn't under the vampiric treant's control, it takes the vampiric treant's requests or actions in the most favorable way it can. Each time the vampiric treant or the vampiric treant's companions do anything harmful to the target, it can repeat the saving throw, ending the effect on itself on a success. Otherwise, the effect lasts 24 hours or until the vampiric treant is destroyed, is on a different plane of existence than the target, or takes a bonus action to end the effect.

Animate Trees (1/day). The vampiric treant magically animates one or two trees it can see within 60 feet of it. These trees have the same statistics as a treant, except they have Intelligence and Charisma scores of 1, they can't speak, and they have only the Slam action option. An animated tree acts as an ally of the vampiric treant. The tree remains animate for 1 day or until it dies; until the vampiric treant dies or is more than 120 feet from the tree; or until the vampiric treant takes a bonus action to turn it back into an inanimate tree. The tree then takes root if possible.

Children of the Vine (1/day). The vampiric treant magically calls 4d6 awakened shrubs. The called creatures arrive in 1d4 rounds, acting as allies of the vampiric treant and obeying its spoken commands. The creatures remain for 1 hour, until the vampiric treant dies, or until the vampiric treant dismisses them as a bonus action.

LEGENDARY ACTIONS

The vampiric treant can take 3 legendary actions, choosing from the options below. Only one legendary action option can be used at a time and only at the end of another creature's turn. The vampiric treant regains spent legendary actions at the start of its turn.

Move. The vampiric treant moves up to its speed without provoking opportunity attacks.

Slam. The vampiric treant makes one Slam attack.

Rock. The vampiric treant makes one Rock attack.

Entangle. The vampiric casts an *entangle* spell (spell save DC 17) without the need for material components or concentration.

Volt (Bolt Wurm)

Small aberration, unaligned
Armor Class 13
Hit Points 13 (3d6 + 3)
Speed fly 30 ft.

STR	DEX	CON	INT	WIS	CHA
10 (+0)	16 (+3)	12 (+1)	2 (–4)	10 (+0)	6 (–2)

Damage Immunities lightning
Skills Acrobatics +5
Senses darkvision 60 ft.
Languages —
Challenge 1/4 (50 XP)

ACTIONS

Bite. *Melee Weapon Attack:* +5 to hit, reach 5 ft., one creature. *Hit:* 5 (1d6 + 2) piercing damage and the volt enters the target's space and grapples the target (escape DC 13). The volt can't move a creature it grapples, but it moves with the grappled creature. If the grapple is broken, the volt immediately moves 5 feet into an adjacent, empty space. The volt can't use its bite attack while it is grappling a creature.

Lightning Jolt. A creature that is grappled by the volt at the start of the volt's turn takes 5 (1d6 + 2) lightning damage. A creature reduced to 0 hit points by this attack is unconscious and stable, not dying.

Voltar

Medium elemental, neutral
Armor Class 14 (natural armor)
Hit Points 65 (10d8 + 20)
Speed 30 ft.

STR	DEX	CON	INT	WIS	CHA
18 (+4)	15 (+2)	14 (+2)	10 (+0)	12 (+1)	16 (+3)

Skills Arcana +2, Perception +3, Stealth +4
Damage Vulnerabilities cold
Damage Resistances bludgeoning, piercing, and slashing from nonmagical attacks
Damage Immunities lightning, poison, thunder
Senses darkvision 60 ft., passive Perception 13
Languages Auran
Challenge 4 (1,100 XP)

Death Burst. When the voltar dies, it explodes in a blinding flash of lightning. Each creature within 10 feet of it must make a DC 14 Dexterity saving throw. On a failure, a creature takes 14 (4d6) lightning damage and is blinded for 1 minute. On a success, a creature takes half the damage and isn't blinded. A blinded creature can repeat the saving throw at the end of each of its turns, ending the effect on itself on a success.

Elemental Nature. The voltar doesn't require air, food, drink, or sleep.

Lightning Weapons. When the voltar hits with any weapon, the weapon deals an extra 1d6 lightning damage (included in the attack).

ACTIONS

Multiattack. The voltar makes two Longsword attacks.

Longsword. *Melee Weapon Attack:* +6 to hit, reach 5 ft., one target. *Hit:* 8 (1d8 + 4) slashing damage, or 9 (1d10 + 4) slashing damage if used with two hands, plus 3 (1d6) lightning damage.

Lightning Bolt. *Ranged Spell Attack:* +5 to hit, range 120 ft., one target. *Hit:* 10 (3d6) lightning damage.

Water Weird

Large elemental, chaotic evil
Armor Class 14 (natural armor)
Hit Points 90 (12d10 + 24)
Speed 30 ft., swim 90 ft.

STR	DEX	CON	INT	WIS	CHA
17 (+3)	14 (+2)	14 (+2)	11 (+0)	14 (+2)	10 (+0)

Skills Perception +6, Stealth +6
Damage Resistances fire; bludgeoning, piercing, and slashing from nonmagical attacks
Damage Immunities poison
Condition Immunities exhaustion, grappled, paralyzed, poisoned, restrained, prone, unconscious
Senses darkvision 60 ft., passive Perception 16
Languages Aquan
Challenge 4 (1,100 XP)

Ambusher. In the first round of a combat, the water weird has advantage on attack rolls against any creature it has surprised.

Surprise Attack. If the water weird surprises a creature and hits it with an attack during the first round of combat, the target takes an extra 14 (4d6) damage from the attack.

Water Invisibility. The water weird is completely invisible while fully submerged in water.

Water Bound. If the pool to which it is bound is destroyed, or the water weird leaves the pool, it dies.

ACTIONS

Multiattack. The water weird makes one Slam attack and one Constrict attack.

Slam. *Melee Weapon Attack:* +5 to hit, reach 5 ft., one target. *Hit:* 10 (2d6 + 3) bludgeoning damage.

Constrict. *Melee Weapon Attack:* +5 to hit, reach 15 ft., one target. *Hit:* 13 (3d6 + 3) bludgeoning damage. If the target is Medium or smaller, it is grappled (escape DC 14) and pulled 10 feet toward the water weird. Until this grapple ends, the target is restrained, the water weird tries to drown it, and the water weird can't constrict another target.

Wind Walker

Wind Walkers use the statistics of an **air elemental**, except for the following changes:

- Its Challenge Rating is 7 (2,900 XP).

- It has telepathy out to 120 feet, and the following new traits:

  Innate Spellcasting. The wind walker's innate spellcasting ability is Constitution (spell save DC 13). It can cast the following spell without material components.
  At will: *detect thoughts, gust of wind*

  Magic Resistance. The wind walker has advantage on saving throws against spells and other magical effects.

  Magic Weapons. The wind walker's weapon attacks are considered magical.

Witch Tree

Huge plant, chaotic evil
Armor Class 16 (natural armor)
Hit Points 94 (9d12 + 36)
Speed 20 ft.

STR	DEX	CON	INT	WIS	CHA
21 (+5)	10 (+0)	19 (+4)	7 (–2)	12 (+1)	16 (+3)

Skills Perception +4
Damage Vulnerabilities fire
Damage Resistances cold; bludgeoning, piercing, and slashing from nonmagical attacks
Damage Immunities acid
Condition Immunities charmed, exhaustion, frightened
Senses darkvision 60 ft., tremorsense 60 ft., passive Perception 14
Languages Abyssal, Common, Goblin, Sylvan
Challenge 8 (3,900 XP)

False Appearance. As long as the witch tree remains motionless, it is indistinguishable from a normal willow tree.

Innate Spellcasting. The witch tree's innate spellcasting ability is Constitution (spell save DC 14). It can cast the following spells, requiring no material components.

5/day: *enthrall*
1/day: *dominate monster*

Tendrils. The witch tree's tendrils can be cut, have an AC of 15, 10 hit points, immunity to poison and psychic damage, and the witch tree's damage vulnerabilities, resistances, and other immunities. Cutting a creature free of the tendrils deals no damage to the witch tree. The tendrils can also be broken if a creature takes an action and succeeds on a DC 17 Strength check.

Actions

Multiattack. The witch tree uses its Constrict ability and makes four Tendril attacks.

Tendril. *Melee Weapon Attack:* +8 to hit, reach 15 ft., one target. *Hit:* 15 (3d6 + 5) bludgeoning damage and the target is grappled (escape DC 16). A grappled creature is restrained.

Constrict. All grappled creatures must make a DC 16 Constitution saving throw, taking 15 (3d6 + 5) bludgeoning damage, or half as much damage on a successful saving throw.

Woods Ape

Medium monstrosity, unaligned
Armor Class 11 (16 with *barkskin*)
Hit Points 82 (11d8 + 33)
Speed 30 ft., climb 30 ft.

STR	DEX	CON	INT	WIS	CHA
17 (+3)	13 (+1)	16 (+3)	11 (+0)	18 (+4)	7 (−2)

Skills Nature +6, Perception +7, Stealth +4 (+7 in forested terrain), Survival +10
Damage Immunities poison
Condition Immunities poisoned
Senses darkvision 60 ft., passive Perception 17
Languages Druidic
Challenge 5 (1,800 XP)

Land's Stride. The woods ape can move through nonmagical difficult terrain without using extra movement and can pass through nonmagical plants without being slowed by them and without taking damage if they have thorns, spines, or a similar hazard. In addition, the woods ape has advantage on saving throws against plants that are magically created or manipulated to impede movement.

Innate Spellcasting. The woods ape's innate spellcasting ability is Wisdom (spell save DC 15, +7 to hit with spell attacks). It can cast the following spells, requiring no material components:

At will: *guidance, mending, create or destroy water, detect poison and disease, entangle, speak with animals, speak with plants, tree stride*
3/day each: *animal messenger, barkskin, call lightning, locate animals or plants, pass without trace*
1/day each: *awaken, commune with nature, conjure animals, plant growth*

Multiattack. The woods ape makes two claw attacks.
Claw. *Melee Weapon Attack:* +6 to hit, reach 5 ft., one target. *Hit:* 10 (2d6 + 3) slashing damage.

Woods Ape, Advanced

Medium monstrosity, unaligned
Armor Class 12 (16 with *barkskin*)
Hit Points 112 (15d8 + 45)
Speed 30 ft., climb 30 ft.

STR	DEX	CON	INT	WIS	CHA
17 (+3)	14 (+2)	16 (+3)	12 (+1)	20 (+5)	7 (−2)

Saving Throws Int +4, Wis +8
Skills Nature +7, Perception +8, Stealth +5 (+8 in forested terrain), Survival +11
Damage Immunities poison
Condition Immunities poisoned
Senses darkvision 60 ft., passive Perception 18
Languages Druidic
Challenge 7 (2,900 XP)

Land's Stride. The woods ape can move through nonmagical difficult terrain without using extra movement and can pass through nonmagical plants without being slowed by them and without taking damage if they have thorns, spines, or a similar hazard. In addition, the woods ape has advantage on saving throws against plants that are magically created or manipulated to impede movement.

Innate Spellcasting. The woods ape's innate spellcasting ability is Wisdom (spell save DC 16, +8 to hit with spell attacks). It can cast the following spells, requiring no material components:

At will: *animal messenger, create or destroy water, barkskin, detect poison and disease, entangle, guidance, hunter's mark, mending, speak with animals, speak with plants, tree stride*
3/day each: *call lightning, conjure animals, conjure woodland beings, cure wounds, lightning bolt, locate animals or plants, pass without trace*
1/day each: *awaken, commune with nature, conjure fey, dominate beast, plant growth*

Multiattack. The woods ape makes two Claw attacks.
Claw. *Melee Weapon Attack:* +6 to hit, reach 5 ft., one target. *Hit:* 10 (2d6 + 3) slashing damage.

Woods Ape Druid

Medium monstrosity, unaligned
Armor Class 11 (16 with *barkskin*)
Hit Points 172 (23d8 + 69)
Speed 30 ft., climb 30 ft.

STR	DEX	CON	INT	WIS	CHA
17 (+3)	13 (+1)	16 (+3)	11 (+0)	20 (+5)	7 (−2)

Saving Throws Int +4, Wis +9
Skills Medicine +9, Nature +4, Perception +9, Stealth +5 (+9 in forested terrain), Survival +13
Damage Immunities poison
Condition Immunities charmed, frightened, poisoned
Senses darkvision 60 ft., passive Perception 19
Languages Druidic
Challenge 15 (13,000 XP)

Land's Stride. The woods ape can move through nonmagical difficult terrain without using extra movement, and can pass through nonmagical plants without being slowed by them and without taking damage from them if they have thorns, spines, or a similar hazard. In addition, the woods ape has advantage on saving throws against plants that are magically created or manipulated to impede movement.

Innate Spellcasting. The woods ape's innate spellcasting ability is Wisdom (spell save DC 15, +7 to hit with spell attacks). It can cast the following spells, requiring no material components.

    At will: *create or destroy water, detect poison and disease, entangle, guidance, mending, speak with animals, speak with plants, tree stride*

    3/day each: *animal messenger, barkskin, call lightning, locate animals or plants, pass without trace*

    1/day each: *awaken, commune with nature, conjure animals, plant growth*

Spellcasting. The wood ape druid is a 12th-level spellcaster. Its spellcasting ability is Wisdom (spell save DC 17, +9 to hit with spell attacks). It has the following druid spells prepared.

    Cantrips (at will): *druidcraft, resistance, shillelagh*

    1st level (4 slots): *cure wounds, fog cloud, thunderwave*

    2nd level (3 slots): *barkskin, enhance ability, gust of wind, spider climb*

    3rd level (3 slots): *call lightning, dispel magic, plant growth*

    4th level (3 slots): *control water, divination, freedom of movement*

    5th level (2 slots): *commune with nature, greater restoration, reincarnate, tree stride*

    6th level (1 slot): *heal*

ACTIONS

Multiattack. The woods ape makes two Quarterstaff attacks or two Claw attacks.

Quarterstaff. *Melee Weapon Attack:* +6 to hit (+9 to hit with *shillelagh*), reach 5 ft., one target. *Hit:* 6 (1d6 + 3) bludgeoning damage, 8 (1d8 + 3) bludgeoning damage if wielded with two hands, or 9 (1d8 + 5) bludgeoning damage with *shillelagh*.

Claw. *Melee Weapon Attack:* +6 to hit, reach 5 ft. or range 10/20 ft., one target. *Hit:* 10 (2d6 + 3) slashing damage.

Woods Ape Warrior

Medium monstrosity, unaligned

Armor Class 11 (16 with *barkskin*)
Hit Points 97 (13d8 + 39)
Speed 30 ft., climb 30 ft.

STR	DEX	CON	INT	WIS	CHA
18 (+4)	15 (+2)	17 (+3)	12 (+1)	18 (+4)	7 (−2)

Saving Throws Str +7, Con +6
Skills Athletics +7, Nature +4, Perception +7, Stealth +5 (+8 in forested terrain), Survival +7
Damage Immunities poison
Condition Immunities poisoned
Senses darkvision 60 ft., passive Perception 17
Languages Druidic
Challenge 8 (3,900 XP)

Brave. The woods ape warrior has advantage on saving throws against being frightened.

Improved Critical. The woods ape warrior scores a critical hit with a weapon attack on a roll of 19 or 20.

Land's Stride. The woods ape can move through nonmagical difficult terrain without using extra movement, and can pass through nonmagical plants without being slowed by them and without taking damage from them if they have thorns, spines, or a similar hazard. In addition, the woods ape has advantage on saving throws against plants that are magically created or manipulated to impede movement.

Innate Spellcasting. The woods ape's innate spellcasting ability is Wisdom (spell save DC 15, +7 to hit with spell attacks). It can cast the following spells, requiring no material components.

    At will: *create or destroy water, detect poison and disease, entangle, guidance, mending, speak with animals, speak with plants, tree stride*

    3/day each: *animal messenger, barkskin, call lightning, locate animals or plants, pass without trace*

    1/day each: *awaken, commune with nature, conjure animals, plant growth*

Martial Advantage. Once per turn, the woods ape warrior can deal an extra 13 (3d8) damage to a creature it hits with a weapon attack if that creature is within 5 feet of an ally of the warrior that isn't incapacitated.

ACTIONS

Multiattack. The woods ape makes two Claw attacks.

Claw. *Melee Weapon Attack:* +7 to hit, reach 5 ft. or range 10/20 ft., one target. *Hit:* 13 (2d8 + 4) slashing damage.

Woolly Rhinoceros

Large beast, unaligned

Armor Class 14 (natural armor)
Hit Points 172 (15d10 + 90)
Speed 30 ft.

STR	DEX	CON	INT	WIS	CHA
21 (+5)	10 (+0)	22 (+6)	3 (−4)	13 (+1)	2 (−4)

Skills Perception +7
Senses passive Perception 17
Languages —
Challenge 6 (2,300 XP)

Improved Critical. Gore attacks score a critical hit on a roll of 19 or 20.

Keen Smell. The wooly rhinoceros has advantage on Wisdom (Perception) checks that rely on smell.

Charge. If the wooly rhinoceros moves at least 20 feet straight toward a creature and then hits it with a gore attack, the target takes an extra 9 (2d8) piercing damage. If the target is a creature, it must succeed on a DC 15 Strength saving throw or be knocked prone. If the target is prone, the wooly rhinoceros can make one stomp attack against it as a bonus action.

ACTIONS

Gore. *Melee Weapon Attack:* +8 to hit, reach 5 ft., one target. *Hit:* 14 (2d8 + 5) piercing damage.

Stomp. *Melee Weapon Attack:* +8 to hit, reach 5 ft., one target. *Hit:* 18 (2d12 + 5) piercing damage.

Wraith, Oblivion

Large undead, lawful evil
Armor Class 18
Hit Points 209 (22d10 + 88)
Speed 0 ft., fly 60 ft. (hover)

STR	DEX	CON	INT	WIS	CHA
6 (–2)	27 (+8)	18 (+4)	17 (+3)	18 (+4)	23 (+6)

Skills Perception +8, Stealth +12
Damage Resistances acid, cold, fire, lightning, thunder; bludgeoning, piercing, and slashing from nonmagical attacks not made with silver
Damage Immunities necrotic, poison
Condition Immunities charmed, exhaustion, grappled, paralyzed, petrified, poisoned, prone, restrained
Senses darkvision 60 ft., passive Perception 18
Languages Abyssal, Common, Giant
Challenge 12 (8,400 XP)

Incorporeal Movement. The oblivion wraith can move through other creatures and objects as if they were difficult terrain. It takes 5 (1d10) force damage if it ends its turn inside an object.
Sunlight Sensitivity. While in sunlight, the oblivion wraith has disadvantage on attack rolls, as well as on Wisdom (Perception) checks that rely on sight.
Chill of the Grave. The oblivion wraith radiates an aura of unnatural cold in a 60-foot radius. All creatures in this area must succeed on a DC 14 Constitution saving throw or have their speed reduced by half. A creature that touches the oblivion wraith or hits it with a melee attack while within 5 feet of it takes 10 (3d6) cold damage.

Actions

Life Drain. *Melee Weapon Attack:* +12 to hit, reach 10 ft., one creature. *Hit:* 26 (4d8 + 8) necrotic damage and 21 (6d6) cold damage. The target must succeed on a DC 14 Constitution saving throw or its hit point maximum is reduced by an amount equal to the necrotic damage taken. This reduction lasts until the target finishes a long rest. The target dies if this effect reduces its hit point maximum to 0.
Create Specter. The oblivion wraith targets a humanoid within 10 feet of it that has been dead for no longer than 1 minute and died violently. The target's spirit rises as a specter in the space of its corpse or in the nearest unoccupied space. The specter is under the oblivion wraith's control. The oblivion wraith can have no more than ten specters under its control at one time.

Xill

Medium aberration, lawful evil
Armor Class 15 (natural armor)
Hit Points 90 (12d8 + 36)
Speed 40 ft.

STR	DEX	CON	INT	WIS	CHA
17 (+3)	17 (+3)	16 (+3)	15 (+2)	12 (+1)	11 (+0)

Skills Acrobatics +5, Arcana +4, Insight +3, Stealth +5
Senses darkvision 60 ft., passive Perception 11
Languages Common, Infernal
Challenge 4 (1,100 XP)

Implant. The xill can use an action to implant up to 7 (2d6) xill eggs in one unconscious or incapacitated creature within 5 feet of it. The xill's eggs hatch when the target takes its next long rest, at which point the young consume the host from within. After each long rest, the target must make a DC 15 Constitution saving throw. On a failed saving throw, the target gains one level of exhaustion.
Xill eggs can be removed individually by the target or another creature by making a successful DC 15 Wisdom (Medicine) check. Each check deals 1d8 slashing damage to the target. The eggs can be destroyed by magic such as *lesser restoration.*

Actions

Multiattack. The xill makes one Bite attack, two Shortsword attacks, and two Claw attacks.
Shortswords. *Melee Weapon Attack:* +5 to hit, reach 5 ft., one target. *Hit:* 6 (1d6 + 3) piercing damage.
Bite. *Melee Weapon Attack:* +5 to hit, reach 5 ft., one target. *Hit:* 7 (1d8 + 3) piercing damage, and the target must make a DC 13 Constitution saving throw or be paralyzed for 1 minute. A paralyzed creature can repeat the saving throw at the end of each of its turns, ending the effect on a success.
Claws. *Melee Weapon Attack:* +5 to hit, reach 5 ft., one target. *Hit:* 6 (1d6 + 3) slashing damage.
Longbow. *Ranged Weapon Attack:* +5 to hit, range 150/600 ft., one target. *Hit:* 7 (1d8 + 3) piercing damage.
Etherealness. The xill magically enters the Ethereal Plane from the Material Plane, or vice versa.

Xill Leader

Large aberration, lawful evil
Armor Class 16 (natural armor)
Hit Points 127 (15d10 + 45)
Speed 40 ft.

STR	DEX	CON	INT	WIS	CHA
18 (+4)	17 (+3)	16 (+3)	15 (+2)	12 (+1)	11 (+0)

Skills Acrobatics +6, Arcana +5, Athletics +7, Insight +4, Stealth +6
Senses darkvision 60 ft., passive Perception 11
Languages Common, Infernal
Challenge 7 (2,900 XP)

Implant. The xill leader can use an action to implant up to 7 (2d6) xill eggs in one unconscious or incapacitated creature within 5 feet of it. The xill's eggs hatch when the target takes its next long rest, at which point the young consume the host from within. After each long rest, the target must make a DC 15 Constitution saving throw. On a failed saving throw, the target gains one level of exhaustion.
Xill eggs can be removed individually by the target or another creature by making a successful DC 15 Wisdom (Medicine) check. Each check deals 1d8 slashing damage to the target. The eggs can be destroyed by magic such as *lesser restoration.*

Actions

Multiattack. The xill leader makes one Bite attack, two Shortsword attacks, and two Claw attacks.
Shortswords. *Melee Weapon Attack:* +7 to hit, reach 5 ft., one target. *Hit:* 11 (2d6 + 4) piercing damage.
Bite. *Melee Weapon Attack:* +7 to hit, reach 5 ft., one target. *Hit:* 13 (2d8 + 4) piercing damage, and the target must make a DC 14 Constitution saving throw or be paralyzed for 1 minute. A paralyzed creature can repeat the saving

throw at the end of each of its turns, ending the effect on a success.

Claws. *Melee Weapon Attack:* +7 to hit, reach 5 ft., one target. *Hit:* 11 (2d6 + 4) slashing damage.

Longbow. *Ranged Weapon Attack:* +7 to hit, range 150/600 ft., one target. *Hit:* 8 (1d8 + 4) piercing damage.

Etherealness. The xill magically enters the Ethereal Plane from the Material Plane, or vice versa.

Xilyat Xaygon Xill

Medium aberration, lawful evil

Armor Class 15 (natural armor)
Hit Points 165 (22d8 + 66)
Speed 40 ft.

STR	DEX	CON	INT	WIS	CHA
17 (+3)	17 (+3)	16 (+3)	15 (+2)	18 (+4)	11 (+0)

Saving Throws Wis +8, Cha +4
Skills Acrobatics +7, Arcana +6, Insight +7, Religion +6, Stealth +7
Senses darkvision 60 ft., passive Perception 14
Languages Common, Infernal
Challenge 9 (5,000 XP)

Implant. The xill can use an action to implant up to 7 (2d6) xill eggs in one unconscious or incapacitated creature within 5 feet of it. The xill's eggs hatch when the target takes its next long rest, at which point the young consume the host from within. After each long rest, the target must make a DC 15 Constitution saving throw. On a failed saving throw, the target gains one level of exhaustion.
Xill eggs can be removed individually by the target or another creature by making a successful DC 15 Wisdom (Medicine) check. Each check deals 1d8 slashing damage to the target. The eggs can be destroyed by magic such as *lesser restoration*.

Spellcasting. Xilyat is a 10th-level spellcaster. His spellcasting ability is Wisdom (spell save DC 16, +8 to hit with spell attacks). He has the following cleric spells prepared.

Cantrips (at will): *acid splash, guidance, resistance, thaumaturgy*
1st level (4 slots): *bane, cure wounds, detect magic, shield of faith, thunderwave*
2nd level (3 slots): *blindness/deafness, enhance ability, silence, spiritual weapon*
3rd level (3 slots): *bestow curse, dispel magic, protection from energy, spirit guardians*
4th level (3 slots): *black tentacles, blight*
5th level (2 slots): *dispel evil and good, insect plague*

Actions

Multiattack. The xill makes one Bite attack, two Shortsword attacks, and two Claw attacks.

Shortswords. *Melee Weapon Attack:* +7 to hit, reach 5 ft., one target. *Hit:* 6 (1d6 + 3) piercing damage.

Bite. *Melee Weapon Attack:* +7 to hit, reach 5 ft., one target. *Hit:* 7 (1d8 + 3) piercing damage, and the target must make a DC 15 Constitution saving throw or be paralyzed for 1 minute. A paralyzed creature can repeat the saving throw at the end of each of its turns, ending the effect on a success.

Claws. *Melee Weapon Attack:* +7 to hit, reach 5 ft., one target. *Hit:* 6 (1d6 + 3) slashing damage.

Longbow. *Ranged Weapon Attack:* +7 to hit, range 150/600 ft., one target. *Hit:* 7 (1d8 + 3) piercing damage.

Etherealness. Xilyat magically enters the Ethereal Plane from the Material Plane, or vice versa.

Aura of Evil (1/short or long rest). Xilyat radiates an aura of evil out to a range of 15 feet. Creatures of his choice are unaffected. Other creatures that enter or end their turn in the area must make a DC 16 Constitution saving throw. On a failed saving throw, the target takes 10 (3d6) necrotic damage.

Turn Undead (1/short or long rest). Each undead that can see or hear Xilyat within 30 feet of him must make a DC 16 Wisdom saving throw. On a failed saving throw, if the undead's Challenge Rating is 2 or lower, it is instantly destroyed. If the undead's Challenge Rating is 3 or higher, it is turned for 1 minute. While turned, the undead must use its turns trying to move as far away from Xilyat as it can, and it can't willingly move into a space within 30 feet of him. It cannot take reactions, and can only take the Dash action, or try to escape from an effect that prevents it from moving.

Reactions

Divine Intervention (1/long rest). If Xilyat is reduced to 10 hit points or less, he can use a reaction to enact one of the following options:

- Cause himself or another creature within 30 feet of him to regain 36 (8d8) hit points.

- Teleport to a location he is familiar with up to 1 mile away.

- Restore one dead creature back to life, as long as that creature has been dead for no more than 1 minute.

Xorn, Elder

Large elemental, neutral

Armor Class 19 (natural armor)
Hit Points 91 (9d10 + 42)
Speed 20 ft., burrow 20 ft.

STR	DEX	CON	INT	WIS	CHA
18 (+4)	10 (+0)	22 (+6)	11 (+0)	10 (+0)	11 (+0)

Skills Perception +8, Stealth +4
Damage Resistances cold, fire, lightning
Damage Immunities acid, poison; bludgeoning, piercing, and slashing from nonmagical attacks not made with adamantine
Condition Immunities poisoned
Senses darkvision 60 ft., tremorsense 60 ft., passive Perception 18
Languages Terran
Challenge 9 (5,000 XP)

Earth Glide. The elder xorn can burrow through nonmagical, unworked earth and stone. While doing so, the elder xorn doesn't disturb the material it moves through.

Stone Camouflage. The elder xorn has advantage on Dexterity (Stealth) checks made to hide in rocky terrain.

Treasure Sense. The elder xorn can pinpoint, by scent, the location of precious metals and stones, such as coins and gems, within 60 feet of it.

Actions

Multiattack. The elder xorn makes three Claw attacks and one Bite attack.

Claw. *Melee Weapon Attack:* +7 to hit, reach 5 ft., one target. *Hit:* 11 (2d6 + 4) slashing damage.

Bite. *Melee Weapon Attack:* +7 to hit, reach 5 ft., one target. *Hit:* 26 (4d10 + 4) piercing damage.

Y'Cart Chi'Namk

Medium undead, lawful evil
Armor Class 27 (natural armor)
Hit Points 660 (40d8 + 480)
Speed 100 ft.

STR	DEX	CON	INT	WIS	CHA
32 (+11)	25 (+7)	34 (+12)	21 (+5)	25 (+7)	27 (+8)

Saving Throws Dex +15, Int +13, Wis +15, Chr +16
Skills Arcana +13, Insight +15, Investigation +13, Perception +15, Religion +13
Damage Vulnerabilities fire
Damage Resistances cold, lightning
Damage Immunities necrotic, poison; bludgeoning, piercing, and slashing from nonmagical attacks
Condition Immunities charmed, exhaustion, frightened, paralyzed, poisoned
Senses truesight 120 ft., passive Perception 25
Languages all languages
Challenge 25 (75,000 XP)

Legendary Resistance (3/day). If Y'Cart Chi'Namk fails a saving throw, he can choose to succeed instead.
Innate Spellcasting. Y'Cart Chi'Namk's innate spellcasting ability is Charisma (spell save DC 24, +16 to hit with spell attacks). He can innately cast the following spells at will, requiring no material components: *chain lightning, dispel magic, haste, knock, passwall, plane shift, scrying, teleport, weird.*
Regeneration. Y'Cart Chi'Namk regains 20 hit points at the start of his turn. If Y'Cart Chi'Namk takes fire or radiant damage, this trait doesn't function at the start of his next turn. Y'Cart Chi'Namk dies only if he starts his turn with 0 hit points and doesn't regenerate.

ACTIONS

Slam. *Melee or Ranged Weapon Attack:* +19 to hit, reach 5 ft., one target. *Hit:* 21 (3d6 + 11) bludgeoning damage. If the target is a creature, it must succeed on a DC 19 Constitution saving throw against disease or become infected with Hunefer Rot. While infected, the creature's Constitution score is reduced by 1d6 at the start of each of its turns until the disease is cured. The reduction lasts until the target finishes a long rest. The target dies if this effect reduces its Constitution to 0. An afflicted creature that dies shrivels away into sand in 3 rounds. On the third round the dust swirls and forms a **mummy lord** with the dead creature's equipment under Y'Cart Chi'Namk's command.

LEGENDARY ACTIONS

Y'Cart Chi'Namk can take 3 legendary actions, choosing from the options below. Only one legendary action can be used at a time and only at the end of another creature's turn. Y'Cart Chi'Namk regains spent legendary actions at the start of his turn.
Move. Y'Cart Chi'Namk moves up to his speed without provoking opportunity attacks.
Slam. Y'Cart Chi'Namk makes one Slam attack.
Despair (costs 2 actions). Any creature within 60 feet of Y'Cart Chi'Namk that can see him must succeed on a DC 21 Wisdom saving throw or be paralyzed for 1 minute. A creature can repeat the saving throw at the end of each of its turns, ending the effect on itself on a success. If a creature's saving throw is successful or the effect ends for it, the creature is immune to Y'Cart Chi'Namk's Despair for the next 24 hours.

Yasiel

Yasiel uses the statistics of a **planetar**, except for the following changes:

- His Challenge Rating is 17 (18,000 XP), modifying Yasiel's saving throw modifiers (+13, +12, and +13, respectively), and making his Perception modifier +12 and his passive Perception 22. He has a +13 to hit with his Greatsword. The spell save DC for his Innate Spellcasting is 21.

- His creature type is Fiend and his alignment is lawful evil.

- He no longer has resistance to radiant damage, but instead has resistance to acid and cold damage. He wears a *ring of immunity* (fire), as well.

- His Angelic Weapons ability deals 22 (5d8) necrotic damage instead of radiant.

Yeti

Large monstrosity, neutral
Armor Class 14 (natural armor)
Hit Points 95 (10d10 + 40)
Speed 30 ft., climb 30 ft.

STR	DEX	CON	INT	WIS	CHA
19 (+4)	12 (+1)	18 (+4)	9 (−1)	12 (+1)	10 (+0)

Skills Perception +5, Stealth +3
Damage Immunities cold
Condition Immunities frightened
Senses darkvision 60 ft., passive Perception 15
Languages Yeti
Challenge 4 (1,100 XP)

Keen Smell. The yeti has advantage on Wisdom (Perception) checks that rely on smell.
Pyrophobic. If the yeti takes fire damage, it has disadvantage on attacks, saving throws, and ability checks until the end of its next turn.
Camouflage. The yeti has advantage on Dexterity (Stealth) checks made to hide in mountainous and snowy terrain.

ACTIONS

Multiattack. The yeti can make two Claw attacks and use its Icy Glare ability.
Claw. *Melee Weapon Attack:* +6 to hit, reach 10 ft., one target. *Hit:* 11 (2d6 + 4) slashing damage plus 3 (1d6) cold damage.
Icy Glare. The yeti glares at one creature within 30 feet of it. If the target can see the yeti, the target must succeed on a DC 13 Constitution saving throw or take 14 (4d6) cold damage and be frightened for 1 minute. The target can repeat the saving throw at the end of each of its turns, ending the effect on itself on a success. If the target's saving throw is a success, it is immune to the Icy Glare of the yeti for 1 hour.

Zombie, Spellgorged

Medium undead, neutral evil
Armor Class 10
Hit Points 108 (12d8 + 36)
Speed 20 ft.

STR	DEX	CON	INT	WIS	CHA
13 (+1)	10 (+0)	16 (+3)	3 (−4)	6 (−2)	5 (−3)

Saving Throws Wis +0
Damage Immunities poison
Condition Immunities poisoned
Senses darkvision 60 ft., passive Perception 8
Languages understands the languages it knew in life but can't speak
Challenge 1 (200 XP)

Spell Storing. The spellgorged zombie can store any spells cast into its mouth as if it were a *ring of spell storing*. The zombie can store up to 5 levels worth of spells at a time. The spells stored in the zombie uses the slot level, spell save DC, spell attack bonus, and the spellcasting ability of the original caster. Once the spell is released by the zombie it is no longer stored in it, freeing up space for additional spells.

Undead Fortitude. If damage reduces the spellgorged zombie to 0 hit points, it must make a Constitution saving throw with a DC of 5 + the damage taken, unless the damage is radiant or from a critical hit. On a success, the zombie drops to 1 hit point instead.

ACTIONS

Slam. *Melee Weapon Attack:* +3 to hit, reach 5 ft., one target. *Hit:* 4 (1d6 + 1) bludgeoning damage.

Hazards

Mold, Brown

Brown mold is an ectotherm and feeds on the warmth of the environment surrounding it. When within 30 feet of brown mold, the temperature is noticeably colder, often to the point of freezing depending on the size of the brown mold patch. It is common for brown mold to cover a 10-foot square, but it isn't unusual for patches to be much larger.

Creatures that come within 10 feet of brown mold, or start their turn within 10 feet of the mold must succeed on a DC 12 Constitution saving throw. A failed save results in 22 (4d10) cold damage, or half as much on a successful saving throw.

Exposure to fire causes the brown mold to rapidly expand and grow in the direction of the fire. Exposure to cold will instantly destroy brown mold.

Memory Moss

Memory moss appears as a 5-foot-square patch of black moss. It grows in temperate or warm climates and is sometimes encountered in subterranean realms. Memory moss cannot abide the cold or the arid clime of the desert and is never encountered in such environments.

When a living creature moves within 60 feet of a patch of memory moss, it attacks by attempting to steal that creature's memories. It can target a single creature each round. A targeted creature must succeed on a DC 15 Wisdom saving throw or lose all memories from the last 24 hours. This is particularly nasty to spellcasters, who lose all spells prepared within the last 24 hours.

Once a memory moss steals a creature's memories, it sinks back down and does not attack again for one day. Any creature who loses its memories to the memory moss acts as if affected by a *confusion* spell for the next 1d4 hours. Lost memories can be regained by eating the memory moss that absorbed them. Doing so requires a successful DC 16 Constitution saving throw, with failure resulting in the creature being nauseated for 1d6 rounds and suffering 5 (2d4) poison damage.

Any creature that eats the memory moss temporarily gains the memories currently stored therein (even if they are not the creature's own memories). Such creatures can even cast spells if the memory moss has stolen these from a previous spellcasting creature. Characters eating the memory moss to regain their own lost memories do not lose them after 24 hours. Ten points of fire or cold damage kills a single patch of memory moss.

When first encountered, there is a 25% chance that the memory moss has eaten within the last day and does not attack by stealing memories. In such a case, the moss contains 2d4 spells determined randomly from a single spell list. When a living creature moves within 60 feet of a sated memory moss, it assumes a vaguely humanoid form and casts the stolen spells at its targets.

Appendix 2
New Magic Items

This appendix details new magic items found throughout this book.

Amulet of Allies

Wondrous item, very rare (requires attunement)

This appears as a bluish-white gemstone inset in a gold medallion attached to a gold chain. Three times per day, you can create an effect akin to the spell *dominate monster* on up to 6 creatures that you can see. Each creature must succeed on a DC 18 Wisdom saving throw to avoid the effects.

Amulet of Shapechange

Wondrous item, very rare (requires attunement)

While wearing this amulet, you can use a bonus action to cast the *shapechange* spell with it. The spell's effects last for 1 hour, and it doesn't require your concentration. The amulet may only be used once per day.

Armaments of Aggression

Armor, artifact (requires attunement)

The complete set of the *armaments of aggression* was forged in the mists of antiquity from the blackest alien metals gathered from a world-killing meteorite. The arms and armor were worked in shadow upon the forges of the elder gods, the fiery panoply tempered in the blood of 100 virgins. Originally crafted for a forgotten demigod destined to rule his world, the armaments granted him a tireless rage upon the field of battle, with each downed foe granting him greater power. With innumerable victories under his belt, the demigod grew more bloodthirsty, but also more careless. Eventually he rebelled and led his forces against the font of his godhood; he was lost to the Abyss in the crossing over. The *armaments of aggression* were scattered throughout the planes. Wherever one of the pieces is recovered, war and strife surely follow.

A helm, greaves, breastplate, shield, and halfspear make up the complete *armaments of aggression*, and it is said whosoever possesses the complete set shall be all but invincible in battle.

The Helm: This grants you protection from the decapitating effects of vorpal weapons and immunity to mind-affecting effects. Further, you gain a +10 bonus on Intimidate checks. Lastly, you may cast *thunderwave* once per day with a spell save DC of 18 and 8d8 base damage.

Each time you don the helm you must succeed on a DC 17 Wisdom saving throw or use the *thunderwave* ability and your alignment shifts to chaotic along the law-chaos axis. This change cannot be undone until you rid yourself of the helm for good.

The Breastplate: This functions as *+5 breastplate armor* and further grants you resistance to nonmagical bludgeoning, slashing, and piercing damage. While wearing the breastplate, you regain 3 hit points at the beginning of each round if you are not at 0 hit points. Upon donning this breastplate each time, you must succeed on a DC 17 Constitution saving throw or lose 2 points of Charisma.

The Greaves: These function as *boots of speed* and further grant you the evasion ability like a rogue. Additionally, you gain a +10 bonus on Dexterity (Acrobatics) checks involving keeping your balance. Each hour the greaves are worn in a non-combat situation, you must succeed on a DC 17 Wisdom saving throw or automatically kick the person or creature nearest you. You continue kicking the same creature until restrained (even then trying to break free and continue the assault) or the creature is unconscious. You can attempt a DC 20 Wisdom saving throw each round to break the effects.

The Shield: The shield is a large steel *+5 shield* and further grants you the ability to create a magic circle against lawful creatures once per day. As long as you carry the shield, you have disadvantage on all Charisma-based checks made against lawful creatures.

The Spear: The spear is a *+4 spear* that sheds light in a 20-foot-radius. It cannot damage undead creatures. If you hit a lawful creature, it does an additional 3d6 necrotic damage. You can use the spear to cast *dispel evil and good* once per day. Each time you enter combat, you must make a DC 17 Wisdom saving throw. On a failed save, you rely solely on this weapon in that battle, foregoing any other weapons or attacks you have (such as spells and spell-like abilities, for example).

Armor of Silent Moves

Armor (any light), very rare

You gain a +1 bonus to AC while wearing this armor and you have advantage on Dexterity (Stealth) checks that rely on moving silently.

Bands of Binding

Wondrous item, rare

After speaking the command word, you can make a thrown weapon attack with this item at a Large or smaller opponent. It has a range of 20/60 ft. On a successful hit, the bands expand and then contract to grapple and restrain the target. The target must use an action to succeed on a DC 18 Strength (Athletics) or Dexterity (Acrobatics) check to escape. You can release the bands with a bonus action, causing them to fall to the ground.

Black Ankh of Set

Wondrous item, very rare
(requires attunement by a follower of Set)

A *black ankh of Set* appears as a cobra in the shape of an upside-down ankh. Such an item is given only to the most devout and wicked followers of Set. This item exudes an unholy aura that grants you a +3 bonus to AC and resistance to poison damage while you wear it. A bearer of a *blank ankh of Set* is not prevented from teleporting outside the Pyramid of Set from within.

Bloody Dagger

Weapon (dagger), very rare

You have a +2 bonus to your attack and damage rolls when you use this weapon. This weapon scores a critical on a 19 or 20. Each wound that you make against an opponent continues to bleed, causing 1 necrotic damage each round until healed magically or staunched with a successful DC 14 Wisdom (Medicine) check.

Boots of Haste

Wondrous item, very rare (requires attunement)

These boots have 3 charges. While wearing them, you can use a bonus action and expend 1 charge to cast *haste* on yourself. The effect lasts for 1 minute and does not require concentration. The boots regain 1d2 expended charges daily at dawn.

Bracers of Defense

Wondrous item, rarity varies (requires attunement)

While wearing these bracers, you gain a bonus to AC if you are wearing no armor and using no shield. The amount of the bonus depends on the rarity of the bracers.

Bracers of…	Rarity	Bonus
Defense	rare	+2
Greater defense	very rare	+4
Superior defense	legendary	+6

Brass Collar

Wondrous item, rare

The brass collars used by the Efreeti of the City of Brass to mark their slave castes are finely fitted collars of living brass. The collars are usually affixed with a red hot bolt that more or less permanently locks the collar into place. The inside of the collar is inscribed with eldritch writing detailing a powerful *geas* upon the wearer of the collar. Wearers of a brass collar are considered to be under the effects of a permanent *suggestion* spell in regards to their servitude to their master. The wearer also gains resistance to fire damage so long as the collar is locked in place.

Individuals wearing a brass collar cannot flee from their captor, take up arms against them, or disobey their will in any way. Attempting to remove the collar by any means (such as cutting, breaking, or use of a *dispel magic* spell) requires the wearer to succeed on a DC 15 Constitution saving throw or die instantly. Each attempt at removing the collar requires another save. The one who fit the collar to the slave can safely remove the collar without any ill effects to the wearer.

A collar can be broken with a successful DC 30 strength check or doing 60 hit points of damage against AC 16. A brass collar ignores all attacks that do less than 10 points of damage.

Wearers of the collar enter a barbarian-like rage if their collar is tampered with (this is an effect of the collar placed upon the wearer), attacking anyone save their master who attempts to remove their collar. This rage is exactly like a barbarian's rage and lasts for one round per Hit Die of the wearer.

Brazen Amulet

Wondrous item, uncommon

Constructed and enchanted by Axam within the Bazaar of Beggars, while you wear a *brazen amulet* you suffer no harm from being in a hot or cold environment. You can exist comfortably in conditions between -50 and 140 degrees Fahrenheit (-45 and 60 degrees Celsius) without having to make Constitution saving throws. Your equipment is likewise protected.

You do not gain any protection from fire or cold damage, nor against other environmental hazards such as smoke, lack of air, and so forth.

Brazen Amulet, Hariph's

Wondrous item, very rare

These amulets are worn by hariphs and high-ranking members of the cult. A set of *hariph's brazen amulets* grants the bearer and anyone within a 5-foot radius immunity to the fires from the **Pillar of Fire** and the **Vortex of Purification**. They provide resistance to all other fire damage. The amulet allows access to all the floors of the tower save the personal dwelling of Sheik Mutastir himself.

Bearers of *hariph's brazen amulets* are immune to the enchantment effects found in the **Mosque of Adoration**

Brazen Amulet, Lesser

Wondrous item, rare

Lesser brazen amulets allow access up to the **Alqamar Mulnajum** (the Hall of Moon and Stars), but is otherwise similar to a *hariph's amulet*. It protects only the wearer from the fires and damaging effects of the **Vortex of Purification** and the **Pillar of Fire**, however.

Bearers of a *lesser brazen amulet* are immune to the enchantment effects found in the **Mosque of Adoration**

Brazen Scimitar

Weapon (scimitar), artifact (requires attunement)

When the last plates of brass were placed, forming the upper walls of the City of Brass, the Sultan thrust his gauntleted hand and scimitar fully into the still burning elemental furnaces. The molten brass fused with the gauntlet and blade, melting them and reforming them fully of brass. The Sultan removed them from the fires and exclaimed, "He who rules the *Brazen Scimitar*, rules the City of Brass."

Magic Weapon. The *Brazen Scimitar* is a magic weapon that grants a +3 bonus to attack and damage rolls made with it. Eternal flames dance along the blade but don't harm you. When you hit a creature with this magic weapon, it deals an extra 4d6 fire damage to any target it hits. If the target is an elemental, the target takes an extra 2d6 fire damage.

Spells. The scimitar has 6 charges and regains 1d4 + 2 expended charges daily at dawn. You can use an action and expend 1 or more charges to cast one of the following spells (save DC 18) from it: *flame strike* (3 charges), *flaming sphere* (3rd-level; 2 charges), *fire shield* (2 charges), or *protection from energy* (1 charge).

You can also use an action to cast the *continual flame* spell from the orb without using any charges.

Bound to the City of Brass. The *Brazen Scimitar* is formed from the same molten brass as the City of Brass and is bound to the city. If it is removed from the City of Brass, it becomes a nonmagical scimitar until it has been returned to the city and stays there for 24 hours. If in the hands of the Great Sultan, the *Brazen Scimitar* remains magical even outside of the City of Brass.

Destroying the Brazen Scimitar. The *Brazen Scimitar* is made of living brass and repairs any damage done to it, no matter how severe. If the scimitar is destroyed while outside the City of Brass, it is reforged anew the next day at dawn out of the *Throne of Brass*. To destroy the *Brazen Scimitar*, a Hawanar, a descendant of the previous Sultan and Sultana, must coat the scimitar in the blood of the dying Great Sultan before plunging the blade into the *Throne of Brass*.

Breastplate of Free action

Armor, legendary (requires attunement)

You gain a +3 bonus to armor class while wearing this. In addition, difficult terrain doesn't cost you extra movement and magic can neither reduce your speed not cause you to be paralyzed or restrained.

Burning Stone

Wondrous item, varies

A burning stone is similar to a *spell scroll*. A single stone can hold one spell cast with a spell slot of level 1 through 9. A burning stone can be activated as an action. The spell has the rarity, spell attack bonus, and spell save DC of an equivalent *spell scroll* but can be used by anybody. Once used, the gem loses its magic and turns dull gray.

The Carnelian Idol

Wondrous item, artifact

The *carnelian idol* is a mysterious magical item that was lost in the ever-shifting terrain of the Plane of Molten Skies as a great curse bound Dahish into a pillar of obsidian. This curse may be broken only through the device of the *carnelian idol* itself. The great curse denies any scrying as to the whereabouts of the *carnelian idol*

By smashing the *carnelian idol* upon the sides of the pillar prison in **Area 3** on the Plane of Molten Skies, the characters may release Dahish from his prison.

Chariot of Narmer

Wondrous item, legendary

This great war-chariot was built for Narmer, an evil titan who made himself pharaoh of Upper and Lower Khemit in ancient times. The chariot is huge and very heavy, requiring at least three beasts of at least Huge size to pull it. Blades spring forth from its wheels, and it is said that the chariot platform itself may act as a firing platform granting excellent visibility over the battlefield while providing good cover. The chariot itself may carry as many as eight Medium, four Large, or two Huge beings.

Cloak of Arachnida

Wondrous item, very rare (requires attunement)

When you wear this cloak, you gain the ability to can climb difficult surfaces, including upside down on ceilings, without needing to make an ability check. You also have advantage on saving throws against poison. Once per day you can transform into a Giant Spider for up to one hour similar to the druid's wild shape ability.

Cloak of Charisma

Wondrous item, rare (requires attunement)

While wearing this cloak, your Charisma is effectively 2 points higher. In addition, if you cast friends or charm person, the target must succeed on a Wisdom saving throw against your spell save DC to know that it was subjected to the spell.

Cloak of Etherealness

Wondrous item, very rare (requires attunement)

This silvery gray cloak seems to absorb light rather than be illuminated by it. As an action, you can command the cloak to make you ethereal. You can dismiss the effect as a bonus action.

The cloak works for a total of up to 10 minutes per day. This duration need not be continuous, but it must be used in 1-minute increments.

Cloak of Protection

Wondrous item, rarity varies (requires attunement)

While wearing this cloak, you gain a bonus to your AC and saving throws. The amount of the bonus depends on the cloak's rarity.

Cloak of...	Rarity	Bonus
Protection	uncommon	+1
Greater protection	rare	+2
Superior protection	very rare	+3

Cloak of Resistance

Wondrous item, rare (requires attunement)

You have advantage on saving throws while wearing this cloak.

Codex of Infinite Planes

Wondrous item, legendary

The *Codex of Infinite Planes* is an ancient text said to have been penned by the lords of creation at the beginning of time and recounts histories lost to the minds of mortals.

The *Codex* is massive in size and scope, and no mortal can ever hope to read it in its entirety. No matter how many pages are turned, another always remains. Anyone opening the *Codex* for the first time must make a DC 20 Constitution saving throw, being utterly annihilated on a failure and taking 35 (10d6) force damage on a sucess. Those who survive can peruse its pages and learn its powers, though not without risk. Each day spent studying the *Codex* allows the reader to make a DC 23 Intelligence (Arcana) check to learn one of its powers (choose the power learned randomly; lower the DC by 1 per additional day spent reading until a power is learned). However, each day of study also forces the reader to make a Wisdom saving throw with a DC of 20 + 1 per day of study to avoid being driven insane (as the *confusion* spell, but permanent).

The powers of the Codex of the Infinite Planes are as follows: *astral projection*, *banishment*, *elemental swarm*[4], *gate*, *planar ally*, *planar binding*, and *plane shift*. Each is usable at will by the owner of the Codex (assuming that he or she has learned how to access the power). The Codex of the Infinite Planes has spell save DCs of 25 and a spell attack bonus of +17. Activating any power requires both a Concentration check and a DC 20 Intelligence (Arcana) check. Any failure on either check indicates a catastrophe befalls the user (roll on the table below for the effect). A character can incur only one catastrophe per power use, even if he or she fails both checks.

A character who reads from the *Codex* for more than 99 weeks is automatically consumed by the power of the book and dies instantly. Such a character cannot be raised or returned to life, even by a *wish*; only a god's magic can restore such a creature to life.

1d4	Catastrophe
1	**Natural Fury:** An *earthquake* spell centered on the reader strikes every round for 1 minute, and an intensified *storm of vengeance* spell is centered and targeted on the reader.
2	**Fiendish Vengeance:** A *gate* opens and 1d3 + 1 balor demons, pit fiends, or similar evil outsiders immediately step through and attempt to destroy the owner of the *Codex*.
3	**Ultimate Imprisonment:** Reader's soul is captured in a random gem somewhere on the plane while his or her body is entombed beneath the earth (as *imprisonment*).
4	**Death:** The reader is subject to a *disintegration* spell. This repeats every round for 10 rounds or until the reader is dead.

Cruelty

Weapon (longsword), very rare

This magical longsword is sharply serrated and seems to resonate with a dark energy that makes one's skin crawl and numbs those around it.

You have a +2 bonus to attack and damage rolls made with *Cruelty*. In addition, if you roll a 20 on an attack roll with the weapon, you deal an additional 20 slashing damage, and the target must make a DC 20 Constitution saving throw or be paralyzed for 1 minute. A paralyzed creature can repeat the saving throw at the end of each of its turns, ending the effect on a success.

Demon Key

Wondrous item, artifact

This key, crafted from the essence of 666 bound demons, was created by the Grand Vizier himself and is among one of his most valuable possessions. The Demon Key is large, easily the size of a magical rod, its handle in the shape of a balor's face with two murky red rubies taking the place of eyes. Good-aligned creatures touching the key gain four levels of exhaustion and must make a DC 20 Constitution saving throw or be stunned for 2d6 rounds. Further, a lawful good creature that fails its Constitution saving throw by 5 or more is slain instantly, its soul consumed by the demonic key. Such a creature can be restored to life only by *true resurrection* or *wish*.

Neutral-aligned creatures on the good-evil axis touching the key gain two levels of exhaustion if they fail at the DC 20 Constitution saving throw.

The demon key may unlock any lock or open any gate to which it is set against. Magical barriers (such as those affected by *hold portal* and *arcane lock*) may also be unlocked so long as the magical lock is of a 9th level spell slot.

Dragons' Tears

Wondrous item, very rare

Each of these glittering diamonds is tear-shaped and may be substituted for any material component of 750 gp or less when casting a spell. Multiple *dragons' tears* may be used for spells requiring more expensive spell components.

If you swallow a dragon's tear you gain the benefits of having consumed a *potion of greater healing*. However, you must succeed on a DC 15 Wisdom saving throw or be overcome with sadness as your mind floods with images of the gold dragons witnessing the destruction of their eggs and being forced to draw the *chariot of Narmer*. If you fail the saving throw, you have a −2 penalty on attack rolls, skill checks, and saving throws for the next 1d6 minutes.

Durbakke of wakefulness

Wondrous item, very rare

This small hand drum is also called a tablah. It is made of angel hide stretched over a vase-shaped drum constructed of bronze and brass. When you play it, the drum automatically dispels any magical *sleep* effect on all creatures within a 30-foot radius.

If you are trained in percussion instruments, you can also use the *durbakke* to break a comatose effect or rouse an unconscious creature including those reduced to 0 Intelligence, Wisdom, Charisma or hit points. It takes 5 minutes and a successful DC 15 Charisma (Performance) check to rouse a comatose creature. Any mental ability scores currently at 0 are restored to 1 when the creature is revived. If the creature had 0 hit points, it has 1 after the *durbakke* has been used. This special ability can be used up to three times per day.

Elemental Diamond

Wondrous item, rare
(requires attunement by a spellcaster)

This rose-colored diamond is seemingly flawless and worth at least 1,000 gp on that alone. While you carry or wear this diamond, you cast all fire-based spells as if they were cast at one spell slot higher than you use. Further, you gain resistance to fire damage.

Eyes of the Sultana

Wondrous item, artifact
(requires attunement per below)

The eyes of Cirrishade gleam with sadness and tragedy yet possess a wondrous beauty. Saddened by the loss of his beloved sister, Saaid al Djinn[1] enchanted her eyes upon her death. Further powered by the spirit of the Sultana herself as she slipped into the world of the dead and finally sanctified by the will of Anumon, the glittering eyes of Cirrishade glow forever with an eldritch light.

To use these magnificent magical items, you must first pluck out you own eyes, effectively causing permanent blindness and 1 point of Constitution damage per eye removed. Once the eyes are plucked free, the *eyes of the Sultana* may be placed within the empty sockets.

Upon placing the eyes in the sockets, you regain eyesight and gain command of great and powerful magic. Many effects are continuous, while many can be used only once per day or week. Both eyes must be used or you gain none of the benefits. The effects and side effects of wearing the *eyes of the Sultana* are as follows:

• You see as if you are under the continuous effect of a *true seeing spell*. Once per month, you must succeed on a DC 18 Wisdom saving throw or go insane from constantly seeing things as they truly are.

• Each time one of the eye's powers is used, there is a 50% chance your alignment changes to chaotic good or lawful neutral (50% chance of either).

• Once per day, you may unleash a *prismatic spray* (save DC 18).

• Three times per day, you can use a gaze attack that turns anyone meeting your gaze to stone (as by a *flesh to stone* spell). A DC 18 Constitution saving throw negates the effect.

• Once per day, you may cast the *eyebite* spell (save DC 18).

• Once per week, you may use *scrying* (as the spell) with a duration of one hour, using the eyes as your focus (save DC 18).

Falchion of Law

Weapon (longsword), legendary
(requires attunement by a lawful character)

You gain a +2 bonus on attack and damage rolls when you use this weapon. If you hit an aberration or demon, you do an extra 3d6 damage. When you attack a creature that has at least one head with this weapon and roll a 20 on the attack roll, you cut off one of the creature's heads. The creature dies if it can't survive without the lost head. A creature is immune to this effect if it is immune to slashing damage, doesn't have or need a head, has legendary actions, or the GM decides that the creature is too big for its head to be cut off with this weapon. Such a creature instead takes an extra 6d8 slashing damage from the hit.

Fire Armor

Armor (any), very rare

While you wear this armor, you gain a +2 bonus to your AC and you have resistance to fire damage.

Flail of wounding

Weapon (flail), rare (requires attunement)

Hit points lost to this weapon cannot be regained through regeneration, spells, or other magical means. In addition, when you hit a creature with this weapon, the target gains a wound. Each wound causes the creature 1 hit point of damage at the beginning of its turn. A wounded creature can attempt a DC 15 Constitution saving through, ending the effects of all wounds on a success. Alternatively, a creature within 5 feet of the wounded creature may use an action to attempt a DC 15 Wisdom (Medicine check), ending the effects of all wounds on a success.

Flaming Weapon

Weapon (any), rare

You gain a +1 bonus to attack and damage rolls with this weapon. When you hit, the weapon does an additional 1d6 fire damage.

The Flask of Sulymon

Wondrous item, artifact

The flask and its holy contents could prove the Sultan's undoing or grant him a station among the thrones of the greater gods.

The flask can be unstoppered and opened only in the presence of the Sultan, and only then if his true name is spoken as the seal is broken. This knowledge is not readily apparent, and even an *identify* spell will only provide some information about its true nature. A *wish*, *legend lore*, or other sources of information may provide more, at the GM's discretion.

Frost Weapon

Weapon (any), rare

You gain a +1 bonus to attack and damage rolls with this weapon. When you hit, the weapon does an additional 1d6 cold damage.

Gauntlets of Dexterity

Wondrous item, rare (requires attunement)

Your Dexterity is 20 while you wear these gauntlets. They have no effect if your Dexterity is already 20 or higher.

Girdle of Touch Me Not

Wondrous item, very rare

This thin girdle of fine pearls causes anyone who touches you unbidden to make a DC 14 Wisdom saving throw, taking 22 (4d10) cold damage on a failure or half as much on a success each time contact is made.

Golembane scarab

Wondrous item, rare (requires attunement)

While you wear this item, constructs have disadvantage on attacks against you and you have advantage on saving throws versus effects caused by constructs.

Hands of Pang Goy

Wondrous item, artifact (requires attunement)

These appear as metal gauntlets shaped for humanoid hands that reach almost to the elbow. To attune to the *hands of Pang Goy*, you must lop off both of your hands, the gauntlets grafting themselves to the stumps and then becoming a pair of functional appendages. They can only be removed if you die, and are useless if one gauntlet is separated from the other.

The *hands of Pang Goy* provide you with the following benefits:

• Your Strength and Dexterity scores become 20, unless one or both are already 20 or higher.

• You have a +3 bonus to attack and damage rolls made with any melee weapon attack you make, with the *hands* themselves as an unarmed attack or by wielding a weapon. In addition, you deal an extra 2d8 force damage on a hit.

• The *hands of Pang Goy* has 6 charges. You can use an action and expend 1 charge to create one weapon of your choice that you are proficient with, causing the gauntlet to magically transform. You can create two weapons if you are capable of wielding both, such as wielding two light weapons and engaging in two-weapon fighting. The created weapons last for 1 hour, or until you dismiss them (no action required).

Harmonious Lash

Weapon (whip), legendary

This weapon functions as a *+6 whip*. It is a coil of alloy constructed from an unknown metal and lined with barbed spikes. Damage from the *lash* does not heal normally. Wounds can be healed magically but only by a *wish* or a *heal* spell. No other form of magical healing (*cure* spells, *potions*, and so on) works.

As a bonus action, you can speak a command word causing the *lash* to drip a powerful and debilitating venom. A creature hit by the venomous *lash* must succeed on a DC 18 Constitution saving throw or take 55 (10d10) poison damage. One minute later, a new save must be made (same DC) to avoid another 55 (10d10) poison damage. This damage also can only be healed with a *wish* or a *heal* spell.

A creature hit by the whip must succeed on a DC 16 Dexterity saving throw or be grappled by it. The creature must use an action and succeed on a DC 18 Strength (Athletics) or Dexterity (Acrobatics) check to escape.

The first time a non-n'gathau wields the *lash* the character immediately takes 14 (4d6) slashing damage from hundreds of cuts and slices that appear as if the creature is being cut by a thousand invisible razors. Each time thereafter the character uses or attempts to use the *lash*, the character takes 7 (2d6) slashing damage from cuts and slices.

Horn of Alarm

Wondrous item, very rare

This horn has 3 charges. When you use an action to blow on the horn, it emits a resounding note audible up to 1200 feet away. Creatures friendly to you who hear the horn gain +2 on their first subsequent initiative roll, if it is within 1 minute of the horn sounding. The horn regains 1d3 expended charges daily at dawn.

Horns of Power

Wondrous item, legendary (requires attunement)

The horns of power are an ancient magical item from the before the birth of mortals. The horns are from a long-extinct species known for its great wisdom and strength. They have been passed down and even warred over by druidic circles since the dawn of time. On the brow of a non-druid, the horns provide a +1 to Strength, Armor Class, Wisdom, and Saving Throws. When worn by a druid, this bonus doubles. When worn, the horns actually fuse to your head and can be taken off only upon your death or by the use of a *wish* spell.

Icy Burst Glaive

Weapon (glaive), very rare

You gain a +1 bonus to attack and damage rolls made with this weapon. When you hit a creature with this weapon, you do an additional 1d6 cold damage. When you score a critical hit with this weapon, a burst of ice shards explodes from the contact. The target takes an additional 1d8 piercing damage, and each creature within 5 feet of the target must succeed on a DC 15 Dexterity saving throw or take 1d8 piercing damage.

Inhibitor Bands

Wondrous item, rare

While a creature wears this item, it cannot use spellcasting or innate spellcasting abilities, it cannot change form and is immune to having its shape changed with *polymorph* or similar magic, and it cannot teleport, plane shift, or otherwise magically travel or be moved magically. The bands can be open or closed by a creature that knows the magic word and can be broken with a DC 30 Strength check.

Javelin of Freedom

Weapon (javelin), very rare (requires attunement)

You gain a +1 bonus to attack and damage rolls with this weapon. While you carry it, you are unaffected by difficult terrain, and spells and other magical effects can neither reduce your speed nor cause you to be paralyzed or restrained. You can also spend 5 feet of movement to automatically escape from nonmagical restrains, such as manacles or a creature that has you grappled. Being underwater imposes no penalties on your movement or attacks.

Juggernaut of Kil Kath Kesh

Wondrous item, legendary

This construct of unknown metal alloys and wires once served as the guardian of the City-State of Kil Kath Kesh. Roughly humanoid in shape and standing 25 feet tall, the juggernaut has four pairs of huge flails on braided cables running down its back. One arm ends in a tube containing seven large jewels ranging the color spectrum, while its other arm has a huge crab-like pincer with a menacingly sharp razor edge. Legends say that the juggernaut can move upon the ground in a lumbering walk, but that it can also fly, raining death from the skies. It is said that a hidden panel in the juggernaut's back opens to reveal a compartment for up to four passengers. The juggernaut stands lifeless, its brain crystal lost long ago in a battle with its creator. Stats for the *Juggernaut* are listed with the creatures in **Appendix 2**.

Lifestealer

Weapon (shortsword), legendary

Whenever you take the attack action to make an attack with this weapon against a living creature that is not an undead or construct, the target must make a Dexterity saving throw. The DC is 8 + your Dexterity modifier + your proficiency bonus. On a failed saving throw, the target takes 3d8 + 10 necrotic damage. If you use your action to attack with this weapon, you can also use your bonus action to attack with it.

Mace of Ultimate Disruption

Weapon, legendary

This weapon functions as a *mace of disruption*. In addition, you gain a +3 bonus to attack and damage rolls made with this weapon.

Mantle of Faith

Wondrous item, rare

While you wear this item, you have resistance to nonmagical bludgeoning, piercing, and slashing damage.

Mask of Ankev

Wondrous item, artifact
(requires attunement by an evil creature)

This unholy item is purportedly the only likeness of the arch lich Ankev as he appeared in life. Made of solid gold and encrusted with precious gemstones, the mask portrays a handsome face twisted with maniacal cruelty. The mask is purported to have numerous magical powers for anyone with the strength to wear it. It is believed that any creature possessing the *crooked rod of Ankev*, the *sarcophagus of Ankev*, and the *mask* may be instantly transformed into a lich upon the completion of a long-forgotten ritual.

When donned, the mask immediately affixes itself to your face and may be removed only upon your death, or by means of a *wish* spell cast by another. When worn, the mask is completely weightless.

While wearing the mask you have the following bonuses:

- Immunity to gaze attacks

- Immunity to poison, sleep effects, paralysis, stunning, disease, and death effects (spells or spell-like abilities that cause death rather than damage), mind-affecting effects (charms, patterns, compulsions, phantasms, and fear effects)

- +4 to your Intelligence score

- +6 bonus to AC

Undead are drawn to the wearer of the mask. Undead detect the wearer of the *mask of Ankev* even if the wearer is otherwise invisible to them.

Once per day, you may reveal a *symbol of death* that affects allies and enemies alike. Any beings slain by the symbol rise as zombies in 1d4 minutes. These undead beings are not necessarily under your command and are 50% likely to attack you unless halted by means of turn undead.

Good-aligned creatures touching the mask take 27 (6d8) necrotic damage each round. Neutral-aligned creatures take 13 (3d8) necrotic damage each round.

Maul of Hezoid

Weapon (warhammer), legendary

This oversized weapon can only be wielded by a Medium or larger character with at least 18 Strength, and medium creatures can only use it two-handed.

You gain a +3 bonus to attack and damage rolls when you use this weapon. When you use this weapon, you score a critical on a 19 or 20. When you score a critical with this weapon, it does an additional 1d8 thunder damage. A Huge or larger creature may use the Maul of Hezoid as a thrown weapon, in which case it returns to the hand of the thrower at the end of the thrower's turn, unless the creature is unconscious or does not have a free hand, in which case it lands in the creature's space.

Mirror of Duplication

Wondrous item, very rare

This mirror functions like a *mirror of life trapping* with an additional potent power. As an action, you can use the mirror to create a double of one of the creatures trapped within. The creature has all of the knowledge and memories of the trapped creature, as well as its hit points and statistics, but no spellcasting or other class features. The creature is under your control as long as you concentrate. When not concentrating, the creature appears dull and listless. You can have as many duplicates as there are creatures trapped in the mirror, but you can only concentrate on one at a time.

Munir Seif al Shihab (Shining Sword of Flame)

Weapon (longsword), artifact (requires attunement)

A gift from the Sultan, this weapon was specially constructed for Rahib in the forges and factories of the City of Brass. It is exquisite in design, the blade forged of living brass. The hilt is wrapped in the blackened skin of a slain demon lord.

When you use this weapon, you gain a +4 bonus to hit and to damage. As a bonus action, you can choose to charge the weapon with your choice of fire, lightning, thunder, or cold damage. The first hit after the weapon is charged does an additional 3d10 damage of that type. The weapon does an additional 2d10 radiant damage against any chaotic creature that it strikes. You gain advantage on attack against a creature wearing nonmagical armor or wielding a shield. In addition, once per day, you can use the weapon to cast fireball with a spell save DC of 18 and a base damage level of 10d6 fire damage.

Mymr Stone

Wondrous item, artifact (requires attunement)

Roughly the size of an apple, this intelligent liquid crystal is said to be a droplet from the pool of wisdom in which the head of the giant Mymr and the eye of Odin float. The stone is capable of solving the most complex of calculations with the greatest of ease. When set to a task, the *Mymr Stone* continues its work until relieved of its duty or until it is set to a new task.

Sentience. The *Mymr stone* is neutral and has an Intelligence of 19, a Wisdom of 19, and a Charisma of 10 It speaks Auran, Common, Abyssal, Ignan, Infernal, and Terran and has telepathy 100 feet, darkvision 120 feet, blindsense, and hearing.

While you carry the stone:

- You gain a +4 bonus to Intelligence and Wisdom.

- You can use the following, each once per day, as spell-like abilities:

clairvoyance (unlimited range), *legend lore, time stop.*

- You may ask one question of the *Mymr Stone* per day as a *commune* spell.

- You must make a DC 16 Constitution saving throw each time you use one of the *Mymr Stone's* powers. On a failed save, you age one year and lose1 ability point chosen randomly.

Those viewing the *Mymr Stone* must make a DC 18 Wisdom saving throw or be fascinated by its beauty, unable to tear their eyes from it and unable to move from its presence. The fascination is broken if they are attacked or threatened. A creature that makes its save cannot be fascinated by the *Mymr Stone* for one day.

The stone protects itself by attempting to mentally *disintegrate* anyone who would attempt to possess it unless they defeat its ego by making a successful DC 18 Charisma check. The creature being disintegrated must succeed on a DC 18 Charisma saving throw or take 75 (10d6 + 40) psychic damage. If this damage reduces the target to 0 hit points, it is disintegrated as its molecules fly out in an explosion doing 7 (2d6) force damage to any within 30 feet of the creature.

Necklace of Frost

Wondrous item, very rare (requires attunement)

This necklace is a heavy white gold chain with a blue gem medallion. While you wear it, you can use an action to unleash a *cone of cold* to a range of 60 feet. Creatures in the cone must make a DC 17 Dexterity saving throw, taking 36 (8d8) cold damage on a failure or half as much on a success. This medallion can be used three times per day.

Oil of Magic Weapon

Potion, varies

When you coat a weapon with this oil, it gains a magical bonus to hit and damage. The bonus is determined by the item's rarity. The oil can coat one weapon or 5 pieces of ammunition. Applying the coating takes one minute and the coating lasts for one hour, except that the effect on ammunition is removed if it hits a target.

Oil of...	Rarity	Bonus
Magic weapon	common	+1
Greater magic weapon	uncommon	+2
Superior magic weapon	rare	+3

Oil of Magic Vestment

Potion, rare

When you coat an item of outer clothing with this oil, the clothing provides a +1 bonus to Armor Class while it lasts. Applying the coating takes one minute and the coating lasts for one hour. A vial of this oil contains enough to coat one Medium or Small jacket or similar item.

Oil of Paralysis Removal

Potion, rare

There is enough oil in one dose to coat one Medium or smaller creature. When you use an action to spread the oil on a paralyzed creature, the paralysis is removed.

Oilshark Armor

Armor (leather), legendary

You gain a +3 bonus to AC when you wear this armor crafted from the hide of the mighty oil shark. In addition, you gain resistance to fire damage and have advantage on checks made to escape from a grapple.

Oriazier's Key: Muse

Wondrous item, artifact

This beautiful golden grand harp weighs roughly 120 pounds and is 6 feet tall, with the likeness of an elven maiden making up the soundboard. The string arm is curved behind the maiden in the form of diaphanous wings that curl around to the floor. The elf maid, who calls herself *Muse*, opens her eyes and haunting notes begin to chime from her strings. The harp has several magical properties that may be drawn out by a skilled player. *Muse* is, however, generally considered to be much too large to take along in an adventuring campaign, unless of course the individual playing her happens to be more than 18 feet tall.

When you use this harp, you have a +4 bonus on all Performance checks while playing the harp and for 1 hour afterward. This bonus increases to +8 if you are a bard. Those within 30 feet who hear the music gain advantage on skill checks involving writing and composing music, literature, or dance for 1 hour. This ability can be used twice per day.

Potion of Antidote

Potion, rare

When you drink this potion, any ongoing effects caused by poison are halted, and you do not suffer from the poisoned condition. Damage or instantaneous effects (such as blindness) already caused by the poison are not cured.

Potion of Delay Poison

Potion, uncommon

When you drink this potion, you do not suffer from the poisoned condition and any ongoing effects caused by poison are temporarily nullified. At the end of 1 hour, any effects caused by poison, including the poisoned condition, resume unless you have received the necessary antidote or magical healing.

Potion of Hide from Undead

Potion, rare

When you drink this potion, you become difficult to locate for undead creatures. An undead creature must succeed on a DC 14 Wisdom saving throw or be unable to detect or locate you with sight, hearing or smell. Even extraordinary senses such as blindsight and tremorsense are not effective. The effects automatically end if you take an action which uses radiant energy, attempt to turn undead, or attack an undead creature. Otherwise, the effects of the potion last for one hour.

Potion of Protection from Missiles

Ring, uncommon (requires attunement)

While you wear this ring, anybody making a ranged attack against you with a normal missile (thrown weapon or arrow, but not including a giant's boulder) has disadvantage on their attack.

Potion of Remove Fear

Potion, common

When you drink this potion, you are immune from the frightened condition for 1 hour, and if you had the frightened condition prior to drinking it, it is removed.

Ring of Blinking

Ring, very rare (requires attunement)

As an action, you can cause yourself to vanish from your current plane of existence and appear in the Ethereal Plane until the start of your next turn. You return to the space you started from unless that space is occupied in which case you return to the nearest unoccupied space.

While on the Ethereal Plane, you can see and hear the plane you originated from, which is cast in shades of gray, and you can't see anything there more than 60 feet away. You can only affect and be affected by other creatures on the Ethereal Plane. Creatures that aren't there can't perceive you or interact with you, unless they have the ability to do so.

Ring of Comfort

Ring, uncommon

While you wear this elegant band, you and everything you are wearing sheds dirt and sweat as they accumulate. Your clothing retains sharp creases or proper drape despite humidity or wind. You are comfortable in temperatures between 32 and 100 degrees Fahrenheit (0 and 40 degrees Celsius) no matter what type of clothing or armor you are wearing.

Ring of Immunity

Ring, very rare (requires attunement)

While you wear this ring, you are immune to one type of damage. The gem in the ring indicates the type, which the GM chooses or determines randomly.

d10	Damage Type	Gem
1	Acid	Pearl
2	Cold	Tourmaline
3	Fire	Garnet
4	Force	Sapphire
5	Lightning	Citrine
6	Necrotic	Jet
7	Poison	Amethyst
8	Psychic	Jade
9	Radiant	Topaz
10	Thunder	Spinel

Ring of Protection

Wondrous item, rarity varies (requires attunement)

While wearing this ring, you gain a bonus to your AC and saving throws. The amount of the bonus depends on the ring's rarity.

Ring of...	Rarity	Bonus
Protection	rare	+1
Greater protection	very rare	+2
Superior protection	legendary	+3

Ring of Qalb

Ring, legendary (requires attunement)

This ring of iron and brass serves as a *ring of resistance* (fire).

The ring is the phylactery of Qalb al Nar's[1] soul. So long as the ring exists, Qalb reforms within 24 hours of his defeat. The regenerated Qalb is always one HD weaker than it was before its defeat, however. If Qalb is ever reduced to zero hit dice, he truly dies, and the ring turns to dust. For example, if Sparque is destroyed in battle while he has 3 hit dice, he returns the next day as a 2 hit die elemental. If he is then defeated two more times before acquiring any new hit dice, he is lost forever.

Ring of Sustenance

Ring, rare (requires attunement)

While you wear this ring, you do not need to eat or drink. In addition, you gain the benefits of a long rest with half the amount of rest you normally require. You still cannot gain the benefits of a long rest more than once in a day.

Ring of Wizardry

Ring, varies (requires attunement by a wizard)

While you are wearing this ring, the number of spell slots you have available for a given level is doubled. The level is determined by the rarity of the ring.

Ring of...	Rarity	Spell level
Wizardry	rare	1st
Greater wizardry	very rare	2nd
Superior wizardry	legendary	3rd

Robe of Armor

Wondrous item, very rare

If worn over normal clothing, these robes set your armor class to 13 + your Dexterity modifier when you are not wearing any armor.

Robe of Fire

Wondrous item, rare

This yellowish-orange robe allows you to shroud your body in flames up to 10 rounds each day. They need not be consecutive rounds. The flames do not harm you but allow you to deal an extra 2d6 fire damage with melee attacks made while shrouded in fire. Additionally, a creature striking you with a melee attack while the robe is ablaze takes 2d6 fire damage.

Robe of Powerlessness

Wondrous item, very rare

When you don this item, you instantly gain 3 levels of exhaustion. While the cloak can be removed easily, the exhaustion can only be removed after *remove curse* has been cast on you. After that, the exhaustion can be healed normally with time or magic. If *identify* is cast on this robe, its cursed natured is revealed.

Robe of Vermin

Wondrous item, very rare

The cloak appears to be a magical robe that would grant protection from weapons or aid with saving throws and an *identify* spell confirms this. You notice nothing unusual when the robe is donned, and it appears to function normally. However, as soon as you are in a situation requiring concentration and action against hostile opponents, the true nature of the garment is revealed: you immediately suffer a multitude of bites from the insects that magically infest the garment. You must cease all other activities in order to scratch, shift the robe, and generally show signs of the extreme discomfort caused by the bites and movement of these pests.

You have disadvantage on initiative checks, attack rolls, saving throws, and skill checks. You must succeed on a concentration check each time you attempt to cast a spell or lose the spell.

Once the robe has activated its curse, it can only be removed after *remove curse* is cast the wearer.

Rod of Flailing

Rod, legendary (requires attunement)

As a bouns action, you can change the rod from a normal-seeming rod to a magical two-headed flail or back. When you use the flail as a weapon, you gain a +3 bonus to attack and damage rolls. In addition, if you use an action to attack with the flail, you can use your bonus action to attack with the other head of the flail.

Three times per day, you can use a reaction to cast *shield* using the rod, whether it is in flail or rod form.

Rod of Spell Empowerment

Rod, rare

This rod may be used as a spell focus by a wizard, sorcerer, or warlock. Five times per day, when you cast a spell using the rod as a focus, you can empower the spell by rerolling a number of the damage dice equal to your spellcasting ability modifier (minimum of one). You must use the new rolls.

Rod of Spell Enlargement

Rod, rare

This rod may be used as a spell focus by a wizard, sorcerer, or warlock. Five times per day, when you cast a spell using the rod as a focus, you can increase the range of the spell. If the range is 5 feet or more, the range is doubled. If the range is touch, it becomes 30 feet.

Rod of Telekinesis

Rod, very rare (requires attunement)

While holding this rod, you can cast *telekinesis* at will, but you can target only objects that aren't being worn or carried.

Rod of Thunder and Lightning

Rod, very rare

Constructed of iron set with silver rivets, this rod acts as a +2 mace.

In addition, you can use the following powers.

Lightning. Once per day, you can cause a short spark of electricity to leap forth when the rod strikes an opponent to deal an extra 2d6 lightning damage.

Lightning stroke: Once per day you can use an action to cause the rod to shoot out a 5-foot-wide, 200-foot-long lightning bolt. Each creature along the path must make a DC 16 Dexterity saving throw, taking 9d6 lightning damage on a failure or half as much on a success.

Thunder: Once per day, the rod can strike as a +3 mace, and the opponent struck must succeed on a DC 15 Constitution saving throw or be stunned until the end of its next turn. You must decide whether to use this power before you make your attack roll.

Thunderclap: Once per day as an action, you can cause the rod to give out a deafening noise. Each creature within 30 feet that can hear must make a DC 15 Constitution saving throw. A creature that fails takes 3d6 thunder damage and is deafened for 1 minute. A creature that succeeds takes half the damage and is not deafened.

Thunder and Lightning: Once per week as an action, you can combine the thunderclap power with a *lightning bolt*. The thunderclap affects all creatures within 10 feet of the bolt. The lightning stroke deals 9d6 lightning damage, and the thunderclap deals 3d6 thunder damage. A single DC 15 Dexterity saving throw applies to halve the damage from both effects.

Ruby Star of Law

Wondrous item, artifact (requires attunement)

This heart-sized gem made from elemental ruby is star-shaped and seems to pulse and glow with an inner light all its own. The *ruby star of law* was said to have been a gift from Anumon himself to the faithful genie who accepted his law and order of things as their creator. It is claimed that the *ruby star of law* possesses great power to destroy any genie that has not accepted the law of Anumon and is thus a much-feared relic when used in the right (or wrong) hands.

Once per round, up to three times per day, you can can make a ranged weapon attack with the *ruby star of law* to fire a ray to a maximum range of 1,200 feet. Genies hit by this ray must succeed on a DC 26 Constitution saving throw or die. On a successful save, the genie loses 14 (4d6) points of Constitution.

Lawful non-genies are *slowed* (as the spell) for 1d4 rounds (no save). Non-lawful non-genies take 21 (6d6) radiant damage and must succeed on a DC 20 Constitution saving throw or be stunned for 1d4 rounds.

You are shielded from spells and spell-like effects of 5th-level or lower as if protected by a *globe of invulnerability*.

When affixed to a temple of Anumon, the jade colossus of the Sultana, or other structure blessed and consecrated to the god of the gates, the ruby may fire its burning ray up to once per round an unlimited number of times per day.

Saddle of Ooze Riding

Wondrous item, legendary (requires attunement)

When affixed to any ooze, slime, or pudding, this strange saddle-shaped object automatically "tames" the creature and doubles its base land speed. You suffer no ill effects from acid, cold, fire, or other such special attacks while mounted on an ooze. You can use the saddled ooze as a mount.

Sarcophagus of Ankev

Wondrous item, legendary

This ancient stone sarcophagus emanates an unholy evil that terrorizes even the most stouthearted heroes and the most diabolically minded fiends. The true sarcophagus of Ankev the Arch-Lich is said to be powerful enough to transform any divine or arcane spellcaster into a lich should they know the ritual. Some whisper that the sarcophagus may be used as an unholy channel for summoning undead. Others say that the undead appear on their own as a reminder of Ankev's power.

Scepter of Anubis

Rod, artifact (requires attunement)

The mighty scepter of the Khemitian god Anubis rests on display here. Whether this is the true scepter of the god or a replica is unknown. It is known that this scepter would in fact hold great power — if it were complete. The top of the scepter is missing (rumored to be a piece of bronze fashioned into the shape of an ankh). Without the top, the scepter is powerless (albeit still worth a fortune given its presumed origins). When complete, the scepter has the following powers. Spell-like powers have a spell attack bonus of +10 and a spell save DC of 18.

Ten times per day, you can cast *gentle repose*.

Five times per day, you can cast *finger of death* or *raise dead*.

Three times per day, you can cast *resurrection* or *powerword kill*.

Twice per day, you can cast *true resurrection* or *disintegrate*.

Scepter of Attar

Wondrous item, legendary (requires attunement)

This ancient scepter was carried by the first followers of the Lightbringer whom he instructed in the primordial dawn of mortal existence. It is made from the bones of one of the first priests and bound with the skull of one of his first sacrifices.

You may use the scepter as a *+3 morningstar* that does an additional 1d6 necrotic damage on a hit. While carrying to the scepter, you gain +2 to any spell attack rolls.

You may use the scepter to cast the following spells, with a +8 spell attack bonus and a spell save DC of 18:

At will: *bane, fear, inflict wounds*

1/day: *augury, animate dead*

1/week: *raise dead, planar ally* (devil only)

Shirt of the Iron Lion

Armor (chain shirt), legendary

This knee length iron chain shirt has a full coif and sleeves and is adorned with symbols of a rampant lion on the breast and circlet that affixes the coif to the brow. It was the shirt of Lord Yahuth a hero who did great battle against the hordes of Hell and the minions of the Abyss. Yahuth's faith is said to have left him immune to temptation and his iron shirt defended him from claw, fang, and sword of his fiendish foes.

You gain a +3 bonus to your AC while you wear the Iron shirt, and fiends have disadvantage on attacks against you. You have advantage on saving throws against the spells and spell like abilities of fiends.

Shocking Sword of Law

Weapon (shortsword), legendary
(requires attunement by a non-chaotic creature)

You gain a +3 bonus to attack and damage rolls with this weapon. As a bonus action, you can cause the sword to sparkle with electricity. While electrified, it does an additional 1d6 lightning damage on a hit. Against chaotic creatures, this damage increases to 3d6.

The Shroud of Truth

Wondrous item, legendary
(requires attunement by a lawful evil character)

The Prince of Darkness amuses himself with half-truths, innuendo, and the small lies that murder some part of the world. The irony of naming this gift to mortals the *shroud of truth* was not lost upon him.

A yellowish brimstone smoke rises from the edges of this red and black velvet cape. The cape itself is lawful evil and deals 14 (4d6) necrotic damage per round to any non-lawful evil entity who attempts to handle it.

Wearing this cape grants you +3 to your armor class and a +2 to your Charisma score as well as the ability to cast *charm person* and *disguise self* at will with a spell save DC of 18.

Silversheen

Potion, uncommon

One does of this thick cream is enough to coat one melee weapon or 5 pieces of ammunition. A coated weapon acts as if it is a silver weapon for one hour, although ammunition loses its sheen if it hits a target.

Skin of Jhedophar

Wondrous item, artifact

The flayed skin of the lich is inscribed with unholy writs and spells of summoning. Among them are the true names of six demons, six dragons and six devils. Intoning the names of any of the eighteen has a 50% chance of summoning them immediately. The beings, upon seeing the skin of the lich, seek to steal it outright. The dragons and fiends should be selected at random and are likely Challenge 12 to 15, depending on the needs of the GM's campaign.

Sleep Potion

Potion, uncommon

When unstoppered or shattered, the liquid inside reacts with air, becoming a clear, odorless gas. The gas affects 7d8 hit points of creatures within 20 feet, in ascending order of their current hit points (ignoring unconscious creatures). Starting with the creature that has the lowest current hit points, each creature affected by the gas falls asleep for one hour or until the creature takes damage or somebody uses an action to shake or slap the sleeper awake. Subtract each creature's hit points from the total before moving on to the creature with the next lowest hit points. A creature's hit points must be equal to or less than the remaining total for that creature to be affected.

Slippers of Seductive Dancing

Wondrous item, rare

These finely crafted slippers grant you +6 on Performance checks made to dance while you wear them.

Spell Potion

Potion, varies

A spell potion mimics the effects of a spell. Only spells that can be cast on the caster and that have a duration of at least 1 minute may be made into spell potions. The rarity of the potion is based on the level of the spell being mimicked. When you drink the potion, it is as if you had cast the referenced spell upon yourself except that you do not need to concentrate to maintain the effects.

Spell Level	Rarity
Cantrip	Common
1st	Common
2nd	Common
3rd	Uncommon
4th	Uncommon
5th	Rare
6th	Rare
7th	Very Rare
8th	Very Rare
9th	Very Rare

Spell Wand

Wand, varies (requires attunement by a spellcaster)

A spell wand allows you to cast a single spell without material components. While holding it, you can use an action to expend 1 charge to cast the spell associated with the wand. You must be able to speak the command and point the wand at the target. If the spell has a range of touch, then you must touch the target with the wand, although you still use the wand's spell attack bonus to attempt the touch. In general, the wand casts the spell with the lowest possible spell slot. The rarity, save DC, spell attack modifier, number of charges, and charge refresh per 24 hours are shown above, depending on the level of spell stored in the wand.

Spell Wand Information Table

Spell Level	Rarity	Save DC	Attack Bonus	Charges	Charge Refresh
Cantrip	Common	13	+5	10	1d6 + 4
1st	Uncommon	13	+5	10	1d6 + 4
2nd	Uncommon	13	+5	7	1d6 + 1
3rd	Rare	15	+7	7	1d6 + 1
4th	Rare	15	+7	7	1d6 + 1
5th	Very Rare	17	+9	4	1d3 + 1
6th	Very Rare	17	+9	4	1d3 + 1
7th	Very Rare	18	+10	3	1d3
8th	Legendary	18	+10	3	1d3
9th	Legendary	19	+11	3	1d3

Staff of Abjuration

Staff, very rare

(requires attunement by an arcane spellcaster)

This staff has 10 charges. While holding it, you can use an action to expend 1 or more of its charges to cast one of the following spells from it, using your spell attack bonus and save DC: *resistance* (1 charge), *shield* (1 charge), *dispel magic* (3 charges), *banishment* (4 charges), or *globe of invulnerability* (6 charges).

The staff regains 1d6 + 4 charges daily at dawn. If you expend the last charge, roll a d20. On a 1, the staff flies off to a random plane to await the next lucky creature that happens upon it.

Staff of Conjuration

Staff, very rare

(requires attunement by an arcane spellcaster)

This staff has 10 charges. While holding it, you can use an action to expend 1 or more of its charges to cast one of the following spells from it, using your spell attack bonus and save DC: *unseen servant* (1 charge), *conjure animals* (3 charges), *stinking cloud* (3 charges), *cloudkill* (5 charges), or *conjure volley* (5 charges).

The staff regains 1d6 + 4 charges daily at dawn. If you expend the last charge, roll a d20. On a 1, the staff erupts in a bright light and turns to ash, useless.

Staff of Defense

Staff, uncommon

This staff has 5 charges. If you are wielding it, you can use a reaction to expend one of its charges to cast *shield*.

The staff regains 1d4 + 1 charges each day at dawn.

Staff of Illusion

Staff, very rare

(requires attunement by an arcane spellcaster)

This staff has 10 charges. While holding it, you can use an action to expend 1 or more of its charges to cast one of the following spells from it, using your spell attack bonus and save DC: *disguise self* (1 charge), *silent image* (1 charge), *mirror image* (2 charges), *major image* (3 charges), *hypnotic pattern* (3 charges), or *mislead* (5 charges).

The staff regains 1d6 + 4 charges daily at dawn. If you expend the last charge, roll a d20. On a 1, the staff vanishes.

Staff of Necromancy

Staff, very rare

(requires attunement by an arcane spellcaster)

This staff has 10 charges. While holding it, you can use an action to expend 1 or more of its charges to cast one of the following spells from it, using your spell attack bonus and save DC: *chill touch* (1 charge), *ray of enfeeblement* (2 charges), *bestow curse* (3 charges), *vampiric touch* (3 charges), or *circle of death* (6 charges).

The staff regains 1d6 + 4 charges daily at dawn. If you expend the last charge, roll a d20. On a 1, the staff crumbles to dust, useless.

Staff of the Prophet

Staff, legendary

(requires attunement by a cleric or druid)

This staff can be wielded as a magic quarterstaff that grants a +3 bonus to attack and damage rolls made with it and inflicts 5d6 force damage with each hit. While holding this staff, you gain a +3 bonus to Armor Class and saving throws, and you have advantage on saving throws against spells and other magical effects.

The staff has 25 charges for the following properties. The staff regains 2d8 + 8 expended charges daily at dawn. If you expend the last charge, roll a d20. On a 1, the staff retains its +2 bonus to attack and damage rolls but loses all other properties.

Divine Avoidance. When you are hit by a weapon attack, you may use your reaction to spend 1 charge. The attack then misses instead of hits.

Spells. While holding this staff, you may use an action to expend 1 or more of its charges to cast one of the following spells from it, using your spell save DC and spell attack bonus: *arcane hand* (5 charges), *globe of invulnerability* (6 charges), *mass heal* (9 charges), *move earth* (6 charges), *protection from evil and good* (1 charge; elementals and fiends only), *wall of stone* (5 charges).

Staff of Transmutation

Staff, very rare

(requires attunement by an arcane spellcaster)

This staff has 10 charges. While holding it, you can use an action to expend 1 or more of its charges to cast one of the following spells from it, using your spell attack bonus and save DC: *expeditious retreat* (1 charge), *alter self* (2 charges), *blink* (3 charges), *polymorph* (4 charges), or *disintegrate* (6 charges).

The staff regains 1d6 + 4 charges daily at dawn. If you expend the last charge, roll a d20. On a 1, the staff crumbles to dust, useless.

Stone of Sulymon, Air

Wondrous item, legendary (requires attunement)

Also known as the Jawahra min Alriya, Jewel of the Wind, this brilliant sapphire floats inside a brick-sized block of clear crystal.

While you carry this stone, you can fly at your normal movement. In addition, you can cast the following spells without material components with a spell save DC of 17 and spell attack bonus of +9:

At will: *gust of wind*

Once per day: *wind walk, wind wall*

Once per week: *summon aerial servant*[4].

Stone of Sulymon, Earth

Wondrous item, legendary (requires attunement)

Carved from a nodule of pure elemental earth, the stone is shot through with iron, gold, silver, and inlaid in platinum. The stone is warm to the touch and is the size of a hefty brick. It vibrates with a deep inner resonance and glows when it is brought within the presence of another of the elemental stones of Sulymon.

While you carry this stone, you gain resistance to slashing damage In addition, you can cast the following spells without material components with a spell save DC of 17 and spell attack bonus of +9.

1/day: *stone shape, wall of stone*

1/week: *stoneskin, conjure elemental* (earth)

Stone of Sulymon, Fire

Wondrous item, legendary (requires attunement)

This stone, while comfortable to the touch, appears to be made of living magma. It glows and spwarks when it is brought within the presence of another of the elemental stones of Sulymon.

While you carry this stone, you are immune to fire damage. In addition, you can cast the following spells without material components with a spell save DC of 17 and spell attack bonus of +9.

1/day: *burning hands, wall of fire*

1/week: *delayed blast fireball, conjure elemental* (fire)

Stone of Sulymon, Water

Wondrous item, legendary (requires attunement)

This stone functions as a *decanter of endless water* except that it cannot produce salt water. Once per week, you can use it to summon a water elemental like the spell *conjure elemental* cast with a 5th level spell slot.

Sword of Dawaad

Weapon (greatsword), legendary

(requires attunement by a lawful creature)

Sulymon himself crafted this weapon for his champion Dawaad to wield.

You gain a +3 bonus to attack and damage rolls with this weapon. Against chaotic celestials, elementals, fey, and fiends, this bonus increases to +5 and the weapon does an additional 2d6 damage on a hit.

Sword of Hunting

Weapon (any sword), rare

You have a +1 bonus to attack and damage rolls made with this magic weapon. Against one creature or type of creature, you have a +3 bonus to attack and damage rolls.

Sword of Speed

Weapon (any sword), very rare

You have a +2 bonus to attack and damage rolls made with this magic weapon. While wielding this weapon, you gain advantage on Initiative rolls and your speed is increased by 5. If you have a flying or swimming speed, it is also increased.

Sword of the Lightbringer

Weapon (greatsword), artifact

Known as Phosphorus, the sword that the Lightbringer took up against the gods that precipitated the great fall was forged in the highest heavens from elements of the universe and the bones of an archangel who attempted to stop the Lightbringer from raising his hand against the creators.

The gleaming, reddish blade glows with a brilliant white light. The sword is large, being considered a greatsword in the hands of a Medium-sized being.

The blade grants you a +5 bonus to hit. It ignores immunity or resistance to slashing or critical hits. The sword deals 14 (4d6) additional slashing damage on a natural 20, and a second roll of natural 20 dismembers a victim's limb, instantly cauterizing the wound so that it cannot be regenerated without additional magical assistance such as a *heal* spell. The blade casts a bright pinkish light in a 10-foot radius and a dim light for an additional 20-foot radius.

The sword itself generates an aura of intense evil, and a successful DC 18 Charisma saving throw must be made by any non-lawful evil aligned bearer, lest they be unable to wield the weapon due to excruciating pain associated with its touch.

Throne of Brass

Wondrous item, artifact (requires attunement by the Great Sultan of the City of Brass)

The stately *Throne of Brass* sits atop a dais of 42 steps in the center of the back wall of the Hall of Kings in the Grand Palace of the Sultan of the Efreet. High-backed with armrests in the shape of dragons, the entire throne is cast from living brass and encrusted with thousands of elemental gemstones harvested from the volcanic fissures of the Plane of Molten Skies. The *Throne of Brass* is a throne built for an immense figure, a regal chair for an awesome planar power.

Most petitioners granted an audience with the Sultan stand before the Advocates' Throne, where they either make their offering to the Sultan or plead their case. The advocates then repeat this plea to the Sultan who makes his judgment known to the entire court. Rarely is a petitioner granted leave to climb the dais and stand before the Sultan himself. In this event, the petitioner must succeed on a DC 25 Wisdom saving throw for every six of the 42 steps climbed (thus it takes seven saves to reach the top). On a failed save, the petitioner succumbs to the awe and power of the *Throne of Brass*, crawling the remaining way to the top (no more saves are required), and is immediately affected as if a *suggestion* spell had been cast on the petitioner by the Sultan.

The Sultan's Protector. While the Great Sultan is within 5 feet of the *Throne of Brass*, he gains the continuous effects of the following spells: *detect thoughts*, *globe of invulnerability*, and *zone of truth*. The Sultan is exempted from the effects of the *zone of truth*. As a bonus action while within 5 feet of the *Throne of Brass*, the Sultan can create a globe-shaped *wall of force* around the *Throne*. The Sultan must use another bonus action to dismiss the wall.

Symbols of Power. The *Throne of Brass* is inscribed with eight *symbol* spells, one of each kind. These symbols are hidden by magic and only appear when the Great Sultan wills it. As a bonus action while within 5 feet of the *Throne of Brass*, the Sultan can speak a command word and reveal a *symbol*, affecting the area with its effects. The Sultan is exempted from the effects of these *symbols*. Once a symbol has been used, it can't be used again until the next dawn.

Destroying the Throne of Brass. The *Throne of Brass* is made of living brass and repairs any damage done to it, no matter how severe. Its fate is tied to the City of Brass, and it can be destroyed only when the City itself falls. To destroy the *Throne of Brass*, a Hawanar, a descendant of the previous Sultan and Sultana, must coat the *Brazen Scimitar* in the blood of the dying Great Sultan before plunging the blade into the *Throne of Brass*. With the scimitar sheathed thusly in the throne, the City of Brass must then be abandoned by the efreet for one thousand years, at the end of which time the City and the *Throne of Brass* crumble to dust.

Thundering Great Mace

Weapon (great mace³), very rare

You have a +3 bonus to attack and damage rolls made with this magic weapon. When you score a critical hit with this weapon, it creates a thunderous boom and the target takes an additional 2d8 thunder damage and must succeed on a DC 14 Constitution saving throw or be stunned until the end of its next turn.

Tlaunehc Tnek the Wyrm of Bones

Wondrous item, artifact

Said to be the bones of the most powerful dragon that ever lived, they are also believed (by some) to be the bones of the first dragon in existence. These skeletal remains of Tlaunehc Tnek stand menacingly on its platform. The dragon is at least Colossal sized and is missing a single bone from its structure. It is believed that the dragon will animate and follow the commands of the one who made it whole if the missing part is ever reunited with the skeleton.

Unending Scroll

Wondrous item, rare

This magical scroll can be rolled and unrolled in either direction forever. The visible portion is always 8 inches long. Anything written on the scroll remains in its relative location and can be recovered by scrolling back to it. The scroll is immune to normal water and fire damage.

Vest of Escape

Wondrous item, rare (requires attunement)

While wearing this vest, you can use 5 feet of your movement to escape nonmagical ropes, handcuffs, or similar bindings. You gain advantage on Dexterity (Acrobatics) and Strength (Athletics) checks made to free yourself from grapples or magical bindings.

Volcanic Longsword

Weapon (longsword), very rare

When pulled from its sheath and held, this blade glows with a deep red light. You have a +3 bonus to attack and damage rolls made with this magic weapon. When you hit with it, you do an additional 1d8 fire damage.

Appendix 3
New Mundane Items and Diseases

This appendix details new nonmagical items found throughout this book.

Drugs, Tobacco, and Poisons

Some of the more potent drugs can have serious side effects. For these, statistics regarding addiction and recovery are provided. Each detailed substance follows the same basic format.

Description: This details the substance, basic effects, and usual means of ingestion.

Addiction: This is the Constitution saving throw DC you must make upon consuming the drug. On a failed save, you become addicted and take the listed ability score damage each week you don't consume the substance (due to withdrawal). So long as the substance is consumed, no ability damage is taken from it. Ability damage suffered as the result of an addiction does not heal naturally during any week the drug is not consumed but can be healed magically. If the substance is consumed, ability damage heals normally that week.

Recovery: This is a listed with the addiction effects. To break an addiction, you must forego the substance for a number of consecutive weeks (the exact number is listed in the drug's description). Note, the character suffers the withdrawal damage during this time. A Constitution saving throw (DC = addiction DC) must be made at the end of each week. If you succeed on all saves, you have kicked your addiction. If you fail a save, you must begin your recovery anew. A *heal* spell removes an addiction.

Effects: This lists the effects of the substance, both bonuses and penalties.

Side Effects: Any side effects and after-effects of using the substance are listed here.

Black Mamba Venom

A creature subjected to this poison must succeed on a DC 17 Constitution saving throw or lose 2d4 points of Strength and begin to suffocate. The target cannot breathe until at least one point of Strength is recovered.

Blue Lotus Extract

The blue lotus flower on its own is a powerful hallucinatory drug that causes extreme relaxation, a lack of inhibitions and willpower, and blissfulness. Users often take the drug willingly for these effects. The extract of this drug, if distilled and infused with alcohol, has a magnified effect that can cause imbibers to slip into a catatonic state of euphoria where they become lost in a dreamlike world not unlike being trapped in the effects of a hallucinatory maze of pleasure and ecstasy for 2d4 hours. Creatures under the effect of the drug feel little pain, gaining 4d8 temporary hit points for the duration of the drug. The drug does require a successful DC 18 Constitution saving throw to avoid random attacks by shadow creatures.

The shadow creatures are figments of the character's mind, having the same hit points and attack modifiers of a **shadow**. Damage suffered by the character is real in so much as the character damages himself or herself trying to fight things that are not there. Three consecutive failed saving throws results in addiction to the substance. Addicts must take the drug as soon as it wears off or lose complete control of their actions until such time as a new dose of the drug is taken.

Blue lotus extract is 100 gp per dose.

Boomslang Venom

A creature subjected to this poison must make a DC 16 Constitutions saving throw, losing 2d6 Constitution points on a failed save and 16 on a successful one. A creature that fails the saving throw by 5 or more is nauseated for 2d6 minutes. The nausea can be cured by magical healing or a successful DC 16 Wisdom (Medecine) check. While nauseated, a creature is incapacitated.

Cannon

This substance is distilled from a rare herb called kolkis on another plane of existence and is imported to the shop. It can be sniffed or smoked. Its effects are fast-acting, giving you a burst of energy and alertness as well as making you more sociable and talkative, but the effects wear off quickly.

Addiction: DC 20 Constitution, 1d4 Constitution/week; *Recovery:* six weeks.

Effects: For 1d10 + 10 minutes, you cannot be surprised, and you have advantage on all Strength, Charisma and Initiative checks.

Side Effects: You gain a level of exhaustion for 1d4 + 2 hours after the effects wear off. Additionally, you takes 1 point of Constitution damage and 1d3 points of Charisma damage each week the drug is consumed (to a minimum of 1).

Cottonmouth Venom

A creature subjected to this poison must succeed on a DC 15 Constitution saving throw or lose 1d6 points of Constitution until after completing a long rest. A creature that fails the saving throw by 5 or more permanently loses 1 point of Constitution as well.

Death Flower Oil

Death flower oil is a complex distillation of black lotus and deadly nightshade berries that has been boiled down into a syrupy oil. So deadly is it that handling it can cause instant death to the user. The oil kills on contact or by ingestion and forces a DC 18 Constitution save. Those who fail are instantly brought to 0 hit points. Those who succeed still suffer 28 (8d6) poison damage and find their Strength drained by 1d4 points until a long rest is completed.

Death flower oil costs 1,800 gp per dose.

Desert Lotus

This wild plant grows with fiery orange flowers. Wild brigands of the desert consume it in order to enter a narcotic trance that makes them very ferocious and more difficult to kill. Those consuming the desert lotus must succeed on a DC 15 Constitution save or fall into a hallucinatory slumber for 2d12 hours. The slumber is filled with such vivid nightmares that the victim takes 1d4 points of Wisdom and Intelligence damage each from the mental and spiritual exhaustion. Habitual use causes the Fortitude save DC to increase by +1 per month.

Those succeeding on their save gain advantage on saving throws against fear effects and ccharm for the next 1d4 + 4 hours. Lotus eaters are so numb to their own personal pain that the first time they are brought to 0 hit points within 6 hours of eating lotus, they drop to 1 hit point instead.

Desert lotus can be harvested and sold on the market for about 100 gp per dose.

Distillate of Nightmare

Distillate of nightmare is a powerful poison made from the distilled remains of slowly murdered fungus folk. The powdered remains are highly toxic to the central nervous system. Intelligent creatures exposed to the venom must make a DC 18 Constitution saving throw. Those who fail their saving throw are dead within 90 seconds as their mind is filled with an amalgam of their worst nightmares. Those who succeed in making their save suffer 14 (4d6) psychic damage to their central nervous systems and are left comatose for 2d6 hours. They awaken suffering long-term paranoia that lasts 1d10 x 10 hours.

Distillate of nightmare costs 1,000 gp per dose.

Efreeti Smoke

This reddish gold tobacco has a spicy, heady flavor, and produces a thick yellowish smoke from the imbiber. The smoke is said to have been given as a gift to mortals from Iblis. Of course, any gift given of the efreeti can largely be considered a curse as well, and Efreeti Smoke is a highly addictive substance that fills the smoker with euphoria and a heightened sense of self.

Effects: You gain +2 to Charisma-based checks for one hour after smoking.

Addiction: DC 15 Constitution, the Charisma bonus becomes a –2 penalty; *Recovery:* one week.

Side Effects: The stench of the smoke tends to make others wish they were anywhere but in your presence.

Efreeti Smoke averages 140–180 gp per ounce when it is in stock.

Ergos

This substance is harvested from the ergos fungus, crushed and boiled. The resulting liquid is then consumed. The effects are felt almost immediately and last for quite a while, filling your mind with vivid and rich hallucinations, making everything around you seem more vibrant, colorful, and enriching.

Addiction: DC 16 Constitution, 1d4 Wisdom/week; *Recovery:* two weeks.

Effects: Your mind is filled with images and hallucinations for 2d4 hours. During this time, you may be slow to react. Each turn, for the duration, you have a 50% chance to act normally; otherwise, you take no action.

Side Effects: You takes 1d4 points of Dexterity damage after the effects wear off. You recover the loss of points after a long rest.

Hannan

This yellowish tobacco has a sweet taste and odor to it. You experience hallucinations; for 1d2 hours you have advantage on Intelligence and Charisma checks and disadvantage on Strength and Wisdom checks. Hannan is not addictive.

Higdne

A higdne specimen features four green slender leaves tapering slightly as they approach the root. Blue bands stripe each leaf in diagonal rows, much like tiger striping. The space between the stripes decreases closer to the root, until the leaves are solid blue. This plant never flowers. The root itself is the drug. When eaten, you gain the effects listed below.

Addiction: DC 18 Constitution, 1d4 Constitution/week; *Recovery:* four weeks.

Effects: You do not suffer from the effects of gained levels of exhaustion until the drug wears off, after 2d4 + 2 hours.

Side Effects: You suffer 1d3 points of Charisma drain each week the drug is consumed (to a minimum of 3).

Jena

This brownish tobacco has a slightly bitter taste and odor. You feel a rush of energy and adrenalin spread throughout your body. For the next 1d4 hours, you enjoy advantage on all Dexterity and Initiative checks and disadvantage on all Wisdom checks. Jena is not addictive.

Jellyfish Toxin

This toxic venom has been reduced to a powdered form. The venom is a complete paralytic that leaves its victim in excruciating pain for 2d6 + 2 hours on a failed DC 15 Constitution saving throw. Those who make their save are weakened, suffering 1d6 points of temporary Strength damage for 2d6 + 2 hours. The victim is awake and aware the entire time, although seems to all others to be dead. The victim appears to have no pulse, and their body temperature starts to drop. A *lesser restoration* spell or similar ability removes its effects. The venom is most effective when ingested, as it reacts strongly with liquids such as saliva, though it can soak through a victim's skin via sweat glands if needed.

Kesh-aath

This substance can be sniffed, smoked, or eaten — the effects are the same. This is an inhibition-numbing drug made cheaply available and enjoyed by the throngs of visitors to the Bazaar of 1,000 Sins.

Addiction: DC 18 Constitution, 1d2 Strength/week; *Recovery:* three weeks.

Effects: For 1d2 + 1 hours, you gain advantage on Charisma-based checks and disadvantage on Wisdom saving throws.

Side Effects: None.

Libynos Blue

The most common tobacco found on the continent of Libynos, Blue is known for its deep blue-tinted smoke and its sharp, almost acidic bite, that is tempered by smoking in a hookah. Blue on its own is not favored by anyone but is considered an ideal filler tobacco when paired with tobaccos from other lands. Initial use of Libynos Blue forces a DC 14 Constitution saving throw to avoid catching a sore throat that takes 1d4 days to heal. Libynos Blue is used by trekkers of the far deserts because it reduces the desire to eat and drink, allowing its users to travel on half rations.

Libynos Blue averages 5–10 gp per ounce.

Modron

This substance is smoked or sniffed and heightens your sense of awareness.

Addiction: DC 16 Constitution, 1d2 Strength /week; *Recovery:* four weeks.

Effects: You gain advantage on Perception and Insight checks for 1d4 + 1 hours and take 1 point of Strength damage immediately when the substance is consumed.

Side Effects: After the effects wear off, you have disadvantage on Dexterity checks for 1d2 hours.

Najala

This dark brownish-black tobacco is mild in taste and smells like coffee grounds. Smoking najala grants the character a +2 alchemical bonus to Strength for 1d4 hours and a –2 penalty to Constitution for the same duration.

Numedan Blond

This tobacco has a golden-brown color and a very sweet smell. It is considered a smooth smoke, though it is much stronger than most tobaccos found in Akados. Aged in casks once used for palm wine, the tobacco has a sharp sweet smell to it, and is often smoked in a hookah filled with cool water to cut the initial bite.

The tobacco gives a +1 bonus to Wisdom-based checks for 30 minutes after use, and its unique smell can be detected within 30 feet.

Numedan Blond averages 10–20 gp per ounce in the Maighib Desert where it is quite common and may be 5–10 times that price when sold outside of Libynos.

Orange Poppy Blossom Pollen

This intense pollen is taken from primitive orange poppy. Those who breathe in its fumes must make a successful DC 17 Constitution save or drop immediately into a fever-filled sleep that lasts until they are removed from the area where the pollen has been spread. Those who are trapped within the confines of the pollen may eventually become dehydrated and die. Beings removed from the pollen's potency recover in 2d10 minutes, though they are lethargic and gain a level of exhaustion.

Orange poppy blossom pollen costs 600 gp per dose.

Purple Lotus

The petals of the purple lotus are highly poisonous and outright kill most people who eat them. Anyone partaking of the purple lotus must make a successful DC 16 Constitution saving throw or take 17 (5d6) poison damage. This usually results in the eater dying, though if they survive, they are granted incredible psychedelic visions. These visions deal 1d3 temporary Wisdom damage but bestow an effect equal to *legend lore*, pertaining to any one certain subject defined before eating the purple lotus. The visions are hallucinogenic and often surreal, completely interpreted by the GM.

Shun

This orange-brown tobacco has a sweet taste and fragrant odor and is a potent hallucinogen. You gain a +2 bonus to Wisdom for 1d4 hours and a –4 penalty on saving throws against mind-affecting effects for the same duration.

Weapons

Automatic Pistol

An automatic pistol is a one-handed ranged weapon with the reload property. It has a range of 50/100 feet. It uses magazines of 30 bullets. A magazine may be loaded as part of a move action. As an action, an automatic pistol may be shot either in single shot or burst mode. In single shot mode, the shooter makes a ranged attack, doing 1d8 piercing damage on a successful hit. In burst mode, each creature within a 20-foot cone originating with the shooter must succeed on a Dexterity saving throw or take 1d8 piercing damage. The DC for the saving throw is 8 plus the shooter's Dexterity modifier plus the shooter's proficiency bonus, if appropriate. A burst uses 10 bullets.

Automatic Rifle

An automatic rifle is a two-handed ranged weapon. It has a range of 150/300 feet. It uses magazines of 30 bullets. A magazine may be loaded as part of a move action. As an action, an automatic rifle may be shot either in single shot or burst mode. In single shot mode, the shooter makes a ranged attack, doing 1d10 piercing damage on a successful hit. In burst mode, each creature within a 30-foot cone originating with the shooter must succeed on a Dexterity saving throw or take 1d10 piercing damage. The DC for the saving throw is 8 plus the shooter's Dexterity modifier plus the shooter's proficiency bonus, if appropriate. A burst uses 10 bullets.

Grenade

As an action, a grenade can be thrown to a point within 40 feet. All creatures within a 10 foot radius of that point must make a DC 14 Dexterity saving throw, taking 5d6 slashing damage on a failure and half as much on a success.

Great Mace

A great mace is a heavy, two-handed martial melee weapon. On a hit, it does 2d6 bludgeoning damage. It weighs 6 pounds.

Ship's Gun, 6-pound

The 6-pound ship's gun has an AC of 19 and 75 hit points. It takes one action to load the gun, one to aim it, and one to fire it. These actions can be completed in a single round by subsequent actors. The gun can be used to make a ranged weapon attack at +6 to hit, range 600/2,400 ft., one target. On a hit, the gun does 44 (8d10) bludgeoning damage.

Shotgun

As an action, you can shoot one or both barrels of the shotgun. Make a single ranged attack roll. On a hit, each barrel does 1d8 piercing damage. A shotgun is a two-handed weapon with ammunition (range 60/120 ft.) that has the loading attribute.

Diseases

Mummy Rot

Mummy rot first causes desiccation and then a slow decomposition. Vision goes early on as the body loses fluids, followed by ever-increasing weakness. Death comes late, well after the victim is completely incapacitated from weakness.

When a humanoid is exposed to the disease, either by magical means or through inhaling the dust of a former victim, the creature must make a Constitution saving throw. The DC for the saving throw depends on the power of the curse for magical contagion, and is 14 for breathing grave dust.

Mummy rot typically manifests immediately with a strong level of thirst. The victim must double its water consumption or gain one level of exhaustion. Every 24 hours, the victim must make a DC 17 Constitution saving throw. Each failure adds one symptom from the table below until death occurs. Two consecutive passes halts the disease but does not remove existing symptoms. *Remove Curse* destroys the disease and heals all damage. A single casting of *lesser restoration* removes the most recent symptom still present.

Symptoms in order of appearance based on number of failed saving throws

0	Thirst — double water consumption or gain one level of exhaustion
1	Gain one level exhaustion and lose 1d4 points of Charisma*
2	Vision reduced by 30 ft.
3	Gain one level exhaustion and lose 1d4 points of Charisma*
4	Blind
5	Gain one level exhaustion and lose 1d4 points of Charisma*
6	Gain one level exhaustion and Charisma is now 1
7	Lose 2d6 each of Constitution, Dexterity, and Strength*
8	Constitution, Dexterity, and Strength are now 1
9+	Lose 1 hp for each failed save until death

*Charisma does not drop below 1. If Constitution, Dexterity, or Strength drop to 0, the victim is dead.

Miscellaneous

Unholy Water

As an action you can splash the contents of this flask onto a creature within 5 feet or throw it up to 20 feet. In either case, make a ranged attack against the creature, treating the unholy water as an improvised weapon. If the target is a good-aligned divine spellcaster or celestial, it takes 2d6 necrotic damage on a hit.

Appendix 4
New Spells

This appendix details new spells found throughout this book.

Bramble Whip

Transmutation cantrip
Casting Time: 1 action
Range: 30 feet
Components: V, S, M (a small bunch of woven brambles)
Duration: Instantaneous

You create a long, flexible whip of woven brambles that is in long, vicious thorns that lashes out at your command toward a creature in range. Make a melee spell attack against the target. If the attack hits, the creature takes 1d6 piercing damage, and if the creature is Large or smaller, you pull the creature up to 10 feet closer to you.

This spell's damage increases by 1d6 when you reach 5th level (2d6), 11th level (3d6), and 17th level (4d6).

Burning Rain

5th-level evocation
Casting Time: 1 action
Range: 120 feet
Components: V, S, M (a shard of obsidian and an open flame)
Duration: Concentration, up to 1 minute

A sudden squall of molten rain forms in a 20-foot-radius, 40-foot-high cylinder centered on a point within range. A creature who enters the area for the first time on their turn or begins their turn there must make a Dexterity saving throw. On a failed saving throw, the creature takes 6d6 fire damage, or half as much damage on a successful saving throw. Unattended objects and buildings in the area are also ignited.

Chant

2nd-level conjuration
Casting Time: 1 action
Range: 30 feet
Components: V, S
Duration: Concentration, up to 1 minute

For the duration of the spell, as long as you chant, you bring special favor upon your allies and bring disfavor to your enemies. You and your allies that are within 30 feet of you gain a +1 bonus on attack rolls, weapon damage rolls, saving throws, and skill checks while your foes in the same area take a −1 penalty on such rolls. You must chant in a clear voice. Any interruption in your chanting, such as a failed Concentration check, a *silence* spell, or speaking or casting another spell, ends this spell.

At higher levels: When you cast this spell using a 3rd level spell slot or higher, the maximum duration increases by 1 minute per spell slot above 2nd.

This spell is found in the *Book of the Justicars*.

Conjure Aerial Servant

7th level conjuration
Casting Time: 1 action
Range: 60 feet
Components: V, S, M (a clear or blue gemstone worth 50 gp)
Duration: Up to 7 days

You call forth an aerial servant[1] that appears in an unoccupied space within range. The servant disappears when it drops to 0 hit points or when the spell ends.

Once summoned, you may assign the servant one task. It can be sent forth to retrieve an object or creature, deliver a message, or perform some other service. Upon completion of the task, the spell ends. A conjured servant that is unable to complete its mission within the allotted time returns to the caster and attacks it in a mad fury.

Conjure Invisible Stalker

6th level conjuration
Casting Time: 10 minutes
Range: 30 feet
Components: V, S
Duration: 1 year

You summon an invisible stalker to an unoccupied space within range. You may give the invisible stalker one command that involves hunting down and slaying a specific creature or recovering an object. The stalker must attempt to complete the task, although will typically subvert the wording if at all possible. If the stalker has achieved the goal or is brought to 0 hit points, it disappears and the spell is over.

Conjure Swarm

4th level conjuration
Casting Time: 1 action
Range: 60 feet
Components: V, S
Duration: Concentration, up to 1 hour

You summon swarms of insects, rodents, or other tiny creatures that appear in a space within range that you can see. Choose one of the following options for what appears:

- One swarm of challenge rating 2 or lower
- Two swarms of challenge rating 1 or lower
- Four swarms of challenge rating 1/2 or lower
- Eight swarms of challenge rating 1/4 or lower

A summoned swarm disappears when it drops to 0 hit points or when the spell ends.

The summoned swarms are friendly to you and your companions. Roll initiative for the summoned creatures as a group, which have their own turns. They obey any verbal commands that you issue to them (no action required by you). If you don't issue any commands to them, they defend themselves from hostile creatures, but otherwise take no actions.

At Higher Levels. When you cast this spell using certain higher level spell slots, you choose one of the summoning options above, and more creatures appear: twice as many with a 6th level slot and three times as many with an 8th level slot.

Elemental Swarm

9th level conjuration
Casting Time: 10 minutes
Range: 100 ft
Components: V, S
Duration: 4 hours

This spell opens a portal to an Elemental Plane and summons elementals from it. Choose between air, earth, fire, and water.

When the spell is complete, 2d4 elementals appear. Ten minutes later, 1d4 greater elementals[1] appear. Ten minutes after that, one elder elemental[1] appears. Each elemental has maximum hit points per HD. Once these creatures appear, they serve you for the duration of the spell.

The elementals obey you explicitly and never attack you, even if someone else manages to gain control over them. You do not need to concentrate to maintain control over the elementals. You can dismiss them singly or in groups at any time.

Flesh to Brass

6th level transmutation
Casting Time: 1 action
Range: 60 feet
Components: V, S, M (a pinch of brass dust)
Duration: Concentration up to 1 minute

This spell is the same as *flesh to stone* except the target is turned to brass.

Ghoul Touch

4th level enchantment
Casting Time: 1 action
Range: touch
Components: V, S
Duration: 1 minute

Make a melee spell attack against a living creature you can reach. On a hit, the creature is paralyzed for the duration of the spell. While paralyzed, the creature exudes a noxious odor. All creatures other than you within 10 feet of the target must succeed on a Constitution saving throw against or be poisoned while within 10 feet of the paralyzed creature. The paralyzed creature may attempt a Wisdom saving throw at the end of each of its turns, ending the spell on a success.

Greater Arcane Lock

4th level abjuration
Casting Time: 1 action
Range: Touch
Components: V, S, M (gold dust worth at least 50 gp. which the spell consumes)
Duration: Until dispelled

This spell is the same as *arcane lock* except for the following. A *greater arcane lock* is unaffected by the *knock* spell. *Greater arcane lock* can be cast using any spell slot of the 4th level or higher, affecting the difficulty a creature would have to successfully remove it with *dispel magic*.

Greater Geas

9th level enchantment
Casting Time: 1 minute
Range: 60 feet
Components: V
Duration: 1 year

You place a magical command on up to 6 creatures that you can see within range, forcing them to carry out some service or refrain from some action or course of activity as you decide. Each creature that can understand you it must succeed on a Wisdom saving throw or become charmed by you for the duration. While a creature is charmed by you, it pursues the suggested course of action to the best of its ability. A creature that can't understand you is unaffected by the spell.

You can issue any command you choose, short of an activity that would result in certain death. Should you issue a suicidal command, the spell ends. A creature who completes the assigned task is under no further compulsion from the spell.

You can end the spell early by using an action to dismiss it. A *remove curse*, *greater restoration*, or *wish* spell also ends it, although a creature subject to *greater geas* will not willingly allow itself to be released.

Halt Undead

3rd level necromancy
Casting Time: 1 action
Range: 120 feet
Components: V, S, M
Duration: Concentration, up to 1 minute

Choose up to three undead creatures you can see within range. Each creature must succeed on a Wisdom saving throw or be paralyzed for the duration of the spell. The effect on a creature is broken if it is attacked or takes damage.

Lightning Spike

Evocation cantrip
Casting Time: 1 action
Range: 120 feet
Components: V, S
Duration: Instantaneous

You hurl a bolt of lightning at a creature within range. Make a ranged spell attack against the target. On a hit, the target takes 1d8 lightning damage. If the target is wearing metal armor, you can reroll the damage and take the higher of the two results.

This spell's damage increases by 1d8 when you reach 5th level (2d8), 11th level (3d8), and 17th level (4d8).

Magic Tattoo

4th level enchantment
Casting Time: 10 minutes
Range: touch
Components: V, S, M (colored inks worth 50 gp that the spell consumes)
Duration: Permanent

As you are casting this spell, you trace an image on a willing or unconscious creature's skin. At the end of the casting, you cast a 1st-level spell. The magic of the 1st-level spell infuses the magical image on the creature's skin. Thereafter, the creature with the tattoo can use the tattoo to cast the 1st-level spell once per week without material components. The spell attack bonus and save DC are the same as the yours when you cast the spell originally.

At higher levels. When you cast this spell using higher level spell slots, you can imbue the tattoo with higher level spells. If cast with a 6th level spell slot, you can imbue the tattoo with 1st or 2nd level spells, and if an 8th level spell slot is used, you can imbue the tattoo with up to 3rd level spells.

Nightmare

5th level illusion
Casting Time: 10 minutes
Range: touch
Components: V, S, M
Duration: Concentration, up to 1 hour

At the end of casting the spell, you touch a sleeping creature. As long as contact and concentration are maintained, the creature has horrible visions in its sleep. If the visions last the full hour, the creature gets no benefit from its rest and its hit point maximum is reduced by 1d10. If this effect reduces a creature to 0 hit points, it dies. The reduction to the target's maximum hit points lasts until removed by *greater restoration* or similar magic.

Runes of Submission

7th level enchantment
Casting Time: 10 minutes
Range: touch
Components: V, S, M
Duration: Until dispelled

As you cast this spell, magic runes appear on a nonmagical collar, bracelet, or other wearable item of your choosing. At the end of the spell, you pronounce a command word. Thereafter, you can use the command word to open and close the item. If you close the item on a creature, it must succeed on Wisdom saving throw or be subject to your commands while it wears the item. A creature will not perform obviously suicidal commands. A creature that succeeds on its saving throw is immune to those *runes of submission* for 24 hours.

Sound Burst

3rd level evocation
Casting Time: 1 action
Range: 60 ft
Components: V, S
Duration: instantaneous

A burst of sound explodes from a point within range. Each creature within 10 feet of that point takes 1d8 thunder damage and creatures that can hear must succeed on a Constitution saving throw or be stunned until the end of their next turn.

Spell Siphon

7th level enchantment
Casting Time: 1 action
Range: 240 ft
Components: V, S, M
Duration: Concentration, up to 1 minute

Developed by the Grand Vizier of the City of Brass to fuel his arcane aspirations, this spell is a much sought-after incantation that is guarded jealously by its creator.

If the target fails a Wisdom saving throw, you create a mental link with your target, draining it of your choice of up to 6 1st level, 3 2nd level, 2 3rd level, or 1 4th level spell slot and gaining that amount as bonus spell slots that you use to power your magic. You can store no more than 40 total spell slot levels.

The drain continues each round you maintain concentration while the host remains in range. If you choose to drain spell slots from a level that the target is out of, or never had, you gain no spell slots that round.

As a host is drained, the slots are wiped from its mind just as if they had been cast that day.

You cannot use the bonus slots to cast a spell of a level you couldn't normally cast. Bonus spell slots remain until you complete a long rest or until expended.

Touch of Idiocy

3rd level enchantment
Casting Time: 1 action
Range: 60 ft
Components: V, S
Duration: Concentration, up to 1 minute

Make a melee spell attack against a creature you can reach. On a hit, the target's Intelligence is dropped to 1 and the target cannot cast spells or use innate spellcasting abilities for the duration of the spell. The target may attempt a Wisdom saving throw at the end of each of its turns, ending the spell on a success.

Detailed below are a 101 story seeds and elements you can use for your party when they are traveling in the Plane of Molten Skies, the City of Brass, and the surrounding lands.

Plane of Molten Skies

1. Chietan Sky Pirates: These unlicensed raiders sail the low stratosphere of the Plane of Molten Skies searching for any prey which could turn a profit in the City of Brass in their small, fast, two-bowed, lateen-sailed Dhow. Generally crewed by 10 to 12 chietan raiders, the pirates capture their quarry by hanging roughly 30 feet above the ground and dragging a large fishing net beneath their ship. They attack by diving from a few hundred feet before pulling up and literally dragging the ground below them. The attack covers an area of 20 feet by 30 feet. Those trapped within the net are as if trapped in a large fighting net (See *PHB*) requiring a DC 25 Strength check or a DC 20 Escape Artist check to break free. Captured individuals are taken to the Corsair docks and sold into slavery.

Pirate Airship Dhow

An airship dhow is 40 foot long and has two pointed bows fore and aft. They are easily crewed by 10 to 12 and have a carrying capacity of 50 tons. An airship dhow travels at a speed 10 miles per hour (100 ft. per round). An airship dhow is AC 25 and has 100 hp per 10-foot section.

2. Sheik Farha Al Jabarra the Junk Merchant: A line of eight fire drake[1] drawn wagons plies its way across the Plane of Molten Skies with destinations of the Bazaar of Beggars and ultimately the City of Brass. Four caravan scouts ride the cardinal points keeping a lookout for bandits, beasts, and other menaces of the tumultuous plane.

This is the caravan of **Farha Jabarra the Junk Merchant**. Farha and his men explore the planes of Earth, Molten Skies, the Material, and other planes in between in search of "other people's junk". Aside from the collecting and resale of wrecked and ruined treasures, Farha and his tribe are known to occasionally have useful items for sale.

Every member of Farha's tribe is either a wife, son, daughter, nephew, niece, or other close relative and all honor him as their Sheik and master. They do not take sides, nor participate in political debate, finding the Sultan of the City of Brass no better or worse than any other despot. They are however careful not to draw too much attention to themselves from their crueler cousins, the burning dervishes.

Farha may be under attack by some random beast or threat in the Plane of Molten Skies, be broken down along the path, or encounter the characters when they are exhausted from the heat and dying of dehydration and offer a hand in exchange for their service getting his haul of trinkets and trash to the City of Brass. Possibly the characters have something he would find valuable in exchange for magical charms against the intense heat or water to quench their parched throats.

3. Save the Whales: When the party is traveling near the Lake of Fire, a group of volcano giants approaches them and asks for their help in eliminating a large retinue of salamander poachers who are threatening the fire whale population.

4. Shazabar the Leper: Shazabar wanders the Plane of Molten Skies wrapped in his pus-soaked and dust-covered rags. He was cursed by the Great Sultan with his blistering leprosy and may only be healed by one who is a devout worshipper of Anumon. Shazabar was once a learned scholar within the city and a keeper of lore within the forbidden confines of the Great Repository. Should the characters attempt to help or befriend Shazabar he may offer them information on surviving the curses and horrors of the Repository. If the characters are cruel to Shazabar, he gathers a handful of his ichor-soaked rags and hurls it upon them, attempting to pass his disease before *teleporting* to a safer locale within the Plane of Molten Skies.

5. Snowstorm: A random location suddenly sees a drop in temperature and within minutes, heavy snow begins to fall covering a radius of about 1 mile. Onlookers stand staring; others play in the storm or run from it, as many have never seen snow. Fire-based creatures immediately seek shelter from the dropping temperatures and falling snow. The storm lasts 1d6+4 minutes before dissipating. The temperature in the area however, doesn't seem to be returning to normal and the snow generally remains on the ground where it fell. The storm is the result of a powerful spell cast by an ice wizard hidden somewhere in the nearby mountains or plains. The wizard's purpose for the spell — to cool off enough of the Plane so he can amass an army of ice elementals and cold creatures to take control of at least part of this plane and crown himself ruler.

6. Umaadi Bandits: A nomadic troupe of vampiric bandits traverses the Plane atop their nightmares, moving quickly across the land. Due to the harsh light of the Plane of Molten Skies, the Umaadi cover themselves from head to toe in dusty sand-colored robes, and cover any exposed portions of their bodies with the bandages of the dead, including their faces. They leave only a slit for their mouth and eyes open and often wear goggles carved from ivory with a thin slit which serve to block out dangerous light, yet allow them to see over a broad horizon. The Umaadi are nomadic, having no allegiances to the Sultan of Efreet[1] or his minions, or to any of the other lesser powers of this heat scorched realm. Among their treasures is a Writ of Passage allowing entrance into the City of Brass.

7. Rise of the Machines: A portal opens somewhere on the Plane of Molten Skies to a machine-world allowing a horde of construct-like machines to pour through into the Plane, devastating everything in their wake.

The Bazaar of Beggars

8. Crossing the Rubicon: Overnight, a mischievous sorcerer splits the Highway of the Damned with a 200-foot wide channel of water. Chaos ensues as the Bazaar's residents clamor to get their fill of precious, untaxed water. Lady Umau sends in the fire giant and efreeti soldiers under her command to cordon off the channel. Slaves add to the press of people, ignoring their masters for a taste of the water. Accusations and fisticuffs fly. Line cutting becomes rampant. Anarchy threatens to destroy the entire Bazaar, and the adventurers are caught in the middle of it all.

9. Dirty Rotten Scoundrels: The adventurers hire some placeholders while they go into the Bazaar. When they come back, the placeholders refuse to relinquish their places. It turns out the group are adventurers who used the placeholder ploy to cut ahead in line rather than taking places at the end like they should have when they first arrived. The adventurers must remove the others from their space without raising the ire of the Sahoduin peacekeepers patrolling the Bazaar. Alternatively, this doesn't have to happen to the characters but instead happens to another group of adventurers. They ask for the characters' assistance in rectifying the wrong, because the fake placeholders are too powerful for them.

10. The Dog Catchers: A pack of justice-seeking blink dogs keeps the northwestern side of the Bazaar free of crime and corruption. Nobody knows why the pack moved into the Bazaar, or when really, but they do know the dogs are ruining the local economy. The adventurers either have a run-in with the blink dogs because they did something morally questionable, or the Bazaar's residents hire them to kill the dogs.

11. Dust Storm: A sudden dust storm comes in from off the plains. The entire Bazaar locks down for the next 12 hours. People unfortunate enough to be on the Highway must try to survive it as best they can, while outsiders inside the Bazaar proper must try to find shelter. The locals will gladly take them in, albeit for a steep fee. The adventurers wind up in the tent of a family whose patriarch lies sick with a deadly gangrene infection in his leg. If he can't get medicine from the local cleric before the storm ends then he will sadly die.

12. The Fast and the Furious: A gang of young flying carpet riders often race through the dizzying tangle of alleys in the Bazaar, wreaking havoc wherever they go. As the adventurers are minding their own business, the carpet riders come tearing toward them. They douse the characters with indelible red ink as they careen past, laughing wildly at their "awesome" prank. The residents in the area can only sigh and shake their heads. Maybe someday someone will do something about those annoying kids.

13. Festival of Blood: Once a year, the Bazaar's children come to the side of the Highway of the Damned to throw rocks, nails, and barbed sling bullets at those in line. This is the Festival of Blood, commemorating something in the Bazaar's early history, though nobody really knows what anymore. The adventurers can either stay in line, dodging bullets, or they can duck into the Bazaar to avoid the ritual altogether (and possibly lose their places in line). Sahoduin enforcers do nothing to prevent the assault, since it is part of the Bazaar's longstanding tradition.

14. Help me, Abey wan Qanabi: Three ghostly women occupy a random alley in the Bazaar, pleading with passersby to rescue them from their cruel master, a prominent outlander noble. They are dead, unable to rest in peace until someone avenges them and gives their bones a proper burial.

15. Mendicant Wizard: A crippled man with stumps where his hands used to be lies in the middle of an alley path, a worn alms bowl before him. As people pass, he bobs his head up and down pleading for mercy toward a poor old veteran. As the adventurers pass, he begs for a coin or two. If they do indeed donate to him, he thanks them profusely. He also casts a beneficial spell upon them. If the characters don't donate, then their lack of compassion offends him, in which case he creates 4 illusions of himself that follow the adventurers for 6 minutes, berating them loudly.

16. Shakedown: One night in the Bazaar's public tents, the adventurers receive the pleasures of a dancing woman in their room. The next day, the woman's husband shows up with Sahoduin enforcers in tow claiming the adventurers corrupted his wife, seducing her into infidelity. According to local custom, a man who sleeps with another man's wife is to be staked to the ground on the open plain for seven days as punishment. The enforcers let the adventurers off the hook if they pay a substantial fine instead.

17. Yo, Jimbo: Two warring beggars' guilds have thrown the southeastern end of the Bazaar into turmoil. A young boy whose father was killed in the crossfire secretly approaches the adventurers one night to plead for the help. He hopes they can put down one guild or the other so that peace will return to the neighborhood.

The Obsidian Bridge

18. The Bound Efreet: An efreeti and his enslaved wizard run a racket to fleece people of their money and their freedom. The wizard offers the adventurers easy access to the City of Brass. He will sell them forged writs for 100 bp and fake Rods of Embassy for 600 bp. All these items seem to be authentic but are marked in a special way so that the guardians at the Great Gatehouse spot them instantly with a successful DC 15 Wisdom (Perception) and the viewer must have seen and examined an authentic writ or Rod. The guardians confiscate the illegal items and fine their owners 1,000 bp and refuse them entrance into the City for 24 hours.

19. The Mule: The adventurers are approached by a disheveled beggar who offers to help the group (for a few simple coins) with advice about the various intricacies of gaining entrance into the City of Brass. If paid any reasonable amount, he provides the adventurers with basic information about the City. Even if ignored, he walks alongside the party offering various commonly known facts about the City. Once the party has grown accustomed to his irritating presence, he attempts to surreptitiously place a scroll into one of the adventurer's possessions. The scroll is a piece of religious contraband that provides a stirring account of the Dead Sultana's struggles and ultimate defeat and foretells that she will one day rise again in triumph. If the guardians find the scroll, it is confiscated and the adventurers are fined 1,000 bp and delayed several hours, if not days, while they are questioned. Should the players manage to get the scroll through the Great Gatehouse, the rogue attempts to reacquire his belongings from within the City and deliver it to his client, a priest of Anumon, who holds hidden services to his god in various locales amongst the destitute of the basin.

20. Mysterious Palanquin: Three fire giant eunuchs bear a disturbing brass palanquin carved with images of mortal suffering and woe. If the characters investigate, the palanquin holds Mother Superior Caircheval, a beautiful female cleric of Lucifer who travels to the Cathedral to pay homage to her dark master. She converses freely with the characters, regardless of their alignments and expresses carnal interest in any obvious paladin types.

21. Pilgrim Tossing: Four off-duty drunken fire giant soldiers indulge themselves by grabbing random passersby and seeing how far they can throw them from one side of the bridge to the other or at fleeing pedestrians. Particularly good throws mean that the unlucky "projectile" flies off the side of the bridge and into the burning sea below rather than just impacting into the hard obsidian surface of the bridge. One of the fire giant decides that one of the adventurers looks particularly aerodynamic.

22. The Prophet: An ancient wrinkled gnome offers to foretell the party's future for 100 bp. Roll or pick a random encounter anywhere on the Plane of Molten Skies or inside the City of Brass. Relate the encounter to the adventurers in general terms but provide visual clues to a specific location for the encounter. When the adventurers come to that location, the encounter automatically happens.

23. Slavers with a Gold Dragon: One hundred azer slaves, whipped by 4 babau overseers, each astride a fiendish triceratops, pull a massive wheeled cage containing a much-abused gold dragon. The bars of the cage are made of petrified rampant unicorns and lidded by green-hued steel. Bits of flesh and hair cling to the wheels, with fan-like stains of blood spread over the bars and the sides of the wagon. Sickly, swarms of quasits roam the body of the gold dragon, prying away scales from its living flesh, snapping horns and bone ridges from its body. The dragon responds with an occasion swat of its tail, crushing a demon to pulp, where his brethren leave the dragon to devour the corpse. The babau plans to take this subjugated dragon to a slaughterhouse where its flesh carries a high price to discerning consumers.

24. Sudden Appearance: Appearing in front of the line to gain entry into the City of Brass is a cloaked figure bearing a slender staff capped with a brass ram's head. In his other hand, he bears a rod of embassy. The wizard is actually an avoral in disguise. If the heroes uncover the identity of the celestial, they may take the rod for themselves, of course after dispatching the angel — a truly evil act, and enjoy unlimited movement throughout the city. The Rod is a fake, something not even the celestial realized. If an authority figure inspects the rod and identifies it for what it really is, the characters face serious trouble. The avoral intends to infiltrate the City of Brass to acquire intelligence regarding the kidnapping and processing of celestial creatures.

25. Stop! Thief!: Alif Q'Ban identifies one of the characters as an easy mark. The thief follows the characters from a safe distance, watching and gauging the most appropriate moment — such as when the character is alone — to spring forward and snare a loose item, money bag, or the like. If the characters detect the thief and manage to snare him, he vows to be a guide through the city for as long as they stay and spare his life. He follows through his vow until such time as he can make a safe escape.

26. Unruly Wizard: Yuen the Lame, a wizard of great power named for his pronounced limp and slack features, argues with 4 efreeti guards at the Bab al Baquarra regarding the entry of his huge water elemental cohort. As the heroes approach, Yuen's tone rises to a near shriek as he berates the guardians of the gate for not knowing who he is. Heroes intervening and calming the situation receive advantage on all Charisma-based checks made against the efreeti guards within the next hour. If the characters fail to intervene within 1 minute, a pit fiend eunuch arrives with a contingent of 5 horned devils to attempt to destroy the offending elemental, subdue the wizard and transport him to the Minaret of Screams.

27. Wanted!: The party is shocked to discovered placards being put up depicting one of their male numbers, with the message, "Wanted! The head of this adventurer, 2,000 bp Reward." There follows a brief but fairly accurate description of the character, and an address to take the head to to claim the reward. Soon after these appear, the character becomes a hunted man. The reward has been offered by a wealthy dealer in magical bronze items. He recently nearly caught one of his concubines with a paramour. When he demanded an explanation for her disheveled appearance, she claimed the room had been visited by an interloper, and names the first person to come to mind — a passerby on the street, hurrying to get where he is going (the character in question).

28. The Wheel of Fire: A great wheel of green flame appears in the sky one morning, raining down blue sparks like snow. Is this an omen of a god's birth or death? The power of an artifact? A new spell by the ruler of the City of Brass? A scout for an invasion of otherplanar beings?

29. Imitation is the Sincerest Form of Flattery: A group of lower level NPCs tries to pass themselves off as the characters — poorly. Works best if the characters have a reputation for them to trade on.

30. Street Artists: An art fair of fire sculptors is advertised. characters may be asked to judge. The art, must be fire produced exclusively by nonmagical means (can use herbs, different shaped burning receptacles, etc. though).

31. City of Brassmen: A new fad arises in the City: cheap brass humanoid clockwork constructs. They are actually secretly controlled by the Nightfall Concordance, but to what end?

32. Playground: A swirling vortex of interwoven flames dances down the street. This is not a weather phenomenon, but a group of juvenile fire elementals playing tag. When it reaches the characters, it breaks up, with young fire elementals shooting everywhere, chasing one another and getting underfoot. The city residents largely ignore them, except when they get in the way. Those without fire immunity may find them more troublesome.

33. Liquid Sky: Dark, sooty clouds roil overhead, cheering up the locals in the City of Brass. One minute later, it begins to rain molten lead. Characters caught within the downpour take 3d10 points of fire damage each round of exposure unless they are immune to fire. Efreet and other fire-loving creatures come out and stand beneath it, laughing as they enjoy the fresh, tingling sensation of the liquid metal. Those not immune to fire may find the experience less pleasant. The molten shower lasts for 2d6 minutes, and instead of cooling, the fallen lead evaporates within 2d12 minutes unless bottled or contained somehow.

34. Infestation: A local wizard with a fondness for strange life forms recently had an accident in the lab, and his breeding stock of variant al-mi'raj (see the *Tome of Horrors*) escaped. Unlike standard al-mi'raj, this strain is immune to fire, and left unchecked, reproduces at an alarming rate. A bounty of 1 bp per dead al-mi'raj is instated, and characters may make some money hunting these things down, but eventually the problem threatens to escalate beyond anyone's control. To stop the threat, someone needs to investigate the source of the infestation, rescue the wizard who created them from a stasis field, and together figure out a way to end the threat.

35. Out for a Walk: While traveling the streets of the City, the street ahead of the characters clears of traffic. Within moments they are the only ones left visible, though they can hear the click-click sound of claws coming from a side street. Assuming they don't flee, they see a wizened, gnome-like humanoid round the corner, leading a large-sized reptilian beast that they may recognize as being markedly similar to the legendary tarrasque in appearance, though slightly smaller. The gnome-figure leads the beast by a fine golden chain. If he sees the characters, he approaches them. He is a slave to an efreeti noble, whose task is to care for the noble's "minirasque". (The minirasque has all the stats of the tarrasque, with AC and attack rolls adjusted for its smaller size, ability score and natural armors reduced for its smaller size) Though placid at the moment, the minirasque is highly excitable, (and if it goes on a rampage the destruction it can cause is truly terrifying. The gnome is desperate to escape his bondage, and may ask those courageous enough to help him. It seems the efreeti noble keeps the gnome's soul locked up in a small brass urn in his estate. He states that his soul can be freed by simply removing the urn's stopper, but warns that the urn must not be removed from its vault or an alarm sounds. What the gnome does not know is that there are over a dozen such urns in the room, and the identity of each owner is not clearly marked. If characters open them all, they earn an enemy in the efreeti noble and unlikely allies elsewhere.

36. The Planar Ship: An efreeti explorer is planning an expedition in his planar vessel to the Steel Garden. He seeks crewmembers to serve as soldiers and help maintain his brass vessel. The pay is good, but the casualty rates for such expeditions often run 70% or higher, so there are few willing to risk it. The efreeti is not above hiring a pressgang of efreeti thugs to snatch victims from the streets and put them to work on his vessel. Of course, the raid on the Steel Garden itself is only one of many possible perils, and if the planar ship is damaged there's no telling to what strange places it might drift.

37. The Riddleless Sphinx: While in a bar or other public meeting area, the characters note a drunken gynosphinx downing firewine by the bucket. Every riddle she has posed has been answered, starting with her signature riddle, and moving right through the rest of her repertoire. She has become a laughingstock among her kind, and powerful patrons looking for a guardian have heard of her reputation, and regularly pass her over when seeking a guardian beast. Now she is on a quest for new riddles, ones so challenging that even other sphinxes would be stumped by them. If the characters were to help her succeed in this, they would earn her undying gratitude.

38. A Little Humor Never Hurt Anyone: A tall, rangy janni observes the characters from the crowd when they have an unrelated encounter or altercation in the street. Afterwards, he approaches the characters with words of sympathy or congratulations as appropriate, and offers to buy them drinks at a local drink shop and hear more of their exploits. In fact, "Alfiq" is a fictitious name of the troubadour Al-Amasai, master of "Almasai and his Marvelous Troupe of Bunglebobs," a notorious satirist company in the City of Brass. Two to three weeks after pumping the characters for information, he puts on a new performance piece satirizing the characters' exploits as described to Alfiq; the performers all resemble comical versions of the characters. See to it that the characters take in one of these performances, perhaps while on unrelated business, or in the course of an investigation into the derision that greets them on the streets. Assuming the characters are good sports, Al-Amasai might even share his good fortunes with them, granting them a fabulous mysterious magical box whose properties he has been unable to fathom. If nothing else, the characters will gain fame in the town, although perhaps not for their bravery and heroics.

39. Perilous Beauty: A mob of jeering, angry efreet come bustling down the street, nearly overwhelming the screams of a woman in their midst; those with sharp eyes occasionally catch the flash of tanned, smooth human skin at the heart of the pack. The mob proceeds to a nearby square, where the mob spreads out, revealing a captive woman bound in chains being hauled by a group of powerfully muscled efreet. As they throw her in a cage, characters can see that the woman has a pair of small, dainty horns, a long, graceful barbed tail, and batlike wings — a succubus! She was the plaything of an efreeti noble, hoping at first to seduce him and drain his life essence, but instead managed to enrage him, and now faces a week of torture and humiliation, followed by transport to the Abyss and permanent death. Amaya, the succubus, desperately wishes to avoid this, and pleads and begs for anyone to assist her. If the characters listen to these pleas, she offers to serve whosoever frees her faithfully and truly for a year and a day, and swears whatever oaths she needs to get her saviors to agree. She is in fact truthful, and serves out her sentence dutifully for the stated period if freed, though the manner in which she performs this service depends on the alignment of her new masters, and the strength of the oaths she is made to swear. Amaya can be a powerful but headstrong ally, seducing characters if she can (with talk and verbal persuasion only if they tell her not to use her powers against them), even as they possibly try to convert her from evil. Of course, the characters must first free Amaya from her captors.

40. Dreadfire Plague: The characters witness an efreeti staggering down the street covered in azure flames. She looses a scream and dies, her body charred blue. Guards surround the corpse and gathering crowd, letting none leave. The efreeti died of a disease called dreadfire which lowers an efreeti's immunity to fire and causes them to spontaneously combust into blue fire. An efreeti noble offers the characters a handsome reward if they travel to the Para-elemental Plane of Ice and retrieve the cure — a substance known as *icefire*. There they encounter the frost creatures and genies responsible for the latest outbreak of dreadfire.

41. Mistaken Identity: Out of the crowd near the characters an assassin strikes, targeting one of their group. The efreeti assassin was sent to slay one Bertram Balagan, a humanoid of the same type and general appearance as the character. The assassin was hired by an efreeti noble to gain revenge for a betrayal. If characters wish to get to the bottom of this and avoid future assassination attempts, they need to ferret out the truth and help track down Bertram or somehow get the noble to rescind his contract.

42. Alms for the Poor: A blind beggar, calling out for alms, pesters the party. This is actually the Sultan of the Efreet in disguise, keeping an eye on doings in his City. Unlike the classic stories of benevolent kings dressed as beggars, the Sultan has little respect for those who are foolish enough to actually hand over hard-earned coin to the weak. Parties that show more spirit, even roughing him up a little, are more likely to win his approval. During the encounter, the Sultan assesses the characters, and if he decides that they are competent, he may subsequently contact them through an intermediary for clandestine missions on his behalf.

43. Comes the Tax Man: The characters find themselves in a tavern or other food-serving establishment and overhear an argument nearby between the owner of the establishment, a burly efreeti, and a scrawnier efreeti backed up by two hulking efreeti guards. The scrawny fellow is dressed in some kind of official-looking outfit. Though his side of the conversation is too faint to make out, the owner protests in a loud voice that he does not have the money now, he can't access it yet, etc. After a few more threats, the scrawny efreeti and his guards exit, and the owner sits on a stool in an obvious state of anxiety and depression. If approached, he relates that his funds are kept safe in a magical chest, but the key to it has been stolen, and he needs the key to access it. If the characters show interest, he offers them a reward to retrieve either the chest, intact, or find and return the key. The chest is on a pocket plane (a demiplane) and the key was stolen by a thief hired by the tax man himself.

44. The Rage of Angels: Without warning, a host of winged celestials descend upon the City of Brass, weapons in hand, and start laying waste to the populace. These celestials have been sent from their home planes to scourge the city in punishment for a recent action — the capture, imprisonment, and torture of a planetar. They attack anyone they encounter, unless their potential victims can prove they are good-aligned, in which case their foes are captured, escorted to a secure point, and interrogated. When the celestials are satisfied that their prisoners are agents of good, and understand why they are in the City of Brass, they may recruit them to aid in rescuing their captured friend from the palace of the Sultan, or simply have them hold tight until the angelic beings are sated and depart. This entire event could be one swift but bloody skirmish, or the beginning of an ongoing campaign, turning the City of Brass into a three-way war zone between the locals, the celestials, and opportunistic fiends looking to strike at their mortal enemies.

45. Visitation: One night as the characters sleep, one of them has a dream, where an angelic figure presents itself and begs for the their aid. This mission can be just about anything the DM wishes to run — retrieving an item from a local stronghold, investigating a nearby dungeon, taking on an adversarial organization, etc. In fact, the "angel" is a magical projection produced by the witch Abbasa'am, who in turn was hired by Farouk ab-Nassi, a notorious spy and troublemaker. He is currently working for a rival of whoever is in charge of the fortress, group, etc. the angel vision pits the characters against, and is looking to stir up trouble. It is possible, though unlikely, that the characters may learn of the true source of this vision. If they are particularly successful on the mission, they may receive further visions as well, for as long as Farouk thinks he can use the characters as stalking horses.

The Lower City

46. Unfortunate Witness: While traversing the basin, the characters hear the unmistakable twang of a crossbow string, and can make a DC 22 Wisdom (Perception) check to identify the shooter. The shooter is a halfling in the window of a nearby building firing at an unseen target. He

disappears immediately after firing his crossbow. If the assassin knows that a character saw him, a khalafi assassin from the Fahd al An'il picks up the character's trail within 1d4 hours and attempts to silence the character in the most permanent of ways.

47. Impostors: Three mercenaries bearing the symbol of the Bureau of Taxation approach the characters. They examine the characters' equipment, claiming that this is a routine tax collection. Have the characters make a DC 18 Wisdom (Insight) to see through the ruse. Each of the mercenaries is disguised with an *alter self* spell. If the characters refuse to pay, the mercenaries move on claiming that the Sultan will hear about it. If the characters give any clue that they know about the deception, the mercenaries attack in an attempt to silence them.

48. Deathly Chill: As the characters pass by a dark alleyway, they see a body in the alleyway. Closer examination of the body reveals it to be that of an efreeti — dead no more than a few hours. If a character examines his wounds closely, they discover that the wounds appear frostbitten. If they use a *speak with dead* spell, or any other similar mode of communication, the efreeti give them his name, as well as a description of the killer, a frost giant assassin who had been sent to kill an efreeti noble.

49. The Gambit: The adventurers are set upon by a group of six mercenaries. They are all under the effects of an *invisibility* spell, and have a traveling *silence* spell to conceal their approach, as well as to neutralize any spellcasters in the group. They attempt to subdue and detain any character that looks as though she can handle herself in a fight and take them to the House of the One-Eyed Jack. There the characters are sold to Morhidd for use in the Gambit. Any character that is unsuitable for fighting in the pit is left bound and gagged, likely to end up in the infirmary.

50. Fiery Blast: The unsuspecting adventurers stop to inspect the clear liquid of the ditch that surrounds the lower basin. There is a 20% chance that the liquid spontaneously ignites sending a blast of fire 20 feet into the air and likely onto the characters.

51. Collection Patrol: The adventurers happen to be in the path of a patrol unit of three burning dervish wizards[1] and two fire giant enforcers who are in search of slaves and potential members of the Legion of Marmalukes. The patrol uses force only if necessary, as the wizards attempt to *dominate* or *charm* their victims first.

52. Petty Thieves: The adventurers are followed by a rag-tag group of five thieves from The Nest. If noticed, the thieves melt away into the crowd, and there is a 30% chance that they return later with four higher ranking members of their group. If they return, they attempt to corner the adventurers with the ultimate intent of doing whatever is necessary to relieve the characters of their valuables. The thieves do not hesitate to kill to get what they want.

The Heyyab District (Lower City)

53. Slaver Press Gang: Press gangs are common all over the City, but more so in the Lower City. While minding their own business one night in the streets, the adventurers have a run in with a press gang of six thugs and their leader who intend to take them alive and sell them in one of the City's many ubiquitous slave markets.

54. Escaped Slaves: A group of former slaves habitually mugs wealthy looking freemen from a shadowy alcove off the main streets or in the dark, crowded alleys. If a fight turns against them, and it undoubtedly will against a powerful party because of their utter lack of experience, they flee.

55. City Guard: A squad of 4 fire giant soldiers, their sergeant, and an efreet officer stop the adventurers at random to see their travel permits, or papers, or whatever. The soldiers hassle them until either the adventurers fight back or offer them a substantial bribe. If neither happens, they squad arrests them for some bogus irregularity or violation of the law.

56. Hell's Angel: A blackguard falls screaming from the Middle or Upper City, impacting soundly with the ground not 10 feet from the adventurers. Seconds later, a horrifying whinny can be heard above them. Looking up, they see an enraged nightmare flying right at them. It thinks, perhaps, they are friends of the dead man who tried so rudely to break it….

57. Inferno: An explosion at the Agony Forge of the Ziggurat of Fire sends a wall of fire expanding out into the City at a terrifying speed. The blast rolls through the entire Lower City, stopping at the brass walls of the City basin.

58. Stampede: A slaver caravan pulled by brass bulls gets inadvertently caught in a wizard's *ice storm* spell. The bulls go crazy and stampede, running madly through the Lower City streets. The adventurers happen to be on one of the streets they run down. Shopkeepers seal their doors and windows as soon as they hear the stampede (this isn't the first time it has happened).

59. The Ecstatics: The adventurers turn a street corner and find themselves in the midst of a very large religious procession for a specific holiday in which the faithful participants flagellate themselves with barbed whips or slice their own flesh with razor-sharp blades. The adventurers are suddenly confronted with a group of men and women who take offense at the "infidels" defiling the procession with their presence. They intend to take it out of the characters' hides.

60. Monsterfest: A ten-story tall, bipedal, electricity-spitting lizard at one end of the street, a fourteen-story tall, three-headed, fire-breathing dragon at the other end, and the adventurers in the middle. You do the math.

Souk Dhimmi (Middle City)

61. Al-Ajadi's Irregulars: While the party presses through a crowded market, a young human boy bolts through the crowd and between the characters. Within moments, mercenaries who work for Noman al-Ajadi show up and stop them. The mercenary-sorcerer holds up a *scrying stone* and accuses one of the characters of stealing something of value. The penalty for theft in Souk Dhimmi is execution.

62. Tiger, Tiger: A half-celestial dire tiger escapes from his captors, a pair of hunters who want to sell the recently captured predator to the Circus of Pain. The tiger goes on a rampage just as the adventurers exit their favorite tavern. As soon as the tiger catches a whiff of them, he turns on them, for they smell just like the men who captured him in the first place and he does not like that all.

63. Stoned Ghost: There are a few places in the souk where criminals are punished by being stoned to death. At one such stoning wall, a discontent ghost harasses passersby. The ghost, a barbarian warrior called Gorgon, seethes with hatred for the locals because of what they did to him; moreover, he was truly innocent of the crime of which they accused him. When the adventurers come within 10 feet of the wall, he materializes out of it, screams insanely, and promptly attacks them.

64. Hello, Sailor: Mercantile airships from far off cities arrive in the night, docking with the souk along its outside wall. Hundreds of sailors are in town on furlough. Succubi whores that normally reside in the abandoned sewer system in the City come out to ply their trade, using their infernal abilities to procure customers whether they want to be procured or not. One such succubus targets the adventurers, likely the one with the highest Charisma or the most evident wealth.

65. Hot to Trot: A powerful enemy wizard dispels the enchantment that keeps Souk Dhimmi's iron from melting in the heat of the plane. As he flies off on his ornately woven carpet, cackling madly, the affected street turns to molten liquid, possibly injuring or killing those in the area. The characters can chase the wizard, help rescue or tend to trapped and injured victims, or help mend and repair the street.

66. Duck and Cover: An outgoing mercantile airship explodes violently hundreds of feet above the souk, the victim of competitive sabotage. For three rounds following the explosion, heavy pieces of marble statuary fall from the sky. Hours later, reward notices are posted offering a substantial sum of brass money to anyone who can arrest Zoodle the Dastardly, a halfling rogue and professional saboteur-for-hire.

67. Your Money or Your Unlife: A gang of vampire rogues has recently infiltrated the souk. They specialize in extortion and racketeering, threatening to the turn the souk's merchants into undead if they don't meet their exorbitant demands. Adventurers are either hired by the merchant's guild or are targeted by the vampires.

68. Dance, Maggot: As the adventurers walk down the street, or perhaps while they are inside their favorite watering hole, a drunken wizard throws a tantrum because someone didn't show him the proper respect. He screams his indignation at the top of his lungs. During this fit of pique, he points a silver staff at random people, commanding them to dance. If the targets don't dance, or are too slow on the uptake, he fires the staff at them, casting *irresistible dance*.

69. Sniper: An extremely pissed off arcane archer takes to the rooftops, whence she covertly fires enchanted arrows at random passersby. Of course, this includes our itinerant adventurers. This goes on until somebody works up the wherewithal to put a stop to her. Noman al-Ajadi's Irregulars are not skilled enough to do it, so he offers a sizeable reward for the woman's head.

70. Dog Meat: A pack of wild dogs inadvertently ate a forgetful wizard's garbage. Normally, this wouldn't be such a problem, but in this particular instance, the wizard threw away stale bread he had enchanted with experimental magic. The dogs were subsequently transformed into hellhounds. They stalk the adventurers for many hours before finally ambushing them in a dead-end alley.

71. Looking For Love In All The Wrong Places: A brass basilisk crawls out of the sewers desperately seeking its "master". Those who cross its path inevitably get turned to brass after making eye contact with it. The basilisk's master hires the adventurers to go after the creature to put it down once and for all.

72. Take That, Brat: While waiting for water at one of the souk's many public wells, an ogre mercenary loses patience with a woman's young but obnoxious child. He throws the kid into the well then storms off without his water. The woman panics. The adventurers can either save the child or go after the ogre.

The Bazaar of Arcana (Middle City)

73. Wild Magic: As the adventurers make their way through the Bazaar, a low rumbling builds from the direction of a nearby shop. The rumbling reaches a climax as smoke begins to seep from the open windows. Within seconds, the shop explodes in a wintry blast of magic gone wrong. All within 50 feet of the shop are pelted with ice and bitter winds. Within 1d4 rounds, a group of 4 fire giants and an efreeti bey arrive to investigate the atrocity. They find the culprit quite dead in what is left of his shop, but the investigation continues for quite some time, and the characters are questioned extensively.

74. Framed: While in the Bazaar, one random character who has a backpack displayed in plain sight is "accidentally" bumped into by a small, paranoid looking human. Have the character make a DC 18 Wisdom (Perception) check to notice that the man dropped an amulet into the bag. The amulet is a powerful magical item belonging to a balor. Within 6d10 minutes, the balor, who is attuned to the amulet, comes looking for his stolen property.

75. Nimble Fingers: The adventurers find themselves a victim of theft. The thief attempts to remove any single item from a random character's belt. Should the thief succeed, he melts away into the crowd and goes about his business. If the character spots the theft in progress, the thief bolts through the crowd, proving to be very adept at moving and hiding amidst the massive numbers. The thief will not answer any questions, and has no other material possessions if caught.

76. Patrol: Three burning dervish wizards[1] for a routine check for contraband magic items stop the adventurers. Any character that possesses a cold-based magical item that is rare or rarer is immediately apprehended and detained for questioning.

77. Enslaved: The adventurers become the target of a mass *dominate person* effect by a powerful arch-mage who takes them to her lab where she places a *geas* spell on each member of the party. The quest they must undertake is to retrieve a tooth and two vials of blood from a great red wyrm. The closest wyrm of this sort happens to be the commander of the bastion forces in the Palace of the Sultan.

78. Duped: The adventurers are offered a powerful potion by a con artist claiming that his potion will hide the characters from the eyes of the Sultan's meddlesome Secret Police. The con artist says that the potion works for a period of four days, and costs a mere 3,000 bp. The potion, of course, does absolutely nothing, other than taste bad. Each potion is, however, the subject of a *Nystal's magic aura* spell that causes the potions to radiate a magical aura.

79. Robbery: As the characters make their way through the Bazaar, they notice a stern looking human man dressed in chain mail armor, resting both hands on a drawn sword whose tip is resting on the ground. He has taken up a firm stance near the door of the Flame on the Wall. The man does not answer any questions, but he does block the door against entry by any party other than the Sultan's Secret Police.

The man's friends have the proprietor detained and his fire giant guard snoozing soundly while they rob him blind. There is a chance each round the giant wakes up, attacking everyone in sight but the proprietor. If rescued, the proprietor offers the characters a reward.

80. Flawed Circle: A commotion is heard a short distance away, followed by a thunderous crash. The door of a nearby wizard's tower explodes outward as the enormous body of a Nalfeshnee tears its way through. The demon immediately causes all sorts of havoc until slain or banished.

The Terrace of Petitioners (Upper City)

Any number of creatures may be encountered while amongst the petitioners who await their call to visit the Palace of the Sultan and offer tribute. The strange assortment of creatures and dignitaries from the vast multitude of planes that await their summons upon the terrace offer the GM numerous resources with which to fuel their campaign. Set encounters may be placed here by the GM or taken from the list below.

81. Horned Devil Ambassador: A horned devil and his 1d4+1 bearded devil bodyguards await audience with the Sultan, regarding the recovery of a lost object coveted by both the Sultan and Lucifer.

82. Khada the Arch Mage: Khada is seeking entry to the Palace of Wonders, and has been thrice denied. He may be willing to barter with characters to get him entry to the Palace of Wonders by any means necessary.

83. Musical Entourage: Hasafi, a well-known half-elven bard and his entourage of performers have just arrived to perform for the Sultan. Hasafi hopes to gain the Sultan as a new patron.

84. Priest of Set: An envoy from the Pyramid of Set brings news and information given him by the dread lord himself. Agents have information that a special flask that the Sultan desires is located within the Ash Grinder Arcology. Knowing how much the Sultan is willing to pay for the flask, he hires characters to go and find out if the story is true, and if so, to return it to him.

85. Janni Merchant Prince: The Mahab al Jann has over 50,000 bp worth of treasure and one hundred slaves he is offering to the Sultan in exchange for efreeti muscle in overcoming a trade dispute on his home plane.

86. Gloobleblub the Aboleth: Gloobleblub is in a specially designed temperature control water tank, born by dozens of dominated human slaves. He seeks audience with the Sultan concerning the locating of several artifacts of power that the Sultan desires. The artifacts rest beneath the seas of Gloobleblub's home plane, in the hands of a sahaugin king. The characters may be recruited to recover the items.

87. Palathenes the Kolyrat: Palathenes wears the guise of a wealthy merchant of some unknown giant race. He travels alone and without any obvious treasure, but carries what appears to be a writ of passage rolled in his left hand. Palethenes has heard that the Sultan of Efreet[1] is a notorious deal breaker, and seeks to force the Sultan into keeping his bargains.

88. Half-Dragon Senator: A half-dragon senator from a far off world of reptilian and draconic beings seeks to barter for the release of the gold dragons kept in the Sultan's stables. The dragons of his home world rarely mate anymore, and he has been sent to seek dragons from other planes and other worlds to help repopulate the stock. He offers four adult blue dragons, raised specifically for the purpose of drawing the Sultan's fabled chariot in exchange for the golden ones. If the Sultan denies him, the senator seeks the aid of foolhardy adventurers to steal the gold dragons from the Sultan, in exchange for 20,000 bp.

89. Burning Dervish Secret Police: A squad of burning dervish Secret Police keeps a watchful eye on the petitioners. They are disguised as pilgrims, requiring opposed Perception and Deception checks to identify them for what they truly are. Should the characters look like they are up to something they shake them down and demand to search their belongings. Should the characters refuse, the dervishes attack.

90. Adventurers: A party of evil adventurers brings riches to the Sultan of Efreet[1]. They wish to offer their services to him in exchange for permission to visit the Repository Annex and the Palace of Wonders. The DM should feel free to drop in any evil character party of levels and abilities fairly equally matching those of the characters.

91. Pilgrims: A group of humanoid pilgrims who have taken to worshipping the Sultan of Efreet[1] as their God of Fire have come to bask in his presence. Little do the pilgrims know, the Sultan intends to give them to one of his court as a gift.

92. Fire Giants and a Triumph of Salamander Prisoners: A group of ten fire giants hauls a trio of salamander nobles[1] bound in an iron cage before the Sultan of Efreet[1] for punishment.

93. Assassin: Idag of the Knife, a famous half fiend assassin, wears the guise of a janni noble bringing gifts to the Sultan of Efreet[1]. Idag appears as a janni noble with four fire giant mercenaries, bearing a platform containing a Gargantuan dragonne in a golden cage. In truth, the fire giants are actually frost giant barbarians of a secret berserker suicide cult. The dragonne and its cage are actually a frost worm. Idag has no idea that he was secretly hired by the Grand Vizier in an attempt to destroy the Sultan and place himself atop the Throne of Brass.

94. A Merchants Dispute: An efreeti merchant and a lesser efreeti noble are having a dispute over the sale of a *huge vorpal falchion*. Details are sketchy as to the matter of the conflict, the noble claiming that the falchion was not as big as the one he ordered, and the merchant claiming that it is indeed made to the measurement and specifications agreed on. Now the noble is refusing to pay. They seek the Sultan's judgment as to whether or not size really does matter. The pair readily pleads their case to any who listen. If the characters solve the dispute for them, they gain a 20% discount at the merchant's shop, and an *elemental gem* from the noble.

95. Bilsaab the Hunter: Bilsaab, a human ranger, makes fortunes off the Great Sultan. More of a bounty hunter than anything else, Bilsaab finds and captures comely females of any race or background from outsiders to mortals for the Sultan's harem. Currently he has a beautiful Ghael named Ursala trapped within an *iron flask*. If freed by the characters, Ursala readily joins the characters in battle against her former captor(s).

96. Volcano Giants: A trio of volcano giants bears their tribute of a pallet of oilshark skins to the Sultan as part of their yearly pilgrimage.

97. Gorlik the Unclean: A dwarven lich bears an item he claims is the brain crystal of the *juggernaut of Kil Kath Kesh*. He seeks to trade the crystal for a magical rod located in the Palace of Wonders. The crystal is in fact a fake. It seemingly animates the juggernaut, which works normally for 1d4+1 minutes, before going berserk. Although the juggernaut itself is almost completely indestructible, the only way to shut it off is to somehow remove the false brain crystal.

98. Haggis the Night Hag: This twisted beast is given wide berth by evil and chaotic beings that stand in the line waiting to see the Sultan of Efreet[1]. Haggis comes to the Sultan to demand satisfaction in the matter of the execution of a rogue and murderer from the basin. It seems Haggis was in the midst of draining the poor fool prior to his capture. His soul, she claims, should rightly be hers, and she wants it now!

99. Rezzalli the Corrector: Paid by the Great Sultan indirectly through the House of Bayt Al Sikkin, a female doppelganger is petitioning for an audience to make a very public assassination on a high-ranking efreeti noble of a rival house. She plans to make it appear as if the attack is on the Great Sultan, killing her target as collateral damage. What she is unaware of is the Great Sultan plans to double-cross her should the attempt be fumbled or extremely messy in nature–alleviating any involvement by the Great Sultan in this plot.

100. Two-Faced Janni: Fatoosh, a strong, well-kept janni looks to sell information to the Great Sultan or Grand Vizier about a planned djinni threat of valued interest of the Brass Throne. This janni is a double agent, attempting to pass off information that if followed leads efreet forces into a combined djinni and janni ambush.

101. A God's Request: A demigod or lesser deity awaits an audience with the Sultan. The deific being in question desires to move ahead in the divine ranks and seeks the Sultan's aid in making it happen.

Legal Appendix

Designation of Product Identity: The following items are hereby designated as Product Identity as provided in section 1(e) of the Open Game License: Any and all material or content that could be claimed as Product Identity pursuant to section 1(e), below, is hereby claimed as product identity, including but not limited to: **1.** The name "Frog God Games" as well as all logos and identifying marks of Frog God Games, LLC, including but not limited to the Frog God logo and the phrase "Adventures worth winning," as well as the trade dress of Frog God Games products; **2.** Product names of any and all Frog God Games product names referenced in the work; **3.** All artwork, illustration, graphic design, maps, and cartography, including any text contained within such artwork, illustration, maps or cartography; **4.** The proper names, personality, descriptions and/or motivations of all artifacts, characters, races, countries, geographic locations, plane or planes of existence, gods, deities, events, magic items, organizations and/or groups unique to this book, but not their stat blocks or other game mechanic descriptions (if any), and also excluding any such names when they are included in monster, spell or feat names. **5.** Any other content previously designated as Product Identity is hereby designated as Product Identity and is used with permission and/or pursuant to license.

This printing is done under version 1.0a of the Open Game License, below.

Notice of Open Game Content: This product contains Open Game Content, as defined in the Open Game License, below. Open Game Content may only be Used under and in terms of the Open Game License.

Designation of Open Game Content: Subject to the Product Identity Designation herein, the following material is designated as Open Game Content. (1) all monster statistics, descriptions of special abilities, and sentences including game mechanics such as die rolls, probabilities, and/or other material required to be open game content as part of the game rules, or previously released as Open Game Content, (2) all portions of spell descriptions that include rules-specific definitions of the effect of the spells, and all material previously released as Open Game Content, (3) all other descriptions of game-rule effects specifying die rolls or other mechanic features of the game, whether in traps, magic items, hazards, or anywhere else in the text, (4) all previously released Open Game Content, material required to be Open Game Content under the terms of the Open Game License, and public domain material anywhere in the text.

Use of Content from *The Tome of Horrors Complete*: This product contains or references content from *The Tome of Horrors Complete* and/or other monster *Tomes* by Frog God Games. Such content is used by permission and an abbreviated Section 15 entry has been approved. Citation to monsters from *The Tome of Horrors Complete* or other monster *Tomes* must be done by citation to that original work.

OPEN GAME LICENSE Version 1.0a The following text is the property of Wizards of the Coast, Inc. and is Copyright 2000 Wizards of the Coast, Inc. ("Wizards"). All Rights Reserved.

1. Definitions: (a) "Contributors" means the copyright and/or trademark owners who have contributed Open Game Content; (b) "Derivative Material" means copyrighted material including derivative works and translations (including into other computer languages), potation, modification, correction, addition, extension, upgrade, improvement, compilation, abridgment or other form in which an existing work may be recast, transformed or adapted; (c) "Distribute" means to reproduce, license, rent, lease, sell, broadcast, publicly display, transmit or otherwise distribute; (d) "Open Game Content" means the game mechanic and includes the methods, procedures, processes and routines to the extent such content does not embody the Product Identity and is an enhancement over the prior art and any additional content clearly identified as Open Game Content by the Contributor, and means any work covered by this License, including translations and derivative works under copyright law, but specifically excludes Product Identity; (e) "Product Identity" means product and product line names, logos and identifying marks including trade dress; artifacts; creatures; characters; stories, storylines, plots, thematic elements, dialogue, incidents, language, artwork, symbols, designs, depictions, likenesses, formats, poses, concepts, themes and graphic, photographic and other visual or audio representations; names and descriptions of characters, spells, enchantments, personalities, teams, personas, likenesses and special abilities; places, locations, environments, creatures, equipment, magical or supernatural abilities or effects, logos, symbols, or graphic designs; and any other trademark or registered trademark clearly identified as Product identity by the owner of the Product Identity, and which specifically excludes the Open Game Content; (f) "Trademark" means the logos, names, mark, sign, motto, designs that are used by a Contributor to identify itself or its products or the associated products contributed to the Open Game License by the Contributor; (g) "Use", "Used" or "Using" means to use, Distribute, copy, edit, format, modify, translate and otherwise create Derivative Material of Open Game Content; (h) "You" or "Your" means the licensee in terms of this agreement.

2. The License: This License applies to any Open Game Content that contains a notice indicating that the Open Game Content may only be Used under and in terms of this License. You must affix such a notice to any Open Game Content that you Use. No terms may be added to or subtracted from this License except as described by the License itself. No other terms or conditions may be applied to any Open Game Content distributed using this License.

3. Offer and Acceptance: By Using the Open Game Content You indicate Your acceptance of the terms of this License.

4. Grant and Consideration: In consideration for agreeing to use this License, the Contributors grant You a perpetual, worldwide, royalty-free, non-exclusive license with the exact terms of this License to Use, the Open Game Content.

5. Representation of Authority to Contribute: If You are contributing original material as Open Game Content, You represent that Your Contributions are Your original creation and/or You have sufficient rights to grant the rights conveyed by this License.

6. Notice of License Copyright: You must update the COPYRIGHT NOTICE portion of this License to include the exact text of the COPYRIGHT NOTICE of any Open Game Content You are copying, modifying or distributing, and You must add the title, the copyright date, and the copyright holder's name to the COPYRIGHT NOTICE of any original Open Game Content you Distribute.

7. Use of Product Identity: You agree not to Use any Product Identity, including as an indication as to compatibility, except as expressly licensed in another, independent Agreement with the owner of each element of that Product Identity. You agree not to indicate compatibility or co-adaptability with any Trademark or Registered Trademark in conjunction with a work containing Open Game Content except as expressly licensed in another, independent Agreement with the owner of such Trademark or Registered Trademark. The use of any Product Identity in Open Game Content does not constitute a challenge to the ownership of that Product Identity. The owner of any Product Identity used in Open Game Content shall retain all rights, title and interest in and to that Product Identity.

8. Identification: If you distribute Open Game Content You must clearly indicate which portions of the work that you are distributing are Open Game Content.

9. Updating the License: Wizards or its designated Agents may publish updated versions of this License. You may use any authorized version of this License to copy, modify and distribute any Open Game Content originally distributed under any version of this License.

10. Copy of this License: You MUST include a copy of this License with every copy of the Open Game Content You Distribute.

11. Use of Contributor Credits: You may not market or advertise the Open Game Content using the name of any Contributor unless You have written permission from the Contributor to do so.

12. Inability to Comply: If it is impossible for You to comply with any of the terms of this License with respect to some or all of the Open Game Content due to statute, judicial order, or governmental regulation then You may not Use any Open Game Material so affected.

13. Termination: This License will terminate automatically if You fail to comply with all terms herein and fail to cure such breach within 30 days of becoming aware of the breach. All sublicenses shall survive the termination of this License.

14. Reformation: If any provision of this License is held to be unenforceable, such provision shall be reformed only to the extent necessary to make it enforceable.

15. COPYRIGHT NOTICE

Open Game License v 1.0a © 2000, Wizards of the Coast, Inc.

System Reference Document 5.1. Copyright 2016, Wizards of the Coast, Inc.; Authors Mike Mearls, Jeremy Crawford, Chris Perkins, Rodney Thompson, Peter Lee, James Wyatt, Robert J. Schwalb, Bruce R. Cordell, Chris Sims, and Steve Townshend, based on original material by E. Gary Gygax and Dave Arneson.

System Reference Document © 2000. Wizards of the Coast, Inc; Authors Jonathan Tweet, Monte Cook, Skip Williams, based on material by E. Gary Gygax and Dave Arneson.

Original Spell Name Compendium Copyright 2002 Clark Peterson

City of Brass Copyright 2007, Necromancer Games, Inc.; Authors Casey Christofferson and Scott Greene, with Clark Peterson.

Wilderlands of High Fantasy Player's Guide Copyright 2003, NecromancerGames, Inc. and Judges Guild

Swords & Wizardry Complete, copyright 2007-2017 Matthew J. Finch and Frog God Games

Tome of Horrors Complete, copyright 2002-2019 Frog God Games

Bards Gate, copyright 2002-2018 Frog God Games

Rappan Athuk, copyright 2018 Frog God Games

Sword of Air, copyright 2016 Frog God Games

Fifth Edition Foes, copyright 2016 Frog God Games

Book of Lost Spells, copyright 2016 Frog God Games